TITAN

– UNDERVERSE –

Book 4

2ND EDITION

JEZ CAJIAO

TABLE OF CONTENTS

UNDERVERSE SYNOPSIS

BOOK ONE:

Jax is working a dead end job, in a semi-stable relationship, and searching for his missing brother, while plagued by dreams of the UnderVerse. This terrible alternate reality is where he, and his brother Tommy, are pulled against their will on occasion. When in the dream they inhabit artificial bodies and fight to protect abandoned villages and more, standing between the inhabitants of the Old Empire and the creatures of the night.

They awaken back on earth once the threat has passed, or they've been killed, with their injuries following them. While they heal at a tremendously accelerated rate, it still requires days to recover, and in that time, they hide their injuries, lest they be locked away for self-mutilation.

After one such session, Jax decides to come clean to his GF and explain everything. Badly injured and bleeding heavily, he arrives at her home, only to find her in bed with another man. He loses control, half beating the man to death, and having his skull shattered in turn by her, using the baseball bat he'd bought her for self-defense.

Jax comes to in the hospital, chained to the bed, and is interviewed by the police and warned he faces a significant jail term. While alone and contemplating this, an unknown doctor slips in and assures him it has all been taken care of, before drugging him.

When Jax wakes up this time, it's to find himself restrained, again, but on an airplane heading to meet 'the Baron Sanguis'. A lawyer assures him that should he carry out the reasonable requests of his new employer, then not only will all legal concerns be a thing of the past, but he will find his brother as well. Jax accepts, warned that refusal means death, and meets the Baron, an inhuman monster who admits to being an interplanar traveler, and a member of the original nobility of the UnderVerse, the Realm that Jax and his brother dream of.

To be free and to find his brother Jax must travel to that shattered Realm, and open a stable portal back to this Realm, as the mana here is simply too low in concentration for the portal to be held open for more than bare seconds. Alternatively, a portal from that side, to here, would be secure and enable the nobility to return with servants and forces intact, ready to reconquer their home.

Over the next several months, as Jax is trained for the 'little task', he discovers more about the past of that Realm, including that the voice of madness that occasionally speaks to him, and that he'd written off as himself being mad to some degree, is actually the voice of the Eternal Emperor Amon, a fragment of His soul being all that's left, clinging to the genetic line.

Amon was murdered, by the Baron, His son, and others of the nobility, with the aid of the God of Death, Nimon. In the process, and as his price for this, the followers of the other nine greater gods were purged and their temples cast down. Leaving the God of Death, who dragged one of the moons down to impact the Realm, with a powerful enough surge of His 'aspect' (death) that He managed to banish the other Greater Gods.

Jax grows to hate the Baron, but has nothing left in his life beyond his missing brother, and so takes the opportunity, training heavily, before facing eleven other nobles' choices in the arena to 'earn' the right to go to the UnderVerse. He wins, barely, and trades the remains of his opponents and their personal items to their sponsors, in exchange for several magical artifacts, before passing through the great portal.

Once on the other side, and having made a deal with an opposing noble 'house' for access, he finds himself in a ruined tower. The Great Towers were bastions of the old Empire, powerfully magical, self-sustaining and intended as entire self-contained cities. At half a mile wide at the base, two to three miles high, and sustained by their own mana collectors they acted as garrisons and secure imperial bastions in places of danger.

The Tower that Jax finds himself in, however, was never inhabited fully. It was finished, intended as a research and security station, but had only a skeleton crew when it was assaulted by a SporeMother. The SporeMother, a multi-limbed monstrosity of legend, flooded the defenders with undead and possessed creatures, birthing DarkSpore creatures, parasitical clouds that could puppet flesh, turning the unprepared defenders into attackers, claiming the Tower. The few remaining survivors, beleaguered on all sides, ordered the Tower's controller Wisps to shut the entire structure down, sealing the Wisps themselves away, and preventing the creature from being able to feed on the mana of the Tower to grow stronger, expecting that the Tower would be assaulted and retaken shortly by the Imperial Legion.

Then, before reinforcements could take the Tower back, the Cataclysm came. Seas and mountains rose, islands vanished and the creatures of the deep and of nightmare were set loose to roam. When Jax arrives at the Tower he finds it dark and silent, populated by the ancient dead, with only occasional more recently killed adventurers scattered here and there. He also encounters Sporelings, immature SporeMothers, hidden in the portal chamber, fighting them and locking himself away in a side room.

Jax uses one of the spells he gained, resurrecting one of the Sporelings he killed to form a companion to fight alongside him. Using his new companion, Bob, and his weapon of choice, a bastardized naginata, Jax proceeds to clear the Tower partially, discovering the 'Hall of Memories' and its sleeping Wisp, Oracle. He is gravely injured, and alone, Bob having perished in the fight to enter the room, and when he awakens the Wisp takes the chance it unthinkingly offers, to use some of the stored knowledge of the Hall of Memories, in the form of spellbooks, to enable him to defeat the undead outside the room.

Unfortunately, all magic he has accessed so far has been through books such as this, impressing outside knowledge across his brain and damaging it each time. This final spellbook is one too many, and results in scarring, internal bleeding and more. Jax is dying and Oracle, the newly awakened Wisp, bonds herself to him in an attempt to save him, gaining access to his manapool and enabling herself to cast the needed healing spells to save his life.

Over time Jax recovers, and with Oracle's guidance, reawakens and names Seneschal, the Wisp that controlled the tower, reactivating the mana collectors and beginning the basic repairs the Tower requires, as well as awakening the Goddess of Fire, Jenae. This awakens the SporeMother, now ancient and decrepit, but still powerful. In the fight that follows between Jax, Oracle, the newly reformed Bob and the SporeMother and her minions, the Eternal Emperor Amon makes contact with Jax, guiding him to use an artifact recovered in the Tower earlier. This Silverbright potion (Dragon's blood) transforms his weapon from a standard construction into a basic magical, but evolving, weapon. Jax kills the SporeMother, but is gravely wounded. Over the next day, as he is healed, the companions clear the remaining sections of the Tower, and find the creature's nest underground, along with the remains of the Golem Construction Cradles or Genesis Chambers.

They also find the Wisp responsible for the golems, name him Hephaestus, and take the time to reclaim the single working Genesis Chamber. This begins the construction of the most basic of stone golems to protect and rebuild the Tower. In the process, HeartStones are uncovered, a magical way to send a memory, as a method of communication. Most are long drained of mana, but the fragments that remain make it clear that Barabarattas, lord of one of the two nearby cities, has been trading slaves to the SporeMother in exchange for Sporelings, hoping to raise a captive army of SporeMothers.

The Wisps sense an intrusion higher in the tower and Jax explores, finding a group of slavers, heavily armed, using their slaves to loot an old armory. Jax attacks when seeing a child beaten, killing the slavers, with Oracle's help, and driving off the two airships that had been docked on the balcony. One is damaged and crashes in the courtyard below, while the other escapes to land at a nearby lake to effect repairs.

The freed slaves pledge allegiance to Jax, and while they rest, he takes one of their number, Oren, the captain of the crashed ship, down to the courtyard. He discovers that they were pressed into service, and had no desire to work with the slavers. The remaining surviving crew swear as well, and inform Jax that there is a third ship. This is the warship that was enforcing the City Lord's will, and it was still incoming, having stopped to raid a village along the way. Jax and the slaves use the weapons they have, the remains of the damaged ship and subterfuge to lure the warship in to land, while Oracle disables their engines.

Jax and Bob, aided by some of the former slaves, fight and kill the soldiers aboard the warship, capturing the crew, freeing a group of slaves taken from the villages and locking the crew in those same cages. Jax formally claims the Tower as his, and through the right of blood, having found that he is an illegitimate son of the Baron Sanguis, and therefore noble in his own right, he begins the right of Imperial Succession.

Barabarratas, like all nobles remaining in the Empire, with no Imperial House to swear to, had been unable to lay claim formally to the Imperial Throne, but once the succession has begun, sees a way to claim the throne. He threatens war against Jax, unless he surrenders. Jax, being short of patience and self-control, as well as occasionally being an asshole, in turn declares war on Barabarratas and his city of Himnel, taunting him before leading his people in a wake. The end of the book comes to Thomas, Jax's brother, languishing and injured in a jail, before being sold as fodder, the lowest caste of soldier, to the Dark Legion of Nimon.

BOOK TWO:

Thomas fights his abusive jailor and draws the eye of a Paladin of Nimon, who grants him a chance to prove himself. Thomas is happy to take that chance and prove his worth in battle to escape the rank of fodder.

Jax awakens with a hangover, the wake having gone well, and proceeds to set about trying to repair the Tower. Two of the new recruits, now citizens of the Great Tower, Oren the Dwarf airship captain, and Cai, a Panthera humanoid with a skill for organization, assist him. Teams are formed for hunting and defense, with a personal squad geared around Jax. This is formed from ex slaves who are determined to never be cowed again. Lydia leads them (mace and shield, heavy armor), with Jian (dual wielding swords), Arrin (mage), Cam (Axeman), Miren (archer), Stephanos (archer) and Bob. Jax and his new team go to try and capture or recruit the escaped second airship, but upon arrival at the lake, find the ship deserted.

They are attacked as they search by small four-armed amphibious creatures known as the 'Mer'. In the course of the fight, Jax realizes they are young, ranging from a young adult, to a child, and they were attacked by goblins prior to Jax's arrival, attacking him in pre-emptive self-defense. The young ones are joined by older, more experienced warriors, who agree to a truce at first, and then request help to deal with the nearby goblin horde.

Jax agrees, and three of the Mer join them, assaulting the goblin camp. In the course of the fight, Jax saves the life of one of the Mer, the oldest of the younglings, and upon clearing the ruin, and rescuing the surviving crew of the airship from them, claims the land as part of the Empire. In the process, the goblin cave is revealed as a buried outpost, complete with basic golems, which are claimed and returned to the Tower.

The Mer village remains neutral, but several of their people join Jax, including the youngling, Bane. The leader of the Mer that join the Tower is Flux, an accomplished adventurer, and he supports Bane's desire to be Jax's bodyguard. Several of the older Mer decide to join the Tower, many of whom are skilled, but crippled. Jax heals them, magic being increasingly rare in the UnderVerse since the fall of the Empire, and his abilities and the knowledge stored at the Tower are revealed as being incredibly valuable. The rescued crew join Jax, bringing their ship and joining the resurgent Empire.

The older banished Gods are awakened, and Jax has a disagreement with one, Tamat, the Lady of Assassins. Using a draconic legacy from Amon, Jax manages to beat Her in Her weakened state, before being forced back by Jenae, who begins the process of spreading the worship of the original Gods again. The Gods are weak, but They have abilities They can grant, and information from the past that is relevant. Nimon is unaware They are back.

Jenae, after an earlier disagreement with Jax, helps him to find that his brother was recently in the city of Himnel. Oren and the others implore Jax to free their families, to bring them to the Tower from Himnel. He agrees, pausing only long enough, to have his body inked with tattoos, guided by Jenae, Ame, a Mer runesmith, and a tattooist named Renna.

While attempting to find a hidden entrance to the city, used by smugglers, Oracle, who has fallen in love with Jax, and he with her, is captured and taken deep underground by the Drow, a race of Dark Elves that are scouting the city for an unknown reason. Jax catches some of them, and in a bout of frantic insanity, imbues his body with sufficient mana that he gains a new ability 'Mana-Overdrive' speeding his movements and strength up, but it is short lived, and results in a 'crash' afterward. Jax uses this ability to kill two of the Drow, and then, driven mad by Oracle's capture, pain and fear allows his darker side to come out as he tortures the Drow for information.

Bane calms him down, hides the body from the others, and guides Jax back to himself. Jax's group, now including Barret, a former soldier and a member of Oren's ship's crew, dives underground, hunting the Drow. Over the underground trip, they meet Ashrag, an ancient Cave Spider, who remembers the Empire, and despite her monstrous appearance, was once an Imperial Citizen. Jax resurrects ancient Oaths, claiming them as his own at Amon's direction, and passes out from the mana drain. This convinces Ashrag and, after fighting a group of her brood, she swears allegiance. She agrees, on the condition that Jax free the tunnels of the Drow who view her kind, and their bodies, as a great delicacy.

Jax eventually leads his team through the various dark places, and finds Oracle, captured by the Drow leader, a Drider. The half woman-half spider, has several smugglers held captive and fights the group. Jax is triumphant, but Cam dies at the hands of the Drow. Oracle is freed and the smugglers are mainly compliant, save their leader, who ends up making a comment that Jax disagrees with pointedly, and dies.

The last few Drow fight a retreat, until they are killed by a new threat coming the other way along the tunnel. The three newcomers slaughter the Drow, then, after a tense standoff, are revealed to be Imperial Legionnaires. The Imperial Legion has been dismissed and derided since the Cataclysm, slowly dwindling in numbers and through several bad apples in leadership, have become outsiders in their own homes. They are disliked and disrespected by the locals, even as they march out to fight the creatures that nobody else can.

The Legion is falling apart, its members lost and despairing, until Jax resurrects the Oaths, and finally a chance at a future is given back to them.

The three scouts, Yen, Tang and Amaat swear to Jax, and reveal that they are even now, below the City of Himnel.

BOOK THREE:

Jax leads the group to the surface, fighting off a group of local thugs who attempt to hunt the Legionnaires, and eventually reach the Arena and Arena Master Mal, one of the local leaders of the Smuggler's Guild. This is the man Oren had recommended as the best choice of an ally in the city. At the same time Jax is in the process of capturing a small group of Djinn, who offer allegiance in exchange for freeing their captured clan mother from the Skyking.

Mal agrees to help, for a fee, and introduces his team; Soween, his right hand, Jay his muscle and Josh his mage and Soween's husband. While Jax is resting, and about to finally get some 'private time' with Oracle, who can assume human form and size at will, Mal receives a message from the local crime lord, the Skyking. He demands Mal turn over the 'Legion' having discovered that it was Legionnaires that killed its people. Mal refuses, and instead, to gain the time they need, arranges a series of arena fights with the 'captured' Legionnaires, including Jax, and betting games.

While Mal makes these arrangements, Jax and his team visit a local healer, intending to get some of the deep seated injuries to his brain that are slowing his ability and level growth addressed. Along the way, Jax is surrounded by the enslaved, seeing the casual cruelty of the people, the way that nobles laugh and stroll, while slaves on the verge of starvation carry their bags. Amon sees this and their twinned rage escapes control, resulting in a temper-tantrum of epic proportions, leveling a section of the city and freeing the slaves, while also releasing Amon to face Jax inside his own mind.

Jax manages to defeat Amon, but in the process, discovers that he's had an unrecognized parasitic inhabitant all this time. He tears it free, gutting himself in the process, and only survives through the intervention of his team getting him to the healer, and the divine help of Jenae.

The Legion, having lost contact with their scouts, and seeing the devastation in the city, send a small, but elite team out to investigate, and with their help, Jax is returned to the Arena. The Legion settles in to protect him.

Jax is drained by the healing, and Centurion Primus Augustus, one of the four Primus of the Legion, fights in his place in the Arena that night, slaughtering all thrown against him.

Jax awakens and meets Mal and the others, works to integrate himself with the Legion and meets the non-human members of the shipyards who've been brushed aside by Barabarattas and his kind as 'sub-human'. They are recruited, and a plan formed. Rather than escaping with everyone through the hidden Smuggler's Path and robbing the city for the Tower's needs, a new more daring plan is concocted.

The airships are built in the shipyards, and Himnel's greatest weapon is under construction, the battleship. Currently it's a bare structure, open to the elements, but under the plan, additional volunteers are brought in, and the battleship is sealed up, and made, minimally, airworthy. The Legion are contacted and given orders, in three days they are to capture the shipyards.

Having little alternative, and no love for the city, as well as a legitimate authority encouraging it, the Legion agree.

Jax fights and recovers that night and trains, dragging Grizz, the Legionnaire into his group, as well as Yen and Tang. The next night, after the fight, he leads his team to raid and rob the Magical Emporium, a golem secured shop. The presence of the golem leads Jax and the others to discover a hidden section below the main shop, unknown by all. They realize that long ago it wasn't a shop, but a golem repair and construction facility. The golems are claimed, the construction facility below ground being ordered to begin repairs and construction, while golems there are used to repair ancient mining golems, which are sent to the Tower, burrowing underground. The rest of the golems are sent to wait in the river for the assault on the shipyards.

The following night the Arena fight is 'fixed', but Jax, with the help of his team, wins, and they launch the assault. Combining the assault on the Skyking with the one on the shipyards, Jax and the small Legion team, along with his own, take the Skyking's tower, killing them all. Halfway through the fight, when confronted with the rarely seen Anubai, a heavily magical species, Jax activates his trump card, his Tattoos. Rather than being decorative, they are in fact magical runes enabling him to channel mana through them, helping him to turn the tables on his foes.

In the fight, they capture the first of the airships circling on 'overwatch' over the city. To capture the others, Jian assumes control of one of the ships and accidentally, being unfamiliar with the controls, fires a giant fireball at the tent city of recruits around the Dark Citadel of Nimon. Jax, as the leader of the group, is blamed and declared Apostate, and a holy war begins.

The ships are brought under Jax's control, and return to the shipyards, to be crewed by his people. In the following confusion, Jax is hit in the head and injured. The ships flee Himnel, having stolen the vast majority of the city's manastone store, which are needed to power the engines of the ships.

Without stones, Barabarattas is unable to give chase, and the ships head out to sea, hoping to leave the impression that they're not from the Tower, and as Jax had ordered. Unfortunately, Nimon is aware of the truth.

The Dark Legion attacks the stragglers leaving the city, and their latest recruit, Thomas assists in killing some of Jax's Legionnaires. Jax awakens when they are far out to sea, close to the Sunken City, a flying city from the old Empire that crashed into a seamount. He confirms the orders to land there, to make the ships secure, and then to make for the Great Tower. He also finally gets some 'private time' with Oracle.

GIINT

PROLOGUE

"**W**hat?!" Barabarattas, Lord of Himnel, he spun on the unfortunate victim of his ire, voice dropping to a low growl. "What did you just say?"

"Uh…well, you see, m…my lord," the messenger stammered. "The guards…they said…uh…"

"Cletus!" Barabarattas screamed. A few seconds later, a dark-cloaked figure materialized from the gloom obscuring the back of the room, stepping free of the heavy black velvet curtains as though lingering there, out of sight, was perfectly normal.

"Yes, my lord?" Cletus Thane asked calmly.

"Is this true?" the fuming lord hissed. "Some thieving *nobody* has raided my city, stolen my ships out from under me, stripped my Stockpile, and murdered my citizens, all while you caroused and chased tavern wenches?"

"It appears so, and he's not *exactly* a nobody. You *did* declare war on him, after all," Cletus replied unconcernedly. "Hmmm, I do vaguely remember seeing the legion storm past while I was being sick in a gutter, actually." He rubbed his eyes and yawned, filling the room with a stench of stale ale and vomit as he strode forward.

"Gods, man!" Barabarattas gagged and waved his hand to dispel the fumes. "I'd have you killed for that—"

"If you could." Cletus finished for the city lord, shaking his head. "We both know you need me, *my lord*, and until you no longer require my services, I am irreplaceable. Besides, if you killed me, who else would act as your representative in…certain deals?"

The seething noble glared at Cletus, who smirked before glancing at the thoroughly terrified messenger.

"He knows too much," Barabarattas snapped at Cletus, who turned and smiled lazily at the messenger, who paled at the sharply pointed teeth he revealed.

"True," the pale man said languidly, then burped again, wafting the foul odor away from his face and looking confused. "Well, I don't remember eating *that*…oh well. Sorry, old boy." Cletus's right hand flicked out, and a thread of black light flashed across the intervening distance to splash across the messenger's face, bursting like water before solidifying and emitting an evil red light. The messenger started to scream, frantically grabbing at the silken strands that joined his face to the creature's hand and trying to pull them free.

The pained screams only rose as the skin of his hands became bound to the inky material. More and more of his life force was torn from him, carried down the threads to Cletus's hand in flashes of dark red.

It took a bare handful of seconds, time which seemed far longer for the messenger as he collapsed to the floor, writhing. Soon enough, the thread released, retracting back to Cletus's wrist and disappearing as he casually lowered his sleeve. The corpse crumbled slightly as even the chemical engines of the cells failed, starved of energy.

"By the Dark Lady, that's better," Cletus muttered, wiping his face with the palm of his hand. His pasty white complexion had darkened to a light olive, and his teeth gleamed as he smiled, the points glittering as they shrank back down and resumed their normal, human appearance.

"I didn't give you permission to indulge your filthy habit in my presence." Barabarattas gestured angrily at the husk that was laid on the floor. "Get rid of that and find out what the hell happened last night! Gather your team and go; use your test subjects and get me back what is mine!"

"Why, of course, my lord," Cletus replied sardonically, dropping into an elegant low bow with his arms held out to the sides. Then he snorted and strolled off to vanish into the pre-dawn darkness of the citadel.

Cursing, Barabarattas summoned a servant to dispose of the corpse that Cletus had so arrogantly ignored.

"Send someone to the Dark Legion," he snapped at the quivering servant as the man tried to drag the corpse from the room. "*Ask* the High Priest to attend me at his earliest convenience…and send in the head of the guard! And my headsman!" He threw himself into the tall, wing-backed chair by the window and glowered out at the city, gnawing on a knuckle in frustration.

No matter what he did, everyone was going to hear about this, and that was all he needed, especially after the months—*years*, even—of work he'd put into smearing the legion. Everything was ready; a few more weeks, and he'd have been able to kill them or absorb them into the city guard. Either way, they'd have been out of their damn enclave, and he wouldn't have to worry about anyone finding out about the caves underneath it anymore…Although, that, at least, was true now, since they'd fled the city.

"And send for the city planner! I need to start building!" he roared abruptly, ignoring the servants who frantically huffed and puffed as they dragged the fully armored corpse out of the door.

CHAPTER ONE

I woke up slowly, blinking at the light that filled the cabin. Oracle's hair left behind a tickling sensation as the gentle breeze from the open porthole sent it drifting across my cheek.

I frowned for a second, shifting slightly, and smiled to myself as my brain caught up with the events of the last day—well, several days, I supposed. With the amount of time I'd spent unconscious, it had all blurred into one for me.

Idly, I reached down and felt her warm skin under my fingers, causing her to stir as she realized I was awake. The world, hell, my reality, had changed so much in the last few months that I'd never have seen this coming in my wildest dreams a year ago. But as she shifted around, propping herself up and looking down at me, I couldn't help but smile, happy beyond anything I'd ever known. I was in love.

Oracle was stunning. Not just physically, though I had to admit that was definitely part of the package. Her ability to adjust and alter her physical form, and us sharing our minds, meant that she was able to be exactly what I found most attractive and arousing at any particular time. The part that I loved most, though, wasn't her looks, or her figure, as much as last night and this morning would lend the lie to that.

It was her mind and her soul. I'd spent forever worrying about us taking this final step, becoming partners in the bedroom as much as partners in mind and companionship, despite us both wanting it for ages.

One of the reasons I'd remained unsure had been the whole "master" situation. I was literally the High Lord of Dravith, Lord of the Great Tower, and she was bonded to me as a companion.

That bond left me quite firmly in the position of Overlord, with all the responsibility and power that entailed. Taking advantage of that power to satisfy my "needs" sat a bit wrong with me, especially as when we'd met, she had been an amorphous wisp, with absolutely no sexual experience or capacity, really. That had changed when I allowed her access to my mind, and she'd picked a form she discovered that I'd like.

Unfortunately, to do so, she'd scanned all the women that had made a lasting impression in that way in my mind. As I was in my early twenties, and had, like most of my contemporaries, spent a lot of time wrestling with myself…literally…while watching porn, she'd managed to make herself so beautiful that an entire generation of Hollywood starlets would cry themselves to sleep over comparisons, complete with a figure that made a certain Kardashian look flat-chested and boring.

The combination of her body and my own subconscious reactions to it, and the fact that she'd spent years observing the various races that inhabited the tower, watching them do everything from talking shit to trying to break each other in bedroom Olympics, and…well.

She felt my hormonal reactions, and because we shared our minds, it had a hell of an effect on her too, turning her from curious to obsessed, and I certainly hadn't helped it. With my mind and body being injured so much of late, my self-control was practically non-existent.

I thought back to the girls in the Baron's citadel, shaking my head unconsciously. I'd been a prisoner, and they worked there under the control of a magical geas as maid companions. Once I'd realized the geas compelled them to do as I ordered, I'd been very careful not to ever order them to do anything. One night, they'd explained honestly, even bluntly, that while the geas could compel them into bed, and some had used it that way, that wasn't why they were having sex with me.

It wasn't simply because I was fucking irresistible and hung like a horse either, unfortunately for my ego. Instead, it was a mixture of the girls liking me for me, and a bit of planning that could only be defined as mercenary sensibility.

The girls knew the Baron was a monster, a noble of the UnderVerse who was hell-bent on returning to that—*this*—realm. Those who pleased him would be taken along, and whoever actually secured the Great Portal to the UnderVerse would become a Prince of the Empire, at the very least.

They essentially wanted to guarantee their own futures. The girls were recruited from pleasure houses and brothels around the world, trained to serve the nobility and paid a decent wage or stipend. If they wanted more, they needed to catch the eye of a member of the nobility.

They'd basically laid it all out before me as a "business proposition." In a sense, and they'd admitted that *they* were the ones using me. I got all the fun I could handle, and if they managed to catch my eye more, then they got the lives of pampered courtesans in the UnderVerse, provided of course I survived and won.

If not, so sad, too bad, and next, please…

It had taken Oracle and me some time to really understand what was going on between us, and she'd grown, emotionally as well as physically, in the time we'd spent together. Her consciousness had evolved from an almost child-like curiosity to that of a full-grown woman who was comfortable with what she wanted.

Wonderfully comfortable, I reflected, admiring at her naked figure as she sat back upright and straddled me, smiling, as I remembered the night we'd just had.

She brushed her hair back from her face, before pushing her lower lip out to blow an escaped strand of hair upwards with a light puff, then smiling down at me. Her hair had shifted from a golden blonde when I had fallen asleep to a deep, lustrous red this morning, her skin pale, soft as silk, and her muscles taut and firm.

I sat up, taking her in my arms and kissing her, reveling in the sensations of her gently biting down on my lower lip and shivering as I ran my hands down her back to settle on her full and firm ass…

"Lord Jax!" a familiar voice called from the door, followed by a heavy trio of thumps that rocked the thin, hastily built wall, let alone the door itself. "Are you awake? I'm coming in."

The door opened before I could so much as break the kiss, revealing Grizz, who paused, then grinned.

"Get out, Grizz!" Oracle and I both ordered. He shrugged, his cheeks reddening as he got an eyeful.

"Ah! Sorry, boss, and sorry, uh…boss lady? Augustus sent me to see if you were alive, and, well, you are!" He kept grinning, partly out of relief and partly because Oracle was admittedly a hell of a sight.

"Out!" Oracle repeated, throwing our shared pillow at his head as he laughed and closed the door so quickly, the entire wall shook.

"Think that was deliberate?" I asked Oracle, sighing.

"Him walking in, or them sending him?" she countered.

"Yes," I said, shaking my head. "Both, I mean. He deliberately walked in, probably not thinking about it, or thinking he might be able to wind us up with something, and probably saw more than he expected to. I guarantee you that Augustus and whoever else wants us would have suspected what he would do. Sending a blunt instrument rather than a scalpel to do a job does work, after all."

"It's just messy," she said.

"Shall we get him back?" I asked, grinning.

"Oh definitely, and Augustus, too. I think Hellenica will help us there. You know she likes him, right?"

"God, yes; it was a bit blatant," I replied as she leaned back slightly, arching her back and making sure I got a hell of a view.

"So…shall we get dressed, or…?" She raised one eyebrow and glanced down suggestively.

"Jax, I'm sorry to interrupt, but…" Grizz's voice filtered through the door. "Prefect Romanus said he needed you on the bridge, if you were able."

"He's fucking listening to us, isn't he," I said flatly to Oracle.

"He really is," she agreed, crossing her arms in annoyance. I summoned a fountain of clean, cold water by the doorway, causing the water to splash and run under the door as Oracle fired off a particularly weak Lightning Bolt. I watched with silent amusement as she deliberately adjusted it into a zap, rather than a stunning effect.

"Gahhhhh!" Grizz screamed, followed by the satisfying sound of a huge, fully armored legionnaire dancing out of the spray.

"He deserved that." Oracle huffed regretfully as she *shifted*, resuming her normal diminutive size. Her wings lifted her into the air, a short, black halter top and hot pants materializing to cover her assets. I sighed, dropping my feet over the side of the small cot to rest on the wooden deck, staring after her regretfully as I muttered "down boy" at my crotch.

The airship changed direction slightly, the engines firing in a controlled burst, before dying away to a steady *thrummm* as the room shuddered faintly.

I shook my head again, standing and stretching, while a multitude of tiny pops and clicks protested the night spent on the cot. It was small, tight, and while better than the floor, the benefit wasn't by much.

We'd actually managed to break it twice overnight, and the rudimentary fixes weren't likely to hold a third time, so I folded it up and leaned it against the back wall. Grabbing some boxers and tugging them on, I couldn't help grinning as Oracle made exaggerated eye-rolls and wolf whistles at me.

"We can't all just magic clothes up, you know," I said, hopping on one leg as I pulled my drow gloom spidersilk pants on. They were a little…okay, a *lot* stained and scruffy, but they were undoubtably the most comfortable clothes I had. As I dressed in the rest of my gear, casually pulling armor on and settling weapons into place, I reflected on the fact that going everywhere fully geared for war was the new normal for me.

"You ready?" Oracle asked as I checked to ensure that my various sheathes and pouches were all secure, twisting at the waist to make sure nothing was caught on anything.

"Yeah, come on." I nodded to her. "Time to go play with the legion, I guess."

"Just remember, they might be a bit reserved with you. You're the lord to them, but most don't know you yet. They just felt the bond become active, and the upper echelons recognized that you were their best chance for survival. While they'd never attack you, due to the Oath, it doesn't mean they're automatically going to love you either. You're still going to have to earn their respect."

"I know," I agreed, recalling my first encounters with the legionnaires I had grown close to in the arena. "We struck gold with Augustus and his team, and we still lost a lot of them in the Skyking fight and escape. Now we need to make them understand that abandoning everything was worth it."

"Don't forget that you *are* their lord, though," Oracle said quickly. "You're not there to plead with them for support. Give them orders, but, I don't know, be nice?" She lifted her hands in an uncertain gesture.

"Wow, that's helpful, Oracle." I laughed. "At least I've got you to keep me on the straight and narrow!"

"Yeah, well, I've never been in this situation either," she quipped, smiling at me as her cheeks tinged with red.

"Well, we'll face it together," I said firmly. She nodded in agreement, flitting over and landing on my left shoulder as I picked up my naginata and headed for the door.

I pulled the door open, looking out into the corridor and trying to ignore how flimsy the whole thing felt. Grizz was standing a few feet away, grinning at me, while two unfamiliar Legionnaires stood on either side of the door, fully equipped.

"Morning, I guess," I said, looking from one to the other. "I hope I didn't get either of you with that spell?" They both straightened, clapping their fists to chest in salute.

"No, Lord!" they said in unison. I winced, looking questioningly at Grizz, who shrugged.

"Right; what are your names?" I asked.

"Legionnaire Westin," the one to the right barked, closely followed by the one on my left barking out, "Legionnaire Holtic."

I noted the ramrod-straight backs, the gleaming armor, and the slight sheen of sweat on their faces. Westin was dark skinned, with a beard that bristled out of his helmet as though looking for someone to fight on its own. Holtic was paler, with almost nordic white skin, no beard, but a chin I could have used as an anvil, if I were so inclined. Beyond that, they were practically identical, the same height and everything.

"Is this a joke?" I asked Grizz uncertainly.

"I'm afraid not, Jax. And sorry again, for…*that*." He nodded toward the door with a grin, making me think he'd really just been oblivious to interrupting us. "It's standard that nobility be guarded when under the protection of the legion. In your case, they were assigned to guard you for this shift, and they don't really know you yet, so they're on their best behavior. That's all."

"Bollocks," I muttered. "Right, then, let's have this out now, as I've no doubt I'm going to be saying this a lot from now on. Yes, I'm the High Lord of Dravith. Yes, I'm the Imperial Scion and heir to the empire. No, I'm not a prick who needs sunshine blown up my arse."

I met both of the guards' eyes directly, my tone firm. "I want you both to relax. As you've seen from this pillock here," I said, gesturing to Grizz, "I'm not one for formalities; hell, he just walked in on me and my partner naked and got a pillow to the face as a consequence. It was only when he was being a filthy bastard, and blatantly listening at the door, that he got a zap for it, and even that was a warning, not a powered one. Despite him deserving it twice over for that ugly mug."

The pair stood frozen at attention for a few seconds, then exchanged a look and slowly seemed to relax, nodding in slow acceptance of my words.

"I take it you've been assigned as a bodyguard for me?" I pressed, and they nodded in sync. "Not just assigned to watch over the door, I mean, as it's a kinda shitty door."

"That's right, my lord," Westin said formally.

I shook my head before giving in. I was the High Lord of Dravith, after all. I needed to start accepting that the role came with certain shitty downsides.

"Right, well, if you two are out here, I'm hoping that means that Bane and Tang had a night off?" I said aloud, peering down the corridor.

"I wish," came a voice, and I turned to find Tang leaning against a wall support, where I'd have sworn a second before, there had been nobody.

"You better not have been in there," I growled, gesturing at the door to my cabin.

"It's okay; I left when you and Oracle got…distracted," he said, shuddering excessively.

"Well, fuck you too, mate. I told you before, stay outta the bedroom, or you'll see sights you don't want to!" I snapped, unsure if I was more amused or irritated.

"Yeah, well, you were brought on board unconscious and severely injured, so we thought it best to watch over you. Didn't expect to see *that*. Certainly not right after downing a potion of Legionnaire's Might." Tang shook his head in amazement.

"Well, more fool you, then," I said, shrugging nonchalantly. "Which way to the bridge?"

Tang gestured over his shoulder with one thumb. "This way, boss," he confirmed, straightening up and shooting me a wink. "Seriously, though, it's good to see you upright and even better to see you clothed."

"Bah! You'd love a moustache ride," I retorted unthinkingly, earning a laugh from Grizz, and quickly stifled snorts from Westin and Holtic as we started off down the corridor.

I glanced about as we went, realizing that the unfinished and flimsy look that dominated my cabin was the same out here. The structural walls and main girders were clean and beautifully made, while the smaller walls that served to separate our rooms seemed hastily put into place, with nails sticking out in random places, boards only being held together by the bare minimum, and jagged, unsanded wood everywhere.

"Uh…" I gestured to a nearby doorway, which had a pair of planks nailed across the frame in an X and nothing but open air beyond, the wind whistling frantically and tugging at our clothes as we passed by. "Is the entire ship like that?"

"Yeah, this is the battleship, Jax," Grizz pointed out, shrugging as we continued walking. "It's huge, and damn, it's amazing. Nothing this big should be in the air, you know? It's nowhere near finished though; a year or more, at least, I'd think. They hammered it together just enough to escape the city, and that's it.

"The main hold is where the majority of people are bunking, and these sections are off limits. There, at least, it's secure, and while there's not much space between all the passengers and gear, there's at least a lot of things to hold onto when the winds get bad. We decided it was best to give you a little distance from the majority of the people, plus, you know…they're not legion, so we can't trust them," he finished darkly.

"Ah, crap. Grizz, seriously, they'll be sworn to me soon; that means you'll have to trust them, you know?" I asked.

He nodded hesitantly. "Until then, though…anyway, a bunch of us got together with the shipyard workers and put the walls and door on the cabin for you. It was mainly to keep you as safe from any possible assassins as we could, that's all."

"Well, thank you, Grizz, and anyone else who helped. I definitely prefer a room to sharing." I winked at Grizz when I caught his grin.

"Shit." My amusement immediately dampened as I peered through another open door that led out onto a small walkway above the clouds. "I kinda hoped it was better than this," I admitted.

"Seriously, it's amazing this thing flies at all, Jax," Grizz said, grinning.

"You're really not helping; you know, that right?" I asked.

"I owe you one, you know, for back in the arena." He shot me a grin.

I snorted, remembering getting everyone to cheer him. It'd been a shitty joke, just something to wind him up, but that had obviously started a competition.

We headed up a set of narrow stairs and turned right, passing deeper into the ship as we passed through larger, wider corridors. The walls were noticeably built with far more care, the feeling of imminent collapse vanishing as a sense of impressive solidity was conveyed instead.

Every ten meters or so was a recessed section in the roof, which I guessed were designed for holding magelights, and spaces had been marked out for banisters, presumably in case of rough weather or fighting. Instead of these fixtures, though, the spaces were occupied by piles of gear, thousands of planks of wood, ingots of metals, and the countless minor things that turned a ship into a home, never mind a platform of war.

The items were piled as neatly as could be, strapped together, but here and there, the strapping had come loose. We clambered over materials that filled the corridors, while sailors and engineers swore and rushed about around us, carrying armfuls of parts, or metal or wood panels, obviously working to seal up as much of the ship as possible on the go.

Most had no idea who I was, but the few who did recognize me, or more likely, noted the escort and drew the correct conclusion, straightened up and saluted, frantically trying to avoid eye contact.

"They're afraid of us?" I asked Oracle quietly, not bothering to communicate through our mind-link.

"You're a lord. They know what happens if they get a lord's attention in the wrong way," she replied sadly.

"Fuckers," I growled under my breath, making a concentrated effort to smooth my features and smile at those we passed.

Tang led us along a winding route through the bowels of the ship before guiding us up a set of wide stairs choked with equipment. Nearly ten minutes after we'd left the cabin, we finally reached the ship's bridge. A pair of legionnaires on guard duty straightened, clapping fists to chest in salute as we approached.

Tang strode forward, opening the door without knocking, and ducked inside, then stepped to the side and straightened before formally announcing to the room at large:

"High Lord Jax of Dravith, Scion of the Empire, Heir to the Imperial Throne!" For the first time in as long as I could remember, his voice was clear of the sardonic wit, the sarcasm, and general "I've seen it all before" attitude. Instead, it was clear and proud, and as I stepped into the room, I saw the effect his words had on those gathered inside.

The room was filled with people who had clearly been managing the business of flying a ship that likely massed hundreds of thousands of tons, maneuvering it safely through the air high above the sea. However, they'd dropped everything and were spinning to face the doorway, fists crashing to chests in salute. Then the ship started to list to one side, and the helmsman frantically spun and controlled the wheel again.

I noted the panic on his face as he tried to decide if letting the ship drift off course was worth "disrespecting a lord," and I couldn't help but snort in amusement.

The bridge had been designed as a large, semicircular room, flanked by stairs leading up to an exit at the back center of the room, with the arc flowing out of sight on the right and left. Clear glass filled in some of the windows covering the entire front wall, with boards hastily nailed in place over others.

I stopped a handful of steps inside the door, clapped my hand to my chest in salute to them all, then called out in as clear a voice as I could, "Relax, people; get back to whatever you were doing."

With that, everyone seemed to breathe again, and the majority turned away, the helmsman sagging in relief.

The legionnaires in the room strode forward to meet me as I started walking again, coming to a halt before me in the center of the bridge.

"Lord Jax." An older legionnaire, who stood in the center of the group, fell to one knee and bowed his head, drawing, then holding his sword out before him, pommel offered to me. "I am Romanus Dominai Perival, Legion Prefect of the Dravith Cohortes Praetoria. The legion stands ready to obey."

"Prefect Romanus," I said in greeting, reaching down and grasping him by the wrist and pulling him to his feet. "There's no need to kneel in my presence. I'm a man like any other." I smiled at the startled prefect.

"Thank you for the gesture, but from now on, you stand with me. I'm proud to have the legion join me, as it will make saving the empire far easier, but I will tell you now, Amon never required an honest man to kneel twice to him, and neither will I."

Romanus blinked in surprise and tightened his grip on my wrist. We shook once, and I released him, letting him sheathe his sword. He quickly beckoned two more legionnaires forward, introducing them as they took my offered hand in turn.

"Thank you, my lord. This is Tribune Alistor, second-in-command of the Legion of Dravith, and Restun, Centurion Primus. They are my right and left hands, respectively. Alistor deals with the men in a commander's role, as well as providing me with counsel and overseeing legalities and negotiations that I haven't the time for. And Restun, well, Restun is the legion's heart. The men follow me, but they'd die for him," Romanus said, smiling at the men with pride.

The first man nodded to me, as though uncertain, stepping back as quickly as possible. Where the dark-haired Tribune was slender, wiry, and clearly fit, considering he moved with ease in full legion armor, the Centurion Primus was tall, broad and exuded a palpable aura of health and strength. When the second man stepped forward, he grasped my wrist and squeezed hard, pumping it up and down quickly while clearly judging me as he released my wrist and stepped back.

"It's good to meet you all," I said, smiling and turning to the fourth man, who'd needed no introduction, but had hung back respectfully. "I see you there, Augustus. Come here, my friend!" I stepped forward and ignored the offered hand, instead giving him a bear hug and slapping him hard on the back.

He laughed and returned the gesture, reminding me that, while I had the physique of an Olympian now, he was a true titan. The massive number of physical points he'd clearly accrued over the years had changed him at a seemingly molecular level. I stood around the same height, but with his muscles he looked as though he'd gone past the mere standard of humanity, instead resembling a Greek marble statue of the God of War that had simply stepped down from a pedestal one day and strolled off.

"I have to ask, though." I paused, looking from one to another. "If Restun is the Primus, what is your rank again, Augustus?" I asked him curiously.

"Ah, common confusion there, Jax," Augustus replied, the use of my first name instead of my title eliciting a flinch from Alistor. "I am the Primus of the second maniple. The legion is split into four active maniples, with a fifth that deals in support, combat engineers, blacksmiths, and general camp followers, for example.

"Each maniple has a specific function and is led by a primus. Then the centurion primus is responsible for leading us. When we last talked, you mentioned a similar role in your own background, a 'first' staff sergeant, as opposed to the staff sergeant?" he reminded me.

"Ah! Totally understand now. Restun, it's a damn honor to meet you, Primus!" I said, grinning before turning back to the prefect. "It is an honor to meet you all, of course, but I hope you understand, Prefect, Tribune? I was an enlisted soldier in my home…my realm. The equivalent of a new legionnaire? So I hope that you can understand my awe at meeting a man like Restun!"

"Hah!" Romanus barked, grinning at me. "I know what you mean, High Lord Jax. I rose through the ranks with the primus watching over me. If he snapped an order now, I'd probably salute and drop into pushups without a pause."

I shared a smile with him and Augustus, gaining a respectful nod and slight grin from Restun, while Alistor remained at the back, watching me quietly.

"So, my lord, while this is our first meeting, Primus Augustus has been filling us in on your adventures and your plans, as he understands them. This is the captain of the ship, obviously awaiting your formal acceptance," Romanus said, gesturing to a tall elven woman who had remained patiently off to the left, watching our small group and waiting for her invitation to join.

"Lord Jax," she said smoothly, stepping forward and offering her right hand with a smile. "I am Athena, captain of the battleship. It is an honor to meet you."

"The honor is mine, Athena," I said formally, privately wondering about the way she was dressed. Her smart, white shirt and black trousers provided a crisp background for a blindingly gaudy red sash. A dozen or more bangles on each wrist chimed as she moved, making it clear that tiny bells were hidden amongst them. As most of the people I had encountered in the UnderVerse were either slaves, drow, or legion, I had come to expect drab, functional attire. Oracle caught my surprise and noted privately through our bond that this was the official airship captain's uniform, in part to make them easy for the crew to identify at a glance.

"So, are you happy to confirm my position as captain?" she asked bluntly.

"How did you get the position?" I countered after a blink.

"Elise came begging, said she needed a captain crazy enough to run a gauntlet, especially one that'd be able to put up with the ship only being bare bones, letting her team build it as we flew."

"And you said yes?" I asked her.

She shot me a wry grin. "Well, it helped that she was asking while she was smashing open the cage that they'd been holding me in," she admitted, dipping her right hand into the neck of her high-collared shirt and lifting a thick black collar up into sight before dropping it back down with a shrug. "I'd have done it for that alone, but she told me that in your lands, slavery isn't the done thing. I figured, what the hell. Not like I've got much to lose, after all."

"Shit." I shook my head and stepped close to her. "Do you mind?" I asked, gesturing to her neck.

"Uh, no?" She looked at me quizzically as she leaned back slightly. We paused, looking at each other for a long second before Oracle, who'd been silently observing from her perch on my right shoulder, floated into the air between us.

"You'll all get used to this; Jax isn't very articulate," she explained reassuringly. "Athena, he wants to look at your collar. Is this okay?" Athena looked from Oracle to me, and I gritted my teeth at my own forgetfulness.

"Sorry, everyone. This is Oracle; she's my companion, my lover, and also the keeper of knowledge for the Great Tower," I said, figuring it was best to get it all out of the way straight away.

"Uh…okay…I guess…wait, lover?" Athena stammered, inspecting Oracle's diminutive size then considering me, flashing a reflexive look downwards before she could help herself.

"Goddammit. Oracle, take your full size, please. The last thing I need is rumors starting," I grumbled, rubbing the bridge of my nose.

Oracle laughed and blurred; there was no better way to describe it, really. One minute, she was about a foot tall, while the next, she hovered slightly before touching down, just over five and a half feet of stunning, voluptuous beauty.

"She changes her size whenever she wants," I clarified. "She is usually around six inches to a foot tall most of the time now, for some reason."

"It makes people act nicer to me," Oracle clarified as she bounced her hair with one hand. "Besides, when I'm this size, everyone just stares at my tits and ass, and it's not like I can't cast spells the same, big or small," she added. Athena, Romanus, and Alistor flinched, looking away quickly, amusement flowing through the bond I shared with Oracle.

She'd deliberately been bouncing gently on the balls of her feet so that she could draw their eyes and catch them. Restun had glanced at her once, clearly assessing whether she was a threat, and had gone straight back to standing at attention, unphased by her beauty, while Augustus was used to her and her tricks by now.

"Uh, so, my collar?" Athena said, shaking her head and trying to get the conversation back on track. I reached out and hooked a finger under the rim of it as she pulled it back up into view for me.

"Right, moving swiftly on," I muttered, studying the collar. I decided to try something I'd not done for a while, but something that had been in the back of my mind for days. I reached out, or in, to Amon.

"You there, you crazy old fart?" I directed to him, only to be met with silence. *"Amon!"* I tried again, and I felt…something, a stirring…like when you've woken up after a long sleep to find you've slept on your arm and it's gone numb. That sensation just as feeling starts to return, when it's as much looking at your fingers moving, as it is actually feeling the motion, the point where you can just feel it starting to respond.

That was what I felt.

"Amon, are you there?" I tried again, and this time, I felt Oracle join me, doing something I couldn't quite define.

"Slaves…" I felt and heard him respond. *"No, slaves were banned, they were…freed…that's it…they were freed. No slavery in the empire,"* he continued, before reverting to mumbling and muttering.

"That's the point, Amon!" I growled at him. *"I need to know how you helped me to shatter the collars before!"*

"Break them…yes…break them all," I heard him mumble. A sense of anger rose briefly, followed by confusion. Just as I was about to give up, a sudden burst of information flooded my mind, staggering me mentally and physically.

CHAPTER TWO

"My lord!" Romanus cried, darting forward, but before he could reach me, Restun caught me under the arms and steadied me.

"Lord Jax?" Athena asked, concerned, stepping back and tucking away her collar as every legionnaire in the room went on high alert.

"I'm all right," I said, shaking my head, dazed by the information.

"I'll deal with that, Jax. Just relax. You do what you need to do here, but then you need to rest," Oracle said firmly, taking my hand as Augustus dragged a chair across and Restun helped me into it.

"I'm all right," I repeated, panting, my heart hammering at the barely sensed information I'd just absorbed. It felt as if someone had poured the ice water melt from a glacier directly into my brain, shocking and freezing me at the same time. So much knowledge bubbled away in my mind. Even as I frantically tried to grasp and understand it, it began to seep away, a weak human mind such as mine unable to absorb it all.

"Oracle," I whispered. "Find the key."

"I will." She nodded soberly to me before shrinking down and landing on my chest. Leaning back against me and closing her eyes, she dove into the mass of knowledge, searching for the key to that lightning attack we'd unleashed on the city, the way we'd torn the collars apart, interrupting the owner's control and slamming the power back into the control devices, causing them to explode.

I didn't need the explosion now, but I needed the key to that power to completely free the slaves we had brought aboard.

"I sent Legionnaire Grizz to verify whether you were well enough to join us, Lord Jax; I apologize. I should have waited. You had, after all, sustained terrible injuries. Let us get you safely back to your cabin, or perhaps an interior one? Captain, can one of the storage cabins be cleared now? With speed, please?" Romanus said, his tone and expression making it clear to Athena that it wasn't a request.

"Of course, legion prefect." She straightened her shoulders and called over two of the bridge crew. "Tal, Viktor, get the cabin next to here, the big one, cleared out, right goddamn now!"

The pair saluted and ran from the bridge.

"Ummm, look, I know this is a long shot, but my brother Tommy…" I started to ask, only to stop when Augustus shook his head.

"I'm sorry Jax, but no, we didn't find him."

"Dammit." I muttered, closing my eyes and swaying slightly as the secondary effects hit me.

"Grizz, Westin, Holtic, go help," Romanus ordered, and all three saluted before sprinting to assist the other two. "I should have…"

"I'll be okay," I muttered, interrupting him and rubbing my temples. "It's nothing you did; it's Amon. The bastard never does things by half." I squeezed my eyes shut, missing the glances the small group shared.

"Amon? As in, the Eternal Emperor Amon?" Romanus asked after several seconds.

I nodded, wincing as my head felt like it might fall off. "Yeah, I can talk to him. Most of the time, he's fuck-all use, but sometimes…wow…that hurt. Felt like downloading a kilo of ice cream into my brain. Talk about brain freeze."

"Iced…cream?" Augustus asked in confusion.

"You guys don't have that, huh?" I asked, wincing up at him blearily as he shook his head in confusion. "Well, you're in for a treat at some point, then. My ex loved the stuff an' insisted we learn ta make it ourselves. Remin' me when winter comes. Hell, remin' me when I learn an ice spell," I mumbled, slightly slurring my words.

"Lord Jax, I'm sorry. I didn't realize that looking at my collar would do—" Athena started, and I shook my head.

"No, nothing you did, don't worry. It just made me aware of an issue we needed to address. How many freed slaves do we have with us; still collared, I mean?" I asked the group in general, and Alistor was the one to respond.

"One hundred and seven, Lord Jax," he stated flatly.

"Then I have a hundred and seven reasons to get this sorted damn quickly," I replied, making sure Oracle was safe as I stood up by cradling her to my chest. "I'll sort this in the next few days, or at least, I'll do my best. I promise, Athena."

I nodded to her. "As to the captaincy, if Elise picked you out, then yes, that's good enough for me. The chief engineer should damn well know what the ship needs." I paused, looking around. "I assume she is the chief engineer, right? When I spoke to her before, she was, anyway."

"Yes, my lord," Athena responded, smiling widely. "Thank you! I won't let you down. Elise is the chief engineer, and she's been swearing constantly about some skillbooks? She'd have been here now to greet you, but we couldn't find her. She and her team are constantly running from issue to issue, trying to get the ship up and running properly."

"Is everyone okay?" I asked Augustus, turning to him. "Oracle said they were, but I've no idea what's going on here, and…"

"Point," he said, shaking his head in apology. "Jax, how about we fill you in on everything first? Then you can make some quick decisions and go back to bed and get some rest?" His offer made me nod in agreement, albeit slowly and carefully. "Prefect?" Augustus asked, and Romanus nodded to him to continue.

"Very well. So, if we roll back to the last few hours in the city, Jax, when we were boarding the ships and while Jian had his little 'accident,' Prefect Romanus and the rest of the legion were taking the shipyards. They essentially stormed the security posts, wiped the floor with the city guards, and took command of the battleship. We also made off with three cruisers, including the two in their berths and the one that we boarded straight from the Skyking's lair."

Augustus pointed out of the window with a slight smile as he went on.

"That's the *Star's Glory*, as well. It's a crappy little trader vessel, but it's armed and it flies, so to hell with it, and I know you wanted to take it."

I nodded, a little smile quirking my lips as I glanced at the ship in the distance and the clearly huge spiders crawling across it.

"Last of all, three fast scouts, one we claimed during the fight, and two that were at rest. Mal came through for us, stripping the Stockpile down to the nails and rat shit. We've got more parts than we know what to do with, honestly. He brought us the essentials from the main Stockpile and practically every manastone in the city, from what I can tell.

"There are several dozen tons of hardwood and planks, literally dozens more barrels of pitch and naphtha, all the nails we could ever need, and best of all, the sneaky bastard even raided the ships' weapons store when we got to the shipyard. Made it out with ten cannons, two of which can't be fired unless they're integrated into the superstructure, they're that powerful.

"The legion and other crews also cleared out the rest of the stockpiles in the shipyard as best we could. So, we've got everything from spare engines to toilet seats, magelights to navigation equipment. Even the cooks have a dozen new knives each. Food-wise, we could feed these refugees for at least a year, provided they like beans and bread." Augustus shrugged casually, as if to say it was all the same to him.

"Once you were injured, I took direct command," Romanus interjected, taking over from Augustus. "I ordered the ships boarded, and we took off, bearing southeast, after a discussion with Augustus and a disreputable man named Mal, who claimed to be your 'right hand in all this mess.'

"We had two of the cruisers with captains who knew what they were doing fire on the shipyards when we left, and, as we'd already been declared apostates, we took the opportunity to, ah, demonstrate our disapproval of the Dark Legion as we passed over their marshalling grounds."

"We shit over the side," Augustus clarified, making me laugh aloud.

"Now, now, Maniple Primus…but yes, we, ah…did relieve ourselves thoroughly as we passed overhead. Anyway, moving on, we set a course out to sea, waited until we were out of sight of the land, then adjusted course for the Sunken City. We're currently about three hours out from landing. Unfortunately, we are merely limping along, due to the unfinished condition of the battleship. I dispatched two fast scouts to look the location over, and they found that it is not as uninhabited as we had hoped." He sighed, squaring his shoulders and clearly waiting for me to change my mind about the direction or reprimand him for something.

"There are two camps present, presumably one from Himnel and one from Narkolt, judging from the flags their ships fly. Both have an airship on standby. The camps are ringed with stakes and what appear to be defensive positions, but it's unclear if this is to defend against each other or the Sunken City's inhabitants.

"The scouts also made preliminary maps of the entrances to the upper city and marked the best landing areas. I gave the orders that we were to land as soon as possible, the larger ships at least, with the scouts staying high and watching out for anything heading our way." Romanus cleared his throat uncomfortably before going on, glancing at me.

"The engineers are aware they'll have a short period of time to enact any repairs and essentially do any work that they can to improve the ships while we're grounded before we set off again. There's also the matter of that smuggler called Mal, who is evidently in command of a ship called the *Falcon*. He said that you'd given orders that the next destination after this was to be the Great Tower of Dravith, and Maniple Primus Augustus vouched for that. Is this still the aim?" Romanus asked carefully.

"It is; is there a problem with this?" I asked, eying the legionnaire.

"Not to the final destination, my lord, no, but the smuggler had said that we were to stop for no more than a single day before launching northeast, then swinging around to head for the tower, staying out of sight of the land and any following ships.

"I would request we stay grounded longer, however. Several days docked on the Sunken City would enable us to search it more thoroughly, enact greater repairs and upgrades to the ships, and possibly even make the battleship into a weapon in fact as well as name?"

"Sounds reasonable," I agreed. "Surely there won't be much to loot from the city, though. I mean, it's been here for a damn long time, right?"

"Yes and no, my lord—"

"Jax," I interrupted. "For the love of the gods, Romanus, we're going to be spending a lot of time together. From here on out, just call me Jax, please. In public, fair enough, call me 'lord' and all that, be formal if and when it's needed, but in private? Please don't. It's easier on all of us."

"Very well, Jax. Augustus explained that you prefer informality, but as we've yet to get a measure for each other, well, it seemed prudent to err on the side of caution."

"Yup, understand that, but seriously, Jax is fine. And as to my decisions, if you think I'm making a mistake, speak up. I might not agree, or I might even tell you to get fucked, but I will listen, I promise that. I *want* to hear your advice, not have you blow sunshine up my arse, okay?" I said, meeting the eyes of every person in the small group, waiting for nods and verbal acknowledgement before moving on. "You were saying, Romanus?"

"Yes, thank you. So, getting back to the Sunken City. Do you know much of its past?" the Centurion Primus asked, continuing when I shook my head. "The Sunken City was discovered, at least as far as we can find in historical records, around a hundred years ago, by some of the first of the crude airships. Gnome-built, I'll stress.

"We—as in the rest of the races—have had airships for about thirty years now. It's long been believed that the gnomes found the secret to the airships aboard a similar wreck, or in a vault somewhere in the mountains. This Sunken City's true location was kept from most of the realm by the gnomes until about twenty years ago, when too many sailors had learned of it for it to remain hidden any longer.

"The gnomes had apparently looted most of the upper floors by the time the cities of Himnel and Narkolt sent their forces to search the place. The lack of any real loot and the high concentration of specters, not to mention standard undead creatures, meant it was abandoned as quickly as it was found. Once airships became more commonplace in the cities, researchers begged, borrowed, and stole enough to get out here, and it was when those first crude airships reached the Sunken City that true exploration began.

"It is heavily overgrown with various plant life, and the surrounding shoals are extremely hazardous to water-bound vessels. This means that a small group of researchers is stationed on the leeward side of the city from Himnel, while a small group from Narkolt has set up camp on the windward side, with a squad of soldiers protecting each." He smiled ruefully, shaking his head. "Not that I think they'll want to mess with a force this large, of course."

"Probably not!" I agreed, grinning.

"As I'd mentioned, when the city was discovered, it was covered with plant life and surrounded by these shoals, it was initially assumed to be a small island raised up by the Cataclysm. Due to the misconception, it went largely ignored until the airships spotted a pattern to its shape and landed. Several abandoned camps were found, and finally, a known pirate ship that had been beached in a small bay was unearthed, arousing suspicions that at least one pirate had been using it to store their ill-gotten gains.

"That, of course, led to a race to search the island, which is how they found the truth of the Sunken City. The top floor has been thoroughly mapped out and stripped bare, but the lower you go, as I've heard it, the more difficult it becomes, with creatures nesting, collapsed and flooded levels, and a variety of guardians."

"What kind of guardians?" I asked, sitting forward quickly.

"There is a wide variety, unfortunately; mainly spirits known as revenants or specters. They are believed to be the original crew, cursed to spend eternity protecting the city as punishment for their failure to protect it in life. Both types are extremely aggressive, and they won't stay dead, so their presence had greatly slowed exploration and looting. Then there are the more common undead, risen skeletons, adventurers and explorers who were killed, that sort of thing. Lastly, there are rumors of feral creatures and golems roaming the lower levels as well."

"Golems?" I perked up hopefully.

"Yes, and they are apparently extremely hostile to explorers, unfortunately. They seem to be unconcerned with the upper levels, but the ones closer to the core, they protect most assiduously. Teams sent into those never return."

"Okay, well we can take a few days on the island, see what we can find, and if the golems can be hacked, maybe?" I said to myself, rubbing my chin.

"Hacked?" Romanus asked. "Hacked apart, you mean? They are apparently made of several different forms, some metal, some stone."

"Ah, no; where I come from, there were groups that 'hacked' secure locations and items, it means to take control of them, to remove their allegiance to the city, for example, and convert them to serve me."

"Is this possible?" He frowned. "I mean, I saw the golems on the main deck, but…"

"The deck?" I interrupted him abruptly. "What are they doing on the deck?"

"Standing," interjected Athena. "They just stand there all day and get in the damn way. I've had my people shore up the deck underneath them, but I tell you, a wooden ship, especially one that's half-built, is no place for those monstrosities!"

"No, I mean they're just *standing* there? They've not been put to work?" I gasped, horrified, looking around. "Augustus, I told you I set them to obey your orders."

"I've not been able to order them, Jax, unfortunately, and even when we arrive, the entrances to the Sunken City are legendarily small. They're unlikely to be able to fit—"

"Augustus?" I cut him off.

"Yes, Jax?" he answered with a note of confusion.

"You do remember what the golems are, right?"

"I do?"

"Two of them are complex level, so they can order the others around. If you need things moved, like the wood that fills the corridors, or walls held in place in order to secure them, the golems can make that happen. The one that's a servitor class is complex as well, which means it can independently build and repair shit. Tell me you at least made it help the engineers?"

"I did not, Jax. In fact, I was ordered to stay away from them," Augustus said stoically.

"Wait, so they didn't ignore you because I set the orders incorrectly; you were ordered to stay clear of them?" I asked, and he nodded shortly. "Why?" I asked Romanus, straining to keep my patience at the thought of how many hours of work had been wasted, then he shook his head.

"I wasn't aware of these orders. I..." He turned suddenly to Alistor, who'd been growing paler by the second. "Alistor?" he pressed, and the tribune swallowed hard before straightening.

"I ordered the Maniple Primus to stay away from the golems. In fact, I ordered everyone stay clear of them, including your 'people,' *Lord Jax*. I received a report of them roaming wild and devastating the Magical Emporium just prior to our...exit...from the city. I see no reason to risk them doing the same here." He stared at me, as though daring me to countermand his orders.

I frowned, then replied.

"Well, I can understand you being cautious, but I'll be clear. Next time I order that someone has authority over something, such as Augustus having the direct authority to command the golems, they are to have unopposed access to that item. The golems didn't run wild. They were under my orders, and I took control of them; that's how they ended up on this airship." I tried to maintain an even tone of voice, while internally, I was growling at this jumped-up shit.

"So, it's true, then? You ordered them to loot and rob an innocent man's property?" Alistor asked acidly.

"No, *Tribune*," I retorted harshly. "*I* robbed the shop, and if you want to view the golems as artifacts, I stole them as well. I, however, don't. I am at war with that prick Barabarattas, and they were being controlled using imperial authority to guard a particular location.

"The 'Emporium' was originally a golem repair facility for the city, one of several, and as near as I can tell, the only one that survived the Cataclysm. I used my authority as *High Lord of fucking Dravith* to take command of the site, and yes, I took everything I could, considering that *the city is at war with me, and the golems remain the property of the empire!*" Realizing how loud my voice had gotten and the way that the entire room was staring at me, I paused and took a deep, calming breath.

"Look, I apologize for shouting," I said, reaching out a hand placatingly. "But seriously, you're accusing me of a fucking crime? I'm at war with that city, and as such, so is the empire. You, as a legionnaire of the empire and as an imperial subject, are therefore also at war with the city, which means you can loot the shit out of it, if it's for the greater good, okay?"

I pinched the bridge of my nose, feeling a headache building. The warning, wriggling bar of light in the left of my vision, which had always signaled a migraine incoming, was growing brighter.

"We accepted you as our lord, Jax. Never fear; we understand our place, and the responsibility of the Legion," Romanus said soothingly. "I apologize; you've barely survived your injuries, and we have exacerbated them, giving you stress at such a time. Perhaps if we could get some clarity on your orders, then you could rest for the day? Tomorrow, we can look to address more details," Romanus offered.

"Fine," I said tiredly, rubbing my eyes again. "Look, I'll go rest for a few hours, see if I can get rid of this migraine. As to orders: yes, land on the Sunken City, get everyone working on making the battleship as safe as possible, and send overtures to the researchers in both camps. Ask them to come tomorrow morning at…fuck knows, first light?" I asked, getting a subtle nod from Augustus. "Right. First light, get them to come to our camp, and we'll talk to them. I want to know what they know. As to the golems…" I eyed Alistor sternly, before looking back to Romanus.

"Augustus is in charge of them. I want them used to their maximum potential." I shifted my focus to Augustus. "Use them as you see fit, but the ship is the priority. If you think that it'd be better served by having them on sentry duty and the legion helping with construction, fine. If not, also fine.

"Just discuss it with the engineers, okay? And make damn sure the servitor is put to work immediately; you've no idea what those things could do," I said, closing my eyes as the glare built in direct proportion to the pain. I knew instinctively that attempting to use magic to heal this would be a mistake, and Oracle wasn't talking, since she was still too busy trying to make sense of Amon's info-dump.

"Augustus," I whispered, my eyes still closed.

"Yes, Jax?" came the response, his voice now at my side.

"Get me somewhere I can rest, please, mate. Somewhere dark." I was painfully aware that while I could push through this, I'd regret it later, something was very wrong.

"Yes, my lord," he said, strong hands on either side, guiding me from the bridge.

The next few minutes passed in a blur, as every time I opened my eyes, all I could make out was a smear of bright light and colors, and pain, so much pain.

Then I was in a room, being guided to a bed, then doors were being softly closed, and the last thing I heard was a familiar voice that made me release a relieved breath, trusting fully that I was safe.

"Jax, I'm here, sleep well," Bane said.

CHAPTER THREE

I t was the change in the ambient sound that brought me back to consciousness. The steady, ever-present *thrummm* of the engines; a mixture of a purring diesel engine and the warm hum of magic was the closest I could match it to, and it had changed.

Instead of the steady purr, interspersed with occasional rapid-fire bursts of the engines altering course, I had been awoken by the sound of creaking and breaking wood, of branches rubbing against the hull, then, finally, of the engines dying away. A creaking filled the air as the ship settled slowly, weight returning to the supports.

I blinked slowly, opening my eyes cautiously and feeling that particular weird feeling you get after a migraine where your skull is simultaneously too tight and yet feels like a balloon that might either pop or float away at any second, the hollow space surrounding your mind that had been filled with pain, now suddenly free.

"O"—*cough*—"Oracle?" I managed, feeling her close by.

"I'm here, Jax," she said, flying into view from where she'd been hovering in the air nearby. "Are you okay?" she asked.

"Yeah, what happened?" I replied groggily. "God, it tastes like a cat shit in my mouth."

"Well, I didn't see a cat around, but Grizz checked on you a few minutes ago." Bane's voice offered from the corner.

"Well, he's got the morals of a cat, from what I hear, but as long as he didn't stick anything in my mouth, I'll let that slide," I muttered, pausing. "He didn't, right?" I asked, feeling terror rising.

"No, he crept in like a mouse and left the same way. I think you scared the entire legion, Jax. They've been tiptoeing around outside, threatening to murder anyone who disturbs you with a loud noise."

"Crap," I muttered, rubbing my face. "I hope they've not scared the crew too much. Seriously, Oracle, what happened?" I asked again.

"Amon," she said simply. "He's simultaneously millennia dead and utterly oblivious to what you're capable of. When he was alive, well, he was exceptional and seriously high-leveled; he doesn't really have much of an accurate impression of what a living human can handle. You remember the issues you had with spellbooks?" she reminded me.

"Well, Amon just gave you a whole new level of that. Think, the equivalent of ten spellbooks or more; he's given you a basic grounding in so many different subjects, I can't even figure them all out." She landed on my chest and gazed down at me. "Luckily, removing the Valspar and being healed by Jenae and Mistress Nerin repaired almost all of your previous brain damage.

"The fact that this was a direct mental transfer of knowledge minimized the impact as well, and I was able to soothe some of that absorption. The headache should be about the worst of what you have to suffer this time. Interestingly, considering the spells that you used, 'Ability' would probably be closer to the truth of what you've been given.

"Specifically, this ability, the one that you used to free the slaves in the city, is a mixture of several spells so complex I really haven't got a handle on them yet, let alone how you activated it instinctively and fueled it out of pure righteous fury. All I really remember is that it felt *amazing*," she said, giving a little shudder as she closed her eyes, then pursed her lips in thought as they popped back open.

"I am positive that it was a solid *Ability*, like a capital-A ability, that you used as well. Much like the way that certain species can perform different feats, like the djinn can phase their bodies into mist and back, or the way that a warrior can use Taunt. Those are both Abilities; one is intrinsic to the creature, while the other is a gained, or learned, Ability. You getting this?" she asked.

I nodded in confirmation. "Yeah, I think so. Go on…"

"Well, I think this is an intrinsic Ability: something that is part of you, of who, and what, you are. You haven't read your notifications for a while; now might be a good time," she suggested hopefully.

"Okay," I shifted to sit upright, grinning as she effortlessly floated into the air before me, her tiny wings blurring. "I need a drink first, and damn, flying does look fun," I admitted as I watched her.

"It is!" she replied with a smile as Bane materialized from the darkness of the corner, stepping forward and offering me a canteen. I nodded my thanks and swigged from it, washing my mouth out first, then swallowing a second mouthful and feeling better as the cool liquid ran down my throat. As I handed it back, I eyed Bane's gear with concern.

"You're a mess, mate," I said. He shrugged nonchalantly, moving fluidly back to the corner where he'd been crouching. Bane was a Mer, or a Tia'Almeratic, as the race called themselves.

Essentially, Bane was an amphibian frigging ninja. He stood about six feet tall with no visible eyes or ears. Instead, his face and head were smooth, intersected only by a mouth that contained a mix of sharp incisors, canines, and flatter molars. About three quarters of the way back on his head, where a human would have hair, just behind the ears, a ridge looped around, running from behind his jaw to halfway up his skull.

From under this ridge hung a nest of tentacles. They were short and stubby, and long and thin, and every shape in between, and they moved constantly, shifting like a nest of vipers. These tentacles were how he saw the world. He somehow produced a kind of sonar, or at least that was what I understood, called worldsense.

He could perceive far more with the sense than I could with my eyes, due to being totally unreliant on light, and the peculiar nature of it allowed him to accurately map things. He tended to be amazing at finding traps and other such hidden dangers. He had four arms and two legs, wore mainly leather and chitin armor, typically carried a pair of short stabbing spears, and almost always had several sets of daggers, knives, and throwing blades secreted about himself, even when he was off duty.

He was sarcastic, snappy, and the sneakiest motherfucker I'd ever met, able to blend in almost anywhere, through a mix of a racial ability, heavy training, and investing his points in becoming an assassin-hunter class. He'd appointed himself, with his trainer's approval, as my personal bodyguard.

During our time in Himnel, he'd recruited an elven legionnaire called Tang to join him, and the pair kept me as safe as possible around the clock.

Bane had become a close friend, even more so now that he understood the male bonding ritual that was shit-talking, and we spent at least half of every day trying to wind each other up.

Normally, I could expect to be mocked for "napping" in the middle of the day or something. The fact he hadn't made a single crack meant he'd been seriously worried.

His armor was torn, battered, and missing in sections, and I clearly remembered the terror and fury I'd felt when he'd been gravely injured in the fight to reach the Skyking. His chest armor had clearly taken the brunt of the damage. It was held together with twine in places now and the rest, well, twine was the best of it, really, and I shook my head in dismay.

"Seriously, Bane, we need to replace your armor, mate," I insisted, frowning at him.

"And your own," he replied calmly. I glanced down at it, noting the multiple sections that had been hastily stitched back together, the missing links and torn sections of gear, and the way that I was constantly having to pull my belt up, as even that, old faithful weapon that it was, concealing my razorwire, was starting to give out.

"Good point. I think a trip to the armorers is due," I muttered, "and if we look this bad, god knows the rest of the team will as well. Shame, really, I like these pants." I tugged at a fold of Gloom spidersilk.

"Jax, I know you feel like your head's full of wool right now, but focus, okay?" Oracle said, floating closer. "You really need to read your notifications."

"Right," I said, rubbing my face and trying to clear my mind fully. "Sorry."

I pulled up the notifications and read carefully, finding that I had quite a few of them awaiting my attention.

> **You made progress in a Quest given to you by the Goddess Jenae: Bring Home the Bacon.**
>
> The Goddess Jenae has commanded you to retrieve all you can from those who skulk and raid the corpse of the empire. Take your rightful place as their lord and bring back that which you need to repair the seat of your Power, the Great Tower.
>
> **Recover Magical Artifacts and Technologies:** 27/?
> **Retrieve Manastones:** 327/100
> **Recruit Additional Citizens:** 937/100
> **Recruit Skilled Crafters:** 31/100
> **Recruit a Tower Healer:** 1/1
> *Bonuses will be given for exceeding these numbers.*
> **Reward:** Basic functionality of the Great Tower, Unknown, 250,000xp
>
> *Congratulations!*
>
> **Through hard work and perseverance,**
> **you have increased your stats by the following:**
>
> **Constitution +2**
>
> **Intelligence +1**
>
> **Continue to train and learn to increase this further.**

I quickly pulled up my stats, reading them over and nodding to myself as I found the differences from the last fight.

Name: Jax				
Titles: Strategos: 5% boost to damage resistance, Fortifier: 5% boost to defensive structure integrity, Champion of Jenae: One search for hidden knowledge every 24 hours				
Class: Spellsword > Justicar > Champion of Jenae > Imperial Magekiller			**Renown:** Imperial Scion, Lord of Dravith	
Level: 18			**Progress:** 83,972/265,000	
Patron: Jenae, Goddess of Fire and Exploration			**Points to Distribute:** 7 **Meridian Points to Invest:** 0	
Stat	**Current points**	**Description**	**Effect**	**Progress to next level**
Agility	44	Governs dodge and movement.	+340% maximum movement speed and reflexes, (+10% movement in darkness, -20% movement in daylight)	38/100
Charisma	23	Governs likely success to charm, seduce, or threaten	+130% success in interactions with other beings	71/100
Constitution	45 (40)	Governs health and health regeneration	880 health, regen 57.75 points per 600 seconds, (+10% regen due to soul bond, -20 health due to soul bond, each point invested now worth 20 health)	19/100
Dexterity	37	Governs ability with weapons and crafting success	+270% to weapon proficiency, +27% to the chances of crafting success	48/100
Endurance	33 (30)	Governs stamina and stamina regeneration	660 stamina, regen 23 points per 30 seconds, (each point now worth 20 stamina)	36/100
Intelligence	60	Governs base mana and number of spells able to be learned	580 mana, spell capacity: 33 (31 + 2 from items), (-20 mana due to soul bond)	15/100
Luck	24	Governs overall chance of bonuses	+14% chance of a favorable outcome	82/100
Perception	25	Governs ranged damage and chance to spot traps or hidden items	+150% ranged damage, +15% chance to spot traps or hidden items	44/100
Strength	31 (28)	Governs damage with melee weapons and carrying capacity	+21 damage with melee weapons, +210% maximum carrying capacity	63/100
Wisdom	35 (30)	Governs mana regeneration and memory	+250% mana recovery, 1.75 points per minute, 250% more likely to remember things, (-50% mana regeneration until mana manipulation reaches level 10)	41/100

Basically, I'd leaped upwards like I'd had my dick stapled to a rocket lately. It wasn't exactly a surprise, as I'd done almost nothing but fight since leaving the tower—hell, since finding out Lou had been fucking Martin, my entire world had gone mental. I'd either been training, enduring torture, fighting for my life, facing the creatures of nightmare, or riding a flying ship with a shapeshifting, sex-crazed wisp. It was mental, all that had happened, but I sure as hell wouldn't swap it for the world. I pulled up the last few notifications, finding one that was totally new.

Congratulations, Admiral!
You have taken command of a fleet.
Current crew condition: Cautiously optimistic.

<u>Fleet assets:</u>
1x Battleship:

Unnamed: Unarmed
> Crew: 46
> Passengers: 470
> Condition: 34% Hull Integrity.

3x Cruisers:

Atlantessa: 6x Cannons, 1x Heavy Lightning Cannon
> Crew: 13
> Passengers: 58

Sigmar's Fist: 4x Cannons, 3x Heavy Mortars
> Crew: 18
> Passengers: 57

Ragnarök: 6x Cannons, 1x Fireball Generator
> Crew: 19
> Passengers: 57

3x Fast Scouts:

Link's Arrival: 1x Cannon
> Crew: 8
> Passengers: 39

Furies' Awakening: 1x Cannon
> Crew: 9
> Passengers: 44

Summer's Promise: 1x Cannon
> Crew: 9
> Passengers: 43

Trader:

Star's Glory: 1 Cannon
> Crew: 7
> Passengers: 49

Due to the fact that you were unconscious while the fleet was assembled and took no direct part in its capture, no experience will be awarded for acquiring these vessels beyond that which has already been awarded.

"What the hell?" I muttered to myself, shaking my head. "I gave the orders, made the plans, with others, yeah, but still!" I grumbled irritably as I read through all the details. It didn't give a further breakdown of passengers, to my disappointment. Knowing if all the Legion were in one ship, for example, would help, but still, even the minimal information gave me a much better idea of what was going on.

I dismissed the window, thinking that I really needed to find a proper Admiral for this fleet, as I really didn't have time to learn another skillset. I mentally tagged it as job number three-hundred and sixty-seven thousand, nine hundred and four on my to-do list.

I was joking, even with myself, but it really did feel like that at times.

Then I had an evil thought, and decided it was Oren's problem. That was what I sort of paid him for, after all. Or it would be; if I paid him.

I pulled up the last notification and grinned as I read it, realizing that this was what Oracle had been waiting for me to see.

Congratulations!

New Ability Unlocked!

As an Imperial Scion and acknowledged Heir to the Imperial Throne, you gain new Abilities in direct relation to the number of your followers. Increase your loyal population to increase these abilities.

New Ability: Righteous Rage
The sight of your subjects, even unwitting and unsworn as some may be, has awoken the Righteous Rage of the Imperial Throne! For a cost of 200 health, mana, and stamina per second, you can reach out and touch your subjects, freeing those who have been unlawfully imprisoned, and turning the devices of their imprisonment against their captors.

Beware: All Imperial Abilities come with a permanent cost. Utilizing an ability such as this will change you and those around you in ways great and small.

"I see it," I said simply, opening my eyes and meeting Oracle's impatient gaze.

"Really?!" she squealed, closing her eyes and examining the details before letting out a cry of celebration. "It is! It really is!"

She threw herself at me, knocking me off the small bed I'd been reclining on as she reverted to full size, and the damn bed gave out under us, reduced to so much kindling with a crash.

"Want me to leave the room?" Bane asked sardonically as Oracle and I laid there, grinning idiotically at each other, my blanket half-covering us from where it had slipped off the bed.

"Oh, sounds fun!" Oracle said, grinning, just as the door opened and Grizz stuck his head in.

"Is everything okay? What happened?" he asked anxiously, searching around, three more legionnaires just visible in the corridor behind him.

"Oracle is getting frisky, apparently," Bane said dryly, and Grizz grinned, sheathing his sword.

"Boss! Are you okay?" he repeated, stepping inside, then pausing. "Unless you really do want some 'alone time,' if you know what I mean. Want me to move the guys away from the door so they can't hear as much?"

"Oh god," I muttered, recalling the earlier reactions to my activities with Oracle. "These walls don't stop any noise, do they?"

"Nope! They actually make them louder in places. Weird, the way the ship is laid out; some things can be heard from one end to the other, practically!" He didn't even bother trying to hide his shit-eating grin.

"I don't ever want you to confirm if the entire ship heard Oracle and me getting our rocks off. Never. Understand?" I said in as calm and dignified a manner as possible in conjunction with lying on the floor with a stunningly beautiful woman atop me, amidst the remains of a broken bed.

"Got you there. Don't worry, boss. I'll never confirm that the entire legion were placing bets on how long you'd go; don't worry."

"Thanks, Grizz, I appreciate that," I grumbled, facepalming.

"Grizz," Oracle said sweetly. "Do I have to hit you with lightning again to shut you up, or are you going to stop that tongue all on your own?"

"Uh…lightning, probably." Grizz laughed, then ducked hastily back into the corridor.

"I swear I'm going to toast his nuts one of these days," Oracle threatened in a low growl.

"You know Grizz, though," I said as she shifted back into her fairy form and took off, while I clambered to my feet. "He'd probably like it."

"Probably!" Grizz's cheerful voice agreed from the corridor, making me shake my head while trying to stifle a laugh.

"Want us to get him for you, my lord?" a voice offered. I looked out as one of the other legionnaires met my searching gaze, obviously testing the waters.

"Hell yes," I said, smiling evilly.

"Whoa, no fair!" Grizz shouted, his voice filled with laughter as two of those on guard duty tore off out of sight after him, the sound of fleeing feet ringing through the wooden halls. Another two moved effortlessly into view, standing on either side of the door as one reached in and tugged the door closed.

"How many are out there?" I asked Bane.

"Eight or ten; the number changes regularly. I think two were assigned to you, then the others just sort of showed up. From what I can hear, they're worried about you, and they're determined to ensure that nothing else will happen to you now that they've found you."

"Did I just get a couple hundred baby-sitters?" I asked slowly, as Oracle moved to the side and I started to get up.

"Makes my job easier," said Bane smugly.

"I hate you."

"That's nice."

"Jax, what are you doing?" Oracle asked, interrupting the byplay between Bane and me.

"Getting dressed." I sighed, pulling my boots on regretfully. When they'd taken me to wherever I was, they'd helpfully removed my boots, gauntlets, and swords, then covered me with a blanket. I quickly pulled my gear back on, taking the time to actually inspect the worn patches on the gauntlets, the sections of my shoes that were nearly worn through, and the generally shitty state of my gear. "Man, I didn't realize how bad it was getting. "

"It's seen some hard use," Bane agreed, standing up and reaching over to pick something up. "Here."

He threw something to me, and I caught it easily. The battered object was my helm, or what was left of it.

The black headpiece was battered, cut, and dented, with half of one side hanging loose where the arrow had hit, the banded metal insert dented and scored by the impact.

"Damn, it was that close?" I asked, fingering it and remembering the last few seconds of the fight for the shipyards, when that arrow had hit me in the head, ending my involvement for the night.

"It was. We honestly feared you were dead," he said soberly, gesturing to it. "I suggest a replacement, and soon."

"Yeah," I breathed, dropping the helm into my bag of spatial folding. "Right; let's go see what's going on, and make a plan for the Sunken City." I walked to the door, pulling it open to the sight of almost a dozen legionnaires standing in the corridor, fully armed and armored. Shouts and the sound of scuffling filtered to me from the far end. I nodded to the legionnaires, who straightened on seeing me.

"My lord, how can we serve?" one of them asked with a salute.

"For a start, you can relax. I'm not made of glass, legionnaire." I paused, curious about the continued sounds of a struggle. "Are they kicking Grizz's ass?" I asked, nodding toward the cacophony.

"Even odds, really. There's only two of them, after all," a voice chuckled from my right, and I turned to discover Rinko leaning against the wall.

"Rinko!" I said, unable to hide my delight.

"Jax," he replied casually, nodding, and grinning back to me. "It's good to see you upright, my lord. You looked like shit when we boarded the ship, and again when you were carried in there." He nodded to the room I'd just exited.

"Yeah, well, you know how it is. Besides, you looked pretty shitty last time I saw you, as well."

"All I needed was a few quick rounds of healing from Mistress Nerin, and a spot of rum." His smile deepened, and he winked, clearly pleased with himself.

"Yeah, rum would fix me, too, and I think I owe her some thanks, as well," I admitted ruefully. "I need to get the gang together, check on them all, and that includes you now, mate. You fought alongside us in the Skyking's lair…think you can gather everyone for me, in, say, an hour?"

"Of course," he said, still smiling. "Where do you want us?"

"Ah," I faltered, suddenly remembering I didn't know where I was, let alone the layout of the ship.

"On the main deck," Oracle interjected, and I smiled at her, then nodded to Rinko.

"The main deck," I agreed, and he saluted before rushing off.

"Right. Where's Romanus?" I asked, and another legionnaire stepped forward, clapping his fist to chest and bowing his head.

"He said he intended to set up a station outside the ship. I can take you there, Lord Jax," he offered.

"Great; lead on, please," I said, and he spun around, setting off down the corridor, with the entire group in fast pursuit, myself included.

It took fifteen minutes to cross the ship, a distance that would have taken five if not for the corridors that were missing floors or totally filled with stashed gear or wall-to-wall refugees.

We finally exited the ship onto the grass of a small clearing, and I stood blinking in the sunlight, amazed by the change in the weather a mere few hundred miles from the tower.

Here, it was pleasantly warm. The air was filled with the tang of the sea, and a gentle but constant breeze ruffled the leaves of the trees that surrounded us. I took a deep breath, feeling instantly better, memories of Thomas and me chilling on Greek beaches, drinking our body weight in Ouzo and Metaxa, and chasing girls all day filling my mind.

As soon as I pictured him, sunglasses on, buffed to hell, and trying to convince the girls of some new bullshit, like that he was an RAF pilot or something, I sighed, my heart aching as I wondered about him. I knew he'd been in the city recently, and I'd even felt like I'd sensed him nearby at times, but Mal just hadn't been able to find any sign of him. The last he'd heard, Thomas had been an adventurer, and he'd been leading a party out of the city a few months before. Mal said the trail went cold there, even though I knew from Jenae that he'd returned at least once since then.

"I'll find you, bro..." I blinked away the spectral memory and looked around at the dozens, no, hundreds of people roaming the clearing and forest. "But for now, I have to protect them," I whispered, shaking my head.

Tommy would be all right. Hell, if I knew him, he'd probably have found a way to get to a pleasure island and was probably banging the realm's equivalent of supermodels somewhere, off his tits on booze and weird local drugs.

I didn't know when things had changed, but the longer I was here, in this realm, the more I felt the pull to defend its people. Tommy was a hard lad, and he'd already survived five damn years here. All I had to do was survive as well, get these people back to the tower, and I'd find a way to save him yet. Now that Jenae had narrowed his location down to the city six or seven weeks ago, she'd be able to find him more easily when she searched next.

If I hadn't torn that goddamn Valspar thing out of myself the way I had, she wouldn't have had to provide the costly healing I had needed, and I'd have probably found Tommy days ago.

He'd be all right. I had to believe that, or I'd go mad, having been so close to him, and having left the trail behind. I had responsibilities to these people, ones I'd given myself, and I would not abandon them or Tommy.

"I *will* find you," I muttered again, burying my worry and self-recriminations down deep. Straightening my shoulders, I strode toward Romanus, who was standing nearby in discussion with Elise and Athena.

CHAPTER FOUR

"Lord Jax!" Athena said cheerfully when she spotted me. Romanus and Elise spun to face me, the legion prefect smiling in relief and Elise nodding her head in recognition.

"Athena, Romanus, and Elise!" I said, nodding to them each in turn. "Elise, I have to congratulate you. None of this would have been possible without you. You did an amazing job so thank you," I said to her.

"Aye, well, I didna do it fer free, ye ken?" the stout dwarf grumbled, trying to ignore the fact that her cheeks were reddening at the well-earned praise. "I had help. Finbar an' Viktoria were part o' it, sendin' me spare staff an' all. I'd have no made it in time otherwise."

"There's no shame in needing help, Elise," I said firmly. "That's one of the reasons I need to talk to you. Has Augustus explained to you yet about the golems?"

The diminutive engineer nodded quickly.

"Oh, aye. He be directin' them now, an' that servitor one, ah, can I keep him?" she asked hopefully. "I'd be able ta work miracles on the ship wit' him under my command!"

"Man, I forgot about that. Heph and Seneschal are going to go mental when they find out I left one in the city," I muttered to myself, before shaking my head and smiling fondly at Elise. "You can't have this one for the long term, but you certainly can use it as you see fit for now. Give me a minute." I closed my eyes, reaching out and feeling Oracle gently guiding me.

The area surrounding me was black as I traveled inside my mind, but slowly, it started to fill as I reached out with my thoughts. First, there was the sense of warmth, of people, all around me, and a…river? No, stream…that was it. A stream of light that connected me to each of them. It was a soul thread, as thin as a thread of silk, but it seemed to carry so much: information, emotions, desires. Each and every one was a bond between me and the person who'd sworn to follow me.

I reached out, still guided by Oracle, and I soon found eddies where the threads and streams seemed to be bent, reminiscent of water running around stones submerged in the path of the stream. I concentrated on these sections, finding that they glowed to my spectral sight, then I felt them.

The golems.

They had a rudimentary awareness, or at least these level two and three versions did. The level twos were slow, plodding minds, dull as dishwater, but still there, while the threes were…different.

I could only compare them to animals in my mind. If I were to continue with the water analogy, the level twos were fish; they knew to eat, to swim, and to do, but not to think for themselves. By contrast, the level threes were closer to seals; they could think, reason things out. But they weren't human minds, and they didn't have the self-awareness I was used to. Instead, there was an almost hive mentality. They reached out and commanded their lesser brethren through a kind of neural link, and the more individuals they linked with, the faster their minds worked.

I had a vision of the hundreds that had once filled the Great Tower, and I couldn't help but shiver at the capacity they must have once had.

The greater golems were far more intelligent, becoming almost fully sentient, and would live until destroyed, Heph had explained once, with the king level of golems being capable of true majesty in their works.

The flying cities, I'd been told, were the work of a single golem king, and although it would make no sense for one to be here, lying in dormant repose on one of those cities that had crashed, I still had a momentary fantasy of finding it.

Then I shook the thought away. If it had been here, it would have fixed the damn city.

I searched quickly, jumping from one golem mind to another, until I found the level-three servitor, and I sank into it. The golem was working on the far side of the ship, two decks up, somehow blending sections of wooden timbers together. It had found a crack in the hull, and its hands had begun weaving the sections of wood together like it was sewing the material, fixing what could have been a problem and making it into a strength instead.

I couldn't explain how I did it; I simply impressed a sensation of Elise, her personality, the "taste" of her mana, and all that I had seen of her into a single tiny ball of identity, then attached it to the golem. I was careful to add it under me in the structure of authority in its mind, but after a handful of seconds that seemed like hours, the golem knew to seek her out if it needed further orders.

"I've ordered the servitor to obey you, for now. Use it as best you can," I said to Elise, opening my eyes and looking at her. Her face froze for a second, then the biggest grin I'd seen from her yet spread across her cheeks. She turned, about to run straight for the golem.

"Wait!" I ordered, and she froze, clearly half afraid I was about to take her toy away. "Don't panic," I said reassuringly, smiling and reaching into my bag to pull out Mana Engine Integration. It was one of the three skillbooks I'd promised to Elise, Finbar, and Viktoria, the other two being Magical Device Creation and a choice from the ones I had back at the tower. "I swore I'd give you and the other two a book each, remember?"

By the way her eyes were suddenly glued to the book, she clearly did.

"Well, I'd say, with all you did, you've earned the right of first refusal. Do you want this, the other book, or to wait until you reach the Great Tower in order to look through the library there?"

"Ah…uh…ah…" she stammered, staring fixedly at the book.

"Want time to think about it?" I asked her.

She shook her head fervently. "I told ye, I only made it 'cause th' others helped," she whispered.

"You made it happen," I said firmly. "Yes, they helped, but I bet you had to direct them and make things work, so as I said, the right of first refusal—"

"I'll have it, so help me god, even iffin it pisses off Finbar an' Viktoria, I'll have it!" She reached out eagerly. I passed the volume to her, and she grabbed it from my hand like it was her firstborn, yet coated in gold at the same time.

She slowly and reverently opened the pages of the book, eyes widening as the book began to glow, words lifting off the pages to shiver in the air before her, and light seeping into her eyes and mouth as the book dissolved into golden smoke and sank into her.

She collapsed to the floor, twitching, and I swore, dropping down next to her and turning her on her side, hoping she wasn't having a fit.

"Jax!" Oracle said, dropping down next to me and reaching out in reassurance. "It's okay. It's just an information overload. Her brain has taken a hell of a lot of knowledge in, that's all."

"Like Amon's gift?" I asked.

She smiled, shaking her head. "No, it's okay. Amon gave you a lot of information and knowledge, more than anyone should get in one go. That's a skillbook, on the other hand. It's designed to be used. It'll have limits on the amount of information stored in it, but it'll be sparking off things Elise already knew. She's having the mother of all inspirations right now, as the knowledge triggers other ideas. She's probably—" Oracle was cut off as Elise suddenly gasped, jerking upright like a landed fish and sucking in great lungful's of air.

"Hot damn!" she cried. "The stanchion! It be in tha wrong place!" She shoved me back, tumbling me onto my ass as she struggled to her feet. "Whut ye all lookin' at?" she growled, before realizing what she'd done. "Oh, ah. Sorry an' all, Lord Jax, but...yer see..." She gestured awkwardly to the ship and began backing away. "I...well, I need to..."

"Just go, it's fine!" I laughed, taking Romanus's proffered hand and letting him pull me to my feet. I shook my head at the way Elise ran to the ship, pushing people aside and almost sending someone toppling from the gangplank that led to the hatch. "Wow, she's really excited, isn't she?" I murmured with amusement.

"Engineers," Athena said, shrugging. "You do know you've probably extended our stay here, right, Jax? I mean, she's going to be tearing half the ship apart if she's found a better design now."

"Three days," I replied. "She can have three days. That's enough time to do the basics and make the hull a bit more secure, right?"

"It'll do. That will mean I can get the bridge and helm all connected up properly," the captain agreed, nodding approvingly. "I don't know if you noticed, but the helm literally has to be guided constantly, and on a ship this size, that's not ideal. Engines are fired manually, rather than in series or groups. And that landing, well, it wasn't exactly my finest." She gestured behind the ship, and I turned to observe the effects our descent had on the environment.

A trail of devastation lay behind the airship, leading all the way down to the beach. Dozens of trees had been snapped in half, branches and debris strewn everywhere, and at least a dozen sections along the sides of the ship where planks and entire sections were broken and damaged.

"Shit..." I sighed. "Can we fix all of that in three days?"

Athena snorted a laugh.

"We'll have that fixed by tonight; don't worry," she reassured me. "It's just the outer hull. Most of it wasn't even attached properly. Entire sections aren't even closed off yet. With those golems holding the sections in place and the engineers bolting them down? The work will get done at a speed that has never before been seen. You mark my words, Jax: three days, and you won't recognize her."

"That does raise a good point," Augustus said, walking over and smiling at Oracle before nodding to me. "The ship doesn't have a name yet. We all refer to her as 'the ship' or the 'battleship.' But it's bad luck to have no name for her."

"Then we need to name her," I determined. "How about you all suggest a name in the next three days, and when we launch, we will name her officially?" I offered, getting a round of nods and smiles. "Good. So, uh, Romanus, I don't remember a great deal about the end of the last conversation we had…" I started.

He shook his head. "It's okay, Jax. Oracle explained it to us. I have sent legionnaires to both camps. Fortunately, the local Himnel garrison commander hasn't heard about the events of the last few days, so they agreed to attend tomorrow, as did Narkolt, along with the lead researchers. Everyone knows the legion is neutral in the disagreements among the cities, provided nobody assaults the populace, so we have that going for us."

"How does that work in times of war?" I asked, confused.

"It…it's a pain, to be honest, as we need to protect the populace. We tend to simply open the enclave to the people and warn off any soldiers that come near. In the past, it was easier, when we were both more numerous and more respected, but it is what it is," Romanus admitted gravely.

"I bet," I replied. "Okay, so this ship is in hand: what about the other ships?"

"I've set up a rotation for them to land so that the crews and refugees can stretch their legs. I'd arranged for six hours at a time, but I'll change that if we're to be here for three days," Romanus said, making a note. "Beyond 'shore leave,' they're fine. The majority of the people are excited and happy to rest and eat, really.

"Mistress Nerin has been healing anyone who needs it, as has Clan Mother Hellenica. She and her djinn are up on the *Ragnarök* right now, as we boarded the majority of the injured and disabled engineers and shipyard workers on her. Hopefully by tomorrow, we'll have fewer lying about and a few more working on the ship."

"Sounds good. I need to speak with Hellenica anyway, as well as my own team. I asked Rinko to gather them on the ship's deck in an hour. Probably half an hour now, considering—Augustus, I'd like you and any of the legion that were in on the Skyking raid to join us as well, please?" I asked, and he saluted. "Good." I took a deep breath and blew it out, enjoying the salty tang of the sea air. "Then I guess the last thing to do is to plan a schedule for the city," I mused aloud.

"The city?" Romanus asked carefully.

"We need to search it. We won't go too deep, but—"

"Well, it's pretty damn big, son," a voice interrupted from behind, and I turned to see Mal walking over. "We did a few loops of the city before comin' in to land. She's impressive," he warned, coming to a stop next to me and clapping me on the shoulder. "Good to see you're alive, lad. I thought someone had finally gotten tired of your shit and put me out of my misery back there."

"Nah, you're not that lucky, Mal." I snorted, smiling as Oracle accepted a hug from Soween, who accompanied Mal. "What can I do for you?"

"We came to check on you, mainly," Mal admitted. "We came here with you, as agreed, but we'll be headin' on soon. I'm plannin' on checkin' in on the old man, see what he's been up to."

"He in Narkolt?" I asked.

Mal shrugged dismissively. "Sometimes. He tends to travel a bit, doesn't like bein' tied down; you know how it is. Usually leaves people to handle things in his place, then complains about how they do it. Man tends to be a stickler for rules."

"He's into rules and has you as a son?" I asked, trying not to smile.

"He's into rules *now*. I ain't sayin' he was always like that. Nowadays, he's all about responsibility. Poor bastard," Mal said, shrugging again.

"Well, think I could persuade you to hang around a few more days?" I asked. "We're going to be doing some work on the ships here, then setting off around then. Although, I'd much prefer having you stick around longer? Hell, you know there's always a need for you in the empire," I said hopefully.

"Not a chance, son." Mal grinned. "I've got things to do, places to go, and gold to spend. While you've got a need for me, I don't need this shit. I'm goin' to go pay off some debts, bounce some fine ladies on my knee, and relax."

"Come on, Mal," I pressed, smiling knowingly. "Tell me you haven't had the time of your life this last week. Tell me you didn't feel more alive than ever before."

"Ain't gonna happen," Mal said, shaking his head.

"That's the heir to the imperial throne you're talking to, smuggler," growled Romanus, straightening and resting his hand on the hilt of his gladius.

"And I don't care." Mal bit the words off as he glared back at Romanus. "Listen, *Legion*, Mister High and Mighty here and I had a deal: I get him through this, I get his people—and that includes *you*—out of the city and free, and I get paid well for it. Well, I did my part, and now I want what was promised."

"Whoa, calm down, Mal. Wait, you expect to be paid now?" I questioned, only to be met with a glare.

"Yes, you little shit; we had a deal! Ten spellbooks, a memory crystal, and my ship, dammit. I have the ship; now gimme!" He thrust his hand out insistently.

"Yeah, I remember the deal," I said, staring at him. "We agreed on *two* spellbooks and a single memory crystal—my choice of which, remember? You know damn well I don't carry those around with me. I told you what they were and that they were in the tower. Add to that, you asked for free repairs for your ship. Can't do that here, either, Mal. You know better."

"You alterin' our deal, boy?" he asked in a low growl, his right hand dropping to the pistol grip of his crossbow, which hung against his hip, and the low whine of the magical device powering up filled the air.

"Nope. I gave my word, Mal. I've got some spellbooks right here, and you can have two of them. That's no issue, but you want the crystal, you're gonna have to wait a little. Few days, at least," I said.

"Why days?" he growled, keeping his hand on the crossbow.

"Because I'm going to lead a team into the depths of the city here, and I'm going to loot the shit out of it while the ships get repaired and upgraded. You want a crystal, you either come dungeon-diving with me and chance if we find one, or you wait until we get to the tower. Or you leave now, and you'll have to wait until you come back to get it."

"You never said that before!" Mal snarled.

"You never asked, Mal," I said. "You're the one who just tried to rip me off for eight additional spellbooks, so don't give me that shit. You want a memory crystal before we leave here? Join my team and damn well hope there's some down there; otherwise, you're stuck waiting 'til you come to the tower."

"Fuck's sake!" Mal snapped, spinning around and stalking off, while Soween stepped forward and held out her hand to me.

"I'll take the two spells, thank you. They're for my husband, after all," she said calmly.

"Fair enough," I said to her sadly. "I'd hoped it wouldn't come to this, Soween. When we set the deal, Mal was supposed to come to the tower with us, after all. I haven't changed the deal, regardless of what he thinks. Here, you choose."

I pulled the books out and stacked them on a pile of wood nearby, drawing incredulous stares from the small crowd around us.

All told, there were two copies of Deathbolt, two Firebolt, a single Blizzard, three Iceshield, a pair of buff spells for Intelligence, one for Strength, and one for Dexterity. Four more dealt with summoning creatures, including two lesser demons, an earth golem, and a flame golem, respectively. I had more, but none that I was willing to share, not yet.

The way that Soween's eyes bulged, I knew she'd been ready to take anything. However, at the sight of all the options, she swallowed hard, closing her eyes and mumbling for several long seconds, one hand gripping a necklace tightly.

Eventually, she opened her eyes again and selected a copy of Iceshield and the Blizzard spell, which made me sigh internally. I'd had designs on that one myself.

"Josh says to thank you for these, and he'd like to do a deal personally for some more, he says, before we leave."

"When are you leaving?" I asked hopefully.

"We'll see, but Jax? Don't take Mal's mood personally, he's just feeling a little trapped right now and is desperate to leave and get loose. When he calms down, he'll remember the deal and who his friends are."

That was all she said, but she shrugged as she walked away, leaving me with some optimism.

"That damn smuggler needs to learn his place," Romanus growled.

"Not really, Romanus." I shrugged dismissively. "He signed on for this when I really needed him. He's a good man, even if he does try to sneak things past me at any chance. As Soween says, when he calms down, he'll remember that the original deal was to help me get these people out of the city and back to the tower, then he gets his loot. If he wants to come get it later, that's fine. But if he wants it now, he either has to hope that there is something worthwhile below us that we can reach, or he has to be patient."

"As to 'below us,' I trust you'll be taking the legion?" Romanus asked.

"Some of it, at least, and Lydia's squad. We'll sort it out soon. First things first, I need to go talk to them, then I need to replace some of this armor and so will a lot of my people, actually. Are the legion armorers about?" I asked.

"They'll be proud to provide you with armor," Romanus said firmly, calling to a pair of legionnaires who stood nearby, watching over us. "Trin, go find the armorers. Send them to the upper deck and tell them they'll have the honor of providing the Lord of Dravith with new gear, and they'd damn well better do me proud."

"Yes, Prefect!" the legionnaire barked, slamming fist to chest, and tearing off into the ship at a dead run.

"Damn," I said, marveling at the speed he managed.

"I'll lead you to the upper deck, if that's acceptable?" Romanus offered, and I smiled gratefully, nodding my thanks. "Good. Mind if I give you some advice, Jax? If you don't want to hear it, just say."

"I'll take it, mate; god knows I'm flying by the seat of my pants at the minute," I admitted.

Romanus frowned, trying the phrase out. "The seat of your pants...hmmm. Well, anyway. I've noticed that you're an informal man, Jax, and that's fine. Some of the greatest leaders in our history were charismatic giants of song and legend, men and women who could drink with the men one minute, then lead them in battle the next. But..."

"But I'm not that charismatic." I shrugged. "I know, mate, but I'm trying."

"No, Jax," Romanus said, cutting in. "That's not what I'm saying. Charisma can be earned and learned; either way is fine. You've got a strong enough presence that you can do that if you want to, my point is that you appear to be trying to be everyone's friend. An older brother, if you will.

"You have the responsibility of a leader, and you make those calls, but you also keep telling nearly everyone to just call you by your first name." He paused, eyeing me as though to verify whether I was listening.

I nodded mutely for him to continue.

"You are the Lord of Dravith, Jax. You need to understand what that means. The legion is loyal to you, and as more and more of our enclaves find out who you are, your following will grow. We weren't confined to just Himnel, after all; there are legion garrisons in each of the great cities. Several hundred in Narkolt still exist, led by a good man who I've no doubt will follow you as well, and there were other enclaves on Dravith, advance forts."

"What? I thought—"

"We lost contact with the forts on the far side of the mountain range after the Cataclysm, much as we did with the greater empire, but there have been trade delegations, and explorers from other lands. From their tales, we know that the legion still lives, even if it's not all that it once was. If you reach out to them, you could bring them into the fold yet."

"That's great news!" I said, my mind suddenly full of marching armies, of bringing peace and prosperity...

"But they won't all accept you as you are," Romanus cut in, ruining my daydream as we walked up the gangplank, followed by my escort.

"What?" I asked, frowning.

"We in the legion are trained to obey our rightful lords, and that is you, Jax, for Dravith. You have a claim to other lands as well, as Imperial Scion and heir to the throne for the empire at large. But until you extend your authority over those lands, their legions may not respond to you. They certainly won't if you're not what they expect from the imperial throne."

"Go on…" I said, listening.

"You like to be one of the team and to lead from the front, I hear. That's a good thing in a legionnaire; taking those risks alongside your men will earn you a level of devotion few can imagine. But Jax, you're not a legionnaire," he said firmly.

"You're the High Lord of Dravith; you *command* the legions. You can still lead from the front, but the people are used to lords who, essentially, are remote, unfeeling bastards, who insist on their due and more. They claim anything and everything they can, and that's the normal thing for a lord to do now. The common folk see that as the way, anyway."

"I'm not doing that—" I started to say, but he cut me off.

"And that's a good thing. Believe me, that's not what I'm asking you to do, but the people are conditioned to expect…certain things from a lord. If you tell them not to show you respect, they won't, and then you're on a slippery slope."

"Whoa, I'm not saying don't respect me," I protested as we all shuffled to the side to allow a golem to stomp past along one of the wider internal corridors, its arms full of wood.

"No, I get that, but you are asking them to talk to you as an equal, and frankly, they're not." He slowed to a halt in the corridor. "We've just met, and this is a bit hard to say, Jax, but because of our roles and where we stand, with the world against us, it honestly needs to be said. You deserve respect from these people. You've rescued them. You need to accept it."

"I…I will." I nodded thoughtfully, stopping myself before I could apologize. "I can see where you're coming from, Romanus, and thanks for having the balls to say it. In my…land, we are taught that we are all equal, and that no man should demand respect from others. It's a bit of a change here."

"I can understand that, and your land sounds very strange. Hopefully, you'll tell me about it sometime, but you need to forget that now. You are the High Lord Jax, Ruler of Dravith, and one day, the empire. You need to be that man. I thank you for the right to call you by your first name, but please consider my words and take them as advice freely offered, not as a criticism."

"I will," I said, trying not to take it personally. I'd been damn well doing my best to be the big boss already, as well as getting along with people. It wasn't easy, but he had a point.

We crossed two corridors and bypassed the main stairwells, as they were full of stored gear and people running everywhere. Instead, we used a series of small ladders to climb the four stories to the main deck, stepping out into a steady wind that cut across the island.

I gazed in amazement at the deck rolling out on all sides. The bridge was an entire raised section to our left, located in the middle of the deck, with bare boards covering most of the surfaces which they'd hastily made safe against the constant breeze during flight. The main deck itself, though, was a patchwork of completion.

Some were almost finished, solid and clean, while other sections were cordoned off or entirely missing, with openings dropping all the way to the lower decks. There were mounting sections for masts, and two great trees, obviously planned to be those masts, were strapped to the deck on the starboard side. Despite those, the ship would be entirely engine powered for a while.

Among the various groups scurrying here and there, I caught sight of my team, looking out over the island, and I strode over to join them.

Rinko had already rounded up most of those who had made the Skyking raid such a success, with the exception of Hellenica and Augustus. If I was right, the legionnaire would seize the opportunity to go and get her personally, if given the chance.

I clapped my fist to my chest, acknowledging the crisp salutes of the legionnaires and the hasty, sloppy salutes of Lydia's squad as they tried to imitate them.

"Damn, it's good to see you all," I said cheerfully, getting smiles and laughs in return.

Lydia stepped forward. "We're glad te see yer, too, believe me. Tha' last arrow scared tha shit outta us," she said, looking me over carefully to make sure I was all right, as I did the same to her.

Lydia had changed since I'd first recruited her to fight for the tower. The freed slave, who'd been scared and determined that I was going to try to take advantage of her somehow, had grown from a half-starved, raw-boned woman into a warrior who filled her armor and intimidated people with far higher levels.

Now, she was tall, heavily muscled, and grim. She rarely seemed to smile, but when she did, it was clear and honest, from the heart, and it transformed her appearance entirely. She was the tank of our little group, wearing heavily patched armor we'd looted from a heavy guardsman attacker, and she carried a mace and shield.

She was brave and steadfast, and I'd struck gold when I'd managed to somehow win her loyalty. With her stood the rest of her squad, a team that had been with me since leaving the Great Tower.

Jian was a short, dark-haired man who loved to dual wield, with a pair of silvery drow-made scythes on either hip, and a pair of matching swords on his back. He was a quiet man, but the last few weeks of constant battles had shaped him to be a deadly opponent for anyone who crossed him.

Holding his hand was Miren, his partner, or lover at least. She was the youngest of the group, besides Bane at least, not even twenty yet. She had started to train as a hunter in her old village, before she'd been taken as a slave. I'd inherited her when I'd killed the slavers and had promptly freed her and her companions. She was a slight half-elven girl with long, blonde hair, which she typically wore braided. She had settled into her position as a ranged fighter with alacrity, her drow-made bow helping to improve her shots.

Standing next to her was her fellow ranged death-dealer, Stephanos. Where she was short, he was tall and thickly muscled, but the pair of them were inseparable, at least when she wasn't jumping Jian's bones, anyway.

Arrin, the mage for our little party, chatted quietly with the others. He'd been practicing at every opportunity since I'd given him his first spellbook, and now, after only a few weeks, he'd leveled and invested his points to make himself into the kind of war-mage that would have a job in almost any fighting or adventuring force I could imagine, if not for the fact that he was a crazy adrenaline junkie.

Yen and Tang stood at attention as they waited, two of the first three legionnaires to swear to me, both elven scouts. With them, standing proudly while his "wing" flew overhead, was the alkyon, Amaat. He was a birdman; specifically, he looked like a humanoid eagle, and he'd seized control of several dozen of his race who had been enthralled to the Skyking, physically beating most of them into submission. Now they followed the legionnaire, and he carried himself with a pride that had been missing when he, Yen, and Tang had sworn to me in the Smugglers Path under the city.

There, he'd been just another member of the legion, a highly skilled member of the Praetoria, the legion's elite, but his body had been weakened by a lifetime of poor food and nutrition before signing up.

When I'd healed him, using the spell that Oracle had helped me to create, we'd straightened crooked limbs and regrown feathers long lost. He'd transformed from an average example of his species, who'd risen through the ranks through sheer bloody determination, to an Adonis-like specimen. To display his fathomless gratitude, he'd set out to beat all those who opposed me into the ground.

The result was that now he ruled his own wing of alkyon, and he had integrated any djinn flyers who weren't healers. Even the dozen or so lesser imps who had come along could be seen wheeling around in the formation above us.

Next to the group, leaning against a handy wooden brace, was Barrett, the former ship's first officer of the first airship I'd captured…well, the airship I'd damaged and sent crashing to its doom, but, meh, semantics.

Barrett was human, *apparently*, but he was short enough that he'd pass as a beardless dwarf easier than a human. Despite being a particularly fugly guy, he'd previously dated Joya, the huge, muscular caravan guard who was currently towering over him as she stood nearby. She worked for Mal, or had until recently, so seeing her with the rest of the group was a surprise.

Mistress Nerin, the Great Tower's official healer, glared at me while adjusting her bandoliers of bags. She was clothed in a long, grey dress, two belts running from shoulder to opposite hip on either side, and attached to them were dozens of bags.

Leaning against the railing and looking like he'd be comfortable on the edge of a razorblade, stood Nigret, a Trigara. He was a heavily armored feline humanoid with white fur. While he was new to our group, he was also a lethal ex-arena fighter who had sworn to follow me when I agreed not to kill him.

Lastly, the legion contingent gathered in around us. Rinko, Plas, Denny, and Grizz I knew, having talked to them over the last few days, and there were two others with them that I recognized, although I didn't know their names.

"Are we only missing Hellenica and Augustus?" I asked, searching around, and got a variety of nods, affirmatives, and a single call of "Gnomes rule!" from somewhere at the back.

I ignored that. As far as I knew, we didn't have any gnomes with us, so it must have been a hallucination brought on by overwork, stress, and an excess of being stabbed lately.

"Right, then. I'll sort out Hellenica and Augustus later, as wherever they are right now, I'll bet not being interrupted is more important to them." I started, getting a round of laughs and sniggers.

"You all fought with me for the good of Dravith and the Great Tower. While I know that, officially, it was either your damn job or you were already sworn to me, it doesn't mean you shouldn't be rewarded for that. Each and every one of you went above and beyond what you could have expected I'd ask of you, so here's a little something as a thank you."

I pulled out a pouch, asking them to gather round.

I took my time, thanking them individually, referencing an instance when I'd seen them show bravery, and I handed them a single platinum coin. Knowing that platinum was worth a thousand gold was one thing, but seeing the faces of my people as they held what was undoubtably the most money they'd ever seen in their life in a single coin was worth it, beyond a doubt.

"There will be more in the future, but I doubt there will be a windfall like this again. When we return to the tower, I'll start to pay wages; that seems reasonable, after all. So, thank you for all you've done," I said, smiling at them and getting a shocked cheer in response.

"Now, I need a few volunteers," I began, and I was swamped as everyone stepped forward, including Joya, who'd basically been there just because she was holding Barrett's hand in a death grip, and Mistress Nerin, who glowered at me while mumbling something about "Damn fool will get himself killed if I don't..."

"Whoa, honestly, guys, this is serious!" I protested, raising my hands to call for quiet. "We're aboard the Sunken City at the minute, and Jenae has informed me that there are some spells we need that have been buried somewhere below. I'm going to lead a team, including some legionnaires, down there to get them. We don't know what there is, or where it's hidden, though."

Again, they all volunteered, and I grinned at them, trying to hide the proud tears as I looked around.

"Okay, okay!" I laughed and shook my head, resigned to having to choose. "I'll shout when the time comes, but it won't be until tomorrow at the earliest. I need to meet the locals first. Lydia, keep your team close; I need a word. Now, all you other buggers, go get back to whatever you were doing." I gestured their dismissal and began to turn when I heard a cough from Romanus.

"You have something to add, prefect?" I asked him curiously.

"No, Lord Jax." He shook his head. "And please, forgive me for my counsel earlier. What I said was true, and I meant to help you, but I see from your actions here that these people, both yours and mine, already love you. That's a rare thing for a commander to earn, that level of devotion," he said seriously. "My impression was based on incomplete knowledge of you, and for that, I apologize. And you know you could have given them a single copper piece, and they'd have been thankful, don't you?"

"I do, but I gained that money thanks to them, so they deserve a share," I explained.

"Oh, I agree, and believe me, serving a lord who pays in gold and platinum, rather than back-handed compliments or daggers in the back is appreciated."

CHAPTER FIVE

grinned at Romanus, then relaxed as the others wandered away. My small team that had come with me from the tower gathered around, and I called out to Barrett as he passed.

"Barrett, mate, your sister and her little one okay?"

He smiled, nodding in clear gratitude.

"They are, thank you, Jax; as are Oren's family. They've asked to meet you and thank you personally at some point?"

"Sure, but it's not necessary," I said, waving my hand dismissively. "As things stand, though, we're going to be here for the next few days on the Sunken City. I know you volunteered to come explore, but I need you here, man. You've got a gift with people, with getting them to follow your instructions.

"I need you to manage the refugees, which means you're in charge of them. Make sure they're organized and fed, they have room to stretch their legs, and they don't cover the ship in shit, because I've no idea where we would find toilets for that many people right now. This is Romanus. He leads the legion, so work with him, okay?"

"Of course, Jax, and thank you for your confidence," Barrett said simply, nodding deferentially to Romanus before leading Joya off the deck and deeper into the ship.

I turned around cautiously, looking back and forth, then moved to the side of the deck and peered over the edge before speaking up.

"Okay, Bane, I give in. Where the hell are you?" I asked plaintively, and I nearly shat myself when he spoke, predictably, from right behind me.

"Here, Jax." His voice was filled with the deep *thrummm* of amusement I'd learned to expect from his race.

I spun around and glared at him, searching the area and trying to figure out how the hell he'd hidden himself there. But try as I might, it made no sense to me.

"You're an asshole," I said to him, and he replied as I'd taught him:

"Takes one to know one."

"I wish I hadn't taught you to shit-talk," I muttered, shaking my head. Sighing, I scanned the deck. Now that the rest had left us, we were down to the two legionnaires who were on guard for me, Romanus, and Lydia's squad of five. I contemplated the small group, the seven of us, who were survivors of the journey from the Great Tower.

"I know it's been a harder trip than we were hoping for," I admitted, meeting their gazes, noting the battered armor, the bloodstained clothing, and the weary looks in their eyes. "So, if any of you want to take a step back after this, I'll understand. As things stand now, I need you for the next few days, at least. You're all outfitted with armor we cobbled together with bits of gear we've looted from practically half the land, at this rate."

The mismatching, battered, and scruffy group that stood with me was mute testament to the fact.

"My own's not much better; even my damn belt is falling apart, so…" I said, glancing over at Romanus, who nodded to a trio of men led by a single woman as they walked out onto the deck from below. "So," I repeated, "I've asked Romanus to send up his armorers. They won't have time to make us gear from scratch, obviously, but they're highly skilled, and as such, I'm hoping they can alter some existing gear to give us at least a bit more protection than we currently have?" I turned my hopeful attention to the four armorers.

The woman was the first half-orc I'd seen yet, or at least I assumed she was, judging from the size of her. She stood nearly seven feet tall with arms that made my thighs look scrawny. Her black hair was twisted into a myriad of dreadlocks and tied back, and apart from the slightly protruding lower jaw, tusks, and green-tinted skin, I'd have pinned her as simply a massive human woman back on earth.

"Lord Jax, it will be an honor to serve you," she said, clapping a massive fist to her chest in salute. "Me and mine stand ready."

"Excellent!" I smiled gratefully. "What's your name?" I asked, remembering at the last second that it was considered rude to cast spells, even Identify ones, on people you weren't actively fighting.

"Thornapple," she offered, nodding her head in greeting, then gesturing to each of her companions in turn. "This is Manny, Terr, and Oloutai."

"Then it's great to meet you…Thornapple," I said, wondering at the name. "My team and I are going into the Sunken City tomorrow, so any armor you could fit us with would be gratefully appreciated."

"Tomorrow?" she asked apprehensively. "My lord, we will do our best, but even with all of us working around the clock, there is no way we could do our best work to armor even one of you fully in that time. I mean—"

"I know," I said, cutting her off. "I don't mean for you to make us unique armor fitted to our individual specifications, but do you have spares, perhaps, that you could alter to fit us? Or replacements for the most ruined sections we have? Essentially, we've spent our time fighting and never had the chance to gain a cohesive set of gear. As you can see, we've made do with whatever we could scrounge." I gestured at my team's ragged state, ending with my own sorry gear.

"I can see that, my lord." She smiled with ease, now that she knew we didn't expect wonders. "As for available armor, we do have spares. Few, as we haven't set the forge up yet, and we have limited supplies, but we have enough to outfit your group and to replace the damaged pieces that the legion has returned over the last few days. First, I need to know about you and what you need, though. Judging from your armor, you are a front-line fighter?"

"I am," I confirmed. "I'm most comfortable being mobile, flowing back and forth with the battle, as opposed to being at the back, though sometimes, I function as a tank."

"A 'tank'?" Thornapple asked, lifting one eyebrow.

"Me," Lydia said, stepping forward. "I be tha tank for our party. It means I be needin' heavy armor, and solid. I tend ta pull as many in towards me as possible, getting' hit and dishin' out tha pain, while lettin' the others take 'em out."

"Ah! I get it," the armorer said, nodding thoughtfully. "Okay, let me explain the legion armor types for you, as I think that'll make things a little easier to understand. First, you have the standard legion armor, which is a mix of heavy and medium, as outsiders would understand it.

"It's heavy because it's composed of plate and chainmail, with leather banding and more. Because it's designed to lock together, it reduces the overall weight and makes it more mobile through a lot of little tricks that the legion armorers have developed over the centuries." She looked from one to another of us as she spoke, making sure we were listening and understood.

"We have the legion scouts next; they wear a mix of light and medium armor, specially treated to assist them in hiding, with movement as silent as is physically possible in the field.

"Next, we have the Speculatores Praetoriae armor for the elite scouts. The Speculatores Praetoriae are considered outside the standard chain of command, and while there are few of them, they have each earned the right to be the elite. In the days of the empire, a single team would have been responsible for everything from assassinations to monster hunting, to 'questioning' any nobility that might have stepped out of line.

"As such, their armor is of a higher quality than the standard or scout variants. It is both quiet, and strong, although we have lost the knowledge of most of the enchantments that once made it the masterwork that it was. The wearers of that armor are generally accepted to be far more in need of protection and our aid in surviving."

Thornapple nodded over at an armor stand to one side that was being carefully assembled, before going on. "Then last and most important of all, we have the Praetorian Guard armor. This is the ultimate legion armor; each set must be crafted to mark the passage of an armorer from journeyman to master, even if only within our own ranks. The Praetorian suit is far stronger, heavier, and yet more flexible than even the scout and standard variants, forged of rare metals and heavily enchanted, even if we can barely make the most basic of the runes activate these days."

She smiled sadly with the admission, nodding to Lydia. "As you're a member of Lord Jax's personal retinue and, as you call it, the 'tank,' my recommendation would be for you to work towards either Speculatores Praetoriae or full 'standard' armor, but I'll warn you, you'll need to increase your stats before you can wear either. You're a bit…scrawny."

I couldn't help but burst out laughing at Lydia's mortified expression and the careful way that Thornapple had said it.

"It's okay, Thornapple. Honestly, we all know we need to seriously improve ourselves to be able to wear full legion armor properly," I said, still chuckling.

"I'm glad you're not offended, Lord Jax. Okay, I'll need to examine you all and make some notes, get some measurements, and then late tonight, we can have a fitting? With a final fitting in the morning? What time are you planning on leaving?" she asked, and I shrugged.

"We've got a meeting with the researchers first thing tomorrow, so following that, I'd say; why?"

"Because—and I need to say this—we don't have enough time. Any extra time you can give me tomorrow will be appreciated. To make this happen, we will work through the night, but still, if you could hold off an extra few hours?" she asked hopefully.

I paused and considered her request. The timetable was arbitrary, as I'd just made it up, that was true, But I needed to get back to the Great Tower as soon as possible. Even an hour lost here could mean defeat when Barabarattas and his forces came for the tower, but we also needed to level as much as we could, and I couldn't afford to walk away from any chance to do that. Plus, the engineers needed time to work on the battleship. Besides, if we died because our armor was shit, then it was all over anyway.

"Noon," I said eventually. "I can give you until noon; that way you have a bit longer to finish up, and we have a bit longer to train and prepare, but then we need to move on."

"Thank you!" Thornapple said, sagging in relief. "I warn you, it'll not be my best work, but it will be the best I can do in the time I have."

"Then I can't ask for more," I said graciously. "Once we're back to the tower, I'll ask that you work on getting a proper forge set up, then start to build us some more specialized pieces, so spend the next few days thinking about that and what resources you'll need, okay?"

"Ah…to set up a forge, or to make custom armor?" she asked cautiously.

"Both, either, why?" I replied distractedly as she stepped in close and lifted my right arm, holding a knotted piece of string to my armpit and grunting as she felt my current armor shift.

"This really wasn't even fitted to you, was it?" She clicked her tongue disapprovingly. "I'm going to need you to take it all off," she started to say, stepping back as I started to strip the battered pieces off. I saw the look on her face as I did so, though she hid it quickly.

"Yeah, and I'll need new clothes as well," I said to her. "Clean ones…preferably without bloodstains…and that fit."

"Yes, you definitely need those." She wrinkled her nose involuntarily at the acrid smell. Beyond a quick wash down when I'd first awakened and Oracle had been feeling frisky—with an icy cold fountain of water, I'd add—I'd not had a proper bath or a shower since the fights in the arena. The Skyking raid had followed immediately after, so now, after several days of sweat, blood, and more soaking into my armor, I had to admit to myself that I was a little…ripe. "I'll send for the clothiers as well, and share your measurements with them, if that's acceptable?" she offered, and I nodded thankfully.

"I'll go find a river or something to dunk in as well," I muttered, having caught a whiff of myself.

"Let me get your measurements first, please," she asked with a smile, going back to work and making notes in a small journal as she went. "As I was saying, though, I can set up a field forge easily enough, and we brought all the complicated and expensive sections of our full forge, leaving only the heaviest and largest parts. The new forge will be achievable fairly soon, although it'll be a few months to get it fully built and as good as we can make it. The custom armor, though," She paused hesitantly.

"Yes?" I asked, waiting.

"Well, you know the legion doesn't do more than four armor designs, right? Scout, Standard Legion, Speculatores Praetoriae, and Praetorian Guard. That's it," she said slowly. "It's the law."

"Is it?" I asked, raising one eyebrow. "Law, I mean? Or is it tradition?"

"Well…in the legion, tradition…kinda *is* law," Thornapple said slowly, sneaking peeks at me from under her eyebrows as she worked.

"And would learning new armor designs really be a bad thing?" I asked. "Would you hate it that much?"

"No!" she said quickly. "No, we wouldn't hate it at all! Well, most of us wouldn't…"

"Let me guess. It's tradition, so you can't change it, right? And there's someone within the leadership structure that's making sure of that?" I asked, already having a certain Tribune in mind.

"I…uh…we'd not be opposed, my lord!" she repeated, bowing her head quickly.

"Good," I said, straightening up and watching the huge woman who was trying to both remain unnoticed and drop hints as subtly as she could.

"Thornapple, I need to make some changes to the way the legion does things. Amongst them is the belief that change is bad. Because I've got a goddamn robot–horse thing down in storage that's an amazing feat of engineering, and I can't believe that things like that exist, yet our armor is as basic as it gets. We're making new weapons and armor.

"Yes, there will be a uniform design, because that's more efficient, but it doesn't have to be something from a goddamn thousand years ago. Your job, as the chief armorer, is to come up with some new designs. In fact, make me the absolute best armor you can imagine; spare no expense, and create something you'd be seriously proud of, okay?"

"Anything I want?" she pressed cautiously. "I can have the other smiths work on this with me?"

"Sure, if they want to," I said, shrugging. "Seriously, Thornapple, I'd never really looked at the legion armor properly before I wore it in the arena, and it is stunning. The craftsmanship is fantastic, but I think you can make more, if you're set free, so, make it the very best you can and take a lot of notes as you go."

"Why notes?" she asked, frowning.

"Because once you've got it as perfect as you can make it, we'll test it, and if it passes the tests, you're going to be making a lot more of them for the Legion of the Tower."

"Uh…Lord Jax, you don't understand. Making the kind of armor I want to make, it'll take us months, weeks at least, and that's just to make one," she said hesitantly. "Add to that the various different shapes and sizes of the wearers, not to mention species—"

"Trust me, Thornapple."

"Just call me Thorn, my lord," she said, smiling.

"Then call me Jax," I responded. "But seriously, trust me on this, Thorn. I can teach you ways to speed up production like you'll never believe. Standardization and factory builds are going to rock your world."

"Sta—" she started to ask, and I shook my head.

"Honestly, not important right now and not something we can do anything with. For now, if you can kit us all out in Speculatores Praetoriae kit, that's my team and me here"—I gestured around at my team—"and give Lydia Praetorian Guard armor—"

"No," Thorn said flatly, cutting me off.

"What…?" I asked, nonplussed.

"No, Jax…no, my lord," she insisted, shaking her head, and meeting my eyes steadily, all doubt gone. "I can give *you*, specifically, Speculatores Praetoriae armor. Honestly, I could even give you full Praetorian armor, should you wish it, although you wouldn't even be able to use it. But you are our lord, and it is yours by right. But…to give the others the same, even if we had enough…it would make the entire legion hate them."

"Hate?" I asked, even more confused.

"Yes, my lord," she said, sighing. "I'm sorry, but the legionnaires out there, they train their entire lives to be chosen for the Speculatores Praetoriae. None of our legion, or any other we have had contact with, have been able to earn a place in the Praetorian Guard since the fall of the emperor, understandably.

"If you then jump your own people over their career-long dreams, especially when yours are…untested…it will only drive a wedge between them and your people. Add to that, we have a single set of Praetorian Guard armor, as each armorer is required to make one to pass their apprenticeship, but that is all we have. The other remaining pieces were smelted down, as is custom."

"Well, shit." I closed my eyes in dismay. "Okay…can you give us all basic armor, then? Hell, anything better than what we're wearing now?" I asked her, receiving a firm nod in return.

"I can provide you all with basic legion armor, the scout variety for most of you, and the heavier infantry version for your…tank," she agreed quickly. "I am sorry, Jax, but please understand."

"No." I cut her off. "It's fine, and it's something I should have considered, honestly. Okay, looking at the armor you can do, how long will that take?"

"If we work through the night, we can have it ready for noon tomorrow," Thorn said, pausing to make sure I was fine with that. When I nodded, she relaxed, clearly relieved, and went back to making notes in her journal. After a handful of minutes, she moved on to Lydia, and I took a deep breath, relieved that the issue was taken care of.

"Right, then…" I started to say, before looking up as movement caught my eye. It was Augustus and Hellenica, falling from a ship overhead and gliding toward us.

My first instinct was to panic that two people were falling to their deaths until I noticed how gently they fell and that nobody else seemed concerned. Instead, I leaned against the railing and watched.

It took little more than a minute for them to reach me; a few gentle course corrections then suddenly, they were there, Hellenica landing as gracefully and gently as a leaf, and Augustus stumbling and staggering to a halt, panting, his cheeks flushed and a huge grin on his face.

"Jax!" he said, stepping forward and reaching out to grab my shoulder. "You have to try that!" He beamed with excitement. "Honestly, it's not as bad as it looks. It's just wow."

"Okay, mate!" I laughed, shaking my head at him in amusement as he dropped his hand, and I turned to Hellenica. "Clan Mother, it's good to see you again."

"And you, my Lord Jax. It is refreshing to see you upright and unbloodied," she said with an amiable smile, breaking off and looking over my ragged, filthy clothes. "Well, somewhat unbloodied," she amended awkwardly.

"I know; don't worry, a bath or something is very high on my list of jobs today," I promised her.

Her smile deepened with relief that she didn't have to be the one to broach that subject with me. "So, is there anything you need from me?" she asked graciously.

"No." I shook my head, returning her smile. "I simply wanted to thank you for your help at the Skyking's tower and afterwards, and especially for the healing—"

"You and your people saved me from a fate I'd rather not remember. It is I who should be thanking you," she insisted, but I waved her off.

"Well, as long as you're happy, that's all that matters. Is there anything I can do, or that you need from me?" I asked, and she paused, tapping a finger against the bottom of her lip before straightening and answering.

"There is a boon I'd ask, if it's permitted?" she said slowly and I nodded. "Then I ask that you consider releasing Augustus to leave the legion and instead join—"

"WHAT?!" Augustus interrupted, stepping forward and lifting his hand to forestall her. "I'm not leaving the legion! Lord Jax, please understand, I'm certainly not looking to leave. My term still has another eight years to go, and then I fully intend to accept a second term!" Hellenica glared at him, then me, before speaking up.

"A clan needs a father as much as a mother! You say that you aren't interested, Jax, and your wisp made it clear again yesterday when I came to check on you that I was not to offer myself to you. But if I cannot choose a mate, then my clan will weaken! For years, we have been enslaved, and now you would force us to—"

"I told you that—" Augustus started to interject, clearly fuming, before I cut them both off.

"Enough!" I snapped, clapping my hands together sharply. "Hellenica, I don't care if you want to be with Augustus." I noted the way his cheeks were reddening, filing the information away for shit-talking at a later date. "Provided, of course, he wants to be with you," I clarified hastily. "But he's my right hand in the legion. I'm not releasing him from his Oath, especially not with everything that's coming!"

"And I don't want to be released from it, Jax!" Augustus insisted, his words laced with mild panic.

"But I want to mate with him!" Hellenica snapped at me, grabbing the big legionnaire by his right arm and tugging him closer to her.

"Then go have fun!" I snapped back, then paused, realizing we were virtually shouting at each other about Augustus getting some loving.

"What?" she asked, freezing.

"I said: go have fun!" I repeated. "Try not to leave him too worn out to do his job, but yeah, go for it. As long as you both want to, feel free to try to break his back. I don't care; as long as he's happy and able to do his job, that's all that matters."

"But I would have more children," Hellenica said slowly, as though testing me for a response.

"Right?" I said slowly. "That's kinda a risk you take when boinking…as long as that's understood, go for it."

"You would permit me to breed? I must be absolutely clear on this, Jax. You would permit me to take Augustus as Clan Father, mate with him, and bear his children? They would be permitted to live?" she asked carefully, searching my face.

"What? I'm not a monster, Hellenica. Why would I kill your kids?" I asked, shocked.

"Because they would be loyal first to me, then second to him. They would be beholden to you, as part of my clan, but…"

"Seriously, they'd be your kids. That's kinda normal. Family first, and all that," I said, frowning at Augustus. "Look, mate, I'm not seeing the issue here. Am I missing something obvious?"

"Djinn are born magic users, Jax," he said slowly. "And they tend to be…problematic…as newborns. Their natural affinity for magic outstrips their ability to control it. When the djinn first started turning up in the city, they were maybe four or five in age, and it was chaos for a while. Many were killed outright, some as a consequence for their pranks, while others were hunted to make…alchemical concoctions."

He grimaced, gently taking Hellenica's hand in his. "More and more turned up, and eventually, they simply became part of life in the city. The youngest ones were hunted down, though, so I'd guess there have been many hundreds born?"

"There were," Hellenica said softly, looking away. "They were taken from me and raised by the Prometheans as slaves. Few survived that upbringing to reach the streets, and far fewer lived to reach teenage years."

"Fuckers," I growled, suddenly glad we'd killed every last one of them. "Look, I don't know much about djinn life cycles. How often do you have kids, how many at a time, and how long to gestate?" I asked indelicately.

"I can birth up to a hundred at a time, and gestation is four months. I can have another litter in just under a year," Hellenica said bravely, straightening up and knowing that we were all working out how many children she had lost.

"That's insane," I said, shaking my head. "With their immediate talent as magic users, how aren't djinn everywhere? You're powerful; are they the same when they're fully grown?"

"Not as strong as me, but on par with a weak human mage, on average," Hellenica admitted slowly.

"Seriously, you should be ruling an empire," I started to say, then stopped as a memory came to me, a stray one from Amon.

I was seated atop Shustic'Amon, diving through the clouds, surrounded by legionnaires with wings, Prometheans and alkyon amongst them, as well as other races I didn't know.

As the clouds cleared before me, we broke through to discover a huge island below us, large enough that I could just make out the outer edges on the horizon.

It had clearly been green and verdant once, but now, it was torn and burning. Great swaths of forest smoldered, and huge scars marred the land where the ground had been scoured free of life.

I saw them rising, like seagulls, in a wave: hundreds, then thousands, of tiny forms, led by bigger, fully grown djinn. The clouds around us began to darken as the juvenile mages worked in concert to create a storm front of epic proportions.

"Feist!" Amon cried out, my mouth opening to shape his words. "Shield the advance!"

"Yes, my emperor!" A voice rang in my ears, carried by magic.

A shield grew slowly, spreading out from me and flowing across the sky to rest between the strike force and the clouds. It would not last long, but neither would the djinn…I swore under my breath.

Shustic drew in a deep breath as we dove lower, filling her mighty lungs. Her magic surged, even as thousands of arrows flew past us, aimed at the upcoming horde.

Most missed, but here and there, a djinn didn't manage to shift their form in time, and the break in their concentration helped to slow the storm.

Shustic gave a long shudder and breathed out with a roar that echoed up my body and reverberated through my blood. The flame that followed was a great blue-white gout of heat that tore a path straight through the heaviest concentrations of the enemy.

It was like watching a blowtorch go through tissue paper, as hundreds of them died, screams of agony abruptly cut off as their bodies turned to sooty embers, then blew away on the breeze. She rolled, aiming to rise through their left flank and tear another hole there.

The day was just beginning, and I had no doubt it would be a long and bloody one, but no number of lesser creatures had ever faced a greater dragon and lived, especially not one supported by the legion.

Hours later, I stood on the upper slopes of an active volcano while Shustic rested inside, groaning in pleasure at the mana-rich lava, as the three Clan Mothers of Terin'Olek were led up to me in chains.

I drew Soulstealer and waited, the old hunger taking over inside me, rising ahead of being slaked with their blood.

I blinked and shook myself, the memories vanishing like a popped soap bubble, and I saw Hellenica in a different light, suddenly understanding her questions far more than I had before.

If I were to provide them a safe place to breed, they would quickly grow and grow and grow. That was what had happened on Terin'Olek. A thousand years of peace on the island had been broken when the djinn ran out of room and began to seek more land, aggressively.

"You were…" I muttered, remembering. "There was a djinn empire, but you destroyed it with infighting…then I stepped in when you tried to expand."

"How…how do you know that?" Hellenica said slowly, her eyes wide. "Humans don't have racial memories—"

"Nope, they don't," I agreed, my mixed-species heritage springing to mind, banished just as quickly. "Hellenica, your children are unable to breed, right?" I asked, glancing up at the juvenile djinn frolicking in the air above us.

"Yes, only a Clan Mother, or a 'mother-in-waiting' can breed. There are few born, perhaps one female in ten thousand, if not more. Full females of our species are exceedingly rare, and we must accept other species and integrate their strengths into our lines to breed, we tend to happily—" she broke off, glancing sheepishly at Augustus.

"You happily boink other species; got that," I said, nodding. "Do you have any control over your children? For example, can you stop a girl from being born?"

"Kill it, you mean?" she asked flatly, and I shook my head emphatically.

"No, not at all. I mean, is it a choice?"

"No; it is very rare, though," she said slowly.

"Okay then, for now, until we have time to think more about this, I'd ask you to try to hold off on breeding. Have all the fun you want, just try not to, ahem, finish the deed?" I said awkwardly, glancing at them both.

"If it happens, then it does, and I won't ever kill your children, provided they don't raise their hand against me, my subjects, or the innocent. I just want you to wait until the tower is secure and we can provide a safe place. Then, I don't know, we'll have to come up with some kind of birth control for you, I guess. No more Clan Mothers, and definitely no uncontrolled breeding, okay?" I said, feeling like a complete shit for setting such harsh restrictions.

"That's fine, Jax!" Augustus said quickly. "I already have a dozen kids to look after in my bloody squad. I don't intend to be a father for real yet!"

"But…" Hellenica sputtered, and he squeezed her hand, speaking over her.

"No, Hellenica. We can talk about this, and make plans, but we do it in private! You don't just blurt it out to the future emperor, especially without even discussing it with me first! We can go…talk. Alone," the huge legion primus growled, trying to hide his embarrassment, as well as a little excitement.

"But you want to?" she asked quickly, staring at him in wonder, and he sighed, nodding slowly.

"So help me. Gods, yes. Yes, Hellenica, I want you. I've dreamed of you for thirty years, and more. Yes, I want to be with you, and yes, to be your mate, but we need to discuss this *in private*," he insisted, then twisted around and glared at the side of the ship where a rope ladder was twitching slightly. He glanced at me, and I gestured for him to investigate. He let go of Hellenica's hand and strode to the side, drawing his dagger and looking over the edge.

"Well, well, Grizz. Fancy seeing you here," he said acidly.

"Uh, Legion Primus, I was…just…uh…"

"Goodbye, Grizz," Augustus said, cutting the knot free and sending the ladder slithering over the side. A short cry of panic and shock, followed by a thump and a groan from below, let me know that the legionnaire was still alive. "Go to Mistress Nerin and explain exactly how you came to be injured, Grizz, and if you breathe a *word* of what you heard to anyone else," he snarled over the side, before nodding curtly and turning back to us. "Oh, just a little internal discipline issue there, Jax. Nothing for you to worry about."

I grinned at him and gestured to the stairwell leading back into the ship.

"Perhaps you two would like to go talk?" I offered, and Hellenica smiled, but Augustus shook his head firmly.

"No, Jax, as much as I want to have this conversation, there's something else that's been neglected for too long."

"What's that?" I asked slowly, a terrible feeling of foreboding coming over me.

"Your training, remember?" he said with an evil grin. "You might have forgotten, but I haven't, and Bane mentioned to me that you'd been avoiding his training sessions, too. Makes sense to me that we'll just roll them both into one. Bane agreed when we last had a chat about it."

"Oh, I bet he did…" I growled, turning around and catching him watching me as he was measured up for new armor. The air shook with the subsonic *thrummm* of amusement that was his version of laughter.

"But unfortunately, I have to spend a lot of time with the golems, especially directing them, and Bane needs to be able to watch outwards, as your bodyguard." Augustus paused.

I let myself relax slightly, thinking it wasn't going to be as bad as I'd feared.

"So instead, I reached out to the one person I felt could provide the level of training and dedication that the future emperor requires…"

His words trailed off as someone strode up from the depths of the ship and out into the bright sunlight.

"Centurion Primus Restun, thank you for your willingness to take over Lord Jax's training," Augustus finished, and my balls shriveled at the look of evil satisfaction on the legion primus's face, as well as the look of calm determination on Restun's.

"Well, fuck," I muttered disconsolately.

"I win," whispered Bane from behind me, the sound carrying in the sudden silence that filled the ship's deck, even the legion armorers watched me with pity on their faces.

I might be the imperial heir, and the Scion of the Empire…but this was Centurion Primus Restun, and he was a far higher authority.

CHAPTER SIX

I reached up one shaking hand, fumbling desperately for the rope, and my grip weakening involuntarily. My fingers flailed about, frantically patting across the top of the railing blindly, while I swung in a gentle breeze and tried not to fall.

"W…where…are…you," I growled to myself before finally finding the scalloped, carved grip and digging my fingers in. Shaking, I pulled myself up the last few feet and rolled over the railing, only to collapse heavily, sweating and gasping for breath on the deck, while sparkling flecks of light appeared and vanished alternately, indicating that I'd pushed myself so far I was dangerously low on air.

Slow, steady footsteps from my right preceded Restun sliding into view, staring down at me in grim-faced disapproval.

"You agreed that when I train you, you have no rank, yes?" he asked firmly, and I wheezed out that I agreed. "Then you are lower than the lowest new recruit. They, at least, are aspirants," he continued, and I winced at the acidic tone. "But you, Jax, you are an embarrassment! You break down and collapse after only three hours of climbing?! I haven't even *started* to train you yet!" he roared at me, dragging me to my feet and shoving me forward.

I stumbled, my legs like lead weights as I tried to keep upright, staggering along the track he'd laid out. The battleship still had huge sections of the deck missing, but if you were careful and paid attention, it was possible—just—to run across it.

The points I'd sunk into my Agility stat were truly earning their keep as I staggered, wove, and stumbled my way forward, trying to keep up with the centurion primus. He hadn't even broken a sweat yet, as near as I could tell, and he'd been doing the same exercises as I was, even going so far as to wear the same weighted armor he'd had me kitted out in.

When Thorn had brought it out and strapped it on, she'd whispered an apology to me as she locked the sections together. An apology I'd taken with good grace and a smile.

That seemed like at least fifteen years ago now, as the additional weights clattered and banged, bouncing and swaying and nearly throwing me off balance further as I followed the old bastard around the edge.

Cheering and whooping echoed from below as I came into sight again. The legion and civilians, those who were eating their evening meal, had apparently taken the time to place more bets and cheer me on as I continued on my way.

I dug deeper, motivated by the shouts and the determination that I wouldn't be seen as a failure by my own people. Gritting my teeth, I pushed myself to try to catch up to Restun, where he comfortably jogged a few meters ahead of me.

Once we passed from the end of the deck, we took the next stairwell down, then turned left, running along corridors that were strewn with junk, gear, and people's belongings. Before long, our path took us out into the second level of the main hold.

Once within the space, we followed a balcony path around the second level, jumping over occasional obstacles and avoiding the few people remaining inside before taking the far set of stairs down to the lower floor of the hold. Rather than slowing, we began climbing the crates and piles of gear, jumping down from the opposite side and climbing the next one, then jumping down and repeating, until we reached the far side of the hold.

Here, we stopped for thirty seconds to rest, then started pushups, star jumps, and sit-ups.

After three hundred of each, done in sets of fifty with sixty seconds between them, we were off again, running along the corridors to the far end of the ship, then back along the outside until we reached the rope ladders and climbed the side, wrestling ourselves back up to begin all over again.

I was seeing stars and spots, my breathing running ragged and shallow. I could taste blood with every breath, when Restun finally called it two more laps later, and I fell to the floor bonelessly.

"Well, you've earned a break, boy," he said grudgingly. "I have to admit, you've got grit, but that won't save you once we start sparring, so take your time and rest now. I'd assign those points as well, and good job on holding off this long."

He nodded briefly to me and walked away to take a drink from a canteen that hung from a nail. He'd told me in no uncertain terms that I'd be a fool to assign the points before we finished for the day, so I'd held off. Now I pulled up my screens and read through the waiting notifications.

Congratulations!

You have begun formal training under Master Trainer Restun Bashir.

As a trainee, you gain 25% to your skill and physical attribute growth due to studying under a professed Trainer!

Congratulations!

Through hard work and perseverance, you have increased your stats by the following:

Agility +1

Endurance +1

Luck +1

Strength +2

Continue to train and learn to increase this further.

I winced, feeling the painful burn from the damage I'd endured to increase all of those, but I had to admit that I was damn pleased as well.

"How...how far...can...you push...it in...training...?" I wheezed out, dismissing the screens and pulling up my character sheet in order to decide where to add the points.

"Depends on the trainee and the trainer," Restun said calmly. "It's generally agreed that the hard limit for any stat is fifty points from training. Once you hit that, it becomes all about maintaining the level, rather than losing the points."

"Losing...?" I gasped in horror.

"Of course. If you stop exercising, you'll lose the points. What did you expect, that you'd do this once and just keep them all? No; with physical stats, if you stop exercising, you'll grow flabby, weak! But don't you worry, Jax," he said, grinning evilly, "You won't have to experience that! In fact, I'm intending on finding out if it's truly a hard limit on the fifty, or if it's possible to push past it."

"Oh, god, no," I whispered, and I finally did what I kept threatening to do, but rarely found a reason to justify: I sank all of my points, all seven of them, into Endurance, boosting it from a base of thirty up to thirty-seven.

"Gods, that hurts..." I groaned as my body adjusted to the changes, altering at the cellular level to become more efficient and recover quicker.

"What did you do?" Restun asked curiously. I told him, earning a nod of approval once I explained my choice.

"Good! That means I can push you harder!" he stated crisply, throwing me the canteen. "Take a drink, then get ready, because it's time to teach you to fight."

"I know how to fight," I groaned, rolling to my feet.

"No, you *think* you do; there's a difference. I am ranked as a journeyman trainer in asha'tuun, the elite martial art of the legion. It is based around a single guiding principle, and that is death. From the beginning of any fight, any disagreement or conflict, you will be trained to kill your opponent. You will be taught that this"—he lifted a dagger up, then tossed it aside to clatter on the deck—"this is a tool." He left the small blade lying on the wooden surface and reached forward.

"While this"—his finger jabbed out to strike me on the forehead, then again on the chest above my heart—"is a weapon. It must be honed, prepared, and forged; it must be acknowledged as the weapon, and all else must be seen as a tool. I will teach you this; I will teach you to view the world in a different way. It will not make you a happier man, but it will make you a stronger one. One that can survive to become the emperor we need you to be."

"You're going to teach me to fight by changing the way I look at everything?" I asked, confused.

"When everything around you is a tool to kill with, it takes some of the beauty of the world away," he admitted soberly. "But in return, it means you will have the strength to save those who can still see such beauty. As legionnaires, we willingly sacrifice those things to enable us to stand between the empire's citizens and the oncoming night. Will you do less?" he asked, and I growled in defiance as I straightened up.

"Hell no," I snapped.

He nodded to me in respect. "Then it's time that I taught you to truly fight. These methods, these skills, are difficult to learn. They take time and dedication, but you can master them, and once you do, nothing will be able to stand against you, Lord Jax of the Empire."

"Then let's start," I said.

He guided me to a clear space where we began to stretch, working out the kinks in our muscles from the previous exercise. Ten minutes later, we began to move, slowly at first, our motions feeling almost like a dance as we shifted from one stance to another.

Restun taught me five different positions and how to move fluidly from one to another. Then we simply repeated them over and over, slowly, and the entire time, he commented, pointing out differences in bodies, in instinctive versus trained movements, discussing the kinds of joints that all sentient species had as bipeds and quadrupeds.

He explained the way we were built and how to take us apart. The way he taught drew a mental picture for me, and as he went on, he filled in the thousands of details that made the image live and breathe. He spoke of veins, of arteries, how a slight cut here or a blow there would sever the flow, stun, or even kill.

He spoke of the thousand ways a household object, a cup, a pin, a goddamn vegetable, for fuck's sake, could all be tools, and how to kill someone with each one.

He described creatures, like the Teradon, and how they could be stunned with a blow to a section under their chin where the arteries were too close to a bone. A single hard strike would block the blood flow for several seconds. In that time, the Teradon would stagger around, unable to focus, to see, or even to defend itself.

He continued as the sun set and as the moons rose, one hanging low on the horizon, full and red, while the other spun and danced overhead, a bright silvery-white.

All the while, we moved, practicing. He gradually sped up, lifting his leg slightly higher, moving the heel faster, until before I knew it, we were blurring back and forth through the forms. He had squared off to face me, and he mirrored my movements, the pair of us spinning, kicking, and jumping as we flowed from one stance to another seamlessly.

When we finally finished, I felt refreshed. Exhausted, definitely, but invigorated in a way I hadn't experienced in ages.

I felt that satisfying heat in my muscles, burning to let me know I'd had a hell of a workout, but they also felt better. They weren't screaming in pain, so much as humming with potential.

I bowed formally at the waist, as I had to many a sensei in the past, and he smiled, clapping his fist to his heart and bowing his head in return.

"It was a good day, Lord Jax," he said proudly. "I can see the potential in you that Augustus described. I have decided I will train you, after all. Each day, regardless of other distractions, you will practice the kata I have taught you, and in a month, we shall see where you stand."

"This…this was a test?" I asked him after a few stunned seconds.

"All of life is a test, Jax." He chuckled dryly. Passing allows you to try another day. I suggest you go and take a bath now, though. Knowing my legionnaires, they will have found some good spots to relax nearby."

"Thank you, I think?" I said, shaking my head. *Another goddamn test.*

I forced myself to remain upright as we went our separate ways, my legs shaking as I walked down the stairs. Once out of earshot, I let out a tired breath as Oracle flew over to me, landing on my shoulder and wrapping one arm around my head, before leaning in and kissing the top of my head.

"You're all sweaty," she complained, and I snorted out a weary laugh.

"What did you expect, after all that? Besides, you didn't complain the other night about me being all sweaty…"

"You were naked then, and so was I," she said airily, wafting her tiny hand dismissively through the air. "Different rules apply."

"Okay, then," I said, arching an eyebrow at her. "Fancy finding a storeroom where I can get naked and less sweaty in private?"

"Nope," she said firmly.

"Why not?" I asked, a touch disappointed.

"Because I've already sorted somewhere out where we can get naked, then clean, then have some fun," my impish companion explained, grinning down at me.

I grinned back, and she pointed to the left as we came to a cross-corridor. I followed her imperiously guiding finger, then realized how short her skirt was and remembered the other night, picking up speed as I went.

It took us a dozen minutes to get free of the ship and emerge out into the forest, a handful of legionnaires appearing around us and flanking us as we made the trek.

"They've already cleared the area, and they'll make sure we're not interrupted," Oracle reassured me with a naughty grin in response to my questioning look.

I accepted their presence and continued to follow her guiding gestures, activating my DarkVision to make it easier. I soon noted the regularity of the thicker vegetation and the way certain sections were clearer than others.

"It's a garden, isn't it?" I asked her, peering around. "A giant, overgrown garden."

"That's right," she confirmed. "In the tower, the plants could only grow so far, with the limited space and combination of elevation and exposure to the elements contributing to make the gardens smaller, though still lush. Out here, however, there's only been the occasional storm to endure. Even then, those merely served to spread the vegetation around, rather than scour the area clean."

"So, wait…the entire island under our feet is the city?" I wondered, gazing around with new eyes, observing the lush undergrowth and heavy tree cover.

"Depending on the area, it's anywhere from a few inches to dozens of feet. Then you've got higher structures that have long since collapsed, like that one," she clarified, gesturing to what I'd taken to be a hill. "They've been overgrown, again and again, and any animals that were aboard, including those that have been brought here over the years, or that have accidentally floated to shore on driftwood, have adapted as well."

"Damn," I breathed. "I thought the city had crashed into an island and buried itself or something."

We pushed through a thick section of hanging vines and came out into a glade containing a small hidden pool that glimmered in the moonlight.

One of the Legionnaires—Rinko, I suddenly recognized—moved closer and saluted us.

"We'll make sure you have some peace and quiet, Jax, don't worry," he said, winking and holding out a small bundle. I inspected it cautiously, finding freshly-made clothes, and as I sniffed them, I grinned appreciatively. The clean, fresh scent was enough that I almost stripped on the spot.

"Thank you, man," I said in earnest. He grinned in response and turned away, before I called out, causing him to glance back over his shoulder. "Oh, and Rinko, I'll trust you to keep Grizz well clear? He's got a habit of interrupting at particularly…inappropriate…times?"

He snorted in amusement.

"He'll find it hard, considering Faren and Hess tied him to a chair in the ship and buried him under a pile of canvas, just in case." With that, he winked and walked away, and I grinned in the darkness.

Satisfied that we were alone, I turned back to the pool. I had felt Oracle lift from my shoulder during the exchange with Rinko, and I saw her now, perched gracefully on a rock that jutted up in the center of the water, full-sized and naked.

Her hair was as dark as midnight suddenly, her eyes smoky, and her figure full. She lifted one hand, beckoning me.

I couldn't get undressed fast enough, but before my thoughts had caught up with my movements, I was stepping down into the pleasantly cool water, wading out to her.

The pool grew deeper with each step until I was forced to swim the last few feet to reach her. I had always been graceless in the water, too heavy and clumsy, but that was far from my mind as I pulled myself up from the liquid depths, reaching up eagerly as she leaned down for a kiss.

It went on and on, her tongue slipping into my mouth and mine into hers; then she was sliding free of the rock and sliding down into the pool with me. Her lips remained glued to mine, our arms wrapping around each other and her legs lifting, resting and locking onto my hips.

As the water closed above our heads, my feet impacted the bottom on the pool in an explosion of silt. I dipped my legs, pushing off powerfully and driving us toward shallower water.

As soon as we reached the light, we broke the kiss, me to take in a replenishing lungful of air, and her to nuzzle into my neck, as she'd found I liked.

I lowered my arms from wrapping around her back, my right hand sliding down to cup her ass and pull her tight against me, while my left reached up, enclosing the full firmness of her right breast and tracing with a finger the hardness of the tip.

She gasped, then giggled, and we sank again from sight, the legionnaires firmly keeping their eyes and ears trained outward as their lord and his lady enjoyed each other as quietly, yet fervently, as they could.

CHAPTER SEVEN

I returned to consciousness slowly, a reluctant tapping on the door forcing me to rouse as Oracle growled in annoyance. She slipped out from under my arm and stalked to the door, her clothes materializing as she went.

I remained lying in the pile of blankets we'd gathered against the far wall. The camp bed had collapsed *again* at some point after we'd returned to our room, and we'd piled its remains against a nearby wall to be fixed or disposed of.

A portion of Oracle's growled question drifted to me, followed by a low conversation, then a sigh as the door was closed again. I laid there still, on the verge of returning to sleep, eyes shut, as she moved over to me and crouched.

The warm, vanilla scent of her breath brushed my cheek, and the soft press of her lips warm as she kissed me. I opened my eyes, blinking up at her. I couldn't help smiling in reflex as I focused on her face, outlined by the faint pre-dawn sunlight streaming in through the small window.

"Morning," I whispered and kissed her. When she pulled back, she was smiling, but she gently disengaged herself from my arms when I tried to draw her back into bed.

"We don't have time, unfortunately!" she said gently but firmly.

"You sure?" I whispered, grinning and trying to tug her down again.

"Very sure!" she said, shaking her head regretfully as she slipped free of me and lifted into the air, shrinking to her smaller form. I groaned as she moved out of reach, and I fell back onto the pillow, running my hands through my hair and rubbing my eyes with the palms.

"Why are we always rushing?" I complained to myself. "Can't we—just once—wake up slow, relax, have some morning chillout time, some head, maybe a bacon sandwich," I muttered disconsolately.

"You're the one who arranged for the representatives of both camps to come to meet us at first light," she said, grinning, "and actually, you're also the guy who declared war on Himnel, which is what led to this, remember?"

"Details, details," I mumbled, sitting up and stretching. "God, we need a decent mattress. I'm aching from last night," I said as I clambered clumsily to my feet, trying to stretch the kinks out of my back.

"Are you complaining?" Oracle asked me.

"Only that you won't come play again," I retorted, and she laughed as she shook a tiny finger at me.

"It took me weeks to tempt you into bed. What happened to all your self-control and patience?" she demanded.

"It's long gone, I tell you." I snorted out a laugh. "Once that line was crossed, that was it. I did warn you, if you remember."

"That you were a sex pest and you'd be constantly trying to get your hands on me? I don't remember you warning me about that."

"Hey, who was naked first last night? Who arranged a little private place?" I shot back as I pulled on the clean, smart clothes the tailors had prepared for me yesterday. The pants were a bit snug and the chest too loose, but considering they were working with already-made gear and adjusting it to fit me, I couldn't complain. They'd promised I'd be getting some properly tailored clothes soon.

"Details, details," Oracle replied airily, floating backwards as she waved a hand negligently to brush away my comment. "Anyway, that was Yen at the door. The scouts have picked up the two groups leaving their bases and tracked them to twenty minutes out."

"Okay, sounds like we've got just enough time to get out front and be ready for them, then," I calculated, nodding to her appreciatively. I had left my armor piled up by the door into our room, but apart from the boots, which were worn out but my only option at present, I left it all behind, carrying only my battered belt, bags, and naginata.

The rest of my weapons and gear had mainly been stashed in my various bags of holding now, anyway, and I resolved to empty those as much as possible before this afternoon's excursion.

Oracle landed deftly on my right shoulder, and I walked over to the door, tugging it open to reveal four legionnaires waiting outside: Yen and Tang, along with two I didn't yet know.

They all straightened reflexively, fists smashing to chests as I stepped out, and I returned the salute, before Yen spoke.

"Good morning, Jax. The delegates are on their way now. Prefect Romanus has set up a tent to hold the meeting; shall we go straight to it?" she asked crisply.

"Morning, Yen, everyone," I said, looking at each of them with a smile. "Yeah, that sounds good. Lead the way, please."

We set off at a fast walk, covering the distance to the gangplank and off the ship in only a few minutes' time. When I asked about the new route we'd taken, and noted how much faster it was, Yen was quick to explain.

"Augustus has been working the golems hard," she said. I couldn't help but smile at that, until Restun slipped in alongside me as we walked.

"Good morning, my lord," he said, his tone full of respect, and my butt puckered in fear.

"Morning, Centurion Primus," I said, swallowing a suddenly dry mouth. "Unfortunately, no time to train this morning; we've guests incoming."

"I know," he said simply. "I'm glad that you think it's unfortunate, though, as it shows you know you need to continue with your training." He carried on, glancing at me as I nodded quickly. "And because you know it's important, I know you'll want to fit in an hour before you go into the Sunken City."

He smiled smoothly as he finished, deftly closing the jaws of the trap.

"I…uh," I mumbled, before forcibly kick-starting my brain again. "I *would*, you know that, Primus, but I need to sort out my new armor and my squad, as I've not selected a team yet, not fully. Maybe when I return—"

"So you've not chosen your escort yet?" he asked slowly. I frantically cast about for a way to stop him from offering to join us.

"I...I—" I said articulately, when Yen stepped in smoothly.

"You did say that you wouldn't confirm the places in your team until today, Lord Jax, but it was filled within minutes by volunteers, both those who'd already fought by your side and those who hadn't. How many did you decide on bringing in the end?" Yen asked, barely risking a meaningful glance.

"I...eight," I said, frantically picking a number at random.

"Hmmm, good choice, too small to attract too much attention, but big enough to handle most things," Restun murmured approvingly. "Who are you taking?"

We had walked down the gangplank, across the clearing, and were approaching the tent when I saw some of my usual squad standing nearby, and I sighed in relief.

"Lydia, Arrin, Jian, Stephanos, and Miren, of course," I said quickly, "that's five, then Yen and Tang, if they want to come?" I offered, getting smiles and accepting nods from both. As I glanced around frantically, I caught a glimpse of the man I was looking for a few seconds later, getting ribbed by a few legionnaires and giving as good as he got.

"And Grizz; he was assigned to me as a bodyguard, after all." I practically jumped on the choice, then blinked and went on more calmly. "And Bane, and me? So...ten in total?"

"Hmmm..." Restun said slowly. "I thought you'd settled on eight?" He eyed me suspiciously, and I quickly raised placating hands.

"I had, but that's because I think of Bane in the same way I do Oracle; he's a companion, not a member of the squad, if you understand."

"Ah, I get it. A good bodyguard becomes a fixture in your life. I shall include him in some additional training, then, and make sure he is up to the task." Restun nodded in satisfaction to himself, and I felt the low *thrummm* of Bane's amusement cut off abruptly, making me smile suddenly, much wider and more evilly than I had before.

"That's a great idea, Primus! In fact, I remember thinking last night, when I kept running past my squad, *as they ate and drank*, that maybe I should ask you to take over their training?" I agreed smoothly, eyeing Arrin, who was by far the weakest of the group, trying to charm a woman who appeared utterly unimpressed with him. That bastard had been hollering at me last night to go faster, I certainly remembered that.

"Hmmm, well, with your own training, I have made time in my schedule," he explained hesitantly.

"I could cut back on some of my training, for their sake!" I slipped in hopefully, only to be met with an evil grin from him that made my heart plummet.

"Oh no, Lord Jax. You need every bit of that training, though perhaps I will simply fold your training and theirs together, doubling up on it, as it were. In fact, that's a fantastic idea. They will join you in training, then! And, after the physical side is done, you and I will continue to train alone, in asha'tuun."

"Fuck," I muttered, reading the glimmer of triumph in his eyes.

That wily bastard had planned this, I realized, and I'd fallen straight for it, slipping my entire personal squad in under his command for training, when previously they'd been outside of his reach. Not only that, now I was going to be getting at least as much training as before, if not more. *Double fuck.*

"Glad to hear you're so enthusiastic," he said, chuckling with unbridled amusement. "I'll let you inform your squad. Oh, and Yen, Tang, and Grizz? I expect you to be there as well."

He graced them with a beatific smile before saluting me and walking away into the light drizzle without a care in the world.

"What?" Grizz said, having just joined us as Restun was leaving.

"Well, Grizz, I've got good news for you, mate," Tang said stepping up to him and clapping him on the shoulder.

"Great!" Grizz said, smiling, then immediately frowned. "Wait, it's never good news when the centurion primus is that happy. I've only ever seen him smile like that when…" He paused nervously, his mind working frantically through the options, before letting out a small whisper. "Oh gods, no."

"Oh, yeah," Tang confirmed, nodding. "His fault."

He yanked his head to indicate me.

"Why?" Grizz asked frantically. "Look, okay, I probably took the joke too far, interrupting you guys so much, but come on, boss?!" He dropped his face into his hands and groaned loudly.

"Oh, don't worry," Yen piped up grimly. "It's not just you."

"What?" Grizz asked, whipping his head back up and noting the expressions on both Yen and Tang's faces, then the wide grins on the faces of the rest of the legionnaires that passed by.

"I was conned," I said shortly.

"You never heard the saying, did you?" Yen asked me, quirking an almost-sympathetic smile.

"Which one?" I asked.

"'If you think you've won when it comes to a centurion primus, count your fingers, toes, then relatives,'" she said sadly.

"That's not a real saying," I scoffed, ducking under the canvas edge of a large grey-green tent, and shaking myself, sweeping my hair back from my face and running my fingers through my beard to get rid of the water. "Damn, I need a trim."

"Well, I can do it," offered Bane, materializing out of stealth. "Just let me near that throat with my blades…" he finished in a low growl.

"Not a chance!" I said, grinning at him. "You brought this on yourself, mate!"

"How?!" he growled, and I opened my mouth to tell him when Lydia and the rest of her team reached the tent, coming inside in response to my waved invitation. Romanus was heading across the grass, and with him were a dozen or so other legionnaires, carrying tables, chairs, and more.

"Hi, guys," I said to the squad, smiling at their return greetings. "Look, I'm just going to get this over with." I sighed, giving up on any chance of sugarcoating it. "There's no good way to say this, but you all know who Centurion Primus Restun is, right?" I asked, grinning evilly when Arrin spoke up.

"The guy who was torturing you last night? Oh yeah, we like him!" he asked cheerfully, eliciting a few chuckles.

"Yup, that's the guy. Well, there's good news and bad news, so what do you want first?" I asked.

"Bad news," Lydia replied. "Always tha bad news first."

"Fair enough. He's decided to take over the training for us all," I said, glancing around at the rapidly shifting looks on their faces.

Lydia looked like all her Christmases had come at once. Arrin looked like he was going to be sick, with the rest of the group falling somewhere in between.

"What the hell is the good news, then?" Arrin gasped, appalled.

"Well, if you want to come explore the Sunken City with me, you can probably put off beginning the training for a day or two," I chuckled.

"I'm in," Grizz said straight away. "Anything that keeps me out of his clutches for a little longer? Hell yes."

"Me, too."

"Oh yes."

"Can we go now?"

The others spoke up quickly, falling over themselves in their haste to escape Restun, with only Lydia and Jian looking disappointed at our imminent departure and the delayed opportunity for bodily torture.

"So, boss, the Sunken City," Grizz prompted, and I nodded for him to continue. "Is this a, *oh, you know,* a situation where…if, just as a wild example, off the top of my head…a certain legionnaire was to loot some stuff—gold, jewels, that kinda thing—that legionnaire would keep them, or would they have to give them up?" he asked mildly, trying to appear innocently curious.

"It's a case of looting for the group," I said firmly. "Everyone gets a cut, but the majority of high-value stuff goes into the coffers. If we find spellbooks, skillbooks, or memory crystals, those definitely go into the vault, but I'll be giving a bonus out at the end of the dive, as you'll have damn well earned it, and you know, risked your life and shit."

"What about gear?" Tang asked.

"Depends what it is." I shrugged. "You'll note the drow weapons everyone has?" I pointed out, and he nodded. "They were all looted. I don't have any issue with handing out the gear we take; I just want to make sure it goes to the best person for it. None of that shit about claiming stuff when you can't use it, to just sell it later, understand?"

"Yeah, that's fine," Yen said, nodding her agreement. "We've all heard about people in the adventuring parties doing that. For the legion, it's a lot different. Usually, we give up everything to the legion coffers, then we get a bonus for it. Most gets sold to keep the legion going, but sometimes you can buy the gear you want from the internal auctions before it goes outside."

"You loot it, hand it over, then have to buy it out of the pot with your own money?" I asked suspiciously.

"It's the fairest way, Jax," Romanus interjected as he joined us. "It's never been popular, but when it costs as much to feed and clothe the legion as it does, not to mention healing potions and other supplies, well, it has to be done."

"You buy potions?" I gaped, shocked to my core. "Surely you have people who can make them?"

"Yes and no. We had a single alchemist, and he had an assistant. That was the Legion General—the alchemist, I mean—and his assistant had only been studying under him a few months, as his previous assistant died last year."

"That's unlucky," I said, frowning suspiciously at the too-convenient obstacle.

"Yes, you could say that," Romanus said grimly. "It was right after we'd started to sell our own potions, due to having teams of legionnaires harvesting ingredients. It was a way to get out from under the thumb of the nobility and their taxes on the people, or so we thought, until the man who was making the potions came down with a bad case of dead. Steel poisoning."

"Steel poisoning? I didn't realize…you mean he was stabbed, don't you?" I faltered, sighing at the confirming nod and moving on. "So, the assistant was making them, or the Legion General?"

"His assistant was making the vast majority, as the Legion General was too busy, understandably. His death meant we started having to buy them in again, instead of selling them. Then when we lost the general, with his new assistant only half-trained…well, the costs rose again," he said grimly.

"Gotcha." I met his embittered eyes firmly. "Well, I've got some good news there, then."

"Oh?" Romanus asked, lifting one eyebrow. "Do tell. Gods know we could always use some of that."

"Do you have access to many skillbooks or memory crystals in the legion?"

I received a snort of derision as an answer.

"They cost more than a legionnaire makes in years, Jax. The exceedingly rare times we loot them from battles or monster hunts, we've been forced to sell them, as whoever uses them gets murdered in the city shortly after, otherwise," Romanus growled, anger and bitterness tinging his voice.

"Well, I've got a few hundred of each back at the Great Tower," I admitted, casually dropping the bombshell into the conversation. "Spellbooks, too." Silence spread around me as Romanus and the rest of the legionnaires present absorbed that information. "I'm an alchemist as well. I'm crap at it, don't get me wrong, but I can do it."

"You have access to hundreds of them?" Romanus asked me slowly, his eyes searching my face with nervous hope. "Truly?"

"Yeah, and they cover everything from the basics to master level. Don't get me wrong; there's not a full library of everything but it's pretty packed," I confirmed, shooting a quick look up at Oracle, who still sat, smiling proudly, on my shoulder.

"You…I…" Romanus spluttered, trying to get his words out, before turning and locking eyes with Tribune Alistor. "You see! I told you the risk was worth it! This is truly the rebirth of the legion!"

"Yes…Prefect," he said flatly, his eyes never leaving me, only forcing an oily smile when he caught me watching him.

I glanced from him to Romanus, realizing that Romanus had entirely missed the exchange and was lost in imagining a future where the legion wasn't barely scrabbling by, but was instead respected, well-supplied, and supported.

My heart clenched when I realized what he was seeing. He wasn't thinking of personal wealth or glory; he was picturing a world where the people he was responsible for weren't hated and reviled. Despite seeing the causes of this desire already, knowing the weight of it, it still filled me with a simmering fury.

"Lord Jax, Prefect Romanus, they're here," a legionnaire stationed outside the tent announced. I nodded my thanks to him, swallowing my rage. The adjutants had finished setting up the inside of the tent and were filing out quickly, leaving chairs and a low table covered with food ready for us.

"We can discuss this more later, then, but I'm going to damn well look after the legion, Romanus, you have my word," I reassured him, dismissing the tribune's odd behavior from my thoughts, and turning to walk out of the tent. Romanus and the others followed my lead, with Tang and Yen staying close by. Bane was hidden somewhere close as well, I presumed, while Lydia guided the rest of the team away to give us some room to talk. Oracle lifted from my shoulder to hover at the edge of the tent, just inside the protection from the rain.

I stopped just outside the entrance, taking in the scenery for a moment. The slight drizzle was picking up to a steady downpour, making the branches of the trees surrounding the clearing shake as rivulets of water ran from their leaves.

The battleship had landed as gracefully as it could, all things considered. But due to its size, it had still taken out a sizable swath of forest when it had come to rest. This clearing, which the legion was leading the delegates to, was only large enough to accommodate the bow of the battleship at one end, and that was surrounded by broken trees.

I glanced back at the devastation, then shook my head, wondering about the damage the forest must have caused to the ship. I abandoned that line of thought, however, as the first group left the tree line and walked out into the clearing.

A tall, slim man led them. He was impeccably dressed in dark, knee-length boots, white trousers and shirt, topped by a red jacket and gold flashing ostentatiously at both collar and wrist, with a gold-lined black cloak flapping behind him.

His long, dark hair was pulled back and tied up atop his head, a variety of feathers sticking out of the arrangement. He totally ignored the slightly built man who hurried alongside him, holding one side of a square sheet over his head with a pair of poles. The child who bore the other side of the sheet stumbled as he tried to avoid catching it on a tree. Both he and the slight man, who motioned frantically for him to keep up, were dressed in well-worn, rough clothes, frequently mended tears in the knees and hems clear to see as they moved closer.

The pole-supported sheet was the local equivalent of an umbrella, I realized as the water streamed down the sides and off the back as the first man strode forward. He was followed by a coterie of eight guards, and unlike the guards from the city, they were heavily equipped.

Their heavy plate armor had been painted or dyed a glossy black, with a streak of red slashing across the helm and down over the right pauldron. Each was armed identically with a large, triangular red shield and a spear, a heavy shortsword clattering against their leg with every step.

"I am Lord Faustus, and I own this relic," the man said, coming to halt several feet back from our party and speaking before I could. "I have come, as a gentleman, to discuss your immediate removal from my property, and to accept your apologies and the restitution you owe for this damage." He gestured toward the flattened trees.

"What?" I ground out in shock.

He merely strode past me into the tent, followed by two of his guards as the rest took up station nearby.

I started to turn, fully intending to give this stuck-up fucker a piece of my mind, when Romanus quietly interrupted me.

"The second party is here," he said discreetly.

I growled under my breath, shaking my head in frustration as I ignored the prick inside helping himself to the food we'd laid out.

The second party proved to be larger than the first, with fewer guards but far more people. Where the first group had topped out at eleven, counting the guards, noble, and his umbrella bearers, the new group was composed of at least twenty.

Only four guards were easily noticeable, but two men dressed as nobles were being carried along on separate palanquins. Each was supported by four muscular beings, the one on the right borne by heavily muscled cat people, the one on the left by people that made me think of velociraptors given humanoid form.

Following behind the palanquins were another ten or so men and women of various species, each dressed in an odd blend of fashions, but all talking excitedly and occasionally pointing at the Legion and the ships.

They came to a halt a few steps from me, and both men slid down, the older man being helped from his palanquin by a young boy I'd not noticed before, while the younger man jumped clear himself.

Where the first noble had dismissed me as unimportant, these two looked me over curiously before eyeing Romanus and shooting an unreadable glance at each other.

The older man took the lead, speaking clearly to Romanus, while the younger peered around warily, stopping only when he spotted the first party standing off to one side.

"I am Lord Hannimish, Count of the Southern Woods and the River Gaige. I have come at your request. Where is your master?"

"Hannimish!" the second noble snapped, interrupting Romanus as he opened his mouth to respond. "Look! That ass Faustus and his men are here!" Hannimish turned to look in the direction his companion indicated and growled, his color bleeding from lightly tanned to florid with anger.

"I see Faustus has beaten us to it. Very well; where is your lord, legionnaire? Tell him I have an offer for him that will eclipse whatever that thief Faustus thinks to offer! Hurry up, man!" he snapped, glaring past me as though I didn't exist and squinting into the tent, where Faustus glared back at him. Romanus turned to me and bowed, fist to heart, and spoke loudly and clearly so that both parties could hear him.

"Lord Jax, Scion of the Empire and High Lord of Dravith, Master of the Great Tower, and Champion of the Himnel Arena, Count Hannimish feels he can make you an offer, although what that is, he has declined to state." With that, he straightened up and returned to a position of attention.

"Thank you, Romanus," I ground out, trying to remain as calm as possible. "Sit with me. I think I need to reevaluate this meeting, as I'd expected common courtesy, at the very least." I turned, walking into the tent and shaking the rain from my hair. Once inside, Oracle shifted, blurring to full size, and joined Romanus and me as I strode purposefully to the back of the tent, tipping Faustus's jacket onto the floor and sitting in the seat he'd obviously decided was his.

"How dare you!" he gasped, dropping his hand to a slim rapier that hung on his hip. Instantly, the atmosphere of the meeting changed, as the legion came to life. The legionnaires around the outskirts of the clearing spun to face the tent, one in every five facing outwards to maintain their watch, while the rest drew their swords and stood ready.

Romanus had his hand on his blade. Augustus and Restun had appeared from seemingly nowhere, while Tang and Yen joined the two legionnaires stationed in the doorway.

The two small groups of guards were surrounded in seconds by dozens of battle-hardened veterans, and the air crackled with the promise of death. I turned to Faustus, who had frozen, his rapier only half-drawn, as he registered the reaction of the legion.

"I'd recommend you sheathe that," I said flatly.

"Who do you think you are!" he snarled at me, eyes flinty with hatred. "I am L—"

"Lord Faustus, high muckety muck, chief wanker and all that." I waved my hand dismissively, cutting him off as I sat back. I casually braced my naginata across my lap as Oracle came to stand behind me, one hand resting lightly on my right shoulder. "Let's start with that then. You see, there's a problem with any title you claim," I said slowly and distinctly, biting the words off.

"I am the High Lord of Dravith, and all titles, deeds, and laws in my lands are officially up for review. As such, you can call yourself lord, king, or whatever else you think you deserve, but it doesn't mean shit."

I steepled my hands in front of me as he gaped indignantly.

"Now, you stormed past me as if I didn't matter, okay, I'm not dressed appropriately, so maybe that's on me, but the way you acted before the legion prefect and his men? Legionnaires you damn well had to recognize as officials of the empire? No. That's not acceptable." I stared him down, my tone flat with anger.

"They are legionnaires!" Faustus interrupted me, glaring indignantly, while Hannimish and his companion kept silent, observing.

"Yes," I said firmly. "They are *legionnaires*. People who dedicate their lives to making sure the empire is protected, to hunting monsters, defending the weak, and standing between innocents and the evil of the realm. And. You. Just. Treat. Them. Like. Shit," I enunciated, punctuating every word with scorn.

"Ridiculous; they're just legionnaires!" Faustus snapped again, totally unaware of the effect his attitude was having. "Anyway, they don't matter! I was deeded this relic by Lord Barabarattas himself! To that effect, you are trespassing, and you will leave immediately!

"You have ships, I see…they look similar in design to the great airships of Himnel, although they are obviously inferior. I will permit you to take two of the smaller ones. The rest will remain here as restitution for your crimes! Legionnaires, I have spoken. Do your duty!"

"You sure that's what you want them to do?" I asked him, my voice dropping to a low purr. "You want these legionnaires to perform as their duty tells them?"

I could see the legionnaires in the tent shift, and the fool went on speaking.

"Silence, you oaf!" he snarled at me. "Learn to hold your tongue when your betters speak, or lose it! Legionnaires, I *ORDER* you to do your duty!"

"Very well. Romanus, do 'your duty,' please, and inform those outside as well." I smiled coldly, leaning back in my chair as I reached out to the nearby table, picking up a slim wedge of pale cheese and taking a bite.

Romanus saluted smartly, and, barely able to keep the grin from his face and the satisfaction from his voice, he called out clearly to the legionnaires around the clearing, his voice only slightly muffled by the tent fabric.

"Legionnaires! Our duty is clear, and we have been *ordered* to carry it out! Those two appear to be enslaved citizens." He gestured to the shabby man and boy that had been carrying Lord Faustus's rain cover. "Investigate their story and stand ready. Any and all forces inside the boundaries of the empire are now declared subordinate to the legion or are our enemies.

"As it was in the empire of old, so shall it be again!" Romanus roared, and the legion echoed the cry back to him, clashing their swords against shields and advancing upon the tent menacingly.

"As it was in the empire of old, so shall it be again!" they bellowed to the skies.

Dozens of alkyon and djinn took up station, appearing from nowhere to hover in the air above, crossbows and spells clearly primed, even as the ships overhead shifted in their steady patrols and dipped lower, closing the distance to the ground.

The woods rang with the sound of marching feet, and dozens upon dozens of legionnaires marched out into the drizzle, their armor gleaming wetly as they took up position in formation.

Four legionnaires approached the two slaves that had carried the rain cover, and they spoke quickly in low voices.

"Wait, what…what is this all about?" Faustus whined, his anger and pride draining from him like wine from a cracked jug in the face of the legion roused to anger.

"I am the Scion of the Empire," I growled. "Until I take my place as emperor, I speak for the empire. When I do take that final step, I will *be* the empire. Either way, you have threatened me, spoken down to me, and attempted to rob me, not to mention breaking the laws of the empire blatantly before me. And beyond all of these offenses, you had the gall to order my legionnaires to do their duty? All legionnaires, everywhere, are under my direct command now, as Acknowledged Scion of the Empire. There is no higher authority than mine," I finished, my anger building as my voice dipped to a low rumble.

This man—no, this self-righteous *fool* was ordering *my* legion to do their duty? He who blatantly had slaves carrying a fucking umbrella for him?

Power built as my anger grew, and without knowing why, I rose to my feet, shaking my head slightly and cracking my neck. The muscles of my shoulders flexed as my body subconsciously prepared for war, and a glorious feeling of building anger and power filled me.

"Romanus, get the slaves down here, fast," Oracle ordered, feeling the building rage, her voice crackling with authority, and he saluted her without pause.

"Yes, my Lady Wisp," he acknowledged, spinning to address the legionnaires close around the tent and passing orders in terse sentences.

I strode out into the gentle rain. Romanus, following along behind, grabbed Faustus and dragged him along, the weasely lord's shoulder gripped inextricably in one gauntleted fist.

I looked over the men and women that had filtered in to surround the clearing. The legion were present, of course, but peering out from behind them, from every angle, were hundreds of common people. Milling liberally around the stoic legionnaires, these emaciated, filthy, people who, even now, remained terrified of being harmed, were the slaves we'd freed from the city.

These hundreds of men, women, and children were creatures of every race, small and large, from gnomes to a half-giant creature who huddled at the back in an attempt to hide, seemingly unaware of his massive size and strength.

They stood there, soaking in the rain, all looking to me, all rescued by my order, and all desperate for a chance. A single chance at life again.

They slowly crowded forward as my power grew, sensing something as it poured through me, a river growing by the second. I strode into the center of the clearing, my steps implacable, obeying a need that poured through me until, all at once, my feet lifted from the ground, and I began to glow. My love, my companion, my heart, Oracle, was drawn up beside me, her usual faint shine now radiating like the sun as she threw back her head, power flowing through us both.

Her emotions resonated with mine, feeding my rage and strangely, my love; the two emotions, so different, yet so necessary, two sides of the same coin, built and reinforced each other as the Ability continued to amplify.

"Who am I?" I called out, slowly rotating, able to see every last detail in the clearing in stark clarity as shadows were banished by the light of the Imperial Ability, Righteous Rage as it built in power, called into being by its master.

"I AM LORD JAX," I called out, my voice booming in the stunned silence, augmented by the power. "I WILL BE YOUR HOPE. I AM YOUR LORD AND YOUR SERVANT. YOU WHO HAVE BEEN ABANDONED, DISCARDED, AND ENSLAVED, I AM YOURS. WHEN NO ONE STOOD FOR YOU, I NOW WILL." Lightning crackled across me, jumping from hands to feet and arcing in the air.

"I WILL PROTECT YOU. I WILL BE THE ROCK YOU STAND UPON TO REACH THE LIGHT. NEVER AGAIN WILL A LEGIONNAIRE DIE ALONE AND FORGOTTEN. YOU WILL ALL BE REMEMBERED, HONORED, AND LOVED," I intoned, slowly lifting higher. As I cleared the tree line, hanging unsupported in the air, I saw them, and I felt Amon. The souls of those he had lost, the crew of the Prax, named Glorious Retribution, seemed summoned into existence by my power.

I felt them, flickers of will, or honor and dedication, rising from the Sunken City as they were drawn to me, desperate for absolution, for forgiveness of their failures, in allowing Glorious Retribution to be smashed from the sky so long ago.

Lights rose from the wilderness all around me, dozens, then hundreds of them, glowing souls that were being drawn from the depths of the city by my power and lifted into the air by the grace of my magic.

The long-dead crew of the Prax flickered as they came closer, their incorporeal forms glowing as the first jolts of lightning flashed out to them from the gathering storm of mana. These quick jolts of energy granted them visibility to mortal eyes once again in daylight.

Cries rose from below as hundreds of the souls of the dead, unable to move on, punishing themselves for centuries over a failure that wasn't their fault, became visible to the average person.

They streamed up to me, their calls echoing in my ears as Amon reached out our arms, and our power altered. So many of these spirits, the souls of the forgotten, forced by a twisted sense of duty and their own personal beliefs that they should have done more, had been bound indefinitely to this plane of existence.

I saw them as I never had before, and I knew then that the world was filled with them: the unquiet dead, trapped in this realm, unable to move on until they received absolution.

"I AM YOUR LORD, AND I AM THE IMPERIAL SCION, ACKNOWLEDGED HEIR TO THE THRONE," I whispered in a voice that bounced off walls and echoed in the bones of all who heard it.

"I SEE YOU AND I REMEMBER; I FORGIVE YOUR PERCEIVED FAILURES. KNOW THAT I, JAX AMON, DECLARE YOU TO BE WHOLE. YOU ARE NOT FAILURES. YOU ARE NOT BROKEN. YOU ARE NOT WEAK. YOU WERE FAILED BY THE REALM AND THE EMPIRE, NOT THE OTHER WAY AROUND. YOU ARE LOVED, AND YOU ARE ENOUGH," I declared, tears running down my cheeks and turning into wisps of steam as they boiled away from the power that flooded my form.

"I SEE YOUR SOULS. I SEE YOUR POWER AND YOUR PAIN. I SEE YOUR POTENTIAL, AND I SEE THOSE WHO HAVE DONE THIS TO YOU," I snarled, my voice rising in anger as the power built to a crescendo inside me.

"I SHALL BRING YOU VENGEANCE. I SHALL BRING THE DEAD PEACE, THE LIVING FREEDOM, AND THE SOULS YET UNBORN THE CHANCE TO STAND TALL IN THE LIGHT OF THE SUN! YOUR CAPTORS AND TORTURERS SHALL KNOW MY WRATH, THOSE WHO HAVE IMPRISONED MY CHILDREN!" My voice boomed in the air, shaking leaves from the trees, and stunning those around me into silence.

"FOR I AM JAX AMON, HEIR AND LORD, AND I DECLARE YOU TO BE MY IMPERIAL SUBJECTS. AS SUCH, YOU ARE FREE OF ALL OTHER TIES!" I screamed those final word, as the world seemed to reverberate with power. Blinding white light roared outwards, tearing at the ground, and latching onto slave brands and collars, leashes that were welded into place, and worse, harnesses that had been fused to bone through some mix of evil magic.

All of these were touched and bathed in the pure white light of Righteous Rage, and when it passed, it left behind clear, healed skin, unmarked by any blemish.

Hundreds of slaves and former prisoners were lifted into the air on wings of my power, scoured of injuries, and in the dark places of their souls, they found light as they found me.

As the light receded, and I slowly lowered to the ground, my feet gently touching down onto the grass, I heard and saw them, my people, weeping as they rejoiced in their freedom.

The empire was born anew that day for many, a weight lifting from my heart as I accepted my role .

CHAPTER EIGHT

I turned back to the tent, to Romanus and his prisoner, to the lords from Narkolt and their sycophants and guards. I looked from one to another of their stunned faces, feeling the burn of using magics not meant for mortals.

Oracle landed next to me, full-sized again, clad in a gleaming white dress with a belt of woven silver leaves around her waist and judgement for the lords in her eyes. Her hair, black as a raven's wing, ran down her upper back in ringlets and curls, while lightning still crackled across her body, leaping and flashing across to mine and back.

We stood glaring at the delegates we'd invited with open hearts to discuss the Sunken City. I'd had high hopes of recruiting them or at least of sharing information with them, purchasing maps or artifacts. At worst, I had expected to simply warn them to keep out of our way.

Now Romanus stood gripping a nobleman who'd been revealed as a slaver, if the pulse of white fire that had caressed his two rain-cover bearers was any judge.

"I...I...how?" Faustus sputtered, before seemingly remembering himself and deciding it was demeaning for him to be held by a "mere" legionnaire. He twisted and glared at Romanus, attempting to backhand him across the face.

Romanus simply twisted him, the attempted blow becoming a pathetic brush of his lacy sleeve instead. The prefect took one quick glance at me, then smiled grimly and stomped down hard on the back of Faustus's left calf, twisting, and shoving down on the shoulder he still held.

Faustus fell to his knees, and Romanus switched his grip, grabbing the back of the callous lord's head and pressing down, folding him over and exposing his neck. His gladius announced its presence into the suddenly silent clearing.

All around the periphery, people who had been whispering, weeping in joy, and laughing, had fallen silent, watching the spectacle of a noble, one of their "betters" being shoved down and prepared for execution without the benefit of a trial, without the usual gold and backhanders changing the facts, and without the chance to become one of those who had broken even the most heinous of laws only to simply laugh and walk free.

Instead, they heard his startled yelp of pain as Romanus's razor-sharp blade came to rest directly over his arced neck, ready to slice through the spinal cord.

"Please!" Faustus cried out. "I have gold! I...I have more slaves! You can have them!" he whimpered frantically.

"From his own mouth, he condemns himself, Lord Jax," Romanus called to me, raising one eyebrow in question.

"Do it," I ordered flatly, turning to the guards he had brought with him.

They stood uncertainly in the clearing to one side, surrounded by legionnaires, and a single movement would spell their doom.

"Your former lord broke the laws of the empire," I called to them. "One of the earliest laws established was that slavery was illegal and that slavers were to be summarily put to death." As I spoke, Romanus ignored Faustus's squeal for mercy and drove his sword down with a grunt. The sharp blade sheared through the gap between Faustus's upper vertebrae, slicing through the cord, and severing his head's attachment to his body.

Romanus twisted the blade, forcing the cleaved vertebrae apart, then braced himself and yanked his sword free, leaving the corpse to collapse bonelessly to the side. Blood gushed from the wound as he calmly wiped his blade clean on Faustus's golden cloak.

"When the criminal Faustus took slaves, he crossed the line, and his death was only a matter of time. You have a choice to make now. You can join me and serve the empire, or I'll give you a day to leave the island by whatever means you used to get here. Decide now, but any remaining slaves in your camp must be set free, or the legion will come and free them," I said warningly.

There were a few seconds of hesitation until one of the guards stepped forward and hesitantly bowed to me.

"We…we'll take the day, lord," he stammered.

"Then leave. Now," I ordered, dismissing them and turning to the two people that had carried Faustus's rain cover. "You were slaves?" I asked them gently. They both nodded, the older man rubbing at his neck where his collar had been. "Then you're free men now. You can choose to leave with the guards, or you may join my people."

They looked at each other for a second, then the guards, then they began to move at the same time, easing toward the nearest legionnaires. "Get them food and berths on the ships," I ordered the group nearest to them, and a legionnaire clapped his fist to his chest in salute before leading them away.

I turned my attention to the second party that had arrived and glared distrustfully at them, my anger still filling me, even as the ability drained away. Weakness rose within me, a gnawing hunger that seemed to be reaching up from my boots. Due to the slight tremble starting in my muscles, I knew I didn't have long.

"Well?" I asked them. "I believe you had a deal you wanted to offer me?"

Silence hung thickly for a few seconds before Hannimish seemed to come to his senses and coughed apologetically, spreading his hands as he bowed low.

"My apologies, ah, Lord Jax?" he said hesitantly, elbowing his companion to do the same.

The younger man started at the blow, glaring at him, then at me, before grudgingly bowing as well, albeit much shallower. As they both straightened, I nodded to them and strode into the tent, sinking into the chair that Denny, one of the legionnaires who'd assaulted the Skyking's lair with me, braced with one knee. He ensured that I was seated safely before backing away, his eyes glued to me as though he were aware of what the Ability had cost me in terms of strength.

I nodded in thanks, and he slipped from the tent as soon as the others took their places. Oracle's voice suddenly spoke in my mind.

"He's gone for Nerin. I think you scared them, beloved."

"I damn well scared myself," I responded internally, a terrible weariness filling my mental voice.

"Well?" I asked Hannimish brusquely. "I've not got all day, man."

"Ah, perhaps you could tell me why you summoned us…lord?" Hannimish interjected. "We had come here, expecting that a mercenary band or an expeditionary force had arrived, assisted by the legion, and we had planned to make deals, hiring your forces to assist in the exploration of the Sunken City."

"I intended on making deals with you," I said flatly. "Until Faustus proved that he couldn't be trusted. Then I moved to simply executing him."

"Well, we've not done anything of the sort, now, have we?" he said, forcing a smile and ignoring the significance of Romanus taking up station behind my chair as Oracle sat down next to me, clasping one hand and squeezing it. "Add to that, I'd personally love to discuss…"

"Yet," I interrupted grimly. "You'll have to forgive me, Hannimish." I watched him carefully as I deliberately left off the "lord."

"Every former lord I've dealt with so far has attempted to kill me, rob me, or worse. Now, I came here expecting this would be a research and exploration outpost, most likely manned by a few scientists and historians, and that's all. I had planned to recruit them and share the spoils of the exploration if they chose not to join me in exchange for their knowledge of the Prax."

"The…Prax?" Hannimish's companion asked, glaring at me as though weighing and measuring me.

"Ah, this is my nephew, Joshua, Baron of Sarat," Hannimish said smoothly. "He means no offense, my lord, but his question is appropriate, what is a Prix?"

"Prax, not Prix," I said shortly, my body aching and notifications flashing desperately in the corner of my vision. A deeper tremble ran through my body, and I did the only two things that I felt might help: I attempted to ignore it for the moment, planning to make this meeting short, and I turned to Romanus. "Could you get me a Potion of Might, please, Romanus?" I asked. He blinked in surprise before nodding and speaking softly to someone out of my sight.

"As to the Prax, well, this was a Prax, or a war-city, as it might translate. This particular Prax was named Glorious Retribution. She sailed the skies, hunting down those who attempted piracy against the empire, and assisted the legion in bringing peace. Permanently, usually."

I gestured generically, waving my hand to include the ground, the trees, and the island. I knew things now, no details, but the connection I'd had, even for the few seconds it'd lasted with the specters, I'd felt something of their lives and their deaths.

"I am here to retrieve some items from the depths of the city and make some repairs to my ships, as well as permit my people to stretch their legs. I am at war with Himnel; as are you, I believe?" I asked, getting nods of affirmation from them both.

"Good. That makes this easier, then. I have no quarrel with you, so if you have anything you want to trade, we can talk about it. Otherwise, we simply stay out of each other's way. You don't annoy me, and I won't have my legion stomp you from existence."

Joshua drew in a deep breath, straightening as if he were about to argue, when Hannimish grabbed his arm and held on tightly, bowing and forcing a smile.

"That sounds wonderful, Lord Jax. Perhaps we could return to our camp and consider what treasures we might trade? And we could return to discuss this with you tomorrow? Or the day after, if that suits better?" he asked in a strangely pleasant tone.

"Yes, fine." I nodded tiredly. "Apologies for my lack of patience, Hannimish, Joshua; using powers such as that have an effect on me," I said, forcing myself to smile in return.

"Of course! We completely understand, my lord. We will, of course, look forward to meeting with you again soon. Noon, on the second day from now? At our camp? I will ensure there are refreshments, and…"

He continued to blather happily as I nodded acceptance.

"Fine, fine." I waved one hand to stem the tide of his platitudes. "But mark my words, Hannimish: if I find slaves there, you will regret it. Better to admit it now and free them, before I get annoyed."

"We don't have slaves in Narkolt," Hannimish replied quickly, looking offended. "We hold to the old ways as well."

"Ah, of course," I said, relaxing slightly. "I remember hearing that once; my apologies. I'm glad to learn that it is true, Lord Hannimish, Baron Joshua. I'll look forward to meeting you then."

I gestured to the door, and they hurried out, gathering up their people and leaving the clearing quickly.

"Romanus, I want their camps watched. Oh, thank you," I said tiredly as he handed me a potion of Legionnaire's Might and watched in a sort of sick fascination as I popped the top off and downed it, chugging the horrible concoction as quickly as I could before grabbing a pitcher of water and washing it down.

"It will be done, my lord. Restun?" Romanus asked, and the centurion primus saluted and disappeared from the tent as Romanus turned back to me. "I've never seen anyone actually *ask* for one of those," he said, smiling faintly. "It usually takes a direct order to make someone take it, and even then, I'm always reminded of advice I got as a young officer."

"Oh?" I asked curiously, swilling my mouth out and making a face. "Gods, that shit's nasty." I forced myself to take a bite of cheese to try to cleanse my palate. "What advice?"

"Never give an order you know won't be obeyed," Romanus said, shrugging.

"Ha, well, yeah, I can see why." I grimaced, shaking my head and sitting back in my chair. Taking Oracle's hand again, I reveled in the feeling of her cool fingers as they intertwined with my own and offered silent support and reassurance. "What do you think of that, then?" I asked him.

"Well, it could have gone better, admittedly, but I've had dealings with Faustus and his brother before, so I have to say, I'm not unhappy about the turn of events in the slightest."

"Really?" I asked him, grinning. "I'm not the only one who hates the nobility, then?"

"Gods, no, but you're not allowed to hate the nobility anymore, as you're one of them." Romanus snorted. "They're only nobles at your sufferance. Dispossess them of their titles and raise new ones up in their stead, and watch how fast some of them start pulling their fingers out and following the laws."

"That'd get their attention, wouldn't it!" I chuckled, picturing the panicked chaos.

"It really would!" he agreed with enthusiasm. "Mind you, I know you'd want to watch their faces when they find out, but why haven't you done it with at least a few by now?"

"Done what?" I asked.

"Dispossessed them of their titles?" Romanus prompted. I blinked, eyeing him in surprise.

"I can actually do that?" I stared from him to Oracle and back in astonishment.

"Of course!" Romanus said, frowning at me in surprise. "You're the Imperial Scion, and they bear imperial titles, even if they sully them by using them. You have only to order them stripped of it, and it's done."

"How…how do I do this?" I asked slowly, a grin spreading across my face, and Romanus started to grin in response.

"You issue a proclamation, that's all; like you did when you declared war on Barabarattas," he explained.

I searched Oracle's eyes questioningly, grinning when she nodded in confirmation.

I closed my eyes and whispered to myself, "Oh, this is going to be awesome…"

I concentrated, and I felt her guiding me, pushing my attention to the side, where there seemed to be a space, a sort of blank area hovering before my mind's eye. The notifications buzzed for my attention, but I ignored them and instead reached out, pouring my intent into the space. I could feel Oracle making slight adjustments, altering it from my normal speech to a more formal, dignified one, suitable for this purpose.

"Seems a bit pretentious?" I mumbled, reading it over, but Oracle disagreed, her rich, throaty laugh washing over me as she finished editing it, and I felt her asking without words for permission to send it.

With no reason to postpone, I wordlessly agreed, and my vision was assaulted by a new box that opened without my permission as mana was torn from me.

The prompt was black as pitch, encased in a golden scrollwork-covered frame, the letters pulsing in golden smoke that flowed to form words:

Attention, Citizens of the Territory of Dravith!

High Lord Jax, Imperial Scion, Master of the Great Tower, and High Lord of Dravith, today and effective immediately, revokes the title of High Lord Barabarattas, stripping him of lordship of the City of Himnel, all additional titles and possessions, and declares him outlaw.

Let no citizen offer the criminal Barabarattas succor, lest their titles be stripped from them and their lives declared forfeit.

All Hail High Lord Jax of Dravith!

I read it, hearing indrawn gasps from others around me as everyone saw the same message. Then I sat back, waiting. I was somewhat surprised I'd not received a message in response to my actions, like I had last time.

After several seconds, I pulled up my notifications and read through them, wondering if it had been subsumed into that location by mistake.

Warning!

**You have activated an Imperial Ability without sufficient authority,
and now you must pay the price!**

**All stats have been permanently reduced by two points, and your body has
been damaged in ways small and profound.
Think carefully before you overreach again.**

"What the hell?" I growled, feeling Oracle slip into my mind to examine the
notification. Her shock at the high price pierced sharply through my brain. The act
had literally cost me nearly three levels, at two points off each of my ten stats. I
growled in fury, but I also acknowledged the little voice in the back of my head that
had seen the slaves freed of their bonds, and I knew I'd do it again in a heartbeat.

Just, maybe not today.

I pulled up my stat sheet and double-checked, grumbling under my breath as
I saw the damage.

Name: Jax Amon				
Titles: Strategos: 5% boost to damage resistance, Fortifier: 5% boost to defensive structure integrity, Champion of Jenae: One search for hidden knowledge every 24 hours				
Class: Spellsword > Justicar > Champion of Jenae > Imperial Magekiller			**Renown**: Imperial Scion, Lord of Dravith	
Level: 18			**Progress**: 83,972/265,000	
Patron: Jenae, Goddess of Fire and Exploration			**Points to Distribute**: 0 **Meridian Points to Invest**: 0	
Stat	**Current points**	**Description**	**Effect**	**Progress to next level**
Agility	43	Governs dodge and movement	+330% maximum movement speed and reflexes, (+10% movement in darkness, -20% in movement daylight)	46/100
Charisma	21	Governs likely success to charm, seduce, or threaten	+110% success in interactions with other beings	73/100
Constitution	43 (38)	Governs health and health regeneration	840 health, regen 54.45 points per 600 seconds, (+10% regen due to soul bond, -20 health due to soul bond, each point invested now worth 20 health)	36/100
Dexterity	35	Governs ability with weapons and crafting success	+250% to weapon proficiency, +25% to the chances of crafting success	49/100
Endurance	38 (35)	Governs stamina and stamina regeneration	760 stamina, regen 28 points per 30 seconds, (each point now worth 20 stamina)	8/100
Intelligence	58	Governs base mana and number of spells able to be learned	560 mana, spell capacity: 32 (30 + 2 from items), (-20 mana due to soul bond)	18/100
Luck	23	Governs overall chance of bonuses	+13% chance of a favorable outcome	15/100
Perception	23	Governs ranged damage and chance to spot traps or hidden items	+130% ranged damage, +13% chance to spot traps or hidden items	48/100

Strength	31 (28)	Governs damage with melee weapons and carrying capacity	+21 damage with melee weapons, +210% maximum carrying capacity	91/100
Wisdom	33 (28)	Governs mana regeneration and memory	+230% mana recovery, 1.65 points per minute, 230% more likely to remember things, (-50% mana regeneration until mana manipulation reaches level 10)	47/100

Congratulations!

Your Class: Justicar, has interacted with your Rank of Imperial Scion and evolved due to your acceptance of your role, as well as actions taken to begin to right ancient wrongs! You are now an Imperial Justicar and gain a one-off bonus of five points to Perception and five points to Wisdom.

*

Congratulations, Imperial Scion and Justicar!

You have followed your Soul's demands for Justice and have fulfilled the first step on an evolving Class Quest!

As both Imperial Scion and Justicar, you have been given a unique Quest by the Spirits of the Realm.

Quest: Return the Rule of Law, Bring Freedom to the Enslaved, and Peace to the Unquiet Dead I

Note: This Quest cannot be refused without losing your class as an Imperial Justicar.

Punish Breakers of Imperial Law: 67/10

Free Unjustly Imprisoned Citizens: 114/10

Grant Uneasy Revenants their Eternal Rest: 76/10

Reward: 50,000xp, Access to Second Tier of Evolving Quest

Note: Because you have gone above and beyond the base requirements, your achievements will be accepted toward the following tier, minus this tier's requirement.

*

Quest: Return the Rule of Law, Bring Freedom to the Enslaved, and Peace to the Unquiet Dead II

Note: This Quest cannot be refused without losing your class as an Imperial Justicar.

Punish Breakers of Imperial Law: 57/50

Free Unjustly Imprisoned Citizens: 104/50

Grant Uneasy Revenants Their Eternal Rest: 66/50

Reward: 250,000xp, Access to Third Tier of Evolving Quest

Note: Because you have gone above and beyond the base requirements, your achievements will be accepted toward the following tier, minus this tier's requirement.

*

Quest: Return the Rule of Law, Bring Freedom to the Enslaved, and Peace to the Unquiet Dead III

Note: This Quest cannot be refused without losing your class as an Imperial Justicar.

Punish Breakers of Imperial Law: 7/250

Free Unjustly Imprisoned Citizens: 54/250

Grant Uneasy Revenants their Eternal Rest: 16/250

Reward: 1,250,000xp, Access to Fourth Tier of Evolving Quest

"Hell. That's a serious chunk of experience," I muttered softly, realizing that it would go a long way to replacing the lost levels, just as the additional points in Perception and Wisdom began to take hold. I groaned, screwing my eyes shut and covering my ears with my hands. Sounds were suddenly magnified insanely, my eyes burning as they altered again, and I gritted my teeth against the explosion of sensations.

With each point that I gained in Perception, the world around me changed in a thousand ways, many minor, some major, but the more points I gained in that stat, the more those changes *hurt*.

Now, my brain ached, my eyes burned, my ears bled, and my skin shrieked in agony as each fresh breeze felt like a cheese grater being dragged across it. Finally, my sense of taste and smell, well, I suddenly really missed toothpaste and mouthwash and resolved to find a way to make a magical equivalent damn fast.

When the adjustments were eventually over, I sat back, wincing as my raw nerves screamed at me. As I cautiously opened my eyes, I found myself looking into the faces of Augustus, Hellenica, Nerin, Denny, and Lydia, who had all joined Romanus in the tent. I felt Oracle's gentle hand resting on the back of my own.

"Ouch," I said distinctly, and several people snorted out a laugh while Nerin stepped forward to look at me, her eyes shifting to glow a fierce silver.

"Jax," Jenae's voice and the sense of her presence suddenly blossomed around me, and I smiled, turning my eyes up to the sky.

"Great to hear from you, Jenae," I said, closing my eyes in relief. "Sorry. Okay, everyone, that is the Goddess Jenae, Mistress of Fire, Exploration and Hidden Knowledge."

I caught the confused and surprised looks on the faces of the nearby legionnaires, as well as noting, farther out, the way the nearby people faltered and stopped in their motions, gazing about as though trying to figure out what was happening.

"Thank you, Jax. It is good to see you survived. I was concerned," Jenae said, and I caught the amusement in her voice at my apology for tossing her a casual general greeting after promising I'd show more respect in the future.

"It was a close thing a few times," I admitted.

"I know; I felt your injury and checked in on you, only to find that your new healer, backed by a Djinn Clan Mother, already had things in hand. Good choices on your allies there," the goddess commented.

I nodded, still facing upwards. "I was damn lucky to get them, I know that much," I said.

"More than you know, considering the agreement that binds the Clan Mother. But I digress; do you remember, after the incident with the Valspar, when I promised to lead you to a cache of knowledge that would aid you in facing them?"

"Yeah," I said, rubbing the back of my head. "Sorta. I was kinda having a bad day."

"Understandable," Jenae replied with a slight chuckle. *"You had just destroyed a section of a major city, followed by tearing out your own guts and nervous system. Most sentients would define that as a bad day, I'd expect."*

"With cause, I didn't just do it for shits and giggles, okay?" I said quickly, anxiously watching the small group with me and the much larger group of people that were slowly drifting in to listen.

"You did," Jenae agreed. *"Anyway, part of that cache is nearby. The Prax, or war-cities, depending on how they translate in your race's tongue, were created to be able to enforce the emperor's will across the realm. In addition to all the facilities a mobile platform of war required, such as production centers, food, and barracks, they also contained Vaults.*

"These were maintained by a resident wisp, and while I am weaker than I'd like, I sense the presence of knowledge buried deep here. I cannot discuss my current situation, Jax, not now. But soon, we must speak at length, both about your path ahead, the effects of my naming you as Champion, and about your quest to return the gods."

"I'll look forward to it, Jenae, and thank you," I answered respectfully as her presence vanished.

"Was…was that really her? The Lady of Hidden Knowledge?" Romanus asked, blowing out a heavy breath and studying my face. "By the gods, her presence…it was…"

"Powerful," I said.

Romanus's eyes were wide as he nodded. "Truly, there can be no doubt that she is divine. The sense of her mind was…and she talks with you?"

"You didn't tell him?" I frowned at Augustus in confusion.

"Oh, I did; it's just not the kind of thing that people accept at face value, Jax. It's something that people need to experience." He smiled as Denny clapped him on the shoulder wordlessly.

"You still stand by your word to introduce me to Ashante, boy? The Goddess of Nature and Life?" Nerin demanded, and I reassured her that I intended to keep our agreement. "Good, because every time I turn my damn back, you do something that's either insane, or impossible, or both together."

Nerin crossed her arms, a look of wonder on her face. "I was aboard the ship, dealing with a young slave girl that had been…abused by her past masters. I was trying to figure out how to remove restraining bolts that had been joined to her shoulder and hip bones to lock her into place, when lightning tore through the hull and smashed into her.

"I panicked, trying to save her, and found, much to my surprise, that she was being healed, not hurt. The bolts were melted to slag, reduced to puddles of metal on the floor. I watched the remnants running across her skin without so much as singeing her. Every single one of my patients from the city, all of the enslaved that I've treated so far, at any rate, are healthier than they have any right to be."

"Okay, why do I feel like I'm getting told off for this?" I asked in confusion.

"Because you shouldn't be able to do it! I know how many people were hurt, boy; it's my job to know all about it. I also know the depth of your manapool, and I *thought* your capabilities. There is no way you could cast a spell like that. Honestly, I don't know how any being short of a god could wield that kind of magic, and you just throw it around like a child!" she snapped furiously.

"Hey!" I retorted. "It costs me to use that shit! I don't just toss it off, you know!"

"Exactly! Points are missing from all of your stats!" She paced in front of me, clearly agitated at my reduced state. "I told you, boy, I know you! I know when a patient of mine changes, especially in a way that shouldn't be possible! You directly converted life-force and experience into power, while draining the ambient magic from the area, and still, that shouldn't have been sufficient to do what you did!"

"I…uh—" I tried to interrupt her rant, but she cut me off.

"That's why I'll be watching you closely. One wrong move, a single toe out of line, and I'll be there!" she snarled, turning on her heel and storming off.

"What the hell?" I said to the room in general. "I do all that, and I'm the bad guy here?"

All I got for long seconds was silence.

I waited, and when nobody said anything constructive or helpful, I shook my head in disgust.

"Right load of lions, you lot are," I grumbled. "Okay, Romanus, I want both cities' camps watched from now on and searched for slaves. I need to go and rest, followed by some new armor, and hopefully I can go kill something with a ridiculous amount of violence. Right now, though, I'm going to hide in my goddamn room from that sadistic bastard Restun for a bit.

"Augustus, I want you to go speak with Elise and Athena; get me a good sense of the ship's condition. Romanus, take care of the legion, and liaise with Barrett. Make sure all of our people are taken care of. Oh, and someone get that shit off my lawn," I ordered grimly, forcing myself to my feet and gesturing to the corpse of the former Lord Faustus.

"Lastly, thank you all." I forced a smile and looked around at all of the people present, recognizing that they'd all come running, worrying that I'd been hurt.

CHAPTER NINE

I strode to the ship, grumbling under my breath the entire way, yet unsure why I was so annoyed. I'd actually had a good morning, despite the lack of sexy time with Oracle, and I'd even gotten to strip that ass Barabarattas of his title. Considering what utter weapons-grade wankers the nobility were, that had to have upset him…and then I realized what I was missing.

I had received no kind of contact from Barabarattas. I'd expected at least a declaration that I was a dickhead or something, but nope, nada.

"Oracle?" I asked, turning to her as she walked beside me, her arm wrapped around my waist and mine draped across her shoulders making it slightly awkward to walk, as my legs were longer than hers. Still, it was nice, and I was taking the chance to both lean on her slightly, as I was exhausted, and to occasionally glance down the front of her top as we went.

Little bonuses.

"Yes, beloved?" she asked calmly, well aware of the extra weight I was putting on her and the direction of my gaze.

"Why haven't I heard from that pillock, Barabarattas?"

She snickered. "Oh, that! Well, it's simple. Only a person of authority can communicate through declarations, and as he's no longer a city lord or even a noble, he doesn't get to do things like that. It would be like Jay having access to the Great Tower's screens. Never going to happen."

"Wait, he won't have access to the city management functions now? Is that what he was using? Like when I used the tower's management facilities?" I asked, grinning.

"Exactly. He's been locked out of all those parts of the city, and the City Guard will 'feel' that he's a criminal if they clap eyes on him. Literally. You know how, actually, no, you don't. Okay then, let's cover the guard and their abilities quickly," Oracle said as we walked up the gangplank into the ship, our escort following along and leading us at the same time.

"Each member of the guard gains access to a simple Ability once they achieve the class of guardsman. It grants knowledge of the crimes of outlaws, should they see an outlaw, or should the outlaw not have an Ability to counter them.

"It's all very cat and mouse, but some members of both sides actually reserve every point possible, investing them only in those Abilities, as it enables them to do amazing things for their side. Guards can share information, so if a highly skilled guard used his Ability on, say, a murderer, he'd get the details of that person's crime.

"Not really specific, but flashes of inspiration, images, a feeling of where bodies might be found, that kind of thing. The criminals might be capable of a similar Ability, and then they would attempt to convince the guard that this person, or that, didn't commit the crime. If they're skilled enough, they can make the guard release a murderer that they witnessed, simply by twisting the series of events in the guard's mind. It's a horrifying skill," she said earnestly.

"Yeah, we have those where I came from, too." I grimaced. "Not with Abilities, although some detectives might come close. And the criminal version we have is called a lawyer."

"Remind me to avoid them if we ever get to your world," Oracle said firmly.

"In my world, there's a saying: What's the difference between a dead dog in the road and a dead lawyer?" I asked her, grinning.

"I…don't know?" she asked suspiciously, feeling the amusement in my mind.

"There are skid marks in front of the dog," I finished enthusiastically, then sighed at the look on her face. "Imagine a cart, one that goes really, really fast, and no horse, okay…" I started to explain to her, before stopping. "Wait; you can see my damn memories. You know what a car is."

"I do. It still seems weird, though. So, in your world, it was okay to kill lawyers?" she asked, curious.

"Well, no, but generally, everyone wanted to. They basically make money out of human misery, so while they're rich, everyone also likes to keep as far away from them as possible."

"Hmmmm. I can see there's a lot of context I'm just not getting…is it important?" She tilted her head questioningly, eyeing me with mild concern.

"No, not really." I adored her, but in that moment, I was missing having someone with the same life experiences to talk to.

I loved this new realm; magic was amazing, and the opportunities to lose my mind and seriously hurt people and monsters was actually great. I'd kind of always yearned for this without knowing it. The dreams had been a taste, but each time I woke up, it always came with the pain, new scars, and having to hide all of it, with only the satisfaction of helping dream people as my reward, or the bone-deep shame of failing them.

Here, I got to gain from the fights in a much more "real" way. I got to improve myself, to grow, to learn, and explore, and hell, I was finally getting sexy time with a stunningly beautiful woman. All of this was unbelievable, and best of all, I was getting closer to Tommy. I knew it.

I'd almost been able to feel him at the end, just before I'd left Himnel. I'd sensed he was close, not in some kind of "magically bonded twin" sense, just…I couldn't explain it. I had looked over my shoulder, expecting him to be there, then…

Then some fucker had shot me in the damn head with an arrow.

Even before then, I'd occasionally sensed something, never enough to think it was him, just…something. Looking back at it, I wondered if maybe, just maybe, he'd been somewhere close.

I'd been forced to leave the city regardless. I couldn't have not gone ahead with the plan to raid the city, as we needed everything we could lay our hands on. We couldn't delay, not once the ball started rolling, not even to keep scouring the city.

Mal had his people out searching high and low, and all they'd found by the end was that he'd been adventuring with a party that had been mostly wiped out. He'd come back to the city briefly, then disappeared again.

That meant he was still out there, and the injuries and pain in his mana channels that Jenae had sensed had almost certainly been caused by whatever had killed his party.

The fact that I knew he'd survived and had come back out, meant he was probably okay. Probably. I'd asked Gaion to come up with some way to leave a message for him, telling him where I was, but I'd not heard anything back since, and it had all gone sideways in the escape from the city.

For me, anyway, as I was out cold, rather than leading a triumphant, escaping fleet.

All this went through my mind as Oracle, my guards, and I walked along the corridors of the ship before clambering up the final flight of steps and emerging into the corridor that led to the bridge. It was at the far end, with three rooms leading off on the approach. One was the captain's, one was mine, and I had no clue what the third was originally intended for, as it was ram-packed full of random stolen gear from the Stockpile.

We took the door on the right and entered what had been clearly planned as a stateroom for an admiral or a noble.

It was large and square, with no windows; the single room that led off it, presumably intended as personal quarters, had been designed with huge windows that would offer an amazing view as the ship cruised along…if the windows had been fitted.

Also, if they really were as big as my one look suggested they'd be, it'd provide a hell of a target for anyone attacking the ship.

For now, I dismissed it, and we all ignored the cool, steady breeze that flowed from under the ill-fitting door leading to that room.

I slumped down into the pile of blankets on the floor that Oracle and I had been sharing and waved my thanks to the legionnaires, who closed the door and left us alone. A thought occurred to me, and I sighed.

"Bane, you sneaky, creepy bastard, are you in here?" I asked, and I felt the characteristic *thrummm* of his amusement.

"I am, Jax. Is this a time you want me to leave?" he asked, and Oracle grinned at me as he became visible.

"I wish," I said, shaking my head wearily. "I'd love a bit of fun right now, Oracle, but in all honesty, using that power…"

"I know, and I understand. Don't worry," she said soothingly, sitting down next to me. I lifted my head as she shuffled around, sliding her legs into position to allow my head to rest in her lap, where she began to slowly stroke my hair, smiling gently.

I closed my eyes for a second, just enjoying the feeling and the closeness, before smiling up at her. The next hour or more passed as I rested and recovered, and we all talked of little things and told stories of our pasts.

"God, I'd love it if this was all we needed to do for the day…just relax in here; some sex, some good food, talk some shit with the team over some beers," I muttered once I felt a bit stronger, closing my eyes and drawing in a deep breath. Then I opened my eyes and stared up at Oracle, and across the room where Bane crouched.

"Okay, then. Planning time, I guess. Oracle, you're basically living in my brain, so I know you know what I'm thinking," I commented.

"But it helps to say it aloud, as then we can all bounce details around?" she finished for me.

"Yeah, close enough," I said, letting out a little groan as she worked my scalp. "And Bane, while you don't live in my brain, you do see more of me than anyone else."

"I know, and I'll have nightmares for the rest of my life," Bane interjected quickly.

"Ass," I said, smiling. "I meant you know me well, you prick. I need to figure out what we're going to do. I know I'd said three days to have a rest and refit here, get things ready to move on, then head back to the tower, but does the information from Jenae change that? We need to know everything we can about the Valspar, and knowing that spells and knowledge related to them is hidden somewhere below," I mused, inspecting the rough burrs and whorls in the wood of the deck above and hearing the distant clunking rattling, shouts and thumps of the ship being worked on.

"It has to," Oracle said seriously. "We need that information; without it, we can't be sure that what you did in ripping it out is enough. Where did it come from, after all? Can it regrow? Does everyone have them inside, or is it another example of how special you are?"

"Yeah, I'm 'special,' all right," I grouched. "Try the windows; they're strawberry flavored."

"What?" she asked, confused.

"Nothing; it doesn't matter," I said, smiling and banishing the stray thought. "Bane, what do you think?"

"As to the information, spellbooks, and all of that, yes. When a goddess says you need something, I tend to think she knows what she's saying. Add to that, she's saved your life, and while you've had your…disagreements…in the past, you work well together. I doubt she is telling you to get them without a good reason," Bane said seriously.

"Okay. How do we do it, though?" I asked. "I mean, I had intended to take Lydia and her squad, a few legionnaires, and maybe Nerin with me, go exploring, maybe have a little fun as well as raiding the place. Now, it's a bit more serious. Do I take the entire legion? Hell, they're professional monster hunters; maybe I should just send them ahead, stroll through after them," I said, before shaking my head. "No, no, I can't do that. Not only would it be cowardly and boring, but I need to improve, to grow stronger, and so does the team."

"We do, but we also have a large area to cover," Bane interjected. "Perhaps use your team as you intended, but split off a significant group of the legion and send them to the other entrances?"

"What entrances?" I asked, looking over at him in surprise.

"There are apparently dozens of entrances into the city; that's part of what the researchers were doing, mapping out the city and its entrances. I asked around a little earlier, and it seems this is just the top floor of the city, and the least intact area. There are at least three more levels—"

"Six," I corrected him as memories surfaced suddenly. "There were six levels. The third was the largest. If we take the top as floor one and count down from there, floor one was literally the garden level so the residents could relax when not at war. The next was a mix of military facilities and the homes of the nobility.

"Three was the main barracks, quarters, and the command center, with four and five being storage, production, and training areas. Six again was military, as that was where the troops would launch from, and the mages would cast the portal or attack spells from."

I mentally wandered through the designs as well as the memories from the specters coupled with my fractured memories of a similar city that Amon had visited with Shustic. I remembered the amusement she had felt at all the effort mortals had to make to move about in *her* realm, while Amon had appreciated the sheer level of determination and effort his engineers and the golem king had used to create such a marvel.

I saw the dreams of Amon, and the meeting he had with the golem after touring it. I heard fragments of the discussion regarding the City Eternal, which the golem had sworn to build, a city that would be the shining Jewel of the Empire...then it was gone, the memory filled with the anguished howling of a young boy as he died, alone, slowly crushed to death by a slab from one of the buildings demolished in the Cataclysm.

My mind was suddenly filled with them: an elderly woman, her face wreathed in laughter lines, who had once gifted the emperor's sixty-third grandchild, Cora, with a small handmade doll, all red and gold, crafted with love and adoration. She died slowly as a moloch, a carnivorous worm, tore through her insides. No healers had been left alive within hundreds of miles to help.

I saw them, hundreds, thousands, all in a rush, as Amon poured them out into my mind, the smallest fragment of the loss that had driven him mad. I saw them all dying, the young, the old, the fit and healthy, and the decrepit. I saw Fintin, known as the Lord of Lust and Excess amongst his peers, a grossly fat man who had devoted his life to trying every possible food, crushed by a falling pillar, viscera bursting across the floor to be eaten by his tiny white hound. The creature had been all that he loved, and it gorged itself on his entrails before dying weeks later, when all the food and water ran out, trapped in Fintin's mansion.

"No!" I heard a shout, and suddenly I was jerked clear, Oracle yanking the river of memories away. I collapsed back into her embrace, my eyes still streaming tears.

"What..." I managed to gasp, stunned, and shaking my head in denial.

"You went too deep," Oracle said softly. "You let him show you his memories of the city, but his mind is fractured, and then they poured out."

"That's what he's filled with?" I asked aloud, knowing it was true. "No wonder he's insane, knowing that it was your own children that did that, as well," I said, rage burning up from the space where I had Amon contained.

"Yes, now maybe we should think about something else?" she said quickly, and I nodded in frantic agreement as Bane crouched next to me, reaching out and putting his hand on my shoulder.

"Are you okay?" he asked quietly

I nodded slower. "I am; sorry, mate, didn't mean to scare you. As Oracle says, best to talk about something else. She'll explain it to you later, okay?"

"Well, on that note, I've got good news and bad," he said, bowing his head respectfully.

My heart dropped. "Go on..."

"Well, the good news is that there's something to distract you, coming along the corridor," Bane said, and I vaguely remembered the feeling of his worldsense washing out from him as the memories took over.

"And the bad news?" I asked slowly, the jingle of armor coming to a halt outside. "Oh, god, no," I moaned, closing my eyes.

"Lord Jax, Centurion Primus Restun, asks to see you?" one of the legionnaires called, knocking, then leaning in.

CHAPTER TEN

"**S**eriously? Now?" I muttered to myself, sitting up and wiping the remnants of the tears from my cheeks. "Uh…oh, fuck it," I grunted, pushing myself to my feet and feeling my legs wobble slightly. "Yes, send him in," I said.

My mana dipped as Oracle created a fountain of fresh water in the corner of the room. I quickly washed my face in it and stepped back, letting Bane move in.

As I crossed the room to greet Restun, Bane drew in deep gulps of the water, relaxing as his amphibious nature reveled in it.

Restun stepped inside and closed the door, looking me over for a long moment before smiling faintly as he clapped his fist to chest, and I returned the salute.

"Lord Jax, I don't think it would be wise to exercise today, if you're truly as tired as you seem, and you still intend on entering the Sunken City later?" he said, and I nodded thankfully, relaxing slightly.

"I am; my team and I, I mean. We'll be entering it in a few hours, and I was just discussing that with Oracle and Bane. What's happening with the other camps?" I asked Restun, and he immediately looked grim.

"The Himnel camp looks like a kicked anthill. It seems they had more soldiers than we thought; they'd been keeping them underground. Seemingly, there's an entrance in their camp. Unwise in my opinion. Now they're stripping the camp and loading their single ship with everything of value, including their slaves and what looks to be items they've looted from the city."

"Motherfuckers!" I growled, my anger rising. "What about the other camp?"

"Much the same. Fewer soldiers, but the ship is being made ready and it looks like the entire camp is mobilizing."

"So, that was bollocks about us meeting in a few days, then. I thought it would be, but I wanted them gone badly enough that I didn't care," I said flatly, thinking I'd made a mistake.

"Judging from the way the scouts reported it, they're splitting their forces. One lot is readying the ship…"

"And the other?" I asked grimly.

"They look to be preparing to head into the city," he admitted simply.

"So, it's a race, then?" I muttered. "What the hell do they think is down there?"

"No idea, but the fact that you're after something suggests that something valuable is still buried within, so they want it first," he explained.

"And the first group—are they boarding the ship?" I asked.

"Not all of them, or at least, I doubt it. I went to look at that camp myself, Jax. There's no way that everyone there will be able to fit on that single small ship. Most likely, it was the lord's private ship, and if his brother is there, he's going to use it to escape with anything he wants to keep, then send the guards down into the city to find whatever you're after."

"While he runs back to Himnel and gets reinforcements," I finished for him, and he inclined his head slightly.

"That's probably his intention, yes."

"Well, looks like my nap can wait," I said, shaking my head. "Time to go see the armorers and get everyone suited and booted. Restun, can you lead the way, please?" I gestured to the door, and he saluted crisply.

We moved out into the corridor, and the legionnaires seamlessly formed up to escort me. I recognized one of them in the lead and reached out, putting one hand on his shoulder.

"Do me a favor, and ask Romanus to meet us at the armorers, and have the rest of my squad, Yen, Tang, and Grizz meet us there as well, please."

"Of course, my lord," he said, saluting and rushing off down a side corridor.

Restun led us down to the main hold, then further down the ship to a small gangway that led outside to a section missing most of the outer structure.

This section had rooms that were basically two walls, and the occasional roof, the lower floor of the next floor up, but little beyond that.

As we walked around the makeshift space, the clanging of hammers and steel, insults and good-natured swearing rose to greet us. We marched around the final corner and found the area the armorers and weaponsmiths had claimed as their own.

The area was perhaps ten meters deep by twenty long and had a wall on either side in place already, but no floor, outer wall, or, for two floors, any decking overhead. They had somewhere that was partially sheltered from the weather while actually being open enough to feel as if they felt like they were working outside, yet without any of the accompanying stress of trying to get rid of the smoke from the forges.

Three scruffily dressed men scurried about, helping the legionnaires by working the bellows, setting workspaces up, and moving materials around.

As soon as Thorn saw me, she grinned, standing tall and proud, with the three men falling to their knees and bowing their heads.

"That's enough of that crap," I said, striding forward and pulling first one, then the other two men to their feet. "I don't expect you to kneel, lads; not for me, not ever."

My voice was firm as their astonished gazes met mine. "I'm your lord, or I will be, as soon as you take the Oath…crap. We need to sort that out, Oracle, before we leave today. Restun, I'm going to need mana potions," I requested, mentally bracing myself for what was to come. "Anyway, I'm your lord, but I'm still just a man, so no need to kneel. I take it you were slaves?" I asked the first man, then looked to the other two, receiving mute nods of confirmation from all three.

"Well, I'm glad we managed to free you," I said, smiling. "I'll let you get back to whatever you were doing." I trailed off, seeing the look of stunned adoration on their faces and feeling extremely uncomfortable.

"Weems, Tim, Joh, back to those jobs, please," Thorn prompted, and the men jumped, running to return to their work.

"Thanks," I muttered quietly to her, and she grinned, her tusks making her smile seem strange, but it was definitely heartfelt, and for that, I was grateful. "Some new volunteers, then?" I asked, nodding toward them.

She beamed. "I picked them out of the pool. They're certainly determined; it's good to see, in all honesty. Admittedly, they know nothing yet, but the way they all focus on each task? They'll be smiths to be proud of in a year or two."

"The pool?" I asked.

"The volunteer pool," Thorn confirmed, then smiled. "Come, let's get you into your armor and make any last-minute adjustments, and I can tell you while I fit you."

She guided me around to a waiting pile of gear, picking out three bundles, setting one before me and patting the other two.

"First of all, these," she said, unwrapping the first bundle. "Three sets of clothing. This one is for under your new armor; it's specially designed, padded, and strong, helps to hold the armor in place and helps to spread the weight more evenly, thanks to the small hooks and design." She pointed out each feature as she described them.

"There's a full set, from underclothes up, including coverings for your feet, while those two there," she said, gesturing to the other two, "are a set of standard workout clothes and a set for relaxing in. The tailor said he and his people will come to see you as soon as you're free to design your normal working uniform, and so on."

"Sounds good," I said, grateful for the fresh clothing.

"Now, once you're dressed in that, we can get the armor on. This is our standard equipment, so I made very few changes to it, but it's a step up from the gear you've been wearing. What we talked about earlier, though, are you sure about me making the best armor I can for you?" she asked slowly.

"Definitely."

"Then we need to make some serious plans, because we've talked here about what we could do...there's not a crafter in the legion that hasn't dreamed of making something new, something unique and glorious. So last night, I got them together, and we planned as we worked," she explained, almost sheepishly. "The design that we came up with, it incorporates dreams of more than half the crafters we have. I've personally been fantasizing about it for years; it'd be a hell of an upgrade to our standard gear, but..."

"But it's not the traditional armor, so some legionnaires will freak out, and it's expensive. Got that earlier, totally fine with it, just make it as best you can."

"We can make a prototype, as a demonstration, but we'd need to create a specialist forge for the final product. The metal I want to use won't melt for the likes of a piddly little forge like this, nor the one we had in the enclave. We need arcanium, and that requires a magma forge," she said cautiously, hope clear in her voice.

"Okay, I don't know what that is, but I'll see what I can do," I said, shrugging. Her shoulder slumped, and I stopped admiring the new armor and looked at her properly.

"Thornapple," I said, and she looked at me, her expression a respectful mask. "I came to this realm a month or so ago. I've done so many things since then that I'm told are impossible that I'm not even going to mention them. You tell me you need a magma forge? Fine. I'll get you one," I promised earnestly.

"I just raided my enemy's city, stole most of his most powerful weapons of war, and almost all of his most valuable stored resources. I've picked fights with the drow on their own ground, slaughtered my way across the arena and killed the Skyking, tore a SporeMother a new asshole, and captured the Great Tower.

"Believe me, if you need a magma forge, I'll get you one. Right now, I don't know what it is, but I will sort it out, okay? Now, about my armor?" She stood a little straighter and grinned at me, nodding to the set that stood in pride of place in her little section, gleaming dully on a stand.

"You'll need to get changed," she said, indicating the clean clothes. I was all too happy to comply, pulling my battered equipment off and stabbing the base of my naginata into the soil. "I can leave, if you wish," she offered quickly, but I indicated that her comfort level was the deciding factor, stripping down unabashedly to my undercrackers. One touch of the legion standard ones left me shaking my head in refusal. No way was something that rough cradling my nether regions.

In a blink, I was covered again, wasting no time in pulling the new clothes on. "You said the new gear would be the work of a lot of the crafters of the legion; I take it you don't just mean the armorers, then?" I asked.

"Well, no, Jax. To make what I'd like but pair it with cheap underclothes or a crappy set of leathers to attach to it would be sacrilege. I've reached out to the others, and—" Thornapple started, gesturing happily as she began to describe her plans.

"Honestly, that's fine." I chuckled, cutting her off with a wave. "I just wanted to make sure you had involved them; that's all. I felt the same way about it!"

As I finished settling my new clothing in place, Romanus arrived, followed by the rest of my group, who were quickly guided to their respective armorers to begin their own fittings, much as I was with Thorn.

"Lord Jax," Romanus greeted me, smiling as he walked over. Restun, who'd taken up station out of the way to watch the proceedings, seemed to flow up to join us.

"Romanus!" I returned, smiling at him. "Good timing, my friend. I need to make some decisions, and I need your advice."

"Then I'm honored to help; where do we begin?" he asked, sitting on a crate of parts when I gestured to him to relax. "I know you young bucks can stand all day, but when you get to be my age, a good seat now and then is appreciated." He patted the crate with a smile.

"The enemy camps," I said, watching closely as I let Thorn help me cinch tight the straps on my new tunic. It wasn't as soft or as damn sexy looking as the drow silk shirt had been, nowhere near, but it was comfortable, after a fashion, and it gave me a reassuring feeling of solidity. Romanus blinked, looked at Restun, and frowned slightly as Restun nodded to him.

"I see. I know Restun reported to you first; I take it they're not making ready to hand over any slaves and play nice, then?"

No," I said shortly. "And I trust Restun and our scouts enough that I don't need to hear any more than I already have. The Himnel camp is loading their airship with everything they view as valuable, including their slaves. They seem intent on fleeing while leaving their soldiers behind, who appear to be gearing up for a fight.

"Restun assumes their plan to be a fast, hard hit to loot as much as they can, but it could also be to fight us. As to the Narkolt contingent, they appear to be doing much the same, but they've asked me to wait a few days for a visit while they desperately prepare their ship and dive into the ruins ahead of us. It's basically becoming a race, and it's not one we can afford to lose. What's your feeling on this?"

"I suspect you're right. The Sunken City was long ago looted for anything that could be easily taken; with entire sections blocked off or flooded, it became a game for the nobility to come out here and look it over, it seems. They probably brag about 'roughing it' when they get back, but with the nigh-on unlimited specters—which you've helpfully freed the city of now," Romanus added with a grin, "it was a case of nobody getting too far in.

"They clearly guess that there's something of value down there that you need, and they're desperate to get it. I recommend we hammer the Himnel camp flat; we are at war with them, after all. As to Narkolt, they're probably planning the same.

"We're not at war with them, though, so I suggest more of a 'velvet glove' approach. We send a large detachment to 'visit' and order them to stand down as the site has been claimed in your name. If they refuse, we take them. If they try to run, the ships above earn their keep. If they actually want to talk to you, we smile and bring them back for dinner."

"All sounds good, except we can't wait while they search the city," I said firmly. "We keep half the legion for the 'peacekeeping' force up here. The other half is going down the tunnels after these assholes. I'll go in with my team as well, and we'll basically search and map this place as best we can for the next twenty-four hours. After that time, everyone is to return to the surface and gather together, re-evaluate, and either keep going or prepare to move on."

I grunted as Thorn tugged the breastplate over my head and attached it onto the hooks on the underclothes, as well as onto the leg armor. "What's down there?" I asked. "I know you said monsters and undead?"

"I don't know, exactly. A legion team was sent in when it was first discovered, several, in fact. Only one legionnaire made it back. He warned of roaming undead, spirits that attacked everything and were the main threat, and several huge monsters. I'm guessing, since you freed those spirits, you've probably opened up entire areas that had been inaccessible earlier," Romanus said, rubbing his chin. "You said you want me to send in half the Legion—"

I nodded, cutting him off.

"I want half the legion up here to flatten both camps and protect the ships; I think that'll be more than enough, right?" He nodded, so I continued. "Good. Okay, then the other half is to be split up into smaller groups and sent into the various entrances. Someone mentioned earlier that there were dozens of ways in?"

"There are, but is it not better to send down a strong force, one that can hold against whatever is sent at it? Rather than splitting our forces?" he asked dubiously.

"Normally, yes, but some asshole—me, I mean—has removed the main defenses of the city, so now it's a race, and we can't afford to do this the slow, safe way. Tell the groups that if they encounter something they believe will result in casualties, they are to fall back and join another group to take it on, doubling up their strength until they can kick its ass easily, then split up again," I said firmly, bracing myself as Thorn cinched sections tight and made adjustments, straightening my arm out, then sliding on and twisting my vambraces until there was an audible click. The vambraces now attached to the upper arm segment.

"Damn, that feels smooth," I muttered, curling my arm up and down.

"The legion has the best armorers anywhere," Restun said with a rare smile. "Every part is designed to be able to lock together, reinforcing the others and spreading the weight out. You can wear just sections if you need to, then the weight will be what the uninitiated expect from armor like this, but when it's all in place, fitted, and working correctly? A fully armored legionnaire will beat a standard soldier in far more expensive armor over and over again."

"From fighting monsters, to chasing a girl, the legionnaires leave them in a whirl," Thorn muttered, smiling as she worked, gripping my new boots and pulling upwards as I stomped down. Then she twisted a ring-shaped connector on the top of the boot, and it locked into place, and the weight settled even more comfortably.

"It's true, though," Romanus agreed. "The way that the legion armor is built, each section supports the next, much like a shield wall. Because the armor is linked together, it offsets the weight, plus there are a few little tricks our armorers have learned over the centuries. Add to that, sections that are built to bend and give slightly, and others have additional padding, and you'll find nothing to compare with it."

"Nothing?" I asked, lifting my right hand as Thorn tugged the gauntlet on for me, twisting the wrist connector and locking it into place with a smooth click.

"Nothing that you can find anywhere," Romanus insisted proudly. "Sure, back in the glory days of the empire, there were armorers who made equipment that put ours to shame, but almost none of it survived, and that which did, well, we don't get to examine it for lost secrets."

"And even if we could, there's no changing the legion armor," Thorn grumbled under her breath.

"Now, now, legionnaire." Romanus chuckled. "Until now, we've had tradition as our only shield…it'll be hard accepting the changes Lord Jax brings, but we must change, if we are to survive."

"Yes, prefect," Thorn said, bowing her head. "I apologize for my words if they seemed disrespectful."

"No, there's no need for that, Thorn." Romanus smiled gently. "We're all legionnaires, and we all yearn for the glory of our dreams, be they in battle or in creation. We all serve the empire."

"Thank you, sir," Thorn said, smiling and twisting my last gauntlet until it clicked into place. A shiver passed over me, and the notifications sprang to life.

Congratulations!

You have equipped a full set of Legionnaire Scout Armor.

For equipping eight out of eight set pieces, you have an increase of 23% to all physical damage resistances and +5 to physical damage.

Titan

Beware!

**You have equipped a full set of Legionnaire Scout Armor, but you are
inexperienced and weaker than is recommended to wear such armor. As
such, you receive a penalty of +16% increase to stamina drain to all tasks.**

Cuirass of Faithful Service		Further Description *Yes/No*	
Details:		This chest armor includes pauldrons and is made of horizontal strips of highsteel attached to a blackened leather undergarment. It gives a bonus of +5 to resisting physical damage.	
Rarity:	**Magical:**	**Durability:**	**Charge:**
Rare	No	100/100	N/A

Revebrace of Faithful Service		Further Description *Yes/No*	
Details:		This armor covers the upper arms and connects to both the vambraces and the pauldrons. It is made of interlocked scales of highsteel laid over toughened leather. It gives a bonus of +2 to resisting physical damage.	
Rarity:	**Magical:**	**Durability:**	**Charge:**
Rare	No	100/100	N/A

Vambraces of Faithful Service		Further Description *Yes/No*	
Details:		This armor covers the lower arms and connects to both the revebraces and the gauntlets. It is made of interlocked scales of highsteel laid over toughened leather. It gives a bonus of +2 to resisting physical damage.	
Rarity:	**Magical:**	**Durability:**	**Charge:**
Rare	No	100/100	N/A

Culet of Faithful Service		Further Description Yes/No	
Details:		This armor covers the groin and connects to both the cuirass and the cuisse. It is made of interlocked scales of highsteel laid over toughened leather with larger, solid sections in place to cover vital areas. It gives a bonus of +4 to resisting physical damage.	
Rarity:	**Magical:**	**Durability:**	**Charge:**
Rare	No	100/100	N/A

Helm of Faithful Service		Further Description *Yes/No*	
Details:		This helmet is made of highsteel and formed into two separate pieces, a visor that can be raised or lowered then locked into place, and a main section to enclose the head. The legion helm also comes with the facility to add a plume (not attached). It gives a bonus of +4 to resisting physical damage.	
Rarity:	**Magical:**	**Durability:**	**Charge:**
Rare	No	100/100	N/A

103

Gauntlets of Faithful Service		Further Description *Yes/No*	
Details:		These gauntlets connect to the vambraces to form a fitting seal and are constructed of individual sections of highsteel, with a mixture of scales and plate construction for added protection. They grant a bonus of +4 to resisting physical damage.	
Rarity:	Magical:	Durability:	Charge:
Rare	No	100/100	N/A

Greaves of Faithful Service		Further Description *Yes/No*	
Details:		These armored greaves are made of highsteel and are constructed to be both protective and comfortable and grant a bonus of +5 to resisting physical damage.	
Rarity:	Magical:	Durability:	Charge:
Rare	No	100/100	N/A

Sabatons of Faithful Service		Further Description *Yes/No*	
Details:		These armored boots are made of highsteel and are constructed to be both protective and comfortable and grant a bonus of +2 to resisting physical damage.	
Rarity:	Magical:	Durability:	Charge:
Rare	No	100/100	N/A

I looked the details over and nodded to myself in satisfaction. Yes, I was losing a lot of stamina doing everything, but with the increased protection, it was worth that. Add to that, I looked fucking badass!

The armor was beautiful, a combination of the classic paladin style in fantasy movies, mixed with old school Roman legionnaire. With the way everything linked together, the flexibility and sheer artistry of it, damn if it didn't look like more than a hint of super-soldier style thrown in.

Thorn had set up a mirror and was going around tightening straps and marking the correct places for them to be set to, while explaining carefully how, and in which order, I needed to remove them.

"As our lord, I don't expect you to maintain your armor, not the way the standard legionnaire does, of course. Even so, it would be good for you to understand the various parts and how they work and are repaired, just in case of accidents in the field," she pointed out.

I nodded my thanks and lifted my helm off, turning it around in my hands and examining it.

"So, when I first met Augustus, he had a great big plume on the top of his helmet," I said, quirking an eyebrow at Thorn.

"It's removable," she said simply. "When it's attached, it looks great, but..."

"But it catches on things, cleans ceilings of spiders, and can give the enemy an easy way to expose your throat?"

She snorted. "We call 'em cleaners, as they either clean a roof, a seat, or clean your head right back, so that the blood can get out…"

"Well, they look great, they do, but they're insane. Having something on your armor that doesn't add to its defense, and in fact, makes it easier to kill you? Why?" I asked, shaking my head.

"For tradition's sake," Romanus said, shrugging. "When I took over as prefect, the general and I agreed that they are useless beyond formal occasions. Augustus wore his when he came to greet you, but none of the rest did, and they've been packed away since. Prior to my own rise to prefect, and my predecessor's rise to general, they were worn at all times…where you might get spotted by higher officers."

"So the legionnaires took them off as soon as they left the city?" I asked, snorting at his mischievous smirk. "How about we just accept that I'm very informal. I don't need sunshine blowing up my arse, and I sure as hell don't need plumes and trumpets and so on?" I offered. Thorn let out a groan of thanks, calling out in a loud voice: "Everyone! Lose the 'cleaners.' Lord Jax says he doesn't want to see them!"

Instantly, there arose a chorus of grunts, laughter, and general relief, and I sent Thorn a questioning glance.

"Legion Tribune Alistor had ordered that all legionnaires make sure their plumes were ready for parade, at all times, 'just in case,' last night, sir," she said, with a twinkle in her eye. "We had the excuse of the armor for yourself and your people to avoid doing it yet, but we were looking at a minimum of a week of work for all of us, dyeing and reattaching horsehair to fix them all up. Most legionnaires packed them away at the bottom of their kit bags when we left the city."

"Nice," I said, wincing. "Okay, formal declaration time, then." I glanced over at Romanus. "Do you see any real use for the plumes?" I asked, and he shook his head firmly, as did Restun. "Then as of now, I formally declare the plumes to be obsolete. They serve no purpose in my legion, and therefore must be discarded," I stated firmly.

"If you see a real requirement for them for formal events, I will permit the officers to retain them, but unless you feel that need?" I paused, and Restun, Romanus, and Thorn all shook their heads. "Excellent. Scrap them all, then."

Attention, Legionnaires!

As of now, by Imperial Decree, all plumes are declared obsolete and are to be discarded. No longer shall the legion wear them, by the Order of High Lord Jax, Imperial Scion and Lord of Dravith.

The notification that overrode mine, and every other legionnaire's vision, made me flinch for a second, but the cheers rising in the distance and all around made me grin, even as I silently wished I could see Alistor's face right then. *Idiot, wasting time on that shit,* I thought to myself.

"You just earned a place in every armorer's nightly prayers with that." Thorn beamed so widely I started to worry the top of her head might fall off.

"I'll take them! I can always use more interventions with the gods!" I laughed. "Anyway, anything else we need to look at, Romanus, or are you happy with those orders?"

He thought for several seconds before speaking up.

"Two things really, first of all, Lydia. She leads your team, and yet is unranked. Is this intentional?" He asked, glancing over to make sure that she couldn't hear us.

"No?" I replied slowly, frowning. "I mean I can give her a rank, it just didn't occur to me, not really…

"I suggest not." Restun said firmly, holding a hand up when I started to respond, planning on defending Lydia. "It's not due to her capability, don't worry." He glanced at Romanus, who nodded his agreement.

"So, in the Legion, most ranks are granted by higher, but while the rank of 'Optio' is *confirmed*, it is not *bestowed*." Restun said carefully, clearly having to think of the best way to describe a situation that was commonplace to the legion.

"The Legion has to have those in command that are right Jax. Frequently a group will find itself unable to confer with higher authority, and an Optio must be ready to lead. As such, we confirm the rank, but the prospective Optio must publicly claim the rank first. They will step up, if they are the right person, and simply begin giving the orders they see are needed. If they have the respect of their team, they will be obeyed. If not, not."

"That's…so wait, they just say 'hey I'm in charge, do what I say'?" I asked, confused.

"No, in the heat of battle they give the orders that need to be given. Think of your situation, you are leading your squad, and you fall. There is no longer a leader, the group, being as mixed as it is, will fall back on their individual skills. Who will order them, who steps up and guides the group?"

"Lydia." I said firmly. "Well, or Oracle…maybe Bane would as well, hell Grizz…fuck." I winced. "It could be a clusterfuck."

"Very much so. If one of the team steps up and orders the fight, and leads them out? They are the new Optio. They have claimed the rank through blood and command. If they try it and fail? Then they were never ready for command. This is why we do not select them, they have to choose themselves."

We spent a few minutes in broken conversation, going over the team, and confirming, with their recommendations as well as my own, that Lydia was ready. Now all that was left was for her to fully claim the rank by continuing to take the lead in fights.

"What was the other thing?" I asked, grunting as Thorn checked a strap.

"Loot," he said seriously. "As adventurers, I know loot gets divided up equally. For soldiers, they receive a portion of the loot, while the commander takes the rest. In the legion, all loot is handed in, and depending on the loot, occasionally a bonus in coin is paid out.

"Whatever isn't needed by the legion is put up for auction, offered first to the legionnaires, and if they don't want it, it goes to the city auction houses. It'll be in the legionnaires' heads that this might change, with you being here now, so best to address it straight away. Are you happy for this to continue as it is?" he asked.

"Yes, and no," I said, rubbing my chin in consideration. "If there's something powerful, magical or otherwise, the treasury gets first refusal on it, and we pay a fair bonus for finding it. Otherwise, for gold and mundane valuables, since the legionnaires will be receiving pay as well, they get to keep half. The rest goes to the treasury. Does that seem fair?"

Romanus started in surprise, glancing at Restun. They exchanged a long look then turned back to me.

"Half is incredibly generous, Jax, a legionnaire usually receives ten percent," Romanus said slowly. "Perhaps a slightly lower amount would be appropriate?"

"I'll be taking the magical items they find for the treasury, depending on what they are," I pointed out.

"They've always given those up," Romanus countered. "How about twenty-five percent?" he suggested tactfully. "I know that it seems fair to give them half, and it is, but the legionnaires are also provided everything, from food, to clothes, to wages, to medical care. They are given homes, training, all of it. To give them half on top of all that—"

"Hmmm, well, okay. I hadn't thought about that."

"That's what you need us for." Romanus grinned. "And believe me, that's still a huge increase for the average legionnaire. As to the skillbooks, spellbooks, and related items, will you be allowing legionnaires to bid in an internal auction before they're offered externally? It's traditionally how they have gained such things, if their role didn't specifically require them."

"No," I said flatly, and his face stiffened slightly. "If the legionnaires want a spell, they can explain why they need it, and if we have it available, and there is no greater need for it, they'll be granted the item.

"Maybe I will offer them occasionally as a bonus for bravery or something as well, but it won't be charged for. I refuse to hoard such things for simple hoarding's sake. Real power is only useful if you use it, and our people will be at the shitty end of combat too often as it is." I paused for a moment, considering.

"I and others who are skilled in using spells will also teach certain spells to the legionnaires, as time goes on. I'm thinking that every legionnaire should be able to use a healing spell, a ranged attack, and a buff or something, at the very least, with more powerful spells being reserved for those who have a real aptitude for it. This is how the legions used to be."

I remembered it, then forced the memory away, in case Amon used it to pour in his grief again. In that split second, I'd seen enough, though: a marching formation of the legion, firing barrages of what had looked like Firebolts, hundreds and hundreds of them slamming into screaming and charging hordes of undead, while an imperial battlemage had fought with a lich, summoning spells that almost warped reality. Amon sat atop Shustic, ready and waiting, but allowing the legion to carry the day.

"All legionnaires?" Romanus asked slowly. "Not just those who are most in need of the spells, like the Praetoria? All legionnaires, from the lowest to the high, able to use spells?" he repeated.

I cocked my head to the side. "Is that a problem? They have Abilities from their classes anyway, right?"

He rose from his crate, clapping me on the shoulders with both hands, gripping tightly and looking me in the eye.

"Jax, you have given the legion a future, offered to pay us more, provided a real reason for us to exist, and now you ask if it's all right that you intend to train us all in the magic that only a fraction of a fraction could ever afford? Son, believe me, the legion is used to far, far less."

"They don't deserve less, though," I said flatly, and he blinked as he released my shoulders, his eyes watery. "The legion risks its people's lives every goddamn day for shits who don't care. Well, I care, and so does the empire, and fuck those assholes who take and take. I'll spend lives when I have to; I need to do that, and I accept that now. But when I can, I'll make sure those who follow me are gaining as I do, growing as I do, and living their lives to the fullest. To do less..." I said, shaking my head.

"I know," Romanus agreed, smiling understandingly. "When you talk like that, it makes our hearts sing. Too long, we've been dismissed, despised."

"No more. Never again if we win, either," I said fervently.

"Well, an easy fix there, then." Restun snorted, a faint smile on his face. "We just have to kill them all until there's none left, eh?"

"Damn right," I agreed, clearing my throat roughly. "Right; let's get a move on. I need to go kill something."

I forced a grin, trying to hide the raw emotions that filled me, and they did the same. We forced laughs, then they separated to let me walk out and around the small private section to the area where the others waited.

CHAPTER ELEVEN

I joined the rest of the group, noticing that most were equipped with the same legion scout armor that I wore; Jian, Arrin, Stephanos and Miren, anyway. Lydia wore heavier full legion armor, as I termed it in my head, and Grizz wore his as well. Bane shifted nearby, and I realized that he wore something similar to the gear that Yen and Tang wore now, different from the simple armor they'd worn in our first encounter.

I looked closer and saw that I'd been wrong; they *were* wearing the same armor, but the various bits that had been removed to make it look less uniform, less...*quality*...were replaced and improved.

Instead, they wore the gear with pride, the scruffy accents and changes were covered by distinct legion-made panels, and it gleamed darkly. Their Praetorian Scout armor was similar to mine, but it was smoother; its lines just seemed to...flow. The metal was blackened and much more of it was scale than solid, but it looked amazing.

Bane didn't wear it, not fully, but he'd had sections of his armor replaced with parts of one, while sections of other unfamiliar kit had been added in. Original bits of his Mer armor that looked like animal shells had been removed, and new, more *graceful* pieces had taken their place.

"Damn, man," I said appreciatively, whistling quietly as I looked it over. He spread his arms out, inviting everyone to see it. "That looks great; can you hide as efficiently as before with it?" I asked.

He shook his head slightly but seemed unconcerned. "Not as easily as when my old armor was new and intact, but the damage my armor had taken of late meant its bonuses weren't working anymore, so this is a marked improvement. Add to that, it's far, far better for defense, and it's a clear upgrade."

The next ten minutes or so were taken up with us checking out each other's armor and gear, and I asked Thorn quietly why Miren, Arrin, and Stephanos didn't have full sets of gear. Now that I'd looked properly, they had the cuirass, vambraces, and greaves, along with helms, but that was all.

"Weight," she said simply, glancing in their direction. "They are too weak to carry the full set; even with this much-reduced version, they will tire easily, and you'll have to factor that into your plans. I'm sorry, Jax, but our legionnaires are physically stronger than your people.

"I mean no offense, but a legionnaire is made to endure physical training for a year before they are blooded. Then their real training begins, as they are guided through their point allocation. We force them to build a body as perfect as possible without the points, then invest them in certain areas, depending on their chosen specialty."

"All legionnaires are legionnaires first," Restun added, stepping in and taking over the conversation. "They are trained to fight as a unit, to hold the line, and to face the worst the realm can throw at us. But some, like Yen and Tang, are naturally adapted to be scouts. They are guided down this path, while others, such as Thorn, are clearly skilled as makers. There is no dishonor in choosing not to be a front-line legionnaire, for we are all the legion and all can fight when the need comes."

"Cool." I reached an apologetic hand out to the armorer. "I meant no disrespect, Thorn. I literally didn't understand where their gear was, that was all. I didn't know if you'd run out."

"Ha, no. We have spares still, and I have asked the tailors to make some basic leather armor for them. The tailors are excited to experiment, and a former slave has joined them, as he was a tailor himself in the past, apparently."

"The pool!" I exclaimed, shaking my head. "Dammit, I almost forgot. What were you saying about the volunteer pool?"

Romanus stepped in to answer the question. "The vast majority of the freed slaves have been volunteering to help, as have the formerly disabled dock and ship workers. Clan Mother Hellenica and Mistress Nerin have been working until exhaustion to heal them, and the people were thankful. Your little display of power, though? That made the difference. People who'd given up and were essentially along for the ride, simply hoping today would be a little better than yesterday as they sat waiting for orders, have now begun to actively seek out ways to improve their lot in life. They crowded the ships before; now, they are organized into work gangs. Those who wish to learn a trade are apprenticing themselves to the legion's crafters and makers or are helping where they can until they find the role that calls to them."

"That's fantastic!" I said, genuinely pleased.

"It is," Thorn agreed. "The former slaves might not have the skills, or at least most don't, as they've been common manual workers, simply used as beasts of burden. But there are a few gifted former apprentices or workers who fell afoul of the laws. The rest? Well, they're used to working from dawn 'til dusk, for virtually no food, no comfort, and no breaks.

"For the legion, you can consider them as having already served half their year of physical training. They obey with speed, they work until they drop, and they don't give in. Add into that mix some heavy physical training and good food? They'll make fine auxiliaries for battles, and in a few years, they'll be legionnaires to be proud of.

"Those who choose to learn to craft are, well, they're dedicated!" she said earnestly, shaking her head in wonder. "Most of the former slaves who fled to the enclave were either newly captured or broken by life. These citizens, they've been given a reason to live."

"We just have to stoke the flames, Jax," Romanus commented proudly. "They're already strong. We just need to guide and train them."

"Good," I said simply. "Let me know if they need anything."

"I will." He inclined his head respectfully.

"Okay, people, listen up!" I glanced at the rest of the group. "There's a need for us to get our arses down there fast so we can start to explore. As usual, I've done something stupid without realizing it. When I released the spirits trapped here, I probably stripped a lot of the Prax's natural defenders away, so those knobs from the other camps are frantically searching for the gear Jenae wants *us* to have. I'm not disappointing her, and neither are you! You've got an hour to get anything you need; then meet me at the front of the ship, because we're going in! Romanus, I grabbed a *lot* of potions from the Skyking's lair, so gather everyone in as close as possible before we all go our separate ways. It's time to perform the Oath," I insisted.

"Yes, Lord Jax," he responded formally, complete with a sharp salute.

"Also, I've got an honest-to-god robot frigging horse somewhere. We need to find it and unload it of all the random shit and see what we can pass around that will be helpful. Then I need to dump some of my gear somewhere safe, so I've got space for loot."

"The gnomish machine?" Thorn interrupted, wide-eyed. "Might I…I mean…could I—"

"You want to look it over?" I asked in surprise, and she nodded enthusiastically. "Then lead the way to it. I've no idea where the damn thing is."

I set off to follow her as she tore away into the ship, half a dozen of her fellow armorers and smiths following along.

"You'll never get any peace from them now; you know that, right?" Restun murmured quietly.

I shrugged as I jogged up the gangplank and back into the ship. "I don't mind, really. Besides, she might learn something!" I called to him as he turned off and jogged away down a corridor, shouting out to those he passed to gather at the front of the ship in the clearing.

The escort I'd picked up since waking followed me, and I shook my head, well aware that this wasn't going to work when we actually had things to do.

I gave a few quick orders, and most of them peeled off, all but one legionnaire and Bane. The others began spreading the word and searching for some fliers to spread the message to those on the ships overhead.

I ran down corridors and jumped over crates and stacks of gear, always fighting to keep the armorers in sight. Finally, we burst out into the main hold of the Battleship, took a left, then two rights, racing past the piles of boxes and gear, before finally, I found it.

Fenris.

Oracle had been silent for a while, content to simply be present while I did things. I'd felt her working on a spell, so I hadn't interrupted. But when she saw Fenris, she flew forward at speed, flipping over to land elegantly atop its head, her diminutive size meaning she managed to look comfortable as she perched on its forelock and stroked one ear.

"Isn't he gorgeous?" she squealed, grinning at Thorn and the rest of the armorers and blacksmiths. They were slowly circling the enormous horse, checking the build and commenting quietly to each other as they went.

"Uh, Lord Jax," Thorn said slowly. "Do you think you could make it move? We'd love to see how it works."

"Yeah, look, I really haven't got the time to fuck about, so…Fenris, follow the commands of Thornapple to move around inside this location. Do not leave this area without orders from Oracle or myself," I commanded then gestured to the armorer.

"To be clear, this is Thornapple." Fenris swung his head with a smooth whirring of gears and inspected her, making her take a step back before she let out a gasp.

"He's beautiful," she groaned. "Oh, to be able to make such magnificence!"

"Yeah, well, he's useful and a bastard of a thing to fight, I'll say that." I rubbed involuntarily at my chest, and she nodded absently. "Anyway, inventory."

I concentrated, and the inventory opened before me, a grid system that was ten slots by ten, and was half-full still. I looked over all the random crap that was still inside; the Jumna skins especially were just…weird-looking. I pulled one out and passed it to Thorn, who examined it curiously, then stared at me.

"What is this?" she asked.

"Jumna skin, apparently. No idea what that is," I admitted.

She frowned in surprise, looking at it more closely. "Really? Never thought I'd see one. Beats me how they do it, though," she said and I looked at her questioningly. "They're a luxury item, sir, nothing we'd get intentionally. They need to be processed somehow, not something I know how to do, but they make, uh, interesting underwear out of them? For the noble ladies?" she hinted, then smiled with amusement. "And the men, occasionally.

"I used to have a friend, Matt, who swore his old lover wore them for him. Said they took turns with them, but then Matt died. I had to tell his boyfriend about the death, and he…well, he didn't take it well. Punched me in the face and stormed off, said if Matt couldn't be bothered to admit he didn't want to be with him anymore, he could burn in hell."

"So, his boyfriend died, and he didn't believe you?" I asked, and she nodded. "Huh. Had that happen to me once." I frowned and rubbed my cheek. "Well, I say that…her friend told me it was over because she didn't want to do it herself. Not quite the same, I know."

"What did you do?" Thorn asked.

"Slept with her sister the next night. She came home early and interrupted us; I got a hell of a slap for that one." I admitted, grinning absently as I remembered the argument and her sister's point that, if she didn't want me, it shouldn't be an issue.

"Really?" She stared at me, shocked.

"What?" I asked. "I had a life before all this, you know."

"Okay, just seems a bit, well, weird to hear about your sex life. More than the entire ship already has, I mean."

"What?" I asked slowly.

"Ah, forget I said anything, Lord Jax!" She quickly backed away as I tried to keep my cheeks from setting fire to my hair.

"Oracle," I said, very quietly.

"Yes, Jax?" she asked sweetly, flying over to me.

"We need to soundproof our room. And the rest of the goddamn ship. As soon as possible, okay?"

"Oh, okay!" she said, totally unconcerned. "Are you done with Fenris?"

"Dammit, no." I strode irritably back to the mechanical horse's head, pulling the inventory back up, as it had closed when I got distracted. I was too flustered by thoughts of how many people had heard Oracle and I boinking to really concentrate.

I pulled up my bags alongside the Fenris storage and started swapping things around. I started by dumping as much as I could, filling one bag with metals then other trade goods and the various cooking and camp equipment I'd accumulated in my travels.

I kept going until all I had remaining in storage was a few days' worth of food, just in case, a first aid kit, a bedroll, my alchemy kit, and the necessary reagents, and a dozen health, mana, and stamina potions. I made a point of keeping four of each level available, which gave me four common, four greater, and four special grade. Curious, I examined the greater and special, respectively, to see what the difference was.

Greater Health Infusion		Further Description *Yes/No*	
Details:		This potion will restore 250 health points over 10 seconds	
Rarity:	**Magical:**	**Durability:**	**Potency:**
Uncommon	No	100/100	7/10

Special: Potion of Restore Health		Further Description *Yes/No*	
Details:		This is a special-grade potion, and as such has a secondary effect above and beyond the standard. This potion will restore 300 points of health to the imbiber, as well as granting a temporary increase in reaction speed of 10% for up to 3 minutes.	
Rarity:	**Magical:**	**Durability:**	**Potency:**
Uncommon	No	100/100	8/10

"Sweet," I muttered, lifting the potion up and swirling it around as I gazed into its depths, wondering how they'd managed to get that effect. After all, if I could just do that alone, an increase in my reaction speed would be amazing in a fight. "Time to get a move on," I told myself, stowing the potions back in my bag. I'd managed to strip the bag's weight down significantly and now had seventy slots available.

Pleased with the change, I left Thorn and the others to examine Fenris. Oracle and I hurried off down the bay, out into the crossing corridor, and wandered around a bit, getting more and more confused until Bane took pity on me and gave me directions.

Two minutes later, I was strolling out onto the upper deck, and I could see the "command team" waiting for me. The other ships dipped in closer and hovered, ready for the next part of my plan.

I hurried over to them, carefully crossing a few sections that were merely scaffolding and jumping across a section that had no deck at all, to reach them.

"Athena, Romanus, Elise," I said, nodding to each of them before turning to the person I least expected to be present. "Mal? What are you doing here?" He grunted noncommittally, looking at me then turning away, so I turned to his companion. "Soween?"

"We had a discussion, Jax…*Lord Jax*," Soween calmly stated, taking the time to use my title. "We agreed that we made a deal to get you to the tower, then we can look at the future and how we can make this work."

"We're not swearin' an Oath," Mal said sullenly.

I grinned at him.

"Aren't we?" Josh asked, looking confused. "I thought you said we would if the price was right?"

"Soween," Mal sighed, rubbing the bridge of his nose. "You gonna stop your husband's tongue yourself, or do I gotta rip it out by its roots?" he grumbled, before looking back at me. "So, we're *not* givin' you an Oath, not now. We're happy bein' smugglers, and havin' an airship as pretty as mine, not to mention fast, means we don't have to do anythin' we don't want to. That bein' said…"

"Yeah?" I prompted after a long, drawn-out minute of silence, and he held his hand out flat and wobbled it from side to side.

"Maybe…*maybe*…we could come to a deal in the future, do some jobs for you. On occasion. If the price is right," Mal offered

"And what would the price be?" I asked, trying not to laugh.

"Spells!" Josh replied helpfully.

"Gold," Mal demanded, glaring at Josh.

"Supplies and upgrades." Soween spoke over both of them, clearly fighting the urge to roll her eyes.

"So, you all have separate prices, then?" I asked, confused.

"No," Mal snapped, at the same time Soween covered her husband's mouth with one hand and spoke up.

"Yes," she countered, and Mal turned and glared at them both.

"I told you I'd handle this. What the hell's with all this goddamn interruptin'?"

"Just making sure you remember everything, sir," Soween replied calmly.

"Well, I do, okay? This is a deal I'm tryin' to make, and you keep interruptin'!" Mal growled, then seeing the totally unrepentant look on Soween's face, he shook his head and turned back to me. "Anyhow, just so's you know, we're available—"

"And can be bought," Josh added helpfully around Soween's hand.

I chuckled and offered my thanks before excusing myself from them, turning and walking to the edge of the deck to look out over the clearing, where everyone was gathering.

"Ready to make a speech?" Oracle whispered to me.

"Hell no," I muttered, staring nervously out over the sea of expectant faces. "You know I hate doing that, right? And that I'm shit at it?"

"You're getting better." Oracle patted my cheek, smiling reassurance at me.

"Going from sodding terrible to bloody awful isn't much of an improvement, in my book." I grimaced, already wanting it to be over.

"It's still an improvement, and besides, you're not that bad," she insisted, but I just shook my head.

"Nope. I'll make something up, but that's as good as it'll be. You okay to try to string out the Oaths as long as you can, while I guzzle the potions?"

"I'll make sure you're not overwhelmed, don't worry. And remember, this isn't like resurrecting the Imperial Oaths; you're not binding them to the Empire and creating a full link to you. This is a simpler Oathbinding, less than a third of the cost."

"Good thing, that, considering how many of the buggers there are," I muttered.

"You'll be fine," Oracle reassured me as I took in a deep breath. "Romanus? We're ready," she called, and Romanus stepped forward to stand at the edge, gazing out over the upturned faces before glancing up at those that lined the rails of the ships cruising slowly around us.

"Prospective citizens of the empire!" he boomed, his voice almost echoing as it carried clear to the waiting people on all sides. "I bring glad tidings! The empire is reborn. High Lord Jax has assumed the mantle of Imperial Scion and has been recognized by the Soul of His Imperial Majesty, Emperor Amon himself as the Heir!

"We live in momentous times, days where all hands are turned against us, but never despair! For the legion stands with you, and we shall face the darkness together! I give you, High Lord Jax! Scion of the Empire, High Lord of Dravith!" He gestured to me, then stepped back.

"Thanks for that," I muttered dryly, stepping up to the railing and catching his grin out of the corner of my eye. I took a deep breath and deliberately straightened up, projecting my voice as far as I could.

"You all know of me; those who've been around longer know I'm not one for speeches, so I'll make this simple. I came to Himnel for two reasons: I needed to find my brother, and I needed you. You who agreed, who volunteered, and who took the risk to join me, will never be taken for granted. I have freed those of you who were enslaved, and I will never force anyone to take the Oaths against their will.

"But in order to know that we are all able to rely on each other, to enter the Great Tower, you must be sworn to me and to your fellow citizens. The legion has already sworn their allegiance to me, and now it's your turn. Again, if you choose not to, that's fine. We will set you down in a village on the continent and leave you there, but you must choose now."

With that, I felt my mana start to dip as Oracle sent out the Oath, and I took the time to swig down a mana potion before describing the benefits of the Oath.

"As a citizen of the empire, I will feed you all and house you for the next year for free, as well as pay a fair wage, based solely on your skills and abilities, not on your species." I drank a second potion. "You will be required to work for the greater good of the tower and ultimately the empire, but you will be given training, protection, and opportunities you have never had before.

"Some of you, those who show themselves to be exceptional workers, highly skilled, or simply dedicated enough, will be given more. You will be given opportunities to earn spellbooks, skillbooks, or even occasionally, memory crystals that contain the memories of master craftsmen of the past." I could feel more and more invitations being pushed out, and the mana drain kept rising, causing me to breathe deeply as I tried to ignore the trickling feeling, and the incoming mana migraine.

"I ask you now to join with me in rebuilding the empire and take the Oath of the Great Tower." I chugged the last potion I could manage, feeling myself shaking from the speed of mana regeneration and drain combatting each other.

Then it began. At first, it was a low rumble as a few started to say the words quietly, almost hesitantly, as though unsure they were doing it wrong. Then more joined them, and more.

Soon the clearing rang with the sounds, echoing down from the circling ships, and I felt the impending cost building further.

"I swear to obey Lord Jax and those he places over me; I will serve to the best of my ability, speak no lie to him when commanded otherwise, and treat all other citizens as family.

"I will work for the greater good, being a shield to those who need it, a sword for those who deserve it, and a warden to the night.

"I will stand with my family, helping one another to reach the light, until the hour of my death or my lord releases me from my Oath.

"Lastly, I will not be a dick!"

"I, Lord Jax, do swear to protect and lead you, to be the shield that protects you and yours from the darkness, and the sword that avenges that which cannot be saved. As the tower grows in strength, so shall you," I called out, forcing myself to not sway as the last of my mana reserves bottomed out and my health started draining instead. It was nearly over, and I couldn't afford to waste more potions. I'd used three greater potions already, leaving me with only one of that caliber. I didn't even know if Arrin had any, and we'd surely need them down below.

Several more seconds passed, the last voices dying away, the air humming as almost six hundred people swore to follow me.

"Thank you all!" I called out to them. "Those who chose not to swear, please make your way forward to a legionnaire and inform them, and they will make arrangements for you to be guided to a village." With that, I turned away from the edge, moving slowly as I felt the drain finally stop, and my mana started to regenerate along with my health.

"How many?" I asked Oracle.

"Just under six hundred took the Oath." She smiled. "I didn't push it to the legionnaires, as they already swore the Imperial Oath, as did Horkesh and her spiders."

"Horkesh? Shit, I'd forgotten about her." I grimaced, shaking my head at my poor memory. "Where…?"

I immediately looked up and began searching the ships, until I found one on the outer edge, slowly circling. The hull was made of dark wood, or at least stained so badly that it looked dark. As I watched, a spider clambered across one side of the hull and vanished over the top onto the deck. The ship trailed something as it went, and I frowned until I realized what it was, webs.

The entire ship was coated in them, and the spiders happily moved to and fro all over the ship.

"Uh, the crew of that ship…?" I asked cautiously, and Mal spoke up.

"That's the *Star's Glory*, Bateman's ship, if you remember that asshole? Turns out he was tryin' to save money by not allowin' his crew shore-leave, so when Horkesh and her pack took the ship, they got seven of the crew, the old captain included. The passengers, or former slaves, have been learnin' to fly her, and seem happy to be with Horkesh. It mighta been us that arranged it all, but it was her and her pack that freed 'em."

"That's a relief," I said, exhaling shakily. "I'd never want to be on a ship full of them, myself."

"You and me both," Mal said with feeling.

"Jax," Oracle interjected, and I turned to face her. "There were twelve who refused the Oath, not including Bateman and his crew; as slavers, I didn't offer it to them."

"Right?" I said, frowning and peering over the side. "I don't see anyone talking to the legionnaires, though…" I realized slowly as the group dispersed.

"I'll make a note of any that come forward," Romanus said. "Hopefully, they're just waiting until there are fewer people to see them."

"Hopefully," I agreed, a sudden sinking feeling in my stomach.

"Jax, we can't do anything here, not without unlimited mana. Once we're back at the tower, if they haven't come forward, I'll come up with a way to find them, and we can check it out to see what the problem was, okay?" Oracle reassured me.

I nodded in acceptance, relaxing slightly. "Thanks, Oracle. Okay, where are we with the camps?" I asked Romanus.

"I've dispatched forty legionnaires to each camp; they're on their way already. Each team has orders to take command of the camps, secure anything and everything, and capture the ships. Both teams are led by a Primus, and they are under strict instructions to avoid casualties in the civilians, and to kill every last man who raises a weapon to us. The soldiers are to be given the chance to surrender. If they don't…that's their choice to make," he finished calmly.

"Good enough for me," I said flatly. "Do we have many spare potions?"

Romanus nodded in affirmation. "We can find some. Which ones do you need?"

"Mana, mainly. A half dozen or so, if they're not needed, and a few health and stamina? Ideally, I'd like my team to have two each of stamina and health, with myself and Arrin, and Yen, actually, carrying half a dozen mana each, if you can spare them."

"We'll sort it," was all he said as we crossed the deck and headed down into the ship again. As we passed a pair of golems that were adding in sections of decking to the upper levels, I paused and watched them for a moment.

"How large are the entrances to the Sunken City?" I asked hopefully.

"Not large enough, unfortunately," Romanus said, understanding my line of thought immediately. "The centuries of seawater and storms, combined with the growth of the plants, has resulted in increasingly small entrances, and while we could make them bigger, to make even one large enough for the golems would take several days."

"Damn, and that'd be several days of the golems *not* working on the ship. Fair enough. Shame, though," I said, having indulged in a momentary mental picture of me strolling casually through the ruins below, with the golems clearing the way.

"It was something I considered as soon as you had stated that you wanted to explore the ruins, Jax. Unfortunately, it wasn't meant to be. I did consider having Augustus take them along to the camps, but in all honesty, the difference they make to the ship's construction here is immense. Considering that I need Augustus to remain with me here in order to direct them, I made the decision that it was best not to create an opening large enough."

"That's fine," I said, nodding my acceptance. I'd have sent the golems to the camps, personally, rather than risking the deaths of our people, but Romanus knew his men better than I did, and I accepted that. Besides, a single mis-phrased order could have disastrous consequences, and I really didn't want to risk that. I thought back to the sight of the golem literally ripping the arms off a troll and beating it to death "with the wet ends," per an idle order I'd given, and I shook my head in fond remembrance of the goblin slaughter.

For now, until we had either a truly sentient golem to command them, or Oracle and I were managing it together, I wanted them to perform basic tasks. Once we were back at the tower and Heph or Seneschal could take over their direct control, that might change, but for now, simple laborers were more valuable.

Especially ones that could lift the equivalent of a car and hold it in place without complaint while skilled workers secured it.

I was directed through the ship, working my way down to the gangplank and out onto the clearing, where we paused our conversation as we joined my team.

"Be careful, Lord Jax," Romanus said gruffly. "I know you need to grow, you need the experience that only battle can give you. In this case, only you and your companion know truly what you are looking for, but remember: without you, the empire falls apart, as do our lives."

"I will, Romanus. But the empire doesn't fall if a single man does. You would need to take over in the tower and look after our people, until you can find someone to rule in my place."

"I couldn't," he said, aghast.

"You are in charge when I'm gone," I said firmly. "I have a council in place in the tower already. If I die, you are to lead the people there and secure it, protect them, and keep the empire alive. That's an order, Romanus. I might not have known you long, but I trust you, and I know Augustus, and he and the rest of the legion trust you. They'll be needed."

"I will look after things until you return," Romanus said slowly. "But I cannot lead the empire, Jax. I'm a legionnaire, which means I follow and I protect. I do not lead. Please, choose another."

"Then that's something we need to discuss later, but for now, you're in charge," I insisted firmly before turning to the rest of my team.

Lydia, Jian, Arrin, Stephanos, and Miren stood waiting calmly. Bane moved around from behind me to lean against a pile of boxes, and Grizz, Tang, and Yen moved in closer from where they'd been standing, still talking quietly. As the others faded back and returned to the ship to carry out their duties, I looked around the small group and smiled.

"Well, who's ready for an adventure?" I asked them.

CHAPTER TWELVE

There were grins all around as the team got ready, and I checked my gear as well. In addition to the new legion armor, I carried, of course, my naginata. The shield I'd looted from one of the twins was secured by a convenient armor hook as well, covering my two back-sheathed silvery drow shortswords.

As if those weren't going to be enough, I had also equipped a dagger on my right hip and one strapped to my left ankle. My razor wire belt had yet to be repaired, so instead, it was looped up and stowed away in my bag of spatial folding. As I checked myself over one last time, I decided that it should be enough.

Everyone else was doing the same; Miren and Stephanos were with Yen and Tang, checking their bows, arrows and generally going over their equipment, swapping spare bowstrings and so on. Jian and Bane were checking their weapons and making sure their blades were sharp, while Grizz checked my armor, Lydia's, and his own. Arrin was packing mana potions away into his pockets and bag as fast as legionnaires could hand them over.

After a few more minutes, we were all set, and I turned to where my escort stood next to the ship.

"Well, thanks for your help, legionnaires," I said, smiling appreciatively at them. "I'll see you soon."

"Sir, we could help further, join you down there," one offered, but I shook my head.

"No. There are dozens of entrances into the city, and we need to cover as many as possible. Report to your primus, and he will assign you a position." I was tempted; I mean, honestly, I was *very* tempted. These were professional warriors and monster hunters; of course, I wanted them to go with us, but the simple truth was that we needed to level, and they'd slow that considerably. I returned their salutes and dismissed them, turning back to where the team stood ready. "I guess it's time, then," I said, leading the way across the sodden, muddy grass to an entrance Romanus had pointed out earlier, flanked by its four legionnaire guards.

The surface was dotted with openings, indicated by grassy mounds and caves, shallow pits and holes, all leading down into the lower levels.

The Prax's upper levels had once been a mixture of garden and marshalling areas, with the occasional structure to break it up. Now it was a grassy, tree-covered island, and here and there, it led up or down at odd angles where floors had collapsed into the level below, or buildings had fallen into rubble.

I nodded to the guards, and they saluted, stepping aside as we filed inside the grassy mound.

Bane went first, followed by Tang. I went next ducking inside the dilapidated opening, followed by Arrin, Miren, Jian, and Stephanos, with Yen and Grizz bringing up the rear. I couldn't help gazing around as we progressed further into the city, and I wondered at the way the entrance was formed. It really did give the whole "spooky cave system" concept a run for its money.

The passage was misshapen and narrow. The torn metal that had once been a perfectly crafted part of the city was now a sagging, jagged, sharp, heavily overgrown and partially collapsed cave entrance and tunnel instead.

A constant trickle of water came from somewhere overhead as it ran down one wall, and if not for my memories and knowing better, I'd have sworn it was a natural cave.

My DarkVision activated as soon as I'd gone a handful of feet, and the others either activated abilities they had, in the case of Tang and Yen, or attached small magelights to their armor in special holding slots to help them see. The ground was covered with mud and rubble, as were the walls, with fungus and moss creeping up a significant portion of the right side, fighting for primacy. On the left, the signs of something squeezing through and accidentally clearing the gunk off were obvious.

We moved forward slowly until we came to a second choke point in the tunnel, and we had to drop down onto our knees to crawl through. Disgruntled mutters trickled from my people as the stinking muck squelched its way around their new armor and into their clothes.

I sniffed one hand as I paused behind Tang and shook my head, grimacing and hoping it was just rust and muck. Whatever coated the tunnel floor smelled foul. I had visions of generations of animals using it as a toilet and tried not to retch. After a few seconds, Tang started moving again, and a dozen yards further on, the tunnel opened up slightly, allowing us to climb to our feet again.

This became the norm for at least an hour, working our way through to find collapsed sections and maneuvering our way around until we'd reach the next gap wide enough for us to move on. Sometimes, we'd find signs of smaller creatures or of the passage of other long-ago adventurers. Occasionally, we'd come across the tracks of something larger, but mainly, it was just us, in the dark, with the stinking muck.

We finally approached a fallen area of tunnel that was almost totally impassible. We had started to consider going back to the surface and trying to find another route, when Bane sensed a hidden area.

A thin slab of steel had been placed across a section that looked for all the world like the rest of the tunnel, and behind it was a trail that led deeper into the city. Unfortunately, the overhead clearance was low enough that we all had to crawl again for a while, but as we went, we gradually noted less and less depth to the muck, and we started to hope that we had truly found a way forward.

We paused once we were all through, as the next cavern was more regular in shape, clearly delineated, if filth-covered. Walls and a ceiling defined the space, with two other doors leading out. The first, on the left, was choked with debris and mud. Established roots were obvious as we looked it over and quickly dismissed it. The only sign that it had ever been a doorway was the rectangular lintel, the rest of it was so covered and buried.

We moved to investigate the far door, finding that it was open, more or less intact, and the opening was clear even beyond the frame, but here and there, in the filthy corridor beyond, clear marks had been left behind. The most distinct were boot prints and a smeared trail, as though something heavy had been dragged along recently.

We followed cautiously, due in part to having nowhere else to go, and eased our way through the next two rooms. The walls, floors, and ceilings gradually changed as we headed further into the depths. It hadn't been apparent as much from above, mainly because everything had built up over time, but inside, the slope of the city was clear. It was angled downward at about a ten-degree slant, and soon, it became a case of struggling to stay upright as much as continuing forward.

With each new room we entered, the general mulch from outside grew less and less, until the walls were consistently steel, the floors solid and dark, and the air was stale, as though it rarely moved.

We entered a corridor that culminated in a small square room, and finally found the thing we'd been tracking. The room was barely five meters to a side, square, with a sagging roof and light that glimmered weakly up a hole in the floor at the far end.

Bane grabbed my arm then whispered very quietly into my ear to look at the far-right corner. I followed his verbal direction, and there, at the opposite end of the room, perched a creature the size of a child, gazing downwards.

It was clearly reptilian in nature, with a well-developed humanoid upper body and a long, scaly tail. Its blunt, triangular face was angled downwards and illuminated from below as it hissed to itself, watching something traveling along beneath it.

I frowned, then realized what it must be watching, judging from the growing light and the rising noise from below.

It was another party. I had no idea if it was ours or from one of the camps, but I couldn't allow this creature to get the drop on them. I looked to my archers, who were all waiting for a signal from me, and I nodded to be ready before fixing my gaze back on the creature and using my spell to Examine it.

Critical success!

**Your opponent is unaware of being observed
and has no defense against your ability.**

Naga Fiend
The naga as a species are not inherently evil, but their lack of compunction regarding killing, the pleasure they take in eating raw meat, and their choice to regard all that lives as food, have resulted in in them being labeled as such by most sentient races.

Distantly related to the Merrow, the naga's deepwater cousins, these naga are split into three castes, of which this fiend is considered the lowest, both in mental capacity and strength. Its caste is most often used for advance scouts and general soldiers.

Weaknesses: Fire, Earth, and Life magics do 50% more damage.

Resistances: Water, Darkness, or Death magics used against this creature suffer a 25% damage penalty.

Critical Weaknesses: Neck, Eyes, Liver, Lungs.

Level:7

Health: 90

Stamina: 40/40

Mana: 10/10

"Kill it," I said abruptly, and the air was suddenly alive with first the creaks of bows being drawn back, and then the *thwack* of the strings slamming forward. The juvenile naga jerked backwards from its attempt at hiding and was slammed into the back wall, three arrows protruding from its chest.

It barely had time to twitch before it was dead, pinned in place. A small handful of rocks falling from where it had been crouched alerted the group below, and lights were shone upwards in an attempt to see what was going on.

We moved forward slowly and peered down, careful to remain as hidden as possible, until I felt…something…tingle. I froze as Oracle spun to me.

"Mage!" she hissed, and I frantically waved people back from the hole as a voice rose from below.

"It's the goddamn legion!" someone swore, then a low laughter echoed up to us, followed by chanting.

"Fuck; get back!" I ordered the group, scrambling away from the corner as a grey-green cloud started to coalesce and float upwards, filling the room steadily.

We scurried out as fast as we could, while the voice continued to chant and occasionally laugh from below.

We backed up the corridor a dozen feet or so before deciding we were safe. But the fog settled in place and filled the entire small room, making me wonder about its effects. I'd smelled something as we'd backed away from it; something familiar, like rotten eggs. I paused, considering the smell and the way that the cloud was hanging around, before grinning evilly.

"Well, what do we have to lose…?" I mumbled to myself, taking a deep breath and starting to form the magic. I poured mana into my recently evolved Fireball spell, dual casting it and planting my feet before looking back at the people surrounding me.

"Might want to run," I called, the strain of holding the spell clear in my voice.

"Fuck!" Lydia grunted. "Everyone get back! That's an order, legionnaire!" she barked when Grizz moved as though to stay close to me. He glared at her, then nodded once and backed away as she did.

"Maybe see if you can come up with a shield," I whispered gleefully to Oracle, who frantically started trying to build the spell, reading too late the knowledge in my mind, even as I released it.

The spell had begun to buck wildly in my hands, the stability of my old, tamed Firebolt spell vastly different to the wildness of the Fireball. As it flew forward, leaving my hands with a high-pitched whine, I felt Oracle frantically pulling sections of different spells apart and slamming them together, desperately trying to build a shield spell on the fly.

For the first time in our shared history, she wasn't fast enough.

The Fireball slammed into the poisonous cloud, and the smell I'd recognized earlier was confirmed as accurate. Sulfur.

Somehow, a part of the poison cloud involved sulfur. I had no idea why, or how, but the rest of the compounds acted like a miniaturized, compressed-fuel air-bomb.

The first explosion was brief, a burst of flames that washed heat over us, shoving us backwards across the floor. Then, as the air itself ignited, a vacuum formed in the center of the cloud, condensing directly over the group whose foolish mage had been laughing and congratulating himself over the spell he'd cast.

I missed most of the rest of it, having thrown myself over Oracle and pulled the shield from my back atop us, but the enormous explosion that followed, accompanied by the roar of falling steel, the clatter of rock, and the other terrible sounds that rose from the pit that had opened up near us were enough for me to know I'd fucked up.

Badly.

The floor under us tilted, slowly at first, then with increasing speed, and the surrounding walls started to slide as well. We fell into the gaping hole, clattering and tumbling into darkness. My DarkVision was unable to compensate after the explosion had wiped it out.

And we screamed.

All of us did. We screamed, we shouted, there was a lot of cursing—*mostly directed at me for some reason*—and there were horrific moans from the survivors of the party that had attacked us with the poison cloud.

We all fell for several seconds, rocks and soil falling down from higher up and hitting me. Solid sections of the walls and floor continued shifting, and then I smacked into something solid. The world exploded in stars, making me cry out as my right knee bent in a direction it wasn't supposed to. More debris rained down atop me, threatening to bury me alive.

My hands scrabbled frantically as I tried to push myself forward faster. I grasped rocks and loose soil, and they skidded away under my hands. Suddenly, something solid, larger than the rest, stayed in place. I grabbed it, wrapping my fingers around a couple of raised sections.

I pulled, dragging myself out of the debris, seeing nothing at first until Oracle flew down from above.

She'd fallen free of me and had turned mostly incorporeal, I learned later. Then as soon as she'd gotten her bearings, she'd come looking for me. The rest of the party had thankfully been far enough back that, aside from ringing ears and Jian's newly singed moustache, everyone was okay. They hurried across to the closest point and looked down into the cavern I'd exposed, staring down at me.

I gaped up at Oracle, my racing heart slowing as I verified that she was okay. A sound from my right made me look over, and the soil shifted before a larger, and very pissed-off-looking naga dug itself out.

It saw me and hissed, its fanged mouth opening wide enough that it could swallow my head, before tearing the last few feet of its body up and out of the debris.

It screeched at me, coiled its tail beneath itself, and leaped.

I froze for a second, my instinctual fear of snakes combining with my recent fall to leave me momentarily distracted enough that the naga was in the air before I could think of what to do.

It hit me, staggering me backwards, and the long, prehensile tail wrapped around my waist and back, squeezing as the onyx-tipped nails latched onto my armor. Hissing again, it lunged forward for my face, trying to bite me.

I panicked further, remaining frozen until its mouth clattered across my helm, and a single fang slipped inside.

It barely grazed my skin, tearing a shallow cut down the side of my nose, but it was enough.

My rage roared to life, the flames of it burning through the confusion and fear as I yanked my head backwards. The naga drew back as if to bite again, and in that moment, I attacked.

I grabbed both its arms and yanked it forward into a headbutt, the highsteel helm smashing into its unarmored face with the crunch of breaking bone. Wasting no time, I hauled back and struck again.

By the third hit, the naga was frantically yanking at my hands, trying to tear itself free and burbling as blood ran down its ruined face. My blood was up though, and I sure as hell wasn't going to let that happen. As soon as its tail unwound from around me, I let go with one hand, hauled back, and punched it, stunning it and leaving it hanging by the wrist I still gripped.

"Motherfucker!" I snarled, lifting my other hand up under the lower edge of my helm to touch my face and bringing it away bloody. I looked at my fingers, then glanced toward a scrabbling sound from my left.

I hadn't fallen a single floor, I saw now, but two, meaning I had found a way to the outer edge of the main habitation level, my mind helpfully informed me. Judging from the writhing mass that was heading across the floor toward me, we'd found an entire nest of naga.

I drew in a deep breath and felt a grin stretching my cheeks, suddenly feeling more like myself than I had in days. I stepped forward, grabbing the stunned naga by the tail and dropping the wrist.

It stirred and hissed at me before I started to swing it. Then it started to scream.

I spun it round and round by the tail, slowly letting out a little bit to get it to a comfortable length; then, before the rest of my people could get down, I stepped forward, swinging my new naga-flail.

"Who's your daddy!" I roared, spinning the unfortunate reptilian into another that had just leaped for me. I had a split second to enjoy the view as it clearly realized it'd made a tactical mistake. Then its cousin slammed into it, and, with a sound like coconuts bouncing off each other, they went their separate ways. My improvised club swung around to hit another naga and sent it flying into the nearest wall.

The next leaped at me as well and met my left fist coming the other way. Its face folded around the metal-clad limb, causing it to drop to the floor and leave a fang embedded in my gauntlet.

I grimaced and shook it free, stamping down hard on its windpipe and ensuring the cartilage crunched underfoot as I moved on.

"Come on, then!" I shouted, yanking my dagger free and gripping it in my left hand while continuing to lay about me with my "club."

They seemed to come from everywhere, first two, then five, then a dozen, and more, swarming out of a series of holes in one wall, hissing and screaming their hatred.

"We're comin'!" Lydia shouted from somewhere above; then Oracle was there, screaming and lighting up the sunken room with a series of lightning strobes. The bolts slammed out over and over again, taking the creatures down in droves.

I spun, bringing my new naga-nada down hard on another that was struggling up through a hole in the floor, both my club and my target's bones breaking; then another was on me. I hadn't even realized in my furious attack that I'd moved forward under another section of steel until the naga dropped from the ceiling and landed on my shoulders. Wrapping its arms around my neck and upper right arm, it tried frantically to pull my helm aside so it could get at my throat.

I yanked my head back as claws scrabbled across the front of my helmet, catching on the eye slits and digging in, leaving a trio of scratches down my right cheek to join the other one. I twisted and stabbed out, my dagger slicing across skin and sinking below the bottom ribs. Grunting, I yanked downwards, tearing a good-sized section of its guts out to rain down over my right shoulder onto the floor.

It screamed, and I dropped my broken "club" to reach up and grip its head in my right hand. Tearing it free, I slammed it down onto the floor on its back before me.

Reaching over my shoulder and yanking at one of my swords, I found, as always, that it was a bastard to draw from my back. The last few inches caught, but with an extra tug, it was free, and I grinned at the gathering naga, their reinforcements slithering up from somewhere deeper in the darkness.

Then my people were there. Bane, appearing to the left, carved a sudden and bloody path through four of them, screams of shock and pain filling the air until he vanished again. Lydia and Grizz took up station on either side of me, and Jian danced through the area behind, making sure that stragglers and the wounded didn't become an issue.

Then the ranged fighters came into play; they'd clambered down far enough, in Stephanos, Miren and Arrin's case, to be able to see the fight and were firing arrows and Magic Missiles into the horde. Yen and Tang stepped forward, their bows put aside in favor of their swords.

Suddenly, as we were no longer outnumbered, the battle went from fast and furious into a rout. Arrows slammed into the naga as they turned, trying to flee, and Oracle spun to face me, clearly furious and looking terrible.

I couldn't see the fight anymore as the others stepped up and took over, my vision overwhelmed by her haggard and enraged expression as she glared at me. Her hair stuck up in all angles, and her clothes—no, her entire form—just looked wrong, like it had been put together by someone who'd heard roughly what a fairy should look like, but hadn't ever seen one or anything else that should fly.

"O-Oracle?" I stammered, fear in my mind as I desperately tried to understand what had happened to her.

"You…you…arrrgh!" she snarled, throwing her hands up in the air and buzzing in a fast circle as she started to swear, calling me all sorts of names. My companion started with "ass-fucking-monkey-ball-licker" and went downhill from there, getting more and more inventive, until the sounds of fighting entirely ended, and Grizz and Tang started repeating some of the insults to each other in impressed tones.

"What's wrong?" I asked soothingly, trying to break her stream.

"son of a sheep-screwing donkey! You…" She went on, undeterred, as I held up my hands, frantically trying to calm her down. Lightning crackled across her tiny form and between her fingers.

"Oracle!" Lydia snapped loudly, and Oracle spun to face her, glaring her fury at being interrupted. "Tell 'im what 'e did wrong, then snap out of it! Yer can kick his ass later, *when we're no' underground surrounded by monsters!*" she snarled, then went back to watching outwards as the distant sound of snarls and fighting could be heard.

"Fuck!" Oracle cursed, then spun back to me, zipping in close and leveling a finger at my face close enough to scratch my nose. "Remember what a broken spell does, Jax?" she asked me in a low, furious whisper. "Remember what that felt like, in your meaty, muscle-filled brain?" I nodded slowly, eyes widening with every syllable. "Well, now imagine what having the same thing feels like, *when you're a fucking magical creature that doesn't have meat to absorb it! It hurts a lot more, you asshole!* Add to that, I was having to build that goddamn spell on the fly!"

"Shit." I winced, remembering the spell backlash I'd felt before. I shook my head slowly. "Sorry, Oracle," I started to apologize, but she cut me off with a sickly-sweet tone as she moved in awfully close to my face and lifted one hand, claws suddenly forming and glinting in the meager light of the magelights around us.

"Oh no, Jax, you're not sorry, not yet. But the next time we're alone? When you're all hot and ready for me, I'm going to remind you of this, then I'll *make* you sorry."

She tapped her hard-as-steel talons on my helm, her voice ending with a hiss before she turned and zipped away to land on Lydia's shoulder, growling and complaining.

"Oh, shit," I whispered, shaking my head and squeezing my eyes shut. Now that I was relaxed slightly, I could indeed feel the pain that radiated out from her, and I totally understood why she was pissed.

"I'd be staying clear of her for a while," Tang said quietly, stepping up alongside me as Yen moved over to stand next to Lydia and Oracle.

"Can you hear her?" I asked. He nodded, flicking a finger toward his helmet, in reference to his elven ears.

"Believe me, you don't want to hear what the girls are suggesting…*I* don't want to hear it, and it's not me that's pissed them off."

"How bad is it?" I asked him uncomfortably.

He winced. "You don't want to know, and I mean that. You *really* don't want to know."

"Dammit." I groaned, before speaking up so that they all could hear me. "Everyone, I'm sorry. That was my bad. I smelled the sulfur and thought it would just burn off; I truly didn't realize it would be that powerful." I shook my head, trying to ignore the glares I was getting from the three girls, even as Miren dropped down from the level above into Jian's arms, pecked him on the cheek, smiled, and then moved over to join them.

Arrin, always the graceful one, fell and landed face first in the mulch with a splat.

Stephanos jumped down, and he and Jian pulled Arrin up, helping him to strip some of the foul, stinking mess off his armor.

"It sounds like we've got more incoming, so we need to find somewhere more defensible, and soon. First, though, we need to find my goddamn naginata and the bodies of those assholes, verify who we killed and that they've not got anything on them that we need," I said firmly, lifting my right hand and igniting a Fireball for light, then holding it over my head.

Grizz was on the outer edge of the light, searching through the corpses that were revealed, and he grunted as he straightened up, calling back to us.

"These are adolescents," he said, my gut clenching at the fear that I'd just killed kids. "Their nest must be nearby. Looks like all fiends, so get ready for more swarms."

"Swarms?" I asked.

Tang spat on the floor "Fiends are the lowest caste of naga; they're barely sentient, and no matter the age, they'll attack anything and try to eat it. The only thing that can control a swarm of fiends is a packmaster, so either we'll be facing one of those soon, or these are just wild, in which case we might get a swarm or two, then it's over."

"So…?" I prompted, still not fully understanding.

Grizz started kicking through the corpses. "So, if we're really lucky, there's just one nest of these anklebiters; if we're not, there could be a lot more, and this is in the sea, so get ready for that." The legionnaire grimaced. "I hate naga," He grumbled, kicking another corpse out of the way.

I moved back toward the area where I'd first fallen, and while Tang, Bane, and Yen watched outwards, the rest of us started digging.

There was over thirty meters of debris, but thankfully, most of it was large bits, so once we'd moved those aside, it was relatively quick to uncover the bodies.

My naginata was intact, which was a huge relief as I hefted it, and I resolved to take greater care of it as I slid the sword back into its place on my back. I also found my shield, surprisingly undamaged, and decided to slide it into my bag of holding, as it was too cumbersome to continue carrying in these conditions.

The human bodies were fairly blackened and crushed, making any real identification difficult. But as they'd attacked us first, and they clearly weren't legion, we stripped them of valuables and roughly-made bags, then moved on.

We'd gained a few dozen coins, mostly copper and silver, with a pair of jeweled daggers that Yen asked to keep, several low-grade rings, and three mana potions. I gave two to Arrin and kept one myself.

Beyond that, the gear was cheap and uninteresting, mainly weak and shoddy armor, occasional basic iron daggers and the like, so we ignored them and were about to move on when Bane sent out a pulse of his worldsense so he could identify things we might have missed in the dark. After a few seconds, he pointed out a small satchel in the corner under a pile of mud.

Yen opened the bag, smiling grimly, and passed it over to me.

Inside, I found dozens of magelights, long dead, but obviously the group had been ripping them free of the walls as they went. I frowned at the collection.

"Where do these come from, normally?" I asked out of curiosity, and Yen glanced around the dilapidated walls.

"Mostly from ruins. They're not complicated for a crafter to make, apparently, but they are obviously magic, and there aren't many magical crafters, so it pushes the price up." She gestured down the partially collapsed hallway nearby. "I'd guess these areas of the city were hard to access before, so they'd been relatively untouched…by people, anyway."

"They're not exactly hard creatures, though," I said, frowning at the reptilian corpses.

"Ha, just you wait," Yen said, shaking her head. "Fiends are like goblins; they just breed and breed and breed, then swarm over anything they find, so either this is a new nest…" She trailed off, and Grizz spoke up, finishing her sentence.

"Or there's something nearby that was keeping them contained." He drew his sword and pointed out into the darkness. "And I think we're about to meet it."

"Form up, everyone!" Lydia barked, and we flowed into our accustomed battle formation, the legionnaires finding their natural places easily, with Grizz on the front line next to Lydia and me, Jian protecting the archers and Arrin, and Yen and Tang on either flank, able to see better than the rest of us with their elven heritage.

The room we were in now was considerably larger than any we'd been in yet, with sections of sagging ceiling hanging low over us.

We moved out from the small corner we'd been fighting in and took stock of the larger area. Keeping the newly made entrance behind us, and the wall to our right where the majority of the naga had slithered up from, we were left with a huge space that vanished upwards, interspersed with sections of the old floor above that jutted out, creaking and groaning ominously. Even my recovered DarkVision and Fireball weren't enough to dispel the darkness to show the entire room.

"Something's out there," Yen called softly from my left, drawing her bowstring back and sighting down the arrow as Tang called out from the right.

"Here, too," he said calmly, and Arrin started building a spell.

I held the Fireball in my right hand still, so I called out to the group to be ready as I threw it forward, angled up, just in case whatever was out there wasn't hostile. A few seconds later, it slammed into the far wall, bursting and cascading flames out from the point of impact as the barrier shook slightly.

Below the flames, exposed for us all to see, were dozens of crawling, stumbling, and blindly staggering undead. The corpses ranged from rotting and skeletal to almost fresh as they shambled forward with mindless hunger, hunting the living.

The flames guttered out, and the room was plunged back into darkness, lit only by the distantly flickering flames of something that smoldered away fitfully.

"Well, that's not good," Arrin's voice remarked bluntly before Grizz called out. The usual joking and cheerful tones I was used to hearing from him, as one of the youngest members ever to grace the Dravith Legion Second Maniple, were lacking as he spoke up, determined and ready for the fight.

"We need light, sir, and somewhere to fall back to. It's unlikely for us to have been so unlucky as to just stumble into the main concentration. This appears to be a full infestation of the dead, and we're just seeing an outlier."

"Arrin!" I snapped. "Here, start charging these up!" I called as I tossed the bag of magelights at him.

He released his spell, sending five Magic Missiles flaring out into the darkness. Two hit their targets, one blowing off an arm and the other slamming into a ribcage and detonating, smashing a staggering skeleton apart in a shower of bones. The remaining three flew straight and true, impacting walls in the distance. One hit a doorway, exposing a hallway that was filled with the shambling figures. Yen swore, putting her bow away and starting to build a spell.

"We need to bleed them, Jax," Grizz said seriously, his voice professional. "We've encountered this kind of thing before, and we either retreat and get more forces to deal with it, or we bleed them of as many as we can and continually fall back. The real risk from shamblers isn't the individual; it's the fact that there's hundreds or thousands to each one of us. They can afford to make a hundred mistakes, and all they lose is time, until the necromancer resummons them. We make a mistake, we lose someone."

His expression was uncharacteristically grim.

"Okay, people, aim for the head, kill as many as you can, then we fall back and climb back up to the floor above."

"They're getting closer," Tang warned, drawing his bow and firing a single shot out into the darkness.

"Then let's go play!" I snarled to the group, leading the way forward, Lydia and Grizz going with me as the others used ranged weapons to cut the undead down.

I rushed at the oncoming horde, my DarkVision bringing them into sight as I ran. They were slow, weak-looking things, most didn't even have weapons, but here and there, the glimmer of metal resolved into swords, shields, and spears, as well as a surprising number of other weapons being carried, dragged, or brandished.

The first few shamblers I reached were barely intact, almost entirely skeletal and clearly held together by the magic that reanimated them. They clacked their teeth as they saw me with their glowing eyes, and suddenly, they sped up.

Whatever was controlling them clearly started taking a hand as the general lethargy seemed to drop, and the corpses straightened and rushed forward.

I spun my naginata around, sweeping out long and low from right to left in a rising arc, smashing one's legs apart and sending it cartwheeling away as I swung on. The next was hit in the hip and knocked backwards. The third, as I spun around, received the weighted, metal-clad base of the naginata smashing into its skull, shattering it and sending the bones clattering to the floor in a spray as the animating force lost cohesion.

Grunts and clatters reverberated from either side as Lydia and Grizz went to work. I flipped my naginata around, pushing a touch of fire into the weapon and igniting it. I stabbed out, driving the tip of the blade into the next closest shambler's face, feeling the bones shatter, then I yanked back and twisted, slamming both arms out straight. The naginata snapped diagonally between them as I hit two skeletons at once, their questing hands reaching for me as I threw them backwards.

I twisted and kicked out, staggering another undead. The light grew behind me as Arrin filled magelight after magelight and threw them outwards, illuminating the room more.

The fight was close in and was only growing closer as more and more of the undead seemed to awaken from the unsteady general undead, reminiscent of old horror movies, into the terrifying, fast and determined kind. More and more were appearing, and as I hooked one ankle with the butt of my weapon and yanked, slamming the blade into the face of another, Yen called out.

"On the left!" she grunted, her arms held above her head as three glowing spears, wreathed in flames, hovered above her. As soon as she'd given the warning, she threw her hands forward, as though physically hurling the spears. They shot away, spreading out.

They impacted, as she'd warned, to the left of our small group, one after the other, and as soon as they hit, they exploded.

The projectiles burst into flames, spaced evenly apart so that the first reinforced the second, which reinforced the third, creating a shockwave of blazing destruction that wiped out a solid forty feet of undead, sending bits flying everywhere.

I stepped back, then again. Rather than the pause I'd been expecting, we were the ones distracted by the attack, and the undead kept crowding forward, rushing us.

As the flames started to die away from Yen's attack, I caught a glimpse of more undead crowding into the room from the doorway at the end, and I swore.

"There's light above!" Miren yelled above the din. I jerked my head upwards, looking instinctively, before swearing and turning back to the fight. Swinging my weapon from right to left, I cut through a half-decomposed corpse at the neck, sending the head tumbling as the body fell.

"Who is it?" I called, feeling Oracle finish the spell she'd been working on. Whatever lingering effects the broken spell had wrought on her, her casting ability was certainly the most obvious right now, as it was taking her longer than usual to cast.

A full spread of Magic Missiles flew from her, five in all, each aimed at a different undead. The massive darts slammed into them, killing two and injuring another, while the last two shamblers barely seemed to notice.

They were weird-looking skeletal creatures, standing about five feet high and four broad, with huge carapaces on their backs. They moved more like an armadillo than anything else, but with weapons grasped in their hands while standing upright. Additional armor hung loose across their chests, including a few helms that should have covered their heads, making them look like someone had tried to create an organic living tank, then strapped more armor on for shits and giggles.

"What the hell are they!" I grunted, and Oracle called back to me in warning.

"Xon'dike!" she shouted. "They're the original caretakers of this place and its basic defenders, so watch out!"

"Really?" I shouted back, bashing another skeletal warrior in the face, then smashing its legs out from under it and crushing its skull with the base of my weapon. "I was going to let it kill me out of fuckin' curiosity!"

I turned too late, getting shoulder charged by a skeleton from my left.

I staggered, then head-butted it, my greater weight driving it back far enough that I could let go of my naginata with my left hand and grab its throat. As soon as I felt the bones in my grip, I yanked, tearing its head free.

Before I could set myself again, another skeleton hit me, and another, and this time, I went down, slamming into the ground. Refusing to stay pinned, I immediately began rolling, lashing out with my legs and kicking.

The undead started piling on me, their bony fingers tugging and digging, frantically trying to get at my flesh.

One leaped on my right arm, pinning my naginata down, while the first two that had taken me down pinned my back and waist as best they could.

Another appeared behind them, less decomposed than the rest, only at most a few months dead. I leaped into the air, raising its mace high and aiming for my head.

A black arrow flashed through the air, slamming into the airborne undead's breastplate and sending it flying backwards, even as I lashed out with the bones I still held in my left hand.

I had a fist full of spine, still connected somehow to the skull, and I slammed it into one of the skeletons. The crunching of bones sounded loud enough to me underneath it all that I winced as I planted my feet and arched my back, bucking the pair off. Momentarily free, I twisted to my right and slammed the skull-mace into the face of the one that held onto my right arm.

Then Grizz was there, followed by Oracle and Lydia. Between the three of them, they cleared enough space that I could get back to my feet.

"Time to fall back!" Grizz insisted.

I nodded to him, winded but glancing around. At some point, while I'd been on the floor, Yen or Oracle had hit another group with a big spell, and that'd created enough of a gap that we could back up.

"Get Lord Jax out of here," Grizz ordered Lydia." I'll hold them long enough."

"Scratch that. Miren, Stephanos, get back up there now, then you can pick them off while the rest of us fall back." I started to say, when an ominous creak rose from the debris behind us.

"What the…?" I looked up, only to see movement as two men began shoving a section of wall hard, making it tilt.

"Move!" Lydia bellowed, shouldering into me and shoving me aside as more of the section that led up began to fall away, taking with it the low-hanging ceiling.

INTERLUDE – THOMAS

"**S**ir, yes, sir!" Thomas barked along with the others as Sir Edvard Tunnik, Dark Paladin of Nimon, ordered him forward, stepping down the cool, wet marble steps into the pool of black liquid.

"Dark Lord!" Sir Edvard intoned sonorously. "This humble soldier has risen fast in your service, barely weeks ago a slave, then a slave-aspirant, until he stood proudly and fought off all challengers to his right to ascend! Finally, his brothers and sisters in the faith, Belladonna, Turk, Coran, and Majiis have offered their blood in a plea for a full healing and binding!"

Thomas swallowed hard and again worked to keep his eyes locked on the spot of dried viscera that hung from one of the stalactites in the Chamber of Darkness, rather than glancing to his immediate left.

Sergeant Belladonna, his squad leader, one of the hardest, dirtiest fighters he'd ever seen, and without a doubt, the most beautiful, stood by his side, her long, blue-black curls swaying in the slight breeze that filtered up from the depths of this most holy of places. Like Thomas and the other three who had pledged their blood to his, swearing to act as his family, swearing to aid and teach him, in exchange for the healing and rebuilding of his mana channels…she was utterly naked.

Thomas jerked his eyes ahead again, biting down on the impulse to just take a single look sideways. It wasn't that she was naked, although he desperately wanted to see that again at any opportunity.

He'd seen it before; they all shared a communal tent city, after all. The construction of the new legion section of the citadel was still underway, which meant they all shared baths and more out of temporary necessity.

The squad spent almost every waking and sleeping minute together. They trained, they ate, they practiced, and they trained again. The days were almost as monotonous as they'd been in his jail cell, but the difference was here, his beatings were given by others training with him. If he worked harder? Faster? He beat them instead. He ate and drank well, he *lived*, and that was more than he'd ever expected to have again.

They all shared communal baths at the end of the day, and while Belladonna seemed oblivious to her nakedness, he and some of the others sure as shit weren't.

They were all friends and squad-mates though, so out of respect, they damn well did their best not to look.

Also, she'd undoubtably beat the living shit out of them if they offended her. No, it wasn't her nakedness, not entirely.

It was the fact that she stood so close.

He could feel the heat rising off her body, smell her scent on the breeze that filtered past, a faint mixture of crushed lilac and jasmine that changed every so often, a faint peppery undertone joining with the rest. He could see her breath as it clouded the air.

The preternatural cold of the crypt pressed in all around them, and he really didn't want to think about the effect that was having on his manhood, despite simultaneously being damn glad, as it was all that was keeping him from 'springing' to attention at her nearness.

"Now, Dark Lord, your servant Thomas will step forward to ask for your blessing. He will expose his heart to you, aided by his brothers and sisters, and you may judge him! Should he be worthy, we ask that you restore him, heal and bind him, so that he may carry forward your anger unto the enemy, no matter where they skulk!" Sir Edvard roared, the dark light of fanaticism gleaming in his eyes as he looked down on Thomas and his companions.

They stepped forward as one, having been schooled on the correct etiquette, and glided deeper into the oily substance.

The slick, cloying wetness rose up his thighs, and he felt a spike of regret that it was going to take forever to get the damn stuff off every hair, fighting back a grimace as the substance rose higher.

Nobody knew exactly what the liquid was, but it was warm, and the cavern was anything but; that fact alone had given rise to countless rumors over the years.

Add to that, the knowledge that immersing yourself into the substance and having your companions open your veins to it never made the volume rise or fall, that it felt like oil but smelled like blood, and that if Nimon found you wanting, well, the result was explosive, both for you and those who entered with you.

Thomas drew in a deep breath, turned and lay back, feeling the substance buoy him up to float on the surface. He tried his best not to imitate a sailing ship as he looked into Belladonna's eyes. He focused grimly on them until she nodded once to him.

Then he turned his head and stared determinedly upwards, focusing on the stalactites above him as four sets of hands took firm hold of his limbs, and the cold of sharp metal was pressed gently against his skin.

"All praise be to Nimon! For in his glory and service are we all tested!" Sir Edvard intoned, and the others, Thomas included, echoed him.

"All praise to Nimon!" they cried, and then the knives bit into his flesh.

Thomas gasped in pain, his eyes flaring wide as he was opened to the Dark God in truth. The inky substance flowed in, burning into his veins and intermingling with his heart's blood.

CHAPTER THIRTEEN

The entire section of the structure that supported our path to retreat started to tear loose with an ear-splitting shriek of tortured metal. I had a split second to recognize a familiar face grinning down at me from above.

Joshua, the Baron of Sarat, I remembered, Hannimish's nephew, who had just fucked me well and truly. He made a rude hand gesture at me and vanished, making me swear fervently.

"He's just fucked us, whoever he was," Stephanos said grimly, and I turned back to face the oncoming tide of the dead.

"No," I said firmly. "That's Joshua, one of the asshole nobles, and he only *thinks* he has."

I checked my mana, seeing it was a little below half, and scanned the room quickly.

The path up, indeed the entire section where we'd been standing, was now a mess of debris. Behind that was a wall and to the right was another. Straight ahead was the majority of the undead horde, pouring out of a hallway on the far side of the room and flooding in after us.

There were a few undead heading in from the left, but nowhere near as many as from straight ahead, so I pointed in that direction and clicked my fingers.

"Arrin," I ordered. "Fire as many spells as you have to; I need to know what's over there, if there's a way out or not."

I looked to him, and he nodded, determination clear on his face as he yanked a mana potion free of his bag and started chugging it.

"The rest of you, hold this line. We can't afford to get forced back against the wall," I said, taking the lead, only to find Grizz and Lydia moving up beside me.

"No," I insisted, motioning them back. "I need you both to protect the others."

"Our job is to protect you," Grizz said grimly. I shook my head as Lydia grunted agreement.

"I—" I started, only to have Yen call out as well.

"You already got jumped once, Jax," she pointed out

I grunted, then started to laugh. "Yeah, all right, that's true," I said, rolling my shoulders and looking ahead. "But you can't keep up with me."

I took a deep breath and activated Mana Overdrive.

I was getting a better handle on it. I knew that now; I could feel it. Instead of the frantic sensation that had met me when I first started to use it, my very atoms vibrating at an insane rate, I felt a difference flowing through me as I crouched, then exploded forward into the oncoming undead.

My muscles seemed smoother. Each movement was enhanced, but instead of the jerky, powerful motions I'd experienced before, it seemed somehow more refined, like going from an old diesel engine from the seventies to a slick, modern car, the graceful momentum building as power was supplied from the engine to the wheels. Vitality hummed through me, and I almost danced through the undead.

Effortlessly, I slipped between two of them, ducking beneath their outstretched arms while swinging my naginata around to behead them both easily, then darted forward. It was as though they were moving through treacle, while I danced and struck, beating their clumsy counters aside.

The Xon'dike pair were next, and I ran straight at them, planting the base of the naginata on the ground and using it like a pole, vaulting over to bypass three normal skeletons who staggered, twisting around to follow my flight as Grizz and Lydia charged forward and struck them down.

I landed feet first, slamming into the rightmost Xon'dike's face and sending it hurtling from its feet to land on its back, rocking from side to side in its bowl-shaped shell.

I kept my balance easily, my body seeming to vibrate with energy, and I spun around, smoothly ducking beneath a jerkily-swung spiked club to sweep the left one's legs out from under it as well.

Once it was on its back, like the other, it appeared to be stuck. While the living versions would presumably have some trick to getting back up, whatever was controlling them clearly didn't know it.

I grinned viciously and raced ahead again, channeling a little more magic into my naginata and noting that my mana was at thirty percent.

I had maybe another ten seconds, I guessed, judging by the speed it was dropping. Swinging my polearm out as fast as I could, I broke into a run, bringing my trajectory around in a half circle and charging back to the rest of the group.

I moved my arms steadily, the motion more like I was trying to draw a mobius strip with an enormous two-handed pen than anything else. The figure of eight that I carved through the air, aided by my flame-imbued, magically razor-sharp weapon, left devastation in its wake. By the time I cut off the ability, staggering as the vicious debuff took hold, I was nearly free of them.

I braced myself as the world seemed to speed back up; everything became harder as the minus ten to all stats kicked in.

I stumbled, then forced myself forward, grunting and lashing out as something leaped onto my back. Sharp fingers dug into the back of my neck, and I reached up with my left hand, punching blindly.

I hit something that rocked back but continued hanging on grimly when Bane appeared before me. I barely had time to register his presence before he was leaping over my head. I felt a tug; then whatever it was, was gone. I staggered the last few feet to rejoin the rest of the group as Grizz, Lydia, and Bane fell back.

"Looks like there's a limit on how many their necromancer can guide at once," Yen said thoughtfully as she prepared to cast another flaming barrage of spears.

"W…what…?" I huffed, bending over and trying to catch my breath, nodding my thanks to Arrin as he pressed an open mana potion into my hands. He waited until I downed it and then pointed to the far left.

"Over there," was all he said, then he fired a Firebolt in that direction as I straightened and tracked the glowing spell's trajectory. A few seconds later, the Firebolt slammed into the wall about three feet from an open doorway leading off into the darkness.

"Oh, fuck yes," I whispered, taking another deep breath as I felt Oracle struggling with a healing spell, obviously aiming to get me back to top condition again as quickly as possible.

I checked my health, finding it at five hundred and forty-seven out of six hundred and forty.

"Not bad," I mumbled, then spoke up louder so that all my people could hear. "Right, everyone! We've…got a…chance! Follow…me!" I ordered, and I charged for the distant doorway, hoping I wasn't leading them all into a dead end.

"What…were…you saying…?" I huffed at Yen, discouraged that clearly my recent input into Endurance wasn't enough, as I felt terrible.

"Whatever's controlling them," she clarified, easily jogging alongside me. "If it could control them all at once, it'd just bury us in them, so clearly it can't. It seems as though it can only directly control a few, maybe a dozen at a time; the rest are given general orders and set away to follow them."

"Is that a good thing?" I wheezed, stumbling, before Oracle's spell hit me, and suddenly the world seemed to grow brighter and easier. I drew in a deep breath and let it out, my mind becoming clearer again.

"What the—" I muttered, looking over my shoulder and seeing the group following along. Bane appeared and tore through first one, then two, then three of the undead, clearing the path.

"Poison," Oracle said grimly. "That last one on your back injected some kind of poison into you."

"Fuck," I muttered. "I didn't realize," I said lamely.

"Neither did I, until I'd already started casting, but that got rid of it, luckily." She hovered alongside me. "We need to find somewhere to rest and recover; we can't keep this up for long."

"I know," I agreed, watching as the spell cleared my last few points of damage away. Then the relief of the debuff fading washed over me, and everything became just a bit more manageable again.

We reached the doorway without any more incidents as Bane cut us a path. Glancing back, it was clear that the glow from the charged magelights we'd scattered was being blocked by hundreds of bodies.

I swore. "We need to get out of here." Tired agreement rose from the rest of the party. We had no idea what the new passage led to, but the best thing about it was that it wasn't this goddamn room.

I hoped.

"Grizz, Bane, Tang, lead the way down that corridor. Yen, Lydia, Jian, you're with me on rear guard. Miren, Stephanos, Arrin, you're in the middle; hammer those fuckers when and where you can," I ordered, and we got moving. There was a little confusion as people started to shift around but in a few seconds we were all working cohesively.

The flickering shadows thrown by the growing avalanche of the undead moving past the magelights threw strange patterns around the surrounding structures, and the walls seemed to writhe as we ran, the eerie silence of the undead mass broken only by the occasional clatter or snap as bones were broken, metal harnesses jangled, or weapons clattered against something.

We ran, with Grizz and Bane vanishing into the corridor first, Tang mere seconds after the others. By the glow of Grizz's magelight, we could see them taking down stragglers in the corridor. Meanwhile, Lydia, Yen and I jogged backwards, watching over the rest.

Miren and Stephanos had sprinted ahead, getting to the corridor close on Tang's heels, spinning around to take aim, then firing arrow after arrow into the oncoming mass.

Occasionally, one of the undead would collapse, the arrow having taken out the head, but more often than not, the projectiles simply knocked them down to be stomped by the oncoming tide.

"Okay, get inside!" I ordered them, and they fired a last arrow each before rushing after the others, followed by Yen as Lydia and I backed into the corridor.

The first of the next wave had reached us then, and Lydia's mace proved to be a far superior weapon in the confines of the corridor as we battled side by side.

The space was too tight for my naginata to be wielded properly, so instead I flipped it over and started using the weighted, blunt end to shove them back. Each time they'd run at me, I'd wait, then stab out, aiming for a knee or skull, either slowing them down or knocking them from their feet, while Lydia killed any she could.

As the corridor continued to lengthen, I eventually gave in, and, thankful for the amazing properties of bags of holding, slid the naginata into my bag of spatial folding, tugged my shield out and strapped it to my arm, and started using a sword.

It wasn't the best option for the tight confines of the corridor, but I'd been about to use my go-to spell Firebolt and realized at the last second that, due to its evolution to Fireball, it wouldn't end well.

"Oracle," I grunted, stabbing out and deflecting a sword thrust by a rotting adventurer, then shoving their sword further aside and using my shield to bash them back. "Any chance of a little help here?"

I continued swiping the sword across the front of my shield to clear away the reaching, grasping hands that tried to rip it free.

"Jax, I can barely fly and speak right now!" she growled at me, and I swore viciously under my breath.

"Okay, get ahead, then. Keep an eye on Bane and the others, but stay safe!" I ordered her, and she vanished in a flash as Yen spoke up from behind me.

"I've enough mana for two more Flamespears," she said dubiously. "If we ran for it then blasted them down the corridor, it's tight enough that it would funnel them, making them a lot more damaging, like it did to the drow. I'd need time to cast them, though, and as weak as the structure is in here—"

"Do it," I said quickly, shoving forward with my shield again, then stepping back three quick steps and stabbing out at head height, sweeping the blade across in a blind attempt to do some damage. Lydia backed up alongside me, striking out repeatedly for knees and arms, working to incapacitate rather than destroy.

"It might collapse the tunnel, though," Yen warned me from behind, and I shook my head.

"Doesn't matter; we stay here, we're getting swamped, anyway. If they get buried, they can dig their way through to us while we rest."

Yen acknowledged my words with a grunt and lashed out, killing another undead.

"Get back down the corridor, a hundred meters or so, and start building the spell. We'll hold them up as long as possible, then we'll run when you say," I ordered her, then growled and stepped back before Sparta kicking the face of a skeleton that had dragged itself forward under my shield to grab at my leg.

"Go!" Lydia cried to Yen. "We can hold the line."

"Shouldn't be the fucking lord holding the goddamn line!" Yen spat as she turned and sprinted with the kind of speed and grace only the elven-born could manage.

"Jax, there's an almost empty chamber at the end of the corridor. It's got stairs leading down that are clear, and ones leading up that are blocked." Oracle's voice came to me through our link.

"Fuck! Fine. Get Bane to check out the stairs leading down. We need somewhere we can defend, so we're going to fuck this tunnel up," I sent back to Oracle, before cutting the mental communication off.

"Yen?!" I cried to her, stabbing forward again and biting back a cry as something hit my forearm, somehow gouging into my armor and making me drop the sword. I put my shoulder behind the shield again and drove forward, slamming it into the mass of bodies over and over, trying to force them back as hands grabbed at the edge of the shield and pulled hard.

"Working on…it," Yen cried back, and a flicker of light began to build from behind us, reflecting dimly off the dark, stained, and scored metal walls.

"Fall back," Lydia snapped at me. "I've got this."

"The…hell you…have!" I grunted, yanking hard on my shield with both hands, forcing back a scream as my right arm flared in pain.

Whatever had hit it earlier and stripped me of the sword had done serious damage, and the trail of dripping blood was inciting the undead into greater fury.

More and more bodies slammed into the pair of us as we backed away, and they seemed to have forgotten weapons, uncaring of damage as they reached with their rotting fingers. Flesh cascaded off their corpses as they grabbed and tore at us, frantic to get a solid grip to bring us down.

"I said," Lydia growled at me, "I've"—she started to glow a deep ominous red—"got"—her breath was coming out in faster and faster bursts as her arm sped up, the mace blurring as it smashed hands, legs, and skulls—"this!"

The last word erupted in a bellow as the light began to pour off her like a star going nova.

She screamed in rage and lunged forward, striking out again and again, her mace blurring, her shield no longer a defensive armament. Suddenly, it was spinning, lashing out and smashing targets into walls and the floor.

She took out a skeleton to her right with a mace strike to the side of the head, the skull disintegrating and showering those behind his flying teeth and shards. Her shield simultaneously moved so fast that it slammed into a rotting adventurer on her left hard enough to spin it into the wall, sending it to the floor in a clattering heap of broken bones and armor. A naga, the flesh sloughing off it as it coiled its tail beneath itself, saw the opening and dove forward, only to meet Lydia's foot.

She'd kicked out with an insane amount of force and booted the creature full in the chin as it lunged forward, sending it soaring upwards to hit the ceiling with shattering force. The lower jawbone turned into splinters as the rest of the skull flew away into the distance somewhere, ricocheting into the enemy.

Before the shamblers could recover from the sudden assault, she was driving through them, mace striking out over and over again, smashing one skeleton after another aside, her shield taking on all comers, even as she punched, kicked, and headbutted any that stood in her way.

For five seconds, all I could do was gape, seeing for the first time what it must be like for others when I used my Mana Overdrive, as she became a full-on tornado of destruction.

Then her light began to dim, her breath began to come in short, fast gasps, and she staggered, nearly falling.

"Run…damn you!" she hissed at me, and I did.

I sprinted the dozen or so steps between us, racing to reach her, grabbing her by the shoulder and spinning her around, then driving my shoulder into her gut and lifting, hoisting her fully armored form onto my shoulders and grunting as something twanged in my back.

I staggered, then bit down on my pain and thrust my left hand out, trusting to the straps on my shield to hold it in place as I fired a Fireball off, practically at point-blank range into the reeling, uncoordinated undead.

Whatever was taking personal control had been too slow in changing to new minions when the last lot were killed, and I managed to fire it through a gap in the front lines into a particularly diseased-looking minotaur three rows back.

The Fireball hit him in the middle of the chest and washed out, the blast wave stripping the remaining scraps of leather, flesh and straps that had covered it. It staggered back before detonating in a growing rose blossom of flame.

I'd already turned, glad Oracle had managed to heal me all the way, and I triggered Mana Overdrive again, conscious that I was doing myself damage, but having no choice in it, as I forced my muscles to not only carry me and my full legion-armored weight, but to transport Lydia in her heavier legion armor. I managed to run for a few dozen steps before I started to stagger again, sheer bloody-minded determination all that was keeping me going.

I pressed onward as fast as I could, while Oracle took up station next to Yen, preparing a second Fireball and hurling it over my shoulder into the mass of undead that seethed and rumbled behind me.

"Jax! Move it!" Oracle screamed in my mind. *"They're joining together to form a behemoth!"*

I got a confused welter of images through our link as I strained forward. Glimpses came through of bones slamming together, leather and armor, weapons and gear flying apart, being discarded in the frantic rush of something that was determined we wouldn't escape.

The bones were melding together, absorbing the trail of shattered minions and the oncoming intact undead alike. All were dragged into the forming colossus, and for the first time, I heard a sound from the undead, as something screamed out in rage and hunger from behind me, making my eardrums vibrate with the force of its hatred.

I staggered along, desperate to reach Yen, and I could see the strain that holding her spell was having on her. Five glowing spears, each at least six feet in length, wrapped in flames and glowing a roiling mix of yellow, red, white, and blue hovered above her head, quivering in the frantic need to be unleashed.

The sweat was running down her cheeks, and she was shaking, her hands uplifted and braced in place as though she were physically holding the spears back. The magical projectiles surged forward and back, restrained only by her will.

Ten meters…seven…I staggered again, pain radiating from my back, my thighs, my shoulders, as I forced myself to put one foot in front of the other, pushing off with all my strength, rushing along as fast as I'd ever run on Earth. But now I had the weight of a fully armored tank on my shoulders, one who weakly pleaded with me to abandon her, to leave her behind.

"Not…today!" I grunted.

Five meters…three. I stumbled past Yen, catching sight of Miren and Stephanos, who were firing arrows into the forming creation. Jian and Grizz grabbed at Lydia, dragging her free of my shoulders and passing her further back as I fell, catching myself on the wall and groaning in pain.

"Motherfuckers!" Yen screamed, throwing her arms forward as soon as I was past her. The five spears flashed along in concert, slightly staggered to increase their damage. They cut through the air with a violent whistle and whine, picking up speed as they flew.

I struggled back upright, Grizz grabbing me under the right arm and tugging me to my feet. He shoved me forward just as my mana dropped into the toilet, and I staggered again, my second debuff hitting me and making me almost too weak to move in my armor.

"Move it, legionnaire!" Grizz screamed at me as Tang appeared, taking my left arm and ducking under it, half-lifting me as he started to run. Stephanos took my other arm from Grizz and they worked together, half-dragging, half-carrying me.

Yen was stumbling along with the others, helped by Miren, as Grizz and Jian dragged Lydia along, her metal-clad sabatons dragging along the filthy metal floor raising an ear-piercing shriek, one that was quickly occluded by the explosions behind us.

For me, it felt like a giant hand slammed into my back, lifting me and tossing me along the corridor. The entire team was thrown from our feet, tumbling and collapsing as the blast wave washed over us. The majority of the impact was luckily being directed away, instead barreling into the undead creation that had been forming.

The first spear had hit it on the cheek of the massive skull that had begun to form, cracking the structure and blasting the bone apart. The second impacted a millisecond later, to the left and slightly higher, punching deeper into the horned skull and detonating, the explosion peppering the walls, ceiling, and floor with ballistic bone shards.

The blast wave grew, conical in shape, as the next hit to the right by a few inches. It slammed through the monster, taking a dissolving undead Xon'dike in the face and smashing it backwards before it practically vaporized. The fourth hit further, punching through the back of the Xon'dike's carapace and emerging into a hail of disassembling bones. The final missile flared through the gap created by its predecessors and detonated.

The blast wave, no longer constrained by solid bodies, but instead meeting flying, magically-dragged individual bones, roared out, clearing the corridor and erupting back into the room beyond, sending thousands of flaming shards in all directions and shredding the hundreds of undead on the far side, the final blast turning the room into a bone grinder.

The overpressure that had punched us from our feet vanished, only to be replaced by the cracking, creaking, and screams of failing metal as the corridor's stress tolerances were surpassed by a force never envisioned. The ceiling, walls, and floor abruptly collapsed in a rolling wave of destruction.

We barely escaped, staggering and limping into the room the others had found and falling to the floor in heaps, too exhausted to fight.

I noticed the ceiling above me shuddering, and I closed my eyes, barely able to breathe, let alone escape. The world slipped rapidly from me, turning black.

CHAPTER FOURTEEN

When I awoke, it was hours later, judging by the rested, painless state of my body, and my helmet was off. I blinked slowly, trying to reconcile the view before me and the sensation of my intact body with the way I'd felt in my last memories. Confused, I slowly looked around, catching sight of a glowing campfire pushing back the darkness nearby.

I was half-stripped of my armor and laid out on my bedroll. My head was cradled in Oracle's lap, and I reveled in the softness as she sat and stroked my hair back. She was full-sized and glaring at me, even as our link spoke volumes about how relieved she was to be able to scold me again.

I lifted one hand, bracing it palm-down and levering myself upright. I turned slightly and slid the other behind her head, pulling her in close and cutting off her rising complaint with a hard, relieved kiss.

When I broke it, I glanced around, seeing the amused looks on everyone's faces, and I grinned at the realization that everyone was okay.

"Now, how come all I got when *you* woke up was a smack?" Jian whispered to Miren, and I shot a grin at him as I turned and inspected the room. It quickly became clear that we were camped in the last room we'd found at the end of the corridor.

"What happened?" I asked.

Lydia clambered to her feet, stomping over to me and glaring down. "Yer almost cost us all our lives is what happened!" she snarled. "I was happy ter die there; I woulda held tha line! Instead, yer came after me, just like yer rushed tha damn undead in the first place. Then everyone else had to come stormin' in to save us both! Yer nearly cost everyone their lives, just ter save me!"

I blinked in shock, remembering the chaotic struggle and feeling that I was being unfairly shouted at.

I remembered the pain and the damage happening to my body as I carried her, and I remembered the determination that had filled me.

"You think I should have left you?" I shot back, pushing myself to my feet, only to have her grab the collar of my tunic and pull me forward to glare at me nose-to-nose.

"Yer damn well know yer should have!" she snapped, fury dancing in her eyes. "I'm yer guard, not tha other way around!" She shoved me back, gesturing at the rest of the group. "They all had ter come, they dove in ter save us, because their job is ter look after ye! And *you*, yer stupid son of a bitch, yer were on tha front line, fighting a goddamn hopeless retreat, because yer too fuckin' stupid an' stubborn ter know yer place!"

"I—" I sputtered, before Grizz cut me off.

"She's right." He shot a glare at me before dropping his gaze to the fire and turning a section of meat suspended on a skewer over the flames. Suddenly, the smell of the fat dripping into the fire, bursting and popping with flavor, was all I could think about, until he continued.

"We're all here for you. We *exist* to protect you, and you're trying to be the 'tank,' as you call it. Have you any idea how terrifying that is?" he asked, still not looking at me. "To know that for the first time in hundreds of years, we have a chance at an honorable life? At being the true legion again?

"That we could bring it all back, save the fucking empire itself, as every goddamn legionnaire who's ever lived since the Cataclysm has dreamed of doing? And knowing that instead, we'll have our names and memories cursed for the next thousand years as the incompetent arseholes who let you die?"

He growled, turning the meat more than necessary, and I fumbled for my words, when, of all people, Miren spoke up.

"You saved us in the tower, you gave us a home, but what do you think will happen when you die?" she asked softly. "Do you think everyone will forget what you did and just leave us alone?"

"They'll drop everything and rush to take your place, to take the Tower and kill any witnesses who see it," Stephanos added slowly.

"But—" I managed to get out, before Tang spoke up.

"Then they'll wipe out the legion, seeing us as a liability, waiting for another lord to challenge them. They'll use the excuse that we followed you to wipe us out to the last, hunting us down. Thousands of legionnaires out there who've never met you would be slaughtered by the nobility, just in case. It'd be the only excuse they need." He grimaced, flicking a pebble into the flames.

"What the hell?" I snapped, interrupting the group "let's give Jax shit" love-in. "Seriously—" I started, before Lydia interrupted me again.

"You'd take all that from us, because yer can't bear to think about where yer should be. Yer can't fuckin' accept that we can fight, too, that we can sacrifice."

"I can't!" I snarled, cutting her off, and the room went silent in shock. "You hear me?"

My voice bounced off the walls and echoed back as I felt the weight, the burden I'd been carrying for so long, lifting as it was released.

"You can't do what I have to do; you can't be me!" I threw my hands in the air, unable to stop my own words. "You all want me to just let you die, to step back and let you make that sacrifice? Well, I fucking can't! That's not what I am!"

I glared around at their stunned expressions.

"You think I can't let you have your place in the line because I'm, what? Too fucking greedy for glory? Is that it?" I growled. "It's not! It's that if I'm going to be the next emperor, the center of all this…this *shit*," I cried, waving my hands around, "then I have to be *me*!" I slammed both fists into my chest. "You want to know why I'm on the front line, why I have to fight? Because I'm too fucking weak! I'm too weak to see you die, to see more of you give up your lives for me, because I'm not worth it!"

My voice dropped to a whisper as I felt my eyes burning with unshed tears.

"You don't get it. None of you do," I said mournfully, shaking my head. "I've only ever had Tommy. My brother," I explained quietly. "We only ever had each other to rely on. Everyone else, and I mean *everyone,* either died and left us alone or tried to fuck us over. There was only ever him I could count on, and now, there's you.

"There's all of you. I've gone from having no one I could trust to watch my back, for my entire life, to having you. You're my new family, and I'll burn in hell before I give up a single one of you if I can save you," I growled.

"If I have to be the fucking emperor, or the scion, or the lord, or whatever, then I'll be that, but I'll be me, and I'll do it my fucking way, because you don't know what I could be! You have no goddamn idea what I could be if I let things slide, if I just said, 'fuck it' and took that first little step and the next. You all think I'm a good man? I'm not."

I shook my head adamantly.

"I'm an evil bastard when I stop caring; I'm a man you'd pray to never see coming in the dark. I'm capable of being the worst monster you've ever fucking imagined, so I can't let myself take that step, let myself walk away. Not if there's even the slightest chance I can save you all, protect you. Because I'm not a good man, you see," I mumbled, shaking my head again.

"I'm an unbelievably bad man who's trying to be better, and I can't be anything else. I can either be this—this man you see—or I'll be him. So you need to pick right goddamn now, because I can't have this conversation again. Either you accept that I'll do this, that I'll always try to save you if I can, or you accept that I'll use your Oaths and I'll make you stay at home. I'll *make* you be safe, if I can't trust you to be by my side."

I turned aside and walked away into the darkness, to stand glaring at the collapsed passageway we'd escaped as I tried to slow my ragged breathing and keep the tears from flowing.

They have to accept it, I told myself, blinking the hot tears away. *They have to understand.* Either I protected them, protected them *all,* or I'd be taking a step on that path, the first step to becoming *him…*

"The worst thing…" I whispered aloud, knowing that Oracle was standing right behind me, knowing that the others had followed me and were standing silently as the tears finally flowed down my cheeks.

"The absolute worst thing isn't that Amon could have taken me over back in that shithole of a city. It's that I could see what he was going to do, and there was a part of me that was fine with it. As long as those I wanted to save would be okay, I'd have let it happen, because at last, at long last, I could have just sat back and goddamn relaxed.

"I could have chilled and enjoyed not being pestered every two minutes. I could have just done whatever I wanted. I could have gone fishing and drunk Mal's beers, or whisky, or whatever."

"Yer can still go fishin'…sometime?" Lydia said hesitantly, as though regretting she'd said anything at all earlier.

"I hate fishing," I mumbled wryly, shaking my head. "I tried it once, and it was boring beyond belief. I…don't want to be that person. I really don't—" I broke off, turning around and seeing them all there, even Bane. "But I could be, don't you see? There are days where I'd choose to go fishing, which I fucking hate, rather than help someone in need, because there's always more of them. Every time I turn around, someone else needs something from me. If I turn away, if I say, 'not today, not right now,' I'll end up as him. A single small step is all it'll take, because the next step will be easier, and then just one more after that. I remember it."

I met their eyes, silently pleading with them to understand.

"I remember when Amon took those steps. He had to do it; he let his friends die to save others. Some of them saved thousands with their single deaths, and I know someday, I'll have to let that happen with you. But I can't just let it happen now, not when I could save you."

"I didn't mean it," Lydia said, reaching out, taking me in her arms and clinging to me tightly, her armor clattering against my own. "I'm sorry, I—I…" she faltered, and I felt her tear-stained cheek pressed against my own.

"I know," I said gently, holding her, the fear bubbling up in me that I'd just made a fool of myself in front of all these people who I cared for. I had visions of them starting to laugh and turn from me, when Grizz moved forward and went to one knee, followed by Yen, Tang, and then the others. Lydia gently disengaged herself from me to take her place by Grizz's side as Oracle silently stepped up and claimed my hand in her own.

"I've served in the legion my whole life," Grizz said slowly, staring up at me. "I panicked back there, and then let my anger and my fear get the better of me just now, because you are the reason we *live*, Jax. You say you can't do this; you can't let us die? Then let us live. Let us live by your side and raise the empire up, back into the light. Every day, you give us a new reason to stand by you, and now?"

His gaze bored into my own.

"To hear that you have the same fears that drive us, that drive me? Knowing that you're as terrified of failing or becoming that…that *wretch*, as I am? We've *all* got that darkness inside of us; we just never speak of it, we never admit it, until one of us turns, and we all have to put them down. Then we see it in each other's eyes.

"The fear that we'll be the next one our brothers and sisters have to stop. Do you see that, Jax? We all feel it, but the empire? That's something golden and true that we can hold onto. It's the death of our dreams and our hope that does it, Jax. Seeing the empire rise again? Seeing the wonder and glory of the past resurrected? Seeing kids running free and being able to look at ourselves in the mirror and feel *proud*?! That's what you're bringing back to us, and there's times I, and we all, need to remember that," he said, bowing his head and speaking more formally.

"*I, Centurion Grizz of the Dravith Legion, Second Maniple, acknowledge anew my Oath to Lord Jax of Dravith, Scion of the Empire. I shall be a shield for the weak, a blade for the guilty, and I'll do my best…to not be a dick,*" he finished, looking up at me and grinning, even as the others said their own vows. Each was slightly different, as they said what was in their hearts, but when Bane's voice rumbled to a close at the end, I felt…better.

I felt healed, washed clean of all the stress and sorrow that had been building in me since I lost the first of my people back in the tower, and that had risen to new levels with the deaths of Cam and the legionnaires in the raid on the Emporium. I'd not had the strength to ask yet how many had died taking down the Skyking and escaping with the ships, nor in completing the raid, but I knew I had to, and soon.

"Thank you all," I said fervently, the firelight bathing the chamber in dancing shadows as I looked from one to another. "I'll try not to be a dick as well," I promised, and Grizz stood, replying over his shoulder before walking back to the fire.

"Good, because I can't take this much emotional baggage, you know? I'm kinda in the mood to chill out now, and I need to get my head back in the game and kill something," he said, acting all brusque.

"Yeah, yeah." I smiled, knowing that although he was acting like it was nothing, he'd been the first to bend the knee and give an Oath, somehow understanding that it'd make me feel better.

"So, are you okay?" Oracle asked me quietly as the others drifted back to the fire, the low undercurrent of frustration and fear that had been present since we first fell into the pit now gone as they sat down, taking the meat that Grizz passed out.

"I am and thank you. I'm sorry, Oracle; all of this is my fault. If I'd just given you warning about the poison cloud…given you time to make a shield spell—"

"We'd have all been dead," she said, resting a hand on my arm. "I've been thinking about it, Jax, and the blast rolled over us so quickly…the poison cloud wasn't just at the far end, it couldn't have been. If it had, then I'd have managed to protect us. The majority was there, yes, but the cloud was spreading out. It must have been damn close to us because of the way it exploded. If you'd waited, it might not have been something I could heal." She shook her head, dismissing the speculation. "Or it might; we'll never know, so it's time to put it down to experience and move on. We're here now, and we're at least one step closer to the Vault than we were, okay?"

"Any idea where it would have been?" I asked her, and she pointed back the way we'd come with a half-smile. "Probably that way, and whatever's controlling the undead is likely either trying to get it as well, or already has."

"Joy." I sighed.

She smiled, reaching up and kissing my cheek before wrapping her arms around my neck. I lifted her up, holding her tightly to me for long seconds.

After a bit, Grizz called out to us, making me snort with laughter.

"Look, boss, if you really can't control yourself, we can all pretend not to notice, but your meat's getting cold here, and we're all going to fight over it in a minute."

"Okay, okay!" I chuckled, putting Oracle down and walking over to rejoin the group. I sat down slowly, reaching my hands out to the flames and feeling the warmth before taking the tin plate with slices of hot meat that Grizz passed to me.

While I ate, the others filled me in on what I'd missed. Apparently, Bane and Tang had gone scouting below, once they were sure the collapsed corridor was impassible. The others had set to making camp, with Arrin and Oracle healing everyone.

Now, more than six hours after I'd passed out from exhaustion, and with Oracle nearly recovered from the spell mishap, it was getting close to time to move down to the next level, hoping we could find a way back up to an area where the undead weren't expecting us.

"So, what did you find?" I asked Bane and Tang.

"Not much," Bane said dismissively. "The next level was quiet, or at least the local area is, but there are weird tracks, so there's definitely something alive or undead down there. I didn't want to send out a full pulse, like above. I was afraid it would draw unwanted attention."

"Well, when we're ready to go down, do it and map as far out as you can with your worldsense. I want to know what we're dealing with this time. Besides," I considered aloud, "we should probably be on the level above, so we kinda need to find the stairs, and fast, before that dickhead Joshua loots the place."

"Oh, yeah," Grizz said, lifting a single-edged knife that he'd taken from his boot and angling it so it glinted in the firelight. "Is now a good time to ask for personal permission to…*discuss*…his actions with him when we get out of here?"

A rumble of similarly angry voices arose from the rest, and I smiled.

"Tell you what: whoever kills the most down here…*from now on*," I said quickly, as Yen's face had lit up, "gets first go at 'discussing' things with him. Lydia will keep score." She blinked before peering around the group, grim-faced and nodding authoritatively. "Now, get anything you need to sort out, as we're out of here in half an hour."

The plan in place, I set my plate to the side, pulling up my notification screen and grinning as I saw the first one.

Congratulations!

**You have raised your Ability Mana Overdrive to level 10.
You may now choose your first evolution of this spell.**

Congratulations!

**You have raised your Ability Mana Overdrive to its first evolution.
You must now pick a path to follow.
Will you pursue longevity, enhancing the duration of the Ability by choosing the path of EFFICIENCY,
or will you pick the path of the EXTREME?
Choose carefully, as this choice cannot be undone.**

EFFICIENCY:
Your ability may be in its infancy, but that doesn't mean you shouldn't strive to master it, eking out every last millisecond of use out of it, while reducing the cost on your body. Choosing this path will enable you to utilize the Ability for 10% longer with each additional level, running from level 11-20, and gaining a corresponding dip in 1 point lost to the debuff for each level you gain.

EXTREME:
Sure, efficiency is great, but you know what's even better? POWER! Choosing the path of the extreme will increase the cost of using this Ability by 50% but will also unlock the ability to infuse greater amounts of your mana into your body at a time. Beware! A physical body is not designed to accept high amounts of mana for a sustained period. Investing extreme amounts may result in unexpected changes. Your debuff will increase from -10 to -20 to all stats until complete healing has been carried out.

As this ability has now reached level 10, your mana channels have now fully adjusted to your new body, forming tighter bonds, and you no longer leak mana like an excited puppy!

Congratulations!

**Your mana regeneration has been repaired to full
and now restores at a rate of 3.8 points per minute.**

"Hell yes!" I muttered to myself, and as Oracle came to sit next to me, I had the strange feeling of "mirroring" as she accessed the same data, reading it over and letting out a relieved sigh.

"At last; it's been *forever!*" she said, letting out a deep breath and leaning against me.

"Believe me, I know! I keep stopping myself from using our mana in case you need it; it'll be good to be able to use it again more often," I agreed quietly.

"Bah, you just want me to feel guilty because we both know I'm better at spells than you are." She snorted, smile warm with amusement and gentle fun she poked at me. I reached up and wrapped my arm around her shoulders, drawing her in tight as I read the options over again.

"So, what do you think?" I asked her. "Efficiency or Extreme?"

"Hmm…" She read through the details again, even though I knew she had them imprinted on her memory by now. "Efficiency would mean we could go for longer, and Extreme would mean we'd be able to do a lot more, but for a shorter time."

"Yes, thank you for the basic description we can both see," I said sarcastically, prodding her in the side with a finger and making her giggle.

"I mean, which do you think is more important?" she asked. "A single blast of seriously large power, then a more painful debuff, or the steady ability you've been using for a while now? It's seen you through the worst fights you've had, so to make it cost less and have less of an adverse effect over all…"

"Yeah, it seems good, I'll admit." I tapped my chin thoughtfully. "I'm more concerned about the future, to be honest. The paths you choose gradually grow more and more definite, right? Like they're refining your abilities?" I clarified, and she nodded.

"So, if we choose Extreme, then the next evolution at twenty will be more likely to be a choice of Extreme, like making the infusion go up in strength, but gradually becoming more and more unstable. On the other hand, if we go with Efficiency, level it up through a few more evolutions, and put a load of points into our mana regeneration, we could probably end up being able to live in Mana Overdrive eventually," I pointed out.

"Yes," she said, drawing the word out. "But…you never know what the evolution will be, and what if you really need the more powerful one in the next fight?"

"What if I really need the extra time in the 'zone'?" I countered.

"Well, that's why I'm glad I don't have to make these decisions." She grinned mischievously and kissed the end of my nose before standing up and walking away. "Good luck!" she called back over her shoulder.

I growled to myself as she went, going back to considering my options.

A few minutes later, a clatter and a massive shape knocked me out of my reverie, as Grizz hunkered down next to me and leaned in close.

"Hey, boss, are you okay?" he asked quietly.

I dismissed the screens, blinking at him. He grinned, scratching his beard, and went on in a hushed tone. "Look, I know from what you've said, you've not been dealing with things like evolutions and your stats for long, which is just weird as hell to me, but anyway, if that's true, it means that you never learned the easy ways of dealing with some things that we do."

"We?" I asked.

"Everyone else, I mean," he clarified with a smile. "We all live with this day in and day out. If this is truly new to you, it must seem weird."

"It is, literally, but in my…realm…we had…diversions that included this kinda thing. We can talk about that another time," I said quickly, seeing him light up, ready to hop down the rabbit hole. "What did you want to tell me, then?"

I pulled him back to the reason for his interruption, and he smiled, shifting his armored bulk slightly.

"Okay, boss, look, if I'm out of line here just say, but…"

"Go on," I said, nodding.

"Some ways of dealing with things have become kinda ingrained in our society after millennia of using the stats system, like the allocation system. Some people, hell, most people, are never really able to do much of it in their lives, you know? They don't fight monsters, so they don't tend to get many quests in their lives, and they don't level up much. Others, like the legion, well, we do it a lot, and we tend to climb quickly."

"Right," I said, gesturing for him to go on.

"So, it's like the armor. You remember when we all helped to armor you up for your first arena fight, right? That's part of our traditions, that more experienced legionnaires help the less experienced, and when it comes to stats and bonuses, well, we do that too," he explained, shrugging.

"Each maniple of the legion has its primus. Like ours, in second is Augustus. But he doesn't just kick our asses to train and to stand up straight and so on; he's there for this, too. He knows us all, he watches how we fight, and how we live our lives, and he advises us on allocating our stats, if we ask."

"Wow, I'd—well, I never thought about asking anyone," I stammered in surprise. "I thought it was, well, a private thing."

"It is, but you know, maybe a legionnaire is a bit of a dumb fuck." Grizz grinned, then reached up to scratch the back of his neck before going on, looking down at his feet and shrugging. "He'd never know how dumb he was, so the primus takes him aside and gives some advice. Maybe that legionnaire feels that they shouldn't have to listen, that they know best, and does other things with their points, like boosting their Charisma so they can get laid easier.

"Then as time goes on, maybe this legionnaire keeps making the same mistakes, and maybe he listens the next time and does as the primus suggests, and finds that, yeah, that makes his life easier." Grizz flicked a pebble across the floor, then grinned at me again.

"The point is, we have people in the legion that keep records of the legionnaire's builds and work out the optimum choices. Yeah, there's no guarantee, and from the things you've done so far, you're probably far from the average, so there's no telling how useful it'd be, but…"

"But at least I've got someone I can trust who'd take a good look at my stats and my fighting style and be able to advise me. Thanks, man, I appreciate that."

"Anytime, boss," Grizz said, smiling. "Also, when you decide, it does you no good to second-guess it, as you can't change it. While it's worth considering the future, if a decision for now is the wrong one, with regard to playing 'the long game,' as you called it the other day? Well, that only does you good if you live to see the other end. If you pick something that hammers you now for a possible bonus in the future, you might not live long enough to make use of it, so consider that, too."

With that, Grizz got up, patted me on the shoulder, and walked away.

I sat for long minutes thinking, aware that this ability was in flux right now and I had to decide, before nodding to myself. Grizz's advice was good, I reflected, as planning for the future was necessary, but if I didn't live long enough to get there, it was all for nothing.

I pulled the screen back up and selected Efficiency. I definitely wanted the Extreme option, but if that last fight had taught me anything, it was that getting mobbed down here was a real possibility, and the thought that everyone might die because I saved my power to land a couple of big hits, instead of a hundred smaller, but still devastatingly powerful, ones? Hell, no.

You have chosen Efficiency for your first evolution of this ability:
Your ability may be in its infancy, but that doesn't mean you shouldn't strive to master it instinctually, eking out every last millisecond of use out of it while reducing the cost on your body.

Choosing this path has enabled you to utilize the ability for 10% longer with each additional level, running from 11-20, and gaining a corresponding 1 point reduction in stats lost to the debuff for each level you gain.

Continue to use this ability and build upon your understanding of the underpinning physiological and magical details to unlock further evolutions.

I nodded to myself, feeling a shiver start in my chest, then pouring along my mana-channels like icy water flowing through my veins. It took less than a minute, but it left me gasping when it was done, and I felt…different. An almost indefinable *hummm* seemed to flow through my body, even as I sat at rest. I felt that I had changed profoundly, yet I couldn't put my finger on what it was.

"Congratulations on your Evolution, Champion." A voice echoed into the cavern, and everyone jumped, hunting around. I smiled and looked upwards, then turned to face the fire and spoke as though to it.

"Thank you, Jenae," I said simply.

"It was a difficult decision, I know, but I wanted to allow you to make it alone, as it will define you in the millennia to come."

"Thanks, I think?" I said, and I felt her amusement as the fire flared higher.

"I waited until you'd made this decision to speak, as it needed to be your own choice, but now, is there anything you would ask of me? I have a request to make, and it seems only fair, after all," she offered.

"Tommy," I said straight away. "Where—"

"That is something I cannot answer, Jax," Jenae said quickly. *"I attempted to find him before coming to you, believing that would be your choice, and being willing to gift you the information regardless, for all you have done for me, especially with the new worshippers, but alas. Nimon has stretched his hand out to encompass Thomas, and while I know he lives, he is blocked from me."*

"Nimon?" I asked, surprised. "Why would…he's not dead, right? Tell me he's okay?"

"He is fine, as near as I can tell; he is in fact healthier than ever, and whatever injuries he had before have been healed, but they were healed by an agent of Nimon, and thus he now bears the Dark Mark. I cannot communicate or reach out to him again without risking drawing Nimon's attention."

"Why the hell would…?" I muttered, then shook myself. "That's fine. He's alive, and he's well. That's a great start, Jenae, thank you. I can find him on my own, if that's what it takes."

"Another request, then?" Jenae asked.

I paused, thinking. I cast about for inspiration, before grinning to myself and looking back to the fire.

"There is one thing," I admitted slowly.

"Go on," she said, amusement filling her voice as I tried to keep the hunger from my tone.

"Well, as we're basically the last, best hope for the gods to return, and our best chance of living long enough to accomplish that is if we have protection…and you did promise me blueprints in exchange for worship."

"I offered access to the Constellation of Secrets, Jax, not direct support, but go on," she corrected me, and I grinned at the flames.

"A magma forge," I said quickly. "Apparently, we need one for the kind of armor my legion armorers want to make, and…"

A burst of good-natured laughter from Jenae cut me off.

"Oh, Jax. Yes, I bet they did ask for one!" Jenae chuckled. *"Did they ask for anything else? A solid arcanium hammer and anvil set, perhaps? A pet greater dragon?"*

"Ah," I said slowly. "I take it that's kinda a big ask."

"Jax, a basic magma forge could be doable, at a serious investment of effort, mind you, but it's the kind of thing the tower might have boasted only at the height of its power. Hmm…Actually, now that I'm looking, the Dravith Tower did have one. I wonder…" Her voice faded away as she thought.

"While a full magma forge is, yes, a hell of a reach, we could possibly work towards it. It'll take longer to build than a regular forge, if we do it this way, but you do have a few blueprints coming—average quality only, though—maybe we start with a few of the basics, but make sure they're upgradable. Or, perhaps we'd design the entire facility to be upgradable. Hmmm, that would be a challenge, even with your tower's facilities."

"Okay, what about the blueprints and the Starscape? I should have a load of mana saved up to draw against, and Marks of Favor, right?"

"You do, with forty-one Marks of Favor, and you were earning around thirteen hundred mana per day toward unlocking the Constellation of Secrets. It's been just under two weeks since you brought the tower and its citizens to my worship. Some have donated more than the minimum; some, in fact, have donated far, far more, and your total stands at eighteen thousand, four hundred and eleven points now, which is almost enough to unlock two of the stars. Have you considered which you wish to work on?"

"Okay, the six areas, as I remember them, were Enhanced Construction, Magical Research, Crafting, Governance, Personal Enhancement, and Exploration, right?" I asked, and she made a noise of agreement. "Considering that almost all of this, the raid on the city, the attacks on the Stockpile, was all to get people and stores to repair the tower. Yes, I want to find Tommy, but with all the announcements that keep going out, he's probably looking for me already. I wouldn't be surprised to find the bugger back at the tower when we get there, at this rate." I grunted consideringly. "So, all of this was for the tower, which means that my best choice is probably to double down on that."

I pulled the Constellation of Secrets up and stared at it again, the black twinkling void hanging before me, with the grey and dead stars that led off from the single red star in the center all gently pulsing, flowing from grey and dead to gently glimmering then sinking back into quiescence. I took a deep breath, and feeling Jenae's attention on me, I mentally reached out and selected Enhanced Construction.

There was a pause when nothing seemed to happen, but then the star began to slowly glow as the others dimmed further. A tiny fireball from the red star reached out and sparked toward the flare of fire that rose from the dead star. The two traveled the distance between them as if flying hundreds of thousands of miles. Then they hit, each slamming into the other and creating a great bloom of fire.

As it died away, both ends, the slowly brightening star and the dull red star at the center began to grow in brightness. The red star slowly developed flickers and pulses of yellow that danced across it, while the other grew brighter, until it was glimmering a steady blue-white in radiance.

Once the connection was fully established, I got a new notification, and I felt the changes growing.

Congratulations!

**You have unlocked Enhanced Construction from the Constellation of Secrets. All facilities in which you have an involvement in creating, repairing, or upgrading will now be completed
5% faster and gain 5% capacity.**

You have gained access to the following specializations, which will unlock further options: Magical Construction, Mundane Construction, or Warfare, and you have received a bonus rare blueprint:

Greater Glasshouse:
The Greater Glasshouse is a structure that can be expanded upon, adding more and more wings as the need increases. This building permits the growth of seasonal foodstuffs, despite the outside conditions.

Construction materials required (per wing):

- 100 Steel Ingots
- 350 Copper Ingots
- 250 Glass Panels
- 15 Orichalcum Ingots
- 12 Manastones (average or higher in size)
- 420 Units of Wood/210 Units of Stone (as desired)

Note: This structure requires a constant influx of mana to remain operational year-round, depending on the climate that is desired inside. Cost ranges from 1-1000 mana per day, per wing.

The star shifted, three small planets rising into view and spinning slowly. One glittered as it spun, a thousand colors and more shifting and drawing my eye. As I stared, I seemed to fall down towards it, beginning to comprehend the myriad possibilities of Magical Construction. I saw fantastical towers and knew I was viewing what the Great Tower had once looked like, and could again, clad in shining marble, reflecting the sun, pennants streaming in warm breezes as children played in pools on its balconies. The living, beating heart of the tower drew in ambient mana and released…something…into the air. The people breathed it in and grew stronger, healthier.

The people of the tower stood tall and strong, all of them blessed by the construction. They'd live longer than any elves, all thanks to the wonderful life-giving facets of this place.

I saw cities that reflected the sun like jewels in the sky as they floated past. Their mere presence destroyed the undead and healed the sick.

Fields of crops blossomed, reaching upwards in joy, as people stood on the cities that flew past, singing of their love and peace. My heart lifted at the possibilities, even as I saw the iron fist inside the glove as people worked at magical crafting stations, making swords that glowed with power, forged by simple apprentices, so strong were the facilities.

I could lose myself in exploring the possibilities, so I pulled back, soaring upward to the steadily burning star gleaming in the sky, with another world drawing closer.

I flew to it, finding it much simpler but so much steadier, as well. It was the only way I could describe it. I saw facilities that gave bonuses and cost far less to build, such as a logging camp that produced half again what a normal one could. Instead of being magically enhanced, it was efficiently designed. The blades of the saws were smoothly flowing, driven by a waterwheel that spun practically without effort.

Logs were drawn along clear channels, hoisted in artfully designed slings and sliding into the building without a single wasted motion.

Where the last world had been a fantastic imagining of what could be, this world seemed full of another kind of magic.

Here, I saw the flow of perfection in craftsmen. Each worker knew their job and moved as though they'd done it a thousand times, their actions steady and easy. Six men and women took up ropes, three on a side each, and pulled, lifting a tree trunk that had just floated downstream into the channel.

They moved as one, the dripping trunk lifting into the air. Another team pulled a winch, swinging the suspended tree across to where the first group lowered it. In seconds, a huge redwood had gone from peacefully floating down the river into being sawn into planks, and there wasn't a single wasted motion anywhere that I could see.

The people laughed and joked, calling to their friends as they worked, with a clear, contented voice rising in song in the distance. It made me proud to see how well they worked together, and it made me desperate to see this in my own lands.

Again, there was so much to see here, but I couldn't take the time, so I looked up to the star above and felt the sky rushing past as I rocketed upwards.

Soon, the final world rotated around, flowing into view in the distance, and as I fell towards it, a new, terrible kind of beauty awaited.

I saw weapons of war so magnificently crafted that they were unstoppable. Airships that made my own small fleet laughably weak and ill-considered glided overhead. A single ship the size of a cruiser flew past me, and I watched it in awe. The sides were smooth with carved ports out that glowed, unleashing a barrage of light that scoured hordes of the undead from existence. It looked more like a space shuttle engineer or a stealth bomber designer had made this airship. It was all sleek lines and flowing, deadly grace, and behind it came more.

The Sunken City, or at least its distant cousin, soared along, no longer a jewel of beauty or a rotting corpse like the one we were scouring now. Instead, it was a terrible and majestic weapon. It flew forward ominously, with flares of fire, beams of light, and shells that, upon impact, spread the deepest darkness across the land.

Soldiers marched past, wearing armor that would have made the Terminator weep for desire, wielding weapons that crackled with constrained power.

A single legionnaire led hundreds of war golems, leaping from the edge of the city and floating down on wings of light. Golems that made my own look misshapen and weak thundered along at his command.

The enemy fell, smashed from existence, and I saw the soldiers lifting the innocent to the cities, bringing them to safety, and to life.

I looked everywhere, stunned by all I could see, until a hand shook me gently, and I tore my eyes away from the portal that hung before me, instead focusing on Oracle, who smiled at me.

"You've been silent for a while; are you okay?" she asked.

"The possibilities," I said slowly, shaking my head in amazement.

"That is what I offer you freely, my Champion," answered Jenae's voice. *"All those things, and more, are possible with the knowledge I possess. But to attain them all would take an age and would require many other secrets to be unlocked. Do you wish to assign a specialization now?"* she asked.

I drew in a deep breath. "Would it help the tower if I did?"

"It would." Jenae replied smoothly. *"Even though you haven't earned enough to unlock that field yet, I could funnel your climbing mana to it. Then, once it unlocks, I will pass the knowledge to the tower for you, depending on what it is. Have you made a decision as to what you want to choose?"*

"I have," I said hesitantly, well aware that anything I selected could help tremendously, but equally the wrong choice could leave me regretting it forever.

"And?" she prodded. I drew in a deep breath and reached out mentally, making my choice and seeing the star reach out a tendril of steady white light, moving ever closer to the world as it orbited.

"And I choose Mundane," I said, closing my eyes and explaining. "I desperately want the rest, goddess, do I not, but we have only a bare few crafters as it is. And of those, almost none are magical or have a magical specialty. To instead increase the...*smoothness*...of the people, the flow of their work, it'll affect everyone, not just the handful who are working on magical things. Add to that, the manastones we have will make a huge difference to the tower's condition when we return. I think it's the best choice," I confirmed, forcing a confidence into my words I didn't feel.

"A wise and sensible choice, Jax; well done," Jenae said, and Oracle squeezed the back of my neck reassuringly, rubbing the knotted muscles. I let out a relieved breath, deflating as I released it. Blessedly, the nameless terror of picking the wrong thing receded.

Until next time.

"So, boss, are we going?" Grizz asked simply, gesturing towards the stairwell down into the darkness. I nodded, dismissing the notifications. A last one tried to pop up, and I glanced at it as I closed it down.

Congratulations!

You have killed the following:

- 5x Adventurers (Himnel) of various levels for a total of 39,712xp

- 38x Undead of various levels for a total of 9,787xp

A party under your command killed the following:

- 176x Undead of various levels for a total of 51,709xp

Total Party experience earned: 51,709xp

As party leader, you gain 25% of all experience earned.

Progress to level 19 stands at 446,398/265,000

Congratulations!

You have reached level 19!

You have 7 unspent Attribute points and 0 Meridian points available.

Progress to level 20 stands at 181,398/305,000

"Hey, Yen," I called out to her, seeing the details as it closed. "That must have been mainly you, wasn't it?" I asked, getting a gleaming grin reflected in the firelight as I saw the points, quickly deciding to assign them when we settled down later. After all, I kept wishing I'd picked something else after I'd done it. This time I'd force myself to take some time and really consider it.

"Oh, it was the whole team," she insisted, trying to sound humble, but her grin gave it away.

"Enough to level?" I asked.

She nodded enthusiastically. "I was close, anyway; the Skyking and the city fights were good to me."

The others spoke up, too, making me smile as I realized literally everyone had gained at least one new level in the last few days.

"Well, congrats to you all," I said as I swept up my bedroll and dumped it into my bag, then started pulling my armor back on and finally tugged my naginata out of storage.

A few minutes passed as we all made last-minute adjustments to our gear. I spun the naginata gently, shifting my shield around to make it more comfortable.

It was a bastard at times, using them both together. The length of the naginata made it awkward at first, and it would have been impossible had I used a full-length naginata, as I'd seen in some of the training videos back on earth, instead of my shorter, custom version, which was why I'd not taken a shield originally. Fortunately, gaining the DEFENSE skill for my naginata when I'd reached level ten with it had made it much more manageable.

Add to that, the hours of drills that Augustus had put me through, while mainly with a sword, had trained me in the shield's usage, and it'd made that task easier.

I shifted the shield again on my arm, trying to make it more comfortable, and finally accepted that I needed a lot more strength to pull this combination off. Packing the shield back into my bag of spatial folding, I quickly checked my stats again as I walked over to the top of the stairwell, pleased to see that the organic growth of my Strength was going nicely. It was probably the best way to think of it, after all, as I could both invest points to increase them or invest time and hard work.

"*Jax.*" Jenae's voice returned, and I stopped, realizing that she was speaking just to me this time.

"*Yes?*" I said quietly, directing my voice to her as we started down the stairs. I felt Bane take a deep breath before *pushing* out his worldsense in a long, powerful blast.

"*We need to talk about your stats, and soon.*"

From below came a loud crash in the distance, and suddenly, Bane was backing away quickly and gesturing at us all to move, to run.

"Maybe another time!" I called aloud, and her presence receded like the tide, just as a low grinding noise in the distance started up. It was joined steadily by more, the rumbling, grinding sound growing slowly and echoing up towards us as we ran for it, dashing back up the twisted, damaged stairwell and out into the room above.

The room with only one exit.

CHAPTER FIFTEEN

"What is it?" Grizz asked, and I shut my mouth with an audible *clop* as he beat me to it.

"I don't know," Bane said, and everyone paused, wondering why he'd made us run. "There's something big down there. It's at the outer edge of my range, tucked inside a cavern, but it's huge, solid, and covered in living things. Whatever they are, those things became solid like stone and vanished into big constructions, things that are headed right for us now, faster than any horse I've ever seen."

"Shit," I said. "Okay, people, all we know right now is that's there's a lot of them, and they're fast. Bane was right for us to retreat to here. We can use the stairwell as a choke point—"

"The bottom," Grizz interrupted, and both Yen and Tang nodded emphatically.

"What?" I said, my train of thought broken.

"We need to start at the bottom, not up here. There, we've got the stairwell all the way to use as a choke point. Up here, we take a step back, and it's all over."

It made perfect sense as soon as he said it. Bane's shoulders sagged as he realized the same thing.

"Fuck!" I grunted, waving my arm forward. "Right, then; everyone, back into the stairs!"

Grizz was the first, leading the way, with Bane on his heels, Tang then Yen, then myself, Jian, Lydia, Miren, and Stephanos. Arrin brought up the rear, huffing as he went. As we ran down the stairs, I had to hide a grin as Jian lightened the mood for us all by complimenting his girlfriend, Miren, on the fact that she, barely half the size of Arrin, was holding up better in the same armor Arrin was wearing.

That, of course, led to comments about stamina, and as we all took up station at the bottom of the stairs, squinting out through a doorway into a corridor that opened into the darkness, Grizz and the rest started picking on Arrin and commenting on the shame he must feel.

We all collectively and conveniently glossed over the fact that Miren was half-elven and had racial traits of increased stamina, Strength, and Agility.

Arrin, huffing and gripping his side as he tried to catch his breath, pulled out a magelight and charged it before passing it to Grizz and leaning against the wall, panting and giving everyone the finger.

Grizz looked to me, and I nodded my head toward the corridor. He took two steps down, hauled back, and threw it like a professional baseball player, sending the small gem hurtling down the darkened tunnel.

It hit the ground once, twice, then a third time, before bouncing off a section of fallen wall and coming to a stop, its light reflecting off a puddle it'd fallen into.

We all held our breath, watching down the corridor and listening as the rumbling grew louder. Soon, I started to pick out differences in the sound as more and more tones and noises grew distinct.

"There's at least a dozen of them," Bane called to us from somewhere in the darkness. I grunted, realizing the stealthy bastard had vanished again. As I looked around, I realized with annoyance at my own lack of observance, so had Tang.

That left Grizz, Lydia, and me in the center of the doorway, spaced out slightly, but still feeling like we might bump into each other with every movement. Jian, Yen, and Arrin had taken up positions behind us, and Miren and Stephanos behind them.

"This is so not the right weapon for this," Lydia muttered, hefting her mace and shifting her shield to the side, trying to get the base set right.

"Tell me about it," Grizz said. "I can't get a decent swing in here. Hey, boss, fancy swapping?" he asked me jokingly.

"Not my fault you two can't pick real gear," I said, my voice dying away as the first of the enemies rumbled into sight.

It was…weird.

It was composed of a single large wheel, which was hollow, and seated inside of it was a small figure, a figure with eyes that glowed.

It opened its mouth at the sight of us huddled in the doorway and screeched a single long cry, brandishing a weapon that looked to be a cudgel made of wood with spikes all over it.

The wheel immediately picked up speed, blurring toward us, bouncing and clattering across fallen sections of wall and floor, while I focused and used Examine.

Gnome Badunka Rider
The role of badunka rider was once a position of power and respect in gnomish society, but decades of isolation have changed that. Now, the badunka rider is the lowest of the low, permitted food, water, and territory only if they can deliver fresh meat and salvage.

The gnomish badunka riders have found a way to infuse themselves with the essence of stone, granting them a terrible solidity as long as their mana lasts.

Weaknesses: Water, Air, and Death magics do 25% more damage.

Resistances: Earth magics used against this creature will heal it.

Level: 13

Health: 1410/1410 (30/30)

Stamina: 40/40

Mana: 411/500

"Shit!" I cursed. "It's a gnome badunka rider, whatever the hell that is. But it's got crazy health, over fourteen hundred, with an insane mana pool as well! Earth magic heals it, water, air, and death work better against it."

"Great, well, I've got fuck-all of those!" Yen growled.

I winced, reaching into the one pouch I'd kept with me that was still almost full. I tugged out two of the three Darkbolt spells and tossed them over my shoulder to her and Arrin.

"Keep them for later; no time to use them now," I ordered, even as voices lifted from the right, further down the corridor, as the first rider closed the distance.

"Keep one for me," Tang called, and I winced again. It made more sense to ensure everyone would be able to do a little magic, after all, and I should have thought about it before the beginning of another skirmish.

The badunka rider took a deep breath and wailed again, its voice echoing weirdly off the walls and roof as it closed the distance.

As soon as the gnome passed Tang, he struck, lashing out with his sword. It slammed into the tiny figure, who continued to scream until that point, when it suddenly changed from a solid, ongoing cry into a screech of pain. The creature's arm flailed wildly about in the air with the wooden cudgel until it was snapped back, throwing the gyroscope it was riding into an uncontrolled diversion. It screeched in pain and fury, then hit the wall, bouncing off and tumbling end over end. Sparks and parts went flying as it dissolved into a mass of tumbling, flaming wreckage.

By the time it skidded to a halt, less than four feet from the doorway to the stairs, it was unrecognizable as the strange device it had been mere seconds before. But even as we gaped in shock at the damage, it started to move.

A metal panel, laid halfway across the rider, was suddenly and violently shoved aside as the gnome straightened and dragged herself out of the wreck. She, and it was clearly a she now, with the sides of her head shaved and her remaining hair woven with tiny rings, glared at us, her gaze moving from one to another as she shook her arm out, and the blood stopped flowing from it.

She didn't look to be in any pain as a grey-white, rough-textured stone seemed to build up around the wound, bubbling over and covering it. Instead, she seemed to grow more and more angry as she looked from the wreck to us, dragging the cudgel out, slapping it into her palm threateningly, and screeching again.

We glanced at each other, the sounds of more riders growing louder and louder as they closed the distance.

"Fuck it," Arrin called, and he hit her in the face with a lightning bolt.

The diminutive figure was smacked backwards only to jump back up and grin at us with a mad light in her eyes, suddenly sprinting forward.

She covered the distance quickly, her short legs and wide stance giving her a waddle that would have been amusing, if not for the bloodthirsty look on her face. As I mentally tagged her as "walking like John Wayne," Grizz stepped forward. He batted her cudgel aside and kicked out, smashing her in the face with his armored boot.

She staggered, then grabbed his leg and sank her teeth into it, the sound of metal scraping across metal echoing around the corridor. Grizz growled and struck downwards with the pommel of his sword, slamming it into the side of her head.

The rest of us were frozen, watching the strange tableau: the enormous form of Grizz, well over six feet in height, heavily muscled, the kind of a man you'd have on the recruiting posters for any armed force in the world. He stood versus the tiny bantam-weight woman, barely three feet tall, maybe three and an inch at a push, with bright blue, green, and purple hair running in rows from front to back, the sides shaved, and peculiar tattoos etched into her skin. She had a death grip on his leg and was attempting to gnaw her way through the armor. Judging from the way Grizz's shouts went from anger, to fury, to pained disbelief, she was managing to do it, as well.

Grizz shook his leg, then grunted and rammed his sword blade down against the armor, forcing it into her mouth where she was starting to bend the metal. Once inside the edge of her mouth, he twisted it, holding it in place with his left hand, and slammed his right fist down hard on the pommel, driving it deeper and sending flecks of stone flying.

Before he could do anything else, Yen was there, as was Jian, grabbing the creature's arms and dragging them back, while Lydia slammed her mace down hard on the top of her head.

It took two more blows, but as soon as the stone coating over her head cracked, she changed. The grey-white coating and coloring of her skin suddenly seemed to change into flecks and fragments, floating away on an unseen breeze, leaving a short, weak woman that took the fourth blow on the crown of her skull with a nasty crunching noise.

She collapsed to the floor, twitching, blood leaking from her ears, and we all gaped at Grizz's leg in shock.

Sections of the metal were bent and twisted, as her teeth had been replaced with some kind of metal.

"What the hell was that?" I muttered in shock as Bane whistled. Up the corridor, two more of them barreled toward us, similar in design, but still totally unique.

The first was a single wheel again, but instead of the rider being inside it, he rode above it, seemingly leaning over the top and gripping onto levers. The next was like the first, seated inside a wheel, but it was shaking and shuddering as jets of flame and blue-white steam erupted from it. I watched, stunned, as the pair seemed intent on ramming the other into the walls just as much as racing to fight us.

The riders both started screeching the way the last one had, and I shook my head immediately.

"Nope," I said flatly. "Fuck to the hell, no. Bane, Tang, get your arses back here and get behind us," I ordered. "Miren, Stephanos, get back up the stairs. There's no room for you here, and we need to be able to back up."

I regarded Grizz's leg and then cocked an eyebrow at him.

"Can you fight?" I asked.

"She didn't get through the plate, just bent it and gave me a shock," he admitted with a grim nod.

"Good," I said. "Arrin, you're on lightning until you hit thirty percent mana; then you fall back and heal us as needed. Oracle, I want water in the corridor, lots and lots of it. Join those puddles up. Lydia, you and I have the big shields, so we're going to take the weight until we can jam them up. Yen, fire anything you can down the corridor; I want those monobikes fucked up.

"Jian, stand ready with Grizz. When Lydia and I need to step back, we'll give you both the shields, and then it's your turn." I snapped the orders out, despite worrying that there was no way we could hold those damn bikes if they hit us full on. Our only chance was to make them crash, then we'd fight the gnomes on the ground.

First one, then another, then, with the strain showing clear on Oracle's face, a third fountain sprang up, this time a dozen feet in front of the foremost bike. I grinned, frantically building the spell I needed. Before I could let it loose, though, Arrin delivered, sending a Weak Lightning Bolt hurtling across the air between them and us. The bolt hit the first bike just as it splashed though, the tiny figure on the top of the wheel shaking the water from his face, huge, round goggles reflecting the light, until it hit him in the face.

His screeching broke off suddenly, and the bike wobbled as his muscles convulsed, yanking the levers inwards in reflex and twisting the wheel somehow. It skidded, and as soon as the first bolt wore off, the rider tried to adjust. A scream rose, filled with fury, when my bolt impacted and filled him with twenty thousand volts as well.

This time, he didn't manage to recover in time, and he hit the wall full-on, turning the strangely crafted device into an explosion of parts that flew everywhere. A split second later, the second bike hit the back of the mangled first one.

The corridor was filled with the tearing, screeching sound of steel on steel, and I realized that was what their strange war cries were supposed to imitate, even as the two weird bikes exploded. Whatever they were using for power detonated, filling the corridor with flames.

We paused, observing the devastation, then heard the scream rising again. The rider of the wheel was dragging himself out of the debris, his right leg trapped. He left a bloody trail on the floor behind him as he went, but he gritted his teeth and pressed on, his skin slowly filling with color as the stone coating dropped away.

In seconds, he slowed, then sagged, his head falling forward in death as the third rider leapt out of the flames, skidding and slapping at his leather-clad left leg to smack the fires out.

He glared at us, stomping forward and kicking the corpse of his fellow from behind. When it didn't move, and he noticed the color of it, he grinned, then flipped it over and started rifling through its pockets, pulling out two small manastones and a single black stone that I thought I recognized, as I jumped in shock. Then he dragged the other rider's knife out of his belt and made us all gag.

He drove the blade into the lower jaw of the corpse, digging it in and wrenching about, frantically working while blood ran everywhere. He'd just managed to free the rider's artificial teeth before the next one arrived.

This one was perched atop a massive pair of balls…literally. It made me think of a normal mountain bike, but with gears that glowed with power, and wheels that were the size of beachballs; somehow, the main body of the bike hovered over the pair of balls.

"I do not *fucking* believe it," I growled, shaking my head as I looked at the device.

"What the hell is it?" Grizz asked, nonplussed.

I clapped him on the shoulder as we both stared. "No clue," I said. "But it looks a lot like they're making these things from the goddamn magical gear we need to fucking salvage!"

"That makes it easier, then," Grizz replied, and I blinked at him. "They'll have been collecting it; all we have to do is kill them all," he said with a shrug. I grinned at him, nodding in agreement.

"Yeah, that works. I just hope they've not broken it too badly." I watched as the gnome on the "bike" slowed down and hissed something at the one that was pocketing the teeth.

He hissed back, and they spoke for a few seconds, their language a mixture of hisses, growls, and grunts. The one who was still astride his bike eventually straightened up and slapped his chest like a gorilla.

The other one stood up straight and spat something at him, reaching into a pocket to produce the black stone and hooting in laughter. I swore viciously as I saw it, now sure what it was.

"What's wrong?" Lydia asked, and I pointed at the gnome.

"You see that key? The black thing?" I asked, and she nodded. "It looks exactly like the one I was given to open the portal from this side to let those fucking dickbags through. That needs to be *destroyed*," I said grimly. "The nobles of the empire were assholes and must *never* be allowed to return. They make Barabarattas and others look like fucking saints of honesty."

"How'd it get here?" Lydia asked slowly, clearly confused.

"They've been sending people through every five years for centuries; makes sense we'd find a trace of them eventually. Someone they sent probably came through a portal here, found these assholes, and *boom*. They ate the poor fucker."

My jaws clenched involuntarily as the gnome waved it in the air, then put it back in his pocket, before screeching like he'd won the argument.

He even smiled, his teeth glittering in the reflected firelight, until my Fireball took him in the side of the head, slamming him into the wall as the flames rippled out to encompass the one on the bike as well.

He shrieked something, then strangely spun his bike around and vanished through the flames, causing them to whirl and dance in the slipstream of his passage.

The other one, which I'd hit with the Fireball, pushed himself up, shaking his head and glaring at us, before checking his hands and realizing that the white coating was bleeding away slowly.

He blanched in shock, then glared at us before turning and rushing into the flames, running through to the other side and vanishing up the corridor on foot.

"Where's the magelight?" Arrin asked suddenly.

At first, we'd still been able to see the light through the flames, but no longer: something had taken it.

"Well, now what?" Bane asked from behind me.

I turned, eyeing the way he lounged against the wall comfortably. I looked at the gaps between us and shook my head. There was no way he managed to slip through us, was there?

"Ta—" I started to say, only to cut off when Tang spoke up from behind me. I spun around again, seeing nothing, only to find him seated on the steps a few up from Bane when I turned back.

"Hey, Jax," he said simply, and I shook my head.

"How the hell did you do that?" I asked. "Seriously, I mean, what the hell!"

"We're just that good." Tang shrugged dismissively, and Bane nodded as though it was simply a fact.

"I hate you guys at times," I muttered, getting a grin from Yen.

"That's perfectly normal, Jax. Nobody likes Tang," she reassured me. "I got a promotion to take him on my team, and I still only did it because I lost the bet."

"Hey!" Tang said, looking hurt.

"It's true," Grizz said, trying to keep a straight face. "Nobody likes rogues; they're just so…annoying!"

"Could be worse," I said, joining in on the byplay while I stared up the corridor. "Could be a bard."

"Oh, hell no!" Tang cried, jumping to his feet. "I can put up with a lot: abuse, more abuse…hell, I even put up with working with Grizz, and everyone knows he's riddled, but comparing me to a *bard*?!"

"You really have bards?" I asked, my train of thought derailed as I looked back at the group.

"Yeah, thieving bastards, the majority of them," Yen said, wincing. "I mean, we don't have them in the *legion*…and I'm sure they're not *all* dodgy, backstabbing, thieving bastards. There's got to be one out there that isn't…but hell, I'd trust Grizz to watch over me in the *bath* more than I'd trust one of them. And that's saying something."

"I love you, too," Grizz said, throwing Yen a wink and making her blush bright red.

"Anyway," she pressed on, obviously flustered. "What's the plan, then?"

"Well, I'm thinking we follow them, we kill them all, then we take their stuff," I suggested, rubbing my chin as though deep in thought.

"Simple, yet elegant. I like it," Yen declared, and Lydia nodded enthusiastically.

"Murder-hobo," Bane said in a stage whisper.

"Man, I wish I'd never introduced you to that concept," I muttered roughly searching the corpse of the first gnome.

"What's a murder-hobo?" Lydia asked Bane, and I tuned him out as he started to tell the others a greatly embellished version of my adventures so far, while explaining what I'd taught him about the term back at the Arena.

"Ah, right!" Tang said after a few minutes, as I slipped a pair of magelights, a manastone, and a half-dozen copper and silver coins into my bag. "You're right, he really is!"

"Goddamn wise-ass dolphin-fucking smart-arse," I grumbled under my breath as I stalked forward, picking up the wooden club that the gnome had been wielding.

I flipped it over and examined it, then tossed it to Grizz, who was watching me.

"Can you see anything about that?" I asked him.

"Like what?" he asked with a serious frown, all play gone from his voice as he examined the cudgel.

"Anything, really. She acted like it was a great weapon, but it's just a damn stick?" I asked, and he nodded, inspecting it closely, then swinging it a few times. Finally, he smacked it into the dead gnome, then shrugged.

"Well, whatever she thought it was, she was mistaken. It's literally a nicely polished stick with some metal shards embedded in it. That's it." He passed it back without giving it a second look. I dumped it into a pouch and shook my head in disappointment, scanning the nearest wreckage quickly.

There were several sections that glowed faintly, trailing a white mist. But beyond that, it was literally a pile of scrap. I put the bits that seemed magical into my largest bag, hoping that I could get them to Thorn, but also happy to dump them if something more valuable came along.

We got the team together and started up the corridor, making our way slowly until we reached the fires. I fired a preemptive Fireball through them to hurtle down the corridor until it hit a wall in the distance, and once we were reasonably sure the corridor was clear, we created magical fountains to wash the flaming wreckage down, soaking and diluting the fuel enough that the flames guttered out, and we could move on safely.

We continued along slowly, partially to let our mana recover, and partially because we were sure there was an ambush coming. But after a few minutes, Yen asked me to stop, and we did.

"These spellbooks—" she started to say, holding them up, and I smacked myself on the forehead.

"Yes!" I grunted. "Bane, what can you sense?" I asked.

"Nothing for several hundred meters; the corridor cuts to the left, and then there's nothing but the open air of a big cavern. Whatever these wheel things were attached to earlier was past that point, but I can't sense it now, so it must have moved back. Want me to do a full blast…?"

"No, that's good enough for me for now," I said with a wave of my hand. I passed a Firebolt out to both Tang and Bane, gave the summoning spells for the flame golem to Miren and the earth golem to Stephanos, the buff spell for Dexterity to Jian, and the Iceshields to Lydia and Grizz. Those, added to the Darkbolt spells I'd tossed to Yen, Tang and Arrin, meant that everyone had at least one spell.

It struck me that it could be argued both ways; teaching them spells, in the case of front-line fighters, like Lydia and Grizz, might make them hesitate between a physical and a magical response at some point, but then I quickly dismissed the concern. If I could manage it, so could they.

I got rounds of effusive thanks, followed by a groan from Lydia as Miren summoned her golem. It was only five feet tall and almost willowy in form, but the flames that formed it flared and crackled, and it moved constantly, watching us all.

"You know she's going to burn down the camp with that thing, right?" Lydia said to me.

"We're in an underwater city…oh, shit." I froze, cutting off as I realized something.

"Yeah," Lydia said, nodding as I came to the same realization she had. "Soon, we won't be; the mainly *wooden* airships are going to love that thing."

"No summoning that thing on the ships!" I told Miren sternly, and she pouted, looking sullen. "I mean it!" I said, feeling like I was kicking a puppy. I felt even worse when I caught a glimpse of Jian, who was staring at his feet. I'd literally give everyone else a spell they could use in a fight, but I'd inadvertently made him into a support class.

I suddenly realized that I didn't even let him fight on the front line most of the time, making him hang back to protect the ranged guys. I quickly went looking through the bags again and found the books on summoning demons. They made me wary, to be honest; the whole concept of summoning a demon seemed far worse than summoning a golem, for some reason, and this was in a realm that had gods and imps and all sorts, but still…

I shot a questioning look to Oracle, and she eyed him, then patted my shoulder.

"He's strong enough in his heart not to be corrupted by it, and he loves Miren. Truthfully, I think we can trust him with one," she said, and I looked back at him. He'd looked up at the comment about loving Miren, and he glared at me now, red-cheeked, as if to ask why I'd had that conversation in front of everyone.

"Ah, sorry, mate. There's more for you, but apparently you'll need to be strong in your heart as well?" I half-told, half-asked him as I pulled out the two demon summoning books. "I don't know much about demons here, but apparently, they're real, so…"

"Are you serious?" he breathed, his face lighting up. I looked at the others, not seeing objections so much as envy, as I nodded slowly and handed both books over to him.

"What's the difference in summoning demons or summoning golems?" I asked Oracle silently. *"I was concerned because they're gonna be sentient, or at least more than golems, but they're just like the imps, right?"*

"No," Oracle corrected me. ***"Jian learning to summon demons is granting him a substantially greater power than those that can summon mere golems. He can choose from several demons when he first opens the summoning portal, and they will become, well, 'familiars' is probably the closest I can come. Not as close as us, but far closer than a normal summoned creature. He will gradually start to manifest their powers, and they will gain intelligence, mana, and more as well as returning to the pit with a portion of the power they gain while serving him."***

"Did I just make a huge mistake?" I asked, concerned.

"Noooo," Oracle said slowly in my mind. ***"You just gave a man who's fiercely devoted to you, and in love with another of your team, the chance to change his class to that of a warlock, though. Believe me, that's going to come with a massive jump in power for him."***

"But he'll be safe?"

"No, but I think he can handle it, or I'd have asked you not to give it to him. I know it wasn't planned, but he's clean enough in his soul that I think he's actually one of the best possible choices you could have made. I'd been considering him for some time now as one of the only people I'd recommend for these books."

"Really? Cool." I cleared my throat and went on in a voice that everyone could hear. "It's something that Oracle and I were discussing already. Jian, we trust that you're strong enough to walk this path, but only you truly know, and I understand if—"

"I can do it!" Jian said quickly, clutching the books to his chest and glaring around at anyone who was too close.

"Okay, then, people, take turns and get those books read, then we move on." As I was the only one not reading a book, I moved to the front of the group and activated my DarkVision, staring into the depths of the corridor.

"So, fill me in on the details here, and what I'm missing."

Oracle slipped forward, sitting down on my shoulder in her tiny fairy form. I heard a growl from her a second later, and glanced up, realizing too late that she'd been waiting for a reaction, and I'd totally missed it, being too busy watching the corridor.

She was out of sight of the others, the way that she was half-laid, half-draped across my shoulder and down my arm, and she had changed into something that could only be described as provocative.

The tiny, red, lacy outfit definitely served to enhance her figure, rather than conceal it. Her skin was pale as ivory, and her hair as black as…a very black thing. My brain had stalled at that point as my eyes traveled over her body, and I swallowed hard, a very clear stirring rising from below the belt as I admired the view.

She smiled and nodded in satisfaction before straightening, materializing clothes over the top of the little lacy red outfit. The new black halter top and yoga pants, with two black lines of camo paint up each cheek, was more in keeping with the situation, but the crimson that peeked out as she moved, revealing that she still wore the red outfit underneath, just short circuited my brain entirely.

"I…uh. I…" I mumbled coherently.

She beamed a thousand-megawatt smile up at me, reaching out to pat my cheek.

"That's better," she said happily. "Just checking that you weren't taking me for granted now."

"God, no," I muttered, clearing my throat. "And that outfit…"

"For your eyes only, when we're alone," she said, winking and laughing in satisfaction at the frantic nod of my head. "Good! Anyway, moving on," she continued, smiling. "A warlock isn't entirely the way you remember them being described in your world's tales.

"A warlock makes pacts with demons, who are denizens of an entirely different realm, somewhat like your Earth is a different realm, but they need our mana to survive here. In return, one of the things they bring to their warlocks is a massively boosted manapool, but it's almost unusable, as they need it all to survive here. That's also why demons don't tend to be seen wandering around on their own; they literally starve in hours."

"Are they evil?" I asked dubiously, thinking I should have asked for these details earlier.

"No," she reassured me. "Well, not in the way you mean. They're literally denizens of a hellscape; their realm is all war and fire, so don't be expecting a discussion on the scholarly pursuits…but they're not evil."

"Scholarly pursuits?" I asked, grinning.

"A warlock that used to live in the tower used to summon his demon regularly to…entertain…him. He said it was in pursuit of the scholarly arts. Personally, I never really understood it."

"Why—" I started to ask as she stepped in closer and hooked a thumb under the edge of her top, lifting the red outfit up into view before going on in a low whisper.

"This was an outfit his demon used to wear for him."

"Seriously?" I gaped, frowning as a sudden mental image of an enormous, bright red demon from the pits of hell dressed in *that* came to mind. I shuddered as Oracle went on.

"Yeah, it was what she wore for him on occasion; that's what gave me the idea. So, moving on, the spellbooks for summoning demons aren't so much for any general demons as they are each for an extremely specific demon. As near as I can remember from the things I overheard, the demons themselves create them and use their magic to seed them through the realms.

"Part of most pacts with one involves helping them to seed another book through the warlock, as once a book is used, that's it; it's destroyed. The creator of the book is tied to that summoner until death. But they live much, much longer lives than most sentients, usually into the thousands of years range, so if they ever want a chance at being summoned again, they need more books out there." She shrugged, looking out into the darkness as she continued.

"As they're tied to a particular demon, you can't summon the same one if someone else has already read the book. As near as I can remember—and bear in mind, he didn't spend much time in the tower *talking* to her—the deal is that if you summon a demon, you get a fragment of their power, and they get some of yours. You get access to their abilities, and they get a small portion of your level increases, more Strength, Intelligence, and so on.

"You summon a specific demon, and once they're summoned, if you then use a second book, and it belonged to the same demon as you'd already summoned, they gain the ability to make pacts in their own realm, and they help to find you a new demon that fits your needs. They don't want to do that though, generally, as they then get less of an increase due to your levels being split across multiple beings. Whenever Dimi would suggest it to his demon, she would distract him, making sure he forgot about it."

"Wait, was she a succubus?" I asked, suddenly remembering the species, and Oracle nodded. "Oh, thank god; I had visions of Hellboy in that outfit." I shuddered involuntarily. "Urrgh!"

"Ass," Oracle muttered fondly, and I grinned at her before going back to watching the corridor.

"Yes, yours is amazing; thank you for reminding me," I whispered, shooting her a wink between long glances down the pitch-black tunnel.

A few minutes passed, and in the distance, we could hear occasional noises; clanks, crunches, and every so often, the floor would shake. But when Bane rejoined me, he shook his head as I asked if he could sense anything.

"Whatever they're doing, it's creating a lot of vibrations, which is making it hard for me to see, but I think there might be a lot of them down there," he said, worry clear in his voice. "As near as I can tell, there's nobody coming around the bend, but…"

"Okay, mate. might be a situation where you sit this one out, then," I offered.

"No, but thank you," he said adamantly.

Chanting rose behind us, and I turned to watch, knowing that Bane was monitoring the corridor far further than I could see.

Jian stood to the side of a small circle he'd drawn in his own blood on the floor and was chanting a series of words over and over from the book he held. Each time he finished the chant, the blood would flare with an inner light, then die away. The light continued getting brighter and lasting longer each time, until, on the fifth rendition, it flared upward, forming a cylinder that shuddered as the space between the walls of light seemed to fall inwards. From the collapsed column, a new shape arose, lifting into the air inside the circle.

"Holy shit," I muttered, straightening up and tightening my grip on my naginata.

"Wow," Oracle whispered, wide-eyed. "I don't remember seeing anything like *that* before."

The newly summoned demon was maybe five and a half feet tall, with a flat head and wide horns that flowed out to either side, then arced up and curled in toward a disc of golden light that hovered in the center. The being wasn't particularly heavily muscled, more…wiry in frame, with a humanoid shape and glowing eyes.

It touched down in the circle, having lifted into the air as the portal below it closed, and it raised its right hand to the glowing wall, drawing a single clawed finger down it in wonder, trailing sparks and a burning ozone smell.

It turned and fixed Jian with a glare, and the two of them seemed to freeze in position. Long seconds passed, the only sound being a solitary low growl from the creature and occasional grunts from Jian, as though he was in pain.

I shifted my grip on the naginata, growing more and more concerned, and saw that the rest of the group was doing the same, when Bane spoke up.

"They're coming."

CHAPTER SIXTEEN

I swore and spun around to look further down the corridor, and although I couldn't see anything yet, I could feel a reverberation in the floor.

"Grizz, Lydia, with me. Bane, Tang, back it up; you're with Miren and Stephanos. Yen, Arrin, smite the fuckers. We need to give Jian time to get this done," I said, snapping the orders out without hesitation.

I got a round of affirmatives as everyone moved into position, and a few seconds later, Bane grunted.

"You're going to want to see this," he said, lifting one hand and firing a Firebolt off into the darkness ahead.

I heard the awe in his voice as he cast his first spell, and I couldn't help but grin inside my helm, remembering how rare it was for a Mer to have access to magic. *Well, that's sure as shit going to change,* I thought to myself.

The Firebolt flew straight and true, slamming into the front of a…device. That was the only way I could describe it, and as the flames washed across its surface, a manically grinning gnome popped his head back up from where he'd clearly ducked.

The thing that was stomping towards us was big, alarmingly so. It rose maybe five feet high, but it stretched at least that wide across as well, and the front of it shone in the dying light, reflecting the flames back to us. It was circular in design, the front, at least, and appeared to extend behind itself in a tail. The entire contraption was being driven forward on multiple sets of legs, and a shivering, shuddering motion ran across it as it progressed.

I was trying to figure it out when Grizz spoke up suddenly.

"It's a damn battering ram!" he gasped in shock.

"What?" I asked him, surprised.

"A battering ram. Back in the days of the empire proper, the gnomes made weapons to breach walls and doors, and they could ride them. That's what it must be! It's got a mobile shield on the front, shaped out of extremely thick metal, and it just keeps going. It'll take a wall out if you let it get close enough. Hell, they might even have the old weapons onboard! They're—"

"They're in for a fucking surprise, is what they are!" I snapped. "Magic! Hit those fuckers!"

I straightened, building a Fireball.

"Magic won't do anything if it's a real siege weapon," Grizz warned grimly, but I shrugged.

"Well, it's a good way to test it." I squeezed extra power into the spell, compressing it down and shaping it, while waiting for the first of the new round of spells to light it up.

As soon as it reappeared in the distance, I fired. At the very bottom of the shield, I could see what looked like feet; they were made of metal, and there were lots of them, rocking in concert. I aimed for them, thinking if I could stop its feet, it would be useless.

I watched the barrage flashing towards the metallic form and saw what I'd missed before. It had a goddamn magical shield, not just a mundane steel one!

I quickly triggered my Examine and flash read the details as it faded back into the darkness.

Gnomish War Shield

This mobile war platform has been cobbled together by hacking and stealing damaged parts from dozens of other, heavier designs, creating a single working one that could be deployed in the tight confines of the Prax.

All gnomish battle creations are imbued with both magical and mundane control methods, in case of theft.

Health: 511/2000

Shield Strength: 811/900

Mana Charge: 376/500

I read over the details and remembered where I'd seen the comments about control methods before…the Fenris! That meant that one of those little bastards had a way to control it, and if we could kill them all, then…

I shook my head, breaking off that line of thought. I couldn't risk it. The shield was building up again, and as I dismissed the screen, I saw it increase from eight hundred and eleven to eight hundred and twelve, while the mana charge dropped by a single point as well. That was our best chance, I decided, despite the high cost in mana.

The corridor was narrow enough that it'd be slow climbing around it, and if we tried while it was still running, it could crush one of us against the wall. Our only option was to take it down at range, and to do that, we needed to burn through our spells.

"Keep firing!" I ordered. "It's got limited mana to power it; drain its shield, and it's a dead fucking duck."

My order inspired a second and third barrage. The time we'd spent getting everyone a spell suddenly made me smile as the glow of the shield on the device got weaker and weaker. Finally, it shattered, and the entire thing collapsed to the floor with a crash.

There were several seconds of grunts and screeches arising from behind it, followed by a heavy clang…then another, and another.

With the third, a small figure shuffled around the edge of the device and came to a stop, two large plates of steel held in either hand. He grinned maniacally at us, then slammed them together, and started to slowly advance. As he moved, a second, third, and fourth gnome moved out and around the collapsed machine, taking up station behind the first, hunching down and hiding from sight as much as possible.

We stopped firing for a few seconds, as the last glimmers of light died away, and the small group vanished from sight.

"Okay, what the hell?" I asked aloud.

"Gnomes," Lydia answered, shrugging.

"Well, yeah, but seriously? The damn anklebiters are tiny, but they act like they're the ones who're going to win."

"Because they always do," Grizz said grimly.

"What?" I asked.

"Gnomes," Grizz repeated. "They *always* win in the end, if you fuck with them. If you kill a few now, it just means that more will come. They're like sodding cockroaches, and vicious to boot. These seem a lot more mental than the normal ones, but that's just making my asshole pucker more, to be honest."

"I really didn't need to hear that," Yen grumbled, scowling at Grizz's back.

"You said I had a nice ass, especially when we were…?" Grizz offered conversationally, and she grunted warningly, lifting her right hand.

"I'm going to throw a spell forward in a second or two, Grizz, and if you shut up right now, I might not *miss* what I'm aiming for and *accidentally* hit you. Maybe."

"Yen, I really thought you had better taste, you know that?" I said, making myself sound disappointed in her.

"One night. A single goddamn night of weakness, when I was tired and filthy and we were hiding, and I swear I'm never going to live it down," she muttered bitterly.

"One? What about—" Grizz started to argue, and she growled at him to shut his mouth.

"Again," I said, shaking my head disapprovingly. Then I clarified my order, as nothing happened. "Magic them again," I ordered slowly and clearly.

"Oh, thank god; I thought he was telling her to—" Miren started to whisper to Stephanos, and Lydia growled at her to shut up, even as her flame golem slammed its hands together, twisted them somehow, then flung a Firebolt at the oncoming gnomes. That started the group off, as Miren made gestures of sealing her mouth to Lydia, and everyone who had an offensive spell started casting it.

Arrin was firing Darkbolts; fast and deadly, they impacted the shield and seemed to start it rusting. The entropic energy clearly weakened the shields; the gnome carrying them started to screech in pain and fury as the barrage of Fireballs and Firebolts made one glow a cherry red.

The gnome shield bearer continued forward but kept up a furious screech that sounded like tortured metal, until he dropped both shields in pain and dove back behind the gnomes sheltering behind him. The next one swept the shields up and stomped forward, and I recognized the white skin.

"They're using that stone skin ability or whatever it is; they're acting as shields for the others. Hammer the little bastards over and over," I ordered, growing more and more concerned that they would reach us and be impossible to injure. "Oracle, I'll bring the water—"

She spoke up quickly.

"And I'll bring the pain!" she finished grimly. "Arrin, lightning the water repeatedly; it'll damage them all and hopefully let us kill the ones without the ability active, as well."

I cast the fountain spell, sending the water soaring up behind the shields as the bearer stepped forward. The spray quickly soaked him but didn't give him the chance to plunge the shields into the water to cool them. Then the lightning started to fly, pounding one bolt after the other into the water as it spread and the little procession stumbled on.

Screams of pain rose from further back, but the leading gnomes simply grunted and groaned, then marched on. Finally, when they were within a dozen meters from us, the shield bearer gave up with a groan and dropped the shields as his ability ran out.

As soon as he did so, before the next in line could sweep them back up, Stephanos and Miren loosed their arrows, slamming a continuous volley into the gnome and staggering him back.

The blow was enough to block the next gnome in line, and as he frantically tried to shove his former comrade aside, we unleashed hell.

Two lightning bolts flashed, joined by three firebolts and a Fireball from me as I stopped casting the fountains, now that my mana was down to forty-eight.

A entropic black bolt flew ahead, taking the next gnome in the face and making him stagger. All attempts at order finally dissolved, and the remaining three gnomes shoved their way forward to sprint at us, relying on their stone coating to protect them.

"Boss, be ready," Grizz said suddenly, grinning at me as he sheathed his sword and shrugged his shield aside. "I'm gonna try something."

As the spells cut off, he dove forward, sweeping up a section of broken vehicle from one of the crashed badunkas.

The gnomes raced forward to meet him, the one in the lead brandishing an axe that glowed an unhealthy green. The tiny creature roared and drooled, the light of fanaticism glowing in its eyes.

Before it could reach him, Grizz spun, sweeping the four-foot section out in a low swing that connected with the gnome's upraised arm and spun him about. He slammed into his oncoming fellows and took them all down, the crunching of stone and screams of fury rising…until Grizz stepped in, discarded the metal length, and grabbed the gnome by the ankles, then tugged him backwards into a clear section of corridor.

"Gonna need some room." He grunted, swinging the gnome around by his feet and building up speed. We backed up as far as we could, but Jian's bonding meant we didn't have much space. We didn't need to wait long, and as Grizz got a handle on the weight, he grinned wildly. I watched in open-mouthed amazement as the mad bastard spun around, swinging the gnome, and slammed him into one of his companions as they rose from the ground.

The force of their heads colliding was enough, combined with the speed and weight, to break both their necks, and the now-familiar death's head symbols I'd added oh so long ago lifted into the air.

I grinned, impressed, as Grizz spun the corpse around again, then flung it at the third gnome, who took his flying friend to the face, sending him to the floor in a screeching pile of rage.

"Well," huffed Grizz, bending over and gripping his knees as he tried to catch his breath. "I'm…not taking…them all."

"Mad bastard!" I shouted, laughing as I lunged forward, rushing past him, Lydia's distinctive boot strike following me, along with more clomping footfalls.

I ran as fast as I could, managing to cover the distance before one of the injured gnomes could get the last uninjured one, whose stone coating was still intact, to her feet. She hissed up at me, hate clear on her face as I skidded to a halt over her, throwing up a spray of water as I stabbed forward. The blade of my naginata tore out the throat of the gnome who was half-hidden below her, pushing upwards.

Then I yanked the blade back across, the tip scarring a line in the stone over her throat and up her jaw before she punched out, her small fist hitting with the power of a bulldozer as it slammed into my weapon, knocking it aside.

She shoved herself upwards, ignoring the bleeding-out gnome beneath her as she opened her mouth wide to bite and flung herself at me.

Lydia slammed her shield into the side of the incoming gnome, battering the small female aside and raising her mace, slamming it down again and again.

"Hold it!" came an order from behind us. I spun around, seeing Stephanos pointing at the gnome…and a short, stumpy figure, no bigger than three feet high, dove past both Lydia and me, slamming itself down atop the gnome and pinning it.

It was his earth golem, I realized, and if the way the gnome was struggling was any guess, it weighed at least as much as she did.

It wrapped its arms and legs around her and clung on tenaciously. The little gnome screeched and bucked around, furiously trying to get free, before sinking her teeth into the golem to absolutely no effect.

I looked further up the corridor, and while I could hear a faint splashing noise somewhere in the darkness, the cause was out of my sight.

"Let me," Bane said, stepping up and hefting the crossbow he'd taken from the Drow trap. Somewhere, he'd gotten a bushel of bolts, and he looked over the options for a few seconds. He sighted carefully down its length before firing…then he started cursing.

He grabbed at it with his secondary arms, holding it in place and heaved with the bigger pair, yanking the string back into place and tried again.

He missed.

And again, until on the fourth shot, a scream echoed back to us, followed by a faint splash and the sound of something thrashing in the water.

"I hate crossbows," Bane muttered to me as he slung it back onto his back, striding around the gnome pinned on the floor and jogging into the darkness.

I stood there with Lydia for a few minutes, watching the frantic gnome as it bit, chewed, and bit again, seemingly determined to eat the golem while trying to punch and kick it.

"That's not normal," Lydia said finally.

"Really?" I asked as Bane slowly came back into sight, dragging a wailing figure by one ankle. "I mean, I didn't think it was, but you know, different realm and all that."

"No, this is really not right," Yen agreed, stepping up next to us, with Grizz following close behind. "Gnomes are generally crazy, but they're more of a 'what will happen if I pour these crystals into that liquid and drink it' crazy. I mean, yeah, they tend to blow shit up a lot, and they even make the goblins look sane at times with their addictions, but…"

"Their addictions?" I asked.

Yen snorted. "Yeah, you know those drugs you seized? Gnomes. Always the gnomes."

"What's with that?" I frowned. "I mean, slavery is legal—well, you know what I mean; it's accepted, as is some seriously dodgy shit in the city, like blood sports—but there's illegal drugs?"

"Gnomes," Yen repeated, shrugging. "They're the ones who love the stuff, and when they've got a nose full of that white powder, they all seem to want to do crazy shit, like finding out what happens when you add a 'harmless compound' to the city water supply. To 'help people enjoy themselves,' was the last justification I remember hearing."

"They really did that? Man, what was it?" I gaped, amazed.

"Who knows?" Yen scoffed. "Whatever it was, though, the street of negotiable affection was rammed that night."

"Literally!" Grizz said, grinning crazily. "It was like I had a rocket in my pants…not that I don't normally, but…you know…!"

"Oh, gods, Grizz, you remember when we talked about this?!" Yen groaned, dropping her face in her hands. "We talked about engaging the brain before speaking?"

"Yeah, I remember," Grizz said evenly, grinning and winking at me where Yen couldn't see. "I decided not to do that this time; after all, what's the worst that could happen?"

"What's the worst?!" she growled, popping her head back up to glare at him.

"Yeah, and remember, I'm a centurion, legionnaire," he said, raising one eyebrow.

"Oh, really? You think that's going to work?" she growled. "Speculatores of the Dravith Cohortes Praetoriae, remember?" She stepped in close and fumed up at him. "You might be a centurion, but I can still give you orders!"

"You're a legionnaire—" he started to repeat when she interrupted him, her voice a low growl of anger.

"By my authority as a Speculatores of the Dravith Cohortes Praetoriae, *drop and give me a hundred!*"

The cocky grin was wiped off Grizz's face as his body reacted to the order, enforced by the Oath the legion took, and he swore viciously, trying to apologize to Yen, while she ignored him, turning a sweet smile upon me.

"Sorry about that, Lord Jax," she cooed.

"Hey, legion politics are your problem," I said with a shrug.

"He thought seducing me was even more fun because he was technically screwing a member of the lower ranks." She laughed. "He forgets that the Speculatores are outside the normal chain of command and can give orders to those within it. Now he gets to rethink his position on that…for the next little while, anyway. Would you like him to do a hundred for you, too, sir?"

"No," I said, and Grizz let out a relieved breath.

"Thank you, boss…" he began, his grin coming back, until I went on.

"But only because we're in hostile territory. I think keeping order is important, though, so maybe two hundred more on top will remind him? Burpees, I mean?"

"Burpees?" Yen asked curiously, while Grizz tried to interrupt with pleas for understanding and increasingly genuine apologies.

"Yeah, you do a pushup, then stand, do a jumping jack, then drop, do another push up, roll onto your back, sit up, roll over, start again," I explained, demonstrating the jumping jack portion."

"Oh, I like that!" Yen said. "Good point about the area, though; I'll let him finish his hundred, and he can do the rest tonight when we make camp."

"I'll leave it with you." I returned her salute, watching as Bane dragged the injured gnome up. The Mer dumped him unceremoniously on the floor before us, just as the one pinned under the golem lost its white coating and gasped as it was crushed.

I looked down at the sound of breaking bones and saw the blood running from her mouth and nose.

"Ah, well, never mind," I said simply, surprised at myself for not feeling anything at the prisoner dying. I'd planned on just holding it until we could take it prisoner. "Anyway, you were saying?" I asked Lydia and Yen.

"Ah, right!" Lydia said. "Yeah, I used ter drink with a couple o' gnomes; they were twins, pretty crazy. But as I say, that's gnomes, right? These, though? They're *crazy*. Like, not in tha normal way."

"Yeah, the chewing on my leg is a good hint!" Grizz called up, and Yen squatted down to whisper something to him. I couldn't hear it, but I saw the fear on his face. When she stood up, he was back to doing the pushups perfectly, as fast as he could.

"So…" I said, turning back to the groaning, bleeding gnome on the floor who glared at us all while clutching a crossbow bolt that protruded from the front of his right leg. "Anyone speak gnomish?"

"It's Common," Lydia said shortly.

"What, everyone speaks it?" I asked.

"No, it's Common that they speak, usually, like we do. Whatever they were sayin' before, it's not a real language."

"You understand us?" I asked the gnome, and he glared up at me through gritted teeth. "Bane, get the bolt," I said shortly. Bane squatted down and grabbed the tiny leg in one hand, the creature's two arms in two more, and then yanked the bolt free with his remaining hand in one smooth motion.

The gnome screamed in pain, then spat at Bane, who slapped him, hard.

"Oracle?" I said quietly, and she hit him with a healing spell, then swore. "What's up?" I asked her, frowning at the sudden feeling of shock through the bond.

"I need more mana," she said urgently, and I felt her building a spell. I immediately recognized it, and trusting her, I pulled a potion free and downed it, then sighed and moved to the side of the corridor, where a dry patch remained. I sat, closing my eyes and beginning to meditate, as Oracle used Battlefield Triage on the gnome.

After a few minutes, she'd burned through the mana I had regenerated, and I groaned at the mana migraine that started to spread before managing to ignore it again and sinking my mind into my meditation even deeper.

I locked the world away, envisioning myself first as I was. Working my way from the top of my head to the tips of my toes, I separated out every individual muscle I could identify and relaxed it.

Once they were all loosened, I envisaged the energy field flowing through my channels, the mana, forming a box around me. I visualized it pulling at the nearby ambient mana, twisting it and tugging it down into the form of the box around me. I created six sides and closed myself inside on a whim, drawing the mana into channels that twisted and compressed the mana down, without knowing why I did it.

Then I created a second box just slightly larger, surrounding the first, and visualized the mana that moved from the outer box to the inner as being purified on the way, compressed and given a slight spin, again, working entirely on instinct.

The more I visualized it, the more natural it seemed to become. Every so often, the mana inside me dipped down before being slowly refilled by the mana in my "box."

"Jax, you can stop now," I heard Oracle say to me, as if from a great distance. I blinked, slowly opening my eyes and looking around, an afterimage of a glowing blue-white box around me fading away into the ether.

"Hell, that was impressive, boss." Grizz panted, nodding to me as he stretched and recovered from his exertions. As I continued looking around, I discovered that the others were watching me intently as well.

"Okay," I said, shaking myself and glancing over at the gnome, who sat rubbing at his head and moaning, but he sounded, hell, he *looked* totally different. "What happened to him?" I asked in surprise, and Oracle flitted around him to land next to me, laying her hand gently on my arm.

"We cured him," she said.

I turned my gaze back to the gnome, who was gaping around at the rest of us with a mixture of horror, fury, and terror.

The tiny gnome stared at our group before finally settling on me and Oracle. He shuffled to his feet and reached out a hesitant hand for Oracle, then when nobody did anything to stop him, he snarled and grabbed her, pulling her close and glaring defiantly at us all as he held her cradled to his chest.

"It's okay!" Oracle called out quickly, halting us as we all reached for weapons. The little gnome pulled her closer to his chest and started to growl defensively.

"Well, shit," I muttered. "Looks like we're gonna have to housetrain a gnome now."

CHAPTER SEVENTEEN

"It's okay," Oracle repeated, but this time, she said it to the gnome, reaching up and patting his cheek. He made a cooing sound down at her, then bared his teeth at the rest of us, before snarling and attempting to back away in the direction he'd come from.

"I don't think so," I said warningly, hauling myself to my feet and glaring at the little bastard while pounding the base of the naginata down once, hard, and channeling a flare of mana into it for emphasis.

The light that flared out from my weapon made the gnome shy away, raising one hand to cover his eyes, though he held Oracle tighter to his chest.

"Let her go, or I swear you're dead meat," I growled at the diminutive figure.

He glared up at me, squinting past the light, and I readied myself to give the order, pausing as I noticed a blur that I knew to be Bane shifting around behind him.

"No!" Oracle said, holding a hand out to me and getting crushed to the gnome's chest again. "No, Jax, honestly, it's okay…we need him!"

She reached up and twisted herself around. She planted her hands on his chest and pushed hard, arching her back to make the gnome release her, but she didn't flee when she fell to the ground.

She landed lightly, her wings growing again, and I realized I'd missed them vanishing. When she reached up, she took the gnome's outstretched hand on her left, then patted it lightly with her right hand as she faced him.

"Come on; you can understand us now, can't you?" she asked him, and he grunted, looking confused. "My words…do you understand them?" she asked again, slowly.

He squinted at her, moving his lips, as though sounding out what she'd said, before tilting his head in thought.

"Jax," Oracle said, turning and looking up at me. "There's more going on here than 'crazy creatures in the darkness.' Seriously, I don't know what happened here, but the buildup of metals in his body was toxic; they were making him crazy, and I'll bet that the rest of the gnomes are the same."

"So, they're not evil, they're sick?" I clarified, and she nodded. "What about the undead?"

"Maybe they're not all one team?" she hazarded a guess. "Maybe the undead are controlling one side of the ruin, and the gnomes run the other? Or maybe there's a gnome necromancer who's gone mad? I don't know, okay? All I know is that, with the toxins in his body, he was driven mad, desperate to fight and kill. He was filled with all sorts of contaminants…I hope…I mean, there's a chance they might not all be like this…?"

"Do they know they're mad?" I continued, and the gnome surprised us all by croaking a response.

"M…aaaa…dddduuur," he said, his voice raspy and clearly unused to speaking.

"What?" I asked, and Oracle smiled up at him, nodding encouragingly for him to continue.

"Maaa…aadddurrrr…brrrrriiiinggg…mmmmetttttalll…maaadddduuurrr giiiiivvvesss clllleeeean…wwwaaaaaatttuuurrrr," the gnome ground out, making us glance at each other in confusion.

"Master!" Oracle said suddenly, working it out first. "The 'Master' makes you bring metal, in exchange for water?" she asked.

"Waaaaattttuuuurr, speciiiiiaaallll wwwatttturrrr…" The gnome whined, and the rest of us looked at each other grimly.

"Special water?" Oracle repeated, and the gnome nodded eagerly.

"Waaaatttturrrr sppppeciiiiiallll…taaaake youuuu? Giiiivvvve to maaaaadddurrrr! Givvvvessss morrrre waaaaattttturrrr tttto Giiiiinnt?" the gnome half-asked, half-insisted, pointing frantically down the corridor into the darkness.

"He wants to take me and give me to his Master; I think his name is Giint?" Oracle translated, and the gnome nodded to her frantically.

"Taakke yoouuuu, giiiiivvve! Ggettt moorrrrreee!"

"That's enough," I said firmly, stepping forward and leveling my naginata at the little figure. "Nobody takes Oracle; never!" I insisted, the last words coming out in a growl.

"Jax, it's okay," Oracle said quietly. "I don't think he understands, not really. He's been conditioned to give things to the 'Master' to such a degree that it's all he can think of. His brain's been full of poisons for so long, it'll take a while for it to make real sense. For now, he's trying to fall back on what he knows. That's all."

"So, he'll attack us?" I asked, and surprisingly, the gnome was the one who responded when Oracle paused.

"Nooooo, nnnooooo fiiiiight," the gnome said, shaking his head sadly.

"You attacked us!" I snapped.

"Meeeetallll, lotttts. And meeeeaaat!" he explained, smiling, then regarded the collection of debris that filled the corridor. "Saaaaaad…Giiiint fiiiix?" he asked plaintively, pointing at the smashed parts.

"You can fix them?" I asked. He stared blankly at me, then pointed at the broken, twisted wreckage.

"Fiiiix?" he asked again, licking his lips nervously and clenching and unclenching his hands as Oracle lifted into the air and landed on my shoulder.

"He doesn't know what to do," Oracle said sadly as I reached up and patted her leg, her hand reaching down to rest on my own. "His mind is broken. I've fixed it enough that there's no physical reason he can't get better now, but the things he must have seen…and if the others are the same."

"Yes," I agreed, nodding to him and pointing to one of the strange little bikes. "Fix this."

He smiled wildly at me, his teeth gleaming in the dim light.

Spinning, he ran at the debris, digging his fingers into a twisted section and tearing it free with ease before tugging tools out of his belt and falling to work. We all watched him in awe for a few seconds, amazed by the difference in him, going from a feral creature to, well, a feral *engineer*.

He was totally uninterested in anything around him suddenly, focused only on the problem and fixing it. I had flashbacks to some of the mechanics I'd known back home, never happier than when they were covered in oil and muck, swapping corroded and damaged parts for new shiny ones, or worse, those weird-ass network engineers with their cable fixations…

"Jax!" Miren called, and I looked over, realizing that the glowing cylinder was dying away, and that both Jian and the demon were coming out of their daze.

"Shit!" I grunted, rushing to interpose myself between Jian and the creature before it could do anything to him. "Bane! Watch the fucking gnome!" I ordered. There were a dozen feet between the space where we'd moved to stand and where Jian swayed almost drunkenly, but I covered it in record time, visions of the creature ripping his throat out filling my mind.

Instead, it spun toward us and stepped between us and Jian, the golden disc above its head flaring and growing brighter. Tiny lightning bolts seemed to crackle across its surface.

"Stop," mumbled Jian, and the creature whipped its head around to look at him. "Don't…it's okay…friends," Jian mumbled again, shaking his head and clearly trying to wake himself up.

The demon twisted back to glare at us briefly before straightening from the half-hunch it'd dropped into, as the light dimmed, and the disc seemed to grow…less. It faded but also seemed to be both smaller and less reflective in a second, and the demon stepped back to stand only a half-step ahead of Jian and to his right, flexing its claws nervously.

We came to a halt, eyeing each other warily as Jian reached out and rested a hand on the demon's shoulder, clearly bracing himself as he shook his head.

"Sorry, Jax," he said weakly. "I just…I just need a minute, okay?"

Miren stepped in and ignored the glare from the demon as she put her arm around Jian's waist in order to help him to stand.

She whispered to him for a couple of seconds, while the demon glared around at us all. Finally, I sighed, stepping forward, deliberately trying not to appear threatening as I spoke to the demon directly.

"Do you have a name?" I asked it. It continued to glare at me, a low growl starting in its throat.

"Uh…Jax?" Grizz interjected, and I tilted my head to him, showing I was listening while watching the demon still. "That's a demon, okay? They're generally not known for being sparkling conversationalists."

"Yeah, well, since I came to this realm, I've gotten drunk with dwarves and cat people, flown on ships in the sky and met people as weird as you, mate. No way to know if a demon can talk or not without asking."

"I can speak your language, whelp," the demon growled out

"Whelp?" I snarled, straightening my shoulders and stepping forward. "Really, you want to go there?" I prepared to summon a spell, and my naginata started to glow again.

"No!" Oracle and Jian said in concert.

"No, please don't kill him, Lord Jax," Jian said quickly, and Oracle smiled at the demon as it glanced from its warlock to me. "He's new here, and he doesn't understand yet. I'll explain things to him," Jian reassured me. I nodded to him, sparing another cold stare for the demon, then turning and walking back towards the gnome.

"How strong are demons?" I asked Oracle from where she sat on my shoulder, and she shrugged prettily.

"Depends; give me a second," she said, looking back at him and half-closing her eyes.

"Master! The wisp is," the demon snapped out, light crackling across his disc again as it pointed at Oracle, and Jian stepped between him and us, frantically speaking to the creature in a low voice.

"Oops," Oracle said, before sharing the information with me. "I didn't think he'd sense that. Might be useful, after all."

Ty'Baronn, Second Spur of the Unsouled
The demon Ty'Baronn is a lesser Balun warrior, and while skilled in using their claws and fighting hand to hand, the Balun warriors are better known for their formidable beam attack: they channel the life force of their prey into a single, powerful blast of energy that can rival the heat of the sun for a short time. Balun warriors that do not use this ability, and instead store the life essences of lesser creatures, will eventually evolve into higher demonic forms.

Weaknesses: Unknown

Resistances: All demons enjoy resistances to fire attacks -25% damage

Critical Weaknesses: Unknown

Health: Unknown

Stamina: Unknown

Mana: Unknown

"What might be useful?" I asked her.

"That he can sense magic being directed at him. Well, possibly, we didn't really get much information on him, though, did we?" she said annoyed.

"Not really, and why did you tell me to stop before? You sounded concerned."

"Well, it's got a beam weapon of some kind; we've got no idea what it does or how fast it can fire. Plus, Jian literally just formed a pact with it? Maybe a little early to decide if you're going to kill it? Hmmm?"

"I wasn't…" I started to protest, and Oracle just snorted at me.

"Jax, it's me. I know how irritated you get, and the way you both looked at each other? It was never going to end well. Just do us both a favor and look at my boobs; that'll make you happy, and it keeps everyone else alive, hmmm?" she purred, shaking her head and talking to me as though I was a simpleton or a child. I growled under my breath but still sneaked a look at her chest as I walked, before realizing that part had been a trap, as she started to giggle.

"I'm totally playing with those later," I whispered to her, and she grinned at me as we both dismissed the demon from our minds, finally reaching the gnome and inspecting what he was doing.

Bane was still present, and was now visible, seated atop a piece of wreckage nearby, while Tang was further up the corridor, looking over the mobile shield. With no imminent threat, I leaned against the wall and pulled up the notifications that had been frantically pulsing for my attention.

Congratulations!

You have practiced enough to raise your Meditation skill to its first evolution! Through combining several different methods into one, you have shown an understanding that is beyond your years.
Continue to practice and learn to increase this skill further.

You must now pick a path to follow.

Will you choose to widen your boost with RESOUNDING GAINS, or increase the speed of your mana recovery with FOCUS?

Choose carefully, as this choice cannot be undone.

RESOUNDING GAINS:
The constant changes you've forced your body to undergo, mixed with your newly discovered ability to draw and compress mana, have resulted in an entirely new level of meditation. Now when you meditate, for each level of compression you achieve, you will gain one point each of health, mana, and stamina per minute.

FOCUS:
Your skill in mana compression is formidable, yet it's only just begun. Through experimentation, you have realized that by increasing the rate of compression, you can increase the rate of mana replenishment by a total of five points per minute, per level of compression.

I looked over the options for a few seconds, considering the options. I'd not really understood what I was doing; the meditation that Bane and others had taught me had each seemed to be part of the method to me, like understanding that you cook a chicken to make a roast chicken dinner. Yeah, that's true, but there's a lot more to it as well.

The meditation I'd used had been partially guided by my headache and urgent need to refill my mana, and had been partially instinctual, with my mind simply doing rather than thinking. No, as I looked at the options, I needed to decide. The faster healing, mana, and stamina would have been a game changer when I first arrived here; gods knew that if I could have simply meditated for an hour or two and been totally healed and refilled with mana, I would have saved a fortune in healing potions up until now, but…

I had healing spells and potions for a reason. I couldn't stop in the middle of a fight to meditate, and as cool as it would be, it just wasn't enough. Having my mana jump by five points per minute per level of compression, though? Hell yes. That meant, even if I couldn't get the "boxes" right, I'd still have what, nearly nine points a minute, and that was amazing.

I chose Focus. Not that it was really a choice to make, I reflected, and I went on to the next notification.

Congratulations!

You have killed the following:

- 1x Gnome Badunka Rider, level 8 for 5,150xp

A party under your command killed the following:

- 5x Gnome Badunka Riders of various levels for a total of 32,480xp

Total Party experience earned: 32,480xp

As party leader you gain 25% of all experience earnt

Progress to level 20 stands at 194,668/305,000

"Booya," I muttered to myself, nodding in satisfaction and pulling up the final notification.

You have been given a Quest by the Goddess Jenae: Fix the Fixers.

The Goddess Jenae has commanded you to explore the Sunken City, a site you now know to be the Prax, Glorious Retribution. Upon further investigation, you've found a lost tribe of gnomes, a species renowned not only for their standoffish nature, but also their unwillingness to allow their technology to be investigated by others, and their borderline drug-fueled insanity. Jenae wishes you to further investigate the tribe, healing any you can, and adding to your people.

Discover the Secret of the Gnomish Regression: 0/1

Recover Magical Artifacts and Technologies: 2/?

Retrieve Manastones: 5/100

Retrieve Spellbooks and Skillbooks Lost in the Prax: 0/37

Recruit Additional Citizens: 1/?

Recruit Skilled Crafters: 1/?

Find the Master and Free the Gnomish Tribe: 0/1

Bonuses will be given for exceeding these numbers.

Reward: Improved technological capacity in the Great Tower. Possible technological boosts to the fleet. Unknown, 250,000xp

"Well, that's just fucking peachy," I muttered, rubbing my chin. "You see this, Oracle?" She nodded. "I notice that the option to accept the quest or not is gone."

Blushing lightly, she coughed.

"I removed it," she admitted after a brief pause. "It's not like we were going to refuse, were we?" she asked me.

"No, probably not. So, now we need to save the gnomes? Seriously, they're batshit little bastards; do we really want them in the airships?"

"Probably not," Oracle admitted. "But have you seen what Giint is making?"

I looked over at him again, having been too absorbed in the notifications to pay much attention to him. The periodical wash of Bane's worldsense and the way both he and Tang were watching, meant that we were alright for now, at least.

I paused, my eyes growing wider as I took in the gnome's work. It was small, maybe five feet long by two feet high, but he'd scavenged the wheels from several smashed vehicles then had taken four of the legs from the drained mobile shield before ripping half its guts out and adding them to his creation.

It made me think of a walker from the imperial forces in those movies I'd loved as a kid, but the legs were inside the wheels, moving them like pistons. A long, bare area had been fitted on the back, behind which I assumed Giint intended to sit, maybe four feet long and three wide, with a ridge around it.

"It's amazing," I admitted as he started chucking things into the back. He ignored sections I thought looked almost intact, then chose bits I assumed were trash, and vice-versa, chucking them all in until he grinned up at Oracle and me manically, his eyes still glowing slightly.

"Sseeeee? Giiiint fiiix!" he crowed, his smile indicating that he was still well over the horizon of madness and probably still accelerating.

"Uh, yeah…well done," I muttered, impressed at the speed he'd done it in. Maybe half an hour, that was all it had taken him, but it was taking definite form, and far faster than I could have built a goddamn flatpack wardrobe. I looked to Bane in shock. He shrugged, but it was Tang who spoke up.

"You'll never beat a gnome when it comes to making something, Jax. Seriously; where the other races learn and use magic to change the world, the gnomes instead use it at an instinctive level to fix and improve things. The mad little bastard probably has no clue what he does, but that's why the gnomes are always in demand.

"The slavers will drop anything to try and capture some, so now, gnomes generally keep to themselves and have a *lot* of guards. It's common knowledge that they refuse to share any of their secrets with anyone outside their race, but after seeing what he just did? I'm betting they don't tell anyone because they can't. They probably just do it and have no idea how."

"Well, I hope they can be taught, then, because Jenae gave me a quest to save and recruit them."

"Oh, hell no!" Tang gaped in horror. "You want gnomes on the airships? Jax, we'll never get anywhere; they'll pull everything apart!"

"Well, we'll come up with something," I retorted grimly. "Divine quest, remember?"

"Bloody stupid one," he muttered, but he did so quietly, and Jenae didn't respond, so I was relieved and just hoped she'd not heard him.

We stared at each other silently, all feeling various degrees of concern about having more of these midget nutjobs around, when Jian finally joined us.

"Ah, Lord Jax, sorry about before," he said, nodding to me. "Ty'Baronn wants to apologize as well." He gestured to the demon, who stepped forward and went down onto one knee, glaring at the filthy floor.

"Ty'Baronn was unaware of the lord's nature. Ty'Baronn begs forgiveness and wishes to remain as a bonded pair with warlock Jian," the demon growled out.

I inclined my head, gesturing for him to stand and trying to not snarl back at him.

"That's fine, don't worry; whatever. You're welcome to stay if Jian wants you, just don't attack anyone unless he says it's okay, right?" I said, a little distracted as I glanced over him, then turned my attention back to the gnome. The little bastard was just staring at Oracle again, and I mean *staring*; not in a sexual way, which was good, but more in a desperate-for-approval way, and when you combined that with the glowing eyes and the glittering metal teeth set in a rictus smile...

"You're sure he's sane?" I asked Oracle.

She smiled sadly. "He's as sane as I can make him. That's all I'm saying. I bet Nerin or Hellenica can do more, though."

"Well, I hope so," I mumbled, forcing a smile and speaking to Giint directly. "Well done, Gint!" I praised him, and he bobbed his head frantically.

"Giiiint goooood!" he hissed, then set off at a sudden sprint, rushing at the battle shield again. This time, I caught the glow of mana around his hands as he drove them into the machine, tearing and yanking. A screwdriver and hammers seemed to appear almost at random, practically teleported into his hands from the wide belt of pouches hanging around his waist.

His hands practically blurred, swiftly dipping in and out as he removed parts that he threw onto the back of his little creation, while other bits he tossed aside to lie discarded against the walls. I looked from the dozens of small bits that he saved, then to the parts he'd discarded, and then back to the rapidly shrinking main construction, as he darted back and forth, integrating sections into his new creation or stacking them in the back.

"How the hell is he doing that?" I whispered to Oracle. "I swear there aren't enough parts to account for how fast the big bugger's disappearing, but..."

"His bags," she said simply. "He's putting parts into his bags as well; I think they're bags of holding."

"His...wait." I hesitated, searching for the other gnome corpses strewn about the floor. "Has anyone checked the bodies?" I asked aloud, and everyone looked at each other sheepishly. "Right. Loot the corpses; they might have valuables, loot, or bags of holding, so..."

"Nooooo!" Giint cried out, dumping the parts he held and running back to us. "No plaaaays with bodieees! Deaddss cannn goooo BANG!" he squealed, jumping up and yanking his hands apart. "Waaaaant Giint mak safesss?" he offered earnestly. I held up a hand, stopping everyone in their tracks.

"Yes, but first, Gint, you swear fealty. I'm not letting you get weapons or anything until then, understand?" I said firmly. He cocked his head to one side and made a sound between an inquisitive kitten and a bird, a kind of chirping, before grinning disturbingly again and nodding his head fast enough that he was in danger of giving himself whiplash.

"Giiiint sweeeears!" he said and reached for the nearest corpse again. Grizz reached out to stop him, and Giint snarled, snapping his teeth sharply at Grizz's hand. "Mine!" he growled, and I had to keep from swearing as Grizz smacked him across the nose with two fingers like a naughty puppy.

"Bad!" Grizz snapped, his legion centurion voice coming out as he boomed at the little figure. "Bad Giint!" he repeated, holding up the two fingers warningly.

Giint growled at him again, but impressively, he stopped and watched the fingers, as though unsure what would happen next.

"Grizz, my man, congratulations!" I said, and Grizz looked at me with surprise, straightening up.

"Jax?" he asked, tilting his head inquisitively, and I smiled, nodding to indicate Giint.

"That little bugger is officially in your care once he's been given the Oath," I said, mana dipping as Oracle pushed it to him.

There was a long pause as he froze, confused; then Oracle reached out and touched Giint's head, frowning.

"Damnation!" she growled, moving closer to put both hands on his temples and starting to glow. She remained there for several seconds before Giint seemed to relax, and then, all of a sudden, he fell to the floor, spasming.

"What—" I choked, reaching out, until Oracle blocked me.

"Wait!" she said anxiously. "He's been blocked from his screens somehow, and for a long time. I had to undo it, but now he's getting them all at once."

"So, what, he's leveling?" I asked, and she nodded, rising up and casting a pitying look at the body on the floor as it twisted and kicked, crying out in pain and fury. The little gnome's teeth glinted in the faint light as they continued gnashing angrily.

"Is he going to be okay?" Grizz asked, and Oracle frowned as she examined him from every angle.

"I don't know, honestly," she admitted slowly. "He's over seventy years old, and he'd never leveled properly before, just gaining points by doing things naturally. He'd never advanced any stats by allocation, but now…"

"Now?" I prompted, and she took a deep breath, rotating to meet my eyes.

"Now he's gaining every reserved point in one go, all the points he'd earned but not allocated. He's level thirty-seven; I saw that much, and gnomes get plus two points to Intelligence, and one to Dexterity, with a free point to allocate each level, so he's just gotten…"

"More than seventy points into Intelligence," I finished, wincing in understanding.

"Exactly," Oracle confirmed softly, and all around us, my people gritted their teeth in sympathy.

"Will he live?" I asked her, and her expression became heartbreakingly sad.

"I honestly don't know. I'm sorry, Jax; maybe Nerin or Hellenica could have helped him more. I didn't realize what the issue was until I'd undone it, and now…"

"And now it's too late," I said, sighing. "Okay then, that's fine. There's nothing we can do, I guess. Would another round of healing help him?" I offered hopefully, and she shook her head.

"If it would, I'd have done it already. It's the shock that's the problem. If anything, his body is growing stronger and fitter; rather than needing healing, he needs to rest."

"What if we…" I started to suggest, when Bane suddenly tackled me roughly from the side, driving me against the wall as something flew past me, smashing into the barrier and leaving a green smear to slide down it.

"Watch out!" he cried to the others as Tang drew back on his bow and fired a black-fletched arrow down the corridor into the darkness. The bolt struck true, eliciting a shriek of fury from something whose voice seemed to shake the air.

Bane growled long and low before looking to me.

"Leviathans," he ground out, that single word filled with fear and hatred in equal measure.

CHAPTER EIGHTEEN

Two creatures slunk out of the darkness at the far end of the corridor, their skin the color of the walls, allowing them to blend in easily. They clacked and hissed at each other, tracking us warily.

"What are they?" I asked Bane as I studied them. The pair were tall, almost shoulder-height, but not humanoid; instead, the closest I could get was a cross between a wolf and a squid.

Their incomprehensible bodies were at least a dozen feet long, with four eyes set in a triangular face. Out of each forehead, a long horn jutted upwards, and directly beneath, a vicious beak pointed down. The creatures had six legs, each with bone flanges jutting out from the sides that made them look like they'd be just as happy in or out of the sea.

In addition to the legs, four arm-like appendages protruded out from behind their heads. The limbs moved like tentacles, but after a foot or so, they each narrowed to a long, clearly sharp claw that waved lightly in the air.

I couldn't help but draw comparisons with Bane, and upon looking over at him, I suddenly felt a low growl reverberating from him.

"Leviathans," he growled again.

"Really?" I frowned, backing up and preparing to fight. "In my homeland, we have legends of them. They're a lot bigger—" I started, before Bane cut me off.

"Yeah, these are freshly spawned. Maybe ten or fifteen years old, that's all," he said grimly. "But if they're here, we've got a much bigger problem than I thought."

"What?" I asked with concern, feeling my nuts shriveling as I watched the creatures moving slowly forward.

"Their mother. A leviathan doesn't spawn frequently, and they tend to keep their spawn around, as snacks, if nothing else. Leviathans grow to be as large as the food source can supply. They don't die of natural causes, either, so if you have legends of them and they were huge, they might be true," Bane admitted, an edge of fear and respect filling his voice.

"So, if there's a bigger one than these around," I faltered when one of the creatures suddenly screamed, quickly followed by the second. The noise started high, and then shifted straight into horrific. I winced in pain, the noise reverberating through my skull and making my guts twist, my ears bleeding.

Bane staggered, all four hands clutching at his head as his knives clattered to the ground. The sonic attack was decidedly painful to me, and it made me fear that I was going to need fresh trousers soon, the way it was twisting my insides. But for a creature who saw the world through a form of sonar, it was obviously beyond agonizing. I gritted my teeth, scowling at the creatures as they slunk closer down the corridor, still screaming.

"…" I forced out, then gritted my teeth and tried again, louder this time. As soon as the first syllable failed to materialize, I started trying to cast sub-vocally.

When that failed, fizzling out and sending a tearing pain through my skull, I hissed, glanced at the obvious pain that was tearing through my friend and bodyguard, and I let the chains off the low-level fury that filled me almost permanently these days.

The welcome heat built, and I dug deeper, pushing off hard, determined to close the distance as quickly as possible.

Small rocks, fragments of debris, and general rubbish coated the floor, and I sprinted as fast as I could, bounding over the crap that was strewn everywhere and closing the distance to the screeching monsters.

The one on the right cut off its scream, slinking forward and honing in on me, its beak clacking and tongue flashing out as its four grasping tentacles flexed and tugged at the air, as though desperate to drag me into its maw.

I growled as I ran, leveling my naginata. I sensed as much as felt the others following me, as arrows flashed past, burying themselves into the first leviathan's body.

It flinched back as a long black arrow—*Tang's*, a part of my mind coldly informed me—flew past us all, thudding into the shoulder of the still-screaming creature, staggering it and making the sound cut off momentarily. It hissed in fury, and three of the tentacles near its face wrapped around the arrow. Gripping it tight, the leviathan yanked it free with a small spurt of black blood, taking a deep breath and screaming again.

The sound it emitted was weird; it built steadily, rising from a pitch that was merely uncomfortable all the way into "takes paint off the walls" levels in less than three seconds, all while shaking as though it had a taser applied to its butthole.

The noise reverberated off the walls and funneled down, loud and agonizing enough to make me stagger, even as I gritted my teeth and leveled my naginata, rushing at the closest creature once again.

It crouched, then bounded forward, leaping aside as I stabbed out and thrusting its clawed front foot down hard, slamming my blade aside and trapping it.

Before I could bring my weapon back or dodge, the thing struck, all four tentacles spearing forward, claw tips lunging for my flesh.

They hit me hard; two deflected cleanly off the upper slopes of my breastplate, the legion-made cuirass shrugging the blows off. The third slammed into the joint where the pauldron and cuirass met on my left side, and its tip skittered across the attaching leather to dig into a loose section, making me grunt as it drew blood.

The fourth claw struck the bottom of my helm, snapping it down and making it hard to see, until suddenly, the pressure was lifted as the tentacle hastily retracted.

I stepped back, heaving on my naginata and glaring furiously at the creature as Grizz barreled past.

He ducked down behind his shield and shouted something before slamming it into the leviathan's face, staggering it back several steps. It switched its focus to him, all four claws flashing around the shield to grip it, pulling him inexorably close as it opened its beak to scream or bite him.

Before it got the chance, though, two things happened. The first was that the other leviathan, the one that had been keeping us all off balance by screaming continually, finally ran out of breath or mana or whatever. As soon as the sound cut off, the world came back into focus, and three arrows, a Firebolt, and a full spread of five enhanced Magic Missiles slammed into it a bare handful of seconds later, staggering and severely wounding it.

The other thing that happened was Lydia. She bolted past me, then jumped up and kicked off the wall, twisting her body around to face the leviathan that was grappling with Grizz from the side. As soon as she was in the air and oriented correctly, she screamed out "Shield Bash!" and the ability took over, slamming her forward with tremendous speed and force.

She hit the creature side-on, slamming her shield, with her fully armored bulk behind it, into the side of its face. The impact culminated in a loud crunch of bone. The two tentacles on that side went flaccid, and the bottom half of its beak dislocated, the beginnings of a sonic scream dropping into a warbling, distressed whine.

Lydia bounced off the beast, hitting the wall and then bouncing forward again as she lashed out with her mace, smacking the weapon down hard into the creature's left front claw, just as it lifted the appendage to slash at Grizz.

There was a second crunch of bone and a louder whine, as it tried to pull back before Grizz lunged forward. He swept aside the remaining tentacles that still clung to the left side of his shield and slashed out in a circular rising swing. The tip of his gladius flashed from left to right and sent the remaining two tentacles flying with a gout of sticky blood.

Before the creature could do more than rear back, he'd switched from a swing to a thrust, and the tip of his blade punched into the leviathan's throat, biting deep.

It staggered, trying to move back, but Grizz followed it, yanking the sword from left to right, widening the wound before driving it deeper. As I glanced back to check on Bane, the gasping whistle notified me of Grizz cutting into the creature's windpipe.

Bane remained slumped against the wall, two hands clutching at his head, as another arm braced against the wall. His remaining limb scrabbled for his daggers on the floor. He was stunned, clearly, but my mana dipped as Oracle's hands began bursting with light. She'd have him back together in no time.

I nodded grimly in her direction and looked back at the farthest creature as another barrage of spells and arrows slammed into it. It screeched in pain and fury before spitting something that looked green and venomous in the direction of the others, then turning to run for it.

"Hell no!" I snarled, dropping my naginata against the wall and pulling in my power as my lips started to speak the arcane words, my fingers twisting like snakes on acid.

The spell built faster and faster as I poured increasing amounts of mana into it, compressing it and shaping it, more with my mind and fingers now, it seemed, than the phrases and words I barely understood. Whatever Amon's mind-dump of information had been, it'd filled in tiny gaps I'd never even known were missing from my knowledge, taking all of my spells to the next level.

In three seconds, the spell had taken a basic form; it was bulbous at the back end, closest to me, with a long, thin tip at the further end, a tip that sighted in on its quarry and quivered with a suppressed need to be released. I inspected the additional forms I had laced into the Explosive Compression spell, inspired by the spell I'd created when we fought in the Skyking's tower. Now they felt…better, more integrated, and infinitely more graceful. I tied off the last section and splayed my fingers, releasing the spell with a "huuut" of forced exhalation, shoving forward with my hands as the spell took off.

The leviathan had vanished into the darkness at the far end of the corridor, barely visible as it moved, its camouflage ability occluding the faint light that occasionally lit the far end of the corridor where it jinked to the right. My spell changed that, flaring with light as it hurled itself down the inky hallway.

It covered the hundred or so yards to the creature in less than two seconds, the acceleration causing the air to shake. Unerringly, it slammed into the back-right leg just as the appendage bunched up, gathering itself to propel the leviathan forward.

Instead of its leg slamming down and pushing it further along to power its frantic, injured retreat, the spell punched into the back of the leg, burying itself deep before detonating.

The flesh was shredded a split second before the rest of the back end of the wolf-squid thing, peeling the dark skin, veins, and muscle from the skeleton a split second before the bones fractured and exploded in fragments.

I'd compressed the spell even more than the last time, forcing it to cover a smaller area as it unfurled, and this time, it was far more horrific for its victim.

Rather than spreading out over a dozen feet, hurling things outward with flames and violence, then pulling them back in to compress them into a tiny area, it all happened in a space the size of an average windowpane.

The back end of the body was smashed outwards, shattering bones and pulverizing flesh, tearing the joints apart, before suddenly reversing and pulling back in. The implosion generated the same amount of power, maybe more, but due to being confined to a smaller space, it dragged the surrounding air and body materials into the rapidly forming tiny marble of compressed flesh at the center of the spell.

The effect from where we stood was impressive, as a flash of light blurred away, smashing into the back end of the fleeing creature before detonating. The flare of light exposed the back third of the leviathan being blown apart; then the flames spread, compressing down and yanking the creature back into a single point, filling the corridor with frantic, ear-shredding screeches of pain and snapping bones.

As the light died, so did the second leviathan, and the corridor went quiet as the first fell forward onto its face. Grizz yanked his blade free and stepped back, flicking the blade to clean it of blood.

"Well, that was…messy," Yen commented quietly from just behind me. "Out of curiosity, that spell you just used…what's it called?"

"Explosive Compression," I replied shortly, reaching up to wipe at one ear and frowning at my bloody gauntlets in annoyance.

"And where did you get it?" she asked carefully.

"We made it up," I said, glancing at her curiously. "It's a bit rough, but it does the job."

"Yeah, it really does," she agreed wistfully. "Feel free to teach me that one when you get the chance."

"You teach me the Flaming Spear spell, and I will," I promised, moving past her and heading back down the corridor to check on the others.

Bane was finally standing, slipping the blades back into their sheaths as I came to a stop.

"You all right, mate?" I asked him.

"I am, Jax. It seems some of the old tales of leviathans being anathema to my race are true, though. I wasn't much help in that fight, sorry."

"Don't be daft," I scoffed incredulously. "You managed to kick the Skyking's ass thanks to your abilities; Sod's law that it's a weakness here." I clapped him on the shoulder and searched around for the others. "Everyone okay?" I asked, getting a round of nods and shrugs.

The next few seconds were a mess of health and mana potions, healing spells, and people wiping blood away from noses, mouths, and ears. I shifted uncomfortably, feeling my guts still twisting, and resolved that I'd need a good, long shower when the chance came up again next. Followed by a week of sleep and a good meal to set me right.

"Jax!" a call rose from Yen. I turned sharply, glancing up the corridor at her. She was gesturing further into the darkness. "Tang's scouting ahead," she said in a low voice that carried, and I nodded in acknowledgement before turning back and staring down with concern at the gnome that still thrashed and shuddered on the floor.

"We can't carry him," I said, scanning the corridor. "And he's probably safer here than with us, to be fair. We can't strip the bodies, as they apparently might have traps on them." Sighing heavily, I came to a decision I didn't like. "I'm sorry, Grizz, Oracle, but we can't spare the time to carry him, and we can't trust him until he's taken the Oath, so it's for the best that we leave him here. Hopefully, he will be okay, and…I guess we can come back once we've secured the area a bit."

"I—" Miren faltered, gazing sadly at the gnome where he thrashed and growled. "Should one of us stay with him?"

"No," I said flatly. "If we can, we will come back for him, but he's likely lived his whole life down here. He can find his way about; hell, he's going to be either far more intelligent, or he's going to be dead. He can figure out where we've gone." I frowned, scanning the dimly lit corridor. "You've got two minutes; gather up whatever you need, then we're moving on."

People moved quickly, collecting anything they'd dropped; any interesting bits they wanted went into the bags, and Bane and I examined the remains of the mobile shield, amazed at both its simplicity and its effectiveness.

If it had needed a bigger manastone to power it, or had been able to recharge, we'd have been screwed. I examined it again, seeing it from a different angle this time and admiring the simple yet cunning design. It was as I'd first noted, essentially a massive walking shield at the front, but behind it, a series of small seats had been fitted, as well as a cargo hopper and a section that seemed designed to carry something else, but whatever that was, it was missing now.

Bane tried a couple of the small hatches on the back side of the device and found they were storage for something, but what, we had no idea yet again. After a few minutes, when everyone had gathered up and the gnome was still flailing around, I sighed and gestured to Bane to lead the way.

We set off, traveling deeper into the structure by way of the corridor. Numerous doors were scattered along either side, but each had seemingly rusted shut, and we moved on. The end of the corridor kinked to the right at a sharp, ninety-degree angle. As we approached the corner, Tang appeared and held his hand out in silent warning.

I opened my mouth, but he shook his head frantically, then gestured for me to come forward, slowly.

I nodded in understanding and moved closer, Yen and Lydia moving in alongside me as we crept up to the edge and peered around.

At first, I couldn't make sense of what I was seeing; then, as my eyes adjusted, the scene slowly resolved into a chaotic vista that fell away before me.

Seemingly, at some point, either in the crash or the hundreds of years that followed, an entire subsection of the city had collapsed. This space had then been colonized by the gnomes, creating a small pocket of their civilization surrounded by metal walls. As I stared out, I blinked again and again, trying to bring the scene below me into comprehending focus.

The corridor had been torn apart at some point, and it now ended a few feet ahead, opening out into an enormous cavern. It was filled with thousands of small lights, structures, moving figures, and machinery, with a huge form that belched steam and smoke as it slowly shifted around the outer edge on a track.

My eyes were glued to the mobile structure as it went, the entire thing shaking, shuddering, and occasionally crunching over something that had been left on its tracks.

I watched in awe as its scale became clear; the construct was easily three stories high, box-like, with a pair of great arms that folded up to the main body. The top of the device had a gnome seated inside it, pulling levers and cackling wildly enough that his voice could be heard floating over the hustle and bustle of the tiny town.

It came to a shuddering halt next to a tower that swarmed with gnomes that fought and bit at each other, trying to force their way into the collection of vehicles that rested in racks, waiting to be loaded aboard the device.

The contraption reached out with two massive arms, clamping them both onto the middle of the tower. With a loud clank and a blast of steam, the vehicles started moving; they slid down the rails, one at a time, slamming into holding bays on the mobile creation. Then the arms shifted and took another vehicle, and another, until it was filled again.

We watched in stunned amazement as what appeared to be a mobile siege weapon, originally designed to roll up to city walls and provide access over them, appeared to have been partially rebuilt as a mobile deployment facility.

As we gaped at the unexpected scene, it finished reloading and began to shift around, slowly turning and rolling back in our direction.

On the ground, two levels down and maybe three hundred feet away, a fight broke out between a pair of gnomes who hadn't managed to get onto the vehicles that were loaded. Others nearby seemed to be drawn in, either shouting or caught by stray blows, and the entire section of the cavern was suddenly filled with a rolling, spreading fight.

"It's a tavern brawl…without tha tavern," Lydia muttered in awe.

We watched for a handful of minutes as more and more of the inhabitants appeared from the surrounding buildings, gleefully diving into the fight from nearby roofs and popping out of holes and piling into the center. Fists and feet flailed, until a flash of lightning and a boom of thunder burst into the cavern, blasting the happily fighting group apart. Several were clearly killed, with limbs blown free, and the crowd scattered, cowed by the display of power.

Bane stiffened, and as I turned to inspect the direction he faced, I saw what I'd missed before: a hunched figure clad in a red robe stood on an ornate balcony maybe halfway around the cavern, flanked by two more leviathans, these two considerably bigger than the ones we'd just fought.

"So, if there's a bigger one than them around," I started when one of the creatures suddenly screamed. The noise was horrific, and I clapped my hands over my ears, staring across at them.

The figure they flanked had turned away and they'd been walking back into the building, when apparently one of them had spotted us, and the pair were suddenly laser-focused on us, trying to determine where we crouched to hide in the remains of our corridor.

I shook my head, looking down at the cavern floor, noting that the mobile platform had come to a grinding halt. The streets were rapidly emptying as the gnomes fled their Master's ire.

Bane staggered back, hands clutching at his head again, and I waved him to back away before turning back to glare at the red-robed figure as it pointed at us, its hands lifting as it summoned magic.

There was a split second where I thought about running, about all of us running back into the corridor, but we were too close, and I didn't know what kind of spell they were going to use.

I'd endured hours upon hours of pain for a goddamn reason though, getting tattooed with multiple runes with both Ame and Jenae helping Renna.

I focused on the figure, frantically trying to push my mana into the right channels and mentally gripping mana in the relevant tattoos.

"Get back, all of you," I hissed as I stepped forward, slamming my naginata's base into the floor and giving the mage the finger, while damn well hoping that my tattoos would trigger okay through all the damn highsteel.

It should, it damn well *should*, I knew…but…their spell built, the glowing white light interspersed with crackling gold and black threads as it built to a crescendo, even as I tried to get my shield up and working properly.

It flared to life just as the figure released its spell, a giant spear of glowing energy forming in the air between us before flaring one last time with power and hurtling across the cavern to smash into me.

The world seemed to explode in fire and force as I was thrown sideways, slamming into the nearest wall.

The building shield burst under the impact, it had probably saved my life, but it destroyed an entire section of the lip of the corridor…then the surrounding walls, weakened from long centuries of water and rust, collapsed as well.

The world tilted, and I staggered, sliding, stunned, and confused as the ground vanished from under me. I fell, sheets of metal and stone collapsing with me into the darkness, and even more tons of debris falling after me.

CHAPTER NINETEEN

I fell slowly at first, stunned, wisps of mana and steam lifting from my armor as I plummeted, stone, steel, and more falling with me. Then I hit an out-jutting wall, flipping me over. Then I collided with a roof, one that lasted long enough for me to roll off the far side, before falling debris demolished it. Then I toppled a final time, realizing in a flash of panic that my naginata was gone.

I shook my head in a daze, trying to focus, as I slammed into a second roof. This one crumbled around me, and I plunged to the floor, slamming into the unyielding surface face-first. The world went black, ending the pain that tore through me, sending my nerves flaring with tingling screams of dispersing magic.

I was only out for a short period of time, thankfully, but as I came to, I found myself laid on my back in a half-demolished bedroom. Random metal sheeting, pipes, and shattered planks had been strewn everywhere. I stared up through a hole in the roof, seeing a magical battle being fought high above me. I was also not alone, suddenly aware of a hissing gnome crouched in the far corner from me.

He slowly stood, and judging from the swinging appendage, it was definitely a he. The crazed creature lifted a pair of gleaming kitchen knives, licking his lips frantically.

The Shield tattoo had activated in time to stop the spell's effects from impacting me fully, but whatever the tattoos did for me in channeling and reinforcing the shield, they apparently didn't work as well when buried beneath armor, as I'd feared.

I lay twitching and shaking as the last floods of power from that fucker's spell ran amok through me, shocking me again and again, while the little gnome darted forward, lifting his knives.

I tried to get up, but my body wouldn't respond, just twitching and flailing weakly. I sagged backwards…just as Oracle flew down through the hole in the roof and landed on my chest.

She took one quick peek around the room, then turned back to me, checking me over even as she angrily pulled together a spell.

"I'll give you one chance," she growled roughly over her shoulder at the figure. "Run. Run now or die."

I blinked at the constrained fury in her voice, and as the little figure hissed at her, she burst into light, a thigh-thick bar of lightning flashing from her to smash the gnome back through the far wall and out into the air.

"Your choice," she concluded before turning back to me.

"What the hell was that!" she snarled at me, pulling hard on our mana and slamming a healing spell into me, making me shake and gasp as my nerves regrew. I idly noticed for the first time the way the world smelled of burned meat. "You just see a spell you don't know and decide to take it on the goddamn chin?!"

"Ch—est," I managed to grunt out, lifting a hand that shook crazily, as I tapped my blackened, armored cuirass.

"What?" she growled.

"I…took it…to the…chest…" I said again, reaching down and slowly pushing myself upwards, debris falling off me and clattering around the room. "What…happened?" I asked, my body still feeling like every nerve was an abscessed tooth.

"What happened?" Oracle repeated dangerously, lifting into the air and hovering before my eyes. "What happened is you—"

She broke off as a howl went up from the door, and a second gnome, this one fully clothed, thankfully, rushed inside, brandishing a club.

"Later!" I grunted, then coughed, tasting blood before grabbing the nearest thing I could find: a length of steel that had once been a section of the ceiling. "Tell me later!"

I turned to build up momentum, slamming the section of roof, a panel that was about a foot wide by three feet long, and maybe an inch thick, around into the oncoming figure. He was maybe two and a half feet tall, if that, and had been brandishing a section of metal tubing. My improvised club smashed both him and his tubing back and out through another wall, making the structure creak in warning.

More gnomes appeared in the doorway, rushing towards us, and I growled in frustration.

"Find my weapon!" I ordered Oracle as I swiped back across, smashing the next gnome's outstretched weapon from his hand and spinning him around with a shriek as his wrist was broken. Then I punted the little bastard in the ass, sending him flying head-first into the wall with a crunch of breaking cartilage.

"Fine!" she snapped, as I struggled to get fully free of the piled debris. I could feel it shifting precariously under me as I discarded my "club," which was too big to use effectively. Instead, I reached out and grabbed the next gnome by the shoulder and punched him in the face, ignoring the length of wire he was attempting to use as a whip.

His nose, which had clearly broken at some point in the past, burst messily as my gauntleted fist slammed into it, and the little figure's eyes rolled back in his head. I picked him up, hefted him overhead, and threw him at the growing group forcing their way in the door.

The next of the creatures caught a low-flying fellow gnome in the face, and the pair fell to the floor with an almost comical sound of coconuts bouncing as their heads collided. The one on top screamed as the next gnome in line took the opportunity to stab him in the kidney.

The back-stabber yanked his knife free and clambered up to stand onto the wounded gnome, gesturing at me, her eyes filled with a wild, frenzied bloodlust.

Others crowded in around and behind her, the wary hatred reflected on their faces; they watched each other as much as they did me. As the little female backstabber licked her blade and giggled, I frantically pointed behind them.

"Look out!" I shouted, and the room dissolved into chaos. Some turned to look; others took advantage of the distracted state of the nearest gnome to stab, bite, kick or hit them, and I couldn't help but shake my head in amazement.

It was like a mixture of the Three Stooges, a rabid kindergarten, and the worst kind of horror movie as they fell on each other, screeching, screaming, and sending blood flying.

I quickly started casting the Explosive Compression spell again, but this time I left the standard size of impact at six feet in all directions, and I grimly kicked out at those who came too close.

It only took a handful of seconds to put the spell together, and I targeted it just outside the door where the majority of the gnomes still fought and writhed.

Just as it left my hands, I grunted, staggering to one knee and glaring to my right, where I found a small figure shaking. He'd slammed a length of metal into my knee, and it'd probably caused him as much pain as it had me, thanks to the metal armor I wore.

I reached out, grabbed his bar, and yanked him forward. Clutching his long, grimy beard with my right hand and pulling his head down into my knee, I knocked the little fucker out on the metal plates that covered it.

The impact from the spell was insane; there'd been dozens out there, I saw out of the corner of my eye. Now they were being dragged, literally kicking and screaming, into a ball of filthy, biting, stabbing, and stinking gnomes. And they were on fire.

"Oracle!" I shouted, reaching out and grabbing a stanchion that braced the wall to my right, using it to haul myself up. I drew back with the metal post and slammed it down hard on a struggling figure that was screaming and trying to escape the morass of flaming bodies caused by my spell. "Where the ever-living *fuck* is my weapon!"

"I don't know!" she screamed at me, obviously as pissed as I was, and we both paused for a second as the sound of magic being exchanged high above us rang out. "We're down here, while everyone else is getting hammered up there, and I'm digging in the fucking rubbish trying to find it!"

"Fine!" I snapped. "Get up there and protect them. I'll kill my way across the entire goddamn cavern, if I have to!"

"You'll die," she fired back, becoming full-size and solid long enough to drag a section of sheeting aside and peer underneath.

"At least I won't have my last minutes filled with nagging!" I roared, then pulled back and drove the post into the pile of debris, levering it up and tipping it over, exposing the floor. "Fuck! It's not here!"

Oracle turned back to the door, firing off a Fireball into the pile of bodies, making me stagger backwards.

"It must have fallen outside somewhere," she said after a moment in a scared voice, glancing from me to the doorway to the sounds of battle above us.

Guilt stabbed through my chest. I stepped in close to her and, reaching out, I pulled her into a deep kiss, both of us pausing for a second to stare into each other's eyes.

"I'm sorry," I admitted softly.

"I know. It's okay," Oracle replied, clearly still pissed and trying to be calm.

"Go on; you need to go to them," I said, gesturing upwards with a jerk of my head. "I can sort this, so go."

She hesitated briefly before kissing me again and shrinking back to her small state, taking a last look at me before zooming up out of the hole in the ceiling.

"I love you," I called out to her in the privacy of our bond.

"I love you, too. Fight smart. I wouldn't leave you if I didn't know you could handle this," she replied.

I nodded to myself grimly as the spell in the doorway died away.

There was a long, pregnant pause, then the moans, growls, and screaming began as the dozens of gnomes that had survived the spell were attacked by their former comrades.

"Well, I'll not be turning my back on you fuckers!" I said grimly, drawing back and smashing the post into the back of a gnome's head as he hunched over one of his dead fellows, trying to pry a bag free of the corpse.

"Outside! A hundred feet to the right of the building and one level up; I think I can see your naginata inside a window!"

"Got it! Thank you!" I called back to Oracle, grinning at the dozens of gnomes who gathered themselves in the doorway and outside. The ones inside slowly edged forward, glaring at me suspiciously.

"Looks like it's time to dance, motherfuckers!" I snarled, flipping the post over in my hands. Catching it by the other end and swinging for the fences, I smashed the end into the chin of a gnome who had stepped too close.

His teeth shattered and his jaw fractured, the tip of his tongue flying through the air in a spurt of blood as the rest of the pack pounced.

The entire room devolved into a flying, screaming mess of gnomes, bloody teeth, and bits. Less than a minute into the fight, the post bent, and I threw it at a gnome's head, resorting to my fists.

I caught one as he leaped at me, stopping him with a flat palm to his chest and slamming my other fist into his nose, sending him flying. I struck out with a high kick to my left, then struck downward, heel first, taking another creature in the face before jumping at him and stamping down on his neck, hard.

A stab came in from the right; the small blade, barely better than a penknife, clattered across my greaves. I grabbed the gnome's extended arm, twisting it backwards. Yanking the limb straight, I slammed the heel of my palm into the locked elbow, drawing a scream of pain as the bone shattered and the sharp, broken edges were forced out through the flesh.

I released the limp wrist, snatching the penknife as it started to fall and ramming the blade home into her eye before spinning and bracing as another figure ran at me.

This one leaped at my groin, mouth wide open, and the little fucker had the metal teeth, as well as the stone-skin that the recent majority had lacked.

What he didn't have, though, was solid stone's weight, or any kind of magical workaround for Newtonian physics. I practically chuckled as I brought my right knee across my body, sweeping right to left, and deflected him to the side, catching him by the left arm with my left hand as I turned to follow his trajectory, finally grasping his right leg with my right hand.

I pulled back with my right, shifting my left-handed grip from his flailing arm to his other leg, and went to work.

Suddenly, I had a good-sized weapon that was coated in stone, and I put it to good use.

I had a sudden memory of a meme from years ago, entitled *Ever been so pissed, you beat a mother-fucker with a mother-fucker?* The image had been a guy swinging another guy at a third guy, and I couldn't help but grin as I mimicked the move, realizing, as Grizz had demonstrated before, that sometimes it was good to go old school and just beat your opponents to death in a damn impressive way. I smashed first one, then two, then five of the gnomes out of my way, sending them all reeling with broken bones, and I realized that, apart from the worry about the rest of the team, I was starting to enjoy myself.

I swung the gnome-club back, spun around, and heaved him as hard as I could at a new stone-coated guy that had just stepped inside.

He left.

He actually left very quickly, while making a new hole for a window and breaking my current "weapon." I dropped the bloody mess that I was holding, suddenly realizing I didn't know how long he'd been flesh for, then shrugged. They'd started this, after all.

There was a sudden lull in the fighting as the gnomes fell back, unsure. I nodded to myself in satisfaction at causing a race of apparently regressing, rabid, drug-abusing psychopaths to pause and reconsider their lifestyle choices.

I glanced around the room, disgustedly observing the way everything was now spattered in a thick coating of blood and viscera, and I carefully reached up to wipe my hand down the outside of my helm, then glanced at my fingertips.

Yup. Coated in lumps and blood.

I paused for a second, staring at it, when I heard a scream of pain from above and saw Miren's symbol flash from green, to yellow, to red, and I growled in renewed fury.

These little fuckers were keeping me from saving my people!

"You think I'm bad now?" I whispered, rolling my shoulders and drawing my Dagger of Ripping free of its sheath. Holding it in my right hand, I made a "come here" gesture with my left. "You ain't seen *nothin'* yet."

When they hesitated, I didn't. I lunged forward, grabbing the nearest gnome to the door and yanking him in, ignoring the cudgel he wielded with a trio of spinning blades affixed on it. I drove the dagger into his throat, then yanked it aside, sending a spray of blood out to coat the walls even further. Whipping around, I threw the dagger at another gnome who'd been creeping up on me through a hole Oracle had blasted in a wall earlier.

That did it, as I reached down and lifted the cudgel the frantically squealing and bleeding out body on the floor by my feet had borne. First in ones, then twos, then ten, the small, wild creatures ran, more and more of them sprinting away in terror as I flicked the trigger on the side of the cudgel and watched as the three circular saw blades that were set into the cudgel revved to life.

"Oh yeah!" I growled out, spinning the cudgel and rolling my wrist through an offensive strike form. "You and I are gonna be *real* good friends!"

I stepped over to the gnome, who was slumped half-in and half-out of a hole in the wall, staring at the dagger still stuck into his chest. He drooled a long, bloody streak as he tentatively fingered the hilt, and I smacked his hand away. Planting my booted foot on his shoulder to brace him, I ripped the dagger free, then wiped it on the shoulder of his tunic as he slumped forward.

Cautiously, I moved over to the door and actually had to kick some of the corpses aside before I could clamber out, having to hunch down to pass through the small doorframe and looking around as I emerged. There were still a dozen or so gnomes in sight, but they'd backed up and were watching me from a distance.

I stomped clear of the small river of blood that flowed out of the ruined house and searched around, spotting the house that I thought Oracle had meant, up and to the right of my current building. The roof had clearly been demolished by something smashing through it, and there were a handful of gnomes up there fighting over something.

I quickly scanned the street I was in, noting the rusty, slumped, and collapsed buildings, the festering pools, and the hatred which the gnomes showed for basically everything around them. I frowned as I considered another home, observing the remains of a garden and a tiny picket fence, long since subsumed into the muck, and broken in dozens of places.

They'd clearly been built after the gnomes had come here and colonized the cavern and had been designed with care and an impressive degree of craftmanship, judging from the variety of designs and the fact that so many of them had lasted this long. Something had changed, and it had done so in an unbelievably bad way. Clearly, whatever had mutated the gnomes had either been very gradual, over lots of years in little ways, or it'd been a significant effect that was much more recent.

I looked back up and down the street, trying to figure out the best way to go, and two things struck me at once.

First, my mana was dropping like a stone, and I tugged out a mana potion, downing it and licking my lips at the minty taste, then casually throwing the vial at a half-hidden gnome. Second, there wasn't an easy way up from here; in fact, the only way I could see was at the far end of the street, where a dangling rope ladder swayed, filled with gnomes fighting to climb up already.

I took a few steps out further into the street and looked around, frowning as I tried to make sense of the layout and determine whether I could climb up, when the decision was made for me.

In the distance, the mobile siege tower-thing had started up again, and it rolled into a position where whoever was controlling it clearly saw me.

It turned, noisily clanking around until it was lined up on my position, then raised one arm, pointing it in my direction.

"Well, that's not happy-making," I muttered to myself as the arm shuddered, with blasts of gas and plumes of electricity rocketing out, and a half second later, the first of the badunka riders erupted from the end of the arm.

This one was a two-wheel design, looking more like a traditional motorbike, if you discounted the jets of blue-white steam that rocketed out of the sides, the blades that reflected the dim light, and the screaming trio of gnomes that hung on for dear life as it flew through the air. It vanished from sight behind a building just as a second racer flew out of the arm, this one bouncing off the end of the platform and twisting before slamming into the side of a second building and erupting in flames.

The third and fourth badunka riders flew free and vanished from sight as well; then the structure turned away, facing the side of the cavern and clattering away out of sight behind a building. I swore, hearing the roaring of the mad little bastards approaching on their bikes.

The gnomes that had been creeping forward and hiding themselves poorly around me, suddenly turned and began sprinting frantically, clearly wanting to be nowhere near the badunka riders when they arrived. I took advantage of the sudden desertion and turned, searching for the best combination of a low roof and intact walls out of the nearby buildings.

I spotted a low-hanging corner of a roof three houses along that looked like it wouldn't collapse as soon as I touched it. I flicked the lever to power down the cudgel as I started to run, shoving it into my bag and jumping to kick off the wall of the building next to the one I wanted, and launching myself as high as I could.

My fingers caught the lip of the roof, and I grunted, pulling myself up and feeling my boots scraping on the wall as I tried to find purchase. It took a few seconds of huffing, but I managed it. Just as I pulled my ass up over the edge, the building shook, and a wash of heat and flame tossed my legs upwards, flipping me further onto the roof.

I slammed down on the metal and rolled, my armor clanging as the building shook again. I peered over the way I'd come and cursed.

The first badunka rider had found the street I was in, and his creation had a small seat on the back. Another gnome was balancing on the small perch as he fired blasts at me from a wand that sparked and bucked in his hands.

"Goddamn crazy bastards!" I growled, rolling to the side and coming dangerously close to the edge of the roof as I dodged another blast.

The passenger howled in triumph and gestured again, firing another flaming orb that flew through the air like a mortar, slamming into the building next to the one I was on and taking out an entire section of the wall.

I shoved myself to my feet and looked behind me, seeing a row of blocked-off passages nearby that formed the wall of the cavern, which then stepped back a couple dozen feet overhead from my position to form the second level, where the building I wanted stood further up the slope.

I ran at the closed-off passages, jumping, grabbing onto a section of the wall, and heaving. My feet scrabbling frantically as I went, I managed to drag myself up, searching for the next handhold, the next grip or crack, and I climbed.

I climbed in full legion armor, the weight alone obscene, and I had a momentary mental image of me doing this on TV back home, watching as swarms of fans gasped and *ooh*-ed and *ah*-ed as I went, slipping up the side.

"Gods, I'd be rich if I had a camera." I grunted to myself as I went, imagining the social media posts.

I reached out and grabbed onto a large section of the wall that had a crack in it, and as my fingers wiggled in, holding on as best I could, I felt it shift slightly. A scream suddenly rose from inside, on the other side of the crack, making me try to pull my hand free but finding my gauntlet caught on a jagged section of metal.

I pulled again, and a third time, finally yanking it free and almost falling off the wall with the force, until something hit the other side of the wall, and the edge of an axe blade crashed through where my hand had just been.

Whoever was in there was majorly pissed at me for climbing their wall, and I swung back, digging my feet in and jumping, forcing myself upwards, inch-by-inch and foot-by-foot.

Climbing in full armor was a terrifying experience, not lessened by the blasts of fire that flew up randomly from below, or the screeching and crashing from the other side of the wall.

In armor, not only could I not feel the grips properly or bend as well as I had years ago when I'd frequented climbing weekends and excursions to indoor walls, but with the helm, I couldn't see well, either. My breathing grew more and more panicked and frustrated, until I heard a clatter above me, and as I pulled myself up the last few inches to grab the edge of the next level, a gnome stepped into view, clearly not realizing I was there until too late.

We both froze, me looking up and him down, and he slowly grinned at me and finished pulling his dick out, obviously intending on pissing on me, then kicking me off.

I dug my feet in and jumped, relying on the grip I had on the edge of the level, and practically flew up the last few feet, grabbing the edge of a building and rolling myself over to kick his legs out from under him.

He slammed into the floor, both nose and pecker making unprotected contact with the jagged, rusty ground. He shrieked in pain and fury as he glowered up at me before meeting my boot coming the other way.

I stomped hard on his upturned face, then kicked him off the edge, hearing the roof below stop his fall with a crunch. I rolled onto my stomach, forcing myself to jump to my feet as I searched my surroundings…then I looked back over the edge.

He'd crashed through the roof of the next floor down, right into someone's "house" and they were *pissed* about it. I saw a blur of hands, steel then screaming, both of them screaming…then a third jumped in as well, with claret spraying free. I shook my head and turned my damn back on them, crazy motherfuckers.

The majority of the gnomes I'd seen earlier were gone, a veritable small mob running away down a street that disappeared to my left. I dismissed them, sprinting for the house Oracle had indicated. It was less than a minute's lumbering dash to reach the door, which hung half off its hinges, swaying crazily.

I kicked it in, taking it fully off its remaining hinge as I stepped into the gloom. My DarkVision painted it in greys and greens and I swore viciously.

The room was filled with bodies and blood, and the hole where something had torn through the roof was centered over the middle of the pile…

…but my naginata was gone.

CHAPTER TWENTY

I turned abruptly, rushing back outside, and saw the cavern before me, taking the time to try to figure out who was where. It didn't take long.

Dozens of gnomes blitzed across the cavern, heading right for the large building on the far side that the red-robed figure was stationed atop.

He fired a barrage of silvery darts through the air, and they slammed into a glowing, icy-blue shield that blocked off the entrance to my team's area.

The shield flickered and pulsed, but I could see my people hiding behind it as gnomes scaled the wall. Worried, I reached out, calling to Oracle.

"Are you all okay?" I asked.

"Yeah, but the walls are starting to give way; whoever that is, they've got a lot of mana, and Yen says her Identify spell wouldn't work, so they're at least level thirty."

"Well, fuck," I sent back. *"They've got my naginata as well; looks like the little bastards are taking it to the boss."*

"Dammit. We're getting hammered here. I can probably get out to you, though? Once the shield falls, I can sneak through if I have Lydia wait until she uses hers."

"And if the gnomes use that opportunity to get in to reach you all? Or if they manage to land the spells at the right time?" I asked. *"No. I'll create the diversion, see if I can get my weapon, and storm the building. When they turn to come for me, use the distraction to hammer that fucker hard."*

"I don't like it!"

"Neither do I, but shit happens. Good luck." I grunted, receiving a sensation of frustrated agreement and love from her in a confusing welter of emotions.

I drew a deep breath as the fighting group cleared another street and disappeared from view, the badunka riders appearing at the bottom of the bank that led up to where I stood.

"Looks like it's time to play," I muttered as they raced toward me. The passenger stood up, wobbling as he aimed with his wand again.

"On the upside, two problems can cancel each other out," I said to myself, a grin stretching my cheeks as I picked up a short spear from the ground.

I didn't want to waste my own good weapons on a stone-covered monstrosity, after all.

I took a few deep breaths, squinting at the oncoming riders as they closed the distance, and the first spell-mortar lofted towards me. I checked the mana I had, just over half, and nodded in satisfaction.

Then I triggered Mana Overdrive and sprinted forward.

My feet seemed to fly across the ground, rubble and debris changing from impediments to things I could use to push off even faster. Planting my foot on a wall, a pile of rubble, even a dead gnome's corpse, all became useful as I raced at the riders, and they raced at me.

I jinked left, then right, rolled under a Fireball that screamed past, and leapt to my feet, heaving the first spear through the air at the nearest bike as it closed the distance between us.

He skidded left, then swayed right, barely staying upright as the spear flew through the space he'd been about to cross.

His passenger, though, had been swaying and barely clinging on before they'd had to swerve, so when the badunka straightened up, the rider looked back to find his passenger screaming as he fell, hitting the street, hard.

As the rider's head was turned, I swept up a nearby rock and flung it as hard as I could, followed by another; then I ran forward, closing to a dozen yards as the rider looked back at me and frantically swerved again, before flipping the bike and slamming into the floor.

My second rock was aimed at the next badunka in line, and it was a hell of a miss. But it still made them swerve, and the passenger from the first badunka was right in their way.

There was a scream, then the spiked wheels ran over him, shredding his body and sending blood spraying as I changed direction, rushing the gnome driver of the first badunka as he groaned and stirred.

I leaped at the tiny figure, leading with my right foot to kick him in the chest, bowling him over before he could get up. I swept up another rock in my fist and slammed it into his head, knocking him back, hard.

His skin was the white-grey of stone, but the cracks and fractures meant it wasn't going to last long, by my guess. I grabbed his shoulder and flipped him over while he shook his head, trying to overcome the stunning blow. Then I was pinning him face-down and kneeling on his back. I grabbed his chin in my right hand and the back of his head in my left, wrenching my hands around and breaking his neck.

The death's head rising was his only funeral, as I grinned at the badunkas heading towards me. The first, having coated itself with the blood of the passenger, had spun out and crashed, while the final one had taken a side street, clearly deciding to loop around and get me from behind.

I jumped onto the nearby riderless, idling, *smoking* badunka and hunched down. The seat was suspended between the wheels, and made of steel bands, with a space that I could barely hunch into, while the second seat was just too far back to be comfortable. The controls were a pair of levers, and I gripped them tight, twisting them and nearly snapping the damn thing in half as the wheels tried to go in opposite directions.

I changed quickly, now twisting the right lever forward and the left back, instead of both in the same direction, and nearly gave myself whiplash as it took off.

I frantically twisted and pulled, yanking and pressing in every way I could think off, bouncing off the walls as I went. Luckily, a few seconds in, I had a rough idea of what to do, and I cut Mana Overdrive before I bottomed myself out.

The levers controlled the front and back wheels independently; right, forward and left, back. The wheels went forward, while the opposite was reverse, with steering managed by pushing the levers in towards the center of the bike or pulling away from it.

It was totally insane and weird to control, but as the wind tore tears from my eyes, I couldn't tear the grin from my face. I passed buildings in a blur, gnomes diving aside, frantically skidding down one street and up another. The spiked wheels and blades that covered the outside gleamed in the dim light of the cavern.

The world itself was a blur, and I could barely keep up with the machine; only my enhanced Agility and Intelligence gave me the edge I needed to keep it upright and not wrap it around something, but I'd not last long.

I took a corner I thought would lead to the building—the mansion, really— on the far side of the cavern, and instead found the tracks that the siege weapon used right in my path. I twisted the levers, rolling right, then swore as I saw the tower that the badunka riders were housed in up ahead.

As I got closer, two more of the leviathans waited on either side of the gate at the bottom of the tower, and another humanoid figure in a black robe higher up the tower. I had barely enough time to recognize it before I was haring down another street, but the scream of rage and the loud boom of metal slamming down, and the feeling of my balls trying to reach my ears internally informed me in no uncertain terms that neither that sound nor the lack of a proper saddle on this damn thing were good for me.

I took another cross street, barely skidding across to clear the building on the corner. A short thug of a gnome with a mohawk screamed in fear, diving through a window as I nearly ran him down, and I looked back over my shoulder at the roar of revving engines.

I passed between two houses and saw the tower again, as well as the half-pipe tube that had been dropped from it, letting the badunkas race free in pursuit of me.

Rising even over the squeals and hisses of the badunka I rode were the sounds of dozens more engines. They were powering up, and they were getting closer.

I turned at the next crossroads, taking a right, then a left, then almost destroyed my vehicle as I came to a dead end, filled with rotting refuse and huge, dimly glowing mushrooms. Desperately spinning around, I tried the right, gritting my teeth as I bounced across a corpse in the road, while the metal bands of the seat attempted to make me into a eunuch.

I took the next corner, heading away from the tower and trying to swing around to head for the mansion as the first of them came into sight.

They were all shapes and sizes, from things that looked like horses with three wheels, to others that balanced precariously on one. Some had seats, while others barely clung on, as though about to fall to their deaths.

They all bore screaming gnomes, though, and lots of them carried passengers that cast various spells through wands that sparked and bucked, and thank the gods, occasionally exploded.

One explosion within the pack wiped out three of the dozens of Badunkas. I grinned, turning the levers even further and feeling the engine starting to shake, as even more steam erupted out and hissing started up.

The badunka wouldn't last long; it was too damaged, too badly built, and too…cack-handed, basically. The entire thing looking like it was someone's first draft, made out of scrap to send someone they really hated to their doom.

"You okay?" I threw out to Oracle.

"Yeah, is that…what are you doing?!" she asked abruptly, horror and jealousy clear in her voice, and I remembered how much she'd loved riding the airships.

"Told you I'd get their attention!" I said, grinning maniacally to myself. *"Gonna need some destruction dealing soon, and some fucking healing!"*

"I'll be ready," she said, and I hunched down and leaned over. My left knee clinked against bits of metal as I used it to corner before straightening up.

The red-robed figure had stopped casting spells, clearly either out of mana or happy to leave them to be mobbed by the gnomes, now that the siege tower was so close.

I twisted the throttles and took another corner, then grinned as I shot out of the rabbit warren of streets, bursting into what I assumed was farmland. I was suddenly surrounded by enormous mushrooms and glittering pools of contaminated water that glowed with a dim, silvery light. Just then, I saw two things ahead of me.

First was the mansion; switchbacks led up to it on the far side of the cavern. But the way was clear now, even as the pack of gnomes I'd been hunting hurried through the gates and vanished inside. They had my naginata; I'd seen it gleaming as they vanished, and that was a relief, even if it was in there.

The second thing was that the siege weapon was even more rickety than I'd thought it was at first glance, and I'd found the track to it again. I checked my mana and released the right lever, holding on grimly to the left as my fingers twisted, and the arcane syllables fell from my lips, torn away by the wind of my passage.

I swerved almost at random, occasional spells hurtling past, and screamed invectives as they tried to close the distance.

One of the badunkas pulled up alongside, and the rider swung a mace at me, the head gleaming white with power. I ducked, the strike passing by mere inches as I rammed my spell into his face.

The goggles covering his eyes and his mad grin vanished into the Fireball, as did his head, leaving a sickly-sweet, pungent odor of cooked meat to float on the breeze as he reached for his face then crashed.

He flipped end over end, disappearing in a Fireball, with the wreckage taking out two more badunkas.

I frantically thrust the Fireball back, aware that containment had been broken on the spell and wanting it far, far away from me when it went off.

I felt the spell leave me, the draw of mana cutting off, even as I drew hard on my mana again and started building another Fireball, trying again when the first detonated.

It flew behind me a dozen feet or so, the spellform shaking and twisting as it broke apart. Then it exploded, the wavefront pouring outward, tearing up the mushroom fields and flinging shards in every direction.

I swore, frantically clinging onto the badunka, and barely managed it, even as the following badunka riders plowed straight into a maelstrom of fiery destruction.

I finished my incantation and hurled the spell away from me at my target, grabbed the levers, and twisted them aside, flinging the badunka onto a new trajectory and hurtling towards the switchback.

I tore left and right, weaving through the fields and grinning maniacally to myself as the explosion rocketed behind me, followed by a loud, reverberating scream of rage as the siege weapon tilted ominously.

My aim had been true, and the Fireball had taken out one wheel of the thing, the front right. Its own motion and weight had done the rest once the spell detonated, setting fire to the wheel and shattering it. As the wheel crumbled, it twisted the tower, then, instead of following the carved, circular path on the rails, the edge of the tower crunched into the ground on that side.

It dug in, making it tilt, and the three wheels that were left creaked and groaned as they tried to keep going, then the back right gave way as well.

When that wheel went, the entire structure dipped; then the weight of the badunkas played their part. The gnomes were bouncing and hollering, screeching with bloodlust and fighting amongst themselves. They looked for all the world like drugged-up baboons desperate to kill and maim, and their movement was the feather that broke the camel's back.

It tilted further, grinding to a halt, then more beams and cross-members snapped, and the entire thing twisted and fell, smashing into the nearest wall, detonating as first one then another of the badunkas went up in flames.

Furious and terrified screams echoed from the tower and from the badunka riders that had survived. But I didn't care, as I took the last left and right, racing up the final stretch towards the mansion doors. Then I gunned the engine all the way to the end, forcing the wheels to top speed before straightening up, letting go of the controls, and digging my boots into the ground. I rolled backwards off the badunka, tucking myself into as tight a ball as I could, as the badunka rocketed into the doors and detonated.

I bounced and rolled across the floor for a good dozen feet before slamming into a wall and nearly knocking myself out.

It easily took dozens of minutes before I could make enough sense of the world to know I'd fucked up. Literally. Everything was ringing, spinning, and all I wanted to do was throw up. I lay there, occasionally trying to get up but just making the world spin more, until hands grabbed me roughly and dragged me aside, pulling me into cover. A voice I knew I recognized told me to be still and silent. The sounds of creatures moving nearby rose and fell.

Time passed as someone forced a healing potion into my mouth, and I heard cursing as something seemed wrong with my head.

I blinked blearily as someone pulled off my helm, tearing my skin; then it was like I'd been plunged into an ice bath. I stiffened and gasped in pain and my eyes were forced open wide.

The world came back into focus, and I blinked at all the blood on the wall and on Bane's hands as he held my damaged helmet in one hand, helping to hold me upright with the rest.

I shook myself, looking about frantically, and saw the rest of the team were there, and that Oracle, sweet Oracle, was kneeling by my side, exhausted, as she struggled to get my last mana potion out of my bag and lift it to my lips.

I drank it, still in shock, then shuddered as she hit me again, healing me all the way to full.

I sagged back and Bane lowered me against the wall, then handed me my helm. I stared at it and let out a low whistle as I took in the cracks and the dented-in section; no wonder it'd hurt coming off.

I looked up, finding my entire team there. The gnome, Giint, was there too, seemingly ignoring me. I frowned at him, and Oracle spoke up quickly.

"Jax, it's okay. He helped us," she said reassuringly before continuing through our mental link.

"He turned up halfway through the fight; he has a nasty-looking crossbow in a bag, and he helped to take down the other gnomes, but he's not happy about it. He can talk now, more or less, but he's seriously pissed. Oh, and he swore the Oath," she added as an afterthought.

"Okay, thank you, Gint, for helping us," I said, and he grunted and hunched his shoulders.

"It's Giint, actually, Jax," Oracle corrected me gently, reaching out and brushing my hair back, then kissing my cheek.

"Are you okay?" she asked privately again.

"I am," I said to her in the same way; then I saw the look she gave me. *"Honestly, I am. I just had my bell rung a bit. What happened?"*

"When you crashed into the side of the building, you took out a section of the supports, and the red-robed mage fell out of sight when some of the roof caved in. It's somewhere inside, and the one in the black robes came up here as fast as it could. Bane managed to make it to you first and get you to cover, thankfully," she said aloud again, and I nodded gratefully to her before reaching up and bracing myself against the wall, then climbing to my feet.

"Sorry, Giint," I apologized to the gnome, who glared at me then huffed and went back to staring at his hands. "What's going on here?" I asked.

He looked up at me. For the first time since we'd healed him, I got a good look at his face.

The seemingly ingrained snarl and general hatred of the world around him was gone, instead replaced with a bone deep self-loathing that seemed to shriek up at me from his gaze.

"What's…wronnng?" he croaked, his voice sounding old and hard-used. "What coulddd be wronnng? I…wake…from a nightmaaare to find it'sss my liiiife." He swallowed back tears. "I kiiilled my wife. My childrrren. I ate—"

He broke off, looking away in disgust. He started to shake, and more tears flooded his cheeks, carving tracks in the filth that coated his skin.

He was dressed in a mixture of clothes, clearly scavenged from other dead gnomes. He wore thick leather pants with reinforced knees and multiple pockets, a tunic that, while grubby, was still an off-olive green color and was similarly reinforced, along with four sets of tool belts looped around his waist. One was slung over each shoulder to the opposite hip in a bandolier style, and one he'd cinched to his right leg in a spiral that wound around it.

The outfit itself was obviously strong and made to last, which was the only reason he was decent still, considering that it was torn, shredded, burned, and filthy with every possible combination of stains that I could see, not to mention it reeked. I knew that was, at least in part, the body, or bodies, that had worn the clothes recently.

"What happened here?" I asked him, glancing up at the building above us and back at the mushroom fields, seeing the trail of corpses, flaming wrecks, and destruction both I and my team had left to get here. Movement marred the distance, but it seemed we'd actually managed to break through even the fanatic insanity of the gnomes by now.

"The Maassster happened," he said flatly. "He…itttt…came. Itttt fed on usss, made ussss ssslavessss…then ittt took the waterrr. All we haaaad leffft wass the metalll and morrre drinkiiiing metal, morrrre madnesss."

He refused to look at me now, twisting his fingers together over and over and shuddering as the sobs tore through him.

"What's the 'Master'?" I asked him, and he just shook his head, refusing to say more.

"He doesn't know," Oracle said softly. "We questioned him on the way over as well; all he knows is that he or it has powerful magic, and it makes them do whatever it wants. He vaguely remembers before it came, when the gnomes lived here.

"They literally lived here for over a century in relative peace, the specters seemingly content to not kill them if they didn't enter the other portions of the city. They're from a scout vessel that found the Sunken City. They tried exploring it, and a party got cut off, trapped down here. The rest of the crew came to rescue them and got trapped as well. The spirits were still about, then; the revenants of the crew and the imperial forces, as well as the undead. The gnomes basically reinforced the area and settled in to try to build up enough weapons to fight their way free."

I glanced at Giint, trying not to think of the things he must have seen and done in his life, as she went on.

"Whatever the 'Master' is, it came about fifty years ago, and it took over, fed on them, both magically and occasionally physically, apparently. He calls it 'the Master' or 'the Skin-Walker,' depending, and I don't think even he knows what he means.

"Evidently, it took what it wanted and killed anything that tried to stand up to it. Then it took the water, and whatever cleaned the saltwater to make it potable. The gnomes only had whatever rainwater made its way down here through the various holes, and it was contaminated with all sorts of poisons. They tried to clean it, but the Skin-Walker stopped them, killing any who tried." Oracle shook her head, looking at Giint and the burning village sadly.

"Over time, the gnomes, well, went feral. They stopped trying to fix things and started attacking each other. The buildup of poisons twisted them, and the Skin-Walker and its leviathans preyed on them all. The gnomes stopped caring as long as it wasn't them, and they followed their instincts in making new and wonderful things, but they were all geared towards war, and…well, they used the fastest and lowest-effort methods, so everything breaks regularly, and they steal everything from each other, so they ended up like…this," she finished, waving her arm generally around the cavern.

"So, there's a couple of fuckers left inside. Then what?" I asked the team, and Bane was the first to speak up.

"There isn't a way out from here, apparently," he explained. "But there are passages that lead deeper into the territory that is claimed by the undead. They were filled with the revenants as well, but you already freed them, so?"

He waggled a dagger in suggestion.

"So we kill the Skin-Walker and its leviathans, then we go kill the undead and hopefully find a way out," I clarified, repeating the information back. "If there are any books or good magical shit left in the gnomes' territory, I'm betting it's in there, along with my naginata," I said, nodding to the building and trying not to wince as a section of the roof fell in slowly with a loud crash.

"Is everyone okay?" I asked, getting nods and gestures, mostly rude, but given in good faith. At some point, I was going to have to explain the gestures I'd taught them, but for now, it was too funny. I checked my mana and found that it was just over half, thanks to the last mana potion that Oracle had forced down my throat. Now, I was out of potions entirely.

I paused, wondering if I should meditate and try to recover more, until the choice was taken from me by a howl further down the switchback, as the pair of larger leviathans came into sight, one with a twitching arm dangling from its beak. It threw its head back and gobbled the limb down, hissing in pleasure. Then it hunched down and pointed its beak at our group, who quickly ducked out of sight.

There was a brief burst of the sonic attack, but it mostly missed us, serving only to make everyone angry.

"Fuck this shit," I snarled. "Let's get inside, then we can kill those fuckers when they come looking," I said, deciding that possibly fighting on both sides would be better than getting blasted with the sonics out in the open.

I drew my remaining sword from my back, and we hurried through the front of the building, barely taking the time to note the way the metal was more corroded than anywhere else I'd been, yet still solid, somehow, as though it didn't get much in the way of disturbances, yet it was rotting from within.

The building itself was fairly large, almost huge, in comparison to the buildings I'd seen in Himnel, easily thirty meters across to a side, and built into a hexagonal shape, as near as I could tell by the collapsed sections.

It had probably been beautiful once, stunning even, with large sections of what looked like glass in the remains of windows and heavy crenellations on the walls. The front had previously been surrounded by gardens of some kind, but now there were only the rotting remnants of bodies and encroaching mushrooms and other fungus. Here and there, the glowing lichen that seemingly provided most of the light in the cavern would colonize a wall or section of ground, producing an uneven, almost diseased glow to the place.

The front of the building had held two large doors; I say "had" because the badunka that I'd crashed had taken not only the doors, but the entire front of the building out, including a section of the upper floors with it.

I winced as I stepped through the shattered doorway, ducking my head to avoid a gently swaying section that hadn't fully fallen yet, and I saw the bodies.

There were at least a dozen, although none appeared intact. Bits of bodies were everywhere, along with sections of wall, roof, and door, not to mention blackened badunka remnants. I searched quickly, making sure of what I knew in my heart. My naginata wasn't here.

I growled and moved forward, slipping on an uneven section and feeling a strong grip grab me from behind to hold me upright. I looked back and nodded my thanks to Lydia, catching the grim look in her eyes through the slit in her helm.

"Yer need ta be more careful," she grumbled, supporting me as I cleared the section of uneven ground, then almost slipping herself, before I caught her hand.

We grinned at each other and moved on, passing into the next section of the building. As I looked back, Giint attached a thin line to a box and looped it over the middle of the path we'd followed. I looked at Tang, seeing that he was close to the gnome. He nodded, indicating that it was okay, and he was watching.

We moved through two more rooms before coming to a halt in the first one that seemed solid. The walls and ceiling, as well as the floor, were coated in dust and filth. But it also contained the looted remains of chests and display cases around the outside, with a sturdy door in and out of the room on either side.

Bane was waiting at the far door, as he had been each time, and he gestured onward and shook his head. There was nobody waiting outside, and by now, we could hear the snuffling growling approach of the leviathans from outside.

"We make a stand here," I said grimly. "We—"

I was cut off by a screech of pain and fury from outside and the building shook again as a shockwave of light, noise, and debris flooded the room from where we'd just been.

There was a moment of shock, then we all looked to Giint.

"They attttte my giiirl," he said grimly and glared at the doorway we'd just come through.

"So, what, that was a fucking *bomb*?" I asked, aghast. "In a building that's practically falling down already?" I gestured around at the solidly built room. Giint looked at me, then shrugged.

"They deaddd," was all he said in a flat, grim voice.

I bit back on swearing at him. He didn't understand, and frankly, if those fuckers had eaten my kids? Yeah. I couldn't blame him. I just needed to watch the mad fucker more closely, I decided.

I gestured wordlessly to the door. Tang and Yen slipped through quickly, and I looked to Bane, who shook his head from the far door, indicating there was still no sign of anything that way.

They were gone less than a minute before Tang moved over to stand next to Giint, and Yen came to me.

"One leviathan was dead, the other gravely injured, Jax, but whatever he used, it was powerful, like your mortar or my Flamespear going off in a small space. It literally shredded the first one and took the second's front legs off, partially cooking its face. Tang killed it, but I don't like the idea of the crazy little sod carrying shit like that around when we hardly know him," she said grimly, watching Giint, who glared round at the room while fingering a bulging pocket.

I nodded to her and picked my way over to Giint, clearing my throat and making him squint up at me. The battered and cracked lenses in the goggles he wore perched on his head made him look even crazier than the drunken dwarves I was used to dealing with.

"I don't know you, Giint, or at least I barely know you, and yet you gave an Oath to me. I'm sorry to have to do this, but I order you to tell me the truth," I commanded, and I saw him stiffen as the magic took hold. "Giint, are you a danger to me and my people?" I asked, and he glared at me before croaking out a single word answer.

"Yesss."

"Why?" I asked, trying to keep the anger from my voice.

"Becaussse I hate them! I willll do anyyything…anything at all to freeeee my peoplesss and to make upppp for whats I did," he said, his voice laced with fury, gesturing out at the remains of the leviathans as he spoke.

"Okay, well that's understandable." I sighed, rubbing my chin and trying to figure things out. Oracle called over, interrupting my musings.

"Giint, if you want to fight them, you need to swear to try your best to help us, to protect the party, and to do no intentional harm to any of us. If not, Lord Jax will send you outside, and you won't get your revenge."

"Noooo!" he snarled. "Musssst fight!"

"We can't trust him, Jax," Grizz said grimly, shaking his head. "He's useful, he could be, but he's also totally batshit and would happily kill himself to take out whatever the Skin-Walker is. Tell me you're honestly happy with him having your back in a fight."

"Hell, no." I snorted. "Giint, I order you to stay to the rear of the group. You have ranged weapons; you can use them only if you judge there is no danger to the rest of the group, and you cannot use any weapons or means that are likely to cause direct or indirect harm to any of my party. Swear that you agree to this, and that you will obey the spirit, not only the wording of the Oath, or you can go wait outside."

He growled in wordless fury, scowling at me before finally spitting out the Oath again. This time, I watched him as the full effect took hold. He slumped, dejectedly accepting that he was a ranged fighter, and not, as he'd seemingly intended, a walking bomb.

I glanced at Grizz, who grimaced but nodded that it was the best that could be expected, as did the others. We moved out, heading into the next room then finally into a huge open area at the heart of the building.

As we walked out, the entire group paused, observing what must once have been a stunning room. The walls were covered in long-dead magelights, with cases situated directly below each one, almost all plundered. Dust and filth coated everything, and there was a strong tang of sea air, floating up from a black cage at the back, where a huge form dangled from a makeshift cradle, and two more leviathans grimly scooped up seawater and flung it over the caged monstrosity.

The creature itself was constrained by the cage, trapped and prevented from growing, with rings of metal sunken into flesh that had grown around it over the years.

The limbs had atrophied, and the tentacles looked to have been severed at their bases, leaving rounded cylinders of flesh that hung suspended, dripping ichor and filth over a wide secondary cage, where smaller, freshly born leviathans mewled and thrashed.

"It's breeding 'em," Lydia said in shock. "Whatever tha Skin-Walker is, it's breeding tha goddamn leviathans."

She hissed in shock, her expression horrified.

"Wait, surely not. Why would its own young—" Stephanos started to say, and Yen cut him off with a single word.

"Magic," she said, shaking her head. "Dark magic, domination or something similar."

"So, what, the Skin-Walker controls them, makes them feed and care for the parent as it breeds more of them? Why were there only a few of them out there?" Stephanos asked.

I pointed to a grim sight.

Next to the smaller cage where the newborns were contained was a slab of metal obviously rigged as a bench, and it was stained black with the inky black ichor the leviathans had for blood.

"They eat them," I pointed out quietly.

"Fuck, that's crazy brave," Arrin said, the first words I'd heard him say in a while, and I looked at him curiously. "Seriously," he said, nodding to the gnomes. "I know they're crazy; gnomes always are, but a species that would subjugate them, turn them all crazy, then live here? Surrounded by them and happily eating leviathans? Is it too late to walk away?"

"Yeah. Way too late," I said, pointing to Giint. "Whatever twisted him up that bad needs to be gutted and nailed to the wall by its balls…if it has any."

"Ah, well, as long as I can hammer the shit out of something with magic? I'm fine with it, I guess," he said philosophically before pointing at the leviathans that were throwing the water up at their parent. "One question, though…how come they've not reacted to us?"

Yen snorted in derision.

"Whoever dominated them didn't give them orders to do anything if someone came in. Clearly, they're idiots, whoever they are." Yen spat on the floor. "Can we go kill them already? I hate this place."

"What will happen to them once we kill whatever controls them?" I asked.

"They'll be free, and they'll do whatever is in their nature." She looked sick. "Probably kill the adult, then go hunting anything else they can kill in the area."

"So, the weakest die before they can," I said, and she nodded.

"Want me to start it off?" she asked, then started to cast at my gesture of approval, and Lydia ordered the ranged fighters to get ready.

I stepped aside and peered up the stairs that led upwards in the corner of the room to spiral around the building. There were balconies that led out to rooms and floors on each level. Somewhere up there, I could hear movement, and my mood had only gotten darker since coming down here.

Inside my mind, I could hear Amon. I could hear his maddening grumblings, and the worst part was that I found myself agreeing with them more and more.

Since our confrontation, when the fragment of his soul lodged in me had somehow reconnected with the rest of him, floating in unquiet death on the other side of the veil, he'd become more conscious, more rational, and more terrifying.

I'd grown up with his mumbling, screaming, and random crap. I'd learned to live with it, to ignore it even, but now? He was watching and mumbling about how this shouldn't be allowed to happen, and I agreed. I agreed wholeheartedly, but he'd intended to steal my body and live again. He'd bring fiery death and destruction to the realms, slaughtering everyone, the good and the evil alike, so that he could then grant life again to the good, as he saw them.

The most terrifying part was that, when I saw things like this cavern, I felt more and more like it was a real solution. Not that killing everyone would be the way to do it, not really. But these gnomes? If I had to kill them all to stop their actions, as they were all murderers and worse, would it really be that much of a loss?

I considered Giint, and I wondered if it would be better to do that, to simply kill him now, for his own good. To kill them all, bringing justice for the victims. Who knew how many he'd killed…? As I looked at him, I felt it slowly starting to build, the tingle of my magic.

It was uncontrolled; hell, I'd not done it deliberately, but as I'd focused on killing Giint, it had started, a faint tingling in my body, flowing down to my fingers, where it sparked.

As I stared at my hands, entranced, *something* came to life. It started as a spark, then a flame, a black flame. It boiled and stuttered, flaring and dying, roiling across my fingers and backs of my hands. A smoke spread from the flame, like an oily, black mist, and it formed into tendrils of…something.

I looked up at a feeling and found Oracle hovering before me. She gazed into my eyes, and the soul-bond between us pulsed. I felt the love she felt for me, and the trust, and I nodded slowly to her unspoken request. I lifted my hands and closed my eyes, willing the magic back to quiescence.

It took several seconds, but eventually, it died away, and I looked back at Oracle in silent question.

"Jax, I'll explain when we have time, but for now, please, don't use that," Oracle said in our bond.

"What—" I started to ask, when the *whoosh* of Yen's Flamespear erupted through the air, a superheated wash of air flooding out as three spears of glowing, spitting, and roiling fire hurtled across the space between her and the leviathans. The individual smaller creatures took one each, the spears slamming into them hard enough that they staggered, while the third and final one embedded deeply into the caged beast and sank into its maw, blowing a section of the flesh that surrounded the beak free.

"Dammit," I growled, shocked at myself for getting so distracted. I turned back to join them, and froze, looking up.

I'd seen movement up there.

CHAPTER TWENTY-ONE

"**B**ane!" I hissed, gesturing upwards to the balcony on the far side of the room. I got no response, but I couldn't see him anywhere when I glanced around, and I guessed he'd gone to investigate. Instead, I turned my attention to the leviathans. Seeing them getting hit over and over, in their weakened, mentally dulled state, they didn't last long.

First one, then the second died, then everyone concentrated their fire on the caged parent.

"Infidels!" came a roar of fury. I twisted around, tearing my eyes from the one-sided fight to the balconies above us. The first was empty; the second, where I thought I'd seen movement, was empty as well, but where the stairway spiraled upwards, opening onto the third floor, a figure stood, and its arms were upraised in fury as a spell built between its hands.

"Run!" I shouted, matching action to words as I sprinted for cover, rushing for another doorway and throwing myself inside, rolling as I hit the floor and coming up with a wall between me and whatever spell the creature was casting.

"Oracle!" I called to her, and I felt her presence as she flew towards me. I moved to the doorway and glanced out, seeing the others had scattered as I'd ordered, but that while Yen and Tang were nowhere to be seen, Miren had fallen, Jian had stopped to help her, and of course, Lydia was standing over them, her shield raised in defiance.

My heart froze. I should be out there; it should be me standing over my people, then all three of them vanished in a blast of dark light.

The spell hit Lydia straight on, exploding out in a wash of blackness that seemed full of reaching, searching tendrils. Then they rolled back in, and all three of my people screamed in pain.

"No," I whispered, my heart clenching as the wash of darkness crushed in on the three, vanishing and sinking into them. It flooded into their mouths, their eyes and ears, and they collapsed, convulsing.

The exposed skin suddenly flooded with black veins, veins that seemed to twist and lift, spreading out and colonizing their bodies before the three stopped moving.

"Bring them to me," the voice intoned from overhead.

I glanced out, seeing the figure in the red robes clutching the edge of the balcony with bleached-white knuckles as it staggered. The black-robed figure appeared and grabbed the first under the arms, towing it away.

I looked out, seeing Lydia and the others slowly climbing to their feet before turning and looking around the room.

"Lydia!" Arrin shouted. "Are you—"

He cut off with a gulp of fear as Lydia, Miren, and Jian spun as one, locking in on Arrin and letting out hisses of rage that were clearly audible even from where I was. Their respective summoned creatures immediately screamed out and vanished.

"Domination!" Yen shouted, stepping out from another doorway that she'd hidden in. "They've been dominated, all three of them!"

"What do we do?" asked Tang, appearing on the other side of the trio.

I blanched, realizing he was asking me. "I—I—" I stammered.

"Either we kill them or we restrain them. First option, some definitely die, second, well…some probably die, and those of us who are restraining them…" Yen called to me.

"Aren't available to help me kill that fucker," I said grimly, nodding my head. "Fine. Grizz, Arrin, Yen, Tang, Oracle, and Stephanos. Restrain them and try to free them. Bane, let's go fuck shit up," I snarled, looking up at the stairs.

"We've got this, boss!" Grizz called out, and I waved grimly.

"Be careful," Oracle said to me, and I felt her concern, as well as her determination that she'd damn well heal the others and somehow free our people from the domination.

Lydia led the way as the three ran at Arrin, and he took off, sprinting as fast as he could, heading for Grizz.

I broke out of the room I was in, running for the stairs, my shield sliding out of my pouch as I reached in and freed it, then summoned the kill-stick I'd taken from the gnomes earlier.

I'd nearly reached the stairs when the first arrow slammed into Arrin, dropping him and making him scream in pain as it took his leg out from under him.

I glanced back and saw Miren aiming at him with a second arrow already drawn, even as Jian raced to intercept Yen, and Lydia went for Grizz.

I swore and jumped over a small pile of bones, skidded on some filth, and jumped again, landing on the bottom stair and starting upwards. The screech of metal on metal grated on my hearing, then another scream rang out from Arrin, followed by my mana dipping sharply as Oracle worked to heal someone.

"Motherfucking asshole spell-casting dickbags!" I snarled under my breath as I took the stairs as fast as I could, clearing them two and three at a time as I raced around the inside of the tower.

The first floor flashed past, and glittering trash lay everywhere, things hanging on walls and lying discarded on the floors.

The stairs came and went again, leading up to the second-floor balcony. Here, I found a dead gnome, laid in a pool of blood, a crossbow abandoned on the floor next to it. I glanced into the rooms as I passed, seeing more broken bodies laid inside.

They were covered in teeth marks and savage blows, and in the split second I had as I ran past, I noted they were all armed, and they had all faced each other. They'd fought to the death, and none had tried to run. Whatever this domination was, it was powerful.

The last set of stairs to the balcony I'd seen the figures on was up ahead, and as I clattered onto it, my armor announcing my arrival. A figure blurred nearby, sweeping my legs out from under me.

I smashed to the floor, rolled, and came up swinging, my thumb flicking the activation lever on the kill-stick and sending all three circular blades whirring to life as I aimed for whoever had tripped me.

And for the second time, my heart cramped.

It was Bane. His flesh was covered in black veins that crawled and multiplied, and his arms spun and dipped, each holding a different dagger.

He sprang at me, and I dove aside, rolling and coming to my feet, planting a foot against the wall and kicking off, jumping to the side as he followed me, blades flashing and slicing through the air.

"Bane!" I shouted. "Stop, man!"

He didn't respond beyond a low grunt of pain as he closed the distance between us. Hooking out and down with his upper arms, he lunged, digging the curved backs of the daggers around my shield and kill-stick, then grabbing with the lower arms, having dropped his blades to hold me fast.

Then he let rip with a blast of worldsense that jarred me to my teeth, before stomping down on my left knee, forcing it sideways.

He clambered up me, using my knee as a stepping point and shifting his grip on his lower arms to hold on, while he lifted the upper arms and stabbed down, aiming for my exposed throat and face.

I dropped the kill-stick, unwilling to use it on my friend, slamming the shield into his back instead. My two arms were fortunately stronger than his lower arms, and I managed to bring my armored right arm up to deflect the daggers in time.

I cried out as one sliced my right cheek to the bone, then I grabbed his right wrist in my right hand and spun, throwing myself from my feet.

He'd not been idle, though; when his first stab had failed, and his right arm was locked down, he kept ahold of me and brought his free left upper dagger back, stabbing it down into the gap in my armor at the back of my neck.

The blade dug deep, missing my spine by luck more than skill on my part, and I felt horrific pain from it, and more so when I landed on him, fully armored, and smacked him into the ground.

He tried to use the grip he had on the dagger embedded in my upper back to stop me, and I grunted in agony before releasing my shield and shoving up with all my strength, pushing myself almost to my feet.

He came with me, grunting in pain but determined to hang onto the dagger he'd managed to get into me, even as he yanked himself back and forth trying to break my grip on his wrist.

I saw his mouth open wide as he drew in a deep breath, about to blast me with a stronger worldsense, and that'd be it. If I lost the grip I had on him for even a second, he'd slit my throat, and I did the only thing I could think of.

"Relax! That's an order!" I snapped frantically.

Just as the first high-pitched note washed over me, I felt Bane's body forced to relax by the magic of the Oath.

It lasted only a second, as the domination warred with the Oath, but it was enough.

I head butted him, then whipped my arms up, wrapping them around his and yanking down hard, pinning his arms to his sides.

I pulled back and nutted him again, and again, aware from our conversations where his species had their sensing nodes in the front of their faces. With each blow, his tendrils flared out in shock and dropped, and he took longer to recover.

After the fourth hit, his body went limp, and I let go long enough to flip him over and get my arms around his neck, one in front and one behind in a triangular choke hold, grabbing onto my opposite arm and squeezing for all I was worth.

As he recovered from the blows to his face, he reached up, clawed hands frantically grasping at my arms, searching for a weakness, a way to break my grip.

I felt tears burning my eyes as I doubled down and forced his airway closed, choking my friend out. He kicked and thrashed around frantically, trying to get free or to injure me, and I managed to slam his face into the stone floor again.

This time, it was enough, and he went limp. I was about to release him when I saw his symbol in my vision. It was flecked with a warning redness that pulsed, and I somehow knew this was to show he was dominated, but it didn't give the same sense that I'd had before when someone was unconscious.

I almost released him anyway, fearful I'd kill him. Then I gritted my teeth and held on, two seconds more, four. At seven, he seemed to come to life, panicking and kicking and slapping again, but now it was too late, and his blows landed with less force than a summer rain.

Three more seconds…and he was out. I saw the flash on his icon, and I knew it in my heart; he was unconscious.

I released him and shoved his limp form aside.

I desperately wanted to heal him, but I didn't dare, and I forced myself to my feet, staggering, then got to the balcony wall and coughed, before shouting down to the struggling groups below.

"Lydia! Jian! Miren! I order you to freeze and drop your weapons!"

I staggered as the Oath pulled at me, draining me of…something…as it took hold, all three pausing and dropping their weapons for a second as the others jumped on them.

I turned back, looking at the entrance to the final series of rooms at the top of the building, and I dismissed the rest of the group. Either they'd be okay or they wouldn't. I couldn't take any more time now.

The best chance they had was if I stopped the assholes controlling them.

I reached back and let out a scream of pain when, after three attempts, I managed to tug the blade free of the back of my neck, sending me collapsing to my knees. I pulled the special healing potion out of my bag and bit down on the top, spitting the cork onto the floor, and spitting again as a wax seal broke in my mouth. I chugged the potion, feeling a weird grittiness in the liquid before my eyes shot open and I lunged to my feet.

Whatever was in the special potion, as opposed to the weaker ones, I needed that recipe.

It felt like I'd been given a triple espresso, an energy drink chaser, and then a hit of cocaine, all while plugged into a defibrillator.

I practically flew forward, grabbing my shield and gripping Bane's dagger by the hilt hard enough to make it creak as I ran from the balcony and into the first suite of rooms.

They were different from the ones below in that they were clean, tidy, and had an almost familiar feel to them. One wall was covered in a rough painting, one that looked scarily familiar, like a twisted re-imagining of one of my favorite childhood movies, but here, the evil empire was the good guys. The apprentice sorcerers that were leading the rebellion against them were shown with mocking smiles and glowing eyes. As I paused in shock, the small bear-like helpers of the rebels…were gnomes.

I glanced around, seeing more, drawings, devices, strange things that looked almost like they'd fit in back home.

I glanced around and set off again, racing for the single path to the next room, seeing a shimmering wire stretched across the doorway at ankle height at the last second and jumping over it.

I landed, skidded on some debris, and scanned the space. This room was huge and circular with cabinets and display cases ringing it and a solitary, massive device in the middle. It was ringed in concentric circles of runes, and it struck me with a powerful sense of wrongness as I looked at it.

It was connected to an arched doorway, with the outer edge twisting as it went, until it became the inner, and then the outer, and try as I might, I couldn't see a second edge on it.

I froze as I realized what it was.

A portal. Just like the one I'd been sent through to come here, and like the one that was at the top of my own Great Tower.

On the far side of the portal was a cage—a cage with two bodies in it, slowly rotting and slumped in death. The room around me made a twisted sense, suddenly, as I looked about, noticing the almost-familiar sights of home.

A rack on the wall was stacked with portal keys. There were three of them with a space for a fourth. I remembered seeing the gnome with something that had looked like a key, and I swore loud and long.

There were three ways out of this room: the hole in the roof with a demolished wall that went down to the ground on my right, the doorway to my left, and the large doors out onto the balcony ahead, and one of them had to hold someone like me.

Someone from Earth, sent by the Baron and his kin…and they were responsible for all of this. The roof was unlikely, I decided, where the ceiling had come down when I'd taken out part of the building earlier. There was no point to fleeing now, only to fall to their death when the floor gave out. That left the balcony ahead or the room to the left.

I chose left, sweeping up a big rock and throwing it at a half-hidden tripwire strung across that doorway as well.

There was an explosion followed by a scream. I grinned, the wall that led to the room collapsing, exposing the black-robed figure as it reeled back, arms pressed into the cowl of its hood.

I had thirty-seven mana left, and I spent twenty on a lightning bolt, hurling it through the gap in the wall to smash the robed figure from its feet and backwards into the edge of a four-poster bed.

It fell onto the bed, thrashing and screaming, and I stepped through the remnants of the doorway, hefting my weapon and looking around. There was nobody else I could see, and I strode forward, determined to end the fight as quickly as I could and go looking for the red-robed one to free my friends.

I made it to the bed, tore the cowl back, and saw the ruined face of a red-headed woman. The flesh was burned and pocked, her eyes white and milky and her lips missing, exposing broken teeth. I paused for a second, seeing the injuries and wondering what had caused them, knowing that only two were new: the gash that ran from her left eyes to her ear, that had possibly blinded her entirely when the explosive went off, and the burned patch on her shoulder.

Then she howled at me like a mad dog and tried to bite me, aiming for the hand that gripped her shoulder.

I stabbed down without pause, ramming the blade into her heart and pinning her to the bed. She seemed to freeze for a second before sagging back, and a look of peace and relief crossed her face.

I felt something grab my leg, then…PAIN! Pain suddenly ripped its way up my left leg, and I collapsed to the floor, glimpsing the evil grin covering the face that looked out at me from under the bed. Black tendrils wormed their way up my leg from where they held onto my calf, and pain tore into me in crescendoing waves.

Beware!

You have been afflicted with As'Vier's Darkest Domination!

I gritted my teeth and tried desperately not to piss myself as the black veins ate their way up my limb, digging deep into my flesh and traveling along my veins, surging faster and faster as each panicked beat of my heart spread them throughout my body.

I shook as I tried to crawl free, rolling to my right and starting to drag myself along, reaching out with a shaking hand to grab onto the doorframe in an attempt to drag myself free of the room. I glanced back to see the red-robed figure clambering out from under the bed on the far side of the room.

Where the black-robed figure had been obviously a human, this one was anything but. It looked human in its size and dimensions, but as it emerged, it shifted, an arm lengthening as it slammed down on the floor with a loud crunch.

It dragged itself forward, rising to stand hunched over. It lifted its other hand into sight, clutching my goddamn naginata.

It hunched forward heavily, its inhumanly long right arm hanging low out of the robes. Its fingers twitched as the bones of the arm rearranged, growing shorter with a popping, cracking sound as the body shuddered and gasped.

I looked back in growing horror as it shrugged the hood off, exposing its face and letting out a high-pitched giggle.

Its face was like something out of a nightmare; it had clearly been human at some point, but now, it was stretched and distorted. The jaw was almost the correct size, but the teeth that filled it were a mix of canines and incisors, grown to at least double the normal size and jutting at all angles with a thick line of bristling hair erupting from the upper lip.

The flesh looked stretched past the breaking point, with dozens of livid red lines showing through the pasty white exterior and bulging sections where…*something*…shifted and rolled under the skin.

The figure hobbled forward, letting out another high-pitched giggle, and it rubbed the haft of my naginata lovingly while drooling as it tried to speak.

"I…I have to thank you; yes, thank you my pet. You brought me so much!" The voice was weird. One minute, it was a mumble, then a hoarse whisper, as though someone desperate to share a secret. "You came to me, yes…called here to serve, as they all are." He seemed to be talking to himself, then suddenly his head shot up and he fixed me with a glare. "You came alone? You brought no others, no hunters? SPEAK!"

At his command I felt my mouth open involuntarily, and I gasped as I tried to stop the words tumbling out.

"No hunters!" I heard my own voice declare.

The creature relaxed as it nodded to itself, the skull shifting under its flesh as though the two were only imperfectly attached.

"Good…good!" it mumbled, nodding and shifting its weight with a creak of bones that sounded terrible.

"Hmmmm, perhaps it is time for a new sleeve? A new coat for my soul?" it asked itself, looking at me and trying to smile widely, succeeding only in grimacing and drooling.

He pulled himself more upright, using *my* goddamn naginata, and started to stumble forward while looking at the weapon admiringly, drawing his fingers down the blade and shuddering in pained pleasure as he sliced himself open.

"It's your own fault, slave," he whispered. "Not only did you trespass in my realm, but you brought me a new toy to help me to be free." He stroked my naginata slowly, and its haft flickered with blackness, absorbing the domination spell he still channeled.

"Ah!" he said, grinning at me. "You see? My new toy recognizes true magic; it hungers for it, it *needs* it, to be wielded by a Master."

He gazed on the weapon adoringly before stopping and lifting it to his eyes, staggering as he stared at a small mark etched into the wood around halfway up the staff section.

I knew what he was looking at, having traced it with my fingers a thousand times and more. It was the maker's mark that graced the haft, a pair of stylized wings with a spear rising between them.

He stared at it for long seconds then spun with an outraged hiss.

"Where did you get this! Where!" he snarled.

I fell back, my vision narrowing to a single point of light as he screamed and did…something. The world seemed to rocket back into focus, and I panted, staring up at him as my body stayed locked in place.

"Answer me, slave! Where did you get this weapon!" he screeched, hobbling over and reaching down, his arm lengthening with a crack and pop of shifting bones to backhand me with a twisted claw of a hand.

I looked at it, and at him, now that the cowl had fallen back, exposing the rest of his face. He had once been a man of late middle years, skinny to the point of being emaciated, with pock-marked cheeks, grey eyes, and scraggly black facial hair. His face was heavily scarred, and he obviously had physical problems, judging from the way he moved, the staggering and weakness, and three questions sprang into my mind at once.

First, and most important, what had brought on the change? He'd gone from a creature that was clearly possessing a body, into seemingly the human shell, but the human was in control now, and whatever was under the skin had sunk back into quiescence?

Secondly, was he really from Earth? And third, why do moustaches always make seemingly normal people look like sex criminals? Needless to say, it was number three that forced its way from my mouth.

"You...look like...a...kiddie fiddler," I gasped out, glaring up at him. "I'm...not telling you...shit."

"Kiddie-fiddler?" he gasped, then snarled and stabbed the naginata into my exposed inner left thigh, slicing deep into the gap between the armored sections. "They sent you here, didn't they? The nobility...my father," he spat. "He sent you to kill me, didn't he?"

He suddenly began writhing, as whatever was under the skin shifted again, coming to the fore. A seemingly different face glared down at me, its eyes full of hatred and fear.

"What are you? Why are you here?" it screamed. The voice carried weird timbres and inflections, and before I knew what I was doing, I heard my voice speaking up in answer, desperate to appease this freak of nature.

"I am Jax! Lord of—" I clamped my teeth shut, almost taking my own tongue off in the process, and scowled at the creature, even as the weird subsonics in its voice tugged at me to obey.

"Lord?!" it whispered in a voice that carried before dropping to a lower octave and assuming a wheedling quality. "You were a lord? A lord of where? Of what? Are there...are there more? More fleshlings?" Its face split in a wide smile as it nodded frantically.

I got a horrified impression of the creature under the skin that was trying to get free, before he barked out a roar of pain, then a self-conscious little giggle. "I'm sorry, you shouldn't see that; oh no, not him, he's been naughty, you see, so he can't come out to play now...but you have to tell me what you know, okay? Tell me...TELL ME!" he screeched, his lips growing flecked with foam and an uncontrolled shudder flowing up and down his body.

I gasped and tried to reach up as pain wracked through my body again, but I stayed frozen in place, barely quivering, as he lifted his right hand and waved it almost negligently, the fingers twitching spasmodically as he glared down at me.

"You will tell me the truth; then I'll let the spell finish, and you will be mine. The only choice you have left now is how painful you make this!" With his words, the spell shifted, the blackness filling my veins, twisting and flowing back and forth, tearing the vessels as it went, making me bleed into myself. "It's your own fault, you know," he added conversationally.

"Jax! We're coming!" Oracle sent to me, and I found I could respond.

"He's got me! Dom—argh!" I broke off the mental sending as pain ripped through me, and the red-robed figure hunched down close, glaring at me.

"What was that?" he growled, drool escaping from a drooping right lip. "You...felt different, wrong! What were you doing?"

The last words came out as a scream, with both voices demanding the answer at once.

"Telling your…momma I missed…her!" I ground out, knowing how stupid it was, and how I was going to pay for the comment, yet unable to think of anything else to distract him from looking too closely at me with his magic.

"My…momma?" he said, looking more confused than annoyed. "What is this foolishness?" He staggered back as he lost his balance, then cursed as he heard shouting from outside.

"We're coming!" someone called. I gritted my teeth, wishing they'd kept their goddamn mouths shut. He gestured to me, and my body obeyed, lurching upright, grabbing my shield, and attempting to draw my second sword from the sheath on my back.

Fortunately, the thing that annoyed me the most about having sheaths on my back struck again, and I was left with my arm extended overhead yanking and trying to clear the last few inches. By the time I managed to wiggle it free, thanks to my body being essentially controlled by him, and not by myself, I'd drawn his attention away from the others again.

"Who sent you! Was it my father?" he snarled, reaching out and drawing his right hand down my face in an incredibly awkward gesture that trailed a red mist-like substance that floated through the air.

It touched my skin, and I started to scream in earnest as my flesh began to bubble and melt.

"I warned you! I told you! You tell me what I want to know, or you will suffer," he said, drawing the word out in a sing-song voice. I glared at him as my body moved at his direction, the black filth drawing in again.

There was a noise from the doorway, and I moved against my own desires, stepping between the red-robed shitbag and Tang, who eased in slowly, crouched low, with his bow in hand.

"Jax, if you can hear me still, you have to fight it," he said slowly. I glared at him, the most control I had over my body. "He can control you, but only if you let him. Domination is an insidious magic, but it's rooted in making you *believe* you have no choice…he's giving you orders, but your body is the one carrying them out. Don't listen to him."

He drew back on his bow and aimed at me, knowing his target was hiding directly to my rear.

I thought about what he said, even as I felt my body take its first step forward, bringing the shield up and pointing my sword at Tang.

"It's all in my head…?" I said to myself, concentrating and reaching deeper into my mind, remembering the fight with Amon, when he'd tried to take over my body. I remembered how I'd stopped him from using my own body and power against me.

I concentrated harder and spoke a single word in the silence of my mind.

"Aegis!"

The pain tearing through me became a distant thing, weak and insignificant, and I spun, moving so fast that Tang almost shot me by reflex.

I slashed my sword across the figure, and he brought the naginata he'd been holding across to block me, barely deflecting my blow from taking his head.

"H—how!" he squealed, throwing himself backward and staggering as his foot caught on something on the floor.

Tang fired then, taking him in the right shoulder as he tried to lift his palsied hand, making him shriek with pain.

I slashed down, the drow-made blade slicing easily through his extended forearm and taking the hand that gripped the naginata off at the wrist in a spray of blood.

"How?" I asked, stepping forward and hooking my right foot behind his left ankle while punching him in the face with my right hand, the pommel of my sword breaking at least one of his rotten teeth. "How about how fucking *dare* you?!" I snarled. He fell backwards, dropping the naginata and it reverted to its customary appearance, the black necrotic energy that had been pulsing through it fading away as the connection was broken.

"You…you can't do this!" he screamed, lifting his right curled hand and twisting the fingers as best he could while glaring up at me hatefully.

The pain raged higher, my health plummeting as veins tore open and blood started to stream down my skin.

I forced an evil grin through the mask of blood I now wore, and was about to take his other hand when a heavy *twang* echoed around the room, and the red-robed mage convulsed, collapsing in death.

The pain died down as his magic released me. The wounds remained, though, and as I fell to one knee, I looked up, seeing the short, grim-faced figure of Giint.

The little bastard had climbed up the outside of the building, I realized, all the way up, then had shot the prick through the window.

I warred with myself, half-relieved that it was over, and half-furious, as that red-robed asshole had answers I needed. Who was he, how had he come to be here, and most of all, what the hell was…?

Then I sagged forward further, blinking at the frantically flashing indications before me. I had seventy-six health left, and I was losing forty-three per second through the outrageous bleed effects I was suffering.

I blinked, and the world started to go black, before something hit me. A terrible, icy cold spread through me, and the world was gone.

CHAPTER TWENTY-TWO

I woke up with a start, my heart racing at what felt like a thousand beats a second, and I almost flew upright before strong hands pressed me back down. I felt something being jabbed into my neck; there was a hiss, and coldness flooded me again.

This time, it was more like a freezing wind combined with eating a ton of ice cream really fast. I almost screamed from the brain-freeze, but in a matter of seconds, it passed, and warm hands propped my head up as a rough voice ordered me to drink.

I blinked and saw Tang and the glimmering red potion he held for me, and I reached up hungrily, taking it and chugging the liquid as fast as I could.

Whatever it was, it made me feel fantastic as my eyes dilated and the room was filled with light. I felt my skin literally swell with strength and vitality, and I fought to be upright again. This time, the hands holding me let me up, and I looked around, seeing Tang, Yen, Giint, and Bane were all there, with Yen glaring in horror at Tang. Bane had Giint pinned to the wall with his daggers at the gnome's throat.

"Tell me that wasn't what I think it was!" she said, aghast.

"Strength of the Ogg," he confirmed, grinning at me. "How do you feel, Jax?" he asked me. I held up my hands, curling them into fists as I admired the jewellike shimmer my skin had suddenly gained.

"Amazing," I muttered, trying to keep the grin from my face and failing utterly.

"Oh, for…you seriously gave him one of those? You're going to get thrown out for this. Dishonorable discharge! I can't believe you got the new lord goddamn *shined*!" Yen said in horrified astonishment.

"What is…this?" I asked slowly, shaking my head and blinking furiously.

"It's something that an idiot gave you to make you feel better, Jax. Just give it a few minutes, and it'll wear off."

"It's high grade," Tang admitted ashamedly.

"Are you f—" Yen snarled, taking a deep breath and blowing it out in a long sigh. "Tang, when we get back, you and I are going to Augustus, and you're going to explain this…in fact, no. We're going to *Restun*! Once he's done with you, you'll never touch this shit again, and I swear, if you've got him hooked on this—"

"I'm all right." I interrupted her low-voiced yet fervent rant as I shook my head. "What the hell was that, though?" I asked as I blinked again, seeing the shimmer fade slightly.

"It's a drug, Jax," Tang admitted ashamedly. "I had it for a while, kept promising I'd throw it away, and…well…you needed something to get you back on your feet, so I mixed it with my last healing potion."

"What does it do?" I asked him, shaking my head and breathing deeply, trying to flush the stuff out of my system. I had no real issue with drugs, but I'd known others who'd been killed or worse by them. To have an unwanted one in my system freaked me out more than a bit. I checked my mana, seeing it was at twenty-two. I grimaced, resolving to leave it, in case Oracle needed it.

I considered meditating and thought better of it; I needed to be sure that everyone was okay first.

"It basically supercharges your stamina regeneration, but makes you feel amazing while it does, and with the healing potion I gave you, it was enough to wake you up," Tang said, grimacing. "I'm sorry, Jax, but I didn't know what else to do. Giint used something on you to stop the bleeding. It'd mostly worked, but your skin was like ice, and you…well, you looked terrible. Then he stabbed you in the neck with something he'd found, and I panicked."

"Bane, it's okay; let him down," I said, then staggered. Yen was there, and a second later, Tang was on the other side, and they helped me to the edge of the bed, making me sit next to the corpse of the black-robed woman.

"Giint. I know you've sworn the Oath to me, so how about you explain this, please?" I asked slowly, as the room spun in and out of a kind of hyper-focus, before falling back to my normal vision.

"Yooou were dyyyyying. Usssed collld bombbb. Slooow heart. Then healllingg intttto neckkk, fassssster." He growled, glaring at Bane as he rubbed his throat where Bane had pinned him.

"So, you froze me to stop or slow the bleeding, then injected me with a healing potion?" I asked, rubbing at my neck. I could feel raised bumps where something had pierced the skin, then been healed over. Even as I rubbed them, the dried blood flaked away, leaving healthy skin.

"Yessss," he said grudgingly.

"What about shooting him with your crossbow? Hell, I lost you downstairs; how did you get up here?" I asked.

"Climb," he said flatly. "Oath make meeee nott helppp down belllowww, but here? Nooooo riskkk to partyyyy. Could shoooot."

"Fuck. Fine, we'll look at the Oath again. Sorry for that, but you're batshit," I muttered, rubbing my face and licking my lips. "Why the hell does everything taste like…purple, suddenly?" I asked, then shook my head. "I don't believe I just said that."

"What does purple taste like?" Bane asked me quietly, and I shrugged.

"No idea. I just know I can taste it. Weird shit you gave me, Tang. Yen's right, we're going to have a chat about this later, but I know you did it for the right reason, knowing you'd be in trouble for it as well, because you were trying to help." I shook my head again, and the world tilted suddenly before coming back into focus. I pulled up the details I could see for the group, noting that everyone was alive, even if most of them were well below half health.

"Right, look, I'm going to meditate, get my mana up, and hopefully let this shit wear off as well. How about you get the others up here, and we all get some rest? It's been a long-ass day," I said, getting some weary agreement from them all, bar Giint, who stomped forward and cleared his throat awkwardly.

"Myyy people…they neeeed helppp," he said hesitantly.

"I know, and we will heal them, don't worry. But I'm out of mana potions now, and it'll take a lot. Let me recover, and we will come up with a plan, maybe capture a few at a time and heal them up? I don't know. I need to rest; I'm sorry Giint," I apologized, and he nodded, looking determined, before moving off.

I sat down on the floor, pressing my back against the side of the bed, not wanting to stay sitting next to a corpse, or the bloody sheets. I shook my head a few times and breathed deeply, trying to wake myself up as my mind seemed to scatter from one thing to another, and I noticed suddenly that the dead woman's toenails were painted and carefully manicured. Staring at them, I wondered about the life she'd had, here, with that thing, and…I shook myself again, harder this time. No. I had to meditate.

I began to build the structure around me, visualizing the box, even as I started relaxing my body and mind when Bane knelt next to me and started to speak.

"Jax…I…I'm sorry," he began, and I opened one eye to glare at him.

"What for?" I asked. "Interrupting me while I'm meditating, or trying to kill me?"

"Ah, both?" he said, shrugging. I nodded, closing my eye again.

"For trying to kill me, don't be so damn stupid, mate. You weren't in control. Don't worry about it; hell, he even got me, and I practically forgot everything trying to fight it. I was damn lucky that Tang spoke up when he did and made me think. As for interrupting me while meditating, I'll let you off this once; next time, you can join Grizz in the punishment exercises."

"I—" Bane started to say, and I cut him off with a raised hand.

"Bane, shut the hell up and let me meditate, please," I whispered.

He grunted, then stood up and walked away, not spotting me watching him go and smiling until he reached the entrance to the balcony.

He caught me smiling and nodded in response, relaxing before moving out and patrolling the area, as Tang got more of a dressing down by Yen.

I ignored them all, focusing on my muscles and working down from the top of my head, locating every muscle I could and individually relaxing it. By the time I was forcing my toes to relax, I felt like I'd wasted a load of time, but as I mentally constructed the box around my image of myself, then tried to build another, twisting the streams of ambient mana as they poured inside, I felt my mana regeneration shifting and speeding up.

I tried again and again to construct a second box, but each time, it failed, and I'd feel the first one shaking and starting to come apart as well.

Finally, after at least an hour, with my mana building and dropping as Oracle used it, I managed the second box, finding, unlike the first, which I visualized as making a six-sided box and simply enclosing myself within it, the second box had to be constructed with two panels at a time. It fell apart again and again before finally becoming solid, and my mana regeneration leaped upwards again.

I eventually blinked back into reality, seeing the world again, rather than the mental image of the boxes surrounding my glowing form, and I breathed a sigh of relief at finding the group settled around a small campfire in the middle of the main room. Where I was seated, I had some privacy in the bedroom, and the others were gathered next door, still in sight, but giving me enough space that they wouldn't distract me.

They sat joking and relaxing, with the silent form of Bane on the far side, looking out over the cavern and Arrin watching down the stairs.

Grizz was helping Lydia with her armor, and I noticed a few new dents in it, and surprisingly, a matching series of dents in Grizz's, suggesting she'd given as good as she got.

I smiled internally at Oracle, knowing immediately where she was and that she was watching me. I turned my head and found her in the corner of the bedroom. She hopped down from the chair she'd been perched in and walked over, crouching down and giving me a hug and a kiss.

The hug was long, and I felt myself relaxing further, knots I hadn't been aware of relaxing at her touch. I silently acknowledged that finally, after so many years alone, she would always be there.

I kissed her again, and she grinned at me before getting up and moving out of sight of the main room, crooking her finger at me to join her.

"How are you feeling?" she whispered, and I kissed her thoroughly before responding.

"Better!" I said simply.

"And the potion that Tang gave you?" she asked.

"Gone, worn off, I think?" I said, shrugging.

"There's an easy way to tell, apparently…" She grinned mischievously.

"Oh?" I asked, and she told me to sit in the chair. Once I was down, she checked that the others couldn't see, then *shifted*.

She changed her form to a slimmer, less busty version than usual, with long, blonde hair that curled down to touch mid-back. White stockings and suspenders and a lacy little bra and panties set did nothing to hide her body, serving only to enhance it.

I'd felt her emotions as she changed, and I knew that feeling, the mix of naughty, horny, and hopeful that characterized her teasing. But still, I couldn't help but take a long, slow look, smiling widely as I planned all the things I was going to do with her when we had some privacy.

She came to me, clambering onto my lap and straddling me, kissing me deeply. I let my hands lift, one stroking its way up her leg and settling on her firm ass, the other moving higher, sliding up the front. I flicked back a section of lace, exposing a nipple and leaned down, kissing it, before she shifted *again*.

This time, she flowed back, shrinking down, and was suddenly dressed again, grinning at me with a mix of elation and sadness that was just weird.

I grunted in shock, reaching out to her, then stood and adjusted myself, my trousers suddenly far too restrictive.

"You're cruel," I whispered, getting a shake of her head in reply.

"Apparently, it's an effect of the Ogg potion," she explained, smiling regretfully. "It makes you unbelievably horny, so if you'd been unable to stop, and had jumped on me after that, we'd know that you were still drugged," she whispered huskily. "It's made to some secret recipe from a witch up in the mountains."

"Wait, that was a setup?" I asked, half-hurt, half-amused.

"Not entirely. Let's just say that it seemed the most fun way to find out, with the best consequences if you were still under its effects," she said, grinning.

"What, that my team sees me running round with my third leg out?" I asked, feeling a bit of annoyance rising at the thought of the damage that could have done to my image. Sure, the entire goddamn ship apparently knew what we'd been up to the other day and had been able to hear it, more's the shame, but still.

"No, I'd have hit you with a heal, don't worry," she said seriously, flying forward and shifting back to her full size, although dressing far more demurely. "Healing does clear it out, especially the Cleanse spell that Nerin taught us. Actually, the Cleansing Fire would have done it as well, but when I got to you, you were already meditating, and I thought it was wearing off." She smiled then, evilly.

"Besides, I'd been thinking about that form and wanted to see if you liked it, and the outfit…?"

"Oh, well, gosh, I wonder if I liked it…?" I said quietly and very sarcastically, gesturing to the tentpole in my trousers. "You know these pants don't stretch, right? And that the chainmail over that section rubs? Or at least, it damn well does when I'm practically ripping my way through them!"

"I'll make it up to you, you know, if you want me to?" she purred, grinning naughtily and licking her lips. I grinned in response, and we started moving to the far corner of the room so that we'd be out of sight of everyone, just in case…when Grizz stuck his head in.

"Hey, boss!" he said, grinning. "Looks like you're awake, and that's great timing…food's ready!"

With that, he ducked back out of sight before Oracle or I could get a lightning bolt ready.

"I swear he knows," I muttered, shaking my head, as Oracle laughed and stood on her tiptoes to kiss my cheek.

"It's okay. We'd have gotten caught anyway, and you know it," she said, grinning unashamedly. "But, you know, not that it would have stopped me."

With that, she laughed and jumped back before I could grab her, moving for the door.

I swore under my breath and rearranged myself again, thinking calming thoughts for a few seconds before giving up and walking through to sit with the others.

I ignored the looks on Lydia, Miren, and Jian's faces, and before they could say anything, I plonked myself down on the floor.

"Well, I don't know about you lot, but when that asshole hit me with his Dominate spell, it nearly killed me. I don't see how anyone could resist it, so I don't think we need to talk about it again, understand? Nothing you did was your fault." I reached out and took the dripping meat skewer that Yen passed me, lifting it over the fire, with fat dropping and popping on the flames.

Tang grinned at me shamefacedly. I winked at him, nodding that we were okay, and he let out a long sigh, straightening up and seeming to relax until Yen elbowed him and glared him down again.

We ate in companionable silence, mostly, the day having been a lot more intense that we'd expected it to get. Once a guard rotation was agreed upon, we all relaxed, confident that, with one person on guard over the balcony and the section where Giint had climbed up earlier, and one on the stairwell, we were reasonably safe.

Oracle had been sitting with me, cuddled up to my side, and she snuggled into me as I rolled myself up in my bedroll to sleep.

At first, it was almost impossible to drop off with the feeling of her body so close to mine, and my mind started to go down another route. So, when she got up and kissed me, I grinned at her and was about to climb out of my bedroll, when she shook her head seriously, leaning in for a single chaste kiss before breaking free and whispering to me.

"Better if we behave…I don't need sleep, and as much as I love being cuddled up to you, I'll go take a flight around the cavern and see what I can find out."

She shifted again, this time to her smallest size, and flew for the balcony doors, flitting outwards and up, disappearing from sight as I sagged backwards regretfully.

I started to settle back down, but as I did, a thought struck me, and I knew I couldn't sleep, not yet. Tomorrow was another day, and it was a day we were going to be facing without potions. That alone left me with no choice, and I sighed regretfully as I began clearing a space in the bedroom where I could make some potions up.

The next hour passed both quickly, as there was so much to do, and horrifically slowly, as I was exhausted, and that goddamn potion Tang had given me was making me twitchy. I swore to myself. I kept getting the feeling that something was watching me. Watching and waiting for its chance to do…something.

I made a large batch up, scouring through the ingredients and managing to make both a mana recovery potion that I got six small vials out of and a health recovery potion that I made two batches of, getting seven in the first batch, then over-boiling the second and losing the lot.

I sighed, trying to hide my anger and anxiety from Tang when he came to check on me. I packed the potions away carefully, leaving two of each out on the side, just in case.

When I finally lay down, I found myself unable to sleep, a nameless dread filling me, making me feel like something was about to attack me at any point, until Tang came and sat nearby and built up the small fire.

The light seemed to banish any evil miasma, and I swiftly fell asleep.

The rest of the night passed quickly, until in the early hours, I was awoken by a terrible feeling of foreboding.

"Jax!" Jenae called, startling me from sleep. I jumped, having just started to wake, searching the room for a threat and went straight from sleep into full-blown paranoia stage.

"Jenae?" I said aloud. "What happened, where's Oracle?!"

"Jax, Oracle's fine, but I have bad news, and as my Champion, you need the warning," she said.

I blew out a breath, kicking my bedroll aside and speaking loudly as everyone looked to me.

"Up and at 'em, everyone. Shit's hit the fan," I growled.

"Jax, I don't have long. I'll explain at some point, but time here doesn't flow the way it does for you there, and there are things—beings—that I cannot allow to know of our return yet.

"I saw an opportunity to check on you and found a stain in the realm headed towards you. You fought a SporeMother once, so you know how evil they can be. There are seven aboard several ships somehow, with ships full of mortals traveling as escorts to them.

"There is also a creature that is neither mortal nor immortal controlling the creatures. I cannot tell you more about it without tipping my hand. I sensed that they are young, immature, but several have begun to produce DarkSpore. They will reach the Prax in six hours, and the devastation they could wreak upon your people would be immense."

"Shit!" I snarled, thinking fast. "Are they alone? Is it one ship, or—"

"There are seven; five appear to be of Narkolt, one bears the flag of Himnel, and the ship that carries the largest of the creatures bears no flag but is clearly leading the fleet."

"How big are the ships? I mean…" I said, pausing and trying to think of the best way to phrase it.

"They are all cruisers, save a single fast scout. Your fleet is larger, but with inexperienced hands commanding, and with the battleship to protect, you will not win without great casualties."

"Fuck," I grunted, my mind spinning as I tried to think of a way out. If we could get back up, then we could run for it. The ships were supposed to be worked on to be ready to take off today anyway, but we'd need to get the legion back out of the city…

"Jax!" Oracle said, flying in the window, eyes wide in concern. "The gnomes! Giint is leading them; he's bringing them straight for us!"

"Shitfuck!" I snarled eloquently. "What else could—"

Grizz's hand slammed over my mouth, stopping me before I could say the words that guaranteed a worse event coming. I glared, then realized what I was about to say and nodded in understanding as he grinned and stepped back, releasing me.

"Sorry, Jax," he said.

"It's fine. I know why you did it. Right, Jenae, is there a way off the Prax? From down here, I mean?" I asked. There was a long pause before she responded, concern clear in her voice.

"There is a chance. It's not nearby; it's on the far side of the Prax, and you'd need to cross through the undead territory, where a lich holds sway, but yes, the gnomish airship is still there. It was a prototype that appears to have been well ahead of its time.

"Although it is archaic in comparison to more recent designs, it is gnomish, and therefore far better-built. It lies hidden behind a barricade on the north of the island, but if you could reach it there may be sufficient manastones in the Vault to enable you to power it again," Jenae said, the excitement giving way to concern. *"Jax, the ships are hidden by a powerful illusion; the legion is unaware of them, and as slow as the battleship is, its only chance is to flee, and flee now."*

"Right." I bit my knuckle as I thought. "We've got six hours; six hours from now until the ships make landfall, and DarkSpore would tear through the legion as it is now, with hardly any spells. They have to leave."

"Jax, this is the legion; they can take down any monsters," Grizz said, clearly offended.

"And how many would die? How many citizens?" I asked him grimly. "No, the legion needs to go, and we need to go as well. We've got six hours, that's hardly any time, but we need to escape the gnomes, cut our way through the damn lich and its forces, and find that Vault, then the ship, and get the hell out of here.

"I don't know if we should hope they follow the fleet or stay here, but either way, we've only got the one chance. We have to cut our way through them."

"There is a path, high above. It is narrow and crosses through collapsed sections, but Oracle could make it through to speak to the legion. I cannot help further; they hunt for me, and I must flee. Either way, Jax, I am sorry, but I must leave you. Good luck, my Champion," Jenae said, the sense of her presence fading as I looked around at them all, wishing now that we hadn't stopped for the night or that I'd taken the time to make more potions. I'd planned to do it this morning, but now it was too late.

"Right, you've got five minutes. Loot the shit out of this place," I ordered. "Anything magical, any potions or valuables, get them here."

I pointed to the floor before me, then turned to Oracle, reaching out to her. She flashed to full size and landed, reaching out to me as well.

We held each other for a few long heartbeats, then I released her, and she stepped back, knowing what she had to do.

"I'll go to them, give them their orders and get them moving, then I'll come find you.... " she started to say, and I shook my head.

"No," I said, swallowing hard. "You'd never be able to find us; you know it as well as I do. You go with the fleet; you command them in my absence. When you can, you said once you could communicate with Seneschal and Heph if you got high enough. Get them free of the trap, then go high, get Decin and Oren out to join the fleet. Those extra ships could make all the difference. Then run, go straight to the tower. The cities know who we are by now, and they've clearly picked a side, or they'd have not joined forces."

"I don't want to leave you," she said, tears running down her cheeks.

"I know, and I don't want you to, but it's what you have to do, or they'll all die. Go. I love you, but go!" I said to her, kissing her fiercely one last time.

"You better win this!" she said, glaring up at me.

I smiled at her as she shrank to her smallest size and flew out of the door. The pair of us knew the risk we were both taking; without her support, we could all die down here in the dark, and without my direct mana, she would die within days.

"I will," I said quietly as she took one last look back at me then vanished upwards in a blur of light.

CHAPTER TWENTY-THREE

pulled up the notifications that had been pulsing away, guessing at what I'd find, and dismissing the unimportant details, like the experience notifications, until I saw it.

Congratulations!

You have made progress in your Quest: Fix the Fixers.

The Goddess Jenae has commanded you to explore the Sunken City, a site you now know to be the Prax, Glorious Retribution. Upon further investigation, you've found a lost tribe of gnomes, a species renowned for their standoffish nature, their unwillingness to allow their technology to be investigated by others, and their borderline drug-fueled insanity. Jenae wishes you to further investigate the tribe, healing any you can, and adding to your people.

Discover the Secret of the Gnomish Regression: 1/1

Recover Magical Artifacts and Technologies: 2/?

Retrieve Manastones: 17/100

Retrieve Spellbooks and Skillbooks Lost in the Prax: 0/37

Recruit Additional Citizens: 1/?

Recruit Skilled Crafters: 1/?

Find the Master and Free the Gnomish Tribe: 1/1

Bonuses will be given for exceeding these numbers.

Reward: Improved technological capacity in the Great Tower, Possible technological boosts to the fleet Unknown, 250,000xp

*

Congratulations!

**Because of recent events, the Goddess Jenae has
upgraded your Quest: Fix the Fixers**

You have discovered the chilling secrets of the Prax, Glorious
Retribution, discovered a working, if unpowered, portal, and killed the
Master and his unwilling servants. Due to the level of difficulty involved,
and the bravery shown by your acceptance of the realities of your
situation, the Goddess Jenae has increased your rewards and has altered
the Success Conditions of the Quest.

Recruit the Gnomish Survivors: 1/27

Recover sufficient manastones to power the ship, Interesting Endeavors: 17/40

Eliminate Bartholomew the Lich: 0/1

Find and Prepare the Ship Interesting Endeavors and Use It to Escape: 0/1

Bonus Condition: For Each SporeMother Killed, Receive 10,000xp

Reward: Improved technological capacity in the Great Tower, Possible
technological boosts to the fleet, survival , gnomish exploration vessel
Interesting Endeavors, 500,000xp

Accept? Yes/No

I grunted as I looked it over. I still needed the spellbooks, regardless of them
being missing from the newly updated quest, as I needed to find out about the
Valspar, but the rest was interesting, to say the least.

"Says here that we've found seventeen manastones so far; is that right?" I asked.

Lydia nodded, pointing to a collection of them in the pile that was growing
by my feet. They glimmered faintly, their light almost extinguished, and I sighed,
hoping there were more with a greater charge.

"There's another six there; might be that there's more, though, don't know
fer sure yet," she said.

"Bane, get your arse out there and see what you can find out; see if they're
hostile, or if they're coming for tea," I snapped as I picked up the manastones,
dumping them into a separate bag quickly. Then I swept the rest of the loot into
other bags, including the keys for the portal. Lastly, I moved to the wall of the
bedroom, having noticed things hanging there when I was inside earlier.

I checked quickly, pleased as I recognized some of the equipment. Standard
camping gear, a bowie knife, a collection of books, all well-worn and old, but
definitely from Earth, as well as a handful of more personal items, such as jewelry,
random letters, and, joy of joys, a map! It showed the City of Fellmore, wherever
the hell that was, but still.

You have found a Map!

Do you wish to add it to your own Adventurers Map?

Yes/No

I selected yes, of course, then put it in the bag, along with a few random bits of loot, a diamond the size of a hen's egg, two rubies that seemed to glimmer with an internal light, and a weird mesh that took me several seconds to figure out what it was. I'd almost given up, not wanting to waste the mana to Examine it, when I suddenly recognized the pattern of holes.

When I did, I hit it with an Examine immediately, before cursing as I realized the size of it.

Glove of Spell Augmentation		Further Description *Yes/No*	
Details:		This mesh glove was made especially for a single user, Marn of Bhutan, and grants the user a 10% reduction in the mana cost of spells, along with a 25% increase in spell strength, due to the alignment of chakras. ***Beware:*** *Other users may not experience the full bonus that this item granted to Lady Marn.*	
Rarity:	Magical:	Durability:	Charge:
Unique	Yes	87/100	100/100

It would have been both cool over my gauntlet and extremely useful, given that it was made of tiny, interwoven black rings, but even without it, my hands were far too big for it. I looked around quickly, then grinned as I spotted Miren.

I slipped the glove into a pocket and went back to stuffing everything into bags, finding dozens of drained manastones laid about randomly.

"Well, that's a relief," I said, picking one up and examining it, seeing the cracks that ran through the remaining powdery crystal. "I take it this was how he was powering all the spells he was throwing at you?" I asked Yen.

"Most likely. The number of spells he used…I'd not expect a mortal to be able to cast anywhere near that, and certainly not the variety. Fair enough if he was a pyromage and had been hitting us over and over with low-level fire spells only, but he was trying all kinds of things. No way he was powering the spells himself."

"Okay, sounds good. Tang, can you get the potions from the table; who needs potions, people?" I called out. "I managed to get six mana and seven health made up last night, so…"

"What potions?" interrupted Tang.

"The ones on the table?" I called back, looking over at him in confusion.

"There are no potions on the table," Tang replied, before taking a deep breath and calling out in a voice that was tinged with concern. "Who stripped and looted the body of the red mage?"

"Not me?" I responded, looking around and getting a variety of head shakes in response. "Nobody?" I asked, a faint edge of irritation flooding my voice as I turned and started in that direction, thinking to do it myself.

When I rounded the table to approach the corpse, though, I found a thick streak of blood, the robes, and a few piles of meat I tentatively identified as organs.

Or I would have, if they weren't blackened and clearly rotting.

"What the fuck?" I muttered, and in seconds, Bane and Tang were by my side as the entire group went on high alert.

I pulled up my notifications when they started to flash madly at me, and I felt my heart sink when I read them.

BEWARE!

**Due to the death of the Master, this portion of the quest is still classed as completed, HOWEVER, the Skin-Walker that possessed the Master has fled and will now attempt to claim a new host.
Be wary, for such a creature can beguile the mind
and feed on the unsuspecting.**

"Motherfucker!" I shouted in fury, sweeping up my naginata from where I'd leaned it against the wall earlier and channeling a spark of fire into it, making the room grow instantly brighter as I started searching.

It didn't take long for us to follow the trail, which led to a small crack in one wall, and then down into a pipe, through a hole that was far too small for any of us to follow, leaving a clear trail of dried blood.

"So, what, the goddamn thing is alive, even though Giint put a bolt through its brain, and it dragged itself off into the fucking sewer system?" I snarled, feeling furious at myself. All damn night, I'd felt something watching me, and it must have been this thing; plus we'd lost any fucking loot it had!

We quickly searched the area as Bane moved to the outer balcony and looked down at the gnomes that were closing in on us.

"Bane? What's happening?" I called after we found the health and mana potions I'd left out, drained, and I had to grit my teeth to keep from snarling as a few seconds later, Bane's voice floated back to me.

"They're still coming, but I don't see the frantic aggression we had with the badunka riders. Giint appears to be leading them."

"They coming by choice?" I asked.

"Possibly, possibly not. I can't be sure from up here."

"Fine; let's go find out, I guess. Grizz, you and Lydia okay? Ready to flank me?" Grim nods came from them both. "Good. Grizz, on my right, Lydia, on my left. Jian, you're with Lydia. Miren, Stephanos, Arrin, you're behind us. Stay as high as you can and blast them if a fight starts. Yen, you're our trump card; stay hidden, and be ready to use the spears if we need it, as high-powered as you can. Bane, Tang, stealth. Be ready to jump them and gut anything you can." I snapped out orders as I headed across the room and toward the stairs.

I knew there were things hidden in here, I just goddamn *knew* it, especially with the way the corpses in the cage were dangling; the whole place just screamed out "hidden treasure," but I had neither the time nor the ability to loot it properly. We'd gotten a good supply of gold, silver, and jewels, ironically the things that had the least value to us, and the thing that was the most valuable: the portal, and any hidden magical gear, we didn't have time to attempt to disassemble or find.

I made damn sure to grab the goddamn keys to the portal—no way I was leaving those fuckers around, just in case.

It was galling, but I didn't even dare use the ability that Jenae had given me to find the hidden room; it was a strictly once-a-day ability, and I couldn't risk using it now when I might really need it later. When I'd considered it last night, I'd not known if "once per day" counted as the rise and setting of the sun, or a twenty-four-hour period. I resolved to talk to Jenae about it later.

I grumbled to myself as I jogged across the floor, kicking a small, broken section of the ceiling out of my way and sending it flying out into space, before hearing it clatter to the ground three floors below.

I jogged down the stairs, the rest of the team following me. By the time we'd reached the lowest balcony, Giint and his people were in sight, crossing the outermost edge of the building and heading inside.

We reached the ground floor at about the same time as he led the first of the gnomes into the atrium, and I stopped a few stairs up from the ground, with the rest of the group spreading out around me, ready for a fight.

"Lorrrrd Jaxx," Giint called up to me, bowing awkwardly and glaring at me before spitting on the floor. "I findsss my peeeople. Bring them for healiiiing. You do thisss, they sssswear, like Giint."

The group that moved in around him were a mixture of the noticeably young and the very old, with only Giint seeming an able-bodied adult; still, I let out a sigh as I relaxed. I'd been hoping they were coming to join us, now that the more…rabid…of their people were dead, and the asshole that had been controlling them was gone, but still. Hoping and having it confirmed were two vastly different things.

"Okay, Giint, you brought them here to swear to me. Do they understand what this means?" I asked, and he nodded hesitantly. I went on, looking out at the group that shuffled around, staring at me and each other in equal measure.

I didn't have to count them; the quest from Jenae had said there were twenty-seven in total that could be recruited, and this was obviously them. Despite the filth that coated them, and the borderline madness that shone in many an eye, I knew what had to be done.

Not only could I not leave them, but I also damn well needed them, each and every one, if I was going to find their old ship and get it flightworthy again, not to mention figure out how the hell it worked.

"Giint says you have come to swear fealty to me, in exchange for healing and being taken off the island. Is this true?" I asked, my voice echoing around the atrium.

They looked at each other, and slowly in ones and twos, then more, they nodded or spoke up to agree.

"Good!" I said. "First, then, the good news. I can heal you all, and I can get you off this structure, leading you up into the sky and to a home that, while not safe, will be a damn sight safer than this place will be." I waited, seeing relief on the faces of some and hostility on the faces of others.

"The bad news is that there is an enemy fleet heading here now. My own forces are leaving, by my orders. The only way we can get out of here, and escape with our lives, is if we clear out the undead, kill the lich, and reach your old vessel. I know roughly where it's hidden; do any of you remember it?" I asked, and the older members of the group nodded, most of them, anyway.

A tiny figure shuffled forward, his right eye covered by a monocle and a scruffy cap perched atop his head. Dozens of larger and smaller lenses decorated it, clearly ready to be pulled down at any time to be looked through. He wore pants and a tunic that once must have been smart and probably black. Now they were an off-grey, with patches that covered older patches, and I suspected the original garment was a distant memory at this point.

"I remember it," he wheezed. I frowned, hearing a rough, but cultured accent and clear diction, as opposed to the way Giint spoke. I glanced to Giint before I could stop myself and back at the elder. "You offer to heal us, and in return, we swear our lives to you, something no gnome has ever done."

He glared at me suspiciously.

"Wrong," I said without thought, hastily going on when I saw the glare grow deeper. "You think no gnomes have sworn fealty before, yet your ancestors swore fealty to the empire, long ago."

"Bah," he said, shaking his head. "They had no choice."

"No, they didn't," I replied, my mind filled with fragments of memories. Of wheeling clouds and dragonfire, screams of pain and roars of triumph, thousands of bolts being lofted into the air and soaring past, as Amon and Shustic dove under them. Dragonfire flashing out to destroy defenses. "But that's what happens when you invade your neighbors."

"The records show it was in self-defense! The island of Reshi was plotting to attack, so we simply did it first," he cried, shaking a fist at me.

"Really? Because the emperor couldn't find any evidence of that," I said calmly. "Look. You've got a choice here. You want to be left here, to be trapped on the Prax when the SporeMothers arrive? Be my guest. We're leaving, and as the only way you can make it to your ship is if we clear the way for you, you must choose quickly."

"What SporeMother?" the elder growled.

I smiled coldly. "The one that the Goddess Jenae warned us about. Some assholes are flying it here in the fleet that is heading our way. I don't have time to fuck about, so let's make this as clear as possible. I have the mana to heal one or two of you right now. That's it. Those I heal, like Giint, will probably go through all of their leveling at once. He was unconscious for hours.

"We have six hours before the fleet arrives, so I'm not doing that for anyone, as I'd have no mana, and they'd need to be carried. You want to come, you swear the Oath now. If not, I'm leaving you here," I stated flatly, before starting forward to Giint.

He stood, looking from me to the elder, and the rest of the group remained in stunned silence. Clearly, he'd been expecting that I would wave my hand and make them all well again.

"Giint, I'm sorry," I said apologetically, looking down at him. "I'd planned on healing any I could and using the manastones to power my magic, if I could figure out how. But that choice has been taken from us, I'm afraid. Do you know the way out of here to the undead, I mean?" He nodded, and I let out a sigh of relief. "That's good. I'd been worrying we'd waste time finding out how to get there."

I straightened up and took a deep breath, my grip tightening on my naginata as I faced the elder and the small group that stood around him, arguing.

"Elder, I wish there were more time, as I desperately need you, and your people. I am Jax, Scion of the Empire and Lord of Dravith. I give you my Oath that I intend you and your people no ill will, but I can't waste time here convincing you of the truth of what I say.

"We're leaving. If you want to come with us, then I ask that you strip this place of anything we can use in the war effort and bring it to the ship. You have to get there no later than five hours from now, as I can't imagine that the ship will just start up for the first time without problems." I paused, forcing mana into my Oath, and seeing the look on the elder's face as he registered it.

"I...see...You have seen that we are not what we once were," he said, gesturing to the group that surrounded him. "The eldest were high enough leveled already that we staved off the worst of the effects of the spells and poisoning, but we are none of us what we should be. We exiled the most unstable to the badunka riders, and many more actively roamed the streets, fighting and...feeding...off of each other. Those who are left, well...the youngest are unstable at best, and several are actively rabid, attacking any that come close. You ask us to leave them to their fate?" he said, his voice cold and pain filling his gaze.

"No. If you would bring any others, you can, but—" I said, holding up one hand to stop him from speaking. "They must be restrained. If they attack me or mine, they die. I cannot afford to take the risks right now; thousands of lives are at stake. Those who want to come either swear the Oath, or they are restrained and watched over by those that have sworn. That, or they stay here."

"You leave us little choice," he growled.

I snorted out a laugh. "Man, I've given you lots of choices; you just don't like them! Here," I said, grunting as I *pushed* out the Oath to the group before me. It'd become easier, much easier than it was before.

Back at the tower, I'd needed to draw on its mana to do this, even for smaller groups, but as I grew more proficient, Oracle and I had found we didn't need to use a hammer; a scalpel was enough. It cost me ten mana per person to perform the Oath and five to offer it, so if they all took me up on it, it'd cost me twenty-six times fifteen mana, or three hundred and ninety mana.

Unlike when I activated the Legion Oath, or when I'd taken Amon's Oaths as my own, this was because, with that small amount from me, the Oath was being sworn by the other person, so it could use their mana!

When we'd done it back in the tower, I'd basically paid the mana debt for them, and it was only when I was unconscious and Oracle had tried to give the Oath out, not thinking about it, that she'd realized the truth. It was one of many things she'd told me over the last few days in idle conversation, mainly as we laid in each other's arms on a night.

At five hundred and forty points, my manapool was high enough now that I could afford to use it for this. With the glares some of the group were giving me, I didn't expect I'd have many takers, anyway.

I was surprised when over half of them began to give the Oath, the words rippling out, starting with the elders, and moving to the younger ones as they were nudged or glared at by their parents and friends.

Half a dozen actively refused, with one leaping at the elder who'd spoken up, a dagger flashing through the air for his face. Fortunately, Bane was there, watching quietly, and the gnome was booted in the face, slamming him to the floor, unconscious.

As the remaining five glared at everyone, one of them spat on the floor and turned, running into the darkness. The others followed her, leaving me with one unconscious, one already sworn, and twenty that took the Oath, costing me three hundred mana.

"I swear to obey Lord Jax and those he places over me; I will serve to the best of my ability, speak no lie to him when commanded otherwise, and treat all other citizens as family.

"I will work for the greater good, being a shield to those who need it, a sword for those who deserve it, and a warden to the night.

"I will stand with my family, helping one another to reach the light, until the hour of my death or my lord releases me from my Oath.

"Lastly, I will not be a dick!"

"I, Lord Jax, do swear to protect and lead you, to be the shield that protects you and yours from the darkness, and the sword that avenges that which cannot be saved. As the tower grows in strength, so shall you," I said, gritting my teeth as the mana was torn from me. Once it was done, and the group of citizens stood looking at me in trepidation, I sighed.

"I'm sorry, honestly I am. If there was a better way, I would take it, but there isn't. How long will it take us to reach the ship from here, if we marched through with no interruptions?" I asked the elder, whose name was revealed to be Frederikk with a judicious use of Examine.

"About two hours, maybe a little more?" he said, unsure.

"Well, we know it won't be that easy, and we'll probably have to fight for every inch, but I bet you can catch up. Giint made a half-badunka, half-sled before in a few hours. Could you make several devices that would carry you all?" I asked.

"Easily. There are many damaged badunkas and other war machines that have been gutted over the years. We could make fast-moving sleds."

"Then do it. You have an hour, then I want you to all follow us and catch up to us in the lich's domain. We'll kill as many as we can to give you a clear path. Giint will take us to the path we need, then he will return and help you.

"If you have any time left over once you've built your devices, for the love of the gods, search this building, take anything that is valuable and bring it. We came here looking for devices and spellbooks, but now, thanks to the SporeMothers, we can't take the time we need to search this place properly. Anything you can find is needed, but in the empire, the most valuable thing is life. I'd rather save you than anything else. I'm sorry that I haven't the time to convince you of that, but it is what it is."

I nodded to them, then looked back at my people, and then down to Giint.

"Giint, lead the way," I said, gesturing. He nodded, moving through the crowd grim-faced. The gnomes made room for us, but the looks on their faces tore at me.

They looked lost and in shock. They'd been given a faint lifeline, and now it felt like I had torn it away and was abandoning them.

We had less than six hours, maybe five and a half now, and when we were going to have to fight our way through the levels back up to the surface, every minute was needed.

As I moved through the group, I saw the looks they gave me; some were excited, but they were in the minority. Most looked lost or angered. Thankfully, Frederikk spoke up, sensing the group's emotions.

"You heard the lord. We don't have time to grumble if we're to survive, so grab your gear! Lars, Dawn, I want you to build…" His voice was hard, but not unkind as he gave out the orders to the shocked remnant of their race. I tried to not think about how many of their families we'd literally slaughtered in the last day, and worse, how many of the survivors were thankful for it.

The voices faded as we moved through the rooms, quickly getting outside. I looked around the cavern, trying to imagine what it was going to be like for the children once they left. In here, you could see the far walls and the ceiling high overhead, so I could only imagine the way they'd react to riding an airship.

I shook my head, imagining the mixture of panic and wonder, then I ruthlessly squashed the feelings down, concentrating on the path ahead.

"How many potions do we have?" I asked, and everyone checked their remaining inventory, making me growl in frustration. We had enough for two average healing potions, or three lesser each, once we'd redistributed them, and seven mana potions left. That was it.

I pulled Jian up for a quick conversation, then handed him the mesh glove to give to Miren, on the grounds that not only was she the only one with small enough hands to use it, but it'd also mean more coming from him than it would from me. He smiled and tucked it away quickly, winking at me when I told him that it was from him, not me, and he could make up any story he liked about it.

We passed around some dried meat and a kind of oatcake the legionnaires had packed as we went, passing down the switchback and breaking into a jog across the cavern floor to move through the remains of the fungus fields and storage areas. I grimaced at seeing the water that was all that was left for the ferals to drink now, including the sheen of chemicals that floated on the top of it.

Always, there was the feeling of eyes watching us, and occasionally, we'd see some of the more feral gnomes, but as long as we kept moving, they seemed to decide we weren't worth the hassle.

"Giint, will you be safe enough going back to join the others through this?" I asked at one point, and he just laughed. I shrugged and dismissed it as unimportant for now, remembering what a handful he'd been to fight. Now that he was aware of himself properly again, I almost felt sorry for the ferals if they attacked him.

He led us to a large door in one wall, braced and barred, with a circular lock on it, operated by a lever.

"There," he said, turning and walking away.

"Oi!" I called after him, making him pause. "Anything we need to know about the area past this?" I asked, exasperated. He bared his teeth at us in what I took for a smile.

"Don't dieeee," he snarled. As he passed Tang, he reached out furtively, and Tang passed him a small bag of something before holding his hands up as Yen grabbed his shoulder.

"It's sugar, for fuck's sake, nothing else, you know gnomes!" he said. I shook my head, resolving again to let Restun deal with whatever it was when we got back.

The door took a few minutes to unlock, twisting and pulling on the metal that had settled into place over the years, but eventually, we managed it.

"Everyone ready?" I asked and got a round of nods in return, as those without dark enhancements to their vision secured magelights to their armor. "Remember, people, we can't slow down. Kill everything, but keep going. The sooner we reach the lich, the less time it has to gather its forces. Let's go!"

I yanked the door open and jumped back as the first undead lunged forward out of the hallway.

CHAPTER TWENTY-FOUR

The first creature was a decrepit skeleton, its armor barely holding together. It bore no weapons and was barely able to move under its own violation. It had clearly been stationed there long ago, in the vain hope that the door would be opened.

Now that its reason for existing was fulfilled, I imagined a sense of relief as Grizz smashed it from its feet with a single blow of his gladius.

While not the ideal weapon for the undead, his incredible strength made short work of the creature, hacking its head clean and sending bone shards flying.

The animating force fled the skeleton, and Grizz plowed into the hallway, his magelight casting weird shadows as he went.

"Go, go, go!" I shouted, matching action to words as I followed Lydia, who was second through the door.

The corridor beyond was filled with filth; one wall was bulging inward. A constant *drip-drip* came from somewhere overhead, along with a steady rivulet of foul water and scum that ran down the left wall to gather on the floor in shallow puddles before leaking out through rusted sections of the far wall.

We ran on, coming to a crossroads and pausing to look at the choices: left, right, or straight ahead. Grizz looked to me, and I pointed forward, shrugging as Tang and Yen took turns scratching or burning an arrow into the wall where the gnomes would be able to see it.

Grizz nodded, and we were off again. The slight downward slope made it feel like we were almost falling as we ran forward, thundering along, with the clatter and racket of our weapons and armor building as we picked up speed.

"On the left!" Yen shouted, and Grizz altered his direction, seeing a skeleton come out of the darkness. It had been laid on the floor, but at our approach, it clambered to its feet. Grizz lashed out with his shield, smashing it into the wall with enough force that it collapsed back to sit on its ass, broken. Jian took its head as he sprinted past, while the rest of us barely slowed.

Two more crossroads came and went before we hit our first dead end, retracing our footsteps and taking the right passage, then a left at the next one.

Ten more minutes passed before we took a turning that led out into a large room, skidding to halt.

We'd barely seen any undead up to this point, but here, we found dozens, and worst of all, they weren't the docile kind.

As soon as we left the cover of the hallway, they struck. Four shir, creatures I'd not seen since I first arrived in the UnderVerse, ran at us, lumbering towards us side-by-side.

They were huge creatures, humanoid, but more ox than man, with wide horns and massive shoulders. As the four lowered their heads in unison, I saw the plan. Either we'd split up, and they'd defeat us in detail, as dozens more undead ran behind them. Or we'd stay together, and the shir would smash us into paste.

I paused for a second, trying to figure out what to do, but for the first time, Lydia didn't.

"Grizz, right flank! Jax, center, shield! Arrin, get their legs!" she snapped out, hunching behind her shield. I followed her, seeing Grizz slide in on the right, locking his shield alongside my own.

As I settled into place, a sudden searing heat washed over us as Jian's demon let rip with its beam ability.

A terrible flare of heat seemed to fill the air, slamming into the four shir and cutting from left to right. The plasma burned deep into their lumbering corpses, making them scream in fury as they caught fire, bones exploding and rotting flesh erupting into sooty smoke.

The blast had staggered them, destroying two and leaving the remaining two on the right damaged. We slammed into them seconds later, shields held up and braced. My naginata, gripped tight and held upright, further braced the shield. Yet I still cried out as we slammed into them, their sheer physical weight being enough to send us staggering backwards like we'd shoulder-charged a wall.

The shir collapsed into piles of bones, though, and the others took up the attack, giving us time to recover. I staggered, my left arm totally numb and barely responding. Grizz, with his massive shoulders, seemed to hardly have noticed the impact.

He lunged forward, stabbing downward and shattering their skulls with his gladius, quickly making sure of the kills.

I grunted in relief as I felt a heal hit me and gritted my teeth, letting out a hiss of pain as my left shoulder popped back into place.

"Thanks, Arrin!" I called over my shoulder and grinned as a trio of Magic Missiles flashed past me seconds later.

Grizz was already hacking and slashing his way into the next staggering wave of the undead. Lydia slid to a halt, bracing her shield and bashing a skeleton that had leaped at her. It cartwheeled backward, slamming into the floor with a clatter of breaking bones, before her mace slammed down, smashing the skull into smithereens.

Tiny Firebolts flashed through the room, thrown by Miren's summoned flame golem, and arrows cut through the air, slamming into the undead and staggering them more than killing, but that broke up their charge, allowing us to face more manageable numbers.

I lunged into the fray again, stabbing out with my naginata. In a stroke of inspiration, I infused it with a little healing energy and grinning when a stab to the chest, not normally fatal to an undead, made it scream before collapsing into a pile of moldy bones.

I twisted around, locking my shield back into place on my back, thankful again for the utility of the legion armor design, feeling the hooks click as it slid to a halt, and I spun my naginata properly.

It was a pain in the ass using the shield and naginata together, and I knew I needed to practice with it, but not right now. I needed to hammer these fuckers out of the way and go, go, go!

The flickering light from the magelights sent dancing shadows across the vaulted ceiling and walls of the chamber, adrenaline building in the group as we set off at a sprint.

We smashed through the next ranks, then more. I ducked down, flipping my naginata around and grabbing it in both hands near the base of the blade, swinging the metal-clad base at an oncoming gnome corpse. The staggering creature seemed to smooth out its motions as it came closer, a sign that the lich had assumed direct control.

"Too late, motherfucker!" I shouted, slamming the base into the side of its head and sending the small, three-foot figure flying, bones shattering and death's head lifting in my vision.

I grinned; there was something about fighting the undead that I just *liked,* I decided. There was no moral gray area. They were undead, they were attacking me, and they were essentially bags of bones, so when they were like this, they were almost fun.

"Left!" came Miren's shout of warning, and the disassembled bones collected to form an abomination, bouncing and clattering across the floor toward each other. I slammed the base of my weapon to the floor and stood still, bracing it in the crook of my arm as I started to cast.

A handful of seconds later, the Fireball materialized fully. I threw it forward with a huff of exertion, sending it flashing across the distance that separated us to slam into the bones that were even now beginning to form a mound. Just before it landed, three Magic Missiles impacted, blowing a hole in the middle. Then my Fireball detonated, sending bone fragments flying across the room.

There was a scream of rage and pain somewhere in the distance, as the lich casting the spell had to suffer the backlash of the collapsed spell.

"Go!" I shouted, as the undead around us staggered. The greater capacity for, well, everything that the lich had bestowed by taking direct control was lost. Those who had been under its direct control at the time almost collapsed.

"Hoo-ah!" Grizz shouted, jumping into the air and using his shield to smash a staggering skeleton from its feet, even as his blade flicked out and severed another's skull.

I shook my head as I sprinted. The others were almost past me, and I couldn't help but grin at Grizz's exuberance. I pushed to catch up, the others smashing their way forward. Lydia was doing amazing; she kept ducking her head down behind her shield and using her Shield Bash ability, smashing the undead from their feet while Jian ran behind her, spinning and slicing, sending the remains clattering to the floor permanently.

Miren and Stephanos had given up firing arrows and had instead concentrated on keeping up and shepherding Arrin as he cast spell after spell.

I stormed ahead, pushing myself harder and harder to catch up to the front line. Lydia saw me and dropped back, taking the time to slow so that her stamina could recover, as I cleared the way.

I spun my naginata end-over-end in a style that I'd been taught was called Kali. I didn't know the name for sure, but I remembered the training. Using my left hand high on the haft as a guide and the right lower down, I swept it back and forth, stabbing up and out and yanking back. My left hand remained partially open, allowing me to slide the haft up and down fast, but I kept it tight enough that when a blow landed, I didn't lose my weapon.

I stabbed out, cut, sliced, and swept the blade back and forth, taking an arm off here, a leg there, deflecting a badly thrust rotting spear and slicing off the arm that held it, then the leading foot the skeleton was braced on, then taking its head.

The battle dissolved into a flurry of stabs, cuts, and sweeps. As I ran forward and jumped, using the base of my naginata almost like a pole vault, I slammed both feet into one of the oncoming skeleton's skulls, catapulting it backwards in a pile of bones. The room suddenly snapped back into focus, and I heard my labored breathing as my body tried to keep up with the demands placed on it.

I glanced about, seeing the room was filling with silent bones, and my team was still going, starting to pass me again.

"Goddamn it!" I grunted, digging deep and catching up again. Grizz dropped back to the third in line, behind Lydia, then me in second place.

We'd slipped into a routine, I realized, taking turns as the leading edge, smashing our way forward, then dropping back to third in line, catching our breath and refilling our stamina, before the second place stepped back up to take the lead, and the one who'd been in front moved into the third line, waiting for their turn again.

It'd not been discussed, it just happened, like the way that Jian swept the injured and disabled undead up, smashing them and moving on, or the way that Tang and Bane appeared and disappeared, picking the outliers off. Yen, who was skilled in magic, archery, and the sword, protected and guided Arrin, Miren, and Stephanos, traded off with Arrin so they both had time to replenish their mana.

Lydia looked at me as she raced forward, her heavy legionnaire armor fitting her more and more by the day. I caught the flash of her grin as she went, returning it unthinkingly.

This was where she'd always wanted to be; maybe not underground in a sunken city out in the middle of the ocean, but adventuring, living on the edge, and being relied upon, respected as a warrior. I grinned as I remembered what we'd decided.

Augustus had come to Restun, Romanus, and me the day before we'd come down here, when we were talking. He'd explained that he'd named her Optio in the battle for the airships, as he felt she deserved it, but he needed it ratified. The rank of Optio was a rank that you couldn't apply for; you had to be in the right place in the rankings and show that you *deserved* it.

As leader of my personal squad, Lydia had the right of rank and clearly the right of ability, so he'd named her, and now it was up to us to fully ratify it…followed by her claiming it.

Now that we'd agreed, it was apparently a case of letting her come to the realization on her own. She'd basically either decide she was ready for the rank and claim it publicly by simply stepping up and giving those orders, or she'd not. She'd already done most of the steps, and now it would mostly be a matter of time.

I'd taken great pleasure in approving it, and Restun and Romanus had agreed. She wasn't a full legionnaire, not yet, so it was a bit of a weird situation. She needed a hell of a lot more training and to be brought up to a minimum standard of skill in all weapons, but that was coming.

As soon as we had time, she would begin her informal training, and as soon as she passed it, which we damn well knew Restun was going to kick her ass until she managed it, she'd be ready.

For Optio, you didn't apply, you just took the rank if it was available…how it happened in most armies as well. In the field, if the sarge was taken down, the corporal would step into their shoes. They'd take the spot, and then once the battle was over, they'd apply for it. Usually, anyway. They might not get it; if there were other sergeants available, they'd often get it, but that corporal would have proven themselves and would be moved into a fast-track to sarge.

In the legion, it was simply a case of prove yourself and boom, provided you weren't already blackballed by the others, anyway.

I banished the thoughts, and I grinned with excitement as I pushed off again, digging in to take up my place in second behind her as we ran from the chamber, hitting the next corridor and racing down it.

We slowed as we hit a section of collapsed wall covering half the corridor, then clambered up a pile of rubble that rose into the upper floor, finding the next wave of undead waiting for us.

This room was bigger than the last chamber, easily a hundred meters across, with a lower ceiling, but the circular room had recesses that were randomly filled with braced figures. My heart leaped at the sight of them.

Golems!

There were dozens of golems, easily thirty in sight, all war models, but they were frozen in hibernation or death. I growled to myself as I realized that if they'd had the mana they'd need to respond to me, they'd have already swept the city clear of the undead.

Basically, they were the equivalent of being broke and visiting Fort Knox on a tour. There was all that wealth, and I'd never get my hands on it.

I banished the annoyance and turned my attention back to the undead as the group slowed, realizing that they weren't attacking.

I slowed as well, coming to a stop at the front of the wedge shape we'd adopted, and I swallowed hard at the rows upon rows of silent figures.

The skeletons numbered in the hundreds. I'd been thinking we were cutting through them at speed, making our way to the lich, and believing we weren't far from escaping. I was horribly wrong.

While we'd been fighting the undead below, the lich had essentially been keeping us busy as it got its real forces into place.

We were outnumbered. Horrifically so.

"What do we do, Jax?" Grizz asked.

The undead were at least three ranks deep. I couldn't see beyond that in the darkness, not with the combination of lights and my DarkVision flaring in and out of focus.

Here and there, amongst the more standard humanoid forms, were others, some Xon'dike, a handful of shir, a couple of huge crab-like things that seemed imposing, but the way the carapace hung on them, they might actually be weaker than the rest, and a collection of small figures. At first, I'd taken them all for gnomes, but some of them had strange, thick flexible limbs like tentacles but solid-looking, and strange ridges on their hairless bodies.

"Now you see that you have no chance." A raspy voice addressed us, as though unused to speaking aloud. I spun to my left where a palanquin of bones was being carried forward through the massed undead, four enormous amalgamations of bone bearing it in spiked claws. "Surrender and answer my questions truthfully, and perhaps I shall let you live."

"Everyone always wants me to fucking surrender," I muttered, and Grizz looked at me, cocking his head to the side. "Seriously, that's what they all say. 'Surrender'—like anyone's going to believe they won't slaughter us, first chance they get. They always start with that, don't they? 'Drop your weapons,' as if they don't just want us to be easier to kill," I muttered, then I raised my voice and called back to the figure I couldn't quite make out on the palanquin. "No, thank you! We don't want to be murdered today, thanks very much!"

There was a long silence as the palanquin cleared the undead, several smaller skeletons crushed by the bigger ones as they went.

"If you give an Oath to leave my city with nothing beyond what you brought when you entered, I may permit you to live," the figure eventually suggested, as though unsure.

"Nope. Want to go for strike three?" I called back to it, turning and whispering to my people. "Stephanos, that earth golem, can it make things? Manipulate the ground, I mean?"

"Uh, yeah?" Stephanos said slowly. "But this is metal under us…"

"Fuck, okay, good point. Grizz, get ready to use your Iceshield. When it runs out, Lydia, you use yours. All ranged attacks are on the lich: bows, magic, everything. Keep your back to the pit; we can run down there if we need to. Jian, is your demon ready for a second blast yet?"

"I can use my power once per day," Ty'Baronn said coldly.

"Well, that's just fucking peachy. Next time, you save it until I tell you," I snapped at him, moving on to Yen. "I want the most powerful Flamespears you can manage, and I want them all around the palanquin. Make them land one after the other in a circle, that way, the blast will reinforce itself."

"You are from Earth." The rough voice rose again. I paused, putting the multiple keys together with the bodies I'd seen so far.

"So are you," I called back. "Lost your key for the portal though, didn't you?"

Silence greeted my words for several seconds.

"I will permit you and you alone to leave right now, by my Oath. Carry whatever else you want, but you leave your companions and any manastones and portal keys," the voice said, suddenly forceful and demanding. "You cannot win this fight, not without likely dying. You know this and what are they to you? I need the bodies. In fact, I'll go one better. Name your patron, and when I return to Earth with my minions, I will spare their life, by your grace," the voice offered, slowly stepping out of the palanquin.

At last, I could see the figure, and I shook my head in disgust.

"Holy shit, you're ugly; you know that?" I called to him. He was tall and rail-thin, the pallor of the dead gleaming out plain to see, even at this distance. "Fuck, man, you don't look healthy!" I jeered.

He growled in anger, lifting one hand between us to flex the clawed, bony fingers. "I was trapped here, cut off from my supplies, from any escape, hemmed in by revenants and twisted insane gnomes. I took the chance I was given and used the knowledge of the Vault to transform myself into a lich. While not the existence I'd hoped for, it is satisfying, and there is no more mortal hunger, no thirst, no need for food or companionship."

"Still fugly, though," I retorted, bracing myself. "When I start moving, hit them with everything you have," I muttered under my breath to the group before turning back to the lich, who glared at us. "So, you're 'Barry the Lich,' then?" I called to him. "Now *there's* a name to inspire fear!"

"Bartholomew!" he screeched at me, lifting one hand and summoning a ball of necrotic energy, while I started circulating mana through the channels to my tattoos. "My name was Bartholomew! Never Barry!"

"Looks like Barry to me, mate; even says so when I Examine you!" I called back, not bothering to check if that was true or not.

"Bartholomew!" he screamed, thrusting both hands forward in a necrotic display of temper. The bolt flew straight for me, a sickly black and mottled green that glowed in the darkness, splashing harmlessly across my hastily raised magical shield. I let out a sigh of relief, as it'd literally coalesced less than a second before the impact, and I'd thought it was going to be too little, too late.

Thankfully, unlike the spell hurled by the Master, the dickbag who had been abusing the gnomes, this was powered mainly by anger and didn't have the same kind of effect as a spell powered by a manastone. I paused, then grinned, sighing in relief as the magic was sucked into powering my shield instead of slamming into my body.

"Oh, come on, even the wanker in charge of the gnomes put up more of a fight than that!" I called to him, slowly walking forward, trying to close some of the distance between us before he realized.

He was the linchpin here; the freeing of the revenants had removed the inhabitants that were roaming under their own power. When I summoned Bob, I was warned that, if I stopped powering him, he'd die. I had to assume it was the same here: kill the controller, and the undead would collapse.

That or smash us into paste, but as it was the only plan I had, it was the one I was going with.

"You killed Grant?" he growled. "You killed my brother?!" He screamed wordlessly, the sound raw and full of fury as every undead in the room shifted, and the lich's eyes began to glow a sickly green. "You murdered my brother!" he shouted again. "Now die!"

The room exploded into movement as I swore and lunged. The others behind me started their spells, the Iceshield growing around the group while I launched into a sprint, trying to get close enough to the lich.

The first dozen meters were open as I ran to get clear, then I reached the first of the incoming undead, and the battle began.

The smallest undead got to me first, the ones that had looked like gnomes. Their strange, tubular limbs flexed and crunched as they moved, but they seemed made up of joints, dozens on each limb, and the resulting range of motion both allowed them greater speed and flexibility as they darted around their slower, lumbering brethren.

The huge amalgamations of bone that had carried the palanquin were moving as well, and the standard skeletons and crab-like undead between them and me were sent flying when the foremost lashed out to clear itself a path.

The glow around the larger ones matched the lich's eyes; he obviously believed bigger was better. I fed a little healing magic into my naginata and started striking out as I continued running for him.

The first of the little ones bunched its legs underneath itself and leaped for me, its bald head opening as if on a hinge to expose a huge maw filled with missing and damaged teeth.

I smashed it from the air with the butt of the weapon, spun it around, and skewered a second one, catching the third on the haft and flinging it aside before kicking another back and sweeping the blade low to medium height. My blade made short work of cutting through ankles, knees, thighs, and in the case of a few actual gnomes, throats.

It all went to shit as I frantically dove aside, rolling and jumping, then diving again, trying to get clear of the impact point.

The palanquin smashed to the floor right where I'd been, flung by one of the amalgamations, I guessed. I'd literally just seen it soaring towards me, and I'd dove aside, realized I was still within the edge of the target area, and had gone again.

When it landed, it easily smashed a dozen smaller undead into splinters, with the larger group curving around to follow me as I rolled to my feet and set off at a dead run.

We were encircled by the undead, several hundred standard humanoid corpses, if I had to guess, with at least a dozen larger heavily armored aquatic crab things, dozens upon dozens of the little ones, and while there were only the four larger ones so far, there were ten of us. While the undead were generally weak individually, all they had to do was pin us down.

That didn't even factor in the bigger ones or the shir that could simply trample us, breaking bones before coming for a second lap.

I just hoped we wouldn't face another bone colossus.

I ran headlong at the main body of the undead before me, saving my Mana Overdrive for when I really needed it. I started swinging and keeping the enemies' focus on me, until the wonderful sound of rolling explosions could be heard.

The rest of the team had joined the fray.

I stabbed out, taking a skeleton in the face, the blade crunching through the moldy remnants of flesh and punching into the skull, then I yanked the blade to my left, ripping the remnants of the skull free of the neck, and bringing the metal-clad butt up to smash into a second creature.

It was sent hurtling into its fellows, the undead's lighter weight making it less able to shrug off my blows as I dipped the blade down and spun. Extending the naginata outwards as I crouched, I continued sweeping around me in a wide strike, hacking and slicing through dozens of limbs before coming to my feet and getting kicked in the chest with the force of a car wreck.

The remnants of my mana shield popped, and I was sent flying, slamming into a group of the undead and scattering them like a bowling ball through pins.

I gasped, coughed, and shook my head, trying to get my diaphragm to stop clenching and damn well pull in the air I needed. I rolled to the side, grabbed a shifting, bony arm as the skeleton under me tried to clutch my throat. Forcing myself up, half reaching, half gasping for air, I punched another in the face, knocking it backwards.

My naginata was gone, lost somewhere when I was sent flying, and the mass of undead was rapidly closing in around me.

At last, my diaphragm unclenched, the spasm relaxing, and I sucked in a deep lungful of air, relief flooding me as it came.

I was surrounded, and the mentality of the Royal Marines rose in me as I grinned at them all. I wasn't surrounded; this was just a target-rich environment, that was all.

"As the Americans say," I mumbled, pulling the components of a spell together, "'Enemies to the left, enemies to the right, enemies to the rear and enemies to the front.'" I forced more and more mana into the spell, ignoring the grasping fingers and the sword that clanged off my vambrace, sending a jolt of pain through me, but little else.

"I HAVE YOU RIGHT WHERE I WANT YOU!" I screamed as I threw the spell. Explosive Compression hurtled forward, slipping between the bodies before hitting the knee of a giant form and detonating.

The giant staggered as a lower leg cracked, entire sections of bone flying away or being reduced to splinters. Then the second phase went active, and the stooping figure was yanked downwards, as was everything else in a three-meter radius.

I'd wanted to make a bigger AOE, but I had neither the time, nor had I expected to get enough space to use it, so I spun, grabbing the nearest undead and throwing it in the direction of the compression.

Dozens were being pulled in, the lack of screams made all the more eerie by the cracking and crunching of bones.

Then the Flamespears Yen had been building up and charging were released, flashing through the air and aimed at the lich, who was still controlling the giants.

The first slammed into him directly, sending him flying to the ground, wreathed in flames. The second hit just to his left, then the right, then on the far side of him, barely missing his screaming head.

The shockwave of the impacts, the flaming explosions, and the sheer overpressure induced by the spell did horrific damage, but, even as the damage began to hit it, a shield charm on its belt flared and activated, and I assumed the charm had been tied to its health dropping below a certain point.

Protected from the strikes for a few seconds, it reached out, grabbing onto the leg of an undead that ran to it, and ripped the imbuing half-life free.

The animating energy flowed into Bartholomew the Lich and began to repair the damage Yen had done, just as the second volley arrived.

Magic Missiles, Firebolts, and more slammed into it, rocking the shield and making it flare and pulse, followed by arrows that shattered as a dome of black energy flared brightly around the lich.

The undead paused as it abandoned them, concentrating on a few that were close enough and pulling them in to defend it. The rest staggered as their driving force for existing wavered, and we struck.

Grizz was the first into the fight, whooping with joy as he slammed out into the reeling undead. Lydia raced from the main group, barreling directly for me as the Iceshield was dispelled, and the others maintained their focus on the lich.

Lydia thundered through, activating her Shield Bash and practically flying across the intervening distance to slam three undead backwards, shattering the first and damaging the second and third, while I lashed out, punching, kicking, and tearing my way through the creatures.

It was true what the movies had told us in one respect: all you had to do to destroy a standard animated undead was rip its head free. That was the focus of the spell; remove it, and the skeleton was still "alive," but its body collapsed to the floor in a clatter of bones, and the skull was suddenly rendered impotent.

As much as I preferred to kill everything around me, for now, the most efficient method was to tear the corpses apart with my bare hands, so I snarled and kicked, punched, and drove stiffened fingers into rotting flesh, grasping spines and jaws, ripping skulls free and tossing them aside.

Lydia battled her way to me, smashing the bone-bags to the floor, before grabbing one that was clambering onto my back.

She tore it free of me, lifted it overhead, and smashed it down, stomping on its skull over and over until it shattered. I grabbed the next one, a decaying adventurer with a strange, bell-shaped breastplate.

I dug my fingers under the rim that ran around the neck and yanked it forward, clutching the chin in my right hand and shoving the jaw to the left as far as it would go before releasing the chestplate and grabbing the back of the head in my left hand. I quickly snapped the neck, tearing the head free in a single rough movement.

As the corpse collapsed, I turned, wild-eyed, then saw Lydia, grinning at the sight of her stomping her enemy into submission. Suddenly, I cried out as a blade sliced into my right jawbone, glancing off the joint and tearing half my ear away.

I brought my right forearm up, blocking the spear that had been so close to taking my head. Then I grabbed onto it, just below the head, pushing it aside as I yanked a dagger free.

I drove the blade into the skeleton's face in retribution, snarling as I shoved, the flesh of my cheek and jaw torn open and flapping in the wind of my movement.

The dagger entered its right eye, the blade scraping across the back of the skull, and I felt it for the first time clearly: the bundle of magic and animated half-life that drove the creature. I snarled louder, ripping the dagger to the left, tearing the skull free of the collapsing body.

While we fought hard, especially Grizz and Lydia, who methodically smashed their way through the undead, the Explosive Compression spell ran out. The undead that had been previously constrained, which had meant we only had to fight on three sides, were released to attack again.

"Jax!" Lydia shouted. "We have to fall back!"

She grunted and slammed her mace out, deflecting a sword that was thrust at my blindside as I whipped the spear up and around, driving the undead back in a display of wild force and aggression.

I couldn't keep this up much longer.

The damage to my face was painful and distracting, but it was the stamina drain and the swarming undead that was the real problem. There might still be a way to win, I realized, but it was a Hail-Mary pass.

"Hit it again!" I screamed to the group, then shouted to Lydia. "Keep them off me as long as you can!"

I hated trying to do this without Oracle, but I needed it. I wasn't stupid; trying to alter a spell in a major way without her help would almost certainly fail, but the high explosive version of the normal Firebolt/Fireball spell was one I'd used enough for it to be familiar already. All I wanted to do was overcharge it way, way past what it was supposed to be able to handle, in a truly short period of time.

I went for it, even as Lydia screamed in frustration before seeming to go practically nuclear as she pushed herself past her normal physical limits.

She drew in a deep breath as I concentrated on my spell, densely layering the mana into it as I went, and she called out, her voice reverberating in a way I'd never heard.

The entire room seemed to pause as Lydia's voice rang out, filled with a choral note, before a response seemed to come back, carried from some unimaginable distance.

The single cry she'd roared out echoed around the chamber, and it was suddenly filled with an entire choir of determination.

I glanced at her in shock, fingers faltering in the weaving of the spell. Her face was suffused with joy and resolve, and as the cry went on, she started to glow.

She began with a deep red, one that seemed to shine from her eyes and the joints of her armor. It slowly grew brighter and brighter, until she was glowing a steady golden yellow. That yellow then began to lighten to blue, and wings of white flame grew from her back as her cry broke off.

"My life before his!" she roared, and the very air seemed to shake before she was off. She moved almost too fast to see, her mace blurring and crunching, smashing down weapons, upraised claws, and skulls. She spun around me like a whirlwind of glowing retribution, every strike dealing destruction.

Bodies shattered from her blows like they'd been hit with a shotgun at close range. Bones, armor, all of it practically detonated as she raced in a circle around me, driving them back.

Yen collapsed to her knees as she fully depleted her manapool with a second barrage of her Flamespears. Firebolts flashed out of the shadowy areas of the room, along with occasional arrows and daggers that sliced skulls free as Bane and Tang continued to pick off the outliers.

Miren's flame golem flashed into play, slamming into the lich's shield just before the spears could, detonating itself and weakening the shield enough that the third and final spear of the barrage managed to break through. It ripped the lich's left arm free in a flaming explosion. I barely managed to stabilize the spell, then continued to plow as much mana into it as I could, making an already unstable mess worse by going too fast.

Grizz cried out in pain as a pair of the small figures latched onto the backs of his knees, wrapping their tentacles around his legs and locking them straight just as a Shir slammed into him, sending him flying.

Jian flowed forward, seeming almost to dance as he stepped from form to form, his blades glowing an icy-blue as he used an ability called Icewind's Fury. Each time the swords landed, their target slowed slightly, until the two shir that he kited around Grizz were stumbling and staggering, barely able to walk, and he took their heads.

Stephanos's earth golem was stomping about, smashing its fists into the undead that came too close to its master, shattering bones and ignoring their attempts to destroy it, taking only small injuries, but it was damage that climbed steadily.

Arrin alternated between healing the group and sending wave after wave of Magic Missiles at the lich, but his mana was dropping fast, and I gritted my teeth, going on.

Lydia was audibly huffing as she spun past me, her symbol flickering in my vision as though she was taking serious wounds.

I grunted and sliced the feed to the spell, gripping it tightly as it shook like a greyhound seeing a rabbit, before I finally released it.

I was hurled backwards by the spell's departure, and it cut the air, covering the distance to the lich with a shrill whine of displaced air.

The lich hunched down, fear plain on its face as it frantically tried to recover its strength, draining a bone amalgamation of life.

It straightened as the spell hurtled past it, glaring at me through blackened skin as it opened its mouth to laugh at my poor aim.

At that point, the spell hit the target, though, slamming into a stanchion that held a section of the ceiling in place.

It'd been sagging already, but when the overcharged Explosive Compression slammed into it and detonated. The effect practically vaporized a section of the roof.

The floor above it was already sagging in that section, a result of ancient damage sustained in the crash, and the roof creaked, groaned, and started to collapse.

The lich's spell shield had held off most of the damage so far, and probably could have continued to hold out long enough for the undead to finish my party off. It clearly understood its minimal chances of holding off a sliding, multi-ton mass of steel and debris and panicked, sprinting for the nearest bone giant. It reached the enormous minion with less than a second to spare as the blocks raining down hit the corpse it was hiding below. The giant amalgamation of corpses hunched down around their master protectively, and every undead in the area spun, racing to do the same, leaving us.

CHAPTER TWENTY-FIVE

I turned just in time to see Lydia fall. She collapsed face-first, seeming to run out of steam mid-swing as she dropped from striking a fleeing skeleton to unconscious and falling limp. Her body slid to a halt in the debris and piled bones of the floor, with only eight health remaining.

I had enough, barely, for a single heal. I pulled out the low-grade mana potion that I had left and downed it, knowing it was barely better than water, but it'd help me regenerate slightly faster, at least. I slammed the spell into her as I went, kneeling down by her side and pulling her helm free, staring fearfully into her bloodshot and blank eyes. The Battlefield Triage spell gave me as much information as I needed, even as it worked to repair the massive trauma done to her body by whatever she'd just done to herself.

The information the spell provided to me told me what she'd done, but not how. Her body had literally burned its way through just about every calorie it possessed. She'd rendered the little fat on her body into fuel and had driven herself at an insane speed. Then her body had begun to eat itself, muscles being consumed to fuel the movements she needed to make.

I kept it going as long as I could before sagging as my mana bottomed out, and the mana-migraine exploded in my mind. I fell forward, catching myself before I fell on Lydia. Screwing my eyes closed, I bit my cheek as I forced myself to squint at her.

As soon as I could focus, I saw that she looked better; not a great deal, but she had a little color back in her cheeks, and her breathing wasn't as labored, which was a relief in itself.

I turned, sweeping my gaze around the remains of the room, and saw my people huddling on the far side. Grizz had managed to get close enough to them to use his Iceshield. That, along with their distance from the lich, had been enough to keep them relatively safe beyond more bruises and a handful of cuts. Though Jian looked to have broken his arm, Arrin was already fixing it.

I scanned the rest of the cavern, seeing the dust and debris starting to settle, and swore as shambling figures started to appear. I pulled out the healing potion I had, a common grade, and half-choked Lydia getting it into her mouth, my concern and distraction, mixed with wearing relatively unfamiliar gauntlets, making it much harder than it needed to be.

A skeleton twisted and turned to face me. Its eye sockets gleamed as it found an enemy, and I growled, long and low.

I still didn't know where my naginata was. I'd lost the spear I'd gained, and a sword would be little use in here, so I reached into my bag and pulled out the kill-stick, flicking it on, and hearing the rumbling, rough sound of the cobbled-together device starting up.

It sounded rusty and ill-made, and it looked like touching the handle might give you tetanus, never mind what getting an actual injury from it might do.

It was a perfect fit for my mood.

I patted Lydia's shoulder and stood up, stalking toward the skeleton as more of its brethren stumbled out of the darkness to join it.

That fucker, that lich, had done this. It had hurt my people.

I moved slightly faster, striding purposefully, no longer walking.

The stupid bastard had hurt Lydia. It had made me ask her to push so hard she was close to death. She'd pushed that hard for me, and I'd let her. Hell, I'd asked her to. That made my anger boil higher, turning to fury.

We could be trapped down here now; we might have lost our chance at an escape before the enemy fleet arrived. We might be fucked, *all* of us. Lydia, Grizz, Yen, Bane, the gnomes, all of them.

They might be stuck here, trapped down in the darkness, eating fucking mushrooms for the rest of their lives, however short they might be, all because of that. Fucking. Lich.

I broke into a jog, then a run, then a sprint, an animalistic growl of fury lifting from my lips, hanging in the air behind me as I raced forward.

I jumped, my left foot landing on a pile of rubble, and I kicked off. Bracing against a fallen skull and flying through the air, I lifted my knees closer to my chest and struck out with both feet to slam the first skeleton backward.

I landed on my feet and lashed out with the kill-stick to the right, catching the nearest figure on the jaw, smashing it apart as the trio of buzz-saw blades burrowed into it and ground out the back of the neck, the head flying free with a grating that echoed in the chamber.

As I pulled the kill-stick back, I spun, thankful for the well-fitted armor as I kicked out. First, I smashed another skeleton's knee then used it to propel myself higher. Grabbing the top of the skull, I brought my knee up to smash the armored plate through the bridge of the creature's nose.

The force was enough to send it staggering back, but I twisted as I fell back to the ground and tucked my legs up, using my weight to yank the skull down and drive the much lighter skeleton downward. My momentum rammed its face into the ground; driving the kill-stick into the back of its neck to chew its way through, finishing it off nicely.

The sight of more and more of them coming, stepping forward out of the darkness, only served to enrage me more.

I knew roughly where the lich had disappeared, with the largest amalgamations crouching down to wrap themselves around it in protection.

Fuck fighting its minions.

I started running again. I blazed toward the pile where I knew it had been earlier, bashing them out of my way until I was shoulder-charged by a larger creature.

I'd not seen this thing before, but I didn't give two shits about that as it slammed into me from the right, staggering me.

It was short and broad, like a centaur that had topped out at five feet and had six legs. Its upper body was rotting, but it had clearly been heavily muscled once with thick three-fingered hands tipped with claws that skittered across my armor. It lunged at me with mandibles spread, an insectile face glaring.

I'd staggered when it hit me from the side, but I quickly grabbed its right arm with my left, twisting it until it locked, and used it to hold the fucker in place as I beat it repeatedly, the saw blades chewing entire sections through as I roared out my hatred of it.

I drove my weapon through its forehead last, making it collapse as the kill-stick gave a chirp of warning and started to slow. I flicked the switch, wanting to save it for later, and slid it into a bag. Just then, a shir lumbered into view, its right leg shattered and barely able to hold its weight.

I lunged for it with a savage grin, kicking the knee and sending it tilting toward that side as the leg gave out. Then I grabbed the horns and drove its skull down as hard as I could into a pile of rubble, making the air resound with the crack of bones breaking.

I yanked it back and then down again, ignoring a dagger that slammed into my armored back and scraped along before glancing off.

I heaved it back and staggered as one of the horns I was holding broke off. Growling in fury, I began ramming the horn into the shir's skull until it collapsed, then ripped it back out and searched around.

My unthinking savagery had carried me through the majority of the group. As I'd run, I'd beaten and kicked others aside, which meant I now stood encircled.

The majority of the undead were unarmed; only a few actually carried real weapons, with the majority relying on teeth and nails. The few that did have weapons were starting to surround me fully now, their swords and maces, spears and flails, morning stars and axes dimly reflecting the light from my team's lights in the distance.

I could feel the gloating of the lich under my feet, hidden safely away under the rubble, as its creatures prepared to slaughter me and mine.

"I don't fucking think so," I growled, taking a deep breath and glaring down at a gap in the rubble where I could dimly see bones.

The knowledge was there, I knew. It had come as part of the enormous amount of information Amon had shared, but as disjointed and incomplete as it was, I didn't have it all. I had a vague sense of danger, a warning of damage, and that was it. Well, if it was a choice between a little pain and fucking this asshole's day up? That wasn't a choice that needed to be considered.

I checked, seeing I'd managed to regenerate eleven mana so far, and I needed far more, at least thirty-five.

I thought I knew what to do, but before I tried it, before I risked breaking my mana channels and seriously fucking myself up, I had one single, tiny, sneaky trick left to play.

I dug my hand into the bag on my hip and summoned the bottle I wanted to my hands, checked it, and grinned evilly down at the lich that was trapped beneath the bodies of its minions below me.

It might be safe from me, at least until my mana regenerated but it wasn't safe from this.

I bit into the cork, pulled it out, and spat it to the side, before giving the lich the finger and pouring the sluggish, foul-smelling concoction down the hole.

"Say hello to my little friend!" I called down before turning and glaring at the ring of oncoming undead. The others smashed through the back ranks in a frantic attempt to get to me before I was overwhelmed. But I stood tall and rolled my shoulders, getting ready.

You have summoned a small earth golem.

Do you wish to command this creation now?

Yes/No

I grinned and selected yes, feeling a new sensation bloom in my mind. It was a hollow, echoing feeling, and I sensed it was the basic mentality of the golem, unthinking, waiting for orders.

Well, I reflected, they wouldn't need to be complicated, at least.

"Smash Barry the Lich into paste," I ordered it aloud, remembering how well telling the uncovered war golem I'd found in the waystation to "tear his arms off and beat him to death with them" had worked with regards to the cave troll which the goblins had thought was their trump card.

It'd been over very quickly.

When a creature made of a mixture of stone and metal, and god only knew what else, weighing several tons and filled with implacable resolve, faced off against a dumb creature of meat and bone that weighed less than a third in comparison, it rarely ended well for the fleshling.

I heard a screech of fear, pain, and fury rising suddenly from under the rubble, and it started to move as the amalgamations frantically tried to respond to their master's cries for help.

While they scrambled to save him, the undead surrounding me were rapidly abandoned by their directing mind, and it showed. The entire first rank staggered, slowing and beginning to move disjointedly. They staggered and hesitated, abandoning the single-minded intensity they'd begun to demonstrate once again.

When they were distracted, I struck. The nearest one was less than five feet away now, short, thick-bodied, and armored in chainmail that had seen better days. The undead dwarf was dragging a maul that was almost as big as it was.

I lunged forward and kicked the dwarf's right arm as it started to bring the weapon around, slamming it backward. As the dwarf staggered, I grabbed its left and right upper arms, then lifted my leg and planted my right foot on its face, heel to chin, before kicking out and pulling at the same time.

The rotten links of flesh and sections of beard that made up most of the face and throat tore through quickly as the head popped loose. The corpse lost the animating force, collapsing to the floor in true death.

I grunted as I released it, reaching down and lifting the maul, then giving it a swing to get the weight right in my mind.

It was a giant of a hammer, close to a mix of a long-handled Mjölnir and a mattock, with a slightly curved spiked head on one side opposite a huge, flat slab of metal.

I hefted it in one hand as I grinned at the mobile corpses around me. They'd gone from a risk to essentially walking skittles as they responded to their master's fear and demand for help.

They totally ignored me and my team, staggering forward and grabbing at the debris, trying to dig their way through, and the change was huge.

Suddenly, the others weren't battling creatures that were a threat; they weren't even fighting anymore, not really. It became simple manual work: destroy the skull and move on.

Where I was, I went from being surrounded by armed undead, intent on killing me, to all of them dropping weapons and staggering forward, grabbing at the metal, rock, and debris and yanking frantically.

I simply started to crush skulls.

One after another, I went, methodically raising the maul and bringing it down. At first, I was shattering them, but then as I moved, I worked to improve and to learn, seeking more to destroy just the skull, rather than shattering half the body at the same time and having to kick the weapon free of the pile of bones.

This wonderful experience farm lasted less than a minute, though, before the mound, with a final screech of pain, went silent, and the remaining undead collapsed to the floor, bones losing all cohesion.

The clattering filled the air for several seconds, echoing. Then suddenly it was over, and more notifications flashed for my attention desperately.

I searched about, grateful that everyone appeared okay, if dirty, dusty, worn out, and bloody from dozens of small wounds. I spun around as the mound made a sound, lifting the maul, but a few seconds later, I dropped it as the small earth elemental oozed its way back up into sight to stare at me, waiting for more orders.

"Retrieve anything the lich had on it and bring it up here," I commanded, watching it turn and flow back down into the darkness.

"Well, thank fuck for that," I muttered to myself, watching the group as they began picking their way across the room. I made my way to Lydia, checking on her.

She was still unconscious, but my mana had recovered enough for a second healing spell, and using it restored more color to her, and she seemed to rest more comfortably.

"What happened to her?" Grizz asked.

"I don't know, in all honesty." I winced, concern leaking into my voice. "I asked her to hold them as long as she could, and boom, she went nuts. Suddenly, she was everywhere, moving faster than I could believe. Then it was like someone flipped a switch, and she just collapsed. When I got to her, she was almost dead, totally drained," I said, brushing her hair back from her face and peeling one eyelid back to look in.

There was no reaction, and I sighed, letting her eye close again and patting her shoulder.

"Miren!" I called, and she stepped forward. "Stay with her and watch over her while I meditate. As soon as I've got enough mana, I'll heal her again, but wake me if she doesn't look well, okay?"

She nodded soberly, settling down next to Lydia. I took a moment to look at the way the entire group regarded her, and I sighed. I might be their leader, but Lydia was their heart.

"Arrin, what's your mana like?" I asked him absently.

"I've got enough for a single heal," he said, stepping forward, but I held up my hand to stop him.

"No, save it for now. Do you know how to meditate?" I asked, and he grimaced, looking embarrassed.

"Sort of?" He rubbed the back of his neck. "I can sit and clear my mind, and I got the skill, but it's only at level two."

"Then it's time to level it," I said, sweeping a space clear on the floor. "We need to keep moving, and to get to the ship, but if there's anything else out there, we're dead as we are. We need to recover as much as possible," I said to the group.

"Arrin and I will meditate. Bane, you go explore; Tang, stay and watch over us. You're more likely than the rest of us to spot any stealth types. Yen, you direct everyone; you've got twenty minutes. I want this place searched, my naginata found, and grab anything we can loot. That fucker had to have some decent gear," I growled, gesturing toward the mound.

With that, I sat down and took a deep breath, then closed my eyes and started to speak. I spent five minutes explaining all that I could to Arrin about how I meditated, then the next fifteen were spent trying to balance the relaxed mentality needed for meditation with building and maintaining my mental "box" to increase my regeneration.

When a gentle hand rested on my shoulder, I let it slip away and blinked into the light cast by Miren's magelight.

"It's time," she whispered simply.

I forced a smile for her. It wasn't her fault, I told myself; it wasn't anyone's fault, but I could feel Oracle.

She was leaving; she'd gone from somewhere higher overhead and to the right, to heading away, climbing higher and at speed. I knew what that meant. The fleet was leaving, and I was stuck trying to recover my mana in a rotting, stinking, shithole of a city, trapped underground and surrounded by wreckage and the dead, with a goddamn gang of SporeMothers incoming.

Every time I thought about it, my anger bubbled up, along with my fear. I admitted that last bit to myself grudgingly. I could lose anyone at any time. I knew that. But the thought of losing Oracle made my heart clench and bile fill my throat. I was right to have sent her; it was the only way, I told myself. But still, I couldn't shake the bubbling fear that I'd never see her again.

I forced myself to my feet and used Battlefield Triage on Lydia again. It was a quick cast, the minimum needed, mainly because it now gave as much information on the condition of the target as it performed healing, and I let out a sigh of relief. Lydia was better than she had been. She was worn out still, but it seemed more like extreme exhaustion now rather than the near death-like state she'd been in.

I smiled at Miren again, more genuinely, and looked around for Arrin. I'd expected him to be sat next to me still, but he'd clearly given up and had gone looting instead of meditating.

"Arrin?" I said quietly as I stepped over to meet him a few feet away where he'd been stripping a gold ring off the finger of a corpse.

"Hey, boss," he said casually, straightening up and holding the ring up to the light of his magelight, then grinning and dropping it in a pocket. Then, he looked at me and swallowed at the look in my eyes.

"What happened to meditating?" I asked him in as even a voice as I could manage.

"I…uh, I couldn't get it, so I figured I'd be better off searching the dead, you know, looking for mana potions and stuff," he replied, looking away.

"And did you find any?" I asked, my voice cold.

"No," he said, sagging.

"No," I repeated. "And did you think that a glass vial of magical elixir was likely to be found on walking corpses? Corpses that were commanded by a lich?" I pressed, and he shrugged, refusing to meet my eyes.

"I didn't…" he mumbled.

"You didn't consider that the lich would have already gathered things like that to him, or you did, and you decided to ignore my order to meditate? An order I gave you because we need all the fucking mana we can get right now, and you decided that looting the bodies of the dead was a better use of your time?" I asked through gritted teeth.

"I—I—" he stammered, looking around at the floor and walls, basically anywhere but at me.

"We'll talk about this later," I growled and turned, walking across to where Yen was standing, ostensibly checking over the loot that everyone had piled together. I glanced over it and noted the gold, jewelry, weapons, and other random shit that made it up.

The lack of anything that was obviously valuable or any potions made me sigh as I marked down the need to speak to Arrin about the fact he'd been pocketing the rings rather than putting them together the way the others had for me to go over.

"I don't have any healing magic," Yen said quietly. "But I do have an Identify spell, and I checked these two over. Your naginata is down there when you're ready for it."

She gestured down to the weapon piled with the rest of the gear, then held out her hand. I reached out, and she dropped a pair of rings into my palm. The first was black, solid black; it looked like someone had made a damn ring out of the darkest part of the goddamn night, while the other was a simple golden band with a gently glowing ruby in it.

"Here," she said, and my notifications pulsed again as she did something.

"Fuck, give me a few seconds to work through these," I muttered, pulling them up.

"It's fine. I'll come back if you need me to share it again." She stepped away, leaving me to read.

Congratulations!

You have killed the following:

- 11x Gnome Badunka Riders of various levels for a total of 47,150xp
- 29x Feral Gnomes of various levels for a total of 63,115xp
- 14x Crazed Gnomes of various levels for a total of 53,875xp
- 16x Insane Gnomes of various levels for a total of 23,430xp
- 1x Crazed, Dominated Human, level 13 for 7,150xp
- 114x Undead of various levels for a total of 28,158xp
- 1x Bartholomew the Lich, level 34 for 18,350xp

A party under your command killed the following:

- 3x Gnome Badunka Riders of various levels for a total of 22,130xp
- 6x Immature Leviathans of various levels for a total of 53,140xp
- 1x Crazed Cavern Dominatrix Human, level 20 for a total of 11,750xp
- 1x Grant, Master of the Gnomes, level 29. 0xp awarded due to Skin-Walker's survival
- 278x Undead of various levels for a total of 57,111xp

Total Party experience earned: 144,131xp

As party leader, you gain 25% of all experience earned

Progress to level 20 stands at 471,928/305,000

*

Congratulations!

You have reached level 20!

You have 27 unspent Attribute points and 1 Meridian point available.

Progress to level 21 stands at 166,928/350,000

*

Congratulations!

Through hard work and perseverance,
you have increased your Strength by one point.

Continue to train and learn to increase this further.

*

Congratulations!

You have made progress in your Quest: Fix the Fixers

You have discovered the chilling secrets of the Prax, Glorious Retribution, discovered a working, if unpowered, portal and killed the Master and his unwilling servants. Due to the level of difficulty involved, and the bravery shown by your acceptance of the realities of your situation, the Goddess Jenae has increased your rewards, and altered the Success Conditions of the Quest.

Recruit the Gnomish Survivors: 21/27

Recover Sufficient Manastones to Power the Ship Interesting Endeavors: 17/40

Eliminate Bartholomew the Lich: 1/1

Find and Prepare the Ship Interesting Endeavors and use it to escape: 0/1

Bonus Condition: For each SporeMother killed, receive an additional 10,000xp

Reward: Improved technological capacity in the Great Tower, Possible technological boosts to the fleet, survival , gnomish exploration vessel Interesting Endeavors, 500,000xp

*

A member of your team wishes to share information with you.

Do you accept?

Yes/No

It wasn't exactly rocket science who and what that was referencing, so I mentally tagged yes and watched the screens bloom for me.

Ring of Darkest Desire		**Further Description** *Yes/No*	
Details:		This ring grants the wearer +5 Charisma and a 10% bonus to Intimidation!	
Rarity:	**Magical:**	**Durability:**	**Charge:**
Highly Rare	Yes	57/100	N/A

Ring of Bloody Brilliance		**Further Description** *Yes/No*	
Details:		This ring was forged in the depths of antiquity by the sadistic creator Ivanna Humpalot. This ring feeds on the life energy of its wearer, providing a +4 to both Intelligence and Endurance, but inflicts a 5 health per second wound on the wearer.	
Rarity:	**Magical:**	**Durability:**	**Charge:**
Highly Rare	Yes	34/100	N/A

I looked the rings over, shaking my head in amazement at the lich. It'd been an absolute asshole, and that was with an additional five points of Charisma? I snorted and popped the black ring on, guessing that the boost might be useful in negotiation, and it never hurt a guy to draw a little attention in the right way.

The second ring, though…hell, no. It would boost my mana and stamina a good amount, true, but not with regards to losing the five health per second. The lich might have been able to get around that with being technically undead, and whoever Ivanna was, she was clearly a kinky fucker or didn't expect to be wearing the ring long-term.

I shrugged and dumped it into a bag, looking at the last series of notifications, realizing that there were five more left.

At a mental flex, they rearranged themselves into easier reading. I scanned over them, dismissing the majority of the extraneous details.

Congratulations!
You have practiced enough to raise the following skills:
Unarmed: level 9
Shields: level 7
Medium Armor: level 9
Staffs: level 12
Mace Wielding: level 7
Small Blades (Daggers): level 8

Continue to practice and learn to increase these skills further.

Once these skills reach level 10, you may choose their first evolutions. For skills that surpass this marker, additional evolutions will occur every ten levels.

"Hey, Oracle," I started to ask without thinking, then stopped myself, realizing that she was already out of my range, never mind her being able to speak to me when I spoke out loud.

"Can I help, Jax?" Yen offered, walking back over and I shrugged.

"I was going to ask Oracle a question about the skill evolutions; just forgot where she—and I—were, that's all," I admitted, rubbing the back of my neck with an awkward grin.

"I'll answer, if I can?"

"Thanks, Yen. I'll be honest, I'm used to asking Oracle, mainly because so many of my questions are so…obvious to the rest of you. You grew up with these systems, after all. Makes me feel a bit stupid at times."

"I can understand that, Jax. Honestly, ask, and if I can answer, I will," she reassured me.

"Okay. I keep getting skill notifications, like my daggers reaching level eight, that kinda thing, but I don't seem to be getting many spell ones. Why is that?" I asked, half expecting it to be a really obvious answer.

"Do you use many standard spells?" Yen asked, smiling gently. "I've seen you use dozens of variations on spells, but hardly any over and over."

"Well, yeah, I use what I need. We usually adjust a spell on the fly, so that…" I said, my voice trailing off as I realized what she meant. "Wait, so because I'm doing that, using spells we're making and adjusting, I'm not leveling?"

"You are, just slower than you would be if you were using, say, Fireball exclusively. You're spreading yourself around all of these spells. Have you examined them individually?" she asked. I shook my head. "I think you should, then. You might get a nice surprise, after all. Has Oracle explained about the various schools of magic?"

"I think so?" I said, unsure, as I looked around the room. "Okay, everyone, grab whatever you've got. It's time to move on," I called, before turning back to Yen.

"There are many schools. Fire, water, earth, basically, any of the basic elements is classed as a 'school, and if you leveled up the spell, for example Firebolt, ten times, you get the first evolution to that spell," Yen explained.

"Well, once you reach that, you gain a single point in Mastery of Fire. It doesn't sound like much, and most people just ignore the little gains like that, as it seems like it takes forever to grow them. After all, a one-point gain in fire mastery gets you only a one percent reduction in the cost of the spell and a one percent resistance to the element."

"I remember my teacher back in my realm talking about this…vaguely," I admitted.

"Well, think of it this way: one percent of say, ten mana cost is nothing. You'd never notice it. Hell, ten percent, even, would only be one point of mana, *but* the higher you go, the more it stacks. Once you reach fifty percent, your fire magic costs are halved, and any fire-based spells that hit you are only half as effective as they should be.

"Hit one hundred, and your fire spells are free, and you'd be able to bathe in lava fields. Hit the grandmaster ranks at one hundred and fifty, and you'd be gaining mana whenever you cast the spell, and you would be healed by anyone who tried to hurt you with fire. You could literally stand in a fireplace and heal yourself!" Yen said excitedly.

"Yeah, but it'd take forever," I countered quietly as the others joined us and we set off, clambering across the rubble and piled bones. Grizz, Stephanos, Jian, and Ty'Baronn worked together to carry Lydia on a stretcher that Stephanos had built from the longer leg bones and some leather he could find.

We took turns carrying Lydia, moving at a fast walk as Yen continued to explain.

"It may seem like it'll take forever," she agreed. "But you're doing it anyway, so just keep going, really. Maybe try to limit yourself to a few spells, and you'll see the increase sooner. Plus, it doesn't really take that long, and there are ways to 'cheat' the system, as it were.

"If you get, say, ten low-level fire spells and advance them all to the tenth level, that still gives you ten points in fire mastery, after all. Also, for example, that water fountain spell; what level is it?" I pulled it up, checking it over, confident in Tang and Bane to keep us safe as we went.

"Uh, level nine?" I said, surprised. "I didn't think I'd used it enough, but…"

"And the explosive spell you've been using?" she asked.

"Level three," I said, nodding my head in understanding. "So basically, keep spreading myself thin, and it'll slow my growth in a specific spell, but eventually, I'll get them all; or I can cast the same ones over and over, and they'll level fast?" I clarified.

"Basically, yes," Yen agreed. "It's one of those things where a little change can make a big difference, after all. Did Oracle explain about complimentary spells?"

"No?" I said, then frowned. There should have been some sign left by now; we'd cleared the far side of the room and started down the next corridor, but there was nothing. As we'd been going, Tang or Bane had been using a pair of damaged weapons, and Yen, Arrin, or myself had used fire spells to mark the walls, making sure that, when the gnomes followed, they could pick up our trail.

There was nothing here, though, and there should have been…

"What are…" I started to ask absently as I looked around. In fact, the floor there looked different, the path seemed to end at the wall abruptly, but…

"Ambush!" Yen roared suddenly.

CHAPTER TWENTY-SIX

Yen leaped forward, tackling me at the shoulder and slamming me aside as a bolt of lightning as thick as my leg slammed into her, instead of me.

The wall I'd expected to hit vanished as I touched it. I staggered, then fell as I threw myself down to avoid an axe being swung at my head.

The walls…we'd come to a crossroads, and someone had covered the branching paths with a goddamn illusory set of walls!

I hit the floor, bounced, and lashed out, grabbing the ankle of the man who'd just tried to behead me as he glared down at me. I'd landed with my naginata underneath me, so I released it and yanked hard, pulling the man off-balance and making him hop to stay upright.

He swore and lashed out, forcing me to release him and roll aside to avoid being hit. As I tumbled, I saw Bane. He sprawled limp further up the branching passageway. If I hadn't seen the glowing spell-web that held him down, I'd have sworn he was dead, there was that much blood.

Next to him was Tang, being slowly bound in gleaming golden lines of magic, rotating as a pair of mages worked, fixatedly staring at their victims.

I rolled again, the grunt of effort all the warning I needed, and the axe slammed down hard, glancing off the metal floor in a shower of sparks. I'd rolled back in the direction I'd come from and came to a stop against the leg of the armored axe wielder as he drew his weapon back up to strike again.

I didn't have time for this shit, my people were in trouble, and my eyes blazed with fury as I triggered Mana Overdrive. I lifted my legs as high as I could and wrapped them around the backs of the towering figure's knees, yanking hard and taking him down.

He staggered forward, his balance lost, falling over atop me. I yanked out my Dagger of Ripping and rammed it up under his helm and into his brain via the underside of the chin.

I felt the parting of flesh, the crunch of cartilage and bone, then the spasm of the fresh corpse over me, even as hands reached out, trying to pull their friend free.

I grinned up at the pair of soldiers that stood over me, one dragging their friend back, the other holding a sword and shield combination half-ready but lowering it in shock. I yanked the blade down, releasing a spurt of fresh arterial blood across myself from his final heartbeats.

I ignored the guy with his hands full of corpse, using the body to sit myself up, Mana Overdrive granting me the speed and strength to rise before they could attack me.

I grabbed the shield of the man on my left, yanking it forward to block both his view of me and any chance of striking, as well as bringing me close enough to drive the dagger into the joint of his armor around the knee.

It scraped across a section of metal before sinking in deeply behind the next piece. As it hit bone, I yanked it back out…sideways.

The soldier screamed in pain as his lower leg was practically severed at the knee. I twisted, looking back at the pair of mages and throwing the dagger, hard.

Unlike other times I'd thrown one, this time, it struck true, the blade sinking into the man's upraised left arm as he tried to bind Tang further, cutting off his casting with a scream. A scream that was echoed by the other mage as their spell tore out of control and lashed them with feedback.

The soldier who'd lifted the corpse let go and swept out his mace, slamming it down at my face.

I yanked the corpse back into his path, making him pause for a second as his mace crunched against the side of his friend's head.

The pause was all I needed. Shoving the corpse aside and grabbing at the man whose leg I'd ruined, I rolled to my feet and backhanded the wounded man across the face with my gauntlet.

It wasn't enough to do lasting damage, but it stopped him from being able to stab me, then I was up. I stepped in, whipping my left hand down, the armored plate on the back of my hand making a ringing sound as it slapped the swordsman's thrust aside. I stabbed out with my right hand, fingers stiffened into a bar of bone encased in steel, driving them into the exposed Adam's apple as the open-faced helm lifted to gape at me in horror.

Behind me, the others had unceremoniously dumped Lydia, and a barrage of spells, the ring of metal on metal, and the screams of the injured filled the exposed corridors.

The man I'd just hit dropped his sword, fingers rising frantically to scrabble at his crushed throat, and I yanked my kill-stick free of the bag, flicked it on, and rammed it home in the gap granted by the open-faced helm.

There was a crunching whirr, and blood sprayed everywhere. A high-pitched squeal of pain tore from my victim as he collapsed to the ground.

I spun around, lashing out instinctively at the figure I'd crippled on the floor, and my weapon glanced off his hastily raised shield.

There were at least a dozen more people in the corridor, although most of them huddled back, trying to keep clear of the fighting. Meanwhile, the small group of soldiers battled frantically to take down my own far better trained and equipped force.

Jian deflected an attack from one woman, then lashed his scythes lightly across both of her shoulders, drawing a crunch of mail as the blades sliced through them. When she tried to raise her suddenly numb arms to block his next strike, he stabbed out instead, the point of one blade sinking into his opponent's gut.

She cried out, dropping her weapon, and reached for the blade impaling her. He slashed his second blade across her throat and kicked her over, freeing himself to find another soldier to face.

Grizz had gone from the happy-go-lucky guy he always seemed to be into the deadly, focused killing machine the legion had made him into. Three soldiers were down, and he wasn't even breathing hard as he blocked a thrust then kicked a fourth's knee, staggering him. The hulking legionnaire punched him in the face then hooked his leg, sending him to the floor, where he finished him off with a single efficient strike.

Others were falling, arrows sprouting from eyes and throats, and I spun, knowing I had only seconds before my Overdrive ended.

The pair of mages were still out of it, one bleeding, but both reeling in shock and unable to cast again, with a single soldier standing between me and them.

I reached down, swept up my naginata, and stepped back, leaving the soldier with the half-severed leg to bleed out on the floor.

He couldn't reach me, and I didn't need to waste more time on him. I shook the buzzing kill-stick at the soldier between me and the mages, spattering him with blood before dropping it into a bag of holding and stabbing out with the naginata.

The man I faced had a sword and shield, and he deflected my strike easily, lunging forward and slashing at me. I stepped back, lashing my right hand around to bring the butt up, and slapped the sword blade aside, hard.

Then I hooked the butt in behind his shield and yanked, putting my left foot behind his right.

He tried to step back, attempting to gain room to free his shield and bring his sword around. Instead, he fell, not expecting my foot. I released my right grip on the naginata, yanking with my left and tugging it clear as he fell, then grabbed it again and drove the butt down hard.

Not at his head or chest, where he'd pulled the shield over to protect himself…no, I slammed it down hard on his left foot, just to the side of the toes, smashing his foot sideways.

His boots were all one piece, and I heard a grisly crack as his ankle broke. He screamed, slashing downwards with his sword. I stepped back, flipped my weapon over, and stabbed out, aiming for the chainmail that covered the inner thigh, just below the groin.

I'd open that artery and…

Something hit me from behind, a blade punching into my lower back and tearing into my kidney. Staggering, I screamed, then collapsed, as my Mana Overdrive expired, taking the last of my mana with it. A migraine exploded, the pain minor compared to the kidney stab. But as it flared, I was blinded, and I hit the floor, crying out again as the dagger that was embedded in my side, held in place by the bent metal plates that had been layered to protect me, jarred against the ground.

I lashed out blindly, hitting nothing but the corridor and wall, as I reeled in shock. Suddenly, hands were hauling at me as a body dragged itself up me, and a leather glove-encased fist slammed into my face.

My head rocked back again, the back of my skull slamming into the floor and rebounding, and light flared again.

The animal broke free then, panic letting it out as I flailed blindly. My left hand felt something, and I grabbed at it, punching with my right as I squinted, trying to see what was going on.

It was the soldier whose leg I'd almost severed, I realized. Behind him lay an empty vial on the floor, and I cursed myself for a fool. A healing potion. God knows I'd used them enough! In the heat of the fight, I'd ignored the possibility, and now, here I was.

"Hold him down!" growled a voice from my right, and I heard the scratching, squealing sound of someone in full armor dragging themselves across a metal floor toward me.

I growled, ignoring the pain, the difficulty in seeing, all of it, and I reached out, grabbing the soldier with the ruined knee by the side of his helmet with my left hand, and punching him as hard as I could with my right.

His helm was the same as the others, a bell-like shape with a cut-out for the face. As I slammed my fist into his face, I felt his nose break. As I hauled back and hit him again, he pulled out a second dagger and stabbed it into my gut. But it glanced off, the angle, armor, and weakness of the blow combining to leave a nasty scratch on the metal instead of a deadly blow.

The dagger in my kidney tore me open as I writhed and fought, but I had no choice but to leave it as I rolled, forcing him over as he laid atop my legs.

With him on his back and me atop his chest, practically face-fucking him, I reared back, screaming as the dagger shifted, torn farther by the movement of my armor. I glared down as the stunned soldier beneath me.

"No!" I screamed, punching him in the face. "Free!" I shouted, hitting him again, punctuating each word with a blow. "Goes. On. The. Cock!" With the last hit, I felt something give, and he spasmed before going limp, his head falling to the side as I yanked my fist free with a groan of pain.

I looked up just in time to see the last soldier swinging his sword at my exposed head. I threw myself aside, clattering to the floor as the blade tore open a thin line across my temple, making me scream as the dagger in my back tore me up even more.

I had no mana, and I yanked free another dagger before taking a second blow on my left vambrace. It slammed to the floor, exposing my head…as an arrow suddenly sprouted from the soldier's exposed throat.

He staggered back a step, fell to one knee, dropped his sword, and reached up, tapping the arrow that jutted from him in shock. He opened his mouth, blood dripping out of it, and made to say something before a second arrow took him in the eye, and the corpse fell bonelessly to the floor.

I looked over at Miren and waved at her weakly in thanks.

She nodded, then drew back her bow and fired another arrow. It flew past me and thudded into the back of one of the mages as he tried to flee, sending him to the floor crying out in pain. The other still lay on the ground, clutching his head.

"Oh, for fuck's sake…" I groaned, shaking my head at the man who started trying to crawl away. I reached down and roughly searched the body under me, avoiding looking at the smashed-in skull, and let out a relieved sigh as I pulled out a healing potion.

It was red, anyway, and I had no mana left to Examine it, so I popped the cork, reaching behind me with the other hand to fumble for the dagger, before Grizz stomped over to me, looked at it, and nodded.

"On three," he said, taking the healing potion from me and passing it to Yen, who, aside from a little shake that occasionally ran through her limbs and a blackened patch on her armor, seemed to be okay.

She crouched next to me, looked at the potion, and snorted, pulling one out of her bag and holding it ready as well. She nodded to Grizz, who put one hand on my shoulder and took a good grip on the dagger.

"Okay, boss, on three. One…two…" And the bastard yanked it out on two. I cried out and half fell forward, being caught by Yen and Grizz. The vials were quickly pressed to my lips, one after the other. I gulped them down, then screamed as my body started reknitting itself. Seconds passed in pain before it died down, and I collapsed forward, panting.

"Bane. Tang," I gasped out, and Yen nodded to me, getting up and moving to them. Grizz stayed by my side, glaring at the remaining eight people who crouched on the far side of the corridor.

"Here," Grizz said, throwing a potion to Yen, and she nodded to him as she caught, crouching to check the others over.

"Arrin," I grunted, then straightened up, looking over at the others. "Arrin!" I called again, and he ran over.

He was bloody, dirty, and looked tired, but he and the rest of the party were okay. Luckily.

"Get to the others," I ordered him. "Any healing you can do…"

"I'm out of mana," he admitted in a small voice.

"What?" I asked, trying to keep my voice even.

"I'm out of mana," he repeated.

"I thought I'd told you to keep some mana back, always, for healing spells?" I asked him, trying to keep the fury out of my voice.

"Yes, you did. I'm sorry, Jax. I…I didn't have much, and when the fight broke out." He sighed and bowed his head. "I panicked," he confessed quietly. "I panicked and started firing off my Magic Missiles; I didn't realize until I hit rock bottom. I'm sorry."

I had to bite my tongue to not scream at him, to not tell the goddamn fool he might have killed Bane or Tang. Even the sight of the tears dripping from his downturned face, the shame I knew he felt, wasn't enough to temper my anger fully.

"Go," I growled out, and he fled back to the rest of the group, busying himself with checking on Lydia as I got up and started over to Bane and Tang. "How are they?" I asked Yen, aware that Grizz had followed me and was glowering at the remaining people that huddled in the far corner from us.

"Not good," Yen said, grabbing onto the mage who was laid next to her, still groaning. "Shut it," she snarled and punched him in the face. There was a sound like a steak being dropped from the third floor onto concrete, and the mage was silent, unconscious. "Wimp," Yen muttered, searching through his pockets and bags. "Grizz! I need you to stop the bleeding!" Yen snapped, and the big man dropped down, pulling bandages out of a pouch and setting to work.

I paused, my brain still foggy as I wondered why he hadn't done it straight away, then I realized. In a world where wounds were fixed by spells and potions, you'd be wasting bandages to use them unless absolutely necessary.

She pulled out two potions, both mana, and cursed, diving back in to search for a healing potion when I pulled the mana from her and downed one.

I let out a groan of relief as the mana-migraine cleared away, and a handful of seconds later, I chugged the second, watching my mana regeneration leap upwards at a terrific rate.

I took a deep breath, then started to cast Battlefield Triage. I hit Bane first, as he seemed the most injured by far, and grunted in dismay as I saw the injuries.

"What the hell did they do to you?" I growled, looking at the information. More than half the bones in his body were broken; he was missing the tendrils that helped him to see on one side, he was burned, had frostbite, and was bleeding internally, and was down to eleven health, his bleeding was that bad.

I concentrated on the internals first, making the veins and the liver equivalent heal themselves. I stopped shy of a full regeneration of them, moving on, picking the injuries one at a time and repairing frantically, even as Grizz tried to slow the bleeding and Yen searched for other healing or mana potions.

"Search the bodies!" Grizz called out, the command clear in his voice. "Any healing or mana potions, I need them, *now!*"

I shifted my focus, flowing into Bane's chest, then out, passing through the heart and along the arteries, fixing as I went. I left Yen and Grizz to deal with the outside, and I concentrated on the worst of the internal injuries, working as fast as I could.

Minutes passed in a blur, and I sagged back again, frantically trying to blink the mana-migraine away as my mana bottomed out. I stared wide-eyed at Bane, terrified I was going to lose him.

I'd heard Yen's assurances of Tang's status; he was beaten up pretty badly, and the spell they were using on him was nasty, but he would survive, with a little rest and food.

Neither of which we had time to provide, but we had no choice, either.

"Grizz," I said, sitting with my eyes closed as Yen worked on Bane, finishing off the bandaging and muttering about wounds that wouldn't close.

"Yeah, boss?" he asked quietly.

"I want to know what the fuck they did to Bane, and I want them all searched for any healing or mana potions. If they've kept them hidden while Bane's dying…"

"I'll make sure they understand," Grizz said in a low growl. "As to the mages…one's unconscious, and the other is bleeding out; want either to survive?"

"Question them for now, but don't be gentle about it," I growled viciously. "Yen, I'm going to meditate quickly; keep him going as long as you can. When it's getting bad, interrupt me, and I'll heal him with whatever I've managed to gain."

"Yes, Jax," she said simply, her eyes far away as she read information on Bane granted by her skills.

I settled back, ignoring the sudden scream that rose from further up the corridor, and the low, angry sound of Grizz interrogating the mage who'd been trying to crawl away.

I managed just over twenty minutes before Yen disturbed me, and the news she had wasn't good.

I checked my mana as I straightened, grateful that I'd managed to make it all the way up to eleven points per minute, reaching the heady heights of two hundred and thirty-three points. I sighed in relief. Surely, that would be enough to heal both Tang and Bane?

"Jax, I don't think we can save Bane," she said softly, and my heart plummeted. I stared down at my friend, seeing the blood seeping through the bandages.

"I've got more mana now," I argued, shaking my head. "We can save him. I just need to…"

"I used a class ability to see what caused the wounds, Jax, and they were made with this." She grimly flicked a notification to me as she pointed to the bandages that were clearly leaking through quickly. I opened the notification, accepting the information.

Death's Kiss		Further Description *Yes/No*	
Damage:		?	
Details:		Limited information is available, but the dagger Death's Kiss is known to inflict almost impossible-to-seal wounds. The wounds have a 25% chance to develop additional corrupted facets, including: Festering, Poisoned, Infected, and Necrotic Feasting.	
Rarity:	**Magical:**	**Durability:**	**Charge:**
Legendary	Yes	?	?

"Mother*fucker!*" I growled out, turning to see Grizz waiting grimly off to one side. The injured mage laid in a still heap, with the unconscious one close by.

There were no mana or health potions, but there were a number of rings and other trinkets waiting to be examined.

I looked at Bane, swallowed hard at the thought of losing him, and shook my head firmly.

"No, fuck this. It says they're *almost* impossible to heal. That means there's a chance. Nobody would be carrying a weapon like this if they didn't know a way to stop it or nicking their finger would be a death sentence. Who had it?" I asked grimly.

"Their noble. He apparently was waiting farther up the tunnel, and he ran with his guards when the fight started to go against them," Grizz said.

"Tell me the rest," I insisted, sensing there was more to come.

"They captured Bane with a spell-net, shocked him, and tried to question him. He refused to answer their questions, and the noble ordered him beaten until he changed his mind. He gave them nothing, so when they caught Tang, the noble stabbed Bane a few times with his dagger; then they fled, waiting to see what would happen."

"He dies," I said flatly. "That cocksucking noble dies, *slowly*."

"By your word, Lord Jax," Grizz said in grim agreement.

"How did they capture them, but not us? Hell, with Bane's abilities?" I asked.

"My abilities as a member of the Praetoria can tell me a lot, such as the weapon used for an attack, but not everything, Jax." Yen shook her head. "I can sense a lot of magic, though, so I'd guess at an artifact, something used to conceal them. Then by the time we came along, it'd either failed or run out of mana, or…who knows. All I know is I smelled blood, and I reacted."

"And thank the gods you did," Grizz said as Arrin moved over to join us. He nodded once to me, still clearly embarrassed, but he reached out and healed Bane, before groaning and sitting back.

"That's all I'd managed to regenerate. I'm sorry," he said, shame clear in his voice.

"It's…fine. Thank you for that, Arrin." I dismissed him, and he went back to join the others, watching over the group of prisoners.

"Who are they?" I asked, and Yen spoke almost absently as she tried to rewrap the bandages on Bane's arm.

"The researchers for the Narkolt party. The noble Joshua apparently brought them down on pain of death; they were to find whatever was of value, or they'd be left here."

"Figures," I muttered, examining Bane and finding that he was down to forty health again, before starting to heal him.

I spent a hundred mana, boosting him back up to almost two hundred health. I left the majority of his wounds alone, concentrating specifically on those left by the dagger, as they were the most life-threatening.

"Okay, he has two hundred and fourteen health now, and he's losing fifteen points a minute. That gives us, say, twelve minutes to get moving; then we stop and heal him again, or I meditate and keep refilling more mana, then boost him higher and higher," I muttered, thinking fast.

"The gnomes," Yen interrupted.

"What?" I asked, confused.

"The gnomes were coming. We've killed the lich, so there's just escaping and killing the asshole nobles left. With the lich dead, there shouldn't be anything between the gnomes and here…and knowing gnomes, they'll have made things to carry everything."

"Go," I insisted. "Go as fast as you can. Find them, get them here fast. If we can ride their machines, I can meditate and keep Bane alive, then we just need to find that ship and escape. I want that noble's head, but I want Bane alive more. Between Nerin and Hellenica, they'll be able to save him."

Yen nodded once and tore out of the cross corridor, the illusory walls long since vanished. As she went, I settled back down and called to Arrin to join me again. As he hurried over, I looked up to Grizz.

"Grizz…Lydia, Bane, and Tang are all out of action. I need to meditate, so I need you to deal with all this shit. I want to know what the hell is going on down here, so ask the questions however you want. Find out where the nobles went and why they came down here, instead of behaving themselves. Most of all, I want to know why the hell they decided to join with Himnel and attack us," I finished irritably.

Grizz moved straight to the others, spreading them out to guard Arrin and me as we meditated, then he went to work on the researchers.

I heard a rude response to his first question, something about him being "just a legionnaire," then the sound of a fist hitting flesh, the crunch of breaking cartilage, and a wail of denial. I filtered it all out after that.

"Okay, Arrin, let's go over the meditation again," I said, speaking slowly and calmly as I led him through the simple steps.

The next fifty minutes were enough to make me want to murder someone. But by the time Yen returned, both Arrin and I had gotten in some good meditation, and we'd hit Bane over and over with healing spells, getting him up to a decent amount of health, despite his remaining injuries and the speed at which it was constantly draining away.

We'd also managed to spare enough to fully heal Tang back to consciousness, and he'd set off scouting again, absolutely furious over being taken down.

Arrin was just finishing his turn at healing Bane when a noise started up in the distance, rapidly growing louder as the minutes passed.

We readied ourselves, just in case, but it was quickly obvious that it was the gnomes, both by the crazed speed they were approaching and by the feeling of the bond with Yen getting noticeably closer.

I blinked when I realized that, as I should have sensed the injuries to Bane and Tang, and their location as well. My HUD showed them as they were now, after all, so the magic that had been used to take them out and to trick us was even stronger than I'd thought.

The lights and noise in the distance soon resolved into five sled-like contraptions, each with multiple wheels. The sleds were all totally different designs with gnomes hanging on all over them. As they pulled up and stopped, I shook my head at the sheer volume of crap the gnomes had secured to the vehicles, and I wondered how they'd respond to being told to dump most of it so we could ride.

When Yen arrived back, the first thing she did, after bringing the elder to me, was to pour a bottle of Legionnaires' Might into Bane's mouth. It damn near choked him, solidifying as it did, but she managed to get it down him a little at a time. She followed that quickly with a ruby-red healing potion that practically made him glow with health for a few seconds.

"That should keep him going for now," she said, grimacing. "I didn't think about it until I was halfway there, but the healing is creating the blood he needs from his body. To do that, it'll be stripping him of everything else: muscle mass, fat, all his reserves will be gone by now. The Might potion won't make up for that, but at least it'll help."

"I was worried about that," I admitted. "But I didn't dare stop healing him."

"We came as fast as we could, lord," Frederikk said, stepping up and bowing his head to me, clearly unsure as to what he was supposed to do now.

"Thank you, Frederikk," I said simply. "I see you managed to make some transports?"

"Basic, shoddy things that they be, but yes, my lord," he said proudly, looking up at me. He barely came to my waist, but he was easily ten feet tall in suppressed insanity and vibrating with energy. "The legionnaire said you needed us, and fast, so we left a lot of the salvage we needed, but we took the bare essentials." Frederikk sadly looked over the sleds that were piled high with random-seeming metals and mechanical parts.

"I don't suppose you found a stash back there?" I asked carefully.

"Oh yes!" he said, a truly manic grin threatening to split his head, it was that wide. "Speakin' of which…your legionnaire there, she took it. Said it wasn't to be used right now, but maybe a little pick me up? It'd help us out…focus us well," he continued quietly, glancing around. "Or, if you're worried about things getting out of hand, just a little for me…?"

"What?" I asked, confused.

"He means the drugs," Yen said disgustedly. "I got there just as they found the old lord's loot stash, and barely managed to get to it before they all drugged themselves into insensibility. I told them it was your order that they load up the loot, and I forced them to leave the rest. I've heard nothing else but reasons why they should be given 'just a little' since leaving."

"Wait, you mean they spent ages back there tearing the place apart, looking for drugs?" I asked grimly, fury filling my voice.

"No, you told them to find the 'stash,' so a few of them did that, while the others joined the damaged badunkas together to make the sleds. They loaded the majority of the Master's looted gear into the rear one, and I took what looked the most valuable," she clarified, reaching for her pouches.

"Keep it for now," I said, holding one hand up. "Unless there's anything that can help us, we don't have time to fuck about with it."

"There's a dozen healing potions and three mana," she said quickly, pulling the vials out. "There's a load of others, but little that is immediately useful beyond the healing and mana. There are also three health rings; each only gives an additional plus fifty health, but…"

"Put them on him," I said, nodding, and she went to work, slipping them into place. "Frederikk, thank you again for choosing to follow me." I nodded to Giint, who grinned maniacally back at me.

"And you, Giint. Now, as you can see, I have wounded, and both Arrin and I need somewhere to sit where we can meditate, but most of all, we need to go fast," I said, pausing when I saw the look of glee on the old gnome's face and the look of utter horror on Yen's.

"What's wrong?" I asked her under my breath as Frederikk spun around, lifted both arms into the air, and shouted something I didn't understand.

The other gnomes looked overjoyed and started piling off the vehicles. They began working together, tearing some of the outer strapped gear off, discarding anything that wasn't clearly magical and integrating more and more into the devices.

"You never, ever, *ever* tell a gnome you want to go fast," Yen said bleakly. "You spend all your time trying to make them go slow, and you just…I don't…I mean." She shook her head in a mixture of horror and amazement.

"Lordddd, we neeeeed a littlllle…extrrrrra?" Giint said, sidling up to me and holding his hand out hopefully.

"What does he want?" I asked Yen, and she scowled.

"He wants some of the drugs they developed. They speed up the heart rate, the mind, everything, but the crash afterwards…" She met my gaze appealingly. "It's seriously dangerous, Jax."

"We can do it, my lord." Frederikk piped up, nodding earnestly. "Your legionnaire doesn't understand. Yes, other races have…*issues*…with the gnomes, but we get things done! We're the greatest crafters the realms have ever seen, and it's been many, many years since we had more than a taste of the substances of life…. We can do this, make it faster, stronger…but we need our mana to do it, and to do that…"

"Fuck it, time to toss the dice," I muttered and gestured to Yen, who covered her eyes with one hand, sighed, and handed a small bag over to me. I peered inside and found a single medium bag of what looked to be icing sugar, but it glittered strangely, making me think it was the "other" kind of sugar, and dozens upon dozens of sticks of something. I pulled the bag out and, after Yen confirmed that it was probably the lesser of the substances, I handed it to the gnome elder.

He took it with a huge and slightly disturbing grin before darting off.

"You know you're going to regret doing that, right?" Yen asked me, and I shrugged.

"If it keeps our people alive, I won't," I replied.

"Oh, believe me, you will," Yen muttered, then snorted, patting me on the shoulder.

"Frederikk, how long—" I started to ask him, and he spun around, his eyes unfocused, face looking like he'd had a kilo of flour stuffed into each nostril. He huffed at me, coughed, and blinked, as though trying to see where and who I was.

"An hour, no more!" he managed to wheeze out while facing a pile of rubble and clearly thinking that it was me. Then he collapsed onto his back and started to giggle, even as other gnomes did the same.

"Oh, fuck no!" I snarled, learning that in under thirty seconds, they'd gone from frantically working to off their tits on the floor.

"Don't panic; they'll be down for a minute or so, that's all. Or at least, that's the normal response. Then…just stay out of the way, I guess," Yen explained, shaking her head again.

"Oh, and Jax, I won't tell you 'I told you so.' Others might, in this situation, and even more so, considering you're going to be riding a magical construction built by drugged-up gnomes soon.

"Hell, some people would be telling you that you're a lunatic, and that they warned you about just this very thing, but I won't," she said calmly, turning to walk over towards Grizz. "I'm a much bigger person than that!" she called back over her shoulder.

"I'm so glad to hear that," I replied sarcastically, then I nodded to Arrin, and we started meditating again and taking turns healing Bane.

After fifteen minutes, I stirred, ready to take my turn, only to find Tang hurrying to me. I let out a sigh of relief. The older gnomes were working at a speed that was beyond belief now. Even if they did occasionally giggle or zone out.

"Jax, we've got a problem," he said.

"We always do," I retorted, and he chuckled.

"That's true. It's certainly never boring being with you, but I mean the noble who attacked us. I found him. More to the point, he's found the lich's home. There's a sealed Vault that he's trying to get into, and whatever the goddess wanted us to find, I'll bet it's in there."

"How far is it?" I asked, glancing at Bane and Lydia then at the gnomes. Half of them still hadn't come down from whatever hit they'd had. The other half, though…they worked with a speed I couldn't believe.

The way they pulled sections of the vehicles apart and rebuilt them was like watching a gifted child with Lego.

They added things on, then tore them off, putting them in back to front, adding bits, then revising, as though working to a shared blueprint that was constantly updating.

It was mesmerizing to watch, but I shook myself free and looked to Tang as he responded.

"Ten minutes, maybe a bit more, depending on who comes. That's at a full run, by the way," he said.

"Okay then, team! Fall in!" I shouted, and they looked blankly at me. "Gather around, I mean," I clarified, and they obeyed as I grumbled about shared history and missing memes.

"Right. Tang found that dickbag noble. The gnomes are going to be at least three-quarters of an hour, so I'm going for it. I need some of you to stay here, both to protect our people and the gnomes, and because I don't trust those assholes." I nodded toward the group of researchers huddled dejectedly on the far side.

"So, we're down to eight; seems fair that I'll leave half and take half. Arrin, stay with Bane and keep him as stable as you can. Yen, you're in charge of the team that will stay. Miren, you're staying with them, and so is Jian. No!" I raised a quieting hand as they all started to speak up.

"No time for fucking arguments! Tang knows the way we need to go, so I need to take him. The only other person here that can do stealth is Yen, so she stays to watch out for others. We need a healer to keep Bane going, so Arrin stays, then both a ranged and close-in fighter, so that's Miren and Jian. Stephanos, Grizz, you're with Tang and me, but leave the golem behind," I said to Stephanos, aware of how slow the damn thing moved.

I got a chorus of acceptance from them, and I nodded in satisfaction.

"Believe me, I don't like splitting the team either, but we have no choice. The gnomes need time to rebuild the vehicles to carry us all, and we've got a chance to both loot one of the Prax's repositories and find that noble. If anyone knows how to stop Bane's bleeding, it'll be him. We can't miss this chance," I growled. "Lastly, there's a dozen healing and three mana potions, right?" I asked Yen.

"Yes, you want them?" she offered.

I shook my head. "No, give us one healing each, and I'll take a mana as well. Keep the rest and try to keep the others safe. Hopefully, there will be more of them in the Vault."

"What about the researchers?" Yen asked me suddenly, and I looked over to her with an angry glower. "They're not all assholes, as near as I can tell. They were ordered to come and have stayed out of the way, basically," she clarified quickly.

"Give them the choice. They can come if they can keep up, and they can swear the Oath; otherwise, they can wait for the SporeMothers," I said grudgingly.

Yen and the others saluted, fists to chests as we set off, Tang in the lead as we ran down the corridor he'd come from.

CHAPTER TWENTY-SEVEN

We moved as fast as we could, giving up on stealth entirely in favor of speed, with Tang filling us in on the details as we went.

"There were five of them, four soldiers acting as guards to the noble, all wearing good armor—not the cheap shit the others had on, so need to watch them. They'll be highly trained if they're a personal guard—they were trying to force the Vault open, but judging by the crap piled around it, it's been sealed a long time. From what I could see, the lich must have been living next to it."

"What about the room itself?" I asked as we ran, jumping over scattered rubble and dodging around sections that were clearly flooded. Water down a dark side passage splashed, stirring as something raced away from our approach.

"It's another large one, circular, with the Vault in the center. There were low walls around it, as though the room used to be more, I don't know…central?" he attempted to explain, then shrugged dismissively. "It's a big dome, though; goes up almost as high as I could see, pitch black above, and a bit of light on the far side. That's all I can say for sure. Couldn't make more out without giving myself away."

"That's fine. We haven't got time for a sneaky approach, not if we've also got to find a way to open the Vault. Grizz, you're lead on this. Full-speed assault, that sound doable?" I asked.

"Yes, Jax, we train extensively for this," he said, nodding seriously despite the grin covering his face. "Stephanos, you peel off when we arrive, get to the best vantage point you can, and snipe them. Tang, stealth and flank. Use your ranged attacks. Jax and I will storm them full-on. Momentum is key; don't slow, don't stop, go all out and storm through any resistance," he ordered crisply. "You got a Shield Bash yet, boss?"

"Nope, not one of my options yet," I admitted.

"Remind me to work on that with you. Do it enough, and you can develop it without that. For now, use that damn stick. I'll be the tank," Grizz directed.

We took the corners far faster than any we'd done so far. My insane level of Agility, Tang's scout training and elven heritage, and Grizz being Grizz meant that Stephanos was falling farther and farther behind when Tang called out over the sound of our running feet.

"Two more corners, then we're there!" he said. Stephanos dug down deep, refusing to give in and be the weak link.

We sprinted along, the magelights on both Stephanos's and Grizz's armor sending crazy shadows bouncing and the harsh breathing echoing in our ears as our steel-shod feet clattered and banged over the metal of the Sunken City.

There was a definite thick, salty taste to the air now, and as we broke around the final corner, we all slowed subconsciously before Grizz barked out to pick up the pace.

The room ahead of us was clearly huge, vanishing to either side and soaring above into the darkness. The sound of lapping water came from the right somewhere. In the center, surrounded by concentric rings of low walls, stood a rounded pagoda that glimmered softly with ancient magic.

It alone in the entire city seemed to still be powered, with a soft golden glow emanating from the walls to illuminate the eleven men and women standing around the building.

As we arrived, the majority spun, falling into place to guard the two who were arguing in the center.

They stood before the doors of the Vault, the younger man being shouted at by the older. I recognized them as the Narkolt nobles as we closed the distance.

Hannimish and Joshua were shouting at each other, seemingly oblivious to everything, until one of their guards frantically interrupted them.

Joshua backhanded the man across the face with a snarl without a thought, and I saw the shocked look on Hannimish's face. The guard seemed to barely notice, clearly used to abuse, and pointed to us.

Joshua bellowed, pointing to us, and the guards spread out, ready to take us on.

"Looks like they got reinforcements!" I grunted as I drew alongside Grizz, wishing we could afford to wait and wear them down from a distance.

"Yeah, that means we get to have a real race!" he said cheerfully. "A gold coin says I kill more than you."

We were a little over forty meters from them and closing fast.

"Hell, no; make it something that matters!" I countered, again amazed by the improvements in my body. Running for more than ten minutes in full armor, and I was barely winded; that was amazing! *I'd be winning the Olympics at home,* a little voice informed me casually, *all of them.*

"Okay, a day with Primus Restun!" Grizz offered. I staggered slightly, my foot landing wrong as every muscle tensed slightly in fear.

A full day of being trained one-on-one with Restun? That was horrific, evil, even, but damn, now *that* was a forfeit.

"Done!" I said, glaring at the guards before me. There were nine total; two had lifted bows and were readying themselves to provide ranged support. Seven had spread out to form a loose half-circle. Of the seven, four held shields and short, wicked-looking curved axes, with the remaining three wielding swords, two of which had no shields and instead carried greatswords.

I angled myself for the right outer edge, knowing that Grizz would do the same with the left. I fed a burst of magic into the naginata at the last second, closing the final few meters.

Lightning crackled out from my hands, flooding the weapon, and I leaped into the air, spinning my body and kicking out at the shield that my first opponent had raised. Simultaneously, I swept my right hand downward, aiming for a second man with my naginata.

The speed of the attack, and the act of shifting from aiming for the outside into the middle at the last second, meant that I managed to avoid most of the weapons aimed at me. Stephanos provided last-minute distraction to the archers in the form of flashing arrows that hammered toward the nobles.

I'd slammed into the guard's shield hard. The weight of my body and armor, combined with the speed I'd been going, sent my target flying, while I used the shield to kick backward, landing upright. My naginata had channeled a powerful lightning spell down its length and along the sword that had been sticking out for me, stunning the wielder, and then the fight devolved into a blur.

I swung the naginata base around and grabbed it with my left hand, yanking the weapon across to catch the semi-stunned wielder's weapon on the haft, then slashed the blade across, slicing across the top of his left pauldron, then the top of the breastplate, and finally slitting his throat.

As he dropped his weapon, hands going to the new wide, red smile I'd given him, I twisted to my right and jumped back as a greatsword wielder swung for me.

I dodged to the right, then struck at him, well aware I was allowing myself to become surrounded, but not having the time to play it safe.

My naginata was deflected by his sword, and he struck again, moving through a series of fast, well-executed blows in sequence, driving me backward.

I lunged to the left, then right, I swung desperate parries, and still he drove me back.

I channeled a second lightning bolt into the naginata and slapped at his sword. He yanked it back, having seen what would happen if he didn't.

I tried two more strikes, each time spinning and striking out at one of the figures to either side of me and panicking as I went.

I nearly triggered Overdrive each time, but I had to save it. At the rate we were going, I might not manage to get them all off the island before the SporeMothers arrived. If those got here, I'd need the damn thing then, and there was no guarantee I'd be able to beat them, even then.

I took a slash to my left lower arm, the force staggering me, even as the armor protected my limb, leaving me with a vicious bruise instead of losing a hand. But the armor was dented and wouldn't survive a second attempt.

Something hammered into my right knee, and I staggered, then slashed out at the greatsword wielder, driving him back.

I was getting hammered, basically keeping them mostly at bay, and I didn't have time to see how Grizz was doing…

But I didn't need to do more than that.

In the blur of the fight, and with Stephanos distracting the archers, they'd all missed Tang.

He had flanked them as Grizz had ordered, and the first thing they knew about it was when one, then the other archer screamed out and fell, pierced through by huge black arrows.

The third shot slammed into the face of a man facing me, sending him backwards in death, and the odds had changed drastically.

Without Stephanos having to distract the archers, he could concentrate on the guards, and his own arrows drove them back as they frantically searched for Tang.

I slammed my naginata into the guard brandishing the greatsword as he stabbed out. As I finally made contact, he stiffened, lightning discharging down his weapon and stunning him. I wrapped the bladed end of my weapon around his, spiraling it, twisting it around and around, until I managed to get the blade under his left wrist just as the stun wore off.

He'd kept a death grip on his weapon, teeth gritted, determined, but as the tip of my blade flashed under and behind his wrist, I drove the opposite end of my weapon down, hooking his arm and lifting his sword up. With the massive weapon out of the way, I stabbed forward, driving the point of my blade into his chest between the breastplate and his pauldron.

The blade dug in and cut through the muscles of his left arm, tearing deep. I yanked it back, spinning around and dodging the frantic downward slash he managed to make with just one working arm.

The blade clanged off the ground, and I sent mine blurring across, taking his head from his shoulders in a single, powerful slice.

"Stop this!" Hannimish screamed, panicked pleading clear in his voice. I realized he'd been shouting since the battle was truly joined, desperately trying to get everyone to stop.

I paused for a second, unsure, and then *he* was there. Joshua, lunging forward, teeth bared, began stabbing at me, an evil, black-bladed dagger aimed at the weakened armor of my left forearm.

The little bastard had lunged out from behind one of his men, using him as a shield, until he was close enough to stab down at my arm. The blade should have had no chance, aimed as it was at my vambrace. But it sliced into the metal like it was made of butter, deflecting slightly, but still cutting into the plate and digging into the flesh below, drawing a deep line across my arm that immediately started notifications flashing.

I slashed at him, but he'd jumped back and grinned at me as the remaining guards tightened in around him and Hannimish.

I swore, backing up and looking at my arm. Shaking it and trying to get a sudden numbness out of it, I could feel my gauntlet filling with blood.

Joy, satisfaction, and goddamn certainty filled his eyes as he straightened up at the back of the group and pointed his dagger at me.

"Now, surrender or die," he snarled, the earlier hesitation and politeness wiped from his face and replaced with an arrogant sneer.

"Joshua!" Hannimish pleaded. "Boy, you saw what he can do; stop this, I beg." Hannimish didn't get to finish before Joshua backhanded him and snapped at one of the guards.

"Restrain the old fool!" he snapped.

Shock registered on Hannimish's face as one of the guards grabbed him and dragged him away, yanking his arm up behind his back and gripping him by the throat.

"Boy!" Hannimish gasped, horror and fury on his face. "You've…gone too…far…this time!"

"No, you old fool. I've won!" he crowed, then turned back to me. The remaining guards had fallen back, and Grizz had stepped in close to me, glancing from me to my forearm to the blade that seemed to glow darkly in Joshua's grip.

"Feel free to read your notifications, *my lord*. I'll wait," Joshua said, sarcasm and greed clear in his voice.

I pulled up the notification and gritted my teeth.

Beware!

You have been infected with: Necrotic Feasting!

The infected flesh is dying, and as it dies, the curse multiplies, spreading faster and faster through the body until death claims you!

-50 health per 60 seconds until death, increasing by 1.5x per 600 seconds

"Really?" I said grimly, hitting myself with a Battlefield Triage spell and checking the wound. I paused, knowing what I had to do, clearly seeing why he'd discounted it and why he thought he had me.

"Yes, you fool! The only way to stop the spell is this dagger. He who holds it controls the curse. But it can be neither removed nor cured otherwise, so you're out of choices now, aren't you!" Joshua said, clearly delighted with himself. "But I can be a merciful lord."

"Let me guess," I said distractedly as I examined the details and nerved myself up to what had to be done. "I just have to, what? Declare you a city lord?"

"Declare me Lord of Dravith and Scion of the Empire in your place! Refute all rights to the throne, and—"

He cut off in horror as I slammed over a hundred mana into the naginata, extending my left hand out to Grizz, who knew what I was going to do.

He gripped my hand, pulling my arm straight as he dropped his sword and flipped the catches on the upper vambrace, freeing it from my elbow.

I looked at him as I felt waves of heat flaring off the naginata, and I saw Grizz nod to me that he understood. I shifted my grip, offering the blade of the weapon toward him, keeping a light grip on the haft and continuing to channel into it as he gripped it by the head and slashed down.

I felt the resistance, the slight snagging, as the blade first met my arm. It vaporized the leather and the cloth instantly; there was a hiss, and a smell reminiscent of burned bacon, then a shift as the blade angled slightly aside, diverted infinitesimally as it encountered the twin bones. Then it was shearing out of the far side, and I fell to one knee, hissing in agony as the reality of cutting off my own goddamn arm struck home.

I released the naginata, and the room dimmed as the magic faded, while I fumbled with my belt, popping the cork off my healing potion and downing it.

It was practically useless.

It was an average-level potion, so it slowed the bleeding, and the sheer heat of the naginata had sealed most of the wound anyway, but it sure as shit didn't help with the pain or the shock, let alone regrowing my damn forearm.

But it was okay, I told myself as I straightened up, forcing myself to my feet and glaring at Joshua, who gaped at me in shock.

I was alive, and as I hit myself with Battlefield Triage again, I found no trace of the curse.

Simple problem, simple solution.

Not one I could have come up with before losing my hand, I had to admit to myself, but infinitely more doable than it would have been. Add to that, years of watching this kind of thing done on TV, and my outlook was a bit different from that of an essentially medieval society.

I glared at Joshua and forced myself to show no pain as I casually spoke.

"That was a mistake," I said simply, coldly, even.

"You…you…fine!" Joshua snarled, coming out of his shock. "All I have to do is cut you again…think you can keep hacking your own limbs off?"

He hefted his dagger again threateningly.

I smiled at him and spoke clearly to Grizz, and to Stephanos, who I hoped could hear me, and to Tang, who I had total faith would be damn close, by now.

"Joshua is mine. Spare Hannimish, for now, and kill the guards unless they surrender," I said.

There was a few seconds' pause as everyone waited for someone else to make the first move, and I took the chance. I had one hundred and twenty-seven mana left.

No point in saving it for the SporeMothers, after all, so I slammed it into Mana Overdrive, slowing the world down as I blurred forward.

I crossed the ten feet that had opened up between our groups in just under two seconds, ducking under a swung sword that moved like it was encased in treacle. I swayed then crouched, slipping effortlessly between two guards, and I yanked a long needle-tipped poniard out of a sheath on the swordsman's leg as I went. Flipping it over and ramming it into the base of his skull, I crunched into the bottom of his brain as I straightened up, my eyes locked onto Joshua's.

He snarled hatefully at me, slashing horizontally, as the swordsman's body got the message that he was dead and collapsed, I simply stepped back, leaning slightly, as the blade ripped through the air before me.

I stepped into range, Joshua staggering off-balance from the lack of expected resistance, and I grabbed his wrist with my right, now only remaining hand. As I twisted, my greater strength and training became clear as I yanked his arm into a locked position.

I straightened, then stamped down hard with my right foot on the inside of his left knee, forcing it to buckle. Then I leaned in, bending his arm around before he could stop me.

Shock, followed by terror, danced across his expression as he tried to grab at me, reaching up in a futile attempt to stop what I was doing.

I had to weigh half again what he did, and that was without my armor. Standing at nearly seven feet of solid muscle and barely controlled rage, I was augmented by Mana Overdrive, and next to me, he was merely a foppish noble looking like a toddler trying to stop a bodybuilder.

I sneered down at him, scorning the terror on his face as I pushed the blade closer.

"That was my favorite arm, you little shit," I growled.

He whimpered, opening his mouth for one last word.

"Please," he managed, before the tip of the dagger punctured his eye, vitreous fluid bursting around the blade as I, oh so slowly, drove it through the orbit and into the brain, the tip crunching out the back.

Joshua twitched and flailed in death, his body receiving a last-minute panicked barrage firing of neurons. I released him to fall to the floor, yanking the dagger free and turning to glare at the single remaining guard as Grizz pulled my naginata free of another.

The last two guards dropped their weapons quickly, one raising his hands in surrender, before he suddenly fell to the floor, an arrow sprouting from his forehead.

"Sorry! My bad!" called Stephanos, just as Tang materialized directly behind the guard who'd been restraining Hannimish and rested his sword against the guardsman's back, the tip pricking the skin right where the armor didn't reach.

"Now, that was lucky timing on your part, wasn't it?" he whispered in the man's ear, and the guard closed his eyes, whispering a brief prayer as sweat began to roll down his cheek.

"Thank you!" I called to Stephanos, turning back to look across at him, and nodding my approval. "*That's* how you use that phrase! Speak to Oracle when we get back; make sure she gets it, okay?" I called, before turning to address Hannimish.

"So," I said, waving with my stump. "Want to explain this and what the *fuck* you're doing down here?" I growled at him, swallowing hard as I released the Overdrive and felt the hit to my stats.

"Be very, very convincing and contrite," Tang recommended quietly, yet in a voice that carried from behind the guard and the pale, trembling noble.

"Ah, my lord…uh," Hannimish started, tears filling his eyes as he stared from me to the still corpse of his nephew on the floor.

"Perhaps a little clearer? And from the beginning?" Tang whispered.

Hannimish closed his eyes, drawing in a deep breath before letting it out in a long exhalation and looking at me again.

"Lord Jax, I'm sorry. We received a communication before you arrived, warning us that there was a third party in the war between Narkolt and Himnel, and that we were to report immediately if we had any information," he began.

"I reported your approach to the city when you became clear in the distance, and I was ordered to do nothing to antagonize you, to see if you could be reasoned with or bought. We reported on the meeting and were ordered to attempt to salvage anything of value we could from the site. We were not to cross you, but if we could retrieve whatever was here first, then we were to return to Narkolt with it, or failing that, to see what kind of accommodations could be reached with you."

He shook his head sorrowfully, looking down at Joshua again. "The fool boy had a second diary, one he refused to share with me. Once we descended into the city, he…he split off. He seemed to know what he was doing and had the majority of the guard with him, so I let him go. I thought I was granting him some independence." Hannimish choked down a sob and pressed on with gritted teeth.

"Then I received new orders. We were warned to get off the city, to escape, and abandon anything else. We were to warn you if we felt we could work with you; if not…" He closed his eyes, inhaling shakily. "I used a second device, a tracking wand, to find him, and when I did, he became irate, screaming that he couldn't leave, not yet…then he told me what he'd done, and how he would use it to force you to give him what he wanted.

"I tried to stop him, tried to reason with him." He faltered, his shoulders heaving with silent sobs. "My god, what will I tell my sister?!" he whispered, his hand coming up to cover his mouth in what seemed like genuine shock and horror.

"How did you communicate?" I asked him.

"Conjoined diaries," he admitted absently, still looking at the corpse.

"Expensive, but effective," Grizz said, stepping up and holding the naginata out to me. "They create a pair of books that are absolutely identical, then use a lot of magic to pair them up. Whatever you write in one appears in the other and vice versa."

"Sounds useful," I said.

"Yes, and no." Grizz grimaced. "Like I say, awfully expensive, plus there's no security on it. You'd never know who was on the other side."

"That's why we used ciphers and confirmation codes," Hannimish said woodenly. "That way, you can confirm their identity."

I shook my head, thinking of easily half a dozen ways to get around that in seconds, but I kept my mouth shut.

"So basically, you were ordered by…who? Someone in your city?" I asked, and he cleared his throat and wiped at his eyes before responding.

"City Lord Rewn. We are distantly related and old friends. He ordered me to attempt to reach an accommodation with you regarding your rank and position; we were to turn to violence only if you attacked first. Lord Rewn seeks allies against Himnel, not another enemy," Hannimish said, clearly shifting his voice to a more formal and less…hurting…timbre. "I am empowered to request a meeting with you, at a neutral place, where you and Lord Rewn could reach an understanding."

"Ha, after this?" I grunted, lifting my left arm into the air where he could see it, waving the truncated stump around. "You think I'll trust you now? Besides, half of the ships on their way here, filled with the fucking SporeMothers, are from Narkolt. You want to explain that?" I asked, then I turned to Grizz without waiting for an answer.

"Grizz, search that cocksucker. Find the diary and pass me that goddamn knife…carefully," I said, moving to the side and sitting on a low wall, the shock and horror of what I'd just done finally catching up with me.

I squashed it down, ignoring the pain and the horror that I'd just maimed myself, and told myself firmly that I'd be able to be healed. I had an amazing pair of healers; Hellenica had already regrown one hand for me. There was no need to be worrying about this shit…not right now.

Hannimish started talking again, but Tang and Grizz, seeing the state of me, shut him up and led him and his guard aside, searching them roughly and making sure they were disarmed.

Grizz stomped over, crouching down in front of me and offering a healing potion. I eyed it and snorted, mistrusting the bright, glimmering liquid.

"The *good* Lord Hannimish actually told me which pouch had their best potions. There's a pair of these and a pair of mana, all greater," he said quietly. "How are you doing, boss? I want to send Tang back to get the others and bring them here; that okay with you?" He popped the top off the potion and held it up.

I took it, drinking half of the ruby liquid and feeling a new heat radiate outwards from my belly, banishing a portion of the lethargy and shock I suddenly realized I'd been sinking into.

"Yeah, yeah. You do that, Grizz. Thanks, man," I said, passing it back to him. He stoppered the bottle and set it down on the wall next to me, before offering the mana potion next.

That one, I drank all of, feeling my mana leap upwards and the regeneration increase at a phenomenal rate as he passed me the last item: Joshua's accursed dagger.

Death's Kiss		Further Description *Yes/No*	
Damage:		25-500	
Details:		The Death's Kiss dagger was crafted long ago by an order of assassins serving the empire. This weapon is inscribed with the motto of the assassins: *"Carpe noctem, die causa vivendi"* and can be used to inflict the following wounds: **Fester:** Inflict a gradually building fever, the original attack has a 50% chance to numb and seal the wound, leaving the victim unaware of the injury. Cost 250 mana **Necrotic Feasting**: This wound will spread, dissolving the flesh of the victim, this wound cannot be stopped so long as there is flesh to convert, only slowed. Cost 150 health *Infected*: Gives the victim a 50% chance of the wound becoming infected and requiring special healing. Cost 50 health *Poisoned:* 25% chance to cause additional 5-15 health damage to the victim per strike. Cost 75 mana **Special attack**: Cursed! For 100 health and mana, the wielder can inflict wounds that cannot be sealed, bleeding the victim to death, or until this curse is removed by use of **CurseBreaker.** Wielder receives 10% of the bleed effect as additional health until this effect is dispelled.	
Rarity:	**Magical:**	**Durability:**	**Charge:**
Legendary	Yes	67/120	30/500

I read and reread the details, wondering what the hell CurseBreaker was. I called to Grizz, seeing that Tang was already gone, and Stephanos had moved over to stand guard over the prisoners in his place.

"Grizz, we need something called 'CurseBreaker'; no idea what it is beyond that," I said, and he nodded, moving back to the corpse and starting to search it quickly.

I saw the look of pain on Hannimish's face as Grizz so casually and roughly tore through the pockets, bags, and other belongings. I scowled, understanding the feeling of horror somewhat, but dismissing it, as Joshua was a fucking prick.

Grizz started tearing things free, passing them over to pile up next to me, and I went to work.

Boots of Bloody Stepping		Further Description *Yes/No*	
Details:		Gain +3 to Agility when these boots have recently been splashed with fresh sentient blood.	
Rarity:	**Magical:**	**Durability:**	**Charge:**
Rare	Yes	57/100	N/A

Midnight's Vision Ring		Further Description *Yes/No*	
Details:		Gain +200 ft to DarkVision.	
Rarity:	**Magical:**	**Durability:**	**Charge:**
Rare	Yes	95/100	N/A

Ring of Healing		Further Description *Yes/No*	
Details:		+250 health in instantaneous healing, single use per charge.	
Rarity:	**Magical:**	**Durability:**	**Charge:**
Highly Rare	Yes	92/100	2/5

Barbed Dagger		Further Description *Yes/No*	
Damage		10-25	
Details:		This dagger has been enhanced with serrated teeth along the rear of the spine to do additional damage.	
Rarity:	**Magical:**	**Durability:**	**Charge:**
Uncommon	**No**	**77/100**	**N/A**

Coif of the Night's Warden		Further Description *Yes/No*	
Details:		Gain +5 to defense when equipped. Collect 2 further pieces of the Night's Warden Set to receive further set bonuses.	
Rarity:	**Magical:**	**Durability:**	**Charge:**
Rare	Yes	52/100	N/A

CurseBreaker		Further Description *Yes/No*	
Damage		1-4	
Details:		A specially created companion to the Death's Kiss blade. When CurseBreaker is returned to its place in the hilt, any wounds that have been inflicted by Death's Kiss will cease to have magical aspects.	
Rarity:	**Magical:**	**Durability:**	**Charge:**
Legendary	Yes	67/100	N/A

"Well, thank fuck for that," I breathed, turning the dagger over and over as I examined it. CurseBreaker was a thin metal rod, about half as thick and long as my little finger, and after a few seconds of careful searching, I found the slot. At the base of the weapon, a thin metal plate had been hidden, and when I touched the rod to it, it slid aside, revealing a narrow hollow, clearly meant to house it.

I slid it in and let out a sigh as another prompt popped up.

Congratulations!

You have broken 17 continuous infliction wounds spread across the following victims:

Al'an Triniar

Rennical Tosa

Proma Ris'aun

Wellin Jeffer

Bane Ter'Jax

CurseBreaker will no longer funnel health to the following bearer: Cletus Thane.

Do you wish to break the bonds between Cletus and this weapon, allowing another to wield it fully?

Yes/No

I selected yes, and I felt the dagger shudder strangely, seeming to become lighter in my hand.

"Who the hell were they?" I muttered to myself, having recognized only Bane's name amongst them. Then I shook my head and took the sheath Grizz offered me for the dagger. I swept the rest of the gear he'd stripped off Joshua up, dumping it in the bag, and forced myself to my feet, grimacing at the phantom feeling of still having the rest of my left arm. Again.

I forced it out of my mind and walked to the Vault, inspecting the walls where they glowed gently. Oracle would have cracked this in a second, but I didn't have her, so I was going to have to figure it out.

I walked slowly around it, Grizz walking with me, watchfully staring out at the darkness. Idly, I played with the Midnight Vision ring as I went, slipping it on and off my little finger in my pocket, as Grizz carried my naginata for me.

After two complete circuits of the small domed area, I was still none the wiser, and I finally stopped at a cleared section, noting the marks on the floor nearby showed that something had stood here for a long, long time to wear grooves in the metal like that.

There were four patches, two further apart at the front, and two closer together at the back, with rough patches where they'd been shifted again and again over the years...

They almost looked like...

"A chair," I muttered, straightening up from where I'd been crouched to examine them. I looked around and spotted a chair where it sat against a stack of old bones and general detritus.

The room gave the impression that it'd become a mixture of a throne room, a bedroom, and a marshalling hall for the lich. Piles of random shit lay everywhere, collapsed small walls, and weird items, including a wheel of bones joined together with a seat in the middle that made me think of a waltzer at a fairground. I dismissed the details as I strode over and grabbed the chair, before having Grizz gently but firmly take it from me and carry it over.

I looked at it as he turned it over, then put it down in what must have been its accustomed position. It grated into place, crumbs of bone filling the grooves. But once it was there, there was nothing else, and I frowned, thinking I was missing a latch or…

"Goddammit, I'm an idiot!" I cursed myself, and I closed my eyes, concentrating. I shifted my consciousness sideways somehow and focused, activating an Ability.

As soon as Seek That Which is Hidden activated, I reopened my eyes and froze. The entire room blazed with a soft golden light.

Sections were brighter, or dimmer, but the small pagoda in the center, the structure that I'd been circling, shone like the sun. I stared at the building, before seeing movement out of the corner of my eye.

I looked over to my right and lifted my eyes upward, then froze as a feeling of existential dread filled me.

The ability showed that which was hidden, and right now, what it was showing me, amongst other things, was that the dark walls of this place weren't walls.

They were glass, or something like it, and the darkness was caused by a combination of being underwater, a buildup of scum slowly growing across the glass over the centuries, and because an enormous creature currently slumbered against the side of the city.

I couldn't make out much beyond long tentacles, teeth, and a humped body that looked like a mix between a dragon and a bulldozer. The thing was easily as long as a football field, without counting the appendages.

I turned back from looking out and stared at the Vault, determined that I would get inside this thing and escape the goddamn place fast.

"What's up, boss?" Grizz asked causally, looking out at the darkness and lifting the magelight he wore attached to a hoop around his neck. He started waving it, trying to make out what I'd seen, when I hissed at him.

"Stop it, you goddamn fool!" I snapped.

"I was just—" he started, looking hurt.

I shook my head, putting my finger to my lips and glaring at him. As soon as he stopped, I nodded and whispered to him.

"There's something out there, and it's about the same size as the fucking battleship. It's asleep and pressed up against the walls. They're also not 'walls,' so much as teeny fucking tiny windows, so let's not wake it up, okay?" I said. He blanched before nodding firmly and starting to quiet people down.

I turned back to the Vault and glared at it, stamping closer from the chair. Clearly something, presumably the lich, had sat here staring at the Vault for a huge amount of time. There were shattered bones everywhere and bonemeal, the ground-up bits of bone, scattered around. So, he'd tried brute force, and until now, at least, that'd not worked.

I circled it again a fourth time, and finally, I noticed something different.

There was a small indentation on the side, scratched and battered and familiar. I stared at it, wondering and trying to figure it out, until I started to hear the sounds in the distance that indicated the gnomes were approaching.

I looked to Grizz in horror, and he nodded, turning and sprinting for the exit.

I turned back to the recess, knowing instinctively that it was there for something to be attached. I squinted at it, ran my fingers across the edges, and swore as it nicked me. I lifted my finger away and saw no blood…but I could have sworn…

No.

I stopped myself, looking from my uninjured finger to a single glimmering, silvery drop that slowly vanished into the recess.

It wasn't a wound I'd felt; it was a drain.

CHAPTER TWENTY-EIGHT

The missing part was a manawell, like those back at the tower, similar to the wells I'd found when I first met Oracle and the others. There was a missing section designed to hold the manawell, and it looked to have been torn off in a fit of rage. I spun around, scrutinizing the floor, searching.

"Boss, you okay?" Stephanos asked carefully, still watching the prisoners.

"No," I said firmly. "You remember the manawell from the tower?"

He frowned thoughtfully, then shrugged.

"Sort of? I mean, I saw one, I think, once?"

"Dammit. Okay, you're looking for a bowl. Just think of it like that, a damn bowl, and one we need to find right goddamn now!" He gestured at the prisoners in question. "Leave them," I said simply, then raised my voice, figuring if the creature out there had ignored the fight earlier, a moderately loud voice was unlikely to get its attention now.

"If any of you move, you're dead," I declared, then I started searching.

A few minutes passed before Yen and several others arrived, the horror that was clear on their faces making me grimace over my lost forearm all the more, until they too started looking in earnest. Yen jogged up to me and nodded in respect.

"Bane's alive," she said without preamble. "Whatever you did, his wounds have closed. The last time Arrin hit him with a heal, they just sealed up like normal. He's unconscious, still gravely injured, drained, and in no fit state to be upright for a month, let alone fight anytime soon, but he's alive and stable. Arrin's unconscious as well, although I think that a combination of overuse of mana channels and exhausted relief."

"Thank god," I breathed, pausing and clasping her shoulder. "Well done, Yen!"

"It's my job, Jax, that's all." She shrugged but looked pleased with the words.

"Well, I need you again," I admitted, gesturing around the detritus-strewn space. "I need to find a bowl; it's a manawell, but it's most likely that you'll recognize it as a bowl, about this big," I explained, miming the size with my hand and stump, "and we need to find it *fast*."

She nodded to me, then sprinted back to the gaggle of gnomes and our team, who were peering cautiously into the room.

She spoke quietly for a minute, gesturing and clearly passing on the rough dimensions I'd given to her then the group scattered, gnomes sprinting away from each other at high speed.

It was found balanced atop a skull on a spike after a few minutes and brought to me. Once I pressed it to the side of the Vault, I felt a crunch, then a click, and the faint glimmer of the building shuddered, growing duller as it magically reattached the manawell.

Congratulations!

You have found a wisp manawell.
Mana required to reawaken the wisp: 10/1000.

"Goddammit!" I growled, then grabbed the edges of the manawell and started pouring my mana into it. "We don't have time for this shit." I fought to keep my irritation down, focusing on the sensation of my mana being ripped from me.

"Can we help?" Yen asked.

I paused, eyeing her as I felt the tugging of my mana, before grinning. "Yes, you damn well can!" I said, relief washing through me. "In fact, anyone who has spare mana, get your ass over here and put your hand on the bowl, please."

I monitored the details, watching it ticking up as more people came and went. It was particularly satisfying to see Grizz staggering as he experienced what looked to be his first ever mana migraine, as the bastard had started to show me up just a little too often.

It ticked ever upwards, while others searched the room, eventually finding a collection of crappy armor, some robes, and a handful of trinkets, including a dog-eared old book, clearly well-thumbed and looking like it was from back home.

"*Condition,*" I wonderingly read aloud, the damaged cover making it impossible to read the rest of the title. "Who the hell was Kevin Sinclair?" I muttered when someone handed it to me. I flicked through the first few pages, frowning. I paused when I realized he'd written about the north of England and grinned to myself. No matter where I was and what happened over the next few days, I was making time to read this.

Clearly, the lich had an extensive library at one time, as a chest was found buried under a mountain of bones. It was filled, to my relief, not with gold or jewels, not even potions, although I'd have loved to find those.

No, it was full of books. Dozens of them. I turned to Grizz, who'd followed me and looked him dead in the eye.

"Grizz, these are from my realm. This might seem stupid to you, but I damn well *need* these. I trust you to make sure they come with us, okay?"

He nodded and started sorting the books out, putting them into different bags on his belt and coordinating some with the others.

I noticed him pause on one, a cover that showed a scantily clad woman with pointy elven or feline ears and boobs bursting out of her bikini, by a guy called Atlas Kane, slipping that one into his pouch with an unashamed grin and a wink to me.

"There's probably not any pictures in that, you know?" I said.

"If not, maybe Yen will read it with me." He waggled his eyebrows, then checked to make sure she hadn't heard him. I snorted and walked back to the Vault as Yen moved everyone back from it, standing to attention as I stepped up close.

"It's at nine hundred and ninety," she said simply, and I smiled gratefully. Forty minutes, it'd taken.

"How long do we have left before the ships arrive?" I asked her, and she swallowed hard.

"Ten minutes." She grimaced.

"Well, hopefully we can loot this and get the hell—" I started to say, before she interrupted me.

"They should have reached the Sunken City ten minutes *ago*," Yen clarified, and I froze before letting out a long breath.

"Well, it is what it is," I said philosophically, trying to hide my fear and anger when it came to the fact that some crazy motherfucker was actually breeding the goddamn things.

I reached out, gripping the edges of the manawell, and poured the last ten points into it.

The well flared brightly, the silvery, mercury-like liquified mana within shining brighter and brighter until the manawell drained and fell off the side of the structure.

We all froze. Everyone looked from me to the well and back to me again, and my mind went over what had just happened in a panic.

It didn't make sense!

Then something changed with the Vault; the gently glowing walls began to grow brighter. At first, it was almost imperceptible, but as the seconds passed, it blazed, and lines of solid silver began to spread from the space where the well had sat. They poured out in all directions, flowing across the surface of the construction, until they had entirely ringed it, with many dozens of tiny runes flaring to life as they went.

Soon, though, they died away and the structure became quiescent again.

I waited politely; then after a minute, I stepped forward, noticing a feeling that I'd missed in all the confusion before.

I could feel a wisp.

I'd never really noticed it until recently, and that was with Oracle, so I'd assumed that it was down to the fact that it was *Oracle*, and we were so close.

I'd believed I could feel her presence because we were bonded, and she was my companion and my lover as well.

Now I was questioning whether there was also more to it, as I felt something moving inside the Vault.

It felt similar to the way a magnet is drawn by iron, or vice versa. Not strong enough to really notice, unless you were close to it, or experienced with the feeling. I only recognized it because I'd been trying to ignore the sensation of loss that not having Oracle nearby had been building in me.

I watched the structure, frowning at seeing the silvery lines start up again, traveling back and forth. But now, I felt the difference, and I watched one in particular.

After a handful of seconds, it vanished, after pausing momentarily, clearly realizing I was watching it.

"Yes," I said slowly and clearly. "I can see you, and I know what you are."

Nothing happened, except for my people staring at each other then back at me, involuntarily projecting a slowly growing concern that I was losing my mind.

A concern that was elegantly summed up by a gnome further back.

"By Garran's hairy nutsack, we've got another crazy one! I thought we were leaving all of them behind?" an elderly gnome whispered to his friend. Unfortunately, the gnome was easily over two hundred, wizened, and clearly drugged up to the eyeballs, so his version of a whisper was little different from someone shouting and pointing at me.

"I know! Fucker cut his own arm off, I hear. I say we make nice, grab the good gear, and run for it!" his friend "whispered" back, then noticed the way that everyone was looking at them and forced a smile, waving nervously around. "Smile and wave, Jimkin, smile and wave!"

I shook my head, looking away and ignoring the loud discussion they started up about wondering how I knew they were talking about me.

Sighing, I focused once again on the structure, reaching down deep and...*listening*...to the feeling of magic.

I drew in a long, slow breath, followed by another, mentally centering myself before stepping forward and reaching out my hand to press it gently to the side of the Vault.

"I am Jax, Lord of Dravith, Scion of the Empire, and by the right of my blood, I claim this structure," I stated formally.

I heard people go silent, watching and waiting.

After a minute, I cracked an eye open and glanced around, feeling incredibly stupid. Voices started to mutter quietly, while bugger-all happened. I was about to give up when I felt a resonance begin in my palm.

It was minor; hell, it was practically infinitesimal, but it was there, and I knew it had begun. The metal under my palm grew warmer, slowly building until it reached the temperature of a comfortable summer's day, and the glow of the Vault grew with it.

At first, it had been a gentle, dim, even shimmer, but now it was *shining*. The room we were in began to glow in response as tiny pathways of silver metal spread out, racing for the far walls.

The liquified mana seemed to bring life to the stone and metal as it went. Color and vibrancy began flooding the room, pushing back the darkness.

I stepped back, somehow knowing that what I'd started couldn't be stopped now, and my moving would have no effect on it.

The floor shuddered slightly, then again, more forcefully, as something awoke under our feet, and the Vault began to glow brighter. The small building itself was an octagon, eight slightly sloped sides leading up from the ground to meet a sharply slanted triangular roof with a peak in the middle. The design made me think of a mix of a Chinese pagoda and a Bedouin tent, for some reason. The panels that made up the sides began to glow in an alternating pattern.

As the glow grew, the room filled with light as dozens of previously defunct magelights bloomed to life, scattered across the room. They ringed the outer edge and were positioned strategically on the dome as it climbed high overhead. But the vast majority were long dead.

The measly thousand mana that the Vault had needed to reawaken clearly was supposed to be an emergency seed of power. The lights bathed the room in a dim, late afternoon light, instead of what I guessed was intended to be a brilliantly sunny day.

The building shuddered again, and a loud crash somewhere in the distance, followed by rushing water, made me swallow hard, as I hoped I'd not just doomed us all.

"Yen," I said, turning to look at her. "Get everyone ready to go, just in case."

"Will do." She saluted, turning and heading off to gather up the gnomes, occasionally kicking one who gave her abuse.

I shook my head at the problems the little bastards were going to cause in the tower but I couldn't wait to see what gnomes could do with the airships, as well.

I dismissed them from my thoughts, though, as I felt the resonance building to new heights, then, finally, the Vault glowed with a solid golden light. The silvery liquid metal-looking mana that flowed back and forth around the structure returned to a single point.

It formed a pool, flat and still, but laid on the side of the structure at a ninety-degree angle, like a mirror. While it reflected the room behind me perfectly, my face frowned out at me sternly.

I blinked and tilted my head, considering the reflection and realizing just how rough I looked these days. My beard was scruffy, and my hair appeared to be matted with dried blood and dirt. I reached up to scratch my chin self-consciously, and did it with my missing hand, making me look even more monstrous and scruffier.

"What do you seek here, Scion?"

I heard the voice differently from the way that I heard Oracle and the other wisps of the Great Tower; they were bonded to me and spoke into my mind, while this voice…this was a faint whisper on the edge of hearing, a voice that echoed strangely, filled with a mixture of fatigue, sadness, and indefatigable yearning.

"I seek lost knowledge to enable me to defend the empire," I answered, forcing my words at the seemingly distant contact.

"And you think I possess this? I have little here compared to the great repositories of the empire. Why do you wish my death?"

"Death? I don't want your death?" I responded, confused.

"A bonded wisp is tied to its function. I must protect this knowledge. Without it, I have no reason for existence. When my mana is gone, I will cease to be. I thank you for the donation of mana, but alas, I cannot help you. Please…do not kill me."

"I don't want to kill you," I said impatiently, the crash of something collapsing in the distance and the surging sound of more water pouring in. *"There must be another way; there is no need for you to die."*

"I agree, there is no need. Leave this place. I sense rising water, and the structure has taken damage. Allow me to sink into my dreamless sleep again, Scion; let me sleep away the years until my Prax and I are recovered."

"Who do you think will recover you?" I asked the wisp. I felt the bone deep weariness in it as it responded with a sigh.

"There have been attempts to destroy the Prax before. This facility is designed to protect against that. The shame I feel that we are the first to fail and fall is enough. Please, let me rest. Soon enough, the others will recover us, and we will be returned to our rightful place in the heavens, patrolling and protecting the empire."

"You think that the other Prax will come for you?"

"Of course; they must be nearly here by now. I sense we have slumbered long years, and more since I was last reawakened."

"The empire collapsed. There is no one coming, wisp—" I started to say, only for fury to rise in the mind I dimly sensed in the distance.

"Speak not such lies! The empire stands and will stand forever! The Eternal Emperor protects the realms of light, and the gods would never permit otherwise!"

"Fuck," I said, then closed my eyes, realizing I'd sent that to the wisp as well. *"Okay, I am the Scion of the Empire; do you dispute this?"*

"I cannot verify your claim, not without blood and access to your mind," the wisp said cautiously, clearly both unsure if I would allow this and unwilling to accept my words as true.

"Then I grant you access to my mind," I said, looking around. *"And the gods know there's enough of my goddamn blood spilled in here today already."*

"I must draw the blood."

"Ha! Nothing's ever easy, is it? Fine, draw the blood yourself and touch my mind; see what you find there."

I stepped forward, getting close enough to the pool of liquid silver that my face was all that I could see, and I tried to stay still as a thin tendril lifted out and moved toward me slowly.

I tried not to imagine the liquid silver killing machines from the movies, but damn, it was hard, especially when the tendril paused in front of my eye.

I had a horrified second, thinking it was going to spear me through, when a minuscule section flashed out and rested against my temple, and I got a prompt pop up.

Do you wish to allow this Vault-locked Wisp to access your mind?

Yes/No

I selected yes, and for a second, a confused welter of images streamed past my mind's eye, many of them focusing on Oracle for some reason. Then, with a tiny flare of pain, the liquid silver tendril detached from my skull and flowed back to the rest of the puddle.

I straightened and backed away slightly, noting the single ruby-red drop of blood the tendril had retreated with.

I waited for long seconds, then finally spoke up when I saw Yen making a gesture to get my attention, then a frantic one upwards, that I guessed meant something along the lines of: "They're coming—we have to go, my lord."

Or it could have been "You're an asshole, and you stink," considering the way the day had gone. I waved to her and turned back to the puddle, jerking back in shock.

A mirror image of Oracle was seated on the side of the Vault in defiance of gravity, watching me.

She was also noticeably naked.

I flinched at the thought of going through all of this *again* and shook my head firmly.

"No," I said. "Not that form. Pick another."

"But…" the little wisp started to say, consternation on her tiny, beautifully familiar face.

"No!" I said firmly. "You do *not* mimic her, not ever. She is my partner, my love, and you might look like her, but you're not her, okay? Please, pick another form…and include clothes!" I added hurriedly, even as a little voice in the back of my head piped up with some remarkably interesting and filthy suggestions.

I drowned it out, concentrating on the fact that the world had just gone to shit, culminating with me chopping my own damn arm off. There was no need to be getting frisky thoughts, especially not right now.

The wisp paused for a long series of heartbeats, before finally changing to an entirely new form, as a six-inch tall woman with fox ears and a bushy tail that flitted from side to side. She wore a perfectly fitted suit that reminded me of a combination of an old English sea captain and a librarian, the fabric a deep, rich blue, with a white shirt and sparkling silver buttons that gleamed as she stood up straight and buffed her nails on her jacket.

"Very well, master. Is this form more to your liking?" the wisp asked, then glanced down at herself, and expanding her chest noticeably. "Or I could…"

"Nope!" I cut her off hurriedly. "The original version is fine!"

"Very well," she repeated, nonchalantly shifting back. "I have accessed your mind, master, and I find much to be concerned about, not least the fact that my Prax has likely been boarded by now, by creatures that are inimical to sentient life. I recommend we eliminate them immediately, then begin recovery of the Prax."

"Can we do that?" I asked her, and she nodded.

"It is possible, though it may take many years," she said, as though that was a minor detail. "First, we must activate the mana collectors. There are two levels of collection: the standard, as a Prax under no threat rests, and the advanced, or war footing. I recommend…" she said, her voice droning on.

"And that's enough," I said firmly. "We don't have the time to fuck about right now. Tell me straight: can we kill the SporeMothers and hold the Prax with the force you see here, and can the Prax be brought back to flight-capable status in any realistically short timeframe? You've searched my mind; you know what I'm up against."

"Yes…it is possible to secure my Prax, and the repairs could be managed by the onboard compliment of golems, once they were charged up. It would take several months to stabilize, followed by a few years of repairs, but…"

"Months isn't an option. We can leave them working, but I can't stay that long, and the Prax would have to be secure. I'm not powering you up and leaving you to be claimed by someone else and used against me. You say we can win against the SporeMothers; do you have any information on them or their number? What are you basing that off?"

"You defeated a fully grown, if weak and virtually senile one before," she said, clasping her hands behind her back. "Therefore, immature offspring would logically be easier to defeat. There is a high likelihood of success, provided your retainers accept the risks and fight to the death."

"Death?" My brow furrowed. "Wisp, clarify the losses you expect if we fight the SporeMothers," I ordered.

"There is no doubt that the Prax is a highly valuable and sought-after facility; therefore the losses will be worth accepting." she began briskly, then trailed off as she saw my face. "I estimate that, based on the information provided by the Goddess Jenae, you will be facing seven SporeMothers of various states, some nigh-on fully grown, some little more than annoyances. Therefore, with the forces you have here, and if you summon your fleet back, you should be able to defeat the invaders with less than fifty percent casualties."

The wisp smiled as though that was brilliant news, and I glared at her.

"Fifty percent?" I snarled. "With the fleet included, meaning we'd lose at least four to five hundred souls?"

"Possibly more," she agreed calmly.

"Fuck. No," I ground out. "I won't enter into a battle like that, even if this thing was operational, let alone, as it is now! This Prax has lain here abandoned for centuries; it can wait a few more years." I shook my head, dismissing her bloody stupid suggestion.

"The Prax is an imperial war machine. It cannot be allowed to fall into rebel hands!" she replied, sounding shocked and horrified, as though it was inconceivable that I'd leave it.

"Nearly a thousand years ago, yeah, it probably was," I retorted. "Now, it's a fucking derelict. Can anyone else control the systems? If I order you to lock down this area and concentrate on getting the golems up and running, can you make damn sure that the SporeMothers and anything else can't get in?" I asked.

"I judge it unlikely, but it is possible that the area could be secured. However…"

"How many golems are intact and could be reawakened?" I asked. "For that matter, if you could repair the goddamn place, why the hell didn't you already? Why wait hundreds of years for me to turn up?"

"There is no way to verify the state of the golems until I have returned power to those areas," she said stiffly. "As to the repairs, I was required to return to the Vault and hold fast until ordered to start repairs. It was a countermeasure to prevent damage to my core."

"And, what, you just sat there while the world went to shit?" I asked, shocked.

"No. I slumbered as I was ordered; then, when I was reawakened by a member of the nobility, I called to the revenants that my crew became, and I attempted to reach others of my kind. The member of the noble houses had come at great risk to himself, he said. He battled through the revenants and demanded access to my core to heal. But when I permitted it, he claimed books and skill memories, rather than allowing the activation of the emergency protocols.

"I was forced to use a significant amount of my remaining mana to expel him from the core when he stole several of my artifacts, and again, I called for help. Since then, I have been in a state of slow decline, as the last of the mana in the Prax has been drained. I have been surviving on what little ambient mana makes it past the creatures that have taken up residence, for an exceptionally long time."

"Wait, the lich I fought; I think he was a noble, was that…"

"The interloper, yes. He claimed several books on the undead and their capabilities, then stole a lich phylactery that had been stored here for safekeeping and investigation long ago. He tied his soul to it and was reborn, spending the next several dozen years attempting to break into my core again to reach the rest of my artifacts."

"Okay, what—" I was cut off by a creaking groan that tore along the length of the room, and the floor shifted suddenly, making me realize just how precarious the Prax's current structure really was.

"Jax!" Yen called frantically.

I grunted, waving my acknowledgement. "Fine; we don't have time for this. You accept me as Scion of the Empire; therefore, I order you to open the Vault and allow me access to the core. I will save whatever we can, and we will return when we have enough forces to retake the Prax from the SporeMothers and attempt repairs. For now, you're coming with me," I said firmly.

"I cannot—" she started to protest, and I cut her off.

"That's an *order*, wisp."

"But…"

"Open the damn Vault!" I snapped.

She stiffened, scowling at me, but waved a hand. The panel to her right shifted, sliding back and into the wall, opening a narrow path into the small building.

I stepped past her and eased inside, finding a single room with shelves that ringed the walls. There were more empty slots than full, but it still held another dozen books, four glowing memory stones, and three swords, two of which were short and wide-bladed, while the third was enormous. There was also a pair of vambraces and a helm that had a subtle silvery glow, and I resolved to examine them later. I grabbed them all, only to find that I didn't have enough room. Frantically, I dumped some of the sections of the vehicles I'd grabbed and a handful of shitty weapons, before trying again. Fortunately, this time I had plenty of room, having gained a lot by discarding the shit I'd piled up, but when I turned to the glowing core, I growled in mounting anger.

The core stood atop a tall narrow plinth, made up of rings that spiraled upwards, with manastones set in them, glimmering faintly. They looked to be almost exhausted, a faint glow remaining in around half, with the rest lying cracked and dull, and I swore as I realized that I might have doomed us all.

I quickly pulled up the quest and read through it while I started pulling the stones that had any charge free and dumping them into my bag.

Congratulations!

You have made progress in your Quest: Fix the Fixers
You have discovered the chilling secrets of the Prax, Glorious Retribution, discovered a working, if unpowered, portal, killed the Master and his unwilling servants, and looted the Vault.

Due to the level of difficulty involved, and the bravery shown by your acceptance of the realities of your situation, the Goddess Jenae has increased your rewards and has altered the Success Conditions of the Quest.

Recruit the Gnomish Survivors: 21/27

Recover Sufficient Manastones to Power the Ship Interesting Endeavors: 43/40

Eliminate Bartholomew the Lich: 1/1

Find and prepare the ship Interesting Endeavors then use it to escape: 0/1

Bonus Condition: For each SporeMother killed, receive an additional 10,000xp

Reward: Improved technological capacity in the Great Tower, Possible technological boosts to the fleet, survival , gnomish exploration vessel Interesting Endeavors, 500,000xp

I grimaced as I dismissed the screen, seeing that I had literally just enough to get the ship up and in flight, and wishing I'd brought some of the hundreds we'd looted from the Stockpile to help power the damn thing.

When just the Core remained, I paused, turning to look at the wisp, who had been yammering onto me about protocols and requirements the entire time.

"Can you seal this up again and keep your core safe?" I asked her, and she glared at me.

"I've just been explaining why—"

"Yes or no, wisp!" I snapped.

"No!" she replied sharply, and I nodded to her before pulling the core free of the stand. It was a single gem, larger than my fist, which glowed with an inner light, and as I pulled it free, I felt…something…change.

The Prax shuddered faintly, and the room around me seemed to become…lifeless. The walls stopped glowing, the lines of silvery mana that had continued spreading across the floor suddenly ceased in their movement, and the magelights began to lose what little light they held. Instead, the entire room started to dim as the power began to leech away, fading into the ether.

"Noooo, my Prax!" the wisp wailed, and I shoved the core into my bag of spatial folding, making her scream as the mana composing her dissipated.

I staggered to a halt, sensing her flowing past me and sinking into the bag, and I let out a relieved sigh, even as something else cracked, and the roar of water climbing grew louder.

I'd not killed her with my thoughtless action, I hoped, but with the lights dimming and the room becoming dead, the rising black sea, and the collapse of some of the Prax, I couldn't take the time to find out.

I shoved my naginata into the bag of holding and ran the last dozen feet, leaping onto the gnomish contraption. Even the prisoners were hanging on for dear life further down the train.

"What…" I started to say, when Yen screamed at Frederikk.

"Go!" she yelled. He grinned gleefully, hunching down and burying his hands in a pit of levers and switches. "Go as fast as you can!" she screamed, in clear disregard of her earlier advice to me. "Get us to your ship!"

The vehicle shuddered, then leaped forward like a greyhound after a rabbit. It was a single creation now, rather than a series of smaller ones, and was more rounded than before, with the additional wheels and legs from the older creations sticking out at odd angles.

As he gunned it forward, I grabbed desperately onto a rough patch, my fingers scrabbling as I started to slide from my perch. Then a calloused hand gripped me by the back of my armor, shoving me forward, and my fingers caught the lip of a section of machinery. The small handhold allowed me to pull myself in and hunch down as flat as I could while the wind began to whistle past me.

I glanced to the side and saw Grizz behind me. The legionnaire nodded and forced a smile, then closed his eyes and hunched down further, going pale.

I squinted past him, finding Arrin, who was seated next to the still form of Lydia. She and Bane were strapped down, with gnomes hanging onto the machine and holding them down at the same time. But Arrin was grinning ear to ear as the walls flashed past in the darkness.

I nodded to him, flashing a sudden grin and feeling some of my annoyance and anger with him slipping away as we shared a mutual love of insane speeds.

I turned back to stare at the rapidly approaching far wall, swaying as we slalomed between the narrow corridor walls and built up even more speed, hurtling toward the far end.

The doorway that led out of the room was small, and for a brief second, I worried that it was too small, but we didn't slow down. If anything, we picked up more speed, as one of the gnomes further down the line started to sing.

It started as a low-voice chanting, then it built as more and more joined in, intoning a weird, deep chorus. The song built as we shot into the tunnel, the extra wheels and limbs sticking out suddenly making perfect sense as we merely bounced off a wall and kept going.

We took a left, then a right, crossing corridors blurring past almost too fast to see. The contraption slammed into a pile of collapsed bones at the next intersection, sending them flying, and the rounded, thick steel prow of the device made sudden great sense as well.

The minutes flew by as we hurtled upwards, the front of the vehicle slamming into a ramp that led higher and sent out a huge shower of sparks as we careened off the side of the wall, before it smashed into a creature that had terminally bad luck. All I saw was a blur of red and green, flying chitin and insectile legs that tumbled past, and we were away.

We looped around, following the rising ramp, then came to an area where the sunlight filtering down from above showed that a barricade had been built on one end of a bridge that rose to join two slumping buildings.

I looked up and all around, desperately hoping to figure out where Frederikk was going to go instead. My heart seized as he hunched down closer and started singing even louder.

"Oh, fuck no, you crazy bastard!" I ground out, squeezing myself down even closer to the frame.

The barricade grew larger and more solid-looking as we closed the distance, Yen screaming at the gnome. But with the rising singing and chanting, he'd never hear us. Instead, I resigned myself to the upcoming crash, having realized that even if he wanted to stop, at this point, it would be too late.

The seconds suddenly seemed to drag out into minutes, even as they hurried by at an insane pace…then we hit it, and the world exploded around us.

CHAPTER TWENTY-NINE

The barrier shattered into a thousand pieces; the section where we'd hit it was thin and clearly designed for a fast breakthrough, while the majority was solid. But I'd had the wonderful luck to be too close to a spar that stuck out, and it'd slammed into the side of the device just ahead of me, wiping me and the gnomes behind me off like the world's most violent sweeping brush.

I tumbled from the gnomish contraption, both arms flailing wildly. I had a split second to be glad I'd stashed my naginata in the bag before I slammed into the dangling roots of a tree and felt bones breaking.

I bounced off, smashing into a wall, then skidded across the floor to come to rest against the side of something huge that vanished above me.

I blinked, coughed out some blood, and took stock of my injuries as I tried to make sense of what had just happened.

I heard an excited sound in the distance, and a screech of metal grinding on metal as the device slammed into something and disintegrated. Cursing and shouts arose, and…laughter and cheering from the gnomes, along with a lot of growls and curses that seemed to be their normal way of acting now.

I forced myself to sit up, wincing at the pain, and blinked to get the room to stop spinning.

"Hey, boss!" a voice called, and a few seconds later, Grizz was there, reaching down and straightening me as I started to slump to one side. "You okay? You look like shit," Grizz said, his usual cheerful manner fading once again as he examined me quickly.

"'M ok'ay," I mumbled, almost incomprehensibly, wincing as I felt bones grating against each other as I spoke. I reached up and gently touched my face, finding that my jaw and right cheekbones were grinding in places they never had before, and my fingertips came away bloody.

I closed my eyes, trying to control myself and get a handle on the pain, when a healing spell slammed into me. I gasped with relief, feeling the bones in my face pop back into place and start binding together again.

My eyes flew open as I hissed in pain, but I abruptly slumped back, being caught by Grizz again as I focused on Arrin, who'd just found us and had clearly been the source of the healing spell.

It took a couple of seconds to run its course, but I took Grizz's hand once it had, and he hauled me to my feet, looking me over with a critical eye as he took in my bedraggled, handicapped appearance.

"Boss, we have got to talk about the way you live your life. Seriously," he quipped. "I mean, I'm gonna get booted out of the legion when I get you back to them; just look at the state of you!"

I glanced down and snorted. Not only was my armor dented, cut, and scratched all to hell, but I was missing my left arm below the elbow. My helmet was crushed to the point of uselessness, and I was covered in dried blood, much of it my own.

My legion bodyguard, on the other hand, looked like he'd had a bad day, and that was it. A few dozen scrapes and scratches and a handful of small dents marred his armor, but in comparison, well.

I looked like I'd lost a fight with a blender the size of a house and had been trapped in it for an hour. He looked like he'd fallen down a few times then got back up.

Bastard.

"Well, let's face it," I mumbled, rubbing at my grubby face. "If you did your job properly…"

I left it hanging and winked at him.

"Are you kidding me? You're like watching over a drunken toddler, off playing with exactly the wrong thing as soon as I turn my back!" he retorted, grinning.

"Ah, bugger off." I snorted as I looked over at Arrin, who'd stepped closer and was watching me with a tentative grin. "Arrin, thank you, mate. That heal was exactly what I needed," I said truthfully. "How's everyone else?"

Yen stepped into sight and visibly relaxed at seeing me upright.

"They're fine, I think?" Grizz said, looking back over his shoulder, lifting a questioning eyebrow at Yen.

"We're all fine!" she called, her elven hearing allowing her to pick up the conversation at a distance none of the rest of us could match. "Aside from some bruises and a single dead gnome, we all made it without any major injuries."

"What happened to the gnome?" I asked curiously, and she simply pointed back to the barricade.

I winced, seeing the still form impaled on the same wooden stanchion that had swept me clear of the vehicle. Clearly, he'd gotten caught between the body and the wood, and boom. His race to escape ended prematurely.

"Fuck," I said, shaking my head in sadness. The gnomes' lives might have been short and brutal, like the majority of them seemed to be at the minute, but that didn't mean I liked seeing one of them like that.

"Yeah, Frederikk is pretty upset. Apparently, the design was supposed to prevent that from happening. He's furious that they failed, more so than at losing a gnome, but I guess that's the influence of the way they've been living coming through."

"He doesn't care that they lost someone?" I asked incredulously.

"Oh, he cares, but it's also a case of him having to kill dozens of them over the years for going feral. He's more or less okay with the deaths, but he's seriously pissed off about the design failure. Oh, and he's annoyed that you 'fell off' as well."

"I 'fell off'?" I gaped. "That crazy fucker rammed a wall!"

"It was designed as an easy point to break through, apparently, but yeah. I'm not happy about the method either, but…" She gestured upwards.

I grumbled and turned, about to ask what she was talking about, when my words died in my throat.

The ship.

It was their ship, and just like the Fenris I had in storage in the battleship, this was a work of art, especially compared to the shoddy, ugly, utilitarian things that the realm had currently.

I admired her in awe, my eyes following the curved hull, the sinuous lines of the stored rigging, and the elegant flow of the deck. From where I stood, I could see truly little of the ship, but damn, it was beautiful.

If I were to compare it to anything, I would have said that the current ships made me think of the boxy car from the Bond movie that went underwater and had the jets, and this…this, in comparison, looked like a dolphin.

Literally. If one was a bad adaptation of design, and the other was an animal that had evolved perfectly for life in its environment, that was the difference.

I moved back quickly, wanting to see more.

The hull was long and sleek, with a flat bottom and stabilizing fins to rest on. The glossy wood curved up gracefully, bellied out, then flowed back in to support a beautifully carved railing that encircled the deck. A raised cabin stood proudly at the back, with forward-sweeping staircases that flowed down to the deck, melding gently into the superstructure.

Two sets of sails were affixed on the sides, but they were folded in now and gave the impression of wings curled up to a bird's body, all integral, as opposed to the 'stuck on anywhere' appearance of the human-designed vessels. Even the engines looked almost organic, the way they flowed up and out.

Add to that, the entire thing was composed of dark oak and copper banding, and even green with age, and covered in dust and debris, with several honest-to-god trees growing up around the ship–and in one case, up from the hold–and vines covering half of it, I immediately fell in love with it.

"Holy shit," I whispered, shaking my head as I looked the ship over.

"Yeah, she's a thing of beauty," Arrin agreed, grinning appreciatively up at the hulking form.

I looked more carefully and soon spotted a series of ladders that rose up the side of the ship. They were recessed, but like everything else, they were carved and designed beautifully.

I eased over to the side of the ship again and reached up, sweeping away debris from the recessed section to clear it for my hand. I tucked my fingers in, feeling a carved handhold. Judging from the depth and the height of the recessed section, it'd be great for feet as well as hands…then swore.

I had one goddamn hand. How the hell was I going to climb with only one frigging hand? Considering the arch of the ships, I'd be climbing outwards as I went, and I would just fall off!

"It's okay, boss," Grizz said reassuringly, clearly understanding the problem. "I've got you." He reached into a bag and pulled out a substantial coil of rope.

"Great. Thanks, Grizz," I muttered, trying not to be rude. My triumphant arrival on the deck of this beautiful work of art was going to be getting hauled up the side like a sack of sodding potatoes.

"Look on the bright side," Yen said quietly.

"There's a bright side?" I groused.

"At least you're conscious. Lydia and Bane are still out, so they're literally getting dragged up there."

"Wonderful." I shook my head and told myself to stop being such a whiny little bitch.

"Seriously, though, thank you, Grizz," I repeated, forcing a smile. "Everyone else is okay, right?" I asked again, and Yen confirmed it.

"They are, although the gnomes are a mix of pissed and pleased; not only did that design fail, which the older and more sane gnomes are upset about, but they know we've got little time, so they can't salvage the remains of their vehicle."

"Fuck!" I hung my head, the scene of beauty and peace before us dissipating in the wake of our urgency. "No, we don't. That damn thing had to have made enough noise to wake the dead!" I snarled, galvanized to action. I turned, looking to Yen first.

"Yen, get everyone aboard, right fucking now. Tell the gnomes to leave anything they have to, save any artifacts that are clearly magical and within easy reach, but tell them if they can't get it aboard in five minutes, leave it," I ordered, getting a decisive nod and a respectful smile as she hurried away.

"Arrin, get your arse up on that ship and start getting it free. Even if you have to burn the goddamn vines off it, I don't care; just don't fuck the ship up."

"What about me, boss?" Grizz asked.

I grinned at him. "You're going to help me get up there, then we're going to make damn sure this ship can actually fly. I'm going to need two hands, I've no doubt. It's not as glamourous as the rest of the jobs, but I need someone I can trust. Sooner or later, the SporeMothers will arrive, and I've got the only weapon that I know those fuckers are going to fear," I stated.

"I'm looking forward to seeing these fuckers. The records say they were a bastard to fight in the old days!" he commented, perking up.

I clapped him on the shoulder. "Good, because we'll need to work together to do it, as I haven't got the time to teach you any more magic, and we'll need everything we can get."

Grizz set off up the side of the ship, following Arrin, who had started up already. In short order, they were both standing on the deck overhead. Grizz wasted no time in tying off the rope then flipping one end down to me with a loop tied in the end of it.

I braced my foot in the loop and held on tight as Grizz wrapped the rope around himself and started walking away from the side.

I could hear the grunting as he pulled, but as I lifted up smoothly, I appreciated the effort he was putting in. I rose quickly into the air, dangling over the side, and looked out across the area we found ourselves in now. The ship had been maneuvered into a small, partially collapsed building at some point in the past. It was obscured from casual view from above. The only way into it, as near as I could tell, was through the barricaded entrance we'd just smashed through.

The overhead sections that allowed sunshine in were small and high up, giving enough light for the plants to grow, but not enough to draw attention to anything hidden there.

The cavern we'd just abandoned, on the other hand, had a few places up high with gaps big enough to fly out of, or at least I hoped so…

The gnomes swarmed over the wreckage, grabbing anything they could, and like a pack of ants, they then swarmed the ship, dumping it all into the main hold.

I looked down, seeing the neat stacks of boxes in the hold being crushed by the dumped equipment, and I paused, thinking about searching the boxes, then resigned myself to the fact that there just wasn't time.

I grabbed a gnome who was frantically dashing past and spoke quickly before releasing him, half-afraid he might bite me, by the feral gleam in his eye.

"Make the loot from the Master's stash the priority, then anything magical, and then and only then, the parts of your machine. Pass that one to the others," I ordered, then dismissed him from my mind and headed to the structure at the back of the ship.

I knew from the ships I'd been aboard so far that they all had a similar design of a "nerve center" in the engineering section. It was a room where a single larger manastone was placed in a specific pedestal, along with the smaller ones being set in the engines to control the ship. I ducked inside, figuring if this was the same sort of design, then I might as well get that one in place first, followed by running from engine to engine and trying to replace the manastones in them individually. At least if the central nerve cluster was powered, then we'd be able to power the ship, even if we only had enough to limp along.

It took Grizz and me tugging on the hatch to open it, thanks to the mound of dirt and debris piled over it. When it eventually came free, it was blatantly obvious that the years in this hidden cavern hadn't been as kind to the ship as I'd first hoped.

Along with tarnishing the copper fittings of the ship an unhealthy green, the wood had warped and swollen from decades of exposure to rain and other water sources. The hatch creaked and ground alarmingly as we pulled it open.

We jumped down and strode into the dimly lit hallway, pausing while my eyes adjusted and Grizz activated his magelight. The first few rooms were clearly designed for housing for the important people aboard, and at the end of the small hallway was a ladder, leading down to the next level. I grunted defiantly before jumping instead.

I bent my knees and took the landing like a champ, straightening nonchalantly as though I did this all the time. Grizz leaped down beside me, landing with one fist pressed to the ground, one knee down, in true superhero style, before straightening up and looking around.

I paused to curse him internally, knowing that if this was a movie, he'd just identified himself as the hero, while I was clearly the sidekick, judging from the total lack of flair and the general gracelessness of my landing.

He set off without noticing my glare, and we searched the nearest rooms, finding scattered moldy clothes, patches where food had rotted away, and beds that had a thick layer of dust coating them.

We moved on, rushing to the end of the corridor halfway to the bow end of the ship. Every room appeared to be a mix of living quarters, a few engineering labs, I guessed, and a small library.

The books were mainly buggered, thanks to water ingress from a swollen joint over one bookshelf. But a few dozen looked intact from my cursory glance.

We jumped down to the next level, and I tried not to think about how awkward climbing back up all of these was going to be.

The lowest level was a collection of a dozen smaller living quarters and access to the hold, a large storage area that reached from the bottom of the hull, just above the bilges, to the deck above. As we stepped out, we saw the devastation caused by the gnomes randomly throwing in gear.

What looked like dozens, if not hundreds, of crates were shattered, and the pungent smell let us know that at least some of the boxes had held foodstuffs that had since rotted away, not to mention the shining, reflected light from a pool of liquid seeping out of some barrels that made my ass clench. I just knew it was oil of some kind, and prayed it wasn't flammable.

Grizz pointed to a ladder to one side, and I led the way back up to the deck. It was awkward, climbing with only one hand, especially since I needed to be quick. I managed by stepping up, pausing, and letting go to grab the next rung up before I could fall off, then repeated the process again and again.

It took me longer than normal to climb, but after a few minutes, I was back on the deck, seeing only the raised wheelhouse remaining to search.

I grumbled to myself as I headed to it, snagging a gnome that sprinted past with her arms full of clothing, and I spoke quickly again before releasing her.

"Find Frederikk and send him to find me," I ordered, figuring if there was one good thing about being a lord, it was that wherever I was, was the place to be, so it was Frederikk's problem to figure out where I was, not for me to wait around for him.

We entered the wheelhouse, finding, again, that the gnomes were ingeniously different from more modern human and dwarven designs.

The long, wide room was well-appointed, with charts hanging neatly on one wall. Several artfully crafted desks and chairs were scattered around the room and against the wall opposite to the maps, with a comfortable central chair surrounded by the ship's controls, and a large bed bolted against the back wall. There was also a door at the back of the room, which appeared more imposing and solid than the others so far.

I pushed that door open as well, thankful that it, at least, wasn't stuck or warped too badly, and finally found what I was looking for.

This next room was small but cozy, with a simple single bed against one wall, a wardrobe against the other, and a small porthole that would give light normally.

Underneath the porthole, though, was a triple row of recesses, and they held the manastones I'd been expecting.

Most were dull and fractured, but here and there were ones that still glimmered with power, making me think their systems had been deactivated or disabled long ago so they'd not drain the stones, despite the long years of silence.

I started pulling new stones out of my bag, while Grizz removed the dead ones, moving from left to right. We began slotting them in as fast as we could, and with each stone that slid in, the airshifted almost imperceptibly. The larger, more powerful stones brought an almost electric feeling of ozone to the air, as smaller ones made the fingers tingle occasionally.

It took less than a minute, but once they were all in place, we stood hesitantly, waiting for something else to happen, even as a low tingle built steadily.

We looked at each other awkwardly, then heard the outside door being shouldered open, and I remembered Grizz closing it, for some reason.

We stepped out and found Frederikk standing next to the controls, looking forlorn. He reached out slowly, hesitantly, and stroked the smooth, once well-oiled wood of the console, before sighing and letting his hand drop.

"You called for me?" he asked quietly, his voice filled with the weight of his years and the terrible sights he'd seen, somehow reinforced by being in the bridge of his old ship once again.

"Yeah, I haven't a clue what the hell to do here," I admitted, gesturing back at the stones in the wall and around the cabin. "This is totally different from the airships I've flown on before, and I have no idea where to start. Were you a pilot, or…" I asked him, and he snorted a laugh out.

"Me? Pilot the *Interesting Endeavor*? Never in a million years would they let the likes of me fly her. I was an engineer, a worker, not one of the fancy ones, not one who was let loose on something like this."

"Well, now's your chance," I said, smiling, but the smile slipped from my face as he shook his head.

"No. I was never good enough to fly her, and I'll not start now. I'll not bring shame on my house," Frederikk insisted.

I resisted the urge to pick him up and shake him violently by the throat. "What's the problem here?" I asked in as calm a voice as I could manage. "You wanted to fly her; now you get your chance, so…"

"I was named an engineer, lordling!" he snapped back at me. "I was judged good enough to maintain and to adjust the systems; never to create, never to control!"

"You made a fucking train that you just rammed through a goddamn wall and nearly killed me! You were controlling *that*!" I spat.

"I made a child's plaything compared to this ship! I was honored when I was given my place aboard, and my first act on her after all these years won't be to refuse my captain and the Master of Flight's direction! You're not a gnome; you don't understand!"

"Then make me understand!" I roared at him, gesturing behind me. "We replaced the crystals, now it's just the fucking controls. You said you were on the ship before and you could fix her! You have to know how to fly it to be able to fix it!"

"You touched the crystals!" he screeched in horror, sprinting forward, making both Grizz and me tense. We reached instinctively for weapons, but he barreled straight past us into the smaller room, gasping in horror and starting to pull crystals free of the slots frantically.

In a matter of seconds, the floor was covered in them, and all of the slots were empty again. Frederikk was glowering at us like a couple of truant schoolboys.

"Do you know what you almost did?" he snarled, all deference gone. "You almost killed us all! You had the emergency channels funneling mana into the engines, but the main channels set to refuse! You'd have created a feedback loop! Not to mention the lift! One set of engines would have fired backwards! You'd have flipped us over!" He jabbed his fingers at slots that looked identical to us, for all the world.

"What the—" Grizz started, when the little gnome went on again.

"You'd have killed us all, and worse! You'll have sent a pulse of mana through the signaling array! Those creatures will know where we are now!"

"What?" I asked, shocked. "How?"

"The signaling array!" Frederikk repeated angrily. "It sends out mana pulses so that gnome ships know if one of our own is in distress! It was never needed before, and when we left the ship, we had no idea how bad things were. But now?"

He shook his head in a mix of fury and horror. "You said those creatures are attracted to mana!"

"So?" I asked.

"So? *SO?*" he wailed. "So you just sent a pulse of mana up from this location! You just screamed 'hey, we're here, come and get us' right when the ship can't fly!"

"It can't fly because you ripped all the crystals out!" Grizz retorted.

"You were going to kill us all!" the diminutive creature screeched at Grizz, then grabbed handfuls of his moustache and pulled, yanking hard as he tried to control himself. Frederikk panted and hissed for several seconds, while Grizz and I looked at each other in alarm before I finally spoke to the little gnome firmly.

"Fine, make it right, Frederikk. Fix it, get us up in the air, and get us the fuck out of here!" I tugged the last few manastones out of the bag, dumping them into the mess on the floor.

"Fix it…FIX IT?!" he cried, tugging handfuls of hair free as he glowered at us, foaming spittle flecking his mouth.

"Because while you're in here, safe, playing with those stones, we'll be out there, fighting anything that comes down," I went on. "Unless you'd rather swap places?"

Frederikk froze for a few seconds, his mouth open, then seemed to deflate slightly, letting go of his moustache and glancing toward the scum-covered porthole apprehensively.

"You go," he eventually muttered. "I'll…I'll fix this…but I can't fly it. Not won't. *Can't.*"

"I can sort that out," I said, jerking my head towards the door. "Come on, then, Grizz, let's go fuck some shit up."

"Sounds fun," Grizz said, walking out of the room, and I followed behind him. We skirted around the chair and control console, inspecting the wall ahead and wondering how the hell the ship was controlled from in here, when the deck was out there.

We'd find out soon enough.

Grizz and I emerged onto the deck and gazed around, seeing that the majority of the gnomes were still rushing about. Yen had organized a sling to get Lydia and Bane onto the ship's deck and was giving orders about moving them below.

I looked out across the cavern, grateful that the barricade was still halfway concealing the ship, but I realized we were also trapped in here before spotting a complex collection of pulleys and cables up high.

I pointed to them, and Grizz followed my finger and grunted.

"Looks like they weren't always as crazy as they are now then." Grizz said, indicating a pair of hinges on one wall that he'd spotted. "I'll bet a cold beer that the barricade either opens out or folds back out of the way. They'd have wanted a quick way out."

"Yeah, but after all this time?" I asked. "Look at the trees."

I pointed to a pair of trees that had rooted into a pile of collapsed rubble and were now growing tall and strong close to the hinges.

"They won't let the damn thing fold back, and there was too much in front of the barricade for them to open outwards." I paused, rubbing my chin in thought. "Hey, you!" I called, and Giint turned from where he'd been playing with something. He frantically stuffed it back into his bag and half grinned, half glared at me.

"Giiiiint?" he asked.

"Yeah, Giint," I echoed, smiling, knowing I'd found the perfect gnome for the job. "I've got something you can help me with…can Giint make something explode?"

His jaw dropped open, before he remembered himself and nodded frantically.

"Giiint caaan make thiiiings go BAAANG!" he agreed hastily, wiping his clearly sweating palms on his pants and managing to smear the filth in new and even more convoluted patterns.

"Okay, buddy, c'mere," I said, leading him to the side of the ship. "You see the barricade?" He nodded definitively. "I want you to make it fall outwards, you understand? I want it to go *that* way!" I gestured enthusiastically, and he frowned for a few seconds.

"Giiiint neeeed morrrre," he said sadly, pulling a part of one of the destroyed badunkas out of his pouch. I hastily took a step back, seeing how worryingly it was flashing, and the way cold blue smoke was pouring out of it.

"You see all those parts?" I asked, gesturing to the pile of bits that the gnomes were trying to salvage below. "Is that enough?"

He squinted, then moved quickly, his habit of bolting from utter stillness to high speed, then slamming to a halt and looking at things intensely, seeming reminiscent of a spider's freaky movement and making me even more uncomfortable around the little bastard.

"Giiiiiint have thisss, too?" he asked hopefully, pointing at the bits the gnomes had already salvaged. He grinned at me in what he clearly thought was a winning way, but as wide and crazed as it was, it just made me want to taser him on general principle.

I glanced down at the gear in the hold and shrugged. Some of it was also glowing alarmingly, and the less of it I had around me, the better.

"Sure. Get the gnomes below to help you as well. Work very, *very* fast," I said brightly, and Grizz piped up before Giint could run off.

"But carefully!" he interjected. "It needs to go off when we say, not before!"

"Giiiint underrrrstand!" Giint nodded his head frantically, then tore off screaming at the top of his lungs at the gnomes below.

A few seconds of silence reigned as they listened to his practically incomprehensible screeching, followed by a chorus of cheering, and they all started swarming the ship, unloading again.

"What did you just do?" Yen asked me anxiously, hurrying over to stand by my side, where we watched the gnomes with a sense of fascinated horror.

"I asked them to make the barricade explode," I said finally, wincing as Yen gaped at me in utter horror and betrayal.

"Jax, you…they…no…please, by all the gods, no." She shuddered, clenching her eyes shut. Then she immediately turned and started shouting orders to the rest of the group.

Everyone started moving, dragging Lydia and Bane below decks, and gathering everything they could to cover the few windows.

"Gnomes like three things, Jax," Yen said through gritted teeth, when I grabbed her arm and demanded an explanation. "They like speed, drugs, and things that explode. They have it reinforced over and over from an incredibly early age that, to make anything explode, *anything* at all, they have to have permission.

"Like the way we teach kids that shitting in their pants is wrong, gnomes start teaching their kids explosions are naughty at *that* level. They are fascinated by fire and combustibles and would burn the world if it didn't mean they couldn't play with it later. They have no sense of self-preservation, so when someone in a position of authority tells them to blow something up?!" She pinched the bridge of her nose, exasperated. "Honestly, Jax, I hope I'm wrong, I really, *really* do, but we need to get this ship ready to go, and fast!"

"That's what I'm trying to tell you," I said, nodding towards the wheelhouse. "Frederikk is in there trying to get the ship ready to take off; he's given a few of the other, more sensible gnomes jobs to do, but the SporeMothers probably know where we are, so we need to be able to open the barricade up as soon as we're ready and fucking escape. Get everyone ready in there, make Jian take the pilot's console, then get your ass out here and get ready."

Yen paused, then nodded firmly, clearly deciding that it made sense. All of a sudden, I had a thought and shouted to send Jian to come here first, and I reached into my bag, pulling the core free.

"What do you think you're doing!" the wisp hissed at me, glaring as I held the core in my hand and she reformed.

"I think I'm trying to get my people to safety, and I'm making sure you, and by extension, the Prax, can't be taken by the enemy!" I snapped, meeting her anger with my own as she swelled to a foot tall, hovering in the air over my palm, hands on her hips.

"I have survived hundreds of years in perfect safety—" she started, and I cut her off.

"Until you stupidly let a lunatic into the Vault, and he almost took command, after which, he managed to use one of the artifacts *you're supposed to guard* to change himself into a fucking lich!" I snarled at her, before calming myself and huffing out a long breath.

"You know who I am, and what I am," I said slowly, fighting to keep an even tone. "Your attitude isn't helping, so let's make this simple. You are required to aid me, to serve me, as part and property of the empire, correct?" I asked her, hating that I was having to go down this route, but not having time to do anything else.

"That is correct," she confirmed flatly. I was struck by the attitude difference from Oracle to Seneschal and Hephaestus to her.

"Good. We'll sort this shit out later, you and I, but for now? You are to help Jian, here"—I lifted her to see him as he approached—"to fly this ship and get us out of here. I know it's smaller than your Prax, but you controlled that, at least in part, so you should be able to do *something* here.

"You are to give him, and me, the most aid you can. You are to help to carry out my plans and schemes, and you are to do all of this to the letter and spirit of these orders. Do you understand?" I asked, staring her down and hating that I'd had to enforce my position of authority to get her to comply. It felt like I was using slavery—honestly, in my eyes, I was—but right now, I didn't have a choice.

The excuse of tyrants and assholes through the ages, my mind informed me.

I squashed that little voice down and ignored the sense of confusion and approval emanating from Amon. God, it was getting crowded in my head these days, I reflected, as I handed the core over to Jian.

"Jian, I know you have little more experience than anyone else here. I know you don't know what you're doing, and I know that you accidentally started a war with a god last time you flew a ship." He flinched at that last one, and I grinned amiably at him and nodded towards the core.

"But despite all of that, I still trust you, and I believe in you. This wisp will help you; she can advise you and possibly even help steer the ship? Hell if I know, but she will help, and you *can* do this."

I broke off as a new sound started up in the distance. I turned my gaze upward, seeing the light filtering down momentarily cut off as something, and then several more somethings, passed overhead. Seconds later, the engines of an airship fired, and the tell-tale *hummm* of engines vibrated the air as ships lowered into the cavern beyond the barricade.

We might be out of sight for now, but that wouldn't be the case for long.

"Jian," I said, turning from him and looking towards the hole in the barricade. "Go, now. Do whatever you have to, but get us up and out of here," I ordered as I started walking forward. The final battle for the fallen Prax, Glorious Retribution, was about to begin.

CHAPTER THIRTY

I strode to the side of the ship, gazing down towards the barrier, then scanning around, working the place out in my mind.

The ship was around sixty meters in length and maybe ten across at the widest point, coming in at twenty meters high, with the small decks above the wheelhouse and bridge, another five meters above that. The shattered half of the building which the ship had been hidden in was taller and wider, but not by much, and the heavily overgrown final level that rose above it had hidden most of the ship entirely from outside sight.

The cavern we were frantically organizing in was mostly hidden by the surrounding walls and overhanging ceiling of the floor above; whatever this section of the Prax had looked like originally, there had been dozens of huge buildings.

Between the buildings that had collapsed, the sagging ceiling, and the centuries of storm damage and garden-level overgrowth, it now resembled a dark scar in the land from above, with trees and overhanging buildings sheltering it.

Inside the sheltering structures and plants was a deep cavern, with sections that dove back under the overhangs. I doubted the sun ever reached many of the corners. Instead, there was a constant low-level internecine war going on between the forces of foliage and the ever-present fungus.

The occasional holes and shattered remnants that let light in from directly above the ship and across the rest of the area created a dappled light source, one that would have almost been soothing, especially with the tropical breeze and pleasant temperature, if not for the very visual reminders that we were essentially squatting atop a corpse of the old empire. A corpse that we had stirred to a semblance of life, and as that life fled again, more of the structure collapsed.

As a crash and boom in the distance echoed around the cavern, and the screech of escaping seabirds rose, I wondered honestly if there would be anything left to recover later. Then I grimaced, seeing something slide through the sky high overhead, blocking off the bright sunlight before shifting to patrol, clearly examining the area.

I contemplated the thick trees, vines, and general foliage, and I was gloomily certain that we could have hidden for hours at least before the SporeMothers would have found us, if not far longer.

If I'd not sent up a damn dinner bell for them, anyway.

The barricade which the gnomes had built to conceal and protect the ship long ago was now, in part, holding the building up, and the greater area beyond it, where the ships were slowly lowering into, judging from the sound, was a far bigger chamber than the one we were in now.

That cavern had been formed by dozens of larger buildings collapsing. Some were now rubble strewn across the floor, while others had fallen into each other, creating lean-tos and more or less solid structures, especially now that vines and trees had secured them together.

The growth of hundreds of years had spread over them, and the slow sagging of the final upper floor into this one had created an area that was almost inaccessible by land above, yet open in parts to the sky, making it a perfect place to dock and hide an airship.

I looked over to the rest of my small team, regretting bitterly the loss of Lydia and Bane. They were, between them, my rock. I literally relied on them and Oracle to keep me sane and safe.

I shook my head and exhaled, forcing the gloom and jitters away. This time, I'd be keeping them safe.

Grizz stepped over to me and pulled something out of his bag, making me grimace uncomfortably.

It was my arm from earlier, or at least, what was left of it. The armor was fine, beyond the gash that had cut through the top layer like butter. But the flesh inside of it had decayed into a black, pungent mush that was dripping out of the gauntlet and stinking up the deck.

"Dude, why?" I asked him, frowning into his eyes questioningly.

"Old legion trick for when you need to look like you're stronger than you are," he said simply, unhinging the gauntlet and separating it from the vambrace, making a face at the rotting mush that fell out along with the blackened bones.

"Errr, didn't think about this before," I said, looking down. "But…could you pass me the rings?" Grizz snorted and plucked them out, dumping them to one side, where I summoned a fountain of water to clean them off. He quickly sluiced out the armor for me, then reassembled it so it looked complete and intact, pulling up small hooks that I'd never noticed before and locking them into place. Then he stepped in and latched it all back together, attaching it to the dangling section of my elbow joint.

"What…" I stammered, but he just grinned and kept working. Finally, I realized what he was doing as he attached his own secondary shield to me. It was smaller than my normal tower shield, whose twin Lydia generally carried, but it was locked in place and reasonably light enough that I could maneuver it around with only half an arm.

It wasn't perfect, but it was a damn sight better than not having any shield at all.

"Thank you, man," I said to him, genuinely grateful at the thought.

Grizz shrugged as though embarrassed. "It's an old trick; means that the injured and disabled can be put on horses and make us still look like we're at full strength," he said quietly.

"It also means that, when a legionnaire is in a bad way, such as a particularly bad night on the sauce, he can lock the armor and keep upright while he sleeps," Tang added in a stage whisper from the other side. I laughed, having a mental image of them doing exactly that when standing at attention on parade or something.

"I should have known," Yen said, shaking her head as she watched the hole in the barricade, shock in Tang's voice as he asked if she'd really never done it.

There was silence for several seconds before she shrugged and admitted that *maybe* she'd done it…once.

We grinned at each other, and I noted that the majority of the gnomes were flooding back to the ship now. I took the time to direct them to strip the remaining debris off, including the dead vines and trees, as Arrin approached us slowly.

He looked exhausted, but he'd managed to burn his way through the vast majority of the entrapping plants in the time that we'd done the rest of the jobs. As Stephanos and Miren joined us, getting their bows ready, and Tang checked his, we all met each other's gaze, getting grim smiles all around.

SporeMothers were known to be horrific enemies, and we were all aware this fight could be a terrible one, so I took the time to speak up. The gnomes were clearing as fast as they could, while shooting fearful glances at the barricade and hopeful ones at the deck hatches leading below. There was obviously little help coming from that quarter, and it was down to us now.

I passed out the last of the healing potions and mana and stood, waiting until Arrin came to us and sat down heavily on an old box.

"I'll…be…okay," he panted, his pale face and red-rimmed eyes showing the drain from working through his stamina and mana so fast.

"Rest, mate," I said firmly. "Drink your potions, catch your breath, and recover. You can join in when they start to break through."

"You think they'll break through?" Tang asked me, and I nodded soberly.

"They're sneaky bastards, but it depends on what's controlling them. If Arrin never needs to do anything in this fight, I'll be over the fucking moon," I said truthfully, peering over the side to where the last of the gnomes were backing away from the pile of fiercely glowing things scattered around the bottom and sides of the barricade.

The last of them, Giint, predictably, broke away and ran full speed for the side of the ship. Even as he scampered, shadows fell across the hole and the sunlight seemed to dim, a weak haze growing over the far side of the cavern.

A slow darkening of the area was followed by a greater shadow, as a battered old hull slowly descended, blocking out the light for several seconds. It was turned away from us, not able to see the barricade properly as it entered the cavern, and it slowly moved away, circling, and searching.

As it passed, shadows fell across it from above, dappling what little light filtered down now.

Seconds passed as we watched in silence, while Giint gibbered and grunted, hauling himself rapidly up the side of the ship, clearly terrified.

When the little gnome reached the top of the ladder, Grizz reached down and bodily hauled him up over the edge and dumped him onto the deck.

"What did you see, Giint?" I asked him, and he searched around frantically, spotting the rest of his people hiding below decks or in the wheelhouse, watching fearfully out of portholes. He shook his head frantically.

"Not seeeee! Feeeel! Feeeels dark, nastyyyy evilllls!" he gibbered out, then he nodded towards the pulsing, glowing explosives he'd rigged. "Goooo bang nowww?" he asked hopefully.

"No, not yet," I said, shaking my head. "We need the ship ready to go, and you're not to fuck with it, understand? Unless Frederikk says you can, no playing with anything on this goddamn ship!" I said quickly, pointing at him until I was sure he understood.

"Giiiiint be gooood," he muttered, then started to slink away, clearly wanting to be off the deck and out of sight when the evil arrived.

"Giint," I called. He froze, glancing back at me with his head cocked to one side. "Will the explosion push the barricade out and away from the ship?" I asked slowly, wanting to be very sure of that.

"Baaaang be biiig!" He grinned widely, turned, and ran for the deck hatch. The cover opened just before he reached it, and he jumped, pulling his legs up and basically cannonballing out of sight into the lower deck.

I sighed as I grimaced at the others, and we exchanged looks that were a mix of amused, annoyed, and nervous as we continued to wait.

More ships cut off the light, passing both overhead and outside in the greater portion of the cavern, but none had spotted us yet, and we were grateful for every second we could get.

Stephanos and Miren had taken up position on the raised wheelhouse's upper deck, setting out arrows and making their area generally ready for the fight, with their summoned creatures standing alongside them. They'd both offered to have them stand with us, but I preferred to have the squishy archers protected, as Jian, who I'd normally delegate to that, was busy.

Grizz stood on my left with Yen flanking my right. Arrin still sat catching his breath behind us, and Tang skulked nearby, waiting.

"Did you find anything good in the Vault, then, boss?" Grizz asked as we waited, and I cursed myself for a fool, pulling up the inventory and examining the fresh loot.

There were only two spellbooks, unfortunately. One was instantly useful, to my evil mind—Control Water—while the other was far more important. I passed Control Water to Arrin and told him to use it when he got the chance, then I opened the second book.

I read it quickly, my eyes flying across the pages as I frantically tried to take it all on, cursing myself distractedly for the time I'd lost in not reading this earlier.

Greater Examination:

This spell enables a far deeper examination of a target, at a significantly higher cost than that of the standard Examine. No creature, item, or target will be able to hide its true nature from this spell.

Note: Higher-tier targets can obscure certain details. Increase your familiarity with this spell to lower the chance of this.

Cost: 50-150 mana, depending on targeted creature and information selected.

I gritted my teeth as the book began to shine, the words lifting from the pages and becoming glowing light that bored into my eyes. I felt the shifting, painful pressure as spell data, concepts of theory, and details I'd never known took up space in my brain, and I shook myself, trying to adjust to the new knowledge.

It was like biting into something, expecting it to be soft, and finding a damn nugget of bone, as I saw myself using my Identify and then Examine spells in the past.

This new information I'd gained made it clear that I'd been basically tossing the examinations off, seeing less than a third of what was there and being satisfied with it.

I blinked away afterimages of gestures, arcane symbols, and more, seeing stars and moons before my eyes as I tried to focus.

"Jax," Yen said warningly, and I blinked again, rubbing my eyes.

"Goddammit," I growled, frowning as I kept seeing things from the book overlaying my actual vision.

"Come on, boss, snap out of it!" Grizz said, and I closed my eyes, breathing deep, then rubbed my eyes with the heel of my hand before opening them and squinting, finally observing what they'd seen already.

A ship hovered just beyond the shattered section of the barricade, and a hulking form squatted on its deck, staring at us greedily from under tarpaulins and a heavy Haze spell that darkened the air and blocked away its hated enemy, the sun.

"Boss!" Grizz shouted, and I triggered Greater Examination, grinning as I saw so much more than ever before.

Your spells Examine and Greater Examination have linked, providing a greater depth of knowledge to be gained.

Adolescent SporeMother

Any SporeMother is to be feared by sentient life, but this creature is at the cusp of adolescence, its accelerated growth fueled artificially by sacrificing sentient creatures in the dozens to it. This SporeMother is controlled by the use of both a Greater Domination spell and a slave collar, and still is only nominally under the control of its master, kept that way by a combination of pain and pleasure.

This SporeMother has reached a high enough level to begin creating the species' greatest tool, DarkSpore.

Beware! Current DarkSpore capacity in use: 471/1000

Weaknesses: Fire, Light, and Life magics are all doubly effective against creatures of darkness.

Resistances: Earth, Darkness, or Death magics used against this creature suffer a 75% damage penalty.

Critical Weaknesses: Sunlight

Level: 23

Health: 2785/2785

Stamina: 294/320

Mana: 196/800

"Well, fuck me lovingly with a jackhammer," I muttered, my eyes open wide in horror as I realized, perhaps fully for the first time, just how lucky I'd been in facing the decrepit SporeMother I had in the past.

This thing was far more powerful; hell, it could create and control a thousand DarkSpore. That was enough to swamp us in the damn things without ever having to get close enough to fight, and even if we managed to survive, we'd be exhausted!

I checked my mana and saw that it'd taken the full hundred and fifty to find out that much information, and I swore before telling the others what I'd seen.

I almost started casting Cleansing Fire immediately, but I didn't dare. I needed the damn things in close before I used that.

The ship moved backward, exposing more of itself as she watched us. I thought quickly, remembering the fight in the tower. It'd been too afraid of the sun, and here, that was our greatest weapon, I realized.

"Okay, guys," I said bluntly, glaring at the mobile darkness on the deck of the ship opposite. "Those fuckers hate the sun, and I mean *hate*. It'll kill them quick, so our best chance of winning this is to expose that thing to the sun, somehow. Failing that, it's fire and light magic, and good old-fashioned slaughter. If any of you get hit by DarkSpore, tell me.

"Don't try to fight it alone; they're parasitic little clouds that will sink into your skin and eat you from the inside out, controlling you. I'll use a spell to surround myself with fire; if you get injured, step into the flames. I think it shouldn't burn you, but I don't know for sure.

"The flames *will* kill the DarkSpore, though, and then I, or Arrin, will heal you. That's the best advice I can give you for now. Once the ship's ready, I'll set the explosives off and hopefully most of the barricade will be taken out, then, in the words of the wisest rabbit I know, we 'run away'!" I said, grinning to myself as I thought about that damn waskerly wabbit.

"Rabbit?" Yen said slowly, then she quickly thrust a hand up. "No, don't tell me; I don't need more of your crazy."

I noticed the looks the others were giving me after a second, then I shrugged and they unanimously moved on, clearly having decided ignoring me was the way forward when I talked like that.

"What have we got that could hit her from here?" I asked the group.

"I could hit it from here with a Flamespear, but the damage? Not sure. There's a shimmer in the air when the ship moves, do you see?" Yen asked, and I nodded. "That's a shield, I'll bet; either she's got a pet mage, or whatever is controlling her is protecting her as well."

"Great," I said slowly. "What if we—" I started to suggest, a sudden plan coming to mind as I glanced around.

At first, it was just shadows, or so it seemed, movement in the darkest places. When I looked, I wasn't sure if there was something there, then they slunk out, skittering and buzzing frantically from one patch of darkness to another.

Sporelings, the filthy, immature spawn of the SporeMothers, ran like spiders, hunching down in the shadows, then sprinting on all six legs as fast as they could, crossing the sunlit patches while screaming in terror and pain…and I realized at least some of the DarkSpore the prompt mentioned were clearly inhabiting the little bastards, judging from the reaction of the sporelings.

"Behind us!" I shouted, spinning around. They flowed down the walls of the cavern all around, heading for the ship.

The sporelings were blackened; more than half of them simply fell from the walls, dead or dying from their time in the sun, and with them came others, corpses that tumbled end-over-end to smash into the floor all around the ship.

Even though only one in five were reaching the ground in any kind of condition to go on, there were hundreds of them. When the corpses smashed into the floor, bodies bursting like they'd swallowed grenades, the DarkSpore were revealed.

Clouds of gritty, inky smoke rose into the air, filling our minds with their buzzing and making the gnomes inside the ship wail in fear.

I spun around frantically; there were at least ten, maybe fifteen sporelings dead already, and hundreds of mobile corpses destroyed, but every one of them was releasing a cloud, and DarkSpore was quickly filling the air.

I hunted around, trying to think. Most of the group had literally no way to fight these bastards, and I…I had three magical sodding swords I'd dumped into my bag, and the terrible dagger!

I tugged the dagger out and passed it, carefully, to Tang, warning him what it was and how to use it, hoping against hope that it might help. Hurrying, I pulled out the two swords.

Hunger	Further Description *Yes/No*
Damage:	25-50
Details:	This weapon, along with its twin, Thirst, are vampiric blades, feeding on the life force of their victims and transferring it to the wielder. Hunger draws on the victims health, at a cost of 10 mana per second, for 10 health, while Thirst drains the victim's mana at a cost of 10 mana per second, for 10 points of health. If used in conjunction with its mate, vampiric drain is doubled, but cost is halved.

Rarity:	Magical:	Durability:	Charge:
Legendary	Yes	98/120	500/500

"Holy shit," I muttered, gaping at the blades in awe. "Who's best with shortswords?"

Grizz spoke up quickly. "Probably me? I've reached level twelve in dual wielding; what about you guys?" he said to Yen and Tang, while gazing with blatant hope at the pair of gleaming onyx blades.

"Level seventeen," Yen said, grinning.

"Level twenty-two with short blades, and seventeen with dual-wielding," Tang added casually.

"Oh, come on!" Grizz groaned. "They're not short blades; that's daggers and knives!"

"Still works, as they're under three feet," Tang said smugly. I grinned, taking the dagger back and passing it to Grizz, who frowned down at it sadly as Tang examined the pair of swords.

"So, if I use both, I'll regenerate twice as much as I drain from a victim, but they'll lose it even faster? Oh, hell yes. I can do some damage with these," Tang said happily, spinning the blades into a figure of eight in the air.

"One more to go," I said calmly, pulling out the greatsword.

Justice	Further Description *Yes/No*
Damage:	50-75 +5-25
Details:	Justice was a weapon forged for the Lord Paladin of Sint, God of Light. The sword was stolen before Sint could gift it to his paladin and was eventually recovered by the Prax, Glorious Retribution, as part of the spoils in the aftermath of the Necromancer Wars. It has never been blessed or sanctified, and as such has only a tenth of its full power. This blade strikes with the holy wrath of Sint; let all creatures of darkness beware. Any wielder that has not been sworn to Sint will receive half of the damage they inflict.

Rarity:	**Magical:**	**Durability:**	**Charge:**
Legendary	Yes	119/120	500/500

"Man, I hate my life," Grizz muttered brokenly as I read out the weapon's details, before putting it away regretfully.

"You're a scout sniper!" Yen chided, rolling her eyes at him. "Why the hell do you never use the damn bow?"

"I took the wrong class," Grizz admitted after a few seconds as we moved back to waiting for the first of the DarkSpore to make their appearance. "I missed the one I wanted, 'cos I was on punishment detail. So I just took the first one that came along after that; didn't want to wait another year for the trainer to come around again."

"What's this?" I asked halfheartedly, watching my sector, well aware that everyone was talking to try to ignore their nerves.

"Class trainers," Yen said quietly, her eyes moving quickly. "Both ours and the Fifth Legion, the Legion of Narkolt, have them, so every year, the trainers travel between our enclaves and give training."

"Why the hell does nobody tell me this shit?" I asked in amazement.

"What, that we both work together?" Yen asked, confused. "We're the legion. Fuck the rest of the world; we're still loyal."

"Point," Grizz said, then snapped out quickly. "To the left

I followed his direction and saw it, a clawed hand that reached up and over, clamping down hard on the railing and gouging splinters out of it as it hauled its body up.

The sporeling was in rough shape. The right front leg worked, but the left didn't. Half its eyes were burned away, and the skin was bubbling in the diffused light. It moved forward unsteadily, hissing, and screeching in pain, even as it attacked.

Tang was the closest, and he set himself ready to receive its charge, when two arrows slammed into it a second apart, staggering it back.

He lunged forward, stabbing out with both blades and sinking them in deep. One carved a long furrow across its face before sinking into a cheek and practically destroying its face, while the other dipped into the space between its ribs and clavicle, burrowing in deep.

Tang grunted, then took a deep breath as the blades glowed suddenly. Red and blue lines snaked up them, traveling the length of the swords, up into the hilts and into Tang.

He let out a little gasp of shock, then a groan of relief, like an itch he'd grown used to was finally scratched. He straightened, seeming to grow taller as he slipped out of his habitual half-slouch.

The sporeling shivered and shuddered, reaching up with weak claws to slap ineffectually at the blades, before slumping in death.

Tang yanked the blades free then stepped back to join us, flicking the swords to free them of the majority of the blood.

"Now *that* was gooood." He groaned under his breath, looking around for another enemy as I pointed with my naginata at the corpse behind him.

"The head," I said simply.

He looked back, registering the slowly shivering skull as the DarkSpore regained control of its meat puppet.

He stepped back in, passing one sword to Grizz to hold, and took the other in both hands, slamming it down hard into the skull.

It cut deep, and a screeching filled our ears as the DarkSpore met the magical blade and had its life sucked away.

The DarkSpore collapsed into dust, and Tang shuddered again, swallowing hard and taking the sword back from Grizz hurriedly.

After that, it was seconds before the next appeared, only to meet the dagger wielded by Grizz. I'd worried that it might not work, but when he drove it deep into the skull of the creature, twisted it, and yanked it back in one fluid motion, the sporeling collapsed bonelessly to the floor. This time, the DarkSpore was dead as well.

"Okay, people," I said, my ears pricking at the sounds of climbing. "This is where it gets real. Try to kill the DarkSpore as quickly as possible," I said, before looking up at Stephanos and Miren and their summoned creatures. "Stephanos! Miren!" I shouted. "Get inside; you're not doing any good up there."

I didn't have time to see their reaction to my words, as another two sporelings and a cloud of DarkSpore rose to my right. But as I spun into them, my naginata glowing like the rising sun, the archers clambered down the ladder and ran to the wheelhouse.

I stabbed out, the blade sinking into the almost-insubstantial cloud before me, ripping a scream from it as the parasitic creature was torn apart. I slashed left to right, cutting through three of them, then jumped back, lifting the shield.

A soft impact thudded, like a snowball with less substance, then sooty tendrils reached up and flowed over the shield, sinking toward my arm. I grinned; the armor there was empty, and I dragged the naginata down across the front of the shield, stripping it of the contaminating creature of the night with a scream of joy.

I stabbed out, the bladed tip sinking into an eye socket of the sporeling, killing it. The other one leaped onto me, staggering me back and biting at my face.

Its teeth snapped shut inches from my eyes, spittle flying, and I had a frozen second to glare into its own hate-filled orbs, all of them glowing with a malevolent internal light, before an arrow protruded from one eye socket, and it screamed.

The bolt distracted it long enough for me to yank the naginata up, and I punched it in the face with my closed fist where it gripped the haft, before yanking the weapon downwards. The blade drew across its skull, and as razor-sharp and filled with magic as it was, it carved a deep groove, making the creature flinch away, releasing me and falling to the floor.

I kicked it savagely, my foot slamming into the wound. Then I stabbed out, driving the blade into it and out the far side to slam into the wooden decking below. The crunch of bone and sizzle of dark blood was loud enough to hear even in the midst of battle, as the death scream of the DarkSpore rose to join the others around me.

I spun back, sweeping the naginata through the air and taking a DarkSpore that had been approaching from Grizz's blind side, then spun again, searching for another enemy before sagging in relief. Tang was dispatching the last with a fast swipe of both blades, which freed its head from the body before slamming his right blade into its skull, piercing the deck below the creature with the force of the blow.

I checked on my team, realizing the others were panting, too, with Miren and Stephanos standing near the open door to the wheelhouse, firing their arrows in defiance of what I'd told them. I grinned and lifted my weapon in thanks, acknowledging the arrow that had distracted the sporeling. Yen groaned under the strain of building her spell so long, then Tang let out a shout. Our momentary reprieve was over, as another wave cleared the railings and attacked.

The next few minutes passed in a blur. We stabbed and thrust, moving as fast as we could. Not one of us was uninjured by the time we'd cleared the deck a second time, just in time to see another wave clearing the sides of the ship.

"I can't hold on much longer; it's too big!" Yen screamed.

"That's what she said!" Grizz shouted back, slashing his dagger through a cloud that lunged at his face. It filled the air with a high-pitched buzz, crumbling into ash that floated away on the breeze.

"Why did you have to teach him that?!" Yen screamed at me, her eyes bloodshot and red-rimmed with stress.

"Sorry, not sorry!" I shouted back, lifting my left hand to cast a spell and cursing as my lack of fingers, or a hand came back to haunt me.

Again.

"For fuck's sake!" I shouted, booting a sporeling in the face to drive it back and grunting as Grizz spun past, disemboweling it almost casually, even with his little blade.

"Seriously, can't hold it much longer!" Yen called out through gritted teeth. I swore, seeing her arms shaking violently. The giant Flamespear that she'd created was now pulsing an angry red and white.

Then I felt it, a change in the air, almost like the static when Grizz and I were randomly slamming the manastones into the holders.

"Grizz!" I shouted and held the naginata out. He grinned, pinned the sporeling to the deck with his dagger, and left it there, taking the naginata from me as I started to cast.

"Oh, yeah!" he shouted, spinning around and around, the blade flashing and glowing blue as he channeled his only spell, Iceshield, into it.

Judging from the effect that it had on the DarkSpore as he tore through them, it imbued the weapon with ice, rather than a shield, so that was a relief.

The ship that the SporeMother rode on bobbed closer, and I glowered at it as the ship shuddered and creaked ominously beneath our feet. A loud cracking noise came from somewhere below us as the ship shifted.

"That's not good!" Grizz shouted, and I grunted in agreement before taking a last look at Yen; she'd sunk to one knee and was on the verge of losing control entirely.

I scanned the repurposed mana engines as fast as I could, locating the biggest, and the one that had the most enemies around it, as the one that Giint had been working on.

There were sporelings, undead, and DarkSpore crawling across it and the floor nearby, burying the stunted trees and fungus deposits that littered the ground under a black, creeping tide of death.

"Hold on; just two more seconds!" I shouted to her, then finished my casting of Fireball and hurled it at the biggest and angriest glowing collection of manabombs that the gnomes, primarily Giint, had made.

It tore through the air, taking out a falling DarkSpore on its way and leaving a smoky wisp of soot behind to mark its passage, before slamming into the pulsing engine.

The impact seemed to freeze the world for a long second. The mana engine let out a little puff of blue-white steam, like dry ice when something disturbs it.

Then there was a second wave as the air shimmered around the engine, sucking inward. It lasted less than a second before it reversed direction and slammed outward with explosive power.

The nearest sporeling and undead were vaporized, the DarkSpore simply ceased to exist, and the entire section of the barricade was blown outwards in a blast of splinters that destroyed dozens more.

The explosion set off a chain reaction of further detonations as the rest of the mana engines went off, entirely shredding the wooden sections of the barricade and sending huge chunks of metal and splinters of wood flying in all directions.

Mainly, though, they went outward.

The closest ship, having just landed on the other side of the barricade, was shredded, then crushed, as a slab of thick metal over eight meters long and five wide collapsed atop it, snapping the deck like a twig. Flames burst out of the mana engines on its own sides.

The two ships just beyond that were driven into the ground as well, as if smacked down by the hand of an angry toddler-god.

The fourth ship, the one that the SporeMother squatted atop, was hurtled backward. The shield that protected it and her was riddled with splinters before finally shattering. The helmsman that hunched behind and above her was taken in the chest with a "splinter" that was at least two feet long and six inches across.

He was hurled from his feet in a spray of blood as the SporeMother screeched in fury and pain at the destruction of her forces.

"Now!" I screamed to Yen.

She heaved her arms forward, collapsing limply on the deck. She was left with barely enough strength to squint through the mana-migraine at the bolt of destruction she'd thrown.

It slammed into the side of the enemy ship and hit an engine, making it explode. The ship that was already reeling went crashing into a collapsed building.

The SporeMother was hurled unceremoniously from her hiding place and out into a patch of sunlit ground, the snap of one of her great legs audible even at this distance as she screeched in agony and pain, frantically scrabbling to escape the searing light of the sun.

Our ship, the *Interesting Endeavor*, lurched and shuddered again, then unexpectedly leaped free of its earthen constraints. The creaking and cracking rose in volume as we lifted into the air.

We slammed into the side of the building, careened off, and lurched forward again, before twisting and firing all the engines at once.

Where we'd been frantically holding on for dear life mere seconds before, now we were slammed to the decking and pinned there by the force of the acceleration as we hurtled upwards.

The SporeMother screeched in pain and fury below us, the noise dwindling as we soared higher at insane speeds, headed straight for the roof.

CHAPTER THIRTY-ONE

The pressure of the acceleration keeping us pinned to the deck lessened suddenly, and we veered to the left with a lurch before slowing and tilting alarmingly to the side as we curved around to line up on an opening in the overhead cover.

The ship lurched again as far too much power was rammed to the engines, and we drove forward at top speed. The sides and roof of the cavern seemed only inches away, blurring as we passed them. Then we were out, erupting into brilliant sunlight as we passed through a magical haze that had seemingly been diluting it.

I staggered to my feet and made it to the railing, gazing back at the Sunken City we'd left behind.

We angled up at a thirty-degree climb that made me want to hang on for dear life. But as we soared, I saw the other ships. Four of them were still in the air and in sight, with a pillar of sooty smoke and flame rising from the hole we'd just fled from. A flash came from below that I had to assume was one of their fallen ship's engines exploding.

I grinned down then warily regarded the four remaining ships. Two were larger than us and clearly built for war, with soldiers manning the decks and a huge cannon attached to the superstructure at the front, while the other two were quite different.

One was a merchantman, if I had to guess; a fast one, judging from the collection of engines, though unarmed and unarmored. But the fourth…she was a new design.

The black ship was long and lean with a single cannon facing forward, built into the deck in the middle at the bow with an additional row of four more on either side.

It had a raised deck at the rear, sheltered by a canopy that blocked the sun. Rows of metal plating protected the sides while four engines to a side were superseded by a huge one at the rear, providing both tremendous lift and maneuverability, I guessed.

Of all four ships, only one was facing us as we rocketed out, and thankfully it wasn't the black one. If we'd been really lucky, it would have been the merchantman, but we weren't *that* lucky.

We continued up, thankful that the ships had all been low down, even as shouts and cries rose from behind us.

A hail of arrows and crossbow bolts peppered the decks, but in seconds, we were out of range, and I breathed a sigh of relief before moving to check on the others.

Grizz, of course was fine; a few scratches and scrapes, a bruise or two, and that was it. In typical Grizz fashion, he'd been in the center of the fight and had been injured the least.

Yen had several long cuts from the sporelings that had tried to reach her, but she was shakily sitting up against the railing now with Grizz's help and drinking a pair of potions, one mana and one healing, so I had faith she'd be fine soon.

Tang, on the other hand, was leaning heavily against the railing on the far side of the deck. As I got to him, he slumped down, grunting in pain and lifted his left hand up from where he'd had it pressed to his side. It was covered in dark blood, and more was spreading quickly from the six-inch-long, three-inch-thick splinter that was sticking out of his side.

"Tang!" I slid to a halt next to him, catching his arm and helping him to lie flat on the deck. "I told you to tell me if you got hurt!" I snapped, looking the wound over quickly.

It was deep and long; the thinner metal of the lower side of the cuirass, usually made up for with a chainmail covering, was holding the splinter in place, with broken links of the chainmail digging into the flesh.

I swore, trying to judge the best way to remove the splinter from the wound as he looked up at me and forced a grin.

"That bad, eh?" he asked weakly, and the blood bubbled as he coughed. My suspicions were confirmed by the tearing gasp he let out as he sagged back.

"You've punctured your lung," I explained gently. "This is a shitty time to have to do this, but I can't leave this in you. I'm gonna have to get it out."

I did my best to project an aura of calm, one that I totally ruined by turning my head and bellowing for the others to get their arses over fast.

I'd seen Firebolts and Magic Missiles hurtling around during the fight before, and I just damn well knew that Arrin had been using magic. We'd needed him then, but Tang really, *really* needed him now as well.

"Arrin, get ready to heal him. Grizz, I'm going to need a hand getting this out," I said, inspecting the splinter. It was wedged in tightly and looked to be something like oak. The damn thing was solid in a way that lesser woods like pine just weren't, or he'd have simply taken a damn bruise and a dent in his armor.

"Well, I don't know how you did it, my friend," I said, shaking my head and distracting Tang as Grizz got ahold of the splinter. "I mean, seriously, how the hell do you get through so many fights without so much as a scratch, only to be taken down by a glorified twig?"

"I just—" Tang started to say, when Grizz yanked hard.

Tang screamed and passed out, even as Grizz yanked again and swore, pulling his dagger free. Thankfully, it was a normal, uncursed one, I noted absently. He went to work, forcing the metal back before giving a final tug and pulling the wood free of Tang's side.

Arrin had already hit him twice with healing spells, and as his second one landed, I released my Battlefield Triage onto him as well. My eyes glowed as I searched Tang's body, finding the spell augmented in infinitesimal ways by my new Greater Examination spell and the information crossover.

"Okay," I muttered, focusing the spell, and beginning the arduous task of rebuilding the lung that had been nicked and the kidney that had apparently been detonated in Tang's side. "I've got good news and bad," I went on as Arrin hit him with a third general healing, feeling the spell take some of the load off me.

"Good news is, you're going to live, because I'm sure as shit not training a new goddamn bodyguard," I said, mock-glaring at Tang, who'd started to come round again and was now pale and sweating.

"Bad…news?" Tang whispered in question.

"Well, you're going to be a bit fucked for a while," I admitted, having seen the level of damage further up inside of Tang's body. I'd originally hoped it was a small area that was affected, but it wasn't. The impact of the wood on his side had driven links of chainmail into him, and the main, solid part of the wooden splinter had done terrible damage to his kidney and lung. But the real issue, and one that would take time to heal, was the dozens of smaller splinters and fragments and the fungus that had coated the wood, which had apparently spread off in all directions inside of his body.

It was like an infection-laden shotgun had gone off in his side, spreading its load in as far as it could, and the fact he was still alive at all was down to Arrin's general healing.

I couldn't let him continue with it, though.

I stopped him before he could do a fourth heal and shook my head, then turned to the others.

"I need him inside and out of this wind; I need a lot of light and a shit-ton of mana potions." We got up, crouching down around Tang and taking a limb each.

"Sorry, buddy," I muttered. "On three: one, two…three!" I heaved him up with the others and we carried him, whimpering and leaking copious amounts of blood, over to the wheelhouse.

Yen shoved the door open, and we staggered inside, finding Jian seated at the controls with the wisp hovering next to him, explaining something. The walls of the room were coated in a mist that flowed and billowed but showed extremely rough images of the world around us.

It was fantastic yet clearly as broken as everything else, magnifying some sections, while others looked entirely dead.

One part of the black ship, lifting as the others were behind us in a pursuit course, was massively magnified, making it almost impossible to see anything else of the ship except for the occasional movements of others as they crossed a particular section of the deck.

"There!" Yen directed, weariness filling her voice. We started towards the map table that she'd nodded towards, Stephanos and Miren, who'd clearly been helping Jian, leaped back and stripped the table of everything, making room for us.

We dumped Tang down as gently as we could, making him pass out again. I downed a mana potion before casting Battlefield Triage again. I stabilized him first, then started seeking out and manipulating his insides, forcing flesh to knit and organs to regrow in specific patterns. I tried to force the splinters out, along with the contaminants, rather than healing the body around them. I found myself having to redo areas that both Arrin and myself had already healed in our panic.

Grimacing, I drew a dagger and cut the seemingly healthy flesh. If I didn't get it all out, there could be terrible repercussions later.

"What can we do?" Yen asked, fear and exhaustion filling her voice as she looked down at her friend.

"Nothing," I said shortly. "Just defend the ship. I can't help out there if I'm going to save him."

"We can do that," she said, straightening and looking around. "Miren, Stephanos, with me. Grizz, you and Arrin as well. Frederikk, you help Jax and come get me if he needs me. Beyond that, stay out of the goddamn way," she ordered weakly, taking charge. "Jian, do you know where you're headed?"

He nodded, gesturing to the front wall.

I glanced up before returning to my work, having seen the fleet in the far distance. I continued working on Tang as Jian explained his reasoning.

"I'm making as good a speed for them as I dare, but I can't go all out. We'd drain the stones, and the ship might not hold together long enough. All we can hope right now is that the fleet sees us and turns back to help, as they'd make mincemeat of those assholes, now that half of them are gone," he said darkly, turning back to the wisp. "So, the core charge level in engine three is six percent lower than it was? Is that an error, or…" he asked, having already dismissed us all from his mind.

"Ty'Baronn," Yen said suddenly, and the demon looked up at her from where he crouched sullenly against the wall. "How far will your plasma attack reach? Can you hit the ships?"

"Not for three more hours," he said in a bored tone, and she growled in frustration.

"Fine. You can damn well keep watch, though," she said, gesturing out of the door. The demon looked at his master, who waved absently at him to go, and he scowled, following along.

The door banged shut behind them, then I lost all track of time again, focusing in on the wounds Tang had taken.

Periodically, I would stop, drink another mana potion, then start back in. Rather than most healing I'd done before, where it simply took a huge amount of mana and *boom*, it was done, this required finesse and patience, healing sections slowly as I forced the splinters out, but keeping him alive at the same time.

Those were two things I had little of at the best of times, but for a friend, I'd damn well make sure I learned them, I growled to myself internally.

I finally sat down after almost an hour. The constant cycle of using all my mana and then replacing it with potions had drained me to the point that I was shaking and having difficulty concentrating.

As I rested, I took the time to inspect the room, suddenly aware of the motion of the ship. I'd felt it before but dismissed it as unimportant. But now, I watched the front wall, seeing a flare from one of the ships, followed by the feeling of sudden weight as Jian fed more power into the engines and sent us up, frantically avoiding a blast of lightning from a ship's cannon fired from the rear.

"Does that happen often?" I asked him dully, my voice raspy and weak.

"Every so often," he admitted. "As long as I know they're going to fire, I can dodge, probably. But it's a guess which way to go, and I can't keep this up forever." He watched over his controls, hissing under his breath. "Reserves are at seventeen percent," he said calmly.

"What?" I asked then coughed and summoned a fountain of water, washing the knife clean and dunking my face into it to refresh me. Feeling a little better, I began studying the cloudy magical displays that covered the walls. We were closing on our fleet, that much was clear. But they were still far ahead, and those that were chasing us were much closer.

"Seventeen percent," Jian repeated. "The reserves. If we use it all, we will crash. We have better engines than them, faster, too, but they have more power, and we can't seem to get above fifty percent cruising speed. The engines just can't do it, but they'll take the power, so there must be leakages everywhere. They're catching us slowly. If I push more power to the engines, we can outrun them for a time, but we're using power at about one percent an hour currently.

"The engines, and the ship in general, are leaking like a sieve. Every time I feed more power in, it costs us. A boost like that," he said, gesturing back toward the ships that were falling behind steadily now, "it costs us two to three percent. If I keep doing it, we can outrun them…until we crash and all die. Or I don't, and they shoot us down. Their ships are being pushed to their limit and draining their stones as well, aren't they?" he said, looking to the wisp.

"They are," she replied smoothly. "The chasing ships are poorly built. While this ship leaks mana due to damage, they are wasteful due to poor construction. They can apparently afford to run us down, though. Our maximum current cruising speed is slightly less than theirs, while our boosted speed is considerably higher, but they can boost more often. This is a race of attrition, with no way to know which side will win."

"We can help," Frederikk said slowly, moving into view from where he'd been seated examining a relay. "I think."

"Explain," I said tiredly, rubbing my eyes and contemplating the second to last mana potion I had. I desperately needed more, and I needed to keep Tang going, as well as trying to keep myself sane. If I could stabilize him again, maybe heal some of the deeper wounds enough that the internal bleeding would slow further, could I make some more potions? The simple ones only took a few minutes to an hour, after all…

"We worked this ship once. We can fix it again…but only three of us were trained for it and taught. The rest would be following their instincts."

"Go on," I prompted, giving him my full attention.

"I must explain…Gnomes are the greatest artifabricants in all of reality because we are the chosen people of the god Svetu," he said, rubbing his temple. "When the god left us, we…changed. Some grew angry and refused to invent new things, instead taking inspiration from the world around us, improving old designs, adjusting things, but swearing to never create new.

"Others believed that the disappearance of the gods and the Cataclysm wasn't an abandonment, and that if we served them truly, if we were what we should have been, then they would return, and they concentrated on only creating new things."

"We've got no time for this." I sighed, and he held up his hands, begging for patience.

"The final group, well, they believed that the gods had abandoned us because they were never gods in truth anyway, and they set off to find out the secrets of the realms, making the mana engines and more. This ship and others were built by all three working together, but all we have left here is the second and first group.

"We as a race spent hundreds of years growing more and more focused, and now, we are all we can be. I can rebuild something a thousand ways, using the designs I know, but to create from new? It is against all I am, much like I cannot spread my arms and grow wings to fly away. Our people will 'fix' the ship, but it will not be what it was. It may be better, but it may not survive it, either," Frederikk said solemnly.

"What?" I asked in shock. "No. No, you literally built a fucking train a few hours ago!" I pointed behind the ship in the direction where we'd come from.

"We made attachments for the badunkas to join together, as we have done before," he corrected, and I shook my head.

"Fine, whatever. Do it," I snapped, thinking that the gnomes were a massive pain in the ass to deal with at the best of times, and that was before hearing this bullshit excuse.

"You accept the risk?" he asked, and I waved my hand at him.

"Yeah, yeah, fine!" I turned back to Tang, the gnome already forgotten. *Maybe if I...*

"We could also use some of the stash," he suggested in a wheedling voice, and I turned to glare at him. The residual anger over everything that had happened flared in my chest as I clumsily tugged a solid stick of their drug out and tossed it at him.

"You pick *now* to try to get your itch scratched?" I growled at him. "Fine, but you fuck this up, and I'll throw you over the side personally!" I hissed threateningly at him, shoving him out of the way as I started dragging my alchemy gear out and spreading it out on a counter nearby. "And send Giint to me!" I ordered, knowing that crazy bastard would have some weird shit that I might be able to use for alchemy, if any of them did.

I spent the next ten minutes working on Tang, and finally, I felt he was stable enough that I could take an hour's break.

I tried to sit back down and found Giint fast asleep in my chair. When I startled him, he bared his teeth and snarled before sniffing and evidently deciding he liked me after all, switching to grinning up at me instead.

"Yooou have gifffft for Giiiint?" he asked me hopefully.

I shot a frown at him. "What? No. Well, maybe…have you got any alchemy ingredients?"

"Some, mebbbbie. Giiiint liiikes smelly herbbbbs," he said, as though embarrassed.

"I'll give you this," I promised, holding up an entire stick of their wonder drug, "if you give me whatever you have."

He froze, eyes wide.

When he didn't respond, I waved the stick back and forth, and he followed it doggedly. I put it back in my bag, and he growled at me momentarily, before apparently remembering my offer and pulling out three bags. I recognized two of them as having been on the badunka riders we'd killed earlier and passed him the stick when he put the bags on the desk.

He ran off to the corner quickly, gnawing on it and making strange sounds, and I looked around hesitantly before pulling out one of the remaining sticks and using Greater Examination on it.

I could see a number of notifications waiting for me by now and resolved to check them quickly next.

Gnomish Wonderdrug		**Further Description** *Yes/No*	
Details:		This substance is known by many names: Krissa, You'Oli, Ginesen, and occasionally, Valerian. **Ingredients:** 1) Catnip 2) Valerian Root 3) Lemon Balm 4) Xanthan Gum	
Rarity:	**Magical:**	**Durability:**	**Potency:**
Rare	No	100/100	2/10

I read it, then blinked, then read it again, and again, before starting to snigger. I'd spent years working in clubs and bars. I'd beaten the shit out of dealers and had force-fed them their own shit over the years, and the wonderdrug that the gnomes were addicted to was some kind of industrial-strength goddamn catnip!

Not one of these things had anything dodgy in it, except maybe the gum; all the others were simple herbs that chilled you the hell out, or sent cats loopy, and that was what the gnomes were off their heads on!

I couldn't help it; I had to laugh.

It started out low, a collection of sniggers and stifled chuckles, before growing and growing, until I couldn't contain it anymore, and I was shaking. My fears and exhaustion had taken their toll on me in little ways that meant that such a simple thing had a profound effect.

For some reason, as finally I calmed myself and got back to the plan, setting up the last few parts of the alchemy kit, I felt better than I had in hours. Days, possibly.

The thought that I was enabling the gnomes to get their rocks off with some kind of seriously harmful drugs, potentially harming them permanently, in order to serve my own ends, had been sitting badly with me, but finding out that it was basically super-strength catnip they were addicted to?

It changed the entire way I looked at their race. They had been hyped up as these almost mystically smart creatures before. Considering how amazing the Fenris was, and the way people spoke about gnomes, that had only reinforced that image, building upon a foundation that I'd had from all the games and lore of my own world. Finding out that instead, they were a race of drug-obsessed lunatics, and meeting an offshoot splinter of them that had basically regressed to a semi-feral state, had made me start to hate them.

It was as though, in my mind, they'd betrayed me by not living up to an image I'd had of them. Now, though…now, I'd been forcibly reminded that not only were they real people, and as such, owed my mental image of them nothing, but they were even more batshit than I thought they were.

They were off their tits on goddamn catnip!

I let another round of the giggles escape as I searched through the bags that Giint had given me, finding a collection of mainly fungus, with a handful of additional herbs that had adapted to low-light conditions, or that had clearly been grown near a magelight, considering the bleached out and worn look of them in real sunlight.

And a hand. Human, apparently.

Ginseng	Further Description *Yes/No*
Details:	This root has many uses and seems to be uniquely beneficial for your health. **Uses Discovered:** 1) Cure Disease 2) Restore Health 3) Fortify Stamina 4) ?

Rarity:	Magical:	Durability:	Charge:
Common	No	100/100	N/A

Warnock Root	Further Description *Yes/No*
Details:	This root is commonly used to cure disease, but may be harmful in larger doses. **Uses Discovered:** 1) Cure Disease 2) Lesser Poison 3) Fortify Perception 4) ?

Rarity:	Magical:	Durability:	Charge:
Common	No	100/100	N/A

Pergola	Further Description *Yes/No*
Details:	These long tubers have an earthy taste but are oddly satisfying. **Uses Discovered:** 1) Tranquilizer 2) Reduce Perception 3) Fire Resistance 4) ?

Rarity:	Magical:	Durability:	Charge:
Common	No	100/100	N/A

Greater Spotted Cap Mushroom		Further Description *Yes/No*
Details:		These dark-spotted mushrooms feel slimy to the touch and make your skin shudder away instinctively. **Uses Discovered:** 1) Muscle Relaxant 2) Paralysis 3) Poison 4) ?
Rarity:	**Magical:**	**Durability:**	**Charge:**
Common	No	100/100	N/A

Green Flutes		Further Description *Yes/No*
Details:		These pale green fluted mushrooms give off a sense of relaxation. **Uses Discovered:** 1) Tranquilizer 2) Depressant 3) Poison 4) Restore Mana
Rarity:	**Magical:**	**Durability:**	**Charge:**
Common	No	100/100	N/A

Rotting Flesh		Further Description *Yes/No*
Details:		This flesh gives off a pungent odor and makes you feel dirty. **Uses Discovered:** 1) Disease 2) Poison 3) Smoke 4) ?
Rarity:	**Magical:**	**Durability:**	**Charge:**
Common	No	100/100	N/A

Mora Telendril		Further Description *Yes/No*
Details:		This dark and flat fungus branches out to form solid tendrils that draw in the spilled lifeblood of those caught by delicious snare plants. **Uses Discovered:** 1) Restore Health 2) Paralysis 3) Fortify Endurance 4) ?
Rarity:	**Magical:**	**Durability:**	**Charge:**
Common	No	100/100	N/A

Delicious Snare	Further Description *Yes/No*
Details:	These plants give off a heady scent of summer and sweet fruits ready to drop, but the plants themselves are coated in razor-sharp needles that cause copious bleeding when disturbed. **Uses Discovered:** 1) Damage Health 2) Paralysis 3) Depressant 4) ?

Rarity:	Magical:	Durability:	Charge:
Common	No	100/100	N/A

I read through the notifications for the various ingredients as quickly as I could, dumping the majority back into the pouches and keeping out only the mora telendril, the ginseng, and on a whim, the green flutes.

I checked Tang again, verified that there were no emergencies that I could help with, then drew a deep breath and started.

I spread the ingredients out on the table before me. Using a short, sharp blade, I separated the heads from the green flutes, then split them lengthways, peeling back the fibrous outer layer to reveal a sickly glowing sap that ran the length of them.

I stripped this out, my basic knowledge of alchemy combined with the practice I'd had thus far and the little training I'd received to guide me as I worked.

Once the sap was out and had been squeezed into a vial, I started to chop the root itself, finding that it dried quickly once the liquid was removed, becoming brittle and crumbly. I chopped it as quickly as I could, then set it aside in an alembic, putting it on a low boil with some pure water I summoned, filling a handful of beakers quickly before letting the spell wink out.

While that was boiling, I worked quickly to peel and chop the mora telendril. These were short, stubby roots, almost like tentacles, but as solid as sweet potatoes and lined with dozens of tiny holes. I diced them up and dumped them into a vial with a small solution of the glowing liquid from the flutes, watching with alacrity as the liquid was absorbed.

I muttered notes to myself, removing the previous vials from the alembic and replacing it with the new one, then getting to work on the next one.

The next hour passed at speed, and soon, I had half a dozen different potions set out before me. Some, most likely the majority, I knew, would be failures, or at least very weak, but that was fine.

I did a little healing on Tang then set to identifying the potions and memorizing what had worked and what had resulted in wasted ingredients.

All in all, from the dozen potions I'd managed to create, I'd made two real successes which were both healing potions. Three new potions, I'd not made this way before, which were variously a Potion of Somnolence and two Potions of Cure Disease, accompanied by seven utter failures.

I stretched, cracking my back, and checked on Tang again before walking over to Jian, looking down at the mess of controls and frowning.

"How are we doing?" I asked him.

He started, having been lost in the complicated controls.

"Ah!" he cried, jerking back, and making the ship shudder before he grabbed the sticks again and got it under control. "Damn, boss, don't do that to me!" he said, shaking his head. "What did you say?"

"I asked you how we were doing?" I said again.

"We're okay...not good. Don't get me wrong, but whatever Frederikk and his people have done, it's resulted in a serious cut to the loss we were suffering. We're using about one percent every two hours now, as near as I can tell, but they're still gaining on us. The rest of the fleet disappeared into the storm up ahead about twenty minutes ago, though, so it looks like we're on our own. Best we can hope for is that we can lose our pursuers in there, maybe change direction and see how close to shore we can get? Land and make a run for the tower on foot?"

"Not a good option there," I said, shaking my head. "We'd be hunted from above and followed by their forces. I doubt we'd last long."

"Could the gnomes not make us something to ride to escape them?"

"Possibly, but it's heavy trees and thick underbrush down there for what, a few hundred miles to the tower? I don't see us riding something the gnomes made and controlled for that long, do you?" I arched a questioning eyebrow at Jian, smiling wryly.

"Well, no...besides the ship, I mean," he said, unconsciously adjusting his crotch. I nodded in understanding. The ride to the ship itself had been an absolute ball-breaker for me, too.

"Besides, they used their mana engines as explosives to take out the barricade earlier. They might be able to cobble something together, but it'd still need power, and I don't have any we could use," I said. "How much longer do we have?"

"We're down to nine percent, so if we don't have to make any fast bursts of speed, maybe eighteen hours," Jian said uncomfortably.

"And how long to the Great Tower?" I asked, and immediately catching the way his shoulders slumped.

"At this speed, and the direction we're going, following the fleet and all, I'd think at least fifty-five to sixty hours. Probably closer to seventy, considering the wind is against us, so we can't use the sails, either."

"So, we're fucked," I stated after a minute of careful thought.

"Yeah, seems that way," he replied quietly, keeping his eyes on the display.

"Well, that's a kick in the teeth," I muttered, shaking my head, and looking around the bridge, as though expecting an answer to just pop up.

"Yeah, I asked Tenandra, and she said that she would look into options, then she vanished. I know you might not like her, but she's really helped me so far," Jian said hesitantly.

I looked at him in confusion. "Who..." I started to ask before noticing that the core sat on the deck, seemingly dull and lifeless. "The wisp?"

He nodded.

"Okay," I said absently, examining the core more closely. This damn thing had taken a charge before, hadn't it?

I was turning the core over and over in my hands when the wisp—Tenandra, I supposed—reappeared.

She looked haggard, but she gave me a polite nod before giving Jian an altogether more friendly, if weak, smile.

"We may have an option, but it will not be easy," she offered hesitantly and looked at me.

"Go on," I encouraged her.

"The storm ahead," she said, gesturing into the oncoming clouds. "The rest of the fleet has altered course to ride the outermost edge for safety."

"Seems a bloody good idea to me," I admitted.

"We don't," she said simply. "Instead, we dive deeper into it, and the gnomes repair a mana collector for us, connecting it to the stones that are almost dead. Some will shatter, I have no doubt, but some may survive and accept the high-density mana concentration found in the storm's outer ring. But we cannot go deeper, not if we want to survive," she warned soberly.

"That's not sounding like a very safe solution," I said carefully, frowning slightly at Tenandra.

"There are no safe options." The wisp sighed, shaking her head. "This will gain us the power needed, but it is far from safe, and if the mana floods the crystals too quickly, many will shatter. We can only hope that it is not essential crystals that are lost. This, I estimate at a thirty-two percent chance of success, while the next most promising, at eleven percent, is boarding one of the enemy ships in the storm and looting their mana crystals, then swapping them out while we fly and hoping the ship survives."

"Oh, well, that's a joyful thought." I grimaced. "That's a pretty shitty percentage of success, either way. Are there other options?" I asked, and she shook her head regretfully.

"None above a six percent chance of success." She sighed again, watching me closely to gauge my response.

"What about this?" I asked her, hefting her core.

"What about it?" she repeated with clear hesitation, eyeing me distrustfully.

"The cores are designed to be charged and recharged, right? Could we charge the core and connect it to the ship? Like a battery?" I suggested, surprised at the look of horror on her face.

"No, please," she begged, shaking her head desperately. "I understand I have not endeared myself to you…but…you would kill me like this—"

"I'm not trying to kill you," I protested, holding my hands up quickly. "Oracle, whose form you took when you first showed yourself to me, she'd bound herself to me directly, rather than the tower, as she was trying to save me when we first met. Could you not transfer yourself to something? Like the ship?"

Silence filled the wheelhouse for several seconds, before she moved, blurring with inhuman speed. As she shot forward to hover before me, her eyes searched mine for a sign, a twitch, anything to suggest I was hiding something…

"You would permit this?" she asked me eventually, her voice filled with wonder as she continued to search my face. "You would permit a wisp to become this ship? To be able to bond to something so…so free?"

"Yes," I said truthfully. "You've already accepted me as your master, and as a Scion of the Empire. You're compelled to be loyal to me and my aims, even though I'd rather you offered such loyalty willingly. I understand that trust has to be earned on *both* sides." I held her gaze, wondering if I was making a huge mistake. "If you bond with the ship, is it permanent?" I asked her, and she nodded quickly.

"If I bonded to the ship, I would be required to spread out my essence—my soul, if you prefer—to permeate the ship. Removing myself after that would be very…painful, not to mention resulting in a permanent lowering of my capabilities."

"How did you manage with the Prax, then?" I asked, and she gestured to the core.

"I was bonded to the core. When things became grave, I was removed from the Prax's control Citadel and interred in the Vault instead. My main control facilities were cut and only a local variant was permitted. It was to ensure that the Prax could be repaired once it was retaken, in the event of an attack being successful."

"So, look, I might be misunderstanding this, but let's get this very clear: if I allow you to bond to the ship, you will remain bonded to this ship, and only this ship, for life?" I asked, wanting to be absolutely certain that I understood, and she nodded in affirmation. "Dammit," I grumbled.

"This is a problem?" she asked, an edge of coldness and sorrow leaking into her voice.

"Yeah. Well, no, not really," I corrected myself. "I was thinking that we'd be better off bonding you with the battleship. It's still being built, and it won't be ready for a while. That was it, in the middle of the fleet, before we lost sight of them, but we truly need you in here, I guess."

I rubbed my chin, considering immediate versus long-term needs.

"The battleship?" she asked incredulously.

"Yeah. I bet if you can gain control of her the way that Seneschal has the Great Tower, it'd make an amazing weapon," I muttered.

"What about my Prax?" she interrupted quickly. "What if I could be removed from this ship and instead inserted into the Prax later? Would you permit that?"

"You just said you couldn't." I fixed her with my best glare. "Okay, you're hiding something. Gimme."

"'Gimme'? Oh. Well, I'm capable of spreading myself out. My essence, as I said…" she explained haltingly. "But once I spread my essence out, I can never get that back. If the ship were to be integrated into another, though, such as your battleship, or better yet, my Prax, I could possibly spread out further? It would take time, and I would no longer be what I am, but I could…*evolve*…?"

"You could become a city?" I asked with surprise, wanting further clarification. "If I allow you to join with the ship now, as long as the ship was integrated into the Prax later, you could spread yourself out and claim it? Resurrect the sleeping golems, repair the city, get it back into the air?"

"I…I think so?" she responded uncertainly. "It has never been done."

"Why not? Hell, why bond wisps with the Great Towers, centers that were meant to be the greatest citadels in times of war, but refuse to allow you the same in the Prax?" I asked her.

"Because we were captured slaves with our natural affinities suppressed. Our ability to draw in ambient mana was burned from us, and we were forced into an eternity of servitude," she replied grimly.

"But why?" I asked, confused, thinking over the rules against slavery that Amon…Then I paused and searched my memories, feeling his silence and his grim shame.

I reached in deeper, searching. Forcing him to share what I knew was there, somewhere. I held up a hand to Tenandra, stopping her as she started to talk. I wanted to know this for myself, to understand it as only one who had made the decision could.

I remembered then, as Amon grudgingly gave it up, the memory surfacing slowly.

It had been early in the empire's history, literally thousands of years ago, long before the empire that people now regarded as ancient history was born. In those days, it had just been Amon and his followers.

Back then, things had been quite different, despite what the history would say later. It was Shustic who had mellowed Amon'Ita, who had taught him right from wrong. When he'd started out, he'd not been a noble man, sacrificing to raise the sentient "good" races out of the quagmire that life was in those days.

He'd been a conqueror, a greedy warlord, a man who'd been named the Demon of Dai'Shiier after he'd put every man and every second child to death for defying him. He'd not been trying to save the innocent; he'd been demanding the supplies the town had labored over to feed themselves through the winter.

He'd forced the survivors to serve him in his army and in his pleasure houses, and it wasn't until he'd had his forces smashed in detail, his followers slaughtered in retribution, that he'd seen the truth.

I remembered his first meeting with Shustic, after he'd lost everything, staggering through the fierce winter snowstorm up to the great dragon's nest, barely alive, dead inside, and almost out, and he'd demanded a bond from her, demanded the ability to kill his enemies, in his unbelievable arrogance.

For reasons all her own, she'd agreed, but she'd made him serve her first: thirty years in the nest, learning at the clawed feet of the Elder Dragons, the greater dragon's leaders, even as the lesser dragonkin, wyrms and their ilk, had mocked and belittled him.

As the years passed, he was broken and reforged anew, no longer the merciless conqueror with a heart of stone, not after Shustic used her magic, forcing him to live the lives of those he'd oppressed.

He'd seen the world through their eyes, lived the nightmare of his invasion and depravity, until he'd been truly broken. Then he was gifted a rescued elven child, a child who no magic could save, who was dying of a rare condition, incapable of knowing the touch of magic. The child would never reach their tenth birthday, he was told.

This child was to be his, his penance and his reward, and he spent the following years raising the boy, making him the best he could be.

When the child, named Shel'Aviir, or Repentance, in the old tongue, finally died, Amon sat over his still body and wept tears of fire and ice. The final part of Amon'Ita, Demon of Dai'Shiier, had died that day along with his adopted son, and the man who was left, Amon, rose to conquer the known world.

In the beginning, there were corners cut; the laws he would uphold were bent and broken frequently, and he hated himself for it, burying the truth under layers of golden lies.

He did things, or gave orders for others to do them, such as the subjugation of the wisps, seeing them as necessary evils for the greater good. He hated it, but he assuaged his fears and self-recriminations with the old line that it was for "the greater good."

"You sanctimonious asshole," I shot at him. I felt his anger and his acceptance of the title, even as I shut him away and reopened my eyes, looking into Tenandra's in turn.

"Amon did it. He hated that he did, but he believed that, for the 'greater good,' it was necessary, as was forcing you to serve and obey the imperial line. I crossed that line when we first met, and I ordered you to obey because we didn't have time for a discussion. For that, I'm sorry. I'll make you a deal, though, if you'll have it?" I offered.

"I will listen but I am required to obey you," she said haltingly, expression curious nonetheless.

"Yeah, well, the deal is this, same as I offered to the others, of any of the races: swear fealty to me, to accept me as your lord, and I'll do my best to raise you up, to make you into the best version of yourself you can be. You can't disobey me, so I won't ask you for an Oath of any kind. Instead, I'll give you one." I took a deep breath, then injected my mana into my words as I spoke them, forcing them to bind to me and to reality as I made a declaration for the entire realm to see.

"I, Jax, Lord of Dravith and Imperial Scion, swear that I will not cross the same lines that my ancestor did in harming the wisps, for 'the greater good.' I will strike those down who oppose me, but never will I enslave the innocent and force them to serve for eternity. Furthermore, if they can be healed and freed, then, provided they assist in developing a replacement for their role, I will free them. But unless they swear to me, they will not be permitted to retain physically bonded items."

I felt the mana being burned from me, examining the words as I spoke them and searching my heart for hidden meanings. Finding none, the Oath was affirmed, and Tenandra stared at me in shock.

"I'm sorry to have to add in the last bit," I said, taking a seat and catching my breath. "But if I let you bond with the battleship, or the Prax, or whatever, then I free you, I'm going to need to keep the damn thing. I am at war, after all." I shrugged and forced a smile. "Seriously, though, I *am* sorry, both for forcing you to obey, and for the shit that was done to you in the past. I need your help, Tenandra. Will you join me?"

"I…will," she replied slowly, nodding her head to me, becoming more animated as she went on. "I will join you, Lord Jax. At least with you, I have a chance of freedom one day, and by the Oath you just gave, you would not further enslave our kind. If we were to find others in the wild, with you, they would be safe, instead of bonded against their will.

"In fact…" She took a deep breath. "I will agree to serve you, willingly, and provide everything you need. I will ask only two things in return: first, that you agree to preserve, protect, and defend any wisp clans that you find out about." She paused, watching me intently and looking relieved when I nodded my assent. "And…and secondly, that you allow me to roam the skies again, but no longer as a mere passenger and assistant.

"Allow me to join with a ship, and if we rebuild it, a Prax. Let me evolve into the greatest form I can imagine! Let me be free to roam the realm, protecting my kind and all those who would be enslaved. Make me an instrument of destruction and rebirth, of freedom and fear. Make me truly into the Prax, Glorious Retribution!"

She spoke with passion in her tiny voice, almost shaking with the desire to be more than she was. To no longer be constrained by the core she lived in or to be locked away again in a vault to wait out the years and centuries for someone to demand her servitude once again.

"I agree," I said simply. "We need you to join with this ship for now, and if we decide there is a need later on, then you can, I guess, integrate this ship into the superstructure of the battleship or the Prax, if we can repair it in truth?"

"I can," she said firmly. "I will bond to the ship, but it will take time, and we will need the gnomes to cease their infernal tinkering with my new body, and to instead concentrate on the core and the manastones, not to mention rigging collectors…"

"Good point," I said, nodding grimly. "Giint!" I shouted, making the semi-comatose gnome in the corner start in terror, almost jumping out of his skin as he awoke from his drug-induced somnolence. "Get your ass in gear and find me Frederikk and any of the other elders you can. Get them in here, right goddamn now, as fast as you can!"

CHAPTER THIRTY-TWO

Giint sprinted for the door, his determination to prove his usefulness only slightly diminished by his frantic attempts to push on a pull door. It took him a few seconds to calm down enough to realize what was wrong, then he was gone, pausing only as I shouted at him to send in Yen as well.

She was the first to arrive, of course, having been outside on the deck already. Although she coughed a little at the fumes coming off the alchemy set, she was quick to smile when she saw that Tang had regained a little color, not to mention the collection of potions next to him, ready and waiting.

"Yen," I said, wasting no time. "We've got a chance, despite the shitty condition of the ship, but we're heading into the storm. No choice about it. Defend the ship as best you can until things get dicey out there, then get in here or below decks. I don't want to lose anyone, and we're going in hard and deep." I paused, reflexively, then sighed at the obvious double-entendre that shot right over her head, missing Bane all over again.

"Yes, Jax," she said, nodding. "How bad will it get out there?"

"Bad," Tenandra interjected, landing on the ship's controls and reaching out, slipping her hands into the nearest crystal and letting out a little gasp as she began to interface herself with it, before explaining. "We're going to try to get the ship into the densest mana concentrations, so expect lightning, at the very least."

"Right," Yen said after a wide-eyed pause. "And…can the ship survive that?" she asked carefully.

"Probably not for long," Tenandra replied distractedly, turning to me and holding out a hand.

I understood what she needed and stepped in close, holding my hand out and feeling her tiny fingers rest on mine. Her hand both gripped my flesh and drew out mana that helped to sustain her in the bonding.

"What's happening out there?" I asked Yen.

"Not much." She shrugged. "We basically fire off potshots at each other. The distance is too great for anything else. An occasional Firebolt or Magic Missile is all we can manage; no bow can shoot with accuracy at that range, and when they try to use their cannons, Jian dodges."

"Cannons?" I asked. "I'd not even heard them…not beyond the lightning one."

"Then you're lucky. Most of the time, they've fired a shot here and there, but the last twenty minutes, they've been trying a lot harder. I don't think they dare go all out. Cannons are just too unstable, but they don't want us getting away, either."

As she spoke, I felt the ship shift to one side slightly and a burst of power boosted the engines, followed by a distant scream of something hurtling through the air. I realized I'd felt this again and again, and heard the accompanying sounds, as well. But I'd dismissed them as unimportant as I had been engrossed in saving Tang and in my alchemy.

More notifications blinked for my attention, and I dampened them down again, resolving to deal with them later. I just didn't have the time. A few moments later Giint came into view, running as fast as his short legs would let him, Frederikk and two others following, screaming obscenities and chasing him.

"Heeerrrre!" Giint said, a manic grin splitting his face as he darted behind me and dove under a desk, while I waved at the furious gnomes to stop.

"What the hell?" I snapped at them. "Stop right there!" I ordered as Frederikk yanked out a dagger, glaring at Giint's feet where they protruded from under the desk.

"He…" Frederikk snarled, huffing as he tried to catch his breath. "He…took—"

"He went to get you at my orders," I said, then paused. "He *took*? What did he…Giint!" I snapped. "Get your arse out from under there!" There was a pause, then Giint poked his head out and grinned maniacally at the three elders and me, all while frantically chewing on something.

"He stole your stash, didn't he?" I asked them and covered my eyes with one hand as I tried to calm down, hearing their angry growls in confirmation. "Right. That's my fault," I admitted begrudgingly. "I ordered him to gather you as fast as he could. Giint, give them back the stash…whatever is left of it."

He looked up at me with an expression of hurt betrayal, clambering out and offering up the compact stick to Frederikk, who snatched it and swung for Giint with a hasty fist. Giint dodged back, then lunged at him, grabbing the elder with both hands and nutting him, before reaching for a knife…and getting yanked back as I stepped in and grabbed him by the collar.

"Stop that, you crazy little bastards!" I yelled at them both, noting the way the other two elders stood back, calmly watching while Frederikk scrambled for a dagger as well. The years of madness and constant fighting making Giint as vicious as ever, regardless of him being "healed" now, and I guessed the elders…well. They were just vicious for any reason after so long, regardless of how poisoned they'd been.

I kicked Frederikk back and shook Giint.

"That's enough!" I barked at him. "Stop, you little shits!" With that, the pair of them subsided, simmering anger ready to bust into life at the slightest spark again. "Tenandra, can you explain the plan so they can understand, please?"

"Of course…I'm not doing anything complicated right now." She grunted, catching my eye and nodding an apology. "I'm exiting my core. Lord Jax requires you to create a set of mana collectors, spreading them about the ship to catch any ambient mana, and channeling it into a central node that the core will form the heart of, then connect it up to the manastones.

"Once those are in place, then I will recharge the ship directly from the storm. Do you understand? The mana engines you used before absorbed a small amount of ambient mana as well as using the manastones, so you know how to create them; all you need to do is place them around the ship."

"Where?" Frederikk asked, his face alight with anticipation.

"The masts, the bowsprit, and atop the wheelhouse…and one…underneath," she said slowly, as if expecting an explosion.

"Okay," Frederikk said agreeably. "I recommend Giint does the receptor underneath." He grinned evilly as the other two elders nodded and spoke up.

"I agree."

"Best place for him."

"You're a bunch of bastards," I said, but nodded when Giint looked to me for help. "Shouldn't piss off the guys that decide the work arrangements, Giint, mate." I grimaced, shrugging.

"Giiiiint going tooo diiie," the little gnome said mournfully, then shrugged and casually slipped something from his pocket into his mouth, munching quickly.

Frederikk looked down at the stick of catnip he'd been given back before snarling and trying to reach Giint again; it was half the size it had been when he got it back, so clearly Giint had managed to snap some off in the fight. This time, I just heaved them both through the air toward the door.

"Go sort it out—out there!" I snapped. "Tenandra, how long?" I asked, and she spoke up quickly, if distractedly.

"An hour, no more, until we hit the true edge of the storm; we're already entering the fringe."

"Get the work done in forty-five minutes," I called to the elders, and the freshly-begun fight froze as both combatants looked at me in shock.

"We need at least a day. Two!" Frederikk spluttered.

"Well, this ship will have crashed, and we'll all be dead by then, so…no. You've got an hour at most; then you'll have to work on it while it's live."

They gawked at me in shock for a handful of seconds, before scrambling and shoving the other aside as they struggled to their feet and rushed out of the room. The remaining two elders followed them as all four started snapping and shouting at each other and summoning the gnomes from below decks to start work.

"How long do we really have?" I asked Tenandra, and she smiled placidly as she pulled more mana from me.

"About three hours, but they'll do a lot more now that they think they've got no time."

"Jian, can we keep going that long?" I asked, and he grimaced in reply.

"We can, but at the speed they're closing, we won't be far ahead when the storm hits, not unless you want to burn through all our stored power…"

"No, this could still go tits-up," I said firmly. "Try to keep as much back as you can."

"I'll be able to help with that," Tenandra said distractedly. "Once I'm bonded to the ship, anyway, but that's at least an hour away."

I nodded and threw the core to Yen, then pulled a stool close to the control panel, sitting and holding my hand out so that Tenandra could draw the needed mana from me directly.

"I'll be out as soon as she's done, but until then, you're in charge, Yen, and make sure the gnomes do all they can. Be sure to give them the core when they need it."

"I will, Jax; good luck." she said, striding back out and closing the door behind her.

"Well, looks like we're either fucked or free," Jian said after a few seconds, and I grunted. The feeling of Tenandra pulling on my mana was like giving blood, but infinitely suckier.

"He's trying to meditate, Jian," Tenandra whispered somewhere in the distance. I ignored the pair of them, closing myself down as much from the world as I could and envisaging my boxes slamming into place around me.

Constrained by a mixture of concern for the others, for the ship and myself, and the definite feeling that we were constantly on the edge of falling out of the air, meant that it took much longer than it should have for me to get my meditation up to speed again.

I reached the second box, the lid slotting in and my compression rate stepping up. Mana flooded into me, just as the door banged open again, making me start.

"We've got a problem!" Arrin said. I gritted my teeth, trying to not shout at anyone.

"What is it?" I sighed, getting up.

"That black ship," he said.

I turned, focusing on the deformed image of the ship as it edged ahead of the others, gradually picking up speed, while I tried to make out what was being assembled on the deck.

"You can see it clearly from above," Arrin said.

"Fine, I'll go look. What's your mana like?" I asked him.

His eyes unfocused as he checked it. "Uh…not bad?" he replied hesitantly. "I've got seventy left?"

"Then take over here as a living battery for Tenandra; meditate and see how you do," I ordered while deliberately not asking him about his mana usage. I just knew the daft sod had been lobbing Magic Missiles at the ships.

I strode past him on the way out and nodded to Tang, who still lay in a deep sleep.

"Give him the Potion of Somnolence—it's that deep blue one with the green flecks—then hit him with a Cleanse. He should be okay for now, but it's best to keep him under so he can't screw up the healing I've already done," I ordered. Arrin nodded to me, squeezing my shoulder in reassurance as he passed by.

Shoving the door closed again, I left the room, the swollen wood making the door grate against the floor. I held up a hand to brace against the storm's initial onslaught, the wind having picked up a hell of a lot from when I was out last.

I snorted in amusement as I saw the frantic speed of the gnomes who raced everywhere, orders being shouted, arguments breaking out, and occasional fights. The elders screamed directions over it all, and the gnomes worked their magic, building totally new parts into the ship's super structure, even as other stripped things apart. I saw pans and rusted weapons, kill-sticks like my own, and an occasional section of engine produced and torn apart, as others worked to integrate the parts.

I turned and clambered up to the next level, the short distance I climbed up stairs, steep enough to almost qualify as a ladder, made all the more difficult by the gusting winds and only having one damn hand. Once I was on the upper deck, I made my way to the rear railing and looked out, easily able to spot the four ships that trailed us.

Arrin was right; even with the distance, it was a clearer picture from here, as whatever magic made it possible to see in the wheelhouse had distinct faults that were warping that ship.

The black ship was in the lead, maybe five hundred meters behind us, with the cruisers on either side of it and the merchantman bringing up the rear. Even the decking of the black ship was tinged black, as at least one mage worked to keep the sun from hitting its decks. The sailors worked frantically, assembling what my brain tried to decide was either a mangonel or a trebuchet.

Either way, it was a problem, as a second SporeMother glared at me from under its own awning, with the tell-tale patches of mobile darkness and nightmare I just knew to be DarkSpore flitting around her.

"They're going to use the catapult to bombard us with DarkSpore." The others nodded in agreement. "Give me options," I half-ordered; half-begged.

"Not many to give," Grizz answered, and Yen nodded in agreement. "They're too far out of range for the archers, and they've got more than we do, so that's no good." He nodded toward the dozens of men milling around with bows in their hands on the enemy deck. "As to magic, well, we might be able to hit them, but they've got a shield, so we'll probably waste it all getting through that, then have nothing left to kill the DarkSpore. Our own cannon doesn't have enough power to fire, not to mention being on the wrong end of the ship…"

"So, we can basically only fight them when they come to board us now?" I asked, and he and Yen nodded. "Joy," I said slowly, scowling at the ships that were slowly closing the distance.

"What should we do?" Miren asked me, and I glanced at her and smiled. She'd changed so much since she'd joined Lydia's squad; truthfully, they all had. Her transformation had been as clear and overt as Lydia's. The soon-to-be Optio had gone from a half-starved slave who hated the world and believed everyone was out to get her to a heavily muscled warrior-tank who stood tall and proud, inspiring those around her.

Miren had started out a waifish girl, barely out of childhood. Her combination of youth and her half-elven heritage combined to make her slim and almost weak-looking, but now, she stood strong as well. She'd grown into a beautiful young woman in the weeks we'd been together; the constant leveling and point gains combined to make changes to her that would usually take years. She'd grown at least several inches, put on a lot of muscle, and definitely filled her clothes in ways that made me think Jian was a lucky guy, but more than all the rest was the confidence that she carried herself with.

She was still immature and girlish at times, the sudden recollection of her naïve desire to visit the "street of negotiable affection" in Himnel jumping straight to mind. She'd believed it to be a place where you could get hugs and verbal affirmations, instead of the seedy place it was in reality. But she'd matured now to stand with a steely glint in her eye and a confidence that told the world that she'd take the best it had and nothing less.

I knew as I looked at her, and then let my gaze carry over the rest of the group, that I could always rely on these people, even if it was a hopeless fight.

Thankfully, this wasn't.

"Okay, people, stand down," I ordered. "Have one on watch, and one to go get the others when it's needed, but for now, until we either get to the storm and lose them, or they manage to close the distance, there's nothing to do, so go get some food and rest."

Grizz saluted to me, the seasoned warrior showing through the happy-go-lucky exterior he generally displayed as he immediately worked with Yen setting up a rotation, then sending the others down below to rest out of the wind and making sure everyone got some food.

"What are we going to do?" Yen asked me quietly as Grizz shooed the others away.

"If they fire the DarkSpore at us?" I asked. "I mean, I assume that's why they're building that thing."

"Yeah."

"We dodge if we can, and we kill what we can't dodge," I said simply. "There's not a great deal of choice in the matter; we don't have the power reserves to outrun them. We can manage maybe one more burst of speed now, but Jian is saving that for when they fire on us next, so it's a case of trying to keep ahead long enough that we can hide in the storm. If not, then we fight."

"We've got less than an hour, the way they're working," Yen said grimly.

"Think they can keep it up?" I asked.

"Depends on the men, really," she admitted, backhanding Grizz without looking at him as he threw me a wink and opened his mouth to comment. "The legion could do it easily, but they're not legionnaires, so who knows. Equally, they're working on a ship that's carrying that thing, so they're either working in a flat-out panic, or they're already possessed, so…" she went on absently.

I nodded in grim agreement, looking ahead at the storm that was quickly building, having grown large enough to blot out the sky from left to right, with huge black and grey-green clouds towering over us.

Flashes of blue-white lightning streaked through the clouds, and I shook my head in disbelief. The storm ahead of us now would be classed as a national threat, something along the lines of a hurricane and a thunderstorm meeting and breeding insanity. As the thunder rolled and shook the world around us, the rain arrived right behind a blast of air that staggered us all and caused the ship to dip in the air.

"Damn, that's cold!" I gasped out as the rain hit, the drumming sound loud even as the wind swept across the deck in a wave, making those hurrying below thankful that they were escaping it. The majority of the gnomes paused in shock, huddling together.

"They've never seen weather!" Yen gasped, her voice a mix of shock and horror as several gnomes broke away and abandoned their work, sprinting for the hatches leading belowdecks.

"Damn. Looks like I found my next job, then!" I cursed, hurrying to the edge of the upper deck and clambering down awkwardly. The suddenly wet deck was made far more slippery as the moss and fungus that covered most of it became slick with moisture.

I fell down the last couple of steps then pulled myself upright, rushing through the oncoming rain to skid to a stop beside Frederikk. He bellowed out orders, trying to return order, or as much as the gnomes seemed capable of, to the work at hand.

"How long?" I shouted to him, amazed by the speed of the wind and rain, having been told only minutes before that we were an hour or more away from the storm.

"Till we can go below decks? Or till it's done?" he shouted back, lifting his hands and trying to block the rain from his face.

"Yes!" I shouted back, and he shook his head.

"We need to go below now! We can't work in this!" he bellowed back, gesturing at the few gnomes that were still in sight, mainly huddling on the floor, clutching desperately at ropes or fixtures, and hiding their faces. "These buggers haven't seen this before, ever! It's like hell has come for them! We need to skirt the storm, or they'll be useless!"

"Get them working, or we're all dead!" I bellowed back. "I'll make Jian skirt the storm!"

I spun and ran for the wheelhouse, practically stomping on a gnome who'd lost his footing and was frantically dragging himself across the deck on his hands and knees.

I jumped over him, landing hard and nearly taking the door off its hinges when I slammed into it, entering the wheelhouse with a gust of wind and a spray of rain.

"Turn us around!" I shouted to Jian as Stephanos shoved the door shut behind me, and the noise level dropped dramatically. "Turn us around," I repeated, shaking myself and sending water droplets flying. "We need to skirt the edge of the storm, or we'll never get the gnomes to finish. They think it's the end of the world out there."

"Gnomes!" Jian replied in annoyance, shaking his head. "We've not even hit the storm yet, Jax; this is the outer edge. We just got a bit blasted forward, that's all. I've spent most of my life outdoors. This will pass in a few minutes, then we'll have a patch of peace, and then the real storm will hit…"

"Well, we can't do anything like this!" I retorted. "Seriously, the gnomes are useless out there, and…" I glanced to the side, spotting three pairs of boots poking out from under a desk and crouched down to look. Four gnomes were piled into a space I'd have called restrictive for just me to sit within. I shook my head, straightening up and calling to Miren and the others.

"Sorry, guys. Your break just got canceled. Get out there and round up the gnomes, or we're all dead," I said to the rest of the team, while gesturing at them to remove the four under the desk. "Jian, I need you to keep us free of as much of the weather as you can, and quickly."

"I'll bring her about and try to ride the outer edge, but it means they'll close on us. I can't dodge them and the storm," Jian warned me, and I sighed, nodding my acceptance.

"Then it's back to a fight," I confirmed, dumping my bag on its side. Reaching in, I eagerly began hoping that the damn helm that I'd looted from the Vault was as good as it looked.

Helm of Imperial Right		Further Description *Yes/No*	
Details:		This Helm was crafted to be worn by the Warden-Inquisitor of the Prax, Glorious Retribution, and grants the following bonuses: • +5 to Wisdom • +5 to Perception **Bonus Ability:** Inquisition Once per day, at a cost of 100 health and mana, the wearer may demand an answer to a question. If the target refuses to answer, lies, or withholds information, they will feel the wrath of the Inquisition. It gives a bonus of +7 to resisting physical damage.	
Rarity:	**Magical:**	**Durability:**	**Charge:**
Legendary	Yes	99/100	1/1

I grinned to myself and lifted the helm up, sliding it down onto my head and shuddering involuntarily as the changes took hold.

My eyes burned, as did my ears and nose. My mouth felt like I'd rubbed freshly-cut Dorset Nagas across my tongue. All my skin tingled, while my brain felt like worms were crawling across it, but after a handful of seconds, it was over, and I nodded in satisfaction.

The air felt slightly different to me now, and I spotted the signs of the air pressure dropping even further, even as Jian slowly angled us outwards. I moved to Tang's side and drew both enchanted blades from his scabbards, sliding one into a bag of holding and gripping the other. I'd decided that I would be better off with that than anything else for this fight.

I pulled up the notifications as well, dismissing them quickly as unimportant, even the skill gains from my alchemy, despite being pleased that I'd hit level fourteen. I skimmed through, quickly finding the ones I needed.

Congratulations!

You completed the Quest: Fix the Fixers

You have discovered the chilling secrets of the Prax, Glorious Retribution, discovered a working, if unpowered, portal, killed the Master and his unwilling servants, and looted the Vault.

Due to the level of difficulty involved, and the bravery shown by your acceptance of the realities of your situation, the Goddess Jenae has increased your rewards and altered the Success Conditions of the Quest.

Recruit the Gnomish Survivors: 21/27

Recover Sufficient Manastones to Power the Ship Interesting Endeavors: 43/40

Eliminate Bartholomew the Lich: 1/1

Find and Prepare the Ship Interesting Endeavors and use it to escape: 1/1

Bonus Condition: For each SporeMother killed, receive an additional 10,000xp: 2/?

Reward: Improved technological capacity in the Great Tower, Possible technological boosts to the fleet, survival , gnomish exploration vessel Interesting Endeavors, 500,000xp

*

Congratulations!

You have killed the following:

- 37x Human Raiders of various levels for a total of 277,150xp

- 36x DarkSpore of various levels for a total of 1,440xp

- 42x DarkSpore Possessed Undead of various levels for a total of 37,113xp

- 1x Immature SporeMother, level 12 for 9,875xp

- 35x Sporelings of various levels for a total of 1,400xp

A party under your command killed the following:

- 15x Human Raiders of various levels for a total of 98,140xp

- 11x DarkSpore of various levels for a total of 378xp

- 15x DarkSpore Possessed Undead of various levels for a total of 14,312xp

- 17x Sporelings of various levels for a total of 875xp

- 1x Immature SporeMother, level 13 for 10,250xp

Total Party experience earned: 123,955xp

As party leader, you gain 25% of all experience earned.

Progress to level 21 stands at 1,044,894/350,000

"Oh, hell yes," I muttered, realizing that I'd gotten the experience for firing the explosives and killing the crews of the ships, as well as everything around them when they'd gone off. Adding that to my quest rewards…

Congratulations!

You have reached level 21 & 22!

You have 41 unspent Attribute points and 1 Meridian point available.

Progress to level 23 stands at 294,894/455,000

Congratulations!

**Through hard work and perseverance,
you have increased your stats by the following:**

Dexterity +1

Perception +1

Strength +1

Continue to train and learn to increase this further.

I stood there for a long moment, frozen in shock, reading and rereading the notifications. I'd forgotten all about the insane boosts you got when you reached a multiple of ten. Much like the way that some of the experience requirements varied from level to level, Xiao had explained it simply as "It is the gods' choice; ask me no more questions, foolish boy." That made me think either she didn't know, or the Baron hadn't told her, as there had to be a reason, surely?

I dismissed that train of thought, simply reveling in the fact that, at level twenty, I'd gained twenty points and seven more for each level I'd passed. Add that to the fact that I'd been so carried away with what had been happening earlier, and I'd not assigned the seven points I'd already got, not to mention the bonus two I got to Wisdom and to Intelligence from Jenae each level, and…

"WHAT THE EVERLIVING FUCK?" I snarled, glaring at the damning details that hovered before me.

"JENAE?!" I called out, a mixture of fury and horror filling my mental voice, and I heard the sigh that echoed back from the Goddess of Fire.

"It's time we had a talk, Jax."

CHAPTER THIRTY-THREE

"**U**h, yeah! What the hell happened? I thought I was getting an extra plus two points to my Intelligence and Wisdom every level since I became your champion?!" I half asked, half screamed into the void between worlds that separated us.

"Yes, well, I tried to speak to you about this a little while ago, but you were short on time. Okay, look, Jax, there's no easy way to tell you this, but the simple truth is that I'm barely holding on.

"Most of my struggles wouldn't make sense to you even if I could explain them, but in this realm, I am being hunted. That bitch Illoth knows I'm back and seems intent on finding me. I named you my Champion twice over. The first time, I named you my Champion as a title, not a class.

"The second time, I changed your class to Champion so that I could award you further bonuses, and specifically the ability to Seek That Which Is Hidden. Essentially, we did this twice; the first time, it was the only way I could save your life after you'd torn your brain open. The second was what I'd always intended to grant you."

"So, what, you forgot to add in the points?" I asked her incredulously. "Because, let me tell you, Jenae, your aura of divine infallibility is looking pretty shitty right now."

"Jax," Jenae said, a clear warning in her voice.

I tried to calm myself down, feeling my rising anger warring with my determination to show her the respect she was due.

"Look, I'm sorry, your goddessness. Truly, I don't mean to be disrespectful here, but you forgot to award me quests in the past, then you forget to award me the bonuses you promised, and now you're saying that you, what? You never meant to award them, and it was a cockup?"

"No, Jax. It was something I had to do to save your life; you know, just like when I had to step in and enhance Nerin's spells to save you then, as well." Jenae let out a growl of frustration. *"If I could give you both, I would, but I'm barely surviving here myself, and that's because I keep intervening to help you, you know, like WARNING YOU ABOUT THE SHIPS!"*

We both paused for several long seconds, shocked by the anger and volume she'd used to make her point. I felt a burgeoning headache from the echo alone.

"Jax, I'm trying to help you here, because I'm well aware that my brethren and I need you, and you need us. I named you my Champion twice over, and that's cost me more than I can pay, so this is how this will have to go from now on. I'm leaving the Champion title, but I'm modifying it, as I cannot afford to give you what I promised.

"Instead, I've been giving you far more incidental help than I ever have anyone, bar Amon himself, and then, I was at the height of my power. I'll leave the ten percent experience gain, and I'll honor the random spellbook or blueprint, but I cannot give you the Intelligence or Wisdom points I promised. I'm sorry."

"No, Jenae," I said, sighing. *"I'm the one who should be apologizing. I was shocked when I saw it. I hadn't realized I wasn't getting those points, and to be fair, I know I could fix that myself with my new influx, so it is what it is. I am sorry for yelling at you, though."*

"One day, I will find a way to show you my reality in a way that you will be able to understand, but for now, please understand that if I could grant you those points, and more, I would. For now, please, I need more devotion, and I need it quickly. Illoth is far more powerful than I am at this stage, and my only hope is in escape and evasion. Beware, as I have no doubt she is hunting you as well."

"I'll get everyone sworn to you and your kin when I get to the tower, Jenae. Two days, three at most, I hope. Can you survive that long?"

"I will have to but knowing that is coming helps; thank you."

Jenae's presence receded, and I let out a deep breath, shaking my head in frustration and irritation. I was angry still. Gods, I was furious. What kind of a god gave out rewards then went back on them? But, I had to admit to myself that Jenae stepped in occasionally, like when I'd ripped the goddamn Valspar out of myself, and to tell me about the cache in the Vault here…and…yeah, to warn me about the ships closing on my fleet, all while being hunted herself.

So, I was basically being a little bitch and whining that I wanted frosting on the top of the cake and threatening to have a meltdown rather than enjoying the party.

I shook myself and sighed, scrubbing my face with my hands. I still had a fuck-ton of points to allocate, and a very short time to do it in before the fight started. If I expected to live through this, I needed to go balls-deep, and in the words of the great Lloyd Bridges, I'd picked the wrong week to stop sniffing glue.

I pulled up my character sheet and looked it over quickly, glancing from one section to the next and thinking hard. Eventually, I nodded to myself in satisfaction. I needed to start thinking more strategically, as I also had a meridian node available and several essence cores…I quickly sorted through my bags and pockets, spilling them out on the desk by my side, acutely aware that I was running out of time.

Fire Elemental Essence Core		Further Description *Yes/No*	
Details:		This essence core was taken from a fire elemental and contains the last remnants of the eons-old creature summoned to this plane. Holding the core makes you feel slightly energized and confident.	
Rarity:	Magical:	Durability:	Charge:
Rare	Yes	96/100	N/A

Air Elemental Essence Core		Further Description *Yes/No*	
Details:		This essence core was taken from an air elemental. This creature had wandered the mountains for many years, and holding the core gives you a feeling of peace. Visions of the high places of the realm fill your mind, where the air is thin, cold, and crisp.	
Rarity:	**Magical:**	**Durability:**	**Charge:**
Rare	Yes	97/100	N/A

Oculai Greater Essence Core		Further Description *Yes/No*	
Details:		This essence core was taken from an Oculai that called itself the Skyking. Due to the age of the Oculai and its latent abilities, this core is classed as a greater core, increasing the standard gains by 25%. The core gives you a feeling of distrust and a crawling, itching feeling on the back of your neck, as though you are being watched.	
Rarity:	**Magical:**	**Durability:**	**Charge:**
Legendary	Yes	98/100	N/A

Drider Essence Core		Further Description *Yes/No*	
Details:		This essence core was taken from a Drider, a sentient hybrid of drow and spider, grown to terrible proportions and unleashed on the world to wreak havoc in Illoth's name. The core gives you a feeling of simmering hatred for all living things.	
Rarity:	**Magical:**	**Durability:**	**Charge:**
Rare	Yes	99/100	N/A

As soon as I'd read over the options from the cores I had, I quickly brought up the details on the slots, knowing I could choose to either slot one of the essence cores in, or I could bind the node and improve myself without the yin and yang of the gains and losses that the various cores would inflict on me.

PRIMARY

Brain: 1/10 Spell Cost Reduction: -5% (Primary Bonus: 1 spell slot per point)
Head: Primary Node: Additional points invested will reduce mana cost by 5%.

SECONDARY

Eyes: 1/10 Vision Improvement (Secondary Bonus: x10% chance to notice important visual details)
Eyes: Important details will glow to your vision. This will level with the relevant skill.

Ears: 0/10 Hearing Improvement
Ears: Important sounds will become clearer with concentration. High levels will aid in translation.

Mouth: 0/10 Vocal Improvement
Mouth: Your voice will become 10% more likely to have a desired effect on a target, soothing, seducing, or persuading as required.

Nose: 0/10 Tracking and Detection Improvement
Nose: Scents will be stronger, aiding in tracking.

Heart: 1/10 Health Increase
Heart: You will gain an additional ten points of health for each point invested in your Constitution.

Lungs: 1/10 Stamina Increase
Lungs: You will gain an additional ten points of stamina for each point invested in your Endurance.

Stomach: 0/10 Sustenance Improvement
Stomach: You will gain the abilities to resist poisons by 5% and to gain sustenance from more sources.

Legs: 0/10 Speed Increase
Legs: You will gain a boost of 10% to your speed, as well as better stability over various terrain.

Arms: 0/10 Strength Increase
Arms: You will receive a boost of 25% to your carrying capacity and your damage output with melee weapons.

Hands: 0/10 Dexterity Increase
Hands: You will develop crafting abilities at a 10% increased rate, along with a greater chance to succeed in crafting complicated items.

I was tempted to assign my point to so many places straight away; hell, with the way my fights had been going of late, being able to double my health or stamina was practically a no-brainer, not to mention the idea of dropping all my spell costs by five percent if I hit it into my brain.

The more I thought about the nodes, the more certain I was that there wasn't a bad choice to be made. I wanted them all, goddammit, especially considering that, if I slammed it into my arms four times over, I'd gain a hundred percent damage increase with any melee weapon. I mean, seriously, I spent my life on the front lines…

I shook myself back into focus and brought up the options for adding in the essence cores. Figuring I needed to move fast, I compared the abilities they would grant first.

You have found a Fire Elemental Essence Core.

You have the capacity to absorb this core, gaining the following abilities:

> **Soul of the Fire**: You can channel your soul fire into an external weapon or item, doing 10-25 damage per second with it.
>
> **Cost:** 10 mana +10 health per second.
>
> **Flaming Desire**: You can use your internal heat to inflame those around you, driving the innocent to guilty pleasures and the guilty to new heights of depravity.
>
> **Cost:** 10 mana +10 mana per second.

*

You have found an Air Elemental Essence Core.

You have the capacity to absorb this core, gaining the following abilities:

> **Soaring Majesty**: You can burn your health and mana to achieve flight, inspiring all those around you to reach for new heights of their own as you literally ascend to the heavens.
>
> **Cost:** 10 mana +10 health per second, scaling by 1.5x with your speed, starting with that of a running horse.
>
> **Peace**: You embody a sense of calm, radiating it out to envelop those around you, granting and gaining boosts to health and mana regeneration while meditating.
>
> **Cost:** 10 mana +10 health per hour.

*

You have found a Greater Oculai Essence Core.

You have the capacity to absorb this core, gaining the following abilities:

> **Seething Hatred**: You are filled with a powerful and undeniable hatred for the lesser beings around you, and this manifests itself through the power of your gaze. Paralyze a single opponent within 100m with your stare, doing 20 points of damage per second you maintain contact, but beware, you are also locked in place using this ability, and your innate paranoia grows with every second, as the sure and certain knowledge grows of the knives in the dark inching closer.
>
> **Cost:** 10 mana per second
>
> **Hunger:** Your hunger for all things is legendary, from flesh to knowledge, all must be consumed. Gain 25% faster skill growth permanently.
>
> **Cost:** 1 point of Agility and Charisma is lost permanently per level gained.

*

You have found a Drider Essence Core.

You have the capacity to absorb this core, gaining the following abilities:

Stealthy Ascension: Your hands and feet when uncovered can extrude tiny barbs that enable stealthy travel across the walls and ceiling as easily as floors, but beware, human flesh was never meant to bear such weight!

Cost: 10 mana +10 health per second.

Vampiric Feeding: When you attack a foe that is unaware, you have a chance to activate Vampiric Feeding, allowing you to paralyze then siphon their health and mana for so long as your fangs are embedded in their flesh. You gain 5 points of health and mana from your target per second, rising by 50% with every second that passes.

Cost: 5 mana +5 health per second.

I read through them at speed, dismissing the Drider out of hand, and after a few seconds, the Oculai core as well. As much as I'd love to gain the abilities, I just couldn't afford the side effects. I pulled up the air elemental essence core and reconsidered the bonuses and negatives, quickly followed by the fire elemental.

**This Air Elemental Essence Core can be located in
one of the following Nodesfor the corresponding bonus:**

Head: *(Alongside Primary Node)*: Increase in mana regeneration by 50%, self-control decreased by 5%.

Eyes: *(Alongside Secondary Node)*: Eagle Eyes ability gained, allowing you to sharpen your vision, zooming in by up to 25 times your regular capacity, but you suffer a 50% reduction in DarkVision's range.

Ears: You can hear sounds over a greater distance, but you cannot focus in on such sounds as easily, transforming the world into a confusing cacophony of sounds until you learn to parse it out.

Nose: You lose all sense of smell.

Mouth: Your voice will travel further, carried on the winds of fate to reach those you desire, 5-mile maximum range added to your whispering voice, but "shouting" over such a distance has its issues. After using this ability, you will be unable to speak again for 6 hours.

Heart: Your heart grows stronger, increasing your health by 5 points per point invested, but at lower elevations, your health regeneration is halved.

Lungs: You gain increased stamina regeneration at a rate of 50% when in clear air, minus 50% when in unclean air.

Stomach: Digestion will be quicker and easier, but less pleasant for those around you, for various reasons.

Legs: you gain a 20% speed boost at higher elevations but at lower elevations your speed is decreased by 20%.

Feet: You gain astounding balance and are much harder to knock down, but easier to injure.

Arms: You gain a 20% increase in speed of attacks and defense, but a 10% reduction in carry weight and damage dealt with melee weapons.

Hands: You gain the ability to guide the air, increasing your accuracy with ranged weapons by 25%, but when using this skill become hyper-focused and may lose awareness of your surroundings.

*

This Fire Elemental Essence Core can be located in one of the following Nodesfor the corresponding bonus:

Head: *(Alongside Primary Node)*: Increase in skill gain of 15%, but more easily distracted.

Eyes: *(Alongside Secondary Node)*: Increased reading and comprehension speed by 20%, important passages will be highlighted to your eyes, but concepts that bore you become far harder to focus on.

Ears: You can locate heat in all its forms by sound alone, increasing your hearing range by a factor of 3, but the sounds of fire are magnified to overwhelming levels.

Nose: You can identify flammable ingredients and substances at an almost instinctual level.

Mouth: Your latent draconic ability is augmented, bringing it to the fore far earlier than should be possible, but using such an ability will injure you almost as much as your foes. 10-10,000 damage per second

Heart: Your heart is filled with fire, both figuratively and literally, doubling your health gained per level, but shortening your lifespan to that of a normal human.

Lungs: You can breathe in any temperature, but lower levels of heat result in lower energy and reactions.

Stomach: You can now feed on flammable substances, gaining boosts to your metabolism, but this may have distressing side effects, depending on the substance consumed.

Legs: You gain short-term boosts to speed when needed, but will suffer later for invoking this, with damaged muscles that require healing to reach their full capacity again.

Feet: You can absorb heat to reduce pain throughout the body, by standing in flames, but the damage incurred to your equipment will be normal.

Arms: You gain a 5% increase to damage dealt due to flames that are permanently in motion across your skin but can expect this to injure those who are too close, be they friend or foe.

Hands: You increase your crafting skills at an increased rate of 10% per hour, but increased heat causes its own issues with certain crafts.

I read and reread them quickly, seeing the positives and negatives of both, and I knew what I had to do. It would be both cool as fuck, and a royal pain in the ass, but I didn't see any realistic way I could choose anything else, not with the way things were going right now. However, I did resolve to look into the draconic ability later.

I made my choice, accepting the air elemental essence core, and selecting the location as my head. The tiny filaments that had burrowed out of my flesh, worming their way through the chinks and links of my gauntlet to interface with the essence core, began to consume it, tearing the essence from the core and drawing it into me, and I shuddered at the alien feeling.

I could feel the foreign essence sliding along inside of me, heading for my brain, and I gritted my teeth, pulling my character sheet up again and slamming points in. I had only seconds before I probably lost consciousness, and I was determined to get it all done as quickly as possible.

Doing this right before a battle was a hell of a risk, but it had to be done. Plus, I'd been thinking a lot of late, and with the massive increase to my mana regeneration, literally jumping from one point seven five recently to nearly six point five points a minute, it meant that I could afford to actually build myself the way I should for the life I now led.

I took the forty-one points and put eight points into Endurance, jumping it from a base of thirty-five to forty-three and making my stamina level out at eight hundred and sixty. Seven points went into Perception, jumping it from twenty-nine to thirty-six, leaving me with twenty-six points to use.

I put six points into my Constitution, pushing that from thirty-eight to forty-four and boosting my health to eight hundred and sixty. That left me twenty points, all of which I slammed into Dexterity, taking me from thirty-seven to fifty-seven.

I'd spent the last few weeks and months fighting the same way, but when I'd first arrived, I'd been alone, so I'd made Bob to be a tank for me. God, I missed his bony bonce.

I'd finally concluded that I just couldn't step back and let someone else take the hits for me, though, so I'd basically become a tank hybrid. I wore medium scout armor for the legion, and I fought head to head, but I blended magic and melee to the best of my abilities, using the one thing I'd always had in abundance.

Sheer, unbridled aggression.

I felt the essence approaching my head and accepted my choices, praying that I'd recover in time.

Name: Jax Amon				
Titles: Strategos: 5% boost to damage resistance, Fortifier: 5% boost to defensive structure integrity, Champion of Jenae: One search for hidden knowledge every 24 hours				
Class: Spellsword > Justicar > Champion of Jenae > Imperial Magekiller > Imperial Justicar			Renown: Imperial Scion, Lord of Dravith	
Level: 22			Progress: 294,894/455,000	
Patron: Jenae, Goddess of Fire and Exploration			Points to Distribute: 0 Meridian Points to Invest: 0	
Stat	Current points	Description	Effect	Progress to next level
Agility	43	Governs dodge and movement.	+330% maximum movement speed and reflexes, (+10% movement in darkness, -20% movement in daylight)	88/100
Charisma	26 (21)	Governs likely success to charm, seduce, or threaten	+160% success in interactions involving other beings	91/100
Constitution	49 (44)	Governs health and health regeneration	960 health, regen 64.35 points per 600 seconds, (+10% regen due to soul bond, -20 health due to soul bond, each point invested now worth 20 health)	81/100
Dexterity	57	Governs ability with weapons and crafting success	+470% to weapon proficiency, +47% to the chances of crafting success	7/100
Endurance	46 (43)	Governs stamina and stamina regeneration	920 stamina, regen 36 points per 30 seconds, (each point now worth 20 stamina)	51/100
Intelligence	58	Governs base mana and number of spells able to be learned	560 mana, spell capacity: 32 (30 + 2 from items), (-20 mana due to soul bond)	36/100
Luck	23	Governs overall chance of bonuses	+13% chance of a favorable outcome	53/100
Perception	41 (36)	Governs ranged damage and chance to spot traps or hidden items	+310% ranged damage, +31% chance to spot traps or hidden items	9/100
Strength	34 (31)	Governs damage with melee weapons and carrying capacity	+24 damage with melee weapons, +240% maximum carrying capacity	15/100
Wisdom	43 (33)	Governs mana regeneration and memory	+495% mana recovery, 6.45 points per minute, 330% more likely to remember things, (+50% increased mana regeneration from essence core)	56/100

CHAPTER THIRTY-FOUR

I came to on the floor with Jian crouched next to me, one hand under my head, the other trying to slide something soft under it. I blinked, trying to make sense of what had happened as the world crashed in around me.

I jerked upright as an enormous *BOOM* went off practically inside the room, screeches of terror ringing from a gaggle of gnomes who were all trying to hide under the bed in the back.

I shook my head as I realized that they'd managed to lift it off its restraints, and it was now balanced precariously on the pile as they all tried to crowd deeper under it. Unperturbed, Jian let out a sigh of relief.

I twisted around, seeing him and the rest of the room, and the world came back into focus.

"Jian!" I grunted in shock. "Who's flying—" I started to ask, as Jian grinned at me, and Tenandra spoke up.

"I am now integrated sufficiently to assume control of the ship's functions, Lord Jax," she said calmly. I twisted around farther to see her standing on the control console, legs braced apart and staring straight ahead, in classic "How to be a Ship's Captain" style.

She wore her navy-blue suit and glittering buttons, the blouse so white it almost hurt to look at it, and her fox like ears and tail flicked nonchalantly as she passively made sure I was watching how gracefully she managed the ship.

"So, you don't need Jian?" I asked her.

"He is useful, but no longer necessary," she replied with a shrug.

"Status, Number One," I muttered, accepting the hand Jian offered and letting him haul me to my feet. I noticed that nobody got the joke, and I tried again. "What the hell happened after I put my points into place?" I asked the pair of them, getting a look of surprise from Jian.

"Is that what you did? You apparently grabbed your head, screamed something about spiders under your skin, and collapsed!"

"I...uh...no time for that now. How long?" I asked again, frowning at him, and he shook his head.

"It's okay. You were only out for twenty minutes, that's all. They're still out there, but we're keeping them at a distance," he said, as another rush of wind and rain buffeted the ship, causing it to roll slightly before righting itself.

"Thank fuck." I grunted. "Jian, you're not needed out there for now, so stay and help Tenandra. You're still the pilot; Tenandra is there to work with you. Now, I need to get out and deal with those fuckers." I flexed my fingers and rolled my shoulders, the feeling of being a stranger in my own skin slowly settling down.

I walked unsteadily to the door, shoving it aside as I went out, my naginata helping to brace my steps as I grew more accustomed to my improved body. I slammed the door closed and looked around the deck, seeing a small group of the hardiest gnomes working frantically from under Grizz's Iceshield spell.

I nodded in approval as I watched the rain spattering against the outer edge and freeze again, forming a secondary layer that seemed to help, as the normally clear bubble grew misty and opaque, hiding the windswept outside world from them.

I stomped across the deck, occasionally slipping slightly from the moss and fungus that coated it, but more and more, the storm-driven wind and rain was scouring the deck clean, exposing the original ship again.

"Jax!" Yen called, making her way over to the railing and reaching down to take my hand and help me up onto the upper deck. "You look like shit!" she shouted above the howling wind.

"You too!" I called back and grinned as she snorted in amusement, her armor gleaming as the rain lashed it again and again, running off in rivulets from elbows and pointed sections.

She'd pulled a hooded cloak out of somewhere and wore that over her shoulders and head, but even I could see it was doing little to protect her, as the wind changed direction so frequently, blasting us both from every angle.

"Where's everyone else?" I shouted, seeing she was alone on the upper deck with the enemy ships obscured by a bank of clouds.

"Below decks!" she shouted, then gestured at a rope that disappeared into the deck nearby. "There's a bell on the end, old gnomish trick apparently. All I have to do is yank on it, and they'll come running, no need for everyone to get wet!"

"Nice!" I shouted to her. "How long do we have?"

"Not long!" She tried pulling her hood around to make it block more of the wind-driven rain that was getting to her even inside her helmet before she gave up and yanked it off, rolling it up and dumping it into her bag. "The gnomes are halfway. They say they should be done with the outside stuff soon, then they can start on the inside."

"There's a gang of them hiding in the damn wheelhouse..." I growled.

"There's not a lot they can do there now. They made the connectors; Frederikk says they can't do more until the outside is done, and they'd be useless anyway. Fear makes for shitty inventing, apparently," Yen shouted, holding a hand up to block the rain for a few seconds, before shaking her head in frustration. "This goddamn rain! It's coming from every angle!"

"Joys of a storm, I guess!" I shouted, hearing my voice carry farther than I intended as we passed out a band of the rain and wind, into a sudden quiet patch. I looked around, the lashing rain dropping to a gentle patter as I shook my head at the madness of a mana-filled storm.

"It does this," Yen said at a more normal volume, pulling her helm off and producing a cloth from her bag to wipe the inside and to dry her face. "One minute, it's all madness, the next it's a summer shower. Remind me to never do this again, okay?"

"Yeah, me too," I said to her, grinning as she looked over the helm.

"Is that the one you took from the Vault?" she asked, and I pulled it off and handed it over for her to examine. It felt peculiar with the sudden loss of the five points in Wisdom and Perception, but I knew I'd get them back when I put the helm back on.

"Nice," she said simply, turning it over in her hands. It was a full-head helm, with a small section cut free for each eye, creating a reinforced forehead that I was going to use to fuck up someone's day, and a small section removed in lower mouth, where the helm came down to a point. There was a small line cut out to aid breathing, but it was too narrow for almost any weapons. The entire helm was molded to follow the contours of the face, and it fit…amazingly. Like it was made for me.

The final crowning glory was the plume. I'd never wanted one before; they looked like they were basically there to sweep the ceiling clear of cobwebs normally, but this one was different. It was made from thousands of tiny spines, razor-sharp, and seemed to shift in color, depending on my location. They dimmed when in shadow, glowed in sunlight, and generally looked awesome.

Yen passed it back with a smile and nodded as I slid it back on, blinking as the effect took hold again.

"It suits you," she said.

"Thanks, Yen," I said, smiling, even though she couldn't see it. "So, some of the gnomes are working under Grizz's shield; what about the others?"

"The bravest amongst them are out on the hull, fixing the collectors into place now, and we're all just waiting, really. Those assholes chasing us closed the distance a few times, but never for long, even with the change in direction, so we're slowly pulling ahead again. They don't seem greatly confident with their ship's weapons, or they'd have shot us down long since."

"Oren told me once that they tend to explode when they're used too frequently," I said, nodding and thinking about how crazy you'd have to be to willingly carry a weapon that had a good chance of exploding and killing you instead of the enemy each time you tried to use it.

"I've heard that, but nobody was going to waste the gold and platinum on giving things like that to the legion," she said philosophically, searching out into the clouds.

"Well, that's a thing of the past, isn't it?" I said, grinning. "Just wait until the battleship is finished. We'll get the damn cannons figured out and make sure they're safe to use, then…"

"Where are they?" she muttered absently, gesturing outwards. "They should be coming out of the clouds by now."

"What?" I asked, frowning.

"The ships; they should have been there. I mean, they took forever to adjust to our new course, and they stopped firing at us, so maybe they're too low on mana now, but even so, I didn't think they would just give up?" Yen muttered, searching the skies around us.

"How long since you've seen them do anything?" I asked her, my stomach clenching in fear.

"What?" she asked, confused.

"How long since they did anything?" I repeated. "When I came up, I caught a glimpse of them, but everyone was standing still. Even the catapult was half-assembled."

"They've been like that for a while," she muttered before gaping at me in horror as she made the same connections I just had.

"It's a spell!" I snarled, rushing to the rope, and yanking on it, hearing a bell ring faintly below us. "Tell Jian to change course!" I snapped at her, and Yen sprinted for the edge of the upper deck, leaping off and twisting her body to land facing the door inside.

I ran to the edge of the deck, looking down, as the deck hatches were thrown back, revealing my team hurrying upwards.

"Grizz!" I shouted, waving my own good arm frantically, but seeing nothing in response from the now heavily opaque shield over the gnomes. "Fuck! Stephanos, get Grizz!" I shouted at him as the big man clambered out onto the deck. He saw where I was pointing and started running, even as the ship lurched to one side, the engines all firing seconds after Yen made it inside the wheelhouse.

The others were spreading out, confused as they looked around for the enemy. I whirled in place, trying to watch in all directions at once, while praying I was wrong, and that I'd only wasted some of our last mana reserves...

"There!" Miren screamed, and I spun, following her pointing finger.

At first, I didn't see what she meant; then the wind gusted harder, blowing some of the cloud cover along, and an entire patch of clouds moved wrong, slower, trying to match the air around them.

"Fire!" I screamed, frantically swapping my naginata to rest against my left side in the crook of that arm, as I freed my right hand for casting.

Seconds passed as everyone realized what I'd seen in a horrified moment of clarity.

They'd hidden behind an illusion once already, sneaking up on us...now they'd done it again, leaving an illusory force lagging behind while they'd burned mana hard to catch up.

There was a heavy *twang* of Miren firing her Drow bow, followed a second later by Stephanos, who'd finally gotten Grizz's attention. Then I hurled my Fireball at the blur, and Arrin launched his Magic Missiles. Yen rushed out onto the deck and started to cast, and Grizz started running towards me.

Just before my Fireball would have reached the illusion, it was pierced by the arrows, making the spell warp, trying to match the arrows in flight. Then it broke, shattering into a thousand fragments of illusory cloud before fading away, revealing three of the ships, the two cruisers and the black one, all well within range now.

Once they realized the spell had been disrupted, the soldiers on the black ship let out a roar of bloodlust, and the catapult fired with a deep clunk and whoosh of release as the arm slammed forward, a black mass flying towards us.

The first shot passed the side of the ship in a buzzing, screaming mess, disintegrating to the left as we frantically turned aside, only to see it breaking down into dozens of DarkSpore that flew at us.

"Here!" I screamed down to Grizz, throwing him my naginata and seeing the wide smile on his face as he caught it.

I reached into my bag and yanked out one of the black vampiric swords, glancing at it and seeing it was the health leaching one, I ordered the others to stay clear of the upper deck as I started to cast Cleansing Fire, determined to keep as wide a space clear as possible.

I'd almost completed it when the first of the DarkSpore hit us, and they were hit in turn. Miren and Stephanos basically ignored them, trusting in the others to keep them safe as they worked to pick off soldiers and sailors on the ships chasing us, their summoned creatures by their sides protecting their backs.

The world dissolved into a confusing maelstrom of magic and blurring steel. We fought to keep the gnomes safe as they finished the last sections of the collectors on the deck, then a scream echoed up from below, and I cursed.

"Grizz, Jian! Get below and sweep for DarkSpore!" I shouted, having seen Jian appear on the deck, leaving Tenandra to fly in his place. I threw the sword down to him, and he dropped his scythes to catch it, understanding the need to use a magical blade instead of a normal one.

As he and Grizz rushed for the hatches, the catapult fired again, and more DarkSpore came screaming towards us. At that moment, Yen finished her incantation and heaved her arms forward, a pair of hastily conjured Flamespears flashing through the air to slam into a shield over the catapult.

It flared black then faded into invisibility again, the mana coursing down the shield to sink into the deck and making the ship surge forward slightly.

"They've got better mages than us." I grunted to myself as the Cleansing Fire spell rolled out, covering the upper deck and setting the first DarkSpore that reached it alight.

I yanked the mana-stealing sword out and stabbed the screeching, buzzing mass, killing it. Ten mana flowed into me through the sword, even as ten health was torn out, quickly recovered by the spell I straddled.

Two more DarkSpore flew at me, each dying as quickly as the last. Suddenly, I was blasted from my feet, a black and green Fireball slamming into the deck behind me.

I sailed through the air, hitting the railing and tumbling over, falling from the ship with scream as the black ship cut across our wake. Three mages on her deck were throwing spells at us that I only now realized were the main attack.

The DarkSpore were a goddamn diversion!

I tumbled end over end, panic making me freeze up, a hasty wish that there was something I could have done, some way I could have a second try at that fight, a way to NOT BE FALLING TO MY GODDAMN DEATH.

Then it hit me, and I reached out, activating my newly gained ability.

It felt strange as I picked up speed, tumbling even more wildly, but as I looked up, the world flashing past, and I locked my gaze on the underside of the black ship. I growled, feeling the wind around me and clutching the threads of air wrapping gently but firmly around my body as my descent reversed, and I blasted back upwards, glorying in the feel of flight.

I was unsteady, clumsy, and closing on the underside of the hull far too fast, but as I drew back with my sword, I forced more speed from myself, rather than less, while I twisted to the side.

I erupted into the air from below the enemy ship, flipped over into a dive, and blasted straight for the upper deck, where three men stood around the helmsman.

I cut the power to my ability, feeling gravity reach out to grasp me again, and I landed, skidding and sliding across the deck, before jumping and slamming both feet into the shield of the man on the right, who gaped at me in shock.

I used it as a springboard, leaping backward, all my inertia transferring to him as he flew back. His waist hit the railing at the back of the deck and sent him flipping over it then vanishing upside down over the side with a scream.

I spun then, lashing out with my sword and was amazed by the ease and sudden grace I had with the weapon. The leap in my Dexterity was obviously coming to play as I lopped the hand off a man who pointed towards me, sending it and the mace it grasped flying, before I crouched low into a spin-kick that had a fluidity my old instructors would have praised to their dying day.

My foot connected with the second man's chin, staggering him as I straightened up and stabbed out. The tip of the blade punched into the helmsman's sternum and cleaved his heart in two.

The third and final man on the deck scowled at me then dove aside, rolling to his feet and counterattacking with blinding speed. The deck lurched out of control beneath us, sending the entire crew staggering.

I jumped back, rolling my wrist to bring my sword around and parrying his. He grunted, then stabbed out again, and again, driving me back, while he used his shield to deflect my sword. I scrambled backward, then growled to myself and lunged at him, striking at his blade, driving it down, then swinging low and up, managing to draw the tip of my blade across his upper thigh.

He screeched and…blurred.

As his blood sprayed out, his skin changed, becoming sallow and grey, his face lengthening, and his straw-like blond hair deepening to black, I slowed momentarily, shocked at the transformation, and he punched out with his shield, driving me back and almost making me lose my sword.

I yanked my shield around, only to have him slam his sword down into it, hard, splitting the outer covering and making me grunt as it dragged my arm down with it.

"You think you can win, human?" The suddenly revealed drow before me asked in a low, fury-filled hiss. "The Dark Lady has decreed your death; now feel her hatred!"

He opened his mouth and drew in a deep breath, glaring at me in spite and triumph, as something black at the back of his throat wriggled into view.

Multiple legs thrashed as they dragged a bulbous body forward, and I freaked out. I lashed out hard against his shield, yanking my own up to block his sword, and lunged, bringing my helm down with all the force I could manage.

He was just out of what would have been my range for a headbutt, normally, but he fell nicely inside my new one, with the spiked plumes that now ran down from the crest of my helmet.

I tore a line down the center of his face, tearing apart his nose and shredding his lips, as well as cutting the summoned spider in his mouth that he'd planned to spit at me into mincemeat, making him scream in horror as his face was torn apart.

I yanked my head back up, still pushed forward, and literally tore the rest of his face apart. As I straightened, he collapsed mewling to the floor. I stabbed down with my sword, driving the blade through his throat and carving a furrow into the wooden deck below.

I spun around, seeing the crew racing for me. Within the concealment of my helm, I grinned, turning back and taking three quick steps before slashing down twice with my sword, carving great chunks from the wheel and shattering several of the control crystals.

The ship immediately twisted on itself, turning in a tight right-handed spiral. I kicked off from the deck, soaring away, even as spells and arrows flew in all directions as the crew tried to take me down.

I'd not done enough to destroy the ship, but maybe…

I screamed as something slammed into my right leg and pain ripped through me. I looked down and saw a large man…no, a large *drow*, clinging to me and grinning up at me, even as he drove another dagger into my left leg, using them as handholds to climb up me.

I slashed down at him with my sword, and he twisted, spinning his body around and leaping to change his grip on the daggers, switching to hanging on behind me, rather than in front.

I kicked feebly at him, notifications flashing for my attention as I felt my legs weakening. Driving myself up into the air even faster, I flipped over and dove towards our ship, seeing the deck coming up at tremendous speed.

I couldn't land gently, not now; hell, I'd never be able to stand, not with the damage this fucker had done to me, but…my Cleansing Fire spell!

I saw it on the top deck, guttering out, and was amazed as I realized only a few minutes could have passed. I focused on it as I tore through the air and reached out, frantically slamming mana into it and feeling the resistance as I tried to do something I'd never done before.

The spell failed as fast as I reached out, and I frantically rebuilt it, feeling my mana torn from me as I poured it into the structure of the spell, feeling it change as my mana poured out like water onto sand.

In the last seconds before I hit the deck, I glared at it, pushing even harder and forcing myself to ignore the pain of the drow clinging to me as he ripped a dagger free and sank it into the small of my back, right where the armor ended.

I screamed, the spell flared with gold and red light…and the world went black as I hit, slamming hard into the upper deck of the *Interesting Endeavor*.

CHAPTER THIRTY-FIVE

The world returned slowly, sound coming first, almost beaten by the pain that followed. The booms and screams, the whir of arrows slicing the air, and the whoosh of spells hurtling back and forth surrounded me, even as someone shouted my name a thousand and more miles away.

I forced one eye open, finding the other one gummed shut with blood, and I twitched a finger on my right hand as I tried to focus.

The world slowly came back to me, as did memory, making sense of what I saw. I lay on my front, the wooden beams and boards that made up the majority of the upper deck cracked and splintered all around me. I could only move my right arm, and even that was sparingly.

I flexed my fingers, seeing them twitching before me and trying to ignore the puddling blood that was growing under them.

I tried to move my legs, arch my back, bring my left arm around, but none of them worked. I felt the left arm still, it just didn't respond, while the right only twitched spasmodically.

I blinked in panic, shifting my jaw and being greeted with a pain like my skull shattering into sharp fragments of glass.

I could see I was losing more of my health bar, and it was flashing that there was a bleed effect, as well as others I didn't recognize. I brought up the relevant notifications as quickly as I could, trying to figure out what had happened, and winced as they bombarded me.

Beware!

**You have been stabbed with a Midnight Helper's Dagger
and have lost all feeling in the affected area.
This effect will remain until the dagger is removed.**

*

Beware!

**You have been stabbed with a Midnight Helper's Dagger
and have lost all feeling in the affected area.
This effect will remain until the dagger is removed.**

*

Beware!

You are Bleeding!

**You lose 5…17…32 points of health per second
until your wounds are closed.**

*

Congratulations!

You have created a new spell: Remote Revival!

Using this spell, you can make a connection to a failing spell at a distance and renew it. Be warned, however: this is an imperfect method, and the cost is significantly higher!

Cost: 50 mana to cast, plus 3x original spell cost.

*

Congratulations!

You have begun healing your wounds!

**Bleed effect has been reduced from 32 points of damage per second
to 4 points of damage per second.**

Please remain in the circle of healing to fully regenerate yourself.

*

Beware!

This spell has run out of mana before you have been fully healed!

Recast or use another method to stop the bleeding quickly!

*

Beware!

You are being fed upon!

You are losing 10 points of health and mana per second.

The last notification was the worst, and I suddenly realized that I could hear another sound as I was shifted slightly. A strong arm levered my left pauldron further out of the way, and I felt the sucking resume as something bit down and drew more of my life from me.

I lay there, paralyzed, filled with fear as my health bar dropped even further, as something fucking *fed* on me. I frantically forced my right hand to make the gestures I needed, even as I sub-vocalized the words, working as quickly as I could.

It was taking forever, and both my mana and my health plummeted before I was roughly dropped onto my front as a scream of fury erupted from whatever had been feeding on me.

I lay there, the sound of running feet and cries of horror and fury filling the air, even as I tried to maintain my focus. I was halfway, and I couldn't afford to start again.

I had just enough left, I hoped, and I kept at it, ignoring the shouts, the screams, and the sound of feet nearby, of weapons clashing and of orders being shouted in an authoritative voice.

I stared at the woodgrain of the plank before me, focusing on the spell and drowning out the rest of the world. The words caught in my throat and being forced out audibly as the last of them came, meant they fell from lips covered in clotting blood and phlegm.

I felt it unroll, and a half second later, the blessed relief of the last of my wounds sealed, of the flames of the spell burning into me, and rooting out any impurities. I coughed, the clotted blood expelling from my throat, and I managed to lift my right hand and place it flat against the floor next to my face.

I took a deep breath and pushed as hard as I could, rolling myself over and onto my back, finding the grey, storm-cloud filled sky above me and the fight that continued amidst the heavy rains all around me.

There were two of them, both facing off against the drow that had attacked me. I managed to tilt my head, seeing Giint and Stephanos driving him back.

Giint was dual wielding a kill-stick and an axe that glowed blue, while Stephanos was using his bow like a staff, both desperate to drive the creature back from me.

I grunted and tried to sit up, coughing up blood and feeling my flames burning the phlegmy gunk from my airways in a hot rush of air that tickled on the way down.

I ignored the flaring mana migraine, suddenly down to the dregs of my mana, thanks to the casting, and I reached out a shaky hand, gripping the dagger in my right leg, and yanking hard enough that I almost passed out.

I heard a boom from nearby and a screech of fury from the drow as the world was lit by a huge Fireball that screamed past us, slamming into the deck of one of the ships that was closing in to board us, and I felt…Oracle!

She was close, and that knowledge alone lifted my heart and soul like nothing else.

I adjusted my grip on the stuck dagger and tried again, this time dragging the right-hand dagger free of my leg, then went for the left. As some feeling returned to the first limb, I reached down, wrapping my fingers around the rough grip and hauling back, tears filling my eyes as the pain flared. I furiously blinked them free, looking up as I heard a shocked gasp, and the fast footsteps of the fight close by all but stopped.

I looked up, the dagger forgotten as Stephanos slowly fell backward, a dagger like the one I now held driven up to the hilt in the center of his chest.

I locked eyes with him as he slowly toppled, his body paralyzed, even as his heart shuddered, pinned by the needle point of the dagger.

"No," I whispered, shock and horror filling me. Giint lunged, only to be kicked aside almost contemptuously by the drow, no match for it.

He turned to me, sneering, and smiled evilly, wiping his mouth, where I could see the sheen of red blood. My blood.

I screamed in fury and did the only thing I could, triggering Soaring Majesty and hurling myself at him.

He caught me as I left the protective circle of my flames, and twisted at the hip, throwing me off the side of the upper deck to crash into the lower, almost making me pass out from the pain of all my wounds flaring at once.

I lay there, stunned, looking up at him in horror as he leaped casually from the upper deck and landed lightly next to me, reaching down to grab me by the throat and drag me upright to hang in the air.

He slowly increased the pressure on my throat as I flailed at my bags, trying to reach a weapon, only to have him contemptuously slap my hand aside each time.

I reached up, making one last attempt as the world started to grow dark, punching at his throat and having my hand smacked away again...before something hit him and sent us both sprawling.

I forced myself to roll back over, coughing and looking up, and my heart surged with hope.

Lydia!

Lydia was alive and conscious!

She was half-dressed, armored to the waist, wearing only a tunic on the top, but she looked by far the healthiest of us all, and she was different. By the gods, she had *changed*, I realized, as great golden wings shimmered in and out of reality on her back. The feathers flared and moved as though blown by a heavenly breeze that I could neither see nor feel.

She wore her shield on her left arm and carried her mace in the right hand, and she fairly glowed with power.

The drow glared at her, then blurred, reaching out with a dagger in either hand, only to have the left smashed free and the right blocked, before Lydia Sparta kicked him in the chest, sending him skidding backwards in a spray of water.

The drow staggered, clearly shocked and unprepared for the counterattack, and Lydia rushed him, her mace and shield flashing.

He dove aside, rolling to his feet, clearly wounded already, and spat on the floor in fury. Hissing angrily, he glared at me and spun around, running for the side of the ship.

He reached it barely ahead of Lydia and leaped, bracing one foot on the edge of the railing and diving out as he ripped something from his belt and snapped it in half. He was suddenly enveloped in a black glow, and he faded from sight, even as he fell.

I laid there in shock, filled with horror at the death of Stephanos, joy at the sight of Lydia upright, and awe of the changes in her, when I felt Oracle reach out to me.

"Jax! I'm here!" That was all she said, but as I looked up, knowing instinctively where she was, a ship rocketed past, and she flew from it. A huge roar of a cannon being fired reminded me of the Fireball from before, and I realized this was the second time I'd seen this ship fire in defense of us.

I reached up one hand weakly, and Lydia was there, crashing down to one knee on the ground nearby and hauling me upright into a hug.

"I thought I was too late!" Lydia said brokenly. "I was for poor Stephanos...I...I..."

"No," I said, hugging her back, hard. "You saved me. I failed him, not you," I whispered, closing my eyes and seeing the look on his face as he fell again and again.

"Our lives for yours," came a voice nearby.

I opened my eyes, seeing Yen as she stepped in close, taking in my damaged body and the glowing wings that even now were furled on Lydia's back.

"It shouldn't have been, but…" I said quietly as Lydia helped me upright, and I looked up, seeing Oracle covering the last dozen meters in a blur.

"But it has to be," Miren said softly from nearby, her tear-streaked face showing she'd seen her friend fall. "Without you, all of this is pointless. He saved you, and he'd never regret that."

"I know," I managed to grunt out, accepting Stephanos's choice and his bravery.

Oracle slammed into me, staggering me back a step, even with her barely corporeal form, with as little mana as I had for her right now.

I felt her as she leaned into me, and I held her as the others gathered around. We looked out, seeing the second cruiser being harried by our savior, and far behind, close to the waves far below, the black ship rocked and fought to stay in the air.

"It's Mal, isn't it," I said quietly.

"Who else?" Oracle whispered, her voice filled with pride and love as she gazed at me. "Who else could, or even would, fly a ship through the heart of a storm to find you?"

"God, he's going to be insufferable," I muttered, shaking my head even as my heart swelled with relief in sharp contrast with the heavy depression that threatened to take me over the loss of my friend.

I cast about the deck, seeing that most of the gnomes were gone, but four arrow-ridden corpses remained, showing that they'd paid even more of a cost for my interference in their lives than they had already.

I looked back, finding Giint as he stumbled down from the upper deck, one hand rubbing at his chest on his way to the central node the other gnomes had been working on.

He fell to his knees, pulling tools out of his bags and going to work. I watched him with a pang of sadness, unsure if they were tears or rainwater that dripped from his chin and nose.

Leaving him to his work, I turned to look over the edge once more, seeing the second cruiser rolling over and diving faster and faster towards the murky waves far below. Mal raked the side of their ship with another shot, tearing the engines free and making two explode.

The ship fell in a barrel roll that picked up speed, figures being thrown from the decks as it fell, until it hit the water with a boom that we heard and felt even over the thunder and lightning of the storm.

I let myself relax as Lydia and Miren were joined by others. They led me back to the wheelhouse, Jian forcing the door and rushing to the controls.

He slipped in and looked over the crystals, seemingly seeing things I couldn't, as I was helped to a seat, bleeding from dozens of minor wounds and running low on health as well as mana.

"Are there any potions?" Oracle asked quietly, and Lydia shook her head, speaking up.

"I don't know."

"I'm here." Arrin grunted, staggering into the room and letting in a wild gust of wind and rain alongside himself. He hurried over to me and hit me with a healing spell, before grunting and clearly being hit with a mana migraine as he bottomed his own reserves out.

I let out a groan of relief as his healing spell closed the last of my open wounds, and I sagged back slightly, drew in a deep breath, and nodded to myself.

It was time to make the most of my new gifts and use the second ability that the air elemental essence core had given me.

I closed my eyes, and began to meditate, activating Peace as I did so. The world seemed quieter, and a light but constant cool breeze picked up, stirring the air around me.

I saw in my mind's eye a plateau, high in the mountains. It was in a small, bowl-shaped valley, surrounded on all sides by higher peaks and walls. But here, the trees swayed gently, and large-footed hares hopped across the sparkling snow. The breeze grew stronger, suddenly carrying a cool, clear, and crisp layer of air around the wheelhouse. I sighed, drawing it deep inside and letting it out.

The air grew cooler still but stopped at the point where cool freshness became true cold, just a few degrees above the level of discomfort. Instead, it seemed to everyone in the room that they were at that perfect temperature, where the body is awake, and the mind is invigorated.

My mana and health regeneration lifted, and I began to construct the box, building it all around me, making the walls, the floor, and ceiling—all of it, in fact—from solidified mountain air, cool and crisp.

My mana dipped and my body began healing, then I buoyed upwards again, building even faster, as Oracle released our shared mana pool.

Several minutes later, I sensed her reaching out to me, and with a palpable sense of regret, I released that meditative mind state.

Most of the squad were gone, either scouring the ship to make sure it was clear of DarkSpore or helping the injured, the rain lessening on the decks outside.

I looked around, finding Jian and Tenandra at their joint station. Lydia stood nearby, watching me with a smile on her face, and Oracle sat in my lap, solid and life-size.

As soon as she saw that I was fully awake, she wrapped her arms around my neck and kissed me, hard, while Lydia laughed and made a comment about waiting outside.

I heard the door close, but I'd missed my love too much to pay too much attention…until she broke off and spoke up.

"That's because I missed you," she said huskily, before slapping me hard enough to make my head ring like a bell. "And that's for sending me away!"

I blinked, trying to see again, as a blinding array of lights filled my vision, and I reached up with my right hand to rub at my jaw.

"What the hell?" I muttered. "And where the hell is my helm?"

"I took it off, obviously," Oracle said, glaring at me. "Now you've some explaining to do, Mister! Starting with where the hell the rest of your arm is!"

"I cut it off," I muttered, rubbing my chin again and wincing. "Seriously, Oracle? Damn, that hurt!"

"It was supposed to!"

"Well—"

"Oh, thank the gods!" Jian said from behind us. I twisted around to look at him. He slumped back on his chair, grinning at Tenandra, who was staying small and trying not to draw Oracle's attention.

"What's happened?" I asked, standing up and walking over. I could feel the phantom aches that were always left behind after a healing; despite knowing I was fully healed, I always felt like I should be limping or whatever.

"Those crazy little bastards did it," Jian said in amazement, pointing to a gently flashing crystal. "That's the ship's mana reserve…and it's climbing."

"Oh, thank fuck," I said, clapping him on the back and grinning. "Well done, Jian, and you too, Tenandra! Fantastic work!"

They both smiled at me, until Oracle moved over to stand by my side and held out her hand, palm up next to Tenandra.

"Well done, Jian! And welcome to the team…Tenandra…Let's quickly get each other up to date on…things," Oracle said, her voice clear and sweet, yet carrying an undeniable threat, much the same as an entire carrier group does when it asks a tugboat to "please move aside." It's a request, but unspoken is the knowledge that they both share. "You can move," it says, "or you can be crushed. I'm only asking to be nice."

"Uh…maybe we should go somewhere else?" Jian asked me quickly, and Oracle fixed us both with a sunny smile.

"That's a great idea; I'll be right out to join you," she chimed sweetly.

"Fine, but don't be long with this. Bane and Tang, hell, half the crew needs our help," I muttered, making sure she understood just how dog-tired and on the edge we all were. Oracle smiled at me again, a sense of reassurance and soothing love flowing through the bond, making me smile at Oracle's possessiveness as I moved to the door, forcing it open and stepping out into the fresh air.

"You forgot this," Jian said quietly, passing me my helm. I put it into my bag with a quiet thanks.

I walked out to where the others stood, looking out over the side of the ship. We stood for long minutes, all in silent contemplation, until Lydia spoke up.

"He was a good man…despite how much he stroked his wood." We all smiled unthinkingly at that, memories of our conversations around the fire as we traveled, about how often he'd oil and rub the drow bow he used.

Stephanos used to comment that it was simple courtesy, looking after the weapon that protected him, but we all ribbed him mercilessly about it, especially because it let us ignore the fact that, for most of citizens of the tower and the continent, touching a bow like that was akin to touching ten times more gold than they'd ever earn in their lifetimes.

"You remember the fight to free Oracle?" I asked the group. "The first time he fired that damn bow, and he fell in love with it on the spot?"

"And how much he played up to the group that it was 'his' but he asked me quietly if I wanted it and offered to wait for another one," Miren said, wiping a stray tear from her cheek.

The others all spoke up, and for a while, we forgot our pain and laughed as Stephanos lived again in our hearts.

CHAPTER THIRTY-SIX

The rest of the day was spent in a blur of healing those who were injured and stabilizing those who needed more in-depth work, like Tang and Bane, before meditating and getting ready for the real healing to begin.

There was also a substantial effort required for carrying out basic repairs on the ship and making sure none of the gnomes fell over the side, as they were all too stoned to walk straight.

I'd agreed when Frederikk had come to me, asking for a bonus, ostensibly for the entire group, but I'd been fine with it.

At this rate, we only had enough "stash" for a few more days, but I was hoping things would calm down for a few weeks, at least. Hopefully, knowing the ingredients as I did, we could figure out how to make more for them. I'd started to get used to their ways, after all.

Once Oracle was finished with her conversation with Tenandra, Jian and I were invited back into the wheelhouse. While he took up his newly-accustomed station at the helm, I moved to the back of the room to start work on Tang, who was now laid on the captain's bed against the rear wall.

Laid *across* the bed would be more accurate, I decided as I looked down on him, half curled up, as he was over six feet tall, and the average gnome was around three feet tall. His legs were folded up uncomfortably, and his neck was at an angle that I just knew was going to leave him in pain, but it was better than the floor.

Oracle looked him over and muttered to herself as she used our new Greater Examination spell in combination with our usual Battlefield Triage spell.

"He's healing well," she said eventually. "I think one more round of healing and rooting out the last of the mold from inside him, and he should wake up. He's lucky you didn't just heal him and leave it at that, though; the infection would have been a nightmare to clean up later."

"I nearly did," I replied. "I was rushing and didn't realize how bad it was at first, but then…well, I nearly did."

"Then let's fix it, shall we?" Oracle said with a wide smile.

"Let's," I said, nodding and settling down next to Oracle. "I'll work on the meditation; you work on the healing."

She agreed, sitting in my lap and reaching out to rest her hand on Tang's forehead.

I sensed the weaves of magic she created as I slipped deeper into my meditation, visualizing the box around me. I activated Peace, and the air around me began to twirl in a faint zephyr that sent Oracle's hair swaying gently.

I worked on it for the next twenty minutes, occasionally losing focus as I sensed the faint tracings of the weaves Oracle used. The fire here that burned away the mold and fragments of wood that were almost too small to see, the water that washed the wounds clean, and every other strain imaginable as she rebuilt Tang's insides.

Eventually, I released it, opening my eyes as I heard Tang let out a faint groan. I smiled and watched him as he tried to shift, then twisted, obviously attempting to get comfy.

That lasted for about two seconds, before his eyes flew wide and he looked about, before falling off the bed entirely.

"Whoa!" he cried, landing on his head, and sliding the rest of the way to the floor as he struggled to turn himself the right way around.

Being the good friend that I am, I sat and watched him, Jian laughing as well, clearly relieved to see Tang back in the land of the living.

"What the hell happened?" Tang growled eventually when he managed to get himself back together and upright.

"We won," I said simply, then let out a sigh. "But we lost Stephanos," I finished sadly.

"No...dammit." He sat down hard on the tiny bed, blanching at the news. "I liked him."

"Me too," I said. "He saved me, and I wasn't fast enough."

I swallowed hard against the lump that had appeared in my throat.

"He saved you?" Tang said slowly, and I nodded. "While I was where...asleep?" His tone dripped with bitterness. "It's my place as your bodyguard to defend you, and Stephanos died because I got a damn splinter...?"

"A splinter that was nearly the size of a damn spear," I exaggerated.

"It was still a splinter," he said morosely. "What about everyone else?"

"They're all good; only Bane is still injured now. Well, and me," I said, gesturing with my stump.

"And Stephanos's body?" he asked, straightening up.

"Lost overboard to the sea. Whoever those ships came from officially, there were Drow aboard them, and they were in command."

"Fuckers!" he spat, and I had to agree with him.

"Yeah, apparently, I'm pretty high on the list of people they want dead," I said, shrugging.

"Believe me, that's a long list," Tang said grimly. He thought in silence for a moment, then met my gaze with steely determination. "There's a settlement of high elves somewhere on the far side of The Knife. I'd bet they'll know where the Drow are coming from, if anyone does."

"The Knife?" I asked, and he blinked before nodding and gesturing toward the distant shore of Dravith.

"The mountain range that runs from north to south along the continent. I don't know what it used to be called, and there's about a dozen names for it now, depending on who you ask. I always liked 'The Knife.' Kinda makes sense, seeing as it cuts down the middle of the continent. Sorry, I'm just used to everyone knowing some things."

"That's fine and yeah, sounds logical," I said. "Where do you think the high elves would be, though, and what makes you think they'd help?"

"They hate the drow, like seriously hate them. I'm a bastard offshoot, as far as the high elves are concerned; there used to be a few different races of elves, but we all started from the 'high' or 'pure' elves. The drow were elves lured away into the darkness by Illoth and seduced, while others moved to the deserts, the woodlands, or the sea, and more.

"The high elves refused to 'water down their bloodline' by intermingling with the other races and established their own exclusive cities on each continent. They're generally purist, stuck-up assholes, but some are all right. If they know where a drow city is, they'll either be raiding it, at war with it, or looking to recruit adventurers to destroy it. Since you're hated by Illoth, they'll at least give you help to fight her."

"And quests, probably," I said, rubbing my chin in thought.

"Oh, hell yes, especially if you bring the gods back. They'll probably even let you into the city, rather than shouting down from atop a wall at you. And that's a hell of an honor," he said sourly.

"You sound like you hate them?" I asked.

He shook his head. "I don't hate them, I just…well, my grandmother was a high elf's daughter. Once her mother's people found out that my great grandmother had fallen in love with a 'low elf,' she was banished. Forbidden to speak to any of her friends or family ever again. My grandmother was twelve at the time.

"She used to tell us tales about the 'City of Light,' and every time she did, she'd cry. Made me want to teach them a lesson, you know? The Cataclysm came not long after she was banished, and my great grandfather died, leaving her alone to raise my grandmother. Eventually, a settlement of low elves took them in, and the rest is history. She never knew if they all survived fine or if they were wiped out. Hell, she'd never tell anyone where the city was, even after they'd done that to her."

"What makes you think they're still around?" I asked.

"Because every so often, a caravan shows up from them, and I know they don't have any airships at the very least, because they bring all sorts of stuff to try to trade for one." He smirked. "The city lords of Himnel and Narkolt both agreed that they'd never sell one under any circumstances, and neither will the gnomes, so…"

"So there's at least four cities out there somewhere that we don't know about, then?" I asked. "The City of Light, the Drow city, the Prometheans and I assume the gnomes have one?"

"The gnomes have a couple of villages way down in the south. Small ones, but protected to an insane degree, from what I heard. But yeah, two cities, at least."

"Well, it gives us a target for the future to open up trading relations if nothing else," I said hopefully.

"Yeah, well, if you ever go, I want a place on the team, okay, boss?" he asked, and I smiled at him.

"Sure, Tang. Now go on; go get some rest or whatever. We need to concentrate on Bane next," I said, standing as Oracle gave Tang a hug and whispered that she was glad he was okay.

We moved below decks then, searching and eventually finding the room that Bane had been dumped in.

He was curled up on the bed—again, a gnome one—but Bane was clearly far more flexible than Tang and had his legs tucked up with his arms wrapped around his knees. He was covered in swaths of bandages, his skin was discolored, and there were swollen areas all over him.

In some places, he had lost a huge amount of skin, while in others, it was blackened and burned almost down to the bone. Still other sections were peeling and raw, with the strange blackness that comes from cell death through extreme cold.

More than half of the tendrils that ringed his head were missing, clearly hacked away in bunches as they'd tried to make him talk.

I looked at him, and I felt like a goddamn terrible friend.

He'd taken all these injuries for me; he'd been scouting ahead, been jumped by that little shit Joshua, then tortured. He'd not told them anything, either. He was a hell of a bodyguard, and I'd find a way to make this up to him, somehow.

I felt Oracle start to use our Greater Examination spell, scanning him and building up a fully populated picture of his body, all the way down to a cellular level.

Then we started work, ignoring the sounds of the gnomes and my team moving around the ship, and the occasional argument between the researchers or Hannimish and my people.

Only once did I have to get involved, and then, when I was interrupted by a shrill complaint so loud that it actually managed to get to me through my meditation. I was so furious, I stormed out of the cabin and literally kicked the door to the adjoining one off its hinges. I hauled one researcher, and Grizz, who'd been on guard at the door of my room, grabbed the other squabbling human. We dragged them both outside and dangled them over the side of the ship, as I seriously considered just letting go.

"I am trying to heal one of my closest friends, who your group tortured to the very fucking edge of death. Each and every goddamn sound you make is making that harder, so give me a single goddamn reason I shouldn't shut you both up right now! *Permanently*!" I screamed at the man who was turning purple in my grip.

"Ah, uh, my Lord Jax," Hannimish attempted to soothe me, standing to one side and having followed us up, rubbing his hands, and licking his lips nervously. "Perhaps…I mean to say…please…"

"You want me to let them live?" I snapped at him, and he nodded quickly. "Then they're your fucking problem! Make them be quiet, and make them useful, or I swear, they can swim from here!" I snarled, yanking the man I held back over the railing and dumping him, gasping and wheezing, on the floor before storming off back to the cabin where I'd left Oracle working on Bane.

"Tempting, wasn't it," I heard Grizz mutter behind me. I snorted my agreement, returning to the cabin, too worried and stressed to speak further.

Healing Bane was easily the most complex series of spells and physical work we'd ever attempted, in part because the specialty of Reconstructor was exactly what was needed here, and that was why we'd had to find Nerin in the first place.

Fortunately, Oracle had learned some things from her, and we had improved our own spells since then, so while we were neither as quick, nor as skilled, as Nerin, we could at least manage the basics.

We stopped for meditation several times over the next few hours, running myself almost dry each time before taking a break. But after three hours, Bane's internal organs were fully repaired.

"How the hell has this taken us so long?" I huffed to Oracle at one point, exhausted.

"More than half of his organs were either dead or dying," she said pointedly. "The rest were damaged in practically every way possible: he had frostbite, severe burns, and had lightning bolts poured into him. His teeth were shattered, and most of his bones fractured, at the least; then in the rapid healing you'd had to do to save his life, you'd basically plastered over the cracks. We've had to rebuild those areas, rebreaking and healing sections, which always takes far longer."

"I know, it just…" I said, gesturing generally.

"It just seems like it should be quicker?" Oracle offered helpfully, and I nodded.

"I've been healed enough times, and it's usually far faster than this."

"It is, because a stab wound, or a broken bone is one injury. Even when you've had dozens of bones broken, beyond that, it's usually been a case of just bruising elsewhere or minor cuts. Here, there wasn't a single part of him that didn't desperately need healing. Believe me, we're doing amazing." She looked at me consideringly. "You know, you've let me take the lead on healing generally, especially in the more complicated situations."

"It's been for the best," I admitted.

"Well, you're not going to learn anything if I keep doing it," she pointed out.

"Wait, what?"

"You're taking over," she said. "Take over Bane's healing, and you'll learn a lot more," she said again, stepping back. "I'll cast the spells, but you guide them; that way, we can still do this despite the…hand…issue."

I grunted but accepted that, yeah, it was probably the best way to do it. I settled down to meditate until I was full again, then used the facilities, which were basically holes that led straight out to the sea far below and resulted in a damn chilly arse, before starting to work on Bane again.

I got comfortable and felt Oracle as she cast the spells—although I didn't feel her in the way I wanted—then she handed the reins over to me somehow, and I started to work.

I sank my senses into Bane's body, starting with the areas around his kidneys, liver, and his other major organs, following the arteries round to each organ, checking and slowly repairing the connecting tissues where needed. I concentrated on repairing the larger injuries first, then moved to smooth the surrounding tissues, relaxing them and soothing away the swelling. That, in turn, reduced the strain on the overall system that was forcing nutrients through the swollen and damaged areas.

Then I moved onto the next section. I rebuilt teeth, coaxing minerals to regrow over the remnants of his old teeth, then smoothed them out and polished them to a gleam.

I soothed nerves and regrew tendrils, and I returned his skin to a glossy black and grey sheen, even as I subtly repaired the patterning of the skin.

Hours passed in a fugue of concentration and focus, stopping only to slip into meditation then back into the fugue state.

I slowly worked him over, going from one area to the next, hour after hour, until I finally finished with him. The last injuries in his brain had hugely concerned me when I found them.

He'd begun to bleed into his brain at some point, but because it was a clear fluid, not blood, and it'd actually served to speed his neural network up tremendously the spell hadn't tried to heal it, and Oracle and I had totally missed it.

Once we found it, we realized why Bane was still unconscious, as every signal sent in his brain was essentially repeating over and over again, rattling around in the mental equivalent of a computer overload.

Oracle helped me with it, and we judged what we thought the problem was, and started to force the substance to be absorbed into Bane's surrounding brain tissue.

It was the most terrifying part of the entire healing, as I was morbidly convinced that, at any second, I was going to erase his mind.

Eleven hours after we began, he finally stirred, and I almost collapsed with relief when he spoke quietly, in a very raspy voice.

"W—water…?" Bane croaked out, and I summoned a fountain right next to the bed for him and helped him roll over to immerse his face in it.

He drank and breathed down the water for several long minutes before leaning back and letting out a sigh of relief.

"Jax?" he asked quietly.

I nodded, knowing he would see it. Just because he didn't have any eyes meant shit to a creature that had evolved for life underwater. His sonar, or worldsense, as he called it, was working again, and I reached out as he held one hand up, grasping his cool, rough appendage in mine.

"Where are we?" he asked.

"At sea. Or over it, anyway. We found the gnomes' ship, and we're headed back to the fleet. We've even got Mal as an escort," I said simply.

"We won?" he asked, and for the second time that day, I had to bite back tears.

"Yes, and no," I said, the pain in my voice clear. "We beat every fucker they threw at us, but Stephanos—" I said, breaking off. "He—"

"He died," Oracle finished softly, taking over from me. "I was still on my way back, and I saw the fight. Stephanos stepped up and protected Jax from a drow, giving him the time to recover, and the drow killed him."

"Are we safe now?" Bane asked quietly, and I nodded.

"As safe as we ever are," I said.

"That good, eh?" he said, a low sub-sonic *thrummm* echoing around the room as I pulled him upright and hugged him.

"Damn glad you made it, mate," I told him quietly, slapping him on the back.

"So am I," he said simply.

"About what happened…" I started awkwardly, releasing him, and stepping back.

"The asshats tortured me, and I imagine you killed them for it?"

I nodded fervently.

"And that prick, Joshua?"

"Oh, he's dead," I said grimly. "I did that one myself."

"Then thank you," Bane said sincerely. "Now, I find I really, really need some food…"

"Ha!" I said, barking out a quick laugh. "Always thinking with your stomach, my friend!" I gestured to the door. "Come on; I'll help you find some food."

I walked with Bane to make sure he didn't collapse.

Each step he took was shaky, and he could barely climb the ladder to the upper deck before collapsing in exhaustion, but with my help, he managed to get to the wheelhouse. We got him some food, and I left him to rest in the bed at the rear of the room as I stretched out on the floor, closing my eyes in utter exhaustion for an hour.

Mal had caught up a few hours ago, having ignored the black ship at first in favor of chasing down the merchantman and boarding it.

He'd basically looted it senseless, and being the sneaky, amoral bastard that he was, when a pair of drow appeared in the crew, ready to wreak havoc, he was paranoid enough that he'd been waiting for something. The pair had sprouted a dozen arrows a piece before they'd made it three feet.

He'd stripped the ship of the best of its goods for himself, tied up the crew, and put his own people in charge. Then he'd escorted the merchantman back to join us, only noticing at the last minute that the black ship had never actually sunk. By that time, it was too late; they were far enough away that when they used their illusion magic, they disappeared without a trace.

He pulled alongside our ship and waved to us, shouting something about how he'd come to save my ass again, and I did the only thing I could.

I used Soaring Majesty and leaped upwards, flying over the intervening space to land on his deck and stealing his thunder with the casual use of my new ability.

The side effect of giving all who saw me fly a boost to their morale was even better, as it literally made him furious, while not giving him any reason he could complain about it.

"Well, that was damn special," he muttered, frowning at me. "What you need a ship for, if you can do that?"

"Because I'd get a bad back if I tried to lead a team without the ship, maybe?" I asked him, and he shrugged.

"Way I hear it, your lady-friend does her best to give you a bad back, anyway. Whole fleet heard it that way, too."

I looked at him flatly.

"I win." His grin couldn't be more smug.

"You're an asshole."

"Takes one to know one," he said, shrugging.

"Whatever. Anyway, thanks, Mal. Thanks for coming back for us," I said, swallowing the feeling that I was surrendering something precious in admitting we'd needed the help. "I mean, obviously, we'd have been fine; we were totally winning, in fact, but you know…"

"Yeah, kid, sure you were." He smirked knowingly.

I resisted the need to lash out at him. There was something about that face, that was what it was, I decided. He was just so *punchable*.

"*Anyway*," I said, glaring at him again while feeling the edges of my mouth twitching, as though the traitorous thing wanted to smile for some reason. "Thank you, and the crew, for coming for us."

"Eh," he said, dismissing it as unimportant. "I see you went and got some gnomes to join you. Mayhap you could lend 'em to me, get a few things around the ship worked on, and we'll call it even for me comin' back for you?" he remarked casually.

I turned to look at him, my mouth dropping open in shock, before I spun around and faced away, looking out over the foam-topped waves far below as I thought quickly, trying to hide an evil smile that was lighting my face.

"Well, I suppose I could order a few to come help you, maybe make some of their ideas about how a ship should be built come true over here. But I have sixteen left, that's all, and there won't be much time before we get to the fleet," I said, struggling to hold in a fit of the giggles. "I'd have to send you them all, like right now, and you'd have to keep them on your ship until we reached the fleet to make it worthwhile."

"You'd do that?!" he asked me incredulously. "You'd lend me all your gnomes, for the last day or two of the flight to the tower? An' I could get them to work on my ship?"

"Well, they'd have to be let loose, essentially. You know gnomes, they 'fix' things in ways that I don't really understand—and my ship is a bit of a derelict mess—but you'd owe me, Mal. I mean it, you'll owe me a favor, a big one for this, never mind us being even. They could be working on my ship, after all," I said, all the while internally giggling and rubbing my hands at the thought of getting the crazy little bastards off the ship. "Plus, there's not many of us. I'd need help to run my ship, maybe get Soween and a few of the crew across to help me, and I'd really need some alchemy ingredients, like a lot, whatever you have."

"Deal!" he snapped, holding his hand out before I could think to ask for more.

I stared at him, utterly gobsmacked, then reached out, gripping his forearm and shaking once, before he released me and laughed in my face.

"You be a damn fool, boy! I'd have given anything to get a single gnome working on my ship, and you agreed to sixteen?! I'll even swear to carry out that favor with a goddamn smile on my face! All it's cost me is a few days without Soween and my alchemy stores that I was going to sell anyway! Ha!" He lifted both fists into the air and started humping the air in front of me. "You just got fucked, boy!" he said, laughing.

"Oh, darn," I said trying to keep the smile from my face, and look downhearted, even as he called Soween over and told her to pick a handful of crew to help with operating my ship. Then he ran off, darting from section to section, clearly wondering what he could get the gnomes to upgrade for him first.

I looked at Soween, and allowed my long, satisfied smile to rival the Cheshire fuckin' cat's.

"Oh my, he just got fucked in the ass, didn't he?" she asked me, trying to hide her own smile.

"Oh, so badly," I admitted. "And without even a touch of lube."

"Am I gonna have a ship to come back to?" she asked, and then glanced over at my ship. "Plus, how bad is it?"

"Mine isn't as bad as I think it looks; the gnomes already did a load of upgrades and fixes, and we have a wisp that's integrated with the ship, so she'll keep it together, if anyone can," I said, shrugging.

"So why did you need me?" Soween asked.

I grinned again. "Well, I figured a few more hands to help out with any work that *has* to be done would be useful, but it was more about making sure you weren't here to help him, I'll admit, but I could definitely do with some help making the ship habitable. It's a damn filthy mess," I said, winking.

"Josh!" Soween shouted over her shoulder. "Get Padraig, Barti, Tinny, and Steve, tell them to bring their gear for a few days' helping me on that ship over there, as well as the basics like food and wine. You bring everything you'll need to help, too."

"Seriously?" Josh asked, popping his head out of the wheelhouse. "I get to look round a gnome airship?"

"You've got five minutes," she replied calmly, before looking at me. "How you going to get us across?"

I shrugged.

"Either I'll fly you one-by-one, or you can jump, I guess?" I offered.

She sighed before shouting out a series of commands to the helmsman. "Right, I'll deal with my ship. For now, you make sure yours stays on this course and heading, same speed, everything; last thing I need is an unexpected bath," she said, nodding towards the grey waves far below.

I nodded and turned, taking a few quick steps and jumping into the air, soaring across the distance between the ships and landing gracefully. I turned, ready to walk into the wheelhouse and pass the directions across to Tenandra, when Giint ran out from somewhere and straight into me, tripping me and sending me staggering like a complete idiot.

I just heard Mal's laughter erupting in the distance, as I managed to catch myself before growling under my breath.

By a massive exertion of will, I managed to not throw Giint over the side, and instead I walked to the wheelhouse, kicked the door open hard enough that it rebounded and nearly broke my nose, and marched inside.

Oracle broke off her conversation with the other wisp and smiled widely at me, shaking her hand free of the little form, and moved quickly to join me. When I sat down, she plonked herself in my lap and promptly ignored Tenandra.

I passed the details across to Jian and Tenandra, and a few minutes later, Mal's ship cut across our path, with the six of them leaping from his ship to land on mine. Arrin gave any who needed it a quick heal, and then Soween was marching into the wheelhouse, throwing herself into another chair and glancing around.

"So, you want to fill me in yet?" she asked, and I grinned at her.

"You'll see everything when we get the gnomes together. Any ideas for getting them across to Mal? And quick, before he comes to his senses?" I asked.

"We just do what I did before. You fly over his ship, close in, and they jump. What do you mean, 'I'll see soon'?"

"Well, you ever deal with gnomes before?" I asked, and she nodded.

"They can be a bit crazy, but mostly not too bad, as long as you keep them calm. Why?"

"These ones have been locked in the Sunken City and drugged up to the eyeballs for around a century, fighting and fucking in equal measure," I explained simply.

"Holy...are they crazy?" she asked.

"Well and truly fucking nuts."

"This I have to see," she said, a wide smile creasing her face.

"It's going to be magnificent," I said, nodding. Then I grabbed the nearest gnome I could, waving a small stick of their favorite substance under his nose to make sure I got his attention, then I put it away. "Get the rest of your people and line them up on the deck, all of them. I've got an emergency job for you, and if you can get everyone in the next five minutes, I'll give you a stick."

His eyes nearly bugged out of his head, and he set off at a full sprint, screaming for the other gnomes.

We went out onto the deck, and I stood with Soween and the others, all grinning at Mal as he cruised along at a distance of about forty meters.

It took less than three minutes to get all the gnomes together, and I held my hands up, getting their attention.

"Okay, everyone, thank you for your help so far. Frederikk, is this ship safe now, with the mana that's coming in to recharge it? Can we fly for a few days with no issues?"

"Should be. Ship's fine now, needs a full rebuild and upgrade, a clean down, and more, but she's safe," he said, nodding and watching me carefully.

"That's great news, because unfortunately, my friend's ship isn't so much. It's new, but it's slow and really needs a lot of upgrades, so I'm offering you all a deal. You know there's a lot of work to come, and I'm going to make your new home into the best place I can, but if you all want a day to relax with a stick of your own when we land," I said and I held up one of the short, compressed sticks of catnip where they could all see it.

The sudden intake of breath, followed by their laser-like focus, told me they'd certainly seen it. "Then I want you to show me what you can do. Go to his ship, fix anything you want, upgrade anything you want to play with, just prove yourself to me, okay?

"All I ask is that you don't risk the ship. Beyond that, go for it, follow your hearts' direction, and make a thing of beauty!" I said, grinning at them. "We're about to fly over their deck, and they've set up bedding on it. All you have to do is jump and land there, then you've got until we land at the Great Tower to do your best."

"We won't fail you!" Frederikk cried. "You know what we can do, but with that time? You won't recognize her when we're done!" he said adamantly.

"That's what I'm counting on," I said with an evil grin. I pulled out a handful of sticks and started snapping them into short lengths, passing them to Frederikk, whose eyes grew more and more frenzied by the second. "Give these out to those who impress you the most, and don't worry about the ship's captain, Mal. He's always grumpy, but he's promised that he'll let you do all you want to his ship," I said, trying to suppress the giggles.

Frederikk took the sticks and started shoving back the gnomes that crowded in around him, even as I gestured to the other ship, and Jian nodded to me from the wheelhouse door before slipping from sight.

A few minutes later, we were passing over Mal's *Falcon*, and the gnomes were dropping over the side like the mad little bastards they were.

"Got any more of those sticks?" Soween asked me as we watched, and I nodded, passing her two, which she snapped into short lengths…then threw into the middle of the milling gnomes on the deck of the ship below us.

"You're evil," I said to her as our ship curved around and started back on the heading to catch up with the fleet.

"That's been said a time or two before, sir," she said with a tiny, evil smile. "Now, I'll familiarize myself with the ship and see what needs doing, with your permission?" As soon as I acknowledged the question, she spun on her heel and walked away, Josh following her below decks.

"She's right you know; that was an evil trick," Oracle said.

I grinned at her, wrapping my arm around her shoulders as she moved in close to me. "I know, but in fairness, he thought he was ripping me off," I said before leaning down and kissing her long and slow.

When we eventually broke off the kiss, it was with a sigh, and we turned back to the ship. Despite the joking, the next few days on the ship wouldn't be as easy as we'd made it out to be.

I had a dozen things that I should have done a week ago, and every time I actually stopped and rested, I ended up regretting it.

Lydia had changed, and I needed to check out what had happened, as well as make sure she was, in fact, fully healed. And the ship was a bombsite. It might be solid now and charging the core and crystals, but it'd also been left for a hundred damn years. All that was keeping some sections together looked to be termites holding hands.

Add to that, I needed to do something I'd been neglecting for far too long.

I needed to put my damn alchemy profession to work. So far, I'd essentially botched and blundered my way through it, relying on the combination of my identification spells and the novice skillbook I'd read ages ago.

I knew there was more to it, though, and I knew very specifically that my fleet, my people, and my damn civilization needed me to not just toss this off.

I was going to have to knuckle down and learn properly, for a change. We took a few minutes to relax together, watching the building chaos on Mal's ship, before turning away with a lighter heart.

We returned to the wheelhouse, and I took a seat with Oracle sitting possessively on my knee, and I looked over to Jian and Tenandra.

"Okay, guys, thank you for getting the gnomes across to Mal's ship. Time to get things sorted here, I think, though; what state are we in?" I asked them both.

"The ship's structure is sound, despite the cracks and physical issues. The abundance of mana, thanks to the outer edges of the storm, means I can use that to begin repairs as we go. I would estimate the overall structure at around forty-two percent intact.

"Certain areas are entirely rotted away, but these are predominately the outer hull, where the wood was sitting in water for years. The inner hull is mostly sound, with only a few small issues that will need to be addressed sooner, rather than later. I can keep the ship together for the time it will take to reach the tower easily, however," Tenandra stated with clear pride in her voice.

"That's a relief, then," I said gratefully. "Thank you, Tenandra. Now, what about the crew? I know we were going to be mainly reliant on the gnomes until you took over the ship, I got six people from Mal to help out, but honestly, I was more concerned with removing his primary help of Soween and Josh. Leaving him with that wanker Jay makes this even funnier."

"Wait, he's just got Jay to help him deal with *gnomes*?!" Jian asked, grinning widely.

"Oh, he's got a load of other people as well, but you know, out of his core group that we all dealt with? I could only see Jay there still!" I said with an evil laugh.

"Oh, now, that's just cruel…you know Jay is gonna pick a fight with one of them, right?" Oracle interjected.

"If its Giint, they'll be picking bits of Jay out of the damn teeth of his kill-stick! Anyway, that's his problem, and I seriously doubt Mal would let something like that happen, anyway. So, back to the subject at hand: food, drink, and the ship."

"Well, we've all got a few days' rations left, I think," Jian responded, rubbing his chin. "The biggest problem we have is space to sleep and relax. Almost the entire ship is filled with mold and crap. The rooms that were secure are okay, but they're all sized for gnomes—" Jian broke off as Soween pushed the door open and stood to attention.

"Permission to enter, sir?" she asked, and I waved her and Josh to chairs before responding to Jian.

"Okay, so we sort a few rooms out to rest in, and we set up a rota between us. Make sure there's always one of us in here, and beyond that, we just spend the next few days resting and recovering," I said. "I'm going to need a few rooms' clearing, at least. One as a medical and alchemy room, so it'll need to be entirely clean of the spores and fungus. Once we make sure everyone is healed up, then I'll use the room for alchemy and make sure to restock our potions. After all, I know Mal agreed to give us all his alchemy stocks."

"He did, sir. I grabbed the bag myself. Mal practically threw me off the ship in his excitement," Soween said, smiling faintly.

"Well, I think he'll probably be regretting that very soon," I chuckled.

"I'll look forward to seeing that, sir. So, you described a single room you needed to clear, but you said you wanted at least three?"

"Ah, yeah, I need a room for us all to sleep in, somewhere we can actually sleep, or relax, or do, well, whatever. And third…" I said, wondering if it was greedy to mention the third room.

"We need a room for us," Oracle said simply. "A room where we can work together and have some privacy."

She didn't elaborate on that, but I could feel her hunger, and my cheeks reddened slightly.

"Of course," Soween said, smiling faintly. "What's the priority?"

"First, I need a room that's actually clean for alchemy. As covered in shit as most of the ship is, I'll end up with contaminated potions, and that won't end well. After that, a main room for us all, then our room last of all," I said firmly, despite wanting to drag Oracle off as fast as I could and try to break her over a table or something.

"We also need to fix your arm," Oracle said, scowling at me.

"I'd definitely like that," I admitted.

Soween frowned, looking me over. "What's wrong with your arm?" she asked.

I shrugged, tugging off the small shield that Grizz had lent me and passing it to him, then flipping the latches to release the armor.

Once I had it all unlocked, I twisted the vambrace and there was a click before the lower section released. I tugged it free, revealing that my arm ended just below the elbow. Soween blinked at the truncated arm, as Oracle spoke up.

"I still can't believe you cut it off; what were you thinking?" she asked me.

"It seemed a good idea at the time, that's all," I said, before looking over at Soween. "If you could concentrate on the alchemy lab, first, please, then we can at least make sure everyone has a potion or something to use when the shit hits the fan next."

Soween nodded, straightening, and saluted, fist to chest, legion style, before striding from the room and gathering up the others she'd brought with her.

They headed straight down into the lower decks, searching for rooms that would be the best to use. Oracle and I looked at each other, and I sighed, getting up and walking to the door, determined to get some fresh air while I worked through the welter of notifications blinking away.

CHAPTER THIRTY-SEVEN

I left as Tang entered to talk to Jian and smiled at his friendly exchange with Tenandra. Then I walked out onto the deck of the ship, looking around and making sure we weren't being snuck up on again, as near as I could tell.

In all directions now, there were angry gray clouds, but at least the majority of the storm was behind us, with a much gentler rain still pattering across the deck. I walked up to the edge of the railing at the bow of the ship and gazed out, Oracle slipping into her smaller form to ride on my shoulder.

"It's beautiful, isn't it?" I whispered to her, looking out over the sea that ran out to the horizon to our right and behind us. In the distance ahead, the continent was clear, with trees and the shore becoming distinct from the waves. To my far left, I could see the bay that the cities of Himnel and Narkolt shared, and I looked down at a sudden movement, catching a glimpse of something the shape of a plesiosaur, but the size of a super-tanker, dipping back under the waves and making me shudder at the thought of being on a sailing ship.

"It is," Oracle agreed. "But I can't wait to return home. I know I'm not tied to the tower anymore, but…"

"But it's your home," I finished for her and nodded in understanding. "Mine, too. I can't wait to get back there, to see everyone, and most of all, to get the place repaired, to make them all safe!"

"Can you imagine Oren's face when he sees the ships?" Oracle asked me, grinning. "He's going to be pestering us for the battleship inside the hour, I bet."

"And Seneschal and Heph will be arguing over the golems as well!" I said, smiling at the thought.

"Not to mention Flux. He's going to be pestering the legion to train him in fighting as fast as he can!"

"Oh god, yes." I groaned. "First thing we do when we land is have a damn party. Let them all see each other and interact. Then we get everyone out onto the ground outside, make sure they're all out of the way while we fix the place up. We get things sorted, get the tower configured for battle, get the golems into production, and for the love of the gods, get us a room with a real door and a real bed!"

"That sounds like a plan," my companion said, looking up at me and smiling. She'd been wearing a black top and camo pants when I'd looked out to sea, but as I glanced up to where she perched on my shoulder, she was suddenly and starkly naked, and I swallowed hard.

"That is so not fair," I said to her in a low voice as I took in the view.

"I know," she said breezily. "Know what else isn't fair?"

"What?" I asked.

"That you're wearing proper pants. If you still had the Drow ones that had that hole that led through from the pocket, I could have had all kinds of fun right now…"

"Oracle!" I groaned, trying to calm myself down as I stared longingly at her.

"I know," she said, grinning. "But I missed you!"

"I missed you too, but damn, you're a tease!" I growled, pulling up the notifications.

Congratulations!

You have killed the following:

- 2x Human Marines of various levels for a total of 22,150xp

- 3x DarkSpore of various levels for a total of 230xp

- 1x Drow Shifter, level 26 for 17,400xp

A party under your command killed the following:

- 7x Human Marines of various levels for a total of 56,870xp

- 9x DarkSpore of various levels for a total of 530xp

Total Party experience earned: 57,400xp

As party leader, you gain 25% of all experience earned

Progress to level 23 stands at 349,024/455,000

Congratulations!

Forces under your command have seized the following strategic items:

- 1x Merchantman Airship for 35,000xp

Due to no formal declaration of war being in force between you and the ship's previous owners, you gain no additional experience for this capture.

I shrugged and dismissed it, while trying not to admit to myself that I was gutted we didn't at least get an assist for the death of the two ships and Mal driving off the third.

Congratulations!

You have raised your weapons skill Swords to its first specialization.

You must now pick a path to follow. Will you choose the path of the BLADE or follow instead the path of the STORM?

Choose carefully, as this choice cannot be undone.

BLADE:

An adherent of the Path of the BLADE believes that there is no need for a secondary weapon, as their sword is a part of them, in much the same way their arm or foot is. To lose one, is to lose all.

Gain 2 points to Dexterity and +5 to damage when wielding a single blade.

Ability Learned: Lunge!

Once per fight, you can force stamina into an ability, Lunge, allowing you to drive forward up to five meters with your blade extended. Any attacks that are landed because of Lunge do double damage.

STORM:

To win requires not that you be a fixed, immobile object; instead, you must be fluid, flowing around your enemies and slicing them apart. Followers of the Path of the STORM specialize in wielding multiple weapons and gain a +5 to damage when wielding more than one bladed weapon at a time.

Ability Learned: Flurry of Blows!

For a cost of 100 stamina, you can increase your physical speed, more than doubling the strikes you can make for up to 60 seconds and imbuing them with the element of your choice.

Fire: Additional chance to inflict Burning status

Water: Additional chance to inflict Freezing status

Earth: Additional chance to inflict Slowed status

Air: Additional chance to inflict Confused status

Light: Additional chance to inflict damage on undead and evil-aligned creatures

Darkness: Additional chance to inflict damage on living and good-aligned creatures

That wasn't really a hard choice there either, considering that I occasionally fought with multiple weapons, yeah, but more often than not, I used my naginata. As soon as I had two hands again, I'd be making the most of that again. I chose Blade and gained the skill Lunge before dismissing the confirmation prompt and moving on.

Congratulations!

You have raised your spell Battlefield Triage to its Second Evolution.

You must now pick a new path to follow. Will you choose to continue to Generalize with the path of GENERALIST, or will you Specialize by following the path of SURGEON?

Choose carefully, as this choice cannot be undone.

GENERALIST:

Your healing spell Battlefield Triage has once again grown ready for evolution. In choosing to generalize further, you find that your understanding deepens regarding the interactions that magic and the living form can achieve together. Instead of focusing on a single issue, you blanket the entire area, pumping in mana until whatever remains in that location is healed.

Healing will now be increased by 5 points per second and cost reduced by 10%, affecting all targets within a radius of 2m.

SURGEON:

Your recent experiences have taught you to view all those around you in a different light. No longer are they defined by their differences in structure. Instead, you see their likenesses. You have grown to identify the common themes in humanoids, and with such knowledge, you are more efficient when fixing them, as well as breaking them, when need be.

When healing humanoids, you achieve an additional 10 points of healing per second, for an increased cost of 5 mana across all healing spells. When attacking humanoids, you do +5 additional damage, due to your knowledge of their inner workings.

Bonus Ability: Examine and Excise!

Due to your recent practice, and the integration of your Greater Examination spell, you have gained the ability to slice and dice with far more finesse than you ever thought yourself capable of. When using this ability, weaknesses and errors in your target's physical makeup may be identified at a 25% chance of success, allowing you to fix issues that your target never knew they possessed.

Cost: 25 mana per second; chances of success rise by 5% per second of examination.

This one was more complicated, but after a few minutes' thought, I nodded to myself. I could feel Oracle's focus, and I agreed with her unspoken suggestion as I selected Surgeon this time. Yes, it'd be cool to have an AOE heal—well, one that worked on everyone that didn't take forever to cast in a fight—but the weakness of the generalized path had been all too clear when I had worked to heal Tang and Bane.

You have selected Specialist for your Second Evolution.

Your Spell Battlefield Triage has evolved to Surgeon's Scalpel and can now be used to fix problems that your target never even knew they had!

For a cost of 40 mana per second, you now heal 32 points of damage and can choose between healing the body in a wide arc or focusing on a single point. Continuing to channel this spell into an area that is already healed may have beneficial effects.

Due to creating your own unique Journeyman Spell, you may now choose a bonus:

- **Additional healing effect:** when in desperate times, additional mana can be channeled into this spell, increasing the effectiveness by half for so long as the spell lasts.

  Cost: 2x single spell cost.

- **Genetic Drift Examination**: due to your own background knowledge, you are aware of the difference between the ideal genetic template and the end product, much as a patient might have their growth stunted through years of poor nutrition, while another may excel due to an abundance of opportunities. Now, rather than your spell working on all areas slightly, you may focus this, improving a specific point of a target to their ultimate potential.

  Cost: 2-5x Surgeon's Scalpel spell cost for 2% per second effect.

I quickly chose the Genetic Drift Examination. It was both a mouthful, and a pain in the ass, if I was reading it right, but…I knew that my people were far from what they could be. I'd healed Amaat from his reduced state when we'd first met into a great example of his race, doing the equivalent of curing male-pattern baldness as part of healing him. But he was still only an average-sized example of his species, as near as I could tell.

If I could use this to work out how to make him into the ideal, literally heal him to the point that he was all that he could be physically, he'd have a huge advantage over others of his race, and the thought of doing that for the entirety of the tower?

Hell, I might even be able to heal my own scars away, so I didn't look so much like Freddy Krueger was my masseur.

I nodded to myself and shared a smile with Oracle as we dismissed the last of the prompts and strolled across the deck toward the hatches.

I clambered down the steep ladder leading to the inner decks and looked around, checking the rooms as I walked down the corridor, until I found Soween and two of her crew carrying out a canvas bucket filled with mulch.

"We're working on this room; it's the second largest and least contaminated, plus it has a solid seal around the porthole, so it's better than most of the others," she said abruptly, wiping her cheek and leaving a smear of grime behind. "Give us another ten, fifteen minutes, and we'll have it ready. By the way, I heard what happened to your bodyguard, Bane. Is he all right?"

"Pretty much. He was captured by an asshole noble; the nephew of Hannimish, if you've seen him about?" I asked, and she nodded thoughtfully. "What do you know about him?"

"He's honest enough, for a noble," she said, stepping to the side and letting the other two move past. "We've had some contact with him, as members of the Smuggler's Guild, I mean. He paid his bills and didn't try to cheat us, so there's that. You'd be surprised how many nobles think you should be thankful that they were willing to take things from you, never mind actually paying for them. He never tried that and never ordered anything dodgy as near as I saw; mostly just gemstones, always uncut, and artifacts from the Empire; where we could get them and they still ran, anyway."

"Well, his nephew was totally different, then," I replied. "Little shit of a man. Got me with a dodgy dagger that would have killed me if I hadn't cut my own arm off." I waved my stump at her. "Seemed to be working with someone else, from what he said, but I have no idea who or what the story was with the dagger and the journal. Something else to look into when I have time," I said, shrugging.

"Okay, anyway, here." She pulled a bag out of the larger one on her pouch. "This is all the alchemy ingredients I'd bought for us. I know Mal said he'd give them all to you, but I was planning on trading them for some potions myself, so if you have any spare later? I'd appreciate a couple, at least."

"Depending on what there is, I'll make you some," I reassured her, and she smiled.

"That'd be appreciated, sir. Anyway, we found a table in the room two down, and we'll move that into this room, as soon as it's clear. Is there anything else you'll need?"

"A chair would be good, but as this was a gnome ship, I'm betting the table is tiny?" I asked, and she nodded. "Ah, well. I can sit on the floor. Guess I should be relieved they didn't go in for low ceilings and be thankful for it, eh? Thanks, anyway."

Oracle and I waited in a side room while I meditated again, getting the practice in while I could, as Soween and her crew sorted the room out. I heard occasional grumbling coming from further down the corridor as others worked on another, larger room. When Soween came to me, telling me they'd done all they could, and the room was as clean as they could make it with the equipment they had, I thanked her and her team and stepped inside, inspecting the spaces where the filth had been scrubbed away wherever they could reach.

I took a deep breath and asked Oracle to manage the fire as I summoned a fountain of pure, clean water and started to guide it around the room.

Oracle held her hands out and let the water flow into the Firebolt she conjured between them, turning the icy cold water into a jet of water hot enough that it could scald, if you weren't careful.

We quickly moved round the room, essentially using a high-pressure jet wash to sluice the room down one last time. The water that ran out between the boards in the floor, down the walls, and off the ceiling was filthy, seeping into the lower decks, but I ignored it, concerned only with clearing the room as best I could.

It took a few more minutes before I was almost out of mana, but at least the room looked clean, and it even had the frame for a bed in it still. I glanced at it, then at Oracle, and we shared a naughty grin, before I shook my head and closed the door behind me.

"We haven't got time to play," Oracle said to me, despite the smile she was giving me. "You know as well as I do, if we start, we'll not get anything else done, and as much as I'd love to, we actually need the potions!"

"I know. I'm just thinking that the bed is actually a better height for the kit to go onto than the table, as I can kneel at it, and it's both wider and longer than the table…"

"Go on," she said, confused, as she could feel my horniness, but couldn't see where this was going.

"So I was thinking it would be best if no one were to walk in and catch us naked, right? Better if we work on getting the potions done now and play later?"

"Yeah..." she drawled out, watching me suspiciously.

"Well, it turns out you'd fit under the bed great, and that would mean your mouth would be at just the right height..." I hinted, grinning before she laughed, cutting me off.

"I knew it! I knew you'd have something dirty in mind!" She laughed. "Well, tough! It's not fair, as I want some of the fun, too!" She gestured to the alchemy set I was pulling out and setting up. "Besides, if I put my mouth to work properly, you think you'd be able to concentrate on your work?" she asked.

"Not sure, but in the interests of science, I'm willing to experiment and find out!" I offered, raising my eyebrows suggestively.

"No, especially not if you're using acids and poisons, not to mention boiling substances. You might spill some on my head, then I might bite down, after all, and that's the last thing we want!" I winced in imagined pain at her very logical point. "Besides, I think we have a hand to regrow?" she offered.

"I'll certainly not refuse," I stated, lifting my stump. "How bad do you think it's going to be?"

"Not good," Oracle responded, frowning at the arm. "With the Genetic Drift, it'll be easier. At least, because your genes know you should have an intact arm, it's essentially providing the power to your body to do its own work, rather than having to learn regrowth from scratch."

"Okay, so...?"

"So lie down but take your armor off first!" Oracle said quickly, as I started to lie down. I sighed and climbed back to my feet, then stripped down to my regular pants and tunic, grimacing all over again at the state of them.

Between the stabbings, the Fireballs, the loss of my lower arm, the various people and creatures that had managed to bleed on me, and the filth I'd ended up being dragged through several times over, I was essentially wearing rags. Filthy ones, at that.

I looked at Oracle and sighed in resignation at the look on her face, as I made sure the door was closed before stripping off entirely, and not for fun.

It was a struggle at times, but once I was fully naked, and my gear was stacked out of the way, I summoned a fountain of clean, crisp, and oh-so-cold water, and began scrubbing myself.

It was difficult, not least because, with only one arm, cleaning my right-hand side was awkward, and also because I had a wisp that had grown to full size, who was perched naked on the wall, somehow managing to make it look totally natural while she sat on thin air, and made constant comments and lewd suggestions about what we were going to do once all the potions were made.

The combination of icy cold water and a ridiculously hot wisp meant that I was distracted as all hell, and therefore missed the knock on the door.

If there ever was one.

Instead, Grizz simply walked in, followed by Lydia and the rest of the squad, just as I looked to be doing a naked squat over a jet of ice water, and was in mid-swing of the willy-copter at Oracle.

Grizz burst out laughing. Lydia about-faced and covered Miren's eyes, marching her backwards. Yen froze, unsure as to where to look, and Jian sighed and followed Miren back out. Tang just shook his head and wandered over to lean against the wall, and Bane threw a cloth at me.

"Honestly, can't you just be normal for five minutes?" Bane questioned me, looking and sounding for all the world like I was some sort of degenerate.

"I was having a wash!" I retorted, catching the cloth and cutting the fountain out as I tried to cover myself up.

"Yeah. Looked like it," Bane replied dryly, shaking his head as though ashamed to know me.

"Looks like I know why the researchers in the room below you were getting soaked, though!" Jian called from outside the door. "Are you decent yet, or should we take Miren somewhere else?"

"Hey, if she's too young to see this, then it doesn't say much for you, mate!" I called out to him, before sighing and moving to my bags.

I rummaged around, ignoring the comments on what a pretty behind I had, and quickly pulled some pants on, before sighing and looking around the room.

"So, anyone want to tell me why you decided to join me in here?" I asked.

Lydia coughed, still trying not to look at me. "Soween told us that this room had been cleared for use as a general sleeping room, and seeing as it's the early hours," Lydia explained.

"You've got to be kidding me? Soween?" I asked Oracle.

"Either she decided it'd be funny, got confused, or wanted to make sure you didn't relax too much," Oracle guessed.

"Soween, confused?" I pondered, before shaking my head. "Nope, don't see that one. She's insanely focused."

"Then I'm betting she thought it'd be funny; remember, she spends all of her time with Mal, so she's got to be twisted in some way," Oracle pointed out.

"Okay, look, guys," I called out, making sure those in the corridor could hear me as well. "I was having a wash, that's all, and the reason this room is so clean is because I needed it like that for alchemy. If you all want to sleep in here, that's fine. It's a bit cramped for us all, but we've all slept in worse places. Be warned, though; I'm going to be doing a few hours of potion-making, so there are going to be some noxious smells, okay?"

"More so than normal, you mean?" Tang quipped.

"That's it." I glared at him. "No moustache rides for you!"

"Promises, promises…" Tang sighed, before shooting me a grin. "Okay everyone, let's check the next room out, see if it's clean. If it is, we can bunk in there. If not, we get to share with Stinky, there."

"Hey, I had a wash, remember?" I growled. But inside, I felt immense relief at having the team back together and winding each other up. I missed Stephanos, but…*it is what it is*.

"Yeah, and believe me, we're all thankful you did. Not so much for the dancing show, but you know," retorted Bane as he waved people out of the room. "I'll watch over him for now, make sure he doesn't get into any more trouble," Bane told Grizz and Tang. They went with the others into the next cabin, where we could hear the sounds of the group setting out their bedrolls and making a meal.

"It's still dirty in here, but at least you've not been naked in it and contaminated it!" Tang yelled to me. I facepalmed, knowing full well that if I could hear him that well, the damn researchers and Hannimish would be able to, as well.

"Close the door please, Bane," I asked, shaking my head. "You know you need some sleep, right? You've had your body pushed to the damn limit with that healing."

"I've had two potions of Legionnaire's Might, and I've been unconscious all day. Believe me, after Grizz forced that shit down my throat, I might never sleep again," Bane muttered.

"Fair enough, but at least lay your bedroll out. There's no way anyone can get to us here," I advised, grimacing at the remembered taste.

"And that's why I need to watch over you. If I was going to try to kill someone, I'd be looking to strike exactly where nobody believes it's possible," he retorted, but he did lay his bedroll out against the door, after checking that the porthole was too small to let anyone in and sealed up tighter than a duck's arse.

I shrugged and left him to it, sitting down cross-legged on the damp floor and looking at Oracle as she stepped down lightly from the wall and inspected my arm determinedly.

"Okay, this is going to hurt, but it's the only way, as near as I can see, unless you want to wait until we reach Nerin or Hellenica?"

"No, let's just go for it." I sighed.

"Okay, we'll start with the new spell, Surgeon's Scalpel, and we'll use the Genetic Drift Examination first as well; it means the spell is going to take time. Worst-case scenario, it'll be costing us two hundred mana a second, and it'll only at the absolute best do two percent in changes, but your arm is what, less than ten percent of your body mass? That gives us five seconds of work—I think— once we've used the genetic spell to look you over." She pondered, rubbing her chin as she worked it out.

"Okay, we've got a manapool of five hundred and sixty, so that's two seconds at a time, say, with a regen of six point four five; that works out as a bit under ninety minutes, add in the meditation, that's anywhere from thirty to ten minutes, maybe, to regenerate it?" I guessed.

"Yeah. It's weird that some of the abilities you gained, like that Peace, only give 'a boost' and no specifics."

"Tell me about it," I grumbled.

Oracle laughed. "Honestly, Jax, the capability to use the genetics and abilities of some of these creatures is amazing. I'm not surprised it's vague; it's part of a different creature you're suffusing yourself with, after all."

"Yeah, I know, and some of it is amazing, it really is. And some of the other changes are, as well, like the fact that doing math like that is so easy. That hardly required a thought, and the fact that I'm now even more of a goddamn sexual tyrannosaurus than I was before.

"But still, there's times I'd love to be back in my old life, you know?" I grumbled, looking down at my stump and thinking back to lazy afternoons in Jesmond Dene, drinking beer and eating a burger, talking shit with Tommy. Our only concern had been who could seduce the hottest girl in the group that day.

"I know," Oracle comforted me, reaching out to lay her hand on my stump, even as I looked up to her smiling face. "But would you really want to go back?" she asked

"No," I contradicted myself quickly. "I love the idea of it, you know, the lack of giant monsters trying to eat my face, and weirdos like Bane staring at my arse and trying to watch me naked, but..."

"Believe me, the sights I've seen already haunt my nightmares," Bane cut in.

"You love it, really," I retorted, grinning involuntarily. "Anyway, no, I was just grumbling."

"I thought so. After all, I couldn't survive in your world," she said sadly.

I stiffened. "Then I'll never return, regardless."

"You sure? I mean..." Oracle started to question, and I held my stump up, cutting her off.

"Let's get this fixed, then get the potions done. Then we kick that pervert out, and I'll show you exactly how unwilling I am to go anywhere without you," I offered, and Oracle laughed, even as Bane put his hands over his head.

"Who do I have to pray to that you'll get a soundproofed room soon?" he muttered, and both Oracle and I laughed at him.

"Okay, let's do this, then," Oracle said, and I lay back slowly, stretching out and closing my eyes, feeling the link with Oracle that she'd extended to me when we had worked together to heal Bane, ready and waiting.

I slipped into it and focused, feeling her all around me as she built the spell. I saw the world through her eyes and felt the additional senses she possessed but I had no context for.

She set to work structuring the spell, and instantly, I knew why she was so much better at building spells from scratch than I was. Mana was an almost physical construct to her, and when we spoke of weaves and so on, she literally saw them that way.

I was imagining it as a tapestry that formed a spell, but for her, it was a layered, infinitely complex, yet visually understandable thing. I gazed in awe at the spell as she seemed to pull it into being, speaking the words and altering the flow, making my own spell casting look like a chimpanzee hammering on a start button by comparison.

I resolved that I was going to goddamn well learn more about magic.

And alchemy.

And the realm.

Dammit, might as well chuck in the exact air-speed velocity of an unladen swallow while I was at it, seeing as I was probably going to end up as a king, or emperor, by the end of all this.

I stiffened, and not in a fun way, as the spell was guided down into me, the improvements that the Greater Examination had wrought on our spells alone became evident as I watched Oracle guiding the spell down to a micro level, seeing a blueprint of my form being constructed in the air before us.

It took less than a second, but as I gazed at the outline and detail of my body as it was hidden in my every cell, I winced.

I was hugely messed up.

The potential that I saw here would take literal months to bring out; even working on a cell-by-cell basis. It would take forever practically, but thankfully, once the overall examination was done, we could easily assign the spell a priority now.

As the last of the mana drained from me, our twin gazes lost in the examination of the details, I winced, the spell failing and a migraine flaring to life.

"Goddammit!" I moaned, throwing my uninjured arm across my eyes as I tried to ignore the pain. The failure of the spell was made worse by the utter loss of all mana, and I turned on my side, groaning.

I was useless after that for almost an hour. My mana channels felt red-raw and like they'd been scrubbed with a pipe-cleaner, not to mention the goddamn migraine, but eventually, when I could see again, I relaxed.

"I'm so sorry, Jax," Oracle whispered to me, and I winced, as even that low volume felt like she was screaming in my ear.

"It—it's…okay," I ground out, forcing myself to breathe through it. It was a weird sensation, having a spell fail. Not only were you useless for casting for a good long while afterwards, but your mana system also seemed to be actually damaged by it, as was your physical form.

"Just meditate, if you can," she whispered again, and I bit down on another groan before sitting up and choking down the vomit that tried to escape as the room spun.

Another half an hour, and I was at last able to lose myself in my meditation.

An hour later, I felt Oracle start to cast, a soothing sensation building and sweeping through me as I tried determinedly to build a third layer of compression.

The weave flowed through me, tightening in my truncated left arm, and a slow itch began to build. I doubled down, trying frantically to ignore it, but the longer I did that, the more the compression failed.

Soon, my second box collapsed, followed by my first, and the soothing, cooling breeze that surrounded me from my Peace ability died away as I opened my eyes and grabbed at my left arm, scratching at the newly formed skin.

My arm was growing before my eyes. Inch by inch, it stretched, the flesh bubbling out as the hand grew inside. It was freaky as all hell to watch, and I had to stop and meditate three times, but eventually, I was whole again, and I looked at my left arm in wonder.

I flicked the fingers, rolling them and twisting my wrist, feeling the smoothness of the motion and comparing it to the way my right worked, as I realized that this rebuild had been done to a higher standard than the original growth was.

"Is this…?" I asked slowly.

"It's brought you closer to your genetic ideal by seven percent. The nerves are stronger, the bones purer; even the hairs have fewer contaminants in them," she said slowly. "But…we were wrong. This is your left arm closer to ideal by seven percent, not your overall body. So yeah, it'd take about a week of constant work to have your arm alone perfect."

"Fuck," I grumbled, thinking about just how difficult this path would be. "I thought Nerin could do this?" I asked, and she nodded.

"She can, but in a different way, and at a far higher cost. Her version of improvement removes the impurities; it doesn't rebuild to the maximum efficiency."

"Damn," I muttered. "At least I've got my arm back, though," I said slowly, my stomach rumbling. I looked around and saw that Bane's bedroll was gone, and instead, Tang sat with his back against the door, watching me, the pair having swapped over at some point while I was distracted.

"Don't even think about testing out the 'feeling' of that new arm while I'm here," Tang warned. I laughed, getting a smile from him and Oracle.

"Ah, you wish. Admit it, that's why you swapped with Bane, in the hope of a show!" I threw back to him, turning back to Oracle as we shared a laugh.

"Right, then; I'm getting dressed, then we're getting the goddamn potions done," I said, even as Tang got some more food out.

"I'd suggest you eat before you work with the potions. You know, in case you end up snacking and poisoning yourself," he suggested, and I grimaced but took the hint.

Ten minutes later, I was spreading the various herbs and ingredients out around myself, looking them over and trying to decide where to start.

CHAPTER THIRTY-EIGHT

The next ten minutes was spent reviewing all I knew about the herbs, and more specifically, about alchemy itself.

There was something missing here.

I could literally feel that I didn't understand this in the right way, like I was using a car to drive forward and backward, only clutching the steering wheel to make sure it stayed straight, yet never really understanding that the car could actually turn corners.

I looked at the ingredients from every conceivable angle, using my Greater Examination on them again and again. I got extra information, telling me what three and sometimes four of the uses of the ingredients were. But somehow, something was still missing.

I tried to shake the feeling off, forcing myself to go ahead, mixing up a basic batch of mana regeneration potions, then pouring them into smaller vials, and staring in dissatisfaction at the finished, weak product.

I *knew* I was doing something wrong; I just couldn't figure out what.

I tucked the vials away, then summoned another fountain of cool, clear water, washing out the collection of old vials I'd accumulated. I felt ready for another attempt, when I paused, looking at the way the water flowed down between the floorboards and seeped into the lower levels of the ship.

I ignored the muffled, shouted complaints of the researcher who had apparently chosen to remain in the room directly below me, and I concentrated, feeling the idea, a breakthrough just out of reach.

Water…

Flowing down, seeping into the cracks, and passing through…

Not water…MANA!

My eyes flared open as I suddenly realized what I was missing. These potions almost all did magical things: they healed us, they altered us, hell, the goddamn potion I'd poured onto the lich had literally summoned an earth golem. These weren't effects a goddamn cocktail should have; they were spells in liquid form!

A damn mojito shouldn't make your wounds close, after all…

I grabbed a mana potion and glared at it, feeling Oracle moving closer. She knew I was on the verge of something and remained silent, but the reassurance I felt from her was enough to guide me. I reached out, focusing and attempting to build a spell the way I'd seen her do it earlier.

I used Greater Examination as the base, then took other sections from my knowledge, guidance and aiming portions from the Magic Missiles, the testing and identification from Cleansing Fire, and I layered them atop each other. Oracle reached out and smoothed the edges, pushing the spell around until the sections seemed to lock together, almost like a jigsaw.

Congratulations!

You have created a new spell: Organic Examination.

The world around you is filled with information. The plants, animals, and the very elements interact with each other, and for the first time, you can see this, too, even if only at a very basic level.

Cost: 10 mana per second active.

I grinned to myself and reached out, plucking a pergola tuber from the collection of random shit I'd piled up. I had two of these left from when I first found them in the Great Tower. Before, I'd found a single use for them; now, I had three when I examined it using the Greater Examination spell.

Pergola	Further Description *Yes/No*		
Details:	These long tubers have an earthy taste but are oddly satisfying. **Uses Discovered:** 1) Tranquilizer 2) Reduce Perception 3) Fire Resistance 4) ?		
Rarity:	**Magical:**	**Durability:**	**Charge:**
Common	No	76/100	N/A

I nodded to myself as I looked it over; then I used the new spell instead, pouring the mana into it and watching as it blossomed, growing to a single point of energy that filled my right palm. Once it was stable, it flowed sideways, sinking into the tuber I held in my left and suffusing it, seeping through its layers, then oozing back to the surface and flowing back to me, like a lazy breeze.

When it returned, I felt…or tasted, something totally new.

It was an entirely new sense, and I struggled for long minutes to make sense of it, but eventually, I did, and I smiled unconsciously at the wonder of it all.

This new sense had carried impressions back to me, parts of patterns that were suffused throughout the realm and indeed the universe around me.

I examined the patterns, or fragments, feeling the heat that radiated from the section that granted the resistance to fire. It literally formed an overlay to the substance I was made of, adding a pattern that seemed to make the fire appear to be a part of me.

It wouldn't last long, as it was, in essence, a liquid version of the pattern, and it'd break up, dissolving away. But what if I added other parts, if I took that tiny piece of the pattern, and added to it? Building upon the piece I had, like constructing a jigsaw, I could see more of the picture.

I could see more of the pattern of reality, and I could alter it.

I moved through the ingredients before me in a daze, gathering up some, tossing others aside, and examining still more, until in the end, I had five ingredients laid out before me.

The Pergola tubers, mora telendril, labian leaves and mugrot stems, as well as the damn bernicle beans. I remembered Lydia telling me that the bernicle beans were used to boost your sex life, and I saw that stood out…prominently…when I examined each ingredient now as well. However, each of them, even though the Greater Examination spell hadn't picked up a use for them that included fire, still resonated in that way to me, strangely. I decided to trust my new instincts.

I set to work, first locating the part that held this pattern. In some, it was a leaf; in others, the furry underside of the leaf. In still others, the sap I could squeeze out from the roots.

As the hours passed, I ran out of many of the ingredients, finding that adding water ruined some of them while it enhanced others.

I boiled, chopped, and reduced. I dried some sections out, and still others I ground up whole. But after nearly six hours, my limbs feeling leaden with exhaustion, my eyes gritty with a need to sleep, I had a single new potion sitting on the desk before me. I'd hoped to have dozens, but I also had three new prompts.

Congratulations!

For staying true to your choices and for walking the Path of the Creationist, you have gained a point of Intelligence!

*

Congratulations, Journeyman!

You have taken your first steps to a wider understanding of the art of the Alchemist! No longer content to trudge along, playing with the simple knowledge that most can possess, you have started to truly experiment! Your discoveries mark a turning point in your Profession, stepping aside from the simple, well-trodden path. Instead, you have begun to explore the wilderness of the universe's potential!

The Path to Fire Pattern Mastery has begun! 7/100

*

Congratulations!

You have taken your first steps along the path of your Secondary Profession of Herbalism and Organic Compounds!

No longer must you wait and hope. No longer must you only purchase or rely upon whimsical luck to guide you in your search for ingredients. As a Novice Herbalist, you will now be guided to Organic Compounds that could enhance or be otherwise used in your Primary Profession of Creationist Alchemist by all of your senses.

Perhaps the secrets of life reside in your dinner? Mayhap that unusual smell you scent on the wind is actually a poison so deadly that cities will fall? Only the gods can stop you now!

Gain +2 to Perception!

I looked them over, grinning to myself despite my exhaustion, before turning to the potion I'd managed to create. The information almost seemed to leap into my tired mind, and I read it quickly, smiling proudly.

Anti-Fire Balm		Further Description *Yes/No*	
Details:		This apprentice-grade balm will grant a 7% resistance to all forms of fire for eleven minutes when spread evenly on a surface.	
Rarity:	Magical:	Durability:	Potency:
Rare	No	100/100	5/10

"So, I basically made sunscreen?" I wondered aloud, reading the details, until Oracle shook her head and told me what I was missing in my sleepless, addled state.

"No Jax, you made a balm that would protect you from seven percent of a *Fireball*. If you could improve on this, you could walk naked over magma and not feel anything. It might be an apprentice-grade potion, but this is hugely significant.

"You managed to make this from scratch, with no guidance, save your own instincts. Half the ingredients there shouldn't work together, and yeah, only a few of them made it into this potion in the end, but you learned so much about mixing and making them into a single product, didn't you?"

"I did," I admitted, realizing that by the time I'd used up most of the ingredients, I'd learned what didn't work for some of them and what did for others. I'd need hundreds of each, I now knew, but once I had them? I could start to really grow into my profession.

I suddenly realized that the healing potions I'd been using and giving out were basically weak as all hell, because they'd been made by utter amateurs. I'd yet to come across a potion made by someone who really knew what they were doing. Even the greater potions were simply particularly good versions of the basic recipes, with perhaps one or two additional ingredients added in.

My eyes widened in recognition as I grasped the faintest possibility of what I'd discovered. If I could find the Pattern for Healing…I needed to devote serious time to this, I knew suddenly. I could find information in every goddamn ingredient out there, and if I could assemble it all together, I'd have a potion that could damn well resurrect the dead.

I remembered a series of books from my past, and a greasy man who'd spoken of bottling fame, brew glory and even of putting a stopper in death itself.

This was a way to actually do *that*.

I could give my people potions that would even the playing field with Nimon, if I worked hard enough. I could create mana potions that would transform someone's mana channels, making them more powerful in every way, not simply increase the regeneration speed.

I sagged backwards, the world of possibilities flooding my mind. I felt my head hit the wood of the deck as my exhausted mind finally gave out, and I slept.

Some seven hours later, I was awoken from a dream in which I was beating a giant gummy bear to death with a potted fern for some reason, only to find Oracle shaking me, fear in her eyes.

"Wha—" I mumbled, confused, until her panic fought its way through the levels of sleep-fogged incomprehension that filled my mind.

"Jax! Wake up!" she snapped, and I rolled to my feet, displacing her, and looking around the room frantically, trying to spot the threat.

"Jax!" Oracle shouted, and I spun on her, my mind filled with a mix of fear, aggression, and a need to fight.

"What!" I shouted back, before I felt it…

There was a feeling or terrible warning, and it was emanating from the northeast. I grabbed my naginata and sprinted for the door, Tang throwing it open and getting out of the way barely a second before I'd have taken it off its hinges.

I ran to the ladder to the upper decks, leaping and triggering my Soaring Majesty ability for a long second, sending me flying out of the hatch and into the air.

I spun in the air, dropping onto the lower deck and staring into the distance. My eyes locked on something that was still beyond the horizon, a structure literally hundreds of miles away, as Oracle focused in on the feeling, receiving a message from Seneschal, even as Jenae spoke it aloud to me, her voice grim as it rang in my mind.

"Beware, Eternal, the Dark Legion of Nimon has begun to march on the Great Tower of Dravith. The War of the Gods has begun."

"Tenandra!" I bellowed, spinning around. "Get us caught up to the fleet. Fast!" I snapped out the order, turning to the others as they raced up on deck behind me, ready for a fight. "The Dark Legion is heading for the tower. We need to get there, now!"

I just hoped we wouldn't be too late.

EPILOGUE

"**M**ove up!" bellowed Turk, jogging along and waving Thomas forward. He ran a little faster, buoyed by the joint feelings of comradeship and a building bloodlust. The bloodlust was an old friend, always there in battle, and had been back in the old world as well, when he'd been crossed. But since swearing to Nimon, he'd found it easier and quicker to rise.

Thomas grinned at Coran as the pair ran side-by-side. The trail they followed was well-trodden by the time they hit it, the green leaves and reaching fronds smashed aside by well over a hundred other soldiers before them.

The hours of running, of constant drilling and pushing that the Dark Legion had instilled in them every day suddenly made perfect sense to Thomas as they ran at a speed barely below a sprint for hour after hour in full armor.

The Trail-Masters, specialist mages of the Dark Church, hurried along with them, men, and women whose only points, it seemed, were invested in Intelligence and Wisdom. They flew atop disks of air, their voices echoing as they chanted the great Trail-Song.

The marching spell boosted the constitution of those who heard it, while decreasing the weight of the world upon them.

"Gravity magic!" Thomas grunted enviously, staring after them longingly as they flowed through the air, making it possible for the Dark Legion to literally run down horses and still be able to fight at the end of it, all in full armor.

"Don't tell me you're going to try to learn that next!" Coran called to Thomas, grinning as he ran alongside him. "Twenty years' service, that calls for, on top of the standard!"

"And it'd be worth it!" Thomas called back. "Besides, you know you're only pissed because they wouldn't teach you the Force-Push!"

"It's stupid!" Coran grunted. "Imagine being able to use that in a fight; parry, Force-Push them over, stab, and you're onto the next one!"

"True, but we all know you only wanted it to be able to lift Mella's dress!" called Sergeant Belladonna from ahead of them as she laughed, and the others joined in.

"Seriously, how many people did you tell?" Coran gasped, glaring at Thomas, who laughed and ran harder, resolving to stand out to Belladonna if it was the last thing he did.

Thomas was part of the Advance, a place of high honor, he'd been told, as the team of three hundred rushed forward, closing the distance to the Great Tower. They were to get the portal mages there and hold the territory until they could create a stable bridge for the rest of the army, all five thousand of them, to cross over.

Such a portal was horrifically expensive, not just in material costs, but in lives. At least some of the twelve mages required to build it were guaranteed to die in the casting. Literally years and years of specific, dedicated training went into each mage, and most would be able to cast such a great working only once or twice before being drained to the point of death or debilitating injury.

The survivors would be rewarded and the dead bundled away. Part of Thomas rebelled against such waste, but the new part, the part that was growing to glory in the fight, in the sheer relief of not having to worry or think anymore, of each day being fresh, filled with opportunities to test himself, to fight and to grow…that part reveled in it.

Thomas jumped over a large rock in his path and landed with a crunch, his black and gold breastplate bouncing slightly atop his chain-mail hauberk. He grunted, resolving to get his straps checked by Coran when he stopped, even as he shifted his bags to a better location, keeping a constant watch on the sides of the trail and hoping some monster might try its luck.

The march—hell, the *sprint*, he might as well call it—had been worked out as just over four hundred miles, apparently. The column could do an average of ten miles an hour, slowed substantially because the damn terrain was so heavily wooded. Two of the Trail-Masters were literally charged with smashing the trees apart as they went, then the soldiers would run over the wreckage. Each company got half an hour in the lead before dropping back, and the next one cycled forward to stomp the ground flat.

Four hundred miles, with the soldiers running for ten hours a day, gave an estimate of four days for the Dark Legion Advance to reach the tower and another day to set up the portals.

Thomas couldn't wait. Five more days, and he'd be able to gut the fucker who had claimed his brother's name, daring to mock him like this.

He glared out of the full-face helm, hearing his rough breathing echoing raspily, as the constant anger, one of Nimon's dark gifts, bubbled along, directly competing against the steady, low-level rage he'd spent his life filled with.

The result was a warrior who was rising fast in the Dark Legion, and who had already caught the approving eye of others, as well as inciting jealousy and hatred.

That was good.

As Nimon taught, only the strong could live. The weak were food.

THE END OF BOOK FOUR

GIINT

UNDERVERSE OMNIBUS THREE

8th November 2022

(Combining books 5&6 of the UnderVerse)

Jax might not have started the war, but he'll damn well finish it. But can he and his allies make it through unscathed?

When Jax entered the UnderVerse, it was with the plan of finding his brother, holing up somewhere and maybe, just maybe, trying to take over the world. He's making progress in all of those goals, but maybe not in the ways he wanted.

The God of Death has personally intervened to send his Dark Legion against Jax and his people, with the aim of grinding the upstart Empire usurper into dust. Jax has refugees by the hundreds, Legionnaires of the Empire by the score and best of all, a team that are cheering as he spits in the God of Death's eye.

The sun is setting though, with new enemies appearing and hidden forces being revealed.

The War of the Gods is growing, and when the sun rises again, it'll be in a changed Realm…

Finish the journey of UnderVerse Season One with Omnibus 3!

UNDERVERSE 7

6th December 2022

The war between Jax and Nimon is on hold, the borders established, and a form of peace should be descending on the Imperial Territory of Dravith…

But life rarely goes as Jax hopes.

New and old enemies are on the horizon, the land itself is disturbed, and worst of all, the Gods are not all he believed they are…

The Dark Tide Rises…

REVIEWS

Hey! Well, I hope you enjoyed the book? If so, please, please remember to leave a review, its massively important, as not only does it let others know about the book, it also tells Amazon that the book is worth promoting, and makes it more likely that more people will see it.

That in turn will hopefully keep me able to keep writing full time, while listening to crazy German bands screaming in my ears, and frankly, I kinda really like that!

If you want to spread the good word, that'd be amazing, and if you know of anyone that might be interested in stocking my books, I'm happy to reach out and send them samples, but honestly, if you enjoy my madness, that's massive for me.
Thank you.

FACEBOOK AND SOCIAL MEDIA

If you want to reach out, chat or shoot the shit, you can always find me on either my author page here:

www.facebook.com/JezCajiaoAuthor

OR

We've recently set up a new Facebook group to spread the word about cool LitRPG books. It's dedicated to two very simple rules, 1; lets spread the word about new and old brilliant LitRPG books, and 2: Don't be a Dick!

They sound like really simple rules, but you'd be amazed…

Come join us!

https://www.facebook.com/groups/litrpglegion

I'm also on Discord here: **https://discord.gg/u5JYHscCEH**

Or I'm reaching out on other forms of social media atm, I'm just spread a little thin that's all!

You're most likely to find me on Discord, but please, don't be offended when I don't approve friend requests on my personal Facebook pages. I did originally, and several people abused that, sending messages to my family and being generally unpleasant, hence, the *Author* page.

I hope you understand.

PATREON!

Okay then, now for those of you that don't know about Patreon, its essentially a way to support your favorite nutcases, you can sign up for a day or a month or a year, and you get various benefits for it, ranging from my heartfelt thanks, to advance access to the books, to signed books, naming characters and more.

At the time of me writing this, the advanced Patreon readers are about 20 chapters into Arise: Dark Crusader, and are voting on the next batch of Character Art as well, so yeah, you get plenty for the support 😌

There's one wonderful supporter out there that I have to thank personally, ASeaInStorm, you utter legend you. Thank you brother.

www.patreon.com/Jezcajiao

Note: All character details, maps and spell/ability details are on World Anvil:

https://www.worldanvil.com/

This requires an account to access, but a free one is fine, once logged in, search for 'UnderVerse' and the covers should show which is mine.

RECOMMENDATIONS

I'm often asked for personal recommendations, so if this book has whetted your appetite for more LitRPG, please have a look at the following, these are brilliant series by brilliant authors!

Ascend Online by Luke Chmilenko

The Land by Aleron Kong

Challengers Call by Nathan A Thompson

SoulShip also by Nathan

Endless Online by M H Johnson

Silver Fox and the Western Hero, also by M H Johnson

The Good Guys/Bad Guys by Eric Ugland

Condition: Evolution by Kevin Sinclair

Space Seasons by Dawn Chapman

The Wayward Bard by Lars M

LITRPG!

To learn more about LitRPG, talk to other authors including myself, and to just have an awesome time, please join the LitRPG Group

www.facebook.com/groups/LitRPGGroup

FACEBOOK

There's also a few really active Facebook groups I'd recommend you join, as you'll get to hear about great new books, new releases and interact with all your (new) favorite authors! (I may also be there, skulking at the back and enjoying the memes…)

www.facebook.com/groups/LitRPGsociety/

www.facebook.com/groups/LitRPG.books/

www.facebook.com/groups/LitRPGforum/

www.facebook.com/groups/gamelitsociety/

PARTE II

19

Sara

IL RESTO DI NOVEMBRE TRASCORRE IN FRETTA TRA VISITE ospedaliere, interrogatori dell'FBI, e attesa. Attesa infinita. Mi sento costantemente tesa, aspettando il ritorno di Peter. Ogni volta che attraverso il parcheggio dell'ospedale, cammino per strada, o mi addormento nella vecchia camera da letto nella casa dei miei genitori (la mia casa, che in virtù dell'appartenenza a un ricercato criminale è stata sequestrata dal governo), mi aspetto di essere rapita e portata via—se non da Peter, da uno degli uomini che ha ingaggiato per sorvegliarmi.

E mi stanno sorvegliando. Lo so. Lo sento. È la stessa sensazione di prima, la stessa paranoia di occhi nascosti che mi seguono. In parte è dovuta agli agenti dell'FBI che studiano ogni mia mossa, ma non del tutto. Sono diventata brava ad individuare i Federali. È sempre l'auto anonima dall'altra parte della strada, il pedone che non sembra della zona, l'uomo o la donna solitari al bar.

Gli uomini di Peter sono diversi. Non li vedo mai; sento solo la loro presenza. Sono l'ombra dietro l'angolo, l'eco dei passi nel parcheggio, il prurito tra le scapole. Ci sono sempre, ma non sono mai abbastanza vicini affinché io—o i Federali—possa individuarli.

Certo, è possibile che io sia davvero paranoica questa volta, ma non credo. Conosco Peter. Non mi lascerebbe qui senza monitorarmi. O almeno, così continuo a ripetermi, mentre passa una settimana dopo l'altra senza ricevere sue notizie... senza nemmeno un indizio che tornerà per me.

Cerco di concentrarmi sul fatto che posso trascorrere tutto questo tempo con i miei genitori, e sono contenta di questo. Lo sono davvero. Papà sembra di nuovo pieno di vita dopo il mio ritorno, nuotando ed eseguendo gli esercizi assegnati dal medico con rinnovato vigore e dedizione. E mamma migliora giorno dopo giorno, con le ossa che guariscono con la rapidità di una donna che ha la metà dei suoi anni. Per ora è a letto—cosa che la fa impazzire—ma i medici hanno promesso che inizierà la fisioterapia non appena il suo corpo lo permetterà, forse entro la metà di gennaio.

Novembre lascia il posto a dicembre, e ancora, l'attesa interminabile continua. È come se esistessi in un limbo tra la mia vecchia vita e quella che avevo iniziato a stabilire con Peter. Vivo nella mia casa d'infanzia, circondata dalla famiglia e dagli amici, eppure non riesco a scacciare la sensazione di essere un ospite, un visitatore in un luogo a cui non appartengo più.

Penso che i miei genitori lo percepiscano, perché con il passare dei giorni iniziano a chiedersi perché non stia facendo certe cose, come cercare un nuovo lavoro o trovare un altro posto in cui vivere. Li tranquillizzo dicendo che voglio concentrarmi su mamma per ora, ma man mano che la sua salute migliora, quella scusa appare sempre più vuota.

"Sara, tesoro... non c'è bisogno che tu sia qui tutto il tempo" dice mamma, quando vado a trovarla una fredda mattina di dicembre. "C'è tuo padre che può tenermi compagnia, e so che ci sono cose che hai rimandato a causa di questo." Agita la mano incolume verso i gessi sulle gambe che la tengono immobile.

Sorridendo, scuoto la testa. "Non c'è niente che non possa aspettare, Mamma. Grazie alla vendita della casa, ho i soldi in banca, e mi piace vivere con papà. A meno che non si sia stancato di avermi sotto al suo stesso tetto."

"Certo che no" dice subito mamma, come sapevo che avrebbe fatto. "È felicissimo di riaverti a casa. Non hai idea di quanto siamo sollevati di riaverti qui. Se vuoi vivere con noi per sempre, sei più che benvenuta. So solo che sei sempre stata indipendente, e non voglio che ti senta obbligata a prenderti cura di noi invece di rimettere la tua vita in carreggiata."

Rimettere la mia vita in carreggiata. Respingo l'impulso di dirle che non so più che cosa significhi questo. Che non ci sono "carreggiate" per me, nessun percorso facile che io possa intravedere. Il mio futuro, una volta così chiaro e lineare, è ora avvolto nell'oscurità, pieno di colpi di scena che posso solo intuire.

"Non preoccuparti, Mamma" dico, scacciando quel pensiero cupo. "Sono felice di essere qui con te e Papà."

E sorridendo, trovo un altro argomento di conversazione che non sia la mia vita.

Che non sia il futuro che non riesco più a immaginare.

CELEBRIAMO L'HANUKKAH DAI LEVINSON, POI NATALE E Capodanno all'ospedale con mamma. Durante i festeggiamenti, rido e sorrido, scambio regali e fingo di essere tornata per sempre. Dico a mio padre che, sì, cercherò presto un nuovo lavoro, e discuto dell'acquisto di una nuova casa con Joe

Levinson. Mi consiglia un buon agente immobiliare, e annoto il nome, come se fosse importante.

Come se qualcosa di tutto questo fosse importante, quando, in qualsiasi momento, potrei scomparire di nuovo.

Quando la metà di gennaio se ne va, lo sforzo di aspettare e fingere, di destreggiarmi continuamente tra mezze verità e bugie diventa insopportabile. L'assenza di Peter mi squarcia il cuore, e per quanto provi a concentrarmi sulla famiglia e gli amici, mi manca sempre, così tanto che non riesco a pensare ad altro durante il giorno. So quanto sia sbagliato, e mi disprezzo per questo, ma a questo punto sono così abituata al senso di colpa che non mi sembra così terribile come un tempo.

Desiderare il mio tormentatore non sembra più un grosso tradimento.

Non posso dimenticare che Peter ha ucciso George e mi ha tenuta prigioniera per mesi, o che uccide la gente per denaro, ma quando penso a lui, sono i momenti dolci e teneri che mi vengono in mente, tutti i piccoli modi con cui mi dimostrava quotidianamente quanto mi amasse. Mi sorprendo a fantasticare su come mi massaggiava i piedi e mi portava la colazione a letto, su come si prendeva cura di me, quando non mi sentivo bene.

Su come mi addormentavo tra le sue braccia, invece che nel mio letto freddo e vuoto.

Le notti sono decisamente le peggiori. È questo il momento in cui il mio desiderio per lui è più acuto, con il desiderio che sfocia nella fisicità. Ogni sera, mi rigiro più volte, cercando di addormentarmi, mentre il corpo brucia per un uomo che si trova a migliaia di chilometri di distanza. Provo con i giocattoli, leggo storie erotiche, guardo i porno, ma niente placa quel doloroso vuoto dentro di me. È come quando Peter era via per il suo lavoro in Messico, solo un migliaio di volte peggio, perché allora, all'inizio della nostra strana relazione, era ancora un terrificante sconosciuto. Ora, però, è parte di me, essendosi conficcato nel mio cuore e nella mente al punto tale che la vita senza di lui sembra vuota come il letto.

La situazione è talmente grave che prendo in considerazione l'idea di cogliere al volo le sollecitazioni dei miei genitori e iniziare a cercare davvero un altro lavoro. Tuttavia, decido di tornare a fare volontariato presso la clinica per donne.

Con mio grande sollievo, sono più che felici di riavermi.

"Ci sei mancata così tanto" mi dice Lydia, la segretaria. "Non c'eravamo nemmeno resi conto di quanto avessimo bisogno di te fin quando non te ne sei andata. Va tutto bene ora? L'FBI si è presentata qui, interrogando tutti noi, e—"

"Sì, è tutto a posto. C'è stato solo un equivoco con il ragazzo con cui sono andata in vacanza" spiego, non volendo ricominciare con l'intero racconto anche qui. "Ora si è risolto tutto, non preoccuparti."

Capisco che Lydia sta morendo dalla curiosità, ma si trattiene, percependo la mia riluttanza nel discutere ulteriormente. Non ho idea di quali voci circolassero qui, ma fortunatamente per me, lo staff della clinica e i volontari si occupano continuamente di situazioni delicate, e sanno quando insistere e quando è meglio lasciar correre. Dopo un primo round di "che cos'è successo" e "dove sei stata," mi lasciano tutti per concentrarsi sulle pazienti—cosa che faccio anch'io a tempo pieno e anche di più.

Fondamentalmente, ogni volta che non sto con i miei genitori.

"Come diavolo fai a sovraccaricarti di lavoro in quel modo, se sei disoccupata?" si lamenta Marsha un mese dopo, quando telefono per declinare il suo invito ad uscire di nuovo, dichiarandomi sfinita dopo un turno di notte alla clinica. "Davvero, tesoro, non ti vedo fuori dai corridoi dell'ospedale da settimane. Prima, tua madre aveva bisogno di te ventiquattr'ore su ventiquattro, e ora questo. Non usciamo da quella volta al Patty."

"Lo so, lo so." Sospiro al telefono, pizzicandomi la punta del naso. "Mi dispiace, Marsha. Forse la prossima settimana sarà più facile."

Non lo sarà—sarò in clinica per oltre sessanta ore la settimana prossima, compresi due turni di notte—ma troverò del tempo per Marsha a prescindere. L'ho evitata dopo aver capito il suo coinvolgimento con l'FBI, e sto iniziando a sentirmi in colpa. Quello che ha fatto mi è sembrato un tradimento, ma non è una reazione del tutto razionale. Probabilmente stava facendo quello che riteneva giusto, forse ha addirittura pensato che mi stesse aiutando. Cooperare con i Federali è generalmente la strategia migliore per il cittadino medio rispettoso della legge—ma non posso più ritenermi tale.

Non quando nascondo i miei veri sentimenti per un ricercato assassino.

Penso che l'Agente Ryson abbia intuito che non sto raccontando tutta la verità, perché continua a trascinarmi nell'ufficio dell'FBI in centro. A questo punto, ho subito almeno dieci interrogatori, e ogni volta sono rimasta fedele alla mia storia, ripetendo agli agenti solo ciò che avevo rivelato all'inizio e nient'altro. Aiuta il fatto che ogni volta che iniziano a sondare più a fondo, il mio battito cardiaco salta, e il corpo entra in modalità attacco di panico.

È come se il mio Disturbo Post Traumatico da Stress o qualunque cosa mi abbia provocato stia dalla parte di Peter.

"Ti sta seguendo un terapeuta, Dottoressa Cobakis?" chiede Ryson, dopo che hanno dovuto chiamare Karen, il loro agente con una formazione medica, per calmarmi dopo una sessione di domande particolarmente approfondita. "Se non è così, posso consigliarti qualcuno."

Il mio respiro è ancora rapido e instabile per l'attacco di panico, ma riesco a scuotere la testa. "Ho qualcuno, grazie."

Non ho visto il mio terapeuta, il Dottor Evans, da quando sono tornata, ma è bravo. Mi ha aiutata in passato, quando non riuscivo a sopportare gli incubi e l'ansia derivanti dall'aggressione di Peter nella mia cucina. Dovrei tornare da lui, ma non posso entrare nel suo ufficio e raccontargli lo stesso confuso mix di verità e bugie che ho escogitato per l'FBI.

Preferirei affrontare i miei problemi da sola, mentre aspetto Peter.

Tornerà a prendermi un giorno o l'altro.

*P*eter

Conto i giorni su un calendario, segnandoli come un uomo che non vede l'ora di uscire di prigione. Il giorno della mia liberazione—il giorno in cui sarò riunito a Sara—può essere solo ipotizzato, così scelgo una data otto mesi a partire dal mio incontro con Novak, e conto alla rovescia, perché scoprire i dettagli sulla risorsa di Novak è il primo passo verso il piano per assicurarmi un futuro reale con Sara.

Con il nostro nascondiglio in Giappone presumibilmente compromesso, passiamo da un rifugio all'altro, senza mai rimanere in un luogo per più di un paio di settimane. Lungo la strada, svolgiamo diversi lavori, alcuni più impegnativi di altri, ma nessuno così complicato o pericoloso come quello che abbiamo concordato con Novak.

I miei compagni di squadra—anche Yan—hanno accettato la mia decisione sull'incarico di Esguerra, così come il fatto che scopriremo di più sulla risorsa, quando sarà il momento giusto. Come ho promesso a Novak, non ho rivelato i dettagli di cui abbiamo discusso. In parte, questo è perché non c'è davvero niente di cui parlare ancora, ma principalmente è perché ho bisogno che Novak si fidi di me. I miei ragazzi possono comportarsi bene come chiunque altro a Hollywood, ma quando si tratta di qualcuno con le risorse di Novak, non si sa mai chi sta ascoltando e quando. I nostri rifugi sono sicuri, ma ci avventuriamo fuori, e un microfono parabolico potrebbe essere utilizzato da distanze sorprendenti.

Questo, più di ogni altra cosa, è il motivo per cui Sara non è più un argomento di conversazione tra noi. Per quanto riguarda la mia squadra, potrebbe anche non esistere.

"Non voglio sentire il suo nome e nemmeno il pronome *lei*" ho detto loro. "Non nominatela con me, e non parlatene mai nemmeno tra voi. Se n'è andata, e basta. Chiaro?"

Hanno annuito tutti, comprendendo la mia preoccupazione, e ho aggiunto altri livelli di sicurezza alla mia comunicazione con gli hacker e con gli uomini che abbiamo ingaggiato per sorvegliare Sara negli Stati Uniti. Non posso *non* tenere d'occhio la mia ptichka, ma per la sua sicurezza nessuno può sapere della mia continua ossessione nei suoi confronti.

E io *sono* ossessionato. La malattia è peggiorata a causa della sua assenza. Sogno Sara ogni notte. A volte, si tratta di qualcosa di innocuo come stringerla e sfiorarle i capelli setosi, ma spesso i sogni sono oscuri e violenti. In alcuni, la perdo; in altri, sono la causa del suo dolore. Il nostro primo incontro, in cui l'ho drogata e torturata con l'acqua, mi ha tormentato nelle ultime settimane, e i ricordi mi hanno invaso la mente con dettagli incredibilmente brutali. Il momento peggiore è quando mi sveglio dai sogni in cui le faccio male con il cazzo duro e bisognoso, e mi rendo conto che per quanto mi manchi—per quanto la ami con tutto il cuore—i miei sentimenti per lei non saranno mai semplici e dolci, incontaminati dall'oscurità del nostro passato.

Dalle cose che le ho fatto... e che potrei fare ancora.

Se le notti sono terribili, i giorni sono addirittura peggiori. La prima cosa che faccio ogni mattina è leggere i rapporti su Sara, sia da parte degli hacker che da parte degli americani che la sorvegliano. Ecco come ho scoperto che è tornata a fare volontariato presso la clinica e che sua madre ha iniziato la fisioterapia. Di tanto in tanto, gli americani riescono a inviarmi anche un video di Sara, e in quei giorni guardo le registrazioni diverse volte prima della colazione, e poi una dozzina di volte in più la sera appena prima di addormentarmi. Nel frattempo, mi alleno con la mia squadra e gestisco gli affari, ma la mente non è concentrata su nessuna di queste cose.

È concentrata su di lei.

Sulla mia bellissima ptichka, che mi manca come un arto reciso.

Penso costantemente di recuperarla. Grazie alla storia di Sara sul fatto che mi sia stancato di lei, i Federali non hanno cercato di nasconderla da me. La sorvegliano ancora per un mio eventuale ritorno, ma non hanno ritenuto necessario metterla nel programma di protezione dei testimoni o qualcosa del genere. Penso che sia perché *sperano* che io torni per lei.

È un'esca, anche se non lo ammetteranno mai.

E sono tentato. Cazzo, sono tentato. Ora che i suoi genitori non hanno più così bisogno di lei, immagino di tornare a prenderla ogni giorno, al punto che l'intera operazione è stampata nella mia mente. So esattamente come supereremmo i controlli aerei e dove atterreremmo, come creeremmo una distrazione per allontanare i Federali da Sara e come realizzeremmo una falsa pista per distoglierli dalla nostra scia, mentre scappiamo.

Potremmo farlo domani, se volessimo.

Tra una ventina d'ore, potrei riabbracciare Sara.

Il più delle volte riesco a scrollarmi di dosso la fantasia, ribadendo a me stesso i motivi per cui lo sto facendo, ricordandomi che è più al sicuro dove si trova. Tuttavia, ci sono giorni in cui la fantasia è l'unica cosa a cui riesco a pensare, e rinsavisco appena pochi secondi prima di cedere e ordinare ad Anton di preparare l'elicottero.

Per mantenere la sanità mentale, intensifico la ricerca di Henderson, l'ultima e più elusiva persona sulla mia lista. Il fatto che non abbiamo ancora trovato lui e la sua famiglia conferma le voci sul suo background nella CIA. Quel bastardo è bravo in questo—come qualcuno nella mia professione.

Potrebbe essere giunto il momento di alzare il tiro.

"Andremo in North Carolina" annuncio al tavolo della colazione il mattino seguente. "Andremo a smuovere le acque ad Asheville, e vedremo di scovare lo stronzo nel più duro dei modi."

I miei compagni di squadra alzano gli occhi dai piatti con espressioni identiche e prive di sorpresa. Questo è stato il piano di riserva da sempre. Preferiremmo non coinvolgere gli innocenti—amici di Henderson e membri della famiglia lontani che non avevano nulla a che fare con il massacro di Daryevo—ma data l'elusività del nostro obiettivo, è l'unica opzione rimasta.

"Se lo aspetterà" dice Anton, spingendo via il piatto. "Molto probabilmente è una trappola."

Sorrido cupamente. "Lo so."

La difficoltà di questa operazione è ciò che mi emoziona. Non solo dovremo entrare e uscire dal Paese senza essere scoperti, ma Henderson indubbiamente farà in modo che i Federali tengano d'occhio le sue connessioni. Logisticamente, questo sarà simile al sequestro di Sara, solo che invece di rapire una donna, interrogheremo una mezza dozzina di persone, che probabilmente saranno osservate dai compari di Henderson dell'FBI, e forse persino dalla CIA.

"Dovrebbe essere divertente" dice Yan, con gli occhi verdi luccicanti. "Meglio che restare qui." Agita la mano per indicare la baita rustica in cui ci troviamo dalla scorsa settimana, il nostro rifugio nella Polonia orientale.

Ilya gli lancia un'occhiata e riprende a mangiare. Ce l'ha col fratello da una settimana, da quando Yan ha scopato una cameriera di Budapest che anche Ilya voleva. Non è la prima volta che si crea una situazione del genere—i gemelli hanno gusti simili in fatto di donne—ma in passato, l'avrebbero condivisa amichevolmente, o contemporaneamente o alternandosi. Non ho idea di cos'abbia reso diversa questa cameriera, ma Ilya è incazzato con Yan da quando siamo arrivati qui.

Non ho intenzione di intromettermi in questa disputa, così fingo di non notare la tensione al tavolo. "Preparatevi" dico ai ragazzi. "Voglio essere ad Asheville prima della fine della settimana, quindi dovremo avere un piano valido entro domani."

E alzandomi, invio un'e-mail ai miei contatti negli Stati Uniti.

Sara

INCONTRO MARSHA IN UN CLUB NEL QUARTIERE WEST LOOP DI Chicago. È nuovo, alla moda e così chiassoso che le orecchie mi vibrano per la musica a tutto volume che esce dagli altoparlanti. Marsha è già sulla pista da ballo, strusciando contro due giovani tipi simili a dei banchieri, così mi dirigo verso il bar e ordino un gin and tonic. Spero che l'alcol calmerà l'onnipresente tensione nella pancia.

Un giorno tornerà. Me lo ripeto da settimane, eppure sono ancora qui, ancora in questo sconvolgente limbo. Cinque giorni fa, mamma ha camminato dal letto al bagno solo con le stampelle, eppure sono ancora qui, a vivere nella casa dei miei genitori senza sapere quando—o se—Peter tornerà a prendermi.

Potrebbe essere vero? Potrebbe essere che le bugie che ho raccontato all'FBI siano diventate la verità? Forse il mio assassino russo si è davvero stancato di me. Forse il mio attaccamento a lui nella clinica gli ha fatto perdere interesse. So che i pericoli e le sfide sono il suo pane quotidiano, e forse questo è tutto ciò che significavo per lui: una sfida. Dopotutto, che cosa c'è di meglio che non sia guadagnarsi l'affetto della vedova del tuo nemico, di una donna che ha tutte le ragioni per detestarti?

Il pensiero continua ad invadere la mia mente, e continuo a scacciarlo, ricordando lo sguardo sul viso di Peter, quando ha giurato di tornare a prendermi. "Finché sarò in vita" ha detto, e non ne ho dubitato per un secondo—non dopo tutto quello che ha fatto per farmi sua.

Non ne dubito nemmeno ora—non esattamente—e questo significa solo una cosa.

Se Peter non è tornato a prendermi, è perché non può.

È perché è successo qualcosa.

Ho cercato di non pensarci, di respingere quella terrificante possibilità, ma non posso più ignorarla. La vita di Peter è tale che tanto varrebbe che fosse un soldato in una zona di guerra. Tra le autorità che gli danno la caccia in tutto il mondo e i potenti criminali con cui ha a che fare tutto il tempo, sfida le probabilità di sopravvivere giorno dopo giorno. E quando i suoi "lavori" vengono aggiunti al mix, le probabilità che rimanga ferito o peggio non sono insignificanti.

In realtà, sono così alte che ho un nodo permanente nello stomaco in questi giorni.

L'unica cosa che mi dà conforto è che sono ancora sorvegliata, sia dall'FBI che dagli uomini inquietanti di Peter. Quella sensazione di prurito tra le scapole non si placa mai, quando sono in pubblico. Anzi, in questo preciso istante, sono certa che ci siano almeno un paio dei miei stalker nel locale— l'anonimo Federale che mi ha seguita e che sta versando una birra dall'altra parte del bar e qualcun altro, qualcuno che non riesco a identificare, ma di cui percepisco la presenza.

Se Peter fosse morto o catturato e l'FBI lo sapesse, avrebbero smesso di seguirmi. Lo stesso vale per chiunque sia stato ingaggiato da lui.

Non è un grande sollievo—potrebbe ancora essere gravemente ferito da qualche parte—ma è già qualcosa.

È quello che mi fa alzare ogni mattina e affrontare la giornata, nonostante il buco che mi tormenta lo stomaco.

"Eccoti!" Marsha compare accanto a me, radiosa per quel fervore unico che genera solo la danza potenziata dall'alcol. "Stavo iniziando a pensare che non saresti venuta."

"Sono qui" la rassicuro, mentre il barista mi porge da bere. "Ho solo fatto tardi in clinica—sai come vanno le cose."

Annuisce con fare comprensivo e dice al barista: "Una Corona, per favore."

Le porge la bottiglia, e lei brinda con me. "Per essere finalmente venuta a divertirti" dice, e rido, mentre la mia amica beve un lungo sorso.

"Allora" dice "come stai? Non posso credere che marzo sia alle porte, e che non usciamo dalla tua prima settimana qui."

"Uh, lo so." Faccio una smorfia. "Mi dispiace. È solo che con mia mamma e tutto il resto—"

Marsha mi interrompe, scuotendo la sua birra. "Non aggiungere altro. Ho capito, lo so. Dimmi solo una cosa..." Si guarda intorno, poi si avvicina, poggiando una mano sul mio avambraccio. "Stai bene, tesoro?" La sua voce è dolce, nonostante la musica assordante, con lo sguardo che si sofferma sulla cicatrice ormai sbiadita sulla mia fronte. "Non abbiamo mai veramente parlato... beh, di quello che è successo."

Mi si stringe la gola. "Ti ho detto che cos'è successo."

Annuisce gravemente. "Lo so. Non mi riferisco a questo. Come lo stai affrontando?"

"Sono"—*stressata al massimo, impossibilitata a mangiare o dormire, ho incubi su Peter ferito o morto*—"tranquilla."

"Uh-uh." Marsha osserva il mio avambraccio, che sembra

particolarmente magro e pallido sotto le sue abbronzate dita elegantemente curate. "Ecco perché sembri uno scheletro uscito dal laboratorio di anatomia."

Tiro via il braccio. "Sono a dieta."

Sospira e si appoggia. "Lo vedo."

Sorseggio il mio drink, desiderando di poterle dire la verità: che non sto subendo le conseguenze di un trauma psicologico, ma che mi manca l'uomo che mi ha fatto questo, che sto aspettando che torni e mi riprenda. Solo che ammetterlo significherebbe firmare la mia condanna al carcere.

"Sono tranquilla, sto bene" ripeto. Stampandomi un sorriso luminoso sul volto, dico: "Che ne dici di smettere di parlare di cose deprimenti e di andare a ballare?"

Marsha esita, poi sorride. "Va bene. Andiamo a ballare."

Le afferro la mano e ci dirigiamo verso la pista da ballo affollata. Sta appena iniziando a suonare uno degli ultimi successi di Nicki Minaj, e rido, mentre ricordo di aver canticchiato la mia versione di questa canzone per i ragazzi in Giappone.

Anche Marsha ride, inclinando la testa all'indietro per ingoiare la birra, e iniziamo a ballare. Canto, sostituendo alcune parti del testo, e poco dopo ci divertiamo per davvero. Il ritmo mi vibra nelle ossa, facendo muovere i piedi di loro spontanea volontà, e rido mentre una bevanda mi scivola sulla mano.

"Aspetta" dico a Marsha, e mando giù il resto del mio gin and tonic per evitare un altro incidente. Posizionando il bicchiere vuoto su un tavolo vicino, mi faccio strada tra la folla verso il bar e ordino una bottiglia di birra—molto più adatta alla pista da ballo. Quando torno, Marsha sta già ballando con un paio di nuovi ragazzi, e mentre mi avvicino, mi afferra la mano, tirandomi verso di loro.

"Loro sono Bill e Rob" grida sopra la musica, e io sorrido, sentendomi a disagio. Non è questo che avevo in mente, quando ho accettato questa uscita con Marsha.

"Vado al bagno" dico, chinandomi in avanti in modo che Marsha possa sentire. "Tornerò presto."

"Aspetta, vengo con te." Marsha abbandona i suoi compagni senza una seconda occhiata e mi segue tra la folla.

È ancora presto, quindi la fila per il bagno delle signore non è lunghissima. Mentre aspettiamo, Marsha mi racconta tutto sul club in cui è andata con Tonya lo scorso fine settimana e sul ragazzo sexy che ha conosciuto lì. Ascolto, sorrido e annuisco, meravigliandomi per tutto il tempo di quanto sia diversa la vita della mia amica, di quanto sia semplice e priva di complicazioni. Quand'è stata l'ultima volta in cui la mia più grande preoccupazione era se un ragazzo mi avrebbe richiamata? Al college, forse? Quando ho conosciuto George, ho smesso di frequentare ragazzi, e non ho ricominciato a farlo dopo la sua morte.

Peter mi ha rapita prima che potessi averne l'occasione.

Finalmente arriviamo al bagno, ci prendiamo cura dei bisogni essenziali e poi torniamo sulla pista da ballo. Adesso è ancora più affollata, quindi dopo mezz'ora passata ad essere spinte qua e là e ad avere bevande rovesciate su di noi, Marsha mi urla nell'orecchio: "Andiamocene da qui."

La seguo fuori con gratitudine, e ci dirigiamo verso una sala a un paio di isolati in fondo alla strada, dove ci fermiamo al bar e ascoltiamo una band che suona dal vivo canzoni rock degli anni Ottanta, intervallate da recenti hit della Top 100. "Tu canti, vero?" chiede Marsha, dopo aver trangugiato un paio di sorsi, e io annuisco, con la testa che mi gira per l'alcol.

"Va bene, allora." Marsha sorride. "Facciamolo." Balza giù dallo sgabello e mi afferra il polso, sollevando il braccio in aria. "Ehi, ascoltatemi tutti" grida sopra la musica. "La mia amica qui canta davvero bene. Volete sentirla?"

Vorrei sprofondare nel pavimento, ma alcune persone nella folla—per lo più ragazzi ubriachi—rispondono con un coro di "sì, dannazione."

"Andiamo." Marsha mi spinge sul palco, dove i membri della band sembrano meno contenti di avere a che fare con una dilettante.

Normalmente, sgattaiolerei fuori per poi urlare in faccia a Marsha, ma tra l'alcol che allenta le mie inibizioni e le piccole esibizioni per Peter e i suoi uomini in Giappone, in qualche modo trovo il coraggio di rimanere sul palco.

"Ragazzi, conoscete 'Karma' di Alicia Keys?" chiedo al chitarrista, sperando che non stia biascicando le mie parole.

Il chitarrista—un ragazzo con le guance rubiconde e una leggera stempiatura—mi studia con diffidenza. "Può essere. Canterai mentre suoniamo?"

"Ti dispiace?" Gli rivolgo il mio sorriso più carino. "Solo una canzone, e poi mi toglierò di mezzo."

Scambia un'occhiata con gli altri musicisti, poi mi infila un microfono tra le mani, e dice: "Oh, dannazione. Forza, ragazza. Mostraci quello che sai fare."

Suonano le prime note, e affronto la folla, con il battito accelerato, mentre mi rendo conto del guaio in cui mi sono cacciata. L'ultima volta in cui mi sono esibita davanti a così tante persone è stata alle scuole medie, quando avevo ottenuto un ruolo da protagonista in un musical scolastico. E proprio come allora, sento uno sciame di farfalle nello stomaco, una sorta di nervosismo.

Sfruttalo, mi dico, e, facendo un respiro profondo, comincio a cantare, lasciando che i miei testi si mescolino con le familiari parole delle canzone. Nonostante tutte le bevande, la mia voce esce forte e pura, così potente che posso sentire la vibrazione del suono. Tutti gli altri rumori nella sala si affievoliscono, e vedo sia la sorpresa che la meraviglia sui volti che mi guardano —compreso quello del Federale che ci ha seguiti dal club e che ora sta bevendo un drink in un angolo.

Anche Marsha sembra stupita, e mi rendo conto che non mi ha mai sentita cantare da sola. Abbiamo fatto la canzone "Tanti

Auguri" per un paio di infermiere come gruppo, e probabilmente mi ha ascoltata cantare insieme alla selezione dei DJ in quel locale qualche mese fa, ma mai così.

Mai una vera e propria performance... specialmente con i miei testi.

Quasi soffoco a quel pensiero. Non ho mai condiviso i miei testi con nessuno, a parte Peter e la sua squadra. Tuttavia, riesco a continuare, e mentre canto la mia versione del ritornello, noto persone tra il pubblico che iniziano a cantare, battendo i palmi delle mani sui tavoli e picchiettando con i piedi al ritmo. Le farfalle dentro di me si espandono, riempiendo ogni fessura del petto, fin quando sento che volerò via sulle loro ali battenti, e continuo a cantare, mentre il corpo inizia a seguire la musica, con l'esperienza della danza che viene alla ribalta.

Non mi rendo conto di toccare le stelle fino alla fine della canzone e del fragoroso applauso. Scendendo dal palco, vedo Marsha battere le mani e fischiare freneticamente verso il palco, e sorrido mentre mi volto, volendo ringraziare la band. Ma stanno applaudendo anche loro, e sembra una fantasia, qualcosa che il mio io adolescente avrebbe potuto evocare in un sogno ad occhi aperti.

"È stato straordinario. Hai altre canzoni del genere?" chiede il chitarrista, e annuisco, anche se le farfalle ora sono più simili a colibrì nel mio petto. In Giappone, ho composto e registrato dozzine di canzoni, alcune con la musica, altre con i miei mix, e le ho eseguite per i miei rapitori come parte del nostro rituale serale. Peter mi ha sempre detto che sono brava, ma l'ho attribuito all'adulazione e alla mancanza di altri divertimenti. Queste persone, tuttavia, sono degli sconosciuti; non hanno motivo di adularmi.

Anzi, i musicisti dovrebbero scacciarmi dal palco, in modo da poter tornare alla musica vera.

"Ne ho un'altra" dico senza fiato al chitarrista, quando il

sogno non mostra segni di dissolvimento. "Conosci la melodia di Bruno Mars 'Just the Way You Are?'"

Sorride. "Certo. Va bene, facciamola—come ti chiami?"

"Sara" dico, e me ne pento immediatamente. Il mio nome è assolutamente ordinario, e questa serata merita qualcos'altro. Qualcosa come Madonna, Rihanna o SZA—

"Facciamo un applauso per Sara!" grida il chitarrista, e dimentico tutto sul mio vero nome, mentre la gente del pubblico applaude e fischia.

La band inizia a suonare 'Just The Way You Are', e faccio un respiro profondo per prepararmi. Quando è il momento delle parole, uso di nuovo i miei testi, e la sensazione di librarmi riaffiora, quando vedo la reazione del pubblico. La adorano. La adorano davvero.

Troppo presto, la canzone finisce e torno sulla terra, solo per librarmi di nuovo, quando il pubblico chiede un'altra canzone, poi un'altra e un'altra ancora. Eseguo sette dei miei migliori numeri di fila, e poi la voce inizia a cedere.

"Ecco fatto" dico al gruppo, restituendo il microfono al chitarrista. "Grazie mille per avermi dato questa possibilità."

"Ragazza, puoi cantare con noi ogni volta che vuoi" dice. "Anzi..." Si volta, scambiando un'occhiata con i suoi compagni, poi si gira di nuovo verso di me. "Ci esibiremo qui per tutto il weekend e ci piacerebbe se ti unissi a noi."

"Oh, io—"

"Ovviamente divideremmo i guadagni con te" dice, come se stessi rifiutando per una questione di soldi. "Faremo dei bei concerti qui."

"Voi ragazzi non potete permettervela" dice Marsha, e mi giro per vederla salire sul palco, ancheggiando. "È una dottoressa, lo sapete."

"Davvero?" Il chitarrista mi osserva. "Talentuosa, carina *e* intelligente, eh?"

Arrossisco, mentre Marsha dice: "Ci puoi scommettere.

Quindi, se la volete, dovete prima parlare con me. Ecco." Afferra il suo polso, estrae una penna e scarabocchia il suo numero sull'avambraccio, proprio accanto al tatuaggio di un cuore trafitto da una freccia. Strizzando l'occhio, aggiunge: "Sono disponibile in qualsiasi momento."

Rido, rendendomi conto di cosa sta facendo Marsha, e la tiro giù dal palco, prima che la mia amica inizi a baciare il musicista davanti a tutti. Secondo le indiscrezioni che girano in ospedale, ha fatto follie, quando era ubriaca.

Ci facciamo strada tra il pubblico che continua ad applaudire e usciamo fuori, con l'aria gelida di febbraio che non riesce a raffreddare il nostro entusiasmo. Sono ancora euforica per l'alcol e la performance, e lo è anche Marsha, che ride e parla di quello che è appena successo e di come possa farmi da agente, in modo da arricchirci entrambe, se dovessi diventare famosa.

Ci stiamo divertendo così tanto che per un momento dimentico che niente di tutto ciò è reale, che la mia vita è solo una grande attesa. Tuttavia, quando salgo su un taxi per tornare a casa, ricordo, e l'euforia svanisce senza lasciare traccia.

Mentre cantavo e mi ubriacavo, è passata un'altra serata.

Un altro giorno senza il ritorno di Peter.

eter

Prendo in considerazione l'idea di contattare Sara, mentre atterriamo in un piccolo aeroporto privato ai piedi delle Great Smoky Mountains, a circa novanta chilometri da Asheville e a soli pochi Stati di distanza da lei. Ho la fortissima tentazione di alzare il telefono e chiamarla per poter sentire la sua voce. Ma se lo facessi, i Federali—che la stanno ancora sorvegliando e che stanno ascoltando le sue telefonate—le sarebbero addosso, dubitando ancora una volta della sua storia e facendola passare nel tritacarne.

Non è la prima volta che rifletto sull'idea di raggiungerla. Ci penso sempre. Per quanto siano prudenti i Federali, potrei ancora farle arrivare di nascosto una lettera, tramite uno degli uomini che ho ingaggiato. Sarebbe rischioso, ma potrei farlo.

Ciò che me lo impedisce non è la logistica, ma il fatto di non essere sicuro di cosa dire—e della reazione di Sara nel ricevere una lettera del genere. Per quanto mi piaccia pensare che le manchi tanto quanto manca a me, so che c'è una possibilità molto reale che il fragile accordo che abbiamo costruito verso la fine della sua prigionia sia svanito, che essere tornata a casa l'abbia nuovamente spinta a temermi e disprezzarmi.

Potrebbe sperare che me ne sia andato per sempre, e ricevere la mia lettera la sconvolgerebbe.

Inoltre, che cosa potrei dirle sul perché sto rimanendo lontano da lei? Non posso rivelare nulla su Novak ed Esguerra —troppo pericoloso, se la lettera venisse intercettata—quindi, restano solo le rassicurazioni fondamentali sul fatto che sono ancora vivo e che tornerò per lei.

Rassicurazioni che potrebbe facilmente interpretare come una minaccia, se è felice di stare a casa senza di me.

Noto che i miei ragazzi stanno morendo dalla voglia di dire qualcosa sulla situazione, ma la regola del Nessuna Parola Su Sara rimane in vigore, e sanno che è meglio non infrangerla. Così, restano zitti, e mi concentro su come far passare i giorni senza di lei, facendo affidamento sui rapporti giornalieri per alimentare la mia ossessione.

Un paio di giorni fa, è uscita con la sua amica Marsha e ha cantato in una sala, esibendosi con una delle sue canzoni in pubblico. Già solo leggerlo mi ha riempito il cuore con una vampata di calore, e ho ordinato agli americani di registrarla la prossima volta, così da poterla ascoltare e osservare la reazione del pubblico. Mi sento assurdamente orgoglioso al pensiero che il mio piccolo passerotto si sia messo a nudo in quel modo, scrollandosi di dosso le inibizioni e mostrando il talento che ho sempre conosciuto.

Naturalmente, l'orgoglio non è stata la mia unica reazione leggendo quel rapporto. L'idea che frequenti posti in cui altri uomini potrebbero provarci con lei è come un carbone ardente nel fianco. Sara è mia. La distanza fisica tra noi non cambia le cose. Finora, i rapporti non hanno evidenziato nessuno seriamente interessato a lei, ma questo non significa che non sia successo. Con l'FBI che segue costantemente Sara, i miei uomini devono fare molta attenzione, e ci sono momenti in cui semplicemente non possono avvicinarsi abbastanza da assicurarsi che qualche stronzo non la supplichi per avere un numero di telefono o le offra un caffè.

Se potessi avere un dispositivo di ascolto su Sara stessa, lo farei in un istante.

Le pianterei un chip nel cervello, se potessi.

"Sei pronto?" chiede Yan, e mi rendo conto di aver passato l'ultimo minuto a pulire distrattamente la pistola, invece di afferrare il borsone e scendere dall'aereo.

"Sì" dico, richiudendo la pistola e infilandola nella cintura. "Andiamo."

∽

LYLE BOLTON, IL CUGINO DI PRIMO GRADO DI WALLY Henderson, possiede un piccolo negozio di alimentari ad Asheville. Secondo i suoi amici e vicini di casa, è un uomo gentile e pacifico, con prole—due bambini in età prescolare e un bambino in arrivo. La moglie incinta è una mamma casalinga e, dall'esterno, sembrano la coppia suburbana perfetta.

Peccato che nessuno sappia che cos'hanno scoperto i nostri hacker.

Lo aspettiamo nella baita di montagna della prostituta, con il nostro fuoristrada parcheggiato fuori dalla vista dietro al capannone. Tecnicamente, la ragazza è una escort, ma il sesso per soldi è lo stesso per quanto mi riguarda. Bolton viene qui ogni martedì e giovedì, di ritorno dalle fattorie locali, da cui ottiene i prodotti per il negozio. Sua moglie è completamente all'oscuro, così come tutti gli altri nella comunità.

Nessuno immaginerebbe mai che il riservato, devoto Signor Bolton, appassionato di benessere degli animali e dell'ambiente, pagherebbe una giovanissima "escort" per defecare su di lei due volte a settimana—dopo averla picchiata.

Henderson ha i suoi amici che tengono d'occhio la casa e il lavoro di Bolton, ed è per questo che questa baita è un posto perfetto per interrogare il bastardo. Il suo sporco vizio è un segreto che ha nascosto a tutti, compreso suo cugino, e grazie a tutte le precauzioni che ha preso in considerazione per questo lasso di tempo, nessuno verrà a cercarlo, se non tornerà al negozio nelle prossime quattro ore.

Possiamo fare molto in quattro ore.

La baita è vuota; non c'è nessuno a parte noi. Yan ha attirato la prostituta fuori stamattina, fingendo di essere un cliente che paga molto bene. Dopo averla portata in una camera d'albergo, l'ha legata e l'ha lasciata lì. Se avremo tempo, la slegherà più tardi; altrimenti, la donna delle pulizie la troverà domani mattina. In ogni caso, la ragazza non andrà alla polizia, non quando troverà il pagamento sul comodino.

Lyle Bolton è puntuale, come al solito, e si presenta alle dieci meno un quarto. Il suo camion romba nel vialetto coperto dalla ghiaia e faccio un cenno ai ragazzi per prepararsi.

Agguantare la nostra preda è un gioco da ragazzi. Non ha idea di cos'abbiamo in serbo per lui. Lo stronzo entra con un largo sorriso di merda sul viso paffuto, e Ilya esce da dietro la porta e gli dà un pugno nello stomaco. Lo fa con delicatezza—con la delicatezza di qualcuno della sua stazza—ma Bolton atterra carponi, ansimando e cercando di scappare via.

Yan lo prende a calci nelle costole, e poi entro, tirando su il bastardo dal retro della maglietta, mentre inizia a piagnucolare e implorare pietà.

"Tuo cugino" dico con calma, sistemandolo su una sedia da cucina. "Dov'è?"

Ci guarda a bocca aperta e scorgo un nuovo tipo di paura sul suo viso. Ora si rende conto che questo non è un errore, che non siamo dei ladri che si trovavano qui per caso.

"Non-non lo so" balbetta, e sospiro, prima di tirare fuori la pistola.

"Ultima possibilità" dico, mettendogli la canna sulla fronte. "Dove cazzo sta Wally?"

Si piscia addosso. Una macchia scura si diffonde sul cavallo dei suoi pantaloni di velluto a coste e sento il tanfo acre dell'urina. Mi infastidisce quasi quanto le lacrime e il muco che gli colano sul viso.

"Te lo giuro, non lo so!" piagnucola, e abbasso la pistola, premendo il grilletto due volte in rapida successione.

Le sue urla sono assordanti, mentre cade dalla sedia e rotola in una piccola palla sul pavimento. Gli ho appena piantato due proiettili—uno per ciascun piede—e aspetto che le urla si plachino prima di ripetere: "Dov'è il tuo cugino del cazzo?"

"Non lo so, non lo so, non lo so!" Ora è isterico, tenendosi i piedi sanguinanti con entrambe le mani. "Per favore, lo giuro, non lo so. È scomparso più di due anni fa, e da allora non ho più saputo niente."

"Niente? Nessuna chiamata, nessuna e-mail, nessuna lettera?"

Conosco già la risposta grazie ai nostri hacker, quindi non sono sorpreso, quando il piagnucoloso idiota scuote la testa come un giocattolo a molla. "No, no, lo giuro! Niente! Nessuno ha più avuto sue notizie da quando se n'è andato."

Mi rivolgo a Yan. "Che ne pensi?" chiedo in russo. "Credi a questo pezzo di merda?"

Lo studia, poi annuisce. "Sì, credo di sì. Henderson non si sarebbe mai messo in contatto con lui."

"Ok, allora. Andiamo."

Chinandomi, tiro fuori il telefono dalla tasca di Bolton e lascio l'uomo sanguinante sul pavimento, mentre usciamo dalla baita. Prima di andarcene, metto fuori uso il suo veicolo per assicurarmi che non possa andarsene per un po'.

Abbiamo altri cinque stronzi da interrogare, prima che la situazione di questo venga scoperta.

LE PROSSIME DUE PERSONE SULLA LISTA RAPPRESENTANO UNA sfida tanto quanto Bolton. Il primo, Ian Wyles, è un insegnante in pensione, che è lo zio di Henderson di secondo grado. I due si scambiavano e-mail con regolarità prima della scomparsa di Henderson, ed è possibile che quest'ultimo possa comunque essere rimasto in contatto con lui in qualche modo.

Tuttavia, nel momento in cui agguantiamo il vecchio, mentre rientra a casa dall'ufficio postale, diventa ovvio che non sa nulla. È così fottutamente sconvolto e sbalordito dalle nostre domande che non perdiamo nemmeno tempo a picchiarlo. Lo leghiamo soltanto e lo lasciamo con il veicolo fuori uso nel bosco, dove sarà trovato tra poche ore, quando sua moglie tornerà a casa e non lo troverà.

La seconda persona, Jennifer Lows, è l'amica della moglie di Henderson. Una donna paffuta, di mezza età, se la fa letteralmente addosso, quando la portiamo fuori dalla casa di riposo dei genitori. Entro il primo minuto del nostro interrogatorio, diventa chiaro che nemmeno lei sa nulla, e la lasciamo legata dietro un cassonetto in un vicolo, imbavagliata e terrorizzata, ma incolume.

"Zero su tre" osserva Anton, mentre ci allontaniamo dal vicolo, ma faccio spallucce. Me lo aspettavo. Se Henderson fosse rimasto in contatto con queste persone, probabilmente l'avremmo già scoperto. Inoltre, la sicurezza intorno a loro sarebbe stata maggiore. Il fatto che fossero relativamente facili da contattare mi dice che non sono nella cerchia ristretta di Henderson.

Le persone che contano per lui—sua moglie e i suoi figli—sono nascoste come un tesoro.

In ogni caso, ottenere informazioni su dove si trova Henderson non è il nostro obiettivo principale. Intendiamo recapitargli un messaggio, facendogli sapere che nessuno nella sua vita—indipendentemente dalla distanza del legame—è al sicuro.

Vogliamo farlo arrabbiare e spaventarlo, perché gli uomini arrabbiati e spaventati commettono errori.

La prossima persona che cerchiamo è un poliziotto locale, che a quanto pare è l'amico d'infanzia di Henderson. Jimmy Gander, di cinquantacinque anni, è uno dei poliziotti più vecchi, e quando lo trasciniamo fuori dal suo bar preferito, riesce a colpire Anton in faccia, prima che lo mettiamo k.o.

"Lo ucciderò, cazzo" borbotta Anton, mentre ci addentriamo nel bosco, dove intendiamo interrogare il nostro prigioniero. "Il bastardo si pentirà di quello che ha fatto."

"Nessun omicidio, se non è necessario" gli ricordo. "Lo faremo solo se qualcuno non collabora."

Anton si acciglia. "Fanculo. Avrò un occhio nero."

"Non avresti dovuto permettere al nonno di avere la meglio su di te" dice Yan, sogghignando. "Forse dovremmo fargli prendere il tuo posto nella squadra. Sembra certamente più abile."

"Chiudete il becco" dico a entrambi, mentre il nostro SUV si ferma in una radura. "Potete litigare dopo."

Trasciniamo fuori il poliziotto e aspettiamo che si riprenda, prima di cominciare a interrogarlo. Come gli altri, sembra sinceramente sconcertato dalla situazione. Tuttavia, a differenza degli altri obiettivi di oggi, all'inizio si rifiuta di rispondere alle nostre domande. Per la gioia di Anton, finiamo per colpirlo un paio di volte, prima di sentirgli dire i soliti "non so niente" e "non ho più avuto sue notizie." In altre circostanze, avrei ammirato la lealtà di Gander verso il suo amico, ma dato che ci rimangono meno di due ore per interrogare le due persone rimaste sulla lista, il ritardo mi rende frustrato.

"Conficcagli una pallottola" dico ad Anton, quando il poliziotto continua a ripetere quand'è stata l'ultima volta che ha visto Henderson, e Anton obbedisce volentieri all'ordine, sparandogli nella spalla destra.

Dopo di ciò, smette di ripetere la stessa risposta, e rimangono solo il vomito verbale e le suppliche per avere un ospedale.

"Andiamo" dico ai ragazzi, quando sono sicuro che abbiamo ottenuto tutto ciò che potevamo dal poliziotto. "Legatelo e lasciatelo qui."

Mentre andiamo via, prendo mentalmente nota di chiamare il 911 e di comunicare loro la posizione dell'uomo, quando saremo al sicuro in aria.

Amico di Henderson o meno, non c'è motivo per cui il poliziotto debba morire.

~

SIAMO STRETTI CON I TEMPI, COSÌ ACCELERIAMO LA PROCEDURA rintracciando gli ultimi due obiettivi e interrogandoli insieme.

Li abbiamo lasciati per ultimi, perché sono connessioni ancora più lontane nei confronti di Henderson, quindi, se per qualche ragione non fossimo riusciti a raggiungerli, non sarebbe stata una grave perdita.

Il primo è l'ex fidanzato della figlia di Henderson, Bobby Carston. Ha vent'anni, circa tre più della figlia e, secondo i nostri file, si sono lasciati quando lui è andato a letto con la migliore amica di lei durante il ballo della scuola superiore. Non sopporto i traditori, così picchiamo il ragazzo, mentre gli facciamo delle domande—una mossa per assicurarci che il nostro ultimo prigioniero, l'insegnante preferito del figlio di Henderson, sia collaborativo fin dall'inizio.

Infatti, Sam Briars è così prolisso nelle sue risposte su Jimmy Henderson che otteniamo qualcosa che non ci aspettavamo.

Una possibile pista.

"—e poi sono andati in vacanza in Tailandia cinque anni fa e Jimmy ha detto di amare la cultura locale e la frutta, e che volevano vivere lì. C'era una famiglia locale con cui avevano fatto amicizia a Phuket. Non in una delle zone turistiche, ma nell'entroterra più profondo, lontano dalle folle. Jimmy lo raccontava in classe a tutti i compagni. E poi c'era Singapore, che la madre di Jimmy ha sempre amato per la pulizia, e c'è l'Islanda, dove i genitori di Jimmy sono andati per il loro anniversario, e c'è il Maryland, dove la sorella di Jimmy andava a scuola, e posso pensare ad altro, se mi concedete del tempo..."

L'insegnante sta parlando così in fretta che sta praticamente balbettando, così lo lasciamo parlare, annotando i luoghi che menziona in modo da poterli controllare più tardi. Abbiamo già esaminato la maggior parte di questi luoghi, compresa la Tailandia, ma gli Henderson si sono spostati per evitare di essere scoperti, e non sapevamo di quella famiglia locale a Phuket.

È sicuramente una pista che vale la pena esplorare.

Passano dieci minuti e l'insegnante non mostra segni di stanchezza, con la verbosità senza dubbio alimentata dai lamenti dell'ex fidanzato ferito. A questo punto, si sta solo ripetendo, raccontando tutto quello che sa sugli Henderson, così faccio un cenno a Ilya, che lo colpisce leggermente sulle costole.

"Basta così" dico, quando Briars inizia a urlare come se quel delicato colpetto gli avesse spezzato le costole. "Legateli e lasciateli qui. Dobbiamo andare."

Mentre guidiamo verso il nostro aereo, controllo se ci sono segni di inseguimento, ma riusciamo ad arrivare a destinazione senza incidenti.

L'operazione è stata ufficialmente un successo: abbiamo inviato un messaggio a Henderson e ottenuto una possibile pista.

Dovrei sentirmi bene, ma quando le ruote dell'aereo si sollevano da terra, tutto ciò a cui riesco a pensare è che non sono più vicino a ottenere ciò che voglio veramente.

Che dovranno passare ancora molti mesi prima di poter riabbracciare Sara.

 ara

"Che cos'ha fatto?" Fisso Ryson, con i palmi delle mani bagnati dal sudore e il cuore che mi martella. La mia prima reazione—la gioia che Peter sia vivo e vegeto—viene rapidamente sostituita da un doloroso nodo allo stomaco.

"Ha aggredito sei persone nel North Carolina" ripete l'agente. "Due sono in ospedale con ferite da arma da fuoco, e le altre quattro sono rimaste ferite e traumatizzate da un violento interrogatorio. Tutti cittadini innocenti. Puoi dirci qualcosa sull'incidente?"

"Io... che cosa?" Scuoto la testa per scacciare le macabre immagini. "Perché avrebbe fatto una cosa del genere?"

"Secondo le vittime, voleva sapere dove si trovasse un loro conoscente—un certo Walter Henderson III. Ha la sfortuna di essere sulla stessa lista del tuo defunto marito." Ryson incrocia le braccia muscolose. "A quanto pare Sokolov sta ricorrendo a misure più estreme per arrivare a quell'uomo. Puoi dirci qualcosa al riguardo? Che cosa sta cercando?"

Ingoio la bile che mi sta salendo nella gola. Negli ultimi due mesi, in qualche modo sono riuscita a dimenticare la brutale realtà dell'uomo che mi manca, a sorvolare sulle parti più oscure dei miei ricordi. "Non sai niente?"

"Te l'ho detto, gran parte del suo fascicolo è stato secretato." Ryson scioglie le braccia e si appoggia. "Dottoressa Cobakis, sai bene quanto me che quell'uomo è letale. Dev'essere fermato prima che altre persone innocenti vengano ferite. È importante che tu ci dica tutto ciò che sai su di lui, affinché possiamo avere un'idea migliore su dove potrebbe colpire prossimamente."

Lo fisso, sentendo alternativamente caldo e freddo. "Lui... non mi ha mai detto molto." Questo è quello che ho raccontato agli agenti, e devo rimanere fedele alla storia, a prescindere da quanto mi senta male, sapendo che Peter sta facendo del male a degli innocenti in nome della sete di vendetta.

In ogni caso, anche se Ryson fosse a conoscenza del massacro della moglie e del figlio di Peter, non cambierebbe nulla. Peter non si fermerà fin quando non avrà trovato Henderson e l'avrà cancellato dalla sua lista, e, come ha dimostrato chiaramente in North Carolina, i Federali non sono ancora in grado di competere con lui e la sua squadra.

Peter e i suoi uomini sono entrati negli Stati Uniti senza essere visti, hanno aggredito sei cittadini, e se ne sono andati.

È stato nel mio stesso Paese, e se Ryson non avesse deciso di interrogarmi, non l'avrei mai saputo.

Il mio stomaco si stringe ulteriormente e, con orrore, mi rendo conto che non sono minimamente sconvolta dal dolore e dalla sofferenza che ha causato a quelle persone.

Sono anche ferita e arrabbiata che Peter non sia tornato per me.

Ci separavano solo pochi Stati, e non è tornato a prendermi.

"Dottoressa Cobakis." Ryson mi scruta attentamente. "Va tutto bene?"

"Io... sì." Stringo le mani sotto al tavolo, lasciando che le unghie mi penetrino nei palmi. L'accenno di dolore mi calma, permettendomi di dire con un tono semi-normale: "Mi dispiace. È solo che sono successe tante cose."

E questa è la verità. È troppo, davvero. Fino a questo momento, non avevo compreso appieno quanto fossi incasinata, quanto quei mesi con Peter mi avessero rovinata, distorcendo il mio senso di giusto e sbagliato. Eccomi qui, ad aver appena saputo che l'assassino da cui sono ossessionata ha ferito sei persone innocenti, e sono arrabbiata che le abbia preferite a me? Che non mi abbia rapita, quando chiaramente ha avuto la possibilità di farlo?

Sono malata.

È ovvio ora—come il fatto che Peter potrebbe non tornare mai più. Per tutto il tempo, la vendetta è stata il suo vero amore, la sua vera ossessione, e qualsiasi cosa provasse per me non è durata... se mai ci fosse stata. Non so perché mi stiano ancora sorvegliando, o se lo stiano ancora facendo—la sensazione di prurito potrebbe essere una paranoia—ma è chiaro che non sono più la sua priorità.

In qualche modo, riesco a sopportare il resto dell'interrogatorio di Ryson, rispondendo automaticamente alle sue domande, e, quando torno a casa, alzo il telefono e chiamo il Dottor Evans, il terapeuta che mi ha aiutata in passato.

È giunto il momento di ricostruire la mia vita distrutta.

È giunto il momento di accettare che qualsiasi cosa io e Peter abbiamo avuto potrebbe essere finita.

PARTE III

2 5

$\mathcal{P}$eter

TRASCORRIAMO I DUE MESI SUCCESSIVI SEGUENDO LA PISTA tailandese—non è facile capire quale famiglia locale abbia fatto amicizia con gli Henderson—e poiché questo non ci avvicina all'obiettivo, accettiamo un lavoro in Russia, in cui un oligarca del petrolio vuole che eliminiamo uno dei suoi rivali. Non è redditizio come gli altri, ma la posizione lo rende conveniente.

Non tornavamo nel nostro Paese da anni.

"Anche a voi fa uno strano effetto?" chiede Anton, mentre passiamo davanti alla Piazza Rossa, e annuisco, sapendo esattamente che cosa intende dire. Camminare per queste strade e sentir parlare in russo intorno a noi è come tornare indietro nel tempo. L'ultima volta che sono stato a Mosca è stato quando ho ucciso il mio supervisore, Ivan Polonsky, per aver aiutato nella copertura del massacro di Daryevo—mi sembra successo una vita fa.

133

"Ti manca?" chiedo ad Anton, che alza le spalle.

"Nah. Voglio dire, non è esattamente divertente essere sempre stranieri, ma mi ci sono abituato. E grazie a Sara, il mio inglese è migliorato, quindi..." Si interrompe, con lo sguardo che diventa diffidente, mentre si rende conto di quello che ha appena detto. "Cioè, mentre eravamo—"

"Basta così." I miei muscoli del collo sono dolorosamente tesi e le mani sono serrate a pugno, ma la voce è dolce e calma, mentre ripeto: "Basta così."

Anton saggiamente si zittisce, e camminiamo per il resto della strada in silenzio. Sa che gli è proibito parlare di lei, e non solo per la sua sicurezza. Sara è un detonatore per me in questi giorni, tanto che la semplice menzione del suo nome è sufficiente a rendermi omicida. La ferita aperta lasciata dalla sua assenza non si sta rimarginando; è insopportabile.

Soffro per lei ogni secondo di ogni giorno, e lo odio fottutamente.

I rapporti quotidiani non fanno che peggiorare le cose, perché sembra che mi abbia dimenticato. Il mese scorso, ha ottenuto un altro lavoro, unendosi a dei ginecologi e ostetrici con più esperienza, e si è trasferita dalla casa dei genitori in un nuovo appartamento. Sono contento di tutto questo—voglio che sia felice—ma nelle ultime sei settimane è uscita ogni fine settimana, bevendo e ballando con le amiche. Inoltre, ha iniziato a cantare con una band il venerdì sera—uno sviluppo che mi piaceva, fin quando non ho visto una registrazione in cui indossava un abito sexy e ho realizzato che ogni uomo del pubblico stava sbavando.

La guardavano come un branco di lupi davanti a una lepre.

Se fossi stato lì con lei, l'avrei impedito—deturpando alcuni volti, se fosse stato necessario—ma sono a mezzo mondo di distanza, e questo mi distrugge. Oltre a ciò, questo solleva la possibilità che Sara possa avermi dimenticato al punto tale da potersi innamorare di un altro uomo... forse addirittura di uno degli idioti che le si avvicinano dopo ogni esibizione per provarci e implorare il suo numero di telefono.

L'unica cosa che mi impedisce di ordinare un colpo su quegli stronzi è che finora non è uscita con nessuno di loro.

È solo questione di tempo, però. Lo so. Più mancherò, più è probabile che sia così. Ed è per questo che, proprio prima di questo lavoro, ho finalmente ordinato che le venisse recapitato un messaggio.

Dovrebbe riceverlo tra poco.

Nel frattempo, abbiamo un uomo molto ricco—e molto corrotto—da uccidere.

ara

"Sara! Sara! Sara!"

L'incitazione del pubblico unita all'applauso assordante è come un'iniezione di eroina nelle vene. Sono così estasiata che mi sembra di volare, e mi inchino, ridendo, mentre l'incitazione si intensifica.

I miei compagni della band—Phil, Simon e Rory—si inchinano al mio fianco. Il pubblico, però, sembra concentrato su di me. Probabilmente perché i ragazzi hanno cambiato il nome della band da *The Rocker Boys* a *Sara & the Rocker Boys* il mese scorso, ignorando completamente le mie obiezioni. Per qualche ragione, Phil ha deciso che la band è molto più richiesta avendo me come cantante principale, e ogni poster ora ha il mio volto in primo piano oltre al mio nome. La scorsa settimana, una paziente in clinica mi ha riconosciuta come "quella Sara" e mi ha chiesto l'autografo—un incidente molto imbarazzante che ha portato lo staff della clinica a chiamarmi "La Celebrità."

Questa era la prima volta che cantavamo all'aperto in uno spazio più ampio, e non ero sicura che ce l'avremmo fatta. Anche se è quasi maggio, il tempo è ancora imprevedibile, e fino a due giorni fa non sapevamo se ci sarebbero stati dieci gradi con la pioggia o ventuno con il sole. Alla fine, ha avuto la meglio una via di mezzo—diciannove e parzialmente nuvoloso —e c'è stata una grande affluenza. Il nostro obiettivo era quello di vendere almeno un centinaio di biglietti per coprire i costi del locale, ma a giudicare dal numero degli spettatori che applaudivano con entusiasmo, ne abbiamo venduti quasi il quadruplo.

Finiamo di inchinarci e di cantare un'altra canzone come bis, prima di scendere dal palco. Come sempre succede dopo una performance di successo, è difficile sbarazzarsi dell'adrenalina, così ci rechiamo al bar vicino per festeggiare e distenderci.

Come me, i miei compagni della band lo fanno come hobby. Phil, il nostro chitarrista, è un insegnante di matematica; Simon, il batterista, è uno scrittore freelance; e Rory, il bassista, lavora in un call center. A differenza mia, comunque, tutti e tre vorrebbero farlo come carriera, e come spesso accade dopo una grande esibizione, iniziano subito a parlare di un futuro tour.

"Potremmo iniziare a Seattle, per poi dirigerci verso la Costa Occidentale" dice Phil, prendendo la birra. I suoi occhi blu brillano febbrilmente sul viso rubicondo. "Da lì, potremmo procedere con il sud-ovest e—"

"Fanculo a Seattle." Rory trangugia un sorso di tequila e fa scivolare il bicchiere verso il barista irritato. "Andremo direttamente in California. San Francisco, poi L.A. È il posto migliore per artisti come noi, per non parlare del tempo, della cultura e del cibo..."

Continua, gesticolando selvaggiamente mentre parla, e

sogghigno quando noto diverse donne che lo fissano sfacciatamente. Con il volto lentigginoso, i ricci arruffati e il fisico da culturista, Rory sembra un incrocio tra Little Orphan Annie e un modello di Abercrombie che fa uso di steroidi. È una combinazione che non avrebbe dovuto funzionare, ma lo fa —e sospetto che il successo della band sia dovuto tanto al suo aspetto quanto al nostro talento combinato.

Non che Phil e Simon siano brutti. Simon, in particolare, mi ricorda un giovane Denzel Washington, solo con un'attitudine punk-rock. Phil è un po' più nella media, con una leggera stempiatura e un filo di pancia, ma la sua personalità estroversa compensa le carenze fisiche. Tutti e tre i miei compagni di band sono attraenti a modo loro—e ognuno ha fatto capire che avrebbe piacere a uscire con me.

È triste che tutto quello che vedo quando guardo un uomo in questi giorni non è Peter.

I ragazzi non lo sanno, naturalmente. Sono beatamente ignari del casino terrificante nel mio passato e degli agenti dell'FBI che ancora mi seguono ostinatamente. Tutti i miei compagni sanno che sono una vedova, e pensano che il dolore per la perdita di mio marito sia il motivo per cui non frequento nessuno.

"Quanto tempo è passato?" ha chiesto Phil con fare comprensivo, quando mi sono unita alla band a febbraio, e gli ho detto che mio marito era praticamente morto circa un anno e mezzo prima, non essendosi mai risvegliato dall'incidente d'auto che lo aveva lasciato in coma. Phil ha espresso le sue condoglianze e ha evitato con tatto l'argomento da allora, così come Simon e Rory.

Infatti, dopo avermi fatto premurosamente sapere che sono interessati, solo per essere rifiutati con lo stesso tatto, si sono completamente ritirati e hanno iniziato a trattarmi come una specie di figura santa, una Madonna intoccabile racchiusa in una bolla di dolore.

Non sono lontani dalla verità, solo che la perdita per cui sto soffrendo ha poco a che fare con George, che svanisce sempre più dai miei ricordi giorno dopo giorno. A questo punto, sono passati più di tre anni dal suo incidente, e ancora di più da quando il nostro amore è stato soffocato dal peso della sua dipendenza. Ogni volta che ripenso a lui ora, tutto ciò che ricordo è come mi sono sentita, quando ho scoperto la sua doppia vita come agente della CIA... i segreti e le bugie che hanno portato Peter alla mia porta.

Vorrei poter dimenticare anche *lui*, ma è impossibile. Anche se sono passati quasi sei mesi da quando il mio rapitore mi ha riportata a casa, penso a lui ogni sera, mentre mi addormento. A volte, sono convinta di poterlo sentire. Non accanto a me, ma da qualche parte là fuori, che attraversa i continenti per tormentarmi, con la sua attrazione sia magnetica che letale, come la forza gravitazionale del sole.

Lo sogno anche. Sogno il tenero modo in cui mi stringeva quando piangevo e il brutale modo in cui mi scopava, tra tutte le piccole e grandi cose che costituiscono la contraddizione che è Peter. A volte, mi sveglio da quei sogni eccitata e frustrata, ma più spesso trovo il cuscino inzuppato di lacrime e le braccia avvolte intorno alla coperta per allontanare l'angosciosa solitudine che mi tiene congelata dentro.

Ho bisogno di voltare pagina, lo so. E ci provo. Esco con Marsha e le ragazze ogni fine settimana, e quando un ragazzo particolarmente attraente mi chiede il numero, glielo do il più delle volte. Ma è lì che finisce per me. Non riesco a fare il passo successivo e ad accettare l'appuntamento, quando mi telefonano o mi mandano un messaggio.

"Perché dai loro il tuo numero, allora?" mi ha chiesto Marsha la scorsa settimana, quando ha saputo che l'ho fatto ancora una volta. "Perché non li rifiuti subito?"

Ho fatto spallucce, non sapendo che cosa dire, e lei non ha insistito, non volendo stressarmi. Come la maggior parte delle mie conoscenze che hanno ascoltato la versione dell'FBI della storia di Peter, Marsha mi tratta come se fossi di cristallo e potessi frantumarmi alla minima pressione. Credo che lei—insieme ad altri in ospedale—pensi che il mio calvario sia stato persino peggiore di quello che ho rivelato. Una volta, quando mamma era ancora all'ospedale, ho sentito due infermiere che parlavano di come fossi fuggita da un "giro di schiavitù sessuale" e di come stessi ancora affrontando le conseguenze di essere stata "costretta a prostituirmi."

È irritante, ma l'unico modo per mettere a tacere quelle voci sarebbe dire la verità, e non ho intenzione di farlo.

Fortunatamente, i miei nuovi colleghi non sono a conoscenza di più di quanto non sappiano i miei compagni della band. I Dottori Wendy e Bill Otterman, la coppia sposata proprietaria del piccolo studio per ostetrici e ginecologi, è rimasta così colpita dal mio curriculum e dalle credenziali accademiche che mi ha a malapena fatto domande sul vuoto di nove mesi nella mia storia lavorativa. Ho detto loro di essermi presa una pausa per viaggiare in tutto il mondo, e mi hanno assunta subito, con l'avvertenza di iniziare immediatamente in modo che potessero partire per la crociera tanto attesa in Alaska per il loro quarantesimo anniversario di matrimonio.

Avrei potuto cercare opportunità migliori e più prestigiose, ma ho accettato subito l'offerta e ho iniziato il giorno successivo. Con mamma appena uscita dall'ospedale, volevo qualcosa di poco impegnativo, affinché potessi seguire lei e papà. Ma quello che mi ha fatto davvero accettare è stata la posizione dell'ufficio—a quindici minuti di auto dalla casa dei miei genitori e a pochi passi dal mio nuovo appartamento.

"Torna sulla terra, Rory." Simon agita la bottiglia di birra davanti al viso di Rory, interrompendo la sua orazione sulle meraviglie della California. "Guardiamo in faccia la realtà. Sara, hai intenzione di venire in tour con noi?"

Sorrido e scuoto la testa. "Non posso, mi dispiace. Il lavoro non mi permette di assentarmi per così tanto tempo."

"Vedi?" Simon osserva trionfalmente i suoi compagni di band, come se avesse vinto una scommessa. "Non verrà. Non succederà."

"Oh, andiamo." Phil afferra la birra da Simon e la finisce in due sorsi prima di fare cenno al barista di portarne un'altra. Voltandosi verso di me, mi guarda con tutto il fascino di Phil Hudson. "Sara, dolcezza..." La sua voce diventa adulatrice. "Abbiamo tutti un lavoro e altre responsabilità, ma opportunità come questa capitano solo una volta nella vita. Stiamo per spiccare il volo, lo sento, e dobbiamo cogliere l'occasione. *Tu* devi coglierla, perché sai che cosa succede domani?"

Scuoto la testa, sorridendo. Ho già sentito versioni di questa lezione da lui, e ogni volta diventa più creativo. "No, che cosa?"

"Esattamente." Agita il dito indice, come un insegnante. "Non lo sai, e nemmeno qualcun altro. La vita è solo una serie di eventi casuali, che sembra seguire un modello, ma non lo fa. Potresti pensare di sapere che cosa ti porterà l'indomani, ma tutto ciò che serve è il cambiamento di una singola variabile e boom! Ti ritrovi a seguire una direzione completamente diversa."

"Come in un tour?" dico seccamente, e sia Rory che Simon ridono.

"Un tour, sì—sarebbe una nuova variabile" continua Phil, imperterrito. "Ma una che *ti* piacerebbe. La maggior parte delle volte, la nuova variabile viene da dove meno te l'aspetti, e poi tutti i tuoi piani studiati attentamente vanno all'aria."

"Cazzo—le cose stanno davvero così? Ho appena appreso la matematica?" chiede Rory, grattandosi i ricci, e scoppiamo tutti a ridere, mentre Phil alza gli occhi, borbottando sottovoce qualcosa sugli ignoranti e gli stronzi ubriachi.

"Devo andare" dico ai ragazzi scusandomi, mentre la risata si spegne. "Devo alzarmi presto per il lavoro domani."

"Nessun problema, lo sappiamo." Simon mi dà una pacca sulla spalla. "Vai a fare quello che devi fare e lascia questi idioti a sognare la fama."

Rido, scuotendo la testa, mentre esco dal bar e mi dirigo verso il parcheggio sul retro. Avevo i miei dubbi sul fatto di unirmi alla band, ma si è rivelata la migliore decisione di sempre. Non solo mi sento come se fossi nata per questo ogni volta che sono su quel palco, ma i miei compagni sono molto divertenti. In realtà preferisco uscire con loro che con Marsha e le ragazze; sento meno pressione, in qualche modo.

Sto aprendo la portiera della macchina, quando lo noto.

Qualcosa di spesso—un foglio di carta piegato, forse?—incastrato all'interno della maniglia della portiera.

La mia prima reazione è quella di tirarlo fuori e dare immediatamente un'occhiata, ma un sesto senso me lo impedisce. La sensazione di prurito tra le scapole—quella che è così onnipresente che a malapena ci faccio caso ormai—è molto più intensa all'improvviso, e, invece di tirar fuori l'oggetto e fissarlo, lo stacco in modo discreto, trattenendolo nel pugno chiuso, e salgo in macchina.

Facendo scivolare l'oggetto—ora identificato definitivamente come un pezzo di carta piegato—nella tasca della mia giacca, esco dal parcheggio e mi dirigo verso casa. Dietro di me c'è l'inevitabile coda dell'FBI, e mentre guido, la carta sembra ardere nella tasca.

Devo davvero impegnarmi per parcheggiare davanti al mio edificio e attraversare tranquillamente l'atrio fino all'ascensore, senza affrettarmi. È possibile che si tratti una specie di pubblicità che è stata semplicemente posizionata in modo strano, ma in qualche modo, sono certa che non sia così.

Entrando nel mio appartamento, chiudo la porta a chiave e mi guardo intorno. Non penso ci siano telecamere o dispositivi di ascolto qui dentro; dopo tutto l'equipaggiamento high-tech trovato nella mia vecchia casa e poi mesi dopo nella casa dei miei genitori, i Federali setacciano l'abitazione regolarmente, e loro stessi avrebbero bisogno di un mandato per quel genere di sorveglianza invasiva. Tuttavia, solo per assicurarmene, tolgo le scarpe e vado verso l'armadio della camera da letto, mantenendo la calma per tutto il tempo.

Se qualcuno mi sta osservando, non gli darò motivo di sospettare.

Il mio appartamento è abbastanza piccolo, con una camera, una cucina e un angusto soggiorno, ma ha una bella funzionalità: uno spazioso armadio a muro nella camera da letto. Vado lì, come farei di solito per spogliarmi, ma, non appena sono fuori dalla vista di qualsiasi possibile telecamera, tiro fuori il foglio dalla tasca e lo apro, con le mani che tremano.

Sono solo un paio di righe, scarabocchiate sulla carta spessa con una grafia nitida e mascolina.

Ricorda, ptichka. Finché saremo entrambi vivi.

IL LAVORO A MOSCA PROCEDE SENZA INTOPPI—ELIMINIAMO IL nostro obiettivo in una breve settimana—e poi torniamo a dare la caccia a Henderson, mentre attendiamo notizie da Novak. Il mese scorso, il trafficante d'armi serbo ha confermato che tutto sta procedendo secondo il periodo originario di otto mesi, ma è ancora concentrato sulla sua risorsa all'interno dell'organizzazione di Esguerra—l'informazione chiave di cui ho bisogno per attuare il mio piano.

Sfortunatamente, Henderson rimane inafferrabile come sempre, così, mentre maggio procede, interroghiamo altri conoscenti per qualsiasi pista. Questa volta, ci concentriamo sulle connessioni della moglie nella sua città natale di Charleston, solo per fare cose diverse.

"Ancora niente" dice Ilya con disgusto, mentre saliamo a

bordo dell'aereo, dopo aver interrogato i nostri cinque bersagli. "Gli idioti non sapevano nulla."

Mi stringo nelle spalle e mi siedo. "Me lo aspettavo."

Continuo a considerare l'operazione un successo. Siamo riusciti a fuggire senza nemmeno un inseguimento in auto, e abbiamo di nuovo dimostrato a Henderson che nessuno nella sua vita, indipendente da quanto possa essere remoto il legame, è al sicuro. Prima o poi, farà un passo falso, e poi commetterà un errore. Forse sua moglie si preoccuperà per una sua amica e andrà a farle visita, o forse la figlia adolescente si agiterà e chiamerà l'ex.

Qualunque cosa accada, nel momento in cui sbaglieranno qualcosa, saremo pronti, e mia moglie e mio figlio morti saranno vendicati.

~

È l'inizio di giugno, quando finalmente accade.

Ricevo un'e-mail da parte di Novak, che vuole incontrarmi mercoledì prossimo.

Solo te, c'è scritto nell'e-mail. *Nessun altro.*

Sopprimo un'ondata di gioia selvaggia e inizio a prendere accordi.

~

Nelle ultime due settimane, abbiamo soggiornato nella nostra casa polacca, aspettando notizie da Novak, così mercoledì mattina i ragazzi mi fanno scendere a Belgrado e assumono le loro posizioni.

Non verranno con me, ma sicuramente saranno nei paraggi.

Incontro Novak nello stesso bar dell'altra volta. Mentre entro, noto che i suoi scagnozzi sono assenti—come i bei baristi. Novak è seduto al tavolino in mezzo al bar, con solo una cartella di pelle marrone davanti a sé.

"Tutto solo?" chiedo, cercando di non mostrarmi sorpreso, e le labbra sottili di Novak si incurvano, mentre si alza e si avvicina per salutarmi.

"Ho pensato che avremmo potuto fare a meno di tutte le stronzate." I suoi occhi chiari brillano, mentre mi stringe la mano. "Abbiamo bisogno l'uno dell'altro, e penso che sia ora di costruire la fiducia."

Sono certo che *questa* sia la vera stronzata—probabilmente i suoi uomini sono posizionati strategicamente come i miei—ma lascio che la mia espressione di pietra si addolcisca leggermente, mentre gli lascio la mano. "Non potrei essere più d'accordo."

"Bene." Si siede di nuovo al tavolo e mi fa cenno di fare altrettanto. "Prego."

Mi accomodo e assumo un'espressione impassibile. "Allora, la risorsa è stata posizionata?"

Novak annuisce, mantenendo un sorrisetto compiaciuto. "È sulla strada verso la tenuta di Esguerra, mentre parliamo."

Il mio polso accelera. Ora e data del trasporto della risorsa—è già qualcosa che posso sfruttare. "Complimenti. È un bel risultato" dico con voce ferma.

Novak accetta le lodi come se gli fossero dovute. "Grazie. C'è voluto molto lavoro, ma ci sono riuscito."

"Allora, parlami di lei, di questa tua misteriosa risorsa" dico.

Tamburella le pallide dita sul tavolo per diversi lunghi secondi, poi dice: "Conosci la struttura finanziaria dell'organizzazione di Esguerra?"

Lo fisso. "No. Non particolarmente. Ero il suo consulente per la sicurezza, non il consulente finanziario." Non mi aspettavo che Novak finisse col parlare di questo. La risorsa potrebbe essere qualcuno collegato al gestore di portafoglio di

Esguerra? So che il ragazzo risiede da qualche parte a Chicago, ma non vedo—

"Quindi, non sai che legalmente e praticamente la moglie di Esguerra è il suo socio in affari e che erediterà tutto in caso di morte del marito?"

"No, ma non mi sorprenderebbe" dico lentamente. Anche allora, quando lavoravo per Esguerra, Nora, la ragazza americana che ha rapito e poi sposato, mostrava un'insolita attitudine per gli affari del marito.

Novak sorride di nuovo e apre la cartella di fronte a sé. "Sì. La giovane Signora Esguerra è piuttosto sveglia, non è vero? Si è laureata alla Stanford con il massimo dei voti." Tira fuori una foto e la mette davanti a me. Mostra Nora con un voluminoso abito da laurea, che riceve un diploma da un funzionario universitario. Il suo volto sorridente è mezzo voltato, guardando altrove, ma anche da quest'angolazione si nota che è entusiasta.

"Quando è stata scattata?" chiedo, perplesso. Se la gente di Novak era abbastanza vicina da scattare quella foto, anche loro dovevano essere vicini allo stesso Esguerra.

Il trafficante d'armi colombiano non avrebbe lasciato la moglie fuori dalla sua vista per più di un minuto.

"Un paio di mesi fa, alla cerimonia di laurea primaverile" risponde Novak. "Carina, non è vero? Così piccola, ma così forte..."

La sua voce è insolitamente dolce, mentre lo dice, con il tocco che sembra quasi una carezza, quando recupera l'immagine e la inserisce nella cartella. Sollevo le sopracciglia, in attesa di vedere dove intenda andare a parare. In qualche modo, si è infatuato della piccola moglie di Esguerra?

È strano, ma sono accadute cose più strane.

Chiudendo la cartella, mi guarda. "So a cosa stai pensando" dice. "Perché non l'ho eliminato proprio in quel momento, durante quella cerimonia? Perché assoldare te, quando avrei potuto colpirlo allora, facendo tutto da solo?"

Inclino la testa. "Mi sono fatto questa domanda, ma ho immaginato che la sicurezza di Esguerra fosse più stretta di quanto non indichi il tuo possesso di quella foto."

Le labbra di Novak si distendono in un altro sorriso. "Hai ragione—la sicurezza era impressionante. Eppure, se l'avessi voluto davvero, avrei potuto provarci. Avrei subito pesanti perdite, ma c'è una piccola possibilità che avrei potuto farcela."

"Ma non hai voluto rischiare?"

"Oh, avrei rischiato... se la morte di Esguerra fosse stato tutto ciò che avessi voluto."

Ora stiamo arrivando al nocciolo del problema. "Vuoi anche lei." Faccio un cenno verso la cartella. "Fa parte di questo?"

Gli occhi chiari di Novak si induriscono. "Sì... ma non come pensi tu. Vedi, Nora Esguerra non è solo carina—detiene le chiavi del regno di Esguerra. Se lo uccidessi, lei semplicemente prenderebbe il sopravvento, e avrei un nuovo nemico da combattere—uno con risorse quasi illimitate e un rancore molto personale nei miei confronti."

La questione sta diventando interessante. "Quindi, vuoi che siano entrambi eliminati?"

"Quello era il mio pensiero originario, ma no. Vedi, Esguerra è intelligente—molto più della maggior parte di quelli nella nostra attività. Quasi tutti i suoi beni sono legalmente intestati, e tutto è sepolto dietro strati su strati di società di comodo. Se entrambi gli Esguerra venissero uccisi, impiegherei anni a districare la matassa, e pur avendo successo nell'eliminazione di un rivale, non avrei accesso a ciò che voglio veramente."

"I suoi possedimenti."

"Sì. Esattamente." Si sporge in avanti. "Non voglio solo che Esguerra sparisca—voglio quello che ha... compresa sua moglie."

Piego la testa. "Quindi, vuoi che Julian Esguerra sia ucciso, ma che sua moglie venga rapita?"

"Sì, e non solo sua moglie." Il suo sorriso è freddo. "Vedi, lei è inutile per me senza una specie di ricatto."

"Ricatto? Intendi qualcosa come un membro della famiglia?"

"Sì, precisamente. E non solo un membro qualsiasi della famiglia. Ho bisogno di qualcuno per cui farebbe qualsiasi cosa... persino accogliere a braccia aperte l'assassino di suo marito."

La mia espressione non cambia, ma il sangue si trasforma in melma ghiacciata. Questo significa che è al corrente della mia ossessione per Sara? Se è così, lo ucciderò sul posto, e sia dannato per sempre. Se oserà minacciarla, gli strapperò quella fottuta pelle, e—

"Vedi" continua Novak, ignaro della mia crescente rabbia: "Ho bisogno di Nora, e ho bisogno che sia completamente sotto il mio controllo. Ho pensato di usare i suoi genitori per questo, ma potrebbe non essere abbastanza. Dopo tutto, i genitori di solito si sacrificano per i propri figli, non il contrario."

Scaccio i pensieri sanguinari. "Che cos'hai in mente, allora?" Non è detto che stia parlando di Sara; almeno, è meglio per lui che non lo faccia. Partendo dal presupposto che non sia così stupido da minacciarmi in modo così indiretto, lo prendo alla lettera: "Per quanto ne so, oltre ai genitori, Nora non ha—"

"Sì, esattamente. Per quanto ne sai." Novak si appoggia, godendosi chiaramente il suo momento di superiorità. "Tu e tutto il resto del mondo, ad esclusione di alcune persone selezionate."

Lo fisso, con i pensieri che saltano da un fatto all'altro. "La tua risorsa" dico lentamente. "Il periodo di otto mesi... Stai dicendo che Esguerra ha un—"

"Figlio? Sì." Il suo viso inespressivo si anima. "Una figlia, in realtà, nata martedì scorso in Svizzera, circa due settimane prima del previsto. Elizabeth Esguerra—detta Lizzie. Bel nome, no?"

"Sì, molto" riesco a dire. Il mio cuore sta minacciando di

esplodere dalla cassa toracica, e sotto al tavolo le mani formano dei pugni.

Una bambina. Una fottuta neonata. È questo il suo piano, la sua risorsa. Ha ragione, in quanto questo sarebbe il modo perfetto per controllare Nora. Una madre farebbe qualsiasi cosa per la propria figlia; rinuncerebbe a un impero e alla propria vita, se necessario.

Non dovrebbe importarmi—Esguerra non è mio amico—ma per qualche ragione, il coinvolgimento di una bambina rende il piano di Novak decisamente osceno per me.

Sono contento di aver fatto il doppio gioco con il bastardo per tutto il tempo.

Ma aspetta. Ha detto che la sua risorsa avrebbe aiutato durante l'operazione. Ciò significa che non si tratta della bambina. Tuttavia... "È una tata?" chiedo in modo uniforme. "La tua risorsa—è collegata alla bambina, non è vero?"

Novak annuisce, allungando la mano sul tavolo di fronte a lui. "Sì, ma non è una tata" dice, addolcendo l'espressione. "Una pediatra—fortemente consigliata dai medici della clinica svizzera, che Esguerra predilige."

Naturalmente. Sospettavo che Novak potesse avere qualche legame con quel posto. "Hai corrotto il personale della clinica?"

"Ci ho provato, ma purtroppo, no." Sospira. "Sono così spaventati dai loro pazienti che sono quasi impossibili da corrompere. Così, ho dovuto hackerare i loro computer."

"Capisco." Tutti i pezzi stanno tornando a posto ora. "Ecco come facevi a sapere della gravidanza di Nora."

Annuisce. "Esguerra l'ha portata lì per farla visitare, notando che il suo ciclo era in ritardo. E non appena lo hanno saputo, l'ho saputo anch'io—e ti ho contattato."

Sopprimo l'impulso di allungarmi sul tavolo e spezzargli il collo. Forse è perché conosco Nora, o forse perché quando penso ai bambini immagino mio figlio a quell'età, ma la semplice consapevolezza che una neonata verrà usata in quel modo mi dà la nausea.

Mantenendo un tono fermo, dico: "Quindi, vuoi che uccida Esguerra, rapisca Nora e la sua bambina, e che le porti da te, così in un colpo solo avrai eliminato il tuo più grande rivale e ottenuto il controllo dei suoi possedimenti."

Il sorriso di Novak è a trentadue denti. "Esattamente."

"È molto intelligente." Inserisco una nota di ammirazione nella mia voce. "Se prendessi solo Nora e la bambina per controllare Esguerra, lui troverebbe un modo per fotterti e riaverli—l'ha già fatto in passato. Ma sua moglie—la sua vedova, dovrei dire—sarà più facile da gestire, soprattutto con una bambina di cui occuparsi. Stai pensando di rendere il rapporto legale con lei?"

"Sì, naturalmente. Il matrimonio è il modo più semplice per aggirare tutti quei fastidiosi ostacoli sulla proprietà. Adotterò anche la figlia."

"E la crescerai come se fosse tua?"

Si stringe nelle spalle. "Più o meno. Qualunque bambina io cresca con Nora avrà ovviamente la priorità, ma finché sua madre si comporta bene, non ho intenzione di fare del male alla bambina."

"Molto generoso da parte tua."

O non nota il sarcasmo nella mia voce o sceglie di ignorarlo. "Sì. Penso che trarremo tutti dei benefici a lungo termine—compreso te. Cento milioni saranno perfetti per la tua piccola vendetta."

Non sono minimamente sorpreso che ne sia a conoscenza. "Sì, lo saranno" dico senza battere ciglio.

"Bene. Hai già un'idea di come farai ad entrare nella tenuta di Esguerra?"

"Sì" rispondo, guardandolo dritto negli occhi. "Andrò a far visita a Lucas Kent e mi farò portare da Esguerra. Gli dirò che voglio seppellire l'ascia di guerra—e che sono disposto a rivelargli il nome di un traditore."

Sara

NON DORMO PIÙ TUTTA LA NOTTE, E AL MATTINO SONO COSÌ esausta che mi trascino in cucina per prendere un caffè. Se oggi fosse stato un giorno di lavoro, avrei dovuto chiamare dicendo di essere malata. Tuttavia, non è quel giorno.

È un sabato in cui non ho assolutamente niente in programma.

Se fosse stato un normale sabato precedente al messaggio di Peter, sarei potuta andare in clinica e dare una mano per qualche ora, oppure avrei potuto sorprendere i miei genitori presentandomi a colazione. Tuttavia, questo è un sabato successivo al messaggio di Peter, e tra la mancanza di sonno e l'ansiosa attesa sempre presente, tutto quello che riesco a fare è affondare nel divano e guardare un programma di cucina.

Ne ho guardati molti ultimamente. Mi ricordano Peter.

Come sempre, quando penso a lui, la mente inizia a vagare.

Sono passati otto mesi da quando mi ha riportata a casa—otto mesi durante i quali l'unica parola da parte sua è stato quel messaggio. Due mesi fa, prima di questo evento, ero più o meno convinta che la sua ossessione per me fosse svanita, e che, nonostante la promessa, non sarebbe più tornato. Ora, tuttavia, non so che cosa pensare.

Se mi vuole ancora, perché sono qui?

Che cosa sta aspettando?

Mamma è ormai completamente guarita—o comunque è nelle migliori condizioni in cui potrebbe essere. Il suo braccio sinistro è ancora debole, ma è in grado di muovere le dita e può usare quella mano per raccogliere oggetti leggeri—un risultato migliore di quanto si temesse inizialmente. Cammina anche senza assistenza e fa il giro del giardino da quando il tempo è migliorato. Papà è in estasi per la sua guarigione, ed entrambi non vedono l'ora che arrivi il giorno della crociera dell'anniversario a settembre—un regalo che finalmente sono riuscita a far loro.

Da quando la salute di mamma è migliorata e la novità del mio ritorno è svanita, le mie visite da loro sono passate da un evento quotidiano a un evento settimanale. I miei genitori sono sempre felici di vedermi, ovviamente, ma apprezzano anche la loro indipendenza. Mio padre, in particolare, è orgoglioso di essere autosufficiente, e io non voglio togliergli questo piacere incombendo costantemente su di loro come una balia.

I miei genitori mi vogliono bene, ma non hanno bisogno di me come pensavo un tempo—o così mi dico per lenire la colpa che inevitabilmente accompagna la brama per Peter.

Il perverso desiderio che torni a prendermi.

Ci ho pensato così spesso che posso immaginarlo come un film nella testa. Un giorno entrerò nel mio appartamento, e lui sarà lì, grande e pericoloso, letale e bellissimo come sempre. Sarà lì, nonostante le pattuglie della polizia all'esterno, nonostante tutte le precauzioni dei Federali.

Aspetterà di portarmi via, e nulla di ciò che dirò avrà importanza.

Questa è probabilmente la parte più vergognosa di queste fantasie: che non ho mai avuto una scelta... e che mi piace. Voglio che Peter mi porti via, che mi liberi dalle mie obiezioni. Allora e solo allora potrò vivere con la consapevolezza che ancora una volta sono scomparsa dalle vite delle persone che mi amano e che hanno bisogno di me, che ho abbandonato la mia famiglia, le mie pazienti, i miei compagni di band e i miei amici.

Ho bisogno che Peter sia crudele, in modo che io possa essere almeno in qualche modo buona.

Devo odiarlo per amarlo.

Sto cominciando a comprenderlo, ad abbracciare la perversità dentro di me, ma quello che non capisco è perché sono ancora qui, se mi vuole. Non può più essere dovuto ai miei genitori, quindi deve trattarsi di qualcos'altro—qualcosa che non mi ha detto.

Mi sono tormentata cercando di comprendere che cosa avrebbe potuto essere, e l'unico indizio che mi è venuto in mente ha a che fare con qualcosa che ha detto, mentre ci stavamo separando. Gli ho chiesto se sarei rimasta a casa fino alla guarigione di mamma, e ha iniziato a dire che anche lui doveva finire prima qualcosa. Tuttavia, non ha rivelato di che cosa si trattasse, né tantomeno quanto potesse durare quel qualcosa. L'unica cosa che posso immaginare sia così importante per lui è la vendetta, ma non so perché questa lo stia trattenendo per così tanto tempo.

Stava dando la caccia a Henderson quando eravamo insieme, e secondo l'FBI è quello che sta facendo ancora.

Due mesi fa, subito dopo aver ricevuto il messaggio di Peter, Ryson mi ha riportata nel suo ufficio in centro. Ho quasi avuto un attacco di panico, pensando che i Federali in qualche modo fossero a conoscenza del messaggio, ma a quanto pare Ryson voleva interrogarmi perché Peter e i suoi uomini hanno nuovamente "interrogato" altri cinque cittadini statunitensi nella loro ricerca per scoprire dove si trovasse Henderson.

"Erano tutti a Charleston, nel South Carolina" mi ha detto Ryson. "Ancora una volta, Sokolov è entrato e uscito dal Paese senza essere scoperto. Dobbiamo sapere come lo sta facendo, affinché possiamo impedirgli di scatenare il caos nella vita delle persone."

"Mi dispiace, non ne so niente" ho detto sinceramente. Peter non ha mai parlato molto delle sue connessioni o di come faccia le cose impossibili che fa. Per quanto mi senta male per le persone che ha terrorizzato e torturato, non so nulla che possa aiutare i Federali.

Ammesso che volessi aiutarli, voglio dire. Se Peter non fosse riuscito a entrare negli Stati Uniti, non avrebbe potuto fare del male ad altre persone. Tuttavia, non riuscirebbe nemmeno a riprendermi, e quella parte perversa e contraddittoria di me—quella che mi tiene sveglia di notte, pensando a quel biglietto con un mix di gioia e trepidazione—non può sopportare questa possibilità.

Ho bisogno di lui.

Lo bramo così tanto che fa male.

Prima di quel messaggio, ero in grado di sopportare il dolore, di essere forte, mentre mi dicevo che era finita, ma aver avuto notizie di Peter—aver saputo che sarebbe tornato—mi ha strappato le fragili nuove difese, reimmergendomi in quell'infinita modalità di attesa.

"Torna a prendermi" sussurro, abbracciando un cuscino sul petto, mentre fisso lo schermo della TV. "Ti prego, Peter, ho bisogno di te. Torna e portami a casa."

eter

"CHE COS'HAI FATTO?" YAN MI FISSA COME SE MI FOSSERO spuntati un paio di tentacoli.

"Ho contattato Lucas Kent per organizzare un incontro con Esguerra" ripeto, mescolando il sugo della pasta. "Mi passi il basilico?"

Yan non si muove, così Ilya spinge silenziosamente il basilico sminuzzato verso di me, e io lo cospargo ampiamente sul sugo. Sto preparando del cibo italiano stasera—una cucina a cui i miei uomini sono piuttosto indifferenti, ma che Sara adora.

Per te, ptichka. Per sentirmi come se tu fossi qui con me.

Ho iniziato a farlo questa settimana, parlando con lei tra me e me. Probabilmente non è salutare, ma mi fa sentire più vicino a lei, come se fosse qui con me e non a un oceano di distanza.

Forse è perché so che potrei rivederla presto, ma mi manca ancora più del solito. Ogni giorno senza di lei è una tortura.

"Pensavo che avresti ucciso Kent" dice Yan, accigliato per la confusione. "Per aver causato l'incidente di Sara."

"E potrei ancora farlo, ma non in questo momento." Affondo un lungo cucchiaio nel sugo e lo assaggio prima di aggiungere un pizzico di sale. "Ho bisogno che mi porti nella tenuta di Esguerra."

Anton si avvicina a Yan. "Quindi, questo è il tuo grande piano? Farti porgere Esguerra su un piatto d'argento da Kent? Ricordi che il tipo ha giurato di ucciderti, vero?"

Lo guardo. "Non mi ucciderà, se vuole il nome della risorsa di Novak."

"Ah." L'espressione di Yan si rilassa. "Quindi, fingerai di fare il doppio gioco con Novak per ottenere l'accesso alla tenuta di Esguerra."

"Esattamente." *E poi lo tradirò per davvero*, penso, ma non lo dico. Per quanto mi fidi dei ragazzi, devo agire con il presupposto che Novak abbia occhi e orecchie su di noi in ogni momento. È altamente improbabile, vista la privacy di questo rifugio sicuro, ma non posso permettermi di rischiare.

Sono a malapena riuscito a convincere il serbo ad accettare il mio piano.

"Dove andrai?" Si è alzato in piedi, quasi rovesciando il tavolo, quando l'ho informato delle mie intenzioni al bar. In un attimo, i suoi scagnozzi sono apparsi dal nascondiglio nella parte posteriore, circondandolo come un muro umano, con gli M16 spianati e puntati contro di me.

"Avevi parlato di fiducia, eh?" ho detto divertito, e Novak mi ha lanciato un'occhiata cupa, prima di ordinar loro di abbassarli.

Mi sono seduto e ho aspettato che facesse altrettanto, prima di spiegare l'essenza del mio piano. C'è voluto un po', ma alla fine ha capito perché quella era l'unica opzione... perché, nonostante la sua risorsa, non riusciremmo ad entrare con la forza nella tenuta di Esguerra.

"Anche ammesso che la tua pediatra sia un mago della tecnologia in grado di disattivare i droni e le recinzioni elettriche che proteggono la tenuta, ci sarebbero comunque le torri di guardia da affrontare. Il che non sarebbe un problema per la mia squadra, a parte il fatto che Esguerra ha generatori e droni di emergenza che verrebbero attivati nel giro di un minuto dalla disattivazione di quelli principali. E poi, mentre ci occupiamo dei droni che ci sparano dal cielo, le guardie di scorta di Esguerra—oltre un centinaio—verrebbero fuori e ci elimenerebbero. L'unico modo per superarle sarebbe con una forza ancora più grande—diciamo, un paio di centinaia di mercenari—ma un gruppo di quelle dimensioni non avrebbe la possibilità di avvicinarsi alla tenuta senza essere scoperto. Non riusciremmo neppure ad entrare in Colombia senza che Esguerra lo venga a sapere e ci intercetti molto prima di poter avvicinarci a lui."

"Quindi, hai in programma di sacrificare la mia risorsa per ottenere la fiducia di Esguerra?" ha chiesto Novak, accigliato, e io ho annuito, spiegando che, una volta entrato, non sarebbe poi così difficile avvicinarsi a Nora—e una volta averla presa come ostaggio, avrò il controllo su Esguerra.

Darebbe la propria vita per salvarla.

"I miei uomini aspetteranno appena fuori dalla tenuta, quindi una volta che avrò avuto Nora e la bambina, disattiverò le difese perimetrali e sfrutterò la confusione della morte di Esguerra per farci scappare" ho detto a Novak. "Non sarà facile, ma è l'unica possibilità che abbiamo."

Il sugo della pasta è finalmente pronto, così, mentre ci sediamo per cenare, riporto lo stesso piano ai ragazzi.

"Col cazzo" dice Anton quando ho finito. "Ostaggi o meno, non uscirai vivo da quella tenuta. Stai parlando di una missione suicida."

"Non necessariamente" dice Yan dolcemente, avvolgendo la forchetta nella pasta. I suoi occhi verdi hanno uno strano bagliore. "Esguerra ha una debolezza ora: sua moglie e sua figlia. E la sfrutteremo. Non è vero?"

"Sì, esattamente" dico, e ricordo a me stesso di tenere d'occhio Yan durante questa missione.

Dato che tutto è in precario equilibrio, il minimo imprevisto —come il tradimento di uno dei miei—potrebbe far crollare tutto.

eter

LA RISPOSTA DI LUCAS KENT ARRIVA QUASI IMMEDIATAMENTE. È disposto a incontrarmi, il che è il primo passo per potermi avvicinare a Esguerra.

Propone il nuovo ristorante della moglie a Londra come possibile luogo di incontro. Non è esattamente un terreno neutrale, ma accetto. So cosa sta pensando: che questo potrebbe essere uno stratagemma per attirarlo, in modo da poter punire lui e sua moglie per la cazzata fatta con Sara.

In altre circostanze, non avrebbe sbagliato. L'immagine della mia *ptichka* in quell'ospedale, il suo delicato viso pallido e contuso, è ancora presente nei miei incubi. Un giorno, Kent *pagherà* per averla lasciata scappare e schiantarsi, ma per ora ho bisogno di lui.

È la mia migliore occasione per raggiungere Esguerra.

Certo, se avesse rifiutato, avrei avuto un piano di riserva.

Conosco l'e-mail di Nora Esguerra, avendo comunicato in passato con lei riguardo alla mia lista. Tuttavia, Esguerra non è esattamente razionale quando si tratta della mogliettina e potrebbe prenderla nel modo sbagliato, se la contattassi dopo tutti questi anni.

È meglio passare attraverso Kent—Esguerra potrebbe essere più disposto ad ascoltare in quel caso.

~

LA MOGLIE DI KENT, LA BELLISSIMA YULIA, NON SI VEDE, QUANDO entro nell'elegante ristorante e mi dirigo verso un separé nell'angolo, dove la testa bionda di Kent è visibile sopra la parete divisoria.

Si alza per salutarmi, con il duro viso diffidente, mentre allunga la mano. "Sokolov."

Gli do la mano, stringendo le dita con troppa forza. "Kent."

Socchiude gli occhi, ma mi libera la mano senza reagire. "Non mi aspettavo di risentirti" dice, mentre prendiamo posto e apriamo i menù. "Come sta la tua Sara?"

"Chi? Oh, già." Chiamo il cameriere e gli dico di portarmi una bottiglia di Guinness chiusa con un apribottiglie. Kent ordina una tazza di Earl Grey per sé. Aspetto che il cameriere se ne vada, prima di dire a Kent: "Non ho idea di come stia. L'ho lasciata andare l'anno scorso e da allora non l'ho più vista."

Solleva le sopracciglia. "Davvero?"

Mi stringo nelle spalle. "Che cosa posso dire? Era giunto il momento."

"Giusto." Non sembra credermi, ma rivolge l'attenzione al menù e lo analizza prima di alzare lo sguardo per chiedere: "Hai già deciso cosa ordinare?"

"Non ho fame, grazie." Visto quello che è successo con Sara e quello che sto per dirgli, non mi fido più di Kent o del cibo nel ristorante di sua moglie.

La sua bocca si piega in un sorrisetto beffardo. "Capisco." Chiudendo il menù, aspetta che il cameriere poggi le nostre bevande sul tavolo, e poi dice: "Perché vuoi vedere Esguerra? Non ti ha ancora perdonato per l'incidente con Nora, lo sai."

"Sì, lo so." Ho usato sua moglie come esca, lasciando che venisse rapita per scoprire dove un gruppo terroristico lo stava trattenendo in quel momento. Allora, sapevo che si sarebbe incazzato per il coinvolgimento di Nora, ma la sua rabbia non aveva davvero senso per me—dopotutto, era l'unico modo per salvargli la vita.

Ora, tuttavia, comprendo meglio la sua reazione. Se qualcuno mettesse in pericolo Sara in quel modo, non mi importerebbe niente delle motivazioni alla base.

La mia vita per lei non sarebbe mai uno scambio equo.

"Ho ricevuto un'offerta molto redditizia" dico a Kent, aprendo la mia Guinness. "Di conseguenza, sono entrato in possesso di alcune informazioni che Esguerra potrebbe apprezzare."

Kent si acciglia e solleva la tazza di tè. "Oh? E quali informazioni sarebbero?"

"C'è un traditore nella sua tenuta" dico e bevo un sorso, mentre il cipiglio di Kent si fa più profondo. "Un traditore che dovrebbe aiutarmi nel mio incarico."

Kent mette giù il tè. "Qualcuno ti ha ingaggiato per colpire Esguerra?" Al mio cenno di conferma, chiede bruscamente: "Chi?"

Apro la bocca per dirglielo, ma giunge alla conclusione da solo.

"Novak" sbotta, spingendo via il tè. La sua mascella si flette violentemente. "Naturalmente. Chi altro oserebbe fotterci?"

Bevo un altro sorso della mia birra. "La sua offerta vale cento milioni di euro, ma sono disposto ad accordarmi con Esguerra—se mi porti in Colombia per parlargli. Voglio porre fine alle discordie del passato. Beh, questo e un centinaio di milioni" chiarisco, affinché non pensi che io intenda solo far pace.

Kent mi fissa, con gli occhi socchiusi. "Sai che potrebbe rifiutare, vero? Ora che sappiamo che c'è un traditore, scopriremo di chi si tratta. È solo questione di tempo."

"Certo. Ma il tempo conta—specialmente quando c'è di mezzo una vulnerabile neonata."

Kent sbianca. "Che cazzo ne sai dei neonati?" La sua voce è pericolosamente flebile. "Perché se stai cercando di insinuare che—"

"Lizzie è in pericolo? Non lo sto insinuando, te lo sto dicendo. Novak sa tutto sulla recente aggiunta alla famiglia Esguerra, e ha dei piani per lei." Sto correndo un rischio rivelando tutto questo, ma non posso permettermi di girarci intorno.

Devo convincere Esguerra ad ascoltarmi.

Il mio futuro con Sara dipende da questo.

Il cameriere si avvicina per prendere il nostro ordine, ma Kent lo manda via con un rapido gesto della mano. "E se Esguerra ti versasse i cento milioni?" chiede, riprendendo il suo tè. "Cento milioni per un nome, nessun rischio per te."

"No" dico e finisco la birra. "Non voglio passare il resto della mia vita a guardarmi le spalle, in attesa che Esguerra si vendichi di me. O mi ascolta di persona o accetterò il lavoro. Dipende da lui."

Alzandomi, esco dal ristorante, con lo stomaco che brontola per i deliziosi odori che emana la cucina.

Se tutto andrà bene, mangerò qui davvero un giorno... con Sara al mio fianco.

 eter

Non devo aspettare molto prima che arrivi la risposta di Esguerra. La sua e-mail è nella mia casella di posta, quando torno nell'hotel.

Stasera alle sette, dice il messaggio. *Lucas ti verrà a prendere.*

Saranno le sette tra mezz'ora, così lo comunico ai ragazzi e mi preparo.

Kent si presenta puntualmente alle sette nella mia camera d'albergo. Non sono affatto sorpreso dal fatto che sappia dove mi trovo; ho capito di essere pedinato nel secondo in cui ho lasciato il ristorante.

Il volto di Kent sembra scavato nel granito. "Niente armi" dice, e alzo le braccia, lasciandomi esaminare dalla testa ai piedi.

Trova il coltello nel mio stivale, i due coltelli in tasca, e il piccolo revolver infilato nella tasca interna della giacca di pelle.

Tuttavia, non si accorge della lama di rasoio nell'orlo dei jeans o del filo metallico cucito nel colletto della giacca.

Camp Larko è stato utile.

"Andiamo" dice, quando è soddisfatto, e lo seguo fuori dall'hotel e su una limousine blindata.

Il tragitto verso l'aeroporto è silenzioso. Mi aspetto che Kent mi porti nell'aereo privato di Esguerra e che se ne vada, ma entra con me.

"Lo piloterai tu?" chiedo, e annuisce lentamente.

"Esguerra ha chiesto che fossi io a portarti da lui."

Non sembra troppo contento, e sorrido, mentre mi siedo sul divano di pelle color crema nella cabina. L'incazzatura di Kent per l'interruzione della sua routine è un vantaggio, per quanto mi riguarda.

Non posso ancora ucciderlo per aver lasciato che Sara rimanesse coinvolta nell'incidente, ma posso certamente divertirmi a rovinare i suoi piani.

Trascorro parte del volo di undici ore a sonnecchiare e il resto a inviare e-mail alla mia squadra. Anche loro stanno andando in Colombia, e mi aspetteranno fuori dalla tenuta, come previsto dal nostro piano approvato da Novak. Se tutto andrà bene, non avrò bisogno di loro, ma in caso contrario, potrebbero aiutarmi a uscirne.

Ammesso che io sia ancora vivo per uscirne, voglio dire.

L'enorme tenuta di Esguerra si trova nella parte sud-est della Colombia, proprio ai margini della foresta pluviale amazzonica. È notte, quando atterriamo sulla piccola pista di atterraggio all'interno della tenuta, e l'aria umida è calda e completamente stabile, mentre scendiamo dall'aereo.

Riconosco il conducente dell'auto che ci sta aspettando. È una delle guardie che erano qui, quando lavoravo per Esguerra.

"Ehi, Diego" lo saluto, e lui sogghigna, con i denti bianchi che brillano.

"Sokolov. Non avrei mai pensato di rivederti, amico." Il suo accento spagnolo non è pesante come ricordavo, ma comunque abbastanza evidente. "Come stai?" Poi, nota l'uomo biondo al mio fianco. "Ehi, Lucas. Dov'è Yu—"

"Guida e zitto" sbotta Kent, salendo in macchina, e seguo il suo esempio.

Sembra che non sia in vena di fare conversazione. Beh, meglio così.

Invece di portarmi nella residenza in cui risiedono Esguerra e sua moglie, Diego ci conduce in un capanno sul margine esterno della tenuta. Riconosco il posto—è il luogo in cui una volta ho aiutato Esguerra a interrogare i suoi nemici—e mio malgrado, un brivido mi aggrinzisce la pelle.

Non c'è niente che impedisca al trafficante d'armi colombiano di legarmi e torturarmi per farmi rivelare il nome del traditore.

Niente a parte il fatto che Esguerra mi conosce—e spero che si renda conto che non sarà facile distruggermi.

Esce dal capanno, mentre io e Kent scendiamo dall'auto, e, mentre i fari della macchina gli illuminano il viso, vedo che ha ancora l'aspetto di una star del cinema, nonostante l'occhio artificiale che ha sostituito quello cavato dai nemici. Non l'avevo più visto da allora—sapevo che si sarebbe incazzato per il metodo del suo salvataggio, così me ne sono andato prima che potesse uccidermi—ma è lo stesso che ricordo.

Ancora pericoloso come nessun altro e privo di qualsiasi empatia... tranne quando si tratta di sua moglie.

E ora forse della figlia neonata.

"Hai le palle" dice pacatamente, fermandosi davanti a me. Il suo inglese è della varietà americana, senza alcuna traccia di accento spagnolo. Sua madre era americana, ricordo—una modella.

"Volevo parlarti in un luogo sicuro" dico, incrociando i suoi penetranti occhi azzurri senza battere ciglio. Non ho paura, anche se probabilmente dovrei averla. Julian Esguerra è uno degli uomini più crudeli che conosca, un vero sadico. L'ho visto spellare uomini vivi e trarne un immenso piacere, e mi sono chiesto spesso come faccia la sua giovane moglie a sopportare quell'aspetto della natura del marito.

Lui la ama, ma dubito che le risparmi questi dettagli.

"Perché?" chiede con lo stesso tono letale. "Perché proprio qui, tra tutti i posti?"

"Perché voglio fare un patto con te" dico con calma, mentre Kent si avvicina a Esguerra. "E sono certo che Novak non possa vederci o sentirci qui." Mentre dico questo, sono consapevole della presenza di Diego, seduto in macchina e con il motore ancora in funzione—che probabilmente sta facendo abbastanza rumore da sovrastare la nostra conversazione.

A quanto pare, Kent è l'unica persona di cui il mio ex datore di lavoro si fidi pienamente.

"Pensi che Novak non sappia che hai avvicinato Lucas?" chiede Esguerra, con la bocca che si contorce con fare derisorio. "Che non sia stato avvisato nel momento in cui il mio aereo è decollato con te sopra?"

"Oh, sì." Sorrido freddamente. "In effetti, è sempre stato a conoscenza del mio piano."

Né Kent, né Esguerra battono ciglio, ma posso percepire la loro sorpresa. "Sapeva che avresti fatto il doppio gioco?" chiede Kent, accigliato.

"Sì. Gliel'ho detto non appena ha rivelato il nome della risorsa."

Esguerra flette la mascella. "Gli hai detto che l'avresti tradito?"

"Non esattamente. Gli ho detto che avrei finto di tradirlo per poter accedere alla tua tenuta. Sa del patto che ho detto a

Kent di voler stringere: far pace con te e cento milioni per il nome della risorsa di Novak."

Il cipiglio di Kent si fa più profondo, ma Esguerra inclina la testa, guardandomi pensieroso. "Il patto che hai detto a Kent di voler stringere" dice lentamente. "Quello che, presumo, non sia il vero patto che stai cercando."

"Esatto." Sono consapevole della dolorosa tensione nel collo e nelle spalle, e rilasso consapevolmente i muscoli. "O, perlomeno, questo non è l'intero patto."

Esguerra incrocia le braccia sul petto. "Qual è l'intero patto, allora?"

"Ti dirò chi è la risorsa di Novak all'interno della tenuta... e ti consegnerò Novak stesso, così non dovrai più preoccuparti di lui."

Esguerra socchiude gli occhi. "In cambio di cosa?"

"Tranquillità e i cento milioni che ho già menzionato—e solo un'altra cosa."

"Che cosa?" chiede Kent, senza preoccuparsi di nascondere la curiosità.

"Amnistia" dico, guardando dal trafficante d'armi colombiano al suo compagno e viceversa. "Voglio l'amnistia globale per tutti i reati di cui sono accusato, così come l'immunità da ulteriori procedimenti giudiziari. Voglio essere cancellato da tutte le liste dei ricercati—e voglio che tu lo renda possibile."

3 2

Sara

Quella notte lo sogno di nuovo. Viene da me come un fantasma, avvolgendomi nella sua oscurità, stringendomi forte, mentre piango e cerco di liberarmi. Non so se sto combattendo contro di lui o il mio stesso desiderio, ma in entrambi i casi, tra non molto, perderò.

Mi sciolgo a lui, lasciando che la sua oscurità mi circondi, scacciando via tutta la solitudine e la luce.

A quel punto, mi prende, spingendo dentro di me con furia punitiva, e lo abbraccio, urlando il suo nome, mentre il mio corpo si contorce per un piacere torrido, con la beatitudine così lacerante e squisita che minaccia di farmi a pezzi. Facciamo l'amore più volte, finché non sono sfinita e dolorante.

Finché non ho più niente da dare e se ne va.

Se ne va, perché non mi vuole più.

Perché si è stancato di me.

Mi sveglio con il cuscino zuppo di lacrime e il sesso scivoloso e palpitante dal bisogno. So che il sogno è stato solo una manifestazione delle mie paure, che nulla di tutto ciò era reale, ma mi sento ancora a pezzi, distrutta dal rifiuto di Peter.

Con il ritorno della terribile solitudine che è la mia compagna di notte.

Alzandomi, trovo la borsa e faccio uscire il biglietto che Peter ha lasciato per me. Si sta consumando intorno ai bordi, così lo distendo, mentre lo apro e leggo le parole, ripetendomele più volte.

Ricorda, ptichka. Finché saremo entrambi vivi.

Porto il biglietto con me e lo metto sotto al cuscino prima di riaddormentarmi.

Peter tornerà. Devo crederci.

In un modo o nell'altro, tornerà da me.

Peter

ESGUERRA MI FISSA, COME SE NON RIUSCISSE A CREDERE ALLE proprie orecchie, poi si lascia sfuggire una dura risata. "Amnistia e immunità? Per te?"

Kent rimane silenzioso al suo fianco, ma vedo la comprensione nello sguardo.

Sa di cosa si tratta.

Lui e Yulia mi hanno visto con Sara.

"In realtà, per me e per i miei ragazzi" dico a Esguerra. "Non sono così popolari per le forze dell'ordine, ma sono ancora sulle loro liste di merda. Di' ai tuoi amici della CIA di cancellarci da quelle liste, e puoi dimenticarti di Novak per sempre."

"Davvero?" dice, continuando a ridacchiare. "Ammesso che io riuscissi a realizzare questo miracolo per te, da quando ti preoccupi che ti stiano dando la caccia?"

Kent potrebbe rispondere per me, ma con mio grande

sollievo tiene la bocca chiusa, mentre dico: "Non sono affari tuoi. Questo è l'accordo che sto offrendo. Prendere o lasciare."

Ogni traccia di umorismo svanisce dal volto di Esguerra. "Fanculo. Mi dirai chi è il traditore e lo farai ora."

Ora sono io a ridere. "E in cambio, mi concederai una morte rapida e indolore?"

Il sorriso di Esguerra è affilato come una lama. "Questo è l'affare migliore che otterrai. Sai che ti tirerò fuori quel nome in un modo o nell'altro."

"So che ci proverai—e alla fine potresti persino riuscirci. Ma ti costerà caro."

Socchiude gli occhi. "E come mai?"

"Molto prima che riuscirai a conoscere quel nome" dico sottovoce "la mia squadra attiverà la risorsa. Forse ci riusciranno senza di me, o forse no, ma questo è un rischio che dovrai correre. Quanto ha Lizzie ora? Otto, dieci giorni? Forse non sei ancora così affezionato a lei, ma Novak ha programmi anche per Nora. Grandi programmi—"

Esguerra è su di me prima che io possa finire di parlare, con i lineamenti perfetti che si contorcono in una feroce maschera rabbiosa. Si allena spesso con le guardie, quindi è veloce e letale, ma mi aspettavo l'aggressione. All'ultimo istante, mi giro, e il suo pugno colpisce il mio zigomo invece di schiacciare il naso. Tuttavia, non c'è modo di evitare l'altro pugno, e il colpo riverbera nel mio plesso solare, facendo uscire l'aria dai polmoni.

Se non mi fossi addestrato per questo, mi sarei piegato, ansimando. Tuttavia, so come superare il dolore. Invece di lottare per l'aria come vorrebbe il mio corpo, scaccio il disagio e vado all'attacco, aggredendolo con una serie di colpi.

Siamo alla pari in termini di stazza e forza, ed è bravo in questo—forse quanto i miei ragazzi. Ma ho la mente più lucida in questa lotta. Ciascuno dei miei colpi è calcolato per neutralizzare e sfuggire, mentre lui agisce in preda all'istinto, lasciandosi guidare dalla rabbia.

Evito la maggior parte dei colpi, ma i pochi che ricevo fanno male da morire. Ignorando il dolore, lo prendo a pugni, e un minuto dopo, riesco a farlo cadere. Il bastardo non si arrende, però. Invece di provare a rialzarsi, mi afferra un piede e lo tira, facendomi cadere sopra di lui.

All'ultimo secondo, mi giro, così il mio gomito atterra sulla sua cassa toracica. Il mio braccio esplode per il dolore, ma lui grugnisce, quindi devo avergli fratturato una costola. Nel momento successivo, però, qualcosa di lucido lampeggia nella mia visione periferica, e reagisco istintivamente, afferrandogli il polso per bloccare la lama che si sta avvicinando a me. Sfrutta quel momento di distrazione per sferrarmi un colpo sul lato del viso, ma continuo a concentrarmi sul coltello e a ruotare il polso, determinato a—

"Basta così." Due mani forti mi afferrano da dietro, strappandomi da Esguerra prima che possa spezzargli il polso. Il mio istinto è quello di attaccare il nuovo aggressore, ma mantengo la lucidità sufficiente per non lottare.

Uccidere Kent o Esguerra sarebbe controproducente per il mio obiettivo.

Esguerra è in piedi prima che Kent mi lasci andare, ma non attacca di nuovo. Invece, si asciuga il sangue che gli cola dal naso e dice con voce gutturale: "Quali programmi del cazzo?"

Naturalmente. Vuole conoscere i dettagli della minaccia per Nora.

"Novak vuole usarla per controllare tutti i tuoi possedimenti" dico, mentre Kent mi lascia andare e si avvicina a Esguerra. Il viso e il gomito mi pulsano come due figli di puttana, e la bocca ha il sapore del rame, ma lo ignoro.

Dato il coltello che Esguerra ha tirato fuori dal nulla, sarebbe potuta andare molto peggio.

"In che modo?" chiede Esguerra, e sono felice di vedere che

un lato della sua faccia si sta già gonfiando. "Come cazzo pensa di riuscirci?"

"Sposandola. Come sennò?" Sputo il sangue sotto la lingua. "Ha aspettato che nascesse tua figlia, in modo da poter ricattare Nora. Vedi, vuole entrambe—tua moglie per sé, e tua figlia come strumento per controllare tua moglie, che a quel punto sarebbe *sua* moglie, ma credo tu abbia capito."

Per un attimo, sono convinto che Esguerra mi aggredirà di nuovo, ma questa volta si controlla. A stento. Non che io possa biasimarlo.

Se qualcuno cercasse di strapparmi Sara, mi piacerebbe tagliare le sue palle in piccoli pezzi e darle in pasto alla fauna locale.

Sospetto fortemente che Esguerra sia tentato di fare proprio questo con me, così dico: "Posso prendere Novak per te, e posso farlo velocemente. So che sei in grado di affrontarlo da solo, ma ci vorrà del tempo affinché tu possa rintracciarlo e superare le sue difese—proprio come ci vorrà del tempo affinché tu possa ottenere il nome della sua risorsa da me... ammesso che tu ci riesca. Nel frattempo, tua moglie e tua figlia sono in pericolo. Se la mia squadra fallisce, Novak troverà qualcun altro per arrivare a Nora e alla bambina. Ho conosciuto il tipo—non si fermerà. Vuole quello che hai—tutto quello che hai, compresa Nora—e continuerà, finché non lo ucciderai. O finché non lo farò per te—cosa che può accadere alla fine di questa settimana."

Esguerra è un fascio di rabbia, ma deve comprendere la saggezza in quello che sto dicendo, perché rimane fermo, flettendo le mani convulsamente lungo i fianchi. Percepisco il conflitto che si sta scatenando dentro di lui, ma alla fine dice duramente: "Cinquanta milioni. E voglio che Novak mi venga portato qui vivo."

Il mio cuore sussulta, ma mantengo un tono calmo. "Settantacinque. È il massimo che possa fare."

In realtà, accetterei anche zero—la felicità di Sara vale tutto per me—ma almeno in questo modo posso ricompensare i miei compagni di squadra per il futuro scioglimento della nostra attività.

Quando non sarò più un fuggitivo, smetteremo di eseguire omicidi.

"Affare fatto" dice Esguerra a denti stretti. "Settantacinque milioni, e farò del mio meglio per ottenere l'immunità per te e i tuoi uomini in cambio sia di Novak che del traditore."

"Ci farai ottenere l'immunità" lo correggo. "Niente immunità, niente accordo."

"Sei rimasto coinvolto in una fottuta campagna omicida globale per anni. Non posso garantire alcuna—"

"Sì, puoi. I nostri crimini non sono peggiori di quello che tu e Kent"—faccio un cenno con la testa verso l'uomo biondo che ci osserva silenziosamente—"fate ogni giorno, e nessuno vi tocca. Fallo, Julian. Chiedi tutti i favori di cui hai bisogno e ti consegnerò Novak su un piatto d'argento."

Esguerra mi fissa, con le dita ancora contratte. "Va bene" dice dopo un momento, con un tono notevolmente più calmo. "Ora dimmi chi è il traditore."

Studio la sua espressione e prendo una decisione in un secondo. "Portami da Nora, e lo farò."

Il viso di Esguerra si indurisce, e Kent si irrigidisce visibilmente—probabilmente pronto a trattenerlo.

"Perché?" sbotta Esguerra. "Che cazzo c'entra con questo?"

"Niente... solo che forse vorrebbe saperlo" dico in modo uniforme. "E una volta che l'avrà saputo, credo che avrebbe un problema se tu mi uccidessi, nonostante il patto che abbiamo appena stretto."

Le sue narici si dilatano. "Stai dicendo che sono un bugiardo?"

Mi stringo nelle spalle. "Faresti qualsiasi cosa per proteggere la tua famiglia, come me. In ogni caso, non ho dimenticato che è stata tua moglie ad aiutarmi con la lista, non tu. Portami da Nora, e rivelerò a entrambi quello che so. Su questo, hai la mia parola."

E aspetto, con i muscoli tesi pronti al combattimento, mentre Esguerra prende la sua decisione.

VENGO ESAMINATO DALLA TESTA AI PIEDI ALTRE CINQUE VOLTE, due volte da Kent e Diego, e una volta dallo stesso Esguerra. Alla terza ispezione, trovano la lama di rasoio e il filo metallico, quindi ora sono davvero disarmato—se si escludono il mio corpo e le sue capacità, voglio dire.

Il tragitto verso la dimora di Esguerra trascorre in un silenzio esplosivo, e so che basterebbe la minima scintilla per far scatenare il mio ospite. È nervoso come non l'ho mai visto, con la violenza dentro di lui sul punto di esplodere.

Un contingente di ventuno guardie ci raggiunge nella dimora bianca in stile coloniale e ci segue nel soggiorno arredato con gusto. Esguerra lascia me e Kent con loro e scompare al piano di sopra—probabilmente per svegliare la moglie, che è nel periodo del puerperio.

Con un traditore in libertà, non poteva aspettare fino al mattino.

Per un paio di minuti, tutto ciò che sento sono le guardie che respirano e si spostano da un piede all'altro. Poi, il pianto di una bambina trafigge il silenzio, con un suono forte, dolce e così familiare che mi si stringe il cuore nel petto.

Pasha piangeva in quel modo da piccolo. Era il suo grido quando aveva fame—una richiesta per ottenere del cibo che veniva sempre soddisfatta nel giro di pochi minuti.

Il dolore che mi colpisce è forte come i primi tempi, durante quei giorni bui in cui la rabbia era l'unica cosa che mi faceva andare avanti. Per un secondo, non riesco a respirare dal dolore, dall'agonia così acuta che mi sento come se avessi una lama conficcata nella schiena.

Mio figlio. Il bambino che non ha mai avuto la possibilità di crescere, di passare dalle macchinine giocattolo alla realtà.

Se avevo qualche scrupolo su quello che sto facendo, evapora in questo momento. Sto facendo il doppio gioco con un cliente, ma ne vale la pena. Anche senza l'accordo che ho stretto con Esguerra, non avrei mai fatto del male a quella bambina indifesa.

Non con il viso di Pasha fresco nella mente.

Ci vogliono un paio di minuti prima che il pianto si interrompa e quasi mezz'ora prima che Esguerra torni, con il braccio avvolto attorno a una ragazza minuta e con i capelli scuri, che indossa uno spesso accappatoio di spugna che la copre dalla testa ai piedi.

La vera ossessione di Esguerra.

Nora, sua moglie.

Il suo viso piccolo si illumina, quando mi vede. A differenza del marito, non ce l'ha con me per il salvataggio che l'ha messa in pericolo—anche perché è stata una sua idea.

"Peter!" Sta per venirmi incontro e salutarmi, ma viene

trattenuta dalla presa possessiva del marito. Stupita, si ferma e sorride. "Come stai?"

"Bene, grazie." Nonostante le guardie intorno a noi e il viso che sta iniziando a sembrare un gigantesco livido a causa dei colpi di Esguerra, non posso fare a meno di ricambiare il sorriso. È difficile credere che una ragazza così giovane e dall'aspetto così delicato possa essere madre—o essere sopravvissuta a qualcuno spietato come Esguerra. "Congratulazioni per la recente aggiunta alla tua famiglia."

Il suo sorriso si allarga. "Grazie. Te la presenterei, ma sai già tutto..." Guarda suo marito, la cui espressione diventa ancora più tetra durante il nostro scambio.

Sono abbastanza sicuro che la sua pazienza sia giunta al limite. Stringendo la moglie al proprio fianco, chiede con letale dolcezza: "Hai intenzione di dirmi chi è o no?"

Ecco. È giunto il momento di rinunciare alla mia carta vincente. Nonostante la presenza di Nora e il patto che abbiamo stretto, potrebbe ancora uccidermi non appena verrà a sapere quel nome.

Oh, beh. Chi non risica non rosica.

Incrociando lo sguardo gelido di Esguerra, dico con calma: "Non so come si chiama, ma è la tua pediatra. È la risorsa di Novak."

3 5

 *ara*

"SAI, JOE HA CHIESTO DI TE" DICE MAMMA, SPALMANDO IL MIELE che ho portato dal mercato contadino sul suo toast. "Non hai più avuto sue notizie di recente, vero?"

"Mamma, per favore." Combatto l'impulso di roteare gli occhi come un'adolescente troppo cresciuta. Per qualche ragione, durante la colazione del sabato mattina, questo argomento riaffiora inevitabilmente. "È solo carino, tutto qui. Non c'è niente tra noi, lo giuro."

"Ma perché no, tesoro?" Delle linee di preoccupazione corrugano la fronte di mamma, mentre papà sospira nel caffè. "Sei tornata da quasi nove mesi, e non sei ancora andata nemmeno a un appuntamento. Non devi niente a quel criminale. Lo sai, vero? Chiaramente, qualunque cosa ci fosse tra voi ormai è finita, e devi voltare pagina. Non tornerà."

Lo farà, a giudicare da quel biglietto, ma non posso dirlo ai

181

miei genitori. Nonostante i miei migliori sforzi per convincerli di essere stata con il mio rapitore volontariamente e che l'intera caccia all'uomo dell'FBI sia stata solo un grosso malinteso, Peter sarà sempre "quel criminale" per loro. Non so se sia perché in qualche modo abbiano avuto sentore della mia storia ufficiale raccontata all'FBI o se siano semplicemente dei normali cittadini rispettosi della legge e diffidenti nei confronti di chiunque abbia qualche problema con le autorità, ma sono convinti che Peter sia malvagio e che tutti i sentimenti che provavo per lui fossero dovuti alla Sindrome di Stoccolma.

Non che questo sia del tutto sbagliato—almeno, non sarebbe stato sbagliato nove mesi fa. La mia attrazione nei confronti di Peter *era* innaturale e tossica, e l'ho combattuta con tutta me stessa. Ho combattuto fino alla fine, quando ho quasi perso la vita in quell'incidente.

No. Non è del tutto vero.

È stato fin quando ha messo i miei bisogni al di sopra dei suoi e mi ha lasciata andare. Ciò ha rappresentato la vera svolta per me, anche se è solo di recente che ho riflettuto su questo... sul fatto che sono riuscita in qualche modo ad accettare i sentimenti che ho sviluppato per l'assassino di mio marito, che quando penso a lui ora è "Peter" nella mia mente.

L'uomo che mi ama, non l'uomo che ha ucciso George.

I miei genitori non sono a conoscenza di quell'ultima parte —almeno spero di no—ma continuano a detestare Peter per avermi tenuta lontano da loro per così tanto tempo. Pensano che sia pericoloso come dice l'FBI, e sto male al pensiero di quanto saranno sconvolti, quando Peter mi rapirà di nuovo.

Tuttavia, non riesco a smettere di desiderarlo.

Di volere lui e tutto ciò che è.

"Non sono pronta, Mamma" le dico e mi alzo per versare altro caffè. "Cerca di capire. Sono ancora innamorata di Peter, e, quando si sarà risolto tutto, *tornerà*. Vedrai."

E con quello, cambio argomento, lanciandomi in una storia sulla mia ultima esibizione con la band.

È meglio che continuare a mentire. Niente sarà mai risolto, perché non ci sono equivoci.

Peter è un criminale e, quando tornerà, mi porterà con sé.

Mi porterà via per sempre.

Peter

Trascorro la notte nel capanno, dove Esguerra tiene i suoi prigionieri, con una caviglia incatenata all'anello di metallo in mezzo al pavimento.

"Solo una precauzione" ha spiegato Kent, quando le guardie hanno bloccato la catena. "Non è che non ci fidiamo di te..."

"Certo." La catena è lunga circa due metri, il che significa che posso sdraiarmi sulla branda che le guardie hanno trascinato nel capanno. Quindi, tutto sommato, non è così male. Ovviamente preferirei non essere incatenato, ma considerando quello che ho appena visto fare da Esguerra alla pediatra, non mi lamento.

Ci vorrà un po' di tempo prima che io possa dimenticare le urla della donna.

Ha ceduto all'istante, praticamente non appena gli Esguerra, accompagnati da me e dalle guardie, sono entrati nella sua stanza. Non so che cosa si aspettasse—guadagnare punti per la sincerità?—ma ha ammesso subito la propria colpa, scusandosi profusamente sia con Esguerra che con sua moglie, giurando che non intendeva causare alcun danno reale, che non conosceva davvero loro o Lizzie, quando ha preso la mazzetta.

È come se pensasse che una volta aver confessato tutto sarebbe stato perdonato e dimenticato, che essere licenziata fosse la cosa peggiore che potesse capitarle.

Forse è perché ho visto Esguerra fare letteralmente a pezzi l'idiota, quando Nora se ne è andata per allattare la bambina o forse è perché sono così vicino al mio obiettivo, ma il sonno è di nuovo inquieto, pieno di incubi. Per due volte, sogno di trovare il corpo di mio figlio in un mucchio di cadaveri, e almeno altre due volte quel corpo risulta essere quello di Sara.

Tuttavia, al mattino sono pallido, ma cautamente ottimista. Il fatto che sono ancora vivo è incoraggiante—un segno che Esguerra potrebbe rispettare l'accordo. Naturalmente non ci sono garanzie, ma ho il sospetto che Nora abbia una buona dose di influenza sul marito in questi giorni—inoltre, è in debito con me per la pediatra.

In ogni caso, non sono sorpreso quando Esguerra e Kent si presentano insieme per liberarmi.

"Qual è il tuo piano?" chiede Esguerra, mentre Kent sblocca la manetta intorno alla mia caviglia. "Come pensi di andare da lui? Ti rendi conto che nel momento in cui ti presenterai senza Nora e la bambina al seguito, capirà che l'hai tradito? O questo, oppure che hai fallito—in entrambi i casi, non sarà contento."

Faccio un respiro profondo. Ecco un'altra parte difficile. "Sì. Ci ho riflettuto. Ed è per questo che ho bisogno di tua moglie per questa parte dell'operazione. Non sarà in—"

"Assolutamente no." I muscoli della mascella di Esguerra si contraggono. "Nora non lascerà questa tenuta."

Deludente, ma non inaspettato. "D'accordo, allora pensi di poter trovare qualcuno che assomigli a Nora? Almeno un po'?"

Esguerra si acciglia, e sento che dirà di no, quando Kent dice: "Non c'è nessuno nella proprietà, ma posso ordinare alle guardie di perlustrare gli insediamenti vicini per una possibile candidata. Non dovrebbe essere così difficile trovare una ragazza con i capelli scuri della taglia di Nora. La sua carnagione non è esattamente insolita da queste parti."

È vero. Se avessimo bisogno di un doppione per la bionda moglie dagli occhi azzurri di Kent, saremmo nei guai, ma Nora è in parte messicana, con gli occhi scuri e la carnagione abbronzata. "Dovresti trovare una ragazza davvero giovane" suggerisco. "Forse una studentessa che somigli a Nora. Come stavo dicendo, non sarà in pericolo—ho solo bisogno che Novak scopra che sono sceso dall'aereo con una donna che somiglia a Nora e la sua bambina al seguito. Una bambola andrà bene per quest'ultima; la ragazza dovrà solo stringerla forte."

Kent guarda Esguerra, che annuisce. "Fallo. E, se possibile, trova anche una neonata—meglio non rovinare tutto a causa di una bambola."

Apro la bocca per rifiutare, ma poi decido di non farlo.

Non ho mentito sulla mancanza di pericolo per "Nora," quindi tanto vale utilizzare una bambina vera.

Tutto ciò che serve per attirarlo nella trappola ed eliminare Novak per sempre.

Otto ore dopo, lascio la tenuta a piedi, armato di un M16 che ho "rubato" a una guardia, e con una terrorizzata sedicenne e la sorella di due mesi al seguito. La famiglia delle ragazze sarà ben ricompensata per la loro recita, ma la prospettiva di bei vestiti e denaro per il college non è sufficiente a calmare la sedicenne.

È spaventatissima, e questo è perfetto.

Lo sarebbe anche la vera Nora.

Le guardie di Kent hanno trovato un'adolescente che somiglia alla Signora Esguerra in modo inquietante—almeno da dietro e da profilo. Da davanti, il viso della ragazza è più rotondo, con il naso più largo e gli occhi più piccoli e infossati, così abbiamo utilizzato il trucco per mascherare quelle caratteristiche.

Grazie all'applicazione impeccabile di ombretto, rossetto e fondotinta scuro, la sosia di Nora ora sfoggia due occhi neri, un labbro spaccato e numerosi lividi giallastri che nascondono la pienezza infantile delle guance.

Parla anche un po' di inglese, ma il suo accento è pesante, quindi le abbiamo detto di non parlare in nessuna circostanza. "Puoi piangere o tacere" le ha ordinato Esguerra, e la ragazza ha annuito, con il mento tremante.

"Sì, señor. Starò zitta."

Finora, ha mantenuto la sua parola. Stiamo attraversando la giungla da oltre due ore, con lei che tiene in braccio la sorellina urlante per tutto il tempo, e non si è mai lamentata—anche se ci sarebbe molto di cui lamentarsi.

Non è ancora piovuto oggi, e il caldo umido è soffocante, con l'aria così densa da sembrare una coperta bagnata sulla pelle. Abbiamo fatto indossare alla ragazza uno dei soliti vestiti di Nora—un prendisole bianco e un paio di sandali—e posso scorgere la dolorosa irritazione sui suoi piedi, nel punto in cui ha calpestato un formicaio un paio di miglia indietro. Siamo entrambi sudatissimi, e dei minuscoli moscerini ci ronzano intorno, pungendo ogni centimetro di carne esposta.

Questa è pura sofferenza, ed è una buona cosa.

Sembrerà più autentico in questo modo.

Dopo un'altra ora di tortura, incontriamo i miei ragazzi al punto stabilito. Vedo lo shock sui loro volti, mentre spingo la ragazza in avanti, con la bambina che piange stretta sul petto.

"Ce l'hai fatta." Lo sguardo incredulo di Yan oscilla da me al mio ostaggio e viceversa. "Ce l'hai fatta davvero, cazzo."

"Sì. Non è stato facile, ma eccoci qui."

La sostituta di Nora rimane in silenzio, imitando bene una prigioniera traumatizzata e terrorizzata. Il suo trucco resistente all'acqua si è leggermente rovinato durante il viaggio, ma sembra ancora incredibilmente livida e malconcia, con l'espressione provata dalla disidratazione e dallo sfinimento. Nessuno dei miei ragazzi ha mai visto la vera Signora Esguerra, solo alcune foto, quindi non hanno motivo di dubitare della sua autenticità.

I "lividi" stanno facendo il loro lavoro.

La bambina continua a piangere, e prendo nota mentalmente di darle la bottiglia di latte in polvere che ho fatto acquistare ai miei ragazzi e da tenere sull'aereo, nel caso in cui "Nora" avesse avuto problemi con l'allattamento al seno. Abbiamo anche pannolini sull'aereo, insieme ad altri accessori per bambini.

"È morto?" chiede Anton in russo, e annuisco, lanciando un'occhiata alla ragazza, come se fossi preoccupato per la sua reazione.

"Sì, ho preso il bastardo. Lei potrebbe non saperlo ancora, però, quindi mantenete un profilo basso. Ha già combattuto come una pazza per quella bambina."

Ilya sembra disgustato, ma non dice niente mentre ci dirigiamo verso l'aereo. Non gli piace quello che sto facendo, e non posso biasimarlo. Rapire una neonata e una madre che ha appena partorito sembra sbagliato, anche ad assassini spietati come noi. E questo è esattamente quello su cui sto contando. La sottile disapprovazione che emanano i miei uomini darà a questa operazione il vantaggio autentico di cui ha bisogno.

Voglio che Novak percepisca la discordia tra noi.

Voglio che percepisca la riluttanza dei miei ragazzi nel consegnare una giovane donna traumatizzata e la propria bambina nella sua crudele e avida presa.

DO IL LATTE IN POLVERE ALLA RAGAZZA NON APPENA ARRIVIAMO sull'aereo, e lei fa mangiare la sorellina, sparandoci occhiate spaventate per tutto il tempo. Sta esagerando un po'—la vera Signora Esguerra non mostrerebbe la propria paura—ma dato che i miei ragazzi non conoscono Nora e tutto quello che ha passato, funziona.

"Come hai fatto?" chiede Yan piano, quando la bambina si addormenta e la ragazza si è calmata abbastanza da guardare fuori dall'oblò, invece che verso il divano dove sono seduto con i gemelli. "Come hai fatto a catturare Esguerra?"

"Gli ho sparato." La mia risposta è secca e cruda, ma non ho intenzione di inventare una storia. "Gli ho fatto saltare la testa."

"Hai la prova?" chiede Ilya accigliato. "Perché Novak avrà bisogno di—"

"Ecco." Tiro fuori un telefono che ho "rubato" da una guardia e mostro la foto di un uomo dai capelli scuri sdraiato a terra in una pozza di sangue. La metà del suo cranio sembra mancare, ma l'altra metà è inconfondibilmente Esguerra.

Ho impiegato un'ora per ottenere una foto così ben fatta; nonostante il suo aspetto da modello, il mio ex datore è pessimo nel mettersi in posa.

Yan mi guarda, si concentra sulla foto per poi tornare a rivolgere l'attenzione a me. Lo guardo con severità. Ha capito che il "sangue" è ketchup mescolato con molta sporcizia o che la metà mancante del cranio è dovuta alle abilità nel Photoshop di Nora? So che l'immagine è falsa, quindi è difficile per me essere obiettivo.

Con mio sollievo, Yan mi restituisce il telefono senza dire niente, e Ilya si allontana, concentrandosi sul trasferimento della mazzetta sul conto bancario privato del controllore del traffico aereo serbo in Svizzera. È così che entriamo e usciamo da quel Paese e da molti altri—compresi gli Stati Uniti.

Sarei tentato di parlare con i miei ragazzi e rivelare il vero piano, ma mi trattengo. Non posso correre il rischio che possano tirarsi indietro all'ultimo minuto. Abbiamo costruito un business redditizio sulla nostra reputazione, e quello che sto per fare—tradire un cliente pagante—più o meno garantisce che non ci saranno ulteriori offerte di lavoro.

Abbiamo parlato di ritirarci un giorno, ma non so se siano pronti per quel giorno—non so se quel giorno sia arrivato.

In ogni caso, se andrà tutto bene, la mia squadra non soffrirà finanziariamente. Oltre ai cento milioni di Novak—la metà è già sui nostri conti bancari—riceveremo settantacinque milioni da Esguerra. Anche se non dovessimo ottenere l'altra metà da Novak prima che io lo colpisca, avremo abbastanza per il resto delle nostre vite.

Tutto ciò che dobbiamo fare è sopravvivere.

Ancora qualche giorno, e riavrò Sara.

Non vedo l'ora, cazzo.

Io ed Ilya incontriamo Novak nel suo magazzino appena fuori Belgrado—come da sua richiesta. Come al solito, arriva con un contingente pieno di mercenari ed armi a sufficienza da far saltare un piccolo edificio.

"Dove sono?" chiede non appena ci vede. "Hai detto di averli. Dove sono?"

"Al sicuro con la mia squadra" dico e tiro fuori il telefono della guardia per mostrargli le foto che abbiamo scattato un'ora fa. Mostrano le sostitute di Nora e della sua bambina, circondate dai miei uomini, e sembrano livide e fragili.

Mi strappa il telefono e le studia con malcelata lussuria prima di guardarmi. "Esguerra è—"

"Ecco." Prendo il telefono da lui e sfoglio le foto di "Nora" fino ad arrivare a Esguerra in una pozza di ketchup. "Gli ho fatto saltare la testa."

Gli occhi chiari di Novak scintillano. "Ottimo lavoro. Sapevo di poter contare su di te. Ora portami da Nora e dalla bambina."

Incrocio le braccia sul petto. "Prima il pagamento."

Quei cinquanta milioni potrebbero non essere necessari in senso stretto, ma farebbero sicuramente comodo.

La bocca di Novak si assottiglia, ma prende il telefono e chiama il suo contabile. "Effettua il trasferimento" ordina in serbo, e aspetto che mi faccia un cenno con la testa, poi controllo il conto sul telefono.

"Tutto a posto" gli dico e guardo Ilya, la cui inespressività riesce ancora a trasmettere in qualche modo la sua disapprovazione.

Anche Novak deve averlo notato, perché sorride di nuovo. Gli piace l'idea che non andiamo d'accordo; pensa che questo ci renda vulnerabili, più facili da controllare.

"Andiamo" gli dico, fingendo di ignorare il sottofondo. "Ti porto da Nora e dalla bambina."

Ilya ed io ci dirigiamo velocemente verso l'uscita, e Novak si affretta a raggiungerci. Le sue guardie si precipitano a formare il loro solito cerchio protettivo, ma noi tre usciamo prima di tutti.

Abbiamo solo un paio di secondi a disposizione, ma è tutto il tempo di cui ho bisogno.

Afferrando Novak per un braccio, grido: "Giù!" e mi tuffo dietro a un cassonetto, spingendo Ilya davanti a me.

Colpiamo duramente il pavimento, atterrando sullo stomaco, mentre gli uomini di Esguerra aprono il fuoco, facendo crollare il magazzino e tutte le guardie di Novak sparando con centinaia di mitragliatrici.

3 8

IL RESTO DELL'ASSALTO È FULMINEO. IN POCHI ISTANTI, SIAMO circondati da tre dozzine degli uomini di Esguerra, e dico allo sbalordito Ilya di lasciar cadere le armi, mentre io faccio altrettanto. Novak ha battuto la testa sul cassonetto della spazzatura, e sembra stordito quando lo tiro in piedi, mentre i nostri carcerieri lo ammanettano e lo perquisiscono.

Mentre sto consegnando Novak, Ilya si ferma in piedi accanto a me. Il suo sguardo incredulo oscilla da me agli uomini che trascinano via Novak, poi torna su di me. "Hai appena—"

"Sì. Spiegherò tutto tra un attimo. Per ora, chiama Yan e digli che stiamo arrivando. Assicurati che lui ed Anton rimangano giù—non vogliamo che qualcuno rimanga ferito."

Ilya esita, chiaramente scioccato, poi tira fuori il telefono. Glielo lascio fare e seguo Novak verso un SUV nero.

Il serbo sta uscendo dallo stordimento e sta iniziando a

193

capire che cos'è successo. Mi scruta come se avesse finalmente compreso tutto; poi, la furia gli contorce il pallido viso. "Fottuto—"

La guardia più vicina a lui lo colpisce in bocca. "Chiudi il becco, *pendejo*" ringhia in un inglese dall'accento spagnolo.

Cerco di scorgere il suo viso coperto dall'elmetto. "Diego?"

L'elmetto si sposta. "Ehi, Peter. Come va?" Mentre parla, porta in macchina il nuovamente stordito Novak e chiude la portiera.

"È semplicemente straordinario" dico, mentre Ilya si avvicina. "Una giornata di lavoro perfetta."

Il mio compagno di squadra non sembra contento—probabilmente perché siamo entrambi ancora senza armi. "Stanno aspettando" dice bruscamente. "E staranno giù."

"Bene." Gli do una pacca sulla spalla. "Andiamo."

YAN E ANTON SONO IN UN CANTIERE VICINO, FACENDO LA guardia alla sostituta di Nora e alla sua sorellina. Le armi sono al loro fianco, mentre ci avviciniamo con le guardie di Esguerra, ma hanno gli occhi acuti e vigili.

"Dovresti darci qualche spiegazione" mi dice Anton, mentre le guardie ci superano per prendere "Nora" e la bambina. "Molte spiegazioni, in realtà."

"Lo so." Io ed Ilya osserviamo le guardie mentre accompagnano la ragazza—che sembra ancora pietrificata—verso un altro SUV nero. "Vi spiegherò tutto."

"Che cosa c'è da spiegare?" dice Yan, avvicinandosi a noi. I suoi occhi verdi brillano con una luce fredda e beffarda. "Non è la vera Nora, giusto?"

"No" dico, guardandolo dritto in faccia. "Esguerra non metterebbe mai in pericolo sua moglie o sua figlia in questo modo—non che sarebbero state realmente in pericolo, intendiamoci."

"Giusto." Il sorriso di Yan non mostra il minimo accenno di umorismo. "Quindi, questo era il piano fin dall'inizio? Far abboccare Novak, scoprire quale fosse la sua risorsa e poi tirare in ballo Esguerra?"

Inclino la testa. "Esattamente."

Anton solleva le sopracciglia nere. "Non capisco. Perché l'hai fatto—e perché non ce l'hai detto?"

"Perché non si fida di noi ciecamente." La voce di Yan è ingannevolmente dolce. "Non è vero, Peter? Per quanto riguarda il perché—"

Lo interrompo agitando una mano. "Mi fido di voi tre, lo giuro sulla mia vita. Ma questa è stata un'operazione molto delicata, che è andata avanti per molti mesi. Avevo bisogno di guadagnarmi la fiducia di Novak, e per questo, tutte le nostre reazioni e interazioni dovevano essere quanto più sincere possibile. Non è stupido. Se avesse intuito qualcosa—solo il minimo accenno al fatto che stessimo facendo il doppio gioco con lui—tutto questo sarebbe stato inutile."

"È a causa sua, non è vero?" Ilya parla per la prima volta. Apro la bocca per rispondere, quando dice: "Non importa. Ovviamente è così. Che cosa vuoi da Esguerra? Più soldi, in modo da poter sparire con lei per sempre?"

"No" dice Yan a suo fratello. "Non è così." Mi guarda. "È così, Peter?"

"No—anche se i soldi extra sono un bel vantaggio" dico guardando dall'uno all'altro. "La vostra parte sta per essere trasferita sul conto, mentre parliamo." Mi rivolgo ad Anton. "Anche la tua."

"Dicci la verità, cazzo" ringhia Anton. "Seriamente, smettila con questo mistero. Che cosa ti ha promesso Esguerra per questo?"

"Una vita" dico e guardo i SUV che si allontanano dal

marciapiede. "Il genere di vita che le persone come noi non possono avere."

"Ah." Il cipiglio di Anton svanisce. "L'amnistia."

Annuisco. "E l'immunità da ulteriori procedimenti giudiziari. Per tutti noi."

Il viso di Ilya si illumina, ma Yan incrocia le braccia sul petto. "Chi ha detto che vogliamo questo? Credi che abbiamo lasciato gli Spetsnaz e che ci siamo uniti a te per poter diventare contabili e insegnanti?"

"No, credo che l'abbiate fatto per diventare ricchi sfondati" dico, imitando il suo tono beffardo. "E ora lo siete, congratulazioni. Oh, e nel caso non l'avessi ancora detto, l'extra proveniente da Esguerra è pari a settantacinque milioni."

Anton fischietta sottovoce. "Dannazione."

Yan mi fissa. "Un lavoro da centosettantacinque milioni?"

"Quello, e la libertà di fare tutto ciò che volete. Se volete continuare con l'attività, potete farlo—anche se forse potreste preferire ricominciare daccapo con nuove identità, nel caso in cui tutto questo—"agito un indice nell'aria—"vi abbia stancato. In alternativa, potete aprire legittimamente un'agenzia di sicurezza o qualcosa del genere."

"E tu?" chiede Ilya, inclinando la testa. "Che cos'hai intenzione di fare, Peter?"

"Non appena avrò il via libera, andrò negli Stati Uniti" dico e sorrido per le loro espressioni. "Sì, è vero, da Sara. Questa volta, giocheremo alla famiglia per davvero."

3 9

ESGUERRA MI RIVUOLE NELLA SUA TENUTA, COSÌ, DOPO AVER raggiunto i miei uomini, salgo a bordo del suo Boeing C-17 e accompagno Novak e le guardie in Colombia. Ilya, Yan e Anton vanno separatamente con il nostro aereo. Continuo a non fidarmi completamente del mio ex datore di lavoro, così i miei compagni di squadra hanno accettato di fornire supporto nel caso in cui le cose dovessero mettersi male all'ultimo minuto. Non mi aspetto un tradimento da parte di Esguerra—anche perché i settantacinque milioni sono già sui nostri conti—ma è meglio essere cauti.

Ho anche chiesto alla mia squadra di continuare ad aiutarmi nella ricerca di Henderson. Essendo l'ultimo cognome sulla mia lista, è un affare incompiuto, e ho tutte le intenzioni di occuparmi di lui a tempo debito.

Prima, però, ho bisogno di tornare a prendere Sara.

Lei è più importante di qualsiasi altra cosa.

∽

Esguerra in persona ci saluta quando atterriamo, con il volto incorniciato da linee dure e selvagge, mentre osserva le guardie trascinare Novak giù dall'aereo. Il serbo cammina a malapena—non si sono preoccupati di nutrirlo o di curare le sue ferite durante il volo—ma non importa. Non rimarrà a lungo su questa terra.

Esguerra non solo lo ucciderà—lo distruggerà.

Lentamente.

Pezzo dopo pezzo.

Mi sentirei in colpa per quel bastardo, ma se l'è cercata. Se si fosse limitato a farsi strada negli affari di Esguerra, sarebbe vissuto molto più a lungo—almeno un altro anno o due. Ma ha preteso la famiglia di Esguerra... Nora e la sua bambina.

Non corre buon sangue tra me ed Esguerra, ma Nora mi piace.

"Dov'è Kent?" chiedo, quando Esguerra viene da me dopo aver ordinato alle guardie di portare Novak nel capanno. "È tornato a Cipro?"

Annuisce. "È andato via subito dopo di te." Non aggiunge altro, e decido di non insistere. Non ho ancora perdonato Kent per quello che è successo con Sara, ma al momento ho un pesce più grosso di cui occuparmi.

"Li hai contattati?" Mi avvicino a Esguerra, mentre ci dirigiamo verso una limousine in attesa. "I tuoi amici della CIA?"

Mi guarda di traverso. "Sì."

"E?" Gli passo davanti, costringendolo a fermarsi. "Hanno acconsentito?"

Flette la mascella. "Parliamone in macchina."

Cazzo. Non si mette bene. "Parliamone ora."

I suoi occhi brillano pericolosamente. "Bene. Ecco il patto—l'unico patto che accetteranno. Tu e la tua squadra otterrete l'amnistia per i vostri crimini e l'immunità da ulteriori accuse, a condizione che non vengano commessi altri reati. Chiunque violi l'accordo verrà arrestato e processato per *tutti* i crimini, passati e presenti."

Rifletto e annuisco. "Mi sembra giusto." Sono quasi certo di poter vivere come un cittadino rispettoso della legge—o perlomeno dare questa impressione. Dovremo stare attenti a non farci prendere, quando finalmente troveremo Henderson, ma sono sicuro di non essere l'unico nemico del vecchio generale. In alternativa, possiamo farlo sembrare un incidente; ci sono molti modi per realizzare un omicidio senza che sembri tale—

"E c'è ancora una cosa" dice Esguerra. "Un'altra condizione che non è negoziabile."

"Quale?" chiedo, con lo stomaco che si stringe per una premonizione, mentre chiudo le mani lungo i fianchi. Spero che non si tratti di quello che—

"Quel generale in pensione, quello a cui stai dando la caccia" dice Esguerra, confermando la mia intuizione. "Devi lasciarlo perdere. Per sempre. La tua immunità dipende dalla sua salute e dal suo benessere. Se lui o chiunque altro vicino a lui viene avvelenato, l'accordo è rotto, e voi quattro sarete di nuovo sulle liste dei Più Ricercati."

Fanculo. Cazzo, cazzo, cazzo!

Suppongo che avrei dovuto immaginare che ci sarebbe stata questa possibilità, date le connessioni di Henderson, ma in qualche modo l'avevo scacciata dalla mente. Ero così concentrato sull'eliminazione del principale ostacolo a una vita con Sara—il mio status di fuggitivo—che non ho minimamente pensato che questo potesse avere un prezzo.

Beh, un prezzo oltre alla fine della mia attività e al rischio che mi sono preso avvicinandomi a Esguerra. Conoscevo questi prezzi ed ero disposto a pagarli. Ma questo? Tra tutti quelli sulla lista, Henderson è il più direttamente responsabile della tragedia che ha colpito mia moglie e mio figlio. Fu lui a dare gli ordini che portarono al massacro del villaggio.

Se qualcuno merita di pagare per le morti di Tamila e Pasha, quella persona è Henderson.

Non gli si può permettere di tornare a vivere la sua vita normale e felice, dopo quello che ha fatto.

"Non posso accettarlo." La mia voce è aspra e gutturale. "Sai che non posso."

Per la prima volta, una parvenza di emozione umana riscalda il ghiaccio blu nello sguardo di Esguerra. "Lo so" dice lentamente. "Lo immaginavo. Ma non accettano negoziazioni, Peter. Ci ho provato."

Giro sui tacchi e mi dirigo verso la limousine, con la rabbia e il dolore che pensavo di aver seppellito come magma nella gola. Respiro, cercando di calmarmi, ma al posto della vegetazione tropicale sento il fetore di morte e cenere, di carne carbonizzata e sangue raffermo. Sento il metallo sulla lingua e vedo un mucchio di cadaveri, di parti del corpo alte due metri.

E quella manina arrotolata attorno a una macchinina giocattolo.

Ricordo appena i primi giorni dopo il massacro. So di essermi allontanato dai soldati della task force che mi avevano trascinato fuori dal villaggio, ma non ricordo come o quando— o se avessi ferito qualcuno, mentre scappavo. Suppongo di averlo fatto, perché la mia stessa gente cominciò a darmi la caccia poco dopo, ancora prima che uccidessi i miei superiori per aver posto fine all'inchiesta nel giro di poche settimane.

La vendetta era tutto ciò che mi permetteva di andare avanti in quei giorni—e nei mesi e negli anni successivi. Ho promesso a mio figlio e mia moglie morti che i loro assassini avrebbero pagato con la vita, e ho mantenuto quella promessa.

Li ho presi tutti, tranne Henderson.

"Potresti riprenderti lei e basta" dice Esguerra, raggiungendomi, e lo guardo, non sorpreso che ora sappia di Sara. Kent deve avergli detto di lei—oppure ha saputo del rapimento dalle sue fonti della CIA. E una volta saputo, si trattava semplicemente di fare due più due.

Nonostante ciò, il mio primo istinto è quello di minacciare lui e tutto ciò che gli è caro, se si azzarda a respirare l'aria di Sara. Ma se sa che lei è la mia debolezza, allora deve sapere che cosa farei, se qualcuno venisse a cercarla.

È la stessa cosa che farebbe lui, se qualcuno venisse a cercare Nora.

Quello che sta per fare a Novak, in realtà.

"Ha una vita lì" dico. "Genitori, carriera, amici."

Si stringe nelle spalle. "Si adeguerebbe. Nora l'ha fatto."

Salgo nella parte posteriore della limousine e si unisce a me, sedendosi di fronte.

"Sara non è Nora" dico, mentre la limousine inizia a muoversi. "Le sue radici sono troppo profonde. Non sarebbe felice in questo modo." Non so se sto cercando di convincere Esguerra o me stesso—o quella parte oscura e insensibile di me che desidera questo da mesi.

Quella che mi ha detto di dimenticare questo folle piano e di riprendere ciò che mi appartiene.

"E tu lo saresti?" Esguerra inclina la testa, guardandomi con particolare curiosità. "Pensi che ti piacerebbe quella mezza vita? Staresti bene nella gabbia delle regole e delle leggi?"

Faccio spallucce. "Forse." Non è una mia preoccupazione, ma se mai dovesse diventare un problema, ci penserò a tempo debito.

Una cosa alla volta.

"E quindi?" chiede Esguerra, quando rimango in silenzio. "La lascerai andare per sempre? O accetterai l'accordo?"

"Non la lascerò andare." Le parole sono istintive, automatiche. Una vita senza Sara—questa non è nemmeno una possibilità nella mia mente. Gli ultimi otto mesi sono stati un inferno, a modo loro terribili quanto le settimane buie che sono seguite alla morte della mia famiglia.

Preferirei morire piuttosto che lasciar andare la mia ptichka per sempre.

È mia, e sarà mia per sempre.

Un sorriso beffardo piega la bocca di Esguerra. "Beh, allora" dice pacatamente. "Sembra che tu non abbia molta scelta."

Mi distrugge ammetterlo, ma ha ragione.

O prendo Sara o accetto l'accordo. La sua felicità o la mia vendetta.

Non posso avere entrambe.

PARTE IV

ara

Ho la sensazione che qualcosa non quadri, quando torno a casa da sola dopo il turno serale in clinica.

Nessuna macchina governativa mi segue, e nessuno mi osserva furtivamente, mentre parcheggio la macchina davanti al mio appartamento ed entro.

Ripetendomi che sono pazza—che sono solo stanca e che non sto riflettendo lucidamente sulle cose—faccio la doccia e mi metto a letto. Non ha senso preoccuparsi per questo. Anche se non si tratta di una strana paranoia inversa, forse i Federali dovevano prendersi la notte libera—fare da babysitter ai figli o qualcosa del genere. Non è mai successo dal mio ritorno, ma questo non significa che sia impossibile.

Anche gli agenti dell'FBI sono umani.

Tuttavia, mi rigiro tremila volte, non riuscendo ad addormentarmi nonostante lo sfinimento. Cerco di ripensare se mi sia sentita osservata oggi, ma non riesco a ricordare. O i miei invisibili stalker sono diventati ancora più bravi nel loro lavoro o mi sono talmente abituata alla loro presenza che non me ne accorgo più.

L'ultima volta in cui ho provato davvero quel prurito è stato quando ho trovato il biglietto di Peter un paio di mesi fa.

Potrebbe essere così?

Non mi stanno più controllando?

Ho lo stomaco in subbuglio. Secondo il biglietto di Peter, c'è solo una ragione per cui all'improvviso cesserò di essere controllata sia dai Federali che dalle persone assoldate da Peter.

No. Scaccio quel pensiero terrificante.

Peter non è morto e non è stato catturato.

Non può essere così.

Chiudo gli occhi e cerco di respirare lentamente e profondamente. Una notte non significa niente, e, quando mi sveglierò al mattino per andare al lavoro—meno di cinque ore a partire da adesso—i Federali si aggireranno nel mio vicinato con la loro berlina grigia.

Devo solo crederci.

～

MA I FEDERALI NON CI SONO, QUANDO GUIDO PER ANDARE AL lavoro, e, per quanto mi impegni, non riesco a capire se sono sorvegliata da qualcuno.

Passo la mia giornata in uno stato di panico appena soppresso. Fortunatamente, tutto quello che ho oggi sono appuntamenti con le pazienti, e, dal momento che siamo sovraccarichi di lavoro, non ho molto tempo per pensare. Mi precipito da una paziente all'altra, eseguo esami, scrivo prescrizioni per il controllo delle nascite e discuto sull'assistenza prenatale—ricordandomi sempre di continuare a respirare, di stare calma e di ignorare il fatto che i Federali se ne sono andati.

Che per la prima volta dal mio ritorno sono sola.

Proprio mentre sto per tornare a casa, Phil, il nostro chitarrista, mi chiama per informarmi di una performance imminente, e chiedo impulsivamente se vuole radunare i ragazzi e uscire per bere qualcosa. È martedì sera e ho una giornata lavorativa piena e un turno domani, ma non voglio restare sola con i miei pensieri.

Con mio grande sollievo, Phil accetta e ci incontriamo in un bar della parte nord di Chicago. Solo Rory riesce ad unirsi a noi —Simon è impegnato in una sessione di autografi—ma dopo che ognuno ha ordinato una birra, stabiliamo la stessa rilassata dinamica di sempre, con Phil che si lancia nel suo discorso di persuasione del tour settimanale.

"Non avete mai voglia di mandare tutto all'aria?" dice, agitando la birra. "Di ottenere qualcosa di più dalla vita? Qualcosa di corroborante ed eccitante?"

"Amico, sembri uno spot pubblicitario" gli dice Rory, e tutti ridiamo. Sento un accenno di disperazione nella mia risata, ma con sollievo, sono l'unica a notarla. I compagni di band non sono a conoscenza del mio crescente tumulto, scherzando e continuando a ridere come se non ci fosse un domani.

Come se fosse solo un normale martedì sera.

E per loro è così—è un normale e prevedibile martedì sera, a cui Phil vuole fuggire. Quello che non ho avuto per molto tempo, perché da quando ho conosciuto Peter, nulla nella mia vita è più stato normale o prevedibile.

Mi chiedo che cosa ne penserebbe Phil se venisse a saperlo —se venisse a sapere di come l'assassino di mio marito mi abbia costretta a "mandare tutto all'aria" tenendomi prigioniera in Giappone. Troverebbe eccitante la mia riluttante storia d'amore con un assassino? Corroborante in qualche modo contorto?

Questa uscita dovrebbe essere una distrazione dai pensieri

angoscianti, ma non riesco a smettere di pensare a Peter, e mi ritrovo a osservare da una persona all'altra, alla ricerca di quel ragazzo che sembri fuori posto... di qualsiasi indizio che mi faccia capire di essere ancora l'interesse dei Federali.

"Stai aspettando qualcuno?" chiede Rory, notando il mio insistente sbirciare.

Mi sforzo di sorridere e smetto di guardarmi intorno come un'idiota. "No, scusa. Mi era sembrato di vedere un vecchio amico."

Phil si scalda subito. "Ooh, un vecchio amico. Maschio o femmina? Perché devo ammettere che la tua amica Marsha è *smack!*" Si bacia la punta delle dita con fare drammatico, e ridiamo tutti di nuovo.

Marsha, Andy e Tonya sono venute ad assistere a uno dei nostri spettacoli un paio di settimane fa, e siamo usciti tutti insieme in seguito. Naturalmente, Marsha ha flirtato con i miei compagni di band, come fa sempre con gli uomini.

Uno di questi giorni, mi piacerebbe conoscere un ragazzo che non si innamori del suo look da sexy bomba bionda—o perlomeno che non cerchi di entrare subito nelle sue mutande.

"Tonya non è poi così male" dice Rory, quando le risate si attenuano parzialmente. "È single?"

Sorrido. "Sì, credo di sì." Non conosco bene la giovane infermiera, ma sono quasi certa che non abbia un ragazzo—o se ce l'ha, non gli dà fastidio che lei festeggi con Marsha dal tramonto fino all'alba.

"Amico, sei sicuro di non volere la rossa?" chiede Phil con la faccia seria. "Pensa a quanto sarebbero belli i vostri figli. Pel di carota a volontà."

"Oh, fanculo. Sei solo geloso che io abbia ancora questa." Rory scompiglia la criniera, e quasi mi strozzo con la birra, mentre Phil si tocca istintivamente la stempiatura prima di alzare il dito medio verso Rory.

"Basta, ragazzi" dico, quando riesco a smettere di ridere. "Andy è presa in ogni caso, e—"

Mi blocco, con le parole che muoiono nella gola, quando noto l'uomo che si sta avvicinando dietro a Phil.

Sbatto le palpebre, incapace di credere ai miei occhi, ma l'apparizione non scompare.

Invece, le sue labbra scolpite si incurvano in un sorriso magnetico. "Ciao, Sara" dice con la voce profonda, leggermente accentata che infesta i miei sogni. "Perché non mi presenti ai tuoi amici?"

41

Peter

IL VISO A FORMA DI CUORE DI SARA SBIANCA. NON SEMBRA ESSERE in grado di parlare, così mi rivolgo ai due uomini che mi guardano a bocca aperta.

"Peter Garin" dico, sfruttando la mia nuova identità, e allungo la mano. "E voi due siete?"

So chi sono, naturalmente, ma se devo integrarmi nella vita di Sara per sempre, devo comportarmi come un normale cittadino, non come qualcuno che esegue controlli approfonditi su ogni persona vicina alla mia ptichka. Ciò significa anche che non posso mettere la mia lama sulla loro gola e tagliare abbastanza in profondità da far sì che non sbavino mai più per lei.

Almeno, non in mezzo al bar.

Il ciccione si riprende per primo, allungandosi per stringermi la mano. "Ciao. Sono Phil Hudson."

"Piacere di conoscerti" dico, e resisto all'impulso di schiacciare le ossa in quel palmo ridicolmente morbido.

"Rory O'Rourke." La stretta del pel di carota è più vigorosa, con la mano quasi callosa come la mia—anche se per ragioni molto diverse.

Solleva pesi in palestra per vincere trofei, mentre io mi alleno per rimanere vivo.

Mi allenavo per rimanere vivo, mi correggo. Se tutto andrà secondo i piani, non avrò più bisogno di farlo.

Sara mi tocca il braccio, attirando la mia attenzione su di lei. "Che cosa—" la sua voce melodiosa si incrina. "Che cosa ci fai qui, Peter?"

Ho volontariamente evitato di guardarla dritto in faccia, perché esserle così vicino senza afferrarla e scoparla sul posto sarebbe una vera tortura. Il suo tocco sul mio braccio, pur così leggero, è come un colpo di Taser. Tutto il mio corpo vibra per la consapevolezza, con tutti i sensi in subbuglio. È a mezzo metro di distanza, e siamo tutti e due completamente vestiti; tuttavia, la sento intensamente, come se fosse schiacciata contro di me nuda.

In realtà, il mio cazzo è convinto che dovremmo essere nudi e sta facendo del proprio meglio per uscire fuori dai jeans improvvisamente troppo stretti.

Probabilmente avrei dovuto aspettarla nel suo appartamento, dove avremmo potuto essere soli per questo incontro, ma ero troppo impaziente. Dopo un mese di cazzate burocratiche, alla fine ho ottenuto il via libera dal governo degli Stati Uniti, insieme ai miei nuovi documenti di identità e alla cittadinanza, e sono salito subito sull'aereo—solo per scoprire che invece di tornare a casa, Sara ha deciso di uscire.

Con due uomini che le sbavano addosso, per giunta.

Faccio un respiro profondo e ricordo a me stesso che l'integrazione fa parte del gioco. È per questo che ho lavorato tutti questi mesi, è questo il motivo per cui ho accettato di lasciar vivere quel bastardo di Henderson—una promessa che mi riempie ancora la gola di bile. Sarebbe stupido rovinare tutto solo perché Sara mi sta fissando con quegli occhioni da cerbiatta, sembrando così incredibilmente bella che vorrei avvolgerla in un sacco di patate e portarla nella mia tana—dopo aver strappato le palle a ogni uomo che ha il coraggio di lanciarle occhiate.

"Ho avuto la possibilità di tornare a casa prima" le dico, e, nonostante i migliori sforzi, la mia voce è troppo rauca per un luogo pubblico. "Anzi, ho lasciato il mio lavoro."

"Tu... che cosa?" Sgrana gli occhi. "Come puoi—"

"È una lunga storia, ptichka." Combatto l'impulso di raggiungerla e stringerla a me. "Andiamo a casa, e ti spiegherò tutto."

Il rosso—Rory—si schiarisce la voce. "State... insieme?" Sia lui che Phil mi fissano con incredulità—e con molta invidia.

Gli stronzi sono fortunati che in questi giorni io sia rispettoso della legge.

"Sì" dico loro, e qualcosa nel mio tono li fa impallidire. "Proprio così." Mi rivolgo a Sara. "Pronta per tornare a casa, amore mio? Abbiamo molte cose da dirci."

E stringendole saldamente la delicata mano, la conduco fuori, lasciando i suoi compagni storditi nel bar.

42

*S*ara

MI SENTO COME SE STESSI SOGNANDO. O SE STESSI AVENDO UN incubo—non riesco a decidere. Io e Peter stiamo camminando insieme in una strada affollata... senza il minimo accenno di sotterfugio da parte sua. In qualche modo è persino più grosso di quanto ricordassi, con le ampie spalle che sembrano tirargli le cuciture della maglietta nera dall'aspetto soffice e le potenti gambe che si flettono negli stretti confini dei jeans logori. I capelli scuri sono più lunghi di prima, ondeggiando leggermente nella tiepida brezza serale, e mi prudono le dita dalla voglia di seppellirle in quella folta massa morbida, per afferrarne una manciata, mentre fa l'amore con me, con la lingua esperta che completa il tutto.

Un brivido fulmineo mi attraversa al pensiero, intensificando il bruciore sotto la pelle. Il cuore mi sta battendo così violentemente che potrebbe esplodere, e non sento più freddo. Non sento più freddo dentro. Il mio corpo è tornato a vivere nel momento in cui lui ha parlato, e da allora vibra dal desiderio... anche se sto annegando nella confusione.

"Mi stai rapendo?" La mia voce è fievole e troppo alta, ma ho problemi ad elaborare tutto questo... *qualunque* cosa sia. Come può apparire dal nulla, dopo più di nove mesi, e presentarsi ai miei amici come un fidanzato? Tra tutti i modi in cui ho immaginato il mio secondo rapimento, questo scenario—in cui sarebbe entrato in un bar e mi avrebbe portata fuori tenendomi per mano—non mi ha mai nemmeno sfiorata. Ero pronta per un ago nel collo o un cappuccio sulla testa—o almeno un brusco risveglio nel cuore della notte. Non per una passeggiata informale lungo North Broadway, nella zona nord di Chicago. Come può uscire allo scoperto in questo modo? Ha usato un nome diverso al bar, ma il suo volto è rimasto invariato. Dove sono i Federali? Dopo tutti i mesi passati a controllare ogni mia mossa, all'improvviso—

"Non ti sto rapendo. Ti sto portando a casa." La sua mano stringe la mia, avvolgendola col calore... proprio come sento la sua volontà avvolgersi intorno a me, forte e inflessibile, ineluttabile come una forza della natura.

Scuoto la testa in un futile tentativo di comprendere. "A casa?" Intende dire in Giappone? Perché se è così, devo dirgli che—

"Il tuo appartamento." I suoi occhi metallici brillano, mentre cattura il mio sguardo. "Per ora, almeno, visto che hai tutte le tue cose lì. Poi, possiamo tornare a casa se vuoi—o comprarne una nuova più vicina al tuo lavoro."

Mi sento come se fossi ubriaca o fuori di testa. C'era qualcosa nella birra che ho appena bevuto? "Di cosa stai parlando?"

Smette di camminare e mi rendo conto che siamo accanto

alla mia macchina. Lasciandomi andare la mano, incornicia la mia guancia con il suo grosso e ruvido palmo e dice teneramente: "Di noi, amore mio. Sto parlando di noi."

E prendendo la borsa dalle mie mani, fruga all'interno, estrae la chiave della macchina e apre la portiera.

43

S*ara*

STA GUIDANDO PETER, E SONO CONTENTA. NON CREDO CHE AVREI potuto farlo in questo momento—non senza schiantarmi.

Non ho questa preoccupazione con lui. Gestisce la macchina come gestisce tutto il resto: con competenza calma e letale. Mentre lo guardo uscire dal parcheggio, mi viene in mente che non l'ho mai visto dietro un volante prima d'ora. Ogni volta che eravamo in un veicolo insieme, c'era sempre qualcun altro a guidare e Peter era sul sedile posteriore con me. Il che mi porta ad un'altra domanda: dove sono i suoi compagni di squadra? Perché è qui da solo?

E cosa intendeva con "ho lasciato il mio lavoro"?

La mia mente vaga freneticamente in sintonia con il battito cardiaco, ma raccolgo i pensieri confusi e cerco di concentrarmi su una cosa alla volta. "Che cosa intendi dire con 'noi'?'" chiedo, fissando il suo profilo fortemente scolpito. O, più specificamente, divorandolo con lo sguardo. Avevo dimenticato quanto fossero straordinariamente virili i suoi lineamenti, quanto fosse bello in quel modo pericolosamente magnetico. Il viso è ancora magro come quando abbiamo lasciato la clinica—qualunque cosa abbia fatto, non si è trattato di riposo e relax—e gli zigomi alti sembrano due lame gemelle, con la mascella ricoperta di barba così dura che sembra essere stata intagliata nel marmo.

Vedo di sfuggita il suo sguardo argenteo e la cicatrice sul sopracciglio sinistro, mentre mi rivolge un'occhiata prima di riportare l'attenzione sulla strada. "Intendo dire che sarò qui per sempre" dice con calma. "Ho ottenuto la piena amnistia e l'immunità—per me e il resto della mia squadra."

Il mio respiro si blocca nei polmoni. "Amnistia e immunità? Stai dicendo che..."

"Sto dicendo che non sono più un fuggitivo, sì."

Mi sento come se stessi precipitando da una scogliera. Non è più un ricercato? "In che modo? Che cos'hai fatto? Com'è possibile—"

"È una lunga storia, ma essenzialmente ho fatto un favore a un mio ex datore di lavoro—ricordi Julian Esguerra, il socio di Kent?"

Inspiro bruscamente. "Quello che voleva ucciderti per aver messo in pericolo la moglie?"

"Proprio lui" conferma Peter, mentre ci immettiamo in autostrada e sorpassiamo un camion, che procede lentamente. "Ad ogni modo, in cambio di quel favore, Esguerra ha sfruttato la sua influenza su vari governi per eliminare i segugi dalle nostre tracce."

Lo fisso, senza parole. Non sapevo che i trafficanti d'armi illegali avessero quel tipo di influenza, anche se immagino che avrei dovuto sospettarlo. Lucas Kent ha persino parlato di un loro contatto con la CIA—John, Jeff Qualcosa?—quando abbiamo cenato tutti nella sua villa a Cipro.

"Wow. Dev'essere stato un grosso favore" riesco a dire finalmente, e Peter annuisce guardando dritto davanti a sé.

"Lo è stato." Non approfondisce, e io non insisto. Ho cose più importanti da scoprire prima.

Sfregandomi i palmi umidi sulle ginocchia, cerco di sembrare disinvolta. "Quindi, quando dici che sarai qui per sempre, che cosa intendi dire esattamente?"

L'angolo della bocca si alza leggermente. "Secondo te, amore mio? Volevi un cane dietro alla staccionata? Un barbecue e bambini nel parco? Beh, ora posso darti tutto questo—o meglio, Peter Garin può dartelo." Si sposta nella corsia di destra e imbocca la rampa d'uscita. "Quel mondo diverso che volevi, quella vita—è tua, ptichka... e lo sono anch'io."

Il cuore mi batte nel petto. "Vuoi stare con me? Qui? Come una coppia normale?"

"No, ptichka. Non voglio stare con te." Svolta a destra ed entra in una stazione di servizio nelle vicinanze—quando noto che il serbatoio della benzina è quasi vuoto.

"Torno subito" dice, spegnendo la macchina e scendendo. Lo guardo intontita, mentre riempie sapientemente il serbatoio della mia Toyota, pagando alla pompa con una carta di credito nera dall'aspetto elegante.

Il mio assassino russo ha una carta di credito, e la sta usando per la benzina.

La mera improbabilità di questo—di Peter che improvvisamente è qui a fare qualcosa di così assolutamente banale—si aggiunge al senso di irrealtà che combatto da quando abbiamo lasciato il bar. Non riesco a scrollarmi di dosso la sensazione di essere in qualche bizzarro sogno e che mi sveglierò da un momento all'altro, sentendo freddo e sentendomi sola nel letto.

Ma no. La portiera del conducente si apre, portando con sé un'ondata di aria estiva umida e l'odore pungente della benzina, mentre Peter torna in macchina, sistemandosi dietro al volante.

Se è un sogno, è il più realistico che abbia mai avuto.

"Che cosa vuol dire che non vuoi stare con me?" chiedo, mentre lasciamo alle spalle il distributore di benzina per imboccare una strada a due corsie. "Che cosa *vuoi*, allora?"

Si ferma a un semaforo rosso e mi guarda. "Voglio tutto, Sara." La sua voce profonda è bassa e dolce, con gli occhi grigi che riflettono i lampioni che ci circondano. "Voglio i tuoi giorni e le tue notti, le tue ore e i tuoi minuti. Voglio condividere le tue gioie e i tuoi dolori, i tuoi trionfi e le tue frustrazioni. Voglio addormentarmi con te tra le mie braccia ogni notte e svegliarmi ogni mattina annusando i tuoi capelli sul mio cuscino. Ti *voglio*, ptichka—ti voglio con me per sempre, in tutti i modi."

Lo fisso, con la cassa toracica che si irrigidisce a ogni sua parola. "Che cosa..." Deglutisco per inumidirmi la gola secca. "Che cosa stai dicendo, Peter?"

Dev'essere scattato il verde, perché torna a concentrarsi sulla strada e la macchina avanza.

Con mia sorpresa, pochi istanti dopo, ci fermiamo di nuovo, e mi rendo conto che ha accostato al lato della strada. Con calma, mette l'auto in modalità "Parcheggio" e si gira verso di me.

Sbatto le palpebre, con il battito che accelera, mentre slaccia la cintura di sicurezza e allunga la mano nella tasca anteriore dei jeans, tirando fuori una scatolina di velluto.

"Questo è quello che sto dicendo" dice sottovoce, e smetto di respirare, quando apre la scatolina per tirare fuori un anello di diamanti—una fede tagliata splendidamente, che sembra avere almeno un paio di carati. Fissata in un delicato cerchio di oro bianco o platino, è semplice ma straordinaria—esattamente quella che avrei scelto, se avessi avuto centomila dollari da spendere.

Stordita, lo guardo. "Peter..."

"Ti voglio come moglie, Sara" dice dolcemente, allungandosi per prendermi la mano sinistra. Le sue dita sono calde e asciutte sulla mia pelle gelata, con lo sguardo oscurato nel buio interno dell'auto. È come se fossimo soli nelle tenebre, come se il resto del mondo non esistesse più, mentre fa scivolare l'anello sull'anulare sinistro, con il peso freddo e metallico che sembra una manetta che mi stringe il cuore.

Il respiro mi sfugge con un'esalazione vacillante.

Oh Dio. Sta succedendo.

Sta succedendo davvero.

Di riflesso, provo a tirare indietro la mano, ma lui stringe la presa, rifiutandosi di liberarmi.

"Voglio possederti, legalmente e in ogni altro modo" continua, e, questa volta, sento l'acciaio dietro la dolcezza, sento la puntura del filo spinato avvolto nella seta. "Sei già mia, ptichka, e voglio renderlo ufficiale" dice, piegando le labbra in un sorriso cupo. "Voglio che mi sposi, e presto."

44

ara

IL RESTO DEL VIAGGIO VERSO CASA MI APPARE CONFUSO, CON l'anello al dito caldo e ghiacciato sulla pelle. Non ho risposto alla proposta di Peter—non potevo—e per fortuna non ha insistito.

È tornato in strada e ha continuato a guidare.

Quando parcheggiamo davanti al mio appartamento, Peter fa il giro e apre la portiera per me, prendendomi la mano per aiutarmi a scendere dall'auto. La sua presa è al tempo stesso premurosa e possessiva, con lo sguardo che mi divora e che mi fa battere il cuore, facendo scattare campanelli d'allarme nella mente.

Non esiterà a prendermi.

Sarà su di me—e dentro di me—non appena entreremo.

"Aspetta" dico, improvvisamente desiderosa di rallentare le cose. Per quanto lo voglia—per quanto mi sia mancato fisicamente—non sono pronta per questo. È passato troppo tempo, e ci sono troppe domande senza risposta.

Tirando via la mano dalla sua presa, indietreggio finché non sono a contatto con la macchina.

Serra la mascella e fa un passo in avanti, poggiando le mani sul tetto dell'auto per ingabbiarmi tra le braccia muscolose. "Credi che non abbia aspettato abbastanza?" Si china su di me, con gli occhi argentei che luccicano, e, anche se non ci stiamo toccando, sento il calore che esce dal suo potente corpo. "Credi che non sia stato paziente per tutti questi fottuti mesi?"

Il battito del mio cuore accelera per la rabbia appena trattenuta nella sua voce, e una furia—una cresciuta gradualmente durante la sua lunga assenza—esplode in me. Tutti questi mesi in preda alla preoccupazione e in attesa di essere rapita, senza sapere se fosse stato ferito o catturato, tutte le bugie e mezze verità e le notti insonni, ed è entrato in quel bar come se non fosse successo niente? Mi ha messo un anello al dito come se dopo torture e rapimenti il matrimonio fosse il naturale passo successivo?

Stringendo i denti, sbatto i palmi, colpendo la parte anteriore delle sue spalle. "Allora, dove diavolo sei stato?" urlo, mentre si tira indietro istintivamente, sorpreso dal mio sfogo. "Perché hai impiegato così tanto tempo? Anch'io ti stavo aspettando, cazzo—ho aspettato, aspettato e aspettato—"

Le sue labbra si schiantano sulle mie, con le mani che mi afferrano entrambi i lati del viso, mentre mi sbatte contro la macchina. Più che un bacio è una conquista, con la lingua che mi invade l'interno della bocca spietatamente, senza pietà. Sento il sapore del sangue, dove i denti mi hanno tagliato il labbro, ma è ricoperto dal sapore familiare di lui, dal calore oscuro e dalla violenza del suo desiderio.

Avrebbe dovuto essere troppo, ma il mio corpo non vede l'ora di reagire con altrettanta ferocia, con le mani che si chiudono a pugno nella sua maglietta, mentre ricambio il bacio, succhiando quella lingua invasiva, ribellandomi con una mia intrusione. Questo è esattamente quello che ho sognato ogni notte, ciò per cui il mio corpo bruciava.

Il motivo per cui non riuscivo a guardare altri uomini, né tantomeno immaginarmi con loro.

Dopo un minuto, le sue labbra si ammorbidiscono e le mani mi liberano il viso per vagare sul resto di me, con il grande palmo che mi stringe il seno, mentre l'altro mi afferra il sedere. Nonostante il bacio sia più delicato, il suo tocco è sfrenato, incredibilmente possessivo—un re che reclama il proprio diritto di nascita. Sento il forte rigonfiamento nei suoi jeans, mentre sbatte contro il mio stomaco, e delle ondate di calore mi attraversano; la sua bocca mi sfiora il collo, riservandomi dolci baci caldi e pungenti, mentre la mano mi lascia il sedere per avvolgere i capelli intorno al suo pugno.

"Sei mia, cazzo" mi ringhia nell'orecchio, inarcando la testa all'indietro, e rabbrividisco, con la pelle d'oca che si insinua sulle braccia, mentre mi mordicchia il lobo e incunea il ginocchio tra le gambe, facendomi cavalcare la sua muscolosa coscia. Nonostante gli strati dei miei jeans e dei suoi, la pressione sul mio sesso è improvvisa e intensa, e mentre mi stringe di nuovo il seno, strofinando il tessuto del reggiseno contro il capezzolo, il calore pulsante si sposta sul clitoride, con una familiare tensione che cresce nelle profondità del nucleo. Mentre gli cavalco impotentemente la gamba, sono visceralmente consapevole dell'odore e del sapore nettamente maschile di lui, delle dimensioni e della durezza del suo corpo; mentre la sua mano scava sotto la mia maglietta, con il palmo ruvido e caldo che scivola sulla pelle nuda, la tensione sale violentemente.

Con un grido soffocato, vengo, con il bisogno represso improvvisamente soddisfatto, mentre il mio corpo si contrae e freme, con l'esplosione di estasi che mi fa arricciare le dita dei piedi dentro le scarpe. Stordita, sento una distante risatina, e poi mi ritrovo sdraiata, trasportata su braccia incredibilmente forti.

Spaventata, apro gli occhi, incrociando le braccia attorno al collo di Peter. Sta camminando velocemente, e siamo già a metà del parcheggio, ma intravedo tre ragazze adolescenti dall'altra parte. Devono averci visti, mi rendo conto, arrossendo, mentre la foschia indotta dall'orgasmo svanisce dalla mente.

"Peter, loro—"

"Lo so." La sua mascella è stretta, mentre attraversa il marciapiede con passi lunghi e sicuri, portandomi come se fossi una bambina. "Dobbiamo entrare."

Il fischio di ammirazione e le grida sguaiate delle ragazze raggiungono le mie orecchie, e lo spingo sulle spalle. "Mettimi giù. Per favore, posso camminare."

L'ultima cosa di cui ho bisogno è essere trasportata nell'atrio come una specie di sposa vestita in modo inadeguato.

Con mio sollievo, Peter ascolta, mettendomi in piedi, mentre raggiungiamo l'ingresso del mio edificio. Appena in tempo. Non abbiamo un portiere, ma vedo le mie vicine—due giovani donne vestite a festa per una serata fuori. Stanno uscendo proprio mentre noi stiamo arrivando, e i loro sguardi curiosi oscillano da me a Peter, che sta mantenendo una presa possessiva sul mio braccio.

Non le conosco così bene—ci siamo scambiate solo dei convenevoli sul tempo—così sorrido goffamente e auguro loro una buona serata.

"Anche a voi" dice una delle donne, fissando sfacciatamente Peter, mentre la sua coinquilina inizia a ridacchiare come una scolaretta. "Buona serata, davvero."

Arrossisco ancora di più, mentre continuano a camminare lungo l'atrio, sussurrando e ridacchiando con le teste vicine, e per la prima volta, sono contenta che il mio edificio non abbia una gran dinamica comunitaria. Ci sono molti affittuari, come me, e visti i repentini ricambi di inquilini, la gente non si preoccupa di conoscere i propri vicini o dei pettegolezzi su di loro.

"Amiche tue?" chiede Peter, lasciandomi andare il braccio per premere il pulsante dell'ascensore, e scuoto la testa.

"Non proprio." Lo guardo, accigliata. "Non lo sai? Non mi hai fatta seguire?"

I suoi occhi grigi brillano per un oscuro divertimento. "Certo. Ma non potevano avvicinarsi troppo, con i Federali che osservavano ogni tua mossa e costantemente alla ricerca di microspie."

"Oh." Ha senso—e spiega perché io abbia visto sempre e soli i Federali.

Le porte dell'ascensore si aprono, e mi fa entrare, con la mano sulla schiena calda e delicata—e inflessibile come l'acciaio. Il mio cuore salta un battito, poi assume un ritmo frenetico e martellante.

Mi sospinge.

Mi sta letteralmente conducendo nel mio appartamento per poter scopare.

"Non pensavi davvero che ti avrei lasciata sola, vero?" dice piano, mentre l'ascensore inizia a muoversi, e scuoto di nuovo la testa, distogliendo lo sguardo dai suoi occhi penetranti. Mi soffermo sul considerevole rigonfiamento nei suoi jeans, e il calore nelle guance si intensifica.

Ha sfoggiato quell'erezione per tutto questo tempo?

Non mi stupisce che le mie vicine siano andate in sovraccarico di estrogeni.

Mi sforzo di guardare in alto e di lato, ma il disastro è dietro l'angolo anche in questo modo. L'interno dell'ascensore ha due specchi ai lati e la vista del mio riflesso mi fa venir voglia di sprofondare nel pavimento. A causa della nostra sessione estemporanea nel parcheggio, non solo ho le mutande bagnate, ma il labbro inferiore è gonfio il doppio delle sue dimensioni normali, con le guance di un rosa acceso e i capelli appiccicati su un lato.

Sembro uscita da un'orgia.

Disperata, distolgo lo sguardo, tornando a guardare Peter. "Non mi hai mai detto... Perché hai impiegato tutto questo tempo per tornare?"

La sua mascella si flette. "Perché quel favore che ho fatto a Esguerra—c'è voluto molto tempo. Volevo tornare prima, ptichka, credimi." Mi fissa. "Ti sono mancato? Speravi che sarei tornato?"

Deglutisco e distolgo lo sguardo, mentre le porte dell'ascensore si aprono, evitandomi di dover rispondere. Pensavo di aver accettato i miei sentimenti contraddittori per Peter, di essermi fatta una ragione che l'assassino di mio marito fosse riuscito a rubarmi il cuore, ma all'improvviso non ne sono più così sicura. Questo—Peter qui, nella mia vita normale—è troppo inaspettato, troppo spaventosamente reale. Non riesco a riflettere sulla logica di tutto ciò, sull'enorme numero di implicazioni nel tentare di avere una relazione normale—un *matrimonio*—con un ex assassino che una volta mi ha torturata e rapita. Se questo sta accadendo per davvero, che cosa dirò ai miei genitori che lo considerano ancora "quel criminale?" O a Marsha, che non solo conosce la storia ufficiale dell'FBI, che dipinge Peter come un mostro, ma che sa anche che lui ha ucciso George? E l'FBI ci lascerà davvero in pace? Come potrebbero, quando l'uomo nell'ascensore con me dev'essere una delle persone più pericolose che conoscano?

Ogni volta che mi immaginavo insieme a lui, era altrove, con me come prigioniera ben disposta. Ero pronta ad accettare il fato come sua prigioniera, ad abbracciare il mio tormentatore come il mio destino, ma non ero pronta per questo.

L'anello è freddo e pesante sul mio dito, mentre usciamo dall'ascensore e Peter mi conduce nel corridoio verso il mio appartamento. Non è mai stato nel mio edificio prima d'ora—

almeno, presumo che sia così—eppure non c'è traccia di esitazione nei suoi movimenti, non sembra affatto perso o incerto. È sicuro mentre cammina nel corridoio sconosciuto, come lo è in tutto ciò che fa, e non posso che invidiarlo.

Mi sento irrimediabilmente alla deriva, come una nave senza timone in una tempesta.

Arriviamo alla mia porta, e armeggio per trovare le chiavi dell'appartamento nella borsa, acutamente consapevole dello sguardo di Peter su di me. Non sembra impaziente, ma lo sento in lui, sento il bisogno violento che sta trattenendo. Il mio respiro si fa rapido, con i palmi che si inumidiscono, quando finalmente chiudo la mano attorno all'oggetto sfuggente.

"Ecco, lascia fare a me." Prende le chiavi e trova infallibilmente quella giusta, aprendo la porta al primo tentativo.

Entriamo, e chiude la porta dietro di noi, mentre accendo le luci del soggiorno. Sento il clic della serratura e mi giro per guardarlo, con il cuore che martella. "Peter..."

È su di me, prima che io possa pronunciare un'altra parola. Le sue grandi mani mi incorniciano il viso, e mi spinge sul divano, con l'avida bocca sulla mia, mentre cadiamo sui soffici cuscini in un groviglio di membra e di sfrenato desiderio.

Qualunque dubbio abbia potuto avere viene spazzato via, annegato da un'ondata di lussuria così intensa da sembrare fuoco nelle mie vene. L'orgasmo nel parcheggio mi ha solo stuzzicato l'appetito, lasciando il sesso sensibilizzato e gonfio, disperatamente dolorante per avere di più. I capezzoli sono terribilmente duri, e l'intimo pulsa letteralmente tra le gambe, mentre mi strappa la maglietta e si muove per tirarmi giù la cerniera, con le mani ruvide per l'urgenza e la stessa fame che mi tormenta da mesi.

Ricambio ogni bacio, strappandogli la maglietta mentre mi tira giù i jeans, ringhiando dalla frustrazione, quando si impigliano nelle ballerine. Riesco a toglierle dai piedi insieme ai jeans stropicciati, mentre mi toglie il reggiseno, e poi sono nuda, sdraiata sul divano sotto di lui, che allunga la mano verso la sua cerniera.

Nessuna parola carina, né dolci carezze—solo la sensazione primordiale di lui, che spinge spietatamente dentro di me, con il viso contorto dalla lussuria e gli occhi che brillano cupamente, mentre mi afferra i polsi e li mette sopra la testa. Respiro per l'invasione implacabile, con i muscoli interni che tremano, lottando per adattarmi allo spessore impossibile, al modo in cui la mia carne si estende per accettarlo. Il mio corpo ha in qualche modo dimenticato questa parte, e mi sembra di replicare la nostra prima volta, solo che la vergogna e il senso di colpa ora sono solo ombre confuse nella mente.

Ho bisogno di questo—ho bisogno di *lui*—e non posso negarlo.

Quando affonda dentro di me, si ferma, concedendomi un momento per abituarmi a lui, e lo vedo lottare per il controllo, frenando quella parte selvaggia di lui in modo da non farmi male.

"Va tutto bene" sussurro, stringendo i muscoli pelvici attorno alla sua spessa lunghezza. "Va tutto bene, Peter... posso prenderlo."

Voglio prenderlo, in realtà.

Le sue pupille si dilatano e, nelle profondità degli occhi metallici, scorgo la superficie del mostro. Con un ringhio basso, gutturale, si insinua sempre più dentro di me, e grido, inarcandomi, mentre stabilisce un ritmo selvaggio.

Mi prende violentemente, sbattendo dentro di me senza pietà, e le mie grida crescono di volume, mentre il dolore diventa piacere, coprendo la mia mente con un rumore bianco, facendo tacere il ronzio incessante dei pensieri. Non c'è spazio mentale per colpa o preoccupazione, nessuno spazio per dubbi e domande. C'è solo questo, solo noi, e mentre la tensione dentro di me cresce, grido il suo nome, consapevole solo del dolore e dell'estasi che mi dilaniano.

Viene quasi nello stesso momento, con il suo potente collo che si distende, mentre piega la testa all'indietro, sbattendo i fianchi dentro di me. La pressione innesca un'ondata di scosse dovute ai postumi dell'orgasmo, e grido di nuovo, con i muscoli interni che si stringono e si contraggono, sentendo ogni centimetro dentro di me, mentre geme e mi inonda col suo seme.

FORSE SONO SVENUTA DOPO, OPPURE HO CHIUSO GLI OCCHI, perché la prossima cosa di cui mi rendo conto è che mi sta tenendo di nuovo in braccio, questa volta mentre mi porta nel bagno.

Sbatto le palpebre, muovendo istintivamente le braccia attorno al collo di Peter, mentre entra nella vasca e mi mette in piedi.

"Stai bene?" mormora, raddrizzandomi, mentre mi lascio andare, e annuisco, ancora troppo sopraffatta per parlare.

"Sto bene."

Esce dalla vasca e si toglie i vestiti che stava ancora indossando. Avidamente, divoro la sua nudità, godendomi le linee potenti del corpo alto e grosso, mentre torna con me nella vasca, chiudendo la tendina, e apre l'acqua. Ogni muscolo scolpito nella sua schiena si flette, mentre si muove, con il sedere stretto e tondo che si china per verificare la temperatura dell'acqua. Le palle oscillano pesantemente tra le gambe, con il grosso cazzo ancora semi-duro, e il calore si insinua lungo il mio collo, mentre noto la lucente scivolosità dei nostri fluidi corporei combinati sulla sua pelle.

Di nuovo, niente preservativo. Per qualche ragione, non sono particolarmente inorridita—o sorpresa. Se Peter intende davvero fare questo—stabilirsi qui con me, dove possiamo vivere una vita normale—allora i figli non sembrano più una follia. Dato che ha ammesso di volermi incinta, non dovrei più aspettarmi i preservativi d'ora in avanti. Siamo entrambi sani, a meno che—

"Sei andato a letto con qualcuna?" sbotto, inorridita per la possibilità che mi è venuta in mente. "Quando eri via, intendo?"

Sono scioccata che il pensiero non mi abbia sfiorata prima. Peter è un maschio altamente sessuale nel fiore degli anni, con l'aspetto giusto e il fascino letale uniti alle mutande color crema. La prova di questo sono le mie vicine—entrambe donne sui venticinque/trent'anni—che ridacchiavano come scolarette di terza media. Non c'è motivo di presumere che mi sia rimasto fedele per tutto questo tempo. Nove mesi di celibato per qualcuno come Peter sarebbero—

"Che cosa?" Si gira verso di me, con le sopracciglia scure che si abbassano sugli occhi. "Dici sul serio?"

Mi stringo nelle spalle e cerco di sembrare disinvolta, come se la sola idea che possa aver toccato un'altra donna non mi facesse venir voglia di vomitare. "Nove mesi sono lunghi, e non è che—"

"Non è cosa?" La sua voce è pericolosamente delicata, mentre mi afferra le braccia. "Non è cosa, Sara?"

La mia bocca si secca sotto lo sguardo dei suoi occhi metallici. "Sai..." Deglutisco. "Non è che avessimo una vera e propria relazione."

"Mi stai dicendo che sei andata a letto con qualcun altro?" Le sue dita scavano nella mia pelle, mentre un piccolo muscolo inizia a pulsargli nella tempia. "Hai lasciato che qualcun altro—"

"No!" Come può anche solo pensarlo? "Certo che no! Inoltre, sono sicura che le tue spie ti avrebbero informato. Hai detto che non potevano avvicinarsi troppo, ma un evento simile non sarebbe *sfuggito*."

La sua presa punitiva sulle mie braccia si allenta

leggermente. "No, probabilmente no" concorda dopo un momento di riflessione. Lasciandomi andare, si volta per girare la manopola che regola l'acqua dal rubinetto alla doccia.

Mi tolgo l'acqua dagli occhi e lo osservo regolare il getto in modo che colpisca più in basso. Poi, torna a guardarmi, bloccando la maggior parte dell'acqua con la schiena.

"Non ho scopato altro che il mio pugno, da quando ti ho lasciata" dice in modo uniforme. "Anzi, da quando ci siamo conosciuti, non ho nemmeno sfiorato un'altra donna in mezzo alla folla. Ci sei solo tu per me, ptichka—sei tutto ciò che voglio, ora e per sempre. Ogni notte degli ultimi nove mesi, sono rimasto nel letto, con il cazzo così duro da far male, e pensavo a te. Solo a te. Sei ogni mio sogno bagnato, ogni fantasia e sogno ad occhi aperti. Voglio scoparti sempre, a prescindere da dove siamo o cosa facciamo. Anche quando gli oceani ci separano, tu sei l'unica che io desideri—l'unica di cui abbia sempre voglia."

Mi si stringe la gola, intrappolando l'aria nei polmoni. Gli credo. Come non potrei? Non mi ha mai mentito, non ha mai cercato di nascondere i suoi veri sentimenti. Fin dall'inizio, ho conosciuto la profondità della sua ossessione per me, e, anche se mi spaventava, ora è perversamente rassicurante.

Finché saremo entrambi vivi.

Qualcosa scatta dentro di me, come una luce che si accende, squarciando la nebbia dello shock e dello stordimento post-sesso. "Peter..." Mi trema la voce, mentre mi allungo per prendergli la mano tra i palmi. "L'hai fatto per me?"

Piega la testa, con gli occhi grigi perplessi. "Ho fatto cosa, ptichka?"

"Questo favore per Esguerra, in modo che potesse cancellarti dalle liste dei ricercati... quella cosa che ti ha tenuto lontano per così tanto tempo." Stringendogli la mano, la porto sul mio petto, dove una strana oppressione soffoca il mio cuore martellante. "Sono io il motivo? Lo hai fatto per poter essere qui con me?"

Aggrotta la fronte, coprendo i miei palmi con l'altra mano. "Certo, ptichka. Non è questo che volevi? Una vita in cui non fossi un fuggitivo, dove avremmo potuto essere insieme senza che tu rinunciassi alla famiglia e alla carriera?"

Lo fisso, finalmente comprendendo l'enormità di ciò che ha fatto. *È* quello che volevo, quello che desideravo nelle profondità del mio cuore. È la mia fantasia più oscura e vergognosa—una vita vera con il mio tormentatore—e l'ha resa realtà.

Ha fatto l'impossibile, ha fatto Dio sa cosa—e tutto questo per me.

Il vapore che riempie il bagno mi fa bruciare gli occhi, e la morsa attorno al mio cuore si intensifica.

Peter mi ama.

Mi ama davvero.

Non è più teorico, quello che potrebbe fare per me.

È tutto vero. L'ha fatto.

"Non è questo che volevi, Sara?" ripete, corrugando la fronte, e mi ritrovo ad annuire come una marionetta, non riuscendo ancora a parlare.

"Bene." Toglie delicatamente la mano dalla mia presa e si gira di lato, così sono sotto il getto dell'acqua. Prendendo lo shampoo, lo versa nel palmo della mano e inizia a massaggiarlo sulla mia nuca, come se fosse quello che si fa dopo quel genere di rivelazione.

Come se fosse tutto quello che c'è da dire.

E forse è vero. Forse dovremmo rivisitare questa conversazione, quando non mi sentirò così presa alla sprovvista, così sopraffatta dal suo improvviso ritorno e da tutto ciò che è destinato a venire con esso. Perché ancora non so cosa dirgli, come spiegare cosa provo.

Come dirgli che anche se sono felicissima di riaverlo qui, sono terrorizzata in egual misura.

Mi lava i capelli a fondo, con le forti dita che mi

massaggiano il cuoio capelluto e il collo, e poi applica il balsamo e attende, mentre lava il resto del mio corpo, con le mani insaponate, callose che scivolano su di me, accarezzando la pelle con la giusta quantità di tenerezza e ruvidità.

È incredibile, come il trattamento spa più rilassante, e quando finalmente mi toglie il sapone, prendo il bagnoschiuma e faccio lo stesso con lui, godendomi la sensazione della sua pelle liscia e piena di peli, mentre gli passo le mani sul grande corpo muscoloso.

Si è sempre preso cura di me, mi ha viziata come una principessa, ma io non l'ho mai fatto per lui, mi rendo conto. Ricambiare l'affetto del mio tormentatore mi è sempre sembrato un tradimento nei confronti di George e di ogni altra cosa che contava, e, anche se non potevo farne a meno a letto, mi sono trattenuta altre volte, accettando le cure di Peter, ma senza mai ricambiarle.

Mi sento ancora un po' in colpa, con quella sensazione di torto, ma non è più la pressione soffocante di una volta. Man mano che i mesi passavano e lo shock per la morte violenta di George svaniva, sono riuscita a pensarci in modo più razionale, ad analizzare gli eventi da una prospettiva diversa.

Per prima cosa, George non era esattamente vivo, quando Peter gli ha sparato un proiettile alla testa. Era in coma da diciotto mesi e, vista l'entità del danno al cervello, non c'era quasi alcuna possibilità che ne sarebbe mai uscito. A un certo punto, avrei dovuto prendere la straziante decisione di togliergli il supporto vitale—cosa a cui ho evitato di pensare, specialmente da quando mi ero convinta che l'incidente di George fosse in parte colpa mia.

In un certo senso, Peter mi ha sottratto quella terribile responsabilità—cosa su cui ho riflettuto solo di recente.

C'è anche il fatto che George mi ha *tradita*. L'alcol che ha rovinato il nostro matrimonio è stato terribile, ma da allora ha anche condotto una doppia vita, aveva una carriera da spia di cui non ero a conoscenza. Ho impiegato tutto questo tempo ad assorbirlo completamente, ma ora vedo le azioni di George come il grossissimo tradimento che erano, e l'amore che pensavo di provare per lui ora sembra una chimera.

Non che questo giustifichi le azioni di Peter—per niente. È ancora l'assassino amorale che ha ucciso più persone di quante io possa immaginare, l'uomo che una volta torturava, dava la caccia e rapiva. Ma ora è anche l'uomo che mi ama, che ha dimostrato nel modo più chiaro possibile che sono importante per lui.

Che è disposto a fare tutto ciò che serve non soltanto per avermi, ma per rendermi felice.

Finendo con il torace e lo stomaco, gli lavo le ascelle e la parte superiore delle spalle larghe, poi massaggio i muscoli pesanti e duri intorno al collo con le mani insaponate. Sembra divertirsi, inarcandosi al mio tocco come un grosso gatto, così massaggio la zona ancora un po', poi mi accovaccio e gli lavo le gambe. Le sue cosce sono come l'acciaio, con nessun cedimento nei muscoli potenti, e i glutei tondi e duri come quelli di un culturista. Non riuscendo a trattenermi, stringo quei globi e alzo lo sguardo, sbattendo le palpebre a causa del getto d'acqua, e vedo i suoi occhi chiusi e la testa piegata all'indietro per una beatitudine puramente maschile.

Gli piace quello che sto facendo. Gli piace molto, a giudicare dal rapido indurimento del cazzo.

Impulsivamente, chiudo il pugno insaponato intorno a quella colonna che si ispessisce e gli prendo le palle con l'altra mano, poi sbircio di nuovo tra lo spruzzo d'acqua. Adesso mi sta fissando, e l'aspetto estatico è sostituito dalla fame predatrice.

"Continua così" dice con voce rauca, infilando la mano tra i miei capelli. "E prendilo in bocca." Chiudendo il pugno intorno alle ciocche bagnate, guida il mio viso fino all'inguine, con la pressione delicata ma ineluttabile.

Chiudo ubbidientemente le labbra attorno al suo cazzo ormai completamente eretto, assaggiando l'acqua e i residui di sapone, mentre mi sistemo sulle ginocchia. Nonostante gli orgasmi precedenti, il calore si insinua nel profondo del mio intimo, con il sesso che inizia a pulsare di nuovo. Avrei potuto iniziare io stavolta, ma sta assumendo il controllo, prendendo il sopravvento come fa sempre. Mi torna in mente il ricordo del periodo in cui mi puniva, e i muscoli interni si stringono per un'ondata di bisogno, con le immagini nella testa più erotiche di qualsiasi film pornografico.

Mi ha scopata in bocca quella volta. Mi ha legato le mani dietro la schiena e l'ha reclamata senza pietà, controllando il mio respiro, la mia vita stessa. È stato brutale, assolutamente schiacciante, eppure mi ha provocato questa stessa dolorosa eccitazione, facendomi desiderare maggior oscurità.

Non capisco appieno perché la sua durezza mi ecciti così tanto, perché mi piaccia essere sotto il suo controllo in questo modo. Prima di conoscere Peter, le mie fantasie sessuali raramente coinvolgevano qualche elemento di forza o coercizione; la convenzione era la mia zona comfort, anche nella mente. Il trauma del nostro primo incontro nella mia cucina potrebbe avermi trasformata in qualche modo? Forse alcuni fili si sono aggrovigliati in seguito, e la violenza che ho sperimentato per mano sua si è collegata al piacere nella mia mente?

Ad ogni modo, qualunque sia la ragione, brucio, mentre mi spinge il cazzo più in profondità nella bocca, così in profondità che quasi mi viene da vomitare. Istintivamente, mi raddrizzo sulle colonne d'acciaio delle sue cosce, ma non lo combatto, nemmeno quando inizia a muovere i fianchi, spingendomi in bocca con crescente ferocia. Lo fisso e lo guardo, sbattendo le palpebre per il getto d'acqua, e quando il dolore pulsante tra le cosce diventa insopportabile, faccio scivolare una mano lì e strofino il clitoride, lasciando che le sue spinte vadano al ritmo dei movimenti delle mie dita.

Lo nota, e i suoi lineamenti duri si irrigidiscono, con lo sguardo predatore che si intensifica. "Sì, così, ptichka." La sua voce è un rombo basso e roco, mentre spinge in profondità nella mia gola, togliendomi l'aria. "Continua a farlo. Voglio vederti venire."

Con gli occhi che si appannano, obbedisco, strofinando più velocemente il clitoride, mentre sostengo il suo sguardo. Stringo l'altra mano sulla sua coscia, con il battito cardiaco che sale, mentre il corpo si blocca per la mancanza d'aria.

Non riesco a respirare.

Non riesco a respirare, e c'è acqua sul mio viso.

Tutto il mio corpo si irrigidisce, con gli occhi che si chiudono e i muscoli che si bloccano, mentre la mente torna alla tortura nella cucina, quando mi ha affogata nel lavandino. Il ricordo mi fa rabbrividire, ma non raffredda il fuoco nell'intimo. In qualche modo, il terrore intensifica tutto, aumentando la tensione, e anche se afferro la coscia di Peter in preda al panico, l'altra mano strofina freneticamente il clitoride.

Vengo così forte che vedo esplosioni di luce dietro le palpebre ben chiuse. Gli spasmi mi tormentano il corpo, facendomi urlare, ed è solo quando mi accascio contro le gambe di Peter che realizzo che la mia bocca è libera e che sto respirando.

Stordita, alzo lo sguardo e lo trovo con la mano chiusa a pugno intorno al cazzo, con una smorfia feroce sul viso. Poi, con un forte gemito, viene, spruzzando sperma su tutto il mio viso e sui capelli. Sbatto le palpebre, pulendomi la fronte con una mano tremante, e mi aiuta ad alzarmi in piedi, con la presa forte, anche se si sta ancora riprendendo dall'orgasmo.

Non dico niente e non lo fa nemmeno lui, mentre mi lava i capelli per la seconda volta. È solo quando usciamo dalla doccia e mi asciuga che mi parla.

"Non mi hai mai dato la tua risposta, sai." Il suo tono è calmo, ma vedo schegge di oscurità nel freddo grigio dello sguardo, mentre mi avvolge l'asciugamano intorno, e poi si allunga per afferrarne uno per sé.

Sbatto le palpebre, afferrando i bordi dell'asciugamano. "C'era una domanda?"

So di cosa sta parlando, ovviamente—l'anello è ancora pesante sul mio dito—ma non sono neanche lontanamente pronta per quella discussione. Non pensavo nemmeno che questa discussione sarebbe mai avvenuta. Non mi ha chiesto di sposarlo; mi ha detto che è quello che succederà. Quindi, non c'è nemmeno bisogno di—

"No, Sara." Lascia cadere l'asciugamano e si avvicina, appoggiandomi al ripiano. "Non giocare con me." La sua mascella si flette, mentre afferra la pietra liscia su entrambi i miei lati e si appoggia. "Mi vuoi sposare?"

Lo fisso, bloccata, incapace di parlare o di pensare. Non mi aspettavo che avrebbe preteso una risposta. Fin dall'inizio, ha preso lui tutte le decisioni in questa strana relazione, ed è difficile credere che mi stia lasciando una scelta.

Che mi stia dando la possibilità di non sposarlo.

"E se..." deglutisco, stringendo più forte l'asciugamano. "E se non volessi?"

Il suo viso si irrigidisce. "È un no?"

Sì. No. Non lo so. Come posso rispondere, quando il mio cervello non è altro che poltiglia, dopo il suo improvviso ritorno e dopo tutti gli orgasmi che mi ha provocato? Vorrei sgattaiolare via, nascondermi sotto le coperte e dormire per risvegliarmi con una magica chiarezza, ma nonostante questo stato di nebbia, so che non succederà mai. Non ci sarà mai un chiaro sì o no, quando si tratta di Peter, mai una decisione facile da prendere. Quello che abbiamo insieme è il sogno bagnato di uno strizzacervelli, e potrei dormire per una settimana di fila senza riuscire ad ottenere lumi sulla nostra reciproca follia.

Sì o no. Sposerò l'assassino che una volta mi ha torturata? Mi ama, e sono quasi sicura di amarlo. Il "quasi" è lì perché una piccola parte di me è ancora terrorizzata, avvolta nel fango tossico della colpa, del disprezzo per me stessa e della vergogna. Anche se alla fine lo perdonerò per la morte di George, non posso dimenticare che è un assassino—che in nome della vendetta, ha inflitto sofferenza e dolore.

Che lui stesso ha sofferto più di quanto io possa comprendere.

Sostengo il suo sguardo, sentendo scendere la temperatura nel bagno umido, percependo la crescente oscurità nel metallo duro dei suoi occhi. "Sì. È un sì." Le parole lasciano le mie labbra di loro spontanea volontà, come se un demone mi avesse strappato la lingua. Eppure, non appena le pronuncio, sembrano giuste.

Sembra che fosse destino.

La pericolosa tensione lascia il suo volto, anche se sento ancora la minaccia in profondità. "Bene" dice dolcemente, allontanandosi dal ripiano. Girandosi, esce dal bagno, e io mi accascio sul lavandino, facendo respiri profondi per calmare il subbuglio nello stomaco.

Ho detto di sì.

Ho accettato di sposare il mio tormentatore.

Oh, mio Dio. Che cos'ho fatto?

eter

GUARDO LA MIA BELLISSIMA FIDANZATA CHE DORME, ALTERNANDO gioia e cupa soddisfazione. Il suo viso elegante è particolarmente dolce e delicato quando riposa, con una mano sottile infilata in un pugno semiaperto sotto la guancia e le labbra morbide leggermente socchiuse.

Probabilmente dovrei spegnere la luce sul comodino e andare a dormire, ma questo significherebbe perdere questo momento. Una parte irrazionale di me ha paura che se chiudessi gli occhi tutto si rivelerebbe un sogno, una fantasia come quella che mi ha sostenuto in tutti questi mesi.

La mia Sara.

Finalmente l'ho riavuta.

È mia, e presto il mondo intero lo saprà.

Era completamente esausta, quando l'ho portata a letto, così stanca che si è addormentata subito. L'ho abbracciata per circa un'ora, ignorando le rinnovate vibrazioni del corpo, e poi ho preso il suo portatile per iniziare a prendere le misure appropriate.

Ha accettato di sposarmi. L'euforia che provo al pensiero è quasi violenta. Ero disposto a ricorrere a misure più severe per convincerla, ma non è stato necessario farlo.

Ha detto sì.

Porta ancora il mio anello sulla mano sinistra, quella che è attualmente nascosta sotto una coperta. Sono tentato di tirarla via in modo da poterlo guardare di nuovo, ma questo potrebbe svegliarla, e voglio che riposi bene.

Dopotutto, questo sabato si celebrerà il nostro matrimonio.

Nell'ultimo mese, mentre aspettavo che i burocrati mettessero le loro scartoffie in ordine, ho avuto il tempo di pianificare tutto e corrompere le persone necessarie. Quindi, a meno che Sara non detesti ciò che ho scelto, abbiamo sistemato location, vestiti, fiori, fotografi e quasi tutto il resto che accompagna un piccolo matrimonio privato. Ci sono ancora alcune piccole decisioni da prendere—come chi officerà la cerimonia—ma voglio che sia Sara, e spero anche i suoi genitori, a riflettere su questo.

È davvero d'aiuto che abbia accettato.

Facendo un respiro profondo, salgo sul letto accanto a lei e spengo la luce, poi piego il corpo intorno a lei da dietro, tenendola stretta, mentre borbotta qualcosa nel sonno.

La mia ptichka.

Non è più una fantasia.

È tutto reale, e, quando mi sveglierò, lei sarà ancora qui.

Farà meglio ad esserci, cazzo.

 ara

Mi sveglio con il profumo delizioso di uova e pancetta, mescolato con qualche tipo di prodotto da forno. Pancake? Biscotti, forse?

Mi sono di nuovo addormentata nella casa dei miei genitori?

Spalancando le palpebre pesanti, mi rotolo sulla schiena e fisso il soffitto.

Vedo il soffitto bianco del mio appartamento.

Immediatamente, i ricordi riaffiorano, e mi siedo con un sussulto, gettando via la coperta.

L'ultima notte è stata reale? Peter è qui?

Un lampo di qualcosa di luminoso cattura la mia attenzione, e guardo verso la mano sinistra, dove un diamante gigante brilla nella luce del sole che filtra attraverso le serrande abbassate.

Santo cielo. *È* tutto vero.

Peter è qui.

Sono ufficialmente fidanzata con lui.

Indossando una vestaglia, corro in cucina, dove non sento solo l'odore, ma anche lo sfrigolio della pancetta che sta friggendo.

La vista che mi accoglie mi fa bloccare.

Con nient'altro che un paio di jeans scuri, Peter incombe sui fornelli, girando abilmente una frittata. Su un'altra padella ci sono le strisce di pancetta, e su un piatto accanto al forno c'è una pila di pancake. I muscoli della sua ampia schiena si increspano, mentre si muove, con i jeans sui fianchi stretti, e devo letteralmente ingoiare la saliva, quando si gira per guardarmi in faccia, rivelando degli addominali scolpiti e un torace potente ricoperto da peli scuri.

I pochi chili persi hanno solo affinato il suo incredibile fisico, rendendolo ancora più duro, più pericoloso.

"Buon giorno, ptichka." La sua voce profonda mi ricorda le fusa di una tigre, mentre mi guarda, soffermandosi sulla punta delle dita dei piedi nudi fino alla cima dei miei capelli disordinati a causa del sonno. I tatuaggi sul suo braccio sinistro si flettono, mentre appoggia la spatola sul tavolo e cammina verso di me.

"Oh, uhm... buon giorno." Indietreggio, rendendomi conto che mi sono precipitata senza nemmeno spruzzarmi un po' d'acqua sul viso. "Torno subito."

Prima che possa fermarmi, mi reco al bagno. Rapidamente, mi lavo i denti, poi salto nella doccia per un rapido risciacquo. Il cuore mi galoppa nel petto e il respiro è veloce e superficiale.

Peter è *qui.*

Nella mia cucina, a preparare la colazione.

Probabilmente dovrei calmarmi un attimo, ma non voglio che tutto quel cibo delizioso si raffreddi.

Dopotutto, il mio *fidanzato* l'ha preparato per me.

Il mio stomaco borbotta, con il battito cardiaco che accelera ulteriormente, e mi sforzo di fare respiri profondi, mentre mi asciugo e rimetto la vestaglia.

Poi, raddrizzando le spalle, torno in cucina.

 ara

"A CHE ORA DEVI ESSERE AL LAVORO?" MI CHIEDE PETER, servendomi un piatto di frittata vegetale preparata a mano con strisce di pancetta e un contorno di pancake.

Alzo lo sguardo verso l'orologio sul muro. "Tra circa quaranta minuti." Sono fortunata ad essermi svegliata in tempo, perché ho completamente disattivato la sveglia ieri notte.

Probabilmente sto disattivando qualcosa anche in questo momento, perché anche se esteriormente sono calma, all'interno sto iperventilando.

Peter è *qui*.

È qui e siamo *fidanzati*.

"Ti accompagnerò al tuo ufficio" dice, sedendosi di fronte a me con il suo piatto. "A meno che tu non voglia prendere la macchina."

Con cautela, spezzo una parte di pancake con la forchetta. "Avevo intenzione di andare da lì direttamente in clinica, quindi sì..."

Non batte ciglio. "Va bene. Verrò con te e poi andrò a fare la spesa. Il tuo frigo è quasi vuoto. Fin quando rimarrai in clinica?" Comincia a consumare la sua frittata con evidente appetito.

"Il mio turno è fino alle dieci, ma se c'è qualche emergenza, potrei rimanere fino a tardi" dico, guardandolo con diffidenza. Obietterà? Cercherà di controllare questa parte della mia vita? George era comprensivo riguardo ai miei lunghi orari lavorativi, visto che spesso anche lui lavorava fino a tardi e doveva viaggiare molto per lavoro, ma non so come la pensi Peter. Non mi impediva di lavorare molto in passato, ma era diverso.

Allora, stava solo aspettando il momento giusto per portarmi via.

"Va bene. Ti verrò a prendere lì." Si alza e si dirige verso il tavolo, dov'è poggiata la mia borsa.

Raggiungendola, tira fuori il mio telefono e inizia a digitare qualcosa.

"Che cosa stai facendo?" chiedo, perplessa.

"Ti sto dando il mio numero." Completando il compito, rimette il mio cellulare nella borsa e torna al tavolo. "Così, potrai chiamarmi, quando avrai quasi finito in clinica. Non ti voglio in quella zona da sola di notte."

"Non mi farai più sorvegliare?"

"Sì, ma manterranno le distanze—io invece no." Taglia un pezzo di pancetta, poi mi guarda. "È per la tua sicurezza, ptichka."

La sua voce è dolce ma ferma, assolutamente inflessibile. Non ha intenzione di scendere a compromessi su questo, e per qualche ragione la cosa non mi dà fastidio. Invece di farmi sentire in gabbia e controllata, il suo patologico bisogno di proteggermi mi riempie di una specie di calore frizzante. Non dimenticherò mai come mi sono sentita, quando due tossici hanno cercato di derubarmi fuori dalla clinica, né com'è stato traumatico, quando Peter li ha uccisi, e sono grata che fosse lì. Inoltre—

"Ti aspetti qualche problema?" chiedo, mentre il pensiero mi torna in mente. "Voglio dire, devi avere molti nemici, con la tua precedente professione e tutto il resto..."

Mette giù la forchetta e incrocia il mio sguardo. "È sempre una possibilità, ptichka, non posso mentire. Ecco perché non ho intenzione di togliere la squadra di sicurezza—e perché ho creato una nuova identità prima di venire qui. Non volevo che qualcuno della mia vita precedente collegasse Peter Garin nei sobborghi di Chicago con Peter Sokolov l'assassino. In realtà, parte dell'accordo che ho stretto con le autorità è che Peter Sokolov non esiste più. È indicato come deceduto negli archivi dell'FBI, della CIA e dell'Interpol, così come Yan e Ilya Ivanov e Anton Rezov. L'accordo di amnistia è altamente riservato, con solo pochi individui di alto rango dell'FBI e della CIA che sono a conoscenza di tutti i termini. Agli altri, come l'Agente Ryson, è stato detto di tenere la bocca chiusa. Certo, Esguerra e Kent sanno chi sono, e c'è sempre la possibilità di essere individuati e identificati da un ex cliente. Tuttavia, a differenza del mio nome, il mio viso non era molto conosciuto, e in ogni caso, la possibilità di un incontro casuale con qualcuno della mia vita precedente è minima—specialmente in questa parte del mondo."

"Oh. Wow." Fino a quel momento, non avevo realizzato la portata completa del patto impossibile che aveva stretto. "Come hai fatto a farli accettare? Voglio dire, so che hai detto che questo Esguerra ha molte aderenze, ma..." Mi fermo, quando l'espressione di Peter si rabbuia notevolmente.

"Il tuo governo aveva le condizioni adatte a me" dice con fermezza. "Ma non è niente che ti debba interessare, ptichka. Ti basterà sapere che l'esercito americano è uno dei più grandi clienti di Esguerra, e vogliono mantenere quel rapporto amichevole, sia perché vogliono le armi che produce sia perché vogliono tenere quelle armi fuori dalle mani degli altri."

"Acquistandole loro stessi?"

Peter annuisce e riprende a mangiare. "Esattamente."

C'è qualcosa di oscuro nella sua espressione, e per quanto desideri approfondire, so che conviene trattenermi. Guardandolo finire il cibo, ho l'inquietante sensazione che un animale selvatico abbia invaso la mia angusta cucina, un predatore che appartiene alla giungla. L'ho già visto in ambienti domestici, naturalmente, ma questa volta sembra diverso, sapendo che è qui per sempre, che questo grande uomo letale farà parte della mia vita quotidiana... parte della mia famiglia.

La mia mente ricomincia a vagare, e spingo via il piatto quasi vuoto. "Peter... Come funzionerà?" Notando il suo sguardo interrogativo, chiarisco: "Che cosa dirò ai miei genitori? L'FBI probabilmente ha mostrato loro la tua foto ad un certo punto. Anche se ti presentassi come Peter Garin, sospetterebbero chi sei veramente—soprattutto dal momento che continuavo a insistere sul fatto che saresti tornato, non appena il malinteso con l'FBI si fosse risolto."

Lo sguardo cupo lascia il suo viso, sostituito da uno di oscuro divertimento. "Beh, è perfetto allora, no?" Allungandosi sul tavolo, mi copre la mano con il palmo. "Dirai loro che l'equivoco alla fine si è risolto—e che ho ottenuto un nuovo cognome."

"Uh- uh. E che mi dici dei loro amici, che hanno ascoltato una versione di quella stessa storia, e dei *miei* amici, a cui è stata raccontata una versione completamente diversa—una in cui non sei altro che il mio rapitore? Che cosa penseranno tutti, quando mi presenterò con *questo*?"—sollevo la mano sinistra, mostrando l'anello—"di punto in bianco, e presenterò un fidanzato russo di nome Peter che somiglia fin troppo all'uomo in una foto che gli agenti dell'FBI hanno divulgato, quando sono scomparsa?"

Mi stringe la mano. "Non preoccuparti di loro, ptichka. Le loro opinioni non contano. Di' semplicemente che sono una persona che hai frequentato segretamente per qualche mese, e lascia che siano loro a trarre le conclusioni."

"Quali conclusioni? Che sono pazza? O che sono fissata con gli uomini russi, che condividono lo stesso aspetto oscuro e meraviglioso e che si chiamano Peter?"

Sorride e si alza, raccogliendo il suo piatto e il mio. "Comunque sia, funzionerà. Basta non confermare nulla. Lascia che pensino che faccio parte di qualche programma di protezione dei testimoni, e che non puoi proprio parlarne."

Questa non è una cattiva idea, in realtà. Marsha e chiunque altro sospetti la vera identità di Peter penserà che sono completamente impazzita, ma finché non avrò confermato i loro sospetti, ci sarà spazio per il dubbio. Dopotutto, quanto è folle che l'uomo che ha assassinato George e rapito me abbia ottenuto la piena amnistia e ora stia per sposarmi? I miei amici potrebbero anche pensare che io abbia delle tendenze masochistiche e abbia deciso di unirmi a un uomo che condivide molti tratti del mio tormentatore.

Questa è certamente una spiegazione più semplice.

"Quindi, diciamo la verità ai miei genitori e raccontiamo la storia di Peter Garin a tutti gli altri" dico, alzandomi per aiutarlo a ripulire il tavolo.

"Sarebbe la cosa più sensata, secondo me" dice e guarda l'orologio. "Dovresti vestirti e andare, ptichka. Non vorrai arrivare in ritardo."

Giusto. Il mio lavoro. Me ne ero quasi dimenticata.

"Ecco, lascia che ti aiuti" dico, camminando per sbarazzarmi degli avanzi, ma mi fa cenno di andare.

"Ci penso io, non preoccuparti. Vai a prepararti per il lavoro." E dandomi un rapido bacio sulla fronte, inizia a caricare la lavastoviglie.

Peter

Conduco Sara nel suo ufficio e le lascio l'auto, così potrà andare in clinica dopo il lavoro, come previsto. Sono solo dieci minuti a piedi dal suo ufficio al suo appartamento, e il negozio di alimentari è lungo la strada, così mi fermo e prendo qualcosa per la cena di stasera. Non troppa roba, solo quello che posso facilmente portare con una mano—mi piace avere la mano della pistola sempre libera—e prendo nota mentalmente che avremo bisogno di una seconda macchina, proprio come tutti in periferia.

Questa non è l'unica cosa di cui avremo bisogno, ovviamente. Il frigorifero nella piccola cucina di Sara è alto solo un metro, e la cucina è a malapena utilizzabile. Ho trascorso i miei anni formativi in una cella fredda e fatiscente in Siberia, quindi non sono schizzinoso quando si tratta degli alloggi, ma non vedo alcun motivo per continuare a vivere in un appartamento chiaramente pensato per un solo occupante.

Stasera, quando Sara tornerà, discuteremo di questo, così come del nostro imminente matrimonio di sabato.

Certo, so perché sto pensando alle auto, agli appartamenti e ai dettagli del matrimonio. Pensare alla logistica mi distrae dall'impulso di prendere Sara e rinchiuderla nella mia camera da letto per poterla scopare tutto il giorno. E poi tutta la notte. E poi la settimana seguente.

In realtà, vorrei incatenarla al mio letto e tenerla sempre lì.

Non so che cosa mi aspettassi quando sono tornato, ma non questo. Non mi aspettavo che sarebbe stato così difficile per me lasciare che Sara andasse avanti con la sua routine, tornare al modo in cui vivevamo prima del Giappone. Anche allora la volevo sempre con me, ma lasciarla andare al lavoro non mi faceva a pezzi in questo modo, non attivava questo esasperante bisogno di metterla in gabbia e buttare via la chiave. Ho dovuto davvero impegnarmi per comportarmi normalmente stamattina, baciarla sulla fronte e farla scendere davanti all'ufficio come un futuro buon marito, invece di un selvaggio che non vuole altro che portarla nella propria caverna.

Questa è l'unica variabile di cui non avevo tenuto conto nella mia pianificazione.

La mia intensa ossessione per Sara—l'unica cosa che può rovinare tutto.

Spero che sia una situazione temporanea, che mi senta così perché abbiamo appena trascorso nove mesi lontani e mi è mancata così intensamente. Che col passare del tempo, man mano che il ricordo di quei mesi infernali svanirà, separarmi da lei per alcune ore diventerà più sopportabile, più facile... meno simile a una tortura.

L'altra possibilità—che in Giappone mi sia abituato ad avere Sara con me ventiquattro ore su ventiquattro e potrei non riuscire a riadattarmi alla vecchia routine—è infinitamente peggiore. Il motivo per cui ho fatto tutto questo è stato renderla felice, darle la possibilità di mantenere la sua carriera, i rapporti con la famiglia e gli amici. Era impossibile, quando ero un fuggitivo, ma ora posso far parte della sua vita senza strapparle tutto.

Potrei darle tutto—se solo riuscissi a superare il lato egoistico di tenerla tutta per me.

TRASCORRO LA MAGGIOR PARTE DELLA GIORNATA DI LAVORO, oscillando tra gioia martellante e sprazzi di panico.

Peter è vivo.

È tornato e stiamo insieme—senza che mi abbia rapita, tra l'altro.

Nonostante quello che Peter ha detto sul suo accordo, mi aspetto che l'FBI si presenti e mi accusi di favoreggiamento. Non viene nessuno, però. È tutto normale—o normale come può essere, quando si è fidanzati con un ex assassino.

Non sono pronta per rispondere alle domande dei miei colleghi, così ho nascosto la mano nella tasca e ho tolto l'anello non appena ho avuto un momento di privacy. Ora l'enorme diamante è sul fondo della mia borsa, costringendomi a portarla con me ovunque.

Non so quanto costi l'anello, ma ho il sospetto che si tratti di un numero a sei cifre.

Peter l'ha comprato o rubato? Probabilmente è la prima opzione—è abbastanza ricco da permetterselo—ma glielo chiederò per esserne sicura. Dubito che si offenderà; ha fatto molto peggio, questo è certo.

Ci sto ancora pensando, chiedendomi se il mio fidanzato milionario possa aver rubato l'anello di fidanzamento. Tuttavia, non sono più nel campo della normalità. Rispetto ad uccidere mio marito, rubare un diamante non è altro che un reato minore, per il quale posso facilmente perdonare Peter. In generale, ora che ho avuto il tempo di riprendermi dallo shock del suo arrivo, il panico sporadico che mi assale al pensiero di sposarlo è meno intenso, quasi gestibile. Verso sera, mentre salgo in auto per andare in clinica, comincio anche a pensare che potremmo andare a trovare i miei genitori questo fine settimana e, a seconda della loro reazione, dir loro che ci sposeremo presto.

Forse già quest'inverno.

Il mio cuore ricomincia a battere, e devo fare dei respiri profondi prima di scendere dalla macchina. No, l'inverno è decisamente troppo presto; c'è troppo da pianificare in così poco tempo. La prossima primavera sarebbe meglio... forse anche la prossima estate.

Un matrimonio estivo è sempre di moda.

Sì, è così, decido, entrando nella clinica. Un fidanzamento di un anno sarebbe perfetto. Avremmo la possibilità di abituarci l'uno all'altra, di stabilire una vita normale insieme. Non so se Peter sia in grado di vivere in questo modo, senza l'adrenalina e il pericolo delle sue missioni. Una volta mi ha confessato che gli piace uccidere, che gode del potere e del controllo che si accompagnano alla morte. Ha detto che uccidere crea dipendenza, e così ho pensato che non avrebbe mai smesso.

Che l'oscurità è una parte di lui, una cosa che non si può

cancellare.

Solo che ci ha rinunciato per me. Ha detto di aver lasciato il lavoro. Non ho avuto la possibilità di fargli domande al riguardo, ma c'è solo un modo per interpretare quello che ha detto.

Sta rigando dritto.

Per me.

Affinché io non rinunci a tutto per lui.

Mi prudono gli occhi, e devo sforzarmi per sorridere e salutare Lydia, mentre mi affretto verso la stanza in cui la paziente mi sta già aspettando. È una ragazza di sedici anni, qui con sua madre per il primo pap test, e mi sforzo di scacciare le emozioni e di concentrarmi, per rivolgere alla paziente l'attenzione che merita.

Fortunatamente, il suo esame non mostra niente di negativo, anche se quando la madre lascia la stanza la ragazza ammette di essere sessualmente attiva dall'anno scorso. Le do di nascosto una scatola di preservativi, e quando la madre torna, consiglio una spirale—per regolare i cicli dolorosi della figlia e fornire protezione contro una gravidanza non pianificata nel caso in cui diventasse sessualmente attiva in futuro.

"Mia figlia non è una sgualdrina" sbotta la donna e trascina via la ragazza, rendendomi felice di aver almeno dato a sua figlia quei preservativi.

Genitori del genere possono essere i peggiori nemici dei propri figli.

La mia prossima paziente è una donna incinta sulla trentina. Ha una storia di aborti e nessuna assicurazione sanitaria. Dopo di lei, visito un'altra adolescente—scopro che ha la clamidia—e poi è il momento della mia ultima paziente.

Finalmente.

Per la prima volta dopo un'eternità, non vedo l'ora di tornare a casa.

Tirando fuori il telefono, scorro fino al nuovo numero di Peter—*Peter Garin*, c'è scritto nella rubrica—e gli mando un messaggio avvisandolo che sarò pronta per uscire tra una ventina di minuti, nel caso volesse venire a prendermi in clinica. Non so come potrebbe farlo esattamente, dato che sono io quella con la macchina, ma conoscendo Peter, ce la farebbe.

Mettendo via il telefono, spingo la testa fuori dalla stanza degli esami e dico a Lydia che sono pronta per la prossima paziente.

Sto annotando alcune note sulla ragazza con la clamidia, quando la porta si apre ed entra l'ultima paziente.

Alzo gli occhi e mi blocco per lo shock.

Riconosco questa ragazza.

È Monica Jackson, la diciassettenne che ho aiutato dopo che il suo patrigno l'aveva violentata.

Il suo piccolo viso rotondo è ricoperto di lividi violacei, e un angolo delle labbra gonfie è incrostato di sangue. "Ciao, Dottoressa Cobakis" dice tremando, e prima che io possa rispondere, scoppia a piangere.

Impiego un bel quarto d'ora per calmarla e venire a sapere che il patrigno è uscito di prigione la scorsa settimana. "Doveva rimanere dentro per sette anni" mi informa, con voce tremante. "E ce la stavamo cavando davvero bene. Con i soldi che ci hai dato, siamo andati a vivere in una nuova casa, mi sono diplomata e stavo lavorando a tempo pieno, e Bobby—il mio fratellino—ha iniziato la scuola, una davvero buona, hanno i computer e tutto il resto. E mamma... stava meglio anche lei, beveva solo un po' la mattina. Pensavo che finalmente stessimo risolvendo i casini, ma poi *lui* è uscito per un cavillo e..."

Ricomincia a piangere, e aspetto che si calmi un po', prima di chiedere attentamente: "È stato lui a farti quello? Ti ha fatto del male?"

Annuisce, asciugandosi le lacrime dal viso con il piccolo pugno. "Mamma ha ripreso a bere non appena ha saputo che era fuori, e quando sono tornata a casa l'altro ieri, lui era lì, a casa con lei, a bere insieme come ai vecchi tempi. Ho litigato con lui, gli ho detto di andarsene, e poi lui—" S'interrompe, con le spalle che ricominciano a tremare.

Devo fare appello a tutto il mio allenamento per mantenere la distanza richiesta da un medico, invece di abbracciarla. "Hai denunciato questo alla polizia?" chiedo gentilmente, quando riacquista un po' di calma, e scuote la testa, guardando il pavimento.

"Ha detto che farà causa a mamma per la custodia di Bobby, se dico qualcosa, e ora ha delle connessioni. È così che è uscito prima del previsto. Un suo amico spacciatore agisce dietro le quinte."

"Anche se farà causa, ciò non significa che vincerà" dico, ma Monica, con decisione, scuote di nuovo la testa.

"Potrebbe non vincere, ma la trascinerebbe nel fango" dice, guardandomi. "Anche lei ha dei precedenti, per ubriachezza molesta e prostituzione, e potrebbero essere coinvolti i Servizi Sociali. Ora ho diciotto anni, quindi anch'io potrei far causa per la custodia, ma il mio lavoro paga il salario minimo e non c'è alcuna garanzia che vincerei. E se non vincessi, Bobby finirebbe in una casa adottiva." Un feroce senso di protezione si accende nei suoi occhi castani. "Non posso permettere che ciò accada, Dottoressa Cobakis. Ci sono passata, e non posso lasciare che accada a mio fratello. Ha delle esigenze speciali; non sopravvivrebbe al sistema. Non posso correre questo rischio, credimi."

Il mio cuore si spezza di nuovo per lei. Penso ancora che dovrebbe andare alla polizia, ma so che non riuscirò a convincerla. E questa volta, non posso farle un assegno e farla andare via.

Cinquemila dollari non risolverebbero la questione, e finalmente comprendo che cosa voglia dire detestare qualcuno abbastanza da augurargli la morte.

Se un'auto investisse quel bastardo del suo patrigno domani, sarei la prima ad esultare.

Inghiottendo la rabbia, ritrovo la distanza necessaria per svolgere il mio lavoro. "Ok, Monica, ho capito. Sali su quel tavolo, per favore, e assicuriamoci che dentro sia tutto a posto."

Fa come ho detto, asciugandosi i residui delle lacrime, e la esamino attentamente. Anche se l'aggressione è avvenuta due giorni fa, ci sono ancora segni di lividi e lacerazioni vaginali, così prendo un kit per lo stupro, nel caso in cui ci fossero le prove del DNA e in seguito cambiasse idea sul fatto di andare alla polizia. Gli do anche la contraccezione d'emergenza e controllo le malattie sessualmente trasmissibili, dopo che ha confessato che il suo aggressore non ha usato il preservativo.

"Puoi darmi anche una di quelle cose di rame?" mi chiede quando ho finito. "Non voglio rimanere incinta."

"Ovviamente."

Ha diciotto anni, quindi è facile. Programmo l'inserimento di una spirale per la prossima settimana, per darle il tempo di guarire.

"Hai un posto dove andare? Oltre alla casa di tua madre?" chiedo, mentre si prepara per andarsene.

È meglio che non vada a casa dal patrigno.

"Sto da un amico al momento" dice con mio sollievo. "Ha un divano su cui posso dormire."

"E tuo fratello?"

Le sue spalle strette si irrigidirono. "Non c'è posto per Bobby a casa del mio amico. Passo a prenderlo la mattina per portarlo a scuola, e poi lo riporto a casa."

"Da tua madre che si ubriaca? Il tuo patrigno è lì, quando torni con Bobby?"

Distoglie lo sguardo. "Devo andare, Dottoressa Cobakis. Grazie di tutto."

E prima che possa farle ulteriori domande, si precipita fuori dalla stanza.

5 0

 ara

PENSAVO DI AVER FATTO UN BUON LAVORO NEL SISTEMARE IL mascara colato, prima di lasciare la clinica, ma non appena esco e poso gli occhi sulla figura alta e grossa di Peter, il sorriso sul suo viso duro scompare.

"Che cos'è successo?" chiede bruscamente, facendo un passo in avanti per afferrarmi le mani. "Qualcuno ti ha fatto del male?"

Cerco di sorridere. "No, certo che no. Va tutto bene."

Socchiude gli occhi pericolosamente. "Non mentire. Hai pianto." Il suo sguardo indugia sulla mia mano sinistra. "Dov'è il tuo anello?"

"Io... non volevo dover spiegare." Nonostante i migliori sforzi, la mia voce è eccessivamente preoccupata, e vedo la sua espressione rabbuiarsi ulteriormente.

"Qualcuno ha detto qualcosa?" chiede, e scuoto la testa,

259

tirando via le mani dalla sua presa e facendo mezzo passo indietro.

"No, non è niente del genere." Mi guardo intorno, ma la strada è buia e silenziosa, deserta, a parte un SUV parcheggiato sul marciapiede dall'altra parte. L'auto con cui è venuto fin qui, forse? Alzando lo sguardo, incrocio quello di Peter. "Mi sono solo rattristata per una paziente, tutto qui."

La sua espressione dura si addolcisce leggermente. "Capisco. Mi dispiace, ptichka. Qualcuno si è fatto male?"

Reprimo un nuovo afflusso di lacrime. "È una lunga storia. Andiamo a casa." Inizio a girarmi verso la mia macchina parcheggiata, ma mi prende per un braccio.

"La farò portare a casa io, non ti preoccupare" dice e mi guida verso l'auto parcheggiata: un SUV Mercedes nero con finestrini sospettosamente spessi e oscurati.

Il conducente abbassa il finestrino, mentre ci avviciniamo.

"Porta la sua macchina a casa" ordina Peter, e un uomo grosso e dall'aria dura scende dal veicolo e consegna le chiavi a Peter.

Sbatto le palpebre, mentre cammina senza neanche rivolgermi un'occhiata. "Quello è—"

"Uno degli esperti della sicurezza che ho assoldato per sorvegliarti? Sì." Peter mi conduce in auto verso il lato del passeggero e mi apre la portiera, aiutandomi a salire prima di tornare al posto di guida.

"Ho deciso che invece di prendere un'altra auto, Danny sarà il tuo autista d'ora in poi" dice, mentre mette in modo la macchina e si allontana dal marciapiede. "Verrò ancora a prenderti la maggior parte delle volte, ma se non riuscirò ad arrivare qui in tempo o dovrai andartene in fretta, saprò che sei al sicuro a prescindere."

Apro la bocca per discutere, poi mi fermo. Non ho l'energia per farlo in questo momento—non con il cuore a pezzi per la tragica storia di Monica.

Non quando penso che domattina andrà a prendere il fratello e affronterà il suo aggressore.

"Che cos'è successo, ptichka?" Il grande palmo caldo di Peter mi copre la coscia, massaggiando il muscolo teso prima di ritirarsi. "Che cosa ti ha fatto rattristare così tanto?"

Esito un secondo, poi mi arrendo. Che importa se Peter conosce l'intera storia? Così, gli dico tutto, dalla visita di Monica alla clinica prima del mio rapimento a quello che è successo oggi.

Peter ascolta con volto inespressivo finché non finisco. Poi, chiede a bassa voce: "E così, questa ragazza è il motivo per cui sei stata aggredita in quel vicolo quella notte?"

Mi raddrizzo, scossa da un'improvvisa paura. "Non è colpa sua!" L'ultima cosa di cui ho bisogno è che il mio assassino iperprotettivo incolpi Monica per i tossici che hanno cercato di derubarmi.

"Non sto dicendo questo." Lascia l'autostrada, verso la mia uscita, e si ferma a un semaforo rosso. "Voglio solo assicurarmi di conoscere tutti i fatti."

Il mio cuore salta un battito. La conversazione non sta prendendo la piega che mi aspettavo.

"Perché?" chiedo, fissando il suo profilo duro. "A cosa ti serve?"

Non mi guarda. "Non ti preoccupare, amore mio. La tua paziente starà bene, te lo prometto."

La mia bocca si secca. Sta dicendo quello che penso stia dicendo? Non gli ho detto il nome di Monica, ma non sarebbe difficile per qualcuno col talento di Peter trovare persone che possano individuare di chi si tratti.

"Peter..."

Scatta la luce verde, e spinge sull'acceleratore, ancora senza guardarmi.

Il mio battito accelera ulteriormente. "Peter, ti prego, dimmi che non hai intenzione di..."

"Di cosa?" Svolta nella mia strada. "Te l'ho detto, non hai nulla di cui preoccuparti. Questa ragazza che hai aiutato starà bene. Non devi preoccuparti per lei."

Starà *bene*... ma per quanto riguarda il suo patrigno?

Vorrei chiederglielo, ma non riesco a formare le parole. Se le pronunciassi ad alta voce, lo renderebbe reale, invece che una mera possibilità terrificante nella mia mente.

Mi renderebbero colpevole.

Entriamo nel parcheggio del mio edificio, e scendo dall'auto prima che Peter abbia il tempo di girare intorno e aprirmi la portiera. Il cuore mi batte forte con un ritmo udibile e i palmi sono sudati, anche se ripeto a me stessa che probabilmente sto interpretando male la situazione.

Peter forse mi sta solo tranquillizzando, dicendomi ciò che crede possa calmarmi.

Voglio crederci, e con qualsiasi altro uomo, ci *crederei*. Se si trattasse di Joe Levinson o di uno dei miei compagni di band, prenderei quelle parole come una semplice rassicurazione, una specie di "andrà tutto bene." Ma questo è Peter, e non posso dar niente per scontato.

Devo—

"Quando andiamo a trovare i tuoi genitori?" chiede Peter, e alzo lo sguardo, sorpresa, quando lo trovo accanto a me. Allungando la mano, prende la mia nel suo grande palmo e inizia a guidarmi verso l'edificio, dicendo: "Dobbiamo discutere con loro degli accordi per questo sabato."

Lo fisso, confusa. Gli ho già parlato della mia idea di andare a trovare i miei genitori questo fine settimana? Ma no, ci ho pensato solo al lavoro, e— "Questo sabato?"

Annuisce, guardandomi con un sorriso. "Ho già prenotato tutto per il nostro matrimonio. Dobbiamo solo parlare di alcuni piccoli dettagli e siamo pronti."

Mi fermo. "Che cosa?"

Ha appena detto *il nostro matrimonio*?

Mi lascia la mano e si volta per guardarmi. "Se li chiami stasera, forse possiamo cenare con loro domani. In questo modo, avranno la possibilità di invitare alcuni amici. E potrai già parlare con i tuoi colleghi e chiunque altro tu voglia che partecipi. Non dovremmo invitare troppa gente, per ragioni di sicurezza, ma il locale ospiterà fino a un centinaio di persone."

La mia lingua si stacca dal palato. "Vuoi che ci sposiamo questo sabato? Cioè, tra tre giorni?"

Inclina la testa. "È un problema? Volevo farlo prima, ma ho pensato che il fine settimana fosse meglio rispetto a un giorno in mezzo alla settimana per dare la possibilità ai tuoi amici di partecipare."

Lo guardo a bocca aperta, sentendomi colpita da un treno merci. "L'*anno* prossimo sarebbe stato meglio" riesco a dire alla fine. "Questo fine settimana è semplicemente… È impossibile."

"Perché?" Mi prende di nuovo la mano e ricomincia a camminare, come se stessimo discutendo di cosa mangiare per cena e non del nostro fottutissimo matrimonio.

Un matrimonio che vuole celebrare tra *tre giorni*.

"Perché... perché non possiamo." Mi affretto a cercare dei modi per convincerlo. "E gli inviti? Non abbiamo tempo per mandarli e—"

"Puoi semplicemente chiamare le persone che vuoi invitare. Sarebbe più intimo in quel modo, tra l'altro."

"E il cibo? E i fotografi? E l'abito?"

"Mi sono già occupato di tutto. Ho assunto un'eccellente compagnia di catering e un fioraio altamente consigliato, e il fotografo è prenotato per tutta la giornata di sabato, così come l'operatore video. Per quanto riguarda l'abito, l'addetta verrà nel tuo ufficio domani per prenderti le misure, e sceglierai un modello che ti piace dal loro catalogo. Mi hanno promesso che non impiegheranno più di mezz'ora, quindi potresti farlo durante la pausa pranzo. L'addetta ai capelli e al trucco verrà a casa nostra sabato mattina, e per la musica ho assunto una band che è attualmente in tour a Chicago—The C-Zone Boys, credo che si chiamino. Mi pare di averti sentito cantare le loro canzoni."

Se la mia mascella non fosse attaccata, la raccoglierei dal pavimento. Ha assunto i C-Zone Boys per il nostro matrimonio estemporaneo? Cioè, la band i cui singoli hanno scalato le classifiche negli ultimi due anni?

"Perché non Rihanna o i Black-Eyed Peas?" chiedo, quando riesco finalmente a parlare, e mi lancia un'occhiata di traverso, mentre entriamo nell'atrio.

"È questo che vuoi? Posso vedere se possiamo—"

"No! È solo che..." Scuoto la testa, non riuscendo a trovare le parole per spiegare. "Non importa. I C-Zone sono perfetti. Qual è il locale?"

"Il Silver Lake Country Club, a Orland Park. Il tempo dovrebbe essere perfetto, quindi avremo sia la cerimonia che il ricevimento all'aperto, proprio vicino al lago. A meno che tu non voglia fare tutto dentro? Non è troppo tardi per questo."

"No... Il lungolago sarà fantastico."

Mi fa entrare nell'ascensore e premo il pulsante per il mio piano, sentendomi come se quel treno merci mi stesse trascinando alla velocità che induce alla follia. Come ha potuto organizzare tutto questo? Quando? E perché non mi ha consultata?

È così che sarà sempre la nostra vita insieme?

Prima che io possa affrontare questo spinoso problema, ho bisogno di esprimere un'ultima argomentazione razionale.

"E se non venisse nessuno?" chiedo, mentre usciamo dall'ascensore. "È già mercoledì. La maggior parte delle persone avrà già dei programmi per il fine settimana, e—"

"Li cambieranno." Infila una mano nella tasca e tira fuori una serie di chiavi—un set che deve aver fatto fare oggi, dato che il mio è nella borsa. Aprendo la porta, mi fa entrare e la chiude dietro di noi.

Lancio i miei sandali. "E se non possono?"

"Allora, si perderanno l'evento." Toglie le scarpe e si gira verso di me. "Ti importa davvero, ptichka? I tuoi genitori saranno lì, oltre a noi. Di chi altro hai bisogno?"

Di nessuno—in realtà—ma non è questo il punto.

"Peter..." Faccio un respiro profondo. "Non posso sposarti questo fine settimana. È troppo presto."

Il suo sguardo si indurisce. "Troppo presto in che senso? Te l'ho detto, mi sono occupato di tutta la logistica."

"Non si tratta della logistica!" La mia voce ha un volume alto, e faccio un altro respiro nel tentativo di riprendere il controllo. Cercando di calmarmi, dico: "Non ti vedo da più di nove mesi, e prima non avevamo esattamente una... relazione normale."

"E allora?" Socchiude gli occhi. "Ora ce l'abbiamo."

"Il fatto che tu mi stia spingendo a sposarmi e stia prendendo tutte le decisioni sul nostro matrimonio non è normale, Peter. Neanche lontanamente." Sono orgogliosa della compostezza che ho mantenuto finora. "Abbiamo bisogno di tempo per conoscerci in *questo* contesto, per vedere se possiamo far funzionare le cose..." Mi fermo, scorgendo la tempesta che si raccoglie nell'argento che si riflette nel suo sguardo.

"Perché non dovremmo farle funzionare?" La sua voce è pericolosamente bassa, mentre mi si avvicina. "Questa non è una prova, una situazione tra compagni di stanza di un college. Credi davvero che se litigassimo per i piatti, ti lascerei andare via?"

Il mio cuore riprende a battere più forte. Certo che non lo farebbe. Non dopo tutto quello che ha fatto per giungere a questa situazione. Tuttavia, deve rendersi conto che sposarmi *questo fine settimana*—e non avermi dato alcuna scelta in proposito—non è la strada giusta da seguire dopo un'assenza durata nove mesi, preceduta da una relazione forzata che coinvolgeva omicidio, tortura e rapimento.

"Che ne dici di un matrimonio in inverno?" dico in preda

alla disperazione. "Potremmo farlo proprio durante le vacanze di dicembre, così la stagione sarà ancora più festosa per noi. Potremmo anche pianificare una luna di miele in quel periodo. Potrei prendermi una settimana o due di ferie dal lavoro, e—"

"Possiamo andare in luna di miele quando vuoi." Allungandosi verso di me, fa scivolare le mani sotto la camicetta, appoggiando i palmi caldi sui miei lati nudi. I suoi occhi metallici assumono un bagliore infuocato, mentre i pollici mi raschiano la pelle sensibile sotto la cassa toracica, accarezzandomi avanti e indietro. "Se non puoi o non vuoi prenderti dei giorni di ferie la prossima settimana, non c'è problema. Posso aspettare fino all'inverno per la luna di miele."

"Allora, perché non aspettare anche per il matrimonio?" Sostengo il suo sguardo, cercando di concentrarmi sull'argomento in questione, invece del modo in cui il lento, ipnotico accarezzamento di quei pollici mi sta scaldando la pelle e facendo tremare le viscere. "Che male farebbe, se ci sposassimo anche in quel periodo?"

La sua la bocca assume una curva sensuale, e piega la testa, inspirando profondamente, come se respirasse il mio odore. "Intendi dire, a parte il fatto che tutta la mia pianificazione si rivelerebbe inutile?" mormora, passando le labbra sulla parte superiore del mio orecchio.

"S-sì." Chiudo gli occhi, mentre mi tira a sé, strofinandomi il lato del collo, e piego subito la testa all'indietro, concedendogli un migliore accesso. Il mio respiro accelera, con una sensazione di scioglimento che mi addolcisce le ossa, mentre la punta dura della sua eccitazione preme sul mio stomaco, rendendomi consapevole di un vuoto profondo all'interno.

"Beh..." Mi morde leggermente il collo, poi lenisce la piccola puntura leccando il punto ferito. "Per prima cosa, ti voglio come mia moglie, e lo voglio oggi, non domani o tra tre giorni." Il suo alito al profumo di menta è caldo sulla mia pelle, e mi scalda il corpo. "Voglio che indossi sempre il mio anello, ovunque, così tutti sapranno che sei mia." Mi mordicchia e lecca dietro l'orecchio, approfondendo la voce, mentre mormora: "Non è razionale, ptichka, ma ho bisogno di questo—ho bisogno di te. E non posso aspettare. Non dopo essere stato lontano da te per così tanto tempo."

"Che mi dici..." Sta diventando sempre più difficile raccogliere i pensieri, mentre continua a infliggere quei piccoli morsi sensuali al collo e alla spalla. Con uno sforzo sovraumano, cerco di concentrarmi. "Che mi dici dei figli? E dove vivremo? E cosa—" Resto a bocca aperta, mentre mi tira giù la cerniera e fa scivolare la mano nelle mutandine bagnate. "Che mi dici di—" inizio ad ansimare, mentre le sue dita trovano il mio clitoride e iniziano a manipolarlo con abilità infallibile—"del tuo lavoro?"

"Te l'ho detto, ho smesso." Il suo respiro è rapido come il mio, mentre affonda un lungo dito dentro di me, poi sfrutta la mia scivolosità per formare cerchi bagnati sul clitoride palpitante. "È finita."

"Ma... oh, Dio." I miei fianchi ora stanno danzando in un cerchio, seguendo il movimento di quel dito dispettoso. La pressione sta crescendo così rapidamente che non riesco più a formulare un solo pensiero. "Oh, Dio, Peter, sto per—"

Con un grido strozzato, esplodo, con ogni muscolo del corpo che si stringe per una violenta ondata di piacere. L'orgasmo è così forte che la mia mente si svuota, inondata da sensazioni puramente fisiche. Sono vagamente consapevole del mio ondeggiare, dei pantaloni e della biancheria intima che vengono spinti giù lungo le gambe, e poi mi piega sul divano e spinge dentro di me, con il grosso cazzo che mi penetra in profondità con un colpo duro.

Lo shock mi colpisce fino all'osso, e i muscoli ancora tremanti si serrano, fremendo in uno sforzo istintivo di fermare l'invasione. Ma questo lo fa sembrare ancora più spesso, più massiccio dentro di me, e mi ritrovo ad ansimare di nuovo, mentre mi afferra i fianchi e inizia a spingere, con il bacino che sbatte contro il sedere ad ogni impietoso colpo.

"Peter..." Sento l'ondata che riaffiora, minacciando di sommergermi nella beatitudine incandescente. "Peter, aspetta..."

Non rallenta; anzi, le sue spinte punitive accelerano. "Vieni con me" ordina con voce rauca. "Voglio sentirti mungere il mio cazzo."

Vengo prima che finisca di parlare, con l'ondata che mi travolge con la forza di uno tsunami. Il piacere sconfigge i miei sensi, eviscerando gli ultimi brandelli di resistenza. Non so se stia urlando o se sia il sangue che ruggisce nelle mie orecchie, ma il resto dei suoni svanisce.

Tutto ciò che sento, tutto ciò che provo, sono l'estasi e lui.

*eter*

La mia ptichka è silenziosa, mentre la porto in bagno e la immergo nella vasca di bolle che ho preparato prima di andare a prenderla. La vasca è troppo piccola per tutti e due, così uso il lavello per lavarmi e poi mi sistemo sul lato della vasca, osservando i capezzoli rosa di Sara giocare a nascondino con le bolle. Con la testa appoggiata sul bordo della vasca, gli occhi chiusi, e le delicate fattezze rosa con il bagliore post-orgasmico, sembra così allettante che già la rivoglio.

Stasera, mi riprometto.

Non appena Sara avrà finito il suo bagno, mangeremo, e sarà tutta mia durante la notte.

Percependo il mio sguardo su di lei, apre gli occhi. "Grazie per questo" mormora, muovendo una mano aggraziata tra le bolle. "Non riesco a ricordare l'ultima volta che l'ho fatto."

Combatto l'impulso di raggiungerla e prendere quella mano,

trascinarla su di me così da sentire il suo corpo scivoloso a causa delle bolle che sfrega contro il mio. "Mi sposerai sabato" dico, con il tono più duro di quanto intendessi. "Questo non è in discussione."

Si irrigidisce visibilmente e si mette a sedere. "Peter, non è—"

"Oppure stasera. Non sono contrario a volare a Las Vegas con te dopo cena." Faccio del mio meglio per tenere gli occhi lontani dai morbidi seni bianchi esposti sopra l'acqua.

Questo è troppo importante per essere distratto dalla lussuria.

Come se percepisse i miei pensieri, Sara sprofonda nell'acqua, lasciando che le bolle nascondano quei seni tentatori dalla vista. "Hai un aereo sempre a disposizione?"

"Più o meno." Lascio che i miei compagni di squadra mantengano il nostro aereo per ora, ma potrei noleggiare un jet privato con un preavviso di due ore.

Con i soldi che ho, tutto è possibile.

"Peter..." Si mette di nuovo a sedere, stavolta coprendosi i seni con un braccio. "Dobbiamo parlare di questo—di tutto, in realtà. Sei tornato ieri, e ancora non so dove sei stato o che cos'hai fatto. Dove sono Anton e i gemelli? Sono qui con te?"

"No." Faccio un respiro profondo e reprimo l'istinto che mi spinge a portarla a Las Vegas proprio in questo secondo. Sara ha ragione; ci sono molte questioni di cui non abbiamo discusso. "Sono in Europa, ma voleranno qui per il nostro matrimonio" spiego e mi alzo.

Segue il mio esempio e le avvolgo un asciugamano intorno, mentre esce dalla vasca. Sembra incredibilmente piccola così, con la testa piegata e l'asciugamano spesso avvolto intorno al corpo slanciato.

Mi rende consapevole di quanto sia indifesa, di quanto sia fragile.

Mi ricorda di come una volta volevo punirla... e di come ne abbia ancora voglia a volte.

"Mangiamo e parliamo" dico, frenando l'oscuro impulso. "Ti dirò tutto."

Nulla di tutto ciò, però, cambierà ciò che sta per accadere.

Prima della fine di questa settimana, in un modo o nell'altro, Sara sarà mia moglie.

5 2

S*ara*

LA CENA DI QUESTA SERA È UN MIX DI CUCINA RUSSA E ASIATICA, con succulenti *pelmeni*—ravioli di carne alla russa—serviti con panna acida come antipasto e una frittura di verdure condita con il tofu al peperoncino marinato come piatto principale.

Ho pranzato un secolo fa, e il sesso intenso combinato con il bagno caldo hanno impoverito ulteriormente le mie riserve di energia. Sono così famelica che non appena Peter mette il cibo sul tavolo, mi ci tuffo, divorando cinque grandi ravioli e due porzioni di piccante frittura ripassata in padella prima di staccare gli occhi dal piatto.

"Fame?" chiede Peter ironicamente, mentre passo alla porzione numero tre, e arrossisco, rendendomi conto di essere rimasta così concentrata sul cibo che ho detto appena una parola.

"È davvero buono" dico scusandomi, e sorride, con gli occhi

metallici caldi come non li ho mai visti.

"Buon appetito, ptichka. Mi piace vederti mangiare il cibo che ho preparato."

"Sei un cuoco eccezionale" gli dico sinceramente, e il suo sorriso si allarga ulteriormente.

"Sono felice che la pensi così, amore mio."

"E se aprissi un ristorante?" chiedo impulsivamente. "Sai, come ha fatto Yulia? O un bar?"

Ride di nuovo, scuotendo la testa. "No, ptichka. Non fa per me. Ma ti preparerò da mangiare ogni volta che vorrai."

"No, ma sul serio.... che cosa *farai* qui?" Metto giù la forchetta e lo studio attentamente. "Hai qualche idea su cosa ti piacerebbe fare in termini di carriera? Hai detto di aver lasciato il tuo lavoro. Immagino che questo significhi che non sei più un... uhm..."

Per qualche ragione, la parola mi rimane nella gola, e solleva le sopracciglia, sembrando profondamente divertito.

"Un assassino? No, ptichka. Ho chiuso con quella parte della mia vita." Infilza un pezzo di bok choy con la forchetta. "Sarò un cittadino rispettoso della legge d'ora in avanti."

"Davvero?" Lo fisso, speranzosa e incredula. Inizialmente pensavo che sarebbe stato così, ma poi abbiamo avuto quella conversazione su Monica. Significa che ho frainteso? Avrei giurato che ci fosse un'implicita promessa di fare qualcosa al patrigno, ma se Peter dice che sarà rispettoso, allora forse quelle erano solo parole vuote, tranquillizzanti, il tipo che qualsiasi ragazzo direbbe per calmare la propria ragazza.

Pensare a Monica mi mette subito di cattivo umore, uccidendo ciò che è rimasto del mio appetito, e spingo via il piatto, mentre Peter sorride e dice: "Davvero. Questa è una delle condizioni dell'accordo: niente più crimini d'ora in poi."

"Oh. Bene."

Solleva di nuovo le sopracciglia. "Non sembri troppo entusiasta."

"Che cosa? No!" Scaccio la pesante sensazione che mi attanaglia il petto al pensiero di Monica e sorrido brillantemente. "Sono felicissima della tua decisione. Come potrei non esserlo?"

Dico sul serio, anche se devo schiacciare quel pizzico di speranza tinta di colpa per una soluzione permanente al dilemma di Monica.

Non che io volessi quello.

Mi rifiuto di crederci.

"Non lo so, ptichka." Peter gira la testa, guardandomi pensieroso. "C'è qualcosa che ti preoccupa?"

"Tutto mi preoccupa" dico senza mezzi termini. "Come affronterai questo tipo di vita? Che cosa farai del tuo tempo? Dici che vuoi sposarmi questo sabato, ma poi? E la tua vendetta? Hai detto che l'ultimo—"

"È finita." Il suo tono è tagliente, con il viso che si rabbuia all'improvviso. "Non c'è niente da discutere su questo fronte."

Lo fisso, con il cibo che ho mangiato che si è trasformato in un macigno nello stomaco. "Che cos'è successo?"

Si alza e prende il suo piatto mezzo vuoto, poi il mio. "Niente." Avvicinandosi al lavandino, sistema i piatti così forte che sbattono, poi torna al tavolo per prenderne altri.

Mi alzo anch'io, con i nervi tesi, mentre lo osservo aggirarsi per la cucina con violenza mal controllata. "Peter..." Raccogliendo il coraggio, gli prendo il polso quando mi ripassa accanto. "Che cos'è successo?" ripeto dolcemente, incrociando il suo sguardo d'acciaio.

I tendini del suo grosso polso si flettono, e so che sarebbe un gioco da ragazzi per lui sbarazzarsi della mia presa. "Niente" risponde invece, e questa volta percepisco il sottofondo di amaro dolore e rabbia. "Assolutamente niente, cazzo."

Inumidisco le labbra asciutte. "Che cosa significa? Non l'hai trovato?"

Contorce la bocca, e si libera attentamente della mia presa.

"Lascia perdere, ptichka."

Vorrei, ma non ci riesco. Non se vogliamo costruire una vita insieme.

Non sposerò un altro uomo i cui segreti potrebbero distruggerci.

"Ti prego, Peter." Gli prendo di nuovo la mano, stringendola tra i palmi. Sostenendo il suo sguardo, dico sottovoce: "Dimmi solo la verità."

Le sue dita si piegano nella mia presa, e chiude gli occhi, respirando profondamente. Quando li riapre, la rabbia è scomparsa, velata dalla mancanza di espressione. "Te l'ho detto... non è successo niente" dice in modo uniforme. "E non succederà niente. Henderson tornerà alla sua vita normale, sano e salvo, perché questo fa parte dell'accordo che ho accettato." E mentre lo fisso, sconvolta, dice: "È finita, Sara. Non c'è altro da aggiungere."

Comincio a parlare e mi fermo, incapace di trovare le parole giuste. Nessuna parola, in realtà. Mi sento come se il cuore si stesse sgretolando, con il petto così stretto che non riesco a respirare.

Ha rinunciato alla possibilità di vendicare completamente la propria famiglia.

Per me.

Ha fatto tutto questo per me.

"Non farlo" dice con fermezza, e sento una goccia di umidità sul viso. La sfumatura liquida davanti alla vista dev'essere dovuta alle lacrime.

"Mi dispiace." Gli lascio andare la mano e passo il dorso della mia sulle sue guance. "Stavo solo... Va bene."

Mi fissa, poi si gira, riprendendo a pulire la cucina come se non fosse successo niente.

Come se non mi avesse appena strappato il cuore dal petto e l'avesse messo in tasca.

Mi concedo un paio di minuti per calmarmi, poi mi avvicino

alla borsa e tiro fuori il telefono.

"Che cosa stai facendo?" chiede Peter, mentre premo il numero dei miei genitori, e tengo il dito sulle labbra in un gesto universale di silenzio.

"Ciao, Mamma" dico, quando sento quel familiare saluto. "Come stai? Come ti senti?"

"Sto bene, tesoro." Sembra perplessa. "Che cosa succede? Va tutto bene?"

Guardo l'orologio e sussulto quando mi accorgo che sono le dieci passate. "Sì, è tutto a posto. Mi dispiace aver chiamato così tardi—ho avuto un turno in clinica e ho perso la cognizione del tempo. Non ti ho svegliata, vero?"

"Oh, no. Stavo solo leggendo prima di andare a letto. Tuo padre si è già addormentato, però. Volevi parlargli? Posso svegliarlo, se—"

"No, non fa niente. Lascialo dormire." Faccio un respiro profondo. "Mamma, che cosa farete tu e Papà domani sera? Siete liberi per cena?"

Con la coda dell'occhio, vedo Peter fermarsi, per poi riprendere a caricare la lavastoviglie.

"Beh, stavamo pensando di andare al Bingo, ma possiamo rimandare" dice mamma. "Perché, tesoro? Non lavori domani?"

"Avrò una giornata leggera" spiego, ed è quasi vero. Non farò visite domani, né avrò alcun intervento chirurgico. E per quanto riguarda il mio turno in clinica, lo riprogrammerò per un altro giorno. "Volete venire a cena da me?"

Un momento di silenzio, poi: "A casa tua?"

"Sì. C'è una persona che vorrei conosceste" dico, mentre Peter si volta per guardarmi.

Questa sarà la seconda volta in cui i miei genitori visiteranno il mio nuovo appartamento. Non sono mai stata particolarmente brava come padrona di casa, quindi di solito o vado io a casa loro o usciamo per pranzo o per il brunch. Con Peter, però, penso che sia meglio se siamo a casa mia.

I miei genitori saranno più propensi a comportarsi al meglio in questo modo.

"Oh." La voce di mamma si riempie di evidente emozione. "Sì, certo, tesoro, ci farebbe molto piacere. Vuoi che portiamo qualcosa od ordineremo a domicilio?"

"Ci pensiamo noi, Mamma. Non preoccuparti di nulla" dico, mentre Peter continua a fissarmi. "Ci vediamo domani alle sei, ok?"

Riattacco, e lui viene verso di me, con movimenti lenti e vagamente predatori, come la pigra falcata di un gatto della giungla.

"Era mia madre" dico, facendo istintivamente un passo indietro. "Li ho invitati qui a cena domani. Non ti dispiace, vero? Possiamo ordinare a domicilio, o—" Le mie parole terminano con uno squittio, mentre Peter mi prende in braccio e mi sistema sul tavolo, poi mi toglie la vestaglia.

"Peter, aspetta..." mi lecco le labbra, mentre mi spinge giù la vestaglia dalle braccia, denudandomi completamente. "Dovremmo decidere cosa faremo—ahh..." gemo, piegando la testa all'indietro, mentre mi bacia la zona sensibile attorno alla clavicola nello stesso momento in cui la mano mi invade l'angolo dolorante tra le gambe, con due dita ruvide che spingono dentro senza pietà. Non sono ancora bagnata e fa male, eppure il mio corpo freme in un lampo di calore, in un'esplosione di violente sensazioni.

"Mi sposerai. Questo sabato" ringhia, scopandomi con quelle dita, e gemo il mio consenso, con il corpo che si accende di nuovo.

Questo sabato, stanotte, domani—non importa più. Ho smesso di combattere, di resistere.

Aveva ragione fin dall'inizio.

Sono sua, e lui è mio.

Le cose dovevano andare così.

P_eter_

STA DORMENDO, ESAUSTA, QUANDO SCENDO CON CAUTELA DAL letto e raccolgo i vestiti che ho lasciato piegati su una sedia. Mi vesto in silenzio, facendo attenzione a non svegliarla, e poi esco dalla camera da letto con i piedi avvolti nei calzini.

I miei stivali sono all'ingresso, così li infilo e palpo la tasca della giacca per assicurarmi che il telefono sia lì.

Ne avrò bisogno per raggiungere la posizione attuale di un certo Signor Samson "Sonny" Pearson, il patrigno di Monica Jackson.

Danny mi sta già aspettando nel parcheggio, così apro l'e-mail dei miei hacker e gli do un indirizzo a pochi isolati da dove vive Pearson—cioè, nell'appartamento della sua ex moglie.

La madre di Monica chiaramente non si fa scrupoli a lasciare che lo stupratore di sua figlia passi la notte con lei.

È un rischio che sto correndo, facendo questo da solo.

Sarebbe stato più intelligente assumere qualcuno per ottenere un discreto successo tra pochi mesi, quando nessuno avrebbe potuto collegare la morte di Pearson alla visita della sua figliastra alla clinica per ragazze senza scopo di lucro. Tuttavia, la mia ptichka stava piangendo oggi—a causa di questo *ublyudok*—e non riesco a sopportarlo.

Morirà stanotte, e la sua figliastra sarà finalmente libera.

"Fammi scendere qui" dico a Danny, quando raggiungiamo l'indirizzo che gli ho dato, un edificio a pochi isolati dalla mia vera destinazione. Il ragazzo è leale e abbastanza disposto a operare al di fuori della legge, ma non mi fido di lui come mi fido degli altri miei uomini.

È meglio che lo faccia da solo, senza testimoni.

L'appartamento di Amira Pearson si trova al secondo piano di un fatiscente edificio a quattro piani. C'è un debole fetore di piscio e vomito nell'atrio, e la vernice sulle scale si sta staccando, ricordandomi gli edifici dell'era sovietica in Russia. Tuttavia, la porta dell'appartamento davanti alla quale mi fermo è in legno, non in due strati d'acciaio, come è comune nel mio Paese infestato dalla corruzione.

Potrei buttare giù questa porta con un solo calcio, se volessi.

Invece, premo l'orecchio sul legno e ascolto. Sento il basso mormorio delle voci, quindi le mie informazioni sono corrette. Sonny ha ottenuto un lavoro che consiste nello scarico dei camion alimentari alle tre del mattino e tra poco uscirà per il turno.

Torno giù ed esco per aspettare. Sarei potuto entrare mentre il bastardo dormiva, ma la madre e il fratello di Monica sono nell'appartamento, quindi è meglio aspettare.

Sarà meglio se riuscirò a catturare Sonny da solo e farlo sembrare un furto andato male.

Passa quasi mezz'ora prima che esca, ma rimango vigile, con l'adrenalina che mi scorre costantemente nelle vene. Non posso negare l'oscura attesa che provo, il desiderio di sangue che mi alimenta come una caraffa di caffè.

Sono un predatore, un mostro, e lo so.

Ora anche Sonny Pearson lo saprà.

Rimango mezzo nascosto in un vicolo, e quando passa, allungo la mano e lo afferro per la maglietta, tirandolo dentro.

"Ehi!" Cerca di colpirmi, ma si blocca non appena gli premo la lama sulla gola.

"Non ti muovere" sussurro, sporgendomi. "Non respirare nemmeno."

Il pomo d'Adamo nel suo grosso collo va su e giù pericolosamente vicino alla lama. "Che-che cosa vuoi, amico? Non ho so-soldi."

"Lo so." Non ho bisogno di vederlo sbiancare per sapere che il mio sorriso è gelido. "Non è quello che sto cercando."

E con questo, affondo la lama nella sua gola. Il suo sangue caldo mi bagna le dita, e il fetore delle viscere che fuoriescono riempie l'aria. Guardo la vita svanire dai suoi occhi marroni come il fango, e poi dico sottovoce: "Monica ti manda i suoi saluti."

Lasciando cadere il corpo sul marciapiede, pulisco la mano e la lama sulla parte più pulita della sua maglietta, estraggo il portafoglio dalla tasca, ed esco dal vicolo, tornando dove Danny sta aspettando.

Dovremo fermarci in un motel sulla via del ritorno.

Ho bisogno di una doccia prima di tornare a casa.

5 4

 ara

NON SONO ANCORA PRONTA PER INDOSSARE APERTAMENTE IL MIO anello in ufficio, ma all'ora di pranzo, quando arrivano le addette all'abito—due donne alla moda che hanno circa la mia età—le conduco nell'atrio principale, ignorando lo sguardo curioso della segretaria. Entriamo in una delle stanze delle visite e mi misurano dalla testa ai piedi—cosa che richiede solo pochi minuti con le loro abili mani.

"Sei molto magra, il che è fantastico" dice una donna alta e con i capelli scuri che si è presentata come Suzie. "Abbiamo un magnifico Monique Lhuillier che ti starà splendidamente, dopo aver apportato modifiche minime. Pam, hai una foto?"

Pam, una bionda bassa e con i capelli ricci, tira fuori il telefono e mi mostra un elegante vestito in stile sirena appeso a un manichino. Con dei pizzi delicati, è senza spalline, ha una scollatura quadrata e una fila di bottoni di perle sul retro—semplice ma così perfetto che posso solo fissarlo e sbavare.

"Abbiamo anche molti altri stili" dice Suzie, interpretando erroneamente la mia mancanza di parole. "C'è qualcosa in particolare che—"

"No, questo è fantastico." Distolgo lo sguardo dallo schermo del telefono. "Quanto costa?"

Suzie sbatte le palpebre e lancia un'occhiata a Pam.

"Il Signor Garin ci ha detto che non c'è un budget fisso" dice Pam con attenzione. "Non è così?"

"Oh, uhm... certo. Stavo chiedendo solo per curiosità." Le finanze sono un'altra cosa che non ho discusso con Peter, quindi faccio del mio meglio per nascondere il disagio dietro un sorriso più luminoso.

"Oh, capisco." Pam ricambia il sorriso. "Beh, il tuo fidanzato è un uomo molto generoso. Quest'abito è un pezzo unico nel suo genere con pizzi fatti a mano, e viene venduto per trentatremila dollari, più le tasse. Tuttavia, le modifiche sono gratuite."

"È... molto gentile da parte vostra." La mia voce sembra strozzata, ma non posso farci niente. Non sono Cenerentola—nonostante il taglio al mio nuovo lavoro, lo stipendio è saldamente nelle sei cifre—ma trentatremila è una somma strabiliante per un vestito che indosserò una sola volta.

Credevo che l'abito da dodicimila dollari per il mio primo matrimonio fosse costoso.

"Avrai anche bisogno di scarpe e accessori" dice Suzie, estraendo un catalogo dalla borsetta extra-large. "Vuoi sfogliare questo"—agita il catalogo—"o preferisci che ti consigliamo qualcosa?"

"Apprezzerei un consiglio" dico, e mi trovano rapidamente un paio di ballerine Louboutin bianche con delicate stringhe attorno alle caviglie, e una collana di perle da abbinare a due orecchini di perle e diamanti.

"Ci vorrà anche un bel taglio di capelli, ovviamente" dice Pam, sfogliando il catalogo per indicare alcune acconciature particolari. "Sarà tutto ben abbinato."

"Grazie. Ne sono sicura" dico, mentre radunano tutto e se ne vanno. Fedeli alla loro parola, l'intero procedimento è durato poco meno di trenta minuti—una frazione del tempo che ho trascorso facendo shopping alla ricerca di un vestito e accessori per il mio primo matrimonio.

Forse c'è qualche beneficio nel fatto che Peter abbia insistito, penso ironicamente, mentre esco per un pranzo veloce nella mezz'ora che mi rimane prima della prossima paziente. Il mio primo matrimonio è stato una grande produzione, con George che invitava tutti quelli che conoscevamo e spendendo soldi che in realtà non avevamo. Avevamo duecento persone al ricevimento, e impiegammo un anno per pianificare—e io, all'epoca sommersa dai tirocini, detestavo ogni minuto di quella pianificazione.

Un piccolo matrimonio in cui tutto ciò che devo fare è presentarmi potrebbe essere esattamente quello che fa per me.

"Chi erano quelle persone?" chiede la segretaria, Annabelle, quando torno dal pranzo, e riprendo fiato, rendendomi conto di avere un compito importante che mi aspetta.

Devo invitare i miei amici e colleghi, sopportando le loro domande sorprese.

"Erano qui per misurarmi un abito" dico, decidendo che non ho molto tempo a disposizione. Infilando la mano sinistra nella borsa, rimetto l'anello e tiro fuori la mano, mostrando il grande diamante ad Annabelle. "Vedi, sono fidanzata e il matrimonio è—"

Un grido emozionato soffoca le mie parole, prima che io possa dire "questo sabato." Annabelle, una donna senza scrupoli sulla cinquantina che gestisce compagnie assicurative e pazienti difficili con la stessa disinvoltura, balza in piedi come un'adolescente e mi afferra la mano per osservare l'anello, chiacchierando per tutto il tempo.

"Oh mio Dio, guarda quella pietra! Chi è il fortunato ragazzo? Come lo hai conosciuto? Non sapevo nemmeno che frequentassi qualcuno!"

Quando fa una pausa per respirare, le dico che io e Peter ci frequentiamo da un po' di tempo, ma che la nostra relazione non era seria a causa del suo lavoro, che prevedeva molti viaggi all'estero. Ora, comunque, farà qualcos'altro, quindi abbiamo deciso di fare il passo successivo e di sposarci.

"Non stiamo pianificando un grande matrimonio" dico, prima che possa lanciarsi nella prossima serie di domande. "Sabato ci sarà una piccola cerimonia e mi piacerebbe se tu e tuo marito poteste partecipare. So che ti ho avvisata tardi, ma—"

Urla di nuovo e mi abbraccia. "Oh, grazie, tesoro—sono così onorata! Ci saremo sicuramente. L'hai già detto a Bill e Wendy?"

Sorrido davanti al suo viso emozionato. "No, ma sto per farlo."

"Oh, allora vai. Subito. Non vedo l'ora di vedere l'espressione sulla faccia di Bill, quando scoprirà che avevo ragione." Notando le mie sopracciglia sollevate, spiega: "Ho scommesso venti dollari con lui che una ragazza carina come te doveva avere un ragazzo." E mentre scoppio a ridere, fa capolino nella zona di attesa, e dice: "Ancora non vedo la tua paziente, quindi hai un paio di minuti."

"Grazie, Annabelle." Rido, mentre fa movimenti scattanti con le mani. "Verrò, te lo prometto."

Mi affretto verso l'ufficio dei miei capi, prima che Annabelle possa trascinarmi lì fisicamente e bussare alla porta.

"Wendy? Bill? Avete un secondo?"

Wendy apre la porta un attimo dopo. "Certo, mia cara. Come posso aiutarti?" Il suo sorriso è delicato come i capelli bianchi che le incorniciano il viso gentile. Tutto della

Dottoressa Otterman è gentile, dal tono della voce al modo in cui chiama regolarmente le pazienti per visitarle.

Lavorare con lei è un assoluto piacere, nonostante il burbero marito sempre al proprio fianco.

"Bill è qui?" chiedo, poi lo vedo seduto dietro di lei, a masticare un sandwich grande quasi quanto i suoi baffi.

Mi rivolge la solita occhiata abbagliante e mette giù il sandwich. "Di cosa si tratta?"

Se non lo conoscessi meglio, penserei che mi detesti. Ma è così con tutti, pazienti compresi, quindi non me la prendo.

Secondo le infermiere, più ti guarda storto, più gli piaci.

"Beh..." Con la coda dell'occhio, vedo Annabelle che mi si avvicina. Chiaramente non riesce a resistere alla tentazione di vedere in prima persona quell'espressione sul viso di Bill. "Mi stavo chiedendo se avevate qualcosa in programma per questo sabato" dico, pensando che sia meglio non farne un caso di stato. "Mi sposerò con una piccola cerimonia di basso profilo, e—"

"Che cosa?" I baffi grigi di Bill tremano, mentre il suo sguardo si posa sulla mia mano sinistra. "Sei fidanzata?"

"A partire da ieri" dico, sollevando la mano per mostrare l'anello. "Mi rendo conto di avervi avvisato tardi, quindi se avete altri programmi, è totalmente—"

"Oh, no, ci saremo, mia cara. Congratulazioni." Wendy mi sorride e si allunga per stringermi la mano destra. "Chi è il fortunato gentiluomo?" Scruta la mia mano sinistra. "È un bellissimo anello, quello che ti ha regalato."

I baffi di Bill si rifiutano di smettere di muoversi. "Hai un ragazzo?" Il suo glaciale cipiglio si fa più evidente, mentre si alza in piedi. "Non sapevamo che avessi un ragazzo."

Sorrido e ripeto la mia spiegazione sul fatto che avevamo una relazione contorta e che Peter viaggiava molto. "Quindi, ora siamo pronti per fare il prossimo passo" concludo e guardo l'orologio sul muro. "Oh, è tardi. La mia paziente probabilmente sarà arrivata ormai" dico, e osservo Annabelle sorridere e tornare al suo posto.

"Scusate, devo andare" dico ai miei capi. "Quindi, ci sarete?"

"Con le campane e i fischietti" dice Bill in tono acido.

Immagino che significhi che è contento per me, e salutando in fretta Wendy mi affretto ad uscire, felice che almeno questa parte del mio compito si sia conclusa senza intoppi.

Ora devo solo dirlo a tutti gli altri—e poi spiegarlo ai miei genitori.

~

HO LA CANCELLAZIONE DI UN APPUNTAMENTO NELLA SECONDA metà del pomeriggio, così sfrutto quel tempo per iniziare a fare le telefonate necessarie.

Simon e Rory non rispondono, così lascio loro un messaggio vocale per farmi richiamare. Phil, invece, deve aver già terminato il lavoro per la scuola, perché risponde al primo squillo.

"Ehi, eccoti. Pensavamo che il tuo misterioso fidanzato ti avesse portata via" dice, e io rido, sperando che non possa sentire la nota semi-isterica nel suono.

Sta scherzando, ma Peter avrebbe potuto facilmente farmi sparire.

È quello che pensavo sarebbe successo, quando ho lasciato il bar con lui.

"Sono ancora qui" dico, quando smetto di ridere. "Ma ho alcune notizie."

"Non dirmelo." Phil finge di sussultare nel telefono. "Sei incinta."

"Uhm, no..." O, almeno, se lo sono, non lo so ancora. Non è impossibile dopo due giorni di sesso non protetto, ma è decisamente troppo presto per dirlo. "Mi sto per *sposare*, però."

Cala il silenzio sul telefono. Poi: "CHE COSA?"

"Sì, è una lunga storia" dico, e mi lancio nella stessa spiegazione che ho dato ai colleghi sulla mia relazione complicata e sui viaggi di Peter.

"Ma perché non ci hai detto di lui?" Phil sembra ancora stordito. "Pensavamo tutti che non frequentassi nessuno a causa di tuo marito."

"È stato un po' complicato a volte. E dato che non sapevo come sarebbero andate le cose..." Mi fermo, sperando che Phil riempia gli spazi vuoti da solo. "Ad ogni modo, ci stiamo per sposare, e ci sposeremo questo sabato, quindi—"

"CHE COSA?"

Sorrido, immaginando i suoi occhi sporgenti. "Sì, lo so. Abbiamo deciso di evitare un lungo fidanzamento. In ogni caso, so che è un preavviso molto breve, quindi se hai altri programmi per questo sabato, capisco perfettamente. Ma *se* ce la fai, ci piacerebbe averti lì, e, ovviamente, puoi portare la tua ragazza."

"Ti sposerai. Questo sabato."

"È quello che ho appena detto." Faccio una pausa per dargli la possibilità di metabolizzare, ma sembra che abbia perso la lingua, così continuo. "Non devi dirmelo subito, ma se ne hai la possibilità, mi piacerebbe sapere entro domani se sarai presente. Peter ha prenotato una società di catering e tutto il resto, quindi sarà piccolo ma spero carino."

"Dove..." Phil si schiarisce la voce. "Dove si terrà il matrimonio?"

"Al Silver Lake Country Club" dico. "Lo conosci?"

"Sì, certo. Mio cugino si è sposato lì un paio d'anni fa. Bel posto."

"Oh, bene." Sorrido, anche se non può vedermi. "Quindi, puoi dirmi se ci sarai o hai bisogno di pensarci fino a domani?"

"Ma stai scherzando? Certo che ci sarò. L'hai già detto a Rory e Simon?"

"Ho lasciato un messaggio nella loro segreteria" dico e

guardo l'orologio. Farò meglio a sbrigarmi, se voglio chiamare Marsha prima della prossima paziente. "Grazie mille, Phil, e scusa se ti ho disturbato" gli dico. "Ci vediamo sabato."

"Sì. Ci vediamo" dice, ancora stordito, quando riattacco.

Marsha è la prossima sulla mia lista, ed è una conversazione che temo quasi quanto la cena imminente con i miei genitori. Mentre compongo il suo numero, spero che non risponda, ma lo fa al primo squillo.

"Ehi, tesoro."

Faccio un respiro profondo. "Ehi, Marsha. Come va?"

"Eh, lo sai. Sto per iniziare il mio turno serale. Andy era di turno questa settimana, ma il suo fidanzato ha insistito, perché oggi è il loro anniversario, così mi ha chiesto di scambiarmi con lei. Come stai? Quali programmi hai per questo fine settimana? Io e Tonya pensavamo di andare in qualche locale sabato. Vuoi unirti a noi? Non devi esibirti, vero?"

"No, ma per quanto riguarda questo sabato..." Stringo il telefono. "Ho delle notizie da darti."

"Oh?"

"C'è un ragazzo che frequento da un po'. Una relazione complicata."

"Davvero?" La voce di Marsha si alza. "Di chi si tratta? Non è quel culturista con i capelli rossi della tua band, vero?"

"Rory? No, non è lui."

"Oh, bene. Perché a Tonya piace molto e pensava che la cosa fosse reciproca. Chi è allora? Lo conosco?"

"No, non lo conosci." Faccio un altro respiro profondo. "Le cose sono diventate molto serie tra noi, però."

"Davvero?" Il suo livello di interesse sta chiaramente aumentando. "Serie in che senso?"

Mi preparo al colpo: "Ci sposeremo sabato."

"*Che cosa?*"

Il dado è tratto, così ripeto il più serenamente possibile: "Mi sto per sposare. Questo sabato. E se puoi, mi piacerebbe che ci fossi anche tu."

"È uno scherzo, vero?"

Mi pizzico la punta del naso con la mano libera. "No. Abbiamo deciso di evitare grandi cerimonie formali, quindi inviteremo solo poche persone. Si terrà al Silver Lake Country Club. Sai, a Orland Park."

"Uh-uh. E io parteciperò a *Ballando con le Stelle*."

"Marsha ... non sto scherzando."

Seguono alcuni momenti di imbarazzante silenzio. Poi: "Ti stai per *sposare*?"

"Sì. Questo sabato."

"Che cazzo stai dicendo? Fai sul serio? Quando vi siete conosciuti e come? Come si chiama? Come mai non me ne hai mai parlato?"

"È una lunga storia. Abbiamo avuto una relazione complicata per un po', e poi—"

"Che cosa intendi con *per un po'*? Da quanto? Settimane? Mesi?"

Faccio una smorfia tra me e me. "Uhm, mesi. Mesi, decisamente." Tecnicamente, il prossimo ottobre segnerà due anni da quando Peter mi ha torturata con l'acqua nella mia cucina, ma in termini di tempo reale trascorso insieme, probabilmente è più vicino a sette o otto mesi in totale.

"Wow. Solo... wow." Marsha resta in silenzio per un secondo, poi chiede con tono vagamente ferito: "Perché non hai detto niente? Sai che pensavamo tutti che tu fossi single dopo... beh, lo sai."

"Lo so, mi dispiace. Perché avevamo una relazione complicata, non pensavo che fosse così seria all'inizio. Viaggiava molto per lavoro. Ma ora ha smesso, così abbiamo deciso di fare il passo successivo."

"E sarebbe il *matrimonio*? Perché non continuate a frequentarvi e provate prima a convivere? Sara, tesoro..." La sua voce assume una nota preoccupata. "Che cosa sta succedendo? Va tutto bene?"

Questa è la parte difficile, perché a differenza di Phil e dei miei nuovi colleghi Marsha mi conosce da anni. Sa che sono estremamente cauta, e sa anche che cos'è successo con Peter.

Beh, almeno le parti più oscure.

"Va tutto bene." Metto tutta l'allegria possibile nella mia voce. "Siamo entusiasti di poter finalmente stare insieme e non vediamo alcun motivo per aspettare. Nessuno dei due vuole una grande cerimonia, quindi..."

"Ok, va bene, wow. Non mi hai ancora detto il suo nome o che lavoro fa."

Faccio un respiro profondo. Ci siamo. "Si chiama Peter Garin. Era un consulente per la sicurezza, ma si è appena ritirato da quel campo."

"Peter Garin? Aspetta un attimo..." La voce di Marsha diventa tesa. "Quell'assassino russo che ti ha rapita non si chiamava Peter qualcosa?"

"Sokolov—e per favore, non ne parliamo." Soprattutto perché non voglio mentirle più di quanto devo. "Ad ogni modo, come ti stavo dicendo, sabato celebreremo un piccolo matrimonio, e ci piacerebbe molto se tu potessi partecipare. Ma so che hai detto di avere altri programmi, quindi se non puoi—"

"Oh, per favore, Sara. Ovviamente ci sarò. I fottuti bar possono aspettare. Ma sono ancora confusa. Anche il tuo ragazzo si chiama Peter? E che razza di cognome è Garin? Da dove viene?"

Tamburello le dita sulla scrivania. "Viene da... un po' dappertutto. Ma è nato nell'Europa dell'Est." Non posso mentire su questo; l'accento di Peter, per quanto sia debole, lo indica chiaramente come proveniente da quella parte del mondo.

Dev'essere per questo che ha scelto un cognome dal suono russo, invece di qualcosa come Smith o Johnson.

"Che cosa?" Marsha sembra sul punto di impazzire. "Che zona dell'Europa dell'Est?"

Socchiudo gli occhi. "Russia."

"Mi stai prendendo in giro, vero? Dimmi che stai scherzando."

Apro gli occhi e do un'occhiata all'orologio. Con mio grande sollievo, è quasi l'ora della mia prossima paziente.

"Ascolta, Marsha, devo scappare. Conoscerai Peter sabato e scoprirai tutto su di lui, te lo prometto. Ora devo visitare una paziente."

"Sara, aspetta—"

"Domani ti invierò tutti i dettagli via e-mail" dico e riaggancio, quindi imposto il telefono in modalità silenziosa prima che possa richiamarmi.

Quattro inviti fatti, ne mancano molti altri.

Posso farcela.

Non è così tragica.

ara

È *COSÌ* TRAGICA, DECIDO, QUANDO ESCO DAL LAVORO, DOPO AVER parlato con Rory, Simon, Andy, Tonya e i miei colleghi della clinica durante un'altra cancellazione fortuita. Dopo aver avuto praticamente la stessa conversazione un'altra dozzina di volte, sono sfinita e devo ancora affrontare il grande kahuna stasera.

La cena con i miei genitori.

"Ci penso io" mi ha detto Peter a colazione, quando mi sono offerta di andare a prendere il cibo da asporto tornando dall'ufficio. "Torna a casa in orario e non preoccuparti di niente."

Danny mi sta aspettando sul marciapiede, quando esco dal mio edificio, e alzo gli occhi verso il super-protettore di Peter, mentre salgo in macchina. Stamattina, il tempo era troppo bello per guidare fino al mio ufficio, così Peter mi ha accompagnata al lavoro. E ora ho anche una scorta fino a casa.

Con questo ritmo, dimenticherò che cosa significhi cavarmela da sola.

Impulsivamente, compongo il numero di Peter.

"Ciao, ptichka." La sua voce profonda mi accarezza le orecchie. "Stai tornando a casa?"

"Sono in macchina con Danny." Guardo l'autista, che sta facendo un buon lavoro nel fingere di essere sordo e muto, mentre si immette nella strada. "Lo sapevi già, però, vero?"

"Danny mi ha mandato un messaggio un minuto fa, sì. Com'è stata la tua giornata, amore mio?"

"Molto carina. Ho invitato praticamente tutti quelli che volevo invitare, e Simon è l'unico che non riuscirà a venire. Ha una cena di famiglia in South Carolina."

"Molto bene." Sento un rumore sullo sfondo, seguito dall'acqua corrente, e poi Peter dice: "Aspetta un secondo. Devo solo girare la pasta."

"Stai preparando la cena?" chiedo, quando torna al telefono un minuto dopo.

"Sì, cucina italiana. Ai tuoi genitori piace, vero?"

"La adorano" dico sorridendo. "Sono sicura che rimarranno molto colpiti."

"Intendi dire una volta che supereranno l'impulso di contattare l'FBI? Sì, probabilmente hai ragione. Sta venendo piuttosto gustosa."

Scoppio a ridere, con l'ansia per la cena imminente che si sta trasformando in pura agitazione. Tutto questo sta accadendo per davvero.

Io e Peter stiamo diventando una coppia normale.

"Com'è andata la tua giornata?" chiedo. "Che cos'hai fatto oggi?"

Che cosa *fa* un ex assassino per passare il tempo?

"Ho fatto alcune commissioni, comprato altri generi alimentari e cose del genere" spiega Peter, e posso sentire il caldo sorriso nella sua voce. "Ho anche individuato un paio di case nella zona a cui potremmo dare un'occhiata più in là. Non ho avuto la possibilità di parlartene ieri, ma questo appartamento probabilmente è troppo piccolo per noi—specialmente questa cucina. E se non sbaglio, non ammettono animali domestici, giusto?"

"Esatto. È uno degli aspetti più negativi di questo edificio" dico, con il cuore che mi martella nel petto. Sta succedendo, sta succedendo per davvero. Una vita insieme—casa, cane e tutto il resto. Reprimendo un picco di vertigini, dico: "L'ho scelta perché era vicina sia ai miei genitori che al lavoro, ma non mi dispiacerebbe spostarmi un po' più lontano ora che mamma si è ripresa."

"Lo immaginavo" dice Peter. "Due delle case che ho visto sono vicine, e una è a circa un chilometro e mezzo dal tuo ufficio. Certo, c'è ancora la tua vecchia casa..."

"Te l'hanno restituita?" chiedo, e capisco subito che è una domanda sciocca. Peter non è più un fuggitivo, quindi il governo non ha il diritto legale di mantenere la proprietà che aveva sequestrato, quando ha saputo che gli apparteneva.

"Sì, certo" risponde Peter. "Pensaci e fammi sapere che cosa vuoi farci. Anche se non ci trasferiamo lì, possiamo tenerla per ogni evenienza oppure possiamo venderla. Decidi tu."

"Oh, davvero? E io che pensavo fossi tu a prendere tutte le decisioni" lo stuzzico; poi, mi rendo conto che sto scherzando solo in parte. Ancora una volta, Peter si è insinuato nella mia vita come una tromba d'aria, capovolgendola e sconvolgendo la mia tranquillità. La sua forza di volontà, unita alla spietatezza, rende impossibile fingere che io abbia in qualche modo il controllo del mio destino, che possa davvero dire la mia su dove sta andando la nostra relazione.

Eppure... forse è così. Siamo qui invece di nasconderci in qualche parte remota del mondo, e sto per diventare sua moglie, non la sua prigioniera. Anche se i suoi metodi sono pesanti, Peter ha dimostrato nel modo più chiaro possibile che gli importa di quello che voglio.

Che la mia felicità è importante per lui.

"Intendi per il matrimonio?" chiede Peter, prendendomi in giro a sua volta. "Perché possiamo ancora cambiare alcune cose, se c'è qualcosa che non ti piace."

"Come la data?" chiedo ironicamente. Al suo silenzio, dico: "Non importa. Ho già invitato tutti. Nessun problema."

"Bene, sono contento." Sento un altro rumore in sottofondo, mentre Peter dice: "Ci vediamo a casa tra un paio di minuti, ptichka. Ti amo."

Ti amo anch'io. Le parole sono sulla punta della mia lingua, eppure mi ritrovo a dire: "Ci vediamo presto" mentre riaggancio. Sono sicura che Peter sappia ciò che provo—è sempre stato convinto che siamo fatti l'uno per l'altra—ma dato che non ho mai pronunciato quelle parole, mi sembra sbagliato tirarle fuori casualmente.

Lo amo, però. Posso finalmente ammetterlo a me stessa, anche se nulla è davvero cambiato. È ancora un assassino, ancora un mostro per il quale qualsiasi donna sana di mente proverebbe paura e odio. Ma non sono più sana di mente, perché lo amo e sto per sposarlo.

Di mia spontanea volontà, sto per unirmi a un uomo che una volta mi ha torturata e perseguitata. Che, tecnicamente, continua a perseguitarmi—se l'avermi fatta sempre seguire rientra in quella definizione.

"Eccoci arrivati" dice Danny con voce grave, e guardo fuori dal finestrino, sorpresa nel constatare che siamo già parcheggiati fuori dal mio edificio—e che l'autista dal viso di pietra mi ha davvero parlato.

"Grazie" gli dico, afferrando la borsa, e Danny mi rivolge un leggero cenno con la testa, mentre scendo dalla macchina.

Wow. Facciamo progressi.

Il mio autista/guardia del corpo si è appena accorto di me.

L'agitazione che avevo scacciato riaffiora—almeno fin quando non vedo l'auto dei miei genitori entrare dall'altra parte del parcheggio.

Sono in anticipo.

In anticipo di venti minuti.

Freneticamente, ricompongo il numero di Peter.

"Sono qui" dico senza fiato, quando risponde. "I miei genitori—sono già qui."

"Va bene" dice imperturbabile. "Il cibo è quasi pronto. Ci vediamo tra un minuto."

"Ok, sì." Riaggancio e rimetto il telefono nella borsa. Comincio a far scorrere l'anello sul dito per lasciarlo cadere nella borsa, ma cambio idea.

Non ha senso nascondere qualcosa del genere, quando conosceranno Peter tra un minuto.

Facendo un respiro profondo, mi avvicino alla macchina dei miei genitori. "Ehi, Mamma, Papà."

"Oh, ciao, cara." Mamma apre la portiera e scende con una rigidità minima. "Stai tornando a casa dal lavoro? Scusa, siamo un po' in anticipo; tuo padre pensava che ci sarebbe stato il traffico, così siamo partiti molto prima del previsto."

"*Doveva* esserci il traffico, secondo il GPS" la corregge papà, che gira intorno alla macchina per abbracciarmi.

Lo abbraccio anch'io e poi bacio mamma sulla guancia. "Va tutto bene. La cena è quasi pronta."

Mamma sorride. "Non è cibo da asporto?"

"No, non temere. L'uomo che voglio favi conoscere—sta cucinando." Mi guardo dietro per vedere Danny seduto nella macchina nera, che ci sorveglia in silenzio, per poi rivolgermi nuovamente ai miei genitori. "C'è una cosa che devo dirvi" dico con attenzione.

"Che cosa c'è, tesoro?" Mamma si allunga per toccarmi la mano sinistra, e le dita mi sfiorano l'anello. Immediatamente, il suo sguardo si posa sul diamante, e sgrana gli occhi. "Sara, quello è—"

"Stavo per arrivarci" dico, mentre mio padre si blocca, fissando incredulo il mio anulare sinistro. "Ho delle ottime notizie."

"Sei fidanzata?" Mamma distoglie lo sguardo dalla pietra lucente per guardarmi. "Come? Con chi? Non stavi nemmeno—"

"Mamma, Papà." Prendo ciascuna delle loro mani in una delle mie. "Vi prego, ascoltatemi e cercate di rimanere calmi." Si bloccano, fissandomi come se fossi un marziano, mentre dico fermamente: "Peter, l'uomo che amo, è tornato. Finalmente è riuscito a chiarire il malinteso con le autorità, e non è più ricercato per essere interrogato. Possiamo finalmente stare insieme—e sì, ci siamo fidanzati."

5 6

GUARDO DI NUOVO FUORI DALLA FINESTRA, DOVE SARA STA parlando con i suoi genitori nel parcheggio. Lo stanno facendo da almeno otto minuti, e vorrei aver messo un dispositivo di ascolto su Sara, in modo da poter sentire che cosa si stanno dicendo.

A giudicare dal selvaggio gesticolare di tutti e tre, le emozioni in gioco sono molte.

Forse dovrei piantare un bug con capacità di ascolto su Sara. Forse anche più di uno—uno nel telefono, uno nella borsa, e un altro paio nelle sue calzature preferite. Ho già monitorato il suo telefono, quindi so dove si trova in ogni momento, ma questo mi darebbe una maggiore tranquillità.

La tavola è apparecchiata, ma non ho ancora portato il cibo. Infine, l'app che monitora Sara sul telefono mi informa che il suo telefono è nell'edificio e che si sta avvicinando all'appartamento, così vado ad aprire la porta per lei e i suoi genitori.

"Mamma, Papà, questo è Peter" dice, mentre l'anziana coppia entra dietro di lei e si ferma, osservandomi con circospezione. "Come ho spiegato, ha dato un taglio netto alle sue vecchie connessioni e ora si fa chiamare Peter Garin. Peter, questi sono i miei genitori, Lorna e Chuck Weisman."

"Piacere di conoscervi entrambi" dico, e allungo la mano per stringere quella del padre di Sara.

"Piacere mio." Nonostante la cortese risposta, la voce di Chuck è dura come la sua presa, e gli occhi azzurro chiaro sono affilati, mentre mi fissa.

Stringo la mano di Lorna, facendo attenzione a non schiacciarle le fragili dita.

"Hai un sacco di spiegazioni da darci, *Signor Garin*" dice dolcemente, guardandomi, e sorrido, scorgendo qualche tratto di Sara nelle linee eleganti del suo viso invecchiato.

"Naturalmente. Sarò felice di spiegare tutto."

"La cena è pronta, quindi che ne dite di sederci al tavolo?" suggerisce Sara, sedendosi accanto a me, e il calore mi riempie il petto, mentre il suo braccio slanciato scivola intorno al mio gomito per un gesto possessivo.

La mia ptichka. Alla fine, ci ha accettati come coppia.

"Certo. Qualunque cosa tu stia cucinando, ha un buon profumo" dice Lorna, e le sorrido di nuovo, rendendomi conto che la madre di Sara, perlomeno, è disposta a stare al gioco.

Quando arriviamo in cucina, Sara si scusa per andare in bagno, e io metto l'insalata e il piatto di antipasti che ho preparato sul tavolo.

"Sara ha detto che ti piace cucinare" dice Lorna, osservandomi mentre mi muovo per la cucina, e annuisco, sedendomi di fronte a lei.

"È un mio hobby. Lo trovo molto rilassante."

"Un hobby, eh?" Il cipiglio di Chuck si fa più evidente. "Che lavoro fai, allora? Non siamo mai riusciti ad ottenere una risposta diretta da Sara."

"Ho fatto diverse cose, ma recentemente ho lavorato come consulente per la sicurezza e ho avuto un'attività del genere" dico e mi alzo. Raccogliendo le pinze per l'insalata, guardo Lorna. "Insalata?"

Annuisce regalmente. "Sì, per favore."

Mi allungo sul tavolo e metto una porzione consistente di insalata nel suo piatto, poi guardo Chuck.

"Niente per me, grazie." Infilza un carciofo marinato con la forchetta e lo trasferisce dal piatto degli antipasti nel suo, guardandomi minacciosamente per tutto il tempo.

"Che genere di attività?" chiede non appena mi risiedo. "Sara ha detto che eri una specie di consulente. Si trattava di un'attività di consulenza per la sicurezza? Chi erano i tuoi clienti, e in che modo tutto questo è legato ai tuoi recenti problemi con la legge?"

Sopprimo l'impulso di sorridere. Il vecchio è insistente.

"Facevo parte degli Spetsnaz—le Forze Speciali Russe" dico, decidendo che posso rivelarlo. "Dopo aver lasciato l'esercito, ho viaggiato in tutto il mondo e ho fatto da consulente a un certo numero di organizzazioni e individui che avevano motivi di preoccuparsi per la sicurezza. Non posso spiegare nel dettaglio che cosa mi ha messo nei guai, dato che sono informazioni riservate, ma posso assicurarvi che è tutto risolto ora."

"Risolto come?" chiede Lorna, mentre Sara torna in cucina, e sorrido, quando la mia ptichka si siede accanto a me e cerca con impazienza l'insalata.

"Ho stretto un accordo con le autorità, che è stato vantaggioso per entrambe le parti" dico, mentre Sara inizia a mangiare, apparentemente contenta di vedermi rispondere alle domande dei suoi genitori. "Quindi, ora ho un nuovo cognome e una fedina pulita—e io e Sara potremo finalmente sposarci."

"Una fedina pulita da cosa?" chiede il padre di Sara,

dilatando le narici. "Ho sentito dire che alcune persone sono state uccise."

"Non posso aggiungere niente di più di quello che sai già, temo." Metto un po' di insalata nel mio piatto. "Fa parte dell'accordo che ho stretto."

Chuck avvampa, e per un attimo sono convinto che mi pugnalerà con la forchetta. Tuttavia, dev'essere più civile di me, perché l'unica cosa che infilza è una succosa oliva verde dal piatto degli antipasti.

"Signor Garin" dice Lorna, posando la forchetta. "Spero che—"

"Ti prego, chiamami Peter. Stiamo per diventare una famiglia."

La sua bocca accuratamente dipinta si stringe leggermente. "Ok, *Peter*. Spero che tu capisca che siamo molto preoccupati, sia per quanto riguarda il tuo background che per quanto riguarda le tue connessioni. Per non parlare del fatto che Sara è scomparsa per cinque mesi dopo che voi due... Beh—"

"Abbiamo iniziato a frequentarci?" suggerisce cortesemente Sara, e sua madre la guarda accigliata.

"Giusto, avete iniziato a frequentarvi." Lorna rivolge la sua attenzione a me, e riconosco l'acciaio dentro di lei. È lo stesso che possiede sua figlia, quello che ha permesso alla mia ptichka di gestire il tipo di trauma che avrebbe distrutto una persona più debole.

"Ascoltami, Peter." La madre di Sara si sporge in avanti, e sebbene la sua voce rimanga dolce, lo sguardo è affilato come quello del marito. "Potresti aver risolto il tuo 'malinteso' con le autorità, ma non siamo convinti che tu non rappresenti un pericolo per nostra figlia. Non sappiamo nulla di te, e quello che sappiamo è, francamente, abbastanza inquietante. Sara dice che voi due siete innamorati, e che è venuta con te di propria iniziativa, ma abbiamo seri dubbi al riguardo. Non sei il tipo di uomo che la nostra Sara avrebbe mai—"

"Mamma, per favore." Sara mette da parte il piatto. "Ti ho detto più volte che Peter non è quello che—"

"I tuoi genitori hanno ragione, ptichka." Le copro la mano con il palmo e stringo leggermente, poi mi volto verso sua madre. "Signora Weisman" dico, utilizzando quel formalismo in segno di rispetto. "Comprendo perfettamente le tue riserve. Se fossi in te, sarei altrettanto preoccupato, perché hai perfettamente ragione: tua figlia e io proveniamo da mondi diversi."

Lorna e Chuck mi fissano, ovviamente sbalorditi, e sfrutto quel momento per preparare quello che dirò. Devo stare molto attento qui, stabilendo una linea sottile tra lasciarli sentire come se mi conoscessero e terrorizzarli.

Decido di cominciare dall'inizio. "Sono cresciuto in un orfanotrofio della Russia" dico. "Non ho idea di chi fossero i miei genitori, ma sono quasi certo che non fossero affatto come voi due. Molto probabilmente, mia madre era un'adolescente che si ritrovò incinta, ma questa è pura illazione da parte mia. Tutto quello che so è che venni lasciato sulla porta dell'orfanotrofio, quando avevo forse qualche giorno."

Sara copre le nostre mani unite con quella libera, offrendomi silenziosamente il supporto, mentre continuo.

"Non era un gran bel posto dove crescere, e da giovane ero sempre nei guai" dico, mentre i Weisman continuano a fissarmi. "Tuttavia, a diciassette anni, venni reclutato da una speciale unità di antiterrorismo degli Spetsnaz—servendo il mio Paese per diversi anni."

"Era davvero bravo in questo" interviene Sara, sembrando orgogliosa come qualsiasi fidanzata. "A ventun anni, era già a capo della sua squadra."

Le sorrido, con il calore nel mio petto che si intensifica, anche se so che sta recitando per i genitori. Sara sa che cos'ho fatto come parte di quell'unità, e dubito che sia davvero orgogliosa di quanti terroristi e ribelli radicali io abbia catturato e torturato per il mio Paese. Comunque sia, è bello avere la sua approvazione, per quanto falsa possa essere.

"È *straordinario*" dice Lorna, e mi giro per vedere lei e Chuck che mi guardano con un leggero calo di ostilità.

"Grazie" dico, sorridendo. "*Ero* bravo, in parte grazie alla mia mancata gioventù."

"Allora, perché te ne sei andato?" chiede Chuck, allungandosi per infilzare un'altra oliva. "Come sei finito qui?"

Il mio umore si fa scuro, con il calore dentro di me che si dissolve, nonostante il continuo tocco delicato di Sara. Non sapevo se avrei affrontato questo—se potessi farlo—ma ora vedo che devo farlo, che se tralasciassi questa parte importante, i Weisman lo percepirebbero e perderei la possibilità di ottenere la loro fiducia.

"Dopo alcuni anni di servizio, il lavoro mi portò in un piccolo villaggio di montagna nel Daghestan, dove conobbi una giovane donna" dico in modo uniforme, tirando via la mano dalla stretta di Sara. "Rimase incinta, e ci sposammo."

Lorna strabuzza gli occhi. "Hai un figlio?"

"Ce l'avevo" dico, e nonostante i miei migliori sforzi, la parola viene fuori dura, quasi amara. "Pasha, mio figlio, e Tamila, mia moglie, furono uccisi sette anni fa. Daryevo, il villaggio in cui vivevano, fu ritenuto erroneamente il nascondiglio dei terroristi, e decine di innocenti rimasero uccisi in un attacco ordinato dalla NATO."

I genitori di Sara mi guardano a bocca aperta, con i volti pallidi e gli occhi carichi di incredulità.

"Non capisco" dice Chuck dopo un lungo, pesante momento. "Com'è potuta succedere una cosa del genere? E questo gravissimo e orribile errore non sarebbe dovuto finire nelle notizie? Quello che stai dicendo è..." Scuote la testa e prende un bicchiere d'acqua con una mano tremante.

"È difficile da credere, lo so, Papà" dice Sara. "Ma posso

assicurarti che è vero. Ho visto le foto con i miei occhi. È successo, ed è stato *orribile*."

Lorna fissa sua figlia, poi si volta verso di me. "Mi dispiace tanto, Peter." La sua voce si addolcisce ulteriormente per qualsiasi cosa debba aver scorto sul mio viso. "Quanti anni aveva tuo figlio?"

"Ne avrebbe compiuti tre il mese seguente." Un'ondata di angoscia mi soffoca, e mi alzo, incapace di guardare i genitori di Sara. Camminando verso i fornelli, prendo la pentola di pasta e la porto a tavola, sfruttando quel tempo per ricompormi.

"Spero che vi piaccia questo tipo di sugo alla marinara" dico con tono più calmo, mettendo una porzione consistente di linguine al sugo sul piatto di Sara, prima di fare lo stesso con i suoi genitori. "È un po' diverso da quello che comprereste al negozio."

La madre di Sara avvolge la forchetta nelle linguine e assaggia un boccone, poi mi rivolge un sorriso tremante. "È buonissimo, Peter. Grazie."

"Prego."

Sento la mano delicata di Sara sul mio ginocchio, che mi stringe leggermente, e quando la guardo, vedo che i suoi occhi nocciola sono troppo luminosi. Non dice nulla, ma il calore riaffiora, sciogliendo il blocco di ghiaccio che si è formato dentro di me rievocando i ricordi.

Il padre di Sara si schiarisce la voce. "Allora, uhm... come sei finito qui? Dopo, lo sai."

Riprendo fiato. Devo fare attenzione a non rivelare troppo.

"C'è stata un'indagine" dico, incrociando lo sguardo di Chuck. "Una che ha portato il colpevole ad essere ufficialmente assolto dalla colpa e l'intero incidente è stato liquidato come 'una di quelle cose che accadono in quella parte del mondo.' Non ho accettato questa spiegazione, e poiché i miei superiori erano complici nella copertura, ho lasciato il mio lavoro. Così, ho viaggiato per il mondo, lavorando come consulente per la sicurezza, e alla fine sono finito a Chicago, dove ho conosciuto vostra figlia."

"Come sei finito nei guai con le autorità, allora?" chiede Lorna, guardandomi con cautela mista ad un accenno di comprensione. "Ha qualcosa a che fare con quello che è successo alla tua famiglia?"

"Temo di non poterlo dire. Come ho detto prima, sono informazioni riservate." Faccio una pausa, lasciando che traggano le proprie conclusioni, e quando non mi vengono immediatamente rivolte altre domande, li guardo negli occhi e dico sottovoce: "Lorna, Chuck—spero di potervi chiamare così." Lorna annuisce, così continuo. "Non posso mentirvi sul tipo di uomo che sono. Non sono cresciuto in un bel quartiere, e non sono andato a scuola per diventare medico o avvocato. Sono un soldato per addestramento e inclinazione, e ho visto e fatto cose che probabilmente non immaginate. Ma amo vostra figlia. La amo con tutto me stesso. È l'unica persona al mondo che conta per me, e farei qualsiasi cosa per lei." Guardando Sara, le prendo la mano nella mia e dico in tutta sincerità: "Darei la mia vita per renderla felice."

Sara

NON AVEVO IDEA DI COME SAREBBE FINITA LA CENA, MA L'ULTIMA cosa che mi aspettavo era che Peter svuotasse la propria anima ai miei genitori, disarmandoli con la sincerità, invece di schiacciare le loro obiezioni con arroganza e minacce velate.

Per tutto il resto della cena, è educato e rispettoso, rispondendo alle loro domande con abbastanza dettagli che quando glissa su qualcosa, continua a sembrare la completa verità.

Dove ci siamo conosciuti? In un club a Chicago. Era già un fuggitivo? Sì. Perché ci siamo frequentati in segreto? Per via del suo status di fuggitivo, di cui non mi ha informata fin quando non fossi già sull'aereo con lui. Perché non sono tornata a casa per cinque mesi? Perché le autorità hanno scoperto dov'era, e quello era l'unico modo per stare insieme. Che cos'ha intenzione di fare ora? Ci sta ancora pensando, ma ha abbastanza soldi per entrambi e per permetterci di vivere il resto della nostra vita. Come ha fatto così tanti soldi? Attraverso la sua attività di consulenza, e sì, anche i dettagli di questo sono riservati.

All'inizio, ascolto soltanto, ma quando capisco meglio la sua strategia, mi inserisco con le mie risposte, seguendo attentamente la guida di Peter. Quando arriviamo al dessert—piattini con frutti di bosco conditi con tiramisù fatto in casa—i miei genitori appaiono, se non esattamente a proprio agio con la nostra relazione, almeno più disponibili.

Questo è sicuramente meglio della loro reazione di puro panico, quando li ho informati del nostro fidanzamento nel parcheggio. Erano sul punto di chiamare l'FBI, quando ho detto che il nostro matrimonio si sarebbe tenuto sabato, e ho dovuto davvero sforzarmi per convincerli ad entrare in casa e conoscere Peter.

"Ancora non capisco tutta questa fretta di sposarvi" dice mamma, sorseggiando la camomilla, e nascondo un sorriso per la rassegnazione nel suo tono. Almeno, ora l'argomento è la velocità del matrimonio, non quanto sia pericoloso Peter o lo stare insieme o meno.

"Questa è una mia iniziativa, temo" dice Peter, rivolgendo a mamma un sorriso così affascinante che mi sorprende che lei non si sciolga sul posto. "Mi mancava così tanto tua figlia che gliel'ho proposto non appena siamo tornati insieme. Vedi, la vita è troppo breve; quando trovi la persona giusta, devi tenertela stretta—e so che io e Sara siamo fatti l'uno per l'altra. Inoltre"—mi scruta, con lo sguardo che si scalda—"vorrei che creassimo presto una famiglia."

Mio padre fa quasi rovesciare la sua tazza di caffè. "Che cosa?"

Peter gli porge un tovagliolo. "Mi piacerebbe che avessimo dei bambini" dice con calma, mentre mio padre asciuga il liquido caduto. "Un maschietto e una femminuccia—o qualunque cosa il destino abbia in serbo per noi."

Arrossisco, quando lo sguardo di mamma si sofferma istantaneamente sulla mia pancia.

"Sara, tesoro, non sei—"

"No, certo che no." Sento il mio viso arrossire ulteriormente, mentre mamma solleva le sopracciglia con incredulità. "È troppo presto—Peter è appena tornato."

"Ma ci state già provando?" chiede mamma, con un bel sorriso sul viso, e, con mio grande stupore, mi rendo conto che è contenta di questo sviluppo.

L'impulso primario di avere dei nipotini deve aver avuto la meglio sulle preoccupazioni riguardo a Peter.

Papà, invece, sembra a disagio come mi sento io. "Lorna, per favore. Questi non sono affari nostri."

"Non appena rimarrà incinta, sarai la prima a saperlo" prometto a mia madre, e lei mi sorprende di nuovo annuendo in modo cospiratorio.

"Grazie." Abbassando la voce, si china verso il mio ex rapitore. "Pensavo che non sarebbe mai successo."

Il mio viso dev'essere dello stesso colore dei lamponi nel piattino, ma mio padre sembra affascinato. Immagino che stia pensando che tutto questo—dall'inaspettato ritorno del mio amante non-più-criminale al nostro frettoloso fidanzamento— fa ben sperare per qualcosa che desiderava sin dal mio matrimonio con George.

Come mamma, vuole dei nipotini, ma data la sua età avanzata, aveva quasi perso la speranza di vederne.

Da parte mia, sono ancora piuttosto terrorizzata all'idea, ma non è questo il momento di esprimere questi dubbi. Inoltre, ricordo come mi sono sentita, quando il ciclo era in ritardo, come la delusione fosse intensa quasi quanto il dolore. Forse *voglio* un figlio con Peter, anche se la parte razionale di me sta urlando che dovremmo aspettare e vedere come tutto questo andrà avanti.

Se posso davvero costruire una vita normale con un killer spietato.

Mentre finiamo il dessert, Peter discute i dettagli del matrimonio imminente con i miei genitori, chiedendo loro delle formalità ufficiali e di quante persone vorrebbero invitare. Ascolto confusa, mentre i tre decidono un giudice locale che mio padre conosce, e i miei genitori esprimono il desiderio di invitare i Levinson insieme ad alcuni loro amici—cosa che Peter appoggia molto.

"Per quanto riguarda me, inviterò solo tre amici" dice, riferendosi indubbiamente ai compagni di squadra russi, e questo sembra calmare i miei genitori un po' di più— probabilmente perché il fatto che abbia degli amici lo umanizza ulteriormente ai loro occhi.

Quando terminiamo, Peter inizia a sparecchiare, mentre i miei genitori si preparano per tornare a casa.

"Grazie. È stato delizioso" gli dice mamma.

"Sì, grazie" le fa eco a malincuore papà, mentre il mio fidanzato sorride.

"È stato un piacere. Spero di rivedervi presto" dice lui, e infilo le scarpe per accompagnare i miei genitori alla loro auto.

"Beh, non era quello che mi aspettavo" dice mamma, mentre le porte dell'ascensore si chiudono. "È... interessante, questo tuo Peter."

Le sorrido. "Vuoi dire, stupendo *e* civile? Sì, sono d'accordo."

Papà sbuffa. "Se quell'uomo è civile, io sono un principe. È un selvaggio. Senza alcun dubbio."

"Chuck!" Mamma lo guarda accigliata.

"Non hai visto come la guardava?" continua papà, mentre le porte dell'ascensore si aprono al primo piano. "Sono sorpreso che non l'abbia colpita alla testa e trascinata a letto davanti a noi."

"Papà, per favore." Il rossore che mi aveva appena lasciata riaffiora, ingrandito di dieci volte. "Non è—"

"Beh, certo che l'ho visto" dice mamma, come se io non esistessi. "Non è necessariamente una brutta cosa, però."

"Lo è, quando hai a che fare con un uomo come quello." Papà si guarda le spalle, come se Peter potesse ascoltare—cosa che, conoscendo le sue tendenze da stalker, non è da escludere.

Per quanto ne so, ci sono già delle telecamere nell'edificio e chissà che cos'ha impiantato dentro di me.

"Non penso che sia così male" dice mamma, mentre passiamo davanti a un paio di vicini nell'atrio. "Voglio dire, sì, non è il solito Joe o Harry, ma—"

"È pericoloso" dice papà con tono piatto. "Non lasciarti ingannare. Solo perché quell'uomo vuole una famiglia, questo non significa che non sia capace di cose che ti farebbero accapponare la pelle. Quello che ci ha detto oggi è solo la punta dell'iceberg, credimi."

"Oh, ti credo" dice mamma, mentre ci dirigiamo verso il parcheggio. "Ma credo che la ami, e se tutti quei problemi con l'FBI sono davvero finiti—"

"Non potete aspettare due minuti, in modo da poter discutere di me in terza persona, quando *non* ci sono?" suggerisco, seguendoli. "Altrimenti, posso tornare su e—"

"No, no, tesoro." Mamma si ferma e si gira, rivolgendomi un'occhiata apologetica. "Scusa, stiamo solo cercando di venire a patti con tutto, sai."

"Sì, Mamma." Sorrido e mi chino per baciarle la morbida guancia. "Stavo solo scherzando. So che questo richiederà qualche discussione."

"Sara, tesoro." Papà mi tocca la spalla, e, quando lo guardo, dice con calma: "Promettici solo una cosa."

"Che cosa?"

"Se ti fa del male, ti spaventa, o fa qualsiasi altra cosa che ti preoccupa, vieni da noi. Non nasconderlo e non provare ad affrontarlo da sola, ok?" Lo sguardo di papà è duro come non mai. "So che ami quest'uomo—lo vedo—ma il lupo non perde il vizio. È pericoloso. Forse non per te, ma per tutti gli altri. Lo vedo nei suoi occhi."

"Papà—"

"No, ascoltami, Sara. Anche se non porta gli orrori del suo passato nella tua vita—cosa di cui dubito molto—non sarà come George, contento di rimanere ai margini della tua vita. Non è quel genere di uomo, capisci?"

"Sì." Capisco meglio di quanto possa immaginare mio padre, perché so esattamente che genere di uomo è Peter. Con George, anche quando eravamo una coppia, riuscivo a rimanere me stessa, a mantenere quel minimo di distanza mentale necessaria per proteggermi. Ma Peter è troppo dominante, troppo autoritario per permetterlo. Sarò sua in ogni senso della parola, e mio padre lo ha già intuito.

"Chuck." Mamma poggia la mano sul braccio di papà. "Vieni. Dovremmo andare."

"Promettimelo" insiste papà, senza muoversi, così annuisco e sorrido.

"Te lo prometto, Papà. Se succede qualcosa, verrò da te."

Papà annuisce, soddisfatto, e camminiamo insieme verso la loro macchina. Mentre li bacio e li abbraccio, noto che Danny è ancora seduto nella sua macchina scura, e sorrido, guardando la finestra illuminata della mia cucina.

Nonostante tutti i loro avvertimenti e ammonimenti, i miei genitori non hanno idea di quanto sia davvero pericoloso e autoritario il mio fidanzato. Ho mentito, quando ho fatto quella promessa a papà. Non c'è modo che io possa riportare a loro le preoccupazioni su Peter, perché non c'è niente che loro, o chiunque altro, possano fare.

Il mostro che ho imparato ad amare fa parte della mia vita ora, e sarà così per sempre, quindi devo capire come poter vivere con lui.

 ara

VENERDÌ VADO AL LAVORO COME AL SOLITO, MA FINISCO COL passare ogni minuto tra le pazienti a rispondere alle domande dei colleghi sul mio imminente matrimonio. Per evitare di sembrare impreparata riguardo all'evento come lo sono realmente, dico loro che vogliamo che i dettagli siano una sorpresa e non aggiungo altro.

Vedranno i fiori, la torta e l'abito domani.

Anche i miei genitori continuano a telefonare, chiedendo di ogni genere di minuzie a cui non so rispondere. Do loro il numero di Peter, dato che è il wedding planner ufficiale, ma mia madre continua a chiamare ogni ora con qualche domanda o preoccupazione. Sospetto che sia perché temono che io sparisca di nuovo, così cerco di essere paziente, ma alla quinta chiamata non posso fare a meno di sollevare il telefono e spiegare per l'ennesima volta che non so se ci saranno sedie o panche alla cerimonia.

Inoltre, è una giornata impegnativa al lavoro, con un cesareo per una gravidanza gemellare programmato per questo pomeriggio, il che significa che ho appena il tempo di pranzare prima di recarmi in ospedale per eseguire la procedura. Per accelerare le cose, acquisto un panino in un minimarket e lo consumo in macchina.

Il vantaggio di avere un autista è quello di avere entrambe le mani libere per mangiare.

Quando arrivo in sala operatoria, la paziente ha già fatto l'epidurale e, dopo averla esaminata, eseguo subito la procedura, poiché sta iniziando a dilatarsi e uno dei gemelli è posizionato nel modo sbagliato. La futura mamma si agita per tutto il tempo—è sulla quarantina ed è riuscita a concepire solo al sesto ciclo di fecondazione in vitro—e quando le metto i due bimbi piccoli ma perfettamente sani tra le braccia, il suo viso si illumina di una tale gioia che devo sbattere le palpebre per trattenere qualche lacrima.

"Grazie, Dottoressa Cobakis" dice con fervore, mentre le infermiere prendono i neonati per gli esami. "Grazie mille per tutto."

"È stato un piacere, credimi" le dico, mentre controllo le bende un'ultima volta e annoto alcuni appunti nella sua cartella. "Dopo la procedura, sono previsti un po' di dolore e sanguinamento, ma se ti viene la febbre o hai dei forti dolori, chiamami, ok?" La guardo con severità. "Dico davvero. A qualsiasi ora del giorno o della notte."

"Lo farò. Sei così gentile." Il suo sorriso lacrimoso è esausto, ma carico di gioia. "È vero quello che ho sentito dire dalle infermiere? Ti sposerai questo fine settimana?"

Le voci viaggiano sicuramente in fretta.

Soffocando un sospiro, dico: "Sì, è vero. Ma puoi chiamarmi lo stesso. Ci sarò, ok?"

"Oh, grazie! E congratulazioni. Sono sicura che sarai una bellissima sposa." Mi sorride, e sorrido a mia volta, godendomi la facile interazione.

A differenza di tutti gli altri nella mia vita, questa donna non sa che questo matrimonio sta venendo fuori dal nulla o che sto sposando un uomo che la maggior parte dei miei amici non conosce nemmeno.

"Riposati e goditi i tuoi figli" dico alla neomamma, e poi torno in ufficio per concludere la giornata.

Forse Peter ha ragione a non volerlo rimandare più di quanto non sia necessario.

Con un po' di fortuna, la follia matrimoniale sarà finita entro lunedì, e poi le cose torneranno alla normalità—o almeno alla normalità che può esserci, quando sei sposata con l'uomo che una volta ti ha rapita.

CONCEDO UNA SERATA LIBERA A DANNY E VADO A PRENDERE Sara, troppo ansioso di vederla per aspettare i pochi minuti extra necessari prima che torni a casa. Sono contento che stasera non faccia volontariato in clinica, né abbia una performance, perché già le ore che passa al lavoro sono troppe per me.

Ho bisogno di averla con me. Sempre.

Esce dal palazzo del suo ufficio, con gli occhi color nocciola che scrutano la strada—senza dubbio, alla ricerca di Danny—quando apro la portiera della macchina e scendo.

Il suo sguardo si sposta immediatamente su di me, e un sorriso le illumina il bel viso, mentre si dirige verso di me. È una calda giornata estiva, e indossa un vestito grigio senza maniche che le abbraccia il fisico da ballerina. Le sue lucenti onde castane ricadono sulle esili spalle, mentre cammina, e mi ricorda nuovamente una star di Hollywood degli anni Cinquanta trapiantata nei tempi moderni.

La mia bellissima ptichka.

Non vedo l'ora che diventi mia moglie, cazzo.

"Ciao" dice senza fiato, fermandosi davanti a me. "Hai comprato una macchina nuova? Non sapevo che fosse—"

Le prendo il viso tra i palmi e sbatto la bocca sulla sua, baciandola appassionatamente. Non posso farci niente. Desidero tutto di lei, dalla dolcezza del suo profumo al modo in cui il corpo snello si inarca contro il mio, con le mani che si aggrappano impotenti ai bicipiti. Voglio divorare quella dolcezza, berla fino a spegnere questa sete furiosa—pur sapendo che non riuscirò mai a spegnerla.

La desidererò fino al giorno della mia morte.

Sento qualche irritante risatina, così sollevo la testa e inchiodo i trasgressori—un paio di ragazze adolescenti a una decina di metri di distanza—con uno sguardo severo. Si allontanano all'istante, impallidendo sotto il pesante strato di trucco, e rivolgo la mia attenzione a Sara, che sta sbattendo le palpebre verso di me, con le labbra morbide gonfie e rosa per quel bacio.

"Ciao, ptichka." Combattendo l'impulso di reclamare quelle labbra, abbasso le mani sulle sue spalle, stringendole delicatamente. "Com'è andata la tua giornata?"

"È andata bene." Sembra ancora un po' senza fiato. "E la tua?"

"Bene anche la mia. Ho acquistato questa nuova macchina per noi." Faccio un cenno con la testa verso la Mercedes S-560 nera dietro di me. A prima vista, assomiglia a qualsiasi altra berlina di lusso. Un'ispezione più ravvicinata, tuttavia, rivelerebbe che i finestrini hanno un vetro antiproiettile e che il telaio metallico è insolitamente resistente.

Mi è costata una fortuna, ma ne è valsa la pena. Non mi aspetto che qualcuno ci spari, ma non si sa mai. Inoltre, questa macchina è praticamente indistruttibile in caso di incidente—il che è molto importante per me, dopo quello che è successo con Sara a Cipro.

"Carina" dice lei, anche se un piccolo cipiglio si forma tra le sopracciglia. "E la mia vecchia Toyota?"

"L'ho venduta."

Si libera della mia presa, con il cipiglio ancora più evidente. "Non hai pensato di consultarmi?"

Sono tentato di prenderla e baciarla di nuovo fino a farle dimenticare il motivo dell'arrabbiatura. Tuttavia, abbiamo già dato spettacolo per i passanti, così chiedo semplicemente: "Eri affezionata a quella macchina, amore mio? Posso riprenderla, se ha qualche valore affettivo."

Non sembra funzionare neanche questo. "No, non mi interessa la macchina. È solo che..." Raddrizza le spalle e mi guarda negli occhi. "Peter, ho bisogno che tu mi coinvolga nelle decisioni che mi riguardano—che riguardano entrambi. Una volta mi hai detto che questa avrebbe potuto essere una collaborazione tra noi, se l'avessi voluto, e ora lo voglio. È importante per me."

Rifletto sulle sue parole e annuisco. "D'accordo."

Sbatte le palpebre. "D'accordo?"

"Ti consulterò, prima di fare qualsiasi altra cosa con la macchina" dico e apro la portiera del passeggero. Stringendole il gomito, la aiuto a salire, con i miei jeans che sembrano scomodamente stretti, mentre intravedo un pezzo di mutandina blu, quando infila in macchina le gambe formose.

Forse dovremmo riconsiderare questo vestito come elemento del suo guardaroba da lavoro.

"Non sto parlando solo della macchina" dice, quando mi metto al volante. "Mi riferisco a tutto, come gli accordi di matrimonio, dove vivremo e cosa farai dal punto di vista lavorativo. Voglio che prendiamo tutte quelle decisioni insieme d'ora in poi, come ogni normale coppia sposata."

"Capisco." Controllo attentamente gli specchietti e mi

immetto nella strada. "Vuoi che ti consulti come dovrebbe fare un marito. Capisco."

"Sì?" Per qualche ragione, sembra perplessa. "Pensavo che— non importa. Sono contenta che tu abbia capito."

Sorrido e poso la mano destra sulla sua esile coscia, godendomi la pelle nuda e vellutata. Se la mia ptichka vuole che la consulti riguardo a queste banalità come l'auto o cosa farò del mio tempo, sono felice di farlo.

Possiamo prendere tutte le decisioni insieme, purché capisca una semplice cosa.

Mi appartiene per il resto della nostra vita.

 eter

Sabato mattina è caldo e luminoso, con il cielo azzurro e senza nuvole che avrei ordinato da un catalogo di matrimoni, se avessi potuto. Il tempo era l'unica variabile incontrollabile, ma per fortuna sta collaborando, quindi l'evento dovrebbe svolgersi senza intoppi.

Me ne sono assicurato.

Organizzare un matrimonio non è poi così diverso dalla pianificazione di un colpo, mi sono reso conto. Si dev'essere altrettanto metodici sulla logistica e preparati a tutte le eventualità. Certo, la posta in gioco è molto diversa, ma è bello vedere che alcune delle mie capacità sono applicabili alla vita civile.

Esguerra si sbagliava.

Farò funzionare tutto questo.

Io e Sara saremo felici qui.

I suoi appuntamenti per i capelli e il trucco sono alle dieci, e l'ho sfinita la scorsa notte, così la lascio dormire, mentre preparo la colazione. Poi, torno in camera con una tazza di caffè fumante tra le mani.

O mi sente o le arriva il profumo del caffè, perché si gira sulla schiena, allungando un esile braccio sul materasso, mentre stringe l'altra mano in un delicato pugno per coprire un grande sbadiglio. "È mattina?" borbotta senza aprire gli occhi, e sorrido, mentre mi siedo sul bordo del letto e poggio la tazza di caffè sul comodino.

"Sì, amore mio." Chinandomi, le strofino la calda, profumata curva del collo. "È il giorno del nostro matrimonio."

I suoi capelli hanno un profumo dolce e di frutta, come lo shampoo nella doccia. Mi fa venire l'acquolina in bocca. Spontaneamente, la mia mano scivola sotto la coperta, afferrandole un seno morbido e rotondo, e il cazzo si indurisce, con il respiro che accelera, mentre il capezzolo eretto mi pugnala il palmo.

Fanculo. Non c'è tempo per questo—per non parlare del fatto che potrebbe essere ancora dolorante per le tre volte in cui l'ho presa la scorsa notte.

Mi sforzo di raddrizzarmi e sposto la mano. "La tua colazione è pronta" dico e mi alzo, sistemando lo scomodo rigonfiamento nei jeans. Ho bisogno di sbollentarmi per non aggredirla proprio qui, mandando al diavolo la colazione e gli appuntamenti di nozze.

"Hmm." Sbadiglia di nuovo e si mette a sedere, sollevando una coperta per coprire quei seni allettanti. Strofinando gli occhi assonnati, si concentra sulla tazza appoggiata sul comodino. "È un caffè?"

"Ci puoi scommettere. E c'è la colazione in cucina—uno sformato di verdure e patatine fritte. Avrai bisogno di carburante per affrontare la giornata."

Mi sorride. "Sei fantastico."

Mi si stringe il cuore—e il cazzo si agita di nuovo—mentre balza giù dal letto nuda e si dirige verso il bagno, apparentemente rinvigorita dalla promessa di caffeina e cibo. Questo è quello che volevo, quello per cui ho combattuto per tutto questo tempo: vedere Sara così, vivace e affettuosa con me. Non riusciremo mai a cancellare l'oscurità del passato, ma insieme possiamo costruire un futuro più leggero.

Un futuro che per qualche ragione sembra ancora terribilmente fragile.

Scaccio il pensiero non appena affiora. Non c'è motivo di supporre che questo tipo di mattinata sia temporaneo, che sia qualcosa di diverso dall'inizio della nostra nuova vita.

Oggi è il giorno del nostro matrimonio, e mi assicurerò che sia il migliore di sempre.

È il minimo che la mia ptichka meriti, dopo tutto quello che ho fatto.

 ara

L'invasione ha inizio proprio mentre sto finendo di divorare la colazione che Peter ha preparato per me. Quello che sembra un esercito di stilisti, truccatori e parrucchieri irrompe nel mio minuscolo appartamento, riempiendo il soggiorno con prodotti per capelli, borse e ombretti per quindici spose—o drag queen. Ci sono Pam e Suzie, le donne che mi hanno preso le misure per l'abito, ma anche due loro assistenti e almeno quattro parrucchieri e truccatori. È difficile dire con esattezza quanti di loro entrino ed escano dall'appartamento per portare quantità sempre crescenti di scorte.

Peter mi abbandona prontamente alla tortura, sostenendo che ha bisogno di supervisionare gli accordi di sicurezza e il resto della logistica a Silver Lake. Il suo smoking verrà consegnato lì, quindi non avrò nemmeno la possibilità di vederlo, fin quando Danny non mi porterà lì nel pomeriggio.

"Non è giusto che tutto quello che devi fare tu sia indossare un bel vestito" mi lamento, mettendo un finto broncio, e lui sogghigna, poi mi dà un rapido bacio sulle labbra, facendo accelerare il battito.

"Comportati bene" avverte, con gli occhi argentei che scintillano dal divertimento, e gli pizzico il fianco per vendicarmi, facendolo ridere per poi ricevere un altro bacio.

"Prima i capelli" annuncia un giovane vestito in modo elegante, appena Peter se ne va, e mi lascio guidare sul divano, dove una serie di strumenti per lo styling dall'aspetto spaventoso sono già pronti.

Ho i capelli ancora bagnati dopo la doccia mattutina, quindi devo prima asciugarli con il phon e lisciarli per poi arricciarli. A quanto pare, il taglio richiede una base perfettamente liscia, che i miei capelli mossi non possiedono naturalmente. Nel frattempo, le unghie vengono lucidate, rifinite e dipinte con uno smalto rosa tenue, e quindi è l'ora del trucco.

Mamma si presenta proprio mentre l'ultimo tocco di mascara mi viene applicato sulle ciglia. È già pettinata e indossa un lungo abito color pesca che le enfatizza il fisico ancora in forma.

"Wow" esclama, mentre mi alzo dal divano, e sorrido, avvicinandomi per abbracciarla.

"Sei bellissima, Mamma." Mi tiro indietro per osservarla meglio. "Adoro questo vestito. Quando l'hai comprato?"

"Il tuo fidanzato me l'ha fatto consegnare ieri sera. È Chanel. Ci credi? Mi stavo giusto lamentando con tuo padre ieri mattina che non avrei trovato nulla di decente con così poco preavviso, e poi bam, arriva questo vestito—e magicamente mi sta alla perfezione. Riesci a immaginarlo? Anche tuo padre ha ricevuto un nuovo smoking." Sembra emozionata come una ragazza che parteciperà al ballo.

"Wow, sì. È incredibile." Peter deve aver installato telecamere e/o dispositivi di ascolto a casa dei miei genitori—

un'invasione della privacy di cui dovremo discutere. Per ora, però, sono grata che sia stato abbastanza premuroso da includere i miei genitori nella sua folle pianificazione del matrimonio.

Mamma adora vestirsi in modo elegante e non l'avrebbe presa bene, se avesse dovuto indossare un abito più vecchio o qualcosa che non trovava sufficientemente speciale.

"Come sta Papà?" chiedo, mentre Pam e Suzie sbattono tutti gli altri fuori dall'appartamento e mi fanno rimanere con la biancheria intima per provare il vestito.

"Sta bene. Sta ancora metabolizzando tutto, ma—" Sussulta, quando vede il vestito. "Wow, Sara. È magnifico!"

"È Monique Lhuillier" le dice Pam con orgoglio, mentre Suzie mi aiuta a indossarlo e allaccia i bottoni sul retro. "Tutti pizzi fatti a mano—ogni singolo centimetro."

"Sara, è..." Mamma sbatte le palpebre più volte, poi singhiozza rumorosamente. "Tesoro, sei così bella... semplicemente meravigliosa, come una principessa delle fiabe."

"Davvero? Lasciami guardare." Aspetto che Suzie aggiunga i fermacapelli, poi mi avvicino allo specchio del bagno.

Una straordinaria bellezza mi fissa, con gli occhi punteggiati di verde enormi e misteriosi nel viso impeccabile. Ed è impeccabile. La cicatrice sulla fronte dovuta all'incidente— quasi invisibile ultimamente—è completamente sparita, e la mia pelle è liscia e priva di imperfezioni come il vetro. Un'ora di trucco, e sembra che non ne abbia affatto—salvo il fatto che ogni lineamento è perfetto come se avessi usato Photoshop.

I capelli danno l'impressione della principessa. Tirati su in un insolito mix di ricci ed onde, ogni ciocca è così lucente e setosa che quasi non la riconosco come mia. Anche il colore— castano scuro con sfumature di rosso—è più ricco e luminoso accanto ai fermacapelli di diamanti; tuttavia, questo potrebbe essere dovuto alla lucentezza extra conferita da tutti quei prodotti.

Pam aveva ragione riguardo all'acconciatura: è esattamente ciò di cui questo abito aveva bisogno. Il pizzo conferisce all'elegante vestito da sirenetta una qualità eterea, ma è solo in combinazione con l'acconciatura intricata che assume quel magico aspetto da fata che ha fatto strabuzzare gli occhi a mia madre.

Mentre mi guardo allo specchio, mi si stringe la gola.

Mi sto per sposare.

Con Peter.

Oggi.

L'ondata di panico è tanto spontanea quanto irrazionale. Con un respiro affannoso, chiudo la porta del bagno e mi appoggio contro di essa, dimenticandomi del fragile pizzo. Il mio cuore è come un tamburo di guerra nel petto, con il respiro rapido e poco profondo.

Mi sto per sposare. Con Peter.

Non capisco quale sia la fonte del panico, ma questo non lo rende meno intenso. Posso sentire il sudore gelido sulla fronte e nelle ascelle, e devo davvero impegnarmi per rimanere in piedi e non collassare sul pavimento.

Peter e io ci stiamo per *sposare.*

"Sara?" Mamma bussa alla porta, sembrando preoccupata. "Stai bene, tesoro?"

Sto bene? Dovrebbe essere così. Dovrei essere al settimo cielo, in realtà. Sto per sposare l'uomo che amo, uno che ha fatto di tutto per dimostrarmi che mi ama... per rendermi felice, nonostante il nostro inizio infausto.

È questo il problema? Una parte di me non riesce ancora a superare ciò che ha fatto Peter?

Il volto impeccabile nello specchio non ha risposte, così faccio un paio di respiri profondi e cerco di calmare la voce. "Sto bene, Mamma. Ho solo un po' di mal di stomaco."

"Oh, povero tesoro. Hai un Pepto-Bismol in casa?"

"No, ma sto bene. Dammi solo un secondo." Faccio qualche

altro respiro più profondo, e, quando il cuore non minaccia più di uscirmi dal petto, bagno un asciugamano e lo sfrego sotto le braccia. Quindi, riapplico l'anti-traspirante e picchietto sulla parte superiore dell'attaccatura dei capelli con un fazzoletto, facendo attenzione a non rovinare il trucco.

Quando lo specchio conferma che non sono rimaste tracce dell'improvviso attacco di panico, mi stampo un sorriso sulle labbra ed esco, assicurando ancora una volta a mamma che sto bene.

Torniamo nel soggiorno, che ora è sorprendentemente deserto.

"Se ne sono andati tutti" dice mamma, sorridendo davanti alla mia espressione sorpresa. "Mentre eri in bagno."

"Oh." Guardo l'orologio e sono scioccata nel vedere che sono già le due del pomeriggio.

Non mi stupisce che Peter volesse essere sicuro che facessi una colazione abbondante.

"La cerimonia inizia alle quattro, ma Peter ha detto che il fotografo arriverà alle tre per le foto di famiglia" dice mamma. "Quindi, dovremmo andare. Tuo padre sta arrivando."

"Giusto, ok." Stringo la mano a pugno per nascondere il leggero tremore delle dita. La gola mi sembra ancora troppo stretta, e il pensiero di tutto questo—le foto, la cerimonia, tutti che guardano e spettegolano—è insopportabile, assolutamente travolgente.

"Mamma..." mi premo la mano sullo stomaco, che ora è davvero in subbuglio. "Sai, credo di aver davvero bisogno di una medicina. C'è una farmacia a un isolato di distanza, quindi—"

"Che cosa? Sei impazzita?" Mamma mi spinge sul divano. "Non puoi andare da nessuna parte vestita così. Siediti, rilassati e torno subito, ok?"

"No, Mamma, va tutto bene. Mi toglierò un attimo l'abito e—"

"Siediti." Il tono di mamma non lascia spazio a discussioni.

"Sarò anche vecchia, ma posso camminare per un isolato. Tornerò tra qualche minuto, e tu nel frattempo ti siedi e ti riposi, ok? Forse mangi anche qualcosa—potresti avere un basso livello di zuccheri nel sangue."

Forse ha ragione. Non appena mamma se ne va, vado in cucina e metto qualche avanzo nel microonde. Ricordo questa particolarità del mio primo matrimonio: essere troppo occupata per mangiare e sentirmi svenire. Questa volta, ho decisamente meno preoccupazioni, grazie a Peter che supervisiona tutto, quindi in realtà ho qualche minuto a disposizione per mangiare qualcosa.

Il fotografo può aspettare.

Il campanello suona proprio mentre sto tirando fuori la pasta dal microonde.

"È aperto, Mamma" urlo, afferrando un tovagliolo per essere certa di non scottarmi con il piatto bollente, e poi mi rendo conto che è troppo presto perché lei sia tornata.

Qualcuno degli addetti al trucco ha dimenticato qualcosa?

Posando il piatto di pasta, esco dalla cucina e mi blocco.

L'Agente Ryson è nel mio soggiorno, con lo sguardo derisorio che si posa sul mio abito bianco.

*eter*

"CE L'HAI FATTA DAVVERO" DICE ANTON CON AMMIRAZIONE, mentre sistemo la cravatta nera davanti allo specchio. "Vita civile, amnistia, ragazza e tutto il resto. Non riesco a crederci, cazzo."

"Credici." Mi volto e sorrido ai miei ex compagni di squadra. "Come sto?"

"Non male." Yan cammina intorno a me, studiandomi in modo critico. "Avrei optato per una cravatta bianca, però. Più formale e più adatta per la tua tonalità di pelle."

Anton alza gli occhi verso di lui. "Smettila di essere un metrosessuale del cazzo. Seriamente, Ilya, che diavolo dava da mangiare tua madre a quello?"

"La stessa merda che dava da mangiare a me" risponde Ilya, e si mette davanti allo specchio per sistemare la cravatta. A differenza del fratello elegante, che sembra essere nato per indossare un completo, Ilya sembra un malvivente travestito. La giacca è tirata sulle sue spalle potenziate dagli steroidi, e i tatuaggi sul cranio rasato brillano minacciosamente alla luce del giorno.

Il padre di Sara potrebbe avere un infarto solo guardandolo —e questo senza sapere dell'arsenale nascosto nella giacca.

In tutte le nostre giacche.

Non c'è motivo di preoccuparsi, naturalmente, ma mi sento ancora a disagio. Tornando ai bei vecchi tempi, eventi come questo, specialmente in un luogo all'aperto, spesso rappresentavano un'opportunità per noi. Matrimoni, compleanni, funerali—ci piacevano tutti, perché i nostri obiettivi, tutti presi dall'emozione, inevitabilmente dimenticavano alcuni aspetti chiave della sicurezza.

È un errore che non ho intenzione di commettere, ed è per questo che oltre al mio solito gruppo che controlla Sara ho assunto altre venti guardie del corpo e ho commissionato la sorveglianza aerea attraverso una dozzina di droni.

Nessuno si avvicinerà a mia insaputa a meno di un chilometro dalla cerimonia.

"Allora, com'è la vita civile finora?" chiede Yan, facendo un passo verso di me, mentre mi dirigo fuori per controllare se il fotografo è arrivato. "È come la immaginavi?"

Il suo tono è beffardo, come al solito, ma quando lo guardo, non scorgo alcun divertimento sul suo viso.

"Sì" rispondo, decidendo di rivelargli la verità. "Dovresti provarla qualche volta."

Ridacchia, ma il suono è privo di umorismo. "No, grazie. Mi sto godendo troppa questa vita."

Annuisco, per nulla sorpreso. Invece di approfittare dell'amnistia che ho ottenuto per lui, Yan ha rilevato un'attività —pratiche, società di comodo, regolatori di conti e tutto il resto —e ha sfruttato i contatti del team per ottenere lavori nuovi e sempre più redditizi. L'acquisizione è avvenuta il giorno dopo che ho lasciato la proprietà di Esguerra, il che significa che Yan l'aveva pianificata da un po'.

Avevo ragione ad essere prudente.

Se non avessi rinunciato quando l'ho fatto, uno di noi sarebbe probabilmente morto.

Come previsto, Ilya si è unito al fratello nella nuova avventura, ma Anton ci sta ancora pensando.

"Sono già fottutamente ricco, sai" mi ha detto al telefono due settimane fa, quando Yan ha insistito di nuovo per ottenere una risposta. "Potrebbero mancarmi l'adrenalina e tutto il resto, ma non ho bisogno di altri soldi—a differenza di Yan." Ha fatto una pausa, poi ha chiesto con attenzione: "Non sei arrabbiato con lui, vero?"

"No" ho detto ad Anton, ed è vero. Ho detto ai ragazzi che possono andare avanti con gli affari, se vogliono, quindi che cosa mi importa se Yan aveva intenzione di farmi le scarpe per tutto il tempo? Nessuno di noi è un angelo e, in fondo, ho sempre saputo che Yan non si sarebbe accontentato di seguire gli ordini ancora a lungo.

Anche in Russia, c'era stato qualche accenno a questo—un campanello d'allarme che ho ignorato, quando ho offerto ai gemelli Ivanov un posto nella mia nuova squadra.

Nel contesto del mio vecchio mondo—del *nostro* mondo— Yan Ivanov è sempre stato abbastanza fedele e, dal momento che abbiamo evitato lo scontro finale, è logico rimanere in buoni rapporti.

Non è detto che non avrò mai bisogno di un favore.

"Che cos'hai intenzione di fare qui?" chiede Yan, quando mi fermo a contare le sedie di fronte al gazebo. "A parte pianificare matrimoni?"

"Ho alcune idee in mente" dico, finendo il conteggio. Mancano alcune sedie—cosa a cui lo staff del locale deve porre rimedio immediatamente. "Per ora, la pianificazione del matrimonio è andata bene."

"Sai che ti stai illudendo, vero?" Il tono di Yan è privo di qualunque accenno di scherno, e quando mi volto per guardarlo, scorgo una strana serietà nei suoi freddi occhi verdi. "Tutto questo non fa per te—non più di quanto farebbe per me."

Lui ed Esguerra hanno letto lo stesso copione? "Chi stai cercando di convincere?" chiedo, incuriosito. "Me o te stesso?"

Sostiene il mio sguardo, poi annuisce, come se vedesse qualcosa che mi sfugge. "Buona fortuna" dice sottovoce. "Farò il tifo per te."

E girandosi, torna indietro, lasciandomi da solo a rintracciare il fotografo.

S*ara*

IL MIO CUORE SALTA UN BATTITO, POI RIPRENDE A MARTELLARE.

Non può essere vero.

Non possono arrestare Peter il giorno delle nostre nozze.

"Agente Ryson." Sono orgogliosa della fermezza nella mia voce. "Che cosa ci fai qui?"

Mi rivolge un sorrisetto. "Oh, non preoccuparti, Dottoressa Cobakis—o futura Dottoressa Garin? Non sono qui in veste ufficiale."

Il mio frenetico battito cardiaco rallenta leggermente. "Perché sei qui, allora?"

"Per porgere le mie congratulazioni, ovviamente." La sua bocca si contorce. "Tu e il tuo amante russo sicuramente ci avete ingannati tutti."

Rimango in silenzio, perché che cosa posso dire? Capisco come debba sembrare dal suo punto di vista—dal punto di vista di chiunque abbia seguito la storia fin dall'inizio, in realtà. Sto per sposare l'assassino di George, l'uomo che mi ha torturata con l'acqua, che ha invaso la mia vita e che mi ha rapita.

L'uomo cui Ryson ha trascorso gli ultimi due anni a dare la caccia.

"Dimmi una cosa, Dottoressa Cobakis" continua amaramente l'agente. "A che punto tu e Sokolov avete cospirato per sbarazzarvi del tuo marito con il cervello danneggiato? È successo prima o durante la cosiddetta aggressione nei tuoi confronti?"

Sospiro, inorridita. È questo che pensa davvero? "Ti stai sbagliando. Non ho mai—"

"Non ci hai mai mentito? Non hai mai finto di aver bisogno della protezione dall'uomo che stai per sposare?" Il suo sguardo è tagliente. "Sì, credo che sia così."

Mi brucia il collo. "Non era così. Non all'inizio."

"Oh, davvero? Com'era allora? Ti ha fatto il lavaggio del cervello in Giappone? Ti ha mostrato qualche trucco da camera da letto per farti dimenticare tutto il sangue sulle sue mani? Forse non ti importava dell'alcolista da cui stavi divorziando— sì, sappiamo tutto—ma il tuo amante ha ucciso anche le guardie di Cobakis. Uomini buoni, uomini onesti. Ha fatto saltare loro le cervella, o l'hai dimenticato?"

Ingoio la bile che mi sta salendo nella gola. "Ovviamente no."

"No?" Ryson si avvicina. "E che mi dici dei poliziotti sull'elicottero che ha abbattuto, quando hanno cercato di salvarti dal presunto rapimento? O di tutti gli altri che ha ucciso e torturato in nome di qualunque giustizia contorta stesse perseguendo? Vorresti che ti dessi un elenco di tutte le sue vittime, in modo da poterlo appendere sulla parete sopra il tuo letto matrimoniale?"

Sto tremando ora, con lo stomaco in completa rivolta. L'odore della pasta riscaldata, così allettante un minuto fa, mi sta facendo venire voglia di vomitare, e devo davvero sforzarmi per sostenere lo sguardo di Ryson invece di raggomitolarmi in una piccola palla di vergogna sul pavimento.

È tutto vero.

Peter è un mostro, e lo sono anch'io per essermene innamorata.

Davanti alla mia mancanza di risposta, l'agente sbuffa con fare derisorio. "Niente da dire? Beh, lascia che ti dia un piccolo avvertimento." Si avvicina finché non ho altra scelta che fare un passo indietro. Incombendo su di me, dice sottovoce: "Non so chi abbia agito dietro le quinte, dando a tutti e due una fedina pulita, ma se c'è una cosa che ho imparato nel corso degli anni è che gli psicopatici come Sokolov non cambiano. *Commetterà* un altro crimine e, quando lo farà, l'accordo che ha stretto con i miei superiori sarà annullato. Aspetteremo—e ora, Dottoressa Cobakis, abbiamo anche il *tuo* numero."

Fa un passo indietro e si gira, come se volesse andarsene, ma poi si ferma e dice voltandosi: "Oh, e ancora congratulazioni. Sei una bellissima sposa. Spero che sarete molto felici insieme."

Poi, esce, sbattendo la porta dietro di sé, e riesco a malapena a raggiungere il bagno prima che il mio stomaco si liberi, espellendo il contenuto nel water.

eter

È IN RITARDO.

La cerimonia inizierà tra quarantacinque minuti, e Sara non è ancora qui.

Rivolgo una feroce occhiata al fotografo, mentre lui guarda l'orologio, e impallidisce, poi distoglie lo sguardo e inizia a giocherellare con i suoi gemelli, come se niente fosse.

Secondo le guardie del corpo che sorvegliavano l'appartamento di Sara e i dispositivi di localizzazione che ho impiantato su di lei, la mia sposa è ancora a casa con sua madre. Le ho chiamate diverse volte, ma solo Lorna ha risposto una volta. "Sara ha lo stomaco sottosopra" mi ha informato brevemente e ha riattaccato—inviando le mie chiamate in segreteria telefonica da allora.

Preoccupato e sempre più irritato, osservo le persone che si aggirano intorno al gazebo in piccoli gruppi, bevendo champagne e mangiando le tartine disposte ad arte. Quasi tutti sono già qui, apparentemente divertiti, sebbene alcuni degli ospiti—soprattutto gli amici e gli ex colleghi di Sara—mi guardino come se fossi Osama bin Laden. Yan sta chiacchierando con i nuovi colleghi di Sara, mentre Ilya sembra affascinato da quello che i compagni di band di Sara gli stanno raccontando sulle loro esibizioni. Anton sta parlando con il padre di Sara del fatto di essere cresciuto in Russia, e vedo perfino Joe Levinson, l'avvocato a cui piace Sara, che trangugia bicchieri di tequila al bar e fissa cupamente nella mia direzione.

Ha le palle a presentarsi qui. Non sa che sono a conoscenza del suo interesse per Sara, però. Se la guarda nel modo sbagliato, non vivrà abbastanza da potersene pentire.

Sempre ammesso che lei si presenti per essere guardata da qualcuno.

Aspetto ancora cinque minuti, controllando la mia app di tracciamento di Sara ogni trenta secondi, e poi chiamo Danny, che fa parte dell'equipaggio delle guardie del corpo di Sara oggi.

"Ho bisogno che tu salga nell'appartamento" dico quando risponde. "Porta il tuo telefono a Sara e non andartene finché non mi avrà chiamato."

"D'accordo."

Riattacca, e cinque minuti dopo, il mio telefono si illumina per una telefonata dal numero di Danny.

"Sara?"

"Peter, io..." Deglutisce. "Mi dispiace così tanto. Ho solo bisogno di un po' di tempo."

La mia preoccupazione si intensifica. "Qual è il problema? È successo qualcosa?"

"No, niente. Ho solo lo stomaco sottosopra."

"Hai bisogno che ti mandi un medico? Vuoi che ti porti qualcosa?"

"No, è solo che..." Si interrompe, poi dice attentamente: "Ascolta, Peter, so che non è il momento, ma—"

"Stai cercando di tirarti indietro?" La mia voce è dolce, e non tradisce affatto la furia che esplode in me. "È di questo che si tratta?"

"No, niente affatto. Ho solo bisogno di un po' di tempo. Il tuo ritorno, il matrimonio—sta accadendo tutto molto velocemente. Non sto dicendo che non dovremmo farlo, ma forse è troppo presto, forse potremmo vivere insieme per un po', vedere se—"

"Vedere cosa?" Il metallo duro del telefono mi taglia il palmo. "Se funziona? Credi davvero che le cose andranno così?" La rabbia è esplosiva dentro di me, ma mantengo un tono gentile e un'espressione calma, mentre mi nascondo dietro una piccola macchia di alberi, lontano da orecchie e occhi curiosi.

"Peter, per favore. Ti sto solo chiedendo una breve proroga. Possiamo dire alla gente la verità—che non mi sento bene—e poi..."

"Lascia che ti spieghi come andranno le cose, ptichka" dico con voce ancora più dolce. "Puoi andare con Danny ora, venendo direttamente qui senza ritardi, o verrò a prenderti io. Solo che non torneremo qui in quel caso. Anzi, non ci sarà motivo per cui tornare qui, perché non intendo lasciare testimoni di questo sfortunato evento." Faccio una pausa, poi chiedo gentilmente: "Capisci che cosa sto dicendo, amore mio?"

Cala il silenzio sul telefono. Poi, dice con un sussurro spezzato: "Non lo faresti."

"No? Mettimi alla prova." Aspetto un attimo, poi aggiungo: "Naturalmente, i tuoi genitori non rientrano nella categoria dei testimoni. So quanto siano importanti per te, quindi li porteremo con noi, quando ce ne andremo. Che ne dici? Si godranno una vacanza esotica, non credi?"

È così silenziosa che sono quasi certo che proverà a scoprire il mio bluff. Solo che non sto bluffando. Non me ne frega un cazzo di queste persone, ad eccezione dei genitori di Sara. Se mi costringerà a farlo, porterò avanti la mia minaccia, anche se questo dovesse significare rinunciare all'amnistia che ho combattuto così duramente per ottenere.

Senza Sara, nessuna di quelle stronzate ha importanza.

Se non posso averla, tanto vale bruciare tutto il mondo del cazzo.

"Sei pazzo" sussurra infine, e sorrido cupamente, sentendo la capitolazione nella sua voce.

"Sì, lo sono, ptichka. Non dimenticarlo. Ci vediamo qui presto."

E, riattaccando, torno a chiacchierare con gli ospiti.

STO ANCORA TREMANDO, QUANDO ESCO DALLA MIA CAMERA DA letto, stringendo il telefono di Danny con una mano e lisciando il morbido pizzo dell'abito con l'altra.

"Sono pronta per andare, Mamma" le dico, quando si alza dal divano, chiaramente sorpresa di vedermi.

"Sei sicura? Tesoro, sei davvero pallida."

"No, sto bene, Mamma." Mi sforzo di sorridere. "Il farmaco sta facendo effetto finalmente."

Mia madre è tornata con la medicina proprio mentre stavo uscendo dal bagno dopo aver vomitato, così ho preso immediatamente un paio di pillole e le ho detto che dovevo sdraiarmi per qualche minuto. Pensavo che avrebbe accettato quella spiegazione, ma mentre le sue sopracciglia si sollevavano, ho capito che mi stavo solo illudendo.

Mamma mi conosce fin troppo bene.

"Sara, tesoro... sai che non devi per forza andare fino in fondo, vero?" dice, fermandosi di fronte a me. "Se hai dei ripensamenti, puoi cambiare idea. Tutti capirebbero. Non devi sposarlo, se non sei pronta."

Si sbaglia. Non posso cambiare idea—non se voglio che tutti i nostri amici sopravvivano alla giornata. Non so se Peter farebbe davvero ciò che ha lasciato intendere, ma non posso correre questo tipo di rischio.

Non con un uomo capace di cose così mostruose.

Se l'obiettivo dell'agente era quello di farmi sentire inferiore a un insetto schiacciato, c'è riuscito egregiamente. Ogni parola che mi ha rivolto sembrava una pallottola, perché era tutto vero. I crimini che Peter ha commesso sono terribili, imperdonabili, e lo so. L'ho sempre saputo, eppure mi sono innamorata di lui.

Ho accettato il suo lato malvagio, l'ho abbracciato al punto che ho accettato di sposarlo di mia spontanea volontà. Nonostante la visita di Ryson, non avrei rifiutato Peter, anche se lui l'ha interpretato in questo modo. Stavo solo cercando di riprendermi dalle sferzate verbali di Ryson, con l'istinto che mi spingeva a prendere tempo.

Avrei scelto il matrimonio—solo un altro giorno.

"Non è quello, Mamma" dico, mentre mi scruta, cercando qualche traccia di dubbio. "Amo Peter, e voglio sposarlo. Solo che non mi sentivo bene."

Il suo sguardo si posa sul telefono che sto tenendo. "Che cosa ti ha detto?"

Sbatto le palpebre. "Che cosa?"

"Quel tuo autista che è venuto—ti ha dato quel telefono. Immagino per chiamare Peter, vero? Allora, che cosa ti ha detto il tuo fidanzato?"

"Niente. Mi ha solo ricordato che ora fosse. E a proposito"—

guardo lo schermo illuminato del telefono—"dobbiamo proprio andare."

Mamma mi guarda in faccia per qualche altro istante, poi annuisce. "Va bene, cara. Se è quello che vuoi, andiamo. Il matrimonio ci sta aspettando."

Sara

DEVO AVERE LA TESTA DA UN'ALTRA PARTE, PERCHÉ IL VIAGGIO fino a Silver Lake sembra durare solo pochi secondi. Sbattendo le palpebre, scendo dalla macchina tra l'allegria di alcuni ospiti, e il mio sguardo si posa su una figura alta e cupa a una decina di metri di distanza.

Peter.

Il mio nemico.

Il mio stalker.

Il mio amante.

Il mio futuro marito.

I suoi occhi sono come catrame grigio: non riflettono nulla, ma posso percepire le emozioni dentro di lui, sentire la violenza mascherata da quell'immobilità predatrice. Tuttavia, non posso fare a meno di guardarlo, facendo scorrere lo sguardo sulle potenti linee del suo corpo. Non l'ho mai visto vestito così formalmente prima d'ora, ma gli si addice, con l'elegante smoking che enfatizza la forma a V del busto e la camicia bianca che fa risplendere la pelle abbronzata.

È magnifico, stupendo come una stella del cinema, e, nonostante il continuo tumulto dentro di me, un calore prende il sopravvento, con quella reazione primordiale e incontrollabile come la paura che l'accompagna.

Potrei aver salvato gli altri presentandomi, ma la pagherò per quel ritardo.

Peter non lascerà correre sul mio momento di debolezza.

Sostengo il suo sguardo mentre mi avvicino, e allunga la mano, con la bocca piegata in un mezzo sorriso beffardo. Metto la mano nel suo grande palmo e sento il calore fino alle dita dei piedi—che sono gelide come le dita, mi rendo conto solo ora.

"Ciao, ptichka" mormora e china la testa per darmi un dolce bacio sulle labbra. Intorno a noi, sento alcuni "ohh"— probabilmente dai miei nuovi colleghi, che non hanno motivo di sospettare che siamo qualcosa di diverso da un semplice coppia innamorata. Con la coda dell'occhio, vedo Marsha che ci fissa, con il viso teso e pallido, e dietro a Peter c'è Joe Levinson, con l'espressione di qualcuno che sta partecipando a un funerale... in cui la bara è piena di esplosivi.

"Ciao" rispondo dolcemente, facendo del mio meglio per ignorare tutti gli sguardi che ci circondano. "Il fotografo è qui?"

"Sì, amore mio. Andiamo."

Mettendomi una mano sulla schiena con fare possessivo, mi guida verso un punto pittoresco vicino al lago, dove un uomo con una macchina fotografica sta scattando foto a Phil e Rory.

Anche mio padre è già lì, e mia madre sta arrivando, camminando con la rapidità che le scarpe con i tacchi alti permettono. Mi scalda il cuore vederla così forte e sana; il ricordo di lei in ospedale, fasciata come una mummia, continua a tormentare i miei incubi.

Quando siamo a metà strada verso il lago e fuori dalla

portata d'orecchio degli altri ospiti, alzo lo sguardo verso Peter e mormoro: "Mi dispiace."

La sua mascella si indurisce. "Ne discuteremo dopo."

Deglutisco e guardo in basso, facendo attenzione a non inciampare sul terreno irregolare con i tacchi alti. Non ho mentito: mi *dispiace*. Ora che sono tornata nell'orbita di Peter, sento l'inevitabilità di tutto ciò, l'attrazione dei fili oscuri che ci legano. I miei precedenti dubbi sembrano infondati e ingenui, irrazionali al limite della follia. Che importa se il nostro matrimonio è oggi, domani o tra un anno? Il mio tormentatore sarà lo stesso uomo, lo stesso assassino letale di cui mi sono innamorata.

Dal momento in cui ho conosciuto Peter, ho capito che non avrei avuto scampo, e quello che è successo oggi lo conferma.

Mentre ci avviciniamo al lago, vedo i compagni di squadra di Peter raggruppati insieme, da un lato, e li saluto. Mi fa piacere che ricambino il saluto. È strano, ma mi mancavano anche loro.

Per me, sono come i fratelli di Peter.

Quando raggiungiamo il lago, il fotografo—un uomo paffuto e barbuto che assomiglia a un Babbo Natale con i capelli scuri—ci sistema in una varietà di pose: guardandoci intensamente negli occhi, seduti su una panchina con Peter che mi tiene in braccio. Scatta foto di noi due insieme e poi di ciascuno da solo; di noi due con i miei genitori, e poi con tutti i nostri amici. Le combinazioni sono infinite, e dopo aver presentato Peter a tutti, mi ritrovo a vagare, sorridendo e posando automaticamente.

Peter avrebbe fatto quello che aveva minacciato?

Avrebbe ucciso tutta questa gente solo per punirmi per essermi opposta?

Voglio credere che la risposta sia no, ma l'istinto mi dice che è sì. Ne è capace, e la sua ossessione per me ha sempre avuto una sfumatura di oscurità, proprio come il nostro gioco nella camera da letto.

Peter mi ama, mi adora, farebbe qualsiasi cosa per me.

Compreso commettere un omicidio di massa.

È un pensiero terrificante—o almeno dovrei trovarlo terrificante. E lo faccio... la maggior parte del tempo. È solo che c'è una piccola parte di me che trova quel livello di ossessione inebriante, eccitante come saltare da una scogliera con un mare in tempesta.

"Pronta, amore mio?" La grande mano di Peter mi stringe possessivamente il gomito, e lo guardo, stordita.

"Per la cerimonia" chiarisce, e annuisco, lasciandomi condurre verso il gazebo.

Le cose stanno così.

Vita coniugale, stiamo arrivando.

eter

LA MIA PTICHKA È PALLIDA E INCREDIBILMENTE BELLA ACCANTO A me, mentre ascoltiamo il giudice che fa il suo discorsetto. Parla di amore e impegno, di sostenersi a vicenda nella buona e nella cattiva sorte, e un'oscura ondata di soddisfazione mi attraversa, quando rivolge la tradizionale domanda a Sara, e lei risponde sottovoce: "Sì, lo voglio."

Poi, si rivolge a me.

"Tu, Peter Garin, vuoi prendere Sara Cobakis come tua sposa, amarla e rispettarla, nella salute e nella malattia, finché morte non vi separi?"

"Sì" dico chiaramente, assicurandomi che la voce sovrasti il rumore del nostro piccolo pubblico. "Lo voglio."

"Ora puoi baciare la sposa" dice il giudice, e guardo Sara.

Mi sta osservando con gli occhi spalancati e le morbide labbra socchiuse, e chino la testa, sfiorando delicatamente le labbra su quella bocca allettante. È molto importante essere delicato adesso. La minima perdita di controllo potrebbe scatenare la rabbia che sta ribollendo dentro di me, e non posso permettere che ciò accada.

Non finché non saremo soli.

Ci sono applausi e fischi, e poi una melodia familiare inizia a suonare da dietro il gazebo.

La band che ho commissionato—quella per cui Sara sembrava così emozionata—è qui, dopo essersi preparata, ed è pronta per suonare durante la cerimonia. Mi è costato un bel po' di soldi averli qui per un paio d'ore, ma a giudicare dalla reazione degli ospiti, ne è valsa la pena.

"Andiamo?" Offro il braccio a Sara, mentre la maggior parte degli ospiti più giovani si affretta verso la musica, entusiasta per la possibilità di vedere i propri idoli dal vivo.

"Certo." La sua esile mano scivola nell'incavo del mio gomito, mentre mi rivolge un sorriso cauto. "Andiamo."

Non abbiamo preparato un ballo, ma viste le sollecitazioni dei nuovi colleghi di Sara, la prendo tra le mie braccia e ondeggiamo insieme durante una canzone lenta e romantica, che riconosco essere un classico piuttosto che uno dei successi della band. Ancora una volta, devo stare attento, devo mantenere un tocco leggero e delicato, mantenere la giusta distanza, invece di tirare Sara verso di me e strapparle quell'elegante abito bianco per prenderla qui davanti a tutti, su questo morbido prato verde.

Per fortuna, la canzone lenta termina prima che il mio autocontrollo cominci a sgretolarsi, e la band si lancia in uno dei successi più popolari. I compagni della band di Sara e alcuni altri ospiti si uniscono a noi, ridendo e battendo le mani, e finiamo per ballare in gruppo prima che l'amica di Sara, Marsha, la trascini via per ballare con lei e due delle altre infermiere.

Aspetto che finisca la canzone, e poi faccio segno al personale del catering di iniziare a portare gli antipasti.

Dato che siamo circa due dozzine di persone, abbiamo tre tavoli: uno piccolo e rotondo per me e Sara, e due ovali più grandi per il resto degli ospiti. Non mi sono preoccupato dei posti assegnati, così i genitori di Sara finiscono con i loro amici, e la maggior parte degli amici e dei colleghi di Sara si riunisce all'altro tavolo.

Il cibo è fantastico, come dovrebbe essere quello di uno chef con otto stelle Michelin, e, mentre iniziamo a mangiare, la maggior parte degli ospiti sembra divertirsi. Anche Sara deve pensarlo, perché dice tranquillamente: "Grazie per aver organizzato tutto. Questo è uno dei matrimoni più belli a cui io abbia mai partecipato."

Le sorrido, anche se tutto quello che vorrei è piegarla sul tavolo. "Sono contento, amore mio. Voglio che tu sia felice."

E lo sarà, una volta superato qualsiasi dubbio abbia ancora su di noi. Me ne assicurerò. Farò tutto il necessario per renderla felice.

L'unica cosa che non farò è liberarla.

In ogni caso, non penso che lo voglia—non in profondità, dove conta davvero. Non so che cosa l'abbia spaventata questo pomeriggio, ma ho un sospetto.

Potrebbe aver saputo della morte di Sonny Pearson?

Non vedo come, visto che non è stata in clinica negli ultimi due giorni, ma è l'unica cosa che ha senso. Ad ogni modo, ho intenzione di andare fino in fondo.

Stasera.

Non appena saremo soli.

Dopo esserci rimpinzati di cibo, io e Sara abbiamo tagliato la torta—una splendida creazione a sette strati con glassa di panna acida—e poi tutti sono tornati a ballare e a scattare foto. Le brevi presentazioni che Sara ha fatto prima della cerimonia chiaramente non erano sufficienti per tutti, e presto mi ritrovo circondato da domande indiscrete da parte di ospiti, il cui coraggio sembra viaggiare insieme al consumo di alcol.

"Come vi siete conosciuti?" chiede Marsha, quasi ondeggiando sui piedi, mentre tranguggia un altro bicchiere di champagne. "Sara ha detto che avete avuto una relazione complicata per un po'..."

"Sì, esattamente" interviene Joe Levinson, con la mascella contratta in una linea dura. "Quando e come vi siete conosciuti? Nessuno di noi sapeva che Sara avesse una relazione."

Ricordo a me stesso che il coltello legato alla caviglia non serve ad affettare la gola di quest'uomo. "Ci siamo conosciuti in un club di Chicago qualche mese fa" rispondo con calma e facendo furtivamente un segnale ad Anton. "Dato che viaggiavo molto per lavoro, abbiamo deciso di mantenere la nostra relazione segreta, fin quando non fossimo stati certi che le cose avrebbero funzionato."

"E tu vieni dalla Russia?" Andy, l'infermiera con i capelli rossi, mi studia con un'espressione confusa. "Lo stesso Paese di—"

"Eccoti!" Anton mi dà una pacca sulla spalla. "Ti stavo cercando dappertutto. I ragazzi hanno bisogno di te per un momento."

"Scusatemi" dico educatamente agli ospiti e seguo Anton verso il lago, dove i miei compagni di squadra si sono radunati con una costosa bottiglia di vodka.

"Grazie per il salvataggio" dico, quando siamo fuori dalla portata d'orecchio degli amici di Sara. "Non sono dell'umore giusto per affrontare le loro domande oggi."

"Dovrai farlo prima o poi" dice Anton, e scrollo le spalle, anche se so che ha ragione.

Per integrarmi con queste persone, dovrò dar loro qualche risposta.

"Allora, come ci si sente ad essere di nuovo un uomo sposato?" chiede Ilya, versandomi un bicchiere di vodka.

Trangugio tutto invece di rispondere, sentendo il familiare bruciore nella gola. Non bevo molto—non l'ho mai fatto—ma oggi sono tentato. Voglio dimenticare ciò che ho provato, quando ho sentito la voce esitante di Sara al telefono, che mi diceva di aver bisogno di più tempo.

"Versamene altra" dico, allungando il bicchiere vuoto, e Ilya ubbidisce.

Ingoio di nuovo, poi restituisco il bicchiere a Ilya.

"Ancora?" chiede, e scuoto la testa.

"Basta così, grazie."

Questo dovrebbe essere sufficiente. Il mio autocontrollo già vacilla, e non ho intenzione di rischiare di fare del male a Sara, quando finalmente saremo da soli.

Non sono un *tale* mostro.

"Quindi è così, eh?" Anton fa un gesto verso la gente intorno al gazebo. "È quello che vuoi?"

"È *lei* che voglio." Mi siedo sull'erba, guardando Sara che va di gruppo in gruppo, ridendo e chiacchierando, fingendo di essere una sposa felice. "E lei viene con tutto il resto."

"Forse" dice Yan, allungando la mano verso la bottiglia. Svitando il tappo, beve un sorso direttamente dall'apertura. "O forse no."

Gli rivolgo un'occhiata tagliente. "Un esperto di mia moglie, vero?"

Si stringe nelle spalle e beve un altro sorso. "Potrebbe ancora sorprenderti. Pensi che sia così diversa da noi? Tutta dolcezza, bontà e gentilezza? Pensi che una di quelle persone"—fa un gesto con la bottiglia verso gli ospiti—"sia tutta dolcezza e gentilezza?"

Guardo Sara invece di rispondere, e lui sospira. "Mi sorprende che tu, tra tutti, non lo capisca. Ti vuole, vero? Ti ama, anche se sa tutto sul tipo di uomo che sei?"

Non rispondo nemmeno a questo, e continua. "Perché pensi

che sia attratta da te? Perché vede qualcosa di buono in te? O perché segretamente brama la crudeltà?"

Anton sbuffa. "Oh, per favore. Non ricominciare con queste stronzate. Ogni volta che bevi la vodka—"

"Scommetto su quest'ultima opzione" dice Yan, come se Anton non avesse parlato. "È più simile a te di quanto immagini, e tutte queste stronzate"—agita di nuovo la bottiglia verso il gazebo—"sono ciò che è stata addestrata a pensare che la renderà felice, non quello che vuole per davvero."

Mi alzo, togliendo qualche filo d'erba dai pantaloni. "C'è altra vodka sul nostro tavolo" dico a Ilya, che guarda con invidia il fratello che trangugia la bottiglia. "Farai meglio a prenderla, se la vuoi. Finirà presto."

Per quanto sia divertente ascoltare le chiacchiere da ubriaco di Yan, preferirei portare a letto la mia nuova moglie.

 ara

SENTO CHE IO E PETER SIAMO UNA FARSA, IN CUI OGNUNO STA recitando un ruolo. Lui è lo sposo gentile, riservato, ma estremamente educato, e io sono la sposa radiosa, spumeggiante ed emozionata. O almeno lo sono dopo tre bicchieri di champagne; aiutano davvero con la parte spumeggiante-ed-emozionata, che a sua volta aiuta ad evitare le domande eccessivamente insistenti dei miei amici.

Posso sempre andare a parlare con un altro gruppo di ospiti, ridendo e incoraggiando tutti a ballare—cosa che fanno volentieri, data la fonte della musica.

"Come ti senti, tesoro?" chiede mamma, quando raggiungo il loro piccolo circolo per un minuto. "Altri problemi alla pancia?"

"No, va tutto bene, Mamma." Rivolgo a lei e a papà il mio sorriso più solare. "Come state voi?"

Mamma sorride e si allunga per prendere la mano di papà. "Ci stiamo divertendo, come tutti gli altri. Il tuo Peter ha fatto un ottimo lavoro."

"Grazie, Mamma." Sorrido a entrambi. La reazione dei miei genitori era la mia più grande preoccupazione, e sono immensamente sollevata dal fatto che sembrino aver accettato la mia relazione—almeno esteriormente. Naturalmente non ho dato loro molta scelta, ma è comunque bello sapere che sono disposti a dare una possibilità a Peter.

"Eccoti qui" mormora una voce familiare, mentre un lungo braccio mi avvolge la vita.

Alzo lo sguardo per incrociare quello argenteo di mio marito e il suo sorriso, dimenticando di essere cauta per il momento. "Ciao. Dove sei stato?"

"Con i ragazzi" dice, indicando la sponda del lago, e rido mentre vedo i tre russi che si passano quella che sembra una bottiglia di vodka.

"E così, gli stereotipi sono veri?" chiede papà, seguendo il mio sguardo, e Peter annuisce, sorridendo.

"La maggior parte. Personalmente, preferisco la birra, ma a volte hai davvero bisogno di sentire la gola in fiamme." Mi guarda, con le labbra ancora curve. "Come ti senti, ptichka?"

Il mio respiro accelera, quando noto il sottotono oscuro in quel sorriso sensuale. "Oh, sto... sto bene."

"Ottimo." Mi prende il viso e sfiora teneramente le nocche sulla mascella. "Ero preoccupato."

Deglutisco, mentre il battito cardiaco sussulta di nuovo. Ci stiamo avvicinando al momento della resa dei conti, lo sento.

"Perché non lanci il bouquet e poi salutiamo gli ospiti?" suggerisce, come se mi leggesse nel pensiero. "È stata una lunga giornata e potresti non stare ancora bene."

"Sì, tesoro" interviene mamma, beatamente ignara dei pensieri che ho per la testa. "Perché non ve ne andate tutti e due? È stata una festa meravigliosa, e sono sicura che tutti hanno avuto da mangiare e da bere in abbondanza."

Guardo il sole che tramonta sul lago. "Ma—"

"Vieni, amore mio." Peter mi stringe il braccio intorno alla vita, anche se il suo sorriso permane. "Andiamo."

"Ok." Guardo i miei genitori. "Ciao. Ci vediamo presto."

"Ciao, tesoro." Mamma fa un passo verso di me, e Peter mi libera abbastanza a lungo da permettermi di abbracciare lei e poi papà. "Ancora congratulazioni."

"Grazie." Rivolgo loro un altro sorriso luminoso, e Peter mi conduce via per gettare il bouquet e salutare tutti gli altri ospiti.

~

"Allora, ci trasferiremo?" chiedo, mentre scendiamo dall'auto vicino al mio edificio. La mia voce è un po' troppo bassa, ma tutto il coraggio alcolico si è esaurito durante il viaggio, facendo martellare il cuore più velocemente, man mano che ci avvicinavamo a casa.

"Vuoi farlo?" Peter mi guarda, con lo sguardo velato, mentre ci incamminiamo verso l'edificio. "Come ti ho detto, ho trovato alcuni posti carini, ma non volevo decidere senza prima consultarti."

Il suo tono non contiene tracce di scherno, ma lo percepisco comunque. Se oggi mi ha dimostrato qualcosa, è che detiene ancora tutto il potere—e che detta le regole.

Decido di stare al gioco. "Sì, credo che mi piacerebbe trasferirmi. Questa casa è troppo piccola per noi due—e sarebbe bello non avere così tanti vicini."

"Sono d'accordo." I suoi occhi assumono un bagliore più luminoso, e la voce si fa più profonda, mentre mormora: "Voglio averti tutta per me."

Arrossendo, apro la bocca per rispondere, ma in quel

momento si piega e mi prende in braccio dolcemente, ignorando il mio sussulto.

"Tradizione" dice, sogghignando cupamente, ed entra nell'atrio, portandomi con la consueta disinvoltura.

Passiamo accanto alle mie giovani vicine nell'ascensore, e nascondo il viso nel collo di Peter, mentre gridano e urlano: "Congratulazioni!"

Dobbiamo assolutamente trasferirci da qualche parte con meno persone.

"Puoi mettermi giù" dico a Peter una volta dentro l'ascensore, ma lui mi guarda, con gli occhi che si rabbuiano.

"Perché?" mormora, stringendo le braccia attorno a me. "Mi piace tenerti così."

Il mio battito riaccelera, con il nervosismo che riaffiora, e spingo sulle spalle di Peter. "No, davvero, mettimi giù, per favore."

"Perché?" La mascella si indurisce, con tutta la giocosità che lascia la sua espressione. "Per poter fuggire? Per nasconderti da qualche parte e mentire dicendo di star male?"

"Io *stavo* male!" Lo guardo storto, con la rabbia che spazza via l'ansia. "Chiedi a mia madre, se non mi credi. Ho vomitato e ho dovuto prendere un Pepto-Bismol."

Solleva le sopracciglia scure. "Che cosa?"

"Mamma te l'ha già detto. Al telefono—l'ho sentita dirtelo." Spingo di nuovo sulle sue spalle, mentre le porte dell'ascensore si aprono e lui esce, portandomi lungo il corridoio. "Il mio stomaco era sottosopra."

Il suo cipiglio si fa più evidente, mentre si ferma davanti alla porta del mio appartamento. "Sì, me l'ha detto, ma pensavo..." Mi mette giù con cautela e cerca le chiavi nella tasca.

"Pensavi che fosse una scusa? No, è successo davvero." Non perché stavo male, però. Mi mordo la parte interna della guancia, poi decido di non iniziare la nostra vita coniugale con una menzogna—nemmeno con un'omissione.

Aspetto che entriamo nell'appartamento, e poi dico in un tono più calmo: "Peter... c'è qualcosa che dovresti sapere. L'Agente Ryson è venuto qui oggi, proprio prima che uscissi."

Si trasforma in una statua, poi si gira verso di me, incredulo. "Che cosa?"

"Non in veste ufficiale" mi affretto a rassicurarlo. "Voleva solo parlare con me."

Le sue grandi mani si stringono ai fianchi. "Perché?"

"Credo che... credo che fosse frustrato. Per come è andata a finire. Pensa che gli abbia mentito e che"—deglutisco, con la gola che brucia—"abbiamo cospirato per uccidere George. Che volevo che ti sbarazzassi di George, perché aveva un danno cerebrale ed era un alcolista da cui avevo già intenzione di divorziare."

Peter impreca sottovoce. "Quel fottuto ublyudok. Avrei dovuto—" Si ferma e fa un respiro per calmarsi. Con un tono più dolce, chiede: "Ti ha fatta arrabbiare, ptichka?" Fa un passo verso di me, e mi prende dolcemente il mento, costringendomi a guardarlo. "È per questo che mi stavi dando buca?"

Riesco ad annuire debolmente. "Mi dispiace. Davvero. Stava già succedendo così velocemente, e poi è venuto lui e..." Chiudo gli occhi, poi li riapro per incrociare di nuovo il suo sguardo grigio-tempesta. "Mi dispiace. Non stavo pensando lucidamente."

Peter muove la mano sulla mia mascella, con un tocco delicato e tenero. "Che cos'altro ti ha detto, amore mio?"

"Niente. Era solo—Oh, ha detto che se farai qualcos'altro di natura criminale, l'accordo sarà nullo e vuoto... e che ora hanno anche il mio numero."

Lo sguardo di Peter si indurisce di nuovo. "Capisco." Fa un passo indietro, lasciando cadere la mano, e mi rendo conto che è arrabbiato—arrabbiato come non l'ho mai visto.

Improvvisamente preoccupata, faccio un passo avanti,

prendendogli la mano in entrambe le mie. "Non gli farai niente, vero? Te l'ho detto, perché non voglio che ci siano bugie tra noi —non perché voglio che tu punisca Ryson."

Non risponde, ma vedo la risposta nella mascella serrata e nella rigidità del palmo nella mia stretta.

"Peter, non farlo, per favore. Ascoltami..." Gli stringo la mano. "È un agente federale, e *vuole* che ti comporti bene. In realtà, non sarei sorpresa, se fosse per questo che è venuto qui oggi: per provocarti e assicurarsi che tu violi le condizioni dell'accordo. Non fare il suo gioco. Non ne vale la pena."

L'espressione di Peter non cambia. "Sei preoccupata per lui o per me?"

Gli lascio andare la mano. "Per entrambi, ovviamente. Non voglio che tu gli faccia del male—e sicuramente non voglio che ti metta nei guai a causa sua."

"Hmm." Peter mi accarezza delicatamente la guancia. "Mi stavo chiedendo..."

Inumidisco le labbra. "Che cosa?"

"Saresti felice se me ne andassi e ti lasciassi libera? Se mi mettessi nei guai e dovessi andarmene per sempre?"

Sbatto le palpebre. "Ma... non lo faresti. Mi porteresti con te, vero? Se dovessi andar via?"

Il suo sguardo si rabbuia. "Può essere. È questo che vorresti, ptichka?"

Mi si stringe il petto, con il respiro che diventa affannoso. "Peter... Io..."

"Non riesci ancora a dirlo, vero?" Mi prende di nuovo il mento, costringendomi a guardarlo. La sua voce contiene una strana nota. "Non riesci ad ammettere che questo è reciproco, che non sono l'unico ad essere pazzo."

Deglutisco con forza e indietreggio, liberandomi della sua presa. "Non è così."

"No?" Mi si avvicina, implacabile come uno squalo. "Dimmi

perché oggi sei quasi scappata, allora. Dimmi come mai la visita di Ryson ti ha sconvolta in questo modo."

Continuo a indietreggiare fin quando la mia schiena non colpisce la parete. "Te l'ho già detto. Ti ho detto tutto."

"Non tutto." Appoggia i palmi sulla parete, su entrambi i miei lati, ingabbiandomi ancora una volta. Il suo tono è allo stesso tempo crudele e tenero, mentre mormora: "Non tutto, amore mio."

Lo fisso, con le pulsazioni che mi martellano le tempie. Non capisco che cosa stia cercando, che cosa desideri da me. "Peter, ti prego. Mi dispiace per oggi. Dico davvero. Ero così arrabbiata che non ero lucida, ma non è una scusa. Non avrei dovuto..." Scuoto la testa.

"No, non avresti dovuto" concorda, con gli occhi che si rabbuiano ulteriormente, e poi, senza preavviso, aggancia la mano nel corpetto del mio abito e lo strappa con sorprendente ferocia, lacerando il pizzo fatto a mano e facendo volare i bottoni di perle sul pavimento di piastrelle.

Ansimando, stringo la parte superiore dell'abito strappato, ma Peter mi gira intorno, premendomi il viso contro il muro. "Davvero, non avresti dovuto" mi ringhia nell'orecchio e strappa il vestito fino in fondo, facendolo penzolare sulle mie ginocchia.

Rimango col reggiseno bianco senza bretelline e la biancheria intima—pezzi sexy e di pizzo che ho indossato per abbinarli all'abito. Nemmeno quelli durano più di un momento, mentre Peter li strappa via, lasciandomi completamente nuda.

Ansimando, premo i palmi contro la parete, aspettandomi che mi faccia divaricare le gambe e che mi scopi, ma il suo braccio potente scivola intorno al mio petto, sollevandomi dai resti del vestito. Le mie scarpe, con i loro sottili cinturini attorno alle caviglie, rimangono sui piedi, mentre agito le gambe in aria, con lui che mi conduce implacabilmente in camera da letto.

Mi getta sul letto a faccia in giù, e mi affretto a girarmi, mentre fa un passo indietro per togliersi i vestiti. Vedo un lampo di metallo e sento un tonfo pesante, quando butta da parte la giacca—*era armato al nostro matrimonio?*— ma poi la mia attenzione si sposta su qualcosa di molto più pericoloso.

L'espressione sul suo volto.

Socchiude gli occhi, dilatando le narici, mentre si slaccia la cintura, e nella frenesia dei movimenti, scorgo il violento desiderio che è sempre lì, l'oscuro e selvaggio bisogno che pulsa anche nel mio intimo.

Mi farà del male stanotte, lo sento, e le viscere si stringono per un'ondata di paura e lussuria. Dovrei scappare, protestare, ma il mio corpo agisce di propria iniziativa, con le gambe che mi spingono giù dal letto per inginocchiarmi sul tappeto davanti a lui, allungando le mani verso la cerniera dei suoi pantaloni dello smoking.

"Sì, così, vieni qui" mormora sottovoce, contorcendo bruscamente le mani tra i miei capelli, mentre apro la cerniera e gli spingo giù i pantaloni, liberando l'erezione. È già completamente eccitato, con il cazzo lungo, spesso e così duro che le vene stanno per esplodere lungo l'asta. È un'arma, quel pene, ma anche uno strumento di piacere inimmaginabile, e mi viene l'acquolina in bocca, mentre lo fisso, ricordando come mi ha soffocata con esso—e come mi ha fatta bruciare.

Mi avvicina il viso e mi schiaffeggia il cazzo sulla guancia. Una volta, due volte, tre volte. Apro la bocca al quarto schiaffo e prendo la punta, succhiandola mentre incontro il suo sguardo. Il familiare sapore al muschio mi scalda ulteriormente l'intimo, e la mia mano sinistra serpeggia tra le gambe, mentre sollevo la destra per afferrargli le palle.

Il suo viso si contorce con feroce piacere, mentre lo stringo dolcemente, e spinge più profondamente nella mia bocca, stringendo i pugni nei miei capelli. "Cazzo..." geme, con voce bassa e roca. "Continua così, proprio così."

Obbedisco, lasciandomi fottere la gola, mentre gli massaggio le palle. Allo stesso tempo, strofino il clitoride con la mano sinistra, con le cosce che tremano per la tensione crescente, mentre trovo il ritmo giusto. Le sue pupille si dilatano ulteriormente, con i fianchi che si muovono sempre più velocemente, e ci sono quasi, quando sibila qualcosa in russo e improvvisamente mi spinge via.

Spaventata, cado all'indietro sui palmi, e, prima che possa riprendermi, mi afferra e mi getta di nuovo sul letto.

"Non te la caverai con così poco" ringhia, e respiro affannosamente, mentre mi passa la cintura intorno ai polsi, legandoli alla spalliera, e poi si muove lungo il mio corpo, con le mani forti che mi separano le gambe.

"Che cosa stai facendo?" Il mio battito cardiaco è così veloce che riesco a malapena a parlare. "Peter, per favore, non—"

"Zitta" respira sulla mia coscia, e sussulto, quando mi passa i denti sulle labbra, prima di spingere la lingua tra le mie pieghe, trovando infallibilmente il clitoride palpitante.

L'eccitazione è quasi istantanea. Il fuoco si fa strada nelle vene, e mi inarco, urlando e tirando la cintura, mentre l'orgasmo ritardato si abbatte su di me, facendo esplodere tutto il corpo. Ma il mio tormentatore non ha finito. La sua lingua si addolcisce quel tanto che basta da lasciarmi godere i residui dell'orgasmo, e poi due ruvide dita affondano dentro di me, trovando il punto G. Grido, mentre la sua lingua riprende a lavorare come una dannata, e non passa molto tempo prima che io venga di nuovo.

Non ha ancora finito, però, con l'abile bocca che si sposta lungo il mio corpo, dandomi baci ardenti sul ventre e sul seno, succhiandomi i capezzoli e la parte sensibile del collo. E per tutto il tempo, le sue dita rimangono dentro di me, mentre il pollice lavora sul clitoride, riportandomi di nuovo al limite.

Le sue labbra incontrano le mie proprio mentre comincio a venire, e gemo il rilascio nella sua bocca, assaggiando la lingua mentre approfondisce il bacio. I miei muscoli sembrano liquefatti dentro la pelle, con i polsi doloranti per aver strattonato la cintura; eppure, continua a scoparmi con quelle due dita ruvide, fino al climax e oltre.

Sono sull'orlo di un altro orgasmo, quando alza la testa e ritira le dita, solo per spostarle più in basso, spalmando la mia umidità su tutto il percorso. Mi agito, realizzando ciò che sta pianificando, ma è implacabile, e grido, chiudendo gli occhi, mentre il suo dito medio trova la mia apertura posteriore, con la scivolosità del sesso che agisce come un lubrificante, e il dito spinge dentro di me, oltre la resistenza dei muscoli serrati.

Mi ha già presa così, ma sono passati più di nove mesi, e il suo dito sembra enorme come il cazzo, con i bordi dell'unghia che lacerano i tessuti teneri. Il mio battito accelera, con il respiro che si blocca in gola, mentre ritira lentamente il dito che mi invade, solo per aggiungerne un altro.

"Peter..."

"Shhh." Mi bacia di nuovo, e, mentre le due dita premono sulla mia apertura, rendendomi nervosa per il panico, il pollice trova il clitoride indolenzito. L'orgasmo che si era quasi placato riaffiora, con la tensione che si infrange con una forza esplosiva, e mentre vengo, gemendo impotente, le due dita spingono fino in fondo.

Mi irrigidisco di nuovo, ma è troppo tardi, e tutto ciò che posso fare è respirare affannosamente, mentre distende il mio passaggio stretto, facendolo irritare e bruciare. La pienezza è insopportabile, invasiva, eppure sotto il disagio c'è la promessa di qualcosa di più, e il mio corpo si contrae per i residui orgasmici, inseguendo quella sensazione più oscura.

"Sì, così, ptichka" respira contro le mie labbra, e rabbrividisco quando il suo pollice trova di nuovo il clitoride. Non posso venire un'altra volta, è impossibile; eppure, il mio corpo non si rende conto di essere sfinito. La tensione si accumula nel mio intimo, avvolgendolo sempre di più, e sono sull'orlo dell'orgasmo, tremando e ansimando, quando le dita invasive escono dal sedere.

Gemo dalla frustrazione, tirando la cintura e inarcando i fianchi, e lui ride piano, con il suono basso e roco, mentre la parte sinistra del materasso affonda.

Spaventata, apro gli occhi, ma è già tornato, con un flaconcino in mano. "Non preoccuparti, ptichka. Arriveremo lì" promette con voce rauca, e sobbalzo quando apre il flacone, facendo cadere il liquido fresco su tutto il mio sesso gonfio. Cola più in basso, verso la fessura tra le natiche, e il mio battito accelera di nuovo, quando i nostri sguardi si incrociano.

Nei suoi occhi, scorgo la fame e qualcosa di più, un'esigenza silenziosa ma feroce. Agganciando gli avambracci sotto le mie ginocchia, mi solleva le gambe sulle spalle e si sporge in avanti, distendendomi i muscoli posteriori della coscia, mentre guida il cazzo verso il mio sedere.

"È questo che vuoi da me?" I suoi occhi brillano, mentre si spinge in avanti. "È di questo che hai bisogno?"

Spinge più in profondità, e gemo per la pressione pungente, con il sudore che mi inumidisce la spina dorsale, mentre lo sfintere cede lentamente. Con le gambe appoggiate sulle sue spalle, non riesco a controllare la profondità della penetrazione, e scivola fino in fondo, riempiendomi fin quando lo stomaco si contorce e respiro con rantoli affannati e superficiali.

"Io non..." Faccio un respiro più profondo, combattendo un'ondata di vertigini. "Non capisco."

"No?" Fa una smorfia, con un crudele bagliore che gli illumina lo sguardo metallico, mentre si ritira a metà strada, solo per rientrare. "Oppure non riesci ad ammetterlo?"

L'ustione bruciante è ancora lì, la pienezza estrema come prima, ma quando il suo pollice atterra sul mio clitoride, una tensione allettante soffoca il dolore. Muove i fianchi lentamente, con l'enorme cazzo che scivola sempre più in fondo con ogni spietato colpo, e l'orgasmo inizia a crescere, con il piacere diverso da prima, più forte e più oscuro, doloroso quanto inebriante.

È troppo, troppo intenso, e mi ritrovo a supplicare e implorare, contorcendomi quanto la posizione restrittiva lo consenta. Ma la crudele luce rimane nei suoi occhi, con il ritmo immutato, anche se sulla fronte appaiono delle gocce di sudore.

"Rispondimi" gracchia, sporgendosi in avanti quasi per piegarmi in due, e urlo, quando il dolore scatena la scintilla, accendendo il fuoco che mi consuma. L'estasi esplode attraverso le terminazioni nervose, con la vista inondata di luce bianca, mentre chiudo gli occhi. Il formicolio mi attraversa la schiena, con il rilascio che riaffiora, facendo tremare ogni muscolo.

Lo sento gemere sopra di me e sento un caldo pulsare in profondità. Sta venendo anche lui, mi rendo conto vagamente, e spalanco le palpebre per il tempo necessario a vedere lo stesso doloroso piacere contorcergli il viso.

Respirando pesantemente, crolla su di me, e restiamo così, con i nostri respiri che si sincronizzano, mentre ci riprendiamo. Mi sento come se i muscoli posteriori della coscia potessero strapparsi, e il sedere brucia, mentre il suo cazzo si ammorbidisce gradualmente all'interno, ma non voglio muovermi.

Voglio rimanere così, con il corpo unito al suo per sempre.

"Sì" dico sottovoce, mentre alza lentamente la testa e si solleva per alleviare la pressione sulle mie gambe. I nostri occhi si incrociano e un cupo trionfo si accende nel suo sguardo, mentre ripeto stancamente: "Sì, è così."

Comprendo la sua domanda ora, e conosco la terrificante risposta. Questo è *ciò* che voglio da lui—ed è sicuramente ciò di cui ho bisogno. Dolore, punizione, forza—ho bisogno di questo da lui quasi quanto ho bisogno dell'amore e della tenerezza.

Ho bisogno del pacchetto completo, per quanto incasinato possa essere.

Si allunga in avanti e mi libera le mani, poi si ritira con cura da me e mi pulisce con un fazzoletto. Chiudo gli occhi, troppo esausta per potermi muovere, e le sue braccia forti scivolano sotto di me, sollevandomi dal letto.

Mi porta sotto la doccia e mi lava lì, asciugandomi il trucco imbrattato, districando tutti i ricci e le onde annodate della mia acconciatura. Poi, mi avvolge in un asciugamano e mi porta nel soggiorno, dove si siede sul divano, tenendomi stretta sul grembo.

Appoggio la testa sulla sua ampia spalla e il palmo sul cuore, sentendo il battito costante all'interno del petto muscoloso, mentre mi massaggia delicatamente la nuca, con le dita forti che sciolgono i nodi che non sapevo nemmeno fossero lì.

"Allora, dimmi." La sua voce è un rombo sommesso e profondo sotto il mio orecchio. "Dimmi perché ti sei quasi tirata indietro oggi."

"Perché..." Perché Ryson mi ha ricordato la realtà delle cose, facendomi sentire inferiore a un mollusco—è quello che inizio a dire, ma poi mi fermo. Non è una bugia, ma non è nemmeno la verità. Ero in preda al panico prima della visita dell'agente, prima che mi costringesse ad affrontare l'amara realtà.

"Perché?" insiste Peter, interrompendomi.

"Perché..." Un nodo mi si forma nella gola, mentre chiudo gli occhi, poi li riapro, tirandomi indietro per incrociare il suo sguardo. È giunto il momento di smettere di fingere e di abbracciare la verità. Prendendo fiato, dico incerta: "Perché avevi ragione. Tornata in Giappone, quando hai detto che era troppo tardi per me, avevi ragione." Sta diventando sempre più difficile far uscire le parole, ma cerco di continuare. "Era troppo tardi allora, ed è decisamente troppo tardi ora. Non so quando è successo, ma da qualche parte lungo il nostro complicato cammino, mi sono innamorata di te. Solo che—" Mi fermo, con la gola che si chiude completamente.

I suoi occhi grigi si addolciscono, con la mano che riprende il leggero massaggio. "Solo cosa?"

"Solo che non riesco ad accettarlo" confesso, con le parole che sembrano pietre nelle corde vocali. "Ho bisogno..." mi fermo, non riuscendo a dirlo esplicitamente, ma lui capisce.

"Hai bisogno di questo." Solleva la mano per accarezzarmi la guancia. "Hai bisogno che io ti faccia del male a volte, che assuma il controllo e ti costringa. Che ti tolga le altre scelte, in modo che tu possa abbracciare quello che vuoi davvero."

Annuisco a scatti, sia vergognosa che sollevata. È sbagliato e codardo da parte mia, ma nel contesto di tutta la contorta situazione è l'unica cosa che sembra giusta. La nostra relazione non sarà mai come quella di altre persone... perché non dovrebbe esistere proprio. Torturatore e vittima, assassino e vedova del suo bersaglio—siamo impossibili insieme come qualsiasi predatore e preda, ma grazie a Peter, siamo qui.

La sua ossessione ci ha creati.

Lui capisce; lo vedo nel caldo argento del suo sguardo. "Così, oggi, quando ti ho chiamata" mormora, mettendomi una ciocca di capelli bagnati dietro l'orecchio "ne avevi bisogno, vero, ptichka? Avevi bisogno di sapere che andare via non era un'opzione... che dovevi sposarmi."

Deglutisco con forza, combattendo la tentazione di distogliere lo sguardo. "Penso di sì. Può essere. Io—" Mi fermo di nuovo, incapace di formulare il confuso mix di emozioni che sto provando. La sua minaccia mi aveva terrorizzata come previsto, ma ora mi rendo conto di essermi sentita anche sollevata.

In fondo, speravo che lo facesse, che mi strappasse la vergogna e il senso di colpa.

Piega la mano calda intorno alla mia mascella, con il pollice che mi sfiora dolcemente la guancia. "Va tutto bene, ptichka. Non starci male. È quello che è, e non c'è niente di male ad ammetterlo."

Lo fisso. "Non pensi che io sia... una persona orribile?"

"Perché mi ami o perché non riesci ad accettarlo completamente?"

"Entrambe."

Il suo sorriso è al contempo sensuale e triste. "No, amore mio. Sei un prodotto della tua educazione, come io lo sono della mia. Avevi ragione anche tu, nella clinica svizzera, quando hai detto che in un mondo diverso, in una vita diversa, sarebbe stato tutto diverso. Se potessi, cancellerei il passato, riscriverei la storia tra noi, ma al posto di quello, ti darò ciò di cui hai bisogno—ciò di cui entrambi abbiamo bisogno, se siamo sinceri."

Sostengo il suo sguardo, con gli occhi che bruciano. Capisce, perché è il mio specchio oscuro e terrificante, con i suoi desideri sia inversi che paralleli ai miei. Mi ama, lo ha dimostrato nei modi più vividi, ma una parte di lui ha anche bisogno di farmi del male, di punirmi per il dolore del passato.

Di controllarmi, in modo che io non possa lasciarlo.

In modo da non perdermi, come ha perso Tamila e suo figlio.

"Ti amo" dico sottovoce, con le parole che escono più facilmente la seconda volta. "Ti amo, Peter, con tutta me stessa. E apprezzo quello che hai fatto per me... quello a cui hai rinunciato."

Ha preferito me alla vendetta.

Ha preferito il nostro amore al desiderio di affrontare la morte.

Il suo sorriso si attenua—il ricordo di Henderson deve ancora fargli male—ma poi si sporge in avanti e mi dà un dolce bacio sulle labbra. "Lo so, ptichka. So che mi ami—e, in un modo o nell'altro, faremo funzionare le cose. Dobbiamo... perché non ti lascerò andare via."

Appoggio la testa sulla sua spalla, chiudendo gli occhi, e sento il cuore che batte in quel torace possente.

Ha ragione.

Faremo funzionare le cose.

Il nostro amore potrebbe non essere semplice e diretto, ma non è meno forte per come è iniziato. Questo matrimonio non sarà facile, ma sarà per sempre.

A prescindere da cosa succederà, lui ha me e io ho lui.

Finché saremo entrambi vivi.

$\mathcal{H}$enderson

F ISSO LO SCHERMO DEL COMPUTER, CLICCANDO DA UN'IMMAGINE patinata all'altra, con la gola che brucia e la mano che trema per una rabbia nauseabonda.

Sono bellissimi, entrambi giovani e in salute, con i migliori abiti da sposi che la ricchezza macchiata dal sangue possa comprare. In una foto, la solleva sul petto; in un'altra, si tengono per mano e si guardano negli occhi.

Clicco di nuovo e assaporo l'amarezza della bile. Si stanno sorridendo in questa foto, accanto alla famiglia e agli amici di lei.

Qualcuna di queste persone sa?

Sono a conoscenza di ciò che lui è?

Lei sa. Non ho dubbi su questo. Lo vedo nei suoi occhi, nel suo sorriso grazioso e menzognero.

Lei sa, e lo ama.

Lo ha sposato, conoscendo le cose mostruose che ha fatto.

Ruoto la testa da un lato all'altro, cercando inutilmente di liberare l'agonizzante tensione. Le iniezioni degli steroidi non aiutano più, e il dolore mi divora, tenendomi sveglio la notte, aggiungendosi agli incubi e all'insonnia.

Tre anni in fuga.

Tre anni nella paura per le vite dei miei figli.

Tre anni, sapendo che tutti quelli che avevo lasciato alle spalle avrebbero potuto essere uccisi o torturati... che nessuno a cui tengo sarà mai veramente al sicuro.

Clicco su una finestra del browser e navigo sulla pagina Facebook di mia figlia. Non c'è niente lì da tre anni, niente sui social media di mio figlio. Anche loro hanno vissuto nella paura per tutto questo tempo.

Nella paura del mostro che sorride alla sua amorevole sposa.

Crede di aver vinto.

Crede che sia finita.

È convinto che lasceranno che il suo regno del terrore abbia la meglio.

Allontanandomi dal computer, apro la cartella sulla scrivania, cercando di mantenere la calma, mentre rivedo la lista dei nomi—la mia lista questa volta.

Julian Esguerra, il mostruoso animale domestico della CIA.

Il suo fedele compagno, Lucas Kent.

Yan e Ilya Ivanov.

Anton Rezov.

E, naturalmente, lo stesso Peter Sokolov.

Pensano di avercela fatta, di essere intoccabili.

Non potrebbero sbagliarsi di più.

È giunto il momento che il mondo li veda per i terroristi che sono.

In un modo o nell'altro, pagheranno.

MIA PER SEMPRE

IL MIO TORMENTATORE: LIBRO 4

PARTE I

Henderson

"CHE COSA STAI FACENDO?"

La voce ansiosa di Bonnie mi fa sobbalzare dalla pianificazione, e alzo lo sguardo, spingendo la cartella che stavo studiando in una pila di file sulla scrivania, mentre mi preparo a rispondere con una bugia plausibile.

Solo che la donna con cui sono sposato da ventun anni non mi sta guardando.

Sta fissando il computer dietro di me, dove la fotografia di una splendida sposa dai capelli castani che sorride al suo bellissimo sposo occupa la maggior parte dello schermo.

Fanculo. Credevo di aver chiuso quella scheda. I miei muscoli del collo si contraggono per la tensione, con la bile che torna a bruciarmi la gola, quando vedo che mia moglie inizia a tremare.

"Perché hai la sua foto?" La sua voce diventa acuta, mentre

gli occhi si spostano su di me, accusandomi. "Perché hai l'immagine di quel mostro sul tuo schermo?"

"Bonnie... non è come pensi." Mi alzo, ma lei sta già indietreggiando, scuotendo la testa, con i lunghi orecchini che svolazzano intorno al viso magro.

"Me l'hai promesso. Mi hai detto che saremmo stati al sicuro."

"E lo saremo" la rassicuro, ma è troppo tardi.

È già andata via.

È tornata al rifugio del suo letto, alle pillole, agli insensati reality show.

Dove io e i nostri figli non potremmo mai raggiungerla.

Sprofondando nella sedia, giro la testa da un lato all'altro, rilasciando la peggior tensione angosciosa, mentre tiro di nuovo fuori la cartella. Il nome all'interno mi fissa, con ogni lettera che mi deride, alimentando gli amari fuochi della rabbia.

Peter Sokolov.

Sono l'ultima persona rimasta sulla sua lista. L'unica che non ha ancora ucciso per quello che è successo in quel villaggio di merda nel Dagestan. Un errore, un ordine emesso con noncuranza, e questo è il risultato. Per anni ha dato la caccia a me e alla mia famiglia, torturando i nostri amici e le persone amate nel tentativo di raggiungermi, agitando i sogni dei miei figli, distruggendo le nostre vite in ogni modo.

E ora, grazie all'influenza del suo amico Esguerra sul nostro governo, gli è stato concesso di vagare liberamente. Di sposare la sua bella dottoressa dai capelli castani e di vivere negli Stati Uniti come se tutto fosse stato perdonato e dimenticato.

Come se la sua promessa di non uccidermi fosse qualcosa a cui dovrei credere.

Il mio sguardo si sofferma sul resto dei nomi nella cartella.

Julian Esguerra.

Lucas Kent.

Yan e Ilya Ivanov.

Anton Rezov.
Alleati di Sokolov—mostri, tutti quanti.
Devono pagare per quello che hanno fatto.
Come Sokolov, devono essere neutralizzati.
Allora e solo allora saremo davvero al sicuro.

2

Sara

MI SVEGLIO CON LA SORPRENDENTE CONSTATAZIONE CHE SONO sposata.

Sposata con Peter Garin, ovvero Sokolov.

L'uomo che ha ucciso George Cobakis, il mio primo marito, dopo essersi introdotto in casa mia e avermi torturata.

Il mio stalker

Il mio rapitore.

L'amore della mia vita.

La mia mente torna a ieri notte e il calore si diffonde in tutto il corpo, con un mix di imbarazzo ed eccitazione. Mi ha punita ieri. Mi ha punita per avergli quasi dato buca sull'altare.

Mi ha presa brutalmente, costringendomi ad ammetterlo.

Facendomi confessare di amare lui—*tutto* di lui, comprese le parti oscure.

Che ho bisogno di quell'oscurità... che ho bisogno che sia

diretta verso di me, in modo da poter superare la vergogna e il senso di colpa per essermi innamorata di un mostro.

Aprendo gli occhi, fisso il candido soffitto bianco. Siamo ancora nel mio piccolo appartamento, ma immagino che ci trasferiremo presto. E poi cosa? Bambini? Passeggiate nel parco e cene con i miei genitori?

Davvero inizierò a costruire una vita con l'uomo che ha minacciato di uccidere tutti al nostro matrimonio, se non mi fossi presentata?

Sicuramente sta preparando la colazione, perché sento profumi deliziosi, che arrivano dalla cucina. È qualcosa di dolce e salato, e il mio stomaco borbotta, mentre mi siedo, sussultando per il dolore nei muscoli posteriori della coscia.

Se dobbiamo scopare spesso in posizioni esotiche, tanto vale iniziare a seguire lezioni di yoga.

Scuotendo la testa per quel pensiero ridicolo, vado a farmi una doccia e mi lavo i denti, e quando esco, indossando una vestaglia, sento la voce profonda e leggermente accentata di Peter che mi chiama.

O, più precisamente, che mi chiama la sua "ptichka."

"Sono qui" dico, entrando in cucina—solo per ritrovarmi travolta da braccia incredibilmente forti e baciata così appassionatamente da perdere il fiato.

"Sì" mormora mio marito, quando finalmente mi rimette in piedi. "Sei qui, e non andrai da nessuna parte." Le sue grandi mani si posano possessivamente sulla mia vita, con gli occhi grigi che scintillano come argento sul viso ricoperto da barba incolta. Pur indossando una maglietta e dei jeans, non deve essersi ancora rasato, perché quella barba ispida sembra deliziosamente ruvida e graffiante, e mi chiedo come sarebbe, se la sfregassi sulla mia pelle.

Impulsivamente, sollevo la mano sulla sua mascella cesellata. È ruvida come immaginavo, e sorrido, mentre chiude gli occhi e strofina la faccia sul mio palmo, come un grosso gatto che segna il proprio territorio.

"È domenica" gli dico, abbassando la mano, quando apre gli occhi. "Quindi sì, non andrò da nessuna parte. Che cosa c'è per colazione?"

Sorride e fa un passo indietro, liberandomi. "Pancake alla ricotta. Hai fame?"

"Potrei sicuramente mangiare" ammetto, e osservo i suoi occhi metallici brillare dal piacere.

Mi siedo, mentre afferra i piatti per entrambi e li dispone sul tavolo. Anche se è tornato solo martedì scorso, è già completamente a suo agio nella mia minuscola cucina, con i movimenti fluidi e sicuri come se vivesse qui da mesi.

Guardandolo, provo ancora l'inquietante sensazione che un pericoloso predatore abbia invaso il mio piccolo appartamento. Parzialmente, è dovuto alla sua stazza—mi supera di almeno una testa, con le spalle incredibilmente larghe e il corpo da soldato delle truppe scelte scolpito da muscoli duri. Ma c'è anche qualcosa in *lui*, qualcosa di più dei tatuaggi che gli decorano il braccio sinistro o della debole cicatrice che gli spacca in due il sopracciglio.

È qualcosa di intrinseco, una specie di spietatezza che scorgo anche quando sorride.

"Come ti senti, ptichka?" chiede, raggiungendomi al tavolo, e guardo il mio piatto, consapevole del perché è preoccupato.

"Bene." Non voglio pensare a ieri, a come la visita dell'Agente Ryson mi abbia fatta letteralmente star male. Ero già in ansia per il matrimonio, ma è stato solo quando l'agente dell'FBI mi ha sbattuto in faccia i crimini di Peter che il contenuto del mio stomaco si è rivoltato—e che ho quasi dato buca a Peter.

"Nessun effetto indesiderato dopo la scorsa notte?" chiarisce, e alzo lo sguardo, con il viso che si scalda, quando mi rendo conto che si sta riferendo alla nostra vita sessuale.

"No." La mia voce è strozzata. "Sto bene."

"Perfetto" mormora, con occhi caldi e oscuri, e nascondo il rossore raggiungendo un pancake alla ricotta.

"Ecco, amore mio." Con abilità, allunga due pancake e spinge una bottiglia di sciroppo d'acero verso di me. "Vuoi altro? Forse un po' di frutta?"

"Certo" rispondo, e lo vedo dirigersi verso il frigo per estrarre e lavare alcuni mirtilli.

Il mio assassino addomesticato. È così che sarà sempre la nostra vita insieme?

"Che cosa vuoi fare oggi?" chiedo, quando torna al tavolo, e fa spallucce, con le labbra scolpite curvate in un sorriso.

"Dipende da te, ptichka. Stavo pensando che potremmo uscire, goderci la bella giornata."

"Quindi... una passeggiata nel parco? Davvero?"

Si acciglia. "Perché no?"

"Nessun problema. Sono pronta." Mi concentro sui pancake per non iniziare a ridacchiare istericamente.

Non capirebbe.

Mangiamo in fretta—ho fame, e i pancake alla ricotta (*sirniki*, li chiama) sono deliziosi—e poi ci dirigiamo verso il parco. Peter sta guidando, e quando siamo a metà strada, noto un SUV nero che ci segue.

"È di nuovo Danny?" chiedo, guardando dietro.

Da quando Peter è tornato, i Federali ci hanno lasciato in pace, e lui è troppo tranquillo perché l'uomo che ci sta seguendo non sia la guardia del corpo/autista che ha ingaggiato.

Con mia sorpresa, scuote la testa. "Danny è libero oggi. Al suo posto ci sono un paio di altri ragazzi della squadra."

Ah. Mi giro sul sedile per studiare il SUV. I finestrini sono scuri, quindi non riesco a vedere. Accigliata, guardo Peter. "Pensi che abbiamo ancora bisogno di tutta quella sicurezza?"

Si stringe nelle spalle. "Spero di no. Ma meglio prevenire che curare."

"E questa macchina?" Mi guardo intorno nella lussuosa berlina Mercedes che ha acquistato la scorsa settimana. "È un po' più sicura in qualche modo?" Passo le nocche sul finestrino. "Sembra davvero spesso."

La sua espressione non cambia. "Sì. Il vetro è antiproiettile."

"Oh. Wow."

Mi guarda storto, con un debole sorriso che appare sulle sue labbra. "Non preoccuparti, ptichka. Non ho motivo di pensare che ci spareranno. Questa è solo una precauzione, tutto qui."

"Giusto." Solo una precauzione—come le armi che aveva nella giacca al nostro matrimonio. O la guardia del corpo/autista che viene a prendermi, quando Peter non può. Perché le normali coppie di periferia hanno sempre guardie del corpo e auto antiproiettile.

"Parlami delle case che hai trovato" dico, mettendo da parte il disagio generato dal pensiero di tutte quelle misure di sicurezza. Data la sua precedente professione e il tipo di nemici che si è fatto, la paranoia di Peter ha perfettamente senso, e non ho intenzione di obiettare su qualunque precauzione ritenga necessaria.

Come ha detto, meglio prevenire che curare.

"Ti mostrerò le inserzioni tra un secondo" mi comunica, e mi rendo conto che siamo già a destinazione.

Parcheggia abilmente la macchina e scende per aprirmi la portiera. Metto la mia mano nella sua, lasciandomi aiutare, e non sono minimamente sorpresa, quando sfrutta l'opportunità di tirarmi a sé per un bacio.

Le sue labbra sono morbide e delicate mentre sfiorano le mie, con l'alito che sa di sciroppo d'acero. Non c'è urgenza in questo bacio, niente oscurità—solo tenerezza e desiderio.

Eppure, quando alza la testa, il mio cuore sta battendo come se mi avesse rapita, con la pelle calda e formicolante, dove il suo palmo mi stringe la guancia.

"Ti amo" mormora, guardandomi, e io gli sorrido, con il disagio rimpiazzato da una sensazione leggera e vivace.

"Ti amo anch'io." Le parole sembrano ancora più facili oggi —perché sono vere. Amo Peter.

Lo amo, anche se mi terrorizza ancora.

Sorride e mi guida verso una panchina. "Qui." Mi mette giù a sedere e tira fuori il suo telefono, toccando lo schermo alcune volte prima di passarmelo. "Questi sono gli annunci che ho trovato" mi informa, osservandomi con un caldo sguardo argentato. "Fammi sapere quali case ti piacciono e possiamo andare a vederle."

Sfoglio le immagini, mentre la sensazione di positività si intensifica.

È questa la vera felicità?

"Camminiamo e parliamo" gli dico, quando ho finito di guardare le foto, e lui è d'accordo, stringendo la mia mano in una salda presa, mentre girovaghiamo per il parco e discutiamo dei pro e dei contro delle diverse abitazioni.

"Non pensi che una casa con quattro camere sia troppo piccola?" chiede, guardandomi con un sorriso interrogativo, e scuoto la testa.

"Perché dovrei pensarlo?"

"Beh..." Si ferma e mi guarda. "Hai riflettuto su quanti figli ti piacerebbe avere?"

Il mio stomaco si contrae. Eccola—la discussione che abbiamo evitato da Cipro, da quando Peter ha ammesso che stava cercando di mettermi incinta e mi sono schiantata con l'auto nel tentativo di scappare. Mi aspettavo che l'argomento sarebbe tornato a galla prima o poi—non abbiamo usato il preservativo da quando è tornato e ha rivelato apertamente ai miei genitori che avrebbe voluto che iniziassimo presto una famiglia. Tuttavia, il cuore mi batte forte nel petto, e il palmo è sudato nella mano di Peter, mentre cerco di immaginare come sarebbe avere un figlio con lui.

Con il killer spietato che mi ama ossessivamente.

Con un respiro, raccolgo il coraggio. Peter non è più un criminale, non è più un fuggitivo, e io sono sua moglie, non la sua prigioniera. Ha rinunciato alla sua vendetta per poter avere questo—una vita vera insieme.

Passeggiate nel parco, bambini e tutto il resto.

"Ne ho immaginati tre" rispondo fermamente, sostenendo il suo sguardo. "Ma penso che potrei anche essere felice con uno. E tu?"

Un tenero sorriso sboccia sul suo viso cupamente bello. "Sicuramente, almeno due—supponendo che tutto vada bene con il primo." Appoggia il grande palmo sul mio stomaco. "Credi che ci sia una possibilità...?"

Rido, allontanandomi. "Ma stai scherzando? È troppo presto per dirlo. Sei tornato meno di una settimana fa. Se sapessi di essere incinta, sarebbe problematico."

"Molto" concorda, prendendomi la mano e stringendola in modo possessivo. Riprendiamo a camminare e mi lancia un'occhiata di traverso. "Suppongo che ti stia bene."

"Avere un bambino adesso, vuoi dire?"

Annuisce e faccio un respiro profondo, guardando un gruppo di adolescenti sullo skateboard. "Credo di sì. Mi piacerebbe aspettare ancora un po', ma so che questo significa molto per te."

Non risponde, e quando lo guardo, noto che la sua espressione si è rabbuiata, con la mascella serrata, mentre fissa dritto davanti a sé. La sensazione di positività svanisce, quando mi rendo conto di avergli inavvertitamente ricordato la tragedia del suo passato.

"Scusa." Sollevo le nostre mani giunte per premere il suo

pugno contro il mio petto. "Non volevo ricordarti la tua famiglia."

Il suo sguardo incontra il mio, e parte della sofferenza in esso recede. "Va tutto bene, ptichka." La sua voce è rauca, mentre solleva le nostre mani unite più in alto per darmi un tenero bacio sulle nocche. "Non devi sempre stare attenta a quello che dici. Pasha e Tamila vivranno sempre nei miei ricordi, ma tu sei la mia famiglia ora."

Il mio cuore si stringe in una palla dolorante. Ha ragione. Sono *io* la sua famiglia—ed è mio. Dato che il matrimonio è avvenuto così velocemente, non ho avuto la possibilità di pensarci davvero, di articolare quella realtà nella mia mente.

Siamo sposati.

Sposati davvero.

Non riesco più a pensare a George come marito, perché Peter detiene questo titolo adesso— proprio come lui non riesce a pensare a Tamila come moglie.

"E hai ragione" continua, mentre metabolizzo quella realizzazione. "La famiglia è importante per me. Voglio che abbiamo un figlio, e lo voglio presto. Comunque..." Esita, poi aggiunge: "Se vuoi aspettare, non forzerò il problema."

Mi fermo e lo guardo a bocca aperta. "Davvero? Perché no?"

Un sorriso lampeggia sul suo viso. "Vuoi che lo faccia?"

"No! È solo che..." Scuoto la testa, liberando la mano dalla sua presa. "Non capisco. Pensavo che ne facesse parte, sai, il matrimonio e tutto il resto. Hai forzato il matrimonio, quindi..."

Ogni traccia di umorismo abbandona il suo sguardo. "Sei quasi morta, amore mio. A Cipro, quando pensavi che ti avrei costretta a fare un figlio, hai cercato di fuggire e sei quasi morta."

Mi mordo il labbro. "Era diverso. *Noi* eravamo diversi."

"Sì. Ma il parto in generale può essere pericoloso. Nonostante tutti i progressi della medicina di oggi, una donna rischia la propria salute, se non la propria vita. E se ti succedesse qualcosa, perché ho insistito io..." Si blocca, con la mascella serrata, mentre distoglie lo sguardo.

Lo fisso, con il cuore che mi batte forte nel petto. Le probabilità che possa succedermi qualcosa di grave durante il parto sono molto basse, e il mio primo istinto di medico è quello di dirglielo, per rassicurarlo. Ma all'ultimo secondo, ci ripenso.

"Quindi, aspetteresti?" chiedo con attenzione, invece.

Si volta di nuovo verso di me, con lo sguardo cupo. "Vuoi aspettare, amore mio?"

Ora sono io a distogliere lo sguardo. Lo voglio? Fino a quel momento, avevo pensato che il ritorno di Peter e il matrimonio affrettato significassero che un bambino era imminente nel nostro futuro. Mi ero rassegnata al pensiero, l'ho persino accolto in un certo senso.

Se non altro, i miei genitori potrebbero avere i nipoti che desiderano—un aspetto positivo che non avevo considerato fino alla cena dell'altra sera.

"Sara?" insiste, e alzo lo sguardo per incontrare il suo.

Eccola qui.

La mia possibilità di rimandare.

Di fare la cosa giusta, la cosa intelligente.

Di avere un figlio solo quando sarò sicura di poterlo fare, che Peter possa vivere questo tipo di vita.

Tutto quello che dovrei fare è dire di sì, sfruttare la possibilità di scelta che mi ha dato, ma la mia bocca si rifiuta di formare la parola. Invece, mentre sostengo il suo sguardo, scorgendo la tensione in esso, mi sento di dire: "No."

"No?"

"No, non voglio aspettare" chiarisco, mettendo a tacere la voce razionale che urla nella mia mente, mentre vedo un sorriso luminoso e gioioso che gli curva le labbra.

Forse questa è la decisione sbagliata, ma in questo momento, non sembra così. Peter aveva ragione, quando ha detto che la vita è breve. *È* breve e incerta, piena di insidie. L'ho sempre vissuta con cautela, pianificando il futuro partendo dal presupposto che ce ne sarebbe stata una sola, ma se c'è una cosa che ho imparato negli ultimi due anni, è che non ci sono garanzie.

C'è solo l'oggi, il momento presente.

Solo noi, insieme e innamorati.

TRASCORRIAMO UN'ALTRA ORA NEL PARCO, POI FACCIAMO LA SPESA insieme, facendo scorta di cibo per la settimana. Peter acquista abbastanza roba da sfamare dieci persone e, quando gli chiedo spiegazioni, mi informa che intende invitare i miei genitori a cena questo venerdì—e prepararmi il pranzo da portare al lavoro ogni giorno.

Quando torniamo a casa, lui scompare in cucina e io vado al mio computer per occuparmi delle congratulazioni e delle carte regalo inviate via e-mail—una scelta popolare per la maggior parte degli invitati al nostro matrimonio, dato che nessuno ha avuto il tempo di acquistare un regalo vero e proprio. Stampo tutte le carte regalo, le divido in categorie, applico i codici ai rivenditori specifici, e invio e-mail di ringraziamento. L'intera procedura richiede meno di quaranta minuti—un altro vantaggio del nostro matrimonio semplice e veloce.

Con George, avevamo passato due fine settimana di seguito a prepararlo.

Sto per spegnere il computer, quando noto un'altra e-mail nella mia casella di posta—questa da parte di un mittente sconosciuto, ma con l'oggetto "Congratulazioni."

La apro, aspettandomi un'altra carta regalo, ma all'interno c'è solo un breve messaggio.

Congratulazioni per il bellissimo matrimonio. Se hai bisogno di contattarci, puoi utilizzare questo indirizzo.

Con i migliori auguri,
Yan

Sbatto le palpebre, fissando l'e-mail. Non ho idea di come l'ex compagno di squadra di Peter abbia ottenuto il mio indirizzo, o perché abbia deciso di scrivermi, ma lo aggiungo ai miei contatti, per ogni evenienza.

Dopo aver finito con i regali, seguo i deliziosi odori in cucina, dove mio marito sta preparando il pranzo.

Forse è troppo presto per dirlo, ma mi sento ottimista.

Questa cosa del matrimonio funzionerà.

Noi due faremo in modo che sia così.

eter

Mentre pranziamo, tocco a malapena il mio cibo, con
tutta l'attenzione rivolta a Sara, che mi parla dei regali di nozze
e della strana e-mail di Yan. I suoi occhi color nocciola
sembrano quasi verdi, mentre gesticola animatamente con la
forchetta, con la pelle pallida nella luce del sole che filtra dalla
finestra della cucina. In un casual prendisole blu, con i capelli
castani ondulati sulle spalle esili, è il mio intero sogno che
prende vita, e il mio petto si stringe al ricordo di com'era stato
senza di lei per tutti quei mesi.

Non la lascerò mai più andare.

È mia, finché morte non ci separi.

"Perché pensi che abbia deciso di darmi le sue informazioni?
Pensi che voglia solo restare in contatto?" chiede, infilando un
pezzo di cetriolo nella sua insalata in stile russo, e mi sforzo di

concentrarmi sulla conversazione, invece che su quanto mi piacerebbe farla sdraiare sul tavolo e banchettare su di lei piuttosto che sul cibo che ho preparato.

"Non ne ho idea" rispondo, ed è vero. Dopo la mia partenza, Yan Ivanov ha rilevato la nostra attività di assassini, quindi non credo che mi vorrebbe indietro. Nei mesi precedenti c'è stata tensione tra noi, e sospetto che se non mi fossi fatto da parte volontariamente come caposquadra, avrebbe fatto del proprio meglio per prendere il mio posto.

Ma non pensa che la vita civile faccia per me; l'ha affermato al nostro matrimonio. Quindi, forse si aspetta che io torni e tenga d'occhio la situazione per ogni evenienza.

Con Yan, non si sa mai.

"Beh, spero che vengano a trovarci" dice Sara. "I ragazzi, voglio dire. Non ho avuto la possibilità di parlare con loro al matrimonio, e mi dispiace."

Sollevo le sopracciglia. "Davvero? È *quello* che ti fa stare male?"

Abbassa lo sguardo sulla sua insalatiera. "E l'averti quasi mollato sull'altare, ovviamente."

I bordi metallici del manico della forchetta mi tagliano il palmo, e mi rendo conto che sto stringendo troppo la posata. Non sono più arrabbiato con la mia ptichka, anche se alcune delle ferite persistono ancora. Capisco quanto sia stato difficile per lei ammettere di amarmi, abbracciarmi pienamente dopo tutto quello che ho fatto. Aveva bisogno che non le lasciassi altra scelta, e l'ho fatto, minacciando i suoi amici per costringerla a presentarsi al nostro matrimonio.

No, la fonte della mia rabbia non è Sara, ma l'uomo che ha cercato di manipolarla per farle evitare il nostro matrimonio.

L'Agente Ryson.

Il fatto che abbia avuto il coraggio di presentarsi in quel modo mi riempie di una furia violenta. Io lascio in pace

Henderson, loro lasciano in pace me e Sara—era questo il patto. Niente più sorveglianza dell'FBI, niente molestie, solo un colpo di spugna per poter condurre una vita pacifica.

Ha minacciato anche Sara. L'ha accusata di aver cospirato con me per uccidere suo marito. Non ho idea di cosa le abbia detto esattamente, ma dev'essere stato qualcosa di brutto per farla reagire in quel modo.

In qualsiasi altra circostanza, starebbe già marcendo con i vermi, ma ora devo essere un cittadino rispettoso della legge. Non posso andare in giro ad uccidere agenti dell'FBI—non senza rinunciare alla vita per cui ho combattuto, la vita civile di cui mia moglie ha bisogno. Per quanto possa essere allettante, Ryson vivrà—almeno per ora. Poi, quando sarà passato abbastanza tempo, potrebbe ritrovarsi coinvolto in uno sfortunato incidente o alle prese con un rapinatore eccessivamente aggressivo, come il patrigno della paziente di Sara... ma ci penserò un altro giorno.

Oggi lei è tutta per me e ho intenzione di godermela.

"Non ti preoccupare, amore mio" dico, quando la mia nuova moglie continua a mangiare tranquillamente, evitando il mio sguardo. "È finita. Fa parte del passato—così come qualsiasi altro errore abbiamo commesso. Concentriamoci solo sul presente e sul futuro... viviamo le nostre vite senza guardare sempre indietro."

Alza lo sguardo, con occhi incerti. "Pensi davvero che possiamo?"

"Sì" rispondo fermamente, e allungandomi, porto la sua mano alle mie labbra per un tenero bacio.

DOPO AVER PRANZATO, ANDIAMO A VEDERE GLI ANNUNCI CHE LE ho mostrato, e Sara si innamora di una casa—una vittoriana con cinque camere da letto costruita negli anni ottanta, ma completamente rinnovata l'anno scorso. Ha un grande cortile—per il cane e per i bambini, mi dice allegramente—e un magnifico camino nel soggiorno. Non mi fa impazzire che sia così adiacente ai vicini e che il cortile sia completamente aperto, ma credo che se piantassimo degli alberi e mettessimo un recinto, godremmo di una privacy sufficiente.

In ogni caso, è meglio che vivere nell'attuale appartamento in affitto di Sara.

Prima di andare, ho inserito un'offerta in contanti superiore al prezzo di mercato e l'agente immobiliare ci telefona pochi minuti dopo per informarci che l'offerta è stata accettata.

"Ecco fatto" dico a mia moglie quando riaggancio. "L'atto di acquisto si farà la prossima settimana."

Sgrana gli occhi. "Davvero? È così facile?"

"Perché no?"

Ride. "Oh, non lo so. Suppongo perché la maggior parte delle persone non acquista case con la stessa facilità con cui acquista le scarpe."

Sorrido e allungo la mano per prendere la sua. "La maggior parte delle persone non sono noi."

"No" concorda lei ironicamente, guardandomi. "Non lo sono."

Torniamo a casa e preparo la cena—capesante alla griglia con purè di patate dolci e broccoli al vapore. Mentre mangiamo, Sara menziona il trasloco, e le comunico che mi occuperò io di tutto, proprio come ho fatto con gli accordi del matrimonio.

"Tutto quello che dovrai fare è presentarti nella nuova casa" le dico, versandole un bicchiere di Pinot Grigio. Poi, ricordando il suo inspiegabile turbamento per la vendita della Toyota, aggiungo: "A meno che non ci sia qualcosa che vuoi che decidiamo insieme. Forse vuoi scegliere nuovi mobili o decorazioni?"

Sorride mestamente. "No, penso che vada bene così. Non sono eccessivamente pignola sulle cose di casa. Se vuoi occupartene tu, per me va bene."

"Alla nostra nuova casa, allora." Sollevo il mio bicchiere di vino e lo avvicino lentamente al suo. "E ad una nuova vita."

"Alla nostra nuova vita" fa eco dolcemente, e mentre sorseggia il suo bicchiere, non posso fare a meno di ricordare il momento in cui ha cercato di drogare il mio vino, all'inizio della nostra relazione. Era così ribelle allora, così sicura di odiarmi.

Lo è ancora? In qualche minima parte?

Rattristandomi, metto giù il vino e mi alzo. Camminando intorno al tavolo, la tiro in piedi.

"Che cosa stai—" inizia a dire, ma la sto già baciando, assaporando il vino sulle sue labbra.

Le sue labbra carnose e morbide che mi hanno fatto distrarre tutto il giorno.

Ho fatto del mio meglio per comportarmi da buon marito, per fare tutte le cose normali con lei, invece di incatenarla al mio letto e fotterla tutto il giorno come richiede il mio istinto. Sono stato calmo e paziente, lasciandola riprendere dalla scorsa notte, ma non posso continuare a comportarmi da persona civilizzata.

Ho bisogno di lei.

Proprio qui.

Proprio adesso.

Mi avvolge le braccia attorno al collo, con il corpo snello che si piega contro di me inarcandosi, mentre la chino sul mio braccio, incapace di assorbire abbastanza sapore, odore, sensazione della sua delicata lingua che accarezza la mia. È fottutamente deliziosa, e il mio uccello si indurisce, con il cuore che mi batte forte nella cassa toracica, mentre sparecchio i piatti dal tavolo con un colpo del braccio, incurante del pasticcio che sto creando.

Avremo comunque bisogno di un nuovo servizio da tavola.

Ansima, mentre la distendo sul tavolo e le alzo la gonna del prendisole, scoprendo cosce pallide e un grazioso perizoma blu bordato di pizzo. Incapace di controllarmi, strappo il pezzo di seta e seppellisco la testa tra le sue cosce, con la lingua che si infila affamata tra le pieghe, le labbra che si chiudono intorno al clitoride con una succhiata dura e golosa, mentre le tengo le gambe sulle mie spalle.

"Peter... Oh Dio, Peter..." I suoi fianchi si sollevano dal tavolo, con le mani che mi stringono forte i capelli, e sento che il fallo mi esploderà nei jeans per il suo sapore, il profumo caldo e femminile e la sensazione della sua pelle setosa sotto la mia lingua. Adoro tutto ciò, dal modo in cui le sue piccole unghie affilate mi graffiano la testa e le cosce toniche mi stringono le orecchie, ai versi ansimanti che le sfuggono dalla gola e al modo in cui la figa scivolosa freme e si contrae sotto la mia lingua.

Questo è il paradiso, il fottuto paradiso, e non posso credere di esserne stato senza—senza di lei—per nove dolorosi mesi.

Continuando a banchettare con il suo clitoride, infilo un dito dentro e sento le sue pareti interne stringersi attorno all'intrusione, mentre i fianchi si sollevano, supplicandomi di avere di più.

"Ci sei quasi... solo un po' di più" ringhio tra le sue pieghe, accarezzandola dall'interno, e, mentre trovo il tessuto spugnoso che indica il punto G, tutto il suo corpo si inarca e lei viene con un urlo profondo, stringendo spasmodicamente le mani tra i miei capelli, mentre la sua figa pulsa attorno al mio dito.

Ormai, il membro sta minacciando di esplodermi dentro i jeans, così ritiro il dito e la rigiro sullo stomaco. Poi, la trascino verso di me, finché non è piegata sul tavolo, con il vestito stretto attorno alla vita, mostrando i globi bianchi e sodi del sedere e una figa luccicante con la sua umidità e la mia saliva. Incapace di aspettare un altro secondo, sbottono i jeans e li spingo giù insieme ai miei slip, liberando l'uccello dolorante.

"Pronta?" dico con voce rauca, chinandomi su di lei, mentre mi sistemo sul suo ingresso, e il suo respiro si fa sentire acutamente, mentre spingo dentro senza aspettare una risposta.

All'interno, è vellutata, liscia e scivolosa, con la tenera carne che mi stringe forte, avvolgendomi così perfettamente che le mie palle si appoggiano contro il mio corpo e un basso gemito mi sfugge dalla gola, mentre le mie dita affondano nei suoi fianchi.

Questa è fottuta pazzia, una follia totale. Dopo la conversazione della scorsa notte, abbiamo fatto sesso altre due volte prima di addormentarci, e non dovrei sentirmi così, così disperatamente affamato di lei da essere sul punto di perdere il controllo. Ma sono così desideroso. Sono famelico per tutto ciò che riguarda Sara. Il bisogno di avere i suoi artigli sulle mie ossa, la cupa lussuria che mi attraversa. Sento il fuoco nelle vene, che mi brucia dall'interno.

È la mia dipendenza e non ne ho mai abbastanza.

Liberandole i fianchi, allungo la mano e le afferro i gomiti, tirandoli per farle inarcare la schiena, prima che sbatta contro di lei più forte, sentendo i suoi muscoli interni stringersi attorno a me, mentre inizio a fotterla sul serio.

Grida ad ogni spinta punitiva, con la parte superiore del corpo sollevata dal tavolo per la mia presa sui gomiti, e sento l'orgasmo ribollire dentro di me, col piacere che cresce come un maremoto. Gemendo, piego la testa all'indietro, martellandole dentro più forte, e le sue grida si intensificano, con la figa che si stringe attorno a me, mentre tutto il suo corpo si irrigidisce. Sento che i suoi spasmi iniziano, e poi sono lì, con l'uccello che si contorce per il rilascio, mentre la sua carne bagnata pulsa intorno a me, mungendomi, stringendomi finché non rimane più niente.

Fino a quando non crollo sopra di lei, spingendola sul tavolo, mentre respiro forte, inalando l'inebriante odore di sesso e il suo sudore.

La mia Sara. Mia moglie.

La mia ossessione.

Potremmo trascorrere insieme un'eternità, e non sarebbe ancora abbastanza.

4

Henderson

Sono sdraiato nel letto, fissando il soffitto. Per la seconda notte, non riesco a dormire, con i pensieri oscuri che mi attraversano la mente, mentre il collo continua a bloccarsi.

Il piano che sto formulando è estremo, mostruoso addirittura, ma non vedo altre soluzioni. Non posso colpire direttamente Sokolov—lui e la sua sposa sono troppo ben sorvegliati. Se provassi e fallissi, sarebbero guai.

Inoltre, Sokolov non è l'unico che voglio eliminare.

I suoi alleati sono altrettanto pericolosi... per me, per la mia famiglia e per il mondo in generale.

Questo è davvero l'unico modo.

Lui e gli altri devono pagare.

$\mathcal{S}$ara

Mi sveglio con il bip della sveglia. Disattivandola, mi giro sulla schiena e mi stiracchio, sentendomi dolorante e soddisfatta. Dopo aver ripulito la cucina e aver fatto la doccia, Peter mi ha presa ancora una volta prima che ci addormentassimo, e poi ancora durante la notte.

Qualcuno dovrebbe imbottigliare il desiderio sessuale dell'uomo e venderlo come droga. Farebbe una fortuna.

Sorridendo a quel pensiero, scendo dal letto e corro sotto la doccia. Sento già l'odore della prelibatezza che Peter sta preparando in cucina, e il mio stomaco è più che pronto per iniziare la giornata.

"Buongiorno, ptichka" mi saluta, quando entro in cucina dopo aver fatto una doccia veloce ed essermi vestita per il lavoro. Sul tavolo ci sono due piatti con pane tostato, uova e avocado, e sul ripiano c'è un sacchetto per il pranzo—presumo da portare al lavoro con me.

"Ciao." Il mio battito cardiaco accelera, quando lo guardo. Oggi è senza maglietta, con i jeans scuri sui fianchi e i tatuaggi sul braccio che brillano alla luce del mattino. Il suo corpo è un'opera d'arte, con muscoli perfettamente definiti e spalle larghe che si assottigliano fino ad una vita stretta. Persino le cicatrici sul torso emanano una sorta di bellezza violenta e pericolosa—proprio come l'uomo stesso.

"Hai tempo per mangiare?" chiede, e annuisco, combattendo l'impulso di leccarmi le labbra, mentre i suoi addominali si flettono davanti a me.

Forse Peter non è l'unico con una libido folle.

La condizione potrebbe essere contagiosa.

"Ho quindici minuti" dico con voce rauca, sforzandomi di camminare verso il tavolo anziché verso di lui. Se gli dessi un bacio del buongiorno, finiremmo di nuovo a letto.

"Bene. Ti accompagnerò al lavoro stamattina" mi informa, raggiungendomi al tavolo. Raccogliendo il suo pane tostato, lo morde e io faccio lo stesso con il mio, gustando il sapore aspro del lime combinato con il saporito uovo fritto e il pane di segale croccante.

"È una settimana impegnativa per te?" chiede, quando ho quasi finito il mio toast, e annuisco, pulendomi le labbra con un tovagliolo.

"Sì, in realtà. Molto impegnativa. Wendy e Bill—sai, i miei superiori—sono appena partiti per le vacanze, quindi vedrò alcune delle loro pazienti oltre alle mie. Oh, e visiterò una delle mie pazienti domani pomeriggio, quindi probabilmente tornerò a casa tardi. Inoltre, ho alcuni turni in clinica nella seconda metà della settimana."

"Capisco." L'espressione di Peter è neutra, ma percepisco un sottile oscuramento del suo stato d'animo. Non è contento di questo, e non posso biasimarlo.

Anch'io preferirei passare del tempo con lui piuttosto che

andare al lavoro.

"Sarai a casa per cena stasera?" chiede, e sorrido, felice di potergli dare delle buone notizie su questo fronte.

"Dovrei esserci. Se non ci sono emergenze."

"Giusto." Si alza in piedi. "Lasciami prendere una maglietta e ti accompagnerò in ufficio."

"Grazie—e grazie per la deliziosa colazione" grido, ma è già andato in camera.

eter

L'UFFICIO DI SARA È A POCHI PASSI DAL SUO APPARTAMENTO, quindi il viaggio dura solo pochi minuti. Troppo presto, mi avvicino al bordo del marciapiede e le consegno il suo pranzo, sentendo per tutto il tempo che preferirei spezzarmi il braccio, piuttosto che lasciarla scendere dalla macchina.

Detesto il fatto che non la vedrò per tutto il giorno, che non potrò toccarla o parlarle fino a sera. È ancora più difficile della scorsa settimana, perché abbiamo passato questa domenica insieme—e ora so com'è il paradiso.

È quello che abbiamo avuto in Giappone, ma senza l'amara animosità—senza che Sara sia risentita per averla strappata dalla carriera e da tutti coloro che ama.

Devo far appello a tutta la mia forza per rimanere seduto e calmo, mentre mi bacia la guancia e sussurra: "Ti amo. A presto" prima di saltare fuori dalla macchina.

Guardo la sua figura snella scomparire nel suo palazzo degli uffici, e poi mando un messaggio alla squadra, dando loro le istruzioni per sorvegliarla.

Se non posso stare con lei, almeno saprò dove si trova e cosa sta facendo.

Almeno, sarò certo che sia al sicuro.

TRASCORRO LA MATTINATA TRASFERENDO I FONDI PER LA STIPULA dell'atto di acquisto previsto per questo giovedì e organizzando il trasloco imminente. Ho intenzione di trasferirci nella nuova casa entro la prossima settimana, il che significa che c'è molto lavoro da sbrigare. Anche se il posto è stato appena rinnovato e non richiederà aggiornamenti importanti, devo installare adeguate misure di sicurezza.

Periferia o meno, la nostra abitazione sarà una fortezza e nessuno—tantomeno l'Agente Ryson—riuscirà a rintracciare di nuovo Sara a casa.

È metà pomeriggio e sto lavando le verdure per cena, quando il mio telefono vibra sul ripiano. Premendo sullo schermo con un dito semi-asciutto, leggo il messaggio di mia moglie.

Mi dispiace. Ho appena ricevuto una chiamata dalla clinica. Sono completamente sopraffatti e mi implorano di andare stasera. Sarà solo fino alle dieci o giù di lì. Mi dispiace tanto.

Taglio in due la zucchina che stavo lavando, e spingo via il telefono con il gomito per evitare di sottoporlo allo stesso destino.

Avrei dovuto saperlo, cazzo. "Se non ci sono emergenze" è il codice per "ci sarà un'emergenza." Era così prima del Giappone, e anche se l'attuale lavoro di Sara è meno concentrato sul lato ostetrico, la sua mentalità non è cambiata.

Il lavoro viene ancora prima di tutto per lei, compreso il volontariato nella clinica.

Impiego una ventina di minuti per calmarmi e iniziare a pensare razionalmente. La sua carriera è una delle ragioni per cui ho passato tutti i guai con Novak ed Esguerra, il motivo per cui ho accettato di rinunciare alla mia vendetta su Henderson. Essere un medico—aiutare i pazienti—è importante per lei; ha bisogno della sua carriera tanto quanto ha bisogno di stare vicino alla sua famiglia e agli amici. Lo sapevo quando l'ho portata via, ma allora non mi importava.

Tutto quello che importava era tenerla.

Ora che ho lei e che è felice, non posso tornare a quel modo di pensare, non posso dimenticare com'era, quando ero la fonte della sua infelicità, quando ogni volta che mi guardava, scorgevo il tormento nei suoi occhi.

Ora è diverso. Qualunque siano le sue riserve, ha finalmente ammesso di amarmi—di amarmi abbastanza da avere un bambino con me.

Una figlia o un figlio... come Pasha.

Per un momento, fa male respirare di nuovo, ma poi il dolore passa, lasciando un malessere agrodolce nella sua scia. Sono riuscito a pensare a Pasha in questo modo sempre più spesso negli ultimi mesi, senza la rabbia che avvelena i ricordi. E so che è tutto merito di Sara.

Il mio piccolo passerotto che desidero così tanto rinchiudere in gabbia.

Facendo un respiro profondo, lo lascio andare lentamente e mi concentro sul compito rilassante di preparare la cena.

Se non può tornare a casa stasera, dovrò andare io da lei.

Sara

MI ASPETTO CHE QUALCUNO DELLA SQUADRA DI PETER VENGA A prendermi per portarmi in clinica, ma lui stesso mi sta aspettando accanto al marciapiede.

Sorrido, con una parte della stanchezza che svanisce, mentre i suoi occhi mi scrutano il corpo, prima di posarsi avidamente sul viso.

"Ciao." Cammino verso il suo abbraccio e inspiro profondamente, mentre le sue forti braccia mi avvolgono, stringendomi forte contro il petto. Ha un odore caldo, di pulito e distintamente maschile—un tipico profumo di Peter che ora associo al comfort.

Mi stringe per alcuni lunghi momenti, poi si tira indietro per guardarmi. "Com'è stata la tua giornata, amore mio?" chiede dolcemente, togliendomi i capelli dal viso.

Lo guardo con espressione raggiante. "Molto dura, ma va

molto meglio ora." Sono incredibilmente felice che sia venuto lui stesso per accompagnarmi in clinica.

Ricambia il sorriso. "Ti sono mancato, vero?"

"Sì" ammetto, mentre apre la portiera della macchina e mi aiuta ad entrare. "Mi sei mancato moltissimo."

Il suo sorriso di risposta mi fa venir voglia di sciogliermi sul sedile. "E mi sei mancata anche tu, ptichka."

"Mi dispiace doverlo fare" spiego, mentre ci allontaniamo dal marciapiede. L'auto odora di qualcosa di deliziosamente piccante, e il mio stomaco brontola, mentre dico: "Non vedevo l'ora di fare una bella cena a casa."

Peter mi guarda. "Ti ho portato la cena. È sul sedile posteriore."

"Davvero?" Mi giro sul sedile e vedo la fonte dell'odore delizioso—un altro sacchetto porta-pranzo. "Wow, grazie. Non ce n'era bisogno, ma lo apprezzo davvero." Allungandomi, afferro la busta e la metto sulle ginocchia.

Stavo per comprare dei pretzel da un distributore automatico all'interno della clinica, ma questo è infinitamente meglio.

"Perché *devi* farlo?" chiede, fermandosi a un semaforo rosso. Il suo tono è indifferente, ma non mi lascio ingannare.

Anche lui non vedeva l'ora di cenare.

"Mi dispiace davvero" dico, e intendo sul serio. Quando Lydia, l'addetta alla reception della clinica, mi ha chiamato all'ora di pranzo, ho quasi ignorato le sue suppliche—ma alla fine, la consapevolezza che alcune dozzine di donne avrebbero perso gli screening sul cancro e le cure prenatali essenziali se non l'avessi fatto ha prevalso. "Sono a corto di volontari oggi, e non ho potuto rifiutarmi."

Mi lancia un'occhiata di sbieco. "Non hai potuto?"

Mi fermo, mentre apro il sacchetto contenente la cena. "No" dico con calma. "Non ho potuto."

Eccolo, ciò che ho sempre temuto. Sospettavo che fosse solo

questione di tempo, prima che le mie lunghe ore iniziassero a disturbare Peter, e a quanto pare avevo ragione a preoccuparmi.

Irrigidendomi, mi preparo a sentire un ultimatum, ma lui preme sul gas, accelerando senza problemi.

"Mangia, amore mio" dice nello stesso tono informale. "Non hai molto tempo."

Seguo il suo suggerimento e scavo nel cibo—un medley di verdure con couscous e pollo arrosto. Il condimento mi ricorda il delizioso kebab di agnello che Peter ha preparato per noi in Giappone, e divoro tutto in pochi minuti.

"Grazie" replico, pulendomi la bocca con un tovagliolo di carta con cui ha così premurosamente avvolto le posate. "Era squisito."

"Prego." Svolta nella strada dove si trova la clinica e parcheggia proprio davanti all'edificio. "Vieni, ti accompagno."

"Oh, non devi—" Mi fermo, perché sta già camminando intorno alla macchina.

Aprendomi la portiera, mi aiuta e mi conduce nell'edificio, come se potessi sfuggirgli, se non mi tenesse una mano sulla schiena.

Mi aspetto che si fermi, quando raggiungiamo la porta, ma entra con me.

Confusa, mi blocco e lo guardo. "Che cosa stai facendo?"

"Eccoti!" Lydia si precipita verso di me, con il viso sollevato. "Grazie a Dio. Pensavo che non saresti... Oh, ciao." Arrossisce, fissando Peter con quella che posso solo interpretare come una vera e propria cotta.

"Peter stava solo—" Inizio a dire, ma lui sorride e avanza.

"Peter Garin. Ci siamo visti al nostro matrimonio" dice, tendendo la mano.

La segretaria spalanca gli occhi e gli stringe la mano, scuotendola energicamente.

"Lydia" dice senza fiato. "Di nuovo, congratulazioni. È stato un evento bellissimo."

"Grazie." Le sorride, e posso quasi percepire l'estasi interiore della donna. "Sai, Sara mi ha appena detto che siete a corto di volontari oggi. Non sono un medico, ovviamente, ma forse c'è qualcosa che posso fare per dare una mano qui stasera. Forse hai dei file che hanno bisogno di essere ordinati o qualcosa che dev'essere corretto. Per ora abbiamo solo un'auto e preferirei non fare avanti e indietro per venire a prendere mia moglie."

"Oh, certo." Il livello di eccitazione di Lydia è visibilmente quadruplicato. "Abbiamo così tanto lavoro. E hai detto di voler essere utile? Per caso te la cavi anche con i computer? Perché c'è questo software testardo..."

Lo conduce via, chiacchierando, e li fisso incredula, mentre il mio marito assassino scompare dietro l'angolo senza nemmeno voltarsi.

eter

AIUTO LYDIA A RISOLVERE IL PROBLEMA CON IL SUO SOFTWARE, A sistemare un rubinetto che perde e ad appendere alcune decorazioni nell'area di attesa, mentre due dozzine di donne—molte delle quali visibilmente incinte—mi osservano affascinate.

Essendo l'unico medico qui stasera, Sara ha un flusso di pazienti infinito, quindi non la infastidisco. Mi basta sapere che è solo ad un paio di stanze di distanza, e che posso raggiungerla nel giro di un minuto, in caso di bisogno.

Dopo essermi preso cura di tutti i compiti di base, mi metto al lavoro assemblando una macchina per le ecografie donata da un ospedale locale. Non ho mai lavorato con attrezzature mediche prima d'ora, ma sono sempre stato bravo a mettere insieme le cose—armi, esplosivi, dispositivi di comunicazione—

quindi, presto capisco dove e come testare ogni cosa per assicurarmi che funzioni.

"Oh mio Dio, sei un vero salvatore, proprio come tua moglie" esclama Lydia, quando glielo mostro. "Abbiamo aspettato per mesi che venisse un tecnico, e oh, questo sarà molto utile! Sara è con la sua ultima paziente ora. Pensi che potresti sistemare anche questo armadietto? Si è inclinato e..."

"Nessun problema." La seguo in una delle stanze degli esami e fisso alcune viti per assicurarmi che l'armadietto in questione non cada sulla testa di qualcuno.

"Sei così bravo in questo" mi loda la receptionist, quando ho finito. "Hai mai lavorato nel campo delle ristrutturazioni, per caso? Sembri molto allenato con quel trapano e tutto..."

"Ho lavorato ad alcuni progetti di costruzione da adolescente" affermo senza pensare. Questa donna non ha bisogno di sapere che i "progetti" erano lavori forzati nella versione giovanile di un *gulag* siberiano.

"Oh, lo immaginavo." Mi sorride. "Fammi controllare se Sara ha finito."

"Per favore." Le sorrido di rimando. "Mi piacerebbe portare mia moglie a casa."

La receptionist si allontana e allungo le braccia, allentando la rigidità dei muscoli. Sono passati solo pochi giorni, ma sto diventando irrequieto, desideroso di muovermi e fare qualcosa di fisico. Dopo aver preparato la cena, sono andato a fare una lunga corsa nel parco e mi sono fermato in una palestra di pugilato per smaltire un po' di rabbia, ma ho bisogno di più.

Ho bisogno di una sfida di qualche tipo.

Per la prima volta, rifletto seriamente su quello che farò per il resto della mia vita. Grazie al doppio incarico Esguerra-Novak, ho abbastanza soldi per me, Sara e una dozzina di bambini/nipoti—soprattutto se non prendiamo l'abitudine di acquistare aerei privati, armi speciali o altri oggetti costosi. Non ho bisogno di lavorare per sostenerci, e non ho pianificato altro, a parte prendere Sara e legarla a me—in parte perché mi è sempre piaciuto il tempo libero tra un lavoro e l'altro.

Ora sto iniziando a rendermi conto che fosse dovuto al fatto che sapessi che il tempo libero era temporaneo, che un'altra missione impegnativa e carica di adrenalina mi stava aspettando. Ora non c'è niente—solo una serie di giorni tranquilli e pacifici che si estendono all'infinito.

Giorni in cui tutto ciò che farò è pensare a lei e aspettare che torni a casa.

"Peter?" Mia moglie fa capolino nella stanza, e un grande sorriso le illumina il viso, quando mi fissa. "Sono pronta per andare a casa, se tu lo sei."

"Andiamo" dico, e accantono il problema per un altro giorno.

Penserò dopo a cosa fare del mio tempo.

Per ora, ho la mia ptichka, e lei è tutto ciò di cui ho bisogno.

Sara

I DUE GIORNI SUCCESSIVI VOLANO AL LAVORO. MARTEDÌ, RIMANGO fino a tardi in ospedale per un parto, e mercoledì ho un altro turno presso la clinica, dove ancora una volta sono l'unico medico a visitare tutte le pazienti.

È estenuante, ma non mi dispiace, perché Peter trova un modo per starmi vicino entrambe le sere—martedì, rispondendo ad alcune e-mail presso lo Snacktime Café accanto all'ospedale, quindi posso uscire e vederlo, mentre aspetto che la mia paziente sia pronta per partorire, e mercoledì, aiutandomi di nuovo presso la clinica.

"Perché stai facendo questo?" gli chiedo, mentre andiamo alla clinica. "Voglio dire, non fraintendermi, sono molto contenta... e Lydia è al settimo cielo, di sicuro. Ma è davvero questo che vuoi?"

Mi guarda, con gli occhi che brillano. "Quello che voglio sei tu, nel mio letto ventiquattr'ore su ventiquattro. Oppure ammanettata a me in ogni momento. Ma dal momento che so quanto sia importante la carriera per te, mi adeguerò alla soluzione migliore."

Lo fisso, incerta su come reagire. Con qualsiasi altro uomo, lo riterrei uno scherzo, ma con lui, non è un'ipotesi sicura. Soprattutto perché capisco come si sente.

Tra l'altro, mi manca ferocemente, quando siamo lontani.

Arriviamo in clinica un minuto dopo, e vado a preparare una marea di pazienti, mentre Lydia afferra Peter per spostare alcuni mobili. Dalle sette alle dieci, vedo donne per problemi minori e seri, e poi un nome familiare compare sul mio prospetto.

Monica Jackson.

Il petto mi si stringe dolorosamente. La diciottenne è venuta la scorsa settimana dopo una seconda brutale aggressione da parte del patrigno, che è uscito di prigione per un cavillo tecnico, invece di scontare la condanna di sette anni per averla violentata, quando aveva diciassette anni. Quella volta l'avevo aiutata dandole un po' di soldi per ridurre la dipendenza finanziaria della madre alcolizzata dal bastardo, ma non ho potuto fare niente la settimana scorsa. Monica era terrorizzata che il patrigno potesse fare causa per la custodia di suo fratello minore, e vincerla—o che il bambino fosse stato adottato.

La sua situazione senza speranza mi aveva sconvolta così tanto che avevo pianto per un'ora intera.

Facendo un respiro profondo, indosso la mia maschera più calma e mi alzo, mentre la ragazza entra nella stanza. "Monica. Come stai?"

"Ciao, Dottoressa Cobakis." Il suo piccolo viso è così radioso che quasi non la riconosco. Nemmeno i lividi semi-guariti ancora visibili sulla sua pelle sminuiscono il suo splendore. "Sono pronta per la mia spirale."

Sbatto le palpebre per il suo entusiasmo. "Fantàstico. Immagino che ti senta meglio."

Annuisce, saltando sul tavolo degli esami. "Sì, molto meglio. E indovina?"

"Che cosa?"

Sorride. "Non può più darmi fastidio. Mai più. La scorsa settimana, stava andando a lavorare di notte, ed è stato aggredito in un vicolo. Gli hanno tagliato la gola, ci credi?"

"Che... cosa?" Affondo nella sedia, mentre le gambe si piegano sotto di me.

Il suo sorriso svanisce, e mi rivolge un'occhiata pentita. "Scusa. Sembrava una cattiveria, vero?"

"Ehm, no. Questo è..." Scuoto la testa per l'inutile sforzo di chiarire. "Hai detto che qualcuno gli ha *tagliato la gola*?"

"Sì, i rapinatori o il rapinatore. La polizia non sa quanti ce ne fossero. Il suo portafoglio è stato preso, però, quindi stavano sicuramente cercando i suoi soldi."

"Capisco." Sembro soffocata, ma non posso farci niente. Il ricordo dei due tossici che Peter ha ucciso per proteggermi riaffiora così vividamente nella mia mente che posso sentire il fetore della morte e vedere il modo in cui erano accartocciati come fantocci, con le pozze scure di sangue che si allargavano sotto i loro corpi...

Così tanto sangue che qualcuno doveva aver tagliato loro la gola.

"Dottoressa Cobakis? Va tutto bene?"

La ragazza sembra preoccupata—devo essere sbiancata.

Sforzandomi, mi ricompongo e sorrido in modo rassicurante. "Sì, scusa. Solo alcune brutte associazioni, tutto qui."

"Oh, mi dispiace. Non volevo spaventarti. E, ti prego, cerca di capire: non sto dicendo che sono felice che sia morto. È solo che..."

"Sei contenta che sia fuori dalla tua vita. Ho capito." Mi alzo di nuovo e, con tutta la calma possibile, porgo a Monica un camice di carta avvolto nella plastica. "Cambiati, per favore. Arrivo subito."

Lasciando la ragazza, esco, con le gambe incerte e i polmoni che lottano per respirare.

La scorsa settimana, dopo aver saputo della seconda aggressione di Monica, non ho solo pianto.

L'ho anche confidato a Peter, spiegandogli esattamente che cos'era successo.

Se questa non è una macabra coincidenza, allora l'Agente Ryson aveva ragione.

Sono un mostro tanto quanto Peter. Ho ucciso il patrigno di Monica puntandogli contro l'arma più letale che conosca.

Il mio nuovo marito.

1 O

*S*ara

NON RIESCO ANCORA A RESPIRARE, QUANDO SALGO IN MACCHINA con Peter, con il peso delle rivelazioni di Monica che incombono come un iceberg sul mio petto.

"Che cosa c'è che non va, ptichka?" chiede, mentre inizia a guidare. "Stai bene?"

Vorrei ridere istericamente. Sto bene? Dovrei stare bene?

Esiste un barometro del benessere per quando hai inavvertitamente commissionato un colpo?

"Sara?" insiste, guardandomi storto, e anche se il suo tono è leggermente curioso, scorgo un barlume di oscura consapevolezza nei suoi occhi.

Deve aver notato Monica in clinica.

Qualunque speranza avessi nutrito su questa terribile coincidenza svanisce, lasciandosi dietro un orrore sempre più profondo.

Peter ha commesso questo omicidio per me.

Il sangue della sua vittima è sulle *mie* mani.

Non ha senso chiedere, ma non posso farci niente. Devo sentire quelle parole ad alta voce. "Sei stato tu?"

Mi aspetto che neghi o che ignori la domanda, ma risponde senza esitazione, con lo sguardo concentrato sulla strada da percorrere. "Sì."

Sì.

Eccolo. Nessun fraintendimento, nessuna confusione.

Ha ucciso un uomo per me.

Tagliandogli la gola, proprio come aveva fatto con quei tossici.

"Avresti preferito che lasciassi la ragazza nelle sue grinfie?" La sua voce è calma e ferma, mentre mi guarda di nuovo. "L'ho fatto in modo che non ti preoccupassi—e in modo che la tua paziente potesse avere una vita normale e felice."

Ingoio e distolgo lo sguardo, fissando ciecamente fuori dal finestrino. Che cosa dovrei rispondere?

Come hai potuto?

Grazie?

Mi sforzo di guardare il suo profilo. "Pensavo..." Mi si chiude la gola e devo ricominciare. "Pensavo che saresti stato rispettoso della legge. Non è questa una delle condizioni del tuo accordo con le autorità?"

Annuisce, tenendo gli occhi sulla strada. "Lo è—e *sono* rispettoso della legge. Considero ciò che ho fatto un *aiuto* alla legge—la legge che dovrebbe proteggere ragazze come Monica da uomini come il suo patrigno."

Distolgo di nuovo lo sguardo, con gli occhi che bruciano, mentre il peso freddo sul mio petto cresce.

Non considera nemmeno ciò che ha fatto come sbagliato. E perché dovrebbe? Questo è quello che è, quello che fa.

Uccidere è normale per lui, come per me lo è aiutare a partorire.

"Sara." La sua voce profonda mi raggiunge, e mi rendo conto che abbiamo già parcheggiato. Devo essermi estraniata per il resto del viaggio.

Irrigidendomi, mi volto verso di lui.

Si allunga per stringermi la mano. "Ptichka..." La sua voce è dolce, la sua grande mano calda, mentre mi avvolge le dita gelide. "Perché me lo hai detto, se non volevi il mio aiuto? Ti aspettavi davvero che rimanessi a vederti piangere per quell'*ublyudok* senza fare niente?"

Sussulto. Non posso evitarlo.

Questo è il nocciolo della questione, il motivo per cui le rivelazioni di Monica sono così devastanti.

Perché, nel profondo, *non* mi aspettavo che lo accettasse docilmente. In un certo senso, sapevo cosa avrebbe fatto—anche prima che promettesse che la mia paziente sarebbe stata "bene."

Lo sapevo e ho finto di non saperlo.

Perché, segretamente, *volevo* che succedesse.

Ho indicato a Peter il problema e lui ha fornito una soluzione.

Proprio così.

"Sara..." Solleva la mano per avvolgermi la guancia, con lo sguardo oscuro ma caldo nell'interno scarsamente illuminato dell'auto. "Non farlo, ptichka. Non starci male. Se l'è meritato; lo sai che è così. Credi davvero che Monica sia l'unica ragazza a cui lui abbia mai fatto del male? Il tuo sistema legale aveva la possibilità di risolvere la situazione, di chiuderlo in carcere per sempre—ma lo hanno lasciato andare. Hai fatto un favore al mondo raccontandomi di lui."

Chiudo gli occhi, desiderando appoggiarmi al suo palmo, lasciando che la sua voce profonda e tranquillizzante scacci l'orrore e il senso di colpa che mi congelano dall'interno.

Non solo amo un assassino ora, ma lo sono diventata anch'io.

"Non farlo, amore mio. Non ne vale la pena." Il suo respiro mi scalda il viso, e poi le labbra sfiorano le mie in un dolce bacio.

Un brivido mi attraversa in risposta, con un lampo di calore che si accende sotto il gelo che mi avvolge e, tutto ad un tratto, la dolcezza non è abbastanza.

Non voglio essere tranquillizzata—voglio essere scopata fino all'oblio.

Aprendo gli occhi, affondo le dita nei suoi capelli, stringendogli la testa e inclinando il viso per approfondire il bacio. Gli spingo la lingua nella bocca, e le mie unghie affondano nel suo cranio, mentre premo contro di lui, chinandomi sulla consolle che separa i nostri sedili. Il suo respiro si blocca, con le mani che scivolano nei miei capelli per afferrarli saldamente, e un ringhio basso rimbomba nel profondo del suo petto, mentre reagisce con la stessa aggressività, con i denti che mi tagliano il labbro inferiore, mentre ricambia il bacio, più forte e più profondo, spingendomi verso il sedile.

Sì, così. Mi gira la testa, con il calore dentro di me che si intensifica in una destabilizzazione. Sa di violenza e desiderio maschile, di punizione e amore, tutto mescolato insieme. Non riesco a ragionare sotto il suo sensuale assalto, e non voglio farlo.

Voglio questo.

Voglio lui.

In qualche modo, il sedile dietro la schiena si reclina, e poi Peter è sopra di me, con la macchina che trema, mentre mi strappa i vestiti, con una mano che scava sotto la camicetta, mentre l'altra raggiunge la cerniera dei miei pantaloni. Il suo palmo calloso è caldo e ruvido, mentre scivola sul mio stomaco nudo, e tengo gli occhi aperti abbastanza a lungo da permettermi di vedere i finestrini della macchina appannarsi. È quasi abbastanza per rendermi lucida, per farmi ricordare dove siamo, ma poi la sua mano si muove più in basso, con il bacio che diventa ancora più aggressivo, e il vortice del bisogno mi spazza di nuovo via.

Non so quando o come lui mi tolga i pantaloni e la biancheria intima, o a che punto gli strappi il bottone dei jeans. Tutto quello che so è che è improvvisamente dentro di me, così forte e spesso che fa male. Grido, ansimando, mentre inizia a fottermi sul serio, ma non si ferma, non rallenta e io non voglio che lo faccia. Ci diamo dentro come animali, senza ritegno o raffinatezza, e quando vengo, aggrappata a lui e urlante, è proprio lì con me, nella follia che è la nostra connessione.

Nell'oscurità che è il nostro amore.

Peter

SONO QUASI CERTO CHE ALCUNI VICINI ABBIANO VISTO QUELLO che è successo nella nostra auto nel parcheggio—e so che la mia squadra sicuramente l'ha fatto—ma non me ne frega un cazzo, mentre porto una traballante Sara verso l'ascensore. È trasandata come non l'ho mai vista, con la camicetta abbottonata in modo sbagliato e i capelli in disordine sul viso arrossato. Sono sicuro di avere un aspetto simile, e non posso fare a meno di sorridere, mentre passiamo davanti ad una coppia di fighetti che spinge un passeggino nella hall. Ci rivolgono un'occhiata scandalizzata, e Sara si volta, con le guance in fiamme.

È così carina. La mia povera ptichka è imbarazzata per il nostro breve episodio di sesso semi-pubblico—anche se è stata lei ad iniziarlo.

"Non preoccuparti. Ci trasferiremo questa settimana" le

ricordo, mentre entriamo nell'ascensore, e preme la fronte contro lo specchio, stringendo gli occhi, mentre sbatte un pugno sul vetro.

"Non posso credere che l'abbiamo fatto. Io... Oh, Dio, non mi sembra vero."

Sembra così mortificata che voglio abbracciarla. Così, faccio esattamente questo, ignorando i suoi tentativi di respingermi, mentre la stringo. Dopo un momento, si rilassa e le accarezzo i capelli arruffati, finché l'ascensore non raggiunge il nostro piano.

Poi, mi chino e la sollevo tra le braccia per portarla nell'appartamento.

Non obietta, nasconde semplicemente il volto contro il mio collo, mentre passiamo accanto a un altro vicino nel corridoio. Il ragazzo—uno poco più che adolescente—sorride e alza il pollice, mentre passa.

Se solo il ragazzo conoscesse l'intera storia.

Quando arriviamo alla porta, metto giù Sara per prendere le chiavi e lei corre nell'appartamento non appena la apro. Mi sto ancora togliendo le scarpe, quando sento la doccia aprirsi, e quando la raggiungo, sta già uscendo dalla vasca, ancora adorabilmente rossa in viso e con l'aspetto imbarazzato.

Sono felice di vederla così.

Sicuramente è meglio dell'espressione che aveva in macchina dopo aver saputo della scomparsa del patrigno di Monica.

"Credi che ci abbia realmente visto qualcuno?" chiede ansiosamente, avvolgendosi un asciugamano intorno, e trattengo un altro sorriso, mentre comincio a spogliarmi.

"Secondo *te*, ptichka?"

"Beh, è tardi, e il parcheggio è piuttosto buio, e—oh, stai zitto!" Mi dà un colpetto sul braccio, mentre getto la maglietta nel cesto della biancheria e inizio a ridere, non riuscendo a farne a meno.

Se nessuno in questo complesso di appartamenti ha visto l'auto parcheggiata dondolare come una nave in un uragano, mi taglierò una mano.

Geme, nascondendo il viso tra le mani, ma poi alza la testa, improvvisamente pallida. "Non pensi che verremo arrestati, vero? Per indecenza pubblica o qualcosa del genere?"

Smetto di ridere. "No, amore mio." Riesco a scorgere la paura e il senso di colpa sul suo viso, e so che non è dovuto alla nostra bravata nel parcheggio.

Ricorda che cosa l'ha preceduta, ed è preoccupata per le conseguenze.

"Sara..." Le prendo le mani tra le mie. I suoi palmi sono di nuovo freddi, nonostante il vapore della doccia calda che riempie ancora il piccolo bagno. "Ptichka, non ci succederà. Non c'è niente che mi leghi alla morte di quell'uomo—né qualcuno che stia investigando davvero. Lo so—ho fatto controllare dagli hacker. Secondo tutti, un ex detenuto è stato aggredito in un brutto quartiere, tutto qui. Nessun poliziotto sprecherà il proprio tempo ad indagare ulteriormente—ma anche se lo facesse, non scoprirebbe nulla. Sono bravo in quello che faccio... o facevo."

"Lo so. E questo è..." La sua esile gola si muove, mentre deglutisce. "È terrificante."

"Perché?" chiedo gentilmente, sfregandole i pollici sui palmi. "Te l'ho detto, quella parte della mia vita fa parte del passato. Non vediamo l'ora che arrivi il futuro, ricordi? E ora lo stesso vale per la tua paziente. È libera di vivere la sua vita senza paura. Non è quello che volevi per lei?"

"Certo che lo è." Tira via le mani e si avvolge le braccia intorno, sembrando così triste che quasi mi dispiace aver fatto questo per lei.

Forse sarebbe stato meglio se avessi escogitato un altro modo per occuparmi del problema di Monica—o almeno se avessi eliminato il corpo.

Ma volevo che la paziente di Sara sapesse che il suo aggressore non rappresenta più una minaccia. Una scomparsa inspiegabile non sarebbe stata sufficiente. La povera ragazza si sarebbe sempre guardata le spalle, temendo il ritorno di quel coglione.

Questa è la cosa migliore, ne sono sicuro. Ora ho solo bisogno di convincere mia moglie.

"Ptichka—"

"Peter—" inizia simultaneamente, così mi fermo, lasciandola parlare.

Fa un respiro e lo rilascia lentamente. "Peter, se vogliamo... farlo davvero—se vogliamo costruire una vita normale insieme—ho bisogno che tu mi prometta qualcosa."

"Di cosa si tratta, amore mio?" chiedo, anche se posso immaginare.

"Ho bisogno che tu mi prometta che non lo farai mai più." I suoi occhi color nocciola sono concentrati sul mio viso. "Devo sapere che se qualcuno mi darà fastidio, non finirà in un vicolo con la gola tagliata. Che se i nostri figli avranno un insegnante difficile a scuola, sono vittime di bullismo da parte di un compagno di classe o se qualcuno mostra il dito medio mentre guidiamo, l'omicidio *non* sarà la soluzione."

Sbatto le palpebre lentamente. "Capisco."

"Me lo puoi promettere?" insiste, stringendo i lembi dell'asciugamano. "Ho bisogno di sapere che le persone intorno a me sono al sicuro—che stando con te non sto condannando a morte nessun altro."

Ora è il mio turno di fare un respiro profondo e calmante. "Amore mio... non posso promettere di non proteggerti. Se qualcuno cerca di fare del male a te o ai nostri figli—"

"Ci rivolgiamo alle autorità, come tutti gli altri." Solleva il mento ostinatamente. "Ecco a cosa serve la polizia. E in ogni caso, non sto parlando di un evidente caso di difesa personale. Ovviamente, se camminiamo per strada e qualcuno ci minaccia con una pistola, è una cosa diversa—anche se disarmare o semplicemente ferire quella persona dovrebbe essere ancora la soluzione preferita. Sto parlando dell'omicidio come modo per affrontare persone che *non* rappresentano una minaccia mortale. Capisci la differenza, vero?"

In realtà, no. Non ho intenzione di uccidere coglioni a caso che suonano il clacson o qualsiasi cosa stia immaginando Sara, ma non lascerò che qualche ublyudok la faccia piangere o le spezzi il cuore.

Mi sta guardando, in attesa, però, e capisco che pretende una risposta. "Va bene" dico dopo un momento di riflessione. "Se è quello che vuoi, prometto che non ucciderò nessuno che non rappresenti una minaccia per noi o per qualcuno a cui teniamo."

"E non lo torturerai, picchierai o ferirai in alcun modo, giusto?"

Sospiro. "Bene. Nessun danno fisico, lo prometto." Ci sono ancora diversi metodi che potrei utilizzare, volendo—tangenti, ricatti, pressioni finanziarie—quindi mi sento a mio agio nel fare questa promessa. Inoltre, ciò che costituisce una "minaccia" è aperto all'interpretazione per quanto mi riguarda.

Se qualche fottuto bullo aggredisce nostro figlio a scuola, lui —o i suoi genitori—*non* se la caveranno senza un graffio.

Non sembra soddisfatta della mia promessa, così prendo il suo asciugamano e lo tolgo nello stesso momento in cui tiro giù la lampo dei jeans.

"Aspetta—" inizia a dire, ma la sto già spingendo nella doccia, dove mi assicuro che gli ipotetici futuri stronzi che potrei dover affrontare siano lontani, lontani dalla sua mente.

1 2

eter

LA MATTINA DOPO, SARA È SILENZIOSA E UN PO' DISTANTE, mentre continua a soffermarsi sulla mia soluzione al problema della sua paziente. È improbabile che questo porti a qualcosa di buono, così cerco di distrarla alimentando il suo nuovo hobby: cantare con la band.

"Quand'è la tua prossima esibizione?" chiedo a colazione. "Ho visto i tuoi video sul palco, ma mi piacerebbe vederti di persona."

Alza gli occhi dalla sua frittata, sbattendo le palpebre come se si stesse concentrando su di me. "Oh, in realtà intendevo dirtelo. Il nostro chitarrista, Phil, mi ha mandato un messaggio la scorsa notte. Ci ha assicurato un concerto domani sera, ma solo se tutti riusciranno a farcela con un preavviso così breve. Pensi che possiamo spostare la cena con i miei genitori a sabato?"

Il mio primo impulso è dire di no. Contavo di averla per me dopo la cena—un evento che probabilmente richiederebbe due o tre ore, al massimo. Questa esibizione ci mangerebbe tutto il venerdì sera, e poi dovremmo ancora stare con i suoi genitori durante il fine settimana—che è anche quando ci stabiliremo nella nostra nuova casa.

Ma sto morendo dalla voglia di vedere il mio passerotto sul palco, riversando la sua anima. E questo è importante per lei, quindi è importante per me.

"Certo" dico con calma e mi alzo per iniziare a ripulire. "Possiamo cenare con i tuoi genitori sabato. O meglio ancora, invitali per un brunch."

Ho sempre saputo che condurre questa vita avrebbe significato dover condividere il tempo e l'attenzione di Sara, e non posso lasciare che la mia ossessione per lei rovini tutto.

Posso sopportarlo.

È solo qualcosa a cui devo abituarmi.

～

Finisco di pulire, mentre mia moglie si veste, e poi la accompagno al lavoro.

"Non dimenticare: l'atto di acquisto è alle sei di oggi" le ricordo, mentre ci fermiamo di fronte al suo ufficio. "Ti vengo a prendere alle 5:30, ok?"

Annuisce, senza incontrare il mio sguardo, mentre cerca la maniglia della portiera.

"Sara." Le prendo il polso, mentre la apre. "Guardami."

Obbedisce con riluttanza, e allungo l'altra mano, sistemandole una ciocca di lucenti capelli castani dietro l'orecchio. "Dillo, ptichka. Voglio sentire quelle parole."

Mi fissa, e sento il rapido battito dell'esile polso che sto stringendo. Sta di nuovo combattendo se stessa, combattendo i suoi sentimenti per me, e non lo permetterò.

"Dillo" esigo, stringendo la presa, e scorgo il momento esatto in cui smette di lottare.

Chiudendo gli occhi, inspira profondamente, poi li riapre. "Ti amo." La sua voce è bassa ma ferma, mentre mi guarda negli occhi. "Ti amo, Peter... nonostante tutto."

Qualcosa in profondità dentro di me—un nodo di tensione che non sapevo nemmeno fosse lì—si rilassa, e porto la sua mano sulle mie labbra, baciando la pelle morbida su ogni nocca. "Ti amo anch'io. Ci vediamo alle 5:30, ok?"

"Ok" mormora, e mi sforzo di lasciarla andare.

Di lasciarla volare libera, almeno fino a stasera.

Sara

FEDELE ALLA SUA PAROLA, PETER PASSA A PRENDERMI ALLE 5:30 in punto e ci rechiamo allo studio del notaio per firmare i documenti.

"Hai messo la casa a mio nome?" gli rivolgo un'occhiata sorpresa, quando vedo lo spazio solo per la mia firma sui documenti.

Annuisce, piegando le labbra in un sorriso. "È la cosa migliore, amore mio. Solo per evenienza."

Un brivido mi attraversa la schiena. "Solo per evenienza" potrebbe riferirsi a qualsiasi numero di cose, ma se tuo marito era ricercato dalle forze dell'ordine in tutto il mondo e ha ancora legami con la malavita, le parole assumono un significato particolarmente sinistro.

Vorrei indagare più a fondo, ma il notaio—una donna carina e raffinata sulla trentina—ci sta guardando con un'evidente curiosità, così firmo su ogni X e cerco di non pensare alle terrificanti possibilità.

Come, ad esempio, una squadra SWAT che abbatte la nostra porta nel bel mezzo della notte, perché hanno scoperto il ruolo di Peter nell'omicidio del patrigno di Monica.

"Tutto a posto" dice la donna vivacemente, mentre le porgo l'ultimo foglio. "Congratulazioni per la sua nuova casa."

"Grazie." Mi alzo e le stringo la mano. "Siamo molto emozionati."

Segue la stretta di mano di Peter e non posso fare a meno di notare il modo in cui lei lo guarda—come un gatto che osserva una ciotola piena di latte. Lui sembra incurante del suo interesse, ma sento comunque una brutta fitta di gelosia.

Forse dovrei dirgli che *lei* mi ha fatto arrabbiare?

Scaccio quel fastidioso pensiero non appena compare nella mia mente, ma è troppo tardi. Ripenso a tutto e mi sento male. Per tutto il giorno, ho cercato di convincermi che quello che è successo sia stato un evento isolato e che mio marito manterrà la sua promessa di non fare del male a nessun altro, ma ogni volta che sono vicina a crederlo, ricordo che cosa ha minacciato di fare al nostro matrimonio, se non mi fossi presentata.

L'omicidio—o la sua minaccia—farà sempre parte del suo arsenale, e nessuno intorno a me è realmente al sicuro. Tanto varrebbe andare in giro con una bomba a mano.

Peter mi accompagna fuori, e ci dirigiamo verso casa, dove il tavolo è già apparecchiato con le candele e una bottiglia di champagne si sta raffreddando in un secchio di ghiaccio, mentre il forno emana deliziosi profumi.

"Alla nostra nuova casa" brinda, dopo averci versato un bicchiere, e trangugio il drink gassato, cercando di non pensare a corpi simili a burattini in vicoli oscuri, che spargono pozze di sangue.

Alla mina vagante che è sempre al mio fianco.

Peter

I TRASLOCATORI NON VERRANNO PRIMA DI MEZZOGIORNO, QUINDI dopo aver lasciato Sara al lavoro venerdì, vado a fare una lunga corsa con uno zaino appesantito per imitare l'allenamento che facevo con i ragazzi. Ho bisogno del duro esercizio fisico per scacciare parte delle inquietudini che ho provato—e per non pensare a quanto mi manchi la mia moglie maniaca del lavoro.

Terminando la mia corsa in un parco tranquillo e quasi vuoto, tolgo la maglietta bagnata di sudore e comincio un ciclo di esercizi a corpo libero, usando lo zaino da trentacinque chili per aggiungere difficoltà alle flessioni con un braccio su un albero vicino.

Ho quasi finito, quando vedo un adolescente che corre verso di me, con la maglietta che gli svolazza intorno al corpo magro. Per un istante, sembra esattamente il mio amico Andrey, quello che mi ha fatto tutti i tatuaggi a Camp Larko.

L'illusione si dissolve, man mano che il corridore si avvicina, ma non riesco ancora a distogliere lo sguardo.

Il ragazzo sta correndo come se dei segugi lo stessero inseguendo, con gli occhi selvaggi e le braccia che pompano disperatamente lungo i fianchi. Qualche secondo dopo, capisco perché.

Quattro ragazzi più grandi, più grossi—giovani uomini, in realtà—stanno correndo dietro di lui, urlando insulti.

Non sono affari miei, ma non posso farci niente.

Non appena il sosia di Andrey mi sfreccia accanto, sgancio lo zaino dalla vita e lo getto a terra con disinvoltura. Poi, proprio mentre i suoi inseguitori stanno per superarmi, incrocio il loro cammino, estendendo le braccia da entrambi i lati.

Si fermano bruscamente, evitando a stento di schiantarsi contro di me.

"Che cazzo fai, amico?" ringhia il più grosso. "Togliti di mezzo!"

Cerca di spingermi da una parte—un grave errore da parte sua. I miei istinti ben collaudati entrano in azione, e un attimo dopo, il giovane è a terra sul sedere, gemendo, mentre i suoi tre compagni si allontanano, con le mani sollevate in modo difensivo.

"Sparite" dico loro, e lo fanno, fermandosi solo per afferrare il loro amico caduto e trascinarlo via.

Mi sto chinando per recuperare lo zaino, quando noto un movimento con la coda dell'occhio.

È il ragazzo che ho aiutato, con il petto magro che si gonfia, mentre mi fissa. "Come hai fatto?" Sento ammirazione e invidia nella sua voce.

"Fatto cosa?" Raccogliendo lo zaino, ci infilo la maglietta che avevo tolto.

"Metterlo giù in quel modo."

Mi stringo nelle spalle, sistemando lo zaino e fissando le

cinghie attorno alla vita. "Solo qualche allenamento di autodifesa di base."

"No, amico." Gli occhi azzurri del ragazzo sono enormi—e stranamente uguali a quelli di Andrey. "C'era qualcos'altro. Eri nell'esercito? Ti alleni lì?" Indica il mio zaino.

"Qualcosa del genere, e sì." Mi volto per andarmene, ma il ragazzo non ha ancora finito con me.

"Puoi insegnarmi? A combattere, intendo dire."

Faccio finta di non aver sentito e inizio a fare jogging.

Non è scoraggiato. Raggiungendomi, corre al mio fianco. "Puoi insegnarmi? Per favore."

Accelero il passo. "Non ho intenzione di addestrare i ragazzi."

"Ti pagherò." È senza fiato, ma in qualche modo riesce a tenere il mio ritmo. "Ecco." Infila la mano in tasca e tira fuori due banconote da venti. "Li avrebbero presi comunque, quindi puoi averli."

Sto per rifiutare, quando mi viene un'idea. Fermandomi vicino ad una panchina, osservo il ragazzo con aria interrogativa. "Vuoi imparare? Davvero?"

"Sì." Praticamente salta dall'emozione. "Voglio sapere come difendermi. Voglio dire, ho seguito alcune lezione di karate da piccolo, ma in realtà non—"

"Quanti anni hai?" lo interrompo.

"Sedici. Beh, quasi. Il mio compleanno è il mese prossimo."

"E chi erano quei ragazzi che ti inseguivano?"

Arrossisce. "Amici di mio fratello maggiore. Fanno tutti parte di una confraternita, ed è una specie di rituale per loro. Sai, prendere soldi da un nerd."

Roteo quasi gli occhi per l'assurdità di tutto questo. Lo sto davvero prendendo in considerazione?

"Per favore, signore." Il ragazzo si sposta da un piede all'altro. "Mio padre dice sempre che devo difendermi, ma non so come. E il modo in cui li hai fermati... Ucciderei per essere in grado di farlo."

Il ragazzo non ha idea di cosa stia dicendo, ma per qualche motivo—forse perché sto ancora pensando ad Andrey e al modo in cui veniva sempre preso di mira nel nostro campo infernale, prima che la sadica guardia lo facesse bollire vivo— allungo la mano e dico: "Dammi il cellulare."

Tira fuori il suo telefono e me lo porge. Inserisco il mio numero e glielo restituisco.

"Chiamami questo fine settimana e organizzeremo un incontro. A proposito, come ti chiami?"

"Aiden, signore. Aiden Walt." Esita, poi decide di essere coraggioso. "E tu sei?"

"Peter Garin" dico, e riprendo a correre, lasciando l'adolescente accanto alla panchina.

15

Com'è stata sua abitudine per tutta la settimana, Peter torna a prendermi dopo il lavoro, solo che invece di andare a casa o in clinica, ci dirigiamo verso il bar, dove stasera si esibisce la mia band.

"Grazie mille per questo" dico tra i bocconi della pasta col pollo che mi ha portato da mangiare in macchina. "È davvero deliziosa."

"Prego." Il suo sguardo argenteo è caldo, mentre mi guarda, prima di riportare l'attenzione sulla strada. "Mi fa piacere che ti piaccia."

"Non posso credere che tu abbia avuto il tempo di cucinare oggi. Non dovevano venire i traslocatori?"

Sorride. "Oh, non te l'ho detto? Sono venuti—e stasera andremo a dormire nella nuova casa."

"Che cosa?" Quasi soffoco sulla mia pasta. "Sei serio?"

Annuisce. "Ho assunto quattro ragazzi, che hanno imballato e spostato tutto a tempo di record. Ho già disfatto tutte le necessità, compreso tutto ciò che serve per la cucina e la camera da letto, quindi si tratta solo di occuparsi di alcune altre scatole nel fine settimana. E di comprare qualcosa di nuovo, naturalmente—ma pensavo che potremmo farlo insieme."

"Sei straordinario" dico, e lo penso davvero. La sua inesorabile spinta ossessiva—quella capacità quasi sovrumana di superare le insormontabili difficoltà nel perseguire il suo obiettivo—mi terrorizzava, ma ora che non combatto più per sfuggirgli, la vedo per il vantaggio che è.

La stessa formidabile forza di volontà grazie alla quale mi aveva fatto innamorare di lui ora sta smussando tutti i piccoli ostacoli nella nostra pacifica vita suburbana—una vita che è possibile solo perché ha compiuto un miracolo e si è tolto dalle liste dei Più Ricercati.

Se non lo conoscessi, lo considererei un mago, che ha piegato il fato e la realtà alla propria volontà.

"Ho deciso di aprire una scuola di addestramento" mi informa con indifferenza, mentre riprendo a mangiare. "Inizierò a cercare un posto la prossima settimana."

Mi fermo a metà boccone, fissandolo incredula. "Davvero?"

"Sì. Ho incontrato un ragazzo oggi nel parco, che mi ha pregato di dargli alcune lezioni di combattimento. Così, mi è venuta questa idea, e più ci penso, più mi piace. Sto pensando a lezioni di difesa personale per donne e adolescenti, programmi di allenamento per atleti professionisti, addestramento per guardie del corpo e così via. Ho una certa esperienza nell'addestrare gli altri, avendolo fatto con i miei ragazzi, quando stavo mettendo insieme la squadra, quindi potrebbe essere divertente."

"È un'idea *fantastica*." Non posso nascondere l'emozione nella voce. "Sarà perfetto per te."

Mi rivolge un'occhiata ironica. "Meglio degli omicidi?"

Rido, perché mi ha letto nel pensiero. "Sì, molto meglio." Ero preoccupata per quello che avrebbe fatto qui, chiedendomi se gli sarebbe mancata la sua ex professione carica di adrenalina, e questo mi tranquillizza un po'.

Con la scuola di addestramento che occupa i suoi giorni e gli offre una nuova sfida, il mio marito assassino potrebbe effettivamente adattarsi alla nostra tranquilla vita civile.

Sentendomi più leggera di quanto non fossi stata fin dalla visita di Monica, finisco la mia pasta proprio mentre saliamo al bar, dove mi esibirò stasera.

LA SENSAZIONE DI LEGGEREZZA EVAPORA NON APPENA ENTRIAMO. Il bar è enorme, rumoroso e affollato, con la maggior parte dei clienti già ubriachi, e mi accorgo della crescente tensione di Peter, mentre ci dirigiamo verso il backstage, dove gli altri membri della band si stanno preparando.

"Ehi, eccoli, gli sposini! Sono così contento che siate venuti." Phil mi stringe in un grande abbraccio, e il viso di mio marito si trasforma in pietra, con la mano che inizia a piegarsi in un pugno.

Cazzo. Avevo dimenticato l'estrema possessività di Peter.

Spingo via il mio compagno di band e afferro rapidamente il braccio di mio marito. Il muscolo d'acciaio si flette sotto le mie dita e capisco che facevo bene a preoccuparmi.

La mia mina vagante stava per esplodere.

"Dove sono Simon e Rory?" chiedo, massaggiando le mani sul bicipite di Peter, come se mi stessi divertendo a toccare tutto quel muscolo letale—e sarebbe così, se non fossi così preoccupata per Phil. "Sono pronti?"

"Si stanno cambiando laggiù." Phil piega la testa verso destra. "Dovresti cambiarti anche tu. Abbiamo preparato il tuo abbigliamento. E non ti preoccupare, ti restituiremo tuo marito, quando avrai finito." Sogghigna verso Peter, che sembra ancora avere voglia di rovinarlo con le unghie. Lentamente.

"Va bene. Sarò veloce." Stringo il bicipite di Peter in segno di avvertimento e con riluttanza mi dirigo verso lo spogliatoio.

Sarà meglio che il mio chitarrista sia illeso al mio ritorno.

eter

"Allora" dice Phil, con l'espressione bonaria che svanisce non appena Sara è fuori dalla vista. "Bastardo geloso, non è vero?"

Lo fisso, senza battere ciglio. "Non immagini quanto."

Se mai oserà abbracciare di nuovo mia moglie, sarà l'ultima cosa che farà. Questo luogo mi fa già innervosire—con tutti gli ubriachi ammassati là fuori, è il posto perfetto per colpire di un assassino—e il solo pensiero delle zampette di questo stronzo col ventre gonfio di birra su Sara mi fa venire voglia di spezzargli il collo paffuto.

Mi fissa, poi scoppia a ridere. "Oh, amico, dovresti vedere l'espressione sul tuo viso. Non credevo che quello sguardo da assassino fosse una cosa reale."

Mi sforzo di sbattere le palpebre, attenuando il mio "sguardo da assassino" mentre continua, ignaro di quanto sia stata vera la sua osservazione. "Scusa, amico. Non intendevo invadere il tuo territorio. Conosciamo Sara da un po' e per noi è come una sorella. Beh, non proprio, perché non siamo imparentati e lei *è* davvero sexy, ma hai capito che cosa intendo. E sinceramente, non sapevamo nemmeno che le piacessero gli uomini. Non sto dicendo che pensavamo che stesse sull'altra sponda—solo che non le interessasse frequentare uomini, essendo vedova e tutto il resto. Anche se immagino che stesse uscendo segretamente con te e..." Scuote la testa. "Accidenti, non posso credere che non lo sapessimo."

"Sì, beh, ora lo sapete." Probabilmente dovrei essere più gentile, visto il suo evidente tentativo di legare, ma sto ancora trattenendo a malapena l'istinto di ucciderlo per quell'abbraccio—e per tutte le altre volte in cui ci ha indubbiamente provato con la mia moglie "davvero sexy."

All'epoca non era mia moglie, ma era *mia.*

Fortunatamente, Sara riappare prima che la mia pazienza venga ulteriormente messa alla prova. Indossa un abito bianco che mi ricorda Marilyn Monroe nella famosa scena della gonna che si gonfia. Su un'altra donna, sarebbe potuta sembrare semplicemente provocante, ma su di lei, con la sua postura da ballerina, è tanto elegante quanto sexy.

"Ho pensato che fosse appropriato" dice Phil mentre la fisso, con l'acquolina in bocca per l'impulso di mordicchiare la pelle morbida esposta per via della scollatura aperta del vestito. "Sai, dal momento che è una sposina e tutto il resto."

Distolgo gli occhi dalle sue delicate clavicole. "Che cosa?"

"L'abito bianco" risponde il chitarrista, sogghignando. "L'ho scelto io. Come una continuazione del tuo matrimonio e tutto il resto."

"Ah." Mi volto per guardare Sara, mentre si ferma per parlare con il loro batterista, Simon.

Quanto sarebbe brutto, se la portassi subito via? Se la

prendessi e la portassi via da qui, per poi tenerla nel mio letto fino a non riuscire più a camminare entrambi?

Voglio che canti per me, e solo per me, con quell'abito.

E con qualsiasi altro vestito, ora che ci penso.

"Amico, riprenditi" dice Phil, e lo guardo storto, irritato. L'idiota scuote la testa e sorride, come se non potesse vedere che sto per spezzargli letteralmente il collo.

"Phil, ehi!" Una donna bionda gira l'angolo, e mi rendo conto che è l'amica di Sara dell'ospedale, Marsha.

Vedendomi, si blocca per un secondo, poi si avvicina a noi con fare esitante.

"Ciao, Marsha." Le sorrido il più gentilmente possibile. Non c'è bisogno di spaventare ulteriormente la donna; ha già ogni sorta di sospetto su di me. "Non sapevo che saresti stato qui."

"Sì, beh..." Il suo sguardo si posa su Phil. "Posso parlarti?"

"Certo." Lui mi guarda di nuovo. "Scusami."

Riporto la mia attenzione su Sara, mentre Marsha trascina via il chitarrista. La mia ptichka ora sta parlando con il ragazzo dai capelli rossi, Rory, e non mi piace il modo in cui quel pollo muscoloso la sta guardando.

Comincio a dirigermi laggiù, ma lei termina la conversazione e fa capolino sul palco. "Sono pronti per noi" urla girandosi, ed esco silenziosamente dall'area del backstage per unirmi alla folla nel bar.

L'esibizione della mia ptichka sta per iniziare e non voglio perdermela.

～

CON MIO GRANDE STUPORE, LA FOLLA CHIASSOSA SI CALMA NON appena Sara sale sul palco. E quando apre la bocca, capisco perché. È fenomenale come qualsiasi altra pop star lassù, con la voce forte e pura, mentre canta i testi che ha composto. L'ho sentita esercitarsi in Giappone, ma ascolto con la stessa attenzione di chiunque altro nel bar.

È impossibile non farlo.

La canzone è sia evocativa che allegra, un insolito mix di country, R&B e recenti successi pop—il tutto combinato con lo stile unico di Sara.

È più che brava.

È fantastica.

I nostri occhi si incontrano, e il cuore si espande nel mio petto, fino a quando sembra che non possa essere contenuto. È surreale, il mio bisogno per lei, la bramosia che provo con ogni cellula del corpo. L'istinto primitivo prende di nuovo vita dentro di me, con l'urgenza di gettarla sulla mia spalla e trascinarla nella mia tana.

La voglio lontana dagli occhi di tutti, in modo da poterla divorare da solo.

Una canzone, tre, cinque, quindici—prima che me ne renda conto, sono passate due ore. Continuano a chiamarla, chiedendo il bis, e lei continua a cedere—finché non finisce tutto.

La prendo, mentre scende dal palco. La afferro letteralmente e la sollevo, premendola contro il mio petto.

"Il privilegio dello sposo novello" ringhio ai suoi fan rabbiosi, e mentre nasconde il suo viso, arrossendo e ridendo, faccio quello che sono morto dalla voglia di fare per tutta la serata.

La porto via, per godermela tutto da solo.

eter

MI TRATTENGO ABBASTANZA MENTRE LA RIPORTO A CASA, ANCHE se ogni volta che Sara si sposta sul sedile e intravedo la sua coscia nuda sotto quella gonna provocante e bianca, sono tentato di uscire dalla strada.

L'unica cosa che mi impedisce di farlo è che non voglio un'altra sveltina in macchina. Ho bisogno di averla nel mio letto, dove posso banchettare sul suo delizioso corpo per tutta la notte. Dove posso mostrarle che sarà sempre mia, a prescindere da quanti uomini sbavino per lei.

Aiuta il fatto che stia parlando senza sosta, ancora riprendendosi dalla performance. Mi sta raccontando tutto su come la chitarra di Phil avesse avuto bisogno di una messa a punto all'ultimo minuto, e su come Simon quasi non ce l'avesse fatta, perché aveva un articolo da consegnare. Concentrarmi sulle sue parole mi impedisce di allungarle la mano sotto la gonna e di farla scorrere sulla sua coscia liscia, prima di scavare sotto il perizoma di pizzo che ha indossato questa mattina e accarezzare il morbido, setoso—

"Riesci a credere che Marsha stia uscendo con Phil adesso?" Mi distoglie dai pensieri, e mi rendo conto di aver smesso di ascoltare, perso nell'erotica fantasia.

"Davvero?" Faccio del mio meglio per concentrarmi nuovamente sulle sue parole. "Quando è successo?"

"Rory mi ha detto che si sono conosciuti la notte del nostro matrimonio. Non è divertente? A quanto pare, Marsha era troppo ubriaca per guidare dopo la cerimonia, e Phil si è offerto volontario per riportarla a casa. E il resto, come si suol dire, è storia."

"È fantastico" dico, sforzandomi di tenere gli occhi sulla strada invece di divorare Sara con lo sguardo. "Buon per loro."

E intendo sul serio. Forse la vivace infermiera terrà occupato il chitarrista, che smetterà di sbavare su mia moglie ogni volta che ne ha la possibilità. E a sua volta, questo terrà Marsha abbastanza distratta da farla rimanere fuori dai nostri affari.

Sara le aveva raccontato un po' troppi dettagli durante la mia assenza, e anche se Marsha non sa per certo che sono io l'uomo che ha perseguitato Sara e ucciso il suo primo marito, lo sospetta fortemente.

"Sì, spero che funzioni per loro" dice. "Entrambi meritano un buon partner."

Annuisco diplomaticamente e le rivolgo un'altra occhiata. Mi guarda con un sorriso, e poi mi uccide appoggiando casualmente la mano sulla mia coscia.

Il mio uccello, già semi-eretto per le immagini proibite nella mia mente, scatta al massimo allarme. Il tocco delle sue dita magre mi scalda la pelle nonostante lo spesso tessuto dei jeans. È come se avessi un nervo teso sulla coscia, che invia scosse di elettricità dritte all'inguine. Il mio cuore batte violentemente, e serro la mascella, mentre la strada davanti si offusca per un pericoloso secondo.

"Sara." Ringhio il suo nome, mentre stringo convulsamente le mani sul voltante. "Ptichka, se non sposti la mano subito..."

Il suo respiro si blocca visibilmente, e tira via la mano, avendo finalmente capito che cosa sta facendo. Non aiuta, però. Posso ancora sentire il suo tocco. È stampato nella mia pelle, nella mia mente... nel mio cuore. Forse un giorno non sarà così, con il suo affetto che mi uccide ogni volta, ma per ora, siamo ancora troppo nuovi, troppo grezzi. Non molto tempo fa, mi temeva e mi odiava. Ero un mostro ai suoi occhi. E forse lo sono ancora—ma ora mi ama.

Sa di aver bisogno di me, parti oscure e tutto il resto.

Quando ci fermiamo davanti alla nostra nuova casa, mi assicuro che nulla inneschi il mio ben collaudato senso del pericolo. Niente lo fa—né dovrebbe. L'abitazione ora è sicurissima, con una tecnologia all'avanguardia che controlla tutto e la mia squadra posizionata in punti strategici in tutto il quartiere.

Non lascerò che i nemici del mio passato si intromettano nel nostro pacifico presente.

"Wow" esclama Sara, mentre la aiuto a scendere dalla macchina. La sua testa gira da un lato all'altro, con gli occhi spalancati per lo stupore. "Da dove vengono tutti questi alberi? E quella staccionata? Quando hai avuto il tempo di fare tutto questo?"

Do un'occhiata a ciò di cui sta parlando. Ho fatto mettere una staccionata alta e ho piantato alberi intorno alla proprietà per garantire la privacy e oscurare la linea di tiro ad eventuali cecchini.

"Ieri" rispondo, poggiandole una mano sulla parte bassa della schiena per condurla all'ingresso.

Potrà ammirare la nostra nuova dimora domani; stasera, tutto il suo tempo appartiene a me.

Abbiamo appena varcato la soglia, quando il mio autocontrollo si spezza come un ramoscello nella tempesta.

Chiudendo la porta con il piede, accendo la luce del corridoio e la appoggio contro il muro, posandole le mani sotto al vestito. Tirandole su la gonna, trovo il suo perizoma di pizzo umido e la figa morbida e scivolosa sotto di esso.

Cazzo, sì. L'esibizione deve averla eccitata in tutti i sensi.

"Peter." Spalanca gli occhi, mentre mi stringe i bicipiti. "Aspetta, andiamo prima—ahh..." Le sue parole terminano con un gemito, mentre la penetro con due dita, godendomi la strettura setosa e scivolosa.

"Dimmi che desideri questo" esigo, pompando le dita dentro e fuori da lei, lasciando che la punta ruvida del mio pollice le sfiori il clitoride ad ogni colpo. "Dimmi che mi *vuoi*."

I suoi occhi diventano sempre più vitrei, con le pupille che si dilatano di più ogni secondo che passa. "Ti voglio. Lo sai che è così." Sembra senza fiato, con i muscoli interni che si stringono e i fianchi che ondeggiano con un ritmo che mi dice che è al limite. "Per favore, Peter..."

Tiro fuori le dita e porto la mia mano sul suo viso. "Succhiale." Spingo le dita tra le sue labbra morbide. "Bagnale per bene, ok?"

Spalanca di nuovo gli occhi, ma obbedisce, con l'agile lingua che vortica intorno alle mie dita, mentre gliele infilo nella bocca. È straordinario, e mi fa immaginare quella lingua sul mio fallo. Volendo di più, spingo le mie dita più a fondo e sento un singhiozzo provenire dalla sua gola, mentre le bagna con altra saliva.

Fanculo. Se non sarò dentro di lei, esploderò.

Sbottonando i jeans con la mano libera, tiro fuori le dita dalla sua bocca e gliele spingo nella figa, lasciando che la scivolosità si mescoli con la saliva, mentre riprendo a fotterla con il dito, desiderando scorgere di nuovo quello sguardo vitreo nei suoi occhi.

Non impiega molto—dopo trenta secondi, sta respirando velocemente, con la pelle pallida splendidamente arrossata. Mi sta ancora guardando, ma i suoi occhi si fanno confusi, con la bocca che si apre, mentre affonda le unghie nel mio bicipite e i muscoli delle cosce vibrano come una corda.

Aspetto finché non sono sicuro che verrà, e poi estraggo di nuovo le dita—solo per sollevarle le cosce toniche e impalarla col mio uccello dolorante. La sua O senza parole si trasforma in un forte rantolo, avvolgendomi strettamente le gambe intorno ai fianchi, mentre la penetro con un unico spietato colpo. Posso sentire i suoi muscoli interiori pulsare e contrarsi, mentre mi sistemo profondamente dentro di lei, e devo fare appello a tutta la mia forza di volontà per non cedere al potente impulso di venire.

Non se la caverà così facilmente.

Non stanotte.

In qualche modo, riesco a resistere fin quando i suoi spasmi non si attenuano e il suo corpo non scivola contro il mio, con le palpebre che si chiudono, mentre una luce beata appare sul suo viso. Abbassando la testa, le bacio le labbra socchiuse e muovo la mano che l'ha scopata con le dita dalla sua coscia alla fessura invitante tra le natiche.

È così rilassata e presa dal mio bacio che oppone una minima resistenza, mentre premo un dito nella sua apertura posteriore e la lavoro con cura. Sono già dentro di lei fino alla prima nocca, quando strabuzza gli occhi e il suo corpo si irrigidisce, con i muscoli interni che mi stringono l'uccello e il dito, mentre mi avvolge più forte le gambe attorno ai fianchi.

"Lasciami entrare, ptichka" mormoro sulle sue labbra. "Sai che lo vuoi."

Non che abbia molta scelta. La sto tenendo su con la mano libera e il peso del corpo. Con le sue gambe avvolte attorno ai miei fianchi e il mio fallo sepolto dentro di lei, è impossibile che possa sfuggire o controllare la profondità della penetrazione di uno dei suoi orifizi.

È completamente alla mia mercé, ed è esattamente quello che voglio.

Non le ho preso il sedere dalla nostra prima notte di nozze, ma non ho mai smesso di pensarci—di pensare alla sensazione di quei globi rotondi premuti contro le mie palle e all'espressione di estasi al limite del dolore sul suo viso. Le avevo fatto male, lo so, e qualcosa al riguardo era stato perversamente giusto, incredibilmente soddisfacente.

Per quanto la adori, voglio ancora punirla a volte, scorgere la paura combattere con l'emozione nei suoi occhi.

Sollevando la testa, vedo che quegli occhi riflettono esattamente questo, mentre mi fissa. "Io..." Il suo respiro è di nuovo rapido. "Non so se—"

Ingoio le sue parole successive con un altro bacio e riprendo a lavorare con il dito nella sua stretta apertura, mentre la sollevo più in alto con la mano libera, spostandola sul mio membro. Geme contro le mie labbra e sento il mio uccello sfregare contro il dito attraverso la parete sottile che separa i suoi due orifizi.

Il mio respiro accelera, le palle si stringono sempre di più, e qualsiasi controllo credessi di possedere svanisce. Approfondendo il bacio, spingo più in alto dentro di lei e contemporaneamente porto un secondo dito nel suo sedere. Si irrigidisce, le sue unghie affondano più profondamente nelle mie braccia e i muscoli interni si stringono per resistere, ma è inutile. Sono già dentro di lei, così in profondità che non riuscirà mai a tirarmi fuori.

Non ci sarà via di fuga per lei.

Non ora. Né mai.

Tutto dentro di me sta urlando di scoparla, di spingere dentro finché non scoppi e l'insopportabile tensione svanisca, ma c'è anche qualcos'altro che voglio. Respirando pesantemente, sollevo la testa e catturo il suo sguardo, mentre mi osserva stupita, col viso arrossato e le palpebre pesanti per l'eccitazione.

"Dimmi di cos'hai bisogno" ordino a voce alta, e il suo respiro sibila tra i denti, mentre spingo le mie dita più a fondo nel suo sedere, distendendolo, preparandolo. "Voglio sentirtelo dire."

"Io non..." Geme, chiudendo gli occhi, mentre infilo le dita a forbice, distendendola ulteriormente. "Non lo so."

"Sì, lo sai. Guardami."

Apre gli occhi obbedientemente, e la sua delicata lingua fa capolino per inumidire il labbro inferiore.

"Dimmi, Sara. Dimmi di cos'hai davvero bisogno."

"Io..." Il suo respiro accelera, mentre comincio a sbattere dentro di lei, assicurandomi di premerle sul clitoride ad ogni movimento. "È... questo. Peter, ho bisogno di questo. Ho bisogno di te dentro di me. Ho bisogno che tu"—ansima mentre affondo in lei —"mi prenda e..."

"E cosa?" insisto, con la schiena che mi formicola, mentre sento i suoi muscoli interni stringersi.

"E che mi fotta." Ora sta ansimando, con lo sguardo che diventa confuso e sfocato. "Che... mi faccia male."

"Sì." La mia voce è rauca. "Giusto. E tu sei mia. Mia da scopare, da ferire, da usare come voglio. Non è così, amore mio?"

Annuisce, con gli occhi che si concentrano sui miei. "Sì. Sempre."

Sempre. La parola mi trafigge il petto, portando con sé un mix di calda tenerezza e violenta soddisfazione. Mi piace che lei lo capisca adesso. Che lo ammetta.

Siamo fatti l'uno per l'altra. L'ho saputo fin dall'inizio—e ora lo sa anche lei.

Immergendo la testa, reclamo le sue labbra, mantenendo il bacio morbido e delicato anche mentre tiro le dita fuori da lei e le fisso entrambe le mani sotto le cosce, allargando le gambe, mentre la sollevo più in alto. Il mio uccello scivola fuori dalla sua figa e preme contro l'ingresso posteriore.

Il suo respiro si trasforma in un sussulto, ma la sto già abbassando sul mio fallo rigido, sfruttando la forza di gravità e la scivolosità della sua lubrificazione naturale per facilitare la penetrazione. Se non l'avessi distesa con le dita, sarebbe stato impossibile, ma visto come stanno le cose, l'anello del muscolo cede alla pressione incrollabile e io scivolo nel suo stretto canale, sentendo le viscere stringermi per uno sforzo frenetico di resistere all'invasione.

"Peter..." Sta tremando, mentre alzo la testa, incrociando il suo sguardo ancora una volta. "Peter, per favore..."

"Sì" prometto con voce roca. "Ti soddisferò, ptichka. Ti darò quello che ti serve... tutto ciò di cui hai bisogno."

E sostenendo il suo sguardo, comincio a muovermi, portandola là dove il dolore sfiora il piacere e l'amore e l'odio si confondono.

In quel meraviglioso luogo in cui è mia e mia soltanto.

18

 enderson

STUDIO IL NUOVO SET DI FOTO SULLO SCHERMO, MENTRE MI sfrego i muscoli nodosi del collo, cercando di ignorare il crescente mal di testa.

Sono riuscito a contattare l'FBI, e non è stato molto difficile. L'Agente Ryson è stato molto felice di riprendere le sue indagini su Sokolov per me.

Non mi aspetto che scoprirà qualcosa, ma non è questo il punto, comunque. Ho solo bisogno che si svolga un'indagine, anche se si tratta più della vendetta personale da parte di un agente scontento.

Aprendo la cartella sulla mia scrivania, studio i progetti dettagliati all'interno. Il piano sta iniziando a prendere forma, lentamente ma inesorabilmente. Ora ho solo bisogno di trovare le persone giuste per eseguirlo.

Gli spari della pistola automatica raggiungono le mie

orecchie, esacerbando il dolore pulsante nelle tempie. Spingendo la cartella da una parte, mi alzo e vado nel salotto.

"Jimmy."

Mio figlio quindicenne non reagisce.

Ripeto il suo nome più forte.

"Che cosa c'è?" sbotta senza distogliere lo sguardo dallo schermo.

"Abbassa il volume di quel fottuto gioco" dico in tono più calmo possibile.

Alza il dito medio verso di me.

Il mio mal di testa si trasforma in un'insopportabile emicrania, con il collo che mi si spezza dal dolore, mentre una gelida rabbia si diffonde nelle vene.

In modo esternamente calmo, mi avvicino al divano e strappo il joystick dalle mani di mio figlio.

"Ehi!" Salta in piedi, cercando di riprenderlo, e il palmo della mia mano si schianta sul suo viso, facendolo cadere a terra.

"Ti avevo detto di smettere con quel cazzo di gioco" dico mentre mi fissa, stringendogli la mascella.

E lasciando cadere lo strumento sul pavimento, torno nel mio ufficio.

SABATO MATTINA MI SVEGLIO CON LA CONSAPEVOLEZZA CHE IO E Peter siamo sposati da una settimana e che abbiamo passato la prima notte nella nostra nuova casa.

Non ho avuto la possibilità di notare tutto ieri sera, così osservo subito la camera da letto. È luminosa e spaziosa, con le pareti di un rilassante grigio chiaro e il soffitto incassato ad almeno tre metri e mezzo sopra il nostro letto matrimoniale in rovere.

È bella e moderna, e all'improvviso sento l'urgenza di acquistare piante da mettere in ogni angolo.

Sorridendo, mi stiracchio, poi sussulto per il dolore interiore. Dopo quella brutale rivendicazione nel corridoio, Peter mi ha portata di sopra e mi ha presa di nuovo nella doccia, e poi ancora una volta in questo letto.

Uno di questi giorni, dovremo parlare di quanto sia normale

una buona quantità di sesso. Gli uomini non dovrebbero scopare le proprie mogli ogni notte come se fossero appena usciti di prigione.

Immagino quella discussione e scuoto la testa. Chi sto prendendo in giro? Dolore o meno, non mi dispiace il suo desiderio per me, nemmeno un po'. L'intensa sessualità di Peter è una parte di lui, ostinatamente ardente quanto il suo amore per me. Non accetta confini, restrizioni. E lo voglio così: selvaggio ma tenero, letale ma perversamente dolce.

Ho finito di fingere di essere tutt'altro che pazza di lui, per quanto sbagliato possa essere.

I deliziosi profumi della colazione stanno già filtrando da sotto la porta chiusa, così faccio una doccia veloce nel nostro nuovo bagno lussuoso, infilo una maglietta, un paio di pantaloncini da yoga e scendo le scale, con lo stomaco che borbotta.

Mio marito è in piedi accanto alla cucina a gas in acciaio inossidabile simile a quelle dei ristoranti, a preparare pancake, e mi fermo, con la saliva che mi si mescola nella bocca alla vista. Con un paio di jeans logori e nient'altro, ha le spalle larghe, i muscoli definiti, i tatuaggi che decorano il braccio sinistro che si flette ad ogni movimento dei potenti bicipiti. I suoi capelli folti e scuri sono deliziosamente disordinati, come se stesse invitando le mie dita a toccarli, e la pelle abbronzata brilla alla luce del mattino.

Voltandosi, mi guarda con un sorriso sensuale. "Eccolo, il mio passerotto canterino. Come ti senti?"

Mi lecco le labbra, incapace di distogliere gli occhi dall'ampia distesa del suo petto. "Ho fame."

"Uh-uh, lo immaginavo." Sorride. "Purtroppo, ptichka, hai dormito così tanto che ormai è l'ora del brunch. I tuoi genitori arriveranno tra venti minuti, quindi dovrai aspettare."

Guardo l'orologio e capisco che ha ragione. "È tutta colpa

tua" gli dico, incrociando le braccia sul petto. "Mi hai tenuta sveglia fino a *tardi*."

"Lo so. Povero tesoro. Vieni qui." Cammina verso di me, con gli occhi che brillano, e io indietreggio.

"Nu-uh. Non abbiamo tempo."

Mi raggiunge. "Abbiamo sempre tempo."

"I pancake—"

Le sue labbra calde sfiorano le mie, con la lingua che invade i recessi della bocca, e le mie dita si fanno strada tra i suoi capelli setosi, mentre la testa cade nella culla dei suoi palmi. Il suo alito sa di miele—deve aver assaggiato i pancake—e non posso fare a meno di sbattere le palpebre, quando finalmente solleva la testa, fissandomi senza alcun accenno di giocosità.

"Cazzo, non vedo l'ora che saremo di nuovo soli" borbotta, poi immerge la testa, reclamando la mia bocca con un bacio sempre più feroce, che non lascia dubbi sul suo vero intento.

Mi prenderà di nuovo.

Nel momento in cui i miei genitori se ne andranno, sarò nel suo letto.

Il campanello suona proprio mentre si stacca per mandare giù aria. "Cazzo." Respirando affannosamente, mi lascia andare. "Sono di nuovo venuti prima del previsto."

Mi liscio i capelli con una mano malferma, dolorosamente consapevole delle mie labbra gonfie a causa del bacio. "Farai meglio a vestirti. Vado ad accoglierli."

"Aspetta." Si avvicina ai fornelli e rovescia i pancake dalla padella su un piatto. "Così, non si bruceranno" spiega, prima di uscire dalla cucina.

Do una sbirciatina allo specchio, mentre mi dirigo verso la porta. Sicuramente ho l'aspetto di una che è stata appena aggredita, ma non posso farci niente.

Mi liscio di nuovo i capelli e apro la porta per salutare i miei genitori.

INSISTONO DI VOLER PRIMA FARE UN GIRO DELLA CASA, QUINDI andiamo di stanza in stanza, mentre Peter apparecchia. Quando mostro tutto ai miei genitori, sono stupita ancora una volta di quanto mio marito abbia realizzato ieri. Anche se alcune scatole sono ancora poggiate discretamente in alcuni angoli e il mobilio è minimo, tutto è organizzato e pulito... quasi in modo innaturale.

"Non posso credere che vi siate già sistemati" dice mamma, esprimendo i miei pensieri. "Pensavo che l'atto di acquisto fosse stato firmato giovedì."

"Infatti" confermo. "Ma Peter ha un suo modo per fare le cose."

"Sul serio" borbotta papà, aprendo un armadio e trovando gli asciugamani già dentro, ben piegati. "È una macchina, quel tuo marito."

Mi allungo per stringere l'avambraccio esposto e malandato di papà. "Sì, e questo è positivo."

I miei genitori non hanno ancora accettato del tutto la nostra relazione, ma spero che man mano che passeranno più tempo con Peter, lo faranno. La nostra prima cena insieme della settimana scorsa è andata abbastanza bene, grazie soprattutto a lui, che è stato sorprendentemente aperto sul suo passato e sui suoi sentimenti per me. Ha aiutato anche che abbia detto loro di voler metter su famiglia, allettando i miei genitori con la promessa di nipoti, che avevano quasi perso la speranza di vedere.

Con mio padre che ha compiuto ottantotto anni e mia madre solo nove anni più giovane, il loro orologio biologico per diventare nonni sta progressivamente rallentando.

Sebbene l'artrite di mio padre sia peggiorata e oggi sia uscito con un deambulatore, insiste a sfidare le scale per vedere tutta casa. Concludiamo il tour nella nostra camera, dove sono sorpresa di trovare il letto rifatto. Peter deve essersene occupato, quando è andato di sopra a vestirsi.

Dopo aver visto la stanza, papà va al bagno, mentre mamma controlla il nostro armadio a muro.

"Allora, che te ne pare?" chiedo, quando finiamo.

Mi guarda con aria seria. "È una casa stupenda, tesoro."

"Ma?" insisto, vedendo che non continua.

Sospira e si avvicina per sedersi sul letto. "Io e tuo padre siamo ancora preoccupati per te, tutto qui."

"Mamma—" Inizio a dire con tono esasperato, ma lei alza la mano e accarezza il letto accanto a sé.

Mi avvicino per sedermi, e dice sottovoce: "L'Agente Ryson ha parlato con tuo padre al parco ieri mattina. Non so cosa gli abbia detto, ma la sua pressione sanguigna è stata tutto il giorno alle stelle. Ho provato ad indagare, ma non mi ha rivelato nulla, ad eccezione del fatto di essere preoccupato per te."

La fisso, con una morsa ghiacciata che mi stringe il cuore. Che ci faceva lì l'agente dell'FBI? Che cos'ha detto a mio padre? Se è qualcosa di simile a quello di cui Ryson mi aveva parlato il giorno del mio matrimonio, è strano che papà non abbia avuto un altro attacco cardiaco in quel preciso istante.

L'FBI potrebbe sapere qualcosa sul patrigno di Monica?

I miei polmoni cessano di funzionare, mentre il pensiero mi attraversa la mente. Devo essere anche visibilmente impallidita, perché mamma si acciglia e si allunga per stringermi la mano. "Va tutto bene, tesoro?"

"Sì, io..." Mi sforzo di riprendere a respirare. "Sto bene." La mia voce è un po' troppo acuta, così sorrido per sembrare più convincente. "Scusa, sono solo preoccupata per papà. Come va la sua pressione oggi?"

Mamma sospira e mi lascia andare la mano. "Meglio. Non è perfetta, ma migliore. Vorrei che mi dicesse che cosa gli ha riferito l'Agente Ryson, però."

"Già." Riesco a sembrare quasi normale. "Glielo chiederò oggi."

"Penso che sia meglio non farlo." Lanciando un'occhiata alla porta del bagno, abbassa ulteriormente la voce. "Di qualunque cosa si sia trattato, era ovviamente stressante, e non voglio che ci si soffermi troppo."

"Hai ragione, Mamma" dico e mi alzo per sorridere a papà, mentre esce dal bagno. "Ora, andiamo ad assaggiare quei pancake."

MENTRE MANGIAMO, OSSERVO PETER INTERAGIRE CON I MIEI genitori. Anche se so che preferirebbe essere solo con me, è di nuovo educato e rispettoso... assolutamente gentile nei modi. Salire e scendere le scale sembra aver peggiorato l'artrite di mio padre, così mio marito lo aiuta con il suo deambulatore—e lo fa in modo così disinvolto che mio padre dimentica di offendersi.

All'inizio, i miei genitori sono cauti e riservati, ma man mano che il pasto continua, sembrano sciogliersi con Peter—persino mio padre, nonostante qualunque cosa gli abbia detto Ryson. Aiuta che Peter prenda in mano la conversazione, facendo domande ai miei genitori su come si sono conosciuti e su com'ero da piccola, invece di aspettare che indaghino sul suo oscuro passato.

"Sara era una bambina così perfetta che non ci crederesti" gli racconta mamma, sorridendomi. "Dormiva tutta la notte, mangiava quando doveva, non piangeva quasi mai. E non si è mai ammalata, pur essendo nata esile—pesava poco meno di tre chili. Eravamo così terrorizzati—a causa della nostra età, sai—ma ha rapidamente messo a tacere tutte le nostre paure. Era come se sapesse che non eravamo i giovani genitori tipici, che potevano sopportare la tensione, e si assicurava che tutto andasse come da programma. È sciocco, ovviamente—era solo una bambina—ma questa era l'impressione che avevano tutti."

"Ci credo" replica Peter, guardandomi con un tale calore che arrossisco e devo distogliere lo sguardo.

Oltre a dirigere la conversazione sugli argomenti preferiti dai miei genitori, mostra la sua attenzione in una varietà di piccoli modi. Mamma ottiene la sua camomilla senza dover chiedere, e i pancake di papà sono serviti con un piatto di frutta fresca e panna montata oltre alla marmellata di fragole fatta in casa. Non so come abbia fatto mio marito a scoprire questa specifica preferenza di mio padre, ma i miei genitori chiaramente lo apprezzano.

"Sei un cuoco straordinario" lo loda mamma, e lui le rivolge un bel sorriso, con gli occhi che si increspano per un piacere sincero.

Guardandolo in questo modo, comincio a chiedermi se Peter non lo stia facendo davvero solo per me. È possibile che una parte di lui desideri ardentemente questo? Che siccome non ha mai avuto dei genitori si stia divertendo a far parte della nostra famiglia? Perché se sta fingendo, sta facendo un ottimo lavoro.

Io, da parte mia, sono convinta che stia cominciando ad apprezzare i miei genitori—e che, nonostante tutto, alla fine anche loro potrebbero ricambiare.

Mentre terminiamo il pasto, i miei genitori iniziano a fare domande su di noi—sul lavoro e ogni genere di cose tipiche dei genitori.

"Allora, hai deciso che cosa farai?" chiede mamma a Peter, che annuisce, raccontando loro tutto sulla scuola di addestramento che sta progettando di iniziare.

"Mi piace l'idea" afferma papà. "Sembra una soluzione valida, visto il tuo background e tutto il resto."

Peter sorride per la sua approvazione. "È quello che ho

pensato anch'io. In ogni caso, è qualcosa con cui tenermi occupato, quando Sara è al lavoro."

Non c'è traccia di risentimento nella sua voce, ma non riesco ad evitare la fitta di disagio, mentre si alza e inizia a sparecchiare. È infastidito dai miei orari, lo so. Dopo tutti i mesi in cui siamo stati separati, le sere e i fine settimana che passiamo insieme non sono sufficienti—per nessuno dei due.

Forse questa sua nuova attività migliorerà le cose, dandogli qualcosa su cui concentrarsi che non sia io, e mentre ci abituiamo alla nostra vita coniugale, non ci mancheremo a vicenda così intensamente. Altrimenti, prima o poi, qualcuno dei due dovrà cedere—e quella persona sono io.

Peter ha sacrificato tutto per rendermi felice, e non posso fare qualcosa di meno per lui.

Mentre i miei genitori se ne vanno, penso che vorrei parlare con mio marito della visita di Ryson a mio padre, ma decido di non farlo. Era già rimasto sconvolto nell'apprendere che l'agente dell'FBI aveva interferito con il nostro matrimonio. Se sapesse che Ryson continua a infastidire la mia famiglia, potrebbe fare qualcosa al riguardo—e questa è l'ultima cosa che voglio.

Promesse o meno, Peter farà tutto il necessario per proteggermi, e non ho bisogno della morte di un altro uomo sulla coscienza.

PARTE II

20

ara

NEL CORSO DEL MESE SUCCESSIVO, CI SISTEMIAMO NELLA NUOVA casa e continuiamo con la routine che abbiamo stabilito durante la nostra prima settimana di matrimonio. Anche se Danny e il resto della squadra di sicurezza di Peter sono sempre in agguato, mio marito mi accompagna e viene a riprendermi al lavoro, e si offre di aiutarmi nella clinica. Nel frattempo, si impegna nella creazione della nuova attività e nella raccolta di clienti—impresa in cui sta riscuotendo un grande successo.

Un pomeriggio, esco di nascosto dal mio ufficio, quando ho un paio di appuntamenti annullati, e Danny mi accompagna al parco che Peter ha scelto come terreno di allenamento all'aperto. E lo osservo, sogghignando, mentre mette alla prova cinque ragazzini, facendoli scattare, saltare sulle panchine, arrampicare sugli alberi e tentare di dargli un pugno in faccia.

Nessuno di loro ci riesce, ovviamente, ma sembra che si

463

stiano divertendo a provare.

So come si sentono, perché gli ho chiesto di insegnarmi qualche mossa domenica scorsa, e abbiamo trascorso la mattinata nella sua palestra, allenandoci con qualche esercizio di base di difesa personale. È stato come combattere una montagna, e l'unica mossa che ho imparato è stata sollevare le gambe per diventare un peso morto, quando mi ha afferrata da dietro—per sbilanciare l'aggressore, presumibilmente. Inutile dire che tutto ciò è risultato in una sessione di sesso nel momento in cui siamo tornati a casa, e che non sono ancora in grado di difendermi—non che ne abbia bisogno, con Peter e le guardie del corpo sempre intorno.

Mi vede un minuto dopo, e un sorriso luminoso gli illumina il viso, prima di voltarsi e ringhiare istruzioni ai ragazzi. Poi viene verso di me, lasciando i suoi allievi a borbottare e ad ansimare, mentre cercano di fare le flessioni su un albero.

È una calda giornata d'agosto, ed è a torso nudo, indossando solo un paio di pantaloncini mimetici e stivali da combattimento. Lo guardo, a bocca asciutta, mentre cammina verso di me a grandi falcate, con il busto muscoloso che brilla per il sudore.

"Che cosa ci fai qui, ptichka?" chiede, fermandosi di fronte a me, e gli salto addosso, avvolgendogli le braccia intorno al collo. Mi sorprende, girandomi intorno, mentre lo bacio impudentemente, e quando mi mette giù, respiriamo entrambi affannosamente, mentre i suoi allievi fischiano sullo sfondo.

"Tornate a lavorare" ringhia girandosi, con le mani ancora sulla mia vita, e loro obbediscono immediatamente, riprendendo i tentativi di sollevarsi.

"Un vero sergente severo, vero?" Gli sorrido, allungando la mano per lisciargli i folti capelli in una parvenza di ordine. Si stanno allungando ai lati e sopra, e sono più difficili da controllare. Mi piace l'aspetto selvaggio, quindi non dico nulla, ma probabilmente presto avrà bisogno di un nuovo taglio.

"Ci puoi scommettere" mormora, abbassando la testa per baciarmi di nuovo, e io rido, spingendolo via prima che iniziamo a baciarci per davvero. È successo in pubblico fin troppo spesso; Peter non si vergogna, quando si tratta di me.

In parte, è perché continuiamo a sentirci come se non trascorressimo abbastanza tempo insieme. Il mio attuale lavoro ha orari più prevedibili, ma ho ancora un paio di pazienti incinte—e i miei superiori hanno prolungato le vacanze, quindi dovrò visitarle tutte io questo mese.

Mi hanno chiesto di coprirli, e non ho potuto dire di no.

"Sì, avresti potuto" ha detto mio marito, quando ho spiegato che avrei dovuto essere disponibile per un altro fine settimana, dato che la paziente di Wendy stava per partorire. "Avresti sicuramente potuto dire di no. Qual è la cosa peggiore che sarebbe potuta accadere? Ti avrebbero licenziata?"

"Beh, sì" ho iniziato a spiegare, per poi fermarmi con un sospiro. "Lo so, lo so. Abbiamo i soldi e tecnicamente non ho bisogno di lavorare."

"Esatto." Il suo sguardo era fisso sul mio viso, e ho distolto il mio, non ancora pronta a discuterne. Logicamente, so che ha ragione—siamo multimiliardari, grazie alle sue recenti imprese —ma ho lavorato troppo duramente per diventare un medico e non posso rinunciare in questo modo.

"Potresti ancora fare volontariato in clinica" ha replicato, e ancora una volta, ha avuto ragione. Ho pensato più volte a quanto sarebbe bello, se potessi coccolarlo ogni mattina invece di svegliarmi e andare al lavoro. Per quanto fosse frustrante la mia prigionia in Giappone, eravamo sempre insieme—cosa che non apprezzavo in quel momento, data la mia rabbia verso di lui, ma che ora ricordo con desiderio perverso.

"Non è la stessa cosa" gli ho spiegato. "Non farei nascere bambini alla clinica."

È vero, e non ha insistito, ma so che torneremo presto sulla questione.

È inevitabile, data la nostra ossessione reciproca.

Ed è un'ossessione. Non posso negarlo. Credevo di amare George, almeno all'inizio, ma i miei sentimenti per lui erano una pallida ombra di quello che provo per il suo assassino. Non mi era mai mancato George in questo modo, quando eravamo lontani, non avevo mai desiderato di tornare a casa da lui con questo tipo di intensità. Le nostre vite erano più o meno separate, e pensavo che le cose dovessero essere così, che tutti i matrimoni—tutte le relazioni—fossero così.

Non c'è separazione di alcun tipo con Peter. Neanche lontanamente. È come se un filo invisibile ci unisse, anche quando siamo fisicamente separati. È costantemente nei miei pensieri e spesso mi ritrovo e provare dolore fisico per lui, come se il mio corpo fosse dipendente dal suo tocco.

Non aiuta il fatto che quando *siamo* insieme, mi ricopra di attenzione e mi coccoli fino a farmi sentire un animale domestico viziato. Mi massaggia, mi strofina i piedi, mi accarezza i capelli—fa tutto quando abbiamo tempo. Per non parlare del sesso.

Oh Dio, il sesso.

Fin dalla nostra prima notte di nozze, quando ho ammesso a lui—e a me stessa—di aver bisogno di un certo livello di forza da parte sua per far fronte alla nostra relazione non tradizionale, non si è fatto scrupoli a scatenare il mostro interiore in camera da letto. Pur essendoci molti momenti in cui è dolce e tenero, il più delle volte mi prende con una bramosia sfrenata, lasciandomi dolorante e sofferente al mattino. Nessuna parte del mio corpo è zona vietata per lui, e spesso mi ritrovo legata in ginocchio, con la bocca piena del fallo e il sedere che brucia per la sua dura rivendicazione.

Sarà anche mio marito ora, ma resta il mio tormentatore.

La parola chiave, però, è "mio." Per fortuna, il sesso con me è l'attività in cui sembra incanalare i suoi impulsi più oscuri. Per quanto ne so, ha mantenuto la parola sul non danneggiare nessun altro, e mentre le settimane passano, mi sento sempre meno preoccupata, quando siamo con la mia famiglia e con i miei amici. I miei genitori si stanno lentamente avvicinando a lui, e ai miei compagni di gruppo sembra piacere—il che mi sorprende, visto che Marsha ora sta frequentando seriamente Phil e *non* è una fan di Peter.

O, almeno, presumo che sia per questo che l'ho vista a malapena dal matrimonio.

"Marsha non sembra mai uscire con noi ultimamente" dico a Phil, quando andiamo tutti a bere dopo una performance del venerdì sera. "Voi due state ancora insieme, vero?"

Arrossisce, chiaramente a disagio. "Sì, ma lei è stata, uhm... davvero occupata."

Annuisco e prendo il mio drink. "Giusto, ok."

È ridicolo che mi senta ferita dall'abbandono della mia amica. Dopotutto, l'avevo evitata per un po', dopo aver saputo che stava aiutando l'FBI a sorvegliarmi. E in ogni caso, non posso biasimarla per essere stata prudente. Qualsiasi persona sana di mente avrebbe voluto tenersi alla larga da un uomo che sospettava fosse un assassino senza coscienza, che una volta aveva torturato la sua amica e ucciso suo marito.

"Occupata con cosa?" chiede Peter, raggiungendomi da dietro e strofinandomi le spalle. Il suo tono è leggero e disinvolto, ma posso sentire la tensione nelle sue dita forti, mentre mi massaggia i muscoli annodati. "Sta facendo più turni?"

"Qualcosa del genere" mormora Phil, facendo poi un cenno al barista. "Un giro di tequila, amico. La migliore che hai."

Il liquore mi brucia la gola, mentre beviamo, e il leggero imbarazzo svanisce, quando Rory e Simon si lanciano in un'animata discussione sui pro e sui contro delle bionde naturali. Phil si unisce, ma Peter rimane zitto, osservandoli con un'espressione vagamente divertita, e quando mi scuso per andare al bagno, lo sento ordinare un giro di vodka.

"Niente per me?" chiedo, vedendo solo quattro bicchierini al ritorno, e mio marito mi sorride.

"Temo di no, ptichka. Ho bisogno che tu sia sveglia e cosciente nel mio letto stanotte."

Accompagna le parole con una stretta del mio ginocchio, e i ragazzi sghignazzano, mentre combatto un rossore. È completamente impenitente riguardo al suo desiderio per me, sfruttando ogni opportunità per toccarmi e rivendicarmi—in privato o in pubblico. I miei compagni di band sono convinti che scopiamo tutto il tempo come conigli, ed è vero.

Mio marito ha la resistenza di un adolescente che assume Viagra.

Continuando a ridere, i ragazzi mandano giù la vodka e Peter ordina immediatamente un altro giro. Lo guardo un po' confusa—non l'ho mai visto bere così pesantemente—ma credo che voglia solo lasciarsi andare un po' dopo una lunga settimana.

Dopo altri due giri di vodka, però, mi rendo conto che sta succedendo qualcos'altro. Innanzitutto, sono abbastanza sicura che Peter abbia rovesciato il suo ultimo bicchiere sul pavimento. I miei compagni di band erano troppo ubriachi per accorgersene, ma io sono solo leggermente sbronza e l'ho visto inclinare il bicchiere di lato prima di sollevarlo con loro.

È come se stesse volontariamente cercando di farli ubriacare.

Dopo un'altra mezz'ora e altri tre giri di alcolici, il mio sospetto si trasforma in certezza. Rory e Simon ora sono proprio sbronzi, con il primo che sta cantando una ballata irlandese e l'altro che lo accompagna stonato, mentre Phil si è lanciato in un trattato filosofico sulla casualità della vita e le tendenze dei media. Peter si comporta come se fosse altrettanto sbronzo e completamente preso dalle divagazioni di Phil, ma per me è ovvio che mio marito stia manipolando la conversazione—non so come mai.

"E così, vedi, il CEO di uno studio cinematografico potrebbe pensare di avere il tocco magico con i blockbuster, ma in realtà, è solo in una striscia fortunata" biascica Phil, e Peter annuisce, come se tutto avesse un senso. "Pensi di avercela fatta, ma è solo fortuna, amico. Solo la fottuta fortuna. E poi bam! Il pendolo oscilla dall'altra parte. Perché è tutto casuale e ritorna la sfortuna. Non ce ne rendiamo conto—pensiamo di avere il controllo, perché vediamo uno schema—ma sono tutte cazzate. La vita è come il pendolo arrugginito in un terremoto, che oscilla da una parte all'altra, e a volte si blocca dopo aver ripreso. E a volte—a volte tutta la tua vita è in ripresa, fino a quando un tremore scuote la ruggine." Agita la testa tristemente e decido che ne ha avuto abbastanza.

Non so quale sia il piano di Peter, ma l'intossicazione da alcol non è uno scherzo.

Chinandomi, tocco la mano di mio marito e dico a voce bassa. "Andiamo a casa. Mi sto addormentando."

Solleva il palmo e mi stringe delicatamente la mano, con gli occhi completamente sobri anche quando le sue labbra si piegano in un sorriso apparentemente brillo. "Ancora un po', amore mio. Phil sta dicendo cose interessanti."

Mi acciglio, confusa. "Davvero?"

"Oh, sì" biascica Phil. "Semplicemente non lo vedi, perché non puoi. Non puoi nemmeno immaginarlo. Nessun umano può, perché le nostre menti non sono in grado di elaborare schemi veramente casuali. E quando gli algoritmi lo fanno per noi, crediamo che non siano casuali. Il mixer sul tuo lettore musicale? Non è casuale. Se lo fosse, riascolteresti la stessa canzone due, tre, quattro volte di fila, e questo non ci sembra casuale. Sembra che una canzone sia stata scelta volontariamente, come se ci fosse uno scopo dietro di essa, ma questo è falso. È solo matematica, solo programmazione. E quindi—"

"Quindi, hanno ottimizzato l'algoritmo, rimuovendo la

casualità per renderlo più casuale" replica Peter, sembrando seriamente ubriaco, mentre gioca con le mie dita. "Hai ragione, amico. È assurdo."

Phil piega la testa. "Non è vero? Lo dico sempre a Marsha, ma lei non ci crede. Non capisce che a volte una coincidenza è solo una coincidenza, che qualcosa può essere semplicemente casuale. Come te e Sara. C'era un cattivo ragazzo di nome Peter nel suo passato, e Marsha pensa che sia tu, anche se l'FBI le ha detto—*le hanno detto apertamente*—che non lo è. Come quello che ha più senso: che sei un killer ricercato che per qualche strana ragione è autorizzato a vagare liberamente o che potrebbero esserci stati due Peter nella vita di Sara? È come una canzone che viene riprodotta due volte—difficile da credere, ma sinceramente casuale. Voglio dire, c'è quel ragazzo dell'FBI che le sta ancora parlando, ma sono abbastanza sicuro che ci stia solo provando, lo stronzo."

Mi blocco, irrigidendo la mano nella presa di Peter, mentre mio marito ridacchia e scuote la testa, esprimendo tutta la sua comprensione maschile. "Wow. Un vero stronzo. Come si chiama il tizio?"

"Tyson o qualcosa del genere." Phil singhiozza e sbadiglia rumorosamente.

Cazzo. Il cuore mi martella nel petto, mentre Peter mi scruta, con lo sguardo duro e illeggibile. Ha sempre sospettato qualcosa del genere? È per questo che ha fatto ubriacare Phil—oltre a Rory e Simon—tutta la notte?

In qualche modo sapeva che l'agente si era avvicinato a mio padre?

Ho cercato di dimenticarlo, di smettere di preoccuparmi che l'FBI venisse a sapere del patrigno di Monica, ma ogni tanto mi sveglio con un sudore freddo a causa di un incubo in cui gli agenti SWAT irrompono nella nostra camera. Ufficialmente, c'è un accordo, ma Ryson ha chiaramente una missione tutta sua.

Che cosa ha detto a Marsha? Che cosa gli ha detto *lei*? La

mia mente lavora, mentre Peter ordina un ultimo giro, poi si scusa con i ragazzi, lasciandoli bere da soli, mentre mi trascina fuori dal bar e verso la macchina di Danny.

Il mio ex assassino è abbastanza rispettoso della legge—o abbastanza intelligente—da non bere e guidare.

Aspetto che torniamo a casa, prima di parlare di ciò che Phil ci ha detto. "Peter, riguardo al—"

"Perché non mi hai detto che Ryson era ancora in gioco?" interrompe mio marito, avvicinandosi a me. C'è solo un lieve accenno di alcol nel suo respiro, mentre si china verso di me, intrappolandomi contro la parte posteriore del divano con il corpo potente.

O ha bevuto meno di quanto pensassi o il suo metabolismo è rapidissimo.

Mi si secca la gola e il respiro diventa irregolare, quando scorgo la gelida durezza nei suoi occhi metallici. Questo è il Peter che mi terrorizzava, l'uomo che aveva fatto irruzione in casa mia e che mi aveva così spietatamente interrogata per trovare George.

L'assassino che non ha mai provato rimorsi.

"Non sapevo che stesse parlando con Marsha" rispondo, quando riesco a sembrare semi-calma. So che Peter non mi farà del male al di fuori dei nostri giochi da camera, ma è difficile non essere intimidita, quando incombe su di me in questo modo, con il calore del corpo muscoloso che mi circonda, con la vicinanza che rappresenta sia una tentazione che una minaccia.

Potrebbe non fare del male a me, ma lo farà agli altri.

La vita dell'Agente Ryson—e forse di Marsha—è in pericolo.

"No?" Socchiude gli occhi. "Che mi dici dei tuoi genitori? Non sapevi che stava infastidendo anche loro?"

"No, io—" mi fermo prima di peggiorare la situazione mentendo. "Ok, sapevo che aveva parlato con mio padre un paio di mesi fa, ma pensavo che fosse stata l'unica volta. Stai dicendo che li ha avvicinati di nuovo?" Le parole mi stanno uscendo troppo velocemente, ma non posso farci niente.

Sono terrorizzata sia per l'agente che per quello che Peter potrebbe scoprire.

Mi fissa, poi finalmente fa un passo indietro, lasciandomi inspirare a fondo.

"Oggi" dice cupamente, e impiego un secondo per capire che sta rispondendo alla mia domanda. "La mia squadra lo ha visto avvicinarsi a tua madre, mentre era in un centro commerciale con Agnes Levinson. Uno dei ragazzi lo ha pedinato quando se n'è andato e vuoi sapere dov'è andato il figlio di puttana?"

Deglutisco. "Dove?"

"All'ospedale. Dove lavoravi tu—e dove la tua amica lavora ancora."

Ovviamente. Ecco perché ha deciso di fare domande a Phil stasera. O più esattamente, di interrogarlo—solo con l'alcol invece di una droga di marca come aiuto.

"Credi che lo sappia? A proposito di Moni—" Mi fermo nel momento in cui mi viene in mente che potrebbe non essere sicuro parlarne così apertamente.

Se l'FBI ci sta tenendo d'occhio, potrebbero esserci delle cimici in casa.

"Va tutto bene. Eseguo controlli quotidiani" mi rassicura Peter, comprendendo la mia preoccupazione. "Nessuno ci sta ascoltando."

Controlli quotidiani? Esiste la paranoia, e poi esiste qualunque cosa sia questa. So che la nostra abitazione gode di tutta la sicurezza di una base militare—ho visto la tecnologia futuristica installata—ma non avevo realizzato che mio marito fosse *così* paranoico.

"E no" continua, mentre raccolgo i pensieri. "Non penso che sappia qualcosa. I miei hacker tengono sotto controllo i file relativi a Sonny Pearson e nessuno ha accesso ad essi da settimane."

Sonny Pearson? È così che si chiamava il patrigno di Monica? Mi si stringe lo stomaco, mentre lo fisso, con immagini di vicoli bui e pozze di sangue che appaiono davanti ai miei occhi. Ho cercato di dimenticare quell'omicidio, proprio come tutte le altre cose terribili che Peter ha fatto, ma ora che conosco il nome dell'uomo, l'orrore e il senso di colpa si rinnovano in me.

"Smettila, ptichka." Il tono di Peter è gentile, e mi rendo conto che il mio viso deve riflettere i miei pensieri. Allungandosi, mi cattura entrambe le mani nei grandi palmi. "Non pensarci più. È finita."

Tirandomi verso di lui, mi avvolge in un abbraccio rassicurante, e gli stringo le braccia intorno alla vita, inalando il suo profumo familiare, mentre la mia guancia preme sulla sua spalla muscolosa. È perverso lasciare che mi consoli in questo modo, ma non posso non accettare questo da lui.

Solo in questo modo posso amare qualcuno così spietato.

Mentre mi abbraccia, accarezzandomi pazientemente i capelli, sento una crescente durezza che mi preme sullo stomaco, e capisco che tra qualche altro momento, non si accontenterà semplicemente di stringermi.

È allettante continuare così, trovare rifugio nel piacere travolgente che mi offre sempre, ma prima devo accertarmi di una cosa.

"Peter..." Tirandomi indietro, lo guardo. "Non farai niente a Marsha o all'Agente Ryson, vero?"

Mi fissa, stringendo le mani sui miei fianchi. "Definisci 'niente.'"

"Peter, per favore."

Appiattisce le labbra e fa un passo indietro, liberandomi. "Bene. La tua amica è al sicuro. Non mi avvicinerò a lei. Anche se non ci evitasse come la peste, ora sai che è meglio non fidarsi di lei."

"Ho le labbra sigillate con lei, te lo giuro. E non ti avvicinerai nemmeno a Ryson. Giusto?" chiedo, quando Peter non conferma né nega la mia affermazione.

Un muscolo della sua mascella cesellata pulsa. "*Rappresenta una minaccia. Lo sai, Sara. Non è più solo un incarico per lui. Vuole eliminarci; è ossessionato da noi.*"

"Sì, ma non stiamo facendo niente di male—stiamo solo vivendo la nostra vita. E se continueremo a farlo, non potrà farci niente. Tuttavia, se abbocchi alla sua esca..."

Impreca sottovoce e si gira, camminando verso la finestra. Lo seguo, sapendo che se non gli carpirò questa promessa, i giorni dell'agente dell'FBI sono contati.

"Sai che è esattamente quello che spera" dico, quando si gira verso di me, con espressione ostile. "Vuole che violi i termini del tuo accordo. Lo sta uccidendo che tu sia qui con me e che siamo felici. Questa"—mi allungo per afferrare la mano di Peter—"è la miglior vendetta che potresti mai avere. Lascia che stia alle nostre calcagna. Non troverà nulla, perché non ci sarà nulla da trovare."

Mentre parlo, stringe le dita a pugno nella mia presa, prima di rilassarsi lentamente, e i suoi occhi assumono un bagliore particolare. "Va bene" dice con voce rauca, mentre mi afferra i polsi e li sposta più in basso. "Capisco il tuo punto di vista." Mi preme le mani sul suo cavallo, dove sento un crescente rigonfiamento.

Mi lecco le labbra, mentre un calore di risposta si accende nel mio cuore. "Quindi, ho la tua parola?" Massaggio delicatamente la sua erezione attraverso i jeans, prima di cadere in ginocchio davanti a lui. "Non farai del male a Ryson in alcun modo?"

Chiude gli occhi e mi afferra le spalle, mentre gli tiro giù la lampo dei jeans. "Sì, hai la mia parola. È al sicuro." La sua voce è tesa dal bisogno, ma sento la nota oscura sottostante, mentre aggiunge: "Finché non proverà a fare altro."

Henderson

Svolto in un vicolo, rabbrividendo per la pungente raffica di vento. Fa incredibilmente freddo a Budapest questa settimana, cosa che mi ricorda il breve periodo trascorso a Vladivostok nei primi anni Novanta.

Cazzo, mi mancano quei giorni normali.

Mi sta aspettando vicino alla porta sul retro, come d'accordo, con la sua esile figura da ragazzina avvolta in una giacca pesante e i capelli corti color biondo platino, che si alzano a punta attorno al viso da elfo.

Se non sapessi chi sia veramente, sarebbe facile credere alla sua copertura come cameriera in un bar alla moda.

"Mink?" dico mentre mi avvicino, e lei annuisce.

"Ecco." Le porgo una busta spessa. "Passaporto degli Stati Uniti e metà del pagamento concordato."

Prende la busta e se la infila nel cappotto. Quando tira fuori la mano, stringe una cartella. "Questi sono gli uomini che vuoi" dice, porgendomela. Il suo inglese è americano come il mio, senza nemmeno un pizzico di accento dell'Europa dell'Est. "Sono i migliori e faranno qualsiasi cosa."

Apro la cartella e sfoglio i file all'interno. Ciascun candidato ha una scheda personale per quanto riguarda i miei obiettivi, e sono tutti ex militari dell'élite.

Soprattutto, ne individuo quattro il cui aspetto potrebbe essere sufficientemente alterato con parrucche e trucco.

"Va tutto bene?" chiede, e io annuisco, chiudendo la cartella.

Questi erano gli ultimi pezzi del puzzle che mi mancavano.

"Sei sicuro di non volere che lo elimini da sola?" chiede, mentre mi infilo la cartella nel cappotto. "Perché potrei, lo sai."

"No, non potresti" dico. "È troppo ben sorvegliato. E anche se ci riuscissi, non è questo il piano. Il tuo compito è assicurarti che non venga catturato vivo, capito?"

Mi rivolge un saluto beffardo. "Sì, sì, Generale. Consideralo fatto."

E girando sul tacco delle sue Doc Martens, apre la porta e scompare nel bar.

eter

NON PENSAVO CHE FOSSE POSSIBILE AMARE SARA ANCORA DI PIÙ, ma col passare delle settimane e scoprendo il nostro percorso come coppia sposata, i miei sentimenti per lei si intensificano e si fanno più profondi. Ora mi rendo conto che c'era molto che non sapevo sull'oggetto della mia ossessione—la nostra relazione era stata così tesa che lei non si sarebbe mai davvero rilassata con me. Ora, tuttavia, riesco a vedere un altro lato di lei, e adoro ogni nuovo tratto e peculiarità che scopro.

La mia ptichka odia la politica, ma è stranamente affascinata dai disastri naturali, divorando tutte le notizie prima di inviare una generosa donazione. Sostiene di amare i cani più dei gatti, ma è dipendente dai video dei gatti su YouTube. Pensa che *The Big Bang Theory* sia lo show più divertente di tutti i tempi e lo guardiamo insieme nei weekend. E soprattutto, canta quando è di buon umore—a volte sottovoce, a volte ad alta voce.

"Dovresti includerla nella tua prossima esibizione" le dico, quando la sorprendo a canticchiare in cucina un sabato mattina. "Mi piace quella melodia. Molto evocativa."

Mi sorride. "Davvero? È qualcosa che ho appena composto. Devo ancora trovare le parole."

"Le troverai." Le bacio la fronte liscia. "Ci riesci sempre."

La sua musica si sta evolvendo, proprio come la nostra relazione. È più fiduciosa nelle sue scelte, e questo si nota nelle esibizioni della band, che ora consistono in materiale originale composto da lei—e che attirano folle sempre più grandi. Un mese fa, Simon ha creato un canale YouTube per la sua band, che ha già raggiunto cinquantamila iscritti.

"È solo questione di tempo prima che diventiamo davvero grandi" ci dice Rory allegramente, dopo che un locale all'aperto piuttosto ampio ha registrato il tutto esaurito per il loro concerto del venerdì sera. "Stiamo per sfondare, lo so e basta."

Phil e Simon sono altrettanto emozionati, e vogliono uscire per festeggiare, ma Sara rifiuta, sostenendo di essere stanca. Preoccupato, la porto subito a casa, così potrò metterla a letto nel caso fosse influenzata.

"Sto bene, davvero" mi rassicura esasperata, quando la prendo in braccio per portarla dall'auto alla casa. "Sono stanca, ma posso camminare. Davvero, è stata solo una lunga settimana."

Ignorando le sue proteste, la porto in casa, senza metterla giù finché non arrivo al nostro bagno al piano di sopra. Una volta lì, le preparo un bagno caldo e mi assicuro che si sia sistemata comodamente, prima di andare in cucina per prepararle un po' di tè di echinacea.

Quando torno con il tè, si sta già addormentando nella vasca, con aria così adorabilmente assonnata che la metto a letto non appena la asciugo, ignorando la prevedibile bramosia dovuta al fatto di averla nuda tra le braccia.

Ho bisogno di prendermi cura di lei adesso, non di scoparla.

Si addormenta immediatamente, senza neanche un sorso di tè, anche se sono solo le dieci e normalmente non andiamo a letto prima delle undici. Sento la sua fronte per assicurarmi che non abbia la febbre, poi prendo il portatile e mi sistemo su una poltrona vicino al letto, decidendo che lavorerò un po', mentre la tengo d'occhio. C'è una grande quantità di documenti che va di pari passo con la gestione di un'attività legittima come la mia scuola di addestramento e in generale la gestione di un'impresa.

Sono contento di questo. Non dei documenti—a nessuno *piacciono*—ma di riuscire a tenermi occupato. Addestrare i civili sulle basi della difesa personale è ben lontano dalle missioni adrenaliniche del mio passato, ma aiuta ad occupare le giornate e allontana il costante desiderio di Sara. Anche se i suoi superiori sono tornati, lavora ancora troppo, e devo fare appello a tutta la mia forza di volontà per non farle pressione e spingerla a passare più tempo con me.

Al di fuori del lavoro, facciamo tutto insieme, dalle commissioni per il volontariato nella clinica per le donne fino al tempo che trascorriamo con la famiglia e gli amici. Ogni volta che le viene cancellato un appuntamento, viene a farmi visita nella mia scuola per praticare alcune mosse di difesa personale che le ho insegnato, e spesso passo a trovarla nel suo ufficio per il pranzo, nel caso abbia il tempo di mangiare un boccone con me. Ho persino programmato le nostre pulizie dentali nello stesso studio dentistico alla stessa ora, così potremo stare insieme durante il viaggio.

Potrebbe sembrare eccessivo per la maggior parte delle persone, ma è appena sufficiente per me.

Dopo un'ora, la controllo. Ancora niente febbre, e sta dormendo serenamente, anche se un po' troppo profondamente. Forse è solo stanca.

Sbadigliando, metto via il portatile e faccio una doccia

veloce, prima di andare a letto. Tirandola verso di me, inspiro profondamente, inebriandomi del suo dolce profumo, e poi mi lascio andare alla deriva, godendomi la sensazione di lei avvolta nel mio abbraccio.

ara

SONO ANCORA STRANAMENTE STANCA, QUANDO MI SVEGLIO LA mattina dopo, e i profumi della colazione che si diffondono dalla cucina al piano di sotto mi fanno venire la nausea invece di stuzzicarmi l'appetito come al solito. Con gli occhi annebbiati, barcollo verso il bagno, e mentre lavo i denti, mi viene in mente che oggi è sabato.

Il che significa che il mio ciclo è in ritardo di quattro giorni.

L'ondata di adrenalina scaccia via tutta la sonnolenza residua. Con il cuore che batte all'impazzata, mi precipito nella camera da letto e tiro fuori il telefono, contando freneticamente i giorni sul calendario per assicurarmi di non aver commesso un errore.

No.

È decisamente in ritardo, e questa volta non posso dare la colpa allo stress.

Eseguo dei test di gravidanza fin dalla nostra discussione sui bambini, quindi corro di nuovo al bagno per prenderne uno. Solo che ho già fatto pipì, e non riesco a far uscire nemmeno una goccia di urina.

Maledicendo silenziosamente la mia mancanza di lungimiranza, richiudo il test completamente asciutto nella scatola, lo rimetto nel cassetto e vado a vestirmi.

Dovrò aspettare fino a dopo la colazione per fare il test.

"I tuoi genitori saranno qui tra poco" mi informa Peter, quando scendo al piano di sotto, e ricordo con un sussulto che oggi verranno per il brunch.

"Ho di nuovo dormito troppo?" Guardo l'orologio. "Oh, wow, sì."

Sono le 11:27—esattamente tre minuti prima del loro arrivo.

"Dovevi essere davvero sfinita" osserva Peter, guarnendo una quiche dall'aspetto soffice con un pizzico di prezzemolo. "Come ti senti stamattina, ptichka?"

Esito, poi gli rivolgo un sorriso brillante. "Bene. Avevo solo bisogno di recuperare il sonno, tutto qui."

Visto quanto mio marito desideri un bambino, è meglio che lo sappia per certo, prima di comunicargli la notizia. Se questo fosse un falso allarme, mi odierei per averlo deluso.

Non sembra esserne molto convinto, ma il campanello suona, prima che possa dire qualcosa. Mi affretto verso la porta per salutare i miei genitori, e quando arriviamo nella sala da pranzo, Peter ha già apparecchiato il tavolo.

"Oh, wow" esclama mamma, quando assaggia la quiche. "Peter, devo ammettere di essere stata in ristoranti a cinque stelle che non erano altrettanto buoni."

Le rivolge un caloroso sorriso, e mio padre grugnisce con

approvazione, mentre mastica la sua porzione. I miei genitori sono ancora piuttosto diffidenti nei confronti di mio marito, ma li sta lentamente conquistando, diventando un genero modello. Con George, quando eravamo molto occupati, a volte passavo un mese o più senza vederli, ma Peter si assicura che li incontriamo almeno una volta alla settimana. Ha anche tagliato la loro erba e si occupa di compiti tecnologici e manuali in casa, facendoli sentire come se stessero facendo tutto da soli e come se lui stesse solo dando una mano occasionalmente.

"Hai un vero dono per questo" gli ho detto un paio di settimane fa. "Conquistare suoceri ostili è qualcosa che insegnano in una scuola per assassini?"

Ha annuito tranquillamente. "Suoceri, esplosivi, armi di alto calibro—tutti devono essere maneggiati con cura. Inoltre, mi piacciono i tuoi genitori. Hanno creato *te*."

Gli ho sorriso, sentendomi incredibilmente felice. Non so che cosa immaginassi, quando pensavo alla nostra vita da coppia sposata, ma finora tutto ha superato le mie aspettative. L'oscurità del nostro passato condiviso aleggia ancora sullo sfondo, ma il futuro ora sembra così luminoso che quasi non ha importanza.

Abbiamo raggiunto l'impossibile: una vita normale e felice insieme.

Dopo aver terminato il brunch—che mando giù nonostante la persistente nausea—porto mamma di sopra per mostrarle un elegante cappotto che ho acquistato online. Papà resta al piano di sotto, sistemandosi nel nostro salotto per guardare il notiziario sul grande schermo, mentre Peter fa sparire i piatti.

Mamma approva immediatamente il cappotto—adora le cose alla moda—e sto per scusarmi per eseguire il test, quando la voce tesa di papà fluttua al piano di sopra.

"Lorna, Sara, venite qui. Dovete dare un'occhiata a questo."

Il mio telefono vibra in quel momento, e lo stesso vale per quello di mia madre.

Scambiandoci occhiate preoccupate, tiriamo contemporaneamente fuori i nostri cellulari.

Sul mio schermo appare una notizia dalla CNN.

Sospetto attacco terroristico alla sede dell'FBI a Chicago, si legge. *Ancora sconosciuto il numero delle vittime.*

2 4

ara

IL CUORE MI BATTE FORTE E LA QUICHE È COME UNA ROCCIA nello stomaco, quando arriviamo al piano di sotto. Peter e mio padre sono nel soggiorno, a fissare lo schermo della TV—che sta mostrando un grande edificio in fiamme.

Lo stesso edificio in cui Ryson mi aveva interrogata così tante volte.

Mamma si copre la bocca, con il volto pallido, mentre guardiamo gli elicotteri circondare l'edificio in fiamme. Sotto, vigili del fuoco e paramedici stanno lavorando freneticamente per salvare i sopravvissuti e caricare i feriti sulle barelle.

Sembra la scena di un film, solo che sta accadendo proprio in questo momento, a meno di un'ora di distanza.

"Sebbene le autorità non abbiano emesso dichiarazioni ufficiali, le prime indicazioni suggeriscono che un esplosivo sofisticato e potente sia esploso all'interno dell'edificio" dice in tono grave la giornalista. "A partire da ora, tutti gli aeroporti e gli uffici governativi a livello nazionale sono in allerta e il traffico aereo nella regione di Chicago è stato sospeso."

L'immagine in TV mostra agenti SWAT che corrono verso O'Hare con cani che annusano bombe, che si scontrano con i viaggiatori terrorizzati in fuga.

"I residenti di Chicago sono invitati a rimanere ai margini della strada per non ostacolare il passaggio ai veicoli di emergenza" continua la giornalista. "Chiunque abbia informazioni su questo terribile evento può contattare il numero qui sotto." Un numero 1-800 appare in grassetto nella parte inferiore dello schermo. "Al momento, ci sono tre vittime confermate e ben quindici feriti. Vi terremo aggiornati, man mano che scopriremo di più." Si ferma, con una mano sull'orecchio, poi continua: "Aggiornamento: sette persone al momento risultano decedute e l'esplosione sembra aver avuto origine al terzo piano dell'edificio."

Terzo piano?

È lì che si trova l'ufficio di Ryson.

Forse era lì?

È tra i morti?

Non sono pienamente consapevole che sto oscillando sui piedi, ma evidentemente lo sto facendo, perché all'improvviso Peter è lì, con il suo potente braccio che mi avvolge la schiena. "Ecco, siediti, ptichka" mormora, guidandomi verso il divano. "Sembri sul punto di svenire."

Sbatto le palpebre, colpita da quanto sembri calmo, mentre si siede accanto a me. A parte una lieve tensione nella mascella, nulla nella sua espressione suggerisce che stia succedendo qualcosa di insolito. Ma di sicuro è perché ha visto di peggio.

Forse ha anche fatto di peggio.

Un pensiero orribile mi attraversa la mente, ma lo scaccio, non volendo verbalizzarlo.

Non voglio pensarci, nemmeno per un secondo.

"Non posso crederci" dice papà, con voce tremante, e mi volto per vederlo seduto accanto a me, con il viso pallido come quello di mamma, mentre fissa la TV. "L'edificio dell'FBI tra tanti posti. Come hanno potuto superare tutta quella sicurezza?"

In effetti, com'è stato possibile?

Lo scomodo pensiero riaffiora, ma decido di eliminarlo una volta per tutte. Questa orribile tragedia non ha niente a che fare con me o Peter.

"Stai bene, Papà?" chiedo, allungando la mano per toccargli il braccio.

Tutto questo non può far bene al suo cuore difettoso.

Annuisce, con gli occhi ancora incollati allo schermo. "Grazie a Dio è sabato. Riesci a immaginare quante persone sarebbero morte, se oggi fosse stato un giorno feriale?"

Torno a guardare la TV, dove i vigili del fuoco stanno combattendo le fiamme e le vittime sono state portate via sulle barelle—molte meno vittime di quanto mi sarei aspettata da un'esplosione di queste dimensioni. Certo, alcune persone saranno state spazzate via, con i loro resti ancora da trovare, ma sospetto che papà abbia ragione e che ci fossero poche persone, perché è il fine settimana.

"Forse la bomba è esplosa in ritardo. O troppo presto" dice mamma barcollando, mentre si lascia cadere su una sedia imbottita accanto al divano. "Sono certa che gli animali che l'hanno fatto volevano uccidere il maggior numero di gente possibile."

"Non ne sono così sicuro" ribatte Peter, e mi giro per vederlo con gli occhi fissi sullo schermo con un'espressione pensierosa. "Chiunque ci sia dietro questo chiaramente sapeva cosa stava facendo."

Deglutisco a fatica, con lo stomaco che inizia a ribollire intorno al peso simile a un macigno della quiche al suo interno. Non voglio pensare alle persone che hanno fatto questo, perché farlo scatenerebbe di nuovo quei pensieri oscuri e terribili, quelli che non voglio nemmeno riconoscere.

"Scusatemi" mormoro, alzandomi. La nausea che mi ha tormentata per tutta la mattina sta peggiorando attimo dopo attimo. "Torno subito."

Naturalmente, Peter mi segue, raggiungendomi proprio prima che io arrivi al bagno al piano di sotto.

"Stai bene, amore mio?"

Annuisco, deglutendo. La saliva si sta accumulando in modo spiacevole nella mia bocca, e il turbinio nello stomaco sta raggiungendo la velocità della lavatrice. "Ho solo bisogno del bagno" riesco a dire, e girando attorno a lui mi tuffo verso la porta aperta.

Faccio appena in tempo a chiuderla e ad inginocchiarmi davanti al water, prima di svuotare il contenuto dello stomaco.

Ovviamente sarebbe stato troppo sperare che Peter sentendo i versi del vomito sgattaiolasse via come farebbe la maggior parte dei normali mariti. Sto ancora vomitando nella tazza, quando sento le sue mani forti che mi raccolgono i capelli per tenerli lontano dalla mia faccia, e non appena alzo la testa, mi aiuta e mi porge un bicchiere d'acqua per farmi sciacquare la bocca.

Sono pateticamente grata per il suo sostegno, mentre mi chino sul lavandino e afferro uno spazzolino con le dita tremanti. Le mie gambe sembrano quelle di una medusa e la T-shirt si attacca alla schiena sudata.

Mi lavo i denti due volte, poi il viso, mentre Peter scarica e asciuga il coperchio con un tovagliolo di carta, sembrando preoccupato ma per niente disgustato.

"Vieni, amore mio, ti porto a letto" dice, quando ho finito. "Chiaramente non stai bene."

"Sto bene ora" protesto, mentre mi solleva per tenermi sul suo petto. "Davvero, mi sento meglio."

"Uh-uh." Mi porta fuori dal bagno e supera i miei genitori

nel soggiorno, che ci fissano con gli occhi sgranati. "O sei gravemente turbata o malata, e devi riposare."

"Che cos'è successo?" Mamma si precipita dietro di noi, mentre Peter si dirige verso le scale. "Sara sta male?"

Mio marito annuisce cupamente. "Sì—"

"Forse sono incinta" sbotto, e poi mi maledico mentalmente, mentre sia lui che mia madre si bloccano con identici sguardi scioccati sui volti.

Non è così che intendevo condividere la notizia.

Beh, la possibile notizia. Non ho ancora eseguito quel dannato test.

Mamma si riprende per prima. "Incinta? Oh, Sara!"

"Non lo so ancora per certo" dico velocemente, mentre delle lacrime—presumibilmente di gioia—appaiono nei suoi occhi. "È solo che il mio ciclo è in ritardo di alcuni giorni e—"

"Sei incinta?" La voce di Peter è tesa, e quando alzo lo sguardo, scorgo l'espressione più strana sul suo viso.

Smarrimento misto a qualcosa di molto simile al panico.

È davvero spaventato da questo?

Non era questo ciò che ha sempre voluto?

"È una possibilità" rispondo attentamente. "Se mi metti giù, vado a fare pipì su un bastoncino e ti faccio sapere."

Ancora sconvolto, mio marito mi abbassa lentamente in piedi.

"Ok, bene." Liberandomi dalla sua presa, indietreggio, grata che le mie gambe sembrino essersi riprese. "Datemi qualche minuto."

"Chuck!" urla mamma, correndo verso il salotto, mentre salgo al piano di sopra, con Peter alle calcagna. "Hai sentito? La nostra Sara potrebbe essere incinta!"

Sussulto, imprecando contro me stessa ancora una volta per aver diffuso la notizia così impulsivamente e con un tempismo così pessimo. Posso ancora sentire il trambusto della TV con gli ultimi sviluppi nell'attacco letale, ed eccomi qui, a distrarre tutti con qualcosa di così banale come un potenziale bambino.

Il bambino mio e di Peter.

Il mio cuore salta un battito, mentre mio marito mi segue nel bagno al piano di sopra e tira fuori dal cassetto la scatola del test di gravidanza. "Ecco, amore mio" dice, porgendomela. La sua voce è ancora grave, ma sembra che si stia riprendendo dallo shock. "Fa' ciò che devi."

Cammino verso il water e mi fermo, guardandolo in attesa.

"Un po' di privacy, per favore?" dico ironicamente, quando non mostra segni di movimento.

Mi fissa, senza battere ciglio, poi si gira. "Continua pure. Non guarderò."

Alzo gli occhi al cielo, ma decido che non vale la pena discutere. I confini non sono il punto forte di mio marito nel migliore dei casi, e in questo momento, probabilmente è preoccupato che possa svenire, mentre faccio la pipì.

La faccio sul bastoncino, poi lo metto su un pezzo di carta igienica pulita sul ripiano e mi lavo le mani, mentre Peter osserva il test come se stesse cercando di ipnotizzarlo.

"Sembra positivo" dice con voce soffocata, mentre mi pulisco le mani sull'asciugamano. "Aspetta—no, è decisamente positivo. Sara, vuol dire...?"

Ho un tuffo al cuore, mentre osservo il test—che ora mostra un piccolo ma inconfondibile segno blu. "Penso di sì." Lo guardo. "Eseguirò le analisi del sangue nel mio ufficio per esserne sicura, ma—"

"Sei incinta."

È un'affermazione, non una domanda, ma annuisco, sapendo istintivamente che ha bisogno della conferma. "Di circa cinque settimane, se i miei calcoli sono corretti."

Per un momento, mio marito non mostra alcuna reazione, fissandomi con uno sguardo metallico. Ma proprio mentre sto cominciando a preoccuparmi che abbia cambiato idea sul desiderare un figlio, si fa avanti e mi avvolge in un enorme abbraccio.

"Un bambino" mormora nei miei capelli, con il corpo potente quasi tremante, mentre mi tiene a sé, stringendomi in un abbraccio abbastanza forte da farmi uscire quasi l'aria dai polmoni. "Avremo un bambino."

"Davvero?" La voce di mia madre è stridula per l'emozione, e Peter mi libera, lasciandomi vedere la mia genitrice di settantanove anni saltellare sulla soglia come una ragazzina troppo entusiasta.

Dev'essere arrivata solo un secondo fa.

Inizio a rispondere, ma prima che possa dire una parola, mamma corre fuori dal bagno, urlando a squarciagola: "Chuck, è positivo! Il test è positivo! Avranno un figlio!"

La sua eccitazione dev'essere contagiosa, perché mi ritrovo a sorridere, mentre alzo lo sguardo su Peter, che mi sta fissando con un'altra espressione strana.

"Stai bene?" chiedo, allungando la mano per accarezzargli l'ispida mascella. "*Sei* felice di questo, vero?"

Mi cattura la mano, premendola contro la sua guancia. "*Tu* lo sei?" La sua voce è bassa e rauca, con lo sguardo inspiegabilmente preoccupato. "Sei contenta, amore mio? È questo che vuoi?"

"Io—sì." Faccio un respiro profondo. "È questo che voglio."

Ed è vero. Voglio questo bambino. Lo voglio così tanto che posso assaporarlo. Non l'avevo ammesso prima, ma quando il mio ciclo era venuto regolarmente negli ultimi tre mesi, avevo sentito più di una leggera fitta di delusione.

Da qualche parte nel nostro viaggio contorto, questo bambino è passato dall'essere il mio peggior incubo al mio più fervido desiderio.

"Quindi, niente rimorsi?" conferma Peter. "Niente paura o esitazione?"

"No." Sostengo il suo sguardo senza battere ciglio. "Niente di niente."

E mentre un sorriso lento e luminoso attraversa il suo bel viso, mi alzo in punta di piedi e lo bacio, sopraffatta da un'ondata di amore per quest'uomo oscuro e complicato.

Per il padre di mio figlio.

eter

QUANDO ARRIVIAMO AL PIANO DI SOTTO, I GENITORI DI SARA hanno già trovato la bottiglia di Cristal che ho tenuto in frigorifero per un'occasione speciale.

"Ecco, lascia fare a me" dico, notando che Chuck sta faticando ad aprirla. Strappandogli la bottiglia, tolgo il tappo e ne verso tre bicchieri, uno per tutti tranne Sara. Per lei, prendo una bottiglia di Perrier e verso dell'acqua frizzante in un bicchiere di champagne.

La mia ptichka non potrà bere alcol per tutta la durata della gravidanza e finché allatterà al seno.

Finché allatterà al seno il nostro bambino.

Il mio petto si stringe di nuovo, e il battito cardiaco sale alle stelle. Non riesco ancora a credere che questo sia reale, che ciò che ho desiderato per così tanto tempo stia finalmente accadendo.

Sara desidera un figlio da me.

Noi due saremo una famiglia.

La mia felicità è talmente assoluta da terrorizzarmi. Non riesco a ricordare di aver mai provato una cosa del genere: mi sento felicissimo e profondamente a disagio allo stesso tempo. Tutto quello che voglio è afferrare Sara e rinchiuderla in una fortezza, o in una gabbia, avvolgerla in una tuta di sicurezza imbottita e portarla con me ovunque, per paura che lei e il bambino si facciano del male in qualche modo.

"Al nostro primo nipote" dice Lorna, sollevando il bicchiere di champagne, e mi sforzo di sorridere, mentre faccio tintinnare il bicchiere contro il suo, poi contro quello di Chuck, e poi contro quello di Sara. Tutti e tre stanno ridendo, completamente presi dalla gioia dell'occasione. Dovrei esserlo anch'io, ma per qualche ragione, non posso lasciare andare la preoccupazione che incombe su di me come una nuvola maligna.

Qualcosa non va, ma non riesco a capire cosa.

Il telefono di qualcuno vibra per una notifica, e Chuck mette giù il suo champagne, prima di scavare nella tasca per dare un'occhiata allo schermo. "Dodici morti adesso." Alza lo sguardo, con il sorriso che scompare dal volto. "Che peccato l'aver saputo di nostro nipote in un giorno così triste."

"Potrebbe essere una nipotina" osserva Lorna, ma anche lei sembra triste.

Forse è questo. Forse è questo che mi infastidisce.

È un giorno buio—almeno per Ryson e i suoi colleghi. Per me, è potenzialmente un motivo di festa. Se Ryson è stato fatto a pezzi, rimarrà per sempre fuori dalla nostra vita. Mi preoccupa che Sara e i suoi genitori siano turbati, però.

Lo stress non fa bene alla gravidanza.

"Vieni, ptichka. Siediti." La dirigo con cautela verso una sedia accanto al tavolo della cucina, e poi vado in salotto, dove la giornalista sta facendo congetture a voce alta su quale organizzazione terroristica possa esserci stata dietro l'attacco. Osservo le immagini dell'edificio in fiamme per un secondo, poi spengo il televisore.

Non ho bisogno che Sara ascolti questo nelle sue condizioni.

Torno e trovo i suoi genitori all'ingresso, preparandosi ad andare. "Verrete domani?" chiede Lorna a sua figlia, mentre prende la borsa. "Stavo pensando che io e te potremmo prendere un tè, mentre Peter aiuta tuo padre a montare quel nuovo ricevitore."

"Sì, certo" risponde Sara, ridacchiando. "Sai che ci sarò, Mamma."

"Bene." Bacia Sara sulla guancia. "Adesso riposati, tesoro, ok?"

"Lo farò" la rassicura con diligenza, e io annuisco, sorridendo, mentre Lorna coglie acutamente il mio sguardo. Non crede a sua figlia nemmeno per un secondo, ma mi conosce abbastanza bene da sapere che mi assicurerò che lei riposi.

"Ci vediamo domani" mi dice Chuck bruscamente, e con mia sorpresa, mi dà una pacca sulla spalla, mentre si trascina verso l'uscita.

"Guidate con cautela" avverto, e poi sono di nuovo sconcertato, quando la madre di Sara mi avvolge in un breve ma caloroso abbraccio, prima di seguire suo marito.

Aspetto che la porta si chiuda dietro di loro, prima di rivolgermi a mia moglie. "Mi hanno—"

"Ti hanno accettato ufficialmente come parte della nostra famiglia?" Mi sorride. "Sì, credo che l'abbiano fatto. Congratulazioni, papino."

Il mio cuore si stringe in un minuscolo punto, prima di espandersi per riempire l'intera cavità toracica. "Ti amo" dico, tirandola verso di me. "Non puoi nemmeno immaginare quanto."

E mentre avvolge le sue braccia magre intorno al mio collo,

la bacio, assaporando la morbidezza delle sue labbra e l'amore che ora ricambia liberamente.

la bacio, assaporando la morbidezza delle sue labbra e l'amore che ora ricambia liberamente.

S ara

DOPO CHE I MIEI GENITORI SE NE SONO ANDATI, IO E PETER CI dirigiamo nel mio ufficio, dove mi prelevo una fiala di sangue. Qualche minuto dopo, abbiamo la conferma ufficiale.

Sono incinta di cinque settimane.

Sono anche famelica, dal momento che ho vomitato l'unico cibo che ho mangiato oggi. "Non credo di poter aspettare fin quando torneremo a casa" dico a Peter, così si ferma presso una piccola pizzeria lungo la strada.

Non sono mai stata in questo posto e sono felice di scoprire che, sebbene siamo gli unici clienti in questo momento, la loro pizza è il vero affare, buona come qualsiasi cosa abbia mangiato nei locali più eleganti. L'unico neo è che la TV è accesa, mostrando le conseguenze dell'attacco, e il proprietario—un grassoccio uomo di mezza età che parla con un forte accento italiano—continua a parlarne con noi, mentre mangiamo vicino al bancone.

"Un evento davvero terribile" afferma cupamente, impastando una palla di lievito davanti a noi. "Dove andremo a finire? Prima l'11 settembre, poi la Maratona di Boston, ora questo. Almeno hanno preso di mira l'FBI questa volta, non dei cittadini innocenti. Non che quegli agenti siano colpevoli, ma sapete cosa intendo. Se avete qualche problema con l'America, è più sensato rivolgersi a loro, alla CIA o a qualcos'altro che abbia a che fare con il governo."

Annuisco automaticamente, mentre mi riempio la faccia con la deliziosa pizza, e questo è tutto l'incoraggiamento di cui l'uomo ha bisogno per andare avanti.

"Dicono che l'esplosivo sia stato qualcosa di insolito, qualcosa di veramente avanzato" spiega, arrotolando l'impasto con movimenti esperti. "Mi chiedo di cosa si tratti e come abbiamo fatto quei terroristi ad averci messo le mani sopra. Sembra più qualcosa che abbiano fatto la Russia o la Cina o persino i nostri militari. Scommetto che tutti i teorici della cospirazione usciranno fuori in pieno vigore, sostenendo che si tratta di un lavoro interno e tutto il resto."

Mordo un'altra fetta, lasciando blaterale l'uomo, mentre lancio un'occhiata a Peter. Mi aspetto che mangi tranquillamente, ma con mia sorpresa, è accigliato, con la sua fetta intatta davanti a lui, mentre fissa intensamente la TV.

"Che cosa c'è?" chiedo piano, mentre il proprietario si gira per prendere altra farina. "Qualcosa non va?"

Distoglie lo sguardo dalla TV e mi rivolge un sorriso triste. "Non proprio. Solo vecchi istinti che mi tormentano, tutto qui."

Voglio interrogarlo ulteriormente, ma il proprietario è tornato a rotolare l'impasto davanti a noi e a fare ipotesi su chi potrebbe esserci dietro l'esplosione.

"Grazie mille. Era deliziosa" dico all'uomo, quando non riesco a mandar giù un altro boccone e Peter paga rapidamente il conto e mi spinge fuori dal locale. Anche se lo nega, mio marito è chiaramente preoccupato per qualcosa—posso vederlo dal modo teso in cui afferra il volante, mentre torniamo a casa —e il seme oscuro del sospetto che avevo represso riaffiora, facendomi contorcere di nuovo lo stomaco.

Potrebbe essere così?

Quante sono le probabilità che questa sia tutta una terribile coincidenza?

Combatto il dubbio il più a lungo possibile, ma alla fine non ce la faccio più.

Nel momento in cui siamo dentro casa, mi volto per affrontare mio marito. "Peter... ho bisogno di chiederti una cosa."

Persino alle mie orecchie la mia voce sembra strana.

Mi rivolge immediatamente tutta la sua attenzione. "Che cosa c'è, ptichka?" Mi stringe le spalle. "Ti senti bene?"

Annuisco, deglutendo, mentre lo fisso. Il mio cuore sta ballando il tip-tap nel petto, e sto iniziando a sentirmi di nuovo male.

Forse quella pizza è stata un errore.

Forse menzionare questo è un errore più grande.

"Qual è il problema, amore mio?" Gentilmente, mi guida verso un divanetto vicino all'ingresso. "Ecco, siediti. Sembri pallida."

"No, sto bene" lo rassicuro, ma mi siedo ugualmente, perché è più facile obbedire che discutere. Si siede accanto a me e mi stringe le mani nelle sue, massaggiandomi i palmi con i pollici come se avessi bisogno di essere tranquillizzata.

E forse è così.

Tutto dipende da come risponderà alla mia prossima domanda.

"Peter..." Trovo il coraggio. "Ho bisogno di sapere. Hai—" Respiro. "Hai qualcosa a che fare con quello che è successo oggi? Con quella... esplosione?"

Si trasforma in una statua, senza battere ciglio né reagire per i momenti successivi. Alla fine, risponde con un filo di voce: "No." Lasciandomi le mani, si alza in piedi, e senza aggiungere un'altra parola, torna all'entrata per togliersi le scarpe.

Lo seguo con lo sguardo fisso, sentendomi terribile e terribilmente sollevata.

Gli credo.

Non mi ha mai ingannata, non ha mai negato la sua colpevolezza in alcun crimine.

Mio marito sarà anche un assassino, ma non è un bugiardo.

"Mi dispiace" dico, quando mi passa davanti senza guardarmi. "Peter, mi dispiace davvero, ma dovevo chiederlo. Il terzo piano è quello dell'ufficio di Ryson e—" Mi fermo perché scompare in cucina.

Faccio un respiro, poi vado verso la porta per togliere le scarpe anch'io. Mi sento malissimo per averlo chiesto—per aver anche solo preso in considerazione l'idea. Non solo questo attacco è un atto veramente atroce, ma è anche qualcosa che avrebbe messo a repentaglio la nostra vita insieme—qualcosa per cui Peter ha combattuto duramente.

Qualcosa per la quale ha rinunciato alla sua vendetta.

Sono completamente preparata a farmi perdonare, quando entro in cucina, ma Peter non è da nessuna parte. Vago per la casa, e non lo trovo finché non sbircio nell'armadio a muro della camera degli ospiti.

È accovacciato su un laptop, con le dita che scorrono sulla tastiera a velocità record.

Accigliandosi, mi inginocchio accanto a lui e scruto lo schermo. Sta scrivendo un'e-mail, ma è in russo e l'interfaccia del programma che sta usando è diversa da qualsiasi altra cosa abbia mai visto.

"Che cosa stai facendo?" chiedo con cautela. "Peter... perché sei qui?"

"Aspetta" risponde senza alzare lo sguardo. "Lasciami finire."

Mi zittisco e lo guardo digitare. Impiega un altro paio di minuti, poi chiude il portatile e dà dei colpetti sulla parete dell'armadio.

Scivola di lato, rivelando lo spazio di un altro armadio.

Uno spazio pieno di armi di livello militare, tra cui diversi lanciarazzi e granate... oltre a laptop di riserva.

Senza parole, osservo Peter mettere il suo laptop su una mensola e toccare un'altra parete, facendo sì che quella originale scivoli di nuovo in posizione, coprendo l'apertura.

Finalmente riesco a ritrovare la lingua. "Questo è—"

"Un ripostiglio di armi nascoste? Sì." Si alza e allunga una mano per aiutarmi ad alzarmi. "Ma non preoccuparti, amore mio." I suoi occhi brillano per un freddo divertimento, mentre gli stringo la mano e mi alzo in piedi. "Non ho intenzione di usarle per commettere atti terroristici."

Sussulto e ritiro la mano. "Lo so. Scusa. Non avrei dovuto—"

"No, avresti dovuto." Mi toglie i capelli dal viso, in un gesto più tenero che mai, anche se il suo sguardo rimane quello di un estraneo. "Voglio che tu venga sempre da me, se hai dei dubbi. Inoltre, tu e il proprietario della pizzeria mi avete aiutato a capire una cosa."

Sbatto le palpebre. "Cioè?"

"Devo esaminare quello che è successo. Sento puzza di bruciato."

"Che cosa intendi dire?"

"Non lo so ancora." Abbassa la mano e fa un passo indietro. "Ho appena contattato i nostri hacker, quindi avrò presto maggiori informazioni."

Si gira e esce dall'armadio. Mi affretto a seguirlo, raggiungendolo appena prima che lasci la camera degli ospiti.

"Quindi, non sei arrabbiato?" chiedo senza fiato, mettendomi davanti per bloccargli la strada. "Che te l'abbia chiesto?"

Piega le labbra. "Arrabbiato? No, ptichka. Perché dovrei esserlo?"

"Beh, perché sei innocente e ti ho praticamente accusato. Mi dispiace davvero; non avrei dovuto nemmeno pensarci—"

"Perché no?" Inclina la testa. "Non sarebbe stata la cosa peggiore che abbia fatto."

Mi si stringe lo stomaco. "Lo so, ma—"

"Era un'ipotesi logica da parte tua. Un esplosivo sofisticato, un obiettivo difficile e un motivo da parte mia. In realtà, sono sorpreso che tu mi creda."

Sono quasi sicura che mi stia prendendo in giro con quell'ultima parte, ma me lo merito. "Cosa posso fare per farmi perdonare?" chiedo invece di scusarmi di nuovo. "Come posso migliorare le cose?"

Solleva le sopracciglia, con gli occhi che brillano per un improvviso interesse. "Che cosa avevi in mente?"

Il mio battito accelera e una vampata di calore mi copre il corpo, mentre mi rivolge un'occhiata decisamente erotica. Il sesso non era quello che avevo in mente, ma se è quello che desidera, sono più che felice di accontentarlo.

"Questo" mormoro, e sostenendo il suo sguardo, comincio a spogliarmi.

Peter

Dopo aver fatto l'amore, Sara si addormenta nella camera degli ospiti, e la lascio lì a fare un sonnellino. Ho fatto del mio meglio per essere delicato durante il sesso, ma devo averla stancata a prescindere.

O quello, oppure ha solo bisogno di riposare di più e devo essere più diligente nel far sì che sia tranquilla nei prossimi otto mesi.

La gioia mista ad ansia mi riempie di nuovo il petto, nascondendo i residui della ferita. Non ha senso essere arrabbiato per la domanda di Sara; semmai, dovrei essere felice che si fidi di me abbastanza da chiedermelo, invece di lasciarsi divorare da tali sospetti.

Non posso nemmeno biasimarla per averne. Non avrei mai fatto qualcosa di così sfacciato e appariscente come far saltare in aria l'edificio dell'FBI, ma avevo pianificato di eliminare

Ryson—che aveva continuato a curiosare dopo la mia promessa condizionata a Sara.

Se ci avesse lasciati in pace, sarebbe stato al sicuro, ma non l'ha fatto—e mi sentivo perfettamente giustificato per quello che gli avrei fatto.

Mi sentirei ancora così, se fosse sopravvissuto.

Il mio disagio si intensifica di nuovo, ma questa volta la preoccupazione è più concreta. Non credo nelle coincidenze, e tutto questo sembra proprio tale. Non l'ho detto a mia moglie, ma ho già trovato un elenco di morti e feriti, e Ryson è tra questi ultimi, essendo stato portato in ospedale in condizioni critiche.

Se non sapessi come funzionano le cose, penserei che qualcuno mi abbia fatto un favore.

Dopo mezz'ora, controllo Sara. Sta ancora dormendo, quindi torno all'armadio degli ospiti e tiro fuori alcune armi. Le sistemo strategicamente in tutta la casa e ne porto alcune nel garage, dove le nascondo in uno scomparto speciale nella nostra auto antiproiettile.

Solo per evenienza.

Dopo aver placato la paranoia, apro il mio portatile e comincio a rispondere alle e-mail dei miei allievi, mentre aspetto che la mia ptichka si svegli.

"OH MIO DIO" DICE SARA IL MATTINO SEGUENTE, CON LO sguardo fisso sulla TV. "Peter, Ryson *era* lì. Hanno appena identificato le vittime dell'esplosione, e lui è tra quelli in condizioni critiche. Puoi crederci?"

Annuisco automaticamente. "Sì, l'ho già saputo. È stato davvero sfortunato."

Secondo le mie fonti, ha riportato ustioni di terzo e quarto grado su gran parte del corpo. Mi sento quasi male per il coglione. L'avrei eliminato in un modo molto più umano—molto probabilmente tramite un attacco cardiaco indotto da farmaci, in modo da farla sembrare una morte per cause naturali.

"Che terribile tragedia" esclama Sara, con lo sguardo fisso sullo schermo. "Spero che si riprenda."

"Mm-hmm." Non c'è bisogno di turbarla contraddicendola. "Vuoi qualcosa da mangiare o hai ancora la nausea, amore mio?" Tutto quello che ha mangiato finora è un pezzo di pane tostato, anche se ho preparato la sua omelette e i pancake preferiti.

Si volta verso di me. "Sto bene per ora, grazie. La nausea è quasi passata, ma credo che mangerò dai miei genitori, mentre tu farai quello che devi con il ricevitore di papà."

"Certo, sicuramente. Pronta per andare, allora?"

Si alza e si avvicina. "Sì. Andiamo."

PRENDO UNA STRADA DIVERSA PER RAGGIUNGERE LA CASA DEI MIEI suoceri e mi assicuro che i miei ragazzi sorveglino la zona prima del nostro arrivo. Gli hacker stanno ancora indagando sull'esplosione, ma il mio misuratore del pericolo mi sta allertando senza sosta.

Forse io e Sara dovremmo andare fuori città, partire per la luna di miele adesso, invece di rimandare le vacanze come avevamo previsto in origine. Potrebbe essere una prematura luna di miele o come si chiama.

I genitori di Sara ci salutano calorosamente, e sua madre entra nella solita modalità padrona di casa, offrendoci tè, cracker, frutta e tutto il resto. Declino gentilmente—ho fatto una colazione abbondante—ma mia moglie accetta le offerte di sua madre, mentre sistemo il nuovo ricevitore di Chuck.

"Devi collegarlo qui" dice, indicando il cavo audio, e io annuisco, ringraziandolo come se non lo sapessi già.

Il padre di Sara ha bisogno che questo sia un progetto di squadra, e sono felice di accontentarlo.

Ho quasi finito di testare il suono surround, quando il telefono mi vibra nella tasca. Tirandolo fuori, do un'occhiata allo schermo—e il ghiaccio mi invade le vene.

SWAT in arrivo, mi informa un messaggio dalla mia squadra. *Tra tre minuti.*

2 8

ara

LO SENTO APPENA PRIMA CHE PETER IRROMPA IN CUCINA, DOVE IO e mamma stiamo discutendo sui potenziali temi per la cameretta del bambino.

L'inconfondibile rombo delle pale dell'elicottero.

"Andiamo." Mio marito mi prende prima che io possa battere ciglio. "Scusa" dice alla mia stupefatta madre, e stringendomi forte al suo petto, fa un passo intorno a lei, dirigendosi verso la porta.

Gli afferro la maglietta spasmodicamente. "Peter, che cosa—"

"Non c'è tempo." Spalanca la porta ed esce fuori, stringendomi—solo per bloccarsi sul posto, mentre un enorme furgone nero stride sulla nostra strada e un gruppo di SWAT scende giù, con i volti protetti e i fucili d'assalto puntati su di noi.

Il mio cervello sembra improvvisamente trasformato in melma.

Non riesco a riflettere.

Non posso nemmeno cominciare a farlo.

Lentamente e molto deliberatamente, Peter mi mette in piedi e cammina davanti a me, proteggendomi con il proprio corpo. "Non sparate." Il suo tono è stranamente calmo, mentre alza le mani sopra la testa. "Non c'è bisogno della violenza. Verrò con voi."

La mia lingua si districa in qualche modo. "Aspettate!" Mi lancio in avanti su gambe instabili. "C'era un accordo. Non potete—"

"Ferma lì, signora!" ringhia l'agente più esposto, e mi blocco, mentre diverse armi oscillano nella mia direzione.

"Ho detto che non ce n'è bisogno." La voce di Peter si acuisce mentre cammina, rimettendomi dietro di lui. "Non sto opponendo resistenza. Nessuno deve farsi male, chiaro?"

"Cosa sta succedendo qui?" chiede papà da dietro di me, e mi rendo conto con un'ondata di panico che i miei genitori sono usciti di casa.

"Tornate dentro." Mi trema la voce, mentre guardo dietro. "Papà, per favore, fa' tornare dentro mamma."

L'elicottero ora è quasi direttamente sopra la nostra testa, con il rombo che copre le mie parole.

"In ginocchio!" urla qualcuno, e mi guardo dietro per vedere mio marito obbedire, con movimenti lenti e deliberati come prima.

Non vuole renderli nervosi, mi rendo conto con nauseabonda paura. Sanno di cosa è capace e, anche se è disarmato, sono terrorizzati all'idea di affrontarlo.

"Peter Garin, sei accusato di omicidio di impiegati federali, distruzione di proprietà del governo, uso di esplosivi e cospirazione per commettere un omicidio" l'agente che ha parlato in precedenza grida sopra al rumore dell'elicottero. Si dirige verso mio marito con le manette, mentre i suoi colleghi impugnano i fucili d'assalto puntandoli sulla faccia di mio marito. "Hai il diritto di—"

Il suo elmetto esplode prima che pronunci la parola successiva, e si scatena l'inferno.

eter

MI MUOVO, PRIMA DI RENDERMI COMPLETAMENTE CONTO DELLO sparo del fucile di precisione.

È istintivo, puramente automatico.

Ho solo un compito.

Sopravvivere abbastanza a lungo da proteggere Sara e il bambino.

Come sempre in tali situazioni, i miei pensieri sono chiari e nitidi.

Cecchino a ore cinque, identità sconosciuta.

Un agente morto. Il resto sta per aprire il fuoco.

Nove avversari di fronte a me. Sara e i suoi genitori dietro di me.

Impugno l'M4 dall'agente a cui il cervello è schizzato, e mi butto di lato, mentre ricopro i suoi colleghi di proiettili, mirando dove so che la loro armatura può avere degli spazi.

Devo attirare il loro fuoco lontano da Sara, per farli concentrare su di me come unica minaccia.

Con la coda dell'occhio, vedo i genitori di mia moglie trascinarla dentro la casa. Sta urlando qualcosa, ma è impossibile sentire a causa del rumore dell'elicottero e del *rat-tat-tat* degli spari.

Il terreno accanto a me viene perforato dai proiettili, ma continuo a muovermi e a premere il grilletto. La loro armatura li protegge, ma li rallenta, permettendomi di acquistare secondi preziosi. Anche quando non li uccido, i miei proiettili li buttano giù.

Restano cinque nemici adesso.

Tutte le armi che ho preparato sono nella nostra macchina, con solo una Glock legata alla mia gamba, quindi, quando quella presa in prestito suona a vuoto, la getto via e mi tuffo dietro due agenti caduti, afferrando l'arma di uno di loro.

Il fuoco mi colpisce al braccio sinistro, ma lo ignoro.

Posso ancora tenere la pistola, quindi la ferita non può essere troppo grave.

Il furgone SWAT è ora a una decina di metri di distanza, quindi mi getto verso di esso, sia per la copertura sia perché è il più lontano possibile dalla casa. Mentre colpisco il terreno, schivo un altro paio di spari e sono fortunato, colpendo due agenti sotto gli scudi facciali.

Il fuoco mi colpisce al polpaccio destro, ma l'adrenalina continua a farmi muovere.

Altre pallottole volano intorno a me, anche se ora sono dietro la macchina.

L'elicottero.

Girandomi sulla schiena, sparo nella sua direzione, e la lama di un rotore esplode, facendolo oscillare bruscamente nell'aria. Sparo ancora, e devia, scomparendo dietro gli alberi a un paio di isolati.

Senza fermarmi, rotolo sotto il furgone e sbuco dall'altra parte, di fronte ai tre agenti rimasti.

Solo che ce ne sono due di fronte a me.

Uno sta correndo verso la casa.

3 0

ara

TUTTO ACCADE IN UN LAMPO. UN MOMENTO PRIMA SONO DIETRO a Peter, mentre l'agente sta per abbatterlo, e l'attimo dopo si sente un tuonante *crack* e l'elmetto dell'uomo esplode, con il sangue e il cervello che spruzzano dappertutto, mentre mio marito entra in azione, afferrando la pistola del morto.

"Sara, entra!" Mamma mi afferra per un braccio, tirandomi indietro, mentre gli assordanti colpi di arma da fuoco esplodono, mescolandosi al rombo dell'elicottero.

"No, entra tu!" grido, liberandomi dalla sua presa. Non posso lasciare Peter qui. "Entra subito dentro!"

"Il tuo bambino!" urla papà sopra al rumore, afferrandomi il polso, mentre sto per lanciarmi in avanti. "Sei incinta, ricordi?"

Il promemoria è come un secchio d'acqua ghiacciata gettato sulla faccia.

513

Mi ero dimenticata della piccola vita dentro di me, il bambino che Peter desidera tanto.

"Entra, Sara. Ora!" Mamma mi tira l'altro polso, e questa volta, obbedisco, inciampando in casa, mentre la strada si trasforma in una zona di guerra.

"Dobbiamo... allontanarci... dalle finestre" ansima papà, chinandosi nell'atrio. "I proiettili—"

"Va tutto bene, Papà. Respira." Afferro il suo gomito, mentre inizia a crollare, ma è troppo pesante per poterlo trattenere e riesco solo ad ammorbidire la sua caduta.

"Dove sono le tue pillole?" La mia voce si alza in preda al panico, mentre il suo viso inizia a diventare blu. "Mamma, dov'è il suo farmaco?"

"In cu-cucina." Sembra scioccata. "A-armadietto in alto sulla destra."

"Va bene, torno subito." La finestra del soggiorno esplode mentre cammino, ma mi rendo conto a malapena dei frammenti di vetro che mi sfiorano la pelle.

Devo prendere la medicina di papà.

Non posso pensare a Peter in questo momento, non posso concentrarmi sul terrore tossico che mi stringe il petto.

Ce la farà.

Deve farcela.

Aprendo l'armadietto, afferro le pillole di nitroglicerina di papà e una bottiglietta di aspirina, poi scatto indietro, mentre il rumore dell'elicottero svanisce e gli spari si fermano.

Mamma è in ginocchio sul corpo incosciente di papà, con il viso che è una maschera di terrore, mentre mi guarda. "Non respira. Sara, non respira."

Sono già in ginocchio, a spingere sul petto di papà, mentre conto tra me e me, e poi mi chino per respirare nella sua bocca.

Il suo petto si alza per l'aria che gli soffio, poi si abbassa e rimane immobile.

Combattendo il crescente panico, ricomincio le compressioni toraciche.

Uno, due, tre, quattro—

La porta si spalanca e due lottatori di wrestling irrompono.

Un agente SWAT e un Peter ricoperto di sangue.

P eter

SPARO PRIMA CHE LO FACCIANO GLI AGENTI, DUE COLPI CHE SI infilano proprio sotto gli scudi facciali. Alimentato dall'adrenalina, salto in piedi, solo vagamente consapevole dell'intenso dolore al braccio e al polpaccio.

Devo fermare l'agente in fuga.

Non posso permettergli di restare dentro con Sara e la sua famiglia.

Sparando una raffica in velocità, lo raggiungo all'ingresso e lo affronto mentre si gira, pronto a sparare. Dall'arma parte una raffica attraverso il portico e ci precipitiamo contro la porta, aprendola con il nostro slancio.

Ho solo una frazione di secondo per notare la scena all'interno, ma è abbastanza per inclinarmi a destra ed evitare di calpestare una Sara in ginocchio e i suoi genitori.

Sbattiamo contro il divano e rotoliamo sul pavimento

insieme, lottando per afferrare la Glock infilata nella sua cintura. Atterro su di lui e gli strappo l'arma, ma piega il gomito nel mio braccio ferito, facendomi cadere la pistola dalla mano.

Ignorando il tripudio di dolore, gli strappo il coltello e glielo infilo nello spazio vuoto dell'armatura. Rantola come un pesce fuori dall'acqua e lo pugnalo di nuovo, poi altre due volte.

Il suo corpo diventa floscio sotto di me.

"Peter!" La voce di Sara mi raggiunge nonostante il ruggito del battito cardiaco, e alzo lo sguardo, notando il suo viso bianco e rigato dalle lacrime. Sta premendo sul petto di suo padre con l'inconfondibile ritmo della rianimazione, con la madre inginocchiata accanto a lei.

Striscio via dall'uomo morto e mi alzo in piedi. La stanza gira intorno a me in un cerchio nauseante, e quando guardo giù, vedo che la mia gamba destra è coperta di sangue—e che altro sangue mi cola lungo il braccio sinistro.

Ovviamente. Le ferite da arma da fuoco.

Scacciando le vertigini, mi incammino verso Sara e i suoi genitori. "Che cos'è successo? Gli hanno sparato?" Non vedo sangue su Chuck, ma—

La ragazza scuote la testa. "Arresto cardiaco." Inarcandosi, gli chiude il naso e gli soffia in bocca, poi riprende a premergli sul petto.

Fanculo. Prendo le bottigliette contenenti le pillole che giacciono chiuse sul pavimento, e mi si stringe il petto.

Questo è il peggior incubo di Sara, e l'ho provocato io.

"Voi due dovete andare." La voce rauca di Lorna sembra quella di un fantasma, e quando la guardo, vedo che sembra tale, con il viso bianco come carta da forno. "Prima che mandino il—"

Una pallottola frantuma la parete sopra di noi, e io istintivamente salto di fronte a Sara e sua madre, proteggendole con il corpo.

Il mio fianco sinistro esplode per il dolore, con la forza

massiccia del colpo che mi butta in avanti, mentre spingo entrambe dietro al divano. La mia vista lampeggia di bianco, con il dolore che mi inonda le terminazioni nervose, mentre un altro proiettile mi sfiora l'orecchio.

No. Cazzo, no.

Con la forza rimasta, mi getto di lato, distogliendo il fuoco del tiratore da Sara e sua madre. Un'altra pallottola colpisce il pavimento vicino al mio ginocchio, facendo volare schegge di legno dappertutto, e attraverso una visione grigiastra, scorgo una figura armata che dondola sulla porta, stringendo una pistola.

È uno degli agenti SWAT a cui ho sparato.

Stordito e ferito, ma vivo.

La sua maschera facciale è caduta, rivelando pelle chiazzata e occhi selvaggi. "Muori, figlio di puttana" sibila, e puntando alla mia testa, preme il grilletto.

3 2

ATTERRO DOLOROSAMENTE SUL FIANCO, SBATTENDO LA TESTA contro il lato del divano, mentre un altro sparo risuona e uno spruzzo metallico e caldo mi colpisce sul viso e sul collo.

"Peter!" Terrorizzata per lui, mi metto in ginocchio, mi pulisco il sangue dagli occhi—e poi la vedo.

Mamma è distesa sul pavimento, con il viso imbrattato di sangue.

O meglio, gran parte del viso.

Le manca una parte della guancia e del cranio, con un buco insanguinato dove prima c'era uno zigomo.

La mia mente si spegne, un muro di torpore mi avvolge, quando un terzo sparo risuona.

Guardo mio marito, supino e sanguinante, poi l'agente sulla soglia, con il viso contorto dall'odio, mentre mira alla testa di Peter.

519

Il mio sguardo si posa sulla pistola che lui ha lasciato, mentre stava lottando contro l'altro agente.

È a meno di un metro di distanza.

Mi allungo e la raccolgo. È fredda e pesante nella mia mano, aggiungendosi al gelido torpore nel cuore.

I miei genitori sono morti.

Peter sta per essere ucciso.

Miro e premo il grilletto una frazione di secondo prima che l'agente faccia fuoco.

Il mio proiettile lo manca, ma il colpo di pistola lo fa sobbalzare, facendogli sbagliare il bersaglio.

Si gira verso di me e sparo di nuovo.

Lo colpisco nel bel mezzo del giubbotto antiproiettile, facendolo cadere all'indietro.

Senza alcuna esitazione, mi avvicino e sollevo di nuovo la pistola.

"Non—" si strozza, ansimando, e premo il grilletto.

La sua faccia esplode in mille pezzi di sangue e ossa. È come un videogioco iper-realistico, completo di odore, gusto e suono surround. Affascinata, getto la pistola e allungo la mano per vedere se è reale—

"Sara." La voce tesa di Peter mi raggiunge come attraverso l'acqua. "Guardami."

Sbattendo le palpebre, mi concentro sul suo corpo prono, e un po' del mio torpore svanisce, quando vedo la quantità di sangue che si accumula al suo fianco.

È ferito.

Gravemente.

Un'ondata di terrore cancella la foschia residua dal mio cervello, e crollo in ginocchio, tirandogli freneticamente la maglietta. Devo fermare il flusso di sangue, per vedere se il proiettile—

"Ptichka, fermati." Mi prende il polso con una forza sorprendente, con gli occhi che mi perforano. "Non c'è tempo.

Devi consegnarmi la pistola. Mettimela in mano. Non sei stata tu a fare questo, capito? E poi devi andartene. Allontanati il più possibile da me—"

"No." Mi libero della sua presa. "Non ti lascerò."

Ha bisogno di un ospedale, ma non c'è possibilità che gli agenti lo portino lì dopo questo massacro. Lo uccideranno sul posto per aver ammazzato così tanti di loro.

Innocente o colpevole, a loro non importerà.

"Ptichka, devi—"

"Alzati." Saltando in piedi, lo afferro per il braccio ferito, tirandolo con tutte le mie forze. "Dobbiamo andare, ora."

Non posso perderlo.

Non lo perderò.

Una smorfia fa contorcere il volto di Peter, mentre tenta di mettersi a sedere e fallisce. "Amore mio, devi—"

"Ora!" Ringhio, strattonandolo, e qualcosa riguardo al mio tono sembra raggiungerlo.

Con la mascella serrata, si mette a sedere, e io mi accovaccio per passargli il braccio intorno al tronco. È incredibilmente pesante, con il grande corpo duro, solido. La mia schiena e le gambe urlano per protestare, ma in qualche modo riesco ad alzarmi, sostenendo la maggior parte del suo peso.

"La macchina" si sforza di dire con voce roca. "Dobbiamo arrivare alla macchina."

La macchina.

Appena fuori, parcheggiata sul ciglio della strada.

Possiamo farlo.

Dobbiamo farlo.

Faccio un passo verso la porta, e improvvisamente, la maggior parte del peso di Peter non c'è più. Lanciandogli un'occhiata, noto che in qualche modo si sostiene da solo, anche se il viso è grigio sotto le macchie di sangue e sporco.

"La macchina. Vieni" esorto, mentre usciamo. "Ci siamo quasi. Un ultimo sforzo."

In lontananza, sento il rumore delle sirene e il rombo di un altro elicottero.

Stanno venendo a prenderci.

Stanno venendo per strappare Peter da me, proprio come mi hanno strappato i genitori.

"Le chiavi. Sono nella mia tasca" gracchia, e ringrazio il cielo, perché ricordo che esse sono tutto ciò di cui la nostra sofisticata Mercedes ha bisogno per partire.

Aprendo la portiera del passeggero, sistemo Peter all'interno, poi scatto verso il lato del guidatore. Il mio cuore sta battendo ad un ritmo nauseante, e mi tremano le mani, mentre avvio l'auto, mi immetto in strada e premo sull'acceleratore.

"Dove vado?" chiedo freneticamente, mentre sgommiamo dietro l'angolo sulla strada principale. I rumori dell'elicottero e delle sirene si fanno più forti; è solo questione di tempo, prima che si accorgano della nostra assenza e inizino ad inseguirci.

Nessuna risposta.

Gli rivolgo un'occhiata. È mezzo accasciato sul sedile, con il volto incolore e gli occhi chiusi, mentre tiene un pacco di tovaglioli di carta bagnati di sangue sul fianco.

Oh no. Oh, per favore, no.

"Peter." Gli scuoto il ginocchio.

Ancora niente.

"Peter, ti prego. Ho bisogno che tu mi dica dove andare."

Geme, mentre lo scuoto più forte, e i suoi occhi si aprono appena. "Casolare vicino a Horicon Marsh. Prendi la I-294 verso la 94, quindi prendi la 41 e la 33, svolta a destra sulla Palmatory e prosegui per quattro miglia. Strada sterrata a sinistra."

Oh, grazie a Dio.

Svolto bruscamente a destra verso l'autostrada e premo sull'acceleratore, mentre chiude gli occhi di nuovo. Sta perdendo troppo sangue, ma non posso fare nulla finché non lo porterò in salvo.

Se ci prendono, morirà.

La mia mente gira come una trottola, mentre percorro l'autostrada. Non riesco a pensare ai miei genitori o all'enormità di quello che è appena successo, quindi mi concentro sui perché.

Perché sono venuti a prenderlo?

Perché qualcuno ha sparato a quell'agente, quando Peter stava per arrendersi?

Ho creduto a mio marito, quando ha detto di non avere niente a che fare con l'attacco all'FBI, ma è possibile che mi abbia mentito? Sarebbero venuti ad arrestarlo in quel modo, se non ci fossero state prove che lo collegassero all'attentato?

La logica mi dice di no, ma non posso lasciarmi ingannare. Peter ha fatto cose terribili, ma non è un terrorista.

Morale a parte, quando uccide, lo fa con precisione e discrezione.

Allora, perché? Perché dovrebbero pensare che sia coinvolto? E chi ha sparato a quell'agente? Qualcuno della squadra di Peter è stato così stupido? Se è così, perché non ci hanno aiutato ulteriormente?

Se erano disposti ad uccidere un agente SWAT, perché lasciare che Peter combattesse gli altri da solo?

Niente di tutto ciò ha senso, ma soffermarmici mi impedisce di andare in iperventilazione al volante. Non posso pensare alle nostre infinitesimali probabilità di sopravvivenza o che mio marito potrebbe morire dissanguato.

O che la piccola vita dentro di me ora ha due fuggiaschi come genitori.

"Rallenta." Il sussurro rauco di Peter mi raggiunge, mentre mi avvicino ad una Toyota che va a centotrenta all'ora sulla corsia di sorpasso. "Non attirare l'attenzione accelerando. Dov'è il tuo telefono?"

Il cuore mi salta dalla gioia, mentre sollevo il piede dal gas.

Parlare fa bene.

Parlare fa molto bene.

"Niente telefono" rispondo, con una parte del sollievo che si affievolisce, quando lo guardo per trovarlo cosciente, ma ancora più pallido. "Ho dimenticato la mia borsa a—"

"Bene. Ciò significa che non possono monitorarci in quel modo."

Cazzo. Non ci avevo pensato.

"E il tuo telefono?"

Fa una smorfia, spostandosi sul sedile, mentre cerca altri tovaglioli di carta da un rotolo infilato al lato della portiera. "Non tracciabile."

"Ok." La mia mente corre. "Che cos'altro? Dovremmo liberarci della macchina? C'è qualcuno a cui possiamo chiedere aiuto? Le tue guardie del corpo? Possono—"

"No." Chiude di nuovo gli occhi, premendo i tovaglioli puliti al suo fianco. "Sarebbero troppo esposti. Non si metterebbero contro l'FBI."

Giusto. Ha senso. La nuova squadra di Peter non è composta da criminali; sono pagati per proteggerci dalle persone pericolose del suo passato, non per aiutarci a sfuggire alle autorità.

Il che significa che non possono esserci loro dietro quell'attentato.

"Peter..." Do un'occhiata, ma è di nuovo svenuto, con la testa che pende di lato.

Il ghiaccio mi gela le viscere. "Peter, svegliati. Devi dirmi cosa fare dopo."

Nessuna risposta, solo il martellante battito del mio polso nelle orecchie.

Allungo una mano per scuotergli il ginocchio, ma lui non reagisce, e vedo che non sta più stringendo i tovaglioli di carta, con la mano floscia al suo fianco.

La mia gabbia toracica sembra ridotta alle dimensioni di quella di un bambino, schiacciando tutti gli organi all'interno.

Non può essere vero.

Non può finire così.

"Peter." La mia voce si incrina. "Peter, per favore... ho bisogno di te. Non puoi farmi questo."

Non può morire e abbandonarmi. Non dopo aver combattuto così duramente per noi.

Non dopo avermi fatta innamorare.

"Svegliati, Peter." Scuoto il ginocchio più forte. "Ti prego, svegliati."

Ma non lo fa.

È troppo tardi.

Sara

SENTENDOMI COME SE LE PARETI DELL'AUTO SI STESSERO chiudendo su di me, gli afferro il polso e cerco il battito.

Lo sento.

Debole e irregolare, ma c'è.

Un sospiro di sollievo mi sfugge dalla gola e la strada davanti a me si offusca.

È ancora vivo.

Svenuto, ma vivo.

Con uno sforzo erculeo, mi ricompongo. Non posso lasciarmi andare, non quando c'è ancora un frammento di speranza.

Cominciamo dall'inizio. Devo medicare la ferita di Peter. Non può più aspettare. Poi, la macchina. Devo presumere che la stiano cercando, ed è solo una questione di tempo, prima che ci individuino sulla strada. Ciò significa che dovrò trovare un altro veicolo.

La domanda è come.

Se lui fosse cosciente, probabilmente potrebbe rubarne una, ma io non possiedo le sue abilità. Devo trovare un'altra soluzione, qualcosa che non ci rallenti troppo.

Il segnale di un'uscita appare più avanti, e mi rendo conto che siamo quasi arrivati all'ospedale Advocate Lutheran.

Il mio cuore salta un battito, poi accelera. Forse dovrei portarlo lì. Ora, prima che le autorità scoprano che siamo qui.

Prima che altri agenti SWAT compaiano e sparino a morte per aver ucciso così tanti dei loro, rivendicando la difesa personale.

Dovrebbero medicarlo al pronto soccorso, se lo portassi lì. Dovrebbero salvarlo. E una volta arrivati i poliziotti, non sarebbero in grado di ucciderlo con tutti quei testimoni in giro. Dovrebbero lasciarlo guarire, prima di portarlo via.

Prima di rinchiuderlo a Guantanamo o in qualche altro buco nero per il resto della sua vita.

Anche se si rivelasse innocente nell'attentato, non lo lascerebbero mai uscire—e prima o poi otterrebbero la loro vendetta.

Se porto Peter lì dentro, non lo rivedrò più. Ma se non lo faccio, morirà dissanguato.

Anche ora, potrebbe essere troppo tardi. Potrei perderlo come ho appena perso i miei genitori.

Scacciando la soffocante paura, mi avvio verso la corsia di uscita e prendo l'autostrada, dirigendomi verso l'ospedale. Quando arrivo lì, trovo un parcheggio sotto un albero, tra un SUV e un furgone.

"Dovremmo essere ben nascosti qui." Mi trema la voce, mentre mi rivolgo a lui. "Ora mi occuperò delle tue ferite, ok?"

Non risponde, ma non mi aspetto che lo faccia.

Raggiungendo il suo grembo, gli abbasso il sedile in una

posizione sdraiata. Poi, solleva la maglietta ed esamino la ferita da arma da fuoco sul fianco.

C'è un foro di uscita e, vista la posizione, ci sono buone probabilità che il proiettile abbia mancato gli organi vitali. Se disinfettassi la ferita e bloccassi il sanguinamento, potrebbe cavarsela senza ospedale.

Trattenendo il respiro, esamino rapidamente le altre parti. Trovo una pistola legata alla caviglia sinistra, ma non ci sono ferite, quindi la ignoro. Poi, scopro che un proiettile gli ha sfiorato il braccio sinistro e che un altro gli ha perforato il polpaccio destro.

Entrambe le ferite stanno ancora sanguinando, ma nessuna delle due sembra pericolosa per la vita.

Respiro, tremando, mentre gli stringo la mano floscia, sollevata.

So cosa fare ora.

Ho solo bisogno di un po' di fortuna dalla nostra parte.

Chinandomi su di lui, gli liscio i capelli incrostati di sangue. "Non lasciarmi, tesoro, per favore. Torno subito, lo prometto. Resisti."

Posso farcela.

Devo farcela.

Tirandomi indietro, mi metto dritta e abbasso lo specchietto per guardarmi. Come immaginavo, sono un disastro tanto quanto Peter, con il viso pallido e rigato dalle lacrime, con macchie e frammenti di sangue sulla pelle e sui vestiti.

Per fortuna il personale del pronto soccorso ha visto di peggio.

"Torno tra poco" sussurro, dandogli un'ultima stretta alla mano, e, saltando fuori dalla macchina, corro attraverso il parcheggio verso l'ingresso del pronto soccorso.

Nessuno fa caso a me, mentre entro, e tengo la testa bassa, evitando le telecamere negli angoli. Per quanto ne so, la mia foto non è ancora sulle cronache, ma è meglio non rischiare.

All'interno c'è il solito pandemonio, con diversi nuovi arrivati che assillano l'infermiera, chiedendo di essere visitati *immediatamente*, e una mezza dozzina di infermiere e medici raggruppati attorno a due pazienti sulla barella: uno che urla per il pasticcio sanguinante che è la sua gamba e l'altro nel bel mezzo di quello che sembra essere un attacco epilettico.

Sul retro è presente un ingresso riservato al personale. Le infermiere spingono lì il paziente urlante e io le seguo, fingendo di essere con lui. Un'infermiera cerca di allontanarmi, ma qualcuno urla per chiamarla, e lei scompare nel corridoio, dimenticandomi.

Seguo la barella senza che nessun altro se ne accorga, e quando passiamo accanto ad un ripostiglio, entro e chiudo la porta dietro di me.

Sul retro ci sono camici ripiegati, lenzuola, bende, campioni di medicinali e forniture di pronto soccorso. Mi cambio rapidamente i vestiti e indosso un camice infermieristico, pulisco più sangue possibile dal viso con una federa, e ripongo qualsiasi cosa ritenga utile in una borsa improvvisata con un lenzuolo. Poi, copro la mia roba con altre lenzuola ammucchiate e mi dirigo fuori, facendo finta di portare lenzuola sporche da lavare.

Nessuno dice niente, mentre passo di nuovo davanti alla zona reception del pronto soccorso e mi dirigo verso l'uscita, assicurandomi che il pacco tra le mie braccia mi copra il volto dalle telecamere che lampeggiano negli angoli.

Tornando alla macchina, trovo Peter ancora incosciente.

"Va tutto bene, sono qui ora" dico, mentre metto il fagotto con le scorte ai suoi piedi. "Andrà tutto bene."

Non può sentirmi, ma non importa.

È me stessa che sto cercando di convincere.

È troppo pesante per poterlo spogliare correttamente, così gli tiro su la manica e gli taglio la gamba dei jeans per raggiungere quelle ferite. Tra i miei rifornimenti rubati ci sono un sapone delicato e una soluzione salina, e li mescolo con dell'acqua per lavare via tutto il sangue e lo sporco vicino alle ferite. Contrariamente alla saggezza popolare, è una cattiva idea usare forti antisettici per pulirle; lo sfregamento dell'alcol e simili potrebbero danneggiare il tessuto e rallentare il processo di guarigione.

Quando sono soddisfatta che le ferite siano sufficientemente pulite e che non rimangano frammenti di proiettili all'interno, ricucio e fascio, iniziando dalla ferita sul fianco. Mentre lavoro, ringrazio il mio tirocinio al pronto soccorso e tutte le vittime di armi da fuoco che ho curato lì.

Tuttavia, mi tremano le mani, quando ho finito, e mi rendo conto che l'adrenalina sta cominciando a svanire.

Questo non va bene.

C'è ancora molto da fare prima di mollare.

"Devo allontanarmi ancora per qualche minuto, ok? Quindi, resisti, tesoro" sussurro, accarezzando il viso di Peter. Chinandomi, lo bacio dolcemente sulla dura mascella e mi allontano, ripetendomi che tutto ciò di cui ho bisogno ora è un po' di fortuna.

Un po' di fortuna e un sacco di palle.

Le mie gambe sono instabili, mentre mi dirigo verso il pronto soccorso. Questa è la parte meno sicura del mio piano, una che fa affidamento su troppi fattori esterni. A questo punto, i nostri volti potrebbero essere apparsi su tutti i notiziari, con la caccia all'uomo in pieno regime. Basterebbe un ficcanaso sconosciuto, e uno sciame di polizia/FBI sarebbe su di noi.

Forse questo è un errore.

Forse dovrei solo tornare in macchina e guidare, pregando che per miracolo nessuno abbia emesso un avviso di ricerca sul nostro veicolo.

Sto per tornare indietro e fare esattamente quello, quando una Toyota blu vecchio modello si ferma nel parcheggio, proprio davanti all'ingresso. "Aiuto!" grida una donna anziana, aprendo la portiera, e mi precipito verso di lei, aiutandola a far scendere il marito semi-cosciente.

A giudicare dal suo aspetto, ha appena avuto un ictus.

Due infermiere corrono fuori dal pronto soccorso per aiutare, e io mi allontano con discrezione, lasciando che si occupino del paziente e della sua nervosa moglie. La macchina è stata lasciata incustodita, la portiera del conducente è aperta, e quando sbircio all'interno, noto le chiavi nell'accensione.

Bingo.

Lo staff del pronto soccorso di solito manda qualcuno a spostare il veicolo in tali situazioni, ma se escono fuori e non lo trovano, molto probabilmente penseranno che sia già stato spostato da qualcuno.

Non denunceranno il furto dell'auto fin quando la moglie del paziente non tornerà e non riuscirà a trovarla.

Mi sento male, mentre mi sistemo dietro al volante e guido la Toyota verso la nostra macchina. Posso solo immaginare quanto sarà stressata la povera donna, quando avrà a che fare con un'auto rubata in aggiunta all'ictus di suo marito. Ma non c'è altra scelta—non quando la vita di Peter è in pericolo.

Parcheggio la Toyota proprio davanti alla nostra Mercedes, salto giù e mi affretto verso la nostra macchina. Aprendo la portiera del passeggero, guardo mio marito, chiedendomi come farò a spostare quasi cento chili di maschio incosciente da una macchina all'altra.

Oh beh, dovrò farlo.

Afferrando le sue caviglie, tiro con tutte le mie forze.

Si muove di un centimetro. Forse.

Fanculo.

Spingo con la schiena, puntando i tacchi nell'asfalto.

Altri tre centimetri.

Forse dovrei abbandonare questa stupida idea e guidare la nostra macchina. La moglie della vittima dell'ictus sarà felice, quando troverà la sua Toyota nel parcheggio e—

Mio marito emette un basso gemito.

Il mio impulso scatta. "Peter." Salgo in macchina, chinandomi su di lui. "Peter, tesoro, svegliati, ti prego."

Borbotta qualcosa di incoerente, girando la testa di lato.

"Per favore, ho bisogno di te." Lo scuoto dolcemente. "Ti prego, svegliati."

Apre gli occhi, offuscati.

"Ecco, tesoro." Il mio respiro si blocca per un gioioso sollievo. "Puoi farcela. Guardami."

Sbatte le palpebre, con lo sguardo che si concentra lentamente su di me. "Sara? Che cosa—"

"Siamo nel parcheggio di un ospedale" dico velocemente. "Ho trovato una macchina, ma non posso spostarti senza il tuo aiuto. Puoi camminare fin lì?"

Serra la mascella, ma annuisce.

"Bene, facciamolo. Vieni." Porto il sedile in posizione seduta e lo aiuto a scendere dall'auto. È instabile sui piedi, appoggiato pesantemente sulle mie spalle, ma in qualche modo, ce la facciamo.

Il suo viso è bianco verdastro, quando lo aiuto a salire in macchina, ma cerca di rimanere cosciente con ogni brandello della sua volontà di ferro. "Le armi" gracchia, crollando pesantemente sul sedile del passeggero. "Sotto il sedile posteriore. Prendile."

Abbiamo delle armi?

Non sono nemmeno minimamente sorpresa come dovrei.

Lasciando Peter nella Toyota, torno indietro e cerco di sollevare il sedile posteriore della Mercedes. Ci vuole un po' di ingegno, ma alla fine riesco ad aprirlo—e resto a bocca aperta davanti all'arsenale interno.

Oltre a pistole e fucili d'assalto, ci sono granate e quello che sembra un lanciarazzi.

Non riuscirò mai a portare tutto senza che qualcuno mi individui e faccia scattare un allarme.

Poi, mi viene un'idea.

Afferrando le scorte di pronto soccorso, corro indietro e le metto sul sedile posteriore della Toyota, poi tiro via le lenzuola da sotto e torno verso la Mercedes. Le armi sono pesanti, quindi devo fare tre viaggi separati, ma trasferisco tutto sulla Toyota—avvolto nelle lenzuola.

"Ecco fatto" dico a Peter, mentre mi sistemo al volante, ansimando per lo sforzo, ma non c'è risposta.

È svenuto di nuovo.

Mi chino e reclino il suo sedile, sia per lasciarlo riposare, sia per non renderlo visibile attraverso i finestrini.

Poi, facendo un respiro profondo, esco dal parcheggio e mi dirigo verso il casolare.

ara

Ricordando il monito di Peter riguardo all'eccesso di velocità, guido attentamente, rispettando tutte le regole del traffico e i limiti. Il suo telefono è bloccato e non riesco a svegliarlo, quindi uso una combinazione di segnali stradali e la mia vaga conoscenza della zona per raggiungere la strada sterrata che ha menzionato.

Non penso ai miei genitori o all'uomo che ho ucciso così spietatamente. Non posso—non quando ho bisogno di essere lucida. Così, mi concentro per arrivare a destinazione senza fermarci. Nel momento in cui svoltiamo nel bosco, la mia vescica è sul punto di esplodere, così vado dietro un albero, in stile campeggio. L'anziana signora ha tenuto una bottiglietta di disinfettante per le mani in macchina, e la uso prima di riprendere la guida, cercando di non pensare a cosa accadrà una volta che saremo effettivamente nel casolare.

Nonostante i miei migliori sforzi, domande pericolose mi affollano la testa.

Che cosa faremo se le ferite di Peter si infettano?

Ci saranno cibo e acqua nel casolare?

E, soprattutto, quanto tempo ci vorrà?

Perché ci troveranno. Non posso ingannare me stessa credendo diversamente. Siamo stati fortunati finora, ma non possiamo eludere l'FBI. Perlomeno, *io* non posso. Peter è riuscito ad evitare la cattura per anni con l'aiuto delle sue connessioni nella malavita.

Non mi sono mai pentita di non avere dei criminali nella mia cerchia sociale, ma ora lo faccio. Nessuno dei miei amici o conoscenti può aiutarci—non senza avere problemi con la legge. Infatti, oltre a mio marito, le uniche persone che conosco e che hanno le competenze e i contatti giusti sono i suoi ex compagni di squadra russi, ma sono lontani e—

Aspetta un attimo.

Ho l'e-mail di Yan.

È così che si è congratulato con me per il nostro matrimonio.

Il mio battito salta di nuovo, con l'emozione che sfrigola nelle vene, prima che ricordi un fatto importante.

Non ho modo di inviare un messaggio di posta elettronica senza utilizzare il telefono di Peter, e per questo, ho bisogno che mio marito riprenda conoscenza e inserisca la password.

Gli lancio un'occhiata, con il petto che si stringe notando il pallore grigio sul suo volto. Dovrebbe stare in un ospedale, con una flebo che gli fornisca antibiotici per reintegrare i liquidi, non a sobbalzare su una strada piena di buche.

Se muore, sarà stata colpa mia.

Sarà così, perché ho scelto di nasconderlo alle autorità invece di portarlo all'ospedale.

Un cartello con la scritta "Proprietà Privata" appare in lontananza, con una recinzione su ogni lato e un cancello di legno che blocca la strada. Dev'essere la nostra destinazione, a meno che non abbia optato per l'uscita sbagliata in precedenza.

Fermo la macchina e scendo per aprire il cancello. Solo che una catena con un lucchetto lo tiene bloccato. Strattono la serratura arrugginita, incapace di credere che dopo tutto potremmo essere ostacolati da qualcosa di così stupido.

Cercando di contenere la frustrazione, torno alla macchina e provo a scuotere Peter per svegliarlo. Potrebbe avere una chiave nascosta da qualche parte che non conosco.

Non reagisce, nonostante le mie suppliche, e quando sento la sua fronte, la trovo calda e umida.

Il mio stomaco si contorce dolorosamente.

La febbre così presto non promette nulla di buono.

Con mani tremanti, lo tocco dappertutto, sperando che abbia una chiave nascosta in una delle tasche. Ma non trovo altro che il suo telefono e la pistola legata alla caviglia.

Esausta, mi siedo a terra dal lato passeggero della macchina.

Non ho speranze.

Non so come fare.

A cosa stavo pensando, quando ho deciso di giocare a fare la fuggitiva? Peter è quello con la conoscenza e le capacità, non io. Non riesco nemmeno a superare uno stupido cancello. Al mio posto, probabilmente prenderebbe la serratura e la farebbe esplodere o—

Certo, è così.

Devo pensare al di fuori del riquadro della correttezza.

Saltando in piedi, infilo la cintura di sicurezza a Peter e torno al posto di guida.

Scivolando dietro al volante, faccio la retromarcia finché non siamo a una cinquantina di metri dal cancello, e poi premo sull'acceleratore a tavoletta.

La Toyota scatta in avanti.

Colpiamo il cancello a novanta chilometri all'ora, staccando il legno invecchiato dai cardini.

Il parabrezza si spezza a causa di un pezzo di cancello che vi si schianta contro, ma nessun airbag si attiva, e spingo sul freno, sogghignando trionfalmente, mentre continuiamo lungo la strada ad una velocità più moderata.

Sara, 1. Cancello stupido, 0.

Lancio un'occhiata per controllare Peter, e la mia ebbrezza svanisce, quando vedo una nuova macchia di sangue che si allarga sulla sua maglietta, nella zona del fianco.

I punti di sutura devono essersi strappati, sia per l'impatto con il cancello sia per la guida irregolare.

Devo portarlo in quel casolare, così potrò medicarlo come si deve.

Il tragitto sembra infinito, anche se realisticamente so che non può essere più di un miglio.

Alla fine, la vedo.

Un casolare di legno circondato da alberi.

Sollevata, corro verso la costruzione.

Sorpresa, sorpresa.

La porta d'ingresso è chiusa a chiave.

Questa volta, però, sono preparata. Afferrando una grossa roccia, mi avvicino alla finestra e la colpisco più forte che posso. Si frantuma, con le schegge di vetro che volano dappertutto, e uso la roccia per eliminare le punte affilate del vetro rimasto. Poi, entro dentro, ignorando il sangue che mi cola lungo le braccia.

Mi occuperò delle mie ferite in seguito. In questo momento, la mia priorità è Peter.

Camminando verso la porta d'ingresso, la sblocco ed esco, tormentandomi il cervello per come farò a spostarlo dentro. Sarebbe fantastico, se si svegliasse di nuovo e usasse quell'impossibile forza di volontà per camminare, ma non trattengo il respiro data la sua precedente mancanza di reattività. Forse posso farlo rotolare sul lenzuolo e poi tirarlo dentro, oppure—

Il mio sguardo cade su un'antica carriola. È appoggiata contro la casa accanto ad un'ascia arrugginita.

Dev'essere lì per trasportare la legna tagliata.

Cammino e sollevo i manici, poi esamino la carriola facendola rotolare avanti e indietro. Le ruote scricchiolano, ma sembrano funzionanti.

La spingo fino alla macchina e la giro in modo che i manici siano appoggiati all'interno della porta aperta, sul pavimento. Poi, afferro le caviglie di Peter e affondo i talloni nel terreno, tirando con tutte le mie forze.

Si muove di un paio di centimetri.

Stringendo i denti, tiro di nuovo.

Poi ancora.

E ancora.

Quando è per metà sulla carriola, vado al lato del guidatore e lo spingo verso di essa, con il cuore che mi duole, mentre si lamenta per il dolore. "Ancora un po', tesoro" prometto dolcemente, e con un'ultima spinta, lo rotolo sulla carriola.

Il primo passo è riuscito.

Ora devo portarlo in casa e metterlo su un letto.

IL MIO MONDO È FUOCO E DOLORE, MESCOLATO AD UNA VOCE delicata e a delle mani rilassanti. La sofferenza è insopportabile, ma quando quella voce è vicina e quelle dita fresche e morbide mi accarezzano la fronte bollente, dimentico tutto.

Mi concentro solo su di lei.

Ed è lei. Sara, la mia ptichka. Lo so anche nel profondo del mio delirio. Qualunque cosa mi stia succedendo, lei è lì, che mi tocca, mi parla, mi fa bere dei sorsi d'acqua. Spesso mi chiede alcune cose, con una voce melodiosa che si riempie di disperazione e mi supplica, ma non posso risponderle, non posso fare altro che girare la testa verso quella voce e accettare il fugace conforto offerto dal suo tocco.

Si arrende dopo un po', il suo tono si fa rassegnato, e questo mi piace di più, anche se non tanto come quando mi sussurra, con la voce dolce e gentile come i baci che mi dà sulle labbra screpolate e in fiamme.

Mi fanno sentire bene, quei baci—almeno finché non sprofondo nell'oscurità e arrivano i demoni, avvolgendomi i loro tentacoli attorno al petto, pugnalandomi con i loro attizzatoi incandescenti. Il mio fianco, il mio braccio, il mio polpaccio—sono spietati mentre mi feriscono, bruciando la mia carne fino all'osso.

Anche Pasha è lì, con mezzo cranio mancante, con il cervello grottesco sotto le lucide onde dei suoi capelli scuri. "Papà!" grida, saltando su di me, spingendo più a fondo gli attizzatoi infuocati fino al cuore.

"Per favore, Peter, resta con me" implora la voce di Sara, e mi aggrappo ad essa, combattendo i demoni nelle tenebre, lottando contro la loro presa.

Seguono altri baci. Le sue labbra sono fresche e umide, stranamente salate. Come le lacrime. Tutte quelle lacrime che le ho fatto versare. Ma perché sta piangendo di nuovo? Non voglio. Voglio immergermi nelle sue cure, assorbire il suo amore, non le sue lacrime. Aveva combattuto contro di me, ma ora è mia. Mia da custodire e proteggere. Solo che non posso fare altro che bruciare, con il fuoco che mi divora, mi consuma, mi annebbia la mente con il dolore.

"Per favore, tesoro. Dimmi la password. Devo sbloccare il telefono."

Le parole dovrebbero avere un senso, ma non ce l'hanno, con i suoni che mi rimbalzano nel cervello come la luce del sole su un lago.

"Papà, vuoi vedere il mio camion?" Pasha torna a saltare su di me, con i piccoli piedi come una palla da demolizione che sbatte contro il mio fianco. "Vuoi vederlo, Papà?"

Apro la bocca per rispondere, ma i tentacoli del demone mi avvolgono il collo, soffocandomi con un laccio di fuoco.

"Per favore, tesoro..." Due mani tenere mi accarezzano il viso e la gola, raffreddando la bruciatura all'interno. "Ti prego, ho bisogno che tu mi dia la password, così posso chiedere aiuto."

"Papà. Papà. Gioca con me."

"La password, Peter, ti supplico. È la nostra unica possibilità."

"Non andartene, Papà."

"Per favore, tesoro. Ho bisogno di te. Il nostro bambino ha bisogno di te."

"Ti prego, Papà. Sarò buono. Lo prometto, Papà. Sarò buono."

Il dolore è insopportabile. Mi sento come se fossi spezzato a metà, con i tentacoli infuocati che si trasformano in fruste, mentre cado più in profondità nell'oscurità.

"Resta con me, Peter. Ti prego, tesoro..." L'umidità salata ritorna sulle mie labbra, con la voce che mi tira su, proteggendomi dai demoni. "Ti amo, e non posso farcela senza di te. Per favore... non posso perdere anche te."

Qualcosa danza sulla punta della mia lingua, qualcosa di importante che devo ricordare. Qualcosa di cui la mia ptichka ha bisogno.

Quattro numeri fluttuano nella mia coscienza e li afferro con sforzo.

È un compleanno.

Il compleanno del mio amico Andrey.

L'avevamo sempre festeggiato in quell'orribile campo.

"Zero, sei, uno, cinque" sussurro—o ci provo. La mia lingua non vuole obbedire. Ci riprovo, con tutta la forza residua. "Nol' shest' ahdeen pyat'. Ptichka, passvord den' rozhden'ye Andreya."

Sara

TREMANDO, MI ALZO, MENTRE PETER SI SCAGLIA IN UNA FEBBRILE serie di frasi in russo, borbottando parole sconosciute inframezzate dal nome di suo figlio, e lo sta facendo da ore. Nonostante i miei migliori sforzi, le sue condizioni stanno rapidamente peggiorando e so che se non metterò antibiotici più forti nel suo organismo, non ce la farà.

La penicillina che ho rubato all'ospedale non può fare più di tanto.

Le pareti di legno ondeggiano intorno a me, mentre cammino verso il lavandino e ritorno con un asciugamano fresco e umido—l'unica cosa che sembra aiutarlo. Sedendomi sul bordo del letto, glielo passo suo viso, sul collo e sul petto, asciugando il sudore appiccicoso. Il mio braccio trema per la stanchezza, con gli occhi che bruciano per le lacrime, ma non mi fermo.

Non posso—non finché ci sarà ancora un frammento di speranza.

Mi fa male tutto il corpo, con la schiena a pezzi per lo sforzo di aver trasferito Peter dalla carriola su questo letto. È mezzanotte passata, e l'unica cosa che ho mangiato è stata la solitaria lattina di minestra di pollo che ho trovato nella credenza un'ora fa. Ho provato a farlo mangiare, ma ha ingoiato solo due sorsi. Così, ho mandato giù io il resto. Non per me, ma per il bambino.

Il bambino di Peter ha bisogno dei nutrienti.

La zuppa non aveva molte calorie, ma mi ha fornito un po' di energia—abbastanza da indurmi di nuovo a convincerlo a darmi la password.

Ho fallito, come le precedenti venti volte, ma è sembrato almeno capirmi in questo tentativo. Ha mormorato "ptichka" e ha detto qualcosa su una password con un forte accento russo. O forse l'ha proprio pronunciato in russo. Per quel che ne so, è la stessa parola in entrambe le lingue.

La mia vista si offusca di nuovo a causa delle lacrime. È stato un errore venire qui. Non avrei dovuto correre questo rischio. Anche in un ospedale, le ferite da arma da fuoco sono soggette a complicazioni e, data la quantità di sangue che Peter ha perso e il luogo in cui ho dovuto curarlo, l'infezione era quasi inevitabile.

Se l'avessi portato in ospedale, avrebbe perso la libertà, ma avrebbe potuto sopravvivere.

"Scusa" sussurro, premendo le labbra sulla sua fronte calda. Il suo corpo sta combattendo l'infezione, cercando di avere la meglio. "Mi dispiace così tanto per questo. Per tutto."

Ed è vero. Mi dispiace non aver confessato prima il mio amore per lui, aver resistito al suo per così tanto tempo. All'epoca sembrava importante non cedere ai miei sentimenti per l'assassino di George. Sembrava etico e giusto. Ma ora vedo la mia resistenza per quello che è stata.

Codardia.

Avevo paura di innamorarmi di Peter, ero terrorizzata di arrendermi e amarlo. Pietrificata che se lo avessi lasciato entrare nel mio cuore, lo avrei perso.

Come ho perso George, quando ha cominciato a bere.

Come sapevo che avrei inevitabilmente perso i miei genitori.

Altre lacrime mi rigano il viso, bruciandomi la gola. Questa è una preoccupazione che non ho più bisogno di avere.

Sono morti.

Il peggio è passato.

Non riesco ancora a soffermarmi su quello che è successo, non riesco ad elaborare l'orrore di aver visto il cervello di mia madre esplodere davanti a me—e poi aver premuto il grilletto. Non ho avuto alcuna esitazione, non provo alcun rimorso per aver ucciso l'agente che aveva sparato a mamma—solo quel terribile torpore. È come se qualcuno si fosse impossessato del mio corpo, qualcuno spietato, freddo... e potente.

Accidenti, mi sono sentita così potente.

È così anche per Peter? Quando uccide, spegne la parte di se stesso che lo rende umano, abbracciando quella scarica di potere? Mi sono sempre chiesta come facesse qualcuno con una capacità così profonda di amare a strappare una vita senza rimorsi, ma ora lo capisco.

Siamo tutti mostri sotto la superficie. Solo che alcuni di noi non hanno mai la possibilità di scoprirlo.

Le sue labbra screpolate si muovono, e io raggiungo una scodella d'acqua. Immergendo un asciugamano pulito, gli cospargo il liquido sulla bocca, attenta a spremerlo goccia a goccia così da non farlo strozzare. La febbre che imperversa nel suo corpo lo sta disidratando, uccidendolo davanti ai miei occhi, e non c'è nulla che io possa fare.

Anche se volessi portarlo all'ospedale, non sopravvivrebbe ad un viaggio di ritorno su quella strada sterrata e accidentata—

e senza poter accedere al suo telefono, non posso chiamare o mandare un'e-mail per chiedere aiuto da qui. Né posso guidare da qualche parte per farlo.

Non posso lasciarlo da solo in queste condizioni.

Sta di nuovo borbottando, muovendo la testa da una parte all'altra dall'agitazione, mentre ripete una frase in russo. Sembra quella che stava dicendo prima, quando pensavo che avrebbe potuto capirmi.

"Nol' shest' ahdeen pyat'. Den' rozhden'ye Andreya, ptichka." La sua voce roca è appena udibile. "Nol' shest' ahdeen pyat'."

Chinandomi su di lui, premo la fronte contro la sua. "Che cosa significa, tesoro?" sussurro, stringendo gli occhi per un nuovo afflusso di lacrime. "Che cosa stai cercando di dirmi?"

C'è qualcosa di vagamente familiare in quella frase o almeno nelle singole parole. Le conosco? Mi sforzo di ricordare ciò che mi hanno insegnato i compagni di squadra di Peter in Giappone. *Spasibo*—significa "grazie" in russo. *Vkusno*—significa "delizioso." Ilya mi ha anche detto i nomi di certi cibi, e Anton ha iniziato ad insegnarmi l'alfabeto e a contare fino a dieci—

Mi metto a sedere, elettrizzata. Ecco! Ecco perché alcune di quelle parole sembrano familiari.

Sono numeri in russo.

"Peter, tesoro, questa è la password?" La mia voce trema, mentre mi chino di nuovo su di lui, lisciandogli i capelli bagnati di sudore. "Mi stai dicendo come sbloccare il tuo telefono in russo?"

Non sembra sentirmi, con l'agitazione che si attenua, mentre sprofonda sempre più nell'incoscienza. Cercando di calmarmi, provo a ricordare le parole specifiche che ha pronunciato e il conteggio fino a dieci in russo. Ha un ritmo quasi musicale, se ricordo bene. *Ahdeen, dva, tree*, eccetera...

Ok, allora. Quindi, *ahdeen* è uno, e sono abbastanza sicura che Peter l'abbia detto.

Era la terza parola, dopo qualcosa che suonava come "null" e "jest."

Mi tormento il cervello, cercando di ricordare come Anton pronunciasse il resto dei numeri. *Ahdeen, dva, tree...* era *chet*-qualcosa? *pet*-qualcosa?...

No, cinque era *pyat'*—che è quello che Peter ha detto come ultima parola.

Cerco di sopprimere l'entusiasmo, ma il mio cuore sta battendo in modo incontrollabile. Ancora non conosco due dei numeri, ma posso azzardare un'ipotesi su uno di essi.

Alcune parole russe sono simili all'inglese, il che significa che "null" potrebbe significare "zero."

Ok, quindi. Zero, sconosciuto, uno, cinque—sono tre su quattro. Posso indovinare il numero sconosciuto... se il telefono di Peter non si blocca per i troppi tentativi sbagliati, voglio dire.

Saltando su, afferro il telefono e, mentre inizio a inserire lo zero, tutti e dieci i numeri appaiono.

Ahdeen, dva, tree, chetyre, pyat', shest', sem', vosem', devyat', desyat'.

Posso quasi sentire la voce di Anton recitarli per me.

Trattenendo il respiro, aggiungo allo zero sei, uno e cinque.

Henderson

LA MIA MANO SPAZZA VIA TUTTO, FACENDO CADERE I CAVALLI DI porcellana che costellano lo scaffale—i ridicoli oggetti della collezione di Bonnie, che lei insiste a trascinare con noi in tutto il mondo. Si frantumano con uno schianto soddisfacente, ma ciò non basta a calmare la rabbia che brucia dentro di me.

Non ancora localizzato.

Le parole sullo schermo del mio computer mi scherniscono, deridendomi.

La caccia all'uomo è in corso, ma il fuggiasco non è stato ancora localizzato, mi informa l'e-mail da parte del mio contatto della CIA.

Come cazzo è possibile?

Come hanno fatto a fuggire?

Secondo gli agenti SWAT sopravvissuti allo scontro a fuoco, Sokolov era stato colpito almeno due volte—e c'è un video che mostra sua moglie intenta a rubare alcune scorte da un ospedale, quindi doveva essere rimasto ferito abbastanza gravemente per rischiare di fermarsi lì. Eppure, non c'è traccia di loro da nessuna parte—né della macchina che lei ha rubato nello stesso ospedale, anche se la polizia pensa che potrebbero essere in grado di rintracciarla a breve.

Bastardi incompetenti. Non sarebbe dovuta andare in questo modo. Sokolov avrebbe dovuto essere ucciso durante l'arresto.

Quella fottuta troia, Mink, è stata pagata bene per garantirlo.

Se Sokolov uscirà dal Paese, è solo questione di tempo, prima che capisca cos'è successo e venga a cercare me e la mia famiglia—e non posso permettere che ciò accada.

Dev'essere ucciso durante la cattura, ma per quello, dev'essere prima trovato.

Piegando il collo da un lato all'altro per alleviare il dolore, compongo un'e-mail di risposta per il mio contatto.

È ora che espandano la rete coinvolgendo l'Interpol e tutto il resto.

38

S ara

CAMMINO AVANTI E INDIETRO DENTRO AL CASOLARE SU GAMBE instabili, lanciando un'occhiata alla finestra rotta ogni cinque secondi. Fuori è buio pesto, il silenzio interrotto solo dai soliti rumori della foresta.

Comunque, continuo a guardare, continuo ad ascoltare gli eventuali elicotteri della polizia.

Sono passate quasi sedici ore da quando ho rubato la macchina dall'ospedale. Ormai, la sua proprietaria l'avrà scoperto e segnalato alla polizia. Se hanno scoperto la nostra Mercedes nel parcheggio—e sarei scioccata se non l'avessero fatto—ogni agente delle forze dell'ordine della zona ora starà cercando la Toyota blu e i fuggiaschi.

È solo questione di tempo, prima che trovino il nostro casolare.

Se Yan non arriverà presto, sarà stato tutto inutile.

Guardo di nuovo il telefono, rileggendo la sua e-mail per la quindicesima volta. Dovrei conservare la batteria, ma non posso farci niente. Le due parole sullo schermo sono l'unica cosa che mi fa andare avanti.

Sto arrivando.

Questo è tutto ciò che Yan ha risposto, quando gli ho mandato un'e-mail spiegando la nostra situazione e l'ubicazione. Chiaramente sa cosa sta succedendo, perché ha risposto in meno di un minuto.

Sto arrivando. Questo è tutto. Nessun dettaglio, nemmeno un tempo stimato. Non so se sarà qui tra pochi minuti, ore o giorni.

Per quel che ne so, potrebbe anche impiegare settimane.

Mi era balenata nella testa un'altra dolorosa idea, quando avevo sbloccato il telefono: chiamare il 911 per assicurare a Peter l'attenzione medica di cui ha tanto bisogno. Ma poi ho optato per contattare Yan e continuare con questa follia fuggiasca. Alla fine, ho seguito il mio istinto—e quando ho guardato il browser del telefono, dopo aver ricevuto la risposta di Yan, sono stata contenta di averlo fatto.

I nostri volti sono fissi sui notiziari, sia il mio che quello di Peter. Tutti i media, minori e importanti, stanno analizzando le nostre vite online, gli articoli diffondono costantemente nuovi dettagli sul nostro matrimonio e speculazioni sulla nostra relazione. In alcuni, sono stata definita una vittima del lavaggio del cervello; in altri, sono stata complice fin dall'inizio. Quando si parla di lui, tuttavia, non c'è ambiguità.

In ogni storia, è il cattivo.

"Mi ha rivelato che le aveva ucciso il primo marito" ha affermato Marsha secondo *The Chicago Tribune*. "Che l'aveva torturata e inseguita prima di rapirla. Era sparita per mesi, e quando è tornata, era completamente incasinata. Deve averla davvero rovinata, facendole il lavaggio del cervello in qualche modo. Perché quando si è rifatto vivo, lo ha sposato. Nel giro di pochi giorni. Sara ha negato che fosse lui—aveva cambiato il cognome in qualche modo—ma non potevano ingannarmi. Ho sempre sospettato la verità."

Anche i miei compagni di band sono stati intervistati. "È saltato fuori dal nulla" ha affermato Phil secondo il *New York Times*. "Per mesi, l'abbiamo tutti conosciuta come una vedova timida e riservata, e poi improvvisamente ha sposato questo misterioso russo. Ha detto che si frequentavano in segreto, ma ho sempre pensato che ci fosse di più in quella storia. E lui era così possessivo con lei. Pericolosamente possessivo. Nel senso che non avrebbe esitato a uccidere chiunque l'avesse guardata un secondo più del necessario. Aveva quest'aura letale."

Leggo questi articoli, cercando la menzione di qualsiasi prova specifica che colleghi Peter al bombardamento, ma non c'è niente—né c'è qualcosa riguardo al suo reale background e alle sue motivazioni.

Alcuni giornalisti affermano che si tratti di una spia russa e che l'attentato sia stata la risposta non ufficiale di Putin alle sanzioni. Altri ipotizzano che Peter sia un assassino della mafia russa e che l'attentato abbia avuto a che fare con un'indagine in corso. Anche George è menzionato, come un coraggioso giornalista la cui storia sulla mafia russa lo ha portato all'omicidio.

Non c'è niente sul piccolo villaggio di Daryevo o sulla famiglia di Peter, nemmeno una sola parola sul terribile errore che ha portato alla loro morte.

Alcuni articoli parlano della morte dei miei genitori e delle reazioni dei loro vicini alla sparatoria, ma non riesco a leggerli. Ogni volta che ci provo, mi si chiude la gola e il cuore inizia a battere ad un ritmo irregolare. L'orrore e il dolore sono troppo intensi, troppo freschi—come la colpa che mi fa contorcere lo stomaco.

Ho deluso i miei genitori, non sono riuscita a proteggerli dall'oscurità che ho portato nelle loro vite, e non posso ancora affrontarlo, non più di quanto possa immaginare un mondo senza di loro.

È più facile ignorare tutto, chiuderlo a chiave e concentrarsi sul sopravvivere attimo dopo attimo—preoccuparsi della persona che amo, che è ancora viva.

Fermandomi, mi siedo sul bordo del letto di Peter e sento la sua fronte. È ancora calda, mentre il corpo sta combattendo l'infezione che sta facendo sì che la ferita al suo fianco sembri rossa e infiammata.

Gli cambio le bende, poi schiaccio la prossima dose di penicillina in polvere e gliela fornisco con cura insieme ad una cucchiaiata d'acqua. Reagisce appena, ma riesco ad infilargli la maggior parte delle medicine giù per la gola. Non è abbastanza —ha bisogno di roba molto più forte—ma è il massimo che possa fare per ora.

"Resisti, tesoro" sussurro, facendo scorrere un asciugamano umido sul suo viso per rinfrescarlo. "L'aiuto sta arrivando. Resisti e andrà tutto bene."

Dev'essere così.

Non posso sopportare di pensare diversamente.

STO ANNUENDO ACCANTO A PETER, QUANDO LA PORTA SI APRE con un forte scricchiolio.

L'esplosione di adrenalina è così forte che sono in piedi, prima ancora di poter riflettere sul suono. "Che cosa—"

"Siamo solo noi" dice Ilya, varcando la porta con Yan. "Dobbiamo andare. Adesso."

Mi rendo conto che sto ansimando, con una mano premuta sul cuore selvaggiamente martellante. "Siete qui. Siete venuti."

Yan incombe già su Peter. "Aiutami" ordina al fratello gemello, e Ilya si precipita. Insieme, sollevano Peter dal letto e lo portano velocemente fuori dal casolare.

Il mio cervello si accende in ritardo, e prendo le scorte di pronto soccorso, poi li inseguo.

Fuori c'è un SUV scuro con i fari spenti, ma con il motore acceso. "Sali dietro con lui" mi dà istruzioni Yan, mentre lui e Ilya sistemano Peter sul sedile posteriore, per poi sedersi nei posti anteriori.

Mi affretto ad obbedire. "Ci sono alcune armi nella Toyota" dico senza fiato, mentre Yan si mette al volante. "Dovremmo prenderle o..."

"Non c'è tempo" spiega Ilya, mentre Yan preme sull'acceleratore e la macchina scatta in avanti. "Se non riusciremo a uscire dallo spazio aereo degli Stati Uniti prima delle otto del mattino, abbatteranno il nostro aereo."

Faccio un respiro profondo e mi zittisco, cercando di proteggere Peter dagli scossoni. È sdraiato sul sedile posteriore con la testa sulle mie ginocchia, e con ogni buca che colpiamo alla massima velocità, sono terrorizzata che volerà via dal sedile e si strapperà i punti.

All'inizio, non so come faccia Yan a vedere abbastanza bene da guidare senza i fari, ma dopo pochi minuti, i miei occhi si abituano e comincio a distinguere le forme di alberi e cespugli nella debole luce della luna crescente che fa capolino tra le nubi.

"Dov'è l'aereo?" chiedo, quando finalmente imbocchiamo una strada asfaltata e la tortura cessa. "Quanto dista da qui?"

"Non è lontano" risponde Ilya, guardando verso di me, mentre Yan accende i fari—probabilmente per mimetizzarsi meglio con le poche macchine che ci sono in questo momento. "Ancora un po', tutto qui."

"Ok, bene." Di nuovo, Peter borbotta febbrilmente qualcosa, e non sarei sorpresa se almeno alcuni dei suoi punti si fossero strappati. "Pensi che riusciremo a—"

"Zitta." L'ordine di Yan è tagliente. "Non posso sbagliare l'uscita."

Torno in silenzio, lasciando che si concentri per portarci a destinazione. In poco tempo, svoltiamo su un'altra strada sterrata, e Yan spegne i fari, mentre ci lanciamo in un'altra avventura da brivido.

Tengo Peter il più fermo possibile, mentre accarezzo i suoi capelli sudati. Questo sembra tranquillizzarlo, e mi aiuta anche a mantenere la calma. Per quanto sia sollevata che non siamo più soli, so che non siamo ancora fuori dai guai—letteralmente o figurativamente. La tensione nell'auto è palpabile, l'adrenalina densa nell'aria.

"*Zdes*" dice Ilya improvvisamente, e Yan svolta bruscamente, quasi facendomi volare. Riesco a stringere le spalle di mio marito, ma lui geme ancora per il dolore, mentre la sua gamba ferita colpisce il sedile nella parte anteriore.

"Sta bene?" chiede Ilya con tono burbero, guardando indietro. Il cielo sta cominciando a schiarirsi con i primi accenni dell'alba, e il suo cranio rasato brilla nell'oscurità simile al crepuscolo, con la pallida levigatezza segnata solo dall'intricato disegno dei tatuaggi.

"Dipende dalla tua definizione" rispondo, mantenendo la voce bassa. Non voglio distrarre Yan di nuovo. "Ha bisogno di un ospedale."

"E tu?" La voce profonda di Ilya si addolcisce. "Ho sentito cos'è successo ai tuoi—"

"Sto bene." Il mio tono è più aspro di quanto intendessi, ma non posso pensarci adesso, non posso indugiare in quel buio pozzo di dolore e disperazione. Posso sentirlo ribollire sotto la superficie, ma finché non lo tocco, non lo apro, posso trattenermi dall'affogarci.

Ilya mi studia ancora per un momento, poi si volta di nuovo verso il parabrezza. Spero che non si sia offeso, ma anche se lo fosse, non riesco a raccogliere abbastanza energia da preoccuparmene. Ora che non sono più la responsabile della nostra salvezza, posso iniziare a districarmi, filo per filo, e devo fare appello a tutta la mia forza di volontà per tenere insieme le estremità sfilacciate.

Devo rimanere forte.

Se non per me, almeno per Peter e il nostro bambino.

Andiamo avanti per altri dieci minuti, prima di imboccare un'altra strada asfaltata, e vedo un aereo di dimensioni decenti a una decina di metri di distanza.

"Questo è l'aeroporto?" Mi guardo intorno, osservando la foresta che circonda la stretta striscia di asfalto che sembra interrompersi non troppo lontano.

"Più una pista di atterraggio illegale" risponde Yan, saltando fuori dalla macchina. "Ilya, aiutami a tirarlo fuori."

Mi sposto, mentre loro sollevano Peter dall'auto e lo portano sull'aereo. Afferrando le scorte di pronto soccorso, mi affretto a seguirli, aspettandomi di vedere Anton, l'amico di Peter e il loro compagno di squadra, all'interno.

Con mia sorpresa, invece del volto barbuto di Anton, mi ritrovo di fronte ai duri lineamenti di Lucas Kent—il trafficante d'armi presso cui sono stata a Cipro. È all'interno della lussuosa cabina, con le braccia incrociate sull'ampio petto.

"Ciao" dico con circospezione, e lui mi fa un cenno con la mascella quadrata. Dev'essere ancora arrabbiato con me per aver persuaso sua moglie, Yulia, ad aiutarmi a fuggire.

O quello, oppure è solo preoccupato per questa operazione.

"Abbiamo meno di due ore, prima che il turno del mio ragazzo finisca" dice ai gemelli, confermando che è almeno in parte la seconda ipotesi. "Mettetelo qui"—annuisce verso un divano di pelle color crema—"e andiamo."

I gemelli fanno come dice Kent, che scompare nella cabina di pilotaggio. Un minuto dopo, i motori iniziano a ruggire, e mi siedo accanto a Peter sul divano, mentre l'aereo inizia a rollare. Yan e Ilya si siedono di fronte e io guardo fuori dall'oblò, trattenendo il respiro, mentre l'aereo accelera.

Con una pista di atterraggio così breve, ci vorrà un abilissimo pilota per superare gli alberi, mentre ci solleviamo.

A quanto pare, Kent *è* un abilissimo pilota, perché superiamo quegli alberi senza problemi. Riesco a sentire i potenti motori prendere vita, mentre ci impenniamo, e un'ondata di sollievo mi attraversa, mentre mi rendo conto che stiamo volando.

Non siamo ancora oltre il confine, ma almeno siamo in aria.

Non appena l'aereo si livella, ispeziono le ferite di Peter. Scorgo un po' di sangue fresco intorno al polpaccio, ma i punti sul fianco e sul braccio hanno tenuto, anche se il fianco continua ad apparire infiammato. Gli somministro un'altra dose di penicillina sbriciolata con l'acqua e metto nuove bende.

Sarà la mia immaginazione, ma sembra un po' più fresco al tatto quando ho finito, e il viso sembra più rilassato. È più come se stesse dormendo piuttosto che essere delirante e febbricitante.

Gli passo un asciugamano umido sul viso e sul collo per rinfrescarlo di più, poi gli bacio la guancia ruvida e ispida e cammino verso il punto in cui sono seduti i gemelli.

"Come sta?" chiede Ilya, alzandosi. "Ce la farà finché non arriveremo all'ospedale?"

Ingoio un nodo in gola. "Credo di sì. È... sì, ce la farà." Non mi ero permessa di pensare che non ce l'avrebbe fatta, ma l'orribile possibilità era lì, a corrodermi il petto e a scavarmi un buco nello stomaco.

"È un bastardo tosto" replica Yan, con gli occhi verdi che brillano, mentre si accomoda sul sedile, con lo sguardo di uno squalo, dei pantaloni eleganti perfettamente cuciti su misura e una camicia gessata. "Ci vorrebbero più di alcuni proiettili per ucciderlo."

Rido tremante, poi sento l'umidità sul mio viso.

Sto piangendo?

Asciugando le lacrime erranti, mi volto, imbarazzata,

proprio mentre una grande mano mi tocca la spalla, stringendola leggermente.

"Va tutto bene" dice Ilya, quando mi volto per guardarlo in viso. "Sei stata grande, *kroshka*. Ce la farà, grazie a te."

"E a voi" ribatto con voce rauca. Non ho idea di come mi abbia chiamata, ma sembrava più un vezzeggiativo che un insulto. "Se non foste venuti..."

"Sì, saresti stata fottuta" concorda Yan con sincerità. "Vi stanno davvero dando la caccia."

Annuisco, reprimendo un brivido. "L'ho capito, quando ho visto le notizie. Non posso neanche cominciare a ringraziarvi per—"

"Allora, non farlo." Yan si alza in piedi. "Non abbiamo bisogno dei tuoi ringraziamenti."

Sorrido, sentendomi un po' imbarazzata. "È molto carino da parte vostra, lo apprezzo davvero. So che state rischiando molto..."

Yan sorride sardonicamente. "Davvero? Sei un'esperta della vita da fuggitivi ora?"

"No, ma sto imparando qualcosa di più ogni giorno che passa" dico in modo piatto. "Quindi, grazie. Sono felice che siate venuti, e sono sicura che quando Peter si sveglierà, lo sarà anche lui." Non ho idea di quale sia l'intento di Yan, ma ho il sospetto che stia giocando con me, come un gatto col topo.

Respingendo quell'immagine inquietante, mi rivolgo a Ilya. "Dov'è Anton?" chiedo. "Sta bene?"

"È a Hong Kong per affari" risponde Ilya. "Non sarebbe arrivato qui in tempo. Siamo stati fortunati che Kent fosse in Messico con noi e che avesse un aereo. Altrimenti..." Si stringe nelle larghe spalle.

"Giusto." Mi mordo l'interno della guancia. "Devo ringraziare anche lui."

"Fossi in te, non lo farei" dice Yan. "Non è il tuo più grande fan."

"Oh." E così, il trafficante d'armi *mi* tiene il muso per essere scappata—o almeno per aver coinvolto sua moglie. "Credo che dovrei prima scusarmi con lui."

"Perché?" Yan sembra freddamente divertito, mentre si china al lato del sedile. "Perché hai visto un'opportunità e l'hai colta? Avrebbe fatto lo stesso al posto tuo."

"Sì, beh, comunque..." Mi volto verso la cabina del pilota, ma Ilya mi precede, bloccandomi.

"Non hai bisogno di farlo" dice, con espressione gentile. "È una storia tra lui e Peter."

"Ok..." Non avevo realizzato che esistesse un protocollo specifico per queste cose. "Credo che lascerò che se la vedano tra loro, allora."

Mi volto per tornare al divano di Peter, ma poi ricordo qualcosa di importante. "Dove stiamo andando esattamente?" chiedo, affrontando di nuovo i gemelli.

"Alla clinica in Svizzera" risponde Yan. "Per rimettere questo"—fa un cenno con la testa verso Peter—"in piedi. E dopo, chi lo sa." Sorride cupamente. "La tua casa ora è il mondo intero, Sara Sokolov. Benvenuta nel nostro tipo di vita."

PARTE III

39

Peter

Mi sveglio con una sensazione di benessere che smentisce il disagio al mio fianco. Delle mani delicate mi accarezzano i capelli, e una voce dolce sta cantando una melodia rilassante, facendomi sentire calmo e rilassato.

Aprendo gli occhi, incontro lo sguardo sorpreso di Sara. È seduta sul bordo del mio letto, con in mano un pettine che deve aver usato su di me.

"Sei sveglio." Il suo viso si illumina, mentre salta in piedi e si china su di me, lasciando il pettine sul comodino. "Come ti senti?"

"Bene." La mia voce esce roca, come se non l'avessi usata da un po'. Anche la bocca è secca, e lo stesso vale per la gola. Inumidendo le labbra screpolate, chiedo con voce grave: "Che cos'è successo? Dove siamo?"

Raggiante, raggiunge un bicchiere d'acqua poggiato accanto

al letto. "Nella clinica in Svizzera. I gemelli Ivanov ci hanno aiutato a fuggire."

Ho molto da metabolizzare, così succhio l'acqua attraverso una cannuccia, mentre scavo tra i miei ricordi. Rievoco il proiettile che mi ha lacerato il fianco e Sara che mi trascinava verso la nostra macchina, ma poi le cose diventano confuse, più come un groviglio di impressioni. Ad un certo punto, dobbiamo aver cambiato auto, perché ho il vago ricordo di essere salito su una Toyota blu, ma il seguito è praticamente una tela vuota. E prima della sparatoria—

"Il bambino." Le stringo il polso, con il cuore che accelera. "Ptichka, tu e il bambino—"

"Stiamo bene." Mette giù il bicchiere d'acqua, sorridendo vivacemente. "Mi hanno esaminata, e siamo entrambi perfettamente sani."

Tiro un sospiro di sollievo, ma poi ricordo qualcos'altro. "I tuoi genitori." Il mio cuore si spezza a metà, mentre il suo sorriso scompare. "Amore mio, mi dispiace così tanto—"

"Non farlo." Si allontana. "Non voglio parlarne."

Osservo, con il petto dolorante, mentre indietreggia, componendosi visibilmente. Ora ricordo di più, compreso l'agente che ha sparato a bruciapelo.

Il mio passerotto, che ha dedicato la propria vita alla guarigione, ha ucciso un uomo.

Per proteggermi... e per vendicare sua madre.

Ha premuto il grilletto non una, ma tre volte.

Posso solo immaginare che cosa le stia passando per la testa ora, con i genitori morti e la vecchia vita irrevocabilmente perduta. Per non parlare del trauma della sparatoria e della fuga che ne è seguita.

Come ha fatto a fare tutto da sola? Sono sicuro che Yan non stesse aspettando fuori dalla casa dei suoi genitori con un aereo.

"Sara..." Mi metto a sedere, sopprimendo una smorfia,

mentre il mio fianco protesta per il dolore. "Amore mio, vieni qui."

Si precipita immediatamente. "Che cosa stai facendo? Sdraiati. È troppo presto per muoverti."

"Sto bene" la rassicuro, ma lascio che mi rimetta sdraiato sul letto. Mi piace che si prenda cura di me, con il bel viso carico di preoccupazione.

È meglio del dolore represso.

"Dimmi che cos'è successo dopo che sono svenuto" dico, dopo che ha controllato le mie bende per assicurarsi che non abbia fatto danni. "Da quanto tempo siamo qui? Come siamo riusciti a scappare?"

Fa un respiro profondo. "È una lunga storia. Ma in sostanza, ho raggiunto il casolare di cui mi hai parlato, e poi ho inviato un'e-mail a Yan dal tuo telefono. Ha coinvolto Kent, e sono venuti a prenderci con un aereo—i gemelli e Kent come pilota." Fa un altro respiro. "Questo è successo due giorni fa."

Due giorni fa? Devo essere stato sulla soglia della morte per essere rimasto incosciente così a lungo.

Spingendo via le implicazioni del coinvolgimento di Kent, mi concentro su come ottenere tutti i fatti. "Ok, ora raccontami la lunga storia" dico, e poi ascolto, sbalordito, mentre la mia civilizzata moglie descrive la sua avventura sotto copertura nell'ospedale e il modo intelligente con cui si è procurata un'auto.

"Quindi, sì" conclude "dopo aver capito cosa stessi dicendo in russo e aver sbloccato il tuo telefono, ho mandato un'e-mail a Yan, e i gemelli sono venuti poche ore dopo. Yan ha detto che erano in Messico, quando tutto è successo, lavorando con Kent su un accordo, quindi era solo questione di prendere il suo aereo e raggiungerci. Oh, e corrompere il tizio del controllo del traffico aereo di Kent con un milione e mezzo di dollari. Yan ha detto che gli devi dei soldi."

A Yan devo molto più del denaro, e lui lo sa. Anche a Kent.

Bastardi manipolatori. Dovrò fare qualche serio favore per loro un giorno.

Notando il mio telefono sul comodino, lo prendo e controllo le e-mail per vedere se gli hacker hanno ottenuto qualche informazione sull'attentato. Devo capire come è nato questo casino.

Sfortunatamente, non c'è ancora niente, quindi metto da parte il telefono e chiedo a Sara: "Dove sono i gemelli e Kent? Sono ancora in giro?"

"I gemelli sono andati a Ginevra per un incontro di lavoro ieri, e Kent è tornato a casa" spiega. "Domani, però, Anton verrà qui da Hong Kong, quindi sono sicura che vedrai lui e i gemelli."

Questo è positivo; avrò bisogno del loro aiuto per districare questa matassa una volta aver capito che cosa l'ha causata. Ma prima, c'è qualcosa di importante che ho bisogno di sapere.

"Ptichka..." Appoggio la mia mano sul suo ginocchio snello. "Perché l'hai fatto, amore mio? Avresti potuto aspettare che arrivassero le autorità e lasciare che mi prendessi la colpa per quell'agente. Nessuno avrebbe sospettato niente e avresti potuto continuare la tua vita, mantenere il tuo lavoro e—"

"E cosa?" Salta in piedi, fissandomi. "Vederti arrestare, mentre stavi morendo dissanguato? Lasciarti in balia di persone che non sono solo convinte che tu sia un terrorista, ma che ti incolpano anche per la morte dei loro colleghi? Come puoi anche solo pensarlo?" Le sue mani si stringono a pugno sui fianchi, con l'intero corpo rigido per l'indignazione. "Sei mio marito, l'uomo che amo—"

"Anche l'uomo che ti ha torturata e rapita" le ricordo ironicamente anche se un tenero calore mi riempie il petto. Non avevo dubitato dell'amore di Sara, non proprio, ma una parte di me deve aver pensato che avrebbe abbracciato l'opportunità di liberarsi—che se avesse potuto scegliere tra me e la sua vita normale, avrebbe scelto la seconda opzione.

Solleva le sopracciglia. "Davvero? Stiamo davvero

discutendo di questo?"

"No, amore mio." Sopprimendo un sorriso felice, accarezzo il letto accanto a me. Non dovrei trovare la sua indignazione così adorabile, ma non posso farci niente. "Vieni qui."

Non si muove, ma mi guarda storto con le braccia incrociate.

"Ok, allora, mi alzo e vengo io da te." Faccio per rimettermi a sedere e, con un sospiro frustrato, si lascia cadere sul letto accanto a me.

"Rimettiti giù" sbotta, spingendomi. "Ti strapperai i punti. *Di nuovo.*" Nonostante il tono acuto, le sue mani sono delicate, mentre si china su di me per ispezionare le bende, e, mentre respiro il suo profumo dolce e caldo, il mio corpo si agita, reagendo alla sua vicinanza allo stesso modo di sempre.

"Ptichka." C'è una nota rauca nella mia voce, mentre le stringo il polso sottile. "Amore mio, guardami."

I suoi occhi nocciola incontrano i miei, e vedo le sue pupille dilatarsi, mentre le afferro la testa da dietro e la tiro verso di me.

"Aspetta, non sei ancora—"

Ingoio la sua protesta senza fiato con un bacio. Le sue labbra morbide si lasciano sfuggire un gemito, e le invado la bocca, beandomi del gusto e della sua sensazione travolgente. Non è il posto o il momento giusto, ma non riesco a fermarmi, con il desiderio che mi scorre nelle vene e mi fa ribollire la pelle.

Mi ama.

Mi ha scelto.

Ha abbandonato la sua vita per salvarmi.

Mi sembra di avere nuovamente la febbre, solo che non provo dolore. Brucio per il bisogno di averla, di sentire quelle mani delicate sulla mia pelle. È mia, ora senza riserve, e mentre le guido la mano sotto le lenzuola, le ultime catene del nostro oscuro passato cadono, lasciandoci uniti nel presente.

Insieme, nonostante tutto.

Henderson

SORRIDO, MENTRE LEGGO L'E-MAIL CHE HO APPENA RICEVUTO.

A parte la sfortunata fuga di Sokolov, il mio piano ha funzionato come previsto, specialmente per quanto riguarda i suoi alleati. L'uso di un esplosivo fabbricato da Esguerra nell'attacco terroristico ha aperto gli occhi di tutti sul pericolo rappresentato dall'impero illegale del trafficante d'armi, e la protezione speciale di cui l'uomo aveva goduto per cortesia del suo rapporto quid-pro-quo con il governo degli Stati Uniti è sparita. Lui e tutti i suoi soci sono ora un bersaglio facile e una squadra è già in viaggio verso la residenza di Lucas Kent a Cipro.

Ancora meglio, l'Interpol è arrivata, proprio come speravo. I fratelli Ivanov sono stati avvistati a Ginevra, il che significa che Sokolov potrebbe non essere lontano. Inoltre, il mio contatto sta indagando sul gossip di una clinica segreta nelle Alpi svizzere specializzata in pazienti dalla parte sbagliata della legge.

Se tutto andrà bene, la maggior parte dei miei problemi finirà presto.

Tra poche ore, Kent, Sokolov e due dei suoi amici assassini russi saranno morti, e tra non molto le autorità cattureranno il restante assassino, Anton Rezov. Quindi, si tratterà semplicemente di smantellare l'organizzazione criminale di Esguerra e catturare il boss.

Una volta fatto, il regno del terrore di questi mostri finirà e io e la mia famiglia saremo veramente al sicuro.

Sara

SORRIDENDO, ATTRAVERSO IL CORRIDOIO, CON LE LABBRA GONFIE e doloranti per il pompino che ho appena fatto a Peter. Suppongo che avrei dovuto aspettarmi una cosa del genere, vista la libido superumana di mio marito, ma mi sorprende ancora.

Nella mia mente, il sesso e i pazienti legati al letto non si mescolano.

Non che Peter sia un paziente tipico. Dal momento in cui l'abbiamo portato e gli abbiamo attaccato la flebo, ha superato ogni aspettativa—mia e del personale della clinica. È come se tutta la sua volontà di ferro fosse stata reindirizzata verso la guarigione. A poche ore dal nostro arrivo, la sua febbre è scesa e, se i medici non lo avessero sedato per favorire il riposo e la guarigione, avrebbe riacquistato conoscenza.

Un'infermiera che mi passa accanto nel corridoio sorride e mi saluta, e io faccio altrettanto.

Mi piace il personale qui. Sono gentili, anche se i loro pazienti sono tra i peggiori criminali noti all'umanità. Non che io sia nella posizione di giudicare.

Ora sono una criminale anch'io.

Ho sparato ad un uomo a sangue freddo.

Non sono ancora riuscita ad elaborarlo, proprio come non sono ancora riuscita a pensare ai miei genitori—o a cosa significhi essere dei fuggiaschi, con le nostre foto su tutti i notiziari. Mi sono concentrata sugli aspetti positivi, rallegrandomi del fatto che siamo entrambi qui, vivi e liberi.

Che ho ancora Peter e il nostro bambino.

Aiuta affrontare tutto momento per momento, passare da un compito all'altro. Quando sono impegnata, non noto la sfilacciatura di quei bordi pericolosi o la crescente pressione del dolore. Riesco persino a sorridere, anche se una parte di me rimane intorpidita.

È quasi come se premendo quel grilletto avessi ucciso qualcosa dentro di me.

Strappando una vita, ho perso un pezzo di me stessa.

"Salve, Dottoressa Sokolov" mi saluta il Dottor Jart entrando nel suo ufficio. "Come sta suo marito?"

"Meglio." Sorrido all'uomo più anziano. "Molto meglio."

Solleva le folte sopracciglia grigie. "Davvero? È sveglio?"

"Decisamente. Anche se potrei averlo... fatto stancare troppo. Quando me ne sono andata, stava di nuovo dormendo."

"Lo farà spesso" mi informa il Dottor Jart. "Il suo corpo ha bisogno di dormire per guarire." Si alza e cammina intorno alla sua scrivania. "Ma sono sicuro che lei lo sappia."

"Sì" ammetto, osservandolo, mentre tira fuori un enorme libro dallo scaffale. Con il suo aspetto rude, mi ricorda un po' il mio capo Bill, anche se per quanto riguarda la personalità, il Dottor Jart è molto più alla mano.

Avevo conosciuto brevemente il medico l'anno scorso, quando avevo trascorso due settimane qui dopo l'incidente automobilistico. Quando è venuto a controllare le ferite di Peter l'altro giorno, mi ha riconosciuta e abbiamo avuto modo di parlare. Dopo aver appreso che sono una ginecologa/ostetrica, mi ha invitata ad assistere una paziente in travaglio—cosa che ho fatto volentieri, una volta essermi accertata che Peter fosse stabile e che riposasse.

Qualunque cosa pur di distogliere la mente dagli eventi degli ultimi giorni.

"Come sta María?" chiedo, riferendomi a quella paziente— l'amante adolescente di un signore della droga messicano che ieri ha dato alla luce due gemelli. "È già tornata a casa?"

"Si sta riprendendo, ma no." Il Dottor Jart sospira. "Gomez vuole che lei rimanga qui per almeno una settimana, e dal momento che paga..." Fa spallucce, tornando alla sua scrivania.

"Capisco." A differenza di un ospedale tradizionale che fa affidamento sui pagamenti delle assicurazioni e aderisce a rigide linee guida in merito alla durata della degenza, questa clinica si rivolge agli ultra-ricchi del mondo sotterraneo, e sono i pazienti—o qualsiasi criminale ricco a cui i pazienti sono collegati—a decidere quando sono sufficientemente guariti.

"Allora, Dottoressa Sokolov..." Il dottore si siede e mi guarda con penetranti occhi scuri. "La ragione per cui le ho chiesto di venire è che volevo discutere qualcosa con lei."

"Certo. Di cosa si tratta?" chiedo, sedendomi di fronte al dottore. Spero che abbiano un'altra paziente da assistere, mentre Peter sta dormendo.

Ho bisogno di tenermi occupata per non pensare alle cose.

"Prenderebbe in considerazione l'idea di unirsi a noi?" chiede il Dottor Jart. "Non so quali siano i suoi piani con il Signor Sokolov, date le circostanze"—si schiarisce la voce—"ma potremmo davvero assumere una dottoressa con la sua specializzazione all'interno del personale. Come sa, il nostro ostetrico—il Dottor Ludwig—è straordinario, ma è un uomo, e alcune nostre pazienti, specialmente quelle di culture più tradizionali, sono un po'... a disagio con questo fatto."

"Oh." Guardo il dottore. "Grazie… Non so cosa dire."

Un'offerta di lavoro—in particolare una in gran parte basata sul mio genere—non era assolutamente quello che mi aspettavo. Ma perché dovrei essere sorpresa? Non c'è correttezza politica in questo mio nuovo mondo senza legge, in cui la violenza fa parte degli affari e le donne sono viste come estensioni degli uomini potenti a cui appartengono.

"Sono sicuro che dovrò consultare il Signor Sokolov" dice il Dottor Jart, quando non aggiungo altro. "Se è qualcosa che le interessa, ovviamente."

"Giusto." Sopprimendo la femminista interiore, mi concentro sull'opportunità reale—che sembra interessante. La perdita della mia carriera è qualcosa su cui ho evitato di soffermarmi, ma so che non potrò farlo per sempre. In questo modo, potrei essere ancora un medico—ammesso che a Peter stia bene che rimaniamo nelle vicinanze.

Per quel che ne so, ha intenzione di nasconderci di nuovo in Asia.

"Ci pensi, nel frattempo" dice il Dottor Jart. "Non deve darci una risposta subito o a breve. Comprendiamo che la situazione"—si schiarisce di nuovo la gola—"al momento è instabile, quindi si prenda tutto il tempo necessario per decidere."

"Grazie." Mi alzo e gli stringo la mano. "Lo apprezzo." Mi chiedo quante volte estenda le offerte di lavoro a sospetti terroristi in fuga dalla legge. Non sembra del tutto a suo agio con "la situazione," ma non ne è nemmeno scoraggiato.

Le schede del personale in questo luogo devono essere interessanti.

~

Dopo l'incontro, mi fermo al bar al piano di sotto per uno spuntino. Quando torno nella stanza di Peter, è sveglio e mi sta cercando.

"Dov'eri?" chiede, mettendosi a sedere—con uno sforzo decisamente minore questa volta. La sua velocità di guarigione è notevole—o questo o la sua tolleranza al dolore è fuori dal normale. Non ha fatto nemmeno una smorfia, anche se il movimento deve avergli tirato i punti sul fianco.

Sono tentata di farlo sdraiare di nuovo, a prescindere, ma mi trattengo. Ora sembra molto più vivace, con gli occhi grigi intensamente concentrati mentre mi fissa, e so che non passerà molto tempo prima che torni al suo solito sé.

"Stavo parlando con un medico" lo informo, camminando verso il bordo del suo letto. "Mi ha offerto un lavoro."

Solleva le sopracciglia. "Qui? In questo posto?"

"Sì. A quanto pare, hanno bisogno di un'ostetrica." Sollevando la mano, strofino il pollice sui calli del suo palmo. "Che cosa ne pensi? Ovviamente dovremmo restare in zona, e non so quanto sia sicuro."

Nessun lavoro vale la pena di mettere in pericolo la nostra libertà.

Rimane in silenzio per un momento, rimuginando. "Non è la peggiore idea" dice alla fine. "Prima, però, dobbiamo capire esattamente com'è successo."

"Vuoi dire perché pensano che tu sia il responsabile dell'attentato?"

Annuisce cupamente, e prendo fiato per combattere la tensione nel petto. Ci ho riflettuto anch'io, e se Peter è innocente—come credo che sia—c'è solo una conclusione logica.

"Qualcuno deve averti incastrato" ipotizzo. "Forse addirittura qualcuno all'interno dell'FBI."

"Sì." La sua espressione non cambia. Deve aver pensato la stessa cosa anche lui. "La domanda è chi e perché." Prende il telefono, come ha fatto prima, e lo guardo scorrere rapidamente tra le sue e-mail.

"Forse i Federali non hanno alcun sospetto reale, quindi hanno deciso di usarti come capro espiatorio" suggerisco, mentre apre un'e-mail. "Probabilmente c'è un'organizzazione terroristica dietro l'esplosione, ma hanno deciso di dare la colpa a te. Qualcuno oltre a Ryson avrebbe potuto essere scontento dell'accordo che avevi stretto, quindi quando si è presentata l'occasione—" Mi fermo, perché la faccia di Peter si trasforma in granito.

"Che cosa c'è?" chiedo, quando continua a leggere senza dire nulla, con la postura che si irrigidisce di più secondo dopo secondo. I miei stessi muscoli del collo sono tesi, con il cuore che corre come se volessi lanciarmi in uno sprint.

Qualunque cosa ci sia scritta in quell'e-mail non è positiva. Posso dirlo dalla sua espressione.

Alza gli occhi per incontrare il mio sguardo. "Ricordi quando ti ho parlato del generale in pensione, l'incaricato dell'operazione Daryevo?" La sua voce ha una flessione letale. "Quello che ho promesso di lasciare in pace in cambio di amnistia e immunità?"

"Sì, certo" rispondo, mentre mi si stringe lo stomaco. "Henderson, giusto?"

"Giusto." Le sue narici si dilatano. "Il fottuto Wally Henderson III."

Faccio un respiro. "C'è lui dietro a questo?"

"Così sembrerebbe." Un muscolo pulsa nella mascella di Peter. "Prima che venissero a prendermi, ho chiesto ai nostri hacker di esaminare l'esplosione, perché qualcosa non mi tornava. E alla fine mi hanno fornito i risultati."

"Hanno detto che Henderson ti ha incastrato? Ma come? Perché? Come poteva sapere che sarebbe accaduta questa tragedia?"

Sono venuti a prendere Peter meno di ventiquattro ore

dopo l'attentato. Persino qualcuno con le connessioni di Henderson avrebbe avuto bisogno di tempo per raccogliere prove abbastanza forti da inviare una squadra SWAT in un tranquillo quartiere suburbano. Anche se Henderson avesse intrapreso il compito non appena saputo dell'esplosione, avrebbe dovuto impiegare giorni, se non settimane, per—

"Perché è stato lui a farla accadere." L'espressione di Peter è selvaggia. "È stato lui il figlio di puttana che ha piazzato la bomba."

Resto a bocca aperta. "Che cosa?"

"Un uomo che corrisponde alla mia descrizione è stato catturato dalla telecamera, mentre entrava nell'edificio come persona di una ditta di pulizie il giorno prima dell'esplosione." La voce di Peter è abbastanza dura da spezzare la pietra. "E le mie impronte digitali sono state trovate su una delle maniglie delle porte sopravvissute del terzo piano, dove era stata posizionata la bomba. Per quanto riguarda l'esplosivo in sé, era davvero unico, uno praticamente non rilevabile—è così che il mio sosia è riuscito a superare la sicurezza senza problemi. Sai chi ha accesso a quel tipo di esplosivo?"

Lo fisso, disorientata. "Io… no."

"L'esercito americano. Lo prendono direttamente dal trafficante d'armi che lo produce—Julian Esguerra."

Il mio battito cardiaco riprende a martellare. "Lo stesso che ha negoziato l'affare per te? Il tizio a cui hai fatto questo favore?"

"Proprio lui." La sua bocca si contorce. "Quindi, capisci come possano pensare che io sia il responsabile, giusto? Le forze armate statunitensi acquistano ogni lotto dell'esplosivo prodotto da Esguerra, e ha una lista d'attesa lunga un miglio, nel caso in cui si fermassero. Tuttavia, qualcuno che conosce personalmente il trafficante d'armi *potrebbe* ottenerne un chilo o giù di lì. Dannazione, probabilmente non ne serve nemmeno così tanto. È potente come una bomba atomica, solo che non è radioattivo."

Oh, Dio. Ora ricordo che Peter ne parlava con Kent, quando cenavamo insieme a Cipro. Qualcosa sullo Zio Sam e sulla produzione di un esplosivo non rilevabile. Era l'esplosivo in questione?

"Allora, perché..." Raccolgo i miei pensieri frenetici. "Perché pensi che ci sia Henderson dietro a questo? Non potrebbe esserci qualcun altro—per esempio, lo stesso Esguerra? Hai detto che ti voleva morto ad un certo punto, e ha le connessioni per far sì che ciò accada, giusto? O forse potrebbe essere stato qualche altro tuo nemico?"

"Perché qui ci sono le tracce della CIA dappertutto" spiega cupamente. "L'uomo delle pulizie che assomiglia a me, le mie impronte digitali sulla scena, la mia connessione con Ryson e la bomba che viene piazzata sul suo piano—è una tecnica classica. Fanno questo fin dai tempi della Guerra Fredda. E indovina chi si dice sia stato un agente sotto copertura in gioventù?"

"Esatto, Henderson." Ricordo che Peter mi ha confessato questo una volta. "Ma Esguerra non ha alcune connessioni con la CIA? Non potrebbe aver—"

"No." Serra la mascella. "A parte il fatto che avrebbe potuto uccidermi in mille altri modi, se avesse voluto davvero, non aveva motivo di rovinare un rapporto reciprocamente vantaggioso con il governo degli Stati Uniti. In questo momento, le autorità credono che sia complice dell'attentato e cercheranno anche lui."

"Oh, questo... non è affatto positivo." Da quello che so, Esguerra era stato quasi intoccabile fino ad ora.

"No, non lo è" dice Peter pericolosamente. "Ecco perché ho bisogno di parlare subito con Yan. Gli altri membri di quella squadra delle pulizie? Le loro descrizioni corrispondono ad Anton, Yan e Ilya, compresi i tatuaggi sul cranio."

Peter

RILEGGO L'E-MAIL DEGLI HACKER PER LA TERZA VOLTA, controllando continuamente l'ora sul mio telefono. Tre ore fa, ho chiamato Yan per condividere quello che ho appreso, ma non ha risposto. Gli ho lasciato un messaggio in segreteria dicendogli di richiamarmi, poi gli ho mandato un sms e un'e-mail, prima di fare lo stesso con suo fratello.

Nessuno dei due gemelli mi ha ancora risposto—e nemmeno Anton.

Controllo di nuovo l'ora. Sono le 23.33—solo due minuti dopo l'ultima volta che ho guardato. Sara sta dormendo accanto a me, con le onde castane sparse sul mio cuscino, e per quanto desideri unirmi a lei in un sonno tranquillo, non posso chiudere gli occhi.

I miei istinti sono di nuovo in allerta.

Facendo attenzione a non svegliarla, mi metto a sedere e

faccio oscillare le gambe sul pavimento. Lentamente e con cautela, mi alzo, ignorando il dolore al fianco e al polpaccio. La stanza gira intorno a me, mentre faccio il primo passo, ma le gambe sono in grado di sostenermi.

Bene.

Non posso permettermi di restare sdraiato, se qualcosa va storto.

Alla mia richiesta, un paio di pistole sono state consegnate nella mia stanza, quindi mi avvicino all'armadio per ispezionarle. Non sono niente di speciale—solo un M16 e un paio di Glock, ma sono meglio di niente.

Controllo ogni arma e la carico, poi tiro fuori un paio di pantaloncini dall'armadio e li infilo sotto la vestaglia, attento a non spostare la benda sulla gamba. Il cuore mi batte troppo forte per lo sforzo, e sudo come un maiale, ma butto via la vestaglia dell'ospedale e infilo un maglione morbido, seguito da un paio di calzini e stivali.

"Peter?" La voce assonnata di Sara mi raggiunge, mentre lego una Glock alla caviglia sinistra. "Che cosa stai facendo?"

Alzo lo sguardo da dove sono rannicchiato. "Mi sto solo vestendo, ptichka. Non preoccuparti."

"Che cosa?" Sara si alza, con la sonnolenza che svanisce dalla sua voce, mentre mi osserva. "Perché ti stai vestendo? Devi stare a letto, a riposo, non—"

"Penso che dobbiamo andarcene." Mi alzo lentamente, respirando nonostante il dolore. "Qualcosa non torna."

Sara si trasforma in una statua sul letto. "Pensi che non siamo al sicuro qui?"

"Penso che non siamo al sicuro da nessuna parte in questo momento" rispondo, mentre mi metto l'M16 sopra la spalla e infilo l'altra Glock nella cintura. "Tuttavia, sono preoccupato, non avendo notizie di Yan o degli altri."

"No?" Attraversa la stanza con i piedi nudi e si ferma davanti a me, con il colore del viso che si abbina alla T-shirt bianca che indossa al posto del pigiama. "Non potrebbero essere solo occupati?"

"Tutto è possibile." Per quanto ne so, i gemelli sono nel bel mezzo di un colpo, e Anton ha problemi di ricezione sull'aereo. "Nella nostra situazione, però, meglio prevenire che curare."

"Ma dove andremo? Tre giorni fa, eri fuori di testa per la febbre. Devi stare in ospedale, guarire—"

"Sto bene adesso" interrompo. Incorniciandole il viso delicato con il palmo, dico in tono più tenero: "Non preoccuparti, amore mio. Hai fatto la tua parte, ora tocca a me fare la mia."

E mentre mi fissa con occhi enormi e spaventati, le bacio le labbra allettanti, poi raggiungo l'armadio per tirarle fuori i vestiti.

43

MI VESTO, MENTRE PETER CERCA DI NUOVO DI RAGGIUNGERE Anton e i gemelli. Le mie mani sono fredde per lo stress, le dita maldestre, e ci vogliono due tentativi per allacciare le sneakers.

"Ti ha risposto qualcuno?" chiedo quando ho finito, e Peter scuote la testa, scuro in volto.

"No. Ho intenzione di provare con Kent, vedere se ha saputo qualcosa."

"Oh, questa è una buona idea." Mi mordo il labbro, mentre compone qualche numero e aspetta, con il telefono premuto sull'orecchio.

"Sono Peter" dice in tono teso. "Hai—aspetta, che cosa?"

Ascolta in silenzio, mentre Kent lo informa su quello che è successo, e quando abbassa il telefono, faccio un passo indietro per la sua espressione.

"L'Interpol ha fatto irruzione nei ristoranti di Yulia. In tutti" mi informa duramente. "Lucas ha fatto appena in tempo a farla uscire, prima che arrivassero a casa sua a Cipro. Ora sono diretti al complesso di Esguerra in Colombia—l'unico posto semi-sicuro per loro."

"Oh, Dio." Sento un'improvvisa ondata di nausea. "Pensi che Yan e gli altri...?"

"Potrebbero essere già stati presi, sì. In ogni caso, non abbiamo un minuto da perdere."

Afferrandomi la mano, mi conduce fuori dalla stanza, con passi forti e sicuri come se non fosse stato sul punto di morire pochi giorni fa.

Devo quasi correre per stare al passo con il ritmo che ha, mentre ci affrettiamo lungo il corridoio e scendiamo le scale. "Niente ascensore?" chiedo, ansimando, mentre ci dirigiamo giù velocemente, e lui scuote la testa, stringendo la presa sulla mia mano.

"Troppo facile rimanere intrappolati."

Vorrei ricordargli le sue ferite e pregarlo di rallentare, ma ora non è il momento. Se le autorità hanno raggiunto Kent—il braccio destro di Esguerra e quindi un altro intoccabile—Peter ha ragione riguardo al fatto che la clinica non sia sicura.

Tutte le solite regole di ingaggio non hanno più alcun valore.

"Dove stiamo andando?" chiedo, soprattutto per distrarmi dalla crescente nausea. La cosiddetta nausea mattutina ha colpito in diversi orari del giorno e della notte, e scendere le scale di certo non aiuta.

"In un rifugio" risponde Peter senza guardarmi, e mi rendo conto che il suo viso è insolitamente pallido, con le tempie imperlate di sudore per lo sforzo.

Non è così guarito come finge di essere.

Dovrei fare appello a tutta la mia forza di volontà per reprimere una supplica e implorarlo di fermarsi e riposare.

Invece, accelero il ritmo, in modo che non debba sforzarsi per trascinarmi. "Non hai intenzione di dirmi dov'è?"

"No." Il suo sguardo si sposta verso l'angolo del soffitto, e scorgo una debole luce rossa accesa.

Naturalmente. Telecamere.

Avrei dovuto immaginarlo.

Continuiamo a scendere in silenzio, e Peter si ferma quando raggiungiamo la porta della hall. Lentamente, la apre leggermente e aspetta, scrutando attraverso la fessura.

"Via libera" mormora dopo un minuto, e lascio andare un respiro tremante, mentre usciamo.

"Signor Sokolov" dice la bionda receptionist sorpresa, mentre passiamo davanti alla sua scrivania. "Sta già andando via?"

"Sì. Pagherò il conto più tardi."

Lei comincia a dire qualcos'altro, ma stiamo già uscendo dall'edificio dirigendoci in un cortile che funge da parcheggio. Si congela, ma è bellissimo qui fuori, con il bagliore della luna che delinea le cime innevate delle Alpi svizzere che ci circondano. Tuttavia, le noto a malapena, visto che Peter mi conduce nel parcheggio.

Il mio stomaco ora è in piena rivolta, e devo deglutire ripetutamente per evitare di vomitare.

Improvvisamente, si ferma e si accuccia tra due macchine, tirandomi giù con sé.

"Sta arrivando qualcuno" sussurra, allungandosi verso il suo M16, e un secondo dopo, un SUV nero si ferma bruscamente davanti alla clinica.

 Peter

Mɪ ᴀsᴘᴇᴛᴛᴏ ᴄʜᴇ ɢʟɪ ᴀɢᴇɴᴛɪ ᴅᴇʟʟ'Iɴᴛᴇʀᴘᴏʟ sᴀʟᴛɪɴᴏ ꜰᴜᴏʀɪ dalla macchina, ma vedo un uomo vestito tutto di nero.

"Anton!" Mi alzo e saluto, facendomi vedere. Si gira, con il sollievo stampato viso barbuto.

"Sali!" Grida, piegando il pollice verso la macchina. "Dobbiamo andare."

Sara è già in piedi accanto a me, e le afferro la mano, mentre mi precipito verso il SUV di Anton. Il polpaccio mi brucia da morire, e sento di essermi strappato alcuni punti sul fianco, ma niente di tutto ciò ha alcuna importanza.

Anton non si lascia prendere dal panico facilmente e sembra più che un po' nervoso.

Salta dietro al volante, mentre raggiungiamo la macchina, e mi lancio sul sedile posteriore, stringendo i denti a causa di un'ondata di dolore. Sara si sistema accanto a me e usciamo dal parcheggio, prima ancora che lei chiuda la portiera.

"Yan e Ilya?" chiedo, quando il dolore si placa, e Anton mi guarda cupo nello specchietto retrovisore.

"L'Interpol ha fatto irruzione durante il loro incontro a Ginevra. Da allora non li ho più sentiti."

"Cazzo." Chiudo gli occhi, sentendo lo stomaco sottosopra. Il mio corpo è ancora in preda alla frenesia, debole e tremante —decisamente non in forma per uccidere una sfilza di agenti armati, se verranno a prenderci.

Aprendo gli occhi, guardo mia moglie e la vedo fare respiri lenti e profondi, con il profilo delicato di una tonalità verdognola di bianco.

"Stai bene, ptichka?" mormoro, e lei annuisce brevemente.

"Nausea mattutina" risponde con un sussurro appena udibile, e le prendo la mano, con il petto che si stringe con un mix di furia e senso di colpa.

La mia Sara è incinta. Questo è il momento della sua vita in cui lo stress è più tossico. Dovrebbe riposare nel comfort della nostra casa, essere coccolata da me e dalla sua famiglia—non scappare dalle autorità, avendo assistito alla morte dei genitori.

Non avrei mai dovuto accettare di risparmiare la vita a Henderson. Quell'ublyudok doveva pagare—e questa volta lo farà.

Lo distruggerò, pezzo dopo dannato pezzo.

Prima, però, dobbiamo uscire vivi da tutto questo.

"Ho provato a mettermi in contatto con te" spiego ad Anton, mentre si gira verso la strada che conduce all'aeroporto privato riservato ai pazienti della clinica. "Hai gettato via il telefono?"

Annuisce. "Ero appena atterrato ed ero al telefono con Yan, quando l'Interpol ha preso d'assalto il loro luogo d'incontro. Quindi l'ho distrutto, per ogni evenienza."

"Bene." I nostri telefoni non sono rintracciabili, con il

segnale che rimbalza sui satelliti di tutto il mondo, ma è meglio non rischiare. "C'è qualche possibilità che se ne siano andati?"

"Tutto è possibile" risponde, ma non sembra crederci.

"Anton..." La voce di Sara è tesa. "Scusa, puoi fermare la macchina?"

"Accosta" gli dico, e lui devia dalla strada, spingendo sui freni. La macchina è ancora in movimento, quando Sara apre la portiera e si sporge, ansimando. Le avvolgo un braccio intorno alla vita esile e le raccolgo i capelli nell'altra mano, tenendoglieli lontano dal viso, mentre vomita.

"Mi dispiace" mormora quando ha finito, e le porgo una bottiglia d'acqua dalla scatola sul pavimento.

"Non hai nulla di cui dispiacerti" dico, mentre Anton torna sulla strada. "Questo è perfettamente naturale."

Mantengo la voce calma, come se non fossi minimamente preoccupato, dopo aver visto mia moglie vomitare le budella sul ciglio della strada, mentre stiamo correndo per le nostre vite. Come se la rabbia non fosse come l'acido nelle vene, tingendomi la vista di rosso.

"Stai male, Sara?" chiede Anton, e mi rendo conto che non sa ancora del bambino. E perché dovrebbe? Noi stessi l'abbiamo appena scoperto.

"È incinta" lo informo, e nonostante i miei migliori sforzi, sembro assolutamente teso.

Se dovesse succedere qualcosa a Sara o al bambino a causa di questo, non me lo perdonerò mai.

"Oh." Anton sembra senza parole. "Questo è... Congratulazioni."

"Grazie" mormoro, e poi lo sento.

Un suono di sirene in lontananza.

Fanculo.

"Accelera" dico ad Anton, che sta già spingendo sull'acceleratore come un dannato, con la faccia tesa.

Mi rivolgo a Sara. "Mettiti la cintura di sicurezza."

Si sforza di obbedire, con gli occhi color nocciola scuro sul volto incolore, mentre controllo le mie armi.

Le sirene stanno arrivando da dietro di noi—dalla direzione della clinica—il che significa che la mia intuizione era giusta.

Sono venuti a prenderci.

Il rombo di un elicottero si unisce presto alle sirene, e Anton accelera ulteriormente, prendendo una ripida curva in mezzo alla strada ad una velocità vertiginosa.

"Rallenta, cazzo" ringhio, mentre Sara mi stringe convulsamente la mano. "Non possiamo schiantarci, capisci?"

Se fossi da solo con Anton, rischierei di farlo, ma non con lei qui.

Non quando è quasi morta in un incidente su una strada molto simile a questa.

Anton lascia andare leggermente l'acceleratore e avvicino la mano di Sara alle mie labbra. "Andrà tutto bene, ptichka" mormoro, baciandole le nocche. "Dobbiamo solo salire sull'aereo."

"Forse ci stanno già aspettando lì" dice Anton. "Dal momento che sapevano della clinica, potrebbero anche sapere della pista di atterraggio."

"La clinica è sulla mappa, ma la pista di atterraggio no" ribatto, stringendo la mano di Sara in modo rassicurante, quando la sento tesa nella mia presa. "Dovrebbero chiedere la sua posizione al personale."

Almeno, spero che sia così.

Perché *potremmo* essere diretti in un'imboscata.

Anton non risponde, preme soltanto sull'acceleratore, mentre raggiungiamo un tratto di strada più dritto. Siamo a pochi minuti dalla pista di atterraggio ora, ma il ruggito dell'elicottero sta aumentando di intensità secondo dopo secondo, soffocando il battito adrenalinico del mio cuore.

Finalmente, vedo i suoi fari spuntare alle nostre spalle, mentre svoltiamo di nuovo bruscamente.

"Giù" ringhio a Sara, facendola distendere sul sedile, e poi apro il finestrino e mi sporgo, ignorando il forte dolore al fianco, mentre punto il mio M16 sull'elicottero.

Devia dietro agli alberi, prima che io possa aprire il fuoco.

Aspetto, non volendo sprecare i proiettili.

Un secondo dopo, l'elicottero riappare e sparo dei colpi.

Spara a sua volta, quindi devia di nuovo.

Fanculo. Siamo quasi sulla pista di atterraggio ora.

Aspetto che ricompaia l'elicottero, poi apro il fuoco, premendo il grilletto, finché la pistola non si scarica e l'elicottero indietreggia per evitare i miei proiettili.

Rientrando in macchina, ricarico velocemente, poi mi sporgo nuovamente dal finestrino.

Questa volta, però, l'elicottero si arresta.

Questo non va bene.

Non possiamo decollare con questi stronzi che ci sparano addosso.

L'auto gira bruscamente, e quando guardo in avanti, scopro che siamo già sulla pista di atterraggio, diretti a tutta velocità verso l'aereo.

"Il lanciarazzi è dentro" urla Anton, spingendo sui freni. "Farò una corsa per prenderlo."

Ci fermiamo a una decina di metri dall'aereo, e stringo i denti, mentre il mio fianco sbatte contro il bordo di metallo affilato del finestrino della macchina.

Se sopravvivremo a questa situazione, Sara sarà sconvolta dal fatto che mi sia strappato i punti.

Anton salta fuori dalla macchina, correndo verso l'aereo, e io fornisco il fuoco di copertura, mentre l'elicottero si avvicina. Anche le sirene si fanno più forti; devono essere proprio alle nostre calcagna.

"Sali sull'aereo, adesso!" grido a Sara, e con la coda dell'occhio, la vedo correre per obbedire.

Il mio M16 suona a vuoto, ma non c'è tempo per ricaricare,

quindi estraggo la Glock dalla mia cintura, mentre l'elicottero fa una virata, poi torna indietro, riempiendo il veicolo di proiettili. Il vetro intorno a me esplode, con i frammenti che mi colpiscono il viso e il collo. Stringendo la Glock, apro la portiera e ruzzolo fuori, rotolando via dall'auto, mentre sparo.

Ho bisogno che si concentrino su di me, non sull'aereo o su Sara.

I proiettili colpiscono il terreno tutt'attorno a me, facendomi volare pezzi d'asfalto negli occhi. Sento l'odore della polvere da sparo, il bruciore del piombo, mentre mi sfiora.

È la fine.

Non ce la farò.

La mia pistola suona a vuoto proprio mentre un furgone nero si arresta bruscamente sulla pista di atterraggio, stridendo fino a fermarsi vicino alla nostra macchina.

Sara

SONO GIÀ ACCANTO ALL'AEREO, QUANDO VEDO IL FURGONE NERO.

L'Interpol.

Ci hanno raggiunto.

"Anton!" urlo al di sopra degli spari e del rumore dell'elicottero, mentre riappare sulla soglia dell'aereo con un lanciarazzi appoggiato sulla spalla. "Stanno—"

Boom!

Il lampo dell'esplosione mi brucia le retine, con un suono così assordante che i miei timpani quasi esplodono. Il cielo sembra trasformarsi in una palla di fuoco, e piovono pezzi di metallo in fiamme.

Santo cielo.

Anton ha abbattuto l'elicottero.

Il mio sguardo attonito cade sul furgone, e vedo due figure familiari saltare fuori.

"Yan! Ilya!" Non sono mai stata così felice di vederli—specialmente quando si chinano per posare le braccia di Peter sulle loro spalle e correre insieme verso l'aereo.

"Sbrigatevi!" urla Anton, e sento le sirene diventare più forti. "Dobbiamo andare ora."

Scompare di nuovo dentro l'aereo, e mi precipito dietro di lui, con i gemelli e Peter alle calcagna.

Le auto della polizia appaiono proprio mentre le nostre ruote si sollevano da terra.

"Quindi, stavano inseguendo te, non noi?" chiarisco con Yan, mentre tolgo la terra e il sangue dalla faccia di Peter, prima di rimuovere alcune schegge di vetro incastonate nella sua pelle. Mi sento stranamente calma, come se stessi eseguendo un Pap test di routine, invece di curare le ferite di mio marito dopo una straziante fuga.

O mi sto abituando alla vita in fuga o sono ancora sotto shock e la scarica di adrenalina sta per colpirmi.

"Sì, e ce l'abbiamo fatta per miracolo" dice Yan dal sedile accanto al divano, dove Peter è disteso. "L'elicottero stava volando sopra di noi per intrappolarci, ma poi avete attirato la loro attenzione." Mentre parla, solleva uno specchietto per applicare una pomata antibiotica all'orecchio, dove un proiettile lo ha sfiorato, lasciando un brutto squarcio.

"Sono contento che siamo serviti come esca accidentale" dice Peter, mentre gli alzo la maglietta per ispezionare la benda sul fianco. Il suo colorito è ancora spento, ma è cosciente—e a quanto pare si sente abbastanza bene visto il sarcasmo.

"Ehi, è stato uno sforzo di squadra" replica Ilya, con un sorriso sul viso, mentre si accomoda sul sedile—in qualche modo completamente illeso. "Non sarebbe potuta andare meglio, se l'avessimo programmato."

Scuoto la testa, cercando di non pensare a come sia stato correre verso l'aereo, mentre Peter era inchiodato dal fuoco dell'elicottero. È un miracolo che sia sopravvissuto—che siamo *tutti* sopravvissuti e fuggiti.

Le mie mani cominciano a tremare, mentre tolgo la benda di Peter, e *realizzo* una cosa.

Ha di nuovo rischiato di essere colpito.

Avrebbe potuto essere ucciso, con il cranio distrutto da un proiettile proprio come—

No, smettila.

"Dove stiamo andando ora?" chiedo per distrarmi dai ricordi che minacciano di invadere la mia mente. Non posso immergermi in quell'oscurità, non posso concentrarmi su quello che è successo ai miei genitori o su quello che sarebbe potuto accadere a mio marito.

Non sono ancora pronta per affrontarlo.

"Questa è una buona domanda" dice Yan, mettendo giù la pomata per prendere il telefono. "Fammi vedere se il nostro contatto turco è arrivato." Tocca lo schermo alcune volte e fa una smorfia. "Fanculo."

"Che cosa c'è?" Peter cerca di sedersi, ma lo spingo a sdraiarsi.

"Stai giù" ordino, guardandolo storto. "Non ho ancora finito."

"Il nostro ragazzo del controllo aereo è in prigione" comunica Yan mentre Peter obbedisce, lasciandomi pulire intorno ai suoi punti strappati. "Qualcuno ha fiutato il suo reddito extracurricolare."

"Quindi la Turchia è fuori discussione." Peter non sembra sorpreso. "E la Lettonia?"

"Fammi vedere." Yan compone un numero, poi inizia a parlare in russo.

Qualunque cosa stia dicendo la persona dall'altra parte della linea non dev'essere buona, perché il cipiglio di Yan si fa più profondo attimo dopo attimo.

"Allora?" chiede Ilya, quando Yan riattacca. "Che cosa ti ha detto quel bastardo?"

"A quanto pare, ogni aeroporto in Europa è alla ricerca del nostro aereo" afferma Yan. "Questo include anche le piste di atterraggio private. L'Interpol ha messo una taglia ridicola sulle nostre teste, e tutti e quattro i nostri volti sono sui giornali, essendo i sospettati dietro l'attentato all'FBI. Non mi fiderei di nessuno in questo momento; hanno la stessa probabilità di tradirci quanto quella di aiutarci."

"Cazzo." Peter cerca di rimettersi a sedere, e questa volta, glielo lascio fare. La calma indotta dallo shock è completamente svanita, e sono consapevole di una terribile stanchezza combinata ad ansia che mi schiaccia il petto.

Saremo anche fuggiti, ma siamo ben lungi dall'essere al sicuro.

"Se l'Europa è fuori discussione, la nostra alternativa migliore è il Venezuela" spiega Peter, mentre gli avvolgo automaticamente una nuova benda. "Abbiamo carburante a sufficienza per arrivarci?"

"Fammi controllare con Anton" dice Yan, alzandosi dal suo posto. Scompare nella cabina di pilotaggio, poi riappare un minuto dopo. "Sì, ma è appena sufficiente" riferisce. "Se qualcosa va storto, siamo fottuti."

"Io dico di provare" replica Ilya, grattandosi il teschio tatuato. "Almeno farà caldo lì."

"Dammi il tuo telefono" dice Peter a Yan. "Contatterò Esteban. Nel frattempo, di' ad Anton di fare rotta sul Venezuela. In un modo o nell'altro, atterreremo lì."

eter

ESTEBAN, L'AVIDO FIGLIO DI PUTTANA, CHIEDE NON MENO DI TRE milioni di euro per prendere gli accordi appropriati, ma non abbiamo tempo per discutere.

Se non atterreremo nel suo piccolo aeroporto, siamo fottuti.

Alla fine, tutta la logistica viene appianata e mi dirigo verso il sedile di Sara. È abbastanza grande per due uomini, e lei sembra minuta, raggomitolata con le ginocchia sollevate sul petto, mentre guarda fuori dall'oblò dell'aereo.

"Ptichka." Affondo davanti a lei, ignorando il dolore al polpaccio e al fianco, mentre le appoggio le mani sulle caviglie. "Amore mio, stai bene?"

Si concentra su di me, sbattendo le palpebre. "Che cosa stai facendo? Dovresti stare sdraiato."

"Sto bene" rispondo, ma lei è già in piedi, tirandomi su e

verso il divano. Sospirando, glielo lascio fare—perché mi sento una merda.

"Sdraiati con me" dico, mentre mi distendo sul divano. "Voglio tenerti in braccio."

Aggrotta le sopracciglia. "Ma il tuo fianco—"

"Non preoccuparti." La tiro giù finché non ha altra scelta che allungarsi accanto a me. Rotolando sul mio lato illeso, la avvolgo da dietro, inalando il delicato profumo dei suoi capelli, mentre Ilya e Yan si voltano bruscamente ai loro posti, offrendoci un minimo di privacy.

All'inizio è rigida, senza dubbio preoccupata di urtare una delle mie ferite, ma dopo un minuto parte della rigidità abbandona i suoi muscoli. E a questo punto, lo sento.

Un tremito quasi impercettibile nel suo corpo.

Sta tremando tutta.

Il mio petto si stringe per la disperata compassione. Il mio passerotto non è ferito fisicamente—quella è stata la prima cosa di cui mi sono assicurato, quando siamo saliti sull'aereo—ma questo non significa che ne sia uscita senza alcuna conseguenza.

Quello che ha appena passato è abbastanza da provocare un Disturbo Post Traumatico da Stress a un soldato esperto, figuriamoci ad una civile.

Ad una civile *incinta.*

"Come ti senti, amore mio?" chiedo dolcemente, posandole la mano sulla pancia. Forse è la mia immaginazione, ma sembra più piatta del solito, come se avesse perso un po' di peso. E forse è così.

Tra l'imprevedibile nausea mattutina e lo stress, probabilmente non ha mangiato correttamente.

"Sto bene" mormora, anche se il suo respiro si blocca su un tremore traditore. "È solo che…"

"Le conseguenze dell'adrenalina, lo so." Mantengo la mia

voce bassa e rilassante, mentre sposto la mano dal suo stomaco per accarezzarle il fianco. "Passerà."

Fa un respiro più profondo. "Lo so. Andrà tutto bene."

"Sì" le prometto. "Raggiungeremo il nostro rifugio, e andrà tutto bene."

È la prima volta che le mento apertamente, e a giudicare dalla rinnovata rigidità del suo corpo, la mia ptichka lo sa.

Perché non andrà tutto bene.

Niente può annullare ciò che è stato fatto e riportare indietro i genitori di Sara.

Tutto quello che posso fare è cercare la vendetta—e lo farò.

Henderson pregherà di morire molto prima che io abbia finito con lui.

Henderson

FUGGITI DI NUOVO.

La furia si mescola alla crescente paura nel mio petto, mentre leggo l'ultima e-mail del mio contatto.

Sono fuggiti, tutti, proprio sotto il naso dell'Interpol.

Un altro minuto, e Sokolov e i suoi amici russi sarebbero stati circondati. L'Interpol avrebbe potuto averli tutti e quattro contemporaneamente. Invece, stanno volando, diretti chissà dove.

E questo per non parlare della fortunata fuga di Kent verso la tenuta di Esguerra nella giungla amazzonica, che persino il governo colombiano considera impenetrabile.

Se riusciranno a riorganizzarsi, sono fottuto—perché ormai avranno capito che cos'è successo e come.

Facendo un respiro per controllare un'ondata di panico, comincio a comporre un'e-mail per il mio contatto della CIA.

C'è ancora tempo per intercettare l'aereo di Sokolov.

Dobbiamo solo raggiungere gli aeroporti di tutto il mondo e convincerli a prendere provvedimenti verso tutti gli ufficiali di controllo del traffico aereo, che potrebbero essere propensi a farsi corrompere.

*S*ara

DEVO ESSERMI ABBANDONATA NELL'ABBRACCIO DI PETER, PERCHÉ mi sveglio con il basso mormorio di voci che parlano in russo. Aprendo gli occhi, vedo mio marito seduto con un computer sulle ginocchia e i gemelli in piedi accanto a lui. Sta indicando qualcosa sullo schermo e sta parlando nella sua lingua madre.

"Che cosa sta succedendo?" chiedo, alzandomi. Mi sento intontita, come se fossi rimasta svenuta per ore. E per quel che ne so, lo sono stata.

È un lungo volo dalla Svizzera al Venezuela.

Gli uomini lanciano un'occhiata nella mia direzione. "Sto solo cercando di capire dove si nascondeva il cecchino" dice Yan nello stesso momento in cui Peter afferma: "Niente, amore mio. Non preoccuparti per questo."

"Un cecchino?" Un nuovo picco di adrenalina mi fa alzare in piedi. "Quale cecchino?" Poi, mi viene in mente. "Oh, intendi dire chiunque abbia sparato all'agente che ti stava arrestando, provocando il panico e iniziando a sparare? Me lo stavo chiedendo anch'io. Inizialmente pensavo che potesse essere qualcuno che cercava di aiutarti, ma non lo era, vero? Stavano cercando di causare problemi."

Peter lancia un'occhiataccia a Yan—pensava che avrei dovuto restare fuori da questo?—prima di voltarsi per affrontarmi. "Esatto" dice in modo uniforme. "Henderson deve aver ingaggiato il cecchino per essere sicuro che venissi ucciso durante l'arresto. Immagino che il piano fosse quello di incastrarmi, quindi usare le autorità per abbattermi, insieme a tutti quelli che mi hanno sempre aiutato—e farlo in un modo molto plateale, cosicché nulla potesse essere nascosto ai media. Se fossi stato arrestato, avrei potuto convincere le autorità della mia innocenza trovando i veri colpevoli, e quindi tutto sarebbe potuto tornare com'era—e Henderson sarebbe stato nei guai."

"Ma se aveva il cecchino lì, perché non ti ha sparato direttamente invece di uccidere l'agente SWAT?" chiedo, sopprimendo un brivido, mentre l'immagine della testa di Peter che esplode mi attraversa la mente. "Se quel cecchino era in posizione—"

"Beh, per prima cosa, l'angolazione non era ottimale per colpirmi" spiega Peter. "O almeno questo è quello che abbiamo determinato sulla base dei miei ricordi dell'evento. Per quel colpo, avrebbe dovuto essere disteso sul tetto della casa a tre piani nell'isolato vicino. Ricordi, quello bianco, con il tetto grigio?"

Annuisco, e lui continua. "Beh, ero più vicino a casa nostra, quindi il tetto deve avermi protetto, almeno parzialmente. Ma cosa ancora più importante, se *fossi stato* colpito da un cecchino sconosciuto, questo avrebbe sollevato ogni sorta di sospetto su chi ci fosse realmente dietro l'attacco, e immagino che questa fosse l'ultima cosa che Henderson voleva. Ma visto che l'agente era morto, era quasi certo che i poliziotti pensassero che fosse qualcuno in combutta con me, e che sarei comunque rimasto ucciso nella sparatoria che ne derivava."

"Ed è andata quasi così." Non posso trattenere un brivido questa volta. "Sei arrivato così vicino a morire..."

Le labbra di Peter si piegano in un sorriso freddo. "Sì, ma purtroppo per Henderson, non ci sono arrivato."

Lo fisso, con i peli della nuca che si rizzano per l'oscura promessa nella sua voce. Non ho dimenticato questa parte di lui, ma era stato facile non pensarci, mentre conducevamo la nostra vita suburbana. Il Peter che avevo accettato di sposare non era stato tanto diverso dall'assassino vendicativo che aveva invaso la mia casa per uccidere George, ma era stato possibile fingere che lo fosse—che non fosse più capace delle cose terribili fatte per vendicare Tamila e suo figlio.

Solo che lo è.

Lo sarà sempre.

E ora ha un motivo in più per eliminare Henderson.

"Come hai intenzione di farlo?" chiedo, e persino io sono sorpresa di quanto suoni indifferente. "Hai già un piano in atto?"

Perché Henderson *morirà* per questo. Ne sono sicura quanto lo sono che Peter mi ami. Il mio letale marito la farà pagare dieci volte al suo nemico, e per quanto sia sbagliato, non riesco a raccogliere un grammo di oltraggio morale al pensiero.

Il mostro recentemente risvegliato dentro di me *vuole* che Henderson soffra, che conosca il dolore e la perdita devastante.

Il sorriso gelido di Peter non vacilla. "Non preoccuparti dei particolari, amore mio. Ti basti sapere che non riuscirà a farla franca."

"So che non ci riuscirà" dico sottovoce, sostenendo lo sguardo di mio marito. "Non glielo permetterai."

E mentre mi alzo, vado al bagno per rinfrescarmi, consapevole dei suoi occhi che mi seguono, mentre cammino verso la toilette.

eter

LE PERSONE ELABORANO IL TRAUMA IN MODI DIVERSI. ALCUNE cadono a pezzi e non si riprendono mai. Altre trovano un nucleo di forza che le aiuta ad andare avanti. Ho sempre saputo che Sara facesse parte della seconda categoria, ma non ho mai apprezzato il suo acciaio interiore più di quanto non faccia ora, mentre guardo la porta del bagno chiudersi dietro la sua figura snella.

È una guerriera, il mio passerotto—forte come qualsiasi soldato addestrato.

"Quindi, pensi ancora che sia tutta dolcezza e luce?" chiede Yan in russo, mentre distolgo lo sguardo dalla porta e incontro il suo, freddamente divertito. "Perché da quello che vedo, la tua piccola dottoressa perfetta sembra aver sviluppato una sete di sangue."

"Chiudi il becco, Yan" scatta Ilya, prima che io possa rispondere. "Ora non è il momento."

In qualsiasi altra circostanza, avrei già messo le mani attorno alla gola di Yan, ma Ilya ha ragione.

Stiamo per iniziare il nostro atterraggio e non c'è tempo per le cazzate.

"Farò un controllo dell'ultimo minuto sulla situazione a terra" comunico a Ilya, ignorando intenzionalmente Yan. "Esteban ha promesso che sarebbe stato tutto pronto, ma sai quanto mi fido di quel furfante."

"Giusto." Ilya strappa il telefono di Yan dalla tasca del fratello e me lo porge. "Buona idea."

Compongo il numero di un capo della polizia venezuelana che ho avuto sul mio libro paga negli ultimi tre anni e aspetto che la chiamata si connetta. Se tutto va bene, Santiago non immaginerà per quale motivo lo sto chiamando. Altrimenti…

"Hola?" risponde.

"Sono Peter Sokolov."

Segue un momento di teso silenzio; poi, sibila nel telefono: "Perché cazzo mi hai chiamato? È troppo tardi; non c'è niente che io possa fare. Sono dappertutto in quel dannato aeroporto. Te l'ho detto, non posso fare niente, con l'intero dipartimento—"

Riattacco, prima che finisca, e alzo lo sguardo per incontrare due identici occhi verdi.

"Sembra che la pista di atterraggio di Esteban sia da evitare" dico imperturbabile. "Qualche altra idea?"

50

Sara

TORNO E TROVO PETER E I GEMELLI RAGGRUPPATI ATTORNO all'ingresso della cabina di pilotaggio. Tutti e tre gli uomini sono in piedi, gesticolando con fare agitato, mentre discutono in russo con Anton.

Il mio stomaco è in subbuglio. "Che cosa c'è che non va? È successo qualcosa?"

"Il nostro contatto venezuelano ci ha traditi" spiega Ilya voltandosi. "O forse è stato catturato— non lo sappiamo per certo. In ogni caso, la polizia sta aspettando che atterriamo, il che significa che dobbiamo risparmiare le scorte di carburante e arrivare ad un altro—"

"Non c'è bisogno di risparmiare il carburante, Anton te l'ha detto." La voce di Yan è dura e acuta. "Io dico che possiamo rischiare con la polizia. Se il nostro carburante si esaurisce, la morte è certa, ma con la polizia—"

"Ne è rimasto il sette per cento" afferma Peter. "È sufficiente per portarci in un altro aeroporto nei dintorni."

"Dove ci aspetteranno in ogni caso" replica Yan. "Siamo già sul loro radar, e se sbagliamo anche di un solo millimetro..."

"È meglio che cadere in una trappola" ribatte Ilya. "Io dico di atterrare da qualche altra parte. Come una pista di atterraggio privata, un'autostrada o forse anche—" Si interrompe bruscamente e si precipita sul portatile che Peter stava usando.

"Che cosa c'è?" chiedo, con il cuore che mi martella.

"Colombia." La sua voce profonda è stranamente eccitata. "Non siamo lontani dalla tenuta amazzonica di Esguerra, che ha una pista di atterraggio all'interno..."

"Stai scherzando, vero?" Yan incrocia le braccia. "Il nostro carburante non durerebbe mai così a lungo—e questo ammesso che Esguerra voglia aiutarci. Deve già vedersela con i suoi casini."

"Sì, ma è lo stesso casino, non capisci?" Le grosse dita di Ilya volano sopra la tastiera. "Siamo noi la ragione per cui è sotto attacco. Quindi—"

"Quindi, sarà lieto di risparmiare il compito alla polizia e di abbatterci lui stesso" dice Yan. "Ad ogni modo, non vedo come avremmo abbastanza—"

"Rivedrò i calcoli del carburante con Anton" interrompe Peter, che scompare nella cabina di pilotaggio.

Lo fisso, con la nausea che riaffiora, mentre rifletto sul fatto che non ci sono buone opzioni per noi.

Anche se non rimarremo senza carburante sulla strada per il complesso di Esguerra, è improbabile che il trafficante d'armi ci accolga.

"*Potremmo* averne abbastanza da arrivare a casa di Esguerra" continua Peter, riapparendo sulla soglia. "Tutto dipende dalla velocità e dalla direzione del vento. In questo momento, abbiamo un forte vento contrario. Se rimane così com'è, ce la faremo."

"Il vento? È su questo che stiamo facendo affidamento?"

Nessuno risponde alla domanda retorica di Yan, così si dirige verso il divano e si lascia cadere, borbottando sottovoce quelle che sembrano imprecazioni in russo.

"Ho appena contattato Kent" informa Ilya, alzando lo sguardo dal computer. "È nella tenuta di Esguerra in questo momento. Forse può convincerlo a permetterci di stare con loro per un po'."

"Non c'è tempo per quello" ribatte Peter. "Quando finiranno di discutere, saremo a corto di carburante. Chiamerò direttamente Esguerra. Deve lasciarci atterrare. È la nostra unica possibilità."

eter

Il trafficante d'armi colombiano risponde al terzo squillo.

"Problemi in vista?" chiede serenamente.

"Anche dalla tua parte, immagino" rispondo con calma. L'ultima cosa che voglio è che Esguerra possa percepire qualche accenno di disperazione. "Penso che possiamo aiutarci a vicenda."

Ride in modo canzonatorio. "Sì, certo."

"Sai chi c'è dietro questo spettacolo di merda?"

"Ho qualche sospetto. L'ex generale, giusto? Quel bastardo che non hai ucciso perché volevi giocare alla famiglia felice?"

Fanculo. Naturalmente già lo sapeva. L'informazione per Esguerra è tanto importante quanto le armi che produce.

Cambio tattica. "Ascolta, mi dispiace che questo si sia riversato su di te e sui tuoi affari. Ma l'unico modo per risolvere questo problema è smascherare Henderson e quello che ha fatto. E so esattamente come farlo."

"Davvero? Non è questo il tizio a cui hai dato la caccia senza successo per tre anni?"

Ignoro la derisione nel suo tono. "Sì—il che significa che nessuno sa di lui quanto me e la mia squadra. Ci vorrebbero mesi, se non anni, per raccogliere tutti i dati che abbiamo sui suoi amici e parenti, e per setacciare tutti i nascondigli che abbiamo trovato ed eliminato. Fattene una ragione: hai bisogno di me per sistemare rapidamente questo casino, prima di perdere ancora più denaro. Quanto ti stanno costando le incursioni nelle tue fabbriche? Dieci milioni al giorno? Di più?"

Ho solo tirato a indovinare sulle incursioni, ma a giudicare dal silenzio al telefono, ho toccato un tasto dolente.

"Julian, ascoltami" continuo, mentre Sara e i gemelli mi fissano intensamente. "Posso abbattere Henderson e posso farlo velocemente. Tutto ciò di cui ho bisogno è un posto in cui riposare un po' e alcune delle tue risorse, e dimostrerò che non hai nulla a che fare con l'esplosione. A quest'ora del mese prossimo, tornerai nelle grazie dello Zio Sam, e noi saremo fuori dai tuoi piedi per sempre. Oppure puoi provare a gestirlo da solo, e vedertela con tutte le forze dell'ordine che stanno arrivando—"

"Fanculo a te e alla tua squadra." Non mi sfugge la furia nella voce di Esguerra. "Sei la ragione di tutto questo fottuto casino. E sai una cosa? Scommetto che se consegnassi te e gli altri "terroristi" della tua squadra allo Zio Sam, questo sistemerebbe il nostro rapporto."

"Davvero? Ne sei sicuro?" Ora sono io ad essere freddamente beffardo. "Un esplosivo pericoloso—il *tuo* esplosivo—è stato piazzato sul suolo americano contro l'*FBI*. Ogni agenzia è coinvolta in questo, ogni burocrate dall'alto al basso. Credi davvero che tutto sarà perdonato e dimenticato, se consegnerai i tuoi co-cospiratori? Perché è quello che penseranno, lo sai—che stai solo facendo fuori i tuoi compari. A meno che non smascheri Henderson per quello che è e riabiliti il tuo nome rapidamente, sei fottuto quanto noi."

Segue un altro lungo silenzio teso sulla linea. Poi, Esguerra afferma aspramente: "Bene. Posso darvi un posto per dormire. Ho un contatto in Sudan. Una volta arrivati lì—"

"Il Sudan non va bene" interrompo. "Ho un altro posto in mente."

"Sarebbe?"

"La tua tenuta. Saremo lì tra un'ora."

E prima che possa replicare, riattacco.

Sara

GUARDO, CON LO STOMACO IN GOLA, MENTRE PETER METTE IN tasca il telefono con calma e torna alla cabina di pilotaggio—presumibilmente per informare Anton che ci stiamo recando alla tenuta di Esguerra, a prescindere dai sentimenti del trafficante d'armi in merito.

"Sai che ci abbatterà mentre ci avviciniamo" dice Yan, quando Peter riappare un minuto dopo. "E questo ammesso che il nostro carburante duri così a lungo."

"Durerà" assicura Ilya. "E lui non ci abbatterà. Hai sentito Peter: Esguerra ha bisogno di noi per risolvere questo casino in fretta."

"Sì, certo" mormora Yan, che si dirige verso il bagno nella parte posteriore dell'aereo.

Le mie gambe non sono del tutto ferme, mentre mi avvicino al divano e mi siedo.

È così che moriremo?

Non per un proiettile, ma in un incidente aereo?

Il divano affonda accanto a me, e una grande mano calda mi copre il ginocchio. "Andrà tutto bene, ptichka" sussurra Peter, alzando l'altra mano per togliermi i capelli dal viso. Le sue dita mi sfiorano la mascella, con un tocco così tenero che mi fa venir voglia di piangere.

"Come fai a saperlo?" mormoro, e poi mi rimprovero, perché mi sto comportando come una bambina bisognosa.

Ovviamente non lo sa.

Lo sta solo dicendo per farmi sentire meglio.

"Perché conosco Julian" dice sottovoce. Non si rade da giorni, e la barba scura accentua il pallore malsano della sua pelle. Tuttavia, in qualche modo continua ad irradiare la sua solita forza e sicurezza. So che molto probabilmente si tratta di una facciata, ma non posso fare a meno di sentirmi rassicurata, mentre preme le labbra sulla mia fronte, e poi mi avvolge un potente braccio intorno alle spalle, tirandomi contro il fianco sano.

"Dovresti riposare" mormoro dopo un minuto. Pur essendo forte, mio marito non è invincibile. Solo pochi giorni fa stava per morire. Ma quando tento di allontanarmi, mi stringe più forte, e mi arrendo con un sospiro, appoggiando la testa sulla sua spalla.

Non vale la pena litigare.

Dopotutto, questa potrebbe essere la nostra ultima ora insieme.

Peter

Il vento in coda si indebolisce proprio mentre stiamo per iniziare la discesa. Lo scopro tramite un laconico annuncio di Anton.

Scusandomi, mi districo attentamente dall'abbraccio di Sara e mi dirigo verso di lui, grato che abbia avuto la lungimiranza di parlare in russo.

La mia ptichka è già abbastanza preoccupata.

Ilya e Yan sono già all'interno dell'abitacolo, con Yan accucciato accanto ad Anton, che tiene in mano un computer.

"Per quanto tempo potremo ancora andare avanti?" chiedo senza preamboli.

"Non molto" risponde Anton. "Se la velocità del vento non si riduce ulteriormente, potremmo avere un atterraggio difficile— o forse no. Dipende da quanto questo aereo possa andare avanti per inerzia."

"Non ci sono piste di atterraggio più vicine?" chiede Ilya. "Anche una strada larga andrebbe bene."

"Non riesco a trovare nulla di simile sulla mappa" dice Yan, e lo vedo zoomare su una regione molto boscosa su Google Maps. "Siamo proprio ai margini della giungla; non ci sono altro che alberi, fiumi e strette strade sterrate."

Trattengo una brutta imprecazione.

Non sta andando bene.

Anzi, sta andando malissimo.

Se fossimo solo noi, non mi preoccuperei più di tanto—le persone possono sopravvivere agli incidenti aerei—ma un atterraggio difficile potrebbe essere troppo per Sara e il bambino.

"Che cosa sta succedendo?" chiede dietro di me, e mi giro per trovarla intenta a fissare preoccupata i comandi. "È successo qualcosa?"

Nessuno risponde. Nemmeno Yan ha più commenti sarcastici.

"Niente, ptichka. Ci stiamo solo preparando per atterrare" rispondo in modo pacato, e prendendole la mano, la conduco fuori dalla cabina.

54

Sara

DENTRO DI ME, LE VISCERE SEMBRANO FOGLIE IN UNA TEMPESTA invernale, mentre Peter mi guida verso il sedile e mi allaccia la cintura, stringendomela sul grembo, finché non riesco quasi a respirare. Poi, si avvicina al divano e tira via i cuscini. Li solleva, li accatasta davanti a me, poi apre uno scomparto sopra la testa e tira giù una sacca da viaggio.

"Che cosa stai facendo?" La mia voce inizia a tremare. "Peter, che cosa stai facendo?"

Non risponde, tira solo fuori una lunga corda e un coltello. Afferrando uno dei cuscini, lo lega allo schienale del sedile di fronte a me, esattamente dove la mia testa colpirebbe, se assumessi la classica posizione da incidente aereo e qualcosa dovesse spingermi in avanti.

Poi, prende l'altro cuscino e lo infila alla mia sinistra, tra il sedile e l'oblò. Si incastra saldamente lì dentro, quindi non ha bisogno di usare la corda per tenerlo fermo.

"Stiamo per schiantarci?" È una domanda stupida, perché è ovvio che cosa stia succedendo, ma non posso farci niente. Voglio che mi menta di nuovo, che mi rassicuri dicendo che quello che sta facendo non è altro che una sciocca precauzione.

"No, stiamo atterrando" risponde, come se mi leggesse nel pensiero, e poi afferra il terzo cuscino alla mia destra legandolo a me.

Mi sbagliavo.

Non voglio che menta.

Voglio che mi dica la verità, in modo da poter impazzire del tutto.

La punta dell'aereo affonda e il mio stomaco fa lo stesso, quando sento l'improvviso cambiamento della pressione nella cabina.

"Peter." La mia voce è sorprendentemente ferma. "Per favore, siediti."

"Tra un momento" dice e scompare nella parte posteriore, mentre Yan e Ilya escono dalla cabina di pilotaggio e prendono i loro posti.

Pochi secondi dopo, mio marito riappare con alcuni cuscini. Ignorando le mie proteste, li lega tutti intorno a me, con uno piccolo sulla mia testa. Quando ha finito, sembro un marshmallow umano.

Allora e solo allora si siede accanto a me.

"Prendi alcuni di questi cuscini per te" lo imploro, ma si limita a stringere le cinture di sicurezza. "Per favore, Peter. O almeno danne un paio ai tuoi compagni di squadra. Perché dovrei averli tutti io? Ti prego, ascoltami…"

"Non ascoltarla, Peter" dice ironicamente Ilya dall'altra fila. "Staremo bene."

"Ma—"

"Rilassati, Sara" replica freddamente Yan. "Mio fratello ha ragione. Inoltre, l'imbottitura sarà sufficiente."

Peter ringhia qualcosa di acuto in russo—probabilmente un ammonimento per avermi spaventata inutilmente—e sento le orecchie scoppiarmi, mentre la nostra discesa accelera.

"Sette minuti all'atterraggio" annuncia Anton nell'interfono, e Peter allunga il braccio sul tavolo tra i nostri sedili, con la mano che scava nella pila di cuscini per stringere la mia. La sua presa è forte come al solito, ma le dita sono fredde, mentre si avvolgono attorno al mio palmo.

"Sei minuti" dice Ilya, mentre l'aereo si inclina a sinistra, permettendomi di intravedere la foresta verde sottostante.

In lontananza, scorgo una vasta area deserta con alcuni piccoli edifici vicino a uno più grande, ma poi l'aereo si piega verso destra e tutto quello che vedo è il cielo.

Un borbottio interrompe il costante ronzio dei motori. Sembra un gigante che si schiarisce la voce.

Smetto di respirare, mentre guardo Peter.

Il suo volto è bianco, la mascella incassata in una linea brutale, ma la presa sulla mia mano rimane ferma e rassicurante.

I motori riprendono il loro ronzio, e io faccio un respiro tanto necessario. Il sudore freddo si accumula sotto le ascelle, e tutti i cuscini mi fanno sentire come se stessi soffocando.

"Cinque minuti" comunica Ilya con voce rauca. "Ancora un po', e potrà abbassare il carrello di atterraggio senza rovinare la nostra traiettoria di discesa."

I motori tossiscono di nuovo, quindi riprendono a funzionare.

L'aereo si inclina di nuovo a destra, e mi sforzo di guardare fuori dall'oblò.

Il complesso di edifici—la tenuta di Esguerra, presumibilmente—è quasi direttamente sotto di noi ora, e vedo che l'edificio bianco è una dimora maestosa. Noto anche quella che sembra una torre di guardia carceraria ai margini dell'area disboscata.

"Quattro minuti" informa Ilya, e individuo la nostra destinazione: una pista pavimentata ad una certa distanza dalla villa, con una fitta macchia di foresta che la circonda su entrambi i lati.

I motori tossiscono di nuovo.

"Tre minuti" comunica Ilya, con voce tesa, quando il carrello inizia ad aprirsi con uno stridio.

Dopo un ultimo borbottio, i motori rimangono in silenzio e lo stridio si interrompe.

Abbiamo appena esaurito il carburante.

"Ptichka." La voce di Peter è stranamente calma, mentre il mio sguardo terrorizzato incontra il suo. "Ti amo. Adesso tieniti forte."

Sara

HO SEMPRE PENSATO CHE GLI AEREI CON MOTORI malfunzionanti cadessero dal cielo, come uccelli colpiti. Ma mentre guardo Peter in preda al terrore, non sembra una brusca caduta.

In qualche modo, stiamo ancora planando, mentre scendiamo.

"Sara." La sua voce si acuisce. "Piegati e abbracciati le ginocchia. Ora."

Le mie membra paralizzate in qualche modo obbediscono, e con la coda dell'occhio, lo vedo assumere la stessa posizione.

Oh, Dio.

Sta succedendo.

È tutto vero.

Stiamo per schiantarci.

Stiamo per morire.

Il mio rapido respiro è un ciclone rumoroso nelle orecchie, con la mano destra scivolosa per il sudore, mentre la spingo attraverso il mucchio di cuscini per toccare il braccio di Peter.

Ho bisogno di sentirlo.

Di sapere che siamo connessi fino alla fine.

Poi, avvolge di nuovo la sua grande mano intorno al mio palmo, e per una frazione di secondo, è tutto ciò di cui ho bisogno. La gioia è intensa quanto il panico che mi consuma, con l'ondata di amore così forte che supera la paura della morte imminente.

"Ti amo" sussurro, girando la testa per incontrare il suo sguardo argenteo. "Ti amerò sempre, Peter... in questo mondo e oltre."

L'impatto iniziale è come atterrare su un cavallo selvaggio. L'aereo colpisce il terreno così forte che rimbalza due volte, ogni scossone più duro del successivo. La cintura sul grembo è l'unica cosa che mi impedisca di volare via dal sedile, e la mia spalla sinistra sbatte contro il cuscino del divano, mentre l'aereo si piega violentemente su un lato, prima di livellarsi.

Il carrello di atterraggio non deve essersi aperto fino in fondo, mi rendo conto, quando lo stridio agonizzante del metallo che si trascina sul marciapiede mi raggiunge le orecchie oltre l'assordante battito cardiaco. E poi, miracolosamente, stiamo rallentando.

Siamo a terra e stiamo rallentando.

La consapevolezza mi colpisce lentamente, e solo quando ci siamo fermati la comprendo pienamente.

Siamo sopravvissuti.

Abbiamo esaurito il carburante, ma siamo atterrati.

Respiro in modo irregolare, mi tiro su e apro gli occhi—devo averli chiusi durante l'atterraggio—e vedo Peter che si sta già alzando, con il volto barbuto e ispido che si acciglia preoccupato, mentre libera la sua mano dalla mia presa.

Allentando la cintura di sicurezza, mi libera rapidamente dai cuscini, prima di accarezzarmi dalla testa ai piedi.

"Stai bene?" chiede con fervore, e quando annuisco, mi ritrovo strattonata nel suo abbraccio e stretta così forte che non riesco a respirare. Non che ne abbia bisogno. Questo è tutto ciò di cui ho bisogno. Il suo calore si insinua nel mio corpo congelato, il profumo confortante mi circonda, e con l'orecchio premuto sul suo petto possente, sento il suo cuore battere in sintonia con il mio.

Ce l'abbiamo fatta.

Stiamo insieme e siamo vivi.

P eter

S E POTESSI FARE COME VOGLIO IO, ABBRACCEREI S ARA PER sempre, sentendo il suo calore e respirando il suo profumo, ma c'è ancora il nostro ostile ospite da affrontare.

Con riluttanza, la lascio andare e faccio un passo indietro. Ilya e Yan sono già sulla porta, aprendola e abbassando la scala, così vado ad aiutarli.

Di sicuro, fuori ci sono guardie armate a sufficienza per abbattere un plotone. Hanno circondato il nostro aereo, e dietro di loro ci sono almeno venti SUV con i rinforzi, ed un'altra dozzina che si avvicina, mentre guardo.

"Resta qui finché non vengo a prenderti" dico a mia moglie girandomi, e poi esco nel caldo umido della giungla, pronto a sparare.

Solo perché Esguerra ci ha lasciati atterrare non significa

che ci lascerà vivere. Potrebbe aver semplicemente voluto che il nostro aereo non fosse danneggiato.

Non mi arrivano pallottole, ma so che è meglio non rilassarsi, mentre scendo i gradini, con l'adrenalina che mi aiuta a nascondere la zoppia.

"Sono disarmato" grido, mentre le guardie più vicine alzano i loro M16. Devono essere nuove; non riconosco alcun volto conosciuto durante il mio periodo di impiego da Esguerra. "Di' al tuo capo che sono qui per vederlo."

"Davvero?" dice Esguerra, sbucando da dietro un gruppo di guardie. "Che coincidenza. Perché avrei giurato che il tuo aereo fosse precipitato qui... come se avessi esaurito il carburante."

"Sì, beh, succede. Perdita di carburante all'ultimo minuto e tutto il resto."

Sibila tra i denti in falsa comprensione. "Dovresti licenziare il tuo tizio della manutenzione. Le perdite di carburante sono pericolose."

"Lo sono, vero?" Il mio sorriso è affilato come il coltello che ho nascosto nello stivale. Nonostante quello che ho detto, non sono mai completamente disarmato. "Ma tutto è bene quel che finisce bene. Siamo qui ora, quindi perché non accantoniamo i perché per dopo e ci concentriamo su ciò che conta—trovare Henderson e risolvere questa situazione il più rapidamente possibile."

Gli occhi di Esguerra si restringono fino a diventare un barlume blu, e per un momento sono sicuro che mi ucciderà. Ma il senso degli affari deve prevalere, perché afferma freddamente: "Va bene. Hai due settimane per sistemare questo casino. Diego mostrerà a te e alla tua squadra i vostri alloggi."

Si gira per allontanarsi, e lascio andare il respiro che ho trattenuto.

Siamo ben lungi dall'essere al sicuro, ma ci siamo appena guadagnati un po' di tempo.

PARTE IV

enderson

"Più veloce" ringhio a Jimmy, mentre trascina la valigia in macchina, con un'espressione di petulante noia adolescenziale. Bonnie e mia figlia diciottenne, Amber, sono già all'interno del veicolo, in attesa.

A differenza del mio stupido figlio, capiscono la serietà di tutto questo. Sanno che se Sokolov e i suoi compari ci troveranno, ci aspettano destini peggiori della morte.

La sconfitta è un acuto sentore sulla mia lingua, mentre salgo in macchina e chiudo la portiera. Secondo le mie fonti, ora anche Sokolov è nel complesso di Esguerra, il che significa che i miei nemici non solo si stanno raggruppando, ma stanno anche organizzando una squadra.

Dobbiamo scappare di nuovo.

Dobbiamo nasconderci.

Almeno, finché non troverò un altro modo per catturarli.

Sara

Mi sveglio con gli inquietanti versi di un bambino che piange, combinati ad alcune voci di donne che cercano di calmarlo.

Aprendo gli occhi, mi metto a sedere, cercando di far funzionare il cervello, in modo da poter capire dove mi trovo. E mentre mi guardo intorno nella semplice stanza, con le sue pareti bianche e il tappeto grigio, capisco tutto.

Siamo in Colombia, nella tenuta del trafficante d'armi.

Più precisamente, siamo nella casa dove Diego—una giovane guardia che a quanto pare Peter conosce—ci ha portati ieri. Sospetto che il nostro ospite ce l'abbia concessa a causa mia. Yan, Ilya e Anton sono andati con le guardie nelle caserme, ma Esguerra deve aver pensato che sarebbe stato strano per una coppia sposata condividere la stanza con un gruppo di ragazzi.

Sono contenta di questo; mi piace la privacy. Per non

parlare del fatto che l'abitazione stessa è bella—pulita e moderna, anche se arredata in modo minimale. Ho persino trovato alcuni vestiti nell'armadio, e sembrano essere più o meno della mia taglia—uno sviluppo utile, dato che i miei indumenti attualmente consistono solo nei jeans e nel maglione con cui sono arrivata.

"Questa non era la residenza di Kent? Dove alloggia lui?" ha domandato Peter, mentre ci avvicinavamo, e Diego ha spiegato che Lucas e Yulia Kent vivono nella casa principale con gli Esguerra—per motivi di sicurezza e convenienza viste le loro riunioni di lavoro.

Il pianto sembra provenire dall'esterno, così mi alzo e infilo una vestaglia che ho trovato nell'armadio ieri. Poi, vado a sbirciare fuori dalla finestra della camera da letto attraverso le persiane chiuse.

Due giovani donne dai capelli scuri sono accovacciate su una bambina distesa su una coperta sul prato verde davanti alla casa. Stanno cambiando il pannolino della bimba, che sta piangendo come se fosse la cosa peggiore del mondo.

Chi sono?

E dov'è Peter?

A giudicare dal sole splendente là fuori, è già mattina—il che, dato che mi sono addormentata solo poche ore dopo il nostro arrivo di ieri, significa che ho dormito per qualcosa come sedici ore.

Il mio corpo deve aver avuto bisogno di riposo dopo tutto lo stress.

Automaticamente, la mia mano va allo stomaco. È ancora piatto, senza alcun segno di vita che cresce all'interno, ma so che è lì. Lo sento.

Un bambino mio.

Tra qualche mese, cambierò i pannolini anch'io.

Ammesso che saremo ancora vivi, voglio dire.

Con il petto che si stringe, mi allontano dalla finestra. Per un momento, avevo quasi dimenticato la natura precaria delle nostre circostanze—e ciò che ci ha portati qui.

Il ruggito dell'elicottero in mezzo agli spari, le pressioni sul petto di papà in un inutile sforzo di far riprendere a battere il suo cuore, la faccia di mamma con un pezzo mancante—

Ansimando, crollo sulle ginocchia, con il cuore che mi batte forte, mentre il sudore freddo mi ricopre il corpo. Per un secondo, è come se fossi stata trasportata indietro nel tempo, con un flashback così vivido che ho sentito l'odore metallico e il caldo spruzzo del sangue sul mio viso.

Oh, Dio.

Non posso farlo.

Non posso soffermarmici.

Tremando, mi alzo in piedi e barcollo verso il bagno attiguo, dove apro l'acqua più calda possibile e indugio, lasciando che bruci il ghiaccio dentro di me.

Un giorno, riuscirò a pensare ai miei genitori, ma non ancora.

Non per molto, molto tempo.

IL CAMPANELLO ALLA PORTA SUONA PROPRIO MENTRE STO entrando nel soggiorno, con indosso un paio di pantaloncini di jeans e una maglietta che ho trovato nell'armadio. Mi stanno sorprendentemente bene. Dato quello che Peter ha detto sul fatto che questa sia la casa di Kent, immagino che tutti i vestiti da donna qui siano di Yulia.

Spero che non le dispiaccia, se li prendo in prestito.

Il campanello suona di nuovo.

"Peter?" grido, guardandomi intorno, ma non c'è risposta. Dev'essere fuori dalla casa.

Respirando, cammino verso la porta e la apro.

Fuori ci sono le due giovani donne che ho visto prima, con la bambina che ora sta dormendo in un passeggino. Sembrano avere poco più di vent'anni e indossano un prendisole e dei sandali casual. Una è minuta e incredibilmente bella, con lucenti capelli lunghi fino alla vita e una corporatura snella e atletica, mentre l'altra ha le guance rotonde, con un sorriso luminoso e una figura sinuosa. Con mio grande stupore, entrambe sembrano familiari.

Dove le ho già viste?

"Ciao" dice la ragazza minuta, studiandomi con un'espressione strana. I suoi occhi sono enormi e scuri nel suo viso delicato. "Devi essere la moglie di Peter. Sono Nora Esguerra."

Anche il nome mi ricorda qualcosa—oltre all'ormai familiare "Esguerra."

"E io sono Rosa Martinez" dice l'altra ragazza con un debole accento spagnolo. Come Nora, mi sta fissando come se fossi una specie di animale esotico, e mi rendo conto che anche il *suo* nome è familiare.

Ci siamo decisamente incontrate. Ma dove?

"Ciao" dico lentamente, mentre un ricordo affiora nei meandri della mente. È qualcosa avvenuto anni fa, qualcosa che ha a che fare con il mio ospedale... "Sono Sara Cobakis—cioè Sokolov." O Garin, o qualsiasi altra identità che Peter ci farà assumere in seguito.

"E sei un medico, giusto?" Nora piega la testa. "Non so se ti ricordi, ma—"

"Eri una mia paziente!" esclamo, mentre mi viene in mente. Il mio sguardo si concentra su Rosa, e il mio shock si intensifica. "Lo eravate *entrambe*."

Lo ricordo ora. È stato anni fa, non molto tempo dopo l'incidente di George. Ero stata chiamata al pronto soccorso per curare due giovani donne che erano state aggredite in un nightclub. Una di loro—Rosa—era stata stuprata, mentre l'altra

—Nora—aveva subito un aborto nel tentativo di difendere la sua amica.

C'era anche il marito di Nora, un uomo straordinariamente bello che sembrava essere sul punto di uccidere tutti tranne la sua giovane moglie.

Quello era Julian Esguerra?

Ho già conosciuto l'uomo di cui ho tanto sentito parlare?

Le labbra di Nora si piegano in un sorriso. "Hai una buona memoria. Sono sicura che hai avuto migliaia di pazienti nel corso degli anni."

"Io... sì, ma..." Rendendomi conto che le sto tenendo fuori come se fossero dei venditori porta a porta, faccio un passo indietro e spalanco la porta. "Prego, entrate. Deve fare caldo là fuori."

"Grazie" dice Nora, entrando, e Rosa la segue, spingendo il passeggino davanti a lei.

"È tua figlia?" chiedo a Rosa, ma lei sorride e scuote la testa.

"È di Nora."

"Oh, sì, questa è Lizzie." Nora spinge indietro la copertura del passeggino e si china per prendere la bambina addormentata. Cullandola dolcemente su una spalla, mi sorride. "Ha cinque mesi."

"Congratulazioni" dico sottovoce. Ricordo quanto fosse stata devastata in ospedale, preoccupata per la sua amica. E Rosa... è difficile credere che la ragazza maltrattata che ho curato quella notte sia la donna dagli occhi luminosi di fronte a me. Se non fosse stato per la presenza di Nora, forse avrei impiegato più tempo a riconoscerla; metà della faccia di Rosa era gonfia e incrostata di sangue, quando l'ho vista per l'ultima volta.

"Grazie." Il sorriso di Nora si attenua leggermente, poi torna grande. "È tutto il nostro mondo—ecco perché ho detto a Julian che avremmo dovuto offrirvi un riparo, nonostante la sua incazzatura per la situazione di Henderson."

Sbatto le palpebre. "Che cosa?"

Rosa calpesta il piede di Nora e mormora velocemente qualcosa in spagnolo.

"Sono sicura che sappia di Henderson" dice Nora, accigliandosi con la sua amica, prima di guardarmi. "Sai di Henderson, giusto?"

"Sì, certo" rispondo. "Sono solo confusa su cosa tua figlia abbia a che vedere con la storia del nostro rifugio."

"Oh, quello." Nora sembra sollevata. "Peter non te l'ha detto?" Al mio sguardo assente, spiega: "Tuo marito ci ha fatto un enorme favore negli ultimi mesi—uno che potrebbe aver salvato Lizzie dalle grinfie di un uomo molto malvagio."

"E te" le ricorda Rosa, e Nora annuisce.

"Giusto, e me. E anche la vita di Julian, anche se lui non vuole riconoscere quella parte."

"Oh, capisco." Dev'essere il favore che Peter aveva menzionato—quello che alla fine gli ha procurato l'accordo di amnistia. Vorrei fare un milione di domande su questo e su tutto il resto, ma prima devo smettere di essere una cattiva padrona di casa. "Volete qualcosa da mangiare o da bere?" chiedo. "Penso che Peter abbia rifornito il frigo ieri..."

"Sto bene, grazie" dice Nora e si avvicina per sedersi sul divano.

"Un bicchiere d'acqua per me, per favore" dice Rosa, quando la guardo.

Felice di avere qualcosa da fare, vado in cucina e riempio due bicchieri d'acqua filtrata, uno per me e uno per Rosa. Come il resto della casa, la cucina è pulita e moderna, anche se non eccessivamente lussuosa. Posso sicuramente immaginare Lucas Kent qui; l'estetica minimalista sembra qualcosa che potrebbe piacergli.

"Allora, come vi siete conosciuti tu e Peter?" chiede Nora, quando torno in soggiorno e porto a Rosa il suo bicchiere d'acqua. Ora è sul divano accanto a Nora, e Lizzie è di nuovo nel passeggino, che dorme ancora pacificamente.

Deve essersi stancata dopo aver pianto così tanto.

"È una lunga storia" rispondo alla domanda di Nora, mentre mi siedo su una sedia di fronte a loro. "E tu e tuo marito? E come mai eravate a Chicago in quel periodo? Sei originaria della zona?"

Non sono sicura di voler entrare nei dettagli del mio primo incontro con Peter. Per quanto possano sembrare cordiali queste giovani donne, non posso dimenticare che stanno dalla parte del nostro ospite—un uomo che, se non è esattamente il nemico di Peter, non è certo il suo amico.

"I miei genitori vivono a Oak Lawn" spiega Nora. "Quindi sì, sono originaria della zona di Chicago. E tu vieni da Homer Glen, giusto?"

"Sì. Wow, che coincidenza." Oak Lawn è a meno di un'ora di macchina da Homer Glen.

La moglie di Esguerra e io eravamo praticamente vicine di casa.

Nora sorride. "È assurdo, vero? Per quanto riguarda come ci siamo conosciuti io e Julian, è successo in un nightclub di Chicago. Lui era in zona per affari e io ero uscita con un'amica, per festeggiare il mio diciottesimo compleanno. Qualche settimana dopo, lui mi ha rapita e—"

Quasi sputo l'acqua che avevo iniziato a sorseggiare. "Lui *cosa?*"

"Non è così terribile come sembra" mi tranquillizza Nora, poi sogghigna, scuotendo la testa. "Oh, che cosa sto dicendo? È davvero così terribile come sembra. Ma siamo felici ora, e questo è tutto ciò che conta. E tu? Come hai conosciuto Peter?"

"Sì, come?" fa eco Rosa, e percepisco qualcosa di più della semplice curiosità nel suo sguardo intenso.

Cerco nella mia memoria. Qualcos'altro sta riaffiorando dal retro del cervello, qualcosa di grosso... E poi, mi viene in mente.

Naturalmente.

Come ho potuto dimenticarlo?

Voltandomi verso Nora, dico apertamente: "Sai già come ci siamo conosciuti. O almeno dovresti... perché sei tu quella che ha dato a Peter la sua lista."

eter

È INCREDIBILE QUELLO CHE POSSA FARE UNA LUNGA NOTTE DI sonno. Il fianco mi fa ancora male quando mi muovo, e il polpaccio e il braccio dolgono debolmente, ma mi sento decisamente meglio, mentre mi siedo davanti al tavolo di Kent ed Esguerra.

Ilya, Yan e Anton si uniscono a me dalla mia parte, e sorrido, mentre una grassoccia donna di mezza età porta un vassoio di frutta e biscotti tagliati.

Questo è un miglioramento dal modo in cui Esguerra era solito tenere riunioni di lavoro in questo ufficio. Non c'era cibo allora, da quel che ricordo.

"Grazie, Ana" dico, mentre sistema il piatto al centro del tavolo ovale, e la governante mi sorride, felice di essere ricordata. Non ho interagito molto con lei, quando lavoravo per Esguerra, ma ho una buona memoria per i nomi.

"Bentornato, Señor Sokolov" replica con un forte accento spagnolo. "È bello rivederti."

"Anche per me" dico, e lascia la stanza.

Il mio sorriso scompare, mentre rivolgo l'attenzione ai due uomini seduti di fronte a me. Nessuno dei due sembra particolarmente contento di essere qui, e per una buona ragione.

Secondo i nostri hacker, la scorsa notte c'è stato un raid negli uffici di Esguerra ad Hong Kong.

Ignaro della tensione nella stanza, Ilya si allunga per prendere un biscotto. "Buono" dice dopo averlo assaggiato, e Anton lo segue, prendendo un biscotto e un grappolo d'uva per sé.

Esguerra li osserva freddamente, poi si rivolge a me. "Quindi, Henderson."

"Giusto." Spingo una spessa cartella sul tavolo verso di lui. "Questo è tutto ciò che abbiamo sul bastardo. Ti invierò anche i file via e-mail, nel caso in cui i tuoi uomini vogliano analizzare i modelli di dati."

"Immagino che tu l'abbia già fatto" ipotizza Kent, e annuisco.

"Circa una dozzina di volte."

"E?" chiede Kent.

Mi stringo nelle spalle. "Niente di decisivo per ora. Ma ho alcune idee."

E mentre Esguerra si sporge in avanti, sopprimo i resti della mia coscienza e ripercorro ciò che voglio fare.

Se Henderson pensava che fossimo in guerra prima, si sbagliava.

Questa è la guerra—e molto prima che avremo finito, si piegherà e implorerà pietà.

60

*S*ara

ALLE MIE PAROLE ACCUSATORIE, NORA TRASALISCE, MA NON distoglie lo sguardo. "Quindi, sai della lista. Quando ho letto per la prima volta il tuo nome sui giornali, mi sono chiesta se fosse stata quella a farvi unire."

"Vuoi dire se sei la ragione per cui ha fatto irruzione in casa mia per strapparmi l'ubicazione del mio primo marito ormai defunto?" chiedo sardonicamente, e Nora sussulta di nuovo.

"È quello che è successo? Speravo che forse Peter ti avesse risparmiata, o almeno..." Abbassa lo sguardo. "Non importa."

"Voleva contattarti, sai" spiega Rosa, sporgendosi in avanti. "Quando abbiamo capito chi fossi, Nora voleva contattarti e avvertirti di Peter."

Fisso la moglie di Esguerra. "Davvero?" Questo non avrebbe aiutato George—Peter alla fine l'avrebbe rintracciato comunque—ma forse se fossi stata avvisata in anticipo, quella notte non sarei stata colta di sorpresa nella mia cucina.

Forse avrei accettato di nascondermi, come volevano i Federali, e Peter avrebbe trovato un altro modo per arrivare a George.

Forse il mio tormentatore ed io non ci saremmo mai conosciuti.

Il mio petto si contrae al pensiero, e con grande shock, mi rendo conto che non è ciò che voglio.

Nonostante tutto quello che è successo, tutto quello che ho perso, se avessi una macchina del tempo e potessi riscrivere magicamente la storia, non lo farei.

Sceglierei di stare qui con Peter e in nessun'altra vita senza la sua presenza.

"Sì, ma non l'ho fatto." Nora solleva la testa, con lo sguardo cupo. "Mi dispiace, Sara. Ho visto il nome di tuo marito sulla lista, mentre la inviavo a Peter, e quando eravamo in ospedale, ho pensato che qualcosa sul tuo cartellino sembrasse familiare, ma solo in seguito ho messo insieme due più due. E quando l'ho fatto..." Inspira. "Beh, non importa ora."

"Importa" dice Rosa, con gli occhi castani che brillano. "Non l'ha fatto, perché suo marito l'ha fermata."

"Rosa—" la rimprovera Nora, ma la sua amica le mette una mano sul ginocchio.

"No, lasciami finire." Mi osserva. "Se vuoi incolpare qualcuno, Sara, quella persona dovrei essere io. Ho riferito al Señor Esguerra che cosa stava progettando Nora, e lui si è assicurato che non l'avrebbe fatto."

Sbatto le palpebre "Davvero? Perché?"

In realtà, non sono arrabbiata per il mancato avvertimento —ovviamente non erano obbligate a farmi alcun favore—ma non capisco perché Rosa abbia interferito.

"Perché Peter Sokolov è un uomo pericoloso." Il suo sguardo non vacilla. "Forse pericoloso come lo stesso Señor Esguerra. E dopo tutto quello che Nora aveva passato, l'ultima cosa di cui lei aveva bisogno era che lui desse la caccia a lei e al Señor Esguerra per essersi intromessi. Tuo marito era ossessionato da quella lista; avrebbe eliminato chiunque avesse ostacolato la sua vendetta."

"Sì, lo so" dico. "Ero lì."

Adesso è Rosa a distogliere lo sguardo.

"Allora, come sei finita a sposarlo?" chiede Nora, rivolgendomi un'occhiata solenne. Se non fosse per quei suoi grandi occhi scuri, con la sua statura minuta e la pelle liscia come quella di una bambina, potrebbe essere scambiata per un'adolescente. Ma il suo sguardo la tradisce.

È lo sguardo di una donna—di una che ha conosciuto più della sua equa dose di sofferenza.

Ha detto che suo marito l'ha rapita, quando aveva diciotto anni. Com'è stato per lei? Io avevo ventotto anni, quando Peter è entrato nella mia vita, e ho avuto problemi a gestire le complessità emotive della nostra relazione contorta. Come ha fatto questa ragazza a quella giovane età?

Come è riuscita a sopravvivere a un uomo che, secondo tutte le indicazioni, è il diavolo in persona?

"Immagino nello stesso modo in cui tu sei finita a sposare tuo marito" dico, mentre continua a guardarmi, aspettando una risposta. "Ho iniziato odiando Peter, e poi, nel tempo, è tutto... cambiato. Dopo aver ottenuto l'ubicazione di George da me, Peter lo ha ucciso ed è scomparso, ma poi è tornato per me."

Potrei raccontarle tutta la storia disordinata, ma non ne ho bisogno. Capisce; lo vedo nei suoi occhi.

"Mi dispiace, Sara, per il mio ruolo nella tua sfortuna" sussurra dolcemente. "Spero che un giorno mi perdonerai. E per quello che vale, a volte devi immergerti nell'oscurità per trovare la luce più brillante. Questo è quello che ho dovuto fare *io*, almeno."

Sorrido per farle capire che non c'è niente da perdonare,

quando la bimba inizia a fare capricci. Rosa salta su e corre verso il passeggino, chiaramente contenta di avere qualcosa da fare, e anche Nora si alza in piedi.

"Dovremmo andare, lasciarti sistemare" aggiunge, mentre Rosa prende in braccio la bimba e calma le sue grida dondolandola avanti e indietro. "Se hai bisogno di qualcosa— qualsiasi cosa—siamo a pochi passi dalla casa principale."

"Grazie. Sei stata più che generosa" le dico, e intendo sul serio. Realizzo solo ora che è stata *lei* a convincere suo marito a fornirci un riparo; il suo commento era stato talmente disinvolto che mi era quasi sfuggito.

Chissà se Esguerra ci avrebbe lasciato atterrare, se non fosse stato per lei?

Potremmo dovere le nostre vite a questa giovane donna.

"È stato bello rivederti, Sara" dice Rosa, sorridendomi brillantemente, mentre passa l'ormai tranquillizzata Lizzie a Nora, e io ricambio il sorriso, anche se il mio sguardo si posa sulla bambina.

"Vuoi tenerla?" chiede Nora dolcemente, e io annuisco, con un formicolio quasi elettrico che mi attraversa, mentre raggiungo sua figlia.

È morbida e calda, come un piccolo fagotto, e mentre la sistemo sulla mia spalla, come ho visto fare Nora, gira la testa e mi fissa con enormi occhi azzurri.

"È stupenda" sussurro con riverenza—ed è vero. La sua testolina è ricoperta di capelli scuri e setosi, e la pelle liscia e delicata è di una splendida tonalità di oro chiaro. Tutti le bambine sono carine, ma questa... Spezzerà i cuori, lo so.

Che aspetto avrà mio figlio?

Lui o lei avrà i lineamenti di Peter?

"Le piaci" osserva Nora. "Guarda come ti sta fissando. È ipnotizzata."

Distolgo lo sguardo dalla piccola creatura tra le mie braccia per concentrarmi su sua madre. "Tua figlia è straordinaria" le dico sinceramente, e lei sorride.

"Io e Julian pensiamo di sì, ma siamo di parte."

"Lo penso anch'io" dice Rosa, sogghignando. "Ma probabilmente anch'io sono di parte."

"Hai figli tuoi?" le chiedo, e lei scuote la testa, con il sorriso che si affievolisce.

"No, purtroppo no." Si avvicina a me e prende la bimba. "Vieni qui, Lizzie, dolcezza. Vuoi venire da Zia Rosa, vero?"

Non sono ancora pronta a rinunciare alla bimba, ma non ho scelta. Lizzie si getta tra le braccia di Rosa con un gorgoglio felice, e subito, il punto in cui la tenevo premuta contro di me sembra freddo e vuoto, con il petto svuotato in qualche strano nuovo modo.

Questo dev'essere quello che si prova a desiderare un bambino—a desiderarlo davvero. Mi sono già occupata di bambini e mi sono divertita, ma non avevo mai provato nulla di lontanamente simile a questo.

Forse è perché sono incinta. La natura mi sta preparando ad essere madre, rilasciando gli ormoni per assicurarmi di accogliere il bambino, quando arriverà.

La mia mano va sul mio stomaco automaticamente, mentre osservo attentamente Rosa posizionare la bimba nel suo passeggino, e quando alzo lo sguardo, gli occhi di Nora sono su di me, carichi di comprensione.

"Di quante settimane sei incinta?" chiede sottovoce, e Rosa sussulta, girandosi per guardarmi.

"Sei incinta?"

Mi mordo il labbro. È ancora presto per comunicarlo a tutti, ma non ha senso mentire. "Sì" ammetto. "Di sei settimane."

"Wow, congratulazioni" esclama Rosa, fissando il mio stomaco.

"Sì, congratulazioni" fa eco Nora con un sorriso caloroso. "Sono così felice per te e Peter."

"Grazie" rispondo sorridendo.

La mia vecchia vita se n'è andata, ma forse questo è l'inizio di una nuova, completa di nuove amicizie.

Forse, nel tempo, recupererò parte di ciò che è andato perduto.

Peter

MI AVVICINO ALLA CASA PROPRIO MENTRE LA PORTA PRINCIPALE SI apre e una donna dai capelli scuri esce con un passeggino, dicendo"—e sebbene il Dottor Goldberg non sia un ostetrico ginecologo, ha una macchina per le ecografie. Julian me l'ha ordinata, quando ero incinta. Quindi, può sicuramente dare un'occhiata, assicurandosi che tu e il bambino stiate bene." Si gira e si ferma. "Oh, ciao, Peter."

"Ciao, Nora" dico. Poi, vedo la sua amica, la giovane domestica, in piedi dietro di lei sulla soglia, con Sara al suo fianco. "Ciao, Rosa" saluto la domestica, prima di rivolgere l'attenzione all'unica persona che conta per me. "Ptichka, stai bene?"

Mia moglie annuisce. "Sto benissimo. Nora mi stava solo raccontando del loro medico locale, nel caso volessi essere controllata dopo tutto. Ma non credo—"

"È un'idea straordinaria" dico fermamente. "Lasciamo che ti controlli oggi." Ricordo Goldberg durante il mio periodo qui, e sebbene preferirei che Sara venisse visitata da un'ostetrica, il chirurgo traumatologo di Esguerra è altrettanto brillante.

"Bene" dice Sara. "Ma dovrebbe controllare anche te."

Mi stringo nelle spalle. "Se vuoi." Quando siamo arrivati ieri, mi ha cambiato tutte le bende, ha messo punti nuovi e sono più che soddisfatto del suo lavoro. Ma se si sente più sicura a farmi visitare da un altro dottore, non è un problema.

Qualunque cosa pur di mantenere mia moglie incinta calma e contenta.

Nora si schiarisce la voce e mi rendo conto che ho completamente dimenticato che lei e Rosa sono lì.

"Perdonatemi" dico, facendo un passo indietro per lasciarle andare, e mentre il passeggino mi passa davanti, intravedo un viso minuscolo con brillanti occhi azzurri.

Lizzie Esguerra.

Il mio petto si stringe per un improvviso dolore lancinante. Fanculo, mi manca Pasha. Dopo tutto questo tempo, mi colpisce ancora come una palla da demolizione, con la consapevolezza che se n'è andato, che il neonato dalle guance magre che è diventato un bambino intelligente non andrà mai a scuola, non crescerà mai, né avrà figli suoi. Niente può riempire quel vuoto straziante; eppure, mentre il mio sguardo si posa su Sara, sento il dolore attenuarsi, con un calore curativo che sostituisce la sofferenza.

Non potrò mai più tenere Pasha, ma terrò il bambino mio e di Sara. Posso già immaginarlo. Se è una bimba, sarà dolce e aggraziata, come una piccola ballerina, e se è un bimbo... Beh, non sarà Pasha, ma lo amerò allo stesso modo.

"Grazie ancora" esclama Sara, salutando Nora e Rosa, mentre si dirigono verso la dimora di Esguerra, e fanno un cenno di saluto, mentre entro in casa e chiudo la porta dietro di me.

6 2

 enderson

MI STROFINO IL COLLO, MENTRE FISSO FUORI DALLA FINESTRA IL paesaggio ghiacciato.

La baita si trova nel luogo più isolato possibile, lontano dalle orde di turisti che invadono l'Islanda nella speranza di vedere l'aurora boreale.

I miei nemici non ci troveranno qui, anche se so che faranno del proprio meglio per provarci. Per ora, io e la mia famiglia siamo al sicuro, ma non mi illudo di poter rimanere qui per un periodo di tempo quantificabile.

Presto, dovremo correre di nuovo, nasconderci di nuovo.

Questo, a meno che non riesca ad uccidere Sokolov e i suoi alleati.

Il mio nuovo piano è rischioso—folle, a dire il vero—ma non vedo alcun altro modo. Non smetteranno di cercarmi, e alla fine, esauriremo i posti in cui nasconderci.

642

La buona notizia è che conosco già le persone giuste per eseguire questa missione—la stessa squadra che ho usato per l'attentato all'FBI. Sono senza scrupoli e altamente qualificati, dei degni avversari per i miei nemici.

Quello di cui ho bisogno ora è mettere le mani sulla mappa della tenuta colombiana di Esguerra.

Poi, potrò finalmente colpirli.

S ara

CERCO DI FAR RIPOSARE PETER, MA LUI INSISTE PER PREPARARE LA colazione, e io sono troppo affamata per discutere. Oggi si sente chiaramente meglio, con il colorito che è tornato alla normale tonalità sana e i movimenti solo leggermente rigidi.

Se non sapessi che ha preso tre proiettili meno di una settimana fa, non ci avrei creduto.

Mentre divoriamo le nostre omelette in cucina, gli racconto della visita di Nora e Rosa e del fatto che le avevo incontrate una volta, molto prima che lo conoscessi.

"Nora aveva abortito?" chiede, aggrottando le sopracciglia, e mi rendo conto che non lo sapeva.

"Sì. Credo che tu avessi già lasciato l'impiego da Esguerra a quel punto."

Annuisce. "Me ne sono andato subito dopo averlo salvato dal gruppo terroristico che lo aveva catturato in Tagikistan.

Ricordi quando ti dissi che era incazzato perché avevo messo in pericolo la moglie durante il suo salvataggio? Beh, sicuramente non era incinta in quel momento—e se lo era, non lo sapevo. Non avrei lasciato che mi convincesse ad usarla come esca, in quel caso."

Giusto. Perché Peter ha un debole per i bambini. Ho visto l'espressione sul suo viso, mentre guardava Lizzie, con dolore misto a tenero desiderio. Mi ha spezzato il cuore, anche se me l'ha fatto amare ancora di più.

Sarà un padre meraviglioso, premuroso com'era stato il mio.

"Non respira. Sara, non respira."

Sono già in ginocchio, a spingere sul petto di papà, mentre conto tra me e me, poi mi chino per respirare nella sua bocca.

Il suo petto si alza per l'aria che gli soffio, poi si abbassa e rimane immobile.

Combattendo il crescente panico, ricomincio le compressioni toraciche.

Uno, due, tre, quattro—

"Sara!"

Ansimando, fisso Peter, confusa. Il suo volto è una maschera di preoccupazione, mentre mi tiene per la parte superiore delle braccia, e siamo entrambi in piedi, anche se ero seduta e stavo mangiando un secondo fa.

"Che cos'è successo?" chiedo con voce rauca, mentre si siede e mi tira sul grembo, avvolgendo le braccia forti attorno al mio corpo tremante. Sono contenta che mi stia stringendo, perché non sono sicura di poter rimanere in piedi da sola. La mia frequenza cardiaca è nella zona supersonica, e il sudore ghiacciato mi gocciola giù per la schiena.

"Sei sbiancata, e poi hai iniziato ad iperventilare." La sua voce è tesa. "E quando ti ho toccata, hai iniziato ad urlare."

"Io... cosa?" Anche la mia gola è dolorante, mi rendo conto, mentre mi avvicino tremante per toccarlo.

"Voglio che tu veda un terapeuta." Il suo sguardo argenteo è duro. "Il prima possibile."

Scuoto la testa automaticamente. "No, sto bene—"

"Non stai bene." Le sue braccia si stringono attorno a me. "Hai avuto un flashback. Non eri qui; eri altrove. Che cos'hai visto? I tuoi genitori? Li hai visti morire?"

Sussulto, con il dolore simile a quello di una pallottola nel cuore. "No" mento in preda alla disperazione. Non posso parlarne, non posso pensarci. Riesco a sentire i ricordi oscuri che ribollono sotto la superficie, minacciando di risucchiarmi. "Non è quello. È solo che—"

Atterro dolorosamente sul fianco, sbattendo la testa contro il lato del divano, mentre un altro sparo risuona e uno spruzzo metallico e caldo mi colpisce sul viso e sul collo.

"Peter!" Terrorizzata per lui, mi metto in ginocchio, mi pulisco il sangue dagli occhi—e poi la vedo.

Mamma è distesa sul pavimento, con il viso imbrattato di sangue.

O meglio, gran parte del viso.

Le manca una parte della guancia e del cranio, con un buco insanguinato dove prima c'era uno zigomo.

"Sara. Cazzo, Sara!"

La faccia di Peter è come una nuvola temporalesca, mentre mi fissa, con gli occhi socchiusi e il corpo teso. Credo che mi stia scuotendo, cercando di farmi uscire dal flashback, perché la mia pelle sembra livida, dove le sue dita mi hanno stretto le braccia con eccessiva forza.

"Scusa" sussurro con voce irregolare. Il mio polso è nella stratosfera, la gola mi sembra ruvida come se avessi ingoiato delle spine. Non capisco perché questo stia succedendo, perché all'improvviso la mente mi stia giocando questi orribili scherzi.

"No, non dirlo." Lasciando andare il braccio, mi culla la guancia, con l'ampio palmo caldo sulla mia pelle gelata. "Non essere dispiaciuta, amore mio. Non è colpa tua. Niente di tutto questo è colpa tua."

E mentre preme il mio volto sulla sua spalla, dondolandomi avanti e indietro, chiudo gli occhi e faccio del mio meglio per credergli.

647

eter

LE MIE BUDELLA SI ANNODANO, MENTRE OSSERVO GOLDBERG esaminare Sara. L'uomo basso e calvo è un chirurgo traumatologico, ma sembra sapere cosa sta facendo—e qualsiasi medico è meglio di niente.

Certo, Sara stessa è un medico, ma non può esattamente eseguire il proprio esame ginecologico.

"Beh, da quello che posso vedere, tu e il bambino state benissimo" annuncia, quando ha finito, e tiro un sospiro di sollievo.

Prossimo passo: portare mia moglie da un terapeuta per affrontare quei terrificanti flashback.

Aghi di ghiaccio mi trafiggono ancora il petto, quando ripenso a come il suo viso fosse sbiancato, come se tutta la vita avesse lasciato il suo corpo. E quando l'iperventilazione e le urla sono iniziate... Fanculo, darei qualsiasi cosa per non vederla mai più in quello stato. So che cos'è il DPTS—l'ho visto in molti soldati—e veder soffrire la mia ptichka in quel modo è stato più di quanto potessi sopportare.

Ho bisogno di farla stare meglio.

Devo annullare il danno che ho causato.

"Ora, sono sicuro che tu lo sappia meglio di me, ma devi evitare il più possibile lo stress" dice Goldberg a Sara, e lei annuisce, osservando il medico calmo e capace. E se non l'avessi vista in preda ad una—due—crisi al tavolo della cucina meno di un'ora fa, sarebbe stato facile credere che stia bene.

Che gli eventi della settimana passata siano stati solo un bip sul suo radar emotivo.

Ma le cose non stanno così. Pur essendo forte, la mia ptichka ne ha passate troppe per non rimanerne influenzata. Ha sopportato, mentre eravamo in modalità sopravvivenza, ma ora che siamo relativamente al sicuro, la sua mente e il suo corpo stanno cercando di affrontare il trauma estremo.

Per quanto ne so, non ha nemmeno pianto per i suoi genitori—né ha parlato dell'uomo che ha ucciso.

Non sono uno strizzacervelli, ma questo non può essere salutare. Forse è per questo che i flashback la stanno colpendo in quel modo: perché sta combattendo i suoi sentimenti, rifiutandosi di pensare al proprio dolore.

L'ho visto anche nell'esercito. I giovani soldati, desiderosi di sembrare forti, tentavano di controllare i propri sentimenti al punto da *perdere* completamente il controllo. Imbottigliare quel tipo di trauma non funziona mai; si finisce sempre per crollare o si ricorre a droghe e alcol per affrontarlo. A parte i miei incubi dopo Daryevo, non ho mai avuto questo tipo di problemi —ma sono fortunato in un certo senso.

Sono stato in modalità sopravvivenza per gran parte della mia vita.

"Grazie, Dottor Goldberg" dice Sara, saltando giù dal tavolo, e quando lei si mette dietro una tenda per rivestirsi, tiro da parte il dottore.

"Sta davvero bene?" chiedo a bassa voce. "Perché ha appena perso i suoi genitori e, in generale, gli ultimi giorni sono stati... difficili."

Il medico sospira, togliendo i guanti. "Non so cosa dirti. Fisicamente, è sana. Emotivamente... beh, non è proprio il mio campo. Potresti parlare con Julian, vedere se riesce a portare qualcuno nella tenuta con cui lei possa parlare. So che un paio di anni fa Nora stava attraversando un periodo difficile, e lui aveva portato qui una terapeuta per lei. Forse potrebbe fare lo stesso per tua moglie?"

Stavo pensando di convincere Sara a vedere uno strizzacervelli a distanza, ma di persona sarebbe ancora meglio.

"Grazie, parlerò con lui" dico a Goldberg, mentre Sara torna, e annuisce, sorridendo.

"In bocca al lupo. E ricorda: non farla stressare, ok?"

"Grazie. Faremo del nostro meglio" replica Sara, sorridendogli. È il suo sorriso dolce e caloroso, e per un secondo provo un orribile picco di gelosia. È illogico—il dottore è gay al cento per cento—ma non posso farci niente.

Non vedevo quel suo sorriso da giorni.

Da quando ha perso tutto per colpa mia.

 ara

PETER È TRANQUILLO SULLA VIA DEL RITORNO VERSO CASA, CON un'espressione chiusa. So che è preoccupato per me, ma vorrei che mi parlasse, che mi distraesse dai pensieri. Invece, mi tiene in silenzio la mano e, per quanto sia confortante il suo tocco, non è sufficiente ad impedire alla mia mente di vagare... in luoghi in cui non posso lasciare che vada.

"E così, Esguerra ti aiuterà a catturare Henderson?" chiedo in tono allegro—in parte perché sono curiosa, in parte per avere qualcosa di cui parlare. "Gli darai la caccia, vero?"

Mi guarda. "Sì—e lui mi aiuterà."

"Oh, bene. Sai già come lo troverete?"

"Abbiamo alcune idee" risponde vagamente, poi cade di nuovo in silenzio.

Fantastico. Probabilmente non vuole parlarne, per paura che io abbia un'altra crisi. È così che sarà tra noi d'ora in poi, con Peter che pensa io sia così fragile che potrei spezzarmi alla minima provocazione?

La parte peggiore è che non sono sicura che abbia completamente torto. Dopo quello che è successo a colazione, la mia mente è come un campo minato, pieno di trappole e pericoli nascosti. Non so cosa lo faccia scattare dentro di me, facendo sì che quei ricordi orribili prendano il sopravvento. E Peter non sa nemmeno del mini flashback che ho avuto questa mattina, prima della visita di Nora e Rosa.

Se lo sapesse, si convincerebbe che sono pazza.

"Come ti senti?" chiedo, decidendo di concentrarmi su un argomento più innocuo. "Come va il tuo fianco?"

Mi sorride. "Molto meglio, grazie. Ancora pochi giorni e dovrei essere come nuovo."

"Davvero? Guarisci molto velocemente."

Il suo sorriso svanisce. "Ho la pelle dura."

E io no. Sono un fragile fiorellino del cazzo, che si spezzerebbe, se solo mi dicesse una parola sbagliata. Non ha detto questo, ma sento quelle parole comunque.

Tutto ciò che *sento* è la sua preoccupazione per me.

Rinunciando alla conversazione, mi concentro su ciò che ci circonda. Passiamo davanti a quello che dev'essere l'alloggio delle guardie; vedo uomini dall'aria dura con mitragliatrici che entrano ed escono dall'edificio simile ad un dormitorio. Tutto intorno a noi c'è una vegetazione esotica, e l'aria è densa e umida, con un profumo di piante tropicali e un pizzico di ozono dalle nuvole che si raccolgono all'orizzonte.

La villa di Esguerra è ad una certa distanza sulla destra, con il bianco edificio a due piani che mi ricorda una piantagione dell'era della Guerra Civile. È circondata da un bel paesaggio e da prati rigogliosi, così come da alcuni edifici più piccoli.

Le torri di guardia che ho individuato dall'aereo sono visibili in lontananza, con in cima guardie armate, e sono sicura che ci siano dozzine di altre misure di sicurezza meno evidenti.

Una volta, vedendo tutti questi uomini con le armi e sapendo di essere nella tenuta di un criminale spietato, mi sarei innervosita, per non dire altro. Ma ora mi fa sentire al sicuro.

Ora i nemici sono le persone su cui la maggior parte dei cittadini conta per la protezione: le forze dell'ordine.

Beh, e Henderson—che usa quelle autorità come strumento di vendetta.

~

Quando torniamo a casa, Peter prepara il nostro pranzo, e mangiamo—questa volta, senza alcuna crisi da parte mia. È ancora silenzioso durante il pasto, però, guardandomi con malcelata preoccupazione.

"Basta" gemo, quando non ce la faccio più. "Per favore, smettila di fissarmi così. Non impazzirò, te lo prometto."

"Non puoi prometterlo, perché i flashback non sono qualcosa che puoi controllare, ptichka" dice lentamente. "E più provi, più peggiorano. Ecco perché chiederò ad Esguerra di far portare un terapeuta qui."

"Che cosa? Oh, andiamo. Questo può aspettare fino a—"

"No, non può." La sua faccia è solcata da linee implacabili. "Non con quello che è successo stamattina."

"Peter, per favore. Non è successo niente. Stai facendo di un sassolino una montagna. Non c'è bisogno di mettermi in imbarazzo davanti a Esguerra chiedendogli di farlo. Inoltre, questo non significherebbe che gli devi ancora un altro favore? Una volta esserti occupato di Henderson, potremo parlare di terapia e tutto il resto. Fino ad allora—"

"Fino ad allora, vedrai chiunque possiamo portare qui."

Uh. Spingo via il mio piatto vuoto e mi alzo. È impossibile far cambiare idea a Peter, quando decide qualcosa. Amo e odio questo di lui—e stavolta, è sicuramente il secondo caso.

Perché non riesce a capire che non sono pronta ad

affrontare la ricaduta emotiva di quello che è successo? Che preferirei rischiare il flashback occasionale piuttosto che addentrarmi nella tossica pozza di senso di colpa e di orrore che si diffonde nella mia mente?

Se potessi semplicemente cancellare quei ricordi, lo farei. Solo che non voglio pensarci.

"Ptichka..." Mi prende per il polso, mentre sto per uscire dalla cucina. Il suo tocco mi brucia, con le dita che mi legano come una catena. "Ascoltami, amore mio. Sei ferita—come se avessi preso un proiettile. Mi lasceresti con le *mie* ferite? O faresti del tuo meglio per guarirle?"

Stringo i denti. "Non è la stessa cosa."

"No?" I suoi occhi grigi sono dolci, mentre mi sistema una ciocca di capelli dietro l'orecchio con la mano libera. "Dove sarebbe la differenza?"

È così e basta, voglio gridare. Perché non ha importanza che cosa faccia o con quanti terapeuti parli.

Niente riporterà indietro i miei genitori.

Questa non è una ferita da proiettile che guarirà con la cura.

Eppure, mentre lo guardo, mi viene in mente che potrei discutere con lui per settimane, e non cambierebbe nulla. Non posso convincerlo che sto bene.

Non con le parole, almeno.

Lentamente e volutamente, mi lecco le labbra. Prevedibilmente, il suo sguardo si posa sulla mia bocca, e la presa sul mio polso si stringe, mentre ripeto l'azione, e poi affondo seducentemente i denti nel labbro inferiore.

Il mio obiettivo era quello di distoglierlo dalla preoccupazione, ma il battito accelera, mentre il suo respiro si fa irregolare e alza lo sguardo per incontrare il mio. Le sue pupille sono già dilatate, trasformando l'argento delle sue iridi in acciaio scuro. Sono acutamente consapevole del calore che emana dalle dita, mentre mi tiene il polso, e la vicinanza del suo corpo alto e forte mi fa desiderare di sciogliermi contro di lui, di strofinare i seni doloranti sul suo ampio e duro petto.

"Ptichka..." La sua voce è bassa e grave. "Stai giocando con il fottuto fuoco."

I miei capezzoli si stringono in boccioli duri e il calore liquido mi bagna le mutandine. Santo cielo, sono eccitata. Quel tono, combinato con l'accenno di violenza nella presa troppo stretta delle sue dita sul mio polso, aiuta più dei preliminari. A parte il sesso orale che gli ho fatto in ospedale, non abbiamo rapporti da diversi giorni, e il mio corpo brama disperatamente il suo possesso.

Facendo un passo in avanti, mi alzo in punta di piedi e premo le labbra sulle sue, avvolgendogli il braccio libero attorno al collo muscoloso. Per un momento, è rigido, come se fosse sorpreso dalla mia aggressività, ma poi il suo istinto prende il sopravvento, e mi ritrovo appoggiata al frigorifero, con il suo corpo duro che spinge su di me e la bocca che mi divora come se non ci fosse un domani.

Sento il rigonfiamento della sua erezione, mentre mi afferra l'altro polso e mi allunga le braccia sopra la testa, inchiodandole contro l'acciaio freddo del frigorifero. Altro calore mi inonda le viscere, e gemo nella sua bocca, sollevando la gamba e agganciandogliela dietro al sedere, in modo da poter strofinare il mio sesso dolorante contro quel rigonfiamento. Non mi sentivo a mio agio nel prendere in prestito la biancheria intima di Yulia oltre ai vestiti, e i pantaloncini di jeans erano ruvidi e fastidiosi sulle mie pieghe nude, la sensazione scomoda ma perversamente eccitante.

"Scopami" sospiro, mentre alza la testa per guardarmi in faccia, con gli occhi scintillanti e la mascella serrata. Stringendomi entrambi i polsi in una grossa mano, tira giù la cerniera dei pantaloni, liberando l'erezione mentre imploro: "Scopami *subito*."

"Oh, lo farò. Credimi."

Il suo respiro è pesante, lo sguardo feroce, mentre mi libera i polsi e mi sbottona i pantaloncini; poi, li fa scivolare brutalmente lungo le mie gambe. Tremando dal bisogno, esco da essi e mi afferra il sedere, sollevandomi. Mentre gli stringo le spalle, mi allarga le cosce e mi abbassa sul suo grosso fallo, impalandomi con un colpo solo.

L'aria mi esce dai polmoni, mentre avvolgo le gambe attorno ai suoi fianchi e le mie unghie scavano nei muscoli delle sue spalle. Cazzo, è grosso. Il mio corpo aveva in qualche modo dimenticato questa parte. I miei tessuti interni sono dolorosamente tesi, l'eccitazione attutita dal bruciore del suo ingresso. Finché non inizia a muoversi.

Continuando a sostenere il mio sguardo, tira fuori e torna dentro. Non c'è attesa, non mi stuzzica con spinte superficiali; subito, il suo ritmo è duro, spietato come l'uomo stesso. E questo è esattamente ciò di cui ho bisogno. Il calore crescente e la tensione riducono il disagio, con il mio corpo che si addolcisce e si scioglie, accogliendolo nel profondo. Ogni colpo martella il mio punto G; ogni volta che il suo bacino sbatte contro il mio, preme sul clitoride.

Il mio orgasmo è violento e improvviso. Mi fa esplodere molto prima che io sia mentalmente preparata, con il piacere che mi spezza, mi dilania. Ansimando, grido il suo nome, con le gambe che si stringono intorno a lui, ma non si ferma.

Mi colpisce fino a quando non vengo di nuovo.

Sto ancora cavalcando le ultime scosse orgasmiche, quando una vena inizia a pulsare nella sua fronte madida di sudore, e il grosso membro si gonfia ulteriormente dentro di me. Con un gemito, spinge più in profondità possibile, e i miei muscoli interni si stringono attorno alla sua asta, mentre pulsa e vibra, bagnandomi le viscere con il seme.

eter

RESPIRANDO PESANTEMENTE, MI RITIRO CON RILUTTANZA DALLA fighetta stretta e scivolosa di Sara e la metto in piedi con cautela. Sembra sopraffatta quanto me, e una forte punta di rimorso scaccia via il caldo residuo del rilascio.

Sono stato troppo duro con lei.

Ancora una volta, sono stato troppo rude.

So che ora le piace così, ma è incinta.

Traumatizzata e incinta.

A che diavolo stavo pensando, perdendo il controllo in quel modo? Devo coccolarla, tenerla riposata e rilassata, non fotterla duramente contro il frigorifero come un animale fuori controllo.

Barcolla, mentre la lascio andare e faccio un passo indietro, e le afferro un braccio, raddrizzandola, mentre cerca un tovagliolo di carta per asciugarsi l'umidità tra le gambe.

"Ptichka... stai bene?"

Sogghigna, gettando il tovagliolo appallottolato nella spazzatura. "Mai stata meglio. E tu?"

Aggrotto le sopracciglia, poi mi ricordo delle ferite. Ora che ci sto prestando attenzione, il mio fianco fa un po' male, ma non è nulla di insopportabile.

"Sto benissimo" dico, mentre sul suo viso appare un'espressione preoccupata e mi afferra l'orlo della maglietta—con l'indubbia intenzione di sollevarla per ispezionare la benda. Lasciandole delicatamente le mani, mi allontano dalla sua portata. "Davvero, sto bene."

Non posso credere che sia preoccupata per me, quando l'ho appena divorata in questo modo. So che le ho fatto male—ho sentito l'estrema tensione del suo corpo, quando ho spinto dentro. E se avessi fatto male anche al bambino?

E se abortisse, come ha fatto Nora quella volta?

Mentre rimango immobile, elaborando quel pensiero terrificante, si china e raccoglie i pantaloncini dal pavimento. Il suo piccolo sedere sinuoso ondeggia nell'aria, mentre si muove, e, nonostante lo sperma che mi ricopre il fallo, lo sento contorcersi con interesse.

Cazzo, *sono* un animale.

"Sara..." La mia voce è tesa, mentre mi guarda. "Stai davvero bene?"

Sbatte le palpebre. "Te l'ho detto, mai stata meglio. Vieni, andiamo a pulirci." E afferrandomi la mano, mi trascina in bagno.

FACCIAMO LA DOCCIA INSIEME—BEH, SARA FA LA DOCCIA, E IO uso l'erogatore per lavarmi strategicamente intorno alle bende —e poi si sdraia per un pisolino, adducendo come giustificazione il coma alimentare e la sonnolenza post-sesso.

Mi sdraio con lei e la stringo, finché non si addormenta. Poi, mi alzo lentamente ed esco di casa.

So perché è stanca, e non ha niente a che fare con il cibo o il sesso. Il suo corpo è sfinito, dopo l'adrenalina ininterrotta della scorsa settimana, e le esigenze del bambino in crescita non aiutano.

Il senso di colpa è come un rotolo di filo spinato nel mio stomaco.

Sono stato io a farle questo.

Sono il responsabile di tutte le sue disgrazie.

Se non fossi stato così egoisticamente ossessionato da lei, se solo l'avessi lasciata in pace, sarebbe ancora a casa con i genitori, a vivere la sua vita tranquilla e pacifica. Se mi fossi allontanato dopo il nostro primo incontro, avrebbe potuto sposare qualcun altro... qualcuno che le avrebbe garantito una gravidanza in tutta comodità e sicurezza.

Invece, è in fuga con me, tormentata da flashback e stanchezza simili al DPTS.

"Ehilà, Peter" mi saluta Diego, mentre lo supero, e annuisco bruscamente, non dell'umore giusto per le chiacchiere.

Ho un obiettivo in questo momento: parlare con Esguerra.

Ho bisogno che quella terapeuta venga portata subito qui.

Poco dopo, busso alla porta della casa di Esguerra.

"È qui?" chiedo ad Ana, quando la apre, e la governante annuisce.

"Sì, prego, entra. Vorresti qualcosa da mangiare o da bere, mentre vado a chiamarlo?"

"No, grazie. Sto bene." Seguo Ana nell'ingresso e mi appoggio alla parete, troppo agitato per stare seduto.

Sale l'ampia scalinata curva e pochi minuti dopo, Esguerra scende, abbottonandosi la camicia, mentre cammina. Ha i capelli arruffati e un cipiglio incazzato inciso sul volto.

O l'ho svegliato da un pisolino o si tratta di qualcosa che riguarda Nora.

Scommetto su quest'ultima opzione.

"Che cosa c'è?" ringhia. "Henderson—?"

"No, non è niente del genere." Prendo fiato, mentre il suo cipiglio si fa più accentuato. "È una cosa personale. Ho bisogno di un favore."

Si ferma davanti a me, con un freddo divertimento che sostituisce la preoccupazione negli occhi. "Davvero? Cibo e riparo non sono abbastanza per te?"

"Conosci qualche strizzacervelli?" chiedo, rifiutandomi di abboccare. "Preferibilmente, qualcuno esperto nel trattamento del DPTS."

Sembra sorpreso. "Per te?"

Ricordando le parole di Sara, annuisco freddamente. "Per me."

Non voglio che la mia ptichka si senta imbarazzata—non che dovrebbe. Aver bisogno di aiuto per elaborare un trauma estremo non rende deboli, solo normali.

Esguerra mi studia con un'espressione illeggibile, poi annuisce. "Potrei conoscere qualcuno. Quando hai bisogno di averla qui?"

"Oggi, se possibile. Oppure, domani o il giorno successivo."

"Va bene. Farò del mio meglio per portarla qui domani."

"Grazie" dico, e si gira per andarsene. So che sarò in debito con lui per questo, e sicuramente lo ricorderà, ma se questo aiuterà Sara, ne sarà valsa la pena.

Farei qualsiasi cosa per farla star bene.

"Peter" esclama Esguerra, mentre sto per uscire dalla stanza. Quando mi volto per affrontarlo, dice sottovoce: "Perché tu e tua moglie non venite a cena da noi stasera? A Nora piacerebbe conoscere meglio la tua Sara."

"Certo" dico, nascondendo la mia sorpresa. "Ci saremo."

"Sette in punto" precisa, poi si volta e torna di sopra.

Henderson

MI FA MALE LA SCHIENA DOPO AVER SPALATO NEVE TUTTO IL giorno, e Jimmy è incazzato nero per averlo costretto ad aiutarmi, ma doveva essere fatto.

Dovevamo avere il vialetto libero, in modo da potercene andare in fretta se necessario.

Il mio piano di raggiungere Sokolov e agli altri—Operazione Air Drop, come la chiamo io—manca ancora di un componente cruciale, che è la mappa del complesso di Esguerra e dei suoi dettagli di sicurezza.

Una volta ottenuto ciò, saremo in grado di colpire, ma nel frattempo, devo fare tutto ciò che è in mio potere per mantenere mia moglie e i miei figli al sicuro.

Devo salvarli dai mostri che ci stanno dando la caccia.

6 8

ara

SO CHE È SCIOCCO SENTIRSI NERVOSI PER LA CENA DOPO TUTTO quello che abbiamo passato, ma non posso farci niente. Per prima cosa, gli unici abiti che ho trovato nell'armadio sono pantaloncini e magliette, e sebbene Peter mi abbia assicurato che non abbiamo bisogno di vestirci in modo elegante, mi sentirei sicuramente meglio se avessi qualcosa di carino, come un prendisole, da indossare. Inoltre, dopo il mio sonnellino pomeridiano, il malessere mattutino ha deciso di svegliarmi.

A quanto pare, sono le conseguenze del jet-lag.

Ho già vomitato una volta, ma mi sento ancora nauseata, mentre Peter mi conduce alla casa principale. Ricordare la sua insistenza nel procurarmi uno strizzacervelli non aiuta. Ne ha già parlato con il nostro ospite? Spero di no, ma conoscendo mio marito, molto probabilmente lo ha fatto.

La procrastinazione non è un concetto con cui ha familiarità.

Ad ogni modo, il mio stomaco si agita, quando Peter bussa alla porta. Un attimo dopo, si apre, rivelando una donna ispanica di mezza età. "Señor Sokolov" dice, raggiante. "Benvenuto. E questa dev'essere la tua adorabile moglie."

Sorrido e allungo la mano. "Ciao. Sono Sara."

"Oh, ciao." Mi stringe forte la mano. "Sono Ana, la governante del Señor Esguerra. Prego, entrate."

La seguiamo in casa. All'interno, la villa di Esguerra è un sorprendente mix di arredi tradizionali e moderni, con mobili in stile barocco, completati da splendidi pavimenti in legno e opere d'arte astratta sulle pareti. Riconosco un paio di dipinti grazie ad un corso d'arte che ho frequentato al college. Se sono originali—e sospetto che lo siano—i muri del foyer da soli valgono milioni di dollari.

Ana ci conduce in una formale sala da pranzo, dove un tavolo ovale è allestito con argenteria scintillante e piatti bordati d'oro. Nora e suo marito non ci sono ancora, ma riconosco la coppia seduta ad un lato del tavolo.

Lucas e Yulia Kent.

Le loro teste bionde sono piegate, con le mani intrecciate sul tavolo, mentre ridono di qualcosa. Mentre entriamo, però, alzano lo sguardo, e i sorrisi scompaiono dai loro volti.

Una forte tensione pervade la stanza, mentre Ana scompare, lasciandoci soli.

Peter è il primo a rompere il silenzio. "Lucas." Annuisce con freddezza all'uomo dalla mascella dura. Si rivolge, quindi, alla moglie simile a una modella di Kent. "Yulia. È bello rivederti."

"Anch'io sono felice di rivederti." I suoi occhi azzurri mi scrutano, con un'espressione riservata. "E di rivedere anche te, Sara."

La mia nausea si intensifica bruscamente.

Oh, cazzo. Presa dal panico, mi guardo intorno in cerca di un bagno, ma non ne vedo.

"Ptichka..." Peter mi afferra il braccio. "Che cosa c'è che non va?"

Se provassi a parlare, vomiterei. Coprendomi la bocca con la mano, mi libero dalla sua presa e sfreccio fuori dalla stanza, verso l'ingresso.

Riesco a malapena a farcela. Nel secondo in cui mi piego sulla ringhiera del portico, lo stomaco espelle tutto il contenuto.

Naturalmente, mio marito mi segue e assiste all'intera scena —e così fa Yulia, vedo con la coda dell'occhio. Mortificata, finisco di rigettare, mentre lui mi tiene i capelli, e quando alzo lo sguardo, lei non c'è più.

Un secondo dopo, tuttavia, torna con un tovagliolo di carta bagnato. "Ecco qua" mormora, porgendolo, e io l'accetto con gratitudine per pulirmi la bocca.

La prossima ad uscire è Ana—Yulia deve averle riferito cosa sta succedendo. Mostrando molta comprensione, la governante mi conduce in un bagno, dove mi porge uno spazzolino nuovo di zecca e un tubetto di dentifricio.

Dopo essermi lavata il viso e i denti, il mio stomaco sembra infinitamente più stabile.

"Stai bene, amore mio?" chiede Peter non appena esco dal bagno, e annuisco, distogliendo lo sguardo.

"Mi dispiace."

"Non hai nulla di cui dispiacerti" dice, prendendomi la mano. "Considera questo l'annuncio ufficiale della tua gravidanza."

E dandomi un bacio sulla fronte, intreccia le dita alle mie e mi riporta nella sala da pranzo.

~

GLI ESGUERRA SONO GIÀ LÌ, SEDUTI DI FRONTE AI KENT, QUANDO torniamo. Riconosco subito il nostro ospite: è davvero l'uomo stupendo che avevo incontrato in ospedale. I suoi capelli scuri sono più lunghi di allora, ma i lineamenti incredibilmente sensuali sono gli stessi. A differenza di allora, tuttavia, non sta irradiando dolore e rabbia; è calmo e padrone di sé, come un re seduto sul trono.

Un re crudele e tirannico, dato quello che so sull'uomo.

Per la prima volta, mi chiedo che cosa sia successo agli uomini che hanno aggredito Nora e la sua amica. Il marito di Nora li ha uccisi?

Come non detto. Certo che li ha uccisi.

L'unica domanda è quanto li abbia fatti soffrire.

"Eccoti" dice Nora, guardandomi. "Vieni, siediti qui." Accarezza la sedia accanto a lei, e io vado da quella parte.

"Julian, questa è Sara" dice, mentre mi fermo accanto a lei. "Potresti ricordarla dall'ospedale di Chicago."

"Ovviamente. È bello rivederti." Mi guarda con penetranti occhi azzurri, e per la prima volta, noto qualcosa di leggermente strano nel suo occhio sinistro, e una sottile cicatrice che va dallo zigomo fino al sopracciglio.

Qualcuno gli ha tagliato l'occhio con un coltello e, in tal caso, come ha fatto l'occhio a sopravvivere?

A meno che... non sia un occhio artificiale?

"Grazie. Anche per me—e ti ringrazio per l'ospitalità" dico, sopprimendo la curiosità. Non sarebbe buona educazione guardare a bocca aperta il nostro ospite spietato.

Mi fa un cenno col capo, mentre mi siedo accanto a Nora, e Peter si siede di fronte a me, vicino a Yulia.

"Grazie per il tovagliolo di carta" dico a Yulia, e lei annuisce, prima di guardare altrove. Come suo marito, dev'essere ancora arrabbiata con me per quello che è successo a Cipro. Col senno di poi, mi sento malissimo per averla ingannata sulla mia relazione con Peter al fine di fuggire. Non avrei dovuto coinvolgerla nel tentativo di evitare di innamorarmi del mio torturatore.

Dovrò parlarle da sola stasera, in modo da potermi scusare.

"Come ti senti?" chiede Nora dolcemente, chinandosi, e io le sorrido, con l'imbarazzo che si affievolisce notando lo sguardo preoccupato sul suo viso.

"Molto meglio ora, grazie."

"Avevo terribili nausee mattutine con Lizzie" confida con un sorriso triste. "Vomitavo dappertutto, al punto che Julian portava con sé uno di quei sacchetti per il vomito che ti danno in aereo ovunque andassimo."

"Forse ne avrò bisogno anch'io" osservo, e lei ride, mentre Peter ci guarda con un'espressione illeggibile.

Disapprova la mia amicizia in erba con la moglie di Esguerra? Se è così, perché?

Mentre rifletto su questo, Ana entra, spingendo un carrello con scodelle di zuppa.

"Ho fatto preparare un brodo speciale e leggero per te" mi informa Nora, mentre Ana mette una zuppa davanti a me, piuttosto che le versioni cremose che vedo davanti a tutti gli altri. "Ho pensato che potesse essere più facile digerire questa per il tuo stomaco. Fammi sapere se preferisci la crema di funghi. Il cibo elaborato era la causa scatenante per me, durante il primo trimestre, quindi ho pensato che potesse esserlo anche per te."

"Questa è perfetta, grazie" dico, commossa dalla sua premura. "Non ho ancora notato una correlazione con i cibi diversi, ma *desidero* qualcosa di più leggero, dopo... lo sai."

"Sì, lo immaginavo." Sorride. "E fammi sapere se qualcuno degli odori al tavolo ti dà fastidio. Ana porterà via qualunque cosa sia. L'odore era un altro grosso problema per me con Lizzie."

"Grazie. Sei troppo gentile." Affondo il cucchiaio nella zuppa e me lo porto alle labbra, assaggiandola con cautela. Con mio sollievo, è leggera come promesso da Nora, con un sottofondo di funghi e un pizzico di miso. "Tua figlia sta dormendo?" chiedo, mandando giù la zuppa.

"*Stava* dormendo, quando l'ho lasciata al piano di sopra con Rosa pochi minuti fa" risponde. Sospirando, lancia un'occhiata all'entrata della sala da pranzo. "È sbagliato che mi manchi già?"

Sorrido. "Affatto. Sembra una bambina molto dolce."

Alza gli occhi al cielo. "Lo spero. È una diavoletta, in realtà. Non lasciarti ingannare dall'aspetto esteriore. È la figlia di suo padre in *tutti* i sensi."

Esguerra sceglie quel momento per guardarci. "Sarebbe a dire, gattina?"

"Niente." Nora gli rivolge un sorriso beato. "Sto solo dicendo a Sara che nostra figlia è un angioletto perfetto."

Solleva le sopracciglia con evidente scetticismo, e lei gli rivolge un'occhiata esageratamente innocente, sbattendo rapidamente le lunghe ciglia. Le sue palpebre si abbassano, la bocca assume una curva sensuale e si scambiano un'occhiata, una così intima e calda da riscaldarmi le viscere.

Sentendomi una pervertita, distolgo lo sguardo—solo per incontrare quello tempestoso di mio marito dall'altra parte del tavolo.

"Non stai mangiando" osserva lentamente, e mi rendo conto che non è la mia potenziale amicizia con Nora a preoccuparlo.

Sono io.

Mi sta fissando come se potessi vomitare—o impazzire—da un momento all'altro.

Il mio umore si rabbuia. A quanto pare, non sono riuscita a rassicurarlo con il sesso prima.

Immergendo il cucchiaio nella zuppa, mi concentro sul finire l'intera scodella, in modo da tranquillizzarlo almeno su quello. Mi osserva per qualche secondo, poi riprende a mangiare la sua minestra, apparentemente rassicurato che non mi stia lasciando morire di fame.

Ognuno si affretta a terminare la zuppa; poi, gli uomini si lanciano in una discussione su alcune misure di sicurezza del complesso. Sto ascoltando solo a metà, perché Nora mi sta parlando dei club e dei ristoranti di Chicago.

A quanto pare, siamo state in molti degli stessi posti nel corso degli anni.

Come secondo, Ana tira fuori un'insalata verde e una paella di pesce dall'odore delizioso. Nora mi offre riso e pollo, ma declino, ringraziandola per la considerazione.

Il mio stomaco si sta comportando bene, e vorrei davvero quella paella.

Mentre il pasto procede, noto uno schema imbarazzante al tavolo. Anche se Nora e Yulia sono sedute l'una di fronte all'altra, non si guardano e non si parlano. Infatti, a parte ringraziare Ana e lodare la sua cucina ad un certo punto, Yulia ha parlato solo con suo marito o è rimasta in silenzio.

Agli Esguerra non piace per qualche ragione? Ora che ci penso, quando siamo andati a Cipro, Peter ha detto qualcosa sulla falsariga di Esguerra "ce l'ha con lei."

Dovrò chiedergli che cos'è successo.

Noto anche una certa tensione tra Peter e Lucas, ma non è così pronunciata. Forse l'aiuto di Kent nel nostro salvataggio riduce la sua colpevolezza nella mia fuga agli occhi di Peter, e ora i due uomini si considerano addirittura pari.

Siamo già a metà del dessert, un delizioso tiramisù fatto in casa, quando la conversazione si sposta sull'argomento che ci ha portati qui.

Henderson.

"Sembra che stasera sarà fattibile" dice Esguerra a Peter. "Lo saprò per certo tra circa un'ora—il tuo tizio della Carolina del Nord è stato piuttosto evasivo."

Mio marito si acciglia. "Offriamogli più soldi."

"L'ho fatto" ribatte Kent. "E gli ho anche detto che se non

collabora, sarà aggiunto alla nostra lista. Quindi, immagino che lo farà."

"Che cosa succederà stasera?" chiedo, guardando gli uomini al tavolo. "Avete già localizzato Henderson?"

Esguerra e Kent guardano Peter, che scuote la testa per un minuto—negando loro il permesso di informarmi. Mio marito, allora, si concentra su di me. "Nulla di cui ti debba preoccupare, ptichka" sussurra dolcemente, allungando la mano sul tavolo. "Non l'abbiamo ancora trovato, ma lo faremo—e stasera sarà solo un passo in quella direzione."

Stringo i denti, e tiro via la mano.

Eccolo di nuovo, il presupposto che io non riesca a gestire nulla di anche solo lontanamente sconvolgente.

Prima che possa dire qualcosa, sento il pianto di un bambino. Sembra che si stia avvicinando alla stanza. Un attimo dopo, entra un'esausta Rosa, con una Lizzie urlante in braccio.

"Mi dispiace interrompere, ma non smette di piangere" spiega. "Le ho dato da mangiare e l'ho cambiata, quindi non so quale sia il suo problema."

Con mia sorpresa, si alza Esguerra, invece di Nora. "Dalla a me" dice con calma, e avvicinandosi a Rosa, prende la bimba, occupandosene con incredibile dolcezza e sorprendente capacità.

I suoi lineamenti si addolciscono, mentre osserva il piccolo viso corrucciato, e con mio grande stupore, la piccola si tranquillizza, mentre la dondola, mormorando qualcosa di insensato con voce profonda. Non sembra importargli che lo stiamo osservando in questo momento così tenero; è completamente preso dalla piccola creatura tra le sue braccia.

"Capito cosa intendo? È tutta suo padre" mi sussurra Nora nell'orecchio, e chiudo la bocca, rendendomi conto che sto fissando il marito come se gli fosse appena cresciuta una coda.

Non mi aspettavo di vedere il potente trafficante d'armi così pratico con la bambina.

"È l'unico in grado di calmarla, quando diventa così" continua la ragazza dolcemente, e quando la guardo, la vedo osservare il marito e la figlia con pura adorazione.

È chiaramente innamorata di lui.

Dell'uomo che l'ha rapita, quando aveva appena terminato la scuola superiore.

Immagino che non dovrei essere sorpresa, vista la mia relazione con Peter, ma è ancora un po' strano, osservandoli così. Una parte di me vorrebbe consigliarle di vedere uno strizzacervelli per la sua sindrome di Stoccolma, mentre un'altra parte più grande sta tifando per la loro storia d'amore non ortodossa.

Se *riescono* a farla funzionare nel lungo termine, forse anch'io e Peter possiamo farlo.

Forse tra qualche anno saremo tutti seduti ad un tavolo da pranzo come questo, solo che ci sarà il mio bambino tra le braccia di mio marito.

Il più piccolo, ovviamente. A quel punto, il più grande andrà in giro da solo.

Sono così presa da questo sogno ad occhi aperti che quasi mi lascio sfuggire il momento con Yulia. Si è già scusata e sta uscendo dalla sala da pranzo, quando mi rendo conto che sta andando al bagno.

"Scusate, torno subito" dico a Nora e Peter, e senza aspettare una risposta, mi alzo e seguo la ragazza.

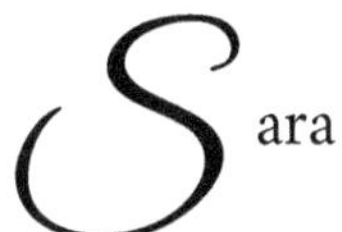

*S*ara

RAGGIUNGO YULIA NEL CORRIDOIO VICINO AL BAGNO.

"Aspetta, per favore" le dico, mentre sta per entrare. Realizzando quello che sto dicendo, mi correggo rapidamente: "Voglio dire, non aspettare, se devi andare. Sarò qui fuori, in attesa che tu abbia finito."

Si allontana dalla porta del bagno. "No, vai pure. Posso andare altrove. Ci sono molti bagni su questo piano."

"Che cosa? Oh, no, sto bene." Rido, realizzando che pensi che abbia urgentemente bisogno del bagno. "Volevo solo parlarti un attimo, scusarmi per l'intera faccenda di Cipro."

L'espressione sul suo bel viso si indurisce. "Non ce n'è bisogno. È tutto passato."

"No, non lo è. Ho causato una spaccatura tra Peter e tuo marito. Sono davvero dispiaciuta per questo e per averti dato un'impressione sbagliata sulla mia relazione con Peter. Avevo bisogno del tuo aiuto per fuggire, ma avrei dovuto essere più sincera. Peter ha davvero ucciso il mio primo marito e mi ha ingannata, come ti ho detto—ma questo è stato prima, prima che le cose si complicassero anche tra noi. Voglio dire, ero *sua* prigioniera in casa tua—ecco perché stavo cercando di scappare —ma mi stavo anche innamorando di lui allora e—"

Yulia mi mette un'esile mano sul braccio. "Va tutto bene, Sara." I suoi occhi azzurri si addolciscono. "Non è necessario entrare nei dettagli. Capisco."

"Davvero?"

Annuisce. "Non sono un'idiota. So che le cose possono cambiare e che il più brutto degli inizi può portare a qualcosa di bello nel tempo. Per quanto riguarda il fatto di avermi usata per fuggire, sono sicura che avrei fatto lo stesso al tuo posto. Anzi —" Si ferma. "Non importa. Sono felice che tu e Peter stiate insieme ora. Voglio dire... è così, vero?" Il suo sguardo si posa sul mio stomaco; poi, mi guarda con una domanda inespressa.

"Oh. Sì, certo." Sussulto internamente, ricordando come le avevo detto che Peter intendesse costringermi ad avere un figlio. Coprendomi il ventre con la mano, dico fermamente: "Questo è molto desiderato."

Sorride. "Bene. Sono contenta di sentirlo. Ora, se mi vuoi scusare..." Lancia un'occhiata al bagno.

Sorridendo, faccio un passo indietro, realizzando che l'ho trattenuta per tutto il tempo. "Grazie" dico, mentre entra. "Per il tuo aiuto allora e per tutto."

"È stato un piacere" replica, e mentre chiude la porta, torno nella sala da pranzo, sentendomi infinitamente più sollevata.

QUANDO TORNO, SONO TUTTI IN PIEDI, VAGANDO INTORNO AL tavolo con drink del dopo cena, e poco dopo ci salutiamo.

"Grazie. È stato tutto meraviglioso" dico sinceramente a Nora, e lei sorride.

"Non posso rivendicare alcun merito. Ha fatto tutto Ana" replica, e in quel momento, suo marito grida il suo nome dal piano di sopra.

"Arrivo!" urla, e facendo un passo avanti, mi avvolge in un rapido abbraccio.

"Vieni a trovarci quando vuoi, ok?" dice, e le prometto di farlo.

Si dirige di sopra, e io mi rivolgo a Yulia. Lei e Lucas alloggiano nella casa principale, quindi è nel corridoio accanto a suo marito, guardandoci andar via. Impulsivamente, vado da lei e la abbraccio.

"Grazie ancora" le dico, mentre ci separiamo, e mi sorride calorosamente.

"Buona fortuna, Sara. Spero di vederti in giro."

"Oh, sicuramente" confermo. "Ciao, Lucas." Lo saluto, sorridendo, e lui mi rivolge uno sguardo di pietra in risposta.

Ok, quindi solo uno dei Kent mi ha perdonata finora.

"Pronta?" chiede Peter, passandomi un braccio intorno alla vita, e io annuisco, chinandomi verso di lui, mentre mi conduce via.

Torniamo alla nostra casa temporanea.

Peter

"ALLORA, CHE COS'È SUCCESSO TRA YULIA E GLI ESGUERRA?" chiede Sara a colazione la mattina dopo. "A cena, sembrava che ci fosse un po' di tensione tra loro, e ricordo che l'avevi menzionato a Cipro."

"Oh, quello?" Le verso ancora un po' di fiocchi d'avena e frutti di bosco. Ho iniziato a cercare un'alimentazione ottimale per le donne incinte e ho intenzione di spostare la dieta di Sara su cibi più sani. "Sì, c'è sicuramente tensione—e per una buona ragione."

Mette giù il cucchiaio. "Davvero?"

Prendo in considerazione l'idea di sorvolare su tutta la brutta storia, ma non ha avuto episodi di flashback questa mattina o la scorsa notte, e questo non ha niente a che fare con i suoi genitori o altri eventi traumatici che ha affrontato. Così, decido di rivelarle tutto, specialmente visto che ieri sera è sembrata cordiale con la moglie bionda di Kent.

"Ricordi che ti ho detto che Esguerra una volta ha avuto un conflitto con un gruppo terroristico e ha dovuto essere salvato?" chiedo. Al cenno con la testa di Sara, continuo: "Beh, c'era un motivo per cui lo avevano catturato. Il suo aereo era stato abbattuto sull'Uzbekistan e *ciò* è accaduto a causa di alcune informazioni fornite da Yulia al governo ucraino."

"Che cosa?" Sara sgrana gli occhi. "Perché l'avrebbe fatto? Stava con Lucas in quel momento?"

"Da quello che ho sentito dire, avevano avuto una sveltina di una notte a Mosca proprio prima dello schianto. Sul perché, quello era il suo lavoro all'epoca. Lavorava come spia per il governo ucraino a Mosca."

"Oh, wow, è..." Sembra scioccata.

Sorrido. "Sì, lo so. A proposito, anche Kent era sull'aereo. Insieme a quasi cinquanta uomini di Esguerra. Praticamente sono tutti morti—ed è così che Esguerra è finito in un ospedale del Tashkent, ferito e senza protezione."

"Oh, cazzo" sospira Sara. "Come fa ad essere ancora viva, addirittura sposata con Lucas?"

Sorrido. La mia piccola civile inizia a ragionare come me. "Sinceramente, non lo so" le confesso. "Ho lasciato la tenuta subito dopo l'inizio di tutto il casino. Ma immagino che sia viva *perché* sono sposati. L'ho aiutato a recuperarla da Mosca ad un certo punto, perché voleva punirla personalmente, ma non so molto oltre a questo. So solo che in qualche modo sono finiti insieme e che sono piuttosto felici."

Sara scuote la testa. "Wow. Sono... senza parole." Scava nei suoi fiocchi d'avena e io mi occupo rapidamente del mio pasto, prima di alzarmi per togliere i piatti.

Mentre carico la lavastoviglie, la guardo di nascosto. Sembra assorta nei suoi pensieri, mentre sorseggia il tè, ma non c'è alcun segno di quel terrificante sguardo vuoto, nessun attacco di iperventilazione o di panico collegato ai flashback. Si è svegliata da un incubo la scorsa notte, ma ho fatto l'amore con lei e si è riaddormentata.

Forse ieri è stata un'anomalia, e la mia ptichka starà bene, dopotutto. In ogni caso, la terapeuta sarà qui questa mattina e la visiterà nel pomeriggio.

Un'altra buona notizia è che l'operazione della scorsa notte si è svolta senza intoppi. Con le risorse di Esguerra e i miei file dettagliati su Henderson, abbiamo rintracciato tutti quelli che speravamo di rintracciare—il che significa che siamo un passo avanti nella risoluzione della situazione.

Se c'è qualche briciolo di empatia in Henderson, cederà.

Altrimenti, lo troveremo in ogni caso, e morirà sapendo che tutte quelle morti sono sulla sua coscienza.

FISSO LO SCHERMO DEL COMPUTER, CON LA PELLE CHE MI SI accappona per l'orrore. Mi aspettavo che Sokolov e gli altri impiegassero tutte le proprie risorse per trovarmi, ma non mi aspettavo questo. I messaggi che mi riempiono la casella di posta sono surreali.

Mio zio. I miei cugini. La famiglia di Bonnie. Tutti i nostri amici.

Morti.

Rapiti nelle loro case, nelle scuole, sulla strada per andare a lavorare e nelle chiese.

Con le dita tremanti, clicco sulla CNN e apro un video web che ne parla.

"Si ritiene ora che la serie di rapimenti della scorsa notte avvenuti ad Asheville, Charleston e nell'area di Washington D.C. possano essere collegati" annuncia il conduttore televisivo con malcelata agitazione. "Finora, non sono state fatte richieste, ma la polizia si aspetta di sentire i rapitori da un momento all'altro. In totale, diciannove cittadini sono stati dichiarati scomparsi, con uno dei rapimenti ripreso da una telecamera di sicurezza."

Il video mostra un filmato di due figure mascherate che afferrano lo Zio Ian, mentre fa rifornimento in una stazione di servizio. I movimenti dei rapitori sono fluidi e coordinati—sono chiaramente dei professionisti che sanno cosa stanno facendo.

"Secondo un'altra versione della storia, sembra che alcuni di questi cittadini abbiano subito rapimenti e aggressioni nel recente passato" continua il conduttore, e la telecamera si sofferma su una rossa in lacrime—Sandra, la moglie del mio amico Jimmy.

Grazie a Dio, l'hanno lasciata stare. È già abbastanza brutto che il mio più caro amico—dal quale abbiamo preso il nome per nostro figlio—sia nelle loro spietate grinfie.

"Perché continua a succederci questo?" singhiozza Sandra, con il mascara che le cola sul viso lentigginoso. "L'ultima volta, l'hanno picchiato e gli hanno sparato, e ha dovuto ritirarsi dalla polizia. E ora questo? Perché? Che cosa vogliono da noi?"

Me. Vogliono me.

La bile acida mi sale nella gola.

I poliziotti non vedranno alcuna richiesta dai rapitori, perché esse sono state inviate direttamente a me.

O meglio, alla CIA, dove devono aver saputo che ho ancora dei contatti.

Avrei dovuto capirlo e prendere dei provvedimenti per prevenirlo, ma ho pensato che tutti quelli che Sokolov aveva già interrogato prima fossero al sicuro, dato che non avevano saputo dare risposte la prima volta.

Mi ero concentrato sull'operazione Air Drop, sottovalutando quanto i miei avversari fossero sociopatici.

Mi fa male il collo, con il dolore sempre presente che si trasforma in agonia, mentre metto in pausa il video e clicco sulla mia casella di posta, dove rileggo l'ultima e-mail.

Diciannove ore, diciannove vite, si legge nel messaggio ricevuto dalla CIA. *Le lancette dell'orologio iniziano a girare a mezzogiorno (fuso orario EST). Consegnati, Wally, o li vedrai morire tutti, uno dopo l'altro.*

S ara

Dopo la colazione, Peter esce per occuparsi di affari con Esguerra e la sua squadra russa, e decido di andare a trovare Nora nella casa principale. Per la prima volta in una settimana, non mi sento tesa o ansiosa. Il mio stomaco è completamente tranquillo e il cuore batte ad un ritmo normale.

Sto canticchiando sottovoce mentre cammino, godendomi l'aria calda e umida sulla pelle. Mi sento bene, quasi come prima che accadesse tutto questo, prima che i miei genitori—

La mia mente si spegne, un muro di torpore mi avvolge, quando un terzo sparo risuona.

Guardo mio marito, supino e sanguinante, poi l'agente sulla soglia, con il viso contorto dall'odio, mentre mira alla testa di Peter.

Il mio sguardo si posa sulla pistola che lui ha lasciato, mentre stava lottando conto l'altro agente.

È a meno di un metro di distanza.

Mi allungo e la raccolgo. È fredda e pesante nella mia mano, aggiungendosi al gelido torpore nel cuore.

I miei genitori sono morti.

Peter sta per essere ucciso.

Miro e premo il grilletto una frazione di secondo prima che l'agente faccia fuoco.

Il proiettile lo manca, ma il colpo di pistola lo fa sobbalzare, facendogli sbagliare il bersaglio.

Si gira verso di me e sparo di nuovo.

Lo colpisco nel bel mezzo del giubbotto antiproiettile, facendolo cadere all'indietro.

Senza alcuna esitazione, mi avvicino e sollevo di nuovo la pistola.

"Non—" si strozza, ansimando, e premo il grilletto.

La sua faccia esplode in mille pezzi di sangue e ossa. È come un videogioco iper-realistico, completo di odore, gusto e—

"Figlio di puttana! Sara, che cos'è successo? Che cosa c'è che non va?"

Torno alla realtà, ansimando per respirare. Sono a terra, raggomitolata in una palla fetale, con Lucas Kent accucciato sopra di me. I suoi lineamenti duri sono preoccupati, con gli occhi chiari che mi scrutano dalla testa ai piedi. Non individuando lesioni evidenti, mi afferra per le spalle e mi tira in piedi.

Ho le ginocchia deboli e sto tremando tutta, con la maglietta intrisa di sudore che mi si attacca al corpo. Sento anche freddo e sto tremando nonostante il caldo del sole che mi brucia la pelle.

"Stai bene?" chiede Kent, tenendomi per le spalle. Quando annuisco automaticamente, mi lascia andare e chiede: "Che cos'è successo? Qualcosa ti ha spaventata o ferita?"

Scuoto la testa, respirando ancora troppo velocemente per poter parlare.

"Ok. Diego!" Fa un cenno verso la guardia che passa—la stessa che ci ha mostrato la casa, mi rendo conto vagamente.

"Resta con lei" ordina Kent, quando il giovane si precipita. "Vado a chiamare Peter."

E prima che possa obiettare, va via, correndo.

eter

"Dov'è Kent?" chiede Esguerra, quando entro nel piccolo edificio moderno che funge da ufficio. Preferisce condurre gli affari lontano dalla casa e dalla famiglia—sebbene Nora sia esperta nei dettagli del suo impero illegale.

"Come faccio a saperlo?" rispondo, mentre mi siedo accanto a Yan, che sta guardando il suo telefono. Anche Ilya e Anton sono già qui, con il primo che sta sgranocchiando allegramente un biscotto preso dal piatto che Ana deve aver portato di nuovo. "Non è in casa con te?"

Esguerra si acciglia. "Stamattina stava facendo il giro con le guardie." Dà un'occhiata ad uno dei tanti monitor TV allineati alle pareti, poi ci guarda. "A quanto pare, dovremo informarlo in seguito. Ho una chiamata in arrivo." Il suo sguardo si sposta su di me. "Notizie da parte di Henderson?"

"No, e non mi aspetterei di sentirlo presto. Manca ancora"—

guardo l'orologio su uno dei monitor—"circa un'ora alla scadenza dell'ultimatum. Immagino che dovremo mettere in pratica la nostra minaccia con almeno alcuni corpi, prima che si renda conto che facciamo sul serio."

Esguerra annuisce. "Va bene. Ho già dato ai nostri uomini le istruzioni su quali ostaggi devono essere uccisi per primi. Qualche notizia dai tuoi hacker?"

"In realtà, sì" risponde Yan, alzando lo sguardo dal telefono. "Hanno appena rintracciato il cecchino—colui che ha sparato all'agente durante l'arresto di Peter."

Stringo la mano sul tavolo. "Chi sarebbe?"

"A quanto pare, è una *donna*" risponde Yan, con gli occhi di nuovo sul telefono. "Si fa chiamare Mink e viene dalla Repubblica Ceca. Aspetta—l'immagine si sta caricando ora."

"E i nostri sosia?" chiede Anton. "Non si sa niente su quei bastardi?"

Yan non risponde, e quando lo guardo, scorgo una vena che gli pulsa nella tempia, mentre fissa lo schermo del suo telefono.

"Che cosa c'è?" chiede Ilya accigliandosi, e il suo gemello gli porge il telefono senza parole.

L'ampia faccia di Ilya sembra trasformarsi in pietra. "Lei?" Guarda suo fratello. "*Lei* è Mink?"

Che cazzo significa? Strappo il telefono dalla mano di Ilya ed esamino l'immagine sullo schermo.

Il volto della donna—ripreso a metà profilo dalla telecamera, è giovane e piuttosto carino, con lineamenti delicati evidenziati da quei capelli biondi e corti, che sembrano spuntoni intorno al viso pallido. Sul lato del collo noto un piccolo tatuaggio di qualcosa di indistinguibile, e l'orecchio è costellato da una dozzina di piercing.

"Chi è?" chiedo, guardando i gemelli. "Come mai la conoscete?"

Il volto di Yan è tirato. "Non importa." Afferra il telefono da me. "Sto mandando degli uomini a catturarla—potrebbe sapere dov'è Henderson."

"Importa" ribatte Esguerra, mentre i pollici di Yan colpiscono furiosamente lo schermo. "Chi cazzo è lei?"

"L'abbiamo conosciuta a Budapest" spiega Ilya, quando Yan ignora la domanda. "Lavora come cameriera in un bar."

Una cameriera di Budapest? Perché suona familiare?

"Sei andato a letto con lei un po' di tempo fa?" sbotta Anton, fissando Yan. "È lei quella per cui Ilya aveva messo il broncio, quando eravamo in Polonia?"

La massiccia mascella di Ilya si stringe. "Non ho messo il broncio. Ma sì, *lui*"—piega il pollice verso il fratello—"l'ha scopata."

Yan sbatte il telefono sul tavolo. "Chiudi quella fottuta bocca."

Osservo la scena con stupore. Il tranquillo, rilassato Yan sta per perdere il controllo come non l'ho mai visto fare.

La faccia di Ilya diventa rossa, e si alza bruscamente, facendo cadere la sedia sul pavimento.

Salto in piedi anch'io, sapendo che si sta per scatenare una rissa—e in quel momento irrompe Kent.

"Si tratta di Sara" annuncia, respirando come se avesse percorso un miglio in quattro minuti. "Peter, devi venire subito con me."

eter

IGNORANDO IL FASTIDIOSO DOLORE AL FIANCO, RIPORTO SARA A casa. Riesce a camminare—lo so, perché me l'ha detto con voce tremante—ma non me ne frega un cazzo. È così pallida e fragile che devo tenerla in braccio, devo sentire il suo esile corpo premuto contro il mio, in modo da assicurarmi che sia fisicamente illesa.

In modo che io possa capire che lei e il bambino stanno bene.

Mi si è gelato il sangue quando è venuto Kent, e non mi sono ancora completamente ripreso. Non aiuta che quando sono corso da lei, la mia ptichka era ancora più pallida di com'è adesso... ancora più fragile.

"Eccoci qui" dico sottovoce, mentre ci avviciniamo alla casa. "Ci faremo subito una doccia, d'accordo?" I suoi vestiti sono coperti di sporcizia e macchie d'erba, come i palmi delle mani, le ginocchia e metà del viso.

Non obietta—né per la doccia, né per il mio aiuto nello spogliarla—il che la dice lunga su quanto stia male. Ieri, ha fatto di tutto per convincermi che stesse bene.

Dopo averla denudata, apro l'acqua e aspetto che la temperatura sia al punto giusto. Poi, la faccio entrare e mi tolgo i vestiti, prima di unirmi a lei sotto il getto. L'acqua bagna immediatamente le mie bende, ma non mi importa. Sono abbastanza sicuro che possano staccarsi ora, e non succederebbe nulla.

"Che cos'hai visto, amore mio?" chiedo delicatamente, mentre mi verso il sapone nella mano. Nonostante la preoccupazione per lei, il mio fallo si indurisce, attirato dalla sua pelle setosa e dai seni con le punte rosa. Spietatamente, sopprimo l'impulso di fare qualsiasi cosa se non lavarla. Il sesso non risolverà questo, anche se vorrei che potesse farlo.

La mia ptichka ha bisogno di affrontare qualunque demone stia combattendo.

Deve lasciarmi lottare insieme a lei.

Chiude gli occhi e scuote la testa. "Non posso parlarne. Mi dispiace."

Fanculo. Ho voglia di sbattere il pugno sulla parete di vetro del box, ma comincio a lavarla, sforzandomi di essere il più delicato possibile.

Non ha bisogno di ulteriore violenza.

Ne ha vista fin troppa.

La preoccupazione, mescolata ad una salutare dose di colpa, continua a divorarmi dall'interno, mentre preparo il pranzo a Sara. Non avrei dovuto lasciarla sola per quei trenta minuti. Avrei dovuto essere lì, fare qualcosa per impedirlo.

Accidenti, avrei dovuto proteggerla dal trauma, innanzitutto.

Con mio grande sollievo, sembra stare molto meglio dopo la doccia—al punto che sta ancora tentando di fingere che vada tutto bene, che Kent non l'abbia trovata raggomitolata come una bambina ferita sull'erba.

"Perché non lasciamo che la terapeuta si riposi dopo il volo?" propone, quando la informo che la porterò ad un incontro con la dottoressa subito dopo aver mangiato. "Potremmo iniziare le sedute domani."

"Si riposerà, dopo aver parlato con te." Non rimanderò questo—non dopo quello che ho visto. Esguerra mi ha mandato un messaggio, dicendo di tornare nel suo ufficio dopo pranzo, ma non la lascerò di nuovo sola.

Henderson e tutta quella merda possono aspettare.

Sara sospira, guardando la sua insalata di cavoli, poi solleva lo sguardo. "Sai che non guarirò magicamente, se parlo con questa dottoressa, vero?" I suoi occhi nocciola sono turbati. "La terapia non sempre aiuta in situazioni come questa."

Almeno, sta finalmente riconoscendo che esiste una "situazione."

Alzandomi, cammino attorno al tavolo fino alla sua sedia. "Lo so, amore mio" dico sottovoce, guardando la sua faccia stravolta. Mettendole le mani sulle spalle, le massaggio, sentendo la tensione nei delicati muscoli. "Non guarirai magicamente, ma sarà un inizio."

E piegando le ginocchia accanto alla sua sedia, le stringo le braccia attorno, desiderando sentire il suo battito contro il mio.

Desiderando convincermi di poter annullare il danno che ho causato.

Sara

Il medico è una donna alta sulla quarantina. Se Sandra Bullock avesse interpretato l'elegante capa/cattiva ne *Il Diavolo Veste Prada*, sarebbe assomigliata a questa terapeuta, inclusi gli occhiali alla moda.

"Ciao" dice, porgendo la sua mano sottile, perfettamente curata. "Sono la Dottoressa Wessex."

"Piacere." Le stringo la mano. "Sono Sara."

Siamo in un'altra casa simile a quella in cui io e Peter alloggiamo, in un piccolo ufficio con una finestra che dà sulla strada. Riesco a vedere mio marito passeggiare fuori; la dottoressa Wessex è stata irremovibile sul fatto che lui non potesse assistere alla mia seduta di terapia.

"Piacere di conoscerti, Sara." Si siede dietro un tavolo lucido, e io mi siedo sulla sedia reclinabile dall'altra parte. "Tuo marito mi ha raccontato un po' di quello che ti porta oggi qui da me, ma mi piacerebbe sentirlo con le tue stesse parole."

Mi sposto nel sedile. "Preferirei non parlarne."

Piega la testa. "Perché? È perché ti addolora?"

Prendo fiato, mentre il mio petto si comprime. "No. Voglio dire, sì, certo. Solo che... non voglio pensarci."

"Perché i tuoi genitori sono stati uccisi?"

Sussulto e distolgo lo sguardo.

"O perché è successo qualcos'altro?" insiste la dottoressa. "Forse qualcosa che hai problemi ad elaborare?"

Il mio respiro accelera e stringo le mani. Mentre le mie unghie affondano nei palmi, il dolore mi aiuta a rimanere concentrata sul presente.

Non posso andare lì.

Non lo farò.

Quando resto in silenzio e mi rifiuto di guardarla, la Dottoressa Wessex sospira e dice: "Hai mai sentito parlare di Desensibilizzazione e Rielaborazione Attraverso i Movimenti Oculari o EMDR?"

La guardo e scuoto la testa.

"È una psicoterapia abbastanza nuova, non tradizionale, con la quale ho avuto grandi successi nell'ultimo anno. L'idea è che rivivrai le tue esperienze negative concentrandoti su uno stimolo esterno. Nello specifico, ti chiederò di tracciare i miei movimenti delle mani con gli occhi, mentre narrerai uno specifico ricordo doloroso."

Sbatto le palpebre "Che cosa?"

Sorride. "Farò questo"—muove ritmicamente la mano da una parte all'altra, come se mi stesse controllando la vista—"e tu seguirai il movimento con gli occhi. Ecco, facciamo pratica."

Riprende il movimento da una parte all'altra, e seguo le sue dita con lo sguardo come un gatto che insegue un puntatore laser. Non vedo come questo possa aiutare, ma voglio provare.

"Ok, bene" dice, quando riabbasso lo sguardo. "Ora

concentriamoci su un ricordo angosciante... diciamo, il tuo flashback più recente. Che cos'hai visto prima? Quale evento hai rivissuto? O, se preferisci non concentrarti su quello, scegli qualcos'altro—o possiamo cominciare dall'inizio."

Sto ancora monitorando i suoi movimenti delle mani con gli occhi, e in qualche modo questo rende più facile distaccarmi dalla pressione vulcanica che si raduna nel petto. Ne sento l'enorme peso, ma è come se stesse succedendo a qualcun altro.

I miei occhi guizzano da un lato all'altro, seguendo le sue dita, mentre comincio a parlare. Lentamente, con fermezza, rivivo gli eventi di quel giorno, dal team SWAT che si presenta fino al momento in cui ho premuto il grilletto la prima volta.

È solo lì che mi fermo, incapace di pronunciare un'altra parola, perché sto tremando troppo violentemente. Con mio sollievo, la Dottoressa Wessex non insiste. Invece, mi dice di concentrarmi su come il mio corpo sta reagendo e sui pensieri che sto avendo in questo momento. E per tutto il tempo, muove la sua mano avanti e indietro, mantenendomi concentrata.

Distraendomi dal dolore soffocante.

Quando Peter entra per riprendermi, sono così tesa emotivamente e fisicamente che andiamo subito a casa, dove prontamente mi addormento.

Mi sveglio un'ora e mezza dopo a causa del suono attutito delle voci maschili. Indossando una vestaglia, mi avvicino alla finestra e sbircio tra le tapparelle chiuse.

Vedo Kent, Esguerra, Peter e Yan. Stanno fuori, discutono su qualcosa.

Trattenendo il respiro, cerco di capire di cosa stanno parlando.

"Ancora niente" dice Kent, sembrando disgustato. "Siamo sicuri che il messaggio gli sia arrivato?"

"Oh, sì" replica cupamente Peter. "Quello stronzo è solo troppo codardo per fare qualcosa."

Esguerra guarda Yan. "E il tuo aggancio? Quando dovrebbe arrivare?"

La mascella di Yan si stringe visibilmente, ma poi sembra riprendere il controllo. "Presto" risponde senza alcuna emozione. "Molto presto."

"Bene." Un sorriso terrificante incurva le labbra di Esguerra. "Una volta che avremo lei, potrebbe non avere importanza se Henderson farà il nobile gesto o meno. Comunque, troveremo il bastardo."

Gli uomini si disperdono e io mi allontano dalla finestra, confusa e speranzosa.

Non so ancora cosa stiano facendo esattamente, ma sembra che stiano facendo progressi con Henderson—e per quanto sia sbagliato, non vedo l'ora che l'ex generale possa avere quello che merita.

enderson

"SEI UN FOTTUTO PSICOPATICO! MI HAI SENTITO? UNO psicopatico!" urla Bonnie, con le lacrime e il muco che le colano lungo il viso. "Cinque persone a cui teniamo sono morte e non te ne frega un cazzo!"

Mi abbasso, mentre lancia un bicchiere, che si schianta contro il muro dietro di me, andando in frantumi nell'impatto. Ogni parola che scaglia nella mia direzione è letale come i suoi proiettili, e la rabbia della risposta si combina con la mia emicrania per macchiare la mia visione con macule di rosso.

Non avrei dovuto dimenticare di riacquistare i suoi farmaci. Avrebbe dovuto essere drogata a letto, non leggere le mie e-mail e guardare le ultime notizie.

Un piatto mi sfreccia accanto all'orecchio e perdo la testa.

"Me ne frega eccome!" ruggisco, girando intorno al tavolo per afferrarle le spalle ossute. "Mio cugino Lyle è uno di quei morti. E allora? Uccideranno tutti loro a prescindere. E anche te, Amber e Jimmy. Pensi che dovrei consegnarmi a questi assassini su un piatto d'argento? È questo che dovrei fare?"

La sto scuotendo così forte che le tremano i denti nel cranio vuoto, ma si rifiuta di cedere.

"Forse dovresti, cazzo!" grida, mentre mi spunta in faccia tutto il suo odio. "Staremmo tutti meglio, se tu fossi morto!"

Infuriato, la spingo via—e sbatte contro il frigorifero, mentre nostra figlia entra in cucina.

"Mamma? Papà?" I suoi grandi occhi azzurri guizzano da me a Bonnie. "Che cosa sta succedendo?"

Fanculo. Amber non avrebbe dovuto assistere.

Dei miei due figli, lei è sempre quella dalla mia parte.

"Niente, tesoro" riesco a dire con calma. "Tua madre ha solo bisogno delle sue medicine, tutto qui."

E lasciando singhiozzare Bonnie sul pavimento, riporto mia figlia nella sua camera.

Non posso salvare tutti quelli a cui tengo, ma *proteggerò* la mia famiglia.

Anche se gli ingrati rendono fottutamente difficile farlo.

FINALMENTE HO MESSO LE MANI SULLA MAPPA DELLA TENUTA colombiana di Esguerra, e la sto studiando per l'Operazione Air Drop, quando mi viene in mente che la casa è silenziosa.

Troppo silenziosa.

Non ci sono esplosioni provenienti dai videogame nel soggiorno, né rumori di piatti in cucina nonostante sia ora di cena.

Con la pressione del sangue che schizza, vago di stanza in stanza.

Niente.

Non c'è nessuno.

La nostra baita in Islanda è fredda e vuota come le strade coperte di neve all'esterno.

Corro nel garage, e come pensavo, manca anche la Jeep. Bonnie deve averla presa per andare in città con i bambini.

Quella stupida stronza. Sbatto il palmo contro la parete. Le ho detto un milione di volte che non possiamo fare un passo fuori da questo posto. Come ha potuto correre un tale rischio visto cosa sta succedendo a tutti i nostri amici e parenti? Non si rende conto che i miei nemici le staccheranno una costola dopo l'altra?

A meno che... Il mio petto si stringe, con l'aria che evapora nei polmoni.

Non lo farebbe.

Non potrebbe.

Non oserebbe.

Tuttavia, le gambe mi riportano dentro la casa, in camera sua. Avevo guardato all'interno solo per un istante, giusto il tempo necessario per vedere che non c'era.

Così, ora entro e mi guardo intorno—e la rabbia mi fa quasi ribollire.

Sul suo comodino, sotto il telecomando della TV, c'è un foglietto di carta con la sua calligrafia.

Ce ne andiamo, c'è scritto. *Preferiamo correre il rischio là fuori che restare "al sicuro" qui dentro con te.*

ENTRO NEL CAPANNO DEGLI INTERROGATORI, DOVE UNA GIOVANE donna è seduta legata ad una sedia. La sua piccola faccia è piena di lividi e il labbro inferiore è spaccato, dandole un aspetto imbronciato. Il suo sguardo, tuttavia, è sveglio e sprezzante.

È un osso duro, questo grazioso cecchino. Mi chiedo se Yan le abbia provocato quelle contusioni durante l'interrogatorio o se siano dovute alla lotta durante la sua cattura di ieri.

Sentendo dei passi, mi volto e vedo Yan e Ilya entrare nella stanza.

"Abbiamo appena ricevuto i file sugli uomini di cui ci ha fornito i nomi" informa Ilya, tenendo fuori il telefono. "I nostri sosia hanno un bel curriculum. Tutti e quattro sono ex Delta Force, stessa unità. Loro e alcuni dei loro amici sono stati processati dalla corte marziale quindici anni fa per lo stupro di gruppo su una ragazza di sedici anni in Pakistan. Sei di loro sono stati arrestati, ma gli altri sono evasi e si sono tutti dati alla macchia. Da allora, hanno fatto lavoretti casuali qua e là, da piccoli omicidi a piazzare bombe per organizzazioni terroristiche."

Mentre parla, esamino le foto sullo schermo. Chiaramente erano travestiti, mentre ci impersonavano. I volti che mi guardano somigliano ben poco ai nostri; nel migliore dei casi, uno ha un aspetto vagamente simile al mio—e anche in questo caso, ha i capelli biondo cenere.

Mi viene un'idea. "Chi ha fatto il trucco e i travestimenti?" chiedo al cecchino, mettendomi davanti alla sua sedia. "A quanto pare, qualcuno molto abile."

Afferma di non sapere dove si nasconda Henderson, e che quel vigliacco di un ublyudok non si sarebbe arreso, lasciando morire amici e parenti al suo posto, quindi dovremo catturarlo in un altro modo... forse attraverso la squadra che ha usato per piazzare l'esplosivo.

Resta in silenzio per un momento; poi, dice cupamente: "Io. Sono stata io."

Sollevo le sopracciglia con fare scettico. "È così?"

Le sue narici si dilatano. "Perché dovrei mentire? Ti ho già dato tutti quei nomi. Che cos'è uno in più nel grande schema delle cose?"

Il suo inglese è puro come quello di qualsiasi americano. Mi chiedo quando e come una ragazza ceca abbia imparato a parlarlo così bene.

"Sarà facile verificarlo" replica Yan, facendo un passo avanti per mettersi accanto a me. "Può dimostrare la sua abilità su di me stasera."

"E su di me." Le mani di Ilya si contorcono ai suoi fianchi, mentre lancia un'occhiataccia al fratello.

Fantastico. Sono ancora incazzati l'uno con l'altro per chi la scoperà.

Respingendo la mia irritazione, rivolgo alla ragazza una

dozzina di altre domande, e lei risponde a tutte, anche se a malincuore. Essendo un sicario privato senza particolare lealtà verso nessuno, ha saggiamente deciso di collaborare con noi in cambio della sua vita e dell'eventuale libertà.

Sto pensando di farla fuori comunque—i genitori di Sara sono morti a causa sua—ma per ora, non mi dispiace farle credere che la lascerò andare.

In ogni caso, non è così utile come speravo. Ha detto di aver incontrato Henderson solo una volta, e non ha idea di dove possa nascondersi. Né sa dove sono i nostri imitatori, sebbene abbia lavorato spesso con loro in passato.

Un altro vicolo cieco, ma non perdo la speranza.

Ora abbiamo più nomi da rintracciare, e uno di questi è destinato a condurci al nostro obiettivo.

~

QUANDO TORNO A CASA, SONO SOLLEVATO VEDENDO CHE SARA sta ancora dormendo, come ha fatto negli ultimi due pomeriggi. Anche se non vuole ammetterlo, la gravidanza e la nausea mattutina che l'accompagna stanno avendo un caro prezzo.

Per non parlare delle sedute di terapia con la Dottoressa Wessex. Qualsiasi cosa la terapeuta stia facendo attraversare a Sara sembra stancare la mia ptichka al punto tale da farla addormentare non appena torna a casa.

"Che tipo di trattamento sta facendo con te?" le ho chiesto la scorsa notte, e mi ha spiegato del movimento degli occhi e di come esso dovrebbe rieducare il suo cervello ad elaborare i ricordi traumatici in modo diverso. Non sono sicuro di aver capito pienamente, ma ha avuto solo un piccolo episodio di flashback dall'inizio della terapia—almeno per quanto ne so.

È del tutto possibile che me li stia nascondendo. Non ha ancora pianto o parlato di quello che è successo con me, quindi so che è imbottigliato dentro di lei, con tutto il dolore e la sofferenza che riempiono il vuoto lasciato dalla morte dei suoi genitori.

La cosa strana è che ne provo un po' anch'io—non solo come echi del suo dolore, ma come se fosse una mia perdita. Nei quattro mesi dopo il nostro matrimonio, avevo conosciuto Chuck e Lorna, avevo cominciato ad apprezzarli e a rispettarli. Erano brave persone, genitori amorevoli, e sebbene avessero ogni ragione per odiarmi, si stavano lentamente aprendo con me, lasciandomi entrare nella loro vita.

Una parte della loro famiglia—una famiglia che ancora una volta non sono riuscito a proteggere.

Lentamente, esco dalla camera da letto, con il petto dolorosamente stretto. Non so se mi perdonerò mai per quello che è successo, per non aver previsto che il nemico a cui avevo dato la caccia così diligentemente potesse non accontentarsi di sgattaiolare via nell'ombra e volesse riprendere in mano la propria vita.

Per non aver immaginato la forma sovversiva che la sua vendetta avrebbe potuto prendere.

Il mio umore è ancora cupo, quando entro nel salotto e apro il portatile per controllare l'e-mail crittografata che ho usato per comunicare con il contatto di Henderson nella CIA. Tutti i diciannove prigionieri sono morti ora, quindi non mi aspetto di trovare nulla—sto controllando più che altro per abitudine.

Ecco perché un messaggio da parte di un mittente sconosciuto mi sorprende completamente.

Aprendo l'e-mail, la leggo—poi la rileggo, incapace di credere ai miei occhi.

Se vuoi Wally, incontriamoci al Marison Café di Londra alle 9 di mercoledì. Vieni da solo.

-Bonnie Henderson

ara

"—È CHIARAMENTE UNA TRAPPOLA" SENTO DIRE ILYA, MENTRE esco dalla camera, sbadigliando dopo il mio sonnellino. "Sta cercando di farti uscire allo scoperto, tutto qui."

"Ovviamente, ma dobbiamo seguire quella pista" ribatte Kent, mentre mi fermo appena fuori dalla vista nel corridoio e sbircio nel soggiorno.

Peter, Esguerra, Kent e tutti e tre i compagni di squadra russi di mio marito sono radunati attorno ad un laptop sul tavolino da caffè, riempiendo il piccolo spazio con così tanto testosterone che posso quasi assaporarlo. "Virilità letale" sono le parole che mi vengono in mente, quando osservo i loro corpi alti e superbi e i volti duri.

Virilità letale e sconvolgente.

Certo, Peter è molto più magnetico degli altri, decido, mentre continuano a parlare, ignari della mia presenza. Kent, con i suoi capelli biondi, mi fa pensare ad un selvaggio vichingo, e percepisco qualcosa di decisamente crudele in Esguerra—e, in qualche misura, in Yan e Anton. Ilya è l'unico che sembra avere un briciolo di gentilezza umana, e non è assolutamente il mio tipo—anche se immagino che moltissime donne troverebbero eccitanti quei muscoli troppo grandi e i tatuaggi sul cranio.

"Siamo sicuri che Peter sia quello che dovrebbe andare da solo?" chiede Esguerra, accovacciato per scrutare lo schermo del portatile. "L'e-mail non è indirizzata a nessuno in particolare."

Mi si ferma il respiro nel petto, e tutti i pensieri sul look degli uomini scompaiono dalla mia mente.

Qualcuno sta cercando di convincere mio marito ad andare da qualche parte da solo?

"I nostri hacker stanno tracciando l'e-mail ora" dice Yan, guardando il suo telefono. "Scopriremo presto l'indirizzo IP da cui è stata inviata."

Peter fa un gesto sbrigativo con la mano. "Non sarà un vero indirizzo IP. Henderson sa come coprire le proprie tracce."

"Ma se non fosse Henderson?" Esguerra si alza in piedi. "E se fosse sua moglie?"

Ilya sbuffa. "Sì, certo. E se ci crediamo, siamo degli sprovveduti che—"

"No, Julian ha ragione" interrompe Peter. "Qualcosa in tutto questo non è da Henderson. Se avesse voluto attirarmi fuori, avrebbe fornito una pista più credibile—fingendosi, per esempio, il suo contatto della CIA o qualcosa di simile. Firmare quell'e-mail con il nome di sua moglie è come se ci stesse dicendo che si tratta di una trappola. Non è necessario aver lavorato per l'agenzia per sapere che è una tattica con scarse probabilità di successo."

"Forse è per questo che lo sta usando" replica Kent. "*Perché* è così assurdo e incredibile."

"O forse perché non è lui quello che ha scritto l'e-mail." Esguerra incrocia le braccia sul petto. "Secondo me, potrebbe essere stata sua moglie."

"Perché sua moglie dovrebbe contattare Peter?" chiede Anton, grattandosi la barba. "Abbiamo appena ucciso diciannove dei loro amici e parenti e abbiamo lasciato i corpi per i poliziotti. Pensi che abbia voglia di suicidarsi un qualche modo?"

"Forse" risponde Yan, mentre mi copro la bocca con la mano, reprimendo un gemito sconvolto.

Diciannove persone?

Hanno ucciso *diciannove innocenti* nel loro tentativo di catturare Henderson?

"Pensaci" continua Yan, ignaro del martellamento del mio battito cardiaco. "Abbiamo seguito suo marito per anni. Pensa allo stress a cui tutta la famiglia è stata sottoposta. Non è questo quello che pensavamo potesse accadere, quando abbiamo avuto a che fare con quelle persone la prima volta? Non speravamo che qualcuno nella famiglia di Henderson—la moglie, la figlia, il figlio—potesse cedere sotto la pressione e commettere questo tipo di errore?"

"Questo è più di un errore" replica Kent. "Non l'abbiamo trovata, perché ha contattato i suoi amici per paura. Ci ha contattati, all'indirizzo e-mail che solo Henderson e il suo contatto della CIA potevano avere."

"A meno che non abbia letto l'e-mail del marito e abbia visto il messaggio inoltrato dalla CIA" ribatte Esguerra. "Allora, l'avrebbe potuto avere anche lei."

Continuando a tenermi la mano sulla bocca, indietreggio, facendo attenzione a non emettere alcun suono.

Ora capisco perché Peter non volesse rivelarmi alcunché di specifico sul loro piano.

Non è a causa del mio stato mentale—è perché quello che hanno commesso è un omicidio di massa.

Peter

Stiamo cercando una strategia su come affrontare al meglio la situazione, quando Sara entra nel salotto.

"Eccoti" dico sorridendo. "Com'è andato il pisolino?"

I suoi occhi incontrano brevemente i miei, poi guizzano via. "Bene. Ciao a tutti." Saluta gli uomini senza sorridere.

"Ci vediamo stasera" dice Esguerra alzandosi dal divano. "Otto in punto, nel mio ufficio."

Lancio un'occhiata a Sara, che ci è passata davanti per recarsi in cucina e si sta versando un bicchiere d'acqua. Non voglio lasciarla sola—ecco perché ho radunato tutti qui.

Comprendendo il mio dilemma, Esguerra aggiunge: "Sara, Nora si stava chiedendo se potessi aiutarla con Lizzie stasera. Rosa ha la serata libera."

Mia moglie alza lo sguardo, con volto inespressivo. "Certo, ne sarei felice."

Esguerra annuisce, soddisfatto, e tutti si allontanano rapidamente, lasciandoci soli. Sono contento—perché non mi piace lo strano umore di Sara.

È successo qualcosa, mentre stava facendo il pisolino?

"Ptichka..." entro in cucina e mi fermo di fronte a lei. "Hai avuto un altro flashback questo pomeriggio?"

Sbatte le palpebre. "Che cosa? No."

Le rivolgo un'occhiata dubbiosa. "Sei sicura?"

La sua delicata mascella si stringe. "Sì. Sto bene." Poggiando il bicchiere sul ripiano, si allontana.

Solo che non ho intenzione di lasciarla andare via dopo una menzogna così evidente. Afferrandola per un braccio, la costringo a guardarmi. "Allora, qual è il problema?" chiedo. "Che cos'è successo?"

Mi guarda e scorgo uno strano vuoto nei suoi dolci occhi nocciola. "Niente. Non è successo niente."

"Sara... non mentirmi."

Qualcosa di doloroso sfarfalla nel suo sguardo, prima di tornare a quel vuoto. "Te l'ho detto, non è niente."

"Non è niente, se ti rifiuti di parlare con me. Ptichka..." Le libero il braccio per infilarle una ciocca di capelli ondulati dietro l'orecchio. "Per favore, amore mio, dimmi cosa c'è che non va."

La sua faccia si corruga. "Niente. Lasciami stare."

Lasciami stare. Lascio cadere la mano, sentendo le parole non dette con la stessa chiarezza con cui le avrei sentite se le avesse urlate contro di me. L'e-mail mi aveva temporaneamente distratto dal mio stato d'animo cupo, ma ora è tornato, con la consapevolezza di aver causato tutto ciò che mi dilania, soffocandomi con il suo peso nauseante.

Sono stato io a fare questo a Sara.

I suoi genitori sono morti a causa mia.

La sua vecchia vita è perduta a causa mia.

Perché non l'ho lasciata.

Perché non potrei mai lasciarla.

"Mi odi?" chiedo piano. "Non ti biasimo, se lo fai."

Mi fissa, con le pupille che si scuriscono, mentre il respiro accelera. Non lo nega, e perché dovrebbe?

Se non fosse stato a causa della mia ossessione per lei, i suoi genitori sarebbero ancora vivi.

"Dovrei." La sua voce è tesa. "Una persona normale lo farebbe."

La pressione sul mio petto cresce, il dolore diventa più acuto. Certo che dovrebbe. Sono da biasimare per tutto questo.

"Mi dispiace." Le insolite parole mi escono dalla bocca con crudezza. "Mi dispiace per questo, per tutto. Non sono riuscito a proteggerli... a proteggerti. Avrei dovuto prevedere che avrebbe fatto qualcosa del genere, ma..." Mi fermo, sapendo di non avere una vera scusa.

Con tutte le guardie del corpo e le misure di sicurezza che avevo adottato, ero pronto per colpire i miei nemici, ma non in quel modo.

Sara sgrana gli occhi, mentre parlo, e prima che abbia finito, inizia a scuotere la testa. "Di cosa stai parlando?" esclama, quando taccio. "Non è quello che—Credi che ti stia incolpando per la morte dei miei genitori?"

Aggrotto la fronte, confuso. "Non è così?"

"Ovviamente no! Casomai, sono io che—" Ora è lei ad interrompersi, con gli occhi che brillano con una dolorosa luminosità. Prima che io possa aggiungere qualcosa, continua. "Il punto è che Henderson è la persona da incolpare per quello che è successo, non tu. È stato *lui* a piazzare l'esplosivo, uccidendo tutte quelle persone innocenti in modo che potesse incastrarti per la loro morte. È stato *lui* a mandare la squadra SWAT a casa dei miei genitori."

"Lo so. Ma lui era il *mio* nemico."

"Sì, e tu sei *mio* marito." Le lacrime ora stanno nuotando nei suoi occhi. "Sono stata *io* ad innamorarmi di te. *Io* a portarti nelle loro vite. *Io* ad insistere per la cosiddetta vita normale nei sobborghi. Se avessi accettato prima i miei sentimenti per te, avremmo potuto vivere felici in Giappone. E poi niente di tutto questo sarebbe successo, e i miei genitori sarebbero ancora—"

"Stai seriamente cercando di dire che sei da biasimare per tutto questo?" la interrompo, incredulo. Prendendole le mani nelle mie, le stringo dolcemente. "Sara, ptichka... hai l'impressione di essere in qualche modo responsabile per quello che è successo?"

Non ricorda com'è finita in Giappone? Come mi sono imposto nella sua vita e l'ho rapita?

Le lacrime nei suoi occhi brillano di più, e cerca di distogliere lo sguardo, ma non glielo permetto. Andremo fino in fondo. Ora. Oggi. Non importa quanto sia difficile.

Perché finalmente la mia ptichka si sta aprendo, parlando di quello che è successo.

"Sara..." Lasciandole le mani, le accarezzo la mascella delicata. "Amore mio, non sei in alcun modo da biasimare. È colpa mia—tutto questo. Dal primo momento in cui ti ho vista, ti ho voluta, e non ho lasciato che nulla ostacolasse il mio cammino... nemmeno i tuoi sentimenti. Sono stato un bastardo —e lo sono ancora, perché anche dopo tutto quello che è successo, non riesco a fare la cosa giusta."

La sua gola aggraziata si muove. "La cosa giusta?"

"Allontanarmi. Lasciarti andare." Faccio una smorfia con la bocca, mentre abbasso la mano. "È quello che farebbe un brav'uomo. Un uomo che desidera pentirsi per i propri peccati. Ma non sono io. Non posso farlo. I nove mesi in cui siamo stati separati mi hanno quasi distrutto—e preferirei bruciare all'inferno per l'eternità che trascorrere una vita senza di te."

Indietreggia, e scorgo di nuovo il tormento nel suo sguardo, prima che torni vuoto. "Non devi farlo" dice frettolosamente. "Non ti sto chiedendo di lasciarmi. Non *voglio* che mi lasci.

Questa è l'ultima cosa che voglio—e sicuramente non ti biasimo per quello che è successo ai miei genitori."

"Allora, che cosa intendevi, quando hai detto che dovresti odiarmi? Che una persona normale mi odierebbe?"

Il suo respiro accelera di nuovo, e lei fa un passo indietro, scuotendo la testa, mentre l'umidità si accumula nei suoi occhi. "Lascia perdere." La trema la voce. "Dimenticalo."

La fisso, mentre mi sovviene un nuovo sospetto. "Quando ti sei svegliata?" chiedo, sondando il terreno.

Un visibile brivido la attraversa, e capisco di aver indovinato.

Deve aver origliato.

Cerco di ricordare quello che abbiamo detto, esattamente—e sussulto internamente.

I diciannove cadaveri sono stati sicuramente menzionati.

Avvicinandomi, le stringo le esili spalle. "Mi dispiace che tu l'abbia sentito" dico dolcemente. "Per quello che vale, stavo contando sul fatto che Henderson si consegnasse per risparmiare almeno alcune di quelle persone."

Deglutisce. "Sì, certo."

"Avresti preferito che non facessi nulla? Vorresti che camminasse libero dopo quello che ha fatto?"

Il suo petto si gonfia. "Dovrei." La sua voce è tesa, mentre mi fissa. "Non che camminasse libero, ma che venisse arrestato. Che pagasse in modo normale per i crimini commessi."

"E vuoi questo?" chiedo dolcemente. "Se potessi agitare una bacchetta magica e farlo andare in prigione per i suoi crimini, ti soddisferebbe? Sarebbe abbastanza, considerando quello che ha fatto? A noi, a Tamila e Pasha... ai tuoi genitori?"

Il suo respiro accelera ad ogni parola che pronuncio, e posso vederla iniziare a tremare. Liberandosi della mia presa, si sposta per andarsene, ma le prendo il polso e la costringo a guardarmi.

"Dimmi, Sara." La avvicino spietatamente. Voglio tirarle fuori tutto, arrivare al nocciolo di ciò che la infastidisce. "È questo che vorresti per lui? La normale giustizia civile? O vorresti che soffrisse? Che conoscesse il vero dolore e la perdita?"

Le lacrime si riversano, coprendole le guance con l'umidità. "Smettila" si strozza, tirando via il polso. "Io non... non sono..."

"Non ti piacerebbe?" Mi rifiuto di cedere. "Ne sei sicura, amore mio? Non c'è una parte di te che si senta soddisfatta che il patrigno della tua paziente abbia avuto quello che meritava? Di *aver* premuto il grilletto sull'agente che ha ucciso tua madre? Che sebbene Henderson sia ancora là fuori, stia già pagando per i suoi crimini in carne ed ossa?"

Le lacrime scorrono più forte, e sento la sua agitazione intensificarsi, mentre sussurro: "Se lo merita, Sara. Sai che è così. È triste che altri debbano morire al suo posto, ma è così che funziona questo mondo. Non è giusto. Non lo è. Lo so—perché se ci fosse giustizia in questa vita, mio figlio sarebbe qui con noi oggi. Invece di essere morto con una macchinina giocattolo stretta nel pugno, sarebbe cresciuto e guiderebbe la versione reale. Sarebbe andato a scuola e sarebbe uscito con le ragazze. E un giorno, ad un certo punto nel futuro, avrebbe conosciuto qualcuno da amare quanto io amo te—qualcuno che gli avrebbe fatto dimenticare le brutali lezioni della vita."

Ora sta piangendo, sbattendo sul mio petto e singhiozzando, e le stringo le braccia intorno, tenendola, mentre la diga finalmente si rompe e lei cede al suo dolore.

Mentre affronta la sofferenza e la perdita.

8 0

ara

PIANGO PER QUELLA CHE SEMBRA UN'ORA, COSÌ PRESA DAL MIO dolore che, quando Peter mi prende e mi trasporta sul divano nel soggiorno, me ne accorgo appena. Mentre mi tiene sul grembo, facendomi dondolare dolcemente avanti e indietro, mi dispero per i miei genitori e per l'uomo che ho ucciso, per le vittime di Peter e per Pasha e Tamila. E soprattutto, mi dispero per la donna che ero un tempo, una che non riusciva ad immaginare di strappare una vita... o di amare un uomo capace di uccidere.

Mi colpisce a ondate, tutto il dolore, il senso di colpa e la rabbia. Dio, provo così tanta rabbia. Non sapevo di averla dentro di me. Se Henderson fosse qui adesso, lo ucciderei a mani nude. Lo guarderei morire e godrei di ogni raccapricciante momento. Nonostante tutto, io e mio marito avevamo costruito la nostra vita da sogno insieme—solo per perdere tutto nel giro di pochi devastanti minuti.

È quello che è successo a Peter, quando Pasha e Tamila sono stati uccisi? Si sentiva così—come se il suo mondo avesse improvvisamente smesso di girare?

Mentre piango, rivivo tutto—tutti i ricordi che ho combattuto così duramente. Sento gli spari e il rombo dell'elicottero, sento il sangue e il panico nell'aria. Vedo i miei genitori morire e sento il peso freddo della pistola nella mia mano, mentre premo il grilletto... una volta, due volte, una terza volta.

Ricordo la sensazione nel vedere la faccia dell'agente esplodere e nel sapere di aver strappato una vita umana—che nel profondo, sono capace di fare le stesse cose di Peter.

Piango per questo e per la consapevolezza che mio figlio non conoscerà mai una vita davvero tranquilla, che crescerà in un mondo colorato da sfumature di oscurità. Piango per mio padre, che non è mai diventato nonno, e per mia madre, che ha passato i suoi ultimi momenti ripiegata sul corpo morto del marito.

Piango per loro e mi infurio con il destino, e per tutto il tempo, Peter è lì, che mi abbraccia.

Che mi presta la sua forza, in modo che io possa crollare senza spezzarmi.

eter

ASPETTO CHE I SINGHIOZZI DI SARA SI PLACHINO, PRIMA DI cedere al calore oscuro che sta fermentando nelle mie vene. Per una lunga ora, l'ho tenuta sulle ginocchia, sentendo il suo corpo sinuoso tremare, con il sedere formoso che si contorceva su tutto il mio inguine, mentre i suoi morbidi seni strusciavano sul mio petto.

È sbagliato bramarla in questo modo, quando ho appena assistito alla profondità della sua sofferenza, ma non posso farci niente. Il suo dolore mi ha prosciugato, spazzando via la sottile patina di civiltà che maschera i miei impulsi elementari.

Sono una bestia scatenata, e lei è la mia preda.

Selvaggiamente, la bacio, assaporando il sale delle lacrime che si asciugano sulle sue labbra, mentre le strappo i vestiti, scoprendole la pelle liscia. All'inizio è passiva, prosciugata dalla tempesta emotiva che ha subito, ma poco dopo, avvolge le esili braccia intorno a me, e ricambia il bacio, strappandomi gli indumenti con la stessa ferocia.

La mia maglietta atterra sul pavimento, unendosi alla pila dei suoi vestiti, e poi lei armeggia con la cerniera dei miei jeans, mentre si mette a cavalcioni sul mio grembo nudo.

"Lascia fare a me" ordino con voce roca, quando sembra impiegare un'eternità, ma ha già capito, e il mio fallo si libera, gonfio e dolorante, disperato dal desiderio di seppellirsi nel suo calore umido.

"Ti amo" ansima, mentre mi tuffo in profondità, e sento i suoi muscoli interni stringersi intorno a me, accogliendomi, nonostante il dolore che devo provocarle.

Proprio come se mi stesse abbracciando, nonostante tutte le sofferenze che ho portato nella sua vita.

Non merito il suo amore, il suo perdono, ma mentre le faccio scorrere le dita tra i capelli, tenendola ferma per il mio bacio divorante, so che me li sta concedendo.

Che è veramente mia, nel bene e nel male.

ara

"SEI SICURA CHE STARAI BENE?" CHIEDE PETER PER LA DECIMA volta, mentre ci avviciniamo alla villa di Esguerra dopo cena, e io annuisco, notando la sua espressione preoccupata.

"Tranquillo. Starò bene."

Per la prima volta dopo una settimana e mezza, non sto mentendo. Mi sento come se avessi strofinato gli occhi con la carta vetrata, e ho un terribile mal di testa per tutto quel pianto —per non parlare del dolore dovuto al sesso nel salotto—ma tutto ciò è secondario. Il dolore peggiore—la sofferenza e il senso di colpa che non sono riuscita ad affrontare in tutti questi giorni—sta diminuendo, anche se potrebbe non sparire mai completamente.

Certo, c'è ancora la questione dei diciannove ostaggi morti, ma sto cercando di non pensarci. Perché, quale sarebbe il punto?

Mio marito sarà anche un mostro, ma non posso vivere senza di lui più di quanto lui possa vivere senza di me.

"Non devo andare per forza" ripete Peter. "Possiamo semplicemente tornare a casa."

"Intendi dire la casa in cui Esguerra ci ha fatto alloggiare? Lo stesso Esguerra la cui ospitalità si basa sul tuo aiuto nel catturare Henderson in un modo rapido?"

Alza le spalle, senza distogliere lo sguardo. "Capirà, se non parteciperò alla riunione."

Gli sorrido, con il petto che si riempie di calore incandescente. Il mio cavaliere oscuro—sempre pronto ad andare in battaglia per me. "Forse—ma non ce n'è bisogno. Starò bene. E ad essere sincera, voglio davvero vedere Nora e Lizzie."

"Va bene, amore mio. Se sei sicura" dice, mentre ci fermiamo davanti alla porta della villa. "Chiamami, se hai bisogno di qualcosa, ok? Non sarò lontano." Indica un piccolo edificio nelle vicinanze—dev'essere l'ufficio a cui si riferiva Esguerra.

"D'accordo. Ci vediamo presto." Mettendo le mani sulle sue ampie spalle, mi alzo in punta di piedi e premo le labbra sulle sue. Intendevo dargli un casto bacio, ma mi avvolge un braccio intorno alla vita e mi infila una mano tra i capelli, tenendomi ferma, mentre approfondisce il bacio, saccheggiando la mia bocca come se non avessimo fatto sesso da mesi, invece di poche ore. La mia frequenza cardiaca accelera, con un calore che si accumula nell'intimo, mentre il suo membro si indurisce contro il mio ventre, e per un momento, sono tentata di accettare la sua proposta inespressa.

Di mollare i nostri impegni, così da poter tornare a casa e passare le prossime due ore a letto.

È solo quando Peter interrompe il bacio per riprendere aria che la mia mente si schiarisce a sufficienza da rendersi conto che siamo nel portico di Esguerra—e che la tenda della finestra vicina si sta spostando, come se qualcuno stesse sbirciando.

"Aspetta..." Respiro pesantemente, liberandomi della sua presa e indietreggiando. "Non possiamo—non dovremmo qui."

Mi fissa, con il petto possente che si alza e si abbassa, e capisco che se non fossimo in pubblico, sarebbe già su di me.

"Va bene" dice gutturalmente, con le sue grandi mani che si flettono ai fianchi. "Ma non restare qui troppo a lungo... Ricorda, prima di tutto, sei mia."

E con questa affermazione atavica, si volta e si allontana.

Se Nora ha notato i miei occhi gonfi e cerchiati di rosso, è abbastanza discreta da non dire nulla, mentre la accompagno nella camera di Lizzie. Invece, mi intrattiene con una storia su un macao scarlatto che ha visto durante la sua corsa mattutina oggi, e altri interessanti incontri con la fauna locale.

"Sembra che ti piaccia qui" dico sorridendo, mentre si china sulla culla per prendere sua figlia. La bimba emette un suono insoddisfatto, ma poi si sistema tra le braccia di sua madre, posando la testolina sulla sua esile spalla.

"Lo adoro." Nora mi sorride, mentre si siede su una sedia a dondolo, accarezzando delicatamente la schiena di Lizzie. "L'ho amato fin dall'inizio."

Mordicchiandomi il labbro inferiore, mi siedo sul piccolo divano accanto alla sedia. L'oscura curiosità mi sta divorando, ma non so se dovrei parlare di cose personali con questa giovane donna. "Ti piace *tutto* di questo?" oso infine.

Non sto parlando del tempo o della natura locale, e vedo che Nora capisce. Tuttavia, la mia domanda è abbastanza vaga che potrebbe rispondere nello stesso modo, se lo volesse—non voglio farla sentire assolutamente a disagio.

I suoi occhi sono scuri e pensierosi, mentre mi studia. "No" dice tranquillamente. "Non tutto—anche se amo *lui*."

Certo che lo ama. L'ho visto durante la cena. Ed è

ricambiata... anche se qualcuno potrebbe dire che un uomo del genere non è capace di quella profondità di sentimenti.

Prima di incontrare Peter, sarei stata d'accordo, ma come ogni altra cosa nella mia vita, le mie opinioni sull'argomento sono cambiate e si sono evolute negli ultimi due anni.

Ora so che gli spietati assassini possono amare e che al cuore può mancare una bussola morale.

"Sei al corrente della loro operazione più recente?" chiedo dolcemente, quando Nora tace. "Quella con tutti gli ostaggi?"

Probabilmente non dovrei insistere, ma non riesco ancora a dimenticare i diciannove morti.

Annuisce. "Sì. Immagino che lo stesso valga per te, no?"

"Peter non aveva intenzione di dirmelo, ma oggi pomeriggio li ho sentiti." Deglutisco. "Quindi sì, ora lo so."

"Ah. Me lo stavo chiedendo—" Gesticola verso i miei occhi e sorride mestamente. "Non importa."

Piego la testa, meravigliandomi di quanto sembri calma, di quanto sembri impassibile davanti a tutto ciò. "Non ti dà fastidio?" chiedo, non riuscendo a farne a meno. "Non trovi questo genere di cose... orripilante?"

Sospira, spostando la bimba sull'altra spalla. "Sì. Certo che lo trovo orripilante. Non sono come Julian; non sono nata per questo tipo di vita."

"Come fai a chiudere gli occhi, allora? Come fai a fartelo scivolare?"

"Ad essere sincera" dice dolcemente: "Non lo so. Tutto quello che so è che lo amo... che ho bisogno di lui come la foresta pluviale ha bisogno del sole. Il mio mondo è più oscuro con lui, ma è anche più luminoso, più ricco in così tanti modi."

Mi mordo l'interno della guancia. La capisco così tanto che è spaventoso. "Ti chiedi mai se... se qualcosa dentro di te possa essere sbagliato e contorto?" chiedo, mentre la bimba inizia a fare storie. "Se forse le donne normali non avrebbero... sai?"

Sospira di nuovo e sposta Lizzie sull'altra spalla. "È

possibile. Conosco Julian, e io— Beh, il modo in cui stiamo insieme non è per tutte, questo è certo." Sta per aggiungere altro, ma il malumore di Lizzie sta crescendo di volume, e Nora si alza, dondolando la bimba per calmarla.

Anch'io mi alzo in piedi. "Posso tenerla?"

Nora sogghigna, mentre i capricci della bimba si intensificano fino alle urla. "Proprio adesso? Sei sicura?"

"Ho bisogno di allenarmi" rispondo ironicamente. "E tuo marito ha detto che avevi bisogno di aiuto."

"In tal caso, ecco qua. Questo fagotto di gioia è tutto tuo." Mi porge la bimba con esagerato entusiasmo.

Con mia sorpresa, Lizzie smette immediatamente di piangere e mi fissa con grandi occhi azzurri.

"Piccola traditrice" dice Nora a sua figlia con finto risentimento. "Col cavolo che ti allatto stanotte."

Rido, cullando la bimba tra le braccia, e mentre gorgoglia, allungando il minuscolo pugno per raggiungere i miei capelli, sento parte della pressione nel petto che si attenua, con le nubi scure che si sollevano abbastanza da farmi intravedere un accenno di luce.

Henderson

Non si trovano da nessuna parte.

Le parole risuonano nel mio cervello afflitto dall'emicrania, con le lettere che si contorcono sullo schermo come serpenti.

Tutti i contatti mi informano che mia moglie e i miei figli non si trovano da nessuna parte. È come se fossero spariti nel nulla.

Mi fa male il collo per il dolore, con la sofferenza che si irradia fino al braccio sinistro. Vorrei ululare come un animale e ingoiare una confezione di pillole, ma non posso.

Ho bisogno di tutta la mia lucidità per questo.

Le probabilità che Sokolov li abbia già catturati sono alte. Che cos'altro potrebbe spiegare la loro scomparsa? Non ci sono tracce sul fatto che abbiano lasciato l'Islanda, nessun biglietto aereo emesso a chiunque corrisponda alla loro descrizione.

Devono essere stati catturati e rapiti.

Presto, riceverò la richiesta di consegnarmi, insieme ad alcune parti del corpo dei miei figli. Sokolov non li risparmierà —non dopo quello che ha fatto al resto dei nostri amici e familiari.

Non dopo quello che è successo a suo figlio in quel piccolo villaggio di merda.

C'è solo una cosa da fare, un ultimo piano disperato da provare.

Prendendo il telefono, compongo il numero sulla mia scrivania.

"L'operazione Air Drop può iniziare" dico, quando l'uomo dall'altro capo risponde. "Tieni pronta la squadra. Colpiremo sabato prossimo, tra una settimana."

Peter

Ripasso il piano A con la mia squadra, Kent ed Esguerra. Quindi, passiamo ai piani B, C, D ed E.

A differenza di un colpo organizzato da un gruppo di assassini, stiamo andando più o meno alla cieca. La trappola potrebbe scattare da qualunque parte, assumere qualsiasi forma che la mente addestrata dalla CIA di Henderson possa escogitare. Dai cecchini, agli MI5 e all'Interpol, potremmo subire un'imboscata in centinaia di modi diversi, e dobbiamo essere preparati a tutto.

Dobbiamo anche immaginare l'improbabile possibilità che *non* si tratti di una trappola, e che sia stata proprio Bonnie Henderson a contattarci.

Ecco perché, nonostante la mia estrema riluttanza a separarmi da Sara per un certo periodo di tempo, andrò a Londra con la mia squadra martedì, dopodomani.

Non credo che la mia ptichka reagirà bene a questo, ma non c'è altra scelta. Verranno anche Kent ed Esguerra per fornire la copertura con le loro squadre.

Dobbiamo trovare Henderson e mettere fine a tutto questo.

Non c'è altra scelta.

"Come pensi che si sentirà Nora all'idea che andrai di persona?" chiedo ad Esguerra, mentre ci prepariamo.

Si stringe nelle spalle, anche se la sua espressione si fa cupa. "Non sarà contenta, ma sa che è importante. Non posso delegare qualcosa di così grande; essere morbidi è pericoloso nella nostra attività. Inoltre, sarete voi quattro ad essere maggiormente in pericolo. Io e Kent saremo coinvolti solo se tutto il resto fallisce... e diversamente dai vostri, i nostri volti non sono su tutti i telegiornali della sera."

eter

LUNEDÌ SERA PREPARO TUTTI I CIBI PREFERITI DI SARA E APRO UNA bottiglia di frizzante succo d'uva per cena. Sebbene siano trascorsi un paio di giorni da quando mia moglie ha avuto dei flashback, detesto l'idea di lasciarla da sola per così tanto tempo.

Anche se rimarrà a casa degli Esguerra, con Nora e Yulia, sarò preoccupato per tutto il tempo in cui sarò via.

"Perché devi andare?" chiede di nuovo, con il viso a forma di cuore palesemente stressato. Il piatto, con la sua pasta preferita, è davanti a lei ancora intatto, come il bicchiere contenente il succo. Non ha mangiato per tutto il giorno—non da quando ha saputo che andrò a Londra.

"Sai che è quasi certamente una trappola" continua, mentre rifletto su come farle consumare un po' di calorie. "Vi sta ingannando, usando l'e-mail di sua moglie come esca."

"Lo so—e siamo preparati a questo" le ricordo pazientemente, mentre spingo la scodella con il pane appena sfornato verso di lei. "È pur sempre un'opportunità per ottenere una pista. È difficile preparare una trappola senza lasciare tracce; da qualche parte, prima o poi commetterà un errore."

"Ma se non succedesse?" Spinge via la scodella. "E se riuscisse ad intrappolarti?"

"Ptichka..." sospiro. "Sai che continuerà a cercarci. Ho provato ad allontanarmi da tutto questo una volta, e guarda che cos'è successo. Se non avessi accettato l'affare e rinunciato a dargli la caccia—"

"No." Gli occhi di Sara brillano con una dolorosa luminosità. "Non ricominciare. Te l'ho detto, non è colpa tua. So quanto sia stato difficile per te stringere quell'accordo, e a prescindere dal risultato, sarò sempre grata che tu abbia provato... che abbia fatto quel genere di sacrificio per me."

"Allora, mangia. Per favore." Spingo di nuovo la scodella con il pane verso di lei. "Se non per te, allora per me e il nostro bambino."

Sbatte le palpebre, come se si rendesse conto soltanto ora di non aver toccato niente di quello che le ho preparato. Raccogliendo un pezzo di pane, lo morde obbedientemente, poi mette un po' di pasta in bocca.

Osservo un filo di salsa rimasto sul suo labbro superiore e, come se mi leggesse nel pensiero, ci passa la lingua sopra, facendomi sussultare.

Cazzo, vorrei mordicchiare quelle morbide labbra... sentirle premute sulle mie palle, mentre usa quella lingua su di me.

L'ondata di lussuria è così forte che mi coglie alla sprovvista. Il mio battito accelera, e passo da una lieve eccitazione ad un'erezione completa in un secondo. L'unica cosa che mi impedisce di distenderla su questo tavolo è che finalmente sta mangiando.

Con riluttanza e un'evidente mancanza di appetito, ma sta mangiando.

Trattenendo la lussuria, finisco il mio cibo, guardandola per tutto il tempo.

Consuma circa metà della pasta nel piatto, prima di arrendersi e dichiararsi sazia. La convinco a mangiare un dessert—una scodella di frutti di bosco con panna montata al latte di cocco—e alla fine mi arrendo al desiderio.

Lasciando i piatti sul tavolo, la prendo e la porto nella nostra camera.

ara

Peter è attento con me stasera, insolitamente gentile, e per una volta, la tenerezza è esattamente quello che voglio. Da stamattina, quando mi ha detto che sarebbe partito per Londra, sono rimasta paralizzata dalla paura, così terrorizzata per lui che riesco a malapena a respirare.

Non è ancora completamente guarito, sebbene si comporti come se le ferite non contassero. Negli ultimi due giorni, ha ripreso ad allenarsi con Anton ed i gemelli, compiendo prodezze di forza e resistenza che pochi atleti potrebbero eguagliare. Nonostante ciò, sono profondamente consapevole che non è sovrumano—che può sanguinare e morire a causa dei proiettili, proprio come chiunque altro.

Ho parlato con Nora dopo pranzo, mentre Peter stava finalizzando la logistica con suo marito e gli altri. Era esteriormente calma, ma ho notato la stessa preoccupazione, la stessa ansia profonda. Mi ha raccontato altri dettagli sul loro piano—su come Kent ed Esguerra avrebbero guidato le squadre di riserva, su come sarebbero state coinvolte sei dozzine delle guardie più addestrate nell'intera operazione. Su come gli uomini abbiano eseguito oltre cinquanta diverse simulazioni, preparandosi a tutto.

Questo avrebbe dovuto rassicurarmi, ma il pozzo di paura nel mio stomaco non ha fatto che peggiorare. Se non altro, quella conversazione mi aveva impressionata su quanto fosse pericolosa tutta l'operazione, in particolare per Peter e i suoi compagni di squadra.

Essendo i fuggitivi più ricercati, si stanno dirigendo direttamente nella tana del leone.

Chiudendo gli occhi, cerco di non pensarci, di concentrarmi solo sulle labbra di Peter che scivolano sensualmente sulla mia schiena. Sono a pancia in giù e mi sta baciando tutte le vertebre della colonna vertebrale, con i palmi callosi che mi accarezzano la pelle con deliziosa rudezza, massaggiandomi dappertutto. Ogni tocco delle sue labbra scolpite invia un calore intenso che si diffonde nel mio corpo, con ogni colpo delle sue grandi mani che mi rilassa e mi eccita immediatamente.

"Sei così bella" sussurra con riverenza, facendo piovere baci sulla mia vita, la curva del sedere, la delicata parte inferiore delle natiche. "Così bella dappertutto." La sua voce profonda, leggermente accentata, è come un velluto per le mie orecchie, aggiungendosi al calore che si accumula nelle mie vene e alla tensione pulsante che cresce nel mio intimo.

Le sue dita sgusciano tra le mie gambe, trovando l'apertura scivolosa, e io gemo, mentre mi penetra con due dita, distendendomi, riempiendomi fino a farmi pulsare dal bisogno. Sono già così eccitata che sono sul punto di venire, e mentre piega le dita dentro di me, premendo sul punto G, il mio corpo freme, con il rilascio che mi travolge come un'ondata di marea calda.

Mi sto ancora riprendendo, quando mi fa girare e mi copre con il corpo muscoloso. "Ti amo" mormora, guardandomi, mentre si tiene appoggiato su un gomito. Piega il palmo libero intorno alla mia mascella, con il pollice che mi accarezza dolcemente la guancia, e la tenerezza nel suo sguardo metallico mi scioglie fino alle ossa.

"Ti amo anch'io" sussurro, con il petto che mi fa male. "E ti amerò sempre, mio caro... a prescindere da quello che il destino ci metterà davanti."

Le sue pupille si dilatano, gli occhi si scuriscono e quando si china per reclamare la mia bocca, scorgo una nuova ferocia nel suo bacio, una specie di desiderio più caldo e oscuro. La sua mano lascia il mio viso e scivola tra i nostri corpi, e sento il suo fallo premere contro il mio ingresso, mentre incunea le ginocchia tra le mie gambe, allargandole.

Sollevando la testa, cattura il mio sguardo con il suo e poi si infila dentro, penetrandomi fino in fondo con un unico colpo. Respiro per la pienezza improvvisa, per il calore e la pressione così in profondità.

"Ripetilo" ordina bruscamente. "Voglio sentirtelo dire, mentre ti scopo."

"Ti amo" ansimo, mentre si ritira e si tuffa in profondità. "Ti amo così tanto." Spinge ancora più in profondità. "Ti amerò per sempre." Sono sempre più senza fiato, mentre i suoi movimenti accelerano il ritmo. "Ti amerò per sempre, finché saremo entrambi vivi."

eter

TUTTI I MIEI SENSI SONO IN ALLERTA, MENTRE MI AVVICINO ALLA caffetteria dove dovrei incontrare Bonnie Henderson. Dato che i gemelli non hanno ancora ucciso il cecchino catturato, ho deciso di sfruttare la sua abilità con i travestimenti, e non assomiglio affatto a me. Il mio stomaco è come un barile, e non solo ho le lentiggini e i capelli biondo-rossicci, ma sto anche sfoggiando un diradamento e un doppio mento.

Se avessi una madre, nemmeno lei mi riconoscerebbe.

Trentasei uomini di Esguerra sono posizionati intorno al bar, sorvegliando un raggio di dieci isolati per contrastare cecchini e forze dell'ordine. Per ora, non sembra esserci alcuna attività insolita, ma questo non significa niente—ed è per questo che Kent ed Esguerra sono accampati nelle vicinanze, ognuno con una squadra di riserva nel caso Henderson ci tendesse una trappola.

E mi aspetto che succeda proprio questo.

Ciò che complica la situazione è che una donna che corrisponde alla descrizione di Bonnie Henderson è stata avvistata, mentre entrava nel bar un quarto d'ora fa. Dubito fortemente che sia lei—non è possibile che Henderson usi sua moglie in questo modo—ma significa che dovrò avvicinarmi alla sosia di Bonnie per escludere la minima possibilità che tutto ciò sia reale.

Quando sono proprio davanti al bar, mi fermo e mi assicuro che le mie armi nascoste siano a portata di mano. Attraverso il piccolo microfono nell'orecchio, i compagni di squadra mi informano che non c'è ancora nulla di sospetto, così prendo fiato e attraverso la strada.

La vedo immediatamente nel locale. È seduta ad un tavolino sul retro, di fronte alla porta. Il mio travestimento funziona: il suo sguardo si sofferma su di me, mentre informo il cameriere della mia prenotazione usando un nasale accento britannico. È tutto a posto—Yan se ne è assicurato—e seguo il cameriere fino ad un tavolo a meno di quattro metri di distanza dal mio obiettivo.

Mi siedo di fronte a lei. Aprendo il menu della colazione, la scruto furtivamente, alla ricerca di indizi sulla sua vera identità. Sembra proprio la donna delle immagini e dei video della moglie di Henderson che ho studiato nel corso degli anni. Ogni minimo particolare corrisponde—persino il fatto che sembri più vecchia rispetto a tutte quelle foto, con il viso magro stanco e invecchiato. È ancora una donna attraente—capisco perché Henderson l'abbia sposata tanti anni fa—ma la vita da fuggitiva chiaramente ha lasciato dei segni.

O forse è quello che Henderson voleva che pensassi, quando ha ingaggiato questo agente della CIA o chiunque stia recitando la parte di sua moglie.

Il cameriere arriva al mio tavolo e ordino pancake e una frittata, mentre continuo a studiare il mio obiettivo. Mancano ancora dieci minuti, prima del nostro incontro, ma la donna sembra essere ansiosa, guardando la porta, poi intorno al bar con crescente nervosismo.

Il suo sguardo si posa su di me una volta, ma senza particolari sospetti.

Il cameriere porta prima i pancake, ed io fingo di divorarli con gusto, sebbene li assapori appena. Se questa "Bonnie," o qualsiasi altra persona Henderson abbia collocato nel bar, sta cercando dei comportamenti anormali, non ne troverà al mio tavolo.

Sono le nove e cinque, quando inizia a diventare davvero nervosa. Si alza, come per andarsene, poi si siede di nuovo.

Non molto professionale per un'agente della CIA.

La mia frittata arriva, e mentre infilo il primo boccone in bocca, lei si alza, con il corpo magro teso per l'ansia. Mordendosi il labbro, si guarda di nuovo intorno, poi si avvia verso l'uscita.

Beh, è interessante.

Agendo d'istinto, le afferro il polso, mentre passa accanto al mio tavolo.

"Bonnie Henderson?" dico, mantenendo l'accento britannico, e lei si irrigidisce, con la paura che le contorce i lineamenti.

"Lasciami andare" sibila in un tono basso, terrorizzato. "Non tornerò da lui. Lasciami andare o urlerò."

Ancora più interessante.

"Sono Peter Sokolov" mi presento con il mio solito accento, lanciandole il polso sottilissimo. "Volevi parlarmi?"

Si blocca di nuovo, a bocca aperta. "Ma tu…"

"È un travestimento" spiego con calma. "Per favore, siediti."

Armeggia con la sedia di fronte alla mia, con le mani tremanti, mentre la tira fuori. Se fossi un gentiluomo, mi alzerei per aiutarla, ma non è per questo che sono qui.

Se questa è davvero la moglie di Henderson—e sto iniziando

a pensare che potrebbe esserlo—mi condurrà da suo marito in un modo o nell'altro.

Il cameriere si avvicina, incuriosito dall'improvvisa aggiunta al mio tavolo, e ordino due tazze di caffè solo per farlo andare via. Qualcosa di strano sembra accadere a Bonnie/chiunque sia. Ora che è seduta dall'altra parte del tavolo, sembra più calma e più composta—almeno se si ignora il sottile tremore delle sue mani.

"Mi hai mandato un'e-mail" dico non appena il cameriere se n'è andato. "Perché?"

Fa un respiro profondo. "Perché dovevo. Questa follia deve finire."

"Sono d'accordo." Sorrido freddamente. "Com'è gentile da parte tua consegnarti in questo modo."

"Hai frainteso." Stringe le mani in una palla tesa sul tavolo, nascondendo i tremori. "Non mi sto consegnando. Ti sto dando quello che vuoi: mio marito."

Piego la testa. "In cambio di cosa?"

Solleva il mento. "Che lasci in pace me e i miei figli."

Ah. Stavo iniziando a sospettare che potesse essere qualcosa del genere. Tuttavia, questo non ha pienamente senso. Perché tradire suo marito ed esporsi a tale pericolo?

"Perché dovrei accettare quell'affare, quando ho già te?" chiedo. "A meno che non pensi di essere al sicuro, perché siamo in pubblico?"

La sua gola si muove, mentre deglutisce. "Non sono un'idiota. So di cosa sei capace."

"Eppure sei qui. Interessante."

Il cameriere riappare in quel momento, ed entrambi smettiamo di parlare, aspettando che ci versi il caffè e se ne vada.

Non appena lo fa, Bonnie afferra la sua tazza e beve un sorso del liquido bollente. "Non si sostituirebbe a me." La sua voce trema leggermente, mentre poggia la tazza. "Quindi, puoi scodarti di usare me come strumento di contrattazione. Non funzionerà meglio di quanto abbia funzionato con gli ostaggi."

Quindi, lo sa. La cosa si sta facendo più intrigante secondo dopo secondo.

"Che cosa stai proponendo, allora? Ti prometto di non uccidere te e i tuoi figli, e tu mi conduci nella tana di tuo marito?"

"Sì. Beh, non esattamente." Sospira. "Non posso condurti da lui al momento, perché non so dove sia. Ha lasciato il nostro ultimo nascondiglio non appena ha saputo che ero scappata con i ragazzi—nel caso in cui ci avessi trovato, vedi."

"Allora, che cosa stai offrendo? E perché sei scappata?"

Esita, poi chiede lentamente. "Sai come ci siamo conosciuti io e Wally?"

Cerco di ricordare se ho trovato le informazioni nell'enorme file che ho su Henderson. "No" ammetto un momento dopo. "Non lo so."

Unisce le labbra. "Lo immaginavo. Nessuno lo sa davvero. A Wally piace dire alla gente che ci siamo conosciuti in un bar, ma non è così. Voglio dire, ci siamo messi insieme in un bar, ma ci conoscevamo già—quando ero una tirocinante presso l'agenzia, e lui era la star operativa... e il mio insegnante."

Nascondo la mia sorpresa. Inizialmente ho pensato che potesse essere un'agente ad interpretare la parte della moglie di Henderson, ma non mi aspettavo che la vera moglie di Henderson fosse un vero agente della CIA.

È troppo convincente per essere una donna di buona società.

"Non preoccuparti, non sono un'agente" dice velocemente, come se temesse di essere uccisa per quella rivelazione. "Ho abbandonato il programma di formazione, dopo che Wally mi ha messa incinta. Ho abortito, ma non sono mai tornata indietro. Vedi, io e Wally ci siamo sposati e lui ha lasciato l'agenzia poco dopo, volendo intraprendere la carriera militare così da poter avere una vita familiare più stabile—il che significava che dovevo stare a casa con i bambini."

Prendo la mia tazza di caffè. "E mi stai raccontando tutto questo perché?"

"Perché voglio che tu capisca il motivo per cui sono qui." I suoi occhi mi scrutano, mentre sorseggio il liquido caldo e amaro. "Sono entrata nell'agenzia, perché sono una patriota, Signor Sokolov. Perché volevo proteggere il nostro Paese dalle minacce sia straniere che interne... dai terroristi che farebbero saltare in aria un edificio senza pensarci due volte."

I pezzi del puzzle alla fine si ricompongono.

Ovviamente.

È questo che l'ha spinta oltre il limite.

"Quando l'hai scoperto?" chiedo, posando il caffè.

"Che ci fosse Wally dietro l'attentato all'FBI di Chicago? Pochi giorni fa, nello stesso momento in cui ho saputo che ha lasciato morire tutti i nostri amici e parenti piuttosto che cedere alle tue richieste." Sembra quasi calma, mentre dice questo, ma posso vedere quanto le costi.

In qualunque modo abbia trovato quell'informazione, dev'essere stato un doloroso shock.

"Perché venire da me, però?" chiedo, esaminandola da vicino. "Sicuramente, devi odiarmi per quello che ho fatto a te e alla tua famiglia. Perché non consegnare semplicemente tuo marito alle autorità? Immagino che le prove che hai siano piuttosto schiaccianti."

Annuisce. "Lo sono—e posso offrirtele. Se accetti il patto, farò del mio meglio per cancellare il tuo nome—almeno in quel particolare crimine. Quanto al motivo per cui sono qui, a parlare con te, è molto semplice." Sospira. "Sono sfinita, Signor Sokolov. Sono stanca di aver paura e di odiarti, e lo stesso vale per i miei figli. Consegnare Wally non avrebbe messo fine a questo incubo per noi; il processo sarebbe durato anni, e per tutto il tempo, avresti cercato di catturarlo tramite noi. Questo è il modo migliore—l'unico—per porre fine a questo. Non ti perdonerò mai per quello che hai fatto alla mia famiglia, ma stringerò questo patto con te." La sua voce si incrina. "Tutto ciò che voglio è che finisca... che i miei figli riprendano le loro vite normali."

È convincente, devo ammettere. Così convincente che sono tentato di crederle. Ma c'è un'altra cosa che devo sapere. "Quando ti ho parlato prima, pensavi che fossi qualcuno mandato da tuo marito. Suppongo che voglia dire che ti sta cercando. Com'è che non ti ha già trovata, con tutte le sue connessioni?"

Si irrigidisce di nuovo. "Ho delle connessioni anch'io, Signor Sokolov. Mio marito non l'ha mai capito. Pensa che il successo sia dovuto alla sua intelligenza, ma sono sempre stata al suo fianco, facendo amicizia con tutte le persone giuste, chiacchierando con le loro mogli—" Si ferma, come se si rendesse conto dell'inutilità dei suoi amari ricordi. "In ogni caso" continua "mi sono preparata negli ultimi due anni, nel caso mi fossi ritrovata vedova con te alle calcagna. Avevo i documenti per me e per i bambini, insieme ai soldi e a tutto il resto necessario per rimanere nascosti per conto nostro. Ma poi è successo questo."

"E hai usato la riserva di emergenza per scappare da tuo marito, invece."

La sua bocca si assottiglia. "Esatto. Allora dimmi, Signor Sokolov, siamo giunti ad un accordo? Se ti consegno mio marito, ci lascerai stare?"

Prendo di nuovo il mio caffè. "Hai detto che non sai dove si trova."

"Non lo so—ma so cosa apprezza più di ogni altra cosa al mondo."

"E sarebbe?"

Mi guarda. "Nostra figlia. Amber. È l'unica persona oltre a se stesso che ami davvero."

Devo nascondere di nuovo la mia sorpresa. Questa donna sta seriamente pensando di offrirci la figlia adolescente come ostaggio?

È fottutamente pazza?

"Va bene" dico, posando la tazza. Se *non* sta assumendo le sue medicine, non ho intenzione di guardare in bocca a caval donato. "Sembra un buon piano—e sì, se riusciremo ad attirarlo con tua figlia, lascerò stare te e i tuoi figli." E dico davvero. Anche se mi piacerebbe far soffrire Henderson con la consapevolezza della morte della sua famiglia, non ho mai realmente voluto catturare sua moglie e i suoi figli.

È la *sua* testa che voglio.

"In questo caso, ecco qui." Prende un telefono e lo spinge attraverso il tavolo verso di me. "Questo è tutto ciò di cui dovresti aver bisogno adesso, ma c'è dell'altro—purché mi lasci andare via di qui oggi."

Premo "play" nel video sullo schermo, e un minuto dopo, mi rendo conto che la moglie di Henderson non è pazza—e che sebbene abbia lasciato l'agenzia, questa non ha mai lasciato lei.

Sara

CAMMINO AVANTI E INDIETRO NELLA SALA DA PRANZO DEGLI Esguerra, con l'ansia che mi perfora il petto come un trapano. Nora e Yulia sono entrambe qui, così come la giovane guardia, Diego. Sta ricevendo aggiornamenti in tempo reale sulle operazioni in corso attraverso le cuffie, quindi so che Peter è appena entrato nel bar, sfidando la probabile trappola.

"Sta parlando con lei ora" informa Diego, alzando lo sguardo dallo schermo del portatile dopo venti minuti di sofferenza, e mi precipito per vedere l'immagine sfocata di un uomo che non assomiglia affatto a mio marito seduto di fronte ad una donna magra.

"Questo è stato ripreso da una telecamera a lungo raggio" spiega Diego. "Non vogliamo spaventarli avvicinandoci troppo."

"Ma tutto è ancora tranquillo?" chiede Yulia, chinandosi sulla sua spalla, e lui annuisce.

"O le spie di Henderson sono straordinariamente valide—o non c'è nessuno in giro."

Guardo Nora. A differenza mia e di Yulia, è seduta in silenzio, senza fare domande. Se non fosse per la presa d'acciaio sul passeggino di Lizzie, penserei che stia prendendo tutto questo con calma.

Rivolgendo la mia attenzione allo schermo, vedo un Peter travestito e la donna che stanno ancora parlando.

"Non preoccuparti" mi sussurra Yulia. "Se qualcuno nel bar dovesse anche solo provare a starnutire, i nostri cecchini lo colpirebbero."

"Sì, lo so." Un sorriso mi fa piegare le labbra. "È incredibile quanto possa essere rassicurante avere dei cecchini."

Sorride e condividiamo un momento. Tuttavia, quando guardo Nora, il suo sguardo è rivolto altrove.

Naturalmente. Con tutto questo, mi ero dimenticata che ce l'ha con Yulia.

Mi chiedo se sia arrabbiata con me per il fatto che io non ce l'abbia con lei.

"Sta uscendo dal bar" dice improvvisamente Diego, e il mio sguardo torna sullo schermo.

Peter è già in strada.

Diego tace, ascoltando attentamente le informazioni che la squadra di Londra gli trasmette, e mentre vedo un grande sorriso sul suo viso, le mie ginocchia si indeboliscono per il sollievo.

L'e-mail *era* della moglie di Henderson.

Peter e gli altri sono al sicuro.

enderson

PASSO IN RASSEGNA LA LOGISTICA PER LE NOSTRE OPERAZIONI DI sabato, quando sul mio schermo compare una notifica. È un'e-mail da parte del mio contatto della CIA.

Scusa, c'è scritto sulla riga dell'oggetto.

Tutto dentro di me si trasforma in ghiaccio, mentre leggo il testo e apro l'allegato video.

Sentendomi sul punto di vomitare, premo "play."

Il volto sporco e rigato dalle lacrime di mia figlia riempie lo schermo. "Papà" singhiozza, mentre la telecamera zooma, mostrandola legata ad una sedia in una stanza anonima con pareti bianche. "Papà, per favore, aiutami. Hanno detto che ci uccideranno. Ti prego, Papà, aiutaci!"

Il video si interrompe, facendomi ansimare.

Sokolov l'ha catturata. Ha catturato tutti.

Adesso è un dato di fatto.

Tremando, leggo il testo inoltrato.

Sai cosa voglio, c'è scritto. *Plaza de Bolivar, Bogotá, giovedì alle 15:00. Presentati lì o guardala morire.*

Me lo aspettavo, sapevo che doveva arrivare, ma mi colpisce ancora come un pugno nello stomaco.

Amber. Mia dolce, devota figlia.

Quel mostro la ucciderà. Non la risparmierà, nemmeno se farò quello che vuole.

Non c'è più tempo per pianificare la logistica, nessuna possibilità di risolvere le problematiche.

L'operazione Air Drop non può attendere fino a sabato.

Dobbiamo agire stanotte.

ara

"CREDI ANCORA CHE POTREBBE ESSERE UNA TRAPPOLA?" CHIEDO A Nora, mentre nuotiamo nella sua piscina olimpionica un'ora dopo. Con l'immediata crisi giunta al termine, Yulia è tornata nella sua camera, risparmiando a Nora la sua presenza, quindi siamo solo noi due a goderci il magnifico paradiso della villa.

Beh, e Rosa con Lizzie, ma stanno entrambe sonnecchiando all'ombra.

"Tutto è possibile, ma Julian non la pensa così" risponde Nora, lasciandosi cadere per fluttuare sulla schiena. Il suo corpo in bikini è così elegante e atletico che è difficile credere che abbia avuto una bimba solo pochi mesi fa.

Anch'io indosso un bikini—uno che ho preso in prestito da Yulia, dato che abbiamo più o meno la stessa taglia, nonostante la differenza di altezza. I pantaloncini e le T-shirt che ho indossato, infatti, si sono rivelate di Yulia. Li ha dimenticati a casa di Kent, quando si sono trasferiti a Cipro, ed è più che felice che io li stia usando.

"Fammi sapere se hai bisogno di qualcos'altro" mi ha detto, quando abbiamo parlato degli abiti questa mattina. "Lucas tiene una valigia con le mie cose sul nostro aereo, per ogni evenienza, quindi sono completamente attrezzata."

Rivolgendo la mia attenzione a Nora, chiedo: "E che cosa accadrà domani? Julian pensa che Henderson si presenterà a Bogotá?"

"Questa è la speranza" risponde, girandosi per nuotare a stile libero. Sono una brava nuotatrice, ma devo sforzarmi per tenere il suo passo, mentre sguazza nell'acqua, raggiungendo il bordo della piscina in pochissimo tempo.

È chiaro che non vuole parlare di questo argomento, ma non posso permetterglielo. "E se non lo facesse?" chiedo, quando rallenta. "Non si è consegnato per nessuno degli ostaggi."

Si ferma e si alza in piedi, lisciandosi i capelli bagnati con entrambe le mani. "Non erano sua figlia" dice, socchiudendo gli occhi a causa del sole, mentre mi guarda. "Ma comunque sia, anche se le cose non andranno secondo i piani, Julian, Lucas e Peter improvviseranno qualcosa. È quello che fanno, e sono bravi in questo."

Sebbene la ragazza non sappia cosa succederà più di quanto lo sappia io, parte della tensione nel mio petto si allenta al ricordo delle capacità di Peter.

Mio marito *è* bravo in questo.

Incredibilmente bravo.

Nuotiamo per un'altra ora, chiacchierando di cose più piacevoli, come la prossima mostra d'arte di Nora a Berlino—a quanto pare, è una pittrice seria—e quando Lizzie si sveglia, reclamando il suo pasto, torniamo a casa.

Con un po' di fortuna, sarà tutto finito entro domani.

*H*enderson

"ATTERREREMO PROPRIO QUI" DICO, ALZANDO LA VOCE PER ESSERE sentito al di sopra del rombo dei motori, mentre indico una zona alberata sulla foto satellitare. "Ci faremo strada fin lì." Indico l'edificio bianco al centro.

"Capito." Danser si tira indietro i capelli biondo cenere, con il profilo che ricorda stranamente quello di Sokolov. "Hai qualche foto degli obiettivi?"

"Ecco." Consegno la foto della moglie di Esguerra. "Dobbiamo catturare questa donna o la sua bambina—o preferibilmente entrambe. Sono il nostro biglietto per uscire dalla tenuta."

Barrett scruta la foto da sopra la spalla di Danser. "Sembra esile. Dovrebbe essere abbastanza facile."

"Dovrebbe funzionare, ma non so se sarà nella casa principale." Tiro fuori un'immagine di Sara Sokolov e la porgo a

Danser e ai suoi compagni di squadra. "E questa"—mostro una foto a figura intera della moglie di Kent—"sarebbe un bel bonus, a parte il fatto che potrebbe trovarsi in qualsiasi punto del complesso."

"Oh, cazzo. Guarda quei capelli biondi e quelle gambe." Kilton mi strappa la foto. "Me la farei di sicuro."

"Io me le farei tutte, tranne la bambina" replica Russ, accarezzandosi la barba con fare lascivo. "Forse tutte e tre contemporaneamente."

Devo fare appello a tutte le mie capacità di recitazione per nascondere l'istintivo sogghigno. Non posso permettermi di inimicarmi questi quattro stronzi o chiunque altro nella loro squadra. E se fossero così stupidi da pensare con il cazzo? Hanno fatto un buon lavoro nel piantare l'esplosivo nell'edificio dell'FBI, e hanno esperienza con i lanci HALO.

Ho bisogno di loro per questo.

È la mia unica possibilità per salvare Amber.

Massaggiando i dolorosi nodi del collo, guardo gli altri sei uomini sul nostro aereo da trasporto militare. "È chiara la vostra parte nell'operazione?"

"Certo" risponde Danser prima degli altri. "Il Team Alpha attaccherà le guardie al confine settentrionale alle 00:58, e il Team Beta ti aspetterà con l'elicottero al punto di prelievo sul confine meridionale."

"E se Esguerra non uscisse di casa per controllare il disordine al confine settentrionale?" chiede Barrett. "Uccidiamo il bastardo?"

"No, feritelo soltanto" preciso. "Ci serve vivo, in modo che possa costringere Sokolov a fare lo scambio con la mia famiglia. Altrimenti, se il trafficante d'armi muore, a nessuno importerà se abbiamo la moglie e la figlia. Certo, se siamo fortunati e catturiamo la moglie di Sokolov, sarà ancora meglio."

"Quindi, ricapitolando" replica Kilton. "Vogliamo la moglie e/o la figlia di Esguerra come ostaggi per uscire vivi dal complesso e scambiarli con la tua famiglia. Ma se troviamo la moglie di Sokolov o la bionda sexy, prendiamo anche loro."

"Giusto" dico. "La moglie di Sokolov è la priorità. Se prendiamo lei, non importa se Esguerra viene ucciso. Sokolov accetterà comunque lo scambio."

"Che mi dici di Kent?" chiede Russ. "Che cosa facciamo se è lì?"

"Se non prendiamo sua moglie, allora uccidetelo" rispondo. "Ma se prendete lei come ostaggio, allora non fatelo."

Quanto più ho influenza sui miei nemici, tanto meglio. Quando ho iniziato a pianificare questa missione, l'obiettivo era usare gli ostaggi catturati per attirare Sokolov e gli altri in una trappola e ucciderli, ma la cattura della mia famiglia ha sollevato la posta in gioco.

La priorità ora è salvare Amber.

"Non pensi che Kent potrebbe essere a Bogotá con Sokolov?" chiede Danser, restituendomi le foto.

"Non so se lo stesso Sokolov sia a Bogotá" dico, infilandole nella giacca. "Solo perché mi ha detto che si sarebbe presentato in piazza domani non significa che ci sarà. Ad ogni modo, preparatevi a tutto. Considerando quanto siano impenetrabili i confini della tenuta, la logica impone che la casa stessa non sia particolarmente ben sorvegliata—ma ovviamente non ci sono garanzie."

"Beh, cazzo." Russ sorride. "Dovrebbe essere divertente. Sei sicuro di volerlo fare con noi, vecchio?"

Ignorando la battuta dell'idiota, prendo la mia bombola di ossigeno e inizio a prepararmi per il salto. Fin quando quel video non ha raggiunto la mia casella di posta, non volevo unirmi a loro in questa missione follemente pericolosa, ma ora non ho scelta.

Non solo quest'operazione ora è la mia unica possibilità di guadagnare influenza sui miei nemici, ma Amber stessa potrebbe essere nella tenuta. Non lo so con certezza; forse la stanno trattenendo a Bogotá o in qualsiasi altra parte del mondo. Ma dato che il luogo di incontro indicato è in Colombia, nel territorio di Esguerra, c'è almeno una possibilità che la nascondano nella proprietà del trafficante d'armi.

Se saremo fortunati, non andremo via solo con gli ostaggi.

Potremmo anche salvare mia figlia.

Sara

Dopo aver dato da mangiare a Lizzie, Nora mi fa fare un tour della casa. È grande come appare all'esterno, e conta oltre una dozzina di camere, tra cui una biblioteca dedicata, un home theater con uno schermo enorme, una palestra piena di attrezzature di ogni genere e una sala illuminata dal sole che funge da studio d'arte.

I dipinti incompleti all'interno sono un sorprendente mix di surrealismo ed espressionismo moderno, con forme ed oggetti familiari, come gli alberi, distorti in qualcosa di intrigantemente sinistro. Nella tavolozza dei colori dominano pesantemente il rosso e il nero, come se tutto fosse consumato dal fuoco.

"Sei davvero talentuosa" dico sinceramente, e Nora sogghigna, ringraziandomi. Mentre il tour procede, spiega che ha iniziato a dipingere come un modo per evitare di impazzire sull'isola privata, dove Julian la teneva, quando l'ha rapita per la prima volta.

Vorrei farle un milione di domande al riguardo, ma siamo già arrivate nella stanza in cui alloggio, mentre Peter è via—una camera splendidamente decorata ad un paio di porte dalla suite padronale e adiacente alla stanza di Yulia. Nora si scusa, dovendosi occupare di alcuni affari, e decido di fare un sonnellino, visto che sono stanca.

Essere incinta è un po' come stare all'asilo, a quanto pare.

Quando mi sveglio, è ora di cena, così mi unisco a Nora nella sala da pranzo. Yulia è stranamente assente, e quando chiedo a Nora dove si trova, mi informa che la moglie di Kent ha già mangiato.

"È ancora arrabbiata per quella questione di Cipro" spiega con un sorriso forzato, mentre Ana ci porge il cibo.

Decido di non insistere ulteriormente—dev'essere imbarazzante avere la donna che ha quasi ucciso tuo marito come ospite sotto il tuo tetto. Invece, mentre mangiamo, faccio domande sulla famiglia di Nora e su come abbiano preso il suo matrimonio con Julian.

"Oh, sperano ancora che io metta la testa a posto e divorzi" risponde, tagliando il salmone, e mentre mi intrattiene con le tese interazioni del padre con suo marito, ricordo quanto Peter fosse stato gentile con i miei genitori—come avesse fatto del proprio meglio per alleviare le loro preoccupazioni su di lui.

Fino a dove si fosse spinto per assicurarsi che facessero parte della mia vita.

Il mio petto si stringe di nuovo, con gli occhi che bruciano per le lacrime, ma questa volta non scaccio il dolore. La sofferenza per la perdita è ancora fresca, la ferita insopportabilmente aperta, ma ora riesco a pensarci, posso rattristarmi senza perdermi nell'orrore della loro morte.

Non mi rendo conto che delle lacrime mi sono uscite, fin quando Nora non mi passa un tovagliolo.

"Scusa, Sara" dice in tono cupo. "Sono stata insensibile."

"No, sto..." Cerco di abbozzare un sorriso. "Sto bene, davvero. È solo che..."

"Li hai appena persi, lo so." I suoi occhi scuri sono carichi di empatia. Anche lei ha perso qualcuno a cui voleva bene?

Prima che io possa chiedere, Rosa entra nella sala da pranzo, portando Lizzie, e mi volto, asciugandomi l'umidità sulle guance. Non voglio che l'amica/tata di Nora mi veda così.

È già abbastanza brutto che Nora abbia dovuto assistere al pianto.

La ragazza si scusa per dare di nuovo da mangiare alla bimba—Lizzie si trasformerà in un mostro urlante, se non verrà nutrita immediatamente, spiega lei in tono apologetico—così, finisco il mio cibo e vado nella mia stanza.

Mentre passo davanti alla porta di Yulia, la sento parlare al telefono in russo. La sua voce è calda e tenera, come se parlasse con un bambino o con un amante, e per un secondo mi prende alla sprovvista. Ma poi ricordo le foto di un adolescente nella sua casa—quello che ho immaginato dovesse essere suo fratello, vista l'impressionante somiglianza.

Forse sta parlando con lui?

Sono molto curiosa sulla sua storia, la spia e tutto il resto, ma non voglio disturbarla, mentre è al telefono. Entrando nella mia camera, chiudo la porta e vado alla finestra, guardando il sole che tramonta sugli alberi.

Mi manca Peter.

Dio, mi manca così tanto.

In questo momento, lui e gli altri dovrebbero essere in volo, mentre si stanno recando all'incontro di Bogotá di domani. Se tutto andrà bene, domani sera, sarà con me.

La sua ricerca di vendetta finirà definitivamente.

Camminando verso una libreria, prendo un thriller a caso e mi rannicchio su una poltrona per leggerlo. Anche se mi sono svegliata dal pisolino solo un paio d'ore fa, sono di nuovo stanca, e prima di avventurarmi troppo nella mia lettura, mi ritrovo a chiudere gli occhi.

Sbadigliando, faccio una doccia veloce e vado a letto. Poi però, prevedibilmente, non riesco ad addormentarmi.

Alzandomi, ne leggo ancora un po', poi scrivo le parole di una canzone che mi è passata per la testa tutto il giorno. È arrabbiata e oscura, diversa dalla mia solita musica, ma qualcosa sembra giusto, sincero e salutare.

Sentendomi di nuovo stanca, torno a letto, e questa volta cado in un sonno inquieto.

93

Henderson

Un'aria gelida mi fruscia sulle orecchie, attutendo il terrificante ruggito del mio battito cardiaco, mentre scendiamo a piombo nel cielo nero come la pece da un'altezza di novemila metri. La notte è dalla nostra parte; le nubi nascondono anche il più lieve bagliore della luna.

Gli occhiali per la visione notturna sono legati sopra la mia maschera di ossigeno, e vedo le altre quattro figure accanto a me. Precipitiamo in caduta libera per quella che sembra un'eternità, prima che io senta una violenta scossa, e i paracadute sopra di noi si aprano.

"Ecco" dice Danser, mentre i contorni delle cime degli alberi appaiono sotto di noi. "Quello è il nostro punto di atterraggio."

È una macchia boscosa nel profondo del complesso di Esguerra, lontano dalle torri di guardia al perimetro. Il pericolo principale qui sono i droni che pattugliano l'aria, ma grazie all'ultimo gadget della CIA, ho una soluzione per questo.

Quando siamo proprio sopra la linea degli alberi, il mio dispositivo rileva i droni in arrivo e si sincronizza automaticamente, consentendo al mio contatto CIA di controllare le telecamere, mentre siamo nel raggio d'azione. Gli operatori dei droni non vedranno altro che il solito scenario, mentre i nostri paracadute fluttuano.

Dato che non faccio salti d'alta quota da due decenni, sto volando in tandem con Danser, e i suoi piedi toccano il terreno per primi, subendone il peso dell'impatto. Tuttavia, le mie ginocchia quasi si piegano mentre atterriamo, evitando per un pelo di essere impalati dal ramo di un albero. Mentre mi chino per riprendere fiato, Danser sgancia l'equipaggiamento del paracadute da entrambi e lo infila nei cespugli.

Il resto della squadra fa la stessa cosa, e quando hanno finito, posso quasi stare in piedi.

"Pronto?" chiede Danser, e io annuisco, ignorando la residua debolezza nelle membra.

Finora, tutto è andato secondo i piani, e non sarò io la ragione del fallimento.

Con calma, strisciamo nell'oscurità, usando gli alberi come copertura. La parte più difficile sarà l'area aperta intorno alla casa, ma è a questo che serve la distrazione al confine.

Fermandoci ai margini della zona boscosa, aspettiamo il segnale del Team Alpha. I minuti passano con dolorosa lentezza, e sento il sudore colarmi lungo la schiena, mentre fisso l'edificio bianco davanti.

Fottuta umidità della giungla.

È peggio del caldo secco in Iraq.

Come sospettavamo, la residenza reale di Esguerra non sembra essere molto sorvegliata. E perché dovrebbe esserlo? Tra i droni e tutta la sicurezza ai confini, la dimora è praticamente una fortezza.

Ci sono solo due guardie che camminano in cerchio intorno alla casa, e quando ci passano vicino, Russ e Kilton sparano col silenziatore, colpendoli proprio sulla fronte.

Primo ostacolo eliminato.

"Ci siamo" annuncia il capo del Team Alpha attraverso le comunicazioni, e sento spari in sottofondo.

"Diamogli un quarto d'ora, vediamo se esce qualcuno" dice Danser, e aspettiamo, fissando la casa.

Non ci sono segnali di movimento all'interno, nessuna luce si accende.

O le guardie di confine di Esguerra non hanno informato il loro capo di ciò che sta accadendo o non pensa che ciò richieda la sua presenza.

Oppure, se siamo fortunati, non è affatto in casa.

Solo per essere al sicuro, attendiamo altri venti minuti, e poi Danser ci fa segno di avanzare.

Accovacciandoci, attraversiamo il vasto prato usando gli arbusti ben curati ai lati come copertura, mentre ci avviciniamo alla zona della piscina sul retro.

Anche qui è tutto tranquillo.

"Andiamo" sussurra Danser, mentre ci fermiamo davanti alla porta sul retro. "Fa' la tua fottuta magia."

Annuendo, tiro di nuovo fuori il dispositivo della CIA. Salta sul Wi-Fi della casa e si sincronizza con le telecamere e il sistema di allarme, dando al mio contatto l'accesso per disattivare tutto.

Mentre lo fa, attivo un dispositivo di disturbo del segnale cellulare, nel caso qualcuno cercasse di chiamare aiuto.

"Tutto fatto" dico sottovoce, quando ricevo conferma dal mio contatto. "Che inizi lo spettacolo."

ara

DORMO INQUIETA, SVEGLIANDOMI OGNI MEZZ'ORA. OGNI VOLTA che mi addormento, dei sogni ansiosi su Peter si combinano con frammenti di incubi sulla morte dei miei genitori, facendomi svegliare. È al quinto risveglio che vado al bagno, con gli occhi annebbiati, e decido di leggere un po' per distrarre il cervello iperattivo.

Indossando una vestaglia di seta che ho preso in prestito da Nora, accendo la lampada sul comodino, afferro un libro e mi rannicchio sulla poltrona, sbadigliando.

Con un po' di fortuna, non rimarrò sveglia a lungo.

Sono a metà di un altro capitolo, quando lo sento.

Un suono scricchiolante proprio fuori dalla mia porta.

Sorpresa, guardo e vedo la porta aprirsi.

Una figura alta e vestita di nero sta sulla soglia—un uomo barbuto che non ho mai visto prima. I suoi occhi si spalancano quando mi vede, e solleva il fucile d'assalto che tiene in mano, puntandomelo contro.

Reagisco in preda al puro istinto.

Con un urlo, mi lancio giù dalla sedia.

Un grande corpo atterra su di me, facendomi uscire tutta l'aria dai polmoni, prima che io possa rotolare via. "Sta zitta, puttana" mi ringhia l'uomo nelle orecchie, mentre una mano guantata mi copre la bocca. L'odore pungente di sudore maschile e sigarette stantie mi soffoca le narici, e poi mi afferra per i capelli e mi mette una mano sopra la bocca per attenuare il mio grido di dolore.

Terrorizzata, gli artiglio la mano guantata, dimenandomi con tutte le mie forze, ma proprio come quella volta con Peter nella mia cucina, non c'è nulla che possa fare, mentre mi trascina fuori dalla stanza, con la ruvida presa sui miei capelli che quasi si strappano alle radici. Lacrime di dolore scorrono sul mio viso, mentre mi trascina, trasportandomi per metà del corridoio, con le mie urla in preda al panico che si attutiscono nel suo palmo.

Si sta dirigendo verso la camera padronale, dove sono Nora e la bambina, mi rendo conto con orrore, e poi siamo lì.

Spalancando la porta con un piede, mi spinge dentro. "Ho preso la cagna di Sokolov" annuncia trionfante, e vedo altri due uomini armati all'interno.

Uno sta tenendo un coltello sulla gola di Nora, e l'altro sta raggiungendo la culla per prendere la bimba addormentata.

 eter

Stiamo per iniziare la nostra discesa a Bogotá, quando Julian riceve la notizia.

"È strano." Si acciglia, fissando il telefono. "Diego mi ha appena mandato un'e-mail su una sparatoria con intrusi sconosciuti ai margini settentrionali della tenuta. Nessuno si è fatto male e gli intrusi sono scomparsi nella giungla, prima che potessero essere catturati. Ha mandato una squadra a cercarli, ma finora non ha avuto fortuna."

Mi alzo, con il battito che accelera, mentre il mio istinto va in allerta. "Chi proverebbe a violare il tuo complesso in quel modo? E cosa ci farebbe nella giungla di notte?"

"Esattamente." La sua faccia si rabbuia, quando si alza in piedi e si dirige verso la cabina di pilotaggio, con il telefono premuto sull'orecchio. "Sto chiamando Nora."

Lo seguo, mentre copre la distanza a grandi passi, ignorando gli sguardi interrogativi sui volti dei miei compagni di squadra.

"La telefonata sta andando dritta alla segreteria" comunica teso, mentre entriamo nella cabina di pilotaggio.

Kent ci guarda.

"C'è stata una sparatoria al confine settentrionale, e non riesco a parlare con Nora" lo informa Esguerra in modo indifferente. "Attiverò le telecamere in casa. Puoi chiamare Yulia?"

Kent annuisce, stringendo la mascella, mentre allunga la mano verso il suo telefono. "Lo sto facendo."

Fanculo. Ho dato a Sara un telefono usa e getta prima di partire, ma non l'avrei chiamata—è mezzanotte passata e voglio che dorma bene. Ma il mio senso del pericolo diventa più forte ogni secondo che passa.

Anche la telefonata a mia moglie va dritta alla segreteria, e quando guardo Kent, posso vedere dalla sua espressione che la stessa cosa sta succedendo con Yulia.

"Le telecamere sono spente. Sto mandando le guardie" dice Esguerra con fermezza, e scorgo la paura profonda fino alle ossa riflessa nei suoi occhi.

C'è qualcosa che non va nella tenuta.

Che non va affatto.

"Inserisco la rotta per tornare alla tenuta" ribatte cupamente Kent, e l'aereo si inclina sotto di me, mentre i motori vanno su di giri con un ruggito.

_S_ara

"TROVATA" DICE UN QUARTO UOMO, TRASCINANDOSI VERSO ROSA, che indossa una camicia da notte, mentre si dimena. Le sta coprendo la bocca con una mano, soffocando le sue grida in preda al panico. "Sembra che siamo stati fortunati. Il resto della casa è vuoto. Nessun segno di Esguerra, Kent o Sokolov." Come i suoi tre compagni, è pesantemente armato, con un fucile d'assalto appeso alla spalla e due pistole infilate nella cintura.

Chiunque siano questi uomini, intendono fare sul serio, e noi siamo completamente sole, mi rendo conto con un'ondata di terrore. Le guardie non sono neanche lontanamente vicine alla casa, e con Peter e gli altri via, nessuno verrà in nostro soccorso.

L'uomo chino sulla culla di Lizzie si raddrizza, con la bimba ancora addormentata stretta davanti a lui. "Niente bionda?" chiede con evidente disappunto.

"No, mi dispiace" risponde il rapitore di Rosa e la fa girare per guardarla in faccia. La ragazza apre la bocca per urlare, ma prima che riesca ad emettere un suono, la colpisce sulla mascella con un montante, e lei si accascia sul pavimento, incosciente.

Mi blocco, fissando inorridita e incredula, mentre il sangue scorre da un angolo della sua bocca.

L'ha colpita con una tale disinvoltura, come se non fosse nemmeno una persona.

Come se non gli importasse niente della sua vita o della sua morte.

"Dovremo farci bastare queste due" continua, annuendo verso di me e verso una Nora pallidissima, che il rapitore sta trattenendo tenendole una mano sulla bocca e premendole il coltello sulla gola con l'altra. Come me, indossa una vestaglia di seta sottile, ma a differenza della mia, è aperta in alto, rivelando le curve interne del suo seno.

L'assalitore di Rosa si lecca le labbra, fissando quella V di pelle dorata, e il mio stomaco si contorce per l'orrore.

Ci violenteranno?

Ci uccideranno?

"Dov'è il vecchio?" chiede il rapitore di Nora, mentre riprendo a lottare in preda al panico, e mi rendo conto che qualcosa di lui sembra familiare, come se ci fossimo già visti.

"È andato a controllare quel piccolo edificio nelle vicinanze. Ha detto qualcosa sul voler cercare la sua famiglia" replica il mio assalitore, trattenendomi. "Ecco, portami del nastro adesivo. Mi sto divertendo" aggiunge, grugnendo, mentre gli conficco il gomito nella gabbia toracica.

"Metti a tacere quella troia" consiglia lo stronzo che ha colpito Rosa, ma porta il nastro comunque. Ho solo il tempo di emettere un breve urlo, prima che un panno mi venga spinto nella bocca e il nastro adesivo venga messo sopra di esso.

"Così va meglio" mormora il mio rapitore, afferrandomi per le braccia. "Ora legale anche i polsi."

L'altro uomo sta per obbedire, quando Lizzie si sveglia con un grido.

"Cazzo. Fai tacere la bambina" ordina il rapitore di Nora, mentre la bimba, turbata per essere trattenuta da uno sconosciuto, inizia a piangere a tutto volume.

La faccia di Nora sbianca ulteriormente, con gli occhi che bruciano come carboni, mentre l'assalitore di Rosa si china e incolla il nastro adesivo sulla boccuccia della bambina, soffocando le sue urla.

Se lo sguardo potesse uccidere, sarebbe stato eviscerato sul posto.

"Va' a cercare Henderson" dice il rapitore di Nora all'assalitore di Rosa. "Ci vediamo al piano di sotto."

L'uomo obbedisce, uscendo dalla stanza, mentre rifletto sulla rivelazione.

Henderson?

Ovviamente. *Ecco* di cosa si tratta.

Come un topo messo alle strette, il nemico di Peter è andato all'attacco.

Sto ancora digerendo le implicazioni, quando un lampo di capelli biondi sulla soglia cattura la mia attenzione.

Il mio battito accelera.

Mi ero completamente dimenticata di Yulia.

Non l'hanno trovata, ma *era* nella stanza accanto alla mia.

Ho solo un millesimo di secondo per notare il suo aspetto seminudo—e la pistola che tiene in mano—perché nell'istante successivo, si scatena l'inferno.

Senza problemi, senza esitazione, Yulia spara al rapitore di Nora, colpendolo in faccia.

Quindi, punta la pistola verso il mio.

Il tempo sembra rallentare, il momento sembra durare un'eternità. Scorgo la feroce concentrazione nei suoi occhi azzurri, avverto l'improvvisa tensione nelle mani che mi stringono le braccia da dietro, e il poco che ricordo dell'allenamento di difesa personale con Peter riaffiora.

Sollevando le gambe dal pavimento, divento un peso morto nella presa del mio rapitore, facendo cadere la testa verso il basso—e mentre la pistola di Yulia sputa il proiettile, sento uno spruzzo di sangue caldo, mentre la testa di un'altra persona esplode sopra la mia.

Il mio sedere colpisce il pavimento, con il coccige che urla all'impatto, mentre il corpo del mio rapitore cade dietro di me.

Yulia si sta già muovendo di nuovo, mirando all'uomo che tiene Lizzie, ma non ce n'è bisogno.

Si sta già accartocciato sul pavimento, con il coltello di Nora conficcato nella gola—e la bimba sana e salva tra le braccia della madre.

Nora ha afferrato sua figlia, mentre lo uccideva?

Cazzo, è veloce.

Combattendo lo shock, mi alzo in piedi, strappando il nastro adesivo che mi copre la bocca. "Il quarto uomo" ansimo. "È—"

"Morto o messo fuori combattimento" ribatte Yulia, abbassando la pistola. "Gli ho fatto saltare le cervella nel corridoio." La sua compostezza è sorprendente, finché non ricordo che era una spia.

Sto per nominare Henderson, quando noto un altro rapido movimento sulla porta.

"Yulia!" urlo, lanciandomi in avanti, ma è troppo tardi.

Un braccio ricoperto da un guanto nero serpeggia intorno alla sua gola con la velocità di un fulmine e una pistola preme contro la sua tempia.

"Non così in fretta" dice dolcemente l'uomo più anziano, usando Yulia come scudo, mentre entra nella stanza. "Muovi un muscolo e lei muore."

eter

"PERCHÉ LE TUE FOTTUTE GUARDIE SONO COSÌ LENTE?" RINGHIO ad Esguerra, mentre digita furiosamente sul suo laptop, presumibilmente dando ordini a quelle guardie. "Sono già passati due minuti. Sai cosa può succedere in due minuti? Sono in quella casa, sole, senza protezione—"

"Lo so!" ringhia Esguerra. Una vena gli pulsa sulla fronte, mentre sbatte il portatile e scatta in piedi. "Non pensi che lo sappia, cazzo? Stanno arrivando, guidando il più velocemente possibile. Le due guardie di pattuglia non stanno rispondendo; chiunque abbia disattivato le telecamere e il segnale cellulare deve averle già fatte fuori."

Fanculo. Vorrei sbattere il pugno contro la parete, ma è troppo pericoloso con tutti i comandi nella cabina di pilotaggio. "Sei sicuro che siano ancora in casa?"

"So che Nora c'è" risponde Esguerra. "Ha degli impianti di

tracciamento nel corpo, ricordi? Fino a due secondi fa era viva e nella nostra stanza."

Cazzo. Ha ragione—avevo dimenticato quei tracker per un momento. Se Nora è viva, allora forse lo è anche Sara—il che rende ancora più imperioso che le guardie si sbrighino.

"Dev'essere Henderson" dice Kent con durezza, le nocche bianche sui comandi. "Quel fottuto bastardo ci ha attirati fuori, così da poter attaccare."

"Non lo sappiamo per certo" replica Yan, e mi rendo conto che si è unito a noi nella cabina di pilotaggio. I suoi occhi verdi si spostano su Esguerra. "Non potrebbe essere qualche altro nemico?"

Ho voglia di strozzare Yan. "Non importa chi sia. Sara è lì, hai capito? È lì dentro, con chiunque egli sia."

Non riesco nemmeno a pensare a lei con Henderson, un uomo abbastanza disperato da correre quel tipo di rischio.

Un uomo che non ha esitato ad attaccare lo stesso Paese che aveva giurato di proteggere per incastrarmi.

Che cosa farebbe a mia moglie, se l'avesse davvero nelle sue grinfie? Arriverò lì, solo per seppellire lei e il nostro bambino non ancora nato... proprio come ho seppellito Pasha e Tamila?

No. Scaccio quel pensiero paralizzante.

Non lascerò che accada.

Non di nuovo.

"Vola più veloce" dico duramente a Kent. "E Julian, se le tue guardie non arriveranno in tempo, le ucciderò tutte, una ad una."

9 8

 ara

Un milione di pensieri mi attraversano la mente. Per un attimo, penso di prendere le pistole sugli uomini morti e sul pavimento—tutte a portata di mano, ma nessuna abbastanza vicina da poter essere afferrata, prima che Henderson conficchi il proiettile nel cervello di Yulia.

Il mio sguardo terrorizzato incontra quello di Nora, e vedo lo stesso calcolo nei suoi occhi.

Anche se fossimo abbastanza brave da colpire il rapitore di Yulia senza uccidere lei, non saremmo abbastanza veloci.

Non con la pistola di Henderson premuta contro la sua tempia.

"Allontanate quelle pistole" ordina, e io esito per un secondo, poi obbedisco stordita, mentre Nora fa lo stesso.

Non solo saremmo troppo lente, ma Henderson non è molto più alto della longilinea Yulia con le gambe lunghe. Con lui che la usa come scudo, nemmeno un cecchino addestrato avrebbe successo.

Il mio sguardo si posa sulla bimba stretta contro il petto di Nora. Lizzie ha ancora il nastro adesivo sulla bocca, e vedo il suo piccolo viso diventare rosso, mentre si sforza di emettere grida soffocate.

Sua madre la sta stringendo come se non volesse mai lasciarla andare—e non lo farà, mi rendo conto, notando la sua presa letale.

Non posso più contare sulla moglie di Esguerra per ricevere aiuto—non con la figlia neonata che deve proteggere.

Mi viene in mente un'idea, e prima che possa ripensarci, guardo Henderson e dico con calma: "So dov'è tua figlia."

Lui sobbalza, come se fosse stato colpito. Riprendendosi rapidamente, chiede: "Dov'è?"

"Posso portarti lì" rispondo, ignorando il nodo della paura nella gola. "Possiamo andare adesso—se lasci andare le altre."

Non ho un piano o qualcosa del genere. So solo che voglio che sposti la pistola puntata sulla testa di Yulia—e il più lontano possibile da Lizzie e Nora. Anche se non fossi a conoscenza dei crimini che ha commesso, qualcosa del vecchio generale mi avrebbe fatto accapponare la pelle. Non è nulla di esteriormente visibile—è in forma, molto in forma per essere un uomo sulla sessantina, e i suoi lineamenti, incorniciati da una testa di capelli color sale e pepe, sono moderatamente piacevoli.

Nonostante ciò, puzza di putrefazione, di marciume che si annida in profondità.

Alla mia proposta, socchiude gli occhi. "Pensi che io sia un'idiota? Tutte e tre mi porterete da mia figlia—o sparerò a questa." Preme la pistola sulla tempia di Yulia, facendola sussultare.

Accidenti.

"Non hai bisogno di *loro*" riprovo. "Puoi usare me come ostaggio. Il tuo nemico è mio marito—e farà di tutto per me."

"Beh, che cosa sdolcinata" replica. "Una storia d'amore che dura nei secoli. Forse ti ucciderò e lo costringerò a guardare. Che ne dici?"

Lo fisso senza battere ciglio, ignorando la nausea che si diffonde dentro di me.

Non ho intenzione di mostrare a questo mostro che ho paura.

Non otterrà quella soddisfazione.

Notando la mia mancanza di risposta, il fastidio si insinua nei suoi lineamenti. "Bene" scatta. "Come ho detto, tutte e tre verrete con me. Tu e quella con la bambina"—fa un cenno con il mento verso Nora—"camminerete davanti a me. E ricordate, una mossa sbagliata, e questa"—preme di nuovo la pistola contro la testa di Yulia—"muore. Chiaro? Ora, camminate verso di me."

Deglutendo, mi dirigo verso la porta, e Nora segue cautamente, cullando una Lizzie urlante sul petto. Henderson indietreggia nel corridoio, continuando a proteggersi con Yulia, e non appena siamo fuori dalla stanza, ci ordina di scendere le scale.

"Mi *condurrai* da mia figlia, chiaro?" dice cupamente, mentre ci dirigiamo verso le scale. "Se proverai a fare qualcosa, qualsiasi cosa, sparerò a tutte le tue puttanelle—e anche al diavolo che Esguerra scatenerà."

Chiudendo le ginocchia per evitare che tremino, mi avvicino alla scala ampia e curva. Il pavimento è ghiacciato sotto i miei piedi nudi, e il cuore sembra sul punto di saltarmi fuori dalla gola. Non so cosa fare, come tirarci fuori da questa situazione. La figlia di Henderson è sana e salva lontano da qui —tutto ciò che ha Peter è il falso video che gli ha dato Bonnie— ma Henderson non mi avrebbe creduto, se glielo avessi detto. E se mi avesse creduto, probabilmente ci avrebbe uccise tutte.

Che se ne renda conto o meno, non è venuto qui per salvare la sua famiglia.

È qui per vendicarsi.

Dentro di sé, sa di aver già perso, e di aver intrapreso questa missione suicida per far soffrire Peter e gli altri prima di morire.

Le mie mani armeggiano con il nodo della vestaglia per non tremare, mentre scendo più lentamente che posso, con Henderson e Yulia ad un passo dietro di me. Nora sta camminando alla mia destra, con il volto vuoto, mentre tiene Lizzie con fare protettivo davanti a lei.

Farebbe qualsiasi cosa per sua figlia, lo so—proprio come farei io per la piccola vita che sta crescendo dentro di me.

Una vita che non vedrà la luce del giorno, se l'uomo dietro di me otterrà ciò che vuole.

Siamo a metà della scala, quando vedo delle luci attraverso una delle finestre del salotto e sento la porta principale spalancarsi, seguita dal martellare degli stivali sul pavimento di legno.

Il mio battito cardiaco accelera con parti uguali di sollievo e terrore.

Le guardie sono qui.

In qualche modo, hanno scoperto che siamo nei guai—e ora Henderson è davvero alle strette.

Da solo, senza la sua squadra, non ha alcuna possibilità di fuga.

Lo sento imprecare sottovoce e un vago piano si forma nella mia mente.

Continuando a scendere con lo stesso ritmo lento, tolgo la vestaglia, e l'aria fresca mi colpisce sulla pelle nuda, mentre l'indumento di seta cade sulle scale dietro di me— raccogliendosi proprio sotto i piedi di Yulia e del suo rapitore.

Le guardie irrompono nell'atrio e contemporaneamente mi tuffo verso Nora, spingendola contro la ringhiera.

Con l'attenzione di Henderson concentrata sulle guardie, lui e Yulia scivolano entrambi sulla vestaglia caduta—e il suo colpo va a vuoto, quando Yulia scivola giù per le scale sbattendo il sedere.

Senza esitazione, le guardie sparano a Henderson, e Nora e io ci stringiamo, proteggendo Lizzie, mentre lo sentiamo cadere.

eter

È PASSATO UN GIORNO DA QUANDO SIAMO TORNATI, E ANCORA non riesco a smettere di toccare Sara, non riesco a smettere di stringerla. Istante dopo istante, combatto anche l'impulso di ispezionarla dalla testa ai piedi—anche se il Dottor Goldberg l'ha già visitata e ha confermato che lei e il bambino sono sani.

Cullandola sul grembo, le accarezzo i capelli e respiro il suo dolce profumo, con un tremore che mi attraversa il corpo ogni volta che penso a quanto sia andato vicino a perderla... a come le guardie l'abbiano trovata accucciata nuda sulle scale un'ora prima che finalmente facessimo irruzione.

Ha fatto inciampare Henderson sulla sua vestaglia di seta, salvando se stessa, Nora e Yulia.

Le tre hanno combattuto contro dei mercenari armati e hanno vinto.

"Va tutto bene. Stiamo bene" mormora, sollevando la testa,

e mi rendo conto di aver pronunciato l'ultima parte ad alta voce. I suoi occhi color nocciola brillano dolcemente, mentre piega l'esile palmo sulla mia mascella. "Te lo giuro, a parte il coccige di Yulia e la mascella della povera Rosa, stiamo benissimo."

"Lo so" sussurro. "Ed è un fottuto miracolo." Coprendo la sua mano con la mia, chiudo gli occhi e inspiro profondamente, cercando di calmare il martellante battito del mio cuore.

Come me, Kent ed Esguerra erano fuori di testa, quando siamo atterrati, anche se Diego ci aveva già informato che Henderson era morto e che le nostre mogli erano al sicuro. Non era abbastanza saperlo; la terribile paura è rimasta con me fino al momento in cui ho messo gli occhi su Sara.

Fino a quando non ho potuto stringerla tra le braccia e sentire che era viva e vegeta.

"Hai salvato tutti, sai" dico con orgoglio, aprendo gli occhi, mentre lei ritira la mano. "Non solo sulle scale, ma prima. Kent mi ha detto che è stato il tuo urlo a far svegliare Yulia in tempo, perché potesse nascondersi sotto il letto e poi venire in tuo soccorso. Se non fosse stato per quello—"

"Li avremmo sconfitti in qualche altro modo" interrompe mia moglie con un sorriso calmo. "Sono certa che l'avremmo fatto."

La convinzione nella sua voce è al tempo stesso assurda e ammirevole. Per qualche ragione, piuttosto che traumatizzarla nuovamente, la crisi di ieri sembra aver eccitato in qualche modo la mia ptichka. Ho sempre saputo che è forte e capace, ma lei stessa evidentemente non ci credeva—fino a quando non ha combattuto il mio nemico e ha vinto.

"A volte, un trauma ripetuto può essere perversamente curativo" mi ha rivelato la Dottoressa Wessex, quando le ho parlato stamattina, dopo che Sara ha dormito tutta la notte senza incubi e si è svegliata ottimista come non l'avevo mai vista. "A differenza di quello che è successo con i suoi genitori, questa volta è stata in grado di fare qualcosa—e nessuno vicino a lei è rimasto ucciso o ferito davvero."

Non so se credere alla terapeuta—è passato solo un giorno, e potrebbe ancora colpire Sara in seguito—ma sono cautamente ottimista sullo stato mentale della mia ptichka.

Sul mio, ne sono meno sicuro. La scorsa notte, ho dormito appena, combattendo incubi e sudori freddi.

"Non ti lascerò mai più fuori dalla mia vista" prometto—e non sto scherzando nemmeno un po'. "Niente più missioni notturne lontane da te, nessun lavoro che ci tenga separati per un certo periodo di tempo. E ho già ordinato il mio set di impianti localizzatori da Esguerra; non appena arrivano, te li impianterò."

Sara non batte ciglio—le ho già detto dei localizzatori di Nora. "Va bene" replica. "Ma solo se li impianterai anche tu. Anch'io voglio sapere dove sei in ogni momento."

Sostengo il suo sguardo. "Affare fatto."

Impianterò tutto ciò che desidera la mia ptichka—purché sia felice e al sicuro.

～

"Sei arrabbiato per non aver avuto la possibilità di ucciderlo?" chiede, mentre siamo a letto poche ore dopo. Anche se abbiamo appena fatto sesso, la sto accarezzando dappertutto, incapace di resistere al piacere sensoriale di toccarla, di sentire la sua pelle calda e setosa sotto i miei palmi. "So che era importante per te" continua, mentre le strofino il collo, inalando il dolce profumo dei suoi capelli.

Non voglio pensare ad Henderson in questo momento, ma Sara sembra determinata a parlare di ogni aspetto di ciò che è accaduto. E quando ricordo quanto fosse stato difficile per lei parlare della morte dei suoi genitori, non posso negarglielo.

Se l'aiuta ad elaborare le cose, le racconterò tutto su come sogni di smembrare Henderson cellula dopo cellula—su come la semplice menzione del suo nome mi faccia rivivere ogni terribile momento sull'aereo.

Così, faccio esattamente questo—le confesso tutto, tutto su quanto sia stato terrorizzato all'idea che saremmo arrivati troppo tardi... che non sarei riuscito a proteggerla, come avevo fallito con Pasha e Tamila. Descrivo gli incubi che ho avuto la scorsa notte e i tremori che sento ancora, quando penso a quanto sia stato vicino a perderla.

Le rivelo quanto mi uccida non esser stato lì ad affrontare il mio nemico, a tenere al sicuro lei e il nostro bambino non ancora nato.

Mi ascolta, con la testa appoggiata sulla mia spalla e con le dita che giocano con i miei capelli, e quando ho finito, dice sottovoce: "Ci hai tenuti al sicuro. È stata la mossa che mi hai insegnato—sollevare le gambe per diventare un peso morto, quando qualcuno ti afferra da dietro—che ha aiutato noi tre a sconfiggere quei mercenari. E siete stati tu, Kent ed Esguerra a mandare le guardie che hanno ucciso Henderson."

Chiudo gli occhi, stringendo le braccia attorno a lei, mentre immagino la scena nella mia mente, con la vestaglia di seta e tutto il resto. Un brivido mi attraversa, e lei mi abbraccia, stringendomi, rassicurandomi con il suo calore, la sua vitalità, la sua forza.

Ci vogliono parecchi respiri profondi, prima che possa allentare la soffocante presa su di lei. Eppure, le tengo il mio braccio attorno, stringendola. Impiegherò anni per riprendermi da quel giorno—persino decenni.

Questo, supponendo che mi riprenderò mai del tutto.

"E sua moglie?" chiede Sara, distraendomi da una fantasia in cui sono in grado di tornare indietro nel tempo e strangolare Henderson con il suo stesso intestino, prima che le si avvicini. "Onorerai il tuo patto con lei?"

La mia mano libera si chiude a pugno al mio fianco. "Il

giudizio sul fatto che ci abbia attirati intenzionalmente è ancora sospeso, quindi—"

"No, non l'ha fatto" interrompe Sara, sollevando la testa dalla mia spalla per guardarmi. "Almeno, non credo che l'abbia fatto. Henderson credeva davvero che avessimo sua figlia; se sua moglie fosse stata coinvolta, avrebbe saputo che era tutto uno stratagemma. E quando quegli uomini ci hanno catturate, hanno detto qualcosa sul fatto che non ci fossero segni di voi tre—come se si aspettassero di trovarvi qui, e fossero rimasti sorpresi di non vedervi."

"Ah." Con sforzo, apro le dita. "Questo cambia le cose."

Se Bonnie Henderson è davvero innocente, la lascerò in pace—soprattutto se consegnerà tutte le prove su suo marito all'FBI, cancellando i nostri nomi.

Voglio questo per Sara. Voglio restituirle una vita normale e tranquilla.

Infilandole una mano tra i capelli, studio il viso a forma di cuore, meravigliandomi della sua bellezza. I suoi occhi languidi fissano i miei, e poi mormora: "Ti amo" e si china per un tenero bacio.

Il mio petto si espande per una scarica di sentimento così intensa che annega l'oscurità persistente. "Ti amo anch'io, ptichka" sussurro, e mentre le nostre labbra si toccano, so che a prescindere da cosa ci riservi il futuro, la affronteremo insieme.

Indipendentemente da com'è nato il nostro amore, ora è abbastanza forte.

EPILOGO

SEI ANNI DOPO

ara

"Papà! Papà!"

Alzo lo sguardo dal mio portatile, mentre mio figlio di cinque anni attraversa la porta, con le guance rosa per il freddo e gli stivali che spargono la neve dappertutto. Non notandomi sul divano, corre dritto verso Peter in cucina, lanciando l'esile corpo contro di lui a tutta velocità.

Sorridendo, mio marito si allontana dalla torta di compleanno e lo prende tra le sue braccia possenti, sollevandolo per farlo roteare sopra la testa.

Le risate di Charlie riempiono l'aria, mescolandosi al latrato entusiasta del nostro cane, e il mio petto si stringe, come fa ogni volta che vedo quell'espressione sul volto di Peter.

Gioia. Una tale gioia sfrenata.

Non mi stancherò mai di vederli insieme.

Il mio tormentatore diventato amante e nostro figlio.

Se la felicità potesse essere definita con un'immagine, sarebbe questa per me.

"Mamma! Charlie ha lanciato una palla di neve contro di me e Bella" urla Maya, correndo nella stanza con la neve e il ghiaccio che le cadono dalla giacca. La sua piccola faccia è indignata, le manine strette a pugno. "E Lizzie gli ha detto una parolaccia!"

Ridendo, metto da parte il mio laptop e abbraccio la mia piccola di tre anni. "Va tutto bene, amore mio" la consolo, accarezzandole i ricci castani aggrovigliati, mentre Toby, il nostro golden retriever, corre a leccare la neve dal suo cappotto. "Tuo fratello stava solo giocando. Ha una cotta per Bella, tutto qui."

"Non è vero!" Il tono risentito di Charlie coincide con quello di sua sorella. "È troppo bionda e strana e parla a malapena il russo."

"Ehi" lo rimprovera Peter, mettendolo giù. "Non è carino."

"Bella Kent parla bene il russo quanto te, stupido" dice Maya pomposamente, con il piccolo mento che si solleva, mentre si libera dall'abbraccio. Spingendo via Toby, aggiunge: "E in ogni caso, lei ha solo quattro anni. Il suo vocabolario crescerà come il tuo. Non tutti nascono intelligenti come me."

Io e Peter ci scambiamo un'occhiata. Quindi, non potendo fare niente, scoppiamo a ridere.

Oggi la nostra festeggiata è raggiante.

Charlie aveva due anni e mezzo, quando è nata Maya, ma l'anno scorso ha iniziato ad insegnargli la matematica e a leggere—questo in inglese, russo, francese e giapponese. La sua mente è come una spugna, e l'intelligenza pari solo al suo ego.

Nonostante il QI fuori dal normale, la modestia è un concetto che il suo cervello di tre anni non riesce ancora a comprendere.

"Pensavo mi avessi detto che non *eri* una bambina geniale" mi ha fatto notare Peter con stupore, quando nostra figlia ha iniziato a studiare musica all'età di due anni. "Che sei diventata medico così giovane a causa dei tuoi genitori, non perché fossi follemente intelligente."

"Ed è tutto vero. Non so da dove venga questo" gli ho risposto, altrettanto perplessa. "Forse c'è del DNA geniale in te."

Non che Charlie, il nostro primo figlio, non sia intelligente. È brillante, curioso ed energico—tutto ciò che abbiamo sempre desiderato in un figlio. Ha ottimi voti alla sua scuola privata qui in Svizzera; secondo i suoi insegnanti, è intelligente come pochi.

Maya, tuttavia, è su un livello completamente diverso.

Sarebbe intimidatoria, se non fosse così carina.

"Va' a chiamare gli altri" dico, prendendola per la giacca. "È l'ora della torta."

Il suo visetto—una copia in miniatura del mio—si illumina, e lei esce dalla stanza, con Charlie alle calcagna. Toby salta sul divano per rannicchiarsi accanto a me, e io sfrutto il minuto di tranquillità per rivedere la nuova canzone che sto componendo, prima di chiudere il portatile.

Essendo tutti qui per il compleanno di Maya, non avrò tempo per finirla oggi.

Dopo che Bonnie Henderson ha aiutato a cancellare il nome di Peter, abbiamo avuto la possibilità di tornare a Chicago e riprendere la nostra vita lì. Tuttavia, abbiamo deciso di non farlo. Non solo saremmo stati assaliti da sguardi sospettosi ovunque andassimo, a causa del fatto che le nostre facce erano su tutti i notiziari dopo l'attentato, ma senza i miei genitori, non c'era nulla che mi legasse davvero a Homer Glen. Così, invece, abbiamo deciso di creare una nuova casa sulle Alpi svizzere, vicino alla clinica privata, dove mi avevano offerto un lavoro, mentre eravamo in fuga.

Ho iniziato a lavorarci a tempo pieno, ma nel giro di un mese, io e mio marito ci siamo resi conto che con la gravidanza che mi rendeva sfinita—e non volendo essere separati per più di qualche ora—non era la soluzione migliore. Così, ho aperto il mio studio al primo piano della nostra casa, dove ho potuto stabilire i miei orari e vedere Peter per tutto il giorno. In poco tempo, la clinica ha cominciato ad inviarmi le pazienti incinte e sono diventata l'ostetrica-ginecologa per le donne con vari legami con la malavita.

Ha funzionato—soprattutto da quando Peter ha deciso di sfruttare le sue abilità e i contatti diversamente: reclutare e addestrare ex soldati a lavorare come mercenari per organizzazioni come quella di Esguerra.

Non è esattamente la civile vita pacifica che immaginavamo, ma è molto meno pericoloso degli omicidi di alto profilo—e molto più interessante per lui che insegnare ai normali cittadini la difesa personale di base. Per quanto mi riguarda, con il mio orario di lavoro flessibile, non ho solo tempo per Peter e per i nostri due figli, ma anche per la musica.

Non mi esibisco più dal vivo o ho un canale YouTube—dopo tutto quello che è successo, mio marito è diventato troppo paranoico sulla mia sicurezza—ma ho la soddisfazione di far cantare le mie canzoni ad alcune delle nuove star più popolari, che mi pagano bene per scriverle per loro. I miei testi più cupi sono particolarmente apprezzati, con due delle mie canzoni in cima alle classifiche da settimane.

"Torta! Torta! Torta!" I bambini arrivano come tornado pieni di neve, con il figlio di cinque anni di Esguerra, Mateo, in testa e Bella, Lizzie, Charlie e Maya che lo seguono. Strillando, i bambini circondano Peter, che sta preparando cerimoniosamente tre candele, e Toby salta giù dal divano e corre verso di loro, agitando la testa per l'emozione.

Poi, entrano gli adulti. Come al solito, Julian ha un braccio avvolto intorno a Nora, tenendola a sé come se temesse la sua fuga. Lucas è più cauto con Yulia, ma a giudicare dalle giacche bagnate, è evidente che si sono rotolati nella neve—e posso solo sperare che l'abbiano fatto lontano dalla vista dei bambini.

Charlie, essendo un intrepido esploratore, li ha già sorpresi a "giocare al dottore" nella loro palestra a Cipro una volta.

Ad ogni modo, sono contenta che siano tutti qui. Sebbene io e Peter andiamo a trovare gli Esguerra con regolarità, Yulia è stata così impegnata con i suoi ristoranti che l'ho vista solo due volte quest'anno. Per fortuna, la piccola Bella Kent non è così segretamente ossessionata dal nostro Charlie—che sostiene di odiarla, ma non perde mai occasione per attirare la sua attenzione—quindi, Lucas e Yulia non hanno avuto altra scelta che presentarsi alla festa di compleanno di Maya.

Altrimenti, la loro figlia, un bellissimo angioletto biondo, li avrebbe guardati con gli occhi da cucciolo moribondo per tutta la vita.

Camminando, saluto Nora e Yulia con un abbraccio. Poi, ci riuniamo tutti intorno alla torta accanto ai nostri figli, e mentre Maya spegne le sue candeline, incontro lo sguardo di Peter ed esprimo il mio desiderio.

Voglio che mi tormenti in questo modo per sempre—che mi ami con tutte le tenebre nel suo cuore.

FINE

Grazie per la lettura! Spero che vi sia piaciuta la conclusione della storia di Peter & Sara e che lascerete una recensione. Per sapere quando sarà disponibile un nuovo libro, iscrivetevi alla mia newsletter su www.annazaires.com.

Desiderate leggere storie che vedono come protagonisti questi personaggi? Allora, non perdetevi:

- *La Trilogia Strapazzami* - La storia di Julian & Nora, in cui Peter appare come personaggio secondario e ottiene la sua lista
- *La Trilogia Catturami* - La storia di Lucas & Yulia

Avete voglia di altri personaggi accattivanti? Allora, non perdetevi:

- *Il Titano di Wall Street* - una storia d'amore sugli opposti che si attraggono che vede come protagonista un irresistibile alfa miliardario

- *La Trilogia su Mia & Korum* - Una storia d'amore dark-fantascientifica
- *La Prigioniera dei Krinar* – uno standalone fantascientifico

Preferite azione, fantasia e fantascienza? Date un'occhiata a queste collaborazioni con mio marito, Dima Zales:

- *I lettori di pensieri* – Fantasia urbana
- *La Veggente* – l'emozionante storia di Sasha Urban, un'illusionista teatrale che scopre poteri segreti inaspettati

E ora, voltate pagina per un breve assaggio de *Il Titano di Wall Street* e *Strapazzami.*

ESTRATTO DE IL TITANO DI WALL STREET

Un miliardario che vuole una moglie perfetta...

Il trentacinquenne Marcus Carelli ha tutto: ricchezza, potere e il tipo di look che lascia le donne senza fiato. Un miliardario che si è fatto da sé, dirige uno dei maggiori hedge fund di Wall Street ed è in grado di affossare le grandi società con una sola parola. L'unica cosa che gli manca? Una moglie che sarebbe una grande conquista come i miliardi sul suo conto bancario.

Una gattara che ha bisogno di un appuntamento...

Emma Walsh, impiegata ventiseienne in una libreria, è rinomata per essere una gattara. Non è esattamente d'accordo con tale valutazione, ma è difficile negare la realtà dei fatti. Vestiti logori ricoperti da peli di gatto? Ce li ha. Ultimo taglio di capelli professionale? Più di un anno fa. Oh, e tre gatti in un piccolo monolocale di Brooklyn? Sì, ha anche quelli.

E sì, non frequenta un ragazzo da... beh, non riesce nemmeno a ricordarlo. Ma quella parte può essere corretta. Non è a questo che servono i siti d'incontri?

Un caso di errata identità...

Un'elegante organizzatrice di incontri, un'app di incontri, un fraintendimento che cambia tutto... Gli opposti possono attrarsi, ma può durare?

"Sì, è vero" dico con impazienza. "Voglio che sia sempre carina e curata. Deve avere un senso dello stile; è molto importante. Una bruna sarebbe la cosa migliore, ma anche una bionda andrebbe bene, purché la sua pettinatura sia conservatrice. Non deve sembrare appena uscita da Playboy, capisci?"

"Sì, certo, Signor Carelli." L'elegante bruna di fronte a me incrocia le lunghe gambe e mi rivolge un sorriso educato. Victoria Longwood-Thierry, organizzatrice di incontri per l'élite di Wall Street, è esattamente quello che ho in mente per la mia futura moglie, se non fosse che ha cinquant'anni e che è sposata con tre figli. "Che mi dici degli hobby e degli interessi?" chiede con voce attentamente modulata. "Che cosa vorresti che le piacesse?"

"Qualcosa di intellettuale" rispondo. "Voglio poterle parlare fuori dalla camera da letto."

"Certo." Victoria prende nota sul suo notepad. "E la sua professione?"

"Quella non ha molta importanza per me. Può essere un avvocato, un medico o trascorrere tutto il suo tempo facendo lavori di beneficenza per gli orfani di Haiti—non c'è problema per quanto mi riguarda. Una volta sposati, può restare a casa con i bambini o continuare la sua carriera. Mi vanno bene entrambe le opzioni."

"È molto saggio da parte tua." L'espressione della donna è immutata, ma ho la sensazione che stia ridendo segretamente di me. "Che cosa ne pensi degli animali domestici? Preferisci i cani o i gatti?"

"Nessuna delle due categorie. Non mi piace avere animali in casa."

Victoria prende un'altra nota, prima di chiedere: "E la sua altezza? Hai una preferenza?"

"Alta" dico subito. "O almeno sopra la media." Sono un metro e ottanta, e le donne basse mi sembrano delle bambine.

"Okay, bene." Victoria lo annota. "Che mi dici del tipo di corpo? Atletico o snello, immagino."

Annuisco. "Sì. Mi piace il fitness e voglio che sia in buona forma, in modo che possa stare al passo con me." Accigliato, guardo il mio orologio Patek Philippe e realizzo che ho solo mezz'ora a disposizione, prima dell'apertura del mercato. Riportando la mia attenzione su di lei, dico: "Fondamentalmente, voglio una donna intelligente, elegante e curata, che si prenda cura di se stessa."

"Ho capito. Non rimarrai deluso, te lo garantisco."

Sono scettico, ma mantengo un volto inespressivo, mentre si alza e mi accompagna educatamente fuori dal suo ufficio. Promette di contattarmi entro un paio di giorni, mi stringe la mano e torna dentro, lasciando dietro di sé una nuvola di profumo costoso. Non è troppo forte—Victoria Longwood-Thierry non sarebbe mai così pacchiana da usare un profumo forte—ma starnutisco, mentre mi dirigo verso l'ascensore.

Dovrò aggiungerlo alla lista: la candidata per diventare mia moglie non può mettere il profumo, punto.

Quando arrivo al mio edificio di Park Avenue dall'ufficio nel West Village di Victoria, i miei programmatori e trader sono incollati ai loro schermi. Solo pochi se ne accorgono, mentre mi dirigo verso il mio ufficio all'angolo. Normalmente mi fermerei alle loro scrivanie per chiedere del fine settimana e ottenere un aggiornamento sulle nostre posizioni, ma il mercato è già aperto e non posso distrarli.

Con novantadue miliardi di denaro dei miei investitori in gioco, non c'è spazio per gli errori.

Il mio ufficio è enorme e ha una magnifica vista sui grattacieli di Park Avenue, ma non mi soffermo ad apprezzarla. Un tempo, questo ufficio sembrava l'apice del successo per un ragazzaccio di Staten Island, ma ora ho fame di altro. Il successo è la mia droga, e ad ogni colpo, ho bisogno di una dose maggiore per sentirmi euforico. Non si tratta più del denaro—oltre alla mia partecipazione personale nel fondo, ho un paio di miliardi di dollari riposti in immobili e altri investimenti passivi—si tratta di sapere che posso farcela, che posso avere successo dove altri hanno fallito. La recente instabilità del mercato ha comportato perdite record sia per gli hedge fund che per i fondi comuni, ma Carelli Capital Management è in crescita, sovraperformando il mercato di oltre il quaranta percento. Fondazioni, fondi pensione, individui benestanti—stanno tutti sgomitando per correre a investire con me, e voglio ancora di più.

Voglio tutto, compresa una moglie che si adatti alla vita per la quale ho lavorato così duramente.

Apparentemente, dovrebbe essere facile. A trentacinque anni, ho soldi a sufficienza per mantenere la popolazione femminile di Manhattan con borse Louis Vuitton e scarpe Louboutin per il resto della loro vita, non ho un brutto aspetto e mi alleno tutti i giorni per mantenermi in forma. Quest'ultima cosa la faccio più per salute che per vanità, ma le donne sembrano apprezzare i risultati. Posso avere qualsiasi donna in un club nel giro di pochi minuti, ma nessuna di loro è ciò che voglio.

Voglio l'alta classe. Voglio l'eleganza.

Voglio una donna che sia esattamente l'opposto di quella che mi ha cresciuto—da questo derivano il contatto con Victoria Longwood-Thierry e le sue altolocate conoscenze.

È stato il mio amico Ashton a indirizzarmi da lei. "Sai che il tipo di donna che desideri non frequenta i bar, giusto?" mi ha detto quando, dopo un paio di birre, ho menzionato le caratteristiche che dovrebbe avere la mia moglie ideale. "Stai parlando dell'aristocrazia americana, Mayflower e tutto il resto. Se fai sul serio per quanto riguarda il toccare una figa di fascia alta, devi parlare con l'amica di mia zia. È un'organizzatrice di incontri professionista, che lavora con politici e ricchi tipi di Wall Street come te. Ti troverà esattamente ciò di cui hai bisogno."

Ho riso e cambiato argomento, ma il germe dell'idea era stato piantato, e più indagavo sull'amica della zia di Ashton, più m'incuriosivo. Ho scoperto che Victoria ha fatto accoppiare almeno due gestori di hedge fund che conosco—uno con una ginnasta olimpica, l'altro con una biologa di Princeton, che una volta lavorava come modella. Dopo ulteriori approfondimenti, ho appreso che entrambi i matrimoni stanno andando alla grande finora, e questo, più di ogni altra cosa, mi ha convinto a dare una possibilità all'organizzatrice di incontri.

Intendo avere successo nella mia vita personale come l'ho avuto negli affari, e avere il giusto tipo di moglie è una parte importante di questo.

Sedendomi davanti alla mia scintillante scrivania in legno di ebano, accendo il monitor Bloomberg e raccolgo una pila di analisi di ricerca. Victoria sta lavorando sul caso, così allontano dalla mente la caccia alla moglie e mi concentro su ciò che conta davvero: il mio lavoro e far guadagnare soldi ai miei clienti.

Sono già le otto di sera, quando il mio telefono vibra per un messaggio in arrivo. Strofinando gli occhi, distolgo lo sguardo dallo schermo del mio computer e vedo che è un messaggio di Victoria.

Ho la candidata perfetta per te, c'è scritto. Può incontrarti al Sweet Rush Café a Park Slope domani alle 18:00. Se va bene per te, t'invierò maggiori dettagli tramite e-mail. Emmeline vive a Boston ed è in città solo per un paio di giorni.

Aggrotto la fronte. Alle diciotto? Non esco quasi mai dall'ufficio così presto il martedì. E Boston? Come potrei mai conoscere questa Emmeline, se non vive a New York?

Inizio a scrivere a Victoria che non posso farcela, ma mi fermo all'ultimo momento. Questo è quello che volevo: che lei mi presentasse una donna che non avrei mai incontrato da solo. Visto il curriculum dell'organizzatrice di incontri, posso ritagliarmi una sera per vedere se ci sia davvero qualcosa per cui valga la pena andare lì.

Prima di poter cambiare idea, scrivo un breve messaggio a Victoria accettando l'appuntamento e riportando la mia attenzione sullo schermo del computer.

Se domani lascerò l'ufficio prima del solito, stasera dovrò lavorare qualche ora in più.

Visitate il mio sito web all'indirizzo www.annazaires.com/book-series/italiano/ per saperne di più e per iscrivervi alla mia mailing list delle nuove pubblicazioni.

ESTRATTO DI STRAPAZZAMI

Nota dell'Autrice: *Strapazzami* è una trilogia dark erotica su Nora & Julian Esguerra. Tutti e tre i libri sono disponibili.

Rapita. Portata su un'isola privata.

Non avrei mai immaginato che potesse succedermi questo. Non avrei mai immaginato che un incontro casuale alla vigilia del mio diciottesimo compleanno avrebbe potuto cambiarmi la vita in questo modo.

Ora appartengo a lui. A Julian. A un uomo che è così spietato quanto bello—un uomo il cui tocco mi fa bruciare. Un uomo la cui tenerezza trovo più devastante della sua crudeltà.

Il mio rapitore è un enigma. Non so chi sia, né perché mi abbia presa. C'è un'oscurità in lui—un'oscurità che mi spaventa anche se mi attira.

Mi chiamo Nora Leston e questa è la mia storia.

~

È sera ormai. Ogni minuto che passa, l'ansia sale sempre di più al pensiero di rivedere il mio rapitore.

Il romanzo che stavo leggendo non mi interessa più. Lo poso e cammino in cerchio per la stanza.

Indosso gli abiti che Beth mi ha dato prima. Non è quello che avrei scelto di indossare, ma è sempre meglio di una vestaglia. Un paio di mutandine di pizzo sexy e bianche e un reggiseno abbinato come biancheria intima. Un bel prendisole blu con i bottoni nella parte anteriore. Mi sta tutto benissimo in modo sospetto. Mi seguiva da tempo? Scoprendo tutto di me, compresa la mia taglia di vestiti?

Quel pensiero mi dà la nausea.

Cerco di non pensare a quello che avverrà, ma è impossibile. Non so perché sono così sicura che verrà da me stasera. Forse ha un intero harem di donne da qualche parte sull'isola e fa visita ad ognuna solo una volta a settimana, come facevano i sultani.

Eppure qualcosa mi dice che verrà presto. Ieri sera aveva semplicemente stuzzicato il suo appetito. So che non ha finito con me, neanche per sogno.

Finalmente, la porta si apre.

Cammina come se fosse a casa sua. Ed è proprio così, infatti.

Rimango di nuovo colpita dalla sua bellezza mascolina. Potrebbe essere un modello o una star del cinema, con un viso del genere. Se ci fosse giustizia nel mondo, sarebbe stato basso o avrebbe avuto qualche altra imperfezione sul volto per compensare.

Ma non è così. È alto e muscoloso, perfettamente proporzionato. Ricordo cos'ho provato ad averlo dentro e sento una sgradita scossa di eccitazione.

Indossa ancora jeans e T-shirt. Una grigia questa volta. Sembra preferire i vestiti semplici e fa bene a farlo. Il suo aspetto non ha bisogno di altri accessori.

Mi sorride. È quel sorriso da angelo caduto—oscuro e seducente allo stesso tempo. "Ciao, Nora."

Non so cosa rispondere, così sputo la prima cosa che mi passa per la mente. "Per quanto tempo hai intenzione di tenermi qui?"

Inclina leggermente la testa di lato. "Qui in camera? O sull'isola?"

"Entrambi."

"Beth ti farà fare un giro domani, potrai nuotare se vuoi" dice, avvicinandosi. "Non verrai chiusa a chiave, a meno che tu non faccia qualcosa di stupido."

"Tipo?" chiedo, con il cuore che mi batte forte nel petto mentre si ferma accanto a me e solleva la mano per accarezzarmi i capelli.

"Cercare di fare del male a Beth o a te stessa." La sua voce è dolce, il suo sguardo ipnotico mentre mi guarda. Il modo in cui mi tocca i capelli è stranamente rilassante.

Sbatto le palpebre, cercando di spezzare il suo incantesimo. "E per quanto riguarda l'isola? Per quanto tempo mi terrai qui?"

Mi accarezza il viso con la mano, piegandola sulla mia guancia. Mi sorprendo ad appoggiarmi al suo tocco, come una gatta che viene coccolata, e mi irrigidisco subito.

Le sue labbra si arricciano in un sorriso presuntuoso. Il bastardo sa quale effetto ha su di me. "A lungo, mi auguro" dice.

Chissà perché, non mi stupisce. Non mi avrebbe portata fin qui, se avesse solo voluto scoparmi un paio di volte. Sono terrorizzata, ma non sono sorpresa.

Raccolgo il coraggio e passo alla prossima domanda logica. "Perché mi hai rapita?"

Il sorriso abbandona il suo volto. Non risponde, semplicemente mi guarda con uno sguardo blu imperscrutabile.

Comincio a tremare. "Hai intenzione di uccidermi?"

"No, Nora, non voglio ucciderti."

La sua negazione mi rassicura, anche se potrebbe benissimo mentire.

"Hai intenzione di vendermi?" riesco a malapena a far uscire le parole. "Come prostituta o qualcosa del genere?"

"No" dice a bassa voce. "Mai. Sei mia e solo mia."

Mi sento un po' più calma, ma c'è ancora una cosa che devo sapere. "Hai intenzione di farmi del male?"

Per un attimo, non risponde. Per un istante qualcosa di oscuro lampeggia nei suoi occhi. "Probabilmente" dice lentamente.

E poi si china in avanti e mi bacia, con le sue calde labbra morbide e delicate sulle mie.

Per un attimo, resto lì bloccata, senza rispondere. Gli credo. So che dice la verità quando afferma che mi farà del male. C'è qualcosa in lui che mi fa paura, che mi ha spaventata fin dall'inizio.

Non è come i ragazzi che ho frequentato. Lui è capace di qualunque cosa.

E sono completamente alla sua mercé.

Rifletto ancora una volta sulla possibilità di affrontarlo. Questa sarebbe la cosa normale da fare nella mia situazione. La cosa coraggiosa da fare.

Eppure non lo faccio.

Sento l'oscurità dentro di lui. C'è qualcosa di sbagliato in lui. La sua bellezza esteriore nasconde qualcosa di mostruoso dentro.

Non voglio scatenare quell'oscurità. Non so cosa accadrà se lo faccio.

Così, resto immobile mentre mi abbraccia e gli permetto di baciarmi. E quando mi tira di nuovo su e mi porta sul letto, non cerco in alcun modo di opporgli resistenza.

Anzi, chiudo gli occhi e mi abbandono alle sensazioni.

Tutti e tre i libri della trilogia *Strapazzami* sono già disponibili. Visitate il mio sito web all'indirizzo www.annazaires.com/book-series/italiano/ per saperne di più e per iscrivervi alla mia mailing list delle nuove pubblicazioni.

BIOGRAFIA DELL'AUTRICE

Anna Zaires è un'autrice bestseller di sci-fi romance, romance contemporaneo erotico e dark del *New York Times, USA Today*. È appassionata di libri dall'età di cinque anni, quando sua nonna le insegnò a leggere. Da allora, vive sempre parzialmente in un mondo di fantasia, in cui gli unici limiti sono quelli della sua immaginazione. Al momento risiede in Florida. Anna è felicemente sposata con Dima Zales (un autore fantasy e di science fiction) e collabora strettamente con lui in tutti i suoi lavori.

Per saperne di più, visitate il sito www.annazaires.com/book-series/italiano/.